EXILES of VALDEMAR

A VALDEMAR OMNIBUS

EXILES of VALDEMAR

A VALDEMAR OMNIBUS

MERCEDES LACKEY

TITAN BOOKS

Exiles of Valdemar Omnibus
Print edition ISBN: 9781785653575
E-book edition ISBN: 9781783296187

Published by Titan Books
A division of Titan Publishing Group Ltd
144 Southwark Street, London
SE1 0UP

First edition: March 2018
2 4 6 8 10 9 7 5 3 1

A CIP catalogue record for this title is available from the British Library.

Printed and bound by CPI Group (UK) Ltd, Croydon, CR0 4YY

EXILES of VALDEMAR

A VALDEMAR OMNIBUS

EXILE'S HONOR

A VALDEMAR OMNIBUS

BOOK ONE
OF EXILES of VALDEMAR

Dedicated to the memory of NYFD crews lost 9/11/2001:

Squad 1:
Brian Bilcher
Gary Box
Thomas Butler
Peter Carroll
Robert Cordice
David Fontana
Matthew Garvey
Stephen Siller
Edward Datri
Michael Esposito
Michael Fodor
James Amato

Squad 18:
Eric Allen
David Halderman
Timothy Haskell
Andrew Fredericks
Lawrence Virgilio
William McGinn

Squad 41:
Thomas Cullen III
Robert Hamilton
Michael Lyons
Gregory Sikorsky
Richard VanHine
Michael Healey

Squad 252:
Tarel Coleman
Thomas Kuveikis
Peter Langone
Patrick Lyons
Kevin Prior

Squad 288:
Ronnie Gies
Joseph Hunter
Jonathon Ielpi
Adam Rand
Ronald Kerwin

Safety Battalion 1:
Robert Crawford

Fire Marshal:
Ronald Bucca

Special Operations:
Timothy Higgins
Michael Russo
Patrick Waters
Raymond Downey

Citywide Tour Commander:
Gerard Barbara
Donald Burns

PROLOGUE

Silver stamped restively as another horse on the picket line shifted and blundered into his hindquarters. Alberich clucked to quiet him and patted the stallion's neck; the beast swung his head about to blow softly into the young Captain's hair. Alberich smiled a little, thinking wistfully that the stallion was perhaps the only creature in the entire camp that felt anything like friendship for him.

And possibly the only creature that isn't waiting for me to fail, hoping that I will, and ready to pounce on me and cut me to pieces when I do. Life for an officer of Karsite troops was spent half in defeating the enemies of Karse and half in watching his own back.

Amazingly gentle, for a stallion, Silver had caused no problems either in combat or here, on the picket line. Which was just as well, for if he had, Alberich would have had him gelded or traded off for a more tractable mount, gift of the Voice of Vkandis Sunlord or no. Alberich had enough troubles without worrying about the behavior of his beast.

He wasn't sure where the handsome and muscular creature had come from; Shin'a'in-bred, they'd told him. The Voice had chosen the beast especially for him out of a string of animals "liberated from the enemy." Which meant war booty, of course, from one of the constant conflicts along the borders. Silver hadn't come from one of the bandit nests, that was sure. The only beasts the bandits owned were as disreputable as their owners. Horses "liberated" from the bandits usually weren't worth keeping, they were so run-down and ill-treated. Silver probably came from Menmellith via Rethwellan; the King was rumored to have some kind of connection with the horse-breeding, bloodthirsty Shin'a'in nomads.

Whatever; when Alberich lost his faithful old Smoke a few weeks ago he hadn't expected to get anything better than the obstinate, intractable gelding he'd taken from its bandit owner. But fate ruled otherwise; the Voice chose to "honor" him with a superior replacement along with his commission, the letter that accompanied the paper pointing out that Silver was the perfect mount for a Captain of light cavalry. It was also another evidence of favoritism from above, with the implication that he had earned that favoritism outside of performance in the field.

Talk about a double-edged blade... Both the commission and the horse came with burdens of their own. Not a gift that was likely to increase his popularity with some of the men under his command, and a beast that was going to make him pretty damned conspicuous in any encounter with the enemy. A *white* horse? Might as well paint a target on his back and have done with it.

Plus that's an unlucky color. Those witchy Heralds of Valdemar ride white horses, and the blue-eyed beasts may be demons or witches, too, for all I know. The priests say they are. The priests call their owners the "Demon-Riders."

The horse nuzzled him again, showing as sweet a temper as any lady's mare. He scratched its nose, and it sighed with content; he wished he could be as contented. Things had been bad enough before getting this commission. Now—

There was an uneasy, prickly sensation between his shoulder blades as he went back to brushing down his new mount. He glanced over his shoulder, to intercept the glare of Leftenant Herdahl; the man dropped his gaze and brushed his horse's flank vigorously, but not quickly enough to prevent Alberich from seeing the hate and anger in the hot blue eyes.

No, indeed, the Voice had done Alberich no favors in rewarding him with the Captaincy and this prize mount, passing over Herdahl and Klaus, both his seniors in years of service, if not in experience. Neither of them had expected that he would be promoted over their heads; during the week's wait for word to come from Headquarters, they had saved their rivalry for each other.

Too bad they didn't murder each other, he thought resentfully, then suppressed the rest of the thought. It was said that some of the priests of Vkandis could pluck the thoughts from a man's head. It could have been thoughts like that one that had led to Herdahl's being passed over for promotion. But it could also be that this was a test, a way of flinging the ambitious young Leftenant Alberich into deep water, to see if he would survive the experience. If he did, well and good; he was of suitable material to continue to advance, perhaps even to the rank of Commander. If he did not—well, that was too bad. If his ambition undid him, or if he wasn't clever enough to see and avoid the machinations of those below him, then he wasn't fit enough for the post.

That was the way of things, in the armies of Karse. You rose by watching your back, and (if the occasion arose) sticking careful knives into the backs of your less-cautious fellows, and ensuring other enemies took the punishment. All the while, the priests of the Sunlord, the ones who were truly in charge, watched and smiled and dispensed favors and punishments with the same dispassionate aloofness displayed by the One God. Karse was a hard land, and the Sunlord a hard God; the Sunpriests were as hard as both.

But Alberich had given a good account of himself along the border, at the corner where Karse met Menmellith and the witch-nation Valdemar, in the campaign against the bandits there. Frankly, Herdahl and Klaus put together hadn't been half as effective or as energetic as he'd been. He'd earned his rank, he told himself once again, as Silver stamped and shifted his weight beneath the strokes of Alberich's brush.

The spring sun burned down on his head, hotter than he expected without the breeze to cool him, hot as Herdahl's angry glare.

Demons take Herdahl. There was no reason to feel as if he'd cheated to get where he was. He'd led more successful sorties against the bandits in his first year in the field than the other two had achieved in their entire careers. He'd cleared more territory than anyone of leftenant rank ever had in that space of time—and when Captain Anberg had met with one too many arrows, the men had seemed perfectly willing to follow him when the Voice chose him over the other two candidates.

It had been the policy of late to permit the brigands to flourish, provided they confined their attentions to Valdemar and the Menmellith peasantry and left the inhabitants of Karse unmolested. A stupid policy, in Alberich's opinion; you couldn't trust bandits, that was the whole reason why they became bandits in the first place. If they could be trusted, they'd be in the army themselves, or in the Temple Guard, or even have turned mercenary. He'd seen the danger back when he was a youngster in the Academy, in his first tactics classes. He'd even said as much to one of his teachers—phrased as a question, of course, since cadets were not permitted to have opinions. The question had been totally ignored. Perhaps because it wasn't wise to so much as hint that the decisions of the Sunpriests were anything other than divinely inspired.

But, as Alberich had predicted, there had been trouble from the brigands once they began to multiply; problems that escalated far, far past the point where their use as an irritant to Valdemar was outweighed by their effect as a scourge on Karse. With complete disregard for the unwritten agreements between them and Karse, they struck everyone, and when they finally began attacking villages instead of just robbing solitary travelers or going after single farms, the authorities deemed it time they were disposed of.

Alberich had spent a good part of his young life in the Karsite military schools and had just finished cavalry training as an officer when the troubles broke out. The ultimate authority was in the hands of the Voices, of course. The highest anyone not of the priesthood could expect to rise was to Commander. But officers were never taken from the ranks; many of the rank-and-file were conscripts, and although it was never openly stated, the Voices did not trust their continued loyalty if they were given power.

Alberich, and many others like him, had been selected at the age of thirteen by a Voice sent every year to search out young male children, strong of body and quick of mind, to school into officers. And there was one other qualification—that at least half of them be lowborn, so that they were appropriately grateful to the Voices for their opportunity to rise in rank and station.

Alberich had all those qualities, developing expertise in many weapons with an ease that was the envy of his classmates, picking up his lessons in academic subjects with what seemed to be equal ease.

It wasn't ease; it was the fact that Alberich studied long and hard, knowing that there was no way for the bastard son of a tavern wench to advance in Karse except in the army. There was no place for him to go, no way to get into a trade, no hope for any but the most menial of jobs. The Voices didn't care about a man's parentage once he was chosen as an officer, they cared only about his abilities and whether or not he would use them in service to his God and country. It was a lonely life, though. His mother had loved and cared for him to the best of her abilities, and he'd had friends among the other children of similar circumstances. When he came to the Academy, he had no friends, and his mother was not permitted to contact him, lest she "distract him," or "contaminate his purity of purpose." Alberich had never seen her again, but both of them had known this was the only way for him to live a better life than she had. And there had been a half-promise— which he had no way of knowing was kept—that if he did well at the Academy, his mother would be rewarded, perhaps with a little house of her own, if she could manage to keep herself from further sin. He had trusted in that particular Voice, though. The priest had no reason to lie to him—and every reason to give his mother that reward. After all, Karse needed officers... *willing* officers, and young boys eager to throw themselves into their studies with all the enthusiasm of youth in order to become those willing officers. Knowing that their parents would be taken care of provided plenty of incentive.

And he had done better than well. He had pushed himself harder than any of his classmates pushed themselves.

Friends? When did I have the time for friends? Up before dawn for extra exercise, all my spare time practicing against the older boys, and after dinner studying by the light of Vkandis' lamps in the Temple until the priests came in for midnight prayers.

Alberich had no illusions about the purity of the One God's priesthood. There were as many corrupt and venal priests as there were upright, and more fanatic than there were forgiving. He had seen plenty of the venal kind in the tavern when they passed through his little mountain village on the way to greater places; had hidden from one or two that had come seeking pleasures strictly forbidden by the One God's edicts. He had known they were coming, looking for him, and had managed to make himself scarce long before they arrived. Just as, somehow, he had known when the Voice was coming to look for young male children for the Academy, and had made certain he was noticed and questioned—

And that he had known which customers it was safe to cadge for a penny in return for running errands—

Or that he had known that drunk was going to try to set the stable afire. Oh, that had been a tricky thing to manage—to stay awake despite aching eyes that threatened to close long enough to be able to "stumble out of bed" and into the courtyard in search of a drink from the pump "just in time" to see the first flames. *No matter how much noise is in a tavern, the sound of a child's shrill scream will penetrate it. No matter how drunk the inhabitants, the cry of "Fire!" will get the appropriate response.*

Somehow. That was Alberich's secret. He knew things were going to happen. That was a witch-power, and forbidden by the Voices of the One God. If anyone knew he had it—

The Fires, and the Cleansing. Oh, of course, those whom the One God favors are supposed to be able to endure the Fires and walk from the ashes Cleansed. Not that anyone has ever seen that happen.

But he had also known from the time that the visions first came on him, as surely as he had known all the rest, that he had to conceal the fact that he had this power, even before he knew the law against it.

He'd succeeded fairly well over the years, though it was getting harder and harder all the time. The power struggled inside him, wanting to break free, once or twice overwhelming him with visions so intense that for a moment he was blind and deaf to everything else. It was getting harder to concoct reasons for knowing things he had no business knowing, like the hiding places of the bandits they were chasing, the bolt-holes and escape routes. But it was harder still to ignore them, especially when subsequent visions showed him innocent people suffering because he didn't act on what he knew.

He brushed Silver's neck vigorously, the dust tickling his nose and making him want to sneeze—

—and between one brush stroke and the next, he lost his sense of balance, went light-headed, and the dazzle that heralded a vision-to-come sparkled between his eyes and Silver's neck.

Not here! he thought desperately, clinging to Silver's mane and trying to pretend there was nothing wrong. Not now, not with Herdahl watching—

But the witch-power would not obey him, not this time.

No—Sunlord, help me, not now! He believed in the Sunlord, in His power and goodness, if not in the goodness of those who said they spoke for Him...

A flash of blue light, blinding him—

Then came sight again, but not of the picket line, but another place.

Where? Where? Sunlord, where?

The bandits he'd thought were south had slipped behind him, into the north, joining with two more packs of the curs, becoming a group large enough to take on his troops and give them an even fight. But first, they wanted a secure base. They were going to make Alberich meet them on ground of their choosing. Fortified ground.

That this ground was already occupied was only a minor inconvenience, one that would soon be dealt with.

He fought free of the vision for a moment, clinging to Silver's shoulder like a drowning man, both hands full of the beast's silky mane, while the horse curved his head back and looked at him curiously. The big brown eyes flickered blue, briefly, like a half-hidden flash of lightning, reflecting—

—another burst of sapphire. And now, *now* he knew where! The bandits' target was a fortified village, a small one, built on the top of a hill, above the farm fields. Ordinarily, these people would have no difficulty in holding off a score of bandits. But there were three times that number ranged against them, and a recent edict from the High

Temple decreed that no one but the Temple Guard and the army could possess anything but the simplest of weapons. Not three weeks ago, a detachment of priests and a Voice had come through here, divesting them of everything but knives, farm implements, and such simple bows and arrows as were suitable for waterfowl and small game. And while they were at it, a third of the able-bodied men had been conscripted for the regular army.

Alberich's own troops had acted as silent guards for the process, to ensure that there were no "incidents" while the conscripts were marched away, while the weapons were taken or destroyed. Yes, he knew this place, knew it too well.

These people didn't have a chance.

The bandits drew closer, under the cover of a brush-filled ravine.

Alberich found himself on Silver's back, without knowing how he'd gotten there, without remembering that he'd flung saddle and bridle back on the beast—

No, not bridle; Silver still wore the halter he'd had on the picket line. Alberich's bugle was in his hand; presumably he'd blown the muster, for his men were running toward him, buckling on swords and slinging quivers over their shoulders.

Blinding flash of sapphire—throwing him back into the vision, showing him what he would rather not see. He *knew* what was coming, so why must he *see* it?

The bandits attacked the village walls, overpowering the poor man who was trying to bar the gate against them, and swarming inside. He couldn't close his eyes to it; the vision came through eyes closed or open. He would look because he had no choice.

It hadn't happened yet, he knew that with the surety with which he knew his own name. It wasn't even going to happen in the next few moments. But it was going to happen soon.

They poured inside, cutting down anyone who resisted them, then throwing off what little restraint they had shown and launching into an orgy of looting and rapine. Alberich gagged as one of them grabbed a pregnant woman and with a single slash of his sword, murdered the child that ran to try and protect her, followed through to her—

The vision released him, and he found himself surrounded by dust and thunder, still on Silver's back—

—but leaning over the stallion's neck as now he led his troops up the road to the village of Sunsdale at full gallop. Hooves pounded the packed earth of the road, making it impossible to hear or speak; the vibration thrummed into his bones as he shifted his weight with the stallion's turns. Silver ran easily, with no sign of distress, though all around him and behind him the other horses streamed saliva from the corners of their mouths, and their flanks ran with sweat and foam, as they strained to keep up.

The lack of a bit didn't seem to make any difference to the stallion; he answered to neck-rein and knee so readily he might have been anticipating Alberich's thoughts.

Alberich dismissed the uneasy feelings that prompted. Better not to think that he might have a second witch-power along with the first. He'd never shown any ability to control beasts by thought before. There was no reason to think he could now. The stallion was just superbly trained, that was all. And he had more important things to worry about.

They topped the crest of a hill; Sunsdale lay atop the next one, just as he had seen in his vision, and the brush-filled ravine beyond it.

There was no sign of trouble.

This time it's been a wild hare, he thought, and his skin crawled at the thought that he'd roused the men and sent them here at the gallop, and there were sure to be questions asked for which he had no answers.

And I answer what? That I wanted to see how quick they'd respond to an emergency? That would hardly serve.

He was just about to pull Silver up and bring the rest of his men to a halt—no point in them running their horses into foundering—

When a flash of sunlight on metal betrayed the bandits' location.

Alberich grabbed for the bugle dangling from his left wrist instead, and pulled his blade with the right. He sounded the charge and led the entire troop down the hill, an unstoppable torrent of hooves and steel, hitting the brigands' hidden line like an avalanche.

Sword in hand, Alberich limped wearily to another body sprawled amid the rocks and trampled weeds of the ravine, and thrust it through to make death certain. His sword felt heavy and unwieldy, his stomach churned, and there was a sour taste in his mouth. He didn't think he was going to lose control of his guts, but he was glad he was almost at the end of the battle line. He hated this part of the fighting—which wasn't fighting at all; it was nothing more than butchery.

But it was necessary. This scum was just as likely to be feigning death as to actually be dead. Other officers hadn't been that thorough—and hadn't lived long enough to regret it.

Silver was being fed and watered along with the rest of the mounts by the youngsters of Sunsdale; the finest fodder and clearest spring water, and a round dozen young boys to brush and curry them clean. And the men were being fed and made much of by the older villagers. Gratitude had made them forgetful of the loss of their weapons and many of their men. Suddenly the army that had conscripted their relatives was no longer their adversary. Or else, since the troops had arrived out of nowhere like Vengeance of the Sunlord Himself, they assumed the One God had a hand in it, and it would be prudent to resign themselves to the sacrifice. And meanwhile, the instrument of their rescue probably ought to be well treated.

Except for the Captain, who was doing a dirty job he refused to assign to anyone else.

Alberich made certain of two more corpses and looked dully around for more.

There weren't any, and he decided, when he spotted a pool of clear rainwater a little farther down the ravine, that he had to wash. He had to get the blood off his hands and the stink of death out of his nostrils.

He picked his way down the rocks to the pool—not rainwater, after all, but fed by a tiny trickle of a spring, a mere thread of clear water that didn't even stir the surface of the pool.

He bent over it, and caught his own reflection staring back at him. A sober fellow, with a face of sharp planes and uncompromising angles; a stubborn mouth, his mother had always said, and eyes that stared unnervingly back at him. "Hawk eyes," said some; with a fierce and direct gaze. Dark hair, cut as short as possible to fit beneath a helm's padding. Skin burned dark by the sun. He looked at the reflection as if he was looking at a stranger, hunting for—what? The taint of witchery?

He saw only a toughened man with eyes that looked—perhaps—a trifle haunted. Suddenly, he didn't want to look anymore—or more closely. *Introspection is for poets. Not men like me.*

He bent quickly to wash, disrupting the reflection. When he straightened to shake the water off his arms and face, he saw to his surprise that the sun was hardly more than a finger's breadth from the horizon. Shadows already filled the ravine, the evening breeze had picked up, and it was getting chilly. Last year's weeds tossed in the freshening wind as he gazed around at the long shadows cast by the scrubby trees. More time had passed than he thought, and if he didn't hurry, he was going to be late for SunDescending.

He scrambled over the slippery rocks of the ravine, cursing under his breath as his boots (meant for riding) skidded on the smooth, rounded boulders. The last thing he needed now was to be late for a holy service, especially this one. The priest here was bound to ask him for a thanks-prayer for the victory. If he was late, it would look as if he was arrogantly attributing the victory to his own abilities, and not the Hand of the Sunlord. And with an accusation like that hanging over his head, he'd be in danger not only of being deprived of his current rank, but of being demoted into the ranks, with no chance of promotion, a step up from stable-hand, but not a big one.

He fought his way over the edge, and half-ran, half-limped to the village gates, reaching them just as the sun touched the horizon. He put a little more speed into his weary, aching legs, and got to the edge of the crowd in the village square a scant breath before the priest began the First Chant.

He bowed his head with the others, and not until he raised his head at the end of it did he realize that the robes the priest wore were not black, but red. This was no mere village priest—this was a Voice!

He suppressed his start of surprise, and the shiver of fear that followed it. He didn't know what this village meant, or what had happened to require posting a Voice here, but there was little wonder now why they had submitted so tamely to the taking of their men and the confiscation of their weapons. No one sane would contradict a Voice.

The Voice held up his hand, and got instant silence; a silence so profound that the sounds of the horses stamping and whickering on the picket line came clearly over the walls. In the distance, a few lonely birds called, and the breeze rustled through the new leaves of the trees in the ravine. Alberich longed suddenly to be able to mount Silver and ride away from here, far away from the machinations of Voices and the omnipresent smell of death and blood. He yearned for somewhere clean, somewhere that he wouldn't have to guard his back from those he should be able to trust.

"Today this village was saved from certain destruction," the Voice said, his words ringing out, but without passion, without any inflection whatsoever. "And for that, we offer thanksgiving to Vkandis Sunlord, Most High, One God, to whom all things are known. The instrument of that salvation was Captain Alberich, who mustered his men in time to catch our attackers in the very act. It seems a miracle—"

During the speech, some of the men had been moving closer to Alberich, grouping themselves around him to bask in the admiration of the villagers.

Or so he thought. Until the Voice's tone hardened, and his next words proved their real intent.

"It seems a miracle—but it was not!" he thundered. "You were saved by the power of the One God, whose wrath destroyed the bandits, but Alberich betrayed the Sunlord by using the unholy powers of witchcraft! Seize him!"

His heart froze, but his body acted, and he whirled. The men grabbed him as he turned to run, throwing him to the ground and pinning him with superior numbers. He fought them anyway, struggling furiously, until someone brought the hilt of a knife down on the back of his head.

He didn't black out altogether, but he couldn't move or see; his eyes wouldn't focus, and a gray film obscured everything. He felt himself being dragged off by the arms—heaved into darkness—felt himself hitting a hard surface—heard the slamming of a door.

Then heard only confused murmurs as he lay in shadows, trying to regain his senses and his strength. Gradually, his sight cleared, and he could make out walls on all sides of him, close enough to touch. The last light of dusk made thin blue lines of the cracks between each board. He raised his aching head cautiously, and made out the dim outline of an ill-fitting door. The floor, clearly, was dirt. And smelled unmistakably of fowl birds.

They must have thrown him into some kind of shed, something that had once held chickens or pigeons. It didn't *now,* for the dirt floor was clean and packed as hard as rock. He was under no illusions that this meant his prison would be easy to escape; out here, the chicken-sheds were frequently built better than the houses, for chickens were more valuable than children. Children *ate;* chickens and eggs were to *be* eaten.

Still, once darkness descended, it might be possible to get away. If he could overpower whatever guards the Voice had placed around him. If he could find a way out of the shed!

If he could get past the Voice himself. There were stories that the Voices had other powers than plucking the thoughts from a man's head—stories that they commanded the services of demons tamed by the Sunlord—and he knew those stories were true. He'd *heard* the Night-demons ranging through the dark, off in the far distance. No dog ever produced those wails, no wolf howled like *that*, and no owl conjured those bone-chilling shrieks from its throat. And once, from a distance, he'd seen the result of one of those hunts. Whatever the demons had left behind wasn't human anymore…

While he lay there gathering his wits, another smell invaded the shed, overpowering even the stench of old bird-droppings. A sharp, thick smell. It took a moment for him to recognize it.

But when he did, he clawed his way up the wall he'd been thrown against, to stand wide-eyed in the darkness, nails digging into the wood behind him, heart pounding with stark terror.

Oil. They had poured earth-oil, the kind that bubbled up in black, sticky pools in this area, around the foundations, splashed it up against the sides of the shed. And now he heard them out there, bringing piles of dry brush and wood to stack against the walls. The punishment for witchery was burning, and they were taking no chances; they were going to burn him now.

The noises outside stopped; the murmur of voices faded as his captors moved away—

Then the Voice called out, once—a set of three sharp, angry words—

And every crack and crevice in the building was outlined in yellow and red, as the entire shed was engulfed in flames from outside.

Alberich cried out, and staggered away from the wall he'd been leaning against. The shed was bigger than he'd thought—but not big enough to protect him. The oil they'd spread so profligately made the flames burn hotter, and the wood of the shed was old, weathered, and probably dry. Within moments, the very air scorched him; he hid his mouth in a fold of his shirt, but his lungs burned with every breath. His eyes streamed tears of pain as he turned, burning, staggering, searching for an escape that didn't exist.

One of the walls burned through, showing the flames leaping from the wood and brush piled beyond it. He couldn't hear anything but the roar of the flames. At any moment now, the roof would cave in, burying him in burning debris—

:Look out!:

How he heard the warning—or how he knew to stagger back as far as he could without being incinerated on the spot, he did not know. But a heartbeat after that warning shout in his mind, a hole opened up in the side of the shed with a crash. Then a huge, silver-white shadow lofted through the hole in the burning wall, and landed beside him. It was still wearing his saddle and hackamore—

And it turned huge, impossibly blue eyes on him as he stood there gaping at it. It? No. Him.

:On!: the stallion snapped at him. *:The roof's about to go!:*

Whatever fear he had of the beast, he was more afraid of a death by burning. With hands that screamed with pain, he grabbed the saddle-bow and threw himself onto it. He hadn't even found the stirrups when the stallion turned on his hind feet. There was a crack of collapsing wood, as fire engulfed them. Burning thatch fell before and behind them, sparks showering as the air was sucked into the blaze, hotter...

But, amazingly, no fire licked at his flesh once he had mounted...

Alberich sobbed with relief as the cool air surged into his lungs—the stallion's hooves hit the ground beyond the flames, and he gasped with pain as he was flung forward against the saddlebow.

Then the real pain began, the torture of half-scorched skin, and the broken bones of his capture, jarred into agony by the stallion's headlong gallop into the night. The beast thundered toward the villagers, and they screamed and parted before it; soldiers and Voice alike were caught unaware, and not one of them raised a weapon in time to stop the flight.

:Stay on,: the stallion ordered grimly into his mind as the darkness was shattered by the red lightning of his own pain. *:Stay on, stay with me; we have a long way to go before we're safe. Stay with me...:*

Safe where? he wanted to ask, but there was no way to ask around the pain. All he could do was to hang on, and hope he could do what the horse wanted.

Through the darkness, under a moonless sky, through cold that froze him as his burns made him feverish. Pain became a constant; he'd have screamed, but he hadn't the strength, wept, but his eyes were too sore and dry. Yet Alberich was no stranger to pain; it could be endured, and he *would* endure it. It could be conquered; he would not allow it to conquer him.

Somewhere in the midst of the living nightmare, came the thought that if he lived through this, his own mother would never recognize him, he'd been burned so badly. He would forever wear a face seamed by scars.

An eternity later—dawn rising as red as the flames that had nearly killed him—the stallion had slowed to a walk. Dawn was on their right, which meant that the stallion was heading north, across the border, into the witch-kingdom of Valdemar. Which only made sense, since what he'd thought was a horse had turned out to be one of the blue-eyed witch-beasts...

None of it mattered. Now that the stallion had slowed to a walk, his pain had dulled, but he was exhausted and out of any energy to think or even feel with. What could the witches do to him, after all? Kill him? At the moment, that would be a kindness, and anyway, it was only what his own people wanted to do to him...

The stallion stopped, and he looked up, trying to see through the film that had come over his vision. At first he thought he was seeing double; two white witch-beasts and two white-clad riders blocked the road. But then he realized that there were two of them, hastily dismounting, reaching for him.

He let himself slide down into their hands, hearing nothing he could understand, only a babble of strange syllables.

Then, in his mind—

:Can you hear me?:

:I—what?: he replied, without thinking.

:Taver says his name's Alberich,: came a second voice in his head. *:Alberich? Can you stay with us a little longer? We need to get you to a Healer. You're going into shock; fight it for us. Your Companion will help you, if you let him.:*

His what? He shook his head; not in negation, in puzzlement. Where was he? All his life he'd heard that the witches of Valdemar were evil—but—

:And all our lives we've heard that nothing comes out of Karse but brigands and bad weather,: said the first voice, full of concern, but with an edge of humor to it. He shook his head again and peered up at the person supporting him on his right. A woman, older than he, with many laugh lines etched around her generous mouth. She seemed to fit that first voice in his head, somehow... she was smaller than he, diminutive in fact, but she had an aura of authority that was all out of proportion to her height.

:So which are you, Alberich?: she asked, as he fought to stay awake, feeling the presence of the stallion (his Companion?) like a steady shoulder to lean against, deep inside his soul. *:Brigand, or bad weather?:*

:Neither... I hope...?: he replied, absently, clinging to consciousness as she'd asked.

:Good. I'd hate to think of a Companion Choosing a brigand to be a Herald,: she said, with her mouth twitching a little, as if she was holding back a grin, *:And a thunderstorm in human guise would make uncomfortable company.:*

:Choosing?: he asked. *:What—what do you mean?:*

:I mean that you're a Herald, my friend,: she told him. *:Somehow your Companion managed to insinuate himself across the Border to get you, too. That's how Heralds of Valdemar are made; Companions Choose them—:* She looked up and away from him, and relief and satisfaction spread over her face at whatever it was she saw. *:—and the rest of it can wait. Aren's brought the Healer we sent him for, when Taver told us you were coming. Go ahead and let go, we'll take over from here. If a Healer can't save you with three Heralds to support him, then he's not worth the robe he wears.:*

He took her at her word, and let the darkness take him. But her last words followed him down into the. shadows, and instead of bringing the fear they should have given him, they brought him comfort, and a peace he never expected.

:It's a hell of a greeting, Herald Alberich, and a hell of a way to get here—but welcome to Valdemar, brother. Welcome…:

PART ONE

EXILE'S CHOICE

1

He was not dead. That much, at least, he was certain of.

At times, between the long moments when he was unaware of anything, he hurt quite enough to be in Hell, but Hell was cold and dark, and he wasn't cold. And the few times he was able to open his eyes, the room he was in was bathed in sunlight.

He couldn't be in Heaven either; if he was in Heaven, he wouldn't hurt. That was one thing that everyone agreed on; in Heaven was an end to all pain and sorrow. Pain he had in plenty, and as for sorrow— well, he'd consider sorrow when the pain ended.

Therefore, he must be alive.

The rest of what was going on around him—well. It was a mix of what he thought was hallucination, and what surely must be madness. Now, that fit with Hell, except that there weren't any demons tormenting him, only his own flesh.

Around him, voices muttered in a tongue he did not understand, but inside his head, another voice murmured, imparting to him the sense of what he heard. And that was where the madness came in. That voice, low and strong and uncompromisingly masculine, informed him that *he*, Alberich, sworn to the service of Karse and Vkandis Sunlord, the One God—

—was now a Herald of Valdemar. And the voice belonged to his Companion, one Kantor.

Impossible.

Not at all, the voice insisted. It began to wear at his stubborn refusal; he could feel his objection thinning. It clearly was *not* impossible because it had happened. He might not *like* it, but it was not impossible.

He slept, woke hurting, was murmured over and moved, fed and cleaned, the pain ebbed, and he slept again. From time to time the bandages on his face were taken off and he could open his eyes for a little. He was in a cheerful room that seemed to be tiled, and the bed he was on was soft and comfortable—which was good, because his face and arms were in agony, his lungs stabbed with every breath he took, and if he didn't have broken collarbones, they were at least cracked. When he could see, there were generally two or three green-clad people in the room with him, and he seemed to recall that outside of Karse, there were Healers who generally wore green. So apparently—if he wasn't delirious—he was being tended to, outside of Karse, by foreign Healers. So whatever had happened, he wasn't in Heaven, or Hell, or prison—which *had* been a third option, after all. Over and over he slept to wake in pain, was given something that stopped the pain, and slept again; there was no way to tell how much time had passed, and no way to sort what he *knew* had happened from what the voice was telling him.

Except that, bit by bit, the words being spoken over his head became more intelligible, as if the language was slowly seeping into his fever-ravaged brain. This tongue—this arcane language—was like *nothing* he could have imagined. The syntax was all wrong, for one thing; these people spoke—backward, sort of. Not that he was any kind of a linguist, but for a long time he was confused as much by the *order* of the words as the words themselves…

He *must* be in Valdemar. The language was as twisted about as the Demon-Riders and their Hellhorses, with the verbs coming in the middle instead of properly at the end. How could you tell what a sentence was truly about if you stuck the verb in the middle? The meaning could be entirely reversed by what came afterward!

How was he learning these things? What demonic magic was putting them inside his brain? Or was this all a fever dream, and was he lying in the embers of the chicken-shed, dying of his burns, conjuring all of this up? He *had* saved the village with his witch-power, he *had* been condemned to burn by a Voice, he *had* been imprisoned and his prison set afire. But after that?

Madness, illusion, hallucination, delirium.

Surely.

But the voice in his head told him otherwise, and as the moments of his lucidity came more and more often, it began to tell him things he could verify for himself—little things, but none of which he could have hallucinated for himself. That, for instance, the reason why he was not able to open his eyes very often was because they had been bandaged shut—at first, the skin of his face hurt so much he hadn't actually felt the bandages. And the skin of his hands was in such agony that he tried not to move them to touch anything, much less his face, which he wouldn't have wanted to touch anyway, given how much it hurt. The voice warned him when he was to be fed, and what they were going to give him—all soup, of course, and juices, and very, very often. The voice warned him when his bandages were to be changed—long before one of those Healer-people even got within hearing distance. And the voice told him about a great many other things.

:There is a large crow outside your window, Chosen,: it would say. *:It is about to sound an alert, so do not be startled and jump, or you will hurt.:* And sure enough, a crow *would* burst out with a raucous shout, but since he'd been warned, he was able to keep still. Or— *:The Healers have come with a new potion for you, to soothe your burns. They think this will hurt so much that they intend to give you an especially strong dose of pain-medicine.:* And indeed, he would then hear footsteps, feel himself tilted up, and he would drink what was put to his lips quickly, because the last time they had come up with a new potion for his burns, the pain had been excruciating.

He had always been a great believer in empirical evidence, and here it was. Slowly, and with great reluctance, he began to sort through his confused memories. With even greater reluctance, he had to accept that what he thought was madness and delirium was nothing of the sort.

So during one of his moments of relative lucidity, he steeled himself, and confronted the voice.

Relative was the operative term—he felt that he *should* be angry, embittered, but there were drugs interfering with those emotions, keeping him oddly detached. Perhaps that was just as well. He needed to think clearly, unemotionally, and this was as close to doing so as he was likely to manage. He coughed, hoping to clear his throat, but the voice in his head forestalled his attempt to speak aloud.

:Don't, Chosen. You don't need to actually say *anything. Just think it.:*

Think it. Well, he talked to himself in his mind all the time; this shouldn't be any different.

:It isn't, except that when you get an answer, you needn't be concerned that madness runs in your bloodline. Not that it's likely that it was true madness that struck your father, all things considered. If it were my case to judge, I would have looked very carefully at his wife's family, and considered all the reasons they might have had for saying he was mad…:

He'd have winced, if he hadn't known how much wincing would hurt. How had this voice—

:Kantor, Alberich. My name is Kantor.:

Kantor, then. *How* had this being known about his past?

:You've been quite generous in sharing your memories.: A hint of dry irony. *:Actually, you've been shoving them down my throat. I know that your mother was not married, that your father was a prominent man in your village and she anything but. I know that he was her only lover and that at some point when you were very young, he was sent away with your priests, supposedly mad.:* Alberich would have been flushing, had his face not been so painful. He was embarrassed—but embarrassed because he had been essentially blurting out every detail of his past life to a stranger, like the sort of drunk who would sit down next to you and begin telling you everything you *didn't* want to know. The very idea made him a little sick. *:Not that I mind, truly.:* the voice continued earnestly. *:It's only that Herald and Companion usually grow to know each other in a more leisurely manner—and as yet, you know very little of me.:*

Another suppressed wince. He didn't really want to know anything about this—Companion—did he? No. He didn't. This was a place full of witches—

—*of which you might be one*—

—and demons, and Vkandis only knew what other sorts of horrible creatures—wasn't it? Surely it was—

:Nonsense. You may be many things, Alberich, but a coward isn't one of them. I've asked the Healers to halve your pain-medicines, so that we can have this little discussion without the drugs interfering. There are several truths that you will have to face today, and the first of them is that virtually everything you think you know about Valdemar is wrong.:

Actually, the unsteady realization of that had been trickling down into his mind for the past—however long it had been. It had probably started when he'd fallen into the arms of those white-clad riders just over the Border. If they'd been half as evil as the Priests painted them, he'd have been roasting in chains right now, with demons nibbling at his soul.

:Excellent. That's another thing that you aren't—stupid. Those weren't just any Heralds, by the way. One was the King's Own Herald Talamir, and the other was the Lord Marshal's Herald, Joyeaus. We stumbled onto the end of a rather sensitive diplomatic mission, it seems.: There was a hint of a chuckle, and Alberich got the distinct impression that they hadn't merely "stumbled" into those particular Heralds—that Kantor had aimed himself quite deliberately in their direction. *:Well, no harm done.:*

He gathered his wits, and *thought* a question. *:I do not suppose that the* rank of our rescuers has anything to do with the speed with which I was taken to further help?:

The impression of a knowing smile. :Not entirely. All Heralds are considered highly important. Even the newly Chosen.:

He let that settle into his mind. :Even Karsites?:

:Well, since we've never had a Karsite Herald before, there's no basis for comparison.: There was a definite undertone there. Alberich decided that he was getting rapidly better at reading around what Kantor was actually telling him to what Kantor would rather just—imply. The undertone was that not everyone would have been as... open to the possibility of an ally out of Karse... as Heralds Talamir and Joyeaus.

:Excellent again. I do believe we are rather well-matched, Chosen. I would not go so far as to say that other Heralds would have run you through on sight—but we have been fighting a rather nasty undeclared war with you for some time, and there are some hard feelings on our side of the Border as well as yours, even among Heralds.: A sense of pondering followed that statement. :In truth, especially among Heralds, since your lot enjoys killing us so very much. Now no Herald would ever slaughter someone who had been Chosen out-of-hand—but there are many, many of them who are not going to welcome you as a long-lost sibling.:

Just his good fortune that he'd never led troops against anything other than bandits, then. At least no one would be holding a personal grudge against him.

He licked lips that were dry and cracked, and stared into the darkness behind his bandages. Inexorably, it was creeping up on him, acceptance that he could never go home again.

He was in the enemy's land, he was exiled inexorably from his own. He had witch-powers, and they were not the curse he'd been taught that they were. And one of the Hell-horses—which were not hellish at all, apparently—had selected him to become one of the Demon-Riders.

:Please, Alberich. Heralds, not Demon-Riders. And as for my being hellish—: a pregnant pause,:—well, although the people of Valdemar would say that we Companions are the sweetest, most marvelous of creatures, I suspect that the several of your men who got in my way would agree that I am "hellish." Assuming any of them survived the experience.:

Oh.

On the other hand, if one of them had been that Voice—

:He was,: came the reply, with a certain grim glee. :Though I am not certain that anyone like that Voice of yours—someone who goes about blithely burning people alive—has any right to make any judgments about who is "hellish" and who isn't.:

Ah...

:The fact that you have never personally fought against us will be useful towards having you accepted,: Kantor agreed. *:And there is at least one thing I can promise you. We will never, ever, under any circumstances, ask or require you to do anything against your conscience with regard to your homeland. I shan't promise we won't ask you to act against those in power there—:*

Just at the moment, he'd rather like to have the skinny or fat necks of some of those in power between his hands.

:Well put.: Kantor seemed satisfied with his answer. *:Now, the Healers will have my tail for a banner if I don't let them drug you again, so I'll ask you to mull this discussion over while you drowse, and we'll have another little talk in a bit.:*

He couldn't have objected if he'd wanted to, and he didn't want to, because the pain was getting unbearable and he heard the welcome footsteps of someone bringing him relief. After a quick, nasty-tasting draught, he was drifting again, cast loose from consciousness and what he'd always thought of as "The Truth"... a state in which it was easier to contemplate a new set of truths—or at least, truisms—in place of the old.

He dreamed.

He sat in the midst of a vast expanse of flowering meadow, flooded in a haze of light that made it difficult to see for any great distance. He was warm, comfortable, without pain of any kind, and—completely alone. He rose, and started to walk, wading knee-deep through wildflowers and herbs that gave off a hundred luscious scents as he brushed them aside. No matter how far he walked, however, the scene never changed, and he never found a path. The only living things were the plants; there were not even insects or birds. He felt no hunger, no thirst, no weariness; this fit every description of Paradise that he'd ever heard—except that there was no one in this Paradise but himself.

As beautiful and peaceful as this place was—he was trapped here. And he came to realize, as he walked on in the thick golden light, that the peace came at the price of *being* unable to escape, and completely alone. Not Paradise. Not even close.

That was the end of the dream. As abruptly as it had begun, it was over, and Alberich dropped out of the meadow and into the usual fever dreams that he had fought since being brought here.

From fever dream, he moved into welcome dreamlessness, and from then into the pain that always woke him when his medicines wore off. But it was not as bad as it had been, and he knew that the drugs being given him were not as strong as they'd been at first. Someone gave him a different-tasting drink, then, and he drowsed for a bit.

Sometime later, he woke to the sound of someone—no, two people—walking into his room.

"Is he awake?" asked a voice that was strange to him.

"He should be. I gave him a draught that should—well—sober him up completely," replied one that was more familiar—one of the Healers who spent a great deal of Alberich's waking time with him. There was a touch on his chest, where there were no bandages other than the ones holding his cracked ribs in place. "Sir, I am going to take off the bandages on your eyes, and leave them off. The skin there is healed enough that you needn't have them on anymore."

"I understand," he said, stumbling over the foreign words. The Healer moved him as gently as could be, propped him up with cushions, and took off the bandages. Alberich blinked, and squinted in the sunlight, taking his first proper look at the room he'd been in for—well, he didn't know how long.

And now that he was thinking clearly, the very first thing he felt was a smoldering resentment.

A shaggy-haired man in stained and well-worn green robes was coiling up bandages at the foot of the bed, but Alberich had very little interest in him, or in the room itself at the moment. It was the other occupant of the room, the one sitting right beside him, that captured his attention.

This was a Demon-Rider.

:This is Talamir, the King's Own Herald,: Kantor corrected gently, speaking into his mind for the first time since he'd awakened.

Alberich's jaw tightened, but he tried to *look* at the man, rather than react to him. What he saw was a tall, a very tall, thin man with graying brown hair, perhaps forty or fifty years old, if Alberich's judgment was any good. His was a careworn, lean face, overlaid with gentle good humor, but with a strong chin that suggested a stubborn streak, and a determination it would not be wise to invoke if you intended to quarrel with him. And, of course, he wore that dreaded white uniform, the emblem of the enemy—a more elaborate version than Alberich thought prudent or practical for a fighting man—

:Those are Formal Whites. Talamir has just come from a Council session at the King's side. Defending your presence here in Valdemar, in Haven, in the ranks of the Heralds themselves, may I add.:

Alberich refused to be distracted from his careful scrutiny.

The uniform—*I would never don anything like this,* he told himself fiercely—a silver-laced, white-velvet tunic, with silver embroidery at the hems, over a heavy white samite shirt with wide sleeves caught in deep cuffs at the wrists, and white satin breeches. A wide, white leather belt ornamented with hammered silver supported a dagger in a matching sheath. He'd have called it foppish, except that it wasn't. But he could not imagine himself ever wearing anything so extravagant.

The fabric alone, if sold, could feed a family for a year—

:Ah. And, of course, the nobles of Karse, the wealthy merchants, the ranking Captains, and above all, the Voices of the Sunlord dress and live so very *austerely.:* came the unwelcome reminder.

"Well, you have been here some two weeks, sir," Talamir said, his hazel eyes scrutinizing Alberich just as closely as Alberich was examining him. "I'm sure you have been wondering."

"Wondering, yes," Alberich replied, giving away nothing, conceding nothing, offering nothing. Talamir sighed.

:You could be more gracious.:

"Alberich—yes, we know what your name is—you must know that *my* Taver has been talking virtually nonstop to *your* Kantor, and what Kantor knows about you, so do I." Talamir's eyes became very penetrating. "I know very well that you have a good command of our tongue now, and furthermore, your Kantor can easily explain anything you don't understand immediately. I should prefer not to spend this entire first interview fencing with you, if you please."

Well, that gave him the opening he'd been looking for. *"My* Kantor, it is?" he asked resentfully. "And when was there asking on my part, for this Choosing, this so-called *honor?"*

Talamir shrugged. "You could be dead right now," he pointed out. "Whether you consider it an honor or not, Kantor saved your life."

"For which blessing, to serve my enemy, I am bound?" There was a sour taste in his mouth, and his stomach muscles were so tight as to make his cracked ribs ache in protest. He'd not only been kidnapped, he had been reduced to simple-mindedness with drugs—but now that he was himself again, he had *no* intention of rolling over like a cowed dog and licking the hands of his captors.

"I was not aware that Valdemar had personally done you harm," said Talamir. "Nor was I aware that any citizen of Valdemar had hurt you. I was under the impression that *everything* untoward that had happened to you was the responsibility of the denizens of your own land. If you can point out to me who and what on this side of the Border has wronged you, I assure you it will be dealt with to your satisfaction."

"Even if it Kantor is?" he asked, and looked Talamir straight in the eyes.

There was silence in his mind.

"Kantor." Talamir gazed on him with astonishment. "Your Companion."

"Who under false pretenses and a disguise attached himself to me. Who carried me off, who brought me *here*, where I would not have gone had I a choice been given. Who—perhaps?—had to do somewhat with my witch-sight coming so clear, and in front of a Voice?" He saw Talamir wince and felt his own mouth tighten in grim satisfaction. "Who therefore could the cause be, that the Voice to the Fires condemned me?"

"You would be dead right now," Talamir repeated uncomfortably. "You couldn't have denied your Gift. With or without Kantor, sooner or later it would have betrayed you, and you would still have gone to the fires—"

"But my own death it was, and mine was the choice to face, or to escape it," he pointed out, anger and resentment coloring every word. "That choice, from me was taken. *Perhaps* the witch-sight I could have fought, taken from me also was the option to try. And in the first place, had not the witch-sight come upon me when and where it did, condemned I should not have been."

A village might have gone under the sword, though—

The silence that fell between them was as heavy and uncompromising as lead.

But it was not Talamir who answered him.

:*I am sorry, Alberich,*: said the voice in his mind humbly and full of contrition. :*You are absolutely in the right. You had a life and choices, and I took them from you. I shan't even bother to make all of the arguments that a Valdemaran would accept. You* aren't *a Valdemaran, and there is no reason you should accept them. For you, my actions were nothing less than arrogance and a smug certainty that I was in the right to run roughshod over you. All I can do is apologize, and try to make it right with you.*:

He closed his eyes, his own heart contracting at the hurt and pain in that voice, armoring himself against it with the anger and resentment in his. "A better way, there could have been found," he said aloud.

"In a sense," Talamir replied quietly, "this is between you and Kantor. But ultimately, all of us are responsible, so I must apologize as well. We take such pride in our freedom here—and then we turned around and robbed you of yours. With the best intentions in the world—"

"Even the Voice that to the Fires sent me, good intentions may have had," Alberich retorted, opening his eyes again. "If not to save *my* soul, then those souls about me."

Again, Talamir winced.

"Served my people, did I, and served them *well*," he continued, bitterness overflowing at the thought that he had been forced to abandon those villagers who depended on him to stand vigilant guard over their safety. "Who now, protect them will? The Voices? Ha! Those who willed, in my place to stand?" He glared, daring Talamir to answer him.

"I do not know," Talamir admitted quietly. "But I have already offered any remedy that you could ask. What do *you* suggest? Name it, and I will do my personal best to see it done."

In the face of such a reasonable answer, Alberich's anger suddenly collapsed, like an inflated bladder with a pin put to it. "I—" he began, and rubbed his eyes, faced with uncertainty of monumental proportions. "I know not."

"Would you have us undo what we have done?" Talamir persisted.

Alberich snorted. "And how? Return, I cannot. *Notorious*, I am, doubtless. If ever a time for remedy was, it now long past is."

Talamir sighed. "We tell our youngsters that Companion's Choice is irrevocable, and for life, but that is not—altogether—true. The bond can be broken between you, if you both want it broken badly enough. It will leave you—damaged. But it can be broken."

That held him silent for a moment. There was a bond between them? And if breaking it would leave *him* damaged, what would it do to Kantor? He thought about the pain in Kantor's mental words when the Companion apologized, and winced away from the very idea. No matter what had happened to him, he could not be responsible for creating more pain. "This moots nothing," he replied, stalling. "Nowhere to go now, have I."

Talamir nodded. "Well, in light of that—*would* you consider giving us—giving life here—a trial period? Surely no choice can properly be made without *all* the information you need. Once you know us as we are, *I* believe you will choose to remain in Valdemar, to choose the Heralds."

He opened his mouth, and closed it again, because, logically and unemotionally speaking, he honestly could not think of a good reason why he *shouldn't* do as the Herald asked.

:*I wish you would,:* said the wistful voice in his mind.

"In the Sunlord, I *still* believe—" he began, bringing up the only remaining stumbling block that occurred to him.

"That is not an issue." Talamir waved that objection aside. "It never was. But perhaps you would rather hear that from a true Priest of the Sunlord?"

He blinked. "A Voice of Vkandis? Here?"

"Not a Voice, Alberich—but I should let him speak for himself." Talamir murmured something to the Healer, who nodded and went to the door of this room. He passed out of it, and another, much older man stepped inside, accompanied by a second about Alberich's age.

Talamir rose, and offered his seat to the older man, who took it. "This is Alberich, Father Henrick," he said. "Alberich, this is Father Henrick, and Acolyte Gerichen, his assistant."

Alberich eyed them both with caution. Neither wore the red robes of a Voice, nor the black of an ordinary priest. Instead, the older man sported a similarly cut gown of fine, cream-colored wool, and the younger, a plainer robe of unbleached linen. Both had the familiar disk of the Sunlord on a chain that hung down over the breast of their robes, however.

"You serve Vkandis Sunlord?" he asked, rather doubtfully.

Father Henrick nodded gravely. "I was born in Asherbeg, Captain," he said, in unaccented Karsite. "I was taken into the service of the Sunlord when I was eight, and made a full priest at twenty. Even as you, I am a child of Karsite soil and I still serve the Sunlord. And at twenty-one—I was ordered to Cleanse three children from the Border village to which I had been assigned."

Alberich went very still. "And?" he asked.

The priest made a rude noise. "What sort of monster do you take me for, Captain?" he asked. "I couldn't of course; they were *children,* guilty of nothing more than having powers that the Voices find inconvenient! Instead of Cleansing them, I took them and escaped over the Border with them, where I met with a Herald who in turn took me to the temple here. We don't call it the Temple of Vkandis, of course; we refer to it as the Temple of the Lord of Light—but those who attend know it, and us, for what we are."

"Powers?" Alberich said, feeling very stupid all of a sudden, as his anger and resentment drained away, leaving nothing behind. "Inconvenient?"

Father Henrick looked as if he had gotten a mouthful of green mead. "Those abilities that *you* have been taught are witch-powers, and signs of the contamination of demons, are nothing more than—than inborn powers that a child has no more control over than he does over whether or not he will be a great musician, or a great cook, or a great swordsman."

"He doesn't?" Alberich asked, dumbly.

"Of *course* not," the priest snapped. "And when these powers are something that the Voices find *useful*, if the child is young enough to be trained, it is whisked into the temple rather than being burned! It is only those whose powers are of no use to the Son of the Sun, or who are too old to be molded into a pleasing shape, that are sent to the Flames!"

Alberich was glad that he was propped up by pillows, else he would have been reeling. The priest looked as if he had plenty more to say, but his assistant placed a cautionary hand on his arm. "Father, enough," the younger man said in Valdemaran. "This poor fellow looks as if you had just stunned him with a club."

In truth, that is exactly what Alberich felt like. "I—" he faltered. "I—had no notion."

"You are not a stupid man, Captain," the old priest said roughly. "And you have a mind young enough to be flexible, if you will it. Try opening it."

He flushed at the rebuke, and felt horribly uncomfortable. This priest reminded him all too clearly of the old priest of his home, a crusty old man who had the respect of everyone in the village, and whose speech was as blunt as his common sense was good. So well was he regarded, despite a short temper and curmudgeonly demeanor, that when a Voice wished to have him replaced by a younger man, the entire village rose up in protest, and the scheme was abandoned.

"But—" he began, in an attempt to explain himself that he knew before he started would be futile.

"But, indeed. You have been given a great gift, Alberich of Karse, a gift that can serve you *and* our people, an opportunity that will lead—well, I cannot tell where it will lead." The old man glared at him from beneath bushy eyebrows. "There is a reason for all of this, I am *sure* of it, as sure as I am that it is men, and not the Sunlord, who have made Karse and Valdemar enemies. You say that you want to help our people? Our people are led by frauds and charlatans! Half, if not more, of the Voices are false, and every high-ranking priest is corrupt! And now this happens, a soldier of Karse is Chosen to be a Herald of Valdemar, and I doubt not it is by the will of the Sunlord himself. Does that not seem like the Hand of the Sunlord Himself to you?"

Alberich was covered in confusion. "I cannot tell—"

"Well, then trust that I can," the old man snapped. "This is a gift, an opportunity beyond price. If you piss it away, I shall be *most* angry with you. And rest assured that when the time comes and you stand before Vkandis' Throne, *He* will ask you why you threw away the gift He placed in your hands. For the God's sake, man, can't you see your sacred duty when it stares you in the face?"

Faced with that stern face of authority—of *legitimate* authority—what could he do or say? He tried to wrench his gaze away from the priest's eyes so that he could think—and found that he couldn't. "But I was given no *choice*—" he tried to protest.

The priest snorted. "Don't be daft," he retorted. "You could have stayed there to die, and you didn't. You made your choice when you sensibly took the rescue that was offered. And as for having your life interfered with, balderdash. If your Companion had never sought you out and *that* particular Voice hadn't discovered your Gift—the thing you call a witch-power—another would have. Only this time, there would have been no rescue. And what is more, your so-called guilt *could* have been used to bring others to the Fires, others who were innocent of anything except supporting you."

Talamir was standing very patiently to one side, pretending to pay no attention to what was going on. Although—Alberich had to wonder, given what he'd said about the Companions talking to one another and to him, if he wasn't managing to follow the entire conversation despite having no working knowledge of Karsite.

The priest glared a moment longer, then abruptly, his expression softened. "Lad, you're angry and resentful that your life has been turned upside down; you wouldn't be human if you weren't. You're bitter and in despair at being betrayed; you should be, but be bitter at the right people, not those who want only your welfare. If you're not frightened at being caught up in something you don't understand, I'd be very much surprised, and I'd suspect that one of those blows to your head had addled your wits. Now you think you're utterly alone. Well, you're not."

"I didn't know about you until a moment ago," Alberich began.

The old man shook his head. "That wasn't what I meant. I've been living here for better than forty years, and I've learned a thing or two about Heralds. No—I meant something else entirely. Open your heart—and I mean, really *open* it—to your Companion, and you'll see what I mean."

Alberich meant to shake his head in denial, but another stern look from the priest killed the gesture before he could make it. "Don't argue," he said. "Don't think of an excuse. Just do it. And while you're at it, open your mind as well as your heart."

The old man rose. "I'll be going now, but if you need me, they know where to find me, or where to send *you* if you'd prefer, once you're on your feet. For that matter, I'm sure your Companion would have no difficulty finding me wherever I happened to be without you having to ask anyone but him."

With that, he nodded to Talamir and shuffled out, followed by his acolyte. The door closed behind them, and Alberich stifled a sound that was midway between a sigh and a groan.

His sacred duty to join the Heralds, was it?

Hard words, thrown in the face of one who had lived his life by cleaving to duty, sacred or not.

Hard words, spoken by one who had been forced to abandon a potentially better life than anything ahead of Alberich, because he could not reconcile *orders* with *duty*. If anyone had a right to be bitter, it was the priest, but there was no bitterness behind that rough-hewn exterior manner. And no duplicity either. Nothing but unvarnished, unadorned truth, as the old man had seen it.

As he sees it—

But with forty years more experience of this place than Alberich had.

He swore under his breath.

"Pardon?" Talamir said. "I didn't quite hear what you said."

Alberich was going to growl "Nothing—" and then changed his mind.

"I said, make a trial of you, I shall," he answered—so brusquely, even rudely, that he was surprised that Talamir didn't take offense.

But the Herald didn't. "Good," he said instead, and moved to follow in the steps of the priest and his helper. But he turned when he got the door opened.

"In that case, there is one thing I should like to ask you to do," he said, with another of those measuring looks. "Before the Healer returns, I should like you to open your mind to Kantor. Completely. I think—I hope it will make a difference to you."

He left the room then, without waiting for Alberich's answer.

But then, given that the priest had virtually ordered Alberich to do the same thing, he probably didn't need to wait. He already knew that— eventually, at least—Alberich would make a trial of that, too.

Eventually. In his *own* time.

2

The Healer fussed over him for a bit, then prepared to leave; on a low table, within easy reach, were a pitcher of water, a cup, and a vial of one of the pain-killing potions. "Take it when you need it and are ready to sleep," the Healer told him. "Or not at all, if that's your choice. But drink the water."

Alberich couldn't tell if the man's brusque manner was his ordinary demeanor, or due to discovering where Alberich had come from. It could be both… and maybe, now that he knew Alberich was from Karse, he might be having second thoughts; maybe that wasn't just an ordinary pain-killing potion.

On the other hand, the man was leaving him with the potion *and* giving him the option of drinking it, or not. Unlikely that it was poison—why waste all that time and effort in healing him just to poison him? If the situations were reversed, a "guest" of the Sunpriests would likely not be treated at all, much less given a comfortable room *and* pain-killing drugs.

"The potion will wear off about dinnertime if you choose to drink it," the Healer continued. "It's about time for you to start feeding yourself again instead of having someone ladle broth into you."

Evidently, they were ready to see the last of him. Well, the feeling was mutual. Alberich was more than ready to do without Healers altogether. Already he'd had more attention for his injuries now than he'd ever had for every other injury in his life combined.

Then the man left, closing the door behind him, leaving Alberich alone in his tiny cell of a room.

Not that his quarters in the barracks—when he'd actually been *in* them, which was rare—were any larger. But the two rooms could not have been more different.

The outer wall of this room held a large window with actual glass panes in it; the wall directly opposite held the door. The other two walls were blank, and the room was tiled in a pale gray-green. A restful color, if a trifle dull. Tiles on a wall, though; that was something odd.

For furnishings, well, there were the bed he was on, a little three-legged table, and a stool to match. Not much need for a clothes chest in a sickroom, he supposed. He was, he discovered, wearing only smallclothes beneath his blankets and sheet. And they weren't even his smallclothes. Everything about him that was Karsite was gone.

On the other hand, perhaps that was just as well. The less to mark him as the enemy, the better.

From where he was lying in bed, all he could see was a single white cloud, a mere wisp of a thing, drifting from one side to the other. Not a very inspiring view. In fact, there was nothing much in this place to occupy the mind.

Suddenly, he wanted to actually look out that window. He wanted to see more than just sky and clouds. He felt stifled; this was the longest period of time that he had spent without seeing the outside world since—well, he couldn't remember. Even when he'd been a cadet, he'd been outside, riding, exercising, training. Even when he'd been hurt before, he'd been in his own quarters, able—indeed, expected—to get about and take up light duties.

His hands were still bandaged, but lightly, and they didn't hurt so much anymore. He could use them—carefully. Well, the sooner he got out of bed, the sooner he'd finish healing. Gingerly, he slid his legs out from under the covers and put his feet on the cold tiled floor, sitting straight up on the edge of the bed. There was a painful twinge in his chest; an ungentle reminder of broken ribs.

Nothing wrong with my legs, anyway. There were some pink patches—healing burns—but at least no one had broken any foot or leg bones when they'd beaten him. A good thing, too—if his leg had been broken, he'd never have been able to get onto Kantor's back, now, would he?

He'd been hurt in the line of duty often enough to know to pause after every movement to see how badly he felt. There was no point in undoing the work of healing by passing out and falling on the floor because he tried to leap out of bed like a healthy person. So he hesitated for a moment with his feet chilling on the tiles, testing for a sign of weakness, waiting for his vision to blur or fade out. But other than those twinges, he was fine. So far, so good.

Now the true test; standing up. If *that* didn't make him pass out, nothing would…

It didn't. Now to get to the window.

Moments later—moments that had felt like far longer, as half-healed bits of him protested his movement vehemently with every step—he stood at the window, sweating, shaking, but looking out.

What he saw was not what he had expected.

He supposed he would look out on an enclosed courtyard, certainly something with high walls around it. Surely they would not have put him inside anything less secure. Instead, he saw gardens, wonderful gardens, and they were extensive enough that he couldn't see the walls that must certainly be there. These were no common pleasure parks or bits of waste ground for just anyone to stroll about on.

Directly beneath his window was a graveled path, bordered on either side with a low herbaceous hedge. To either side of *that* were trees in ornamental clumps, with planted beds of foliage arranged around and among them.

The gardens themselves must have been very old, for the trees looked ancient, the grass as smooth and even as plush, the bushes and flowering plants as if they had been there since the beginning of time. There were stone benches and individual seats placed to best enjoy sun or shade, and lanterns hung from wrought-metal stands beside the benches. Nowhere were there fences to keep people away from the plantings, or even confine them to the paths, except for that little hedge, and it wasn't even knee-high. Once or twice, Alberich had seen gardens like this behind the homes of the wealthy, but never this extensive.

His room was on the second floor of this building, giving him an elevated view; it was a uniquely advantageous one for determining what his surroundings were like. There must have been a door directly below his window, for the path led up to it, and people were entering and leaving from directly below where he stood. *Young* people, he saw with a start. They wore tunics and trews, or long robes, in a paler color of green than the Healer he had seen. Some of them couldn't be older than ten!

:Those are Healer-trainees,: said Kantor tentatively. *:Where we are—it's Healer's Collegium, where young Healers are taught, as well as being a House of Healing. You're on the grounds of a complex that includes Herald's Collegium, where the Heralds are trained, Healer's Collegium, and Bardic Collegium. And the Palace. That's why all the gardens, of course; the pleasure gardens for the Palace, the herb gardens for the Healers, and kitchen gardens. They're open to everyone within the walls.:*

The Palace! They allowed *him*, a Karsite, to be within the same walls that enclosed the Palace? Granted, he was hurt, but still—*if* he were an assassin, he wouldn't let a little thing like that stop him! And most of the time he was unwatched, unguarded—how could they possibly trust him?

:You're with me,: Kantor replied simply.

The simple, bald statement took him utterly by surprise. He was "with" Kantor—and these people considered that to be enough to trust him within reach of the rulers of their land.

He recalled the attitude of the Healer and revised that. *Some* of them considered that to be enough.

Or maybe he is just like that with all of his patients.

He looked out on the gardens for a little, before answering. *:So these people train Healers in one central place?:*

:Mostly. Sometimes they apprentice with an older Healer, or are trained at one of the Temples of Healing, especially if they are uneasy about leaving their homes, but that's rare. We prefer that our Healers come here to learn so that we know that they've gotten a standard education—and any special training that their Gifts and talents might warrant.: Kantor paused. *:Would you rather that I not speak to you this way?:*

He thought about it for a moment; it seemed to him that this sharing of thoughts *should* have seemed like a violation, yet it didn't. He couldn't account for that very foreign feeling—unless, perhaps, he'd gotten used to it while he was semiconscious, so now it just didn't raise the instinctive alarm in him that it ordinarily would have. And he could not deny how useful it was to be able to silently speak and ask questions about this place and these people. *:No—I would rather you helped me. I said that I would give all of you a trial; I don't know that I can manage that without you. But—where are you?:*

:Right here.: He would not have believed that anything as big as a horse could have hidden itself virtually in plain sight—but there was just a little movement, and Kantor stepped into view through a screen of bushes. He was followed by two more of the white Companions, then another two. They all stood just below his window, to one side of the path, looking up at him with eyes so vivid a blue that even from here they struck him with their intensity. *:We're all five of us waiting for our Chosen to heal in there,:* he said, with wry humor. *:Heralds have a habit of winding up in the hands of Healers.:*

These people permitted horses in their formal gardens? He could just imagine the mess that would have caused in the garden of the Son of the Sun...

:We aren't exactly horses,: Kantor reminded him. *:And here, at the Collegia,*

people know they can trust us not to step on or eat the roses—or in this case, rosemary. Everyone here knows exactly what we are, and we can pretty much go where we wish and do what we want. Even into the Palace, if we need to.:

Alberich looked down on them with reluctant interest. Now, with four more of these "Companions" to compare Kantor with, it was very clear that Kantor was distinct among his kind. It hadn't been obvious how powerful he was when Alberich had only been comparing him with ordinary horses—

:There was some illusion on my part as well,: Kantor admitted sheepishly. *:I hid my eye color, for one thing.:*

—but the other four were—well, like graceful acrobats or dancers. Kantor was far more muscular, his head perhaps a bit blockier, his neck arched and strong, his hindquarters and chest definitely deeper and with fantastically developed muscles.

:I am a warrior, Companion to a warrior. My friends need speed and endurance more than they need strength; I need strength and sheer power as well as stamina. No matter where your duties take you, I will always be able to fight at your side and guard your back.: Kantor seemed very proud of that, and for the first time, Alberich felt himself warm to the creature, just a little. They had that much in common, at least.

A warrior, Companion to a warrior…

At the moment, he felt rather less than half of that. There was a growing feeling in his gut, as if he should be trembling, as if, in a moment, he *would.* He knew that feeling; it meant he was coming to the end of his reserves. In fact, it was becoming rather urgent to sit down. He was not going to be able to stand at all, soon. Maybe he shouldn't be surprised, considering all that had been done to him and how recently, but it did seem as if his reserves of strength were not what they should have been.

Then it dawned on him, why it was that he should feel weaker than expected—it had been a Healer, a *real* Healer, in the room with him. Presumably, the others who had cared for him were Healers as well. He hadn't just been physicked and doctored, he'd been Healed, as he would have been under the skilled ministrations of a Healer-Priest in a temple.

And that shocked him. They had actually gone so far as to have him Healed, not just wait for him to get better on his own, as had always happened in the past, except for one single time when he had been badly hurt in training—a pure accident, when a bolt of lightning hit the training field, killed three horses outright, and sent the rest into a blind panic, and he'd been thrown and trampled.

So no wonder he felt shaky, and weak in the knees; Healing took of your own strength and resources, speeding up what normally took days and weeks into hours and days. He probably even weighed a great deal less than he had when they'd brought him here! Small wonder the Healer wanted him to start feeding himself; there was no way that he could get enough nourishment to sustain Healing on broth.

:You should go back to bed,: Kantor admonished.

:I believe that I will. And take that pain potion the Healer left for me while I'm at it.: He knew that part of the drill well enough; it wasn't the first time he'd been hurt, though it *was* the first time it had been at the hands of his own people.

And that—

Well, just at the moment, he would rather go back to bed and to the oblivion promised by the pain potion than think about it.

Herald Talamir finished his informal report on the Karsite, and waited to see what his King would make of it.

"So. Our newest Trainee is not at all pleased about being Chosen, eh?" King Sendar asked—or rather, stated.

This was no formal audience, it wasn't even witnessed by another Herald, unless one counted the presence of Sendar's Heir, his daughter Selenay, who was halfway through her training as a Herald. They were all in Sendar's study, in the Royal Suite in the Palace—the *private* study, not the one where those who were not intimate with the Royal Family would see the King privately. This room had been the Queen's solar until Sendar appropriated it for himself; it faced south and looked out into the Queen's Garden, a courtyard that had no other entrance than the one in this room.

Roses still bloomed out there, beyond the glass, late though it was in the season, and it was home to other flowers and plants that needed tender sheltering from the worst of winter's wrath. It made a tranquil retreat for a harried monarch who wanted some peace—although there really was no way that Sendar could escape altogether from the troubles of the realm.

Talamir shook his head. "No, Sire, he's not," the King's Own replied regretfully. "I must confess, I'm at a loss as to how to proceed with him. This was hardly the response I expected."

He knew Sendar better than anyone else in Valdemar—probably better even than the late Queen had—but Sendar surprised him with his dry chuckle. "I'm not," the King said. "Truth to tell, I'm glad to hear it. I'm not certain I'd trust someone who would abandon everything he's believed in until now just because a talking horse tells him that he's been chosen to join the enemy."

"Oh," Talamir replied, blinking. "But—his own people nearly killed him in their Fires—I thought—"

"His own people had a perfectly good reason to burn him in their Fires, by their lights," Sendar pointed out, raising his eyebrow. "And sooner or later, he'll think of that for himself, assuming he hasn't already. Fine. Perhaps Kantor has managed to insinuate enough into his head while he's been Healing to make him a bit more receptive to us, but a thinking man doesn't just suddenly go over to the enemy without reasoning things through for himself. *And* it will eventually occur to him that just because Kantor is Mind-speaking to him, it doesn't necessarily follow that Kantor is telling him the truth. I would bet on that."

Talamir sensed Taver's surge of indignation at any such notion— and more remotely, sensed Sendar's Lorenil's amusement at both of them. Well, Lorenil always had possessed a strong sense of irony, not to mention a sense of humor that was positively sardonic. Rather like young Kantor in that regard.

"We're going to have to win this young fellow to us, old friend," Sendar said, as if he was completely comfortable with the notion. "We'll have to be completely honest with him, or he'll figure out we've been shading the truth for his benefit—but we'll also have to show him *why* we're trustworthy and his own people aren't. He'll have to come to the conclusion that we're telling him the truth and that he has a real and compelling reason to give us his loyalty all by himself. Anything heavy-handed, and we'll lose him."

Sendar leaned back in his chair—a modest affair of simple design and unornamented wood and leather, chosen for comfort rather than ostentation—and bestowed a penetrating look on the King's Own Herald. He and Talamir had known each other and been friends for a very, very long time.

In fact, their friendship dated from the hour that Talamir had been Chosen by Taver as King's Own Herald on the death of his predecessor—a premature death, brought on by too much stress, too much work, and a brainstorm. Talamir had been so young, uncertain in his office, and disoriented by the bond with Taver, which was *so* strong, and *so* life-altering.

Sendar, on the other hand, had been a very young King, but not at all uncertain in his office. Young, he might have been, but he'd been schooled in his duties since he could toddle. He'd been a handsome young man then, blond and tall and strong, with chiseled features worthy of a god, and an idealistic nature tempered with that finely-honed sense of irony. He was handsome still, though there was as much gray in his hair as gold, and age and care had continued to wield a cruel hand against those features, chiseling lines of worry that gave him a rather stern look. Kingly, but there was no doubt that people found him intimidating on occasion. His own sardonic sense of humor didn't help on those occasions; he rather enjoyed being intimidating now and again.

"He promised that he would give us a trial," Talamir told the King, knowing how Sendar would react. Sendar liked audaciousness; he'd loved it in his Queen, who had boldly proposed to *him* rather than the other way around, who had met every challenge, even the illness that killed her, with spirit and determination.

Sendar laughed as Talamir had expected, a dry little chuckle.

His daughter, Princess Selenay, who had been staring rather fixedly at nothing at all as she listened, made a face. "I don't see what's so funny," she objected.

Selenay might one day grow into the dry wit her father possessed, but at the moment, she was in a stage where she took everything quite seriously and earnestly. Talamir found that uniquely endearing, as did her father.

"Not funny, my dear—ironic," Sendar told her. "A Karsite, of all things, giving *us* a chance to prove our good intentions. If you'll recall your history, you'll know why that seems ironic."

Selenay hesitated, toying with the end of her single braid, then evidently decided to be as forthright as her father. "He must be a man of honor, or Kantor wouldn't have Chosen him, so why should *that* be ironic? Can't Karsites have men of honor, too? It seems to me he has every right to require us to prove ourselves."

"Perhaps because the Karsite leaders have broken every pact they ever made—and have even made war on their own people?" Sendar suggested mildly.

She flushed as Talamir gave her an opaque look, but persisted. "Why should that mean he shouldn't demand we prove ourselves, though? The Karsites—well, how much do we know about them? Next to nothing; maybe in *their* minds they had honorable reasons to break their pacts. I mean, I should think that this man would have *more* reason to be suspicious—"

Sendar shook his head.

:Chosen, don't just dismiss her because she's young,: Taver cautioned. Clearly, this had gone from a discussion of one man to a more abstract problem.

"Well, I still don't see why, just because there are a few bad people in charge of things in Karse, we should assume that nearly everyone that comes from there is bad," she said stubbornly. "Well, look, *one* of them has just been Chosen! I don't see why there shouldn't be as many men of honor there as here."

"The problem with that assumption is that once a man of honor sees what his leaders are doing is wrong, shouldn't it be incumbent on him to do something about it?" Talamir asked the princess, who made a little grimace of impatience. "With the sorts of things that the Sunpriests have been doing, even the most devout worshiper of Vkandis is going to run out of excuses for their excesses."

"What if he can't?" she asked. "Do something about it, I mean."

"If nothing else, he should leave," Sendar pointed out. "By giving his support to a bad leader, he reinforces the position of that leader. People see that *he* is good, and since he continues to act in support of the leader, however inadvertently, they assume there must be very compelling reasons for the leader to act as he is, and they continue to bear the intolerable."

Talamir nodded. Selenay looked uncertain, but not entirely convinced.

She'll learn, he decided. Experience, that was what she needed. "The point is that it's rather ironic, that *this* Karsite, who has already had his own leaders turn against him and try to execute him for the use of a Gift that has been the saving of their own people, should then expect us to prove ourselves to him. Not that we blame him at all, we just find it ironic."

"I can see that," the girl replied with a frown. "But I can also see *why* he has even more reason to want us to prove ourselves."

"What do you propose we do with this fellow?" Sendar asked, changing the subject. "There are bound to be objections to his presence once more people discover where he's from."

"I don't see any point in even trying to keep that a secret," Talamir replied, shaking his head. "It'll be out no matter what we do. It's a pretty problem, and one that isn't easily going to be solved. We can hardly expect people to set aside old grievances."

"It's one I wish we didn't have." Sendar looked as if he was getting a headache. "I suppose all these things happen for a reason, but I would be happy enough for this to be occurring in someone else's reign."

:Everyone always says that,: Taver observed.

Taver should know. *:I suppose they do.:*

"So, so, so. You and I have enough on our plate, I would say, without complicating our lives with this most difficult of Trainees." Sendar pursed his lips. "Who can we delegate to bring the young fellow over to our side and make him admit to himself that his own leaders didn't deserve his loyalty?"

"Gerichen," Talamir said, instantly. "That young Sunpriest. He's—" He groped for words. "He's transparent. Eventually, I suppose he'll learn to mask what he's thinking, but for now his openness will work for us."

"All very well, but what about within the Collegium?" Sendar persisted. "We need a Herald—"

"Jadus, I think. He's taking a turn at instructor this term. And Elcarth. Both of them are so utterly different from anyone Alberich will have encountered before." He thought for a moment longer. "I'll have to keep an eye on things, though. The instructors can hardly be expected to act as nursemaids to him. I'd like to assign another Trainee to him, but there just aren't any that are adult at the moment. I *can't* have anyone younger acting as his guide. He'll resent it—"

Sendar nodded, but Selenay spoke up.

"Make him my bodyguard," she suggested.

They both turned to stare at her.

"Well," she said defensively, "if you make him my bodyguard, *I* can help him to settle in. He won't be offended, and in fact, he'll probably be flattered. After all, it isn't as if a mere Captain would ever be made the personal guard to anyone important in Karse! Making him *my* guard will show that we trust *him,* and I think that could be very important in making him trust *us.* Don't you think?"

"Actually," Sendar said slowly. "Yes. I do."

"And while he's at it, he can teach me Karsite. *Someone* ought to know how to speak it."

:Brilliant,: Taver enthused. *:Absolutely brilliant!:*

"Even if the rest of the Council will have apoplexy?" Talamir asked dubiously.

Selenay raised her chin. "Yes. And I think you ought to tell them that this was my idea. They might as well get used to the notion that I can think for myself. I'm too old to be chucked under the chin and called 'little one' and told not to bother my pretty head about things."

Which is going to come as a shock to no few of them. Talamir kept his sighs strictly mental. Evidently the gods had decided that he was going to have to make do with fewer candlemarks of rest from now on—because he certainly was *not* going to leave all of this to the sole attention of Heralds Elcarth and Jadus, worthy though they might be.

"So be it." Sendar gave his blessing and dismissal all in one, despite Talamir's misgivings. Admittedly, though, the misgivings were all concerned with other people's reactions to Alberich, and not anything having to do with Alberich's trustworthiness. Kantor was convinced; so was Taver. That was all that Talamir needed. "Talamir, I'd like you to organize Elcarth and Jadus. Let them recruit Priest Gerichen, not you."

"Oh, that shouldn't be difficult," Talamir admitted. "I suspect that Gerichen's superior already has something like that in mind, since he brought the fellow along this afternoon on his official pastoral visit."

"Then once he's on his feet and ready to be integrated into the Collegium, Selenay, I'd like you to see to the bodyguard business," Sendar continued. His daughter nodded, her eyes bright.

"Easily done," she replied confidently. She looked like a cat that had just made off with an entire jug full of cream and a brace of trout to boot. *Very* pleased with herself.

:She should be,: Taver put in.

Perhaps—but she still seemed very young to him. Too young to be so closely involved with this potentially dangerous situation. He could readily foresee Council members suspecting that Alberich was subverting the young Heir…

:Yes, but that's supposed to be what she *is going to do to him,:* replied Taver. *:Really, Chosen, if you think that a healthy young* man *is going to be indifferent to an intelligent and attractive young lady, and isn't going to be influenced by her, you're very much mistaken.:*

:You have a point. And I'm sure the thought has crossed her father's mind as well,: he admitted.

He sensed Taver's amusement. *:There you have it. If you take that line with the Council, it will be clear that Sendar believes Selenay can handle the responsibility.:*

:True….: That would be all to the good.

:And if you point out it was her idea, it gives her more validity in her own right.:

:Also true.: He was glad that Sendar was seeing to it that Selenay was brought along as the Heir-in-fact as well as the Heir-in-name, but

it meant a lot of work. Still, better a lot of work now than trying to bring her up to the job later, in a crisis. Because kings, even the kings of Valdemar, were mortal, and no matter what the circumstances, King Sendar's death would precipitate a crisis.

"Now, is there any sign of a repercussion down there along the Karse Border from this incident?" Sendar asked, and Talamir gladly turned the subject to the simpler one of espionage reports and troop movements. Well, relatively simpler.

"At the moment, the best guess is that the incident has been completely suppressed," Talamir replied. "There are no reports, not even rumors, from what our informants can tell us. We don't even really know which little village Kantor won him out of, they're keeping it so quiet. We *think* it's Sunsdale, because that's the only one that recently beat off bandits, but there's no word of anyone escaping the Fires from there."

"It must be an acute embarrassment to them," Sendar speculated. "Good. Let's hope it stays that way. I would rather they didn't have any more excuses to prod at us down there."

"You have a talent for understatement, Majesty," Talamir replied, rubbing his brow absently with one knuckle. "'Prod' is not precisely how I would put it. But the mission you sent me on in the first place is a complete success; Joyeaus has got a Border-watch based on the old fire-watchtowers everywhere along the Border except on Holderkin lands— and there's enough overlap that nothing larger than a bandit troop is going to slip past, even there."

"Then the damned, stiff-necked Holderkin can fight off their own bandits," Sendar growled. "And may they wallow in their pride until they choke on it!"

Her father's outburst caught Selenay by surprise, and she directed a look of shock at Talamir. Talamir just raised his eyebrows in a silent signal that promised *I'll tell you later.* She nodded very slightly.

"Joyeaus promised that she can have word to Haven of *real* troop movements within half a day at the worst," he continued. "It isn't just on our side of the Border that those old watchtowers exist. We can see theirs, and they can see ours, and there has been unofficial cooperation among the foresters for generations about alerting each other to forest fires."

Sendar snorted. "Fire doesn't stop at the Border no matter how many guards you post."

Talamir nodded. "The point is, of course, that we *can* see their watchtowers, and now ours will be manned in or out of fire season. And we've got one more safeguard in place. If one of our informants has a message too urgent to be sent by hand and he can get to one of the fire towers, he'll light a fire beacon or flash a mirror—on *their* side. Not a big one, or for long, but it will be a signal. *That* will warn the local highborn that something is coming, and from what direction, which means we'll have even earlier warning, if not the specifics."

"Remind me to find some appropriate way to thank my idiot South-Border highborn for having the sense to cooperate with each other for a change," Sendar growled, though to Talamir's ears, the "growl!' sounded pleased and relieved.

"Remind me" actually meant "Talamir, go figure it out for me," of course. This time, however, it was a request that had been anticipated from the moment that Joyeaus had gotten all of the heads of the noble families to sit down at the same table and begin ironing out their differences. That young woman had the most remarkable talent for diplomatic maneuvering and soothing ruffled feathers that Talamir had ever seen. A touch of Empathy helped, of course, but mostly it was a knack for saying exactly the right thing at the right time, and being exquisitely sensitive to interpersonal nuances. She'd been utterly wasted on riding circuits…

"I'll see to it, Majesty," Talamir murmured, glad that there was at least *one* small task that would be relatively easy to discharge.

Unlike the untimely arrival of that unlikeliest of Trainees…

"Now, what about that tannery that Lord Wordercan wants to put in?" Sendar continued. "He's been nagging at me for the last week. I know it's something *he* wants, but I'm not sure the market can absorb that much more leather."

Talamir bent his mind to the business of the Kingdom, allowing himself to put the matter of Trainee Alberich aside for the moment—untimely, unlikely, and oh so inconvenient as he was…

3

Alberich looked dubiously into the mirror at himself. The Healers had done a better job on his face than he ever would have thought possible, but nevertheless, he was scarred, and scarred badly. He looked as if someone had beaten his face with a red-hot whip several years ago. At least the scars weren't a livid, half-healed red, or he'd be frightening children and horses. His weathered tan had faded as well in the time he'd spent recovering, and he was thinner, not that he'd been carrying any extra weight before. His cheekbones seemed especially prominent, and his mouth—

Still stubborn, and they'd damned well better read it that way.

He was wearing what was, apparently, the standard uniform for a Valdemaran cadet—

:A Herald-trainee,: Kantor corrected. *:I don't believe that you will find that cadets and Trainees are at all equivalent.:*

This uniform was very new, and in fact, had been made to his measure while he was still staggering about trying to get his strength back. Some strange little fellow had invaded his sickroom one day, asked him to stand, measured him all over, took tracings of his feet, and vanished again. Today, one of these uniforms had appeared, along with a gentle-faced Herald he didn't know, and Herald Talamir.

The cut and design of this uniform was identical to the Heralds' uniforms—well, all of the ones he'd seen other than Talamir's. The difference was the color—a dark gray. Alberich approved of that color; it was a great deal less conspicuous than spotless white. It also suited his own somber disposition.

"You cut a good figure," Talamir said approvingly. "But then again, we don't often tailor a Trainee's new outfits to him; it would be a waste of time and effort, since most of them are youngsters, still growing."

"This isn't the usual color for a Trainee," the strange Herald (who had been introduced as Jadus) said apologetically. "We're apparently out of the usual materials at the moment, and I'm afraid that you're a bit larger than our run of usual newly Chosen, so you wouldn't fit into the old ones from the common stock." The man was older than Alberich, approaching middle age, with sandy hair, and expressive features so open and honest that Alberich knew he would never hold his own in a game of chance. But the one thing that Alberich noticed most about him were his hands, graceful, flexible, strong, but not *powerful*. They were not the hands of a fighter, not even an archer.

The new Herald smiled and shrugged. "I suppose you're lucky, actually. When I say 'common stock,' it's because the uniforms are all parceled out by general sizes. Hand-me-downs, to be honest, worn until they aren't fit to wear anymore, and cycled among all of those who wear the same size. We find that it's not a bad thing, given that highborns or their families might be inclined to embellish any uniforms that were actually their property, which negates the whole point of having a uniform in the first place."

"Keeping to these, I think I will be," Alberich replied, and shrugged. "Conspicuous already, I am."

"True enough," Talamir agreed. "And perhaps by making you a trifle *more* conspicuous, we will at least make it evident that we aren't trying to hide you."

Alberich flexed his arms and legs experimentally. It might be new, but this uniform had been laundered several times to soften the fabric. Linen shirt, a fine pair of well-fitting boots, heavy canvas-twill trews and tunic. At least it was a comfortable uniform, practical and easy to move in. It could have been much worse.

He supposed that these garments would have to be made to take a considerable beating if they were to serve several sets of Trainees in their usual lifespan. Certainly Sunsguard Cadets were hard on *their* uniforms, and he doubted that Valdemaran boys would be any different.

:And girls,: Kantor reminded him.

Talamir excused himself; he had, after all, only come along to effect the introduction of Alberich to Jadus. That left the two men alone, in an awkward moment of silence. Alberich stared at the older man, wondering what *he* saw. Alberich could no more disguise what he was than Jadus could disguise what he felt.

"So," Alberich observed finally. "My keeper, you are?"

To his surprise, Jadus laughed. "Hardly that. No, actually, I'm one of your instructors, and since I have a smattering—a mere smattering, mind you—of Karsite, I was nominated to take you around to the Collegium, get you settled in, and introduce you to the rest of your instructors."

Alberich tried to keep his expression a neutral one, but he still wasn't at all happy about this whole "Collegium" business. *He* was the one giving *them* a trial, after all—so why all this business of putting him into the Collegium? Why couldn't he simply observe, quietly, so he could make an informed decision about what he would do next? Why start him on classes, when in a moon or two he might be shaking the dust of this place from his shoes? It seemed to be an exercise in futility, and one that might have a negative effect on people who would be wondering how much effort they should put into teaching him when the next day he might be gone.

Yet even as he thought that, he wondered. As he recovered, he'd had several visits from the earnest young Gerichen, who seemed convinced that none of this had been an accident, that the Sunlord Himself was behind all of this for some inscrutable purpose known only to the One God. He was trying, in his own self-deprecating fashion, to convince Alberich of this notion. Alberich was in something of a quandary over this.

On the one hand, he had difficulty imagining *why* the Sunlord would choose to put one of His Karsite people in Valdemar as a Herald, when there were better candidates who were *born* here. Surely someone who was Valdemaran was a better choice! He'd speak the language already, he'd know all about Heralds and probably be thrilled to be Chosen, and there would be no question of his being accepted by other Valdemarans.

On the other hand, Vkandis did not move to interfere in the lives of His worshipers often, but when He did—there was a reason. And who was Alberich to try and understand or second-guess the motives and actions of the One God? That would be hubris of the worst sort. If a Sunpriest thought *he* saw the Hand of the Sunlord in this, he might be right. In that case, the wisest and best thing that Alberich could do would be to humbly bow his head and accept what Vkandis intended for him.

But Gerichen was young. He might be right; he might be divinely inspired, but he might well be merely enthusiastic.

As for "settling in," that was proving far more difficult than any Valdemaran would be willing to accept. Alberich felt—well, he couldn't put a name to it. "Dislocated and adrift" was part of it; "unsettled" far too mild. "Utterly alien" came close, but didn't address the feeling of having no support beneath him. As if he were at the halfway point of a blind leap. It was far too late to go back, but he wasn't sure he'd land safely and he certainly didn't know what he'd find if he did. And that went for how he felt about the One God, too. For the first time, he'd had leisure to think about his religion and his own faith. He had questions. A great many of them. And none of them had answers.

For instance, if Vkandis wished to make peace between Karse and Valdemar, *why* not simply appear as He used to in the Great Temple? Why go to the trouble of having one single minor officer in the Sunsguard Chosen? It seemed an unreasonably convoluted path to follow to him.

But on the other hand—once again, the biggest stumbling block— who was *he* to be asking questions like that? He was only one man, one among many, who wasn't even a priest. How could *he* possibly know what was best for Karse?

But why had Vkandis Sunlord left His land to fester on its own for so long? What had happened to all the miracles, the appearances, of the ancient days? Where was the Sunlord, that he allowed his shepherds to turn wolf and prey upon their flocks?

He wrenched his mind away from the doubts and questions, and turned it squarely to face the here-and-now.

"You say, 'the rest of my instructors,'" he repeated carefully. "And it will take how long to learn to a Herald be?"

If I ever wish to do so, that is… There was one clear answer to *why* this Jadus had been chosen to play guide to him. There was nothing intimidating at all about the man, and nothing of duplicity either. At least they were holding to their promise; they would let him decide for himself with no pressure on *their* part.

The Herald rubbed the side of his nose with one long finger. "For the usual Chosen, who come in here at about age thirteen or fourteen, and who are lacking in a lot of skills you already have, it takes about five years. For you, though, I don't know," Jadus replied honestly. "Nobody *will* know until we find out just how much *you* know, plus there is a very great deal about the Heralds and this land that you absolutely must know before you can serve in the field and—" He paused and looked thoughtful for a moment, as if he had suddenly come up with a novel idea. "Actually, that may not quite be true. Something just occurred to me—and we might as well see if my option is a sound one right away." The Herald smiled warmly. "Let's trot you around, Alberich, and see what comes of it. The person I want you to see is on the way to the Collegium anyway."

"Well enough," Alberich replied with resignation. "Lead, I follow."

It was not his first excursion out into the grounds within the Palace walls, but it would be the farthest he had gone since he'd been encouraged to start leaving his bed. The Healers and his own caution kept him close to the building; he had not wanted to risk running into anyone who had the potential to be overtly hostile. He'd already had enough sour or sorrowful looks from some of the Healers and Healer-trainees he'd encountered. Once it was widely known that he was Karsite, well—no one was claiming that Valdemarans were without prejudice or incapable of holding a grudge, though in this case, he could hardly blame them.

So he had gone out, but hadn't taken the kind of long, arduous hikes he *would* have done, had he been conditioning himself at home. Not that he was weak and shaky; he'd been putting himself through a course of physical exercise since that first hour of getting himself out of bed and looking out the window. He knew, far better than the Healers did, what he was and was not capable of, and he knew very well that he was still young enough that his body would respond to being pushed to the limit by increasing where that limit stood. So at this moment he was as fit as he had ever been, if a bit thinner and paler.

As it turned out, it was a very good thing that he was.

Jadus led him through the gardens to a long, low building set off by itself. He had very little attention to spare for what were probably quite lovely gardens, once he realized just what that building *was*.

There was really no mistaking it, not when he saw the practice field laid out beside it, with archery targets, pells, and other equipment. *Then* the lack of ordinary windows, and the placement of clerestory windows instead, made sense.

This was a salle, a building devoted to the teaching and practice of arms. The kind of building that had been home to him for longer than any actual "home"—three years in the little hut he'd shared with his mother, then the rest of the time in the little inn where she worked as a serving girl and cook's helper.

Indeed, he must have spent half his life in a similar building. As a cadet, he had divided all of his waking hours among formal classes, reading and studying on his own, and weaponswork. He had never really taken any time for the recreation that the others did. As a low-born bastard, he was not the social equal of *any* of the others in his year, and he had figured out quite early that if he excelled in fighting, no one would bother him. He had already had a certain advantage in knowing all the dirty tricks he could pick up in the alleys and stables; it wasn't long before the rest of the cadets knew better than to pick on him. And while no one was particularly friendly with him, they treated him with respect. Two of the weapons instructors, seeing his diligence, actually unbent enough to act as his mentors. It wasn't exactly paternal, since they were still very strict with him, but friendly, in a distant fashion, and certainly encouraging. When it came down to it, probably he'd spent the best times of his cadet period in the salle...

There was a line of solemn-faced children in gray uniforms practicing archery under the supervision of an older boy. He clearly knew what he was doing, Alberich noted with approval—correcting the stance of one, the grip of another, the aim of a third. But he hadn't been brought here to watch them; Jadus led him into the building itself without a pause. It was of a pattern with every other salle that he had ever been inside, from the sanded wooden floors to the mirrored wall to the clerestory windows above. It was superior to the salle he had been trained in, for the mirrors were silvered glass rather than polished metal. But the furnishings were exactly the same: dented and chipped wooden benches and storage boxes that doubled as seating. Practice armor, of padded leather, hung on the wall; racks of wooden blades were beside the armor. Even the smell was the same: clean sweat, leather, leather oil, a hint of sawdust.

The salle was empty except for a single Herald, an old, gray-haired man, slightly twisted and with swollen, arthritic joints. He sat on a bench with some of the padded armor over his legs, a threaded leather needle in his hand, and looked up as they entered.

"Jadus," he acknowledged. "That's the new one?"

"Weaponsmaster Dethor," Jadus nodded. "This is Herald-trainee Alberich, Chosen of Kantor."

"Kantor, hmm? Sensible lad, that one; can't see *him* making a mistake. Well, Jadus, what did you have in mind besides the usual?" The Weaponsmaster stood up, and Alberich winced inwardly. The man was in pain—hiding it, but clear enough to Alberich's eyes. He'd seen this before, in men who'd fought too many fights. The joints would only take so much damage; too much, and as the years set in and the pains of old age crept on, all the places that had been abused would suddenly become doubly painful, swelling until it hurt to move even a little.

"Since he was a Captain of the Karsite light cavalry, I did have a notion about him. Test him, and we'll both see if I'm right," was the enigmatic reply. "Isn't Kimel about? He's usually here this time of day."

Instead of answering directly, the old man barked, "Kimel! Need your arm out here!"

Alberich expected another Herald, but instead what appeared from a door at the back of the room was a man in a midnight-blue uniform, similar to the Heralds' in cut, but trimmed in silver. "I was about to go back to the barracks, Weaponsmaster," the man said. "Unless you've found someone to bout with me after all?"

The old man jerked his chin at Alberich. "Don't know. Need this one tested. Jadus seems to think—Well, just arm up, and we'll see."

The man glanced at Alberich, then did a double-take, eyes widening. Alberich braced himself for a negative reaction, but the man showed nothing. "Interesting to see which rumor is true, sir," was all the man said, and motioned to Alberich. "If you would suit up and—"

"Standard sword and shield, first," the Weaponsmaster directed, and put his mending aside, his eyes narrowed and attentive in a lean, lined, hard face. Alberich might look just like him one day. He hoped he would not have the swollen joints to match...

He pushed that thought aside and selected leather practice armor and a wooden sword. There was more of the former to choose from than he'd thought; evidently, this man Kimel wasn't the only adult coming out here to practice. The wooden swords and shields were much of a muchness, nothing to choose among them except for weight, and Alberich picked ones that were the most comfortable for him.

Then he walked warily to the center of the room to face his opponent.

Alberich then went through the most exhausting weapons session he'd had since he'd graduated from cadet training. It began with sword and shield, progressing through every other practice weapon stored in the salle and their corresponding styles. Then, as he waited to see what else the old man wanted him to do, the Herald directed Jadus to lock the doors.

Alberich was sweating like a horse at this point, a bit tired, but by no means exhausted, and he gave the Weaponsmaster a startled glance.

"Live steel next," the old Herald said shortly, in answer to the unspoken question. "I don't want some idiot child wandering in here with live steel out and two real fighters having at each other."

"Ah." Alberich was perfectly satisfied with that answer; the Weaponsmaster was right. If mere untutored children had access to the salle, and he assumed they must (since having a Weaponsmaster implied that all of the young Trainees got some sort of weapons training), there was *always* the chance that one would blunder into the place at the worst possible time. Even in a bout rather than a real fight, he knew his concentration was focused, and he wouldn't necessarily notice anything but his opponent until it was too late. He followed Kimel to the cabinets on the wall and took out real armor and real weapons.

Working with live steel always gave him an extra—the pun was inevitable—edge. His awareness went up a degree, and everything seemed just that much clearer and sharper. Even his reflexes seemed to improve. He suited up, took the rapier in his hand, and faced his opponent with energy renewed.

He assumed that he was expected to pull his blows when necessary, and given the way that the bouts had gone so far, he knew it was going to be necessary. Kimel was good; very, very good in fact. Alberich was better. And Kimel was tiring faster. He wasn't going to be able to ward off everything that Alberich could throw at him.

And he didn't. Alberich had chosen the rapier for that reason; the lightest of the "real" swords, it was the easiest to "pull" when a blow actually fell instead of being countered.

The Weaponsmaster called a halt to the bouting when Kimel was clearly on his last legs. "That enough practice for you, my lad?" he asked, a certain ironic amusement in his voice.

The young man pulled off his helm, showing that his dark hair had gone black with his sweat. "Enough, Weaponsmaster," he admitted. "No matter what else you do, *please* make sure this fellow has a candlemark or so free every couple of days so I have someone to bout with from now on. I'm getting soft, and by the Havens, it shows." He actually smiled briefly at Alberich.

"I'll do that," the old man said with immense satisfaction. "It's about time I found someone to put you on your mettle." He turned to Alberich as the young man dragged himself toward the storage lockers to divest himself of his armor. "Well!" he barked. "Are *you* too tired for more work?"

Whatever was in this man's mind, Alberich was determined not to disappoint him. "No," he said shortly, then added, "sir."

"Good. Jadus, you can unlock the door. Trainee, we'll see how you are with distance weapons."

Ah. Alberich was already impressed with this Weaponsmaster; he had to assume the man had trained Kimel, and Kimel was *good.* Not quite as good as Alberich, but then his own Weaponsmasters had trained many boys that were good, but few as dedicated to their craft as Alberich. There were those that were naturals at the art of war, and Alberich was one of them—but being naturally good at something only took one *to* a certain point. It was dedication and practice that took one beyond that point. Or, as his own Weaponsmaster had said, "Genius will only take you to 'good.' *Practice* will take you to 'Master.'"

Now, this Dethor was a Master; it showed not only in that he had trained Kimel, but *how* he was testing Alberich's level of stamina, strength, and expertise. The point here was that the Weaponsmaster had waited until Alberich was tired to test him at distance weapons, when his aim might be compromised by arms that shook with weariness, and eyes blurred with exhaustion. *Clever. Very clever.*

Now, under the curious eyes of the youngsters as well as the critical eye of the old man, Alberich showed his mettle—with the longbow, with the shorter horse-bow, then finally with spear, javelin, ax, sling, and knife. He always hit the target—not always in the black, but he always hit the target. By now he had an audience of wide-eyed youngsters, ranging in age from child to young adult. It wasn't likely that they were in awe of his targeting skills; it wasn't as if he was putting missile after missile into the same spot. Presumably they were dazzled because they had never seen one man use so many different distance weapons before.

:You're enjoying yourself,: Kantor remarked with pleasure, and to his surprise, Alberich realized that the Companion was right.

:This—is what I do well,: he admitted. *:I am not ashamed of doing it well.:*

:Did I suggest you should be?: Kantor retorted. *:You are what you are: a warrior. Some* must *be warriors, that others may live in peace. You do not enjoy killing, but you are proud of your skill. I see no difficulty with this.:* A thoughtful pause. *:Better that you should be proud of your skill. When need drives, you cannot hold back.:*

Sensible. Quite sensible. He placed a final knife in the center of the target, and turned to Jadus and Dethor. Jadus was looking at Dethor with an expression of expectation.

Dethor was looking at Alberich. "Right," he said. "Karsite. What's the job of a Weaponsmaster?"

"So that those he teaches, killed or injured are not," Alberich said instantly. And bluntly. "However, whatever works, so that learn, they do, and well. Shouts, scolds, b—" He paused. "Not beating, perhaps. *Some*times, gentle. Not often. Out in the world, there will no gentleness be. Better harshness to see here, and live, than softness, and die."

"Na, these're none of your Karsite thugs. No beatings. But all else, aye, and treat 'em gentle only when they're little, scared sparrows.

Gentle pats and cosseting—that's for them as will never need to fight for life." He turned a somewhat grim smile on Jadus, and the eyes of the children—the Trainees—were getting round and apprehensive. "Right. By the Havens, I've got one now, and who'd have thought it'd be soft-handed peace-minded Jadus who'd be the one to find him, *realize* what he was good for, and bring him to me?"

Alberich was beginning to get the glimmer of an idea of what was up, and the Weaponsmaster's next words clinched it. Dethor turned to him. "Trainee Alberich, you're on notice. There'll be no riding circuit for you, and no riding internship. You'll be interning, starting now, with me, as the next Weaponsmaster. Call it—well, it's no apprenticeship, for you're nothing like an apprentice. Call it whatever you like; you're going to be a Trainee in name only."

"But—the classes—" he managed, as the children looked even more apprehensive, if that was possible.

Dethor flapped his hand, dismissing the entire curriculum of the Collegium as inconsequential. "Oh, you'll take 'em. You see to it, Jadus, but no more than three classes in a day, and I'd prefer one or two rather than three. And no housekeeping chores and no dormitory for him either—we'll have him out here, in my quarters, and he can start doing what I can't anymore. Kernos' bones, what you thought you'd be doing, putting a grown man in amongst a lot of boys, anyway—"

"It's been done before," Jadus ventured.

Dethor just snorted, and looked Alberich pointedly up and down—then at the children, who had put a careful space between himself and them.

"Ah," Jadus said, and grimaced. As Alberich had expected, the Herald was utterly transparent when it came to his feelings and what he was thinking, and right now, he realized just how wary, even frightened, all those young Trainees might be of Alberich. "I suppose he's right, Alberich; I don't think you would fit in very well with the rest of the boys."

"I think not," Alberich agreed quietly. Although he did not know this man Dethor—he knew the species. Another warrior. Someone who would think as *he* thought. As comfortable a Valdemaran to share living space with as he was likely to find.

"Then have them fetch his things over. As of now, he's an Internee with classes. I know the rules as well as you, but rules are made to be broken, now and then. Just tell Talamir what I've done, Sendar will decree it, and there'll be an end to argument."

:This is better than I had hoped for,: Kantor said, sounding pleased. *:Dethor*

fought on the Border, you see. We weren't altogether certain what he'd think of you.:.

:Why didn't you ask his Companion?: Alberich asked.

:Because Dethor doesn't have much consistency in the way of Mindspeech. Pahshen doesn't always know what he's thinking. The bond is there, and they do just fine, but when Dethor closes up—well, he's unreadable, and he's been completely unreadable where you are concerned.:

Ah. That put a different complexion on things.

"I'll see to it," Jadus said, and turned to look at the gaping children. "Shouldn't you be practicing?" he asked pointedly.

They flushed and looked guilty, especially the eldest, and gathered up their equipment and went back to the archery field. Alberich followed Dethor back into the building.

At the back wall was a door, half hidden in the paneling, the same door that Kimel, the man in the blue uniform, had come through. Alberich followed Dethor through that door as well, into a long and narrow room with seating and a wall of windows that looked out on a rather unprepossessing stretch of meadow and bushes.

"Come in here, and I'll show you how to clean up," the old man said, waving him on. Apparently there was an entire suite of rooms here, behind the salle. Through another door, Alberich found Dethor waiting in a tiny room tiled floor-to-ceiling in white ceramic, holding a lit fireplace squib.

"Take this, reach up, and light that," the old man said, pointing to a metal container that looked very like a candle with an enormously fat wick. Pipes led up through the ceiling, and also from the bottom of the drum across to a perforated disk suspended from the middle of the ceiling. "Then turn that spigot, and you'll get a warm rain shower out of that plate. There's a box of soap there, and I'll bring you a towel; by the time you're clean, Jadus will have brought your things here and I'll have a new uniform for you. Then we can talk."

Then we can talk. Words both ominous and positive. This man had fought against Karse on the Border—but he had just brought Alberich into his personal quarters, and he was going to talk.

We are both warriors, he reminded himself. *We speak a common language that has nothing to do with Valdemaran syntax and Karsite verbs.*

Alberich stripped off his sweat-sodden uniform and turned the spigot on the wall, and just as Dethor had said, a "rain" of warm water came down from the perforated plate, draining away through a grate in the floor. This was an infinitely faster way of getting clean than a bath. Not as luxurious, but much more efficient. There was a second door into this chamber, but for now, Alberich figured he could wait to discover what lay behind it.

Dethor was as good as his word. By the time Alberich cautiously opened the door to the little room, there was a folded uniform and a towel in a pile beside it. He snuffed the contrivance that heated the water, then lost no time in toweling himself off and getting into a brand new uniform for the second time that day. It felt good to be clean, to have all his muscles aching—just a little—from the exertion. For the first time since he'd come here, he felt entirely like himself. He joined his new mentor in the sitting area, hair still damp.

"Take a seat," the old man said. Alberich gingerly chose a chair facing his new mentor.

"Now, before we start out, I want everything straight between us," said Dethor forthrightly. "I don't particularly like Karsites." He sucked in his lower lip. "Mind, it's the ones in charge I've got a bone to pick with. Your Sunpriests. Just the Karsite ones, mind; we've got a little sect of your lot on this side of the Border, and I've no quarrel with *them.*"

Alberich nodded, cautiously.

"Now, you're a soldier. Reckon that mostly what you did was take orders. Question I've got for you is—just how much did you *think* about them orders when you got 'em?" Dethor gave him a sharp look.

"Much," Alberich replied immediately, without even thinking about it very long. "Look you—my duty—to *what* it was? My God, and my people." He decided that he would leave his duty to Vkandis between himself and the God. "My people to *protect.* Not to the Fires to feed them. Not to bandits to leave them."

"And if them priests had told you to attack us, you'd have done it?" Dethor persisted.

Alberich could only shrug. "Then? You, Demon-Riders, lovers of demons, with witch-powers and witch-ways? Yes. A threat, I saw you."

"Hmph. Honest, at least. Now?" Dethor asked.

"Now—there, I am not. Here, I am." He shrugged. What was the point in asking such a question? Already he was an entirely different person from Captain Alberich of the Suns-guard. Tomorrow he might be a different person from today.

Dethor sighed, with some exaggeration. "All I'm asking is, are you going to knife me in my sleep because I killed a baker's dozen of *your* folk *and* a couple of your Priests a while back?"

Alberich gave Dethor the same answer *he* had given Alberich. "You, a soldier are. And your duty? To your King, and your people. This, I understand."

And if he asked me *about questioning orders, I would suspect he thought about his before he obeyed them...*

"Farmers, killed you?" he persisted. "Craftsmen?" He hunted for the word. Kantor helped.

:Civilians.:

"Civilians?"

"Never," Dethor replied, with such matter-of-factness that Alberich couldn't doubt him. "Unless you count the priests."

Alberich dismissed the Sunpriests out of hand. "Then, no quarrel have I with you."

"Reckon you're ready to help me beat some skill into a pack of puppies that never saw blood?" Dethor asked, the wrinkles around his eyes relaxing, and a hint of ease creeping into his voice.

Some of whom may grow up to slay more Karsites... "A question," he asked, and picked his words with care. "The answer, on your honor, swear. *Do* you of Valdemar—*do* you make war, and unleash demons, my people upon?"

"No!" Dethor said with such force that Alberich started back in his chair, his hand reaching automatically for a knife that wasn't there.

"No," the Weaponsmaster repeated, without the heat. "I swear to you, on my honor, on my gods, on my life, we do nothing of the sort. We'll defend ourselves—and there's bandits along the Border that prey on both sides of it, as I assume you know well enough—but never *once* in my time have we even pursued an invading army past the Border once we reached it. You already know that what you call 'White Demons' are nothing but our Companions. If there are demons preying on your people by night—" and a knowing glance told Alberich that this man *knew* that there were, "—then I say, look to your own priests. We don't have anything or anyone that calls up the likes of demons, and even if we did, we'd not set them on ordinary folk who just have the misfortune to live in the wrong place."

Dethor's suggestion that Alberich look to the Sunpriests for those who let demons prowl the night was not unexpected—and it was true. This was a thought that had already passed through Alberich's mind, more than once. He nodded.

And he thought of those fresh-faced youngsters at the archery field, how unless someone taught them all of the thousands of ways in which

they could die and how to counter their opponents and save themselves—
then they *would* die. For no more crime than serving their people, as he
had. This man would not have taken him, a foreigner, to apprentice as
his replacement, if he'd had any other choice. He could turn Dethor
down, and have all those needless deaths on his own conscience. Or he
could accept the position—

—and accept that he was going to stay.

:You are needed here,: Kantor said simply. *:Perhaps only a handful of people
even among the Heralds know this—but you* are *needed here. Whatever else comes,
whether your God had a hand in bringing you here, whether or not He has further
plans for you here, there is that. No one else can do what you can; Dethor has looked a
long, long time for his replacement, and you are his last, best choice.:*

"Then—yes," he replied, answering both Dethor and Kantor. "Yes.
Learn I will, and teach."

"Then here's my hand on it." Dethor held out his sword-callused
palm, and Alberich clasped it. A powerful and strong hand, that one
had been; it was strong still, under the swollen joints and past the pain.

"Now, let me show you your quarters." Dethor got up out of his
chair; Alberich forbore to offer him a hand. There would be a time for
that later. Right now, Dethor could manage, and as long as he could
manage alone, he would want to. Alberich rose, and followed in the old
man's footsteps.

The quarters behind the salle turned out to be a series of
interconnected rooms, with no space wasted on halls. This was a sitting
room, primarily; the sun came in here on winter afternoons, which
probably made it a good place for Dethor to sit and bask his bones. At
the rear, it led into the "showering room" which had a cistern on the
roof that fed both it and a privy on the other side of the room—which
was where that second door led. On the other side of *that* was Dethor's
bedroom, then a second room, which looked mostly unused, but which
did have a bed and a wooden chest in it. Then storage rooms and an
office, which led, in turn, back into the salle. If one followed a path
around, it would be in the shape of a "u" with the two points of the
letter representing the two doors into the salle.

A pile of clothing and gear lay on the bed in the second room,
which Alberich assumed was going to be his. Jadus worked quickly, it
seemed. The arrangement suited him, actually. And comforted him.
There would be no one sleeping between him and a direct line out of
here. Oh, there were windows to climb out of, but that was awkward

and had the potential to be very noisy.

"This has always been laid out with the idea that the Weaponsmaster shares quarters with his Second," Dethor told him, then grinned evilly. "The Second's closer to the salle, so if there's a crisis in the middle of the night—?"

"The Second, the one who answers, is," Alberich said with mock resignation. "Master."

"Exactly. Just got one question for you. I have 'em bring my meals over from the Collegium—there's a fireplace in the sitting room where things can be kept hot. Wastes my time to be hauling myself over there and back, three times a day. But *you*—you might be wanting to be around people more."

It's too painful for him to be dragging himself back and forth. Alberich found it very easy to read between *those* lines. *But—he's lonely. No, I won't desert him, not even for meals.* "If you, my master and teacher will be here— then going *there* of what use is?" he asked logically. "A waste of *my* time. Asking questions, having advice, I could be. Besides, soldiers are we. Understand each other, we do."

Was it his imagination, or did Dethor actually soften a bit? "You'll find that boy Kimel is another of our sort," he said. "Head of His Majesty's Personal Guard, that boy, and hard on himself. Always after someone to make him better and keener, but he just hasn't what's needed to be Weaponsmaster. Trained him myself, though."

"Then, on himself, he would hard be." Alberich knew that much for certain. "Like master, like man, at home we say."

"We say the same thing here," Dethor replied, and it seemed, with some content. "Not so different after all, in some things, at least."

"No," Alberich agreed.

"Right. *I* have a gaggle of youngsters coming in a moment. *You* get this room arranged to your liking, then come out and give me a hand with 'em. No time like the present to start." Once again, Dethor was all brisk business, and as he limped out, Alberich made haste to follow his orders.

He made up the bed with the linens and blankets he found in the chest, and put his things away. Not that he had a great deal to put away—those uniforms, light ones for summer, heavier materials for winter, a cloak—some toiletries, which he was pleased enough to see. He took the opportunity to give his short-cut hair a good combing, thinking as he did so that he probably ought to let it grow out now. Longer hair seemed to be the fashion in Valdemar, and there was no use in looking more conspicuous than he already did.

:You've decided to stay.: Kantor exuded satisfaction.

:Yes.: He knew he had made up his mind that the so-called "trial" was over, probably the instant that he realized Dethor wanted him to train as a replacement Weaponsmaster. Maybe that was all it had really taken, the knowledge that they weren't going to *make* work for him, and fit him in somehow, but that there already was a place here that was crying out for someone like him.: *Yes,:* he repeated. *:It seems I'm needed.:*

Which was by no means a bad thing. Not at all.

4

Jadus returned about noon, as Alberich and Dethor were picking up the discarded bits of armor and practice weapons in the salle and putting things away. With Jadus was a young man in yet another sort of uniform—this time including a tabard with the Valdemar winged horse on it belted on over his clothing. A servant? It seemed so, since the fellow was carrying a set of stacked metal containers that fitted neatly into a common woven-straw cover. Jadus and Dethor led the young man through the door into the living quarters, while Alberich put the last few bits in a cupboard and followed them.

The young man opened up the straw cover and took out the metal containers one by one, and opened them in turn to disclose the components of their meal, kept hot. Clever, that; Alberich admired the arrangement. Certainly the Collegium was seeing to it that Dethor didn't suffer for taking his meals away from the rest.

By Alberich's standards of camp cookery, it was a sumptuous meal. All of it was laid out in the sitting room, with cutlery and plates that Dethor produced out of a cupboard that Alberich hadn't noticed until Dethor opened it. The servant departed, but Jadus did not; evidently he intended to share their meal. There were four different dishes, plus bread and butter; Alberich took an equal portion of each. Something like a stew, some sliced vegetable, beans, and what appeared to be baked apples. The flavors were good—when in the hands of the Healers, he'd first noticed that the food was good—but not quite familiar. The spices were all different; flavors he was used to were missing, new ones added. And these people didn't seem to use as much spice as Karsites did. It *was* good but—not exactly right. Even the bread was lighter in taste, texture and color than Karsite bread, and not as chewy. As much as the language, the *food* brought it home to him that he was on alien soil.

"Your classes won't start for another three days, Alberich," Jadus said, when the edge had been taken off Alberich's hunger. "Dethor, up at the Collegium we've decided that you should establish a schedule with Alberich first, and we'll work his classes in around that." The Herald sighed gustily. "At the moment, there are so many classes he will need to take, it won't be a problem to work a schedule of three in around whatever you set him up for."

Dethor nodded, and refilled all their cups. Alberich was mildly surprised to find that they were drinking, not beer or common wine, but some rather tasty herb tisane. Tisane—well, that just wasn't what a soldier generally drank. Not that Alberich had any *objections* to the beverage; after all, most of the beer he'd gotten over the years was indifferent at best and vile at worst, and all of the wine had been harsh and rough. Still—tisane. It conjured up images in his mind of little old ladies puttering at sewing and gossiping.

Perhaps it was meant to serve as a good example to all those children populating the place. If so—well, if he was allowed to leave this place, he suspected he would be finding a tavern fairly soon.

Perhaps, if he asked, someone would find him a little cask of some good strong ale.

"At any rate, you won't be seeing nearly as much of me, Alberich," Jadus continued. "You've got another guide coming, a fellow called Elcarth, a bit of a scholar. You see, we reckoned he'd be the best one to help you over some of the classes I'm hopeless at. I'm to bring him around to meet you in the morning."

:Which really means, what?: he asked Kantor. *:What isn't he telling me?:*

:That you aren't everyone's favorite Trainee,: Kantor replied promptly. *:Elcarth is in line to become the Dean—that's the head—of the Collegium within the next ten years or so. He doesn't look like much, but he's as sharp as a poniard, and nothing gets past him. If he approves of you, no one is going to openly contest your being here.:* Kantor paused, and Alberich "felt" him ruminating. *:Our Kings and Queens, you see, don't rule so much as reign, and not at all autocratically. King Sendar will probably have trouble over you with his Council for some time to come. But Elcarth—well, Elcarth comes from one of the most powerful families in the land, and he has a reputation for sharpness, as I told you. The Dean has a traditional place on the Council, but Elcarth is the one who's actually taking the seat for the Dean in absentia. That gives us a majority if we need it.:*

Alberich kept his face straight and showed no sign that Kantor had imparted this amazing information to him, but he had a very hard time doing so. The Priests of Vkandis had things so completely under their hands and wills that he couldn't imagine a ruler who *didn't* rule completely. Oh, of course, there was a King in Karse, too, but he was no more than an impotent figure who didn't rule so much as preside over a gaggle of wealthy aristocrats and would-be aristocrats with nothing better to do with their time than vie for position in a do-nothing Court that was little better than an elaborate social club. It was the Son of the Sun who held the real reins of power, and behind him, so far as Alberich knew, ranged the solid phalanx of the Sunpriests, who fulfilled the Son of the Sun's orders with nary a murmur of discontent.

Then again, what do I know of what goes on behind the closed doors of the Temple? It might be the same there. Really, the most astonishing thing might not be so much that there was contention in the King's court, but that ordinary people seemed to know about it. *That* would be unheard of in Karse.

So much had happened to him in a few short marks. This morning he had been quite willing to walk out of here forever; now he wasn't merely a Trainee, he had a real position here. It felt a bit dreamlike, as if days had passed in the course of the morning. He had gone *straight* into the life of this place without a pause for breath. That wasn't *like* him. It made no sense. There was only one way to account for it. That blasted Kantor.

:Me?: his *(his!)* Companion replied, oozing innocence. :*Don't go laying your so-called conversion at* my *doorstep. I gave you every opportunity to escape. I even had Talamir tell you the great secret—that you could have shaken our bonding loose if you really decided you couldn't bear this life. How many people have been told that in the course of our history?*:

:*How should I know?*: Alberich asked rhetorically.

:*I was about to tell you. No more than a dozen, that's what. You're here now—*:

:*Because you laid a trap for me, you and your precious Heralds, and baited it with the one thing I'd find irresistible.*:

"Then that leaves him free, this afternoon?" Dethor asked, gesturing with a slice of buttered bread. "Good. We'll start you in as my assistant right now, Alberich. Get the youngsters used to seeing you as my assistant first before they start hearing rumors about the evil Karsite Trainee."

Alberich nodded. Well, what else was he to do? He *knew* it was going to happen—the "evil Karsite Trainee" business. How could it not? If the situations were reversed…

Not that they could be. The first sight of a white uniform, and the wearer of that uniform would find himself the object of target practice. Thoughtfully, he bit off a hangnail.

"The difference, I see not," he offered. "The Weaponsmaster, if good he be, always hated is."

Dethor smiled wickedly. "Better to have 'em hating you as the tyrannical Weapons Second, the brutal taskmaster. That way there'll be no room in those rattling little skulls for the evil Karsite Trainee." He finished his bread in a way that suggested the devouring of small children.

Alberich smiled, just a little. The Weaponsmaster was absolutely right, of course. Children—and, to be fair, a great many adults—were apt to label people and stick with the first label they'd come up with. "A brutal taskmaster, I surely will be, as ever," he replied, with a touch of grim humor. "My recruits, ask."

Dethor rubbed his hands together. "I'll keep the small ones, but you—ah! You, I intend to unleash on the older ones. I've been easy on 'em—too damned easy, tell the truth. *I* can't bout 'em anymore, and there's never anyone here consistently that can give 'em proper workouts. And—oh, glory!—*you've* fought real fights. None of this court fencing, oh no! That's the trouble with the teachers the highborn have; they learn to duel, to do fancy court fighting, but not how to *fight*. Plenty of Heralds do, of course, most of 'em trained by me, but they're needed out *there*, and can't be spared." He shook his head reluctantly. "And, truth to tell, it takes more than knowing how to fight to make a Weaponsmaster."

Kantor put in a few words of his own. *:The "older ones," the best fighters among them, anyway, have been getting above themselves lately. We have a flock of them that are one, maybe two years from getting their Whites that were almost all out of the highborn, noble families. Before they were Chosen, they got private swordsmanship lessons, and those continued even after. They think they're masters of the sword now because they're so much better than the rest of the Trainees; Dethor can't give them the sort of workout they need to show them that they aren't.:*

Alberich knew exactly what Kantor meant, and was beginning to warm to his new task. And as for Dethor, well, it was clear that he was doing more than merely "warm" to the task. He bordered on gleeful.

Alberich caught some of his spirit. It wasn't malicious, but there was a certain edge that suggested that there were a couple of these adolescent Heralds-in-training who were due for a comeuppance. Thought themselves immortal and invincible, and it would have to get pounded into their skulls that they weren't. The usual adolescent hubris, of course. Over and over, they came into the Sunsguard, sure of their skill, and thinking only of glory and fame. Time after time, if they *didn't* learn that war against bandits was dirty, perilous, and inglorious, they got their fame by having their names inscribed on the Tablets of the Fallen in the Great Temple. At least none of *these* youngsters would be looking to make a name for himself by taking their officer out in a practice bout—or worse. Worse was an ambitious and unscrupulous recruit who was hoping to advance *himself* by removing the obstacle that Alberich represented. Or to do the same, at the behest of one of Alberich's under-officers.

"That sort, I have seen," he said shortly, and left it at that.

But he did get a bit of a shock when they finished their meal—a relatively light one, appropriate for two men who would be doing very physical work, shortly—and he followed Dethor out into the salle again. Of the six adolescents choosing practice weapons or limbering up, two were female.

Girls! True, one of the Heralds that had first found him had been a woman—he vaguely recalled that now—but it hadn't really occurred to him intellectually, even though Kantor had reminded him of that fact, that he would be teaching *girls.* Females just didn't put themselves forward. Not in Karse, anyway. Females had very clearly defined roles in Karse, which did *not* include being fighters.

:*Don't hold back with them,*: Kantor said instantly. :*You won't be doing them any favors.*: And when he still hesitated, Kantor added sharply. :*There are barbarians in the North, pirates and slavers in the West, and bandits in the South. And they will probably face all three before they're middle-aged, if they live that long. It will be one woman and one Companion out there, alone, and you* have *to prepare them for that.*:

:*Yes, I do see that.*: It made him feel a little sick, but Kantor was right; they *were* Trainees, they *would* be Heralds, and he would do them no favors at all by going easy with them.

In fact, he might well kill them. Or worse. There was always the probability of an "or worse." It was a simple fact that the probability was higher for a female.

:*Or both,*: Kantor added grimly. :*They can't be as strong as the boys; you'll have to give them skill to make up for that. If anything, the girls will need your skills more than the boys.*:

"Well, Trainees, I have a little surprise for you," Dethor said cheerfully. He gestured at Alberich, who lingered near the door. "This is my new Second—and from now on, *he'll* be putting you through your paces, while I watch."

Alberich had no difficulty in keeping his face expressionless. This was no different than facing a line of new recruits. Even the ages weren't *that* dissimilar; he guessed these youngsters to be between sixteen and eighteen years of age. He'd had recruits that young, although, since he'd been in the mounted troops, they'd all come from some background where they'd been riding since they could walk. And, mostly, the cavalry came from recruits rather than conscripts. He supposed Trainees probably fell under the same banner as recruits; surely *he* was the only Trainee who had ever felt as if he'd been conscripted against his will.

:Not exactly the only one, but very nearly.: Kantor said.

In their turn, they eyed him without any shame. Mostly with curiosity, although two of the boys had challenge in their eyes. Well, they'd soon see what he was made of.

They were the two oldest, he guessed. Definitely the two tallest. One very dark, muscular, and blocky, the other half a head taller, with brown hair and knowing eyes. Of the other four, the girls were a pretty creature, blue-eyed, with a smooth cap of brown hair cut no longer than her earlobes, and a smaller, lighter girl with blue eyes, a generous mouth, and blond hair done in a knot on the top of her head. The boys were both brown-haired, one of medium height and one short, both with grave faces.

But it was the first two that held Alberich's attention.

:Just as you thought, those are two of your problem children. Mind, all you need to do is disillusion them. They've got good hearts, they're just, well—:

:Arrogant in some ways, because they're ignorant and don't know it,: he supplied.

:Exactly. I can tell you that they are currently the despair of their Companions. Nothing Trevor and Mik can say shakes them out of their conviction that they are never going to find themselves in trouble that they can't come out of, covered in glory.:

At least he wouldn't have the problem with these boys that he often had with recruits—bad attitude, bad breeding, either spoiled by indulgent parents and thinking that everything should be given to them, or beaten as youngsters, figuring it was every man for himself. Too many of the Sunsguard troops were like that; hardened, with no morals to speak of.

:Why, Chosen—I believe you are beginning to like *your decision to stay with us!:* Kantor said with gentle mockery.

Alberich ignored him.

"I Alberich am," he said gravely, and waited for Dethor to give him his direction. Dethor, after all, was the Weaponsmaster here; it was Dethor who should set the lessons, and Alberich who should carry them out.

He didn't notice any reaction to his name, which was nothing like a

Valdemaran name, or at least, so he supposed.

"It is the new Weapons Second I am," he continued, meeting their eyes, each in turn. "Chosen by Master Dethor. Himself. Who now, direct us will."

Dethor quickly divided the group into pairs and set them working with each other. Interestingly, he paired the girls, not with each other, but with two of the brown-haired boys. The last two—the boys Alberich had marked as being a possible source of trouble—Dethor motioned to join Alberich.

"Sword and shield, and make them work, Alberich," he said shortly. "These lads are ahead of the rest by a bit; treat them as trained, because they are. They can go two-on-one against you."

The boys exchanged a look; the darker, more muscular one with a touch of smug glee, the other (the one who was taller, less blocky, and brown-haired), with a look of dawning misgiving, which was replaced by anticipation when he saw the expression on his friend's face. His friend was wildly optimistic about their chances, and he had come to trust his friend's judgment.

Alberich knew that look of old. Overconfidence, poor young fools, because they were large dogs in a pack of small dogs, and had never been shown any better. They thought that they were the kings of the world, and immortal. An attitude like that would get them killed—

Unless Dethor and I can knock some better sense into their heads.

"Sir," Alberich acknowledged, and picked up a practice sword and shield from the piles at the side of the salle, while the boys did the same. They looked cocky. Alberich figured that they must have had sword training from the time they were barely old enough to hold a practice sword and shield. Five or six, maybe. From families of wealth or the nobility, he figured these were part of that "flock" of youngsters that Kantor had described; they had that particular healthy, confident, well-fed look that only *being* well-nourished from infancy imparted. Maybe only someone who as a child had never been certain whether there would be a next meal would have noticed the difference, but Alberich had learned early which were the well-fed children (and thus, dangerous, for they could bully him with impunity) and which the starvelings like himself (which he could defend himself against without fear of retribution).

"Standard or—special, sir?" he asked Dethor, when the boys had finished arming themselves. *He* had not bothered with padding, arm- or shin-guards, or even a helmet; they had prudently taken advantage of all of these. At least that showed *some* sense of self-preservation. *They* were shortly going to be very glad of every bit of that protection.

"Oh, special, Second," Dethor replied airily—and he must have known or guessed just what Alberich meant by "special." "Tammas and Jahan have had plenty of *standard* training. I believe it's time they learned what real field fighting is like."

"Sir," Alberich replied, and without a pause, whirled and laid into the nearest.

He didn't go at them as if this was a pitched battle, because he'd have taken them both out in moments. They'd been expecting the usual polite exchange of salutes, followed by a measured opening to the bout—not an attack right out of nowhere, with no warning, and that had been enough of a shock for them; he didn't need to go after them full-out.

And the way they reacted was telling; they both stood their ground, but neither close enough to defend each other, nor far enough apart to make him work harder to reach both of them. *They* might think they were trained, but they weren't, not really. So Alberich knocked the first one's shield aside with a brutal blow that nearly knocked it from his arm, without regard for "lines" and the "rules" of swordplay. He followed it up by ramming the boy with his own shield. The lad stumbled backward, and before his friend could come to the rescue, Alberich sidestepped, made a wide, low sweep with the flat of his practice blade, and knocked his legs right out from under him. It was a good thing the boy was wearing shin-guards—though he couldn't have been expecting the low blow, or he'd have guarded against it.

He turned back toward the first as the second scrambled to his feet. Once again, Alberich rushed the boy, this time herding him toward his friend with a flurry of blows. Predictably, they got tangled up with each other, and he backed off to let them sort themselves out, though the next time he did this, he wouldn't give them the respite. Then he simply chased them around the salle for a full circuit of the place, using all the dirty tactics he knew, and hitting them just hard enough that they would have bruises to show for it, even under the padding and protection. He made their ears ring a time or two as well, with unexpected blows to the helm. Neither of them, of course, got so much as a love tap on *him*. He hadn't bothered with a helm, because he wanted to be able to see them easily; he trusted to his reflexes to keep him out of trouble. Oddly enough, he would have worn the helm and padding had they been utterly untrained, for there would be no predicting what they would do.

Part of their problem now was that they were rather too well-trained. If they were going to come up against lads who'd been trained by fighting and killing, instead of by self-styled Masters of the Sword or fellows with equally fancy tides, they were going to have to unlearn some of what was now ingrained. Good habits—if all you were doing was fighting other gentlemen. But very bad if you were going out to kill brigands.

By this time he was just feeling warmed up, and beginning to enjoy himself. Not a chance that they could even get a tap on him; not only because he was a far better fighter, but because they were so shocked by his tactics that they couldn't think. They *were* shocked, the patterns they knew were all disrupted, and they hadn't yet seen that what appeared to be random attacks had patterns of their own, more primitive and brutal, but the patterns were there.

Not that fighting—in the frontline, basic, dirty fighting—had much to do with thinking. It was all muscle memory at that point, because before a mark was up, you'd be so tired that it had better be your muscles that remembered what to do—your mind would be numb with fatigue and no longer working properly. But what Alberich was doing was what any good bandit fighter would do, two-against-one. He certainly wouldn't stand in one place and slug it out, nor would he move forward and back in a single, straight line.

The other Trainees stopped their practice and watched him chase his two victims around the perimeter of the salle. They watched with their mouths hanging open in amazement, and no little shock and surprise. Dethor didn't make them go back to trading blows, so Alberich concluded that *this*, and not what they'd been assigned to do, was the real lesson today.

Good. Let them think about it. Not now—they were as shocked as his two victims—but they would remember, and talk about this in their rooms together, later. If they were smart enough, they would learn from what they watched now, and the next pair he chased around the salle would be better prepared for what he was going to do to them.

He drove the boys back for a good while, which probably felt like an eternity to *them*, taking on first one, then the other; they fought as two separate individuals rather than a pair. Another mistake, for he could hack at one long enough for the other to take heart and try something, then move on the second boy before he'd rightly got his move started. And oh, they were *not* anticipating the shrewd blows to shins, the absolutely *rude* blows to the groin…

The latter he pulled, and pulled *hard;* he didn't want to lay them out, he just wanted them to know what he *could* do if he wished.

And what a bandit *would* do when they came up against him.

And if he'd wanted to lay them out—helmets or no, he'd have had them measuring their length on the floor first thing. The ringing blows he landed on their helms, he hoped, would tell them that. He used the flat of his blade on the helmets, rather than the edge, but one day, when they were better prepared to counter him, he'd use the proper weapon against a heavily armored man, the mace, against them. He'd known men to die of mace blows to the helm with blood pouring from their noses and ears...

Then he feigned getting tired, though he was barely warmed up— which, since they were feeling the strain themselves, they fell for. They pushed him for a few paces right into the position he wanted them, whereupon he turned the tables on them and dashed right between the two of them, catching both of them with blows in the back as he passed. Then he ran them around the salle in the opposite direction.

They had probably thought they were fit, and by most standards, they were. They were no match for a man who had spent the last seven years fighting and riding and living hard, and years before *that* in an infinitely harder "school" than this one. Never mind the past sennights he'd been flat on his back with the Healers; he'd been in top condition before that, and since he'd been allowed up, he'd been regaining what he'd lost.

Besides, these two were nothing like a challenge.

He took pity on them when he caught the telltale signs of true exhaustion—the stumbling, the uncertain aim, the trembling hands. He backed off—and they didn't follow, they just stood there, like a pair of horses that had been run off their feet and just couldn't go another step. Their weapons hung from hands that were probably numb, and their heads drooped. In a moment, if he let them, they'd collapse on the floor where they stood.

"Enough," said Dethor (with immense satisfaction in his voice), the moment before Alberich would have said the same. "Now this, my lads, is what I've been too creaky and gouty and damned old to do to you. You've just faced a *real* fighting man in his full fit trim, and what's more, before luncheon, he was giving one of the Guard a similar workout. *This* is what you'll be fighting, when it comes to it, my children," he continued, raising his voice so that it carried to the rest of the salle. "This is what you'd better be ready to face when you're given your Whites. And this is why Alberich is now my Second, and it will be his job to see to it that you can stand against him before you go out in the field. Any questions?"

Silence, broken only by the panting of the two boys that Alberich had just finished with.

"Right, then. You two—" Dethor gestured at the young men. "Off with the armor, and walk laps around the salle until you're cool. *Then* you can go back to the Collegium and clean up. Not before. You walk out of my door sore, but if you walk out stiff, it won't be my fault."

A groan issued forth from one of the helmets, but both youngsters did as they were told. Alberich almost felt sorry for them; hard luck on them to be used as examples, but they must have warranted the treatment, or Dethor wouldn't have set them up to be knocked down a peg the way he had. Alberich recalled the expressions that they had worn when the exercise began, and stopped feeling sorry for them.

"Now, Alberich—do you note, my children, that he isn't even *sweating* heavily?—take young Theela here, and show her what she's doing wrong."

Young Theela, the girl with the short hair, looked as if she would much rather have died than have Alberich show her anything at all, but her problem of telegraphing certain overhand blows was quickly sorted, and Alberich went on to the next problem, at Dethor's direction. And while Alberich was dealing out lessons to each youngster in turn, Dethor was keeping an eye on the first two recipients of Alberich's attention, making them stop and do stretches at intervals to keep from stiffening up.

As the lesson wore on, Alberich paid attention to what Dethor did and said, and when, whether or not it was addressed to Alberich himself. Dethor was brilliant, really. Despite that Alberich was doing the hands-on work of instructing the Trainees, *he* was in control of the salle and the Trainees, there was never any doubt of that. Alberich was merely an extension of his will, precisely as a good Second *should* be. But Alberich had to admire the man, for he manipulated the youngsters and the situation flawlessly, invisible. They never even guessed they were being manipulated.

By the time the Weaponsmaster was ready to let them go, it was time for *all* of them to return to the Collegium, so if the two young men had thought they were going to get off early and sneak off to some sport or other, they were sadly disappointed.

A great bell rang somewhere outside, which was, evidently, the signal for the next class. This lot was off like a flight of arrows from bows even as the first tone still shivered the air. Alberich looked sideways at Dethor, who chuckled.

"Now, why do I think that my new Second is going to be the *least* popular instructor in the Collegium?" the Weaponsmaster asked the empty air. "Barring me, of course."

"The Weaponsmaster, popularity cannot afford," Alberich said dryly, as he began picking up discarded weapons and returning them to their places.

"True, my friend. Very true. And what did you think of the two young colts who think they're stallions?" Dethor asked.

That was easy to answer. "All spirit, no sense," he replied shortly.

"Ah, but can you drive some sense *into* them? That's what I want to know." Dethor waited for his answer, head to one side, and interest in his eyes.

Alberich snorted. "Not I. *Bruises*. Pain teaches, what I cannot."

And Dethor laughed.

"But yes, learn, they will," he continued. "Stupid, they are not. Nor stubborn. Ill-taught, or *mis*-taught. But unlearn, they can."

The next class was one in archery for younger children, and Dethor took this one himself, although he commended one young lad to Alberich for some special attentions precisely because the youngster was a natural marksman. Alberich soon had him shooting from several different positions and helped him find ways of getting a full draw even when shooting from a prone, partly hidden posture. Following that class was another like the first, weaponswork in the salle, with slightly younger Trainees. This time there was a change in the uniforms, however. Among the Herald-trainee Grays was a boy in pale blue, a boy in a sort of brick-color, and a girl in Healer-trainee pale green. The boy in orange was quick, but not very strong; the girl slow, but patient and deliberate. Neither were very good, but eventually their determination would enable them to hit what they aimed at, though, for now, as many arrows flew over the targets or buried themselves in the grass in front of it as actually hit.

At least they were both trying to the best of their ability, which was more than could be said for the third child that was not in Trainee Gray. The boy in blue looked bored, and not at all interested in trying; he played at the archery, shooting haphazardly, not really aiming. Alberich waited for Dethor to say something or assign more "special attention" to that boy, but Dethor never did, and Alberich concluded that there must be something special about the blue uniform.

:There is,: Kantor said into his mind, startling him, for the Companion had been silent for most of the day. *:He's not a Trainee at all. The students in light blue are the children of some of the nobles in attendance on the King; their parents don't see any reason to hire tutors when the Collegium is here and perfectly capable*

of educating their children. But the Blues don't have any real consequences to not
learning if their parents don't care about their progress, so—: The pause invited
him to draw his own conclusions.

:Ah.: That certainly explained things. *:Are there consequences for beating
their backsides with the flat of a practice blade?:*

:Alas, yes,: Kantor said. *:Political consequences, I fear. Now, the ones in
that orange-red sort of shade are Bardic-trainees. They aren't* required *to learn
weaponswork, but they are encouraged to do so. Bards are often out in the wilds and
in dangerous places—and while most of them* can *talk or entertain themselves out of
trouble, it's a good idea to be able to fight your way out as well. But when you work
with them, be very, very careful of their hands. The last thing you want to do is injure
the hands of a Bard; it would be a catastrophe for them. You could set their musical
training back a fortnight or more, depending on how badly the hand was hurt.:*

He made a mental note of it. Interesting. He knew what Bards were,
of course, but he had never seen one, much less heard one. Something
more to look into.

He ignored the boy in blue, but once it was clear that Alberich wasn't
going to single him out for attention, the boy watched *him* with a kind of
speculation in his eyes. Alberich wondered if rumor had already begun
to spread that the dreaded Karsite Trainee was one and the same with
Dethor's new Weapons Second.

:It has,: Kantor confirmed. *:Although I don't know that he would have heard
it yet; the youngsters from your first class are beginning to put two and two together. I
suspect that it will be one of the main topics of conversation over dinner. Certainly, by
nightfall the whole Collegium will know.:*

Unfortunately, it wouldn't stay there. And once it got out into the
Court, the nobles and the rest who hung about here, well, things were
likely to get very interesting.

:Things are interesting now,: Kantor said.

If Alberich had been a stag, he'd have thrown up his head and sniffed
the breeze at that, trying to find the scent of trouble. The statement
boded no good, no matter what language it was spoken in.

:Just what does that mean?: he thought probingly at Kantor.

:I'll tell you later,: Kantor promised. But that was all that the Companion
would say, and eventually Alberich gave up trying to extract something
from him.

Easier to pound sense into a foolish Trainee. So Alberich set about
doing just that.

But it was going to be a long afternoon.

5

The sunset outside the sitting-room window made a fine backdrop for the meal that another servant had brought them. There were not too many different ways that one could roast a pig, nor stew apples in honey, and beans were beans no matter what you did to them, so at least this dinner had not left Alberich with that particularly odd feeling of dislocation when flavors he expected weren't there.

"A remarkable first day," Dethor said, with more than a hint of satisfaction. "Hand me those plates, would you?"

Alberich handed over the stack of soiled plates, and Dethor packed them neatly in a straw container like the one that their dinner had come in. The servant that had appeared just after darkness fell waited patiently to take it away; the clean plates it contained, evidently meant for tomorrow (so *that* was where they came from!), were already stowed in Dethor's sitting-room cupboard.

Alberich could only shrug. "And I would know this, how?" he asked logically.

Dethor laughed, a sight which would, no doubt, have astonished his pupils. Weaponsmasters, of course, *never* laughed. They also, according to popular repute, never ate, never slept, and were possessed of the ability to know *instantly* whenever one of their pupils had done something he shouldn't, because he was always punished for it with an extra-hard lesson the next day. It obviously never occurred to boys that their guilty expressions always gave them away…

"Don't get coy with me, my lad," Dethor replied. "You know very well how remarkable it was."

Alberich gave the servant a sidelong glance; the man took the hint, picked up the carrier, and took himself off. Dethor sat down beside the fireplace and motioned to Alberich to take his own seat.

"I—I feel—unsettled," Alberich said at last. "I am treated as if I belong—yet I do not. I *should* not. So how comes it, that it is as if I do? And how comes it, that it feels to me as if I should?"

"I wish I could tell you, lad," Dethor sighed, and stared out the window at the darkening trees. "If I could, well, I suspect we'd not be at odds with your land. You're not the first Karsite to come over the Border, as you know—though I suspect you didn't until you found it out here. You're not even the first Karsite to be Chosen, though all of the rest were tiny children when they escaped, and were basically Valdemaran when they became Trainees. But you *are* the first adult Karsite ever Chosen, and I have to think that it's something in you that makes you different from your fellows."

Well, that answered one question—why Vkandis, if indeed His Hand was behind all of this, hadn't arranged for one or another of the former Karsite children to be Chosen. Clearly, he had. And clearly, whatever He wanted from such an arrangement hadn't happened. Alberich stared at the fire in the fireplace. "But it is to Karse—to the Sunlord—that I belong," he said softly. He *knew* that; it was at the core of him. Nothing about that part of him had changed. If that part had changed, he would no longer be himself.

"Your god is no issue to us; we respect a man who keeps to his own gods, and it makes no difference to the Heralds who another Herald gives his soul to. But are you vowed to Karse?" Dethor asked shrewdly. "Or to your people? That's two very different things, my lad. A country— well—that can be a lot of things to different people; some would say it's the land itself. But land can change hands. Some say it's the leaders, but leaders die. Or the religion—but I'll tell you something you'll *never* have heard in Karse—and that's this: religions *change*. I've seen it happen, and I'll bet my boots that if you ask your priestly friends down in the city, they'll tell you that *yours* has changed from what it was."

That was such an astonishing statement that Alberich could only stare at him. Change? How could a religion *change?* Didn't truth come directly from God?

Dethor poked at a log sticking out on the hearth with his toe. "Don't look at me that way. Ask your priests, and see if I'm not right," he said, calmly. "Ah, this is daft. I'm only giving you too much to think about. Look, Alberich, I know this isn't easy for you, and there isn't much I can do about that. You'll have to reckon out what's important to you, and stick to that. Do that, and you'll have *one* thing you can hang onto, no matter how unsettled you feel. That'll give you a bit of firm ground to hold to, as it were, and once you've got that, you can take the time to figure out more." He raised an eyebrow. *"Have* you one thing, right this minute, that's worth everything to you?"

"Honor," Alberich said promptly, without thinking. Without *having* to think. Which meant, he realized, even as the word left his lips, that the choice was *right*.

"Then you stick to that, and you'll be all right, and eventually you'll find your feet under you again," Dethor told him, and yawned. "Me, I'm off for bed. I may not have chased lads around the salle today, but it's been a long one for me anyway." He laughed again. "Good thing I don't get fighting Karsites turn up to become my Seconds every day!"

Alberich immediately got up, but Dethor waved at him to seat himself again. "Now, that doesn't mean *you* need to! Maybe you wear Grays, but you're no Trainee; you set your own hours."

"Only so, I alert and awake will be, when first arrives the class," Alberich replied dryly. Dethor chuckled under his breath, got stiffly out of his chair, and shuffled off into the shadows. Alberich sagged back into his own chair, but in the next moment, he was on his feet, staring broodingly into the fire. He wasn't tired, not even physically—that single workout with the young Guardsman had been good, but he was used to that sort of exercise all day long. When he wasn't drilling or actually fighting, he was riding, in all weathers, without the luxury of hot meals and showering baths. He was used to going perpetually short of sleep; riding before dawn and not finding his bedroll until after he'd stood first watch. When he got a bath, it was usually out of a stream or a rain barrel. When he got a meal, it was field rations augmented by whatever someone had managed to shoot or buy from a farmer.

No, he wasn't tired, not physically, and certainly not mentally. He hadn't heard anything in the back of his head from Kantor for a while, not since that class of children at archery practice. On the whole, that suited him. Kantor was very facile, very persuasive, and he didn't want any interference with his own thoughts right now. He wanted to work through them on his own.

He turned away from the fire, clasped his hands behind his back, and began to pace up and down the long sitting room. He didn't trouble to light any of the lamps; he was used to firelight, and his night vision was very good.

A suite of rooms—even a bed—I haven't slept in a bed for so long that it's going to feel strange. The last time he'd been in a bed—the one at the House of

Healing didn't count—had been just over a year ago, and he hadn't had possession of it for more than a single watch before he'd been turned out by the man he was relieving. It hadn't been much of a bed, just a sack filled with straw in a box on four legs, but it had been better than sleeping in the mud that had passed for ground around there.

Beds, hot meals, willing pupils to teach. Pupils who, with rare exceptions, were singularly devoid of "attitude." Oh, this place, these people—they were so very seductive! If he could have said, "This is what is wrong with my life, and this, and I would change this, and *this* is what I want above all else—" and then have all of that come to pass in a single stroke, *this* is what he would have picked as the way to spend the rest of his life.

The only trouble was, he wasn't where he "should" have been, and he was irrevocably bonded to a White Demon.

He wasn't in Karse. These people were not his people; their gods were not his God. All right, it wasn't a White Demon, it was a Companion, but Kantor was still keeping out of his sight, because he still got a reflexive chill whenever he saw the creature unexpectedly. And yet—

And yet—

If Kantor wasn't the best friend he had never had before, he was certainly the next thing to it. Uncanny, that was—the way they fit together. It was not unnerving, but that was only because Kantor's personality seemed to fit into his without a single rough edge. Strange, yet completely familiar, and the longer that this day had gone, the less possible it seemed that he could ever properly live without the Companion's presence in the back of his mind.

He paused, staring blindly out the window. Full dark it was out there, and as a consequence, what he saw was himself, outlined by the fire, reflected in the glass. Outlined in fire—well, *that* was appropriate. In a sense, he had gone from one fire into another...

As for the life he'd been offered—well. It was all there, virtually everything he could have asked for. Even the fact that he was *not* being asked to fight anymore. At least, not for the moment, though that could change, and he was too wise in the ways of conflict not to know that.

He hated fighting. Oh, not the physical exercise, that he loved; he loved the feel of a solid hit, the surety of a stroke, the way that his body knew what to do without his head having to tell it. Perhaps it would be better to say that he hated killing, despised hurting people. Even when he was ridding the world of bastards that pillaged and raped helpless villagers left without even the means to defend themselves, he hated it. Intellectually speaking, there had to be a better way of dealing with those mad, two-legged dogs than killing them.

Practically speaking, there wasn't, of course, not really. It was kill them or face the consequences of not killing them, and know that they would go on doing what they had been at before you caught them— knowing that even if you locked them up, eventually they'd either get loose or kill themselves and probably others *trying* to escape. Then the deaths of people who absolutely did not deserve it were on *your* head. So he had long ago resigned himself to that fact, and concentrated on ridding the world of murderers as expediently, dispassionately, and humanely as possible.

But there was a part of him that had uncomfortable questions about that, questions he had tried not to think about until this moment. Brigands were not the only creatures that preyed on his people…

Yes, indeed, when tax- and tithe-collectors strip folk of all but the bare essentials, leaving them sometimes not even that. And what of the Sunpriests and their Fires, hmm? Shouldn't you have thought about ridding the world of them, too?

The fire popped and crackled as he passed it, as if his thought of the Sunpriests' Fires had somehow roused it. He shuddered, as the memory of flame licking over his own flesh interposed itself between *then* and *now.*

Before this moment, before he had crossed the Border into this strange land, he had shied away from that question; he had told himself that priestly business was none of his concern—well, except for the uneasy knowledge that they *might* one day come for him. But, in truth, he had tried not to think about that at all, tried to focus on his duty, his men, the job at hand and getting on with it.

Was that cowardice? He had to admit that it probably was, and he was ashamed of it. But what could he, one single man, have done, more than he had *been* doing, other than declare himself against the priests, be denounced, and sent to the Fires himself?

And that was even if they hadn't learned what he was, the powers he harbored. Anathema. Unclean. *If thine eye gaze upon the forbidden, put it out with thine own hand, lest ye be tempted.* That was the Writ and Rule, and he had not obeyed it. Yet how could he have eliminated something over which he'd had no control, except by denouncing himself? And if he'd done that—he'd have done the enemy's work for it, taking a competent fighter, a good officer, out of the fighting.

Had he put so much effort into being a perfect soldier in Vkandis' service so that he might, somehow, expiate the fact that he had those witch-powers?

Which aren't evil. You know they aren't evil, and you knew it then, no matter what the priests claimed. You had no control over those dreams and visions—and what was more, the things they showed you actually helped you to protect Vkandis' people. So why would the Sunpriests say they were evil—unless there was something about those powers that they were afraid of? Was it that they feared one day you might see something about them that you shouldn't?

It was twenty paces from one end of the sitting room to the other, and he measured it a hundred times with his restless walking.

He had prided himself to a certain extent on being brave. He just hadn't been brave enough...

Honor. Dethor asked me what I cherished above everything else, and I said, "honor." But what did I mean when I said that?

He fretted and gnawed at his own soul, tearing into it obsessively, digging deeper than he had ever done before. He had never had so much time to think. Yes, he'd done a fair amount of contemplation while in the keeping of the Healers, but most of *that* had been spent in fighting the assumption that everyone else here had taken as a given that he should be *pleased*, even thrilled, with this whole business of being Chosen. He'd been so concerned with resentment that he hadn't really put any time into thinking about his position. Kicking against the traces—

Oh, what an image that conjured up! The warhorse pulling the cart, and fighting every step of the way.

And such a cart as he was hitched to now; the entire burden of *accepting* Companion, title of "Herald," and all! But it included something he had wanted for so very long.

Yes, I hitched myself to it. I walked into the harness, willingly, because the harness was so handsome. To become a Weaponsmaster—Sunlord! If anyone had ever asked him what he would have chosen to be above all things—to emulate the men he had most admired, from the day he had stepped into the cadet corps.

Those competent, strong men who, when he was a cadet, had offered their own austere brand of distant affection to him, who had counseled him and given guidance and an example to follow—who had given him, when he was forced to bid farewell to his mother, enough to feed his hungry heart.

They must have taken the place of the father he had never known. And he wanted to be like them; had wanted it then, and wanted it now.

Others had called them heartless, but he knew, and he had always known, that they were anything but heartless. They held themselves apart, not because they did not care, but because they feared to care too much. Even for him—though that resolution had not been proof against his need and theirs.

There had been two of them; two he would have done anything for, men he would have rather died than disappoint.

Berthold. Aged Berthold, white-haired but still strong and vigorous, able to hold his own with men half his age—he was the man who was Weaponsmaster to the youngest boys, the ones who barely knew which end of a blade to hold. He was patient, but unforgiving when it came to slackers. He had seen how Alberich was trying, watched him, though Alberich hadn't known it at the time, when Alberich had slipped into the unoccupied salle for extra exercise and practice. He had "chanced upon" one of those practices, and from that moment on, had made certain that Alberich never had to practice alone. A pat on the back or the head, a few well-chosen words of praise or condolence—that was all the physical demonstration of affection he ever allowed himself, but Alberich would have gone through fire for such rewards.

And when Alberich passed out of the junior class into the senior cadets, so Berthold had seen to it that *his* student, Aksel, took up Alberich's education where Berthold had left off.

Aksel, a powerful little man as flexible as he was strong, probably knew more about fighting styles and weapons than any twelve ordinary fighters in the Sunsguard. His first words to Alberich were, "Berthold thinks you have it in you. If it's there, we'll bring it out together."

Alberich had never known just what "it" was supposed to be, but Aksel offered instruction and approval in equal measure, and Alberich had drunk it in as thirsty ground drank rain. They were the finest two men that Alberich had ever known...

And they *taught me what honor was.* Which might be why, when Dethor had asked what he most valued, it was "honor" he had seized on instantly.

He had learned from their example as much as from anything they actually said to him.

Honor was never taking the easy way when it was also the wrong one. Never telling a falsehood *unless* the truth was painful and unnecessary, or a lie was necessary to save others. Never manipulating the truth to serve only yourself. Protecting the weak and helpless; standing fast even when fear made you weak. Keeping your word.

Perhaps that was all part of the problem; serving the Sunpriests had turned him away from the path of honor. How was it protecting the weak and helpless, when he and his troops were turned aside from their duties on the Border to shepherd a tithe collector and his treasure boxes from village to village? How could he keep his word when those about him were making idle promises that *he* was expected to fulfill, promises that again took him away from real duty to satisfy some idiotic whim or moment of vainglory? How could he speak the truth when the truth would simply have gotten him thrown to the Fires?

In the simpler world of the cadet corps, no such compromises had ever entered into his personal equation. They only came when he left that world.

Perhaps that was why Aksel and Berthold hadn't left it themselves… perhaps they had known, in their heart of hearts, that going out into the world would only begin a long train of broken vows.

Vows like the ones he broke when he accepted his place here, his position as the partner of a Companion.

But a vow went both ways. He had pledged himself to the service of Karse and the God; only later were vows required that he pledge to obey the word of any priest, and he'd had misgivings, but it was too late to try and back out at that point. At that same ceremony, though, there had been another set of vows—the priest who administered the oaths to the new officers had pledged on behalf of *all* priests to regard the new officers as Vkandis' chosen, to stand beside them if accused, and succor them in need.

And he had quickly learned how little they honored *those* oaths.

The Sunpriests broke their vows to me long before I ever broke mine to them. Did that mean the pact between him and them was also broken? Was it wrong of him to feel that *their* betrayal released him from his oath? Or was he just trying to rationalize his own sins?

He realized, belatedly, that all this pacing was probably keeping poor Dethor awake. A glance outside showed him that the moon was well up, and there was plenty of moonlight silvering the grass outside; more than enough for him to pace all he wanted to without tripping over something in the dark.

With a silent apology, he let himself out through the salle, pacing across the wooden floor by the light entering through the clerestory windows, opening the outer door and stepping out into the waiting embrace of the night.

The chill air carried a hint of damp and a scent of grass; from the distance came the sounds of voices, too far off to be more than a murmur. But the very cadences were strange to his ear, and he felt an involuntary shiver of alarm he couldn't suppress.

Oh, these Valdemarans! Not four marks into his first real day among them—he couldn't count the time spent with the Healers—and look what had happened. They had told him the one thing he longed to hear, and had not realized that he longed to hear it—that he was *needed*. They offered for his inspection a gaggle of green children, *good* children, and told him that these young people would go out, unprepared, against the kind of animals *he* had fought against—unless he helped train them. And how—*how*—could he *not* have responded to that?

To defend the weak and helpless—how much better could he do that by training others to do the same job? How could he allow anyone to *send* the weak and helpless—well, all right, the half-trained—out to throw themselves down and be trampled on, when he knew he could remedy the situation?

There was nothing dishonorable about taking that job. There was nothing honorable in refusing it.

Yes, but these are not your *people… so where does your honor come into it? Or is there some reason why it doesn't further break your vows to train Valdemarans?*

But then came additional questions. When he already knew, from the evidence of his own experience, how utterly *wrong* some of the things he'd taken as truth were, why should it? When had that definition of "honor" ever demanded absolute adherence to the Sunpriests of Karse?

Just because the Sunpriests would have put any Valdemaran they found to the Fire and sword—well, he knew how wrong the Sunpriests could be. He had found a Sunpriest here, an upright man who everything in him cried out to trust, who had *told* him in no uncertain words that the Valdemarans were good and true, and that it was his duty to Vkandis Himself to ally himself with them. So where did that leave his vows and his honor?

He did not realize how fast he had walked, or how far, until an angry *snort* brought his attention back to his surroundings.

He looked up, and found he was in the middle of a meadow or clearing, ringed with trees. From where he stood, he could see some lights, a few, through the trees to his right, but otherwise he could just as well have been in the middle of a meadow in farming country.

The snort had come from a very large, white, four-legged creature just under the trees in front of him. It moved out into the moonlight, and quickly resolved itself into a familiar shape.

A Companion. It wasn't Kantor; it wasn't stocky enough, and besides, it didn't "feel" like Kantor. There was, in fact, a disturbing absence of feeling about this Companion, as if there was a wall between him and it.

A moment later, it was joined by a second—then a third, a fourth, and a fifth. They moved toward him, slowly, but deliberately, and he hadn't spent most of his life around horses not to recognize the menace in their movement. Every muscle was tense. They weren't so much walking as stalking toward him, their narrowed eyes glittering in the moonlight. There was no mistaking their hostility, and he was the object of it.

A chill ran down his back as he turned slowly, preparing to go back the way he had come—only to find his path to escape blocked by another pair of Companions. He turned back, to see that the rest had spread themselves out, and were encircling him in an all-too-familiar pincer movement. A moment later, he was surrounded.

They were huge creatures, and came armed with their own hooves. Their weight—an ordinary horse in a panic could easily kill and trample a man—a trained warhorse was as formidable an opponent as any warrior that rode him. How much more dangerous would Companions be, who had minds and intelligence of their own? His heart hammered with a surge of fear, and his throat tightened.

"Your pardon, I beg—" he said aloud, cautiously, as all the stories of White Demons rose again in his mind, no longer tales to frighten a child into obedience, but very tangible. "Intrude, I did not intend."

His words had no effect; none at all. These creatures were so full of deadly malice that he could feel it where he stood. He didn't know what they intended to do to him, but their eyes glittered anger at him, and he felt exactly as he had at the moment that the Sunpriest denounced him…

Like the Sunpriest, these creatures looked at him and condemned him. Like the Sunpriest, they fully intended to wipe him from the earth.

Sunlord, shield me—Suddenly he heard the angry trumpet of a stallion and the thunder of hooves behind him, and dropped instinctively to his knees, *knowing* it would do no good, but trying to make himself less of a target anyway.

The trumpet turned to a scream, and as he winced away, a new Companion pounded out of the night, hooves throwing up clods of sod as it pounded toward him.

But the new one charged through the enclosing circle and brutally smashed his full weight into the shoulder of the nearest Companion threatening Alberich. Knocking it half off of its feet, whirling to lash at another with flailing hooves, snaking his neck around to snap at the neck of a third, the new Companion skidded to a halt beside him—

And Kantor stood with his Chosen, snorting defiantly, pawing the torn earth in challenge.

Instantly, Alberich rose to his feet, taking his stance at Kantor's shoulder.

:What did I do? What do they think I did?: he asked as the other Companions laid back their ears and tore the ground with their own hooves. *:Why are they so angry at me?:*

:It's nothing you *did,:* Kantor replied shortly, and rumbled warningly when another stepped forward a pace. His own ears were so flat to his head it looked as if they'd been cropped. *:It's what you are. Karsite. Which they, young fools that they are, will not abide.:*

Kantor whipped his head around, baring his teeth at all of the others, screaming defiance with voice and mind. *:But you are my Chosen, and they will not touch you! Nor will they reach you, except going through me!:*

But the others seemed just as angry—and just as determined. And there were seven of *them* to Kantor's one. They snorted and added their trumpeting to Kantor's, pawing up the sod savagely.

:Come, then!: Kantor "shouted," so that Alberich winced at the strength of the voice in his mind, following the mental shout with a challenging scream. *:Try and take me, if you dare, you impudent young puppies! Try—and see what fools you are!:*

"Kantor, *no!*" he protested, knowing that, no matter how formidable his Companion was, he was still no match for the power of so many. "Don't—"

:Stop.:

The single word rang in his head like a gong, completely driving out everything else, so *powerful* was it. For a moment, it was as if he'd been punched in the gut, unable even to breathe. He was blinded and deafened, and when he was able to think again, he found himself on his knees, as if the Word had driven him there.

He wasn't the only one so affected; Kantor stood with head hanging and eyes glazed, and the others were shaking their heads, staggering about, looking utterly dazed. *He* had recovered first, and so he was the one who saw the final Companion come pacing into the meadow, striding as a king would stride across a royal carpet spread for his pleasure.

This—this newcomer was the very essence of *Companion*. His shining coat glowed pearly and silken in the moonlight, his mane and tail fell like waterfalls of silver, and his eyes held the wisdom of ages past and the knowledge of ages to come—and Alberich knew, in that moment when he looked into the stallion's eyes, that the knowledge held as much sorrow as joy...

The stallion swung his head about to stare at the others—all but Kantor, that is—with the kind of *look* that Aksel and Berthold would give pupils who had gone so far beyond merely disappointing their teachers that even the most irrepressible or arrogant of boys could not have gone unaffected.

:What is this?: the newcomer asked—no—*demanded,* in tones of disgust. *:What do I find here? Companions—threatening someone else's* Chosen? *What were you thinking? How* could *you?:*

One of Alberich's attackers raised his head and stared at the stallion; Alberich "heard" nothing, but he got the distinct impression that the other was trying to justify his actions, rather like a defiant little boy who knows very well he's in the wrong, but simply cannot bear to admit it. The others were making no such attempts; if a Companion could have flushed or paled with shame, these would have done so.

The stallion gave the defiant one short shrift. *:Enough!:* he said, but the effect on the other Companion was as if he'd been struck between the eyes with a hammer. He literally dropped to his knees, as the others winced. *:You, Jasker,:* the stallion said, more in sorrow than anger. *:What you and yours have endured is* no *excuse. What happened to these others is no excuse either. You should have learned that by now.:* The stallion swung his head around, and again Alberich felt the full force of his gaze. *:You, Alberich—Chosen of Kantor—have you, yourself, ever brought harm to a single soul of Valdemar?:*

"Not unless bandits they were, and with a band of brigands riding," Alberich said truthfully. "Claim I cannot, that my men and I did not make it so that others freed were, to come against your folk—but never a Valdemaran I touched, nor did any of those under my command."

:So I thought.: The stallion turned his attention back to the errant one, who had all but shrunk into a mere pony beneath that gaze. *:Well.:*

It was very clear that the defiant one was the target of a scathing lecture. He was not to hear what the stallion said to the other, but it made the formerly defiant one shrink even further. And if something the size and shape of a horse could have been said to "slink on its belly," then that was precisely what the Companion did—toward Alberich.

:I beg your pardon,: the young one said—whispered, rather.

:I can't hear you,: the stallion rumbled, like a storm on the horizon.

:I most humbly beg your pardon and ask your forgiveness—: came the humiliated response. *:Chosen of Kantor, I acted vilely. I am unworthy.:*

:I should say so!: Kantor snorted, ears laid back, and teeth bared. *:Arrogant little beast, I should—:*

:Kantor!: the stallion said warningly.

But Kantor only raised his head and looked the other in the face, with no sign of the profound shame they displayed. *:I only said that I should, Taver. I should thrash this little cretin around Companion's Field twice—but I won't. I won't ever. Because I'm stronger and a better fighter and it would be no contest between us, so long as it was a fair fight, and not a case of a mob against one—:*

Somehow, the other's head drooped even lower.

:Kantor, I beg your pardon, too,: came the sad voice—if a voice in the mind could sob, Alberich sensed that this one was on the verge of just that. Alberich decided that enough was enough.

For whatever reason, this boy—and it might *look* like a horse, but it *acted* like a boy—had a grudge against all Karsites. Apparently he had decided on his own that Kantor had been deceived or subverted.

And he elected to take out his grievances on this Karsite—Alberich—who had somehow come within his reach. Why the child felt this way, Alberich had no idea—but it was apparently a driving passion, and had driven him to gather up a pack of his cronies to act when Alberich had unwittingly put himself in a position where he could be attacked with relative impunity.

But there was also no doubt in his mind that the boy—colt?—had been forcibly shown the error of his ways. And that his contrition was real, his repentance sincere, his shame overwhelming. And there was only one answer that Alberich could make to that.

He stepped forward, and put a hand under the colt's chin. The Companion started at his touch, and began to shake, his skin shivering with reaction, as Alberich forced his head up so that he could look into the colt's eyes.

"Pardon I give, freely," he said, as he felt the colt fighting to keep from bolting. "But more. Forgiveness I give also."

:Jasker?: prompted the stallion.

The youngster blinked, and Alberich was startled to see two crystal teardrops form in his eyes and slide down his pale, moon-silvered cheeks. *:I am so sorry—thank you—:*

"From you, I will have a promise in exchange," Alberich replied grimly.

"Never again to act without due thought, or so terribly without *honor!*"

:*I promise!*: the young one replied fervently—but Alberich was not finished.

"And you—the rest!" he continued, raking them with as stern a gaze as the stallion's. "Never, ever again to let one with passion lead you to unreason!"

He "heard" murmurs of assent, so subdued that he could only hearken back to the day when Berthold had discovered that some of the cadets had slipped into his personal quarters to assuage their curiosity and had been caught rifling through his possessions. Not Alberich—but he had witnessed the tail end of that confrontation, when the miscreants had been brought up before the entire corps.

"Then your punishment to this gentleman, I leave," he said. "My forgiveness you have. *His*—you must earn, I suspect."

The stallion nodded gravely. A few more moments passed, during which there were, no doubt, a few more silent exchanges. Then the others slunk away.

The stallion turned his attention toward Alberich and Kantor. :*Brave, Kantor. And very wise, to call me, rather than take them on yourself:*

:*I am glad you took no longer to arrive!:* Kantor bowed his head. :*Taver, they are children—and we both know how Jasker... Well. One of us elders should have seen to him before this. We are fortunate that nothing worse came of this.:*

:*Probably.:* The stallion's flanks heaved with a sigh. :*One cannot foresee everything.:*

:*No. One cannot. Thank you, Taver.:*

The stallion turned to Alberich, and suddenly he knew why he had that nagging sense of familiarity—

"You are of Talamir bonded, no?" he asked.

:*I am. And the chief of the Companions; and as such, it was by my neglect that this child was able to menace you. So I, too, ask your forgiveness—:*

But Alberich interrupted him with a shaky chuckle. "Nah, who can tell, what in a boy's head will be? No need, there is. And no harm either. But, I think, good it would be to return to my place."

Taver's ears pricked forward. :*You are gracious—:*

"I am tired," Alberich corrected. "And late, it is. Good night, I bid you."

:*Good night. And know that after this, you will find a warmer welcome among us. No matter who else troubles you, you will always be welcome among the Companions.:* The great stallion ghosted off after the others, leaving Alberich alone with Kantor.

"Thank you," he said to his Companion. Kantor tossed up his head and looked satisfied, if still a bit ruffled.

:*Jasker—underwent much horror at the hands of the Sunpriests,*: Kantor explained. :*He, and all his family. All lost, and in great fear and pain—*:

Family? Companions have families? He supposed, on second thought, they had to come from somewhere. And to lose one's whole family—

:*Night-demons?*: he asked, with a shiver. He had seen what Night-demons left behind, or at least, that was what he had been told had happened, and had heard the things only once, off in the far distance. He never wished to come that close again. The Sunpriests claimed that Night-demons were sent only against the traitors and heretics and enemies of Karse—but Alberich could not imagine how those ravening horrors could determine just who was a traitor, or a heretic—

:*Yes,*: Kantor replied, simply.

:*Then I understand.*: The Night-demons did not leave very much to bury; often it was only enough to tell whether the victim had been male or female, and sometimes not even that much. :*I hope that Taver will not be too hard on him. Shall we go back to the salle?*:

:*You do have the first class in the morning,*: Kantor reminded him. :*I believe it would be wise.*: Then, very quietly, :*You are a man of much honor, Chosen.*:

Alberich started. Then, slowly, smiled.

"I hope I may be," he said after a moment, "I only hope I may be."

6

Alberich contemplated a substantial pile of books waiting beside his chair in the sitting room with a sigh. If he'd seen half that number of books in the past several years, he'd have been very much surprised. Lessons. *Classes!* At *his* age—

Still, only a fool wishes to stop learning. And he needed these classes if he was going to understand these Valdemarans.

He had two of these classes (not three!) for now, both of which entailed an enormous amount of reading. In the interests of preserving his authority as Dethor's Second, however, he was not having his classes, his lessons, with the rest of the Trainees. That idea had been suggested and discarded within two days of being officially appointed and functioning as the Weaponsmaster's Second—four days after actually accepting the job. Dethor had been the one insisting on some alternate form of tutoring, though; Alberich hadn't had anything to do with that particular decision. Not that he'd been particularly enamored of squeezing himself into a desk beside a lot of children. It wasn't just that it was undignified, it was that he needed to impress those same children with his authority, and he wasn't going to do *that* if he was bumbling through classes as one of their "peers." Evidently Dethor felt exactly the same, and had gotten rather testy about it.

In fact, he hadn't even *seen* the Collegium yet. All of his time had been spent in or around the salle; when he wasn't kicking youngsters into shape, he was catching up on the thousand and one little things that Dethor hadn't been able to get to for the past few years since the bone-aches got into his hands. He tried, Sunlord knew, but he had to do things slowly and the work built up faster than he could do it. And often enough, he couldn't do it at all.

There was a shed full of practice armor and real armor discarded by the Guard and Heralds that needed only a bit of mending to be useful again. Shoulder plates and elbow and knee protection just needed broken leather straps or the padding replaced, the bit of chain lying about could be repaired with a few new rings and some patient weaving. Practice armor of leather and canvas generally had to have the same treatment, or tears mended. It took a little bit of skill and strong fingers, nothing more.

Then there were practice weapons in need of mending, and archery targets to be salvaged. The things that got mended soonest tended to be in the sizes that everyone could use, which left children who were smaller, taller, or thinner than the usual struggling with poorly fitting armor. *He* was fixing the odd-sized items first, and had the satisfaction of seeing at least two of his smallest pupils looking comfortable in practice.

In the shed he had also uncovered two or three crates of oddments. The oddments were very odd indeed and, unlike the things needing mending, had been packed carefully away. Alberich hadn't had a chance to do more than look into the crates, but it almost appeared as if the Weaponsmasters of the past had been collecting and storing anything that ever came into their hands that *might* have been a weapon, on the chance that someday, someone might be able to add it to the weaponry lessons.

Now, Alberich just might be that someone, for Weaponsmaster Aksel had learned a great many strange forms of weaponswork over the years, and had passed it all on to Alberich—at least in the form of knowing what a particular piece was *for* and how it was handled, if not in expertise. He wanted very badly to go delving into those chests… but the Collegium had other ideas for his so-called "free time."

Those lessons, for instance. The first of which was History; not only of Valdemar, which he had expected, but also some of the history of their neighbors. It was a good thing that the understanding of the written language had come part and parcel with the spoken word, or he *would* have been floundering. Though how something that looked like a horse could come to know how to read—or have any reason to—was beyond him. At the moment, he wasn't asking many questions of his world; he was just taking things at face value and trying not to think too hard about them. It wasn't that he didn't want the answers, it was that the answers only led to more questions, and *those* to more in their turn. He needed to budget his time carefully; he needed to concentrate his mind (and his questions) on the matters at hand.

His History tutor was yet another Herald, a little bird of a man called Elcarth, who had probably read more books in the past year than

Alberich and any two other Karsite officers combined had seen in their lives. He did have a knack with history, though, being able to get at the story behind the history—and breezing right past the things that didn't have a lot of relevance to what was going on in the world at the moment. He'd concentrated on the Founding of Valdemar in regard to Baron Valdemar's issues with the Great Empire and his decision to flee with his people, then skipped over all the years between settling and the coming of the Companions with a dismissive "hardship, suffering, sacrifice, the usual sort of tales of our heroic ancestors that you'd expect to see, and you can read about it all later." Then, stopped on the tale of how Valdemar had prayed to *all* gods for help in ensuring that his Kingdom was well led after his death. The answer had taken the form of the Companions… which had given Alberich a double shock, for Elcarth had unearthed a dusty account of the event, too tattered and ancient to have been created just for Alberich's benefit. If it didn't date all the way back to King Valdemar, it was old enough to have been copied directly from a document of that time. And in that account was the supposed litany of all of the gods that Valdemar had prayed to. One of them had been Vkandis Sunlord…

Which implied that either Valdemar had been familiar with Alberich's God, or the author of the account had been. Now, in either case, the further implication was that Vkandis would be favorably inclined to Valdemar and her King. Oh, there were a lot more implications than just that one, but that single suggestion was enough to undermine everything *he* had thought of as "history."

But Alberich wasn't allowed to dwell on that, for Elcarth had accelerated past the rest of Valdemar's reign, and that of the next few of his descendants with "there are a great many legends, songs, and tales, and you can look into them at your leisure," settling into the point where Valdemarans first encountered folk who were as strong or stronger than they were, who were self-sufficient and self-governing, and had no interest in uniting with them. Up until that point, as they expanded their borders, all they had come in contact with were small and isolated settlements that were perfectly happy to have the protection of the Kingdom of Valdemar, or "countries" (more like "counties," seeing that some of them could have been crossed in a day) that were willing to ally, and later be absorbed by, the greater nation. It was the Kingdom of Hardorn that they initially contacted, in a cautious probe back in the direction from which they had come, and that was the chapter that Alberich was dealing with now.

The other class was concerned with the government of Valdemar and how it worked; a good bit drier, this was. He'd been given the books yesterday by Elcarth, with instructions to read the first twenty pages or so. Apparently, his tutor would turn up this afternoon when Dethor would be instructing the youngest of the Trainees in their first lessons in edged weapons.

He'd read the first twenty pages as he'd been told and found it all rather… different. A complete contrast with Karse, which was ruled by the Son of the Sun who was in turn selected from the priesthood by the Sunlord Himself.

Supposedly. *Alberich* had never been near the Great Temple himself, never seen any of the Priests of the upper hierarchies or their ilk, nor had anyone he had ever met. Not bloody likely he ever would have either; the common folk were not supposed to trouble themselves about such things. Writ and Rule said that the Son of the Sun was selected by the Sunlord, and that was the extent of his personal knowledge. He had suspicions, of course, that the Sunlord had as much to do with the selection of His highest representative in Karse as He did in selecting Dethor's favorite hat. When had there last been a Son of the Sun selected from the village priests, for instance? They all seemed to come from among the high-ranking lot that never stirred out of Sunhame and were ever-increasingly out of touch with what was going on among the common people.

Karse actually had a king, but the position was purely symbolic, and had been for centuries. King Ortrech largely presided over a court concerned with the social functions of the old nobility and moneyed classes; the Sunpriests made all the real decisions insofar as the actual running of Karse. The King merely ratified what the priests decided, and occasionally the priests would in turn implement some small thing that the King wanted, such as the creation of a new tide or the granting of property to make a court noble into a landed one.

This, of course, was probably one of the causes of strife between the two lands—that Valdemar was ruled by a purely secular figure, and Karse by (supposedly) a divinely-guided one. Alberich wished that he was far enough along in the History classes to see what had happened when the Borders of Karse and Valdemar first met. Had *that* been the primal cause of the enmity? Or had it been something else?

The first few pages of the text on Valdemaran law and government had been perfectly straightforward. But then, toward the end of the assigned segment, he encountered a passage that left him blinking.

Of course, in the circumstance (which has only occurred three times in our recorded histories) that there have been no children of the reigning monarch that were Chosen, it falls to the nearest blood relative who is also a Herald to take up the Crown.

The text had gone on to describe how such a selection was made, based less upon the degree of consanguinity than of ability. Most of that had seemed irrelevant to Alberich—until he came to the part that said "*...and the vote of the Heraldic Circle as a bloc in the election of a new Monarch—provided that the candidate is at least a Trainee, if not a full Herald—comprises one third of the total, with that of the Council comprising two thirds.*"

Ordinary Heralds got a one-third vote in the selection of a King? That was tantamount to the officers of the Sunsguard having a say in the selection of the Son of the Sun!

He didn't know quite what to think about that. There was no question, however, that the Heralds had as much to do with creating the laws and government as they did in disseminating and dispensing it.

The morning classes kept him too busy to worry about all that, however, and by the time his putative tutor showed up, theoretical questions about the government of Valdemar had been pushed so far to the back of his mind that they didn't impinge on his thoughts in the least.

Then, when he saw his "tutor," the question foremost was if someone at the Collegium intended to mock him.

The "tutor" was a young woman in student Grays, slim and blonde, with a determined jaw and blue-gray eyes that considered him thoughtfully. He recognized her from the advanced weaponry class held at the very end of the day, although Dethor had never yet assigned Alberich to work directly with her.

"You might not remember me from the afternoon classes, Alberich," the girl said, in a matter-of-fact manner, as she held out her hand. "I'm Selenay."

"My tutor you are?" he replied, clasping her hand briefly. He didn't bother to hide the doubt in his voice.

She laughed, which surprised him a little. "Unlikely, I know, but the powers that be intend for you to get a practical exposure to how things are done in Valdemar, and they decided that we might as well—as the saying here goes—shoot two ducks with one arrow. You see, I'm the Heir. *Princess* Selenay. And every other afternoon, I serve in the City Courts. No one likes me being there without a bodyguard, and with *you* as my bodyguard, you can observe—as Elcarth put it—'government in action.' Anything you don't understand, I can explain, or Kantor can. Meanwhile, your presence will make the Council less nervous about my being there in the first place."

Alberich controlled his expression, and managed not to splutter. "At your side, the presence of the *Karsite* less nervous will make them?"

"But they won't know it's the Karsite who's my bodyguard," she replied, with a bare hint of irony. "Who I pick—with the senior Collegium staff's recommendations, of course—to act as my bodyguard is *entirely* the Collegium's business, not the Council's. All they will know, unless one of them decides to observe me, is that I've got someone in Grays to keep a weather-eye on my safety. They'll rightly assume that since Dethor must have had a hand in picking him, my escort will be quite competent. Oh, eventually they'll find out, you can't keep anything like that a secret, but by that time it will be so long established that objecting to my choice would make them look like idiots."

:Don't spoil her fun; she's been planning this for a fortnight,: Kantor advised.

:But—to trust me with the safety of the Heir—: He was utterly flabbergasted. He might have to look as if all this was just a matter of course, but at least he could drop any pretense of composure with Kantor, and he did so.

:Aren't you trustworthy?: Kantor countered. *:I know you would be the best person for the task; no one would take it as seriously as you will, because the Heralds all have a blind spot where the safety of Selenay is concerned. They believe that no one realizes that "Trainee Selenay" and the Heir are the same person, which is ridiculous—it's not exactly a secret, and even if it was, you couldn't keep information like that secure for very long.:*

Not very bright of them. *:And just because no one has tried to harm her, no one ever will, hmm?:* he replied. *:Perhaps it does take someone from outside to see the danger.:*

:Too true, I fear. And that isn't all, of course. You need to see how we work, so to speak, and you'll learn more from watching a common Herald's court than you ever would from books.:

:But when the great men find out who it is that is standing guard over their princess—:

:By that time you'll have proved yourself, and no one will think anything of it.: Kantor sounded very certain of himself; Alberich wasn't certain of anything except that there would be repercussions.

But who would be the ones facing the repercussions? Not I. No, that would be Dethor—Talamir—

"The King, your father—" he ventured. "Knows he of this?"

"Of course; he was the first one I suggested this to. I suppose you're ready?" Selenay asked, as calm and casual as if he'd asked what time of day it was.

"Ready?" What was he supposed to be ready for?

"You're coming down into the city with me, correct? As my bodyguard. You might as well start right now." She looked him up and down, critically. "That set of Grays should do, I suppose; they don't *look* quite like Trainee Grays, but they'll be all right. Are there any particular weapons you'd like to carry?"

"Weapons I would like to carry?" he repeated, feeling as if he'd been run over by something. "Ah—knives. A sword?"

"Well, let's get them and get on our way." Selenay waited for him to collect a set of plain knives and a common sword that he had just finished working on. He'd found them in that shed, and he had liked the balance immediately and had taken extra care with them, rewrapping the grips, cleaning, polishing, and sharpening. They were of sound make and good steel, and if old and much-abused, at least he knew they were in decent shape, with no hidden weakness in tang or blade. And he had never been the sort who got attached to a particular chunk of metal; as far as he was concerned, one blade was as good as another so long as it was balanced and sharp.

He'd never had any patience with those sagas wherein the hero found, was given, or created a famous blade with a name of its own. Ridiculous! These things were just pieces of steel, not something sentient. And when you focused too much on "my famous blade, Gazornenplatz," you were apt to forget that it was a tool, to be used and as readily left behind if need be. Aksel had felt the same, and when he'd caught cadets naming their blades and refusing to use any other, he often took the weapons in question to the forge himself and had them melted down, if they happened to have come out of the common arsenal. There wasn't a great deal he could do about heirloom blades or gifts, other than to ban them from the salle, but that's exactly what he had done. Fortunately, the question hadn't yet come up here, but if it ever did, Alberich intended to follow Aksel's example.

Alberich got sheaths and a belt and armed himself while Selenay waited with no signs of impatience.

When they left the salle, he discovered that Kantor had managed somehow to get himself saddled and bridled, and was waiting with a Companion mare in similar tack. How had he done *that?*

:Easy enough. When we show up at the stable door, the helpers know to get us tacked up. Don't forget, here *everyone realizes very well that we aren't horses, and treats us accordingly.:*

Alberich shook his head a little and mounted; Selenay was already in the saddle. The two Companions wheeled and trotted away from the salle, toward the Collegium.

"I'm on a long-track internship, just as you are," Selenay explained, over the chime of bridle bells. When he looked at her without understanding, she quickly explained. "When a Trainee is considered ready to become a Herald, *normally* they're given the white uniforms and they're sent out along with an older, experienced Herald as a mentor. At first, all they do is observe and discuss what the mentor did afterward. Then, over the course of a year and a half, they gradually begin to take on every task that the older Herald does, until *they* are doing all the work and it's the mentor that's observing. But I can't do that."

"Not wise, the Heir out alone with only one other to have as guardian, and not possible, *ordinary* to be, a troop of guards trailing," Alberich observed. "Not wise as well, the Heir to be out of reach, the countryside in, but worse, the Heir to be unguarded, a strange city within. Therefore, *here* the only option is."

She nodded. "Exactly. The Heralds and some of the Council assume that staying within the city is safe enough, but not even the most optimistic of them is mad enough to send me out in the field on Internship. And *because* I'm the Heir, once I put on Whites, I need to have every bit of the authority and experience of a seasoned Herald. The moment I'm a full Herald, I'll have a Council seat and a lot of responsibility. So instead of doing a regular Internship in Whites, I'm on a long-track Internship in Grays. I go sit in on Herald Mirilin's sessions of the Court of Justice, and every so often he asks me to make a judgment or take an action. Rendering justice is a lot of what a Herald does, you see, and you can study it all you like in books, but you never really understand it until you see it done and do it yourself. Justice isn't just *laws,* it's *people.*"

By this time they were approaching the graveled road that ran beside the enormous building of the Collegium. A Herald waited for them there, a nondescript man with long brown hair in a single braid down his back, and a small beard. He eyed Alberich with a stony expression.

"The new Trainee, Selenay?" he asked.

"And my bodyguard, Herald Mirilin," she replied, with perfect composure. "This is Alberich, and actually, he's on a long Internship, just like I am."

"I should think so," Mirilin replied, giving him another stone-faced look. "I will be interested in trying a blade against you at some point, Alberich."

Alberich just bowed slightly. The Herald wasn't being actively unfriendly, so there was certainly no point in taking exception with his passive hostility, when all that Alberich was there for was to observe and watch out for young Selenay. "At your convenience, sir," he replied, making certain that his voice was absolutely neutral.

They rode down into the city in silence; Alberich didn't care that Herald Mirilin made no effort at conversation. Most of his attention was taken up with watching for trouble—for if the Council was nervous about Selenay going out in public unguarded, there must be at least *some* reason for their concern. What little of his attention was left over was involved in simple observation.

Even if he had not known very well where he was, he would have known immediately that this was not Karse.

Nearest to the Palace and the Collegium, just outside the complex walls, were the manors of the nobility and wealthy. In Karse, such buildings were the property of the priesthood, each holding the staff and acolytes of one or another of the high-ranking Sunpriests. There was a great deal of difference between these places that held secular families and those manses. For one thing—sounds. *No* sounds of prayer, chanting, that sort of thing. Dogs barking, occasional voices of children and young people, and also the sounds of domestic animals; some homes had music drifting from them, some the sounds of a party or friendly gathering coming out of the gardens.

The farther the three of them got from the Palace, following a road that wound back and forth in a manner of which Alberich strongly approved (defensively, it made sense not to have a direct path to the Palace), the less expensive and more crowded the buildings became. And soon after that, rows of shops anchored by taverns, cookshops, or inns began to displace houses, and temple facades poked in among the shops, with shrines in city squares or on corners. The noise level increased with increasing traffic and population, of course. But again, it was obvious that this wasn't Karse, because there were so many different temples and shrines, and, as he noticed on closer observation, not all of the things that had appeared to be shrines were anything of the sort. Some were public fountains, some statues that (so far as he could tell) had no religious significance whatsoever.

Some were clearly statues of Valdemaran heroes, and it was no surprise that a great many of them were Heralds (who were invariably shown with their Companions). Not all, however, which was interesting. Equally interesting were the statues that almost always surmounted the public fountains, which were not martial in any way. In fact, given that the figures were dressed in quite elaborate clothing and often held tools or implements, he had a guess—a quite astonishing guess, since nothing of the sort would have been permitted in Karse. Common artisans and merchants, no matter how wealthy or talented, should never be allowed to exalt themselves to the point of putting up public statues of themselves. Vkandis frowned on spending money putting up vainglorious statues when the same money could be given to the temple, and at any rate, exalting yourself or your ancestors in such a fashion was an indulgence in the sin of pride.

"That is who?" he asked finally, catching Selenay's eye and nodding at a statue of a round, balding little man, who clutched a plumb-bob and compass and beamed at passers-by. Alberich rather liked his statue, for not only was there the usual spigot and basin of the public fountain, but the upper basin spilled over into a trough at street level, just the right height for dogs and cats to drink from.

Selenay followed his gaze and smiled. "I don't know *who* that is, but I know what he is, and why he's there," she said. "These statues began going up in Elspeth the Peacemaker's time. Valdemar had been pretty much at peace for more than a generation, and a lot of people were getting very prosperous. So they started putting up statues of themselves, which rather annoyed my ancestor, who thought it was a silly waste of money. She made a law forbidding people to put up privately owned statues on public streets, so they'd have the statues put up, then *give* them to the city. So she had another law made that forbade the putting up of anything on public streets unless it served a practical use and was for the public good, and being able to tie a horse to it didn't count. Oh, and you had to leave money in your will to see anything you put up was kept clean and in working order."

Alberich smiled at that. "Clever, that was," he responded. "And good for the city folk."

Selenay grinned. "Especially since the corners in the best part of the city went early, so people who wanted to do things had to take what they could get. Most people went for fountains and water pumps; the Queen said it was a pity that we were stuck with all those statues of a lot of vain old men, but at least now every street had a public water supply without taxes going to pay for it."

Mirilin overheard them, and unbent enough to smile slightly. "A wise woman, your ancestor," he said mildly. "If she had taxed them to pay for such things, they would have been calling for her head. But when they were able to make them into self-aggrandizing statuary, they were climbing all over themselves to oblige."

"Probably." Selenay shrugged. "I think she said something like that herself. At any rate, you'll find statues like that all over Haven now; when they aren't fountains and pumps, they can be almost anything useful. After a while, the artists that people hired to put up such things got to enjoy thinking up practical purposes. There's a clever basin over in the square where Pitcher and Bright cross where women can wash clothing—it was made that way on purpose. And there's dry mangers with stone canopies over them for feeding your horses or whatever at nearly every market square. There are covered benches, too, with inscriptions instead of statues, and an enormous public pigeon cote, which serves the purpose of giving poor people a place for birds for their pot, and gives the birds a place to go besides making nests in people's roofs." Both of them looked at him, clearly expecting some sort of comment from him; he thought about the larger towns in Karse that he had been in. Nothing this size, of course, but the only public sources of water were the wells in temple courtyards, and to use them…

To be fair, there were plenty of Sunpriests who encouraged all comers to take the water freely. But—well, it seemed to him there were fewer of the generous ones from year to year, and more who at the least, if they did not exact a tithe of work, cash, or goods for the water, insisted on daily attendance at one of the services *before* you got your water. That might not sound like much, but in the day of a busy woman, there were not many marks to spare, and in order to fetch her water, she might face a choice between leaving some task undone or walking farther to fetch water from another source. "One wishes," he said slowly, "that all leaders like-minded were."

Selenay beamed; Mirilin grunted, but at least he didn't seem displeased.

The Court of Justice was held in a building over the Corn Market— literally *over* it, for it stood on four pillars above the valuable stall space. If the courtroom was filled, this covered space below—used on market days for the most valuable of merchandise, and food vendors—enabled people who were waiting their turn to wait out of the weather or sun.

Herald Mirilin was the sole arbiter here; those who brought grievances to him either had tried the regular courts and were unsatisfied, or felt that a regular court would not be as responsive to their grievances as a single Herald would. The Herald sat at a table at the back of the room, within a sort of partition that took up the back fifth or so, divided from the rest of room by a low balustrade. Those whose cases were being heard stood before him, while those still waiting, and interested parties, sat on rows of backless benches on the other side of the railing. Selenay sat beside Mirilin, industriously taking notes, while Alberich stood behind them both and attempted to look like a superfluous statue.

As far as Alberich could judge, the people here ranged in income level from well-off to impoverished. In age, they tended to be middle-aged folk, with a sprinkling of elders. The cases were astonishingly petty, which surprised him. Someone had loaned an object, or money, and the person to whom it had been lent now claimed it was a gift. A child had vandalized something, and the parents disclaimed responsibility. A dog was permitted to run loose and had bitten someone. A chicken flew into a yard and ate seeds and young plants; the angry householder caught, killed, and ate it, and the owner claimed compensation.

None of this was earth-shattering, and all of it would have been settled in Karse with some form of personal confrontation among the parties concerned. In a village, it was usually the responsibility of the headman or council of elders to sort it all out—in a city, well, it generally came to blows.

Alberich wasn't quite sure why anyone "official" was involved in these cases at all. And even if the idea was to keep public fighting at a minimum, there *were* courts to handle these cases, according to Selenay. Why were Heralds concerned with these ridiculous little domestic problems at all? More importantly, at least as far as this "bodyguard" business was concerned, what was Selenay learning here that was vital enough to put her here, where she was very vulnerable?

His questions remained unanswered for the moment. But he did, gradually, begin to see the *shape* of what was called "justice" in Valdemar. When a grievance was between a rich person and a poor one, it was settled in the favor of the poor one as often as not. In the villages of Karse, rich men had influence. No one wanted to get on their bad side, for the most part. They might be cordially loathed, but no one dared to offend them. At least, no one dared except the Sunpriests—but even they tended not to upset the best source of their golden tithes. So justice tended, especially in small matters, to weigh in on the side of the fellow with the most coin. And in the cities of Karse, "justice" was for open sale, as often as not.

But here, to his bemusement, justice was simply that.

But the poor man didn't always win. Not when the poor man was in the wrong.

There was a case of a shabby, shifty-eyed fellow claiming that a merchant's horse had trampled him and broken his leg, and the merchant's coachman had agreed that, yes, that was what had happened—when the shifty fellow had thrown himself deliberately under the horse's hooves.

That was when Mirilin glanced over at the Princess. "Truth Spell, please, Selenay," he murmured.

:Watch this, Chosen,: Kantor said instantly. *:This is important.:*

Selenay nodded and closed her eyes, a tiny frown of concentration on her face. And slowly, a faint blue glow began to gather over the heads of both parties, growing stronger and stronger, until it stood out clearly even in the well-lit courtroom. Alberich kept his face expressionless, but he felt the hair standing up on the back of his neck. When anyone in Karse used magic—well, the only people who *did* were Sunpriests, and the very few times they ever did so outside of the inner sanctum of a temple, someone usually died…

"Now," said Mirilin to the coachman. "Tell me again what happened, precisely."

The coachman, an earnest old gentleman who kept his gaze fastened on Mirilin the entire time, repeated his story, virtually word-for-word, while the light about him glowed steadily. He didn't even seem aware of it, although those in the courtroom who were paying attention to this case murmured with satisfaction.

"And now, sir, would you tell me what happened again?" Mirilin continued, with a courteous nod to the shabby fellow.

"Nah, lookit me *leg!*" the fellow bleated indignantly, gesturing at the limb in question, which was splinted and bound with clean rags—the only things that were clean about him. "Any'un with 'af an eye kin tell what's what!"

"Nevertheless, please tell me again," Mirilin replied, with far more patience than Alberich would have shown. The man began his tale with ill grace, but the moment he got to "—an' I stepped inter the street, an' this bastid comes *whippin'* up 'is 'orses—"

The light went out.

Although the man clearly was unaware that anything had happened at all, the onlookers saw what Alberich had. A gasp—not of surprise, but of satisfaction—went up, and Mirilin cut the rest of the man's speech off with a wave of his hand.

"Sir, you are lying, and this man is telling the truth. He owes you nothing." Mirilin glanced meaningfully at the constables that waited just beyond the barrier. "Now, the penalties for perjury are substantial in a regular court, but since this is a Heraldic hearing, and I have discretion, I shall allow you to leave in peace—providing you *do* leave quietly. I suggest that you find a more honest means of employing yourself from here on, because you are now in the official records as a perjurer, and the next court you bring yourself before will take that into account."

The man followed Mirilin's glance and set his jaw angrily, but didn't even try to dispute the judgment. Instead, he shuffled off, quickly getting himself out of the door (or at least, as quickly as a splinted and wrapped leg would allow) while the coachman thanked Mirilin effusively.

But Mirilin waved him off with a slight sign of irritation. "Do not thank *me* for simple justice," he said. "Now, please, we have a heavy docket to see—"

The coachman took the hint and followed in the path of his accuser.

:That was the Truth Spell, Chosen,: Kantor said with satisfaction. *:And it is nearly the only sort of magic that you will ever see a Herald using. There's mind-magic, of course, which is things like Mindspeech, ForeSeeing and FarSeeing, but unless you are the Herald doing the mind-magic, well, you aren't going to actually see anything. Mirilin is better at the Truth Spell than Selenay, but he wants her to have the practice in setting it, because when she needs to use it, she'll be doing so with many more eyes on her.:*

:Is that all it does?: he asked. *:Just show which person is telling the truth?:*

:There is a more powerful version that can compel the truth, but it's not likely to be used here,: Kantor replied, as an old woman with a cat came hobbling up to the table. *:That's saved for things that are a great deal more serious, and not all Heralds can invoke it. You have to have a very strong Gift, and it usually has to be one like Mindspeech.:*

:Will I—: he began, and stopped.

:You will. You'll probably be very good at it.: But Kantor was evidently sensitive to feelings as well as actual thoughts, for he quickly added, *:But given that you're going to be the Weaponsmaster, I doubt you'll be called upon to do it much. If at all.:*

The afternoon trundled on under its own momentum of petty grievances, minor misunderstandings, rancor, greed, selfishness—and bewilderment, hurt feelings, a certain amount of genuine grief, and the genuine trust that a Herald *would* put things right. As the afternoon went on, there were several inheritance cases that came up, and in one, Mirilin worked something like a miracle, not only getting compromise, but in getting all of the aggrieved parties to apologize to each other and reconcile.

Sometimes both parties were equally right and wrong, and it was then that Mirilin truly showed his worth. Somehow he always managed to get both sides to see the rights as well as the wrongs of the case, and for the most part, managed to get *them* to work out a solution without having to have him decree one for them. That was sheer genius, and Alberich did not see how he managed it. Astonishing.

No wonder he's assigned to this! Alberich thought more than once, as Mirilin played near-invisible midwife to yet another compromise.

:In many ways, Selenay will have to do exactly this when she is Queen,: Kantor pointed out. *:A court is a little like a village or a neighborhood; everyone knows everyone else, everyone has his own particular agenda to pursue, there is an entire pecking order within the group that outsiders would never be aware of, and above all, you can never forget that someone has to be aware of all of the undercurrents and keep conflicts from breaking out into actual feuding. The actual complaints here will be different from those within the Court, but the dynamics of personality are fundamentally the same.:*

So *that* was what Selenay was learning here. Perhaps these people weren't as daft as he thought.

The court was closed around dinnertime, with a backlog of people still waiting. But no one complained overmuch, perhaps because Mirilin had kept things moving fairly briskly.

On the way back, Selenay and her mentor discussed the intricacies of case and personality with great animation; Alberich achieved his goal of becoming unnoticeable, as he rode behind them. This was good; he actually learned far more than he had expected as Mirilin offered the fruits of his hard-earned experience to Selenay.

And when Selenay took her leave of Alberich, he found that he was looking forward to the next session down in Haven. If Mirilin hadn't exactly warmed to Alberich, at least he hadn't rejected Alberich out of hand.

He returned to the salle and headed for his shared living quarters with the feeling, on the whole, that he was rather pleased than otherwise with the way that the day had gone. But Dethor's first words, spoken as he walked into the midst of a conversation that had certainly been going on for at least a mark before *he* arrived, put a chill on his good humor.

"There you are," Dethor said, as the other two Heralds in the room looked up at his entrance. "What do you know about a group that calls themselves the 'Tedrel Mercenaries'?"

7

"What of the Tedrels do I know? Huh. Nothing good," Alberich replied, but only after standing there for a moment, blinking stupidly; such a completely unexpected question left him feeling slightly stunned. *The Tedrels?* What on earth could *that* sinister group have to do with Valdemar? And why ask *him* about them?

"Why?" he asked, as the others sat there looking at him, waiting for him to say something more.

"Because there's word Karse is hiring them." Dethor's eyes could have pierced a hole in steel, but evidently Alberich's reaction of further shock pleased him, for his expression softened immediately.

The Tedrels? Why would Karse hire *them?* Who could have learned of them to hire them in the first place? Most people in *Karse* had never heard of them, let alone anyone this far north. The only reason *he* knew anything about them was because of Aksel.

And the only reason that Aksel knew anything about them was because *he* still had contacts within the Mercenary Guild, friendly contacts, which was not within the norm for anyone in the Sunsguard. One evening Aksel had told him that the Mercenary Guild was issuing warnings about the Tedrel Companies; since that was just before Alberich was commissioned out of the cadets, Aksel had seen fit to warn his protégé in case he came up against any Tedrels in the course of his duties. He'd shown Alberich the broadside carrying the message, in fact.

Don't trust them, said those warnings. *Don't fight with them, and don't take a fight against them.* And the reasons for these flat edicts had been chilling…

Now Karse was not in good odor with the Mercenary Guild. The Sunpriests expected men to fight for the glory of the Sunlord, and not for such venial considerations as money and booty. They had, on two separate occasions, hired Guild Companies and then reneged on the contract. They had *paid* for those mistakes; with full Guild backing, enough caravans led by Karsite merchants crossing the southern Border of Karse had been confiscated to pay for the arrears—and since it had been high-ranking Sunpriests who had backed those caravans with their personal fortunes, the bird of ill luck had come home to roost in the right nest. But the Guild Companies now refused any and all overtures from the Sunpriests, and of all of the military leaders in Karse, only Aksel—who was not a "leader" as such—still had friends in the Guild.

That had all fallen out while Alberich was still sweeping out the stables to earn extra coppers for his mother. By the time he was in the cadet academy, Karse was learning that not even non-Guild mercenaries would take their coin. Being cut off from the Guild left Karse without a reliable source for extra troops; being refused by nearly everyone left them forced to supply their needs from within.

And therein lay the rub. The regular troops were few. Standing armies were expensive beasts to maintain. Men had to be recruited or conscripted—and if you took too many men off the land, who would till and plant and harvest the fields or tend the herds? Once you had the men, you had to train them, and house and feed them *while* you were training them. Then, when they weren't actually fighting (which was most of the time) you *still* had to feed and house them. The Sunpriests might be able to induce religious fervor enough to get their men to fight without pay (or at least, with minimal pay), but they still couldn't get by without food and shelter, no matter how fanatic or pious or even desirous of paradise they were.

And besides that, there was a limit to how many troops you could recruit in the first place. Many places in Karse had poor soil; poor soil meant that a great deal of work had to be put into a farm to make it prosper. The boys might get dreams of glory in the Sunsguard, but their fathers would see to it that they didn't run off when they were needed at home. No matter how hungry for the land and riches of other realms the Sunpriests were, they were not mad enough to deplete their own land of the very people needed to keep the farms going. By the time Alberich was about to get his first commission, they had conscripted so many of the poor in the cities that there was an actual labor shortage, and women were taking jobs that once only men had filled. That had been the reasoning behind permitting bandits to use Karse as a base to raid into Valdemar; bandits didn't require the support of the state, and they kept up the ongoing feud with Valdemar without—in theory, at least—costing Karse anything. Except that, of course, bandits didn't keep their bargains, which had required the Sunpriests use all of their Sunsguard to quell them, leaving no fighters for any other little projects they might have in mind.

Which left hiring troops as the only viable option, if troops were needed for a campaign against anyone. That meant either Mercenary Guild companies, which were trustworthy, would not loot or otherwise molest your people, and in general were welcome in the lands of those who hired them—or non-Guild troops, which were unpredictable at best, and a hazard to those who hired them at worst. By betraying the Mercenary Guild, the Sunpriests had shaved those options to a narrow little rind, because not even the non-Guild Companies operating anywhere near Karse would touch a contract.

Of course, the only reason why you would need more troops was if you were going to start a war. The *last* time when the rulers of Karse had reneged on a Guild contract—the war had been internal. Some madman out of the hills had decided that Vkandis spoke through *him* without any evidence or real miracles to back up his assertions. But his cause was convenient for some of the nobles, moneyed merchants, and even a few priests, so they backed him and began a civil war. Both sides of the conflict had been decimated, which was, in part, how a bastard-born peasant like Alberich had managed to get into cadet training. And if it came to more than Border skirmishing, frankly, in Alberich's opinion Karse couldn't possibly raise the troops needed from among its own people.

If Karse was planning a real war again, non-Guild mercenaries were the only way in which an army could be raised in a hurry. But—the Tedrels? Could they possibly be mad enough to use the Tedrels?

A war? With whom? Rethwellan, perhaps. In the last conflict, Rethwellan had seized the opportunity to increase its borders, and the Sunpriests badly wanted the province of Menmellith. Not Valdemar, surely not—surely the lessons learned in the past were enough by now! No matter *how* fanatically the Sunpriests hated Valdemar and the Demon-Riders, surely they knew better than to engage in open warfare. Now Rethwellan—that made more sense, and there was some justification for warfare with that land. Menmellith had once been Karsite. Very, very long ago, of course, but the Sunpriests had long memories.

But—to use the Tedrels! The very idea made him feel a little sick.

Honor…

It was hardly *honorable* to hire creatures like the Tedrels for anything.

They followed none of the laws of combat; they were more apt to turn to massacre civilians than they were to fight the battles for which they'd been hired.

"But little, I know," Alberich said slowly. "And that, hearsay for the most part is."

"Figure we know less," Dethor said, settling back in his chair, and motioning for Alberich to take the one remaining seat left.

Alberich did so, but not with any feeling of ease. He sat on the very edge, back straight, muscles tense. "It is said," he began, "and long ago this was—three, perhaps four generations—that a war there was, in a land south and far, far east of Karse. Brother fought brother, in a cause none now recall. But those who the Tedrels became, lost that war, and instead of surrender, into exile went. Determined they were to gain back what lost had been—a land their own to call, where called they no man 'lord.' But nothing they had—except their skill at arms. And so, mercenaries they became. All of them. Company after company, after company. Which, even in defeat, enough men was, to fill up a country."

Now it was his turn to watch as Dethor's eyes bulged just a little with shock. "An *entire nation* of mercenaries?" the Weaponsmaster asked, aghast.

Alberich nodded; interesting that Dethor had not known that, which was the thing most notable about the Tedrel Companies. "Now, that was long and long ago, and wanderers they became as well. No wives would they take except those who would wander and consent to being the property of who could hold them, and no women in their ranks as fighters at all. Camp followers only, have they decreed that women may be. And—" He found this next part difficult to articulate, but he tried. "They—altered. It is said."

"In what way?" one of the others asked, abruptly cutting into his narrative.

It was the King's Own, Talamir, not in one of his more elaborate uniforms, but in a set of Whites like everyone else's. No wonder Alberich hadn't noticed him until he spoke. *Talamir here, and waiting to hear what I know... it may be rumor, but they are taking the rumor seriously.*

"Once, they had honor and purpose, and things they would not do. Now..." He shrugged. "Nothing there is, they will not do, should the reward be high. *Anything* for loot. War they bring against the unarmed, as well as fighting true-battles. I have heard—dreadful things." He had to pause, shaking his head. "With no wives, only women held by the strongest, no families, their ranks then grew but slowly, and difficult it was, to replace those who fell. So now anyone they take into their ranks, who presents himself—thief, murderer, it matters not, has he a strong arm. And thus, cruelty upon cruelty piles."

Dethor and Talamir exchanged a worried look.

But Alberich wasn't quite finished. "The greatest change is this. No more seeking *the* home, they look only for *a* home. Should any offer a new land in reward, it is said—it is said that there is *nothing* they would not do." He gnawed his lower lip, thinking about the cold-blooded killers that Aksel had described, and what they would willingly do for anyone who was so foolish as to offer them a new homeland. His blood ran cold at the very idea. "But this, hearsay only is," he amended. "None I know has seen them, spoken to them, fought against them nor with them. Should any in Valdemar seek them to hire, warned they should be. It is said, moreover, that no sworn word do they truly hold by but their own, *to* their own, and they can and have turned against those who hired them."

"Someone had better find a way to get that message across to your own people," Dethor replied grimly. "Because word has reached us that they're thinking about hiring the Tedrel Companies. And not just one of 'em. *All* of 'em."

Now Alberich went icy cold all over with sudden dread, and was glad he was sitting down. Hiring one or two of the Tedrel Companies, he could just barely see. Aksel was not high enough in the ranks for his warnings to be heeded overmuch on that score. But all of them? There was only one reward that would tempt *all* of them together. "Madness," he said flatly. "Surely not—" *Surely not even the maddest and most fanatical of priests would hazard all to cast their lot with the Tedrels!* That would be insane. As Aksel had described them, having the Tedrels in one's midst was like playing host to a large pack of wild dogs. So long as they were full-bellied and content, the worst that would happen was that there would be a little damage to small towns here and there, if the scum that now filled out the ranks of the Tedrels grew bored. Perhaps rape, a bit of looting, possibly a few houses burned.

The "worst" that would happen if they are satisfied… rape. Looting. Oh, my poor people… His stomach turned over. He thought about his border villages, and his throat and chest tightened, his gut roiling.

No worse, perhaps, than the bandits were already doing on the Borders.

But to face it from bandits, and then receive worse from those beasts—who in turn were hired *by the Priests supposed to protect them!*

That would be bad enough, But if the paychests were not as full as promised, or stopped altogether—the pack would turn...

And fire and the sword would reign, at least until the paychests came again.

His chest felt too tight; his heart ached at the mere thought.

If this were true, the only way to hire the whole nation *was* to promise a homeland. Would Karse offer Menmellith?

Possibly. Menmellith was no great prize, but would Karse then want the Tedrels as neighbors?

So it would be Valdemar. The priests hate Valdemar enough to allow anything so long as Valdemar is left gutted, Kingless, and without the Heralds...

Karse as a new homeland probably would not tempt them; it was too hard a land. They wanted something like that dream that their land had become for them, a place fat and rich, soft and sweet. But they would take out their spleen on Karse if it promised them such a homeland and failed to deliver it into their hands.

"That's what we've heard," Dethor said, shrugging. "Anything more you can tell us?"

Alberich shook his head; what more *could* he say? Dread was a sickening lump in his belly. "This rumor—I hope it false proves."

"Our sources are good," was all that Talamir would say. The third man, who was *not* in Whites and did not identify himself, only grunted. *He* looked about as friendly as Mirilin—which was to say, not at all. There was no doubt in Alberich's mind that the third man did not trust him.

And why should he, if even some (if not most) of the Heralds were ambivalent about Alberich?

:But we aren't,: Kantor said with some force.

The warmth that followed that pronouncement made the cold nausea lift a little, and eased some of the churning of his gut. It certainly made him feel less as if he was standing alone, facing a suspicious mob.

:I know. Thank you.: Knowing that the Companions now accepted him helped a little, but—

He knew what he wanted to say—that he had given up everything, *everything*, when he was brought here. That he had thrown his lot in with Valdemar, given his *word*, and that word was not given lightly. Couldn't they see that? This unknown man, who watched him from under furrowed brows, didn't he realize that?

And he wanted to say that—if his own people had sunk so low as to hire the Tedrels to do their dirty work, then surely even the Sunlord would abandon them...

But he said none of this, for it would not matter if he did. Instead, he sat stone-faced and silent, and waited for the others to say something.

Even if it was only to "suggest" that he leave.

Finally, Dethor hissed a little between his teeth. "I don't s'ppose," he said carefully, "that you'd know anybody likely to—well—be *helpful?* Inside Karse, that is? We'd like to know more about these rumors from someone with good, hard facts."

That... was a little better. Even if it sniffed around the edges of that promise they'd made him, the promise never to ask him to work against his own people.

But if those who are supposed to lead my people have already betrayed them? How can knowing if that betrayal is true or false be acting against the people?

"Depend it does," Alberich replied, just as carefully, "on what it is, by *helpful,* you mean."

"Information," Talamir said. "Nothing more. And nothing that would hurt Karse. Only what will protect *us* without hurting your people."

Alberich turned Talamir's words over and over in his mind, as the other three watched him. Because he *did* know someone who might—just might—be willing to be "helpful." Of all the people that Alberich knew, Aksel Tarselein was the most likely to be enraged and offended if this tale of hiring the Tedrels was true, and was, because of his own contacts, the most likely to know if it was truth or rumor spread to discomfit the enemies of Karse.

For Aksel Tarselein, trainer of cadets, had already been a deeply troubled man when Alberich knew him. Someone—another young, highborn officer—had once described him, with a sneer, as "one of the old school," as if being a man of honor and integrity, whose word was seldom given and always kept, was somehow unfashionable and old-fashioned. And the shifts to which the Son of the Sun had fallen by the time Alberich had been commissioned had left Aksel profoundly disturbed. He was glad, he had confessed to the younger Alberich when the two of them had shared a farewell flask on the night of Alberich's commission, that he was no longer in a position where he found himself forced to obey orders which went against his conscience. "And it is a harder world today," he had said sadly, staring at the last few drops in the bottom of his flagon. "You may discover that you have to stop thinking—or stop obeying. I hope that the Sunlord will guide you, young one."

He had said no more on the subject, but Alberich *knew* which path he had taken, though not without qualms, and not without remorse.

I stopped thinking, at least until Kantor came to me…

Just as he knew that Aksel had *not* stopped thinking. That was not Aksel's way. But as long as Aksel remained a Weaponsmaster to cadets, he would never be given an order that forced him to disobey either. Aksel held fast to his own honor only by making sure he was in a place where he would not have to sacrifice it.

Which of them had been given the easier path? Was it better to obey and not think, or think and try to ignore and be glad you, personally, *didn't* have to disobey?

"Possible, it is," he said, very slowly, "that there is a man. But possible it is *not*, directly to approach him. Friends he keeps, in the Mercenary Guild. There it is you must go. Speak with you he may, deny you he may." Alberich shrugged. "I cannot say; his own decision, he must make."

"Fair enough. And we've got enough friendly contacts with the Guild to ferret out whoever knows him," Dethor said, nodding agreement. "His name?"

"Aksel Tarselein. Weaponsmaster to the Sunsguard Cadets." Once again, Dethor and Talamir exchanged a look, this time a startled one.

Should he add something from himself, so that Aksel knew who had revealed him?

:Do you think your name would make Aksel change his mind?: Kantor asked.

:It might…: The now-familiar sickness rose in him again.

:And would you want it to?: Kantor continued. *:Or would you rather—:*

:I would rather there was no pressure on my old teacher but that of his own thoughts,: Alberich said firmly. Kantor let the matter drop. And to his immense relief, Dethor made no request for some token from Alberich. Nor did the third man—who felt, perhaps, that a message from one already branded as a traitor would do *his* cause with Aksel no good.

"Aksel Tarselein." Dethor and the third man exchanged a look, and the third man grunted. "That's one name more than we had before. Especially if he decides to talk."

"Yes." Alberich didn't elaborate; Dethor didn't pressure him to. The third man got up to leave.

Dethor poured a tankard full of beer and pushed it across the table to Alberich, as the third man turned at the door, gave Talamir and Dethor a little nod, and walked out. Alberich picked up the tankard and drained half of it in one gulp.

He felt a great need of it, at that moment, and it did a little, a very little, to settle his unsettled stomach and nerves.

:It is only a rumor,: Kantor said suddenly. *:That is all. No matter that this spy of Sendar's has convinced everyone that it is more than that. He has no proof. He has only heard stories and a name, for no one he has spoken to has seen the Tedrels or their Captains, or even an agent that may be said to come from them.:*

Relief made Alberich's hands a little steadier as he put down the tankard. *:If anyone will know the truth of the rumor, it will be Aksel,:* he replied. *:And if it is true, I believe that Aksel will speak.:*

:And in any case, it is out of your hands.:

"Well, no matter what, Talamir, it's out of *our* hands," Dethor sighed, echoing Kantor's words. "This is a thing for those with talents you and I don't have. Nor Alberich either."

Alberich regarded him broodingly. "I *could*. But a pledge you made to me—"

"And we'll keep it," Talamir said with finality. "Though I will admit to you freely, that this is one reason why the Lord Marshal's man was here. He wanted us to pressure you into crossing the Border again, to spy for Valdemar."

Wordlessly, Alberich shook his head.

Dethor snorted. "Aye, we told him as much, then asked him to his face if he'd really *trust* you if you agreed. And he had to admit that he wouldn't, so what's the point? *We* know you're sound as a good apple, but to the likes of him, a man that turns may well turn again. Gods help us, though, I sometimes wonder what we're to do with you."

Alberich eased his dry mouth with another swallow. "What you have done. There is, what else to do, to bring trust where there is none?"

"Not much. Doubters can't accuse you of much, here with my eye on you, and keeping you apart from the rest means that nobody's going to try and make trouble for you. What d'ye think of young Selenay?" An abrupt change of subject, but Alberich answered it quickly enough.

"Steady, thoughtful, careful, and untried." He saw the questions in Dethor and Talamir's eyes, and tried to answer them. "No opposition, has she met. No loss, no pain. No great joys either, no love. With the single eye, she sees now—clearly, in black and white, as young things do. Until she has more wisdom, well, who knows how she will see then? When great events come upon her—*then* will you see, of what she is made. Not until. But the makings of a king, she has. And she thinks, which, with more than most young things, is not the case."

"Told you so," Dethor said in an aside to Talamir. The King's Own just shrugged. Dethor turned back to Alberich. "She came up with this bodyguard notion on her own, but I think it's no bad idea, having you instead of one of the Guard, especially when she's with Mirilin. Lad in a Guard uniform puts people on edge; fellow in Whites makes 'em wonder if the Heralds have some reason to haul in more than one for a simple Herald's Court. But a fellow in Grays? Nah, that makes 'em relax. We want someone with her to keep *her* back covered, without making people nervous that he's there. People don't necessarily *expect* a fellow in Grays to be much of a fighter, and they don't think of him as a fancier sort of constable. They take you, I'll be bound, for another Trainee on Internship, maybe another highborn."

Alberich smiled slowly, seeing what Dethor was getting at. Talamir only looked strained. "But once the Council finds out, there will be difficulties," the King's Own said reluctantly, then shook his head. "Yes, and I admit, it *is* my responsibility to smooth them out. Well, the easiest way will be by simply not saying anything for now, I suppose. I'll have a word with Mirilin—"

:We already have, via Estan, and he won't be mentioning Alberich's presence as the Heir's bodyguard to anyone, not even to other Heralds,: Kantor said promptly, and by the sudden, startled look on Talamir's face, Taver must have said the same thing at the same moment. Dethor laughed aloud; the word must have reached him, as well.

Talamir coughed. "Well. Apparently you have *far* more friends here than I had thought, Alberich. So unless someone from the Council actually sees you at Selenay's back, and realizes who you are, apparently we'll keep that much from their attention for a while." His face grew distant again for a moment, and he added, "Long enough that perhaps by the time the Council realizes just who Selenay's bodyguard is, there will be far fewer doubts about you."

"Occurred to you, had it, that we being managed are?" Alberich asked him, in a moment of stark frankness. "By *them?*"

They knew who he meant—the Companions. He half expected Kantor to be annoyed by the statement, but he sensed instead a dry amusement.

He got a look of startlement, then one of understanding, from both the Heralds. "Oh, always, at least to an extent," Talamir replied, with the same utter honesty. "And in some cases, that's all to the good." His voice took on a different coloring then, a hint of wry tartness. "But let me tell you a bit of home truth, Alberich of Karse—something that I do *not* tell the children, because they *are* children and need managing—it is your right and privilege to tell your beloved Companion just where he can shove anything he tells you or asks of you if it goes completely against your better judgment." He raised an eyebrow. "As even my Taver has found, to his occasional shock and dismay."

Dethor whooped with laughter, and applauded. "By the gods, Talamir, good for you! And well said!"

Now Alberich expected Kantor to be completely offended, but instead, he "heard" an ironic chuckle in his mind. :*Tell the King's Own that it is our right and privilege to do the same with our Chosen, you know.*:

Alberich started to repeat the remark, but Talamir held up his hand. "Never mind. Taver has said the same as your Kantor, I expect. My point is that we are adults, and although the Companions have certain abilities and information that we, their Heralds, may not—well, the reverse is true as well. You've got a mind of your own, and experience that your Companion doesn't have, and, I presume, sound judgment. Don't be afraid to use them, and if you feel strongly about something, be prepared to insist you be heard. The Companions don't know everything. As Taver pointed out to a few of them the other night, they aren't infallible. They can make mistakes, and advice can go both ways. Herald and Companion are meant to be *partners*, not superior and servant."

"In the beginning for most Trainees, exactly 'cause they *are* younglings, that isn't always the case," Dethor put in. "Sometimes Chosen and Companion are the same age and learn together, but sometimes one's full grown while the other's still a child, or just a little older. But in your case, you're both adults, and you start out with a partnership from the beginning."

Talamir nodded emphatically. "We each give, and we each take, and what we do should be the result of cooperation, not dictation. Don't forget that."

"I shall not," Alberich replied. "But for the moment, Kantor it is, who knows this land and people. Not I."

"True enough." Talamir hefted his tankard and looked at Dethor, who poured him (and, without his asking, Alberich as well) another round. The beer foamed up, leaving a pleasantly bitter aroma in the air.

Dethor and Talamir exchanged another pregnant glance. Alberich's neck prickled. Something was still in the air. Talamir was not here *only* because of the rumors coming out of Karse.

"Alberich, I'm here for more than one reason. I think that you already have some inkling of this, so I am going to put it in plain language,"

Talamir continued, rubbing his thumb along the side of the tankard. "As a fighting commander, I suspect that you have, more than once, had to do what was expedient, rather than what was—"

"Ideal?" Alberich suggested. "An idealist, I never was."

:Liar,: Kantor objected mildly. *:Who was it, agonizing over the fate of the border villages just now? Who is it that values honor above everything else?:*

:Hush: He flexed his shoulder muscles; they felt tense. Something was coming; he was just beginning to make out the shape of it, and he wasn't certain he was going to like it. "You have a thought."

"More than one. Actually, I have—we have—a job that needs doing. It's something *I* used to do, before I got too crippled up," Dethor said, with just a hint of… regret? Bitterness, that he was no longer what he had been? "I don't know that you'd have the stomach for it—but I've got to tell you, Alberich, for all your skill you're the *last* person I'd have looked to for this, except for one thing. Taver trusts you. He thinks you can do this, so Talamir says."

"Taver said to ask you," Talamir added, and sighed, his brow furrowed with concern and uncertainty.

:Taver might have made a suggestion, but Talamir is not completely certain how good an idea it is,: Kantor put it.

Well, that was clear enough.

Talamir cleared his throat awkwardly. "You saw the Lord Marshal's man—you know that there are such things as—agents. Well, we Heralds have them as well—and we need another."

He nodded warily, but might have prevaricated, except that in that unguarded instant, Kantor simply edged into his mind and *showed* him what it was that Dethor and Talamir wanted him to do.

"Agent" was too small a word to encompass the task.

In fact, Alberich was more uniquely suited to the job than even Dethor had been, *because* of his foreign origin. There were places where Dethor would always stand out—because Dethor was nobly-born for all that he pretended he was common. What you'd been born and bred to was difficult to hide, especially when you were under stress. But Alberich was as common as clay, and used to moving in the lowest of circles. Under stress, he slipped into that world as easily as a bottomfish slipping into the muddy river bottom.

Mostly, Dethor had collected information—in the Court and out of it, from the servants' common room in the Palace, to the vilest alleys near Exile's Gate, to the scented rooms where courtiers fenced with words.

Mostly—but a time or two, Dethor had done more than collect intelligence and pass it on to Talamir. A so-called "agent" who was also a Herald had an extraordinary degree of freedom to act as he saw fit, and once, Dethor had used his knowledge of traps to cause a single fatal "accident."

And he had agonized over that murder, for murder it was, and never mind that the man had been the hidden heart of a vile trade and no one had been or would be able to bring him to justice. Dethor had murdered and knew it, and *still* agonized over it.

:*As you would. As you would act, if there was no other way, and you would be decisive about it.*:

Yes, he would, on both counts. But although he would regret murder, for he hated killing, he would not allow such a thing to ride him with guilt afterward. He felt his pulse throbbing in the hollow of his throat, and his collar felt too tight. Yes, he would. Some things had to be done— and was it better to stain innocent hands with blood, or add one more stain to the sleeve of one already steeped in it?

The King *could* have "agents" like the Lord Marshal had, men who would take their orders and carry them out, and leave the question of whether the orders were morally justified to someone else. The King did not want that. He wanted a Herald; he wanted someone who did not simply take orders. He *wanted* someone who would think—weigh—and act. And agonize over it afterwards perhaps... because there would be that necessary question when it was all over.

But it had to be a particular kind of Herald, and such folk did not emerge from among the children—children with their shining certainty of right and wrong—that came with their Companions to fill the Tooms of the Collegium every year. He would not besmirch those pure hearts, would not twist them into something that they were not.

It took a Herald like Dethor, like Alberich, who was Chosen as an adult, full-grown, who knew about moral ambiguities and difficult choices. Like Dethor—who had himself been one of the Lord Marshal's agents, before he was Chosen. Like *Dethor's* master, the Weaponsmaster before him, who had grown up a child of poverty, seen the evils of the world very young, wiser than his years, though his parents had sheltered him from what they could.

No such man (or woman, though perhaps it would have been harder for a woman) had come to Dethor and Talamir until now, and they were not altogether certain that Alberich was the right material for this task. But he was what they had... and they were in terrible need of *some* man for the job. Talamir was altogether too recognizable and too desperately needed to have the time for such covert walkings, and as for Dethor, who could barely hobble to the Collegium for a Council meeting or a meal now and again—well.

All this poured into his mind as the other two sat quietly, waiting for him to assimilate it all. Did they know what Kantor was showing him?

:Of course they know. It is our way. I can show you in moments, what would take them days to explain.:

Ah. Expedience… so the Companions knew it, too. Somehow that made him feel more akin to Kantor, not less.

He took a deep breath, and regarded both of them with somber eyes. "It is much of me, that you ask," he said slowly. "It is surprised, I am. When I have here been—how long?"

"Conscious or unconscious?" Dethor retorted and shrugged. "You've been a real part of things for maybe a fortnight. And I would never in a hundred thousand years *think* to trust you with this—except for Taver."

:Why Taver?: he asked Kantor silently. *:Why, if Companions are as fallible as any other?:*

:Because Taver can make mistakes, but never that kind *of mistake. Never, ever a mistake in judging a person's character, his heart, and soul,:* came the reply—and then he got the sensation that Kantor was conferring with someone else.

Talamir and Dethor watched him closely, weighing his least expression, just as Kantor added, *:Come outside, if you trust me. There is something more you need to have that Taver wishes to share with you. And not just for making* this *decision.:*

There were so many overtones to that deceptively simple statement that it was Alberich's turn to start with surprise. There was more than a hint that this was something as important as *anything* that anyone had ever told him in all of his life—something life-shatteringly important. And a subtle shading that this was something Taver had never shared with any other Herald.

Not even Talamir. *Not even Talamir.*

Suddenly, he had to know what this thing was. "Rude, I do not wish to be," he said abruptly. "But think on this—with no eyes on me—I must, for a little." He stood up even as he said this, and the other two Heralds watched him measuringly, but with a leavening of understanding.

"You don't have to give us an answer right away," Talamir said, as if making up his own mind about it. "But if you would consider it—"

"Tedrels—and now this—" Alberich shook his head. "I must think alone. But consider it, with all seriousness, I will. And—I will answer you soon." He did not define "soon."

The other two remained in their seats as he stalked off, head swirling dizzily with a dozen contradictory thoughts.

He wanted to go back to Karse. The very notion of the Tedrels being *near* there made his skin crawl. He wanted to hide here, and never hear of Karse again. He *didn't* want this new job that Talamir and Dethor had suggested, and yet, if he didn't take it, the tasks *would* be done, but by men who left their thinking and their morality in the hands of others, and merely followed orders... and never cared what the repercussions would be, never wondered if they had done the right thing, never thought at all. The bare idea was repugnant.

And he wanted to see just what this secret that the Companion Taver held could be. And how could it possibly, *possibly,* have any relevance to him?

Taver was waiting outside, just out of sight of the windows of Dethor's sitting room, with Kantor beside him. The sun was setting, and the air lay thick and sweet and still among the trees around the salle— but there was a hint of the bitterness of dying leaves in the sweetness, and the poignant suggestion of autumn coming soon, soon.

:Thank you for coming,: Taver said gravely, directly into Alberich's mind, startling him. Taver's mind-voice was distinctive; rich and deep, with a little breath of echo to it. There was a certainty and a stillness to it, as if Taver was a great tree, with his head in the clouds and his roots reaching down to the bedrock. And powerful, without ever making Alberich *feel* the power as anything other than potential.

"You are welcome," Alberich replied awkwardly, pulse hammering in his throat, feeling as if *he* was the one being granted the favor. This was strange. This was *very* strange. Perhaps the strangest thing that had happened to him since he had arrived here. That odd *thing* that they called his Gift fluttered in the back of his soul with something that was not—quite—warning.

:I think—I hope—that what I have to show you will make many things clearer for you,: Taver said, with infinite gentleness. *:Please, come and place one hand upon my neck and look into my eyes.:*

Puzzled, Alberich did as he was told. He touched the electric softness of Taver's neck—looked into living blue—and paradise engulfed him, as the heavens opened up and spilled out glory.

* * *

And when he came to himself again, he was lying on the grass, staring at the hooves of the two Companions—*silver hooves, why didn't I notice that before?*—with a mind so full it felt as if it couldn't possibly fit in the narrow confines of his head.

Mortal men should not look into heaven. If they do, they should not be surprised when all they can remember is that they were there, for one brief, radiant moment. *He* certainly was not.

But that moment had given him something he had needed, and had not known he needed, until the need was not there anymore.

He sat up slowly and felt the back of his skull gingerly. But the lump he expected to encounter, and the headache he anticipated, were not there.

:I took your body, and caused you to lie down, rather than fall down, Alberich,: Taver said, as Kantor whuffed at his ear. *:I knew what would happen, and it was no thought of mine that you take hurt from it.:*

Alberich stared at the Companion—who was more, so *much* more than he appeared that it made him dizzy even to nibble at the edges of the thought. "You've *never* done this to Talamir?"

:Talamir never required it. He is of Valdemar, blood and bone. You—were floundering, drowning, without a foundation. I think you were not even aware of it, except that you sought for it desperately, without knowing what you sought for. Have I given you what you needed?:

He *had* been looking, and yes, desperately—Taver was right. He *thought* that he'd been thinking, but he'd really been cluttering up his head with the minutiae of his new life here so that he didn't have to think about anything deeper. But if it came to that, he'd been looking for that foundation all his life. He'd tried to make his honor into a place to stand, but honor needed something to be based in.

:Ah.: There was contentment in that thought. *:Good.:*

Good? Oh, this was so much more than *good.* He had been drowning, with no land in sight. Yet, suddenly, Taver had put firm ground beneath his feet. Uncertainty that had been with him for so long it had become an uneasy part of him had been dispelled, popped like a bubble, exploded like the inflated bladder that it was. The monster in the closet was gone. And something so much better had taken its place…

Taver nodded his graceful head. *:Alberich, will you trust me again?:*

Alberich blinked at such nonsense. Trust him? *Trust* him? Trust to so pure a spirit—a being so near to the divine that he could scarcely believe there was no glow of holiness about him? Trust a being that he should, by all rights, be worshiping?

Taver shook his head and mane, and whickered a laugh. *:Oh, come now, Alberich, I am not so much as all that—a servant only, nothing more.:*

A servant! "As much a servant as—as the Firecat of legend!" he whispered, hardly daring to speak. "As the Guardian of the Gates of Paradise!"

:Exactly so. No more than that.: Taver bent to touch a soft—and very, very material nose—to Alberich's ear. *:Come, stand—put your hand to Kantor's neck, and look into his eyes as you did mine. And this time, open your heart to him, as you have not yet done. Give up your walls, Alberich of Karse. Take them down, and let him inside.:*

He could fight the command of one of Vkandis' Priests—he could no more stand against the same command as given by Taver than he could have fought a whirlwind. He did as he was told.

He looked deeply into those sapphire eyes, and opened his heart. And Kantor stepped gracefully into it, and filled it, and until that moment, he had no notion how empty it had been, nor how lonely he had been.

And as all of the knowledge and understanding and revelations that had come to him in the past few moments settled into place like doves coming to rest on their proper perches for the night, he knew, truly and completely, that there *was* Something above them all, call it Vkandis Sunlord or any other name. He could no more understand that Something than a flea could understand a man—but it was there. He would continue to have other doubts, other fears, but that one was gone.

And there was something else, much nearer and homelier, that would also be with him as a *certainty* as rock-solid as the earth beneath him and undoubted as the sky above. No matter what happened, in the next moment, or moon, or year, or lifetime—he and Kantor would never be alone or lonely again.

"Chosen—" he whispered, and buried his face in Kantor's mane.

:Chosen,: Kantor replied, with all the love that great heart could hold.

And it was—oh, yes—it was more, so much more, than enough.

PART TWO

THE TEDREL WARS

8

Alberich heard a sound that once would have prompted curiosity, and now only brought a dull, aching despair. Wagons were coming up the road to the Palace Gates, enough of them that the rumbling noise was audible even from the practice ground outside the salle. He knew what that meant. These days, there were no more fetes and celebrations at the Court that needed fancy foods, wines, and decorations. The burdens these wagons bore were grimmer by far. More grievously wounded folk, soldiers and civilians alike, coming from the battlefields to the south, where the forces of Karse grappled with those of Valdemar. People too badly hurt for their own Healers to tend, who had been sent here, in hopes that the masters at Healer's Collegium could make them whole—or, at least, mend as much as could be mended.

All the fault of the Tedrels... the Tedrels, who had been set against Valdemar after all. It had been no rumor that Karse was hiring them, and once the lands lost to the Menmellith Province of Rethwellan were retaken, to be used as the Tedrel base, it had been Valdemar's turn to face them, face Karsite troops and Karsite Sunpriests backing the most ruthless mercenaries this world had ever seen.

All of Valdemar—except himself—was of a single heart and mind in this situation. Everything must be done to defeat Karse. And had the enemy been anyone other than Karse, no doubt he would be feeling the same.

But it *was* Karse, and he was torn, heart and soul, ripped in half between honor and desire. He *wanted* to go to the front lines himself, to put his considerable skill and knowledge to serve Valdemar. But there was a chance if he did, he would be fighting and killing his own people, and he wouldn't know it until it was too late. The Tedrels had no livery except among their own blood; it could be anyone in the front lines. He would not have cared, if only it had been the Sunpriests and the generals that served them that he slaughtered, but it wouldn't be, would it? *They* would be safe in the rear, or far, far away, and he could not depend on anything except that it would not be only Tedrels he helped to kill. No, mixed in among the Tedrels, and certainly serving them in their camps, would be ordinary people, simple people, who had no quarrel with Valdemar and would have been happy if they had been left in peace. His people, the ones he had pledged himself to serve.

And besides, even if he found a way to help without facing his own folk across the edge of a sword, he wouldn't be allowed to go. If he set foot outside of Haven, there were powerful people who would be certain that he was doing so to betray Valdemar. And having deserted Karse, how could he blame them for that assumption? When a man turned his coat once, it took no great stretch of the imagination to think he might do so again.

Whenever his mind wasn't otherwise occupied, it was thoughts like these that came flooding in, and with them, a tide of guilt and depression. People who had become his friends, his brothers and sisters, were going south into danger—and here he was, safe in the sunshine of high summer in Haven.

He was glad that at least he had a task, something he could do honorably. Now he knew, only too well, some of the pain that Aksel must have felt when he remained training the cadets, while his trained cadets went off to do the fighting. And he knew the agony of being torn between desiring the best for his land, and knowing he could not support what the leaders of his land had joined hands with. Aksel himself must be feeling that same agony, for Aksel had given Valdemar's spies some of the information that warned them that the rumors of the Tedrels' hiring was true. It must have been by Vkandis' will, surely, for the information had come well before the first attack on the border of Valdemar, with enough time to prepare for that attack and those that followed.

These were not battles, these were wars—where the Tedrels moved into land opposite the Border, fortified it, then launched campaign after scorched-earth campaign from spring through autumn and then vanished, only to pick and fortify a new spot during the winter from which to pillage a new territory. Each time they did this, they effectively halted all farming, all commerce in that area, decimating it and leaving it barren and trying to recover. It was a diabolical plan, and there was nothing that Valdemar could do to thwart it without crossing the Border into Karse themselves, which Sendar (wisely) would not allow.

And damn-all use my ForeSight is against them. The magic that the Heralds called Gifts and that Karse called "witch-powers," Alberich found less useful than the exaggerated tales had led him to expect. Oh, he had Mindspeech, and very powerful, but it was of use only with other Heralds with Mindspeech and with Companions—and in setting the Truth Spell, which he seldom used. He probably could reach across the length or breadth of the country with it, but he never left the city of Haven; he was never allowed to leave. And he had ForeSight, that ability to glimpse what was to come—but it didn't stretch ahead more than a mark or two. It was a Gift that might be invaluable on a battlefield, except that he wasn't allowed near the battlefields. Of course, it was also an erratic Gift, which manifested irregularly and unpredictably, certainly not one he controlled... certainly nothing he could use from *here* to help in the Tedrel Wars. It seemed to work only in cases where something *he* could do, immediately, would change what was to come.

The Tedrel Wars; everyone called these seasonal blights by that name now. Little wars, leeching wars, stretching now into the fourth year. Every spring, a new little war, more deaths, more fresh-faced youngsters going out to face the foe, and Alberich wondering—as surely Dethor wondered—*had* he trained them well enough, prepared them well enough? Could he? Could anyone? It wasn't only Heralds he trained, it was young Guard officers, those Healers that would accept training in the use of weapons, and even some of the highborn youths who volunteered, out of a sense of duty and with dreams of glory in their hearts. He trained them, and he sent them out, and he never knew if *any* of them would return.

Valdemar bled from a wound that was not allowed to heal, that weakened her steadily. Alberich *knew* this, knew that when the Tedrel commanders judged the land weakened sufficiently, they would turn a little war into an all-out campaign. And there was nothing he could do about it. If it hadn't been for Kantor, he would never be able to sleep at night—but Kantor had his own ideas about what was good for his Chosen, and when Alberich was prepared to spend another sleepless night staring at the ceiling, his gut in a knot and his head throbbing, he would sense Kantor moving into his mind like a storm front, and then—

Well, then the next time he saw the ceiling, it would be morning. Last night had been one of those nights, leaving him singularly irritable, and not at all inclined to be charitable toward any of his pupils. Charity could—would—get them killed. *Especially* the one before him now.

Alberich surveyed his latest pupil, and reflected that Trainee Myste was at least providing one thing for him: a distraction from grief. Although she was providing a little grief of her own, of a different sort.

The middle-aged woman looked right back at him, her hazel eyes unnaturally large behind the thick glass lenses she wore, held to her face by a frame of wood, with leather straps that buckled behind her head, flattening already straight brown hair. She had a set that she normally wore that had lighter frames with sidepieces of wire that hooked over her ears, but those kept flying off during any sort of exertion; this had been the best they could do for weapons' practice, and it wasn't very good. Her peripheral vision was poor enough, and the frames of the lenses made it worse. And they were a handicap in another way; the *first* thing that an attacker would do would be to try to smash them. But she was virtually blind without them, so what could he do? Her short-sightedness was just the first in a string of handicaps that made her woefully unsuited to be a Herald.

He thought she looked particularly aggrieved this afternoon, but it was difficult to tell what her expression was on the other side of that wood-and-glass mask.

Physically, she was utterly unprepossessing, and looked like what she had been before she'd been Chosen; a sedentary scribe and clerk. He had no idea why she of all people had been Chosen, at a time when fighting Heralds were what was needed, not clerks, and how he was going to *turn* her into a fighter he had no clue. He despaired; she—well, he didn't know for certain how she felt. Frustrated, surely, at the least.

She was the single *clumsiest* Trainee he had ever attempted to teach, bar none. He didn't think this was on purpose, though, for even though she clearly didn't want to be here, she did try until she was black and blue. Even if she'd come here as a child, she'd have been clumsy, he suspected, but this business of learning weaponcraft late in life, a task to which she was utterly unsuited, must seem utter madness to her. He didn't blame her for being irritated and unhappy.

What was the point of putting her in this position anyway? She couldn't *see* without those lenses; she would lose them in a fight, and then she would be blind, and how was he supposed to train her to overcome that? Though there were tales of blind warriors with preternatural abilities in both Karse and Valdemar, those had all been about men and women who had been trained since early childhood in their craft, who brought skilled bodies and the finely honed senses of hearing and smell and touch to bear on the problem of being unable to see.

Not a middle-aged clerk who had been bent over a desk all of her life. She would arrive at the front lines only to return in days in one of those wagons. If she returned at all. Which he doubted.

She sighed and shifted her weight from one foot to the other, recapturing his wandering attention. "Weaponsmaster, all due respect, but we both know I'm hopeless at this. It's a complete waste of your time to try and train me to use *this.*"

She gestured at the sword she carried—and she spoke in Karsite.

In point of fact, if it were not for the fact that she couldn't fight, couldn't shoot, and couldn't defend herself, she'd be in Whites at this very moment. Self-defense was the only skill she lacked to enter her Internship, for she'd known most of what a Trainee learned long before she was ever Chosen. There was nothing about the history of Valdemar and the Heralds that she didn't know before she came here. She mastered the fine points of the law with the indifferent ease of someone who had spent years copying legal briefs. In fact, anything having to do with the written word, including no less than four languages, was of no difficulty to her. And she was the only person besides Alberich himself who was a fluent and natural speaker of his own tongue, learned directly from old Father Henrick before Alberich had set foot on the soil of Valdemar.

"There's a saying in Hardorn," she continued. "'You shouldn't attempt to teach a goat to sing. It will waste your time, hurt your ears, and annoy the goat.' I can say without fear of contradiction that the goat is getting annoyed."

He had to smile at that; she blinked behind those thick lenses, and emboldened, continued. "I keep asking this question, and no one will answer me. Can you give me one single, *good* reason why I have to learn weaponswork? And 'because all Trainees have to' is *not* a good reason. After all—" she set her chin mulishly, "—you don't make all *Healers* learn weaponswork, so why should every single Herald have to?"

Since he had just been about to say *because all Trainees have to,* he found himself stymied. He opened his mouth, closed it again, and regarded her thoughtfully. "Just what would you do if you were ambushed in the field?" he asked.

"Run," she replied promptly. "I'd cut loose my saddlebags, if I was mounted, throw away my belt pouch if I was afoot, and run. Chances are, whoever attacked me would be after my things and any money I had, not *me.* I'd let them have what they wanted. Things can be replaced, and while they'd be scrambling after loot, I'd be getting farther away."

:That was a good answer,: Kantor observed.

"And if you had to help villagers with a bandit attack?" he persisted.

She laughed. "Give my advice and go for help!" she replied. "Not that anyone would be likely to take the military advice of a dumpy, bookish female who's half blind, no matter what uniform she was wearing. But riding Aleirian, I'm as fast as any Herald, faster than any other messenger, *and* once I'm within Mindspeech range of any other Herald, I can relay my information."

:Another good answer. She's full of them, isn't she?:

:She's full of… something.: He sighed. She wasn't intimidated by him, not in the least, difficult creature that she was. She didn't *care* that he was Alberich of Karse, only half trusted even by the Heralds. "I know all about you from Henrick. And from Geri as well, of course," she'd said on meeting him, meaning Gerichen, once-Acolyte, now Priest; Geri, who'd become as much of a confidant as Alberich ever made of anyone. Simple sentences, but the *way* she'd said them had left him wondering just what it was that they'd told her. And later, he wondered what, and how much, she had written down, for she seemed to be always writing everything down in little notebooks. She always had one with her. When she wasn't writing things, she stared in a way that made him feel she was memorizing everything, so that she could write it down later.

:So how are you going to answer her?: Kantor prompted. *:She has a good point; you're never going to make her into any kind of a fighter. You were just thinking that the first thing that anyone seeing her would go for is those lenses, and then what?:*

Then she'd *be* blind, of course, and utterly helpless. No, she was right, very right, the best thing she could *ever* do if attacked would be to run away.

Could running be the answer, then?

:It should never be said that Herald Alberich refused to find a better way when one existed,: Kantor said. *:Besides, if she* can't *fight, they won't send her to the front lines; they'll use her to replace a Herald who can fight and send him instead.:*

"Put that away," he said abruptly. "You are right. I would be no kind of Weaponsmaster if I could not match the weapon to the student, not the student to the weapon. And *escape* might be the answer, however unlikely that weapon might be. Come into the salle, into the sitting room, and we will discuss this."

He didn't miss her smile of triumph, not that it mattered. She wasn't going to get off as easily as she thought; there might not be fighting practice, but she was going to find herself training until she was in far better physical shape than she'd ever been in her life. There would be extra riding classes for one thing; if her Companion was going to be running, *she* had better be in shape to stick with him, no matter what he had to do to get away. And if *she* was going to count on being able to run away, Alberich was going to make her into a competitive foot racer, whether she liked it or not.

Some of that clumsiness, at least, can be trained away.

She followed him into his living quarters; Dethor wasn't there at the moment. One of the Healers was trying a new treatment for his swollen joints, a course of bee venom, for beekeepers swore that the stings of their charges kept the ailment away from them. By now, Dethor's bones were painful enough that he was more than willing to tolerate even the stings of angry bees in hopes of getting some relief.

As a reward for his cooperation, he'd get a massage with hot stones and a treatment for his hands of hot sand afterward, something that *did* give him consistent relief, even if it was only temporary.

Myste took one of the chairs in front of the window; Alberich sat opposite her. "We need to think," he told her. "We need to find a way to make the things you *can* do into weapons. Running, for instance." He pondered that for a while. "I'll trade you saying for saying—in the hills in Karse there's a proverb, 'The hound that chases two hares catches neither.' If you are going to run—we need to contrive a way that you can create more than one thing for your pursuers to go after."

"Dropping my packs—" she began.

"But what if there is something in your packs that you've been entrusted with?" he countered. "What if it's in the winter, with no Waystations near? If you drop your packs, you won't have what you need to survive. It won't do you much good to escape from bandits only to freeze to death in a blizzard." He brooded over the idea for a moment, then the answer came to him. "I think we should add a bit of extra equipment specifically for you—packs and belt pouches that you're *meant* to throw away."

"What?" she asked. "Stuffed with straw or the like?"

He shook his head. "No, *not* that, actually. If you drop worthless decoys, it won't be long before bandits and brigands all *know* that the packs you drop are worthless, and they'll ignore them and go for you again. No, that hare won't run—there will be *just* enough in the decoys to satisfy an ambusher without making it look as if you're an especially juicy target, and to make certain that attackers chase the packs, and not you. And the same for belt pouches; from now on, you'll be carrying at least two small extras, both full of coppers, and if someone attacks you, you'll throw them in opposite directions, one to either side of your line of flight."

She was happy enough about the planning, but visibly unhappy when he brought her back outside and put her in front of the obstacle course. "Run the course, then run it again," he told her mercilessly. "And keep running it until I tell you to stop. Running away isn't going to do you any good if you can't actually run any better than Dethor on a bad day."

And he left her to it, with a faint feeling of having—for once—gotten the better of her. Irritating woman. Not that he didn't *like* her; she not only had the advantage of being one of the few people he could converse easily with in his own tongue, she was an interesting and lively conversationalist. And besides not being afraid of him or intimidated by him, he got the feeling that she respected him in a way that was quite flattering, when she wasn't trying to get the better of him. Why was it that she entered every conversation with the goal of somehow trying to *win?*

Well, she could just work some of that out over the hurdles. Meanwhile, he had a class of young archers to put through their paces.

When he told Dethor of his solution to the problem of Myste over dinner, the Weaponsmaster chuckled. "Good solution," Dethor replied. "A very good solution. But I hope it isn't one we need to use. I'd much rather that the Heraldic Circle can find a position for her that makes the best use of her talents here in the city. Whatever those talents are."

"At the moment," Alberich replied, with just a tinge of sourness, having had to find reasons why every single obstacle in the course was one she needed to learn to negotiate, "arguing and writing. Little enough of anything else, have I seen."

"Heh. I've seen those little notebooks of hers—" Dethor blinked. "Now, why didn't I think of this before? Herald-Chronicler, of course! Elcarth's doing it now, but we want him for Dean of the Collegium, and we need to start training him in that—" His voice faded off as he got that faraway look in his eyes that meant he was thinking, and probably Mindspeaking with his Companion. Alberich now knew that look very, very well.

And Dethor was right, of course; with all of his own reading of the Chronicles, he could see how being the Herald-Chronicler would easily be a full-time job. It wasn't just the doings of the Heralds that the Chronicler covered, it was *everything;* anything that had any impact on any part of the Kingdom larger than a small village.

:What do you think?: he asked Kantor.

:That it's probably the reason she was Chosen,: Kantor replied. *:She gets onto a story like a rat-terrier and won't let go of it until she's shaken it free of all the facts.:*

Annoying little dogs, rat-terriers. All yap and idiotic courage—or was that "stubbornness?" Still. Come to think of it, that described Myste rather well... Or, perhaps, she was more like a cat, one of those mouthy ones that wouldn't stop caterwauling, came when you didn't want them, and wouldn't come when you did.

:We're in nasty times. Someone has to be willing to put down nasty facts without editing them,: Kantor continued. *:And you like cats. You like rat-terriers, too.:*

He ignored that last. *:Hmm. Nasty facts like my little exercise tonight?:* he replied.

:It ought to be written down somewhere,: Kantor countered. *:Maybe not for common consumption, but if someone doesn't record everything, no matter how unflattering to the Heralds it is, the next generation is going to get the idea that we're all plaster saints. Then when someone has to do something underhanded for a good reason, nobody will be willing to do it....:*

He sighed. There was that. And plenty of Chroniclers in the past had created "auxiliary Chronicles" that not everyone was allowed to read, Chronicles that recorded mistakes, blunders, errors in judgment, and jobs undertaken that were somewhat less than the letter of the law, all in unflinching detail. Not the sort of thing one gave the children, of course, but these Chronicles, and not just the standard texts, were what Alberich was studying as history. Just now he was in the middle of the very brief Chronicle of Lavan Firestorm; some of the soul-baring on the part of Herald Pol and King Theran was enough to make the heart ache. He could relate all too easily to the litany of "should haves" and "could haves."

Well, if Trainee Myste—who was certainly being allowed to read and study the unexpurgated versions of the Chronicles—was able to combine the qualities of detachment and tough-mindedness that the job required, especially *now*, well done to her. Elcarth probably wasn't; he was too tenderhearted to be unflattering to people he liked, even when it wasn't possible to get to the truth without being unflattering.

Mind, only a handful of people would know *that* for certain within Myste's or Elcarth's lifetime, because the Chronicles weren't written for the present generations, they were written for the future, and very few Heralds other than the King and the King's Own were allowed to see what their current Chronicler wrote. And then it was in terms of editing by similarly tough-minded Heralds, and only to ensure accuracy.

As he knew very well, the Chronicles could be extremely caustic at times, and no one really wanted to see himself, his presumed or even actual motivations, and his failures, stripped bare and put down in uncompromising writing.

In his opinion, a young person didn't have the perspective nor the experience to write what needed to be written. So there, again, Myste was fully qualified. Appointing her as Chronicler Second would solve the problem of what to do with her very neatly indeed.

Dethor abruptly came back to himself. "I believe that will work," he said, as if Alberich had been privy to whatever thoughts were going on in his mind. "You're going out in the city tonight?"

"No other choice, have I," Alberich replied with a shrug. "Much result, I do not expect, but sow silver I must, a harvest of villainy to reap."

In this, at least, he was able to aid Valdemar with a clear conscience. In disguise, one of half a dozen personae he had concocted and established, he prowled the less-savory quarters of Haven, looking for trouble. "Trouble" came in various guises, but money usually lured it out of hiding. The money wasn't bribes—Alberich was more subtle than that. Sometimes he posed as someone looking for a particular sort of creature to hire, sometimes as a bully-boy looking for work himself. Sometimes he bought information, and sometimes sold it. In all cases, there was nothing to connect the less-than-honest characters he portrayed in the seedy drinking houses and alleyways with Herald Alberich, the Weaponsmaster's Second. There was some benefit in having a scarred and scowling countenance that looked the very acme of villainy. If there wasn't a woman born who'd give him a second look, no one looked askance at him in a low-class bar either.

And fortunately, there were enough foreigners in Haven that his accent caused only a little comment, and no one recognized it as Karsite. Most accepted his story that he came from Ruvan, Brendan, or Jkatha. All three were so far away he might just as well have told the inquisitive that he was from the moon. Virtually anything he claimed would be believed. The only people who *might* know better would be true Guild Mercenaries, and so far he'd never seen one of those in Haven. They weren't needed here; Valdemar fielded its own standing army of full-time soldiers, called the Guard, and always had. Even Guild Mercenaries didn't bother to go where there was no need of them.

"Well, you be careful out there tonight," Dethor said, putting down his empty tankard. Alberich automatically refilled it for him from the pitcher on the table between them and raised an eyebrow. Dethor wasn't known for having the Gift of ForeSight, but one never knew. "A reason for the warning, you have?" he asked carefully.

But Dethor only shook his head. "Not really. It's just that it's been quiet, and it's usually quiet just before there's a lot of trouble."

"And trouble then comes in threes," Alberich agreed gloomily. "*And* a full moon there is tonight. I shall walk carefully."

"Full moon." Dethor groaned. "You're going to get into a brawl tonight, aren't you?"

Alberich felt his muscles tighten with automatic anticipation. He suppressed his reaction as much as he could. Dethor was very good at reading body language.

"Probably." Alberich shrugged with an indifference he didn't entirely feel. A bar fight would at least give him something on which to take out his frustration. He always slept better after being able to pound some villain's face into the floor. The wretches that tried to pick on *him* were at least as bad as he pretended to be. The only reason they were at the tavern instead of jail was that they hadn't been caught at anything lately, and they well deserved whatever punishment Vkandis decreed they meet at the hands of His transplanted worshiper.

:*Oh, very nice reasoning,*: Kantor said, with more than a touch of sarcasm.

"Try not to give the Healers any more work, will you?" Dethor requested with resignation. "They had a few words for me the last time you needed patching up, and since I couldn't tell them *why* you'd gotten cut up, they assumed I'd been working you and Kimel with live steel and you'd gotten the worst of it. So, of course, it was *my* fault."

"That, I can promise," Alberich replied, gathering up all the supper dishes and placing them in the empty basket. "For that the wretches whose bones I break, seeking a Healer would not be, ever. Too fearful would they be, that in seeking Healing, it would be justice they found." With a salute to Dethor, he left the rest unsaid, and headed for the door. He couldn't help it; there were frustrations in him that were crying out for release. He wouldn't *look* for a fight, but if one came to him—

He sensed Kantor's sigh.

He left the basket just outside the door to their quarters for a servant to collect, and went out into the flooding light of the full moon to saddle

Kantor. His Companion was waiting for him at the special stable only the Companions used.

Just inside the door was the tack room, but Kantor's gear was all stowed on racks near his stall, just as it was for every Companion who resided primarily at the Collegium. On a warm summer night like this one, all the half-doors on the stalls were open to the night air, and with all of the moonlight pouring in, the lanterns weren't needed at all.

They were quite alone in the stable, which suited Alberich's mood perfectly. *:You've told Taver and Talamir we're going out tonight?:* he asked Kantor, throwing only the plainest and most basic of saddle pads and blankets over Kantor's back.

:Of course.: Kantor looked back over his shoulder as Alberich tightened the girth. *:We're going out the private entrance?:*

:Of course.: Alberich swung up into the saddle, and they made their way across the Field. Kantor's hooves made no sound at all on the soft grass; they moved across the silver expanse like a pair of spirits gliding over the surface of a silent sea.

There was a little gate at the far end of the wall around Companion's Field that would have been a dreadful security hole had it not been closed by three doors—the final one of iron cunningly cast to look exactly like the rusty-brown stone that the wall itself was made of. Only Talamir, Sendar, and Dethor had held the keys to those doors, and Dethor had given his to Alberich. Furthermore, the iron one was so heavy that it required a Companion's strength to haul it open from the outside, and it wasn't likely that anyone with a horse or a mule was going to be able to get along the outer wall of the Palace without a challenge. And *then* a would-be intruder would have to get his mount to push instead of pull. Not too likely, that. It was an amazingly clever door, that actually could swing in an entire one-hundred-eighty-degree arc—but there was a spring-loaded stop on it that worked as a fairly high doorsill to keep it from swinging outward; a stop that could only be dropped down level to the ground from the inside. So Kantor could push it to swing *out* when they were on the inside, but no one could *pull* it out from the outside. Locking the door released it again, and as Alberich turned his key in that final lock, he heard it *smack* up into place on its spring.

There was no one on the road, but several times he looked up to see one of the Guards keeping watch on the wall, so well hidden in the shadows that only he, who knew *every* hiding place along it, could have spotted them. He nodded to them, and got a little hand signal in recognition. The Palace Guard, at least, now knew and trusted him.

Of course, he'd trained a good many of them, and bouted regularly with all of them. You learned a lot about a man, sparring with him. Once Kimel had accepted him, the rest had started coming around.

He wasn't in Whites tonight—and that would have made him instantly recognizable to the Guards no matter what. He could have Whites if he wanted them… but he didn't want them. He'd become accustomed to those dark gray leathers; they suited him, suited his nature, suited his wish to be something less conspicuous.

:As if you could be anything other than conspicuous,: Kantor scoffed.

:When I'm with you, perhaps not,: he acknowledged. *:You are rather conspicuous all by yourself.:*

By alleys and shortcuts that only he knew, he and Kantor slipped quietly among the mansions of the highborn, through the townhouses of the wealthy, and suddenly came out on a side street in a neighborhood of inns and taverns. They were only paces away from the Companion's Bell, a respectable inn that was their intermediate goal.

Alberich felt that tightening of his muscles again, and a quickening of his pulse. It was time to go to work, work that he understood, work that he, and only he, *could* do.

The Bell had several distinct advantages for what he was about to do. Firstly, it was a place often frequented by Heralds, so the sight of a Companion in a loose-box would not go remarked, nor would the sight of Alberich entering the stableyard. Second, the Heralds had a private taproom available to them—Heralds could and *did* mingle with the regular customers, but no one would think twice about Alberich not appearing among them, for plenty of Heralds who came here kept to the private room.

Ah, but then there was the third reason…

He dismounted, and Kantor followed him into the stable. There were two other Companions there already, who whickered a welcome to both of them. *:Excellent,:* Kantor said. *:I shall have reinforcements—if you need them.:*

Alberich snorted, and left Kantor to make himself at home in a third loose-box as he approached the far wall, and the third reason for his being here.

The third reason for his being here and no other place, was that the Bell had a locked room at the back of the stable that contained a trunk, and had a second locked door that let out onto an alley. A very dark alley, and one that, somehow, never had patrols of constables or City Guards at night.

He unlocked the door. He paused just long enough to light a spill at the lantern beside the door, then locked himself inside. There was a second lantern there, which he lit.

In that trunk had been Dethor's disguises; now it held Alberich's.

Someone else—Alberich thought it was probably the innkeeper himself—had a key to that room, for any clothing he left atop the trunk was taken away and laundered and placed back inside it. Some disguises, of course, *shouldn't* be cleaned—the stains and yes, the odor lent verisimilitude to his persona. Those he put back in the trunk himself, wrapped in a waxed canvas bag to keep from stinking up the rest of his gear.

Tonight, however, it was about time for Aarak Benshane, a common enough thug with a reputation for not asking too many questions of prospective employers, to put in an appearance at the Blue Boar. Aarak was not too noisome a fellow; Alberich could get away with cleanliness tonight.

Alberich opened the trunk and selected his disguise with care; leather trews, battered boots and hat, scarred black leather jerkin strong enough to turn most blades, and a shirt of no particular color that was a bit frayed about the cuffs and collar. Over these, he slung a belt holding two knives, but no sword. Aarak did most of his work with his fists.

:That should suit you, considering the mood you're in.: Kantor was not being ironic nor sarcastic this time.

:As a matter of fact,: Alberich replied, *:it does.:*

By day, the tavern that was his goal, the Boar, was a quiet enough tavern, serving manual laborers at the nearby warehouses. At night, however, it took on a rougher clientele. Some of the laborers returned to drink away their earnings, and they were joined by others, for whom the warehouses were of less-than-legitimate interest. Aarak fit right in there; he *might* hire himself out as a day laborer, if he was inclined to do manual labor, or forced into it, but he would far rather serve as the lookout for thugs who planned a little late-night looting.

Alberich let himself out into the alley. It was dark back there, shadowed on both sides by tall buildings, but he knew his way around Haven even in pitchy black. He kept to the alleys for the most part, only crossing streets when he had to, and at length, found himself in the warehouse area where the Boar stood.

There was a lot of coming and going around a warehouse, and no one asked what was being stored there very often. And, of course, warehouses were full of things that were already packed for transportation; what could be more attractive and easier for a bold gang of thieves?

Alberich had been recruited by such gangs, once or twice, though never out of the Blue Boar, and never as Aarak. He had hopes, though, and he nursed his thin, sour beer at a table here several times a moon, waiting to see if his patient fishing would catch him another gang of thieves.

He opened the door quietly. It wasn't a good idea to make any kind of an entrance into the Boar. There were always people there who would take that sort of hubris amiss.

Flash of blue—a tangle of thrashing bodies on the floor—

He paused, just inside the door, and caught himself.

Damn. Come on. Don't show anything, or you're dead. He shoved on inside the door on strength of will, until his vision cleared and he could pretend that he hadn't just had a flash of ForeSight.

The regular servers knew him by now, or at least, they knew Aarak's distinctive hat. He caught the eye of one, nodded at a vacant table off to one side of the room, and took his seat there. Within a reasonable length of time, the server appeared with a jack of beer.

Despite Kantor's needling, he'd had a few hopes that someone *might* try to recruit him tonight—a full moon now meant moon-dark in a fortnight, and moon-dark meant the possibility of work.

But the truth was, from the moment he'd crossed the threshold, he knew that Dethor had been right about a tavern brawl in the offing. Even if he hadn't gotten that brief—very brief—glimpse of a tumble of fighting bodies on the floor of the place from his ForeSight, he'd have known it. There was something in the air tonight, something wild and edgy, something that made Kantor, back in his stall, prick up his ears and ask wordlessly, and in all seriousness this time, if Alberich thought he'd need any help.

Alberich never actually got a chance to reply. He was just starting on the first swallow of his beer, when the fight erupted over a card cheat, three tables down.

The cheater had friends, and the friends waded in, and Alberich saw—

Flash of blue—

The fight was only a pretext to rob the only person here with any real cash. That was the owner of the Blue Boar himself.

Three people swarming the bar, as combat seemed to thrust them toward it by accident.

He came to himself long enough to dodge out of the way of a tumbling body, and shoved his hand into a special belt pouch he always wore as Aarak. It held weighted knuckle guards, his preferred weapon for brawling. He didn't like using blades in a brawl—he was there to immobilize people, not kill them. No point in killing them, when, if they were what he *really* wanted, he wanted them alive, to question.

Another flash of blue, freezing him for a moment.

The three thieves—he assumed that was what they were—waited for the fight to reach the bar and then threw themselves over it, the surprised tavern owner trying to get out of the way as they all three landed atop him. There were short, heavy clubs in their hands.

They clubbed the tavernkeeper senseless.

Alberich shook his head to free it of the vision, as shouts and cries of pain marked the center of the brawl. A drunk, stinking of beer, blundered into him and made a wild swing at him.

And that was just enough. Alberich sprang into motion, like a mastiff held leashed and suddenly released. A savage grin with nothing of joy in it split his face. He ducked under the other's swing and gut-punched the drunk with his laden fist, stepping out of the way and shoving him to one side to topple him before he spewed the contents of his stomach all over everything in front of him.

Flash of blue, and he saw the three thieves vault over the bar and make off with the cash box while a larger fight still engaged the bouncers and everyone else they could draw in.

That was it; that was all his ForeSight showed him. But it was enough. When his eyes cleared for the third time, he saw the three men beginning to make their way towards the bar.

Ha. Another drunk approached, got one look at his face, and flinched away. Alberich shoved him aside, straight-armed another, shouldered into a third.

And when the three would-be robbers reached their goal, he was already there, waiting.

They only saw one more temporary obstacle in their path, and moved to clear it.

They weren't very good with their lead-weighted clubs, which was probably why the clubs were weighted in the first place. And they hadn't practiced fighting as a team either. He managed to get the first two to tangle each other up for a moment, by grabbing the first and shoving him bodily into the arms of the second. They weren't expecting anyone to reach *for* them—

While the first two were shouting and tripping over each other, he stepped in toward the third, came in low, and laid out his target with a brass-laden right to the point of the chin.

His fist connected solidly, with a satisfying impact that snapped the fellow's head back and sent him sailing across the floor to land over a table. It didn't break, of course. The tavernkeeper didn't want the expense of replacing furniture every moon. The Boar's tables and chairs would stand up to a charging bull and the bull would come away second best.

Now he felt it, that heady pleasure—which would be a guilty one, later, when he came to think about it—that rush of energy and unholy glee that only came during a fight. Fighting-drunk; that was what Dethor called it, for it wasn't the berserk rage that wiped out thought and sense. On the contrary, it made him sharper, and he enjoyed it. when he was fighting in a way that would make him feel a bit ashamed of himself later. But now, it widened his manic grin and filled his veins with lightning.

When the first two got clear of each other, he grabbed them both and shoved their heads together with a *crack* that echoed even over the noise of the brawl. One went down; the other didn't.

He was stunned, though—stunned just long enough.

Alberich grabbed his shoulder and spun him around to face forward; pulled back his fist, and delivered a gut-punch that made the fool's eyes bug out as he toppled to the floor.

He looked around for the trio's friends, the ones he'd seen in his vision, but they, seeing that the cash snatchers were down and out and there was no reason to continue the fight any further, began breaking free of their little knots of combat and scuttling away.

He thought about pursuing. His blood was up now, and he was ready to chase down half a dozen of the young thugs.

:*Chosen. Enough. You've ended the problem; that will do for now.*:

Kantor's demand cut across the fire in his veins, and chilled it.

He shook his head and backed up out of the way, against the wall. With the instigators gone, the bouncers were managing to quell the remaining belligerents without any help from him. He slipped his knuckle guards off his hand and back into his pouch.

Part of him regretted that the fight was over. Most of him sighed with relief. When the last of those still trying to fight had been tossed into the street, he gave the bouncers a hand with sending the unconscious after them.

The three *he'd* done for were among them, but he saw no point in saying anything about what might have happened. After all, there was no proof.

He accepted a somewhat better tankard of beer as his reward for helping out, and stayed only long enough to drink it before returning to Kantor. His glee was gone; his guilt had started, and besides, nothing more was going to happen tonight. If anyone was thinking of hiring Aarak, they wouldn't do it tonight. The men he'd downed might have friends watching, who would take it amiss if someone "rewarded" Aarak with a job.

The moon was down by the time Alberich got to his hiding place, and he had to feel carefully for the keyhole to let himself inside. He discovered bruises he hadn't felt when he changed back into his gray leathers.

:Maybe you didn't, but I did,: Kantor sniffed as he mounted.

:They'll heal,: he replied, sending Kantor back up the street toward the Palace. He felt as he always did after a fight; weary and with emotions dulled except for a fierce and bitter satisfaction. The weariness was welcome; he'd sleep well tonight for a change.

:There was someone watching you from the corner,: Kantor went on, giving him a flash of something that the Companion had noted through Alberich's eyes. *:I think you'll be offered a job next time you go there.:*

The bitterness eased a little; Alberich recognized that vague glimpse. It was someone he'd been watching for some time now, a legitimate businessman who somehow seemed to have more goods in his warehouse than he'd actually *purchased*... Now—now he might find out just where those goods came from.

"Good," he said aloud. *:That is why we come here, isn't it?:*

:Not entirely,: Kantor retorted. *:At least, you don't.:*

Alberich started to reply, and thought better of it. Kantor was infinitely better at warring with words than he was. He let his silence speak for him, letting Kantor come to his own conclusions.

Eventually, the ears flattened, and out of the silence came—

:I apologize.:

:And you are also right,: Alberich acknowledged. *:I do seek out fighting more often than necessary. I could go about the same business without getting involved in altercations at all. But it is what I need, right here, right now.:*

Kantor sighed, but his head nodded. *:So be it. If you need it, then we will continue to seek it, and I will say no more about it, except to ask you to take care.:*

Alberich closed his eyes for a moment. *:Perhaps, someday, we will no longer need to go hunting trouble for trouble's own sake.:*

It was all he could offer. But Kantor seemed to find it enough.

9

Dethor had invited Talamir to his quarters tonight, in a way that had been less "invitation" and more "demand." Talamir was fairly certain that he wanted to discuss the current situation with his Second. Alberich, the probable subject of those discussions (now officially a full Herald, though he kept stubbornly to those peculiar gray leathers of his) was gone when Talamir arrived.

Dethor interpreted his curious look correctly; not a surprise, considering how well he and Talamir knew each other.

There was a small fire in the fireplace, although the weather was not yet so cool in the evenings that a fire was necessary. But the Weaponsmaster seemed to crave both the extra warmth and the emotional comfort of a fire more and more often of late.

Come to that, they all craved extra comfort. The Wars seemed both too far away, and too near. A feeling of dreadful tension underlaid everything, no matter how trivial, a frantic feeling as if whatever was being done *had* to be done, or enjoyed, or dealt with *now*, for there was no telling what the next day, or even the next candlemark, might bring. Small comforts took on enormous importance, yet one indulged in them in a spirit of guilt, quite as if throwing on another log was somehow going to deprive the Guard on the Border of heat and light.

Dethor had lit only two lanterns, one behind each of the two hearthside chairs; the fire provided the rest of the light in the room tonight.

The Weaponsmaster's Second was nowhere to be seen. "He's out. In town," Dethor said, as Talamir looked inquiringly at the third seat that Alberich usually used. "He won't be back for a while. I believe he's got something on the boil tonight."

"He's doing good work down there," Talamir observed as dispassionately as he could, and settled himself into the padded chair opposite Dethor's. It was difficult to be dispassionate about Dethor's bland statement. Every time Alberich had "something on the boil," there was usually a great deal of violence involved before it was over. Alberich was directly involved in that violence at least half of the time; if Talamir hadn't been aware of just how much he despised unnecessary force, he'd have suspected that the man was seeking out opportunities to thrash someone.

But—perhaps he is, and he's simply making sure that the opportunity calls for necessary violence. That wouldn't be too difficult in the neighborhoods Alberich had to prowl.

"I wondered how much you'd kept track of," Dethor said. "What with everything else you've got going on."

"All of it, I think," Talamir admitted. "And he's as good as you ever were in the covert work, and better, far better, than I. We are, perhaps, too much the gentlemen. He fits in down there better than we ever could, no matter how much we deluded ourselves about our acting abilities."

The words hung heavily in the air, and Talamir glanced out the window of the sitting room. It was moon-dark, and a Companion ghosted into and out of sight among the trees out there, a glimmer of white in the darkness.

"There's too many bloody bastards taking advantage of the situation to make trouble. Or money. Or both," Dethor muttered. "You cut one down, and two more spring up to replace him. It wasn't like that when I was doing the dirty work. It was never that vile down by Exile's Gate."

Talamir shrugged; they both knew that was true enough. Haven had been stripped of all but a skeleton staff of the Guard; constables and even private bodyguards had gone to join the army. The opportunities for the criminal and unscrupulous were legion. Alberich and a trusted handful of constables and the Palace and City Guard were accomplishing more than even the Council guessed. None of it had anything to do with being a Herald, of course—other than an occasional use of the Truth Spell and his communication with Kantor, Alberich never did anything that could not have been done by an ordinary constable.

Providing, of course, that an ordinary constable had his knack for subterfuge and covert work. Which, of course, none of them did. There was only one Alberich.

He couldn't rid the place of crime forever, but every time he removed a criminal from the streets, it took a while for someone else to fill the void left behind, a breathing space for the constables still at work on the street.

Alberich had a real flair for working clandestinely, something he'd probably never explored back in Karse. Talamir wondered how Alberich felt about this new skill; it didn't seem to match the persona of a simple military man.

As if Alberich would ever be a simple *anything.*

"It was never that vile because there were never that many opportunities," Talamir pointed out. "And what are we to do? Demand some sort of certification of virtue from everyone who passes the gates? Haul them away and question them under Truth Spell as to their motives? I think not. The best we can do is what Alberich's doing, and thank the gods we have him."

The fire flared, revealing Dethor's troubled expression.

"You know the man's in a real mental state," Dethor said, leveling a long and accusatory look at his old friend. Talamir shifted uncomfortably, but his conscience forced him to meet Dethor's eyes. "I have the feeling that he's overworking, just so he can sleep at night. I have the feeling that he's *looking* for trouble just so he can work out his frustration on a legitimate object. The problem is, when you start looking for trouble, it starts looking for *you.* "

Talamir sighed, deliberately looking down at the plate of fruit on the table between their chairs. Slowly and methodically, he picked up an apple and began to peel it. "I know," he admitted. "I wish there was something that I could do about it. But even if we hadn't promised we would never ask him to do anything against Karse—"

"—the Council won't allow him out of Haven." Dethor snorted, and Talamir looked up from his apple with reluctance. The creases and wrinkles of Dethor's face turned his frown into something demonic, and the firelight only amplified the effect. "Dammit, Talamir. Can't you do anything about this? I *know* he wants to do something about the Wars, and I see his face every time he watches another batch of youngsters going south. It's tearing him up!"

"What? Vouch for him? I have, a hundred times and more," Talamir replied, nettled that Dethor would even *think* he'd been doing less than he could for Alberich. "Then there's the little matter of what he calls his honor."

"Which he's damned touchy about," Dethor growled.

"Exactly so," Talamir agreed. "So what are we going to do? Truth here—I'd give both legs for a dozen Alberichs, all willing to go spying back there among his own people. Damned insular Karsites! Strangers stand out among 'em like a chirra in a herd of sheep. Accents, mannerisms, what they know without even *knowing* that they know it—" He threw up his hands in frustration. "—you just can't *teach* those sorts of things!"

"Tell me something I don't know," Dethor said, throwing an apple core into the fire in a gesture of exasperation. "Just how many agents have we lost?"

"Too many." Talamir was just glad that none of them had been Heralds. *He* had argued—successfully—that the Heralds were too few to risk inside the borders of Karse. But the fact was, from the beginning he had doubted the ability of any of them to pass as Karsite, and when the Sunpriests got their hands on Heralds, the results were traumatic for *every* Herald. It wasn't just the Death Bell tolling that sent everyone into a spate of mourning, it was that everyone *knew* what happened to Heralds that got caught in Karse. There was a sick fear behind the mourning, and the same kind of frustration and anger that sent Alberich out looking for a fight.

The Lord Marshal had been perfectly willing to send in his own people, however, and when he did, exactly what Talamir feared happened. Karse devoured agents as a child devours sweets. They seemed to last about a moon before they were discovered; certainly not much longer. What happened to them after that, Talamir was all too aware; he preferred not to dwell on it, for at least all the men had been volunteers and knew precisely what awaited them if captured. Certainly, no more than a handful had returned.

Horrible. And there didn't seem to be a great deal they could do to change that. No matter *how* much information they gathered on Karse, no matter who they spoke to or how many old books they read, they were *not* able to fool real Karsites for long.

If at all.

"What we need," Dethor said glumly, "is what we can't get. Real Karsites. Someone who's got all the little nuances, habits, all the things you just can't study. Someone who *fits.* Someone who can't give himself away, because what's second-nature to him is all based on real Karsite memories. But the few folk who've come over are all too frightened to go back, and I can't say as I blame 'em." The scent of burning apple, sweet and bitter at the same time, added a strange nuance to his words.

Alberich wouldn't be too frightened to go, if he could; Alberich had everything they needed in an agent. If only they could use him—

And—the other stumbling block—if only his sense of honor would allow him to be so used.

It was so intensely frustrating. Sometimes Talamir just wanted to howl with the frustration.

If it was bad for him, it must be worse for Alberich. He was facing enormous pressure from those who didn't know about the covert work and saw only that he spent little time in the company of the other Heralds and less *doing* anything that might help the war effort. There was even more social pressure from those who had no idea that the Council had effectively shackled Alberich to Haven. There was a feeling from some that he had somehow betrayed the land that had taken him in, the brotherhood into which he had been admitted.

But what could they do to change that? Nothing. Everything he was doing, other than his position as Dethor's Second, was covert, and had to remain so.

Especially the work with the Lord Marshal's agents—though for all the candlemarks he spent with them, there was little enough to show in the way of success.

But then, the agents were only men—clever men, facile men, but just ordinary men. They couldn't *be* him for a day, or a week, or somehow pluck the deep memories that made him *Karsite* out of his head and plant them so solidly in their own minds that they *became* Karsite themselves.

Which brought him back to the problem all over again. If only they could make all those agents into little Alberichs… if only they could link those agents into Alberich's head, so that every time they did something wrong, he would catch them and correct them.

And a blinding revelation hit him.

"Good gods—" Talamir exclaimed, staring unseeingly at his reflection in the window. "I do believe I have the solution."

"To which problem?" Dethor asked skeptically.

"To the problem of how we can get effective agents into Karse," Talamir replied, holding his half-peeled apple tightly. "And to the problem of Alberich contributing to the war. You know how MindHealers are able to get into someone's head and do things with their memories? Extract ones we need from someone who's unconscious, and all that?"

Once again, he found it unnecessary to explain to his friend where he was going. "MindHealer. You think they'd be willing to get into our Karsite's head and get *his* memories out, then plant them in someone else's head?" Dethor looked interested, but skeptical. "They're damn near as touchy about what's moral and what's not as *he* is about his honor."

"If he agrees, I can ask," Talamir replied. "I lose nothing by asking, and if I already have his consent, what can they object to?"

"And will those memories be *real?*" Dethor continued. "I mean, you *know* how faulty even trained memory can be. Memory isn't reliable—especially not childhood memory."

"Which doesn't matter!" Talamir responded triumphantly. "Not in this case. What *matters* are the little things that make him Karsite, not the particulars. In fact, I wouldn't be at all averse to some inaccuracy, even a little childish fantasy; if we can make agents who aren't Alberich but *are* common Karsite folk, all the better."

Dethor brooded over the idea for a while. "I'm not sure that could be done with the Lord Marshal's men," he began, sounding very dubious indeed.

But Talamir shook his head. "I'm not talking about the Lord Marshal's men," he replied. "If this works, we can risk Heralds. And we'll have to; I suspect it will only work with those who've got Mindspeech."

"Ah, hellfires." Dethor was clearly dismayed. After a moment, however, he scratched his head and shrugged. "I suppose you're right. And I have to think we'll get volunteers."

"I'd be shocked if we didn't." It was a depressing thought, actually—his yearmates, students, teachers, people he knew, rushing eagerly into the worst danger. It was bad enough for the Lord Marshal to send spies, but if the Karsites found *Heralds* on their soil—

Yet if those Heralds could pass as common Karsites and be able to discover and pass on what the Tedrels were going to do well in advance—

The alternative, though, was not to be contemplated. Alberich was not the only one who thought that the Tedrels were engaged in a campaign to drain Valdemar until it was so weak that one tremendous push would collapse everything.

They don't know us very well if they think we'll just collapse, Talamir thought, grimly.

:They know us not at all,: Taver said, although Talamir had not deliberately used Mindspeech, sounding just as grim as Talamir felt. *:But the cost of holding against them, never knowing when the push is coming—:*

It didn't bear thinking about. *:So we must know what they are about to do before they do it, so that we can appear to weaken without actually doing so. Then we can lure them into making their final push while we are still strong.:*

That, really, was the only possible option. Sendar and the Council had weighed all the others, not that there were many. By emptying the treasury and conscripting every able-bodied man and woman in the Kingdom, they *might* be able to mount a counter-campaign. There wasn't enough money in the entire Kingdom to hire a force equivalent to the Tedrels...

:There is not enough money in all of Karse twice over to hire *the Tedrels,:* Taver reminded him. *:They are fighting for themselves, not Karse. Karse has not hired them, per se—or at least, they offered them something more than just gold. Karse has merely provided them with a platform from which to launch a campaign to conquer a new homeland and the resources to support them while they do so.:*

"Why do the Karsites hate us so much?" Talamir asked aloud, in something like despair. "Why?"

Dethor shrugged. "Religion's at the heart of it, I'd guess," he opined. "But don't ask me, ask Alberich."

Religion. What about Valdemar could *possibly* seem so threatening to a religion?

:There is no one true way,: Taver said. *:That is what threatens the Sunpriests; that is what terrifies them. If you offer that to people, you offer them freedom, and you challenge those who claim ultimate authority. If you offer that, you give people options. The Sunpriests rely on being the ultimate, unchallengeable authority; their lives depend on the very opposite of options. Their rule depends on their followers having no options, and relies on blind belief and even blind obedience.:*

:Perhaps, but how do they expect to keep their people in the dark?: Short of building a wall around the country and guarding every exit point, there was no way of keeping people from finding out what was going on outside their borders.

:Ah, but a war builds that wall, doesn't it?: Taver responded. *:You don't need stones when you've got an enemy.:*

"Interrupting, I hope I am not," Alberich said from the doorway. He sounded exhausted; when he came into the light, Talamir took a good long look at him, and decided that he was at least as exhausted as he sounded.

"Hmm. Another fight?" he asked. The Weaponsmaster's Second was somewhat the worse for wear. He had a bandage across his forehead and another binding his forearm (suggesting that he'd already been to the Healers), bruised knuckles, and other signs that he'd been getting into trouble down in Haven. Small wonder he sounded tired.

"Fruitful," was all Alberich said. "But to drink, something wholesome, if you please?" He made a face. "The taste of sour beer, to remove from my mouth."

"I very much please, lad, and get off your feet," Dethor said quickly, and Alberich limped into the room. Dethor tilted the kettle at the hearth and poured out a mug of mulled wine, handing it to Alberich, who sat down and accepted it, draining half of it in a single go. "So, what'd you net us this time?"

"Smugglers," Alberich replied. "Of vile things in—of information out." He raised a weary eyebrow. "One leak less, there is, and the jail, full." He still looked troubled, though, and Talamir knew why; it wasn't that he hadn't done well, it was just that he was concerned that there were informants who were eluding him. Anyone that Alberich caught down in the slums of Haven would not likely be sending the most sensitive information. Not that there was any sign that there *was* such a leak, but they always had to assume that one could exist.

Finding *those* leaks was Talamir's job; Alberich could not function in Court circles, while Talamir could, cultivating a mild-mannered and quiet demeanor, saying little and all of that agreeable and sympathetic. He came across as unworldly and just a bit absent-minded. People confided in him a great deal, and generally had no idea how *much* they had told him.

Nevertheless, there was no doubt in Talamir's mind that if saboteurs and couriers were to materialize in Haven, they would be living and operating in the area that Alberich was responsible for. Elsewhere, people were curious about their neighbors. In effect, each little quarter outside of the *most* impoverished areas was a kind of village, where everyone knew everyone else and wanted to know what they were up to. Not so around Exile's Gate. The inhabitants were utterly indifferent to the doings around them, and with good reason. Those who were too curious often ended up on—at best—the wrong end of a beating.

"Plenty of damage can come out of Exile's Gate," Talamir assured him. "Anything you do to stop it from traveling to our enemies is another arrow in our quiver."

Alberich sighed. "It seems like not enough." But he leaned back and accepted a refill and an apple, which he peeled with a frown of concentration, getting the entire peel off in one piece. The knife made a crisp sound as it passed through the flesh.

"If you were a maid, you'd be tossing that over your shoulder, and looking for the letters of your husband's name in it," Dethor observed, as Alberich carefully set the long curl of peel aside.

Alberich regarded him somberly. "Is that so? In Karse, such are for the children fried and dipped in honey. I have told you, divination a thing of witchcraft is. No Karsite maiden would dare such a thing, for the fear of the Fires."

Once again, Talamir was struck by how very different the Karsites were. A Valdemaran wouldn't think twice about tossing an apple peel, reading the tea leaves, wishing in a fountain. And that was the essence of the problem that faced the agents sent into Karse.

"Have you eaten?" Talamir asked, instead of commenting. "More than just that apple, I mean."

Alberich shrugged; Talamir took that as a negative, and made up an impromptu meal for him from the remains of supper's meat and salad and some bread. Since Alberich took it with polite thanks, then absently ate it in less time than it had taken Talamir to make it, the King's Own was certain that he must have been famished.

"Glad enough, I am, to be rid of such filth as were locked away," Alberich continued, swallowing the last bite whole and absently licking his fingers. "Only, I wish it were more that I was doing. In the South…"

That was as good an opening as Talamir was likely to get, and he took it, explaining what he had in mind. He knew Alberich very well now; he didn't waste his breath in trying to convince the man of anything, just stated his case. He watched as Alberich's eyes took on that curiously unfocused appearance that meant he was discussing the idea with *his* Companion.

This gave Talamir plenty of time to study Alberich, and he didn't like what he saw.

Besides the bandaged forehead and forearm—*not* his sword arm, which was telling—there was a bulge beneath the sleeve covering the biceps of that same arm that suggested another bandage, perhaps of a previous wound. The scars left from the burns on his face were crisscrossed by others now. That, as Talamir recalled, was a favorite tactic of low-and-dirty street fighting—to go for the face, figuring that the pain and blood that any facial cut produced would be such a distraction that it would be easier to go in for a kill.

Not that facial scars were going to make him stand out in the neighborhoods and the company where Alberich was going at night. The opposite was true, actually; the more scars, the more he would fit in. Beneath the scars, the face was good, if carved on harsh lines—a long oblong with a stubborn chin, high cheekbones, wide brow, heavy eyebrows set in a permanent scowl, aquiline nose, and the eyes of a goshawk, fierce and wild, with the barest hint of something that was not quite sane. Or at least, it was a peculiar sort of sanity, that saw deeper into dark places and could stare into the abyss without flinching. Perhaps it was the curious quality that Alberich's eyes had of never being the same color twice in a row, varying from the gray of a threatening storm through a muddy green-brown, to (as they were tonight) something close to black.

For the rest, well, there was no doubt that even in the company of Heralds, who were a fit and athletic group, Alberich stood out. It was not that he had a perfect body—at least, not in the sculptural sense—it was something else. The practiced eye picked out the quality of muscle, the way every movement was *just* enough and no more, the absolute stillness at rest, and the immediate response when one was called for. Every movement was exact. It was difficult to describe, but easy to see when one knew what to look for. There was a fine economy in Alberich's actions, not a bit of energy wasted, and nothing held back when it was needed.

All of which, of course, came across as predatory and threatening, and probably all to the good down there in the slums.

"So," Alberich said at last. "I will think further on this."

It was a disappointing reply, but Talamir tried not to show his disappointment. There was nothing more he could add to his argument, and anything else would be nothing more than pressure that Alberich would probably respond poorly to.

"Seeking my bed, I should be," Alberich continued, rising, and looking down at them solemnly. "Dethor's Second, I still am, and there Trainees always are."

They bade him good night, and once he was out of the room, Dethor shrugged. "Well, there it is," he said philosophically. "It's up to him now."

"And hope he can find a straight path through all our tangles," Talamir added—wondering if he ought to begin praying to the Sunlord, just for a little help. And whether, if he did, the Sunlord would take it amiss and tangle things up even further.

Alberich lay in his bed, hands tucked behind his head, staring up at the ceiling. There was no fire in his room, but a dim light from the lanterns and torches lighting the gardens came through the curtains at his window and created soft shadows, contrasting with the deeper pools of darkness among the beams. He was acutely conscious of little things, all of them so alien, so very different to the things he found ordinary... The crisp herbal scent of the sheets, *not* Karsite sairel, but Valdemaran lavender. The shape of the room, long and narrow rather than square. The flavors lingering on his tongue. The cadence of conversation in the next room. All these things speaking eloquently of another place than the one he called *home*.

And his mind buzzed with activity, though his body was still. This was a pretty little quagmire that had been set at his feet…

Granted, he *had* been helping the Lord Marshal's men, but he'd done so knowing full well—and having *warned* them all, as well—that no one not born in Karse, or at least raised there from early childhood, could ever pass as Karsite. Now he was punished for that, for that had been sophistry, a way of appeasing both sides of his conscience without having to compromise either, and he had known it. Now he was caught, and there could be no evasion. Either he could aid Valdemar against Karse, or by withholding his aid, help Karse instead, knowing he was handicapping Valdemar.

Such a choice, and at the moment he could see no way of acting, or not acting, that would not cause harm. Violate his pledged word, or effectively cripple the abilities of those who had succored and adopted him to defend themselves. Betray his home, or those who had saved him.

:Talk to me, Chosen,: Kantor demanded. *:You've closed yourself off to me. Trust me as I trust you; let me hear your thoughts.:*

:You won't like them,: he replied mordantly.

:Perhaps not,: Kantor countered. *:But at least you will be talking to me about it. Perhaps we can find answers if we both look for them.:*

He took a moment to frame his thoughts. *:If I do what Talamir asks of me, I go against my oaths. And it is of no use at all to claim that the spies will work only against the Tedrels when my people are working hand-in-glove with them. Act against the Tedrels, and Karsites will bleed.:*

:Little doubt,: Kantor agreed, as he stared at the shadowy ceiling, listening to the indistinct murmur of voices in the next room. *:But how are you being true to your oaths if you withhold help that could shorten this fight? You know that your Sunpriests will not hesitate to add Karsite troops to the Tedrels in order to defeat Valdemar, and the longer the Wars go on, the more Karsites will die.:*

:I have no control over what the priests do or do not do,: he said stubbornly. *:And I do not know, not for certain, that they will order my people into this affray. What they do is in their own hands, and the will of Vkandis. I can only control my own actions, and I am the one who is responsible for what comes of them.:*

He felt Kantor ruminating over that one; well, he'd spent enough time agonizing over the problem himself, and it was the only answer he could come to. No matter what *other* people did, if he was to remain true, he could only do what *he* felt was right.

:Pah,: Kantor said in disgust. *:Why must the right answers be so unsatisfactory? But, Chosen, this might be right by your oaths, but must you remain bound by oaths to those who violated* their *responsibilities, not only to you, but to the people they lead?:*

:If I break those vows,: he replied slowly, painfully, *:I become no better than they. Who will trust me, if I break my vows? How can I trust myself?:*

Silence again, as Kantor considered this as well. This time, his reply was only a frustrated sigh.

:I have no argument for you that would not also be sophistry,: Kantor admitted, after the silence had gone on for what seemed to be a candlemark at least.

Strangely enough, that reply brought him a modicum of relief. Kantor was with him. Kantor was at least as uncomfortable with the situation as Alberich was, but the Companion was *with* him. Kantor, his best and truest friend in the world, was not going to use that friendship to try and persuade him of something against his conscience. Now all he had to do was argue with himself.

He sensed Kantor thinking furiously and waited to see what the Companion would come up with. *:I don't suppose,:* Kantor offered diffidently, *:that you could get some sort of dispensation from the Priests of Vkandis absolving you of those oaths?:*

:Geri won't *give that. He can't offer it on his own authority, and I wouldn't accept it from him even if he did.:* No matter what the Sunpriests down in Karse did, Geri knew that, short of an apparition of the Sunlord Himself, there was *no* way that he could absolve Alberich of previously made vows.

And as for asking for some sort of message from Vkandis Himself— He flinched away from the very notion.

For whatever reason, the Sunlord had elected to permit the Sunpriests to act as they were. Only He knew what was in His mind. Alberich could speculate, but—

Here was the truth of it all: who was he that Vkandis should appear to him to absolve him of his oaths? Only one man in exile, one man who could only prove his faith by remaining faithful...

:Chosen—: Kantor said suddenly, interrupting his thought. *:Let me ask you this. Suppose, just suppose, that you were not bound by those oaths. What would you do in that case, if you were completely free to do what you wished to do?:*

What would he do? *:I haven't thought about it, haven't even considered it. There was no reason to,:* he replied honestly. And then answered just as honestly, *:If I were free, I would aid all those agents without a moment of hesitation. I'd go myself, if the Council could be persuaded to trust me. In fact, I'd demand to go—:*

:Why?: Kantor interjected. *:Why would you* demand *to go?:*

That was an easy question to answer, for it was the sum of all of his turmoil. *:Because no one born and raised in Valdemar could ever be so careful of the lives of the children of Karse as I. No one but I would care enough to take the extra effort to be sure no harm came to them.:*

Alberich was no Empath, but the sudden flood of triumph that welled up from Kantor was a thing so tangible that it felt like the beams of the rising sun, reaching upward into the heavens at dawn. It so surprised him that he felt stunned, too shocked for words.

But Kantor had words enough for him.

:Then, Chosen, Alberich, Herald of Valdemar and Captain of Karse—make *more of you! Make them out of the Heralds that Talamir brings to you! Give them not only the things that Talamir wants, but the memories, good and ill, that have made you what* you *are! Do that*—and they will be as tender of Karsite lives as you, and *you could ask for no better stewards in your absence.:*

He lay blinking for a long moment as the sense of that penetrated. Then he closed his eyes and considered the advice from every possible angle.

And he could find no flaw in it. What better thing *could* he do for his people than this? How could it violate his oath to create *more* protectors of his people? Kantor was right. Kantor was *right!*

Relief flooded into him with such force that he felt dizzy with it, and he clutched the sides of the narrow bed as it seemed to move beneath him. And when the feeling of release ebbed a little, he felt his face wet with unexpected tears—

Oh, my people—oh, my beloved people—I can send you protectors to take my place at last, at long last!

He rubbed the tears away with his sleeve, swiftly controlled himself, and realized that the murmur of voices in the other room had not stilled. Dethor and Talamir, Sunlord bless them, were still deep in their plans, searching for answers—

:—trying to find a way to persuade you without pressuring you—: Kantor pointed out.

Yes. They would be. They had been as careful of his honor as he was. More, perhaps, because they did not understand the reasons behind what he did, they only honored his conviction that he needed to do them.

He got out of bed; it wouldn't be the first time he'd rejoined a discussion while in a nightshirt and sleeping trews. He made his way to the doorway of the sitting room, and stood there a moment, silent, seeing again the strain, the care, the burden of duty weighing both of them down.

At least this time he'd be able to lift some of that, not add to it.

He cleared his throat, and they looked up, startled.

"I believe, my brothers," he said, with a nod to both of them that acknowledged their kinship without unnecessary words, "I believe, help you I can. And must. So speak you with your Healers, and tell them, Alberich of Karse wishes this, most devoutly."

He waited just long enough to enjoy the look of stunned shock and amazement on both their faces. Then he turned and made his way back to his bed—there to enjoy the first untroubled night of sleep he'd had since the Tedrel Wars began.

1 0

The MindHealers, with one adventurous exception, were not happy about the plan, which was not really a surprise. Alberich did not give a toss whether they were *happy* about what he was doing. All he cared about was that they had agreed to the project.

The Heralds he had recruited for his agents were a diverse lot; four of them, which was *all* he would risk on this venture. He didn't know any of them well, which was another good reason for having chosen them. Three of them were too old for him to have trained, and the fourth had been so average that he was entirely unmemorable. One sun-weathered, dark-haired man who *was* a tinker, and thus had all the skills to pass successfully as a Karsite tinker. One, in his late middle-age years, was from a family of herdsman, and thus able to pass as another goatherd who had been displaced from his home in the hills by the war. In fact, he could probably make a fine case for having had his herds confiscated by the Tedrels, leaving him with nothing but the meager possessions he could carry on his own back. The third was a youngster, a lad who had *just* gotten his Whites—but he had three advantages. First, he was from a forester family just on the Border near Burning Pines. Second, he had been an orphan, forced to take responsibility for himself from an early age. As a consequence, he acted more like a young man in his late twenties than one just barely eighteen. And thirdly—thirdly, he was *smart.* He had a strongly developed sense for self-preservation; he thought before he said or did anything. He, of all of them, was the likeliest to be recruited by the Tedrels themselves and the most likely of anyone who had volunteered to be able to keep his head and stay plausible when within their ranks. There was something to be said for being the type that has been knocking about in the world before becoming a Herald, in this case.

The fourth was a woman as old as the old man; she would try to get taken on as a laundress or cook. Alberich didn't hold out much hope for that, but if she could, well, an old woman would hear a lot from the Tedrel camp followers. Even if the Tedrels themselves didn't speak to women, the recruits were of the type that wouldn't be able to keep their mouths shut.

None of them would have their Companions with them; all of them were confident that their Companions could stay out of sight, but within call, so if things began to look the least bit dangerous, they could get out of the camp and escape before suspicion mounted to certainty.

Alberich was quite certain of one thing, at least. When they were done with these sessions, they would *be* Karsite, or he would call a halt to the whole scheme. That was how he had sold his plan to the MindHealers; he had to wonder how much they really understood what he meant, but he had to take a chance somewhere.

No one knew how this was going to work, but the MindHealer who had agreed to mediate the experiment had some ideas of his own that he wasn't inclined to share with anyone, not even Alberich. He had only promised this much: if what he planned worked, the Heralds were not going to get Alberich's memories, *per se,* and Alberich was not going to be reliving his own memories. "I won't say anything more," he'd repeated stubbornly, no matter who asked him or how many times he was asked. "I don't want anyone going into this with any preconceptions to muddle things up. If this works, it will work very well indeed."

Though how they were supposed to enter into the situation "without any preconceptions" was beyond him.

When the time came, Alberich appeared at Healers' Collegium at the appointed hour, with three of the four Heralds he had recruited trailing in after him, one by one. It probably would have been amusing if they all hadn't looked so serious, even apprehensive; he could have been a tutor or nanny trailed by three of his four charges. They were sent to a quiet chamber that held two narrow beds and a chair between them, and stood, as Alberich thought to himself, "like a gaggle of useless idlers," none of them particularly wishing to take a seat either on the couches or the chair. The young man still hadn't arrived there when Healer Crathach, long and lean and sardonic, appeared in the room to which they had been sent.

"Ah, good. I only need one of you volunteers at a time," he said, looking entirely too gleeful for Alberich's comfort. "Hmm—you, I think, Orven. Take a couch. Alberich, you take the other. Try to relax, and close your eyes."

The former herdsman made a bit of a face, and did as he was told, taking the farther of the two couches. In silence, Alberich did the same, taking the nearest. He closed his eyes, and heard a creak as the Healer sat down in the chair, felt a hand laid atop his forehead and suppressed the urge to knock it away, and—

And suddenly, he was in Karse.

But this was not exactly a memory. He had never lived in this cob-built hut—too small to be called a cottage—though he had seen plenty like it over the years. This was a typical mountain hut of the poorest sort, yet there was a poorer state than that in Karse, and that was to be the lowest of the kitchen or stable staff, who had not even a scrap of floor to call their own. Scullery maids, cook's boys—they slept on the kitchen floor and ate what they could scrape out of pots, never washed except what parts of them got immersed in water when they scrubbed things, never changed their clothing until it dropped from their body.

He and his mother had, thank Vkandis, never been *that* lowly.

However, in this incarnation, it appeared that the protagonists of this "memory" *were*.

A little boy, who was him, and was not him, about three years old, was watching a woman who was his mother, and was not his mother, scrubbing the floor of this hut—a floor, made, as was usual in these huts, of the scrap ends of boards gathered and pieced together. She did not own this place; whereas his mother *had* owned, or had at least rented, their little dwelling. This woman was a servant here, the only one; sleeping on the hearth, doing the heaviest of the work, taken on by the mean old woman who owned the place only because, in her outcaste state, she asked nothing but food and shelter for herself and the boy that was him, and not him. He looked through that boy's eyes, yet he did it from an adult perspective.

Now, he recognized the memory from the framework. *If* this had been his real memory, he would have been watching his mother scrubbing the floor of the inn where they lived. But this wasn't his village, it was another, in herding country, where he had served in his first year with the Sunsguard. It wasn't an inn, for this particular village had been too small to have one; this was just one of the many little houses, with a bush above the door to show that it sold ale and food. He didn't recognize the woman; she was something like his mother, but mostly not. And although he somehow knew that Orven was actually experiencing this episode as if *he* were the toddler, *Alberich* was watching it as a sort of dispassionate passenger in Orven's head.

This was fascinating; living fiction. Except that Orven was living it. Had *he* come from a background that was *that* impoverished? It could be; the MindHealer could be taking both sets of experiences and melding them together in a Karsite setting.

The bones of the experience were the same as his own; a group of fellows who considered themselves to be young toughs strolled past, and decided to abuse the woman because of *his* presence, calling her "whore" and worse. True, she was not married, and now had no prospect of ever wedding. True, she had not named his father to anyone but the Sunpriest. But his mother—and, in this manufactured memory, this woman—were hardly whores. They sold themselves to no man, and had been so tight-lipped about the identity of Alberich's father that *nothing* had ever made them reveal it except to their priest.

The boy knew none of this, nor did Orven who was actually living through this instead of observing it—nor had Alberich at the time. Orven, from his childish perspective, only knew that the men were large and loud, and were making his mother unhappy. They frightened him, and he began to cry.

Now all of this came with an incredible load of detail that Alberich had not even known was *in* his memory—the scent of the harsh tallow soap the mother was using and of the wet wood of the floor, the beer smell from the cask just inside the door, the aroma of the pease porridge over the hearth, and woodsmoke, the sharp not-quite-spring scent of the air itself, the sour-sweat smell overlaid with goat and sheep of the men. And that was just scent. There was the quality of the sunlight, thin and clear, giving a great deal of light, but not much warmth. He somehow *knew* the look of the cobbles and the dirt path outside the door, the shape of the hut, with its rough cob walls, whitewashed some time last spring, the whitewash shabby from all the winter storms—the shape of the other houses of the village, of the village itself, a straggle of houses along the road. He even knew the road, cobbled only where it passed through the village itself. Alberich knew where it had all come from; he'd seen dozens of villages like this one over the years. The story came from his life, and the setting, but both were tolerably confused together, creating a new "life" entirely.

It wasn't him. Orven, taken back in his mind to the level of a toddler, was the one feeling all of this; it would be Orven's reactions that counted here.

The flood of external detail was giving Orven plenty to take in; internal, of course, was something a good deal more primal, the uncertainty and all the turmoil of a small and terrified child.

Then *he* came striding up the path, as if the crying had summoned him; tall, bearded, straight-backed, dressed in a long black robe with something bright and shining and immediately attractive to the wailing child on the breast of it. He wasted no time, verbally laying into the men in a voice like thunder, somehow making it clear that it was their good fortune he wasn't going to lay into them physically as well. There was a great deal of what Alberich—from his dispassionate distance— recognized as Holy Writ being quoted, mostly about the poor, the fatherless, and the repentant. There was also a great deal of Writ quoted about the ultimate destination of those who abused the poor, the fatherless, and the repentant.

And a curious thing happened. The more the man spoke, the larger he seemed to become, and the smaller the woman's harassers became. As they shrank into themselves, unable to look either at the woman or the Sunpriest—that was clearly what he was, although it was Alberich, and not Orven, who knew this—the woman took on more confidence. Since none of the thunder was being directed at him or his mother, the child calmed and crept near to her, and she hugged him close.

"Now, go!" the man finished at last, in tones dripping with disgust. "And if you don't wish another taste of my tongue, find yourselves something godly to do for a change!"

They slunk off, exactly like whipped curs. Now the man came to stand over the boy and his mother. "How long has this been going on, woman?" he asked curtly, but not unkindly.

She shrugged. "Since he was born, Holy Father," she replied, in a resigned voice.

Now the Priest looked down at the boy. "Then it is time I took a hand," he pronounced, in a way that said quite clearly that it would be useless to protest. "I will have the boy with me for two marks in the morning, every morning. It is time he learned the ways of the Sunlord, blessed be His Name, and when the village sees that *my* eye is on you, there will be no more of scenes like this."

Then he turned and stalked away again, and the memory—or, more accurately, manufactured memory—was over.

Alberich "woke," suddenly released from the experience, and opened his eyes. *He* was as calm as he had been when he took his place on the couch, but from the tear streaks on Orven's face, it was clear that he had experienced, and quite directly, everything appropriate to that young child in that situation.

The Healer was grinning with great satisfaction, so Alberich had to suppose that what he had planned had worked. But he put one finger to his lips, and motioned to Alberich that he should leave the room for the moment.

Alberich felt a little unsteady, but did as he was "told." The other three were waiting outside, sitting on a long bench, and looked up at him expectantly when he emerged.

"The Healer, pleased is," he said laconically, and left it at that. It was not very much later that Orven left, looking quite composed for a man who'd been dissolved in tears only a short time ago, and the Healer called in Alberich and the young man, Herald Wethes.

The next three sessions were similar, with Alberich serving more as observer than participant, but each setting being appropriate to the persona being created for the people involved, and rich with vivid detail. Wethes had another mountain village, but *his* mother was from a forester clan, for instance, and for the old woman, the village was down in the plain.

Even the identity of the Sunpriest changed, and Alberich had the notion that here, too, the image was coming from the other Heralds, each of them contributing the face and figure of some authority in *their* childhood, trusted and wise.

He was thoroughly exhausted before the sessions were over, but to his surprise, very little actual time had been spent in the enterprise, no more than a mark or two. But if he was tired, the others were completely drained by what was, for them, a highly emotionally charged experience.

And it was just beginning; he wondered if they were already starting to regret volunteering for this.

But although it was as physically wearing as a good, long practice session, this first set was not as emotionally difficult as Alberich had feared. Well, truth be told, although he had known that the only way to make these fellow Heralds into what he wanted to be was to give them bits of his own life, that was entirely what he had feared as well. He hadn't wanted to expose himself and his life to others so nakedly.

But it appeared that, somehow, he wasn't going to. The others had no idea how much of what they were going through was really part of his life, and the emotions they were feeling were theirs, not his.

Perhaps that was what had bothered him the most of all about this whole project; he had not wanted his feelings to be so exposed. If this was the Healer's doing, then he owed the man thanks. More than thanks.

He lingered while the last of his four volunteers collected herself and tottered off, looking dazed. Healer Crathach gave him a knowing look when he didn't leave, and leaned back in his chair, arms crossed.

"I'll save you trying to wade backward through our language, and tell you straight up the answer to what you're going to ask me," the MindHealer said with a grin that had just a touch of smugness about it. "Yes, I planned this whole business of only *using* what you know to build seminal Karsite experiences for our four victims, rather than taking your memories entire. It's all been very deliberate. I've got a lot of reasons for doing it that way, as much for their sake as yours. You wanted them made Karsite, not made into duplicate versions of you. And I didn't want them subsumed into your rather formidable personality, Herald Alberich. But most of all, I did not want *you* to have to expose yourself in a way that would have been difficult for you to come to terms with."

Alberich let out the breath he'd been holding in. "You knew—" he said, with just a touch of hesitation.

"That you didn't *want* everybody and his Companion knowing every sordid detail about your past?" Crathach looked sardonic as well as smug, an odd combination. "I'd be a pretty poor MindHealer if I hadn't been able to pick *that* up, now, wouldn't I?"

Alberich just shrugged; it was only the truth.

"At any rate, things will diverge more from here, in the little life stories we're concocting," the MindHealer continued, and scratched his head with a slight frown. "How to put this? The powerful *incident* that formed you into what you are now will remain the same, and all of your background, but the way our agents will react to it and the details of the incident will be driven by their own personalities. Am I making sense to you?"

"I—" Alberich hesitated.

"Well, never mind, you'll see it as we go along. The point is, the more we do, the *less* it will be anything like your own experience." The MindHealer shrugged, stretched, and got to his feet, then he paused, giving Alberich a long, measuring gaze. "Go, *do* something," he said. "Something purely physical. There's such a thing as thinking too much, especially for you."

Since thinking was all that Alberich had been doing for the past several marks, the advice seemed good to him, and he nodded. "My thanks," he replied, and went off to follow his Healer's orders.

* * *

Sendar coughed unexpectedly. Selenay pressed down too hard on the goose quill, and it leaked, leaving a trail of ink spatters on the parchment. She cursed and tried to blot the damage but only made it worse. She dropped the quill and made a grab for the edge of the parchment in irritation.

Her secretary snatched it away before she could crumple or tear it to pieces, as she had two others. "Let Crance take care of it," her father said, without looking up from his own work. "He has your notes, he has what you've written so far, and he should have been doing this in the first place. You don't need to be here, and you're getting hunched shoulders from sitting at a desk. Go do something purely physical."

When she didn't respond, he looked up at her. "*You* do not need to write every word of your judgments yourself. Crance doesn't have enough work from you as it is. For Haven's sake, you don't need to replace the entire Circle, clerks and all! You've already freed up two Heralds from the city courts so that they can go South, and that is *enough*, Selenay."

He sounded exasperated, and he probably was. She was trying so hard—and in her head she knew he was right, but in her heart, she kept feeling that she should be trying harder still.

She rubbed one of her tired eyes, and let poor Crance take the offending paper away to his own desk. "It doesn't seem like enough," she said; she felt forlorn, but she was afraid she sounded sullen. "I feel like anyone who isn't feebleminded or sick, or afflicted somehow, ought to be *there*, not here."

Her secretary, a young man who was nearly as shortsighted as Herald Myste and afflicted with wheezes when he ventured near anything in bloom, looked at her mournfully. She immediately felt even more guilty for making *him* feel guilty for not being in the fighting.

"My dear—" Her father sighed. "Selenay, you sit in Council with me, you're serving in the city courts, and half the time you don't let Crance do his job. You are doing more than you need to, and probably far more than you should. Get out of here into the sunlight before you forget what it looks like and you turn into a troglodyte."

She stared at him, blinking. He rose, took her hand, pulled her out of her chair, and shoved her forcibly out the door of the Royal Suite as the two guards at the door tried not to stare.

The door closed behind her, and to her astonishment she heard him slide the lock home. "And don't come back until your nose is sunburned!"

she heard Sendar say, his voice muffled by the closed door.

For a single moment, she thought about pounding on the closed door, demanding to be let in…

The right-hand guard made a choking noise, and Selenay swiveled just in time to catch him screwing up his face in an attempt to keep from laughing aloud. She knew him very, very well, indeed; he'd played Companion to her Herald too many times to be counted when she was little. In that, he had been more fortunate than most patient fellows who allowed toddlers to bounce on their backs; Companions were expected to have minds of their own, and didn't wear bitted bridles. And they didn't suffer being drummed upon by little heels when they didn't move fast enough. He'd bounced her off a time or two when she exceeded the bounds of the allowable.

She made a face, but didn't comment, because there was great relief in being *ordered* to do what she wanted, but had been too guilty to pursue.

"Beggin' your pardon, your Highness," the Guard said, composing himself. "But I believe that sounded like an order. I'd obey the King, if I was you."

He stared straight ahead, but his eyes were twinkling.

She gave a theatrical sigh. "Orders are orders," she agreed, and with a wink, turned and headed for the nearest exit.

:Caryo, I'm on my way!: she Mindcalled, feeling just a bit giddy, as if she'd been released from classes for an unexpected half-holiday. *:I'll need—:*

:Done. Your Alberich's been ordered off to gallop out his megrims by the MindHealers,: Caryo replied cheerfully. *:Perhaps your father knew that already when he ordered you out. It wouldn't surprise me. You can both do with an outing.:*

It could well be; there wasn't much that Sendar didn't know. It saved her hunting up her bodyguard and trying to determine whether he could be pried away from duties of his own, of which he seemed to have rather too many. If she'd been ordered away, she wanted to leave Haven altogether. She hadn't been outside the walls in—well, ages. Certainly not since the Wars began. They wouldn't go *far*, not far enough that anyone could rebuke him for leaving the city. Not that he had a choice if he was guarding her, and she would point that out if anyone dared to say anything.

By the time she reached the stables, Alberich was waiting, with both Companions saddled and bridled. As usual, it was impossible to read him, and she had long ago given up trying.

"A destination, you have?" he asked, though it was more statement than question.

"Outside Haven. The Home Farms," she replied. The so-called "Home Farms" actually belonged to the three Collegia, and supplied the needs of hearth and table. There was a separate farm, the Royal Farm, that took care of the Palace; it wasn't much larger, but it had twice the staff, for the Palace tables required something more sophisticated than the vast quantities of plainer fare devoured by the Trainees. Selenay was in the mood for *simple*, and besides, the Home Farms had the river flowing along beside them, and she had a notion to go fishing. After all, Sendar had told her not to come back until her nose was sunburned, and there was no better way of doing that than "drowning a worm," as the old gardener who'd taught her used to say.

Alberich just nodded; evidently both Caryo and Kantor were more than ready for an excursion, because off they set at the trot. They took a shortcut across the velvety lawn, briskly heading for the Palace, curving around the New Palace and getting onto the paved drive in front of the Old Palace. This was the side of the Palace that the working Heralds rarely saw, and the Trainees, almost never. The facade of the building was interesting, showing as it did the old "fortress" face of the building, with its doors meant to hold against a battering ram. But it had been softened by a planting of formal cypress trees in enormous tubs, and was fronted by a paved courtyard centered by an octagonal pool and a geometric granite fountain, and Selenay had *no* idea what the material paving the courtyard and drive were. The paving dated from just after King Valdemar's time, when the need for defense had begun to take a secondary place to other Palace functions. It wasn't cobbles or bricks, for there wasn't a sign of seams or joins. It was a solid pale gray, very nearly identical to the color the Trainees wore, from edge to edge, and the feel of it was slightly springy. The entire pavement was surrounded by a wrought-iron fence, tall and formidable, like a row of linked pikes twice the height of a man, with the wide drive of the same substance as the courtyard leading up to it and through a pair of gates that were usually left ajar. Nevertheless, there were Guards stationed here, on either side of it, with little boxes to keep the weather off them when it was truly awful.

Alberich led her past them, his back absolutely straight, his seat so easy that there was no doubt in anyone who knew cavalry that it was in the cavalry where he'd learned to ride. For their part, the Guards did not seem to pay any attention to them, staring straight ahead. She knew better, though. They weren't there as ornaments.

The drive went toward the tall proper walls that surrounded the entire complex, velvety grass on either side of it, but no plantings other than a row of cypresses right up against the wall itself, the same sort of cypresses that were inside the fence. And there were yet more of them, planted in boxes arranged with mathematical precision on either side of the drive. The cypresses softened the look of the stone wall, and probably helped give the guards up there a little protection from the wind in winter, and shade in summer.

There were more Guards on the wall and on either side of the passage that led through it, both inside and out. This was still defensive; there were portcullises on both ends, and a rather nasty murder-hole in the middle, through which all sorts of unpleasant liquids could be poured down upon a would-be invader. Not so incidentally, the murder-hole had made a good place for a young Princess to drop petals and peas down on unsuspecting visitors, with extra points awarded for the pea that landed squarely in the middle of a fashionable hat without the wearer noticing.

There was no one up there to drop peas upon them now, and they trotted through the cool shadow and out into the sunlight and down into the city.

Nearest to the Palace, predictably enough, were the enormous mansions of the highborn, each a smaller palace in itself. The farther one got from the Palace, the less expensive (and more crowded) the buildings, until by the time they passed out of the final set of gates and walls—for the city had outgrown its walls several times, and a new set had been built around the new construction that had spilled over on the other side—the final set on *this* road were a mix of shops with apartments above, stables for hire-horses, and inns and taverns. The road was not, however, a straight line to the final city gate; there were no straight lines to the complex within Haven. Everything had been laid out like a maze, so that if the city ever did come under attack, the defense could be fought street-by-street.

Before the Wars, that very notion had seemed laughable. Not anymore. Though it would probably take having the Tedrels appear at the gates before the citizens of Haven believed that.

Out yet another set of gates with yet another set of Guards they went, following the river which ran under the walls at this point. Here, the transition went abruptly from the urban to the rural, for this was where all market gardens that supplied the city with fresh eggs and vegetables were located. While the urban had edged out past the final walls outside other gates, here it had not, for the profit to be derived from such well-watered and fertile property was not to be trifled with. And here, in the midst of market gardens, suddenly loomed a true *farm*, the Home Farms, so named in the plural because they *had* been several smaller farms at one time. All of the buildings from each of these separate farms had been thriftily disassembled and reassembled in a central location; all of the cottages joined into one big building where the farm workers lived, all of the barns ranged around a single yard and each allocated to *one* form of livestock. Even the henhouses had been moved, and were lined up in a neat little row, free-ranging chickens efficiently pecking up every bit of stray grain in nearly every weather, and cleaning up insects in summer.

Here the river curved away from the main road, and the lane leading to the Home Farm's buildings ran alongside it. Behind the Home Farms, also watered directly by the river and situated on this lane, was the Royal Farm—but that wasn't Selenay's destination. The Royal Farm was a show-place of its kind, the chickens segregated by meat-birds and layers, kept separate to keep their breeds pure. Everything on the Royal Farm was a purebred, from the chickens to the plowhorses; every building was spotless and immaculate. The hothouses were there, for forcing flowers, fruit, and vegetables out of season. Pens of gamebirds were there and exotic food plants too difficult to grow in quantity. Ponds of delicately-nurtured fish for the Royal table, even.

Too formal for Selenay today.

The lane was clear, with not so much as a turtle on it, and both Companions broke into a canter that took them all the way to the farmhouse. Selenay found herself grinning as they pulled up with a flourish in the yard in front of the building, and even Alberich looked a little less mordant. The farm manager, an ancient fellow indeed, hobbled out to determine what they wanted, and when Selenay explained her wish to fish for the benefit of the Collegium tables, was happy to direct them to a shed where the fishing tackle lay.

"Eels," Selenay muttered to herself, selecting the appropriate tackle, knowing very well that the Collegium cooks made a fine eel pie. She looked askance at Alberich, who was examining the poles dubiously.

"You *do* know how to fish, don't you?" she asked.

He turned solemn eyes on her. "No."

:*Doesn't mince words, does he?*: Caryo chuckled.

"Then it's time you learned," Selenay told him ruthlessly, and with a touch of glee. "It's a standard skill all Heralds are supposed to know. You might have to find your own food in the wilderness, after all."

"And I, in wilderness will be allowed? Not likely, that." He sighed with resignation. Or disgust. Or both, perhaps. She didn't care. He might as well learn to fish; it wouldn't do him harm, and it might do him good.

She spent the next candlemark or so in a position every Trainee ever schooled by the Weaponsmaster's Second would probably have given his last hope of the Havens for. Schooling the infamous Alberich, playing stern and implacable tutor to the Great Stone Heart himself! And it was highly entertaining as well.

She presented Alberich with his pole, and had to show him how to bait the hook—and the formidable Alberich proved to be very reluctant to touch the bait!

"Now don't be so squeamish," she ordered, pulling a worm out of the earth of the bait pail and handing it to him. "I've shown you what to do, it's not that difficult."

He took the worm in his thumb and forefinger, and held it stiffly in front of him. "Must I?" he asked in a strangled voice.

She suppressed her mirth, and instead fixed him with the same sort of gimlet-eyed stare *he* gave reluctant Trainees. She didn't even need to say anything.

He barely skinned the worm onto the hook, and she *knew* it wouldn't stay. Sure enough, the third time he pulled the hook up out of the water to check on it, the worm was gone.

He glanced aside at her; *she* was pulling in eels at an astonishing rate and already had a bucketful. She just gave him that look again, and nodded toward the bait bucket, without saying a word.

With a long-suffering expression on his face, he probed the loam with a reluctant finger for another worm.

By the end of the afternoon, she was highly satisfied with her half of the expedition. She had a fine mess of eels, *far* more than a mere bucketful, certainly sufficient to provide Heraldic Collegium with an eel-pie supper. She had a properly sunburned nose (but not so much that it was going to hurt later) and Alberich was—

Well, it was comic. The incredibly competent Alberich *did* have something that he couldn't do. He had caught exactly two fish, both of them little sun-perch, and neither big enough to keep. He had lost most of a pail of worms, and it was a good thing that he *hadn't* hooked anything large, or Selenay suspected he'd have lost the rod as well. He, who couldn't miss a target, couldn't cast a line to save his life. He, who was so dexterous with any weapon of any sort, tangled his line with appalling frequency.

Mind, he *had* managed to relax, if only by cursing under his breath at his pole, his line, the wretched fish that stole his bait. Practicing with his students out of doors as much as he did, *he* hadn't had a clerical pallor, but there weren't quite as many frown furrows cutting across his scars.

She put up her gear with a sigh of regret; he put his up with a sigh of relief. The old man came to take charge of the tub of eels, which was as well, since she couldn't exactly take them back to the Collegium in her saddlebag. Together they rode—at a walk, this time—back down the lane to the road.

"How did you manage never to learn how to fish?" she asked him, after they rejoined the traffic on the road heading into Haven.

"I should learn, where?" he asked. "When very young, helping in the inn, I was. Then it was in the Academy, and fishing, a sport for gentleman is, or a subsistence for the poor. No part has it in training for a cavalry officer."

He must have been *very* young when he first began to work, then...

:And very poor,: Caryo told her, knowing that she needn't say more. Although fishing was traditionally a way for the poor to add another source of all-season food to the larder, the poor *also* had to have the time to fish. Which, clearly, Alberich had not. The very poor also might not have enough to spare for hook, line, and bait.

"Besides," he added meditatively, "where lived I and served I, no great rivers there are. Swift streams only. Trout, have I heard of, which great skill takes. Wealthy man's sport."

"Well, you've got the knack now," she replied cheerfully, and was rewarded with his sour look.

"Then best it is that to Haven I am confined," he said. "And should fish be required of me, purchased at market they can be. Else, it would be starvation."

She couldn't help it; she tried to hold back her snickers, but they escaped. He looked pained.

"Oh, really, Alberich, it's so nice to find *something* you can't do!" she exclaimed.

"Glad I am, that such amusement given you I have," he told her crossly. "Perhaps a new title, I should have? Herald-Jester?"

She couldn't help it; he looked so irritated now that the giggles just burst out all over again. And finally, one corner of his mouth began to twitch, then both corners, then, although he didn't actually *laugh*, he unbent enough to admit that the joke, although on him, actually was rather funny.

And it wasn't until he had delivered her back to her father, sunburned nose and all, that she realized that she hadn't thought about the Wars once all afternoon. But what was truly satisfying, she also understood in a flash that in wrestling with worms and hooks and poles that would not do what he wanted them to, neither had Alberich. And that Sendar had sent her off to "do something" at the same time that someone in authority over Alberich had evidently decided that *he* needed some distraction.

So perhaps her father was even cleverer than she'd thought. *No, there's no perhaps about it,* she decided, making her way back toward the Royal Suite. *He's much cleverer than I'd thought.*

However, of all the thoughts that had occurred to her today, that was, perhaps, the very *least* surprising.

11

Outside the tavern, a storm raged, effectively ensuring that no one would be leaving or coming in any time soon. Water poured off the eaves of the tavern in sheets, like a waterfall, as the gutters overflowed. The rain spouts added to the mess, spouting like geysers, sending a torrent of water over the cobbles. It was *cold* out there, the temperature had plummeted, and the rain felt like icewater.

Inside the tavern, those who were stuck here nursed the last dregs of their drinks and contemplated another. Or perhaps, a nice pigeon pie or a good slice of mutton... The innkeeper, anticipating the needs of his customers, had started a kettle of mulled cider, even though it wasn't the season for any such thing, and the spicy scent began to drift through the inn, turning heads and sharpening appetites. It was unexpectedly cozy in here, with a small fire going, just enough to take the chill off the air. And the ambiance was a million leagues away from the atmosphere in the last tavern Alberich had been in.

Alberich had come out of the secret room at the back of the stables here at the Companion's Bell, only to find that the storm which had been threatening all day had finally broken. Since he was effectively trapped here *and* starving, he decided to make a virtue of necessity and avail himself of the little private room reserved for Heralds and their guests.

Of course he was starving; he'd left before suppertime, and you just didn't eat what was offered in, say, the Broken Arms. Not unless you wanted to have an intimate and detailed knowledge of the inside of the privy, sooner or later, when your stomach objected to what you'd put there. Granted, the indoor water closets at the Collegium were fine things, but not as a place for an extended stay.

He'd already had his fill of watching people tonight; on the whole, he'd rather just sit back on a comfortable settle alone, and watch the storm. Here, once he was *out* of that secret room where he changed his identity from that of a Herald to any one of half a dozen personae he wore in this city and back again to a Herald, he felt almost as secure as at the Collegium itself.

It wasn't only the wretched neighborhoods he prowled, as a cheap thug-for-hire, as a ne'er-do-well of dubious reputation, as a sell-sword. No, he had some respectable personae as well; he was a small merchant in imported knives, he was a votary of some obscure god whose cult was so tiny that no one had ever heard of it (for good reason, since it didn't exist), he was an honest caravan guard…

But most of his time was, admittedly, spent in places most Heralds never saw but the city constables and Guard were all too familiar with. And most of it was spent accomplishing very little but waiting for one or another of his patiently-laid traps to catch something. Far too much of it was spent in places that could be called "taverns" only because they sold alcoholic drinks. And he thought he'd been served some wretched brews as a Karsite officer! At least those had been *drinkable;* rough, strong enough to lift the hair on your arms, but drinkable.

Tonight had been one of those nights when nothing whatsoever happened, or was going to happen, except, perhaps, a common brawl or two. The threatening storm had made people think twice about leaving whatever cramped little corner they called "home"—people with only a single set of clothing had to shiver in it until it dried on their backs if they got soaked through. The taverns had been half empty, and none of his informants had poked their noses out of their holes. When the sky above the rooftops to the west began flickering with far-off lightning, he had given up. He'd hoped to get back to the Collegium before the rain began, but luck wasn't with him, it seemed.

Then, again, perhaps it was.

Heralds were common enough visitors here in the Bell that no one remarked on their presence. When Alberich arrived here, he didn't wear his trademark gray leathers anymore, he wore Whites, which made him blend in with the other Heralds who frequented the place. Sometimes a Herald just wanted to get away from the Collegium, have a tankard or a glass of wine, flirt harmlessly with a serving girl. And why not? Heralds, as Talamir took pains to remind him, were only human.

Sometimes a number of friends wanted to get together when they all came in at once; there really wasn't a big enough room in the Palace where five or more could put their feet up and talk as long and as loudly as they wanted. You could get food anytime you wanted it, but it tended to be the sort of thing that could be fed to a great many people at once—and a bespoke meal, of *exactly* what one had a craving for, was something even Heralds sometimes fancied.

The innkeeper took him to the Heralds' parlor and showed him to a seat by a window, from which he could see, in the frequent flashes of lightning, rain pouring down as if it would never stop. A moment later, a serving girl brought him hot pigeon pie of his own, and a tankard of the innkeeper's own bitter ale. It wasn't Karsite, but it was close, and unlike the harsh brews of the mountains, it was *good.*

The high back of the settle screened him from most of the room, which, in any event, was empty and likely to remain so if the weather continued to be this bad. There was no closing door to this room, and a low hum, like a hive of drowsy bees, came from the common room, in between peals of thunder. The contrast between inside and outside was so striking; storms like this commonly occurred in the mountains of Karse, but this was the first time he'd ever spent one sitting in a comfortable, warm seat with a hot dinner in front of him and the spicy scent of mulled cider in the air.

He could remember dozens of these storms when he was a tiny child, when he'd huddled beside the smoking, struggling fire on the hearth in the middle of the room, while the roof leaked in a dozen places and more rain dripped down through the smoke hole in the middle of the roof. The shutters would rattle with the force of the wind, and his mother would hold him close as she carefully fed the fire with the driest bits of wood to keep it alive. He didn't remember the ones when he was in the temple, though; that sturdy wooden structure never left him with the fear that at any moment the roof would blow away. But the ones when he was older, helping out at the inn—yes. He'd be in the stable, helping to calm the horses, struggling to get doors closed, running all over with buckets to catch leaks. Or he'd be out *in* it, tying things down, bringing them in, and never mind the lightning striking near—too near!—and the cold rain soaking him through. The Academy was down in the valley, in a place that didn't get storms like *that,* but once he was out with the cavalry—oh, he lived through plenty more of them. Most of the time, out in the open. You *hoped* for a chance to get your tents up first, and you'd wrap every blanket you had around your shoulders and watch the rain stream down off the edges of the canvas and know it would be a cold supper again. Being caught without shelter, though, was worse. The best you could do was get down in a valley, try and find the scrubbiest, lowest stand of trees, and get under them. You'd get off your horse, because with the lighting and thunder, even a trained cavalry horse could bolt. You'd use the canvas of your tent as a raincape, and hope it kept the worst of it off you, standing with your head down, one hand holding your horse's bridle up near his nose, the other holding the canvas just under your chin, shivering, both you and the horse.

Oh, this was better, much better, like so much of his life since he'd come to Valdemar. And yet, it was not enough, and he was not certain if the problem was within himself or Valdemar.

He was glad enough that there was no one here. It allowed him to be left alone with his thoughts. He was rarely truly alone for very long.

"I understand you've lost your first fight," said someone at his elbow.

The voice was female—familiar, but he couldn't put a name to it immediately, for the words startled him so much.

"Eh?" was all he could manage, as he swiveled to see who it was that had interrupted his solitude.

"With a fish," Herald—no longer Trainee—Myste amended, her glass lenses glittering with reflected lightning. She sat down across from him without waiting to be invited. "A rather small fish," she added in Karsite, with a chuckle.

The serving-girl, laden with Myste's dinner, set her dishes down opposite Alberich's, then she whisked back through the door to the common room, leaving them together.

"Ah." He found trying to see past those lenses rather disconcerting. "You have been speaking with Selenay."

He found it a relief to speak Karsite; Valdemaran was still a trial to him, and he had the sinking feeling that it was going to take years, even tens of years, before he was comfortable in it. He managed with his low-class personae mainly by being taciturn, knowing that the people around him wouldn't recognize a Karsite accent anyway.

"It's more-or-less my job," she replied. "It's thanks to you I've got the job, I'm told—training with Elcarth, and Interning in the city courts with Selenay as the senior judge. I'm Elcarth's Second, and Elcarth believes I should be ready to step into the Herald-Chronicler position within a year or two."

"Good," he said, and meant it. "And what has my ignorance of fishing got to do with the Chronicles?"

"Not a thing," she admitted. "It just came up in our discussions. I just let people rattle on, you know; it's the most effective way to learn things." She paused, and tilted her head to the side. "I don't suppose *you* would be willing to rattle on at me?"

He opened his mouth to say no, then closed it again. It was an interesting thought. "And this would go into the restricted Chronicles?" he asked instead.

"Possibly. Some things should be common knowledge, and by the time anyone *reads* my Chronicles, all of those covert identities you've got now are going to be outdated."

So *she* knew about what he was doing! Well, he shouldn't have been surprised if she was Elcarth's Second; she'd be reading the restricted Chronicles that *he* was writing. He wondered, knowing that *she* must know about the secret room here, if she'd come down on purpose to waylay him.

She ate two or three bites, reminding him that his own dinner was getting cold. He started in on it; delicious, as always from the Bell's kitchens. Pigeon pie was a delicacy in Karse; the only pigeons there were the larger wood pigeons and calling doves, hard to catch and reserved for those with falcons to take them. Here in the city, though, there were pigeon lofts everywhere, and the common rock doves bred like rabbits. It was rabbit pie that was the ordinary man's fare in Karse, in fact. Rabbit pie, rabbit stew, rabbit half-raw and half-burned on a stick over the fire…

"I grew up on this—" Myste said, gesturing with her fork to her plate. "We had a loft in the back yard. I find I miss the taste at the Collegium."

"Hmm. It *is* good," he agreed. "Not common fare where I come from."

"Well, here—in the city especially—you make up your pies with whatever you have to eat for supper in the morning, and drop them off at your neighborhood bake shop as you go off to work and pick them up when you return, along with your bread. Most people with small apartments or single rooms don't have a bake oven; in fact, especially in the city, most people only have the hearth fire to stew over and not a proper kitchen at all." Myste didn't seem to want a response; she went back to her dinner, and he followed her example.

"It is much the same in Karse," he offered, "save that there is no bake shop, or rather, the baking place is often the inn. And we steam food as often as stew it." He well remembered the smell of the baking rabbit pies in the kitchen of the inn where his mother worked. They'd come out, and woe betide anyone who touched them, each with a particular mark for the family that had left them, and a star cut into the crust of the inn pies. He'd never gotten a quarter pie like this, hot from the oven.

He and his mother had been on the bottom of the hierarchy of servants, and were treated accordingly. First were the customers, of course, then the innkeeper, his wife, and children. Then came the cook and the chief stableman, who got whatever intact portions the innkeeper's family left. Then the cook's helpers, the serving girls, the potboys who served the drink. Then the grooms in the stables and the chambermaids. *Then*, at last, Alberich, his mother, and the wretched little scullery maid and turnspit boy. Which meant that what *he* got was broken crust, gravy, bits of vegetable. Or anything that was burned, overbaked, or somehow ill-made—too much salt, he recalled *that* pie only too well. But they got *enough* to eat, that was the point; once his mother got that job at the inn, scrubbing the floors, they never went hungry. There was always day-old bread and dripping, the fat and juices that came off the roasts and were collected in a drippings pan underneath. There was always oat porridge, plain though that might be, and pease porridge, the latter being such a staple of the common fare and so often called for that there was always a pot of it in the corner of the hearth. Pease porridge was the cheapest foodstuff available at his inn, and they sold a lot of it; when the pot was about half empty, the cook would start a new lot, so that when the first pot was gone the second was ready to serve. All of the inn's servants could help themselves to a bowl of it at any time, even the scullery maid and the boy that sat in the chimney corner and turned the spit in all weathers. The innkeeper was thrifty, but generous with the food, not like some Alberich encountered over the years, who starved their help as well as working them to exhaustion.

"Ah." Myste stacked her emptied plates to the side with a sigh of satisfaction; Alberich pushed his beside them. "I don't mean you to begin nattering at me at this moment, Alberich. I just meant that when you feel like it, I'd be glad of your addition to the Chronicles. And I don't mind being a listener if all you want to do is talk. Think out loud, maybe. Or just talk to hear Karsite."

He smiled slightly. "Knowing your unending curiosity, I thank you for your patience."

"My curiosity has as much as it needs on a regular basis right now," Myste replied. "You know, before Elcarth took me on, I was never satisfied. I wanted to know, not so much what was going on, but *why*. That was the thing that drove me mad, sometimes. *Why* had this or that law been made, *why* were your people such persistent enemies, *why*—Well, there are always more questions than answers. Now I'm able to find out my *whys,* more often than not, and more to the point, I'm entitled and encouraged to do so." She smiled, and her lenses glittered. "Maybe that's why I was Chosen; I can't think of any other reason."

He laughed. "Is that why you were always such a thorn in my side, as a Trainee? That you could not be told to do a thing without wanting the reason for it?"

She shrugged. "I don't take orders well unless I know why the order is being given. And I'll be the first to admit to you that I'm very lucky and have been unusually favored in that way. Most people can't afford to indulge that particular luxury; they either follow their orders without question, or—well, there are unpleasant consequences for wanting answers." She rubbed her thumb absently against the little "clerk's callus" on the side of the second finger of her right hand, a callus created by hours of pressure from a pen.

He nodded, wondering suspiciously if she was hinting at *his* past.

"The more I'm in the courts, the more I realize that," she continued. "As a clerk, well, I *knew* why I was doing what I was doing. It was obvious. Pointless, perhaps, but obvious." She glanced up at him, sideways. "You know, you have to be a clerk, I think, before you realize just what a pother people make over nothing. And the sheer amount of ill-will that people seem to think *must* go down on paper, or die. Dear gods!"

"What, letters?" he asked.

"No. People mostly write their own vitriol in letters. We're a literate people, Alberich; that's mandated by the Crown. Just as Karsite children are required to go to the temple for religious instruction, ours are required to get instruction in reading, writing, and figuring. No, I meant legal documents, that's mostly what a clerk handles. At least, my sort of clerk. There are others who do things about money, but I've never had that kind of head for figures. I saw a lot of wills." She sighed. "A *lot* of wills. And depositions. And the documents involved in lawsuits. Well, since you've been acting as bodyguard to young Selenay, *you've* seen what happens when something gets as far as the courts!"

He nodded again. "But it is important to them."

"Some people have too much leisure, if that's what's important to them," she said sourly. "Wrangling over dead granny's best bedcover, as if the fate of the Kingdom depended on it, when all the while down there in the South—"

She couldn't finish; she just sat there, shaking her head.

He thought back about all of the things he had observed while

Selenay sat, either in judgment as the principal judge or as an assistant when she was still a Trainee. "I do not understand it either," he said, then added, with a touch of humor, "but then, I never had so many possessions that *things* took on a great importance to me."

She burst out laughing at that. "Whereas I have too many, thieving magpie that I am! So I suppose I *should* understand them! Then again, most of my possessions are books, so I still don't understand why people would get into such a state over a few pence or a set of silver." She looked ever-so-slightly superior.

"And if it was dead granny's library that was in dispute?" he asked shrewdly, to puncture that superiority.

She saw it—and bravely took the blow. "There you have me. Dead in the black." She laughed. "Oh, look. The rain's starting to slacken up!"

He glanced out the window. She was right; the downpour had turned into something lighter, and the lightning had moved off into the far distance. "It could be just a lull," he warned, as she made as if to get up.

"Could be, but I'll take my chances. I need to get back up the hill; I'm tutoring a couple of Trainees." She did get up then, and he found himself wishing she would stay.

He stifled an impulse to catch hold of her hand to prevent her leaving, but she seemed to sense *something*, and turned back toward him.

"I meant that, about nattering at me, Alberich," she said. "You know, I don't put personal things in the Chronicles. Not unless they're reasons for something happening, and it would have to be a pretty important something. And Alberich?"

"Yes?" Something had passed—was passing—between them. Something he didn't recognize and didn't understand. She stared at him; he sensed her eyes behind those lenses, oddly intent.

"You might try talking to Geri as well. After all, that's what he's there for, isn't it?" She had an oddly wry smile on her face. "Well, all things considered, that's part of his job, I'd think—to be talked at."

And with that remarkable statement, she was gone.

He sat there for some time, in the half-dark, wondering why this conversation seemed to have—well—a feeling of *importance* about it.

:Perhaps because it's another Herald?: Kantor asked.

He hadn't ever gotten such an odd feeling from anyone else, not even Talamir. *:No, it's not just that. She's not an Empath, is she?:*

:Not so far as I know,: his Companion replied thoughtfully. *:But she does have one rather odd little Gift. She doesn't have to cast the Truth Spell to know if*

someone is telling the truth, so long as she's in close proximity to them. It's why she's in the city courts, in fact.:

Interesting. Perhaps that was why she seemed to be able to get the people to *tell* her so much. Perhaps that was why she was so focused on needing to know the why of things. If you always knew that something was true or false, maybe your focus shifted from finding out the truth, to finding out the reasons behind it.

If you knew that something was true, maybe that impelled you to talk to others, as well as listen to them.

:Am I needed up the hill?: he asked. Kantor would know; the Companions always seemed to be more-or-less in contact with one another.

Kantor's reply was immediate. *:No. And I've no objection to staying here in this nice, dry stable if you have something you need to do. Shall I tell them you're going to be down here a while?:*

:Please do.: Myste might not be the right person to talk to about some of the things that were troubling him, but she was right about one thing. Gerichen *was*, and if he couldn't take counsel with one of Vkandis' own, who could he speak with? *:Tell them——:*

He hesitated. *:If anyone wants to know, tell them I'm going to visit a friend.:*

The Temple of the Lord of Light in Haven was a small one, situated between a saddlery and a chandler. Alberich thought the chandler a particularly appropriate neighbor, all things considered. Candles—next to the Temple of the Light? He wondered if the chandler knew.

He'd gone back to the secret room and donned the garb of one of his more-respectable personae, in no small part because that persona was possessed of a raincape, an article of clothing that Herald Alberich had forgotten to bring with him this evening. Besides, it wouldn't hurt for Lysander Fleet to be seen here. It was one more layer in the persona.

The duties of a Sunpriest began at sunrise and ended at sunset, but Geri would be accessible for another couple of marks—

Candlemarks, he reminded himself. He *had* to start thinking in Valdemaran terms, or he would *never* get the hang of this confounded illogical tongue…

The Temple itself, though modest in size, did not skimp on illumination. In fact, it showed itself to be a most hospitable neighbor; at the gates of the forecourt, directly under the two large oil torches, were benches that were, in nearly every kind of weather but rain or snow, occupied by one or more of the neighbors taking advantage of the "free" lighting to read by. The forecourt was illuminated by six more torches, and there were benches beneath them as well, although normally only a member of the temple congregation was likely to venture in there to read. Or socialize; Henrick encouraged people to feel as if the temple was an extension of their household, and there were plenty who lived tightly packed into a couple of rooms with their entire family who were happy to use the space in good weather. The forecourt was a good place for meeting friends, taking very small children to play, or just to get away from the rest of one's family.

They weren't uncomfortable benches either; of wood rather than stone (though wooden benches would have been more in keeping with Karsite custom anyway) and constructed with a subtle curve that welcomed a sitter. They glistened wetly in the rain, like great, sleek river beasts looming under the torches that had been extinguished by the first of the downpour. With the torches out, the only illumination came from two lamps on either side of the door of the temple itself. That wasn't a lot, and Alberich cursed the invisible bumps and cobbles that made for unsteady and slightly slippery footing.

He pulled open the wooden door and slipped quietly inside, trying not to disturb anyone who might be there. But the place was empty, holding nothing more but the Presence Flame on the altar, and the sharp scent of the oils used to polish the wooden interior. The aroma sent a shiver and a pang of homesickness over him. All Temples of Vkandis had this scent, since (except for the Great Temple in Throne City), all Temples of Vkandis were made of wood. Polishing some of that wood had been one of his tasks as a child…

Not that his old priest had any notion of taking him in as a novice. It was only too clear from the very beginning that Alberich had no vocation, and at any rate, *he* would not have lasted five marks in the cutthroat game of politics that most Sunpriests played.

But the scent brought back memories of his childhood, pleasant ones, in fact, which would have surprised people had they known it.

Well—not his four agents. Thanks to his memories, they now knew what a Sunpriest *should* be like. A little stern, perhaps, but *not* unforgiving; a truly upright person.

Geri came in after Alberich let the door fall closed again, and it did so with a hollow *thud*. The priest—for Gerichen was a full Sunpriest now, just as Alberich was a full Herald—peered toward the shadows enshrouding the door, and made out at least the basic form enshrouded by a rain-cape. "What can I do for you, my s—" Geri began, as Alberich threw back the hood of his cape and stepped forward so that Geri could see *who* it was.

"Don't call me your son, Geri," he admonished in Karsite. "You're nowhere near old enough to be my father."

"Keep coming at me out of the dark like that, and my hair will soon be white enough to pass for your father," Geri replied. "Of all people, you were the last I would have expected to see tonight."

"A mutual friend suggested that I don't come visit nearly enough." Alberich felt himself relaxing in the familiar surroundings that said *safe haven* to his younger self, no matter what had happened to him later at the hands of Sunpriests.

"Ah?" Geri raised an eyebrow, and then a hand. "Well, in that case, since this is a social call, shall we take this to my quarters?"

"Lead on." Alberich came up the aisle toward the altar. The sanctuary, the entire temple in fact, was a harmonious construction of carved and shaped wood, from the vaulted roof to the parquetry floor. The bench pews were finished with finials carved in the shape of a torch flame, and the Sun-In-Glory was inlaid in very subtle parquetry behind the altar. The several woods used to create it were of shades so near in color that you had to *look* for the pattern, and know what you were looking for, in order to see it. More patterns, geometric this time, were inlaid in the backs of the bench pews, in the floor, in the altar itself—and these were anything but subtle. Every color of wood possible had been used here, and Alberich reckoned that the artisan in question was either now a very wealthy man, or else was a devoted member of the congregation doing it for the glory of the One God, for it was quality work, and wouldn't have come cheaply.

Geri led him in past the altar and the door behind the altar itself. This was a kind of robing room, with vestments hung up all over the walls. A door in the opposite wall led to the priests' quarters.

"Here," Geri said, motioning him into a tiny kitchen. "It's warmer in here than anyplace else. Have a seat; Henrick's asleep, but don't worry about waking him. He could sleep through a war and a tempest combined. Do you want anything to drink? Beer? Tea?"

"Tea, please," Alberich replied, and watched with interest as Geri moved efficiently about the tiny kitchen, heating water in the pot over the hearth and getting mugs for both of them. "I don't know why I haven't come here before, instead of making you come up the hill."

He said that, because the kitchen *smelled* right. Those were Karsite spices he could taste faintly in the air, and a uniquely Karsite black tea that was steeping in that kettle. There were sausages hanging up in the corner of the hearth—both for further smoking and because the smoke kept insects away—sausages Alberich would bet tasted like the ones from the inn where he'd grown up.

"So what is on your mind?" Geri asked.

"A great many things," Alberich replied, now fully relaxed, with Geri's good tea on his tongue. "Tell something, though. What do you think about Myste?"

"I like her, but she's deceptive. I don't mean that she lies, I mean that her appearance is deceiving. She looks and sounds harmless, but she's a hunter," Geri said instantly. "She won't let anything stand in her way once she's on a scent. Though I'm not sure what quarry she's stalking. Probably a lot of things, one of them being answers."

"Ah, but to what questions?" Alberich replied.

"She's stalking those, too. Why do you ask?" Geri responded curiously.

"I'm not sure. Now that I'm not having to browbeat her into training properly, and she's a full Herald *and* Elcarth's Second, we're peers, so we're no longer in conflict with one another; she intrigues me, I suppose. It must be that instinct, one hunter recognizing another. She's the one who sent me here tonight, in fact." He took a sip of tea and savored the flavor. It was the *right* flavor, the one from his childhood, although the flavor from his childhood was a diluted version of this. "I'm hunting answers myself."

Geri regarded him with a somber gaze. "You, of all people, ought to know that you aren't going to find many of those *here*. Questions, certainly, but precious few answers. Ours is *a faith*, Alberich, not a map or a guide, and certainly not a set of certitudes. At least, that is the way it should be—"

"Not what it has become." He said that sadly, and once again, he was back in childhood, with that kind, yet stern priest, who tried to show him in ways a child would understand, just what the Sunlord was and was not. "We are the mirror of Valdemar—"

"More like the twin. Or we were, before things disintegrated." Geri sighed. "I've had this discussion with Henrick, actually. *He* is of the opinion that the long slide began with a will to power. I think it's more complicated than that. I think that the priesthood was corrupted by the congregation."

Alberich blinked. "How, exactly?"

"The laity wanted absolutes, answers, and the priesthood finally elected to *give* them answers, the simpler the better," Geri replied. "The Writ took second place to the Rule, and a poor second at that. The answers took away all uncertainty, and what is more, took away the need to think."

Alberich frowned; not for nothing had he spent so much of his childhood under the tutelage of a priest who knew—and lived—the old ways. "Above all, the Writ demands that a man—or a woman, for that matter—learn how to think."

Geri nodded. "You see? The *old* ways require that each person come to the Sunlord having thought through everything for himself. The current Rule requires that men become sheep, herded in one direction, following one path, pastured in one field, ever and always, so will it be."

"Sheep." It occurred to Alberich that it was probably no coincidence that the Sunpriests of Karse had taken to calling their congregations by the name of "flock."

"Sheep don't *have* to think for themselves, do they?" Geri made a face. "The Sunlord was reshaped from the Unknowable into the remote but predictable Patriarch, from the Whirlwind to the windmill that grinds—exceedingly small. Do this—you are gathered unto His bosom. Do that—you are cast into the outermost hells." Geri shook his head. "Answers are terribly seductive. The simpler they are, the more seductive they become."

Alberich turned that over in his mind, and found it certainly matched some of his own experience. "But that isn't the whole of it," he objected.

"Of course not. I just suggest that *this* was where the corruption started," Geri replied. "*Then* came the power, power that came from giving people what they wanted instead of what they *needed*, and power is just as seductive and even more addictive than any drug. Now—I don't know, Alberich. I don't know how it can be fixed. Or even if it can. It would take the Sunlord Himself in manifestation, perhaps. And someone as the Son of the Sun who is willing to hold to the hard course and be disliked, even hated."

"And loved."

"And loved," Geri agreed. "At one and the same time, and probably by the same people. Because when you demand that each situation be considered separately, and not responded to with the predigested Answer, you are always going to anger *someone* since you're always going to disagree with someone. Probably even someone who agreed with you the last time, and now takes this new response as a betrayal."

Alberich smiled sourly. "It would take the Sunlord Himself to protect someone like that."

"I fear so, and I am very, very glad it isn't me." Geri drained his cup and poured himself another, then smiled. "So, since I am *not* going to give you any answers, what can I do for you?"

"Give me an opinion." He outlined, as best he could, what he was doing with his four putative agents. "They have seen the very best that Karse is, in the form of Father Kentroch, my protector and teacher, and if I'm reading them correctly, they have warmed to him just as I did, and more importantly, responded to his ideas of responsibility and honor. We're just about up to the point where I first learned I had a witch-power; I suppose each of them will have a similar experience, but the witch-power will be his or her own Gift in real life."

"If you're wondering if you have somehow betrayed your vow to protect the people of Karse, let me tell you now that both Henrick and I are *positive* you are doing nothing of the sort," Geri said firmly. "If anything, you are going to put four more protectors in place, just as you had hoped. Did you know that all four of them have been coming down here for practice in the language? Or so they say."

Alberich shook his head, surprised.

"Well, they have—and what Henrick and I figured out after the first two visits was that they didn't want lessons in Karsite—their accents are impeccable, by the way—but an understanding of how *our* version of the Sunlord differs from what they're going to encounter in Karse."

Something about the way he said that made Alberich stare at him. "Oh, no—" he said, feeling his heart sink. "Please do not tell me that they want to convert."

"We wouldn't accept them as they are now if they did," Geri said with a laugh. "No, actually, I think they're integrating their two personae; *then* once they know how things are now, they'll react as a Karsite who was brought up in the old ways would."

Alberich felt a profound relief. The last, the *very* last thing he had wanted to do was to change anyone's religion. "That's sensible. Geri—" He hesitated.

Only now did Kantor interject something. :*Geri is your priest. This is surely a question for your priest.*:

"I'm torn," he said at last. "It feels as if there must be something more I can do, for Valdemar. Valdemar has given me so much—what should I be doing in return?"

Geri considered that question carefully. "Alberich, my friend, it is also my duty to tell you things that are true. You *are* doing as much as any other Herald; someone has to be helping to keep the peace here in Haven, and you are doing that. You still serve as Selenay's bodyguard, and thus free someone else to go South. And in case you were wondering if you should offer your military expertise—no."

"No?" That surprised him. "But—my training—"

"One of the things that is true is that you are *not* a great general. Not yet, anyway. Valdemar has great generals, and it doesn't need you in that capacity." Geri gave him a look shaded with pity and understanding.

"Ah." He felt deflated. But—well—

:We have the Lord Marshal, with decades more experience than you. Perhaps you have the advantage of training at the Academy, but we have the Collegium, which is, dare I say, just as good. It isn't only Heralds who are taught here. Occasionally, among the Blues, there is a young military genius from the Guard, and the Lord Marshal was one of those.:

Ah. Geri was right, then. He stared down at his cup. "So—"

"So other than doing what you are doing—you should be getting *yourself* prepared for the day when the King and the Heir and everyone else that can hold a blade goes down to the battlefields of the South to hold off that last big push that you know is coming." Something about the tone of Geri's voice made him look up—because it was odd. Very odd. It didn't exactly sound like Geri.

Geri stared off into space, his face blank, his eyes looking—elsewhere. And Alberich felt an unaccountable chill on the back of his neck. There was something going on here, something he didn't recognize. "You are Selenay's bodyguard, Alberich, and when the day of that final battle dawns, she is going to need you more than she ever has before—because the last, the very *last* thing she will think about is her own safety, so it is the first, indeed, the only thing that *you* must be concerned about. *That* is what you must be readying yourself for. Nothing else, nothing less. If need be, you must save her from herself on that day, so that you save her for her Kingdom."

Alberich had never believed those stories about how "the hair on the back of someone's neck stood up" when something very, very uncanny happened. Now he did—because he could feel that exact sensation. Geri continued to stare off into space, with that peculiarly blank expression on his face, but something glinting in his eyes. And Alberich had the distinct impression that whatever was speaking, it *wasn't* Geri. Which left—what? Here in Vkandis' own temple, it couldn't be anything inimical… but it sounded almost as if this was a prophecy.

He wanted to speak and ask something for himself; wanted to ask a question, a dozen—but they were all questions he really didn't *want* to know the answers to, honestly—

If I did, I'd be trying to tame that Gift of mine and make it serve me predictably.

The Writ said that the future was mutable and unknowable, until one passed through it and it became the past. That was why the Writ spoke against the witch-powers of those who tried to predict the future—not because the attempt to know the future was wrong in itself, but because being told *a* future closed some people's minds to the possibility of any other and they focused all their attention, their hopes, and their fears, on *that* future to the exclusion of other possibilities… which defeated the entire Prime Principle of Free Will upon which all of the Sunlord's Writ was based.

All this flashed through Alberich's mind in the time it took for the cup to slip out of Geri's fingers and drop to the table with a clatter.

"Botheration!" Geri was back, startled, seizing a cloth and blotting at the spill before it escaped to make an even bigger mess. "Look at me— woolgathering! I'm sorry, Alberich."

"No matter." The hairs on the back of Alberich's neck had settled, but not the uneasy feeling that *something* had wanted him to know more than he should about the future. *A* future.

Except that we know there is going to be a final battle. We're planning for that already. And if I had taken thought about it, I would immediately have known that Selenay would never consider her own safety under battlefield conditions. I haven't been told anything I couldn't have figured out for myself. Have I?

"I should be going. My day starts early, and yours, even earlier," he said, trying not to show any of his unease.

"True enough; good thing for me that I'm a real lark-of-the-morning," Geri said cheerfully as he walked Alberich to the door. "Come by here more often, won't you?"

Alberich almost, *almost*, prevaricated. Then he hesitated.

Because the Writ also said that when Vkandis *wished* the future to be revealed—or steered—He would find a way to do so.

"I will," he promised, and went back out into the cold, dark, and the rain—ordinary things.

Ordinary things.

He didn't think he was going to sleep well tonight. Probably not for many more nights to come.

PART THREE

THE LAST BATTLE

1 2

He had been expecting it for months, with a feeling of heavy dread and sick anticipation that put him off his food and kept him staring at the ceiling at night. All winter he'd worried and wondered. Were the Tedrels going to break with their pattern and attack in the winter? After that strange evening when Geri briefly spoke for—Something Else—how could he not have felt that the storm was about to break?

He'd wished for an inkling that he was doing the right thing—and he'd gotten it. Nothing inimical could have used Geri as a mouthpiece, *not* a Sunpriest, and *not* inside the sacred confines of the temple. Everything in the temple was sacred, no matter how homely it seemed. Vkandis was the Lord of All, from the Sun-fire to the hearth-fire, and he did not scorn the small and commonplace. So even if what had spoken through Geri was not Vkandis Himself, it was *certainly* some spirit that was doing so on behalf of the Sunlord.

Be careful what you ask for. Well, now he had it, and now he knew, well in advance of everyone else, that Sendar and Selenay would go into combat, no matter who tried to stop them. Now he knew… and didn't dare tell anyone.

Now he knew but didn't know when. He only knew it would be soon. But how soon? Every night he went to sleep on edge, and every morning he woke with the feeling that a storm was coming. And certainly this was what everyone, including the now-successful agents, had been working toward, all this time—to lure the Tedrels into thinking that the Valdemaran defenses were a hollow shell, and a single concerted drive would crack through. And thanks to the four that *he* had planted, when that time came, Valdemar would know as soon as the Karsite troops themselves did. They would know days, weeks earlier than they would have before his four demi-Karsites got planted successfully on the other side of the Border.

Yes, he was expecting it. But when the word came, it still hit him like a blow to the gut.

It was Talamir who delivered the blow; that didn't make it *better*, but at least it was from the hand of a friend and delivered as calmly as that worthy could manage.

It was early spring—or tail end of winter, take your choice. Raw weather, in any event, the trees still leafless, though there were a few, *far* too optimistic for his way of thinking, that were swelling into bud. The snow was gone, but a bite in the air and the snarl of the wind suggested that it wouldn't be too wise to tempt fate by rejoicing aloud that it was gone. Half the days were clear and cold, half raining, that miserable, dripping rain that would come up without warning and then stay a week, and by the time it crawled away, half the Collegium would be down with head colds. It never stayed clear long enough for things to dry up, in any event, and it was a good thing that the Trainees' uniforms were gray, because you couldn't help ending up with mud from the eyebrows down by midday, no matter what you did. Tail end of winter, *he* would call it, for all that the days were longer, and you could, if you searched diligently, find a few foolhardy crocus and snowdrops coming up in the gardens.

Spring, and he hated to see it, because it meant at least another season of war. And Spring came sooner, the farther South you went. True, in the mountains at the Border, it actually came *later*, but once out of the mountains, or when you stuck to the valleys, Spring was well on the way.

Spring was no longer a season of hope and renewal, and had not been for some time. But would this be the *last* season of war, or only the latest? That was the question that hung suspended over his head like a sword.

For the past fortnight, he'd been running a cross-class with the Horsemanship teacher, an accelerated course in fighting while mounted, and each day it had taken most of a candlemark to clean Kantor up afterward; all the Companions had been mired to mid-flank and spattered above that line. He was cold as a frog, tired, and every time he licked his split lip, he tasted mud and blood. There was no other way of learning how to fight in this kind of muck except to *do* it, though, no matter how much everyone hated it. *He* was looking forward to a hot bath with utter longing, and he trudged into the quarters behind the salle, expecting only to see Dethor and perhaps get a little commiseration before he went back to see about that long soak in hot water.

It took him aback to see Talamir there—Talamir, sitting in one of the hearthside chairs, and the sun still in the sky, for Talamir *never* was free enough to come back here before sundown. Talamir's expression told him the worst even before the King's Own opened his mouth; he froze, feeling as if something had just petrified him in place. He knew; he *knew*. And it didn't take a Gift to tell him.

For a moment, he couldn't breathe. For a moment, he was stunned. The blow had fallen.

The Tedrels were moving.

"This is the season," Talamir said, and that was *all* he needed to say. So the bait had been taken, the misinformation believed. This season, as soon as the rains stopped, the rivers subsided, and the ground was firm instead of mired, the Tedrels would make their all-or-nothing push.

He'd wanted it and dreaded it in equal parts, and now it had come.

He nodded, for there wasn't much that he *could* say at this point. Other than: "Know where, do we? When?"

"When—well, they're going to take a little longer than usual. They're going to try and browbeat the Karsites into adding troops, and if they can't get troops, they plan to demand money so they can hire whatever non-Guild scum they can hold together under a banner." Talamir sounded quite certain of *that* information, which meant that *someone* had overheard something he (or she) technically shouldn't have. "They want shock troops to take the brunt of battle, so their own can move in behind, undamaged. And they'll want a bigger base to move from than before, one that will hold *all* of their people and possessions in it, ready to move into Valdemar as soon as they take it."

"But *where?*" he persisted. That was critical. When they knew *where* the Tedrels were going to come across, they could set up their own defensive lines on ground of *their* choosing.

"Not yet," Talamir admitted. "Other than that we *don't* think it'll be Holderkin lands. The last taste of them that the Tedrels got didn't seem to agree with them."

Alberich's lip curled a little. He didn't much care for the Holderkin, but they had surely proved to be too tough for the Tedrels to digest. And it wasn't that they'd actually formed any kind of a defensive army either. By law and custom, they kept enough food in storage at each of their Holdings to keep everyone minimally fed for two years—and in that way, no single bad year could bring them to their knees. So when the Tedrels descended last summer, instead of fighting them, the Holderkin had locked every man, woman, child, and beast into their fortresslike compounds and sat the Tedrels out. After looting what little hadn't been locked up, and burning the crops, there wasn't much the mercenaries could do, except circle the walls, trying to get in. That wasn't a very successful strategy, and they wound up getting shot full of arrows for their pains any time they got within range. The places were too small to justify the amount of effort it would have taken to breach those walls, and there was no real loot of any kind if you did. The Tedrel recruits being what they were, they fought for the loot as well as the promise of a land of their own. Yet you couldn't leave the hundreds of Holds intact if you intended to occupy the land; that wasn't merely asking for trouble, it was inviting trouble in and offering it a cup of tea, so to speak. So last season when the Tedrels had tried to take Holderkin territory, the season had been singularly profitless and unsatisfying for them. Perhaps that had added to the impetus that impelled them to put in their final push now. They could not afford two lootless seasons in a row; too many of their recruits were *not* fighting for a new homeland, and would break ranks and desert if they saw no profit coming for a second year. You couldn't even tempt them with the Holderkin women; if the walls were breached, as had happened in one or two instances, the ones that didn't kill themselves were slain by their menfolk.

Given that the Holderkin would only follow precisely the same strategy a second time, it was vanishingly unlikely that the Tedrels would attempt the conquest of the entire country of Valdemar from there. It was far more likely that their plan was to conquer all of Valdemar and then cut off the Holderkin, dealing with them one Holding at a time at their leisure.

"I haven't much else to tell you," Talamir admitted. "Only that they've fallen for our ruse, that they believe we have been beaten down and depleted, and that they are gathering every resource they can for that final campaign."

"ForeSeers?" Alberich asked. He hoped the ForeSeers were getting something, although his own rogue and unpredictable Gift hadn't even warned him of this news.

Then again—hadn't it? How much of the dread he'd felt these past several moons had been due to his Gift? It didn't always give him visions; sometimes it only gave him warnings.

"The ForeSeers just confirm that the agents are right. But since the decision was evidently made in their council a few days ago, and only just announced to the general troops, I expect that will change." Talamir sounded confident, and he had every right to be.

Mutable and unknowable Future…

Well, perhaps. What the Writ had to say on *that* subject was a matter of philosophy rather than reality—meant more to keep people from closing themselves off to all of the possibilities that free will gave them. And this was particularly true when Karsite Writ met Valdemaran reality, and the Gift of ForeSight—which, often as not, showed *many* futures, not just one.

And if Vkandis really abhorred the knowledge of the future, would he have given me *that particular Gift?* For Alberich, like the Heralds, had used it to change the future he saw for a better one…

He began making calculations in his mind, trying to reckon how long it would take the Tedrels to coax or coerce the Sunpriests into adding Karsite troops to their numbers—or, more likely, come up with more gold and silver—how long it would take to get all the supplies together for such a campaign—establish a base four times larger than any they'd had before—

Then he realized that there were better heads than his who were already working on that very problem, and that their agents-in-place would be able to give Valdemar infinitely better information about what was actually happening than *he* could with what was only speculation. But there was one thing he could and *would* do.

"Two targets, and two only, they will have, should the King and Heir the field take," he told Talamir and Dethor. "Sendar to slay, and Selenay to take or slay. Take Selenay, they would prefer, and sword-wed to— whatever leader survives. It is the *land* they want. Behead the leadership, they must, to take the land. Better still, to behead the leadership, and make all right by wedding the Heir. Live with their neighbors, they must—" *Now* he could deliver his warning, the warning that Geri had delivered to him.

Dethor made a sound like a groan, and Talamir nodded. "Just what I thought, and I told Sendar as much," the King's Own replied bitterly. "But trying to keep *either of* them out of the fight at this point is impossible. Stopping the Tedrels now is going to take everything we have, and Sendar believes that if he and Selenay stay safe in Haven, we will lose the fight before it even begins. If they take the field, there isn't a man or a woman who won't fight better for their presence. And much as I hate to say this, I have to concur."

With a sense of sick agreement, Alberich nodded. The warning had been delivered and heeded, but it clearly would make no difference to the King and Heir. So—

The warning was given to me: Therefore, it is I who must act on it.

"Then this, I can do," Alberich said firmly. "Heralds there will be, and Guards, to shield them in a battle guard. So, to *me*, bring them for training. To make the shield-wall for a King, a special skill is, and each man, his place must know, and know that the right- and left-hand comrade will firmly stand."

"And he has to know how to fill in when the man to his side falls," Dethor seconded grimly. "Alberich's right, Talamir. We haven't had a King go into combat in—glory!—over a century. More, I think; I never was much good at history. We haven't had a battle guard in all that time. I don't know the strategy except from books."

"But trained the Sunsguard is, for such a thing," Alberich told them. "Sunpriests, Red Robes, and Archpriests and Hierophants we must guard, if not the Son of the Sun—for into the vanguard they *will* go. When know you Sendar's battle guard, to *me* send them. Selenay's battle guard, *I* will choose. And Selenay's battle guard and bodyguard, *I* will lead. Remain here, I will *not.*" He was slightly appalled to feel his spirits rising a little at the prospect of a fight at last, and something he *could* do. Action, rather than sitting.

But that was just it, really; it was a fight at last. No one could deny him his right to be in the thick of it now. He *would* be the leader of Selenay's battle guard; no one could stop him now.

"So far as the Palace Guard members are concerned, I would just as soon that you chose for both Sendar and Selenay," Talamir said thoughtfully. "You are the best judge of them, since you work with them all the time."

"Then, not solely Palace Guard it will be, but City, too." He honestly didn't think that there would be enough men in the Palace Guard who were young and fit enough to supply what he wanted for two sets of bodyguards. And that wasn't being snide either—so many of the Palace Guard had resigned their posts to serve down South that men who had retired had come out of retirement to fill their places. Those old men were perfectly fit to stand indoor guard duty at a door; if their reflexes were a little slower than in their youth, they had a world of experience to take the place of fast reflexes. They might even be good enough to fight with the army as a whole. But they couldn't march like younger men, couldn't *run* like younger men, and hadn't the stamina that was needed for this job.

"Whatever, whomever you want," Talamir told him. "I'll see to it that you get it. Or him."

"Or her. She-Heralds and she-Guards for Selenay, can I get them, half and half with men," said Alberich, and grinned fiercely to see the surprise on both their faces. "Tcha! *Think*, you! No thanks from the Princess, would there be, for clumsy men in her tent trampling. And with her, they must be sleeping! *And* follow her other elsewheres, that a man should not go!"

"You mean to guard her that closely?" Talamir asked, his face reflecting an interesting mix of shock and approval.

"One man, with a knife, all our efforts can overset," he pointed out to them. "Sendar your charge is, Talamir. Selenay is *mine*. And, say I, guarded she will be in every moment of every night and day. Battle guard there will be, but also bodyguards, will she, nil she, waking and sleeping."

He did not say that he expected Sendar would rebel over being so closely watched and would disregard anything Talamir had to say on the subject. But Selenay would listen and obey his orders once he'd explained them, thanks be to the One God. She wouldn't *like* them, but she'd obey them.

Unlike her father, she could not disregard orders. He could and would have her tied up and locked into a secure tower if he had to. He hoped it wouldn't come to that, but at the moment, he thought he could count on her good sense. Especially when she saw her father being less than sensible.

Tcha. All it takes for a youngling of that age is to see the parent doing one thing, and it is certain they will try and do the opposite. How refreshing to have youthful rebellion working for him instead of against him! And perhaps, when *Sendar* saw his daughter being sensible, he would be shamed into sense as well. Not likely, but he could hope.

"You'll want Heralds Keren and Ylsa," Talamir said thoughtfully. "Neither of them will be in the least impressed with rank and birthright; they saw Selenay as a first-year Trainee and helped me whip her into shape."

"Women there are in the City Guard as well—" And he couldn't help the wry smile. "Locasti Perken, Berda Lunge, and Haydee Delias." His spirit rose a little at the thought of recruiting those three to his bodyguard. Selenay would have to be a deal older and craftier before she could outwit or overawe *them*.

Dethor raised an eyebrow. Talamir chuckled. "Oh, I believe I know those names," the King's Own said, matching Alberich's smile. "They have night patrol around the Compass Rose and Virgin and Stars, don't they?"

"And just last week frog-marched young Lord Realard back to his father, *then* delivered a lecture to the old man that fair pinned his ears back," Dethor said, with a nod. "Or so I heard."

"Correctly, you heard. Impressed with rank, *they* are not, either." Two Heralds, three City Guards, that made five, and with the addition of a Palace Guardswoman who came to his practices who was called Lotte—if she had a surname, he'd never heard it—that would give him two women at Selenay's side at all times. That would do for close bodyguards; for her battle guards, and Sendar's, he'd want another ten or a dozen. Twenty or twenty-four good fighters; he'd have to think long and hard about *who*…

"These, I need—" he said, rattling off the names; Talamir nodded. "—those six at once. Special training, will they need. The rest, from Palace and City Guard, I will make a list."

"Have it to me in a candlemark," Talamir said, getting to his feet. "Send it by page. I'll have Sendar sign on it. That will cut through any objections. I'll have your six women report in the morning, and the rest to you within the week."

He would have liked it to be sooner, but that was probably the best that could be done. Replacements would have to be found, schedules juggled, and all of that took time.

Time—which was now working against them.

"Selenay, I want as well," he added. "Best it is, that she learn her guards to work with."

"Right," Dethor agreed. "And if we can get Sendar down here to work with his—" He stopped at the grimace that Talamir gave.

"Ask for the moon, and you're more like to get it," the King's Own said grimly. "If he sees his bed for more than four candlemarks in a night *now*, I'll be surprised, so don't expect him to come down here for what's 'only' a little arms practice."

"Then his Companion, we shall have!" Alberich said, in a burst of inspiration. "One at least of the pair shall we train with!"

:Done, Chosen,: Kantor said instantly.

"And you'll have Taver to stand in for me, because I *must* be with Sendar," said Talamir in the same moment. "That way at least one half of the pairs will get some practice in this."

:The sensible ones,: Kantor said.

Alberich was not disposed to argue with that assessment.

* * *

Six women—two in Herald's Whites, three in City Guard blue, and one in the darker, near-midnight blue that marked the Palace Guard—stood at attention before Alberich. Three of the six were older than he by three or four years, and were probably at least as tough. But there was not a jot less than honest deference in their expression, and though all six of them looked sober, they did not look anxious. That was good; it meant that they trusted him, his competence, and his orders.

"You six have I selected, as Selenay's bodyguards," he told them. "Two each for each of three watches, day and night. Her side, you will not leave, while on watch, ever."

He saw the two Heralds exchange a glance; noticed a slight frown of concentration on Lotte's face.

"Now will I ask, how paired you wish to be, and which watch you wish to take," he continued. "Sensible you are, and know you that no less honor there is, for the night watch than the day."

"If it's all the same to you, I *think* Ylsa and I ought to be on day watch," Herald Keren spoke up. "Selenay will have to be in on all of the battle plans and councils and the like, and—well, not to be rude, but Heralds will just blend in with the background."

Meaning, no one will object to Heralds being there, when some of the highborn might complain to see City Guard, particularly women that they might have seen hauling their erring sons home drunk.

"Objections?" Alberich asked, looking at the other four, who shook their heads.

"That splits the night with us," said Berda. "I'll tell you what, if it's all the same to you two, I'm used to the late hours after the taverns close, and I know that Haydee and Casti are on—*were* on—first night watch. Lotte, think you could handle the dawn watch with me?"

The Palace Guardswoman shrugged. "It'll take me a bit to get adjusted, but I'll manage."

Well, that sorted itself out painlessly. "Make it so," he told them. "And once satisfied I am that your business you know, those watches you will take at Selenay's side."

"Whether or not we're still in Haven?" Herald Ylsa asked, looking surprised.

"Whether or not. Used to your presence, I wish her to be. Invisible, I wish *you* to be."

Nods, no objections. "What do you want us to do that we haven't done before?" asked Lotte.

He proceeded to show them.

They were used to fighting back-to-back, but *not* when in charge of someone incapacitated, or someone who needed to be kept in cover. They needed to learn how to find safe exit routes, at least two, the moment they entered a room or a situation. They had to practice defensive, rather than offensive, fighting. And later, he would teach them quick rescue techniques, how to dash in and grab the Heir if someone had snatched her, while she was still within reach. Even if that someone had a knife to her throat. The time to get her away was *not* after she was in enemy territory. He hoped that at least one of each pair was a good shot; one of the best ways to rescue someone who was kidnapped was to shoot her in the leg. Someone who had to be carried became doubly hard to take.

But he thought he would save *that* lesson for a time when Selenay wasn't with them.

By midmorning, Selenay had joined them. She was not at all happy about having bodyguards *all* the time, but she was reasonable about it. The same could not be said for her father, according to the terse report he got from Kantor.

But *Alberich* didn't have to deal with her father. That was Talamir's problem, not his.

He was just pleased that his six women were quick studies, a little quicker than he'd hoped, actually. The three from the City Guard were especially adept in defensive strategies, perhaps because of their riot training. Students, crowds of layabouts and troublemakers, and drunks in fair season sometimes turned into mobs, and the City Guards and constables were trained to deal with a mob in every manifestation, whether cheerful and manic or surly and destructive.

The two Heralds had their own set of valuable skills, especially suited to their day watch, in no small part because they were used to letting their eyes skim over a crowd, looking for someone or something that was subtly *wrong.* The two Heralds would have their Companions to help, of course—and the Companions made another good reason to have them on day watch. No one assassin, not even a group of three to six, could get past two Heralds and *three* Companions. And the possibility of getting a group of strangers past sentries and guards and other sharp-eyed sorts by day was vanishingly small.

By night—well, it was possible, but it would have to be very well coordinated, and the number of approaches to get at Selenay would be limited. So once Selenay joined them, Alberich concentrated on escapes— how to get *her* to where her Companion could reach her, for once she was mounted, she was probably safe. Safer, anyway. Her Companion could get her out of reach of *anything* that anyone could use at night, for distance weapons would be severely limited by limited visibility. Night watch did have a different problem, for Selenay would be asleep part of the time. The three City Guards solved that problem for him, though, because they were perfectly used to manhandling semiconscious bodies. Even if Selenay was somehow drugged and couldn't be awakened, with a little luck, they'd be able to get her out of harm's way.

"We won't eat or drink anything we haven't brought with us," they told him, before he even asked. "And we won't eat *or* drink at the same time. That way even if someone's somehow managed to get to our grub, *one* of us will be able to see that something's wrong."

He was quite satisfied with their progress when he dismissed them at the end of the first day. The bones were there of a good set of three pairs of bodyguards and a first-class set of battle guards. Even Selenay was impressed, and had worked as hard as they did, in a role that did *not* come naturally to her—that of hiding behind others and allowing someone else to take care of her.

Lotte was the last to leave, and she helped him to clean up the salle before she did. As the door closed behind her, he sat down on a bench in the salle, suddenly feeling exhausted. It had been a long, long day.

The salle was silent, except for the sounds he made himself. The last blue light of dusk came in through the clerestory windows up above and reflected off the mirrors behind him. He unbuckled the straps of his armor with fingers that ached from holding tightly to sword and dagger, and winced at the occasional bruise.

Training the battlefield guards—ah, that would be another question. He'd thought long and hard about it, and had decided to go with a mix of half Heralds, and half Guardsmen, and had given the list to Talamir last night.

He would head up the group around Selenay, and Talamir would be the commander of Sendar's group. The *most* experienced fighters he chose for Sendar's guards, because on the battlefield, the Tedrels that came after Sendar would be going in for the kill. The ones after Selenay would be handicapped as they would be trying to capture, not kill, so they would hold back somewhat. His people would have no such compunction against *them*.

And he rather expected that Selenay, once she saw fighting, would be eager to stay *out* of it. Not that he doubted her courage…

But she was a young and sensitive person, and battlefields were horrors. *He* was sickened by them, and he was hardened to the death and carnage. Once she got her first taste of real fighting, she should be perfectly willing to stay at the rear of the battle lines with the commanders.

Alberich was not as sanguine about keeping Sendar out of the thick of the fighting.

But then, again, that was *not* his job. It was Talamir's, and if the King's Own couldn't manage it, no one could. Certainly not Alberich, the foreigner, for to some, perhaps unconsciously even to the King, that was an issue. No matter how people felt about him consciously, somewhere down deep inside, the moment he opened his mouth—

:Perhaps if you worked on your grammar,: Kantor suggested.

:Indeed. In my infinite leisure time,: he retorted as he pulled off the armor he'd worn to protect himself. He had been the "assassin" for all of this practice, and as such, had worked harder than all of them combined. He was in good condition, as good as he'd ever been, but—ah, it had been a hard day, as well as a long one.

At least he'd been too busy to think, too busy to worry.

Today he had neglected all of the Trainees, leaving poor Dethor and a couple of the older Trainees to conduct lessons themselves. Tomorrow he would have to do the same.

And the day after, and the day after that—

He sagged down on the bench, suddenly, with an overpowering sense of guilt. He was *supposed* to be Dethor's Second, to take the burden of all of this off of the old man. *:Ah, Kantor, what am I going to do?:* he asked plaintively. *:I can't be in two places at once—:*

:And if you were not here, who would be teaching the Trainees? And who would have seen to it that Selenay had bodyguards? And who would be drilling the King and Heir's battlefield escorts?: Kantor replied. Someone else, of course. Dethor, and someone else. Someone who wouldn't have Alberich's experience.

Someone else—if he could figure out *who* that someone else might have been, maybe he could recruit him (her?) to train the Trainees.

:This last lot of Trainees won't see fighting,: he said, after a moment. *:We've put everyone who is even remotely ready into Whites by now, but there are still the ones that are a year away from becoming full Heralds. There must be a dozen of them, and*

I've personally taught all *of them from the time they came in as Trainees; I can put* them *to teaching the younglings, while Dethor supervises.:*

:Good answer,: Kantor approved.

:And I can see to it that Dethor stays here, no matter how much he wants to go South with the full army,: he decided, clenching his jaw. *:He'll fight me on it, but if the King orders him to stay, then no matter what happens to me, there will still be a Weaponsmaster at the Collegium.:*

:He won't like that, but it's a sensible course of action.: Kantor sighed. *:Mind, all he has to do is try* one *night in a tent to know that he'd only be a handicap and a liability. One night spent in something other than a warm bed would leave him a cripple.:*

By that, Alberich knew that Kantor and the other Companions were already plotting ways to get Dethor to make the experiment. Quietly, of course. Without anyone else knowing, of course. There was no point in embarrassing the old man.

:Or hurting his feelings.:

:Good answer,: Alberich replied, and levered his own stiff, sore body up off the bench. A hot soak, something to eat, and then—*:Do you think I'd be allowed to sit in on any strategy sessions?:* he asked. Perhaps he wasn't a great general, but there was only one way to get that expertise, and that was to watch an expert in the craft of war.

:Just slip in and stay in the background, and we'll see to it that no one notices you,: Kantor replied.

Well! That was interesting.

And he'd better take advantage of it.

He limped toward the door to his shared quarters. It was going to be a long night.

The first of many, he suspected.

:The first of many,: Kantor agreed. *:But it won't be alone, Chosen. Never alone.:*

Talamir clenched his jaw and told himself that it wasn't wise to contemplate strangling his King.

He sat, rather stiffly, in the armchair that Sendar had nodded him toward. He knew that chair of old. It was seductively comfortable, and it was supposed to make him relax. He wasn't going to allow it to.

And he wasn't going to strangle his King. "Sendar," he said instead, "I am fully aware that you are an accomplished King and leader, *and* under most circumstances you are perfectly able to defend yourself, but may I be bold and point out to you that you can neither remain awake from now until this war is over, nor can you do everything that you refuse to delegate, even though there are plenty of your humble servants who are perishing for something constructive to do. *Therefore* you can resign yourself to the fact that you *will* have to sleep now and again and *will* require bodyguards while you do so, and you *will* have to learn how to delegate." He took a deep breath and waited for the inevitable reaction.

The King growled under his breath; something inaudible, but it sounded unflattering.

"Furthermore," Talamir persisted, "if you intend to persuade your daughter to put up with *her* bodyguards, you are going to have to set her a good example."

"That," Sendar said, clearly and distinctly, "is blackmail."

"The blackest," Talamir agreed. "It's also the truth."

He neglected to tell the King that he had pointed out the converse to his Heir. If each of them thought that the good example she (or he) was setting was the reason for the *other* behaving in a sensible fashion, it would make everyone's job much easier.

Although Sendar looked sullenly at him (recalling to Talamir's mind the rebellious adolescent that he'd been as a Trainee), he nodded. "All right. I'll accept the bodyguards. But I want to train with them," he said stubbornly.

"I don't think you're going to have a choice in the matter. I believe Alberich was going to insist on it." Talamir had the satisfaction of seeing surprise on the King's face. "He's a very thorough fellow, is Alberich. He realized immediately that having a bodyguard doesn't do you a great deal of good if someone attacks you, and you don't know what to do but they *do*. The wrong move could put you in as much danger as if you didn't have them at all."

"Selenay—" Sendar began, and was interrupted by his daughter walking into the room.

"Selenay *has* been training with her bodyguards," she said, flinging herself down into a chair with a groan and a wince. Talamir noticed that her hair was wet. She must have just come from the bathing room. "Six of them! And the so-gentle Alberich promises that it's going to get harder from here. I have, in the course of the afternoon, been thrown to the ground, thrown *onto* Caryo's back, hauled about like a sack of wheat, and taught how to dive for all manner of cover. Not to mention done just a trifle of fighting practice myself. I'm quite looking forward to facing the Tedrels; they can't be worse than this."

Talamir decided not to disabuse her of that notion. He just caught Sendar's eye and nodded. Sendar grimaced.

"Well, I'll be doing the same tomorrow," the King said, to Talamir's pleasure. "Though how I'm to squeeze more hours into the day, I do not know."

"I've already told you, and done so repeatedly. By putting the Council meetings and any other business that is not directly concerned with the war into the hands of your Seneschal," Talamir told him, with a little heat, because he had been advising this very move for months now. "That is what he is there for. You can't be two places at once, and if we don't win this thing, there won't *be* a Valdemar for you to reign over! Your Seneschal is competent, unflappable, and far better at obfuscation than you are. If it's something he *can't* do, he is supremely good at stalling things until you have the leisure to deal with it, and what is more, he knows to a nicety what he can and cannot do. Delegate, Sendar! How many times do I have to repeat that?"

Sendar shook his head. "I don't—" he began, then shrugged. "I will. But—"

"And don't tell me that you don't like it," Talamir snapped, deciding to show his King and friend the edge of his anger. After all, Sendar wasn't the only person in the Kingdom who was doing things he didn't "like."

"I won't," Sendar replied, in a way that told Talamir that this was exactly what he *had* been going to say. "What else do you want me to put on my plate?"

"A speech. You're going to have to tell the people—of Haven, at least—what's coming. And I've never been the speechmaker that you are." That was *certainly* something that needed doing that only Sendar could handle. "I can't write it, and I certainly can't deliver it."

"A speech." Sendar sighed. "Yes, that will have to be me. Selenay, I advise you that when you take the throne, find someone else to write the speeches for you."

"I think not," she replied, so somberly that both Talamir and her father shot a look at her. "Speeches aren't just something that we deliver, as if we were mere actors. They have to come from our hearts, father, and there has to be truth in them. If they don't resonate from inside us, and they don't have truth behind them, how can we ever expect people to believe in us and what we say?"

They both focused on her at once. It wasn't so much with

astonishment as—unanticipated pleasure. She sounded like an adult. She *was* an adult. And she sounded like someone who had learned all the right lessons from her father.

She returned their looks gravely. "Platitudes might satisfy for a short time, father—but soon or late, the people will realize they are being fed form without substance. What I tell them must be the truth, and I must believe it, and I must hold to it. That is what you have taught me. I have learned far more from you than that, but that is one of the important things you have taught me by your example."

He nodded, and so did Talamir. *:She knows. We've done our job, haven't we?:* he asked Taver.

:We have. She may not yet have all the skills, but she has the spirit and the heart. Skill will come with time.:

Now—if they could just be certain of *having* the time…

1 3

Alberich stood behind Selenay's chair in an attitude that was a hair less than rigid attention. That slight degree of relaxation, he had noticed, tended to make peoples' eyes slide right over him. He had taught Selenay's Six (as they were calling themselves) that same trick; it was very useful to be ignored, especially for a bodyguard. The fact that he was in Whites rather than his own distinctive gray leathers was helpful there; people didn't *notice* that it was the infamous Alberich there because they didn't expect to see *him* in Whites.

Talamir *would* have been standing the same guard behind Sendar's seat, except that he had his own seat on the Council; in this case, his place had been taken by Herald Jadus. Jadus managed to look as if he was no more than an interested bystander, and his guileless expression reinforced that impression. If one didn't know better—and only a few people *did*—one might well assume that was the case.

Jadus was something of a surprise to Alberich. He would have expected the Bard-turned-Herald to be one of the lot remaining behind at the Collegium, not skilled enough in warfare to be of any use in the coming fight. He would never have guessed that Jadus was as grimly determined to strike his own blow against the enemies of Valdemar as any Guardsman, nor suspected that Jadus was a deadly swordsman. His skill with a blade was not something that had come to light until recently, as he had been out on circuit all this time. Dethor had remembered it since he had trained Jadus himself; he was the one who had recommended Jadus as one of Sendar's bodyguards.

There was an interesting twist to his talent with a blade; Jadus fought with a light rapier rather than the commoner broadsword, but such a weapon was much more useful in a situation of close combat. Useful, too, within four walls, or any other crowded situation. Dethor had called Jadus in to work with Alberich, and both of them had immediately suggested that Talamir assign Jadus as one of the King's six personal guards. The more Heralds they had in *those* positions, the better. Sendar was more likely to listen to a Herald than a Guardsman. Not that the King was "likely" to listen to anyone if their advice went against something he felt strongly about, but a Herald was more likely than anyone else to get him to stop and think before he acted.

But Jadus was not the only surprise; another of Sendar's bodyguards was a Healer. In fact, it was the same MindHealer, Crathach, who had mediated the transfer of all of those memories from Alberich to the four spies.

Crathach was also a wicked bladesman, although he favored a two-handed style with knives instead of longer weapons, and his skill was such that he had been able to teach Alberich a trick or two. *He* came to Alberich himself to demonstrate his skills, and volunteer his services at something besides Healing. "You don't want a Healer angry at you," he'd said, when Alberich questioned him on whether he could bring himself to kill with those knives. "A Healer knows how you're put together, and what will hurt the most. I've been working with the severely wounded ever since all this started—" his eyes had glinted, "—and this Healer is very, very angry at the Tedrels."

Alberich often wondered just what had made Crathach, a Healer, into someone who could say that and look Alberich straight in the eyes while doing so. But he of all people understood a wish to keep one's past private, and unless Crathach volunteered the information, *he* was not going to ask. He probably hadn't expected to be made one of the King's personal bodyguards, but he adapted immediately. And Alberich was not at all unhappy about having someone who was *also* a Healer serving as a bodyguard. Especially a MindHealer, who had ways of dealing with a King who was reluctant to rest when he needed to.

It was a convenient assignment, to have the Healer taking the latest of the two night watches, along with one of Sendar's former squires, knighted just after Alberich had come to the Collegium. The lad had then been sent by his father on some mission or other, and hadn't come back to Haven until a few moons ago. Alberich had anticipated a certain amount of trouble from that one, but all he'd gotten was respect. Evidently the young buck had gotten some of the arrogance knocked out of him...

Just as well; any arrogance the young bucks of Valdemar still had was about to get knocked out of all of them, and for some of them, the experience would be fatal. The less arrogance, the better the chance at surviving until all this was over.

What Sendar and Talamir and the Lord Marshal were doing at this meeting was to give the rest of the Council a thorough briefing on absolutely everything that they had all learned—from spies, FarSeers, ForeSeers, and anyone else whose word they thought was trustworthy.

The Tedrels were in the process of establishing their final base for attack just across the Border in Karse, and the size of it made Alberich grow cold all over. So far they had done nothing *but* prepare; it was not yet a campaign, much less a war, and that did not bode well either. This was to be an invasion, and as such, the preparations were being taken with all of the care that decades of detailed planning could insure.

They had been working toward this moment for—well, years, decades, at least. Alberich had known better than to hope that their focus had diminished over the years. Their shock troops might be a combination of the dregs of the mercenary trade, criminals who sought sanctuary in their ranks, and whatever young men they could recruit with promises of adventure, excitement, and easy money, but the core was the Tedrel nation, whose longing for a new homeland had only strengthened the longer that they went without a home.

If anything, the increase had been exponential with the land of Valdemar in their sight. The bitterness of those thrown out of their homeland by their enemies had been distilled by the years. Now it was as much of a weapon as the swords, spears, and arrows in the hands of the army.

And they had done something very clever this final season; Karse was used to their strategy of making a base from which they could strike into Valdemar, and didn't think twice about it when, once again, the Tedrel commanders had set about establishing yet another. But this time, with the Karsites lulled into complacency, they had built up their own troops and established a base that could be used equally well to strike at Valdemar *or* Karse, then made it clear to their erstwhile allies that they did not particularly care if further aid was delivered voluntarily or wrested from the Sunpriests by force. The Sunpriests must have been shocked to discover the monster they themselves had created, sitting on their doorstep, not to be budged, reasoned with, or countered, demanding that it be fed, and fed royally.

That much, Alberich and the others knew from the spies. And although he could not know this for certain, he was fairly sure that the Karsite treasury had been emptied, literally and completely, into the

Tedrel coffers until even the rapacious maw of their army was sated. Shocked and dismayed, utterly undone and perhaps in a panic when they realized the position they had put themselves in, their first thought would be of self-defense. The coffers could be refilled, but if the Tedrels came in force to take what they wanted, they probably wouldn't stop with taking the gold and silver in the treasury—they would go on to help themselves to the personal treasures of the high-ranking priests... at the very least.

Supplies, the lifeblood of an army, were pouring in. And the means to transport those supplies, just as important, were not lacking either. If there was a cart or a beast in all of Karse that was not in the hands of the Tedrels, it was not for lack of money or effort. Trade had slowed to a crawl as carters, draymen, and teamsters flocked to make a small army of their own in the ranks of the Tedrels. Merchants couldn't find anyone to carry their goods; farmers were having to transport their own foodstuffs to market. The silver lure held out to recruit these notoriously independent souls was augmented by the guarantee that they would be sacrosanct, that no one could or would force them into the ranks of the soldiery. *They* would not fight; *they* would be guarded by fighters. The supply lines would roll, fat and heavy with everything the Tedrels needed. *This* time they would not plunder the countryside because they had to; they would not need to worry about living off the land.

Although Sunsguard soldiers did *not* go into the ranks of the Tedrel forces, there had been movement toward the Border, and now they had formed a line of defense on either side of the Tedrel base, ensuring that the Tedrels could not be flanked, at least on the Karsite side of the Border.

Brilliant. It was all brilliant. He couldn't fault their strategy.

Or their patience. They had waited all this time for their golden opportunity, and they were clearly not going to ruin that opportunity by forgetting that patience now. The Tedrels would move when the Tedrels were ready; not before, and not a candlemark later.

Talamir and the Lord Marshal were revealing all of this to the Council now. It was new to most of them, but only because they hadn't been paying attention. It wasn't as if they hadn't been *warned*, over and over again, that the Tedrels were going to keep coming at Valdemar until it fell, or they were destroyed and dispersed.

Alberich couldn't fathom it. It was as if the moment that the Tedrels retreated in the fall, the members of the Council forgot they existed and would be back in the spring. True, there were plenty of pressing concerns, but none, to his way of thinking, as the inevitability of the Tedrels making that final push. Perhaps, in the back of their minds, they hoped that eventually the Tedrels would give up and go away. After all, they had never yet won so much as a thumbnail's worth of Valdemaran land. But if that were so, then all of the things that all of the spies and ForeSeeing Heralds and historians had been telling them had just gone right past them without being believed.

If they'd been paying as much attention as they should have been to all of the reports that Talamir had given them over the last few moons, they would know most of this. On the other hand, the fact that it was all coming as a horrible surprise was going to work in Sendar's favor. The Council could—and would, as Talamir and Sendar worked together like a pair of clever shepherd dogs—be stampeded into granting Sendar whatever he wanted.

One of those things was Alberich—no longer kept back in the shadows, ostensibly no more than a closely watched underling. Sendar wanted Alberich in the thick of things, at his or Selenay's side, seeing and hearing everything that was most important, most secret. This greater danger would make the members of the Council forget where Alberich came from and remember only the uniform, the quiet work on the seamy underside of Haven, the invaluable help in placing agents in Karse. And presumably, there would be no further objection to Alberich's presence wherever Sendar wanted him.

Granting him authority—well, that was another question altogether. Alberich didn't really need or want overt authority; he had all he could handle covertly.

But he *would* get, by virtue of being Selenay's most visible bodyguard, complete access to every strategy session. No one would think twice about it. If he really saw something important, and knew there was something that needed to be said, it would be said through Selenay, or Talamir, or even Sendar himself.

Ah, the advantage of being a Mindspeaking Herald…

:I think that the position of being behind the Powers that Be suits you better, anyway,: Kantor observed.

:Why? So that no one has to look at my face?: he asked sardonically.

Kantor pretended to be shocked. *:Why, Chosen—was that a joke I just heard?:*

:As you know, I have no sense of humor,: Alberich responded. *:Now, hush, I want to see just how hysterical the Council members get when Sendar talks about the*

leaks of what should have been Council information. And how much of it is feigned.:

Because he had some suspicions that there were a few—a very few, no more than two or three—members of the Council who were not as tight-lipped as they should have been. He didn't suspect any of them of sending information to the enemy *themselves*, but rather, that they gossiped about Council doings to others. They probably thought that their friends and cronies were trustworthy enough—if they actually thought at all, which was doubtful. These highborn Valdemarans seemed to take it as read that *none* of their friends, or their friends' friends, could *possibly* be untrustworthy, and never mind heaps of evidence to the contrary...

And never mind all of the political infighting that went on between factions.

That was probably where leaks were happening, and not an overt traitor. Of course, all of this chattering made them feel very important and in the know, and their friends would be feeding them information *back* so that in their turn, they could impress the rest of the Council members with their knowledge and insight. *They* thought it was harmless, and in any other situation than the one they all found themselves in now, it would have been. But now, such loose-lipped behavior was nothing like harmless. Even without the Tedrels on the Border, there were other hazards, outside and inside of Valdemar, that could (and probably did) use this information to the detriment of poor, ordinary folk.

So Alberich was paying very close attention to the reactions of the Councilors, and he wasn't at all happy with what he saw.

Lord Gartheser. He was oh! so very concerned, shocked, dismayed, and he was acting, Alberich was certain of it. Gartheser headed up a faction that had been particularly nasty about Alberich's presence among the Heralds, but Alberich wouldn't have held a grudge if they hadn't been so underhanded about their opposition. Still, he'd have given Gartheser the benefit of the doubt—

Not with that bit of overacting. Gartheser was up to something. Gartheser knew more than he should. And where had he gotten that information?

:Hmm. Unfortunately, Sendar's old playfellow Orthallen is in Gartheser's coterie...:

That was Kantor, who actually knew far more about these people than Alberich did, which was saying a great deal. The Companions had their own information tree, which was as flourishing as any gossip vine in the Court, and was far more accurate.

Alberich suppressed a grimace. That wasn't good. Lord Orthallen, a few years older than Sendar, had been kind to Sendar when the King was a lonely child in the Court, before he'd been Chosen. Now, Alberich was fairly well certain that the *only* reason the adolescent Orthallen had been kind to and protective of the grubby little child Sendar had once been was because he'd had an eye to the main chance, even then. But you couldn't persuade Sendar of that, and as a consequence, as a child, he had made Orthallen into his hero, and as an adult, his close friend and compatriot. Orthallen had extraordinary access to the Royals for someone who wasn't a Herald. In fact, it was virtually a certain thing that Orthallen was going to get the Council seat soon to be vacated by Lord Tholinar.

Alberich liked Orthallen even less than Gartheser. Lord Gartheser was just pigheaded and prejudiced and interfering. He wanted things *his* way, he didn't trust anyone who wasn't highborn, and he wasn't entirely certain even of those jumped-up commoner Heralds. But although he despised Alberich, he didn't mean any harm. And though he probably had friends who were not at all trustworthy, there was no way yet to prove that to him. To give him the benefit of the doubt, Alberich was fairly certain that if anyone could bring Gartheser proof of his friends' iniquity, there was no doubt that he would drop them without hesitation.

Orthallen, on the other hand...

Well, Alberich had no real evidence against the man, other than the evidence of his feelings. Or perhaps, his Gift. Either way, there was *something* about Orthallen that put his back up, like a cat scenting a snake. He had no evidence against the man, and nothing other than his instincts to go on, but—

:*But I agree with you. There is something altogether ruthless about my Lord Orthallen. As if he doesn't care who or what is ruined so long as he comes out with what he wants.*:

Now that was an interesting observation, coming from a Companion. Was this purely Kantor's feeling, or did he have some other source of information? :*What if you hooved fellows conspire to keep Orthallen safely occupied with something else? Do you think you could organize that?*:

:*I can try, but I'm not a miracle worker. The most difficult part is that no one seems to see anything wrong with Orthallen but me and thee.*: Kantor sounded discouraged, as well he should. :*My fellow Companions don't like him either, but that could be only because he doesn't really like our Chosen.*:

:*Then thee and me will have to do what we can.*: Among a thousand other things...

He pulled his attention back to the Council meeting, and was pleasantly surprised to see that the Council members, after their initial shock, were actually pulling things together. Surprised? No— astonished. He truly hadn't thought they would bury their differences and get straight down to working together, burying feuds and sparring and jockeying for power so quickly—

But they were! The horseshoe-shaped table buzzed with half a dozen overlapping conversations, as the Councilors dropped their political differences and settled down to the task at hand. Sendar somehow kept track of it all; Selenay just kept track of who was in need of a page, of writing materials, or just another pitcher of drink. As the time candles burned down, Selenay sent more pages for food and drink, while the Council organized and coordinated the resources of their territories, Guilds, crafts, and associations. They were tallying up what could be brought down South immediately, what could be collected in a fortnight or a moon, what could be spared, and how much could be done and still leave just enough to keep everyone from starving to death over winter, and no more. Because now, finally, they *all* realized that even if the entire kingdom was left impoverished, that ruthless stripping of resources still had to be done in the face of the enormous threat that the Tedrels posed. Finally, *finally*, they understood. And at least now that they understood, they were prepared to act, and act swiftly, with no argument. The shock over, they were showing their mettle. Even Lord Gartheser.

"Better hungry and cold than dead and cold," said Lady Donrevy grimly. That seemed to sum up everyone's feelings.

Not before time, but at least it was *in* time. Alberich settled his face into a mask of indifference. It was time for him to observe, and nothing more. As the candlemarks passed, the daylight faded, and pages brought and took away laden and empty platters and pitchers, he watched and listened.

His time to act would come later.

"No, and no, and *no!*"

Selenay was in a temper; losing patience with her maidservant entirely, she pulled the useless gowns out of the traveling chest, wadded them up, and threw them on the floor. She did *not* want the creature to try and foist the blasted things off on her again.

"I will *not* take those gowns, or *these* gowns, or any gowns *at all!*" she snapped, as the maid snatched the dresses up with an expression of shock and offense, and smoothed them hastily. Selenay felt a pang of guilt over the crumpled and wrinkled state of the delicate white silks and satins, raimes and linens—but not enough to show that she felt any guilt. "How many times must I tell you? I'm going to a *battlefield*, not a fete, a ball, a state visit, or a festival!"

"But, Highness, you will be surrounded by highborn young men!" the maid protested indignantly. "Your Highness cannot possibly wish to appear the hoyden—"

Great good gods! What part of "battlefield" doesn't she understand? Selenay suppressed a groan, and wondered, what demon had possessed her to accept this foolish woman as her personal servant.

Because Uncle Lord Orthallen sent her to me, of course. And now I can't dismiss her, because he'd feel as if he'd let me down. And I did need a proper lady's maid, one that knows about hairdressing and all that sort of thing...

Unfortunately, the creature did *not* know about Heralds, nor did she care. She cared only about the trappings of rank, the care of gowns, the importance of self-importance, and she could not seem to fathom that there was another set of duties of the Princess and Heir that went far beyond looking handsome, finding a husband of suitable rank, and following the appropriate court etiquette. Yes, she was sheer genius when it came to dressing well and looking exquisite. But that was all she was good for. On the whole, the woman was far more hindrance than help, especially now, and finally Selenay sent her on a fool's errand into the attics just to get rid of her, knowing that *she* would be packed and gone long before the woman got back.

Then she did something she would normally *never* have done. She pulled out everything the maid had packed, and *tossed* it out, all over the furniture, the floor, wherever it happened to fall when she dumped the packs. The maid could do something useful for a change when she returned; she could pick it all up, see that the gowns were pressed and brushed, sort out all the hairdressing nonsense and cosmetics, and put it all away. Selenay could braid her hair by herself very well, and the only "cosmetic" she was likely to use "out there" was soap.

With the maid out of the way, it took just over a quarter of a candlemark for Selenay to pack. It wasn't difficult, she'd learned how to pack for the field long ago, and had watched her friends as they packed up to go out countless times. Wistfully, she had watched them then; she had known it wasn't possible for *her* to go, but she had wanted to, so badly.

Well, now she was going; and she didn't want to. Alberich probably thought that she would be excited about being in the front lines, and anticipate being in the thick of fighting, right up until she got her first real look at it, and only *then* would she lose her taste for war. He was wrong. She had already lost her taste for war, and she knew far more about it than she thought he realized. She had been making it her business to visit the wounded in the House of Healing ever since all this began, to thank them. They seemed to appreciate her attention, though why, she couldn't imagine. Maybe it was just that for most of them, it was their first (and probably last) close-up look at one of the royals.

Well, she knew first-hand what war *really* meant, and she was absolutely terrified. And was not, under any circumstances, going to show it.

She rang for a servant to help her with her trunks, but carried two of her packs herself. And she outdistanced the poor servants in her haste to get down to the stables. Probably she should have waited for an escort of Guardsmen, but she didn't have time. And if she wasn't safe at this moment, with the Palace and grounds alive with Guards, Heralds, and the last of the regiments to leave Haven, she would never be safe anywhere.

She popped out of the nearest door onto the courtyard in front of the Palace, a place that was normally quiet and empty at this time of the morning. Not this morning...

The sun was just above the horizon, a sliver of red in a dusky sky; the air was a little damp, with dew slicking the cobbles rimming the pavement and birds filling the air with their morning calls. It seemed too beautiful a morning to be riding out to war.

The courtyard was awash in white: white Companions, Heralds in their white field uniforms. Selenay fit right in; her uniform was not a whit different from theirs. That was a conscious decision. There was nothing about their clothing to distinguish her or her father from the other Heralds. Of course, the moment she crossed the threshold she was joined by her two shadows, the Heralds Keren and Ylsa, who fell in behind her casually, as if they were just a couple of her best friends who'd been waiting for her to come out. She greeted them with a tense smile, and then spotted Caryo, already saddled and bridled with field tack, waiting with Keren and Ylsa's Companions, who were completely ready, saddlepacks and all.

Her father was already in the saddle, but she saw with a touch of relief that she was by no means the last to arrive. It didn't take long for her to sling her basic field packs across Caryo's rump and fasten them in place; less time to get into the saddle herself. Her remaining packs and trunks would go on the wagons carrying the rest of the supplies, with her tent and her father's.

Caryo (with Selenay's two shadows in close but unobtrusive attendance) moved to Sendar's side without prompting. The King nodded an acknowledgment to his daughter but didn't stop reading the dispatch he'd just been handed. He held out his hand and a page on horseback slapped a graphite stick into it; he scrawled a reply on the same paper and held out his hand again. The page slapped a pre-inked seal stamp into it, which he impressed across his signature. He blew on the ink to dry it and rolled it up; this time he handed it to the dark-haired, somber-faced Herald who'd brought it to him, who in turn slipped it into a message tube.

Then the Herald held the tube up at eye-level, frowning at it. One moment he held the tube, the next, his hands were empty. *He* looked a bit pale for a moment, but recovered quickly; Sendar slapped him on the shoulder.

"Well done," was all the King said, but the young man smiled, blushed, and backed his Companion off to rejoin his fellows.

The young fellow was a Herald with the Fetching Gift, of course; either he, or a Mindspeaking Herald, had told Talamir that there was a message, probably from the front, that needed a written answer. The Fetching Herald had brought it in a heartbeat, and sent it back again in the same amount of time.

Now, with this all-or-nothing war to be fought, the Heralds truly showed how invaluable they were; in fact, without them, Valdemar would have no advantage over the Tedrels at all. Heralds who were Mindspeakers rode with scouts and served to relay news, messages, and battle plans. Heralds who were FarSeers spied on the enemy without him even being aware he *was* being spied upon. Heralds with the Gift of ForeSight tried to predict what would come next; the two lone Weather Witches tried to predict when rain would fall on the enemy and when on their own troops. And those with the rare Gift of Fetching sent things to and from their commanders in the distant South.

There were other, even rarer Gifts, which might or might not come into play, depending on circumstances. At the moment, for instance, the only Firestarters in the Heraldic ranks were not very strong, which was—well, some would think it was a pity. Certainly, if they'd had a Firestarter with the strength of the legendary Lavan Firestorm, they would hardly need an army. On the other hand—the finale of the Battle of Burning Pines had very nearly incinerated both the Karsite and Valdemaran armies together. Selenay was just as glad their Firestarter couldn't do much more than ensure campfires from thoroughly soaked, green wood.

The mood was subdued, as the sun rose a little higher, and the dew began to dry. The Companions, unlike horses, were not restive; they stood rock-steady in their appointed places, with little more than the occasional head shake or switching of a tail. The Heralds themselves spoke very little, and only in a murmur. Perhaps most of them were occupied in Mindspeech—certainly Sendar was, for the King had that faraway look that Selenay knew meant he was deep in conversation with someone.

:More likely a series of someones,: Caryo said quietly. *:He's been talking to the others since he woke.:*

Selenay bit her lip; on the one hand, she wished very strongly that her own Gift was powerful enough for her to hear what was going on. On the other hand, she wasn't sure she wanted to know. She was already afraid; if she knew what her father knew—well, she wasn't at all sure that she could keep up the brave face that she *had* to show.

The last of the Heralds to accompany Sendar to the war ran into the courtyard, packs over their shoulders, to finish kitting their Companions and take their places among the rest. When the very last was mounted, Sendar held up his hand, and what little talk there had been ceased entirely.

"You all heard my speech for the people of Haven," he said, his voice sounding rough and tired to Selenay, but strong nevertheless. He squinted into the morning sunlight; there were dark rings under his eyes, and she wondered how much he had slept—if at all. "I won't bore you with repeating it, and besides, none of you need to be told why we are doing this. Before winter comes, some of us will die; many of us will be injured. No less than myself, your King, *you* are primary targets for our adversaries. Our enemy knows very well how important the Heralds are to our strategy, and as you have been aware, he has made it his business in his past campaigns to eliminate as many of you as he could. Only the fact that I have made it *my* business to withhold as many of you from the front lines as I could has kept our losses to a minimum."

Selenay blinked; she hadn't realized that, but of course it was true. It must be. There hadn't been more than four or five Heralds killed in the Wars for each year that there had been fighting! Now she knew why— and knew that Sendar had not been lulled into thinking that the Tedrels would eventually go away. He had believed Alberich, believed the spies, and planned for this from the beginning.

"This is the fight that I have been holding you for," Sendar continued.

"Now, in my turn, I am going to ask you for something very, very difficult. You would not be Heralds if you were not perfectly prepared to pay the ultimate price for Valdemar, so I need not ask you for courage. Instead, I ask you for caution."

Caution? Selenay thought, surprised, even a little shocked. She was not the only one; she saw eyes widen, lips purse, and brows furrow among those closest to her.

"You are a finite resource," Sendar continued, turning in his saddle so that he could meet the eyes of everyone near him. "It will take four long years, at a minimum, to replace each one of you, and that assumes that enough younglings will be Chosen to do so. And each and every one of you is desperately needed for our strategies to work. You cannot be spared. So I ask you for caution, care, and to remember that although your duty to Valdemar may mean that you face death—your duty also requires you to live and serve, no matter what the cost to you." His voice took on a hard and implacable tone. "You must and *will* face the fact that there is worse than death on the field of combat, and be just as prepared to live with such a fate as you are willing to die. Valdemar can make use of a blind Herald—or an armless or legless one, and all you need to do is to recall the story of Lavan Firestorm's mentor, Herald Pol, to know that this is true. Valdemar can make use of even a Herald who is confined to a litter with a broken neck. What Valdemar can make *no* use of is a dead Herald."

Selenay swallowed, and wondered what was going through the minds of those around her. She hadn't thought about that. Had any of the others?

She glanced to her left, and found herself looking into the grave and grim visage of Herald Alberich. He gave a slight, tight little nod.

If no one else had, *he'd* thought of that. And probably reminded Sendar of it.

The silence within the courtyard was so profound that the twittering of sparrows in the trees and bushes in the neat boxes around the courtyard seemed loud and intrusive.

"This is no war like any we have ever fought," Sendar continued. "The Tedrels have nothing to lose and everything to gain. If they are defeated by us here, they will have lost their last, best chance at the homeland that is their only goal. They have nowhere to retreat to. After the way they have treated their allies in Karse, the Sunsguard will fall on them and destroy them if they lose. *That,* so Alberich tells me, is the message implied in the two flanking forces along the Border. The

Sunsguard will not only prevent us from engaging the Tedrels in a pincer movement across the Karsite Border, it will prevent *them* from coming back into Karse. And never believe that they do not know this. They are probably counting on it to keep their own mercenary shock troops in line and under control."

Oh. Selenay repressed a shiver. *Never corner an enemy who has nothing to lose.* How many times had Alberich drummed *that* into her head? And now the enemy had been *put* into a corner. A bad situation had just gotten infinitely worse.

Sendar paused to let all that sink in. No one moved. No one spoke.

"But *we* have everything to gain by defeating them, and not just for ourselves. When this war is over, and we have defeated the enemy, no one will ever face a single Tedrel Company again, much less the entire nation," Sendar said, into the waiting silence. "They will *be finished,* for all time. And we *will* defeat them!" His voice took on a strength and a surety that suddenly made even Selenay's spirits rise. "We *will* defeat them, for although they call themselves, and think of themselves as, a nation, they are *not.* They have a body, with no heart. They think that the land is the nation. *We* know better. We know that Valdemar is not the land—and it is not just the people. Valdemar is a spirit, a community of spirit that binds a hundred disparate peoples with a hundred different religions and ways of life into a company and a greater whole. It is not a unity, for that would be denying our diversity, and in our diversity and our tolerance is our strength. Even if this enemy succeeded in driving us from this land—which he will *not*—Valdemar would live on. If he slew all of us—which he will not—Valdemar would live on. That spirit is what you fight for, and will live for, Heralds of Valdemar, for you are at the heart of that spirit—a spirit of tolerance, compassion, understanding, and care—all things that our enemy cannot and will never understand. And in the name of that spirit—we *ride!*"

The cheer that rose was as spontaneous as it was heartfelt. Even Selenay felt a cheer bursting out of her throat, and she was so used to the effect that the King's speeches had on people that she had thought herself immune by now. Even grim-faced Alberich was cheering, and his expression had as much of hope in it as she had ever seen. Keren and Ylsa cheered with tears running down their faces, and they weren't the only ones.

Sendar and his Companion surged forward, down the drive that led out the Palace gates, buoyed on the wave of sound, and the rest of the Heralds followed.

And Selenay with them, for once nothing more than another Herald, another weapon, to serve Valdemar to the last of her strength, and even beyond.

14

The King and his company of Heralds and bodyguards swiftly outdistanced the baggage train, those Council members who elected to go to the front lines, and the Royal regiment. They would have outdistanced *anything*, as Alberich soon discovered, because they were all mounted on Companions—even the bodyguards, who were being carried as a matter of courtesy by unpartnered Companions. Carried, just like sets of cooperative baggage—because these Companions would not tolerate even the excuse for a bridle that the partnered ones wore. Alberich had known, as a matter of theory, just how swiftly the Companions could cover ground. Now he discovered it as a matter of practice.

They could have been performing a sort of precision drill, for they *all* used a pace that was as fast as a canter, and as smooth as a running walk. So smooth, in fact, that it was perfectly possible to strap oneself into the saddle and doze, if one were tired enough. Their hooves didn't pound, as Alberich had noted before this; they chimed. Not as loud as bells, and not precisely *like* bells, but the effect of so many of them hitting the ground together was a bit unsettling. Like being in the same room as a thousand wind chimes...

Alberich was astonished; it was his first experience of this ability, unique to Companions—

—or to be honest, it was his first *conscious* experience of this ability. Kantor must have used this pace to get him across the Border into Valdemar from Karse.

Now he knew why Dethor had packed his sleeping roll in his saddlepacks and not with his tent. He wouldn't see his tent—or anything else in the baggage train—for days or weeks. Neither would anyone else in this group; they would have to depend on the army for shelter for a while when they got to the front lines. And he supposed that they would have to hope that the weather stayed good on the way...

It didn't matter; Dethor had overseen his packing, and everything he truly needed was with him. He hoped that someone with similar experience had packed for Selenay and the King.

:Selenay and the King already knew how to pack for this sort of trip.: Kantor said, and left it at that.

Once out of the capital, they moved down the road with a purposefulness that was positively frightening. There was no way to properly convey the effect—they weren't *menacing*, but they seemed to exude a sense of needing to go somewhere in a hurry, a sense that somehow made everyone move out of their way without noticing that it was happening. It was uncanny. The first time he saw it working, he felt the hair go up on the back of his neck, and Kantor's wordless reassurance.

This could have looked like some sort of parade, all of the Companions and their uniformed Heralds, with the single spots of Healer Green and Guard Blue among them. It didn't; Alberich could tell by the faces of those who gathered to watch them pass through their towns and villages that they gave no such impression. The expressions that the common folk wore were uniformly grim. Perhaps the people of Haven had not yet grasped the seriousness of the situation, but the people of the towns and villages knew it. There was no cheering, and the hope he saw in their faces was tinged with desperation.

:They know, don't they?: he asked Kantor.

:Better than those in the cities. Everyone knows everyone in a village; when their youngsters go off into the Guard, everyone knows every word in every letter that comes home. And—everyone knows when someone isn't going to come home again.:

Ah. He shifted in the saddle, careful to do so with Kantor's stride so as not to throw him off. Well, that was something he wouldn't know about—letters from the front lines, and a village's interest in them. His mother couldn't have read a letter even if he'd been allowed to send her one from the Academy.

And he remembered, for the first time in a long, long while, the first line of the oath he had sworn when he joined the Academy. *The temple is your mother and your father is Vkandis Sunlord...*

It was still true. Just not in the way that those who had listened to him swear that oath intended.

They stopped for the night around dusk, outside a village—which one, he didn't know; they went past it too quickly for him to read the faded sign in the uncertain light. The Herald in the lead broke off down a side lane and the entire group followed, slowing as they did so. The lane was overgrown, entirely grass-covered, eventually bringing them to a tiny cabin set off in a clearing, with no sign of any inhabitant about it.

:That's because there isn't *an inhabitant. This is one of the Waystations,:* Kantor told him. *:We're two days' journey from Haven at my usual pace; three or four by horse.:*

Feeling stiff, though not as stiff and sore as he had expected, he slowly dismounted. He had read about the Waystations, though he had never seen one. This one, a little stone hut with a thatched roof, looked solid enough, though it wasn't very big. But sheltering no more than two Heralds at a time, and then not for very long, it didn't need to be, he supposed. The walls were thick, and so was the door; there weren't any windows, but inside he saw that the floor was slate, and there was a stone fireplace. It was a better structure than the one he and his mother had shared before she got her job at the inn.

The building itself was given over to Sendar and Selenay as their shelter. Six of the other Heralds returned to the village for provisions, while the rest, Alberich included, made camp and saw to the comfort of their Companions. Even the Guards and Healer Crathach put in the time to groom and feed and water the Companions they rode.

They completely exhausted the stores of food for the Companions in the Waystation bins, but at least there *was* plenty of grazing. It was fully dark by the time the six Heralds who had gone after provisions returned, and by then there were a couple of small fires going, sleeping rolls had been arranged according to friendships or prearrangements—Alberich's would be across the door of the cabin, and the other bodyguards would be in close proximity—and the steady munching of Companions through grass was as loud as the insects and night birds.

Alberich had expected that they would be cooking some sort of communal meal, but what was brought back from the village was both unexpected and touching. The villagers had given up parts of their *own* evening meals to send them to the Heralds on their way to the front lines. Ham, cold chicken, and bread, cheese and fruit, cold boiled eggs, sausage rolls, and sweet cakes, jars of pickles and packets of tea—

Parcel after paper-wrapped parcel came out of the saddlebags and net bags that the six had taken into the village, to be divided equally among the lot of them, Sendar and Selenay taking no precedence in what they got. There was a bit of trading as people swapped items they didn't care as much for, then things quieted down rather quickly.

"Draw straws over who washes up tonight, and who does in the morning," Sendar suggested, as conversation ceased while jaws were otherwise employed. Most everyone was probably as starved as Alberich; they'd all eaten while on the move, taking out provisions that had apparently been packed by Palace servants, since Alberich didn't recall packing the contents of the little bag on the front of his saddle—a paper-wrapped pair of sausage rolls and a skin of cold tea. But it had been candlemarks ago, and it had been a very long day.

Someone collected enough black-and-white beans from the Waystation to equal the number of riders, and put them into a bag. Alberich was not unhappy to find his was a black bean, and when he was done with his ham and pickled beans, joined the queue of those who were cleaning up now. Water straight from the well felt refreshing after the hard and sweaty day of riding; it was going to feel cursed cold in the morning. Sendar and Selenay got black beans as well, and Alberich insisted they go ahead of him. There was method in this; *they* were in the Waystation and probably asleep by the time he finished, and he was able to stretch himself out across the door without worrying that he'd be inconveniencing them. But he wondered, just before he fell asleep, if there was even the faintest likelihood that a village of Karsites would sacrifice portions of their own meals to a troop of Sunpriests and Sunsguard under similar circumstances.

On the whole, he thought not.

The next day followed the pattern of the first, except that they had to stop at midday in a large town and several Heralds went to each tavern and inn in turn to collect meat pies for all of them. Alberich had an idea that he would be heartily tired of meat pies and sausage rolls before the end of their journey... but of course, that was the least of his worries, and it was better fare than he'd ever gotten with the Sunsguard.

The contrast between their grim purpose and the placid, lush countryside they rode through could not have been greater. Alberich tried not to look too closely at the folk who came out to see them pass, but he couldn't ignore them altogether, and it wrung his heart to see them—middle-aged men and older women either *with* children or as old as the old men. There were a great many children and not very many young adults. He knew what that meant. Those that could be spared, were unattached, had no families to support—they were gone. In the army, facing the Tedrels. And who knew if they'd ever return? He saw that in the faces of those that they rode so swiftly past, in the fear they tried not to show.

But if the Tedrels broke through, these same people would be taking up whatever arms they had to defend their lives—or fleeing back up that road to Haven... And try as he might, he could not but help look at those peaceful villages and imagine flames rising above the roofs, and bodies sprawled in the streets.

It was better when they were riding through the countryside. And maybe the others were cursed with the same sort of imagination as Alberich, for their pace seemed to increase, just a trifle, when they were going through a center of population.

So it went, sunrise to sundown, league after league of it, and no end in sight. It almost seemed to him as if he was caught in a peculiar nightmare, riding inexorably toward a dark and dreadful fate.

Selenay had longed for a day when she might ride out like any other Herald, taking to the road with her packs behind her, leaving the Palace and all of the stuffiness of the Court behind. Now that day had come, and she thought—often—that it might have been a good idea if she had never made that particular wish. She would rather have to suffer being laced into a tight gown and listen to dull speeches every day for the rest of her life than face the Tedrels. And it didn't matter that there would be an army between them and her. She was as much afraid for the people she knew, her friends, the people she'd been with as a Trainee, who would *be* in that army, as she was for herself.

What was more, the *reason* why Alberich had assigned bodyguards to her for day and night was real now. She understood that her life was in genuine, serious danger—and worse than just her life. She had learned in several sleepless nights following a long and somber talk with Alberich that there *was* a fate worse than death. The Tedrels had every reason to want to take her alive, and many more reasons to want to make sure that she was alive, and *outwardly* well, but not in possession of her wits anymore. And there were a great many ways to ensure that she wasn't sane once they got hold of her... the most obvious being to murder Caryo. She was used to a Valdemar where the King could walk unguarded among his people—but her father wasn't going anywhere without his six shadows either, and that shook her to the core. He no longer trusted his own people—or at least, no longer trusted the ones he didn't personally know. It would have made her weep, if she hadn't been too frightened to cry.

The heavy, leaden feeling of fear increased day by day. It hung over all of them, making conversation stilted and unnatural, punctuating the silences, and making it impossible to *enjoy* the fragrant, picturesque countryside through which they rode. The enforced, close presence of her father, quiet and grave with worry, or absent altogether as he Mindspoke with the Heralds relaying a moment-by-moment summary of what was going on with the enemy and with their own forces, was a greater burden than she allowed him to guess. She couldn't lean on him for comfort, for Alberich and Talamir were right; he was already taking on more than he should. She could only thank all the gods that ever were for Caryo; at least she had someone to turn to, even if that someone couldn't actually do any more than she could. It helped, immeasurably, when in the dark of some Waystation, unable to sleep, she could unburden her heart to another who would understand; and in moments when she could steal away a little, with Keren or Ylsa pointedly *not* looking at her, that she could pretend to groom Caryo and cry into her soft shoulder.

There were times when Selenay wondered if they would *ever* reach the army, but more times when she hoped they never would. So long as they rode, she could put off the day when everything would change. So long as they rode, she was safe, safe as only a Herald in the company of Heralds could be.

So long as they rode, the army had not yet met the enemy, and she could pretend that they never would.

Nevertheless, the Companions, even her beloved friend, carried them inexorably to that confrontation, and it was almost a relief when that day did come. Almost. The waiting might be over, but now she was *here*.

She heard the army long before she saw it; the hum of a city many times the size of Haven transported to the rolling hills of the southland. And long before she heard it, there were other signs of it; provisioning wagons going toward it full and away from it empty, messengers pounding up or down the road.

There were other signs; more ominous signs. The countryside was empty. It was empty, because insofar as it was possible to get the people to leave, it had been evacuated. There wasn't a sheep on the hillsides, or a farmer in the fields. The fields that no longer held sheep *did* hold something else, grazing on the rich, emerald grass, grass that the Tedrels desired for their own herds. The horses, the oxen, the mules of the army grazed there—not the horses of the cavalry, which were kept within the camp, but the horses that drew the carts that supplied the army, the horses that carried messengers when the message was not urgent enough for a Herald. Common horses, but for the most part better by far than any that these hills had seen before.

But when they finally reached the outskirts of the encampment, it was something of an anticlimax, for it looked like nothing more than an ordinary army camp. They topped a hill, and saw the edge of the camp below them, across the slow river that split the valley in half, on the other side of a stone bridge. Sentries guarded the road there, the visible token of the ones Selenay could not see. Beyond the sentries, rows of pale canvas tents, rows of tents that were as even as furrows in the soil, that marched up the other slope and crowned the top of the hill, a strange and martial crop of spears and pikes planted in stands beside them. And yet, it was no larger an encampment than ones she had seen before, on the edge of the city.

She knew abstractly that it wasn't possible to *see* all of it from any one point, not in these hills. She knew that in her mind, but the emotional impact of so great a force as they had gathered together *should* leave her breathless, or so she felt. So as the sentries barring the road demanded and received passwords, she felt oddly disappointed.

But then they followed the sentry's directions down the road, with properly arranged ranks of whitewashed canvas tents on either side, each section with a central campfire, each four sections serviced by a larger cook tent. And as they continued to ride forward, the ranks of tents went on, and on, and on until she began to lose count. Over the next hill and down the other side, the tents ranged on before them, interrupted only by trees and hedgerows, the racks of pikes and spears piercing the sky beside them. Then the tents were interrupted by a drill ground, full of Guardsmen at practice, followed by another hill, another little valley, and yet more tents and another drill ground. Then a farmhouse, taken over by officers, full of comings and goings, with the yard crowded with horses, snorting and switching their tails at flies. And when they didn't stop there, at what she had thought was the command post, *that* was when it hit her; just how big their army was…

Selenay tried to imagine it, and failed. She had seen several hundred people at once many times, even several thousand, crowded into one of the huge public squares in Haven for some speech of her father's, but never more than a fraction of the number that must be assembled here now. And that number didn't include Healers and Heralds either—and there were probably a lot of Bards here, too, for you couldn't keep a Bard away from something like this. Then there were all of the support people, cooks and carters, laundresses and tailors, the servants of anyone highborn—

No wonder her father had put off assembling this huge a force until now. Where would he have housed them? How long could he have kept them fed? The logistics were mind-boggling. She couldn't imagine the amount of coordination it took just to feed this army for a single day, let alone care for it for the past several fortnights. How could it have been organized in the first place? Who was doing the training? Who was keeping the place *clean,* for the Havens' sake?

No wonder Talamir kept telling her father to delegate more.

Now she knew why Alberich couldn't be jollied into a better humor. He knew this was coming, of course. Well, so had she, but unlike her, Alberich had known very well how large a force the Tedrels had when they decided to commit all of it. For their army was just equal to the one that the Tedrels were fielding, and only just.

Her heart went cold, and she was suddenly, desperately, urgently wanting to run away, to turn Caryo and go so far north that not even the Tedrels would find her. There were places up there—the Forest of Sorrows, for one—where you could lose an entire regiment of cavalry and not find them for years. One girl on a single Companion could stay hidden until the rivers ceased to flow.

The truth of it was, she could *do* that. And no one would blame her if she did. Some people would even applaud her wisdom in giving the Tedrels one less available target. But if she did that, some people would lose heart, and she had no way of knowing how many. It might be enough to make a difference, and she could not take that chance. She could not do much here but this; by her very presence, one slim girl facing down the enemy, daring him to try and take her, she might give heart to those who were actually doing the fighting. And she could take some of the burden—not much, but some—from her father.

So she couldn't run away. And she dared not show how afraid she was.

But she was very glad that she had reins to hold. They kept her hands from shaking.

She had thought that they would stop at that farmhouse—but no, they went on, past more tents, more drill grounds, until she wondered if they would *ever* make an end.

* * *

The practice grounds were all in use—no slacking going on in this army, and well-drilled these fellows were, too. Alberich's practiced eye ran over the troops, and he was pleased with what he saw.

:Better than anything in Karse, eh Chosen?: Kantor asked smugly, as the men lunged and recovered in time to their leader's chants. Spears, this lot had, with cross-braces like on a boar spear that kept the enemy from coming at you once you'd stuck him. It made them a little awkward to handle in a group, but that was what practice was for.

:Not better trained, but better-motivated,: he admitted. *:That's as important a factor as food and weapons.:*

The trouble was, of course, that the core troops of the Tedrels were just as highly motivated. But *not* the shock troops... and that just might make the difference. The shock troops, the ones meant to take the brunt of the attacking, were the flotsam that the Tedrels had lured to their ranks with promises of loot and blood. Once it was *their* blood that got shed, the question was how well they'd stick: Valdemar had that working in their favor.

In numbers, if all of their ForeSeers and spies were right, Valdemar and the Tedrels were evenly matched. But not, perhaps, in motivation.

:Greed might be motivation enough,: Kantor said, soberingly. *:Don't count on them to turn once the fighting gets bloody. Most of them have seen plenty of fighting; it's not as if they were a lot of sheepherders dragged in by fast-talking drummers.:*

His eye lingered on a group of spearmen and pikemen training—spears in the first two ranks, pikes in the next two. Pikemen were traditionally the positions of the least trained. Although there was some skill involved in handling a pike, it was not much different from handling a boar spear, and involved more following orders than thinking.

There was some clumsiness, but not enough to make him think that they were entirely fresh. There was a great deal of determination. Their clothing, beneath their Valdemaran tabards, told him that they were farmers.

Other men might deride farmers-turned-soldiers. Not he. Farmers knew what they were fighting for; farmers were used to death and killing, for they did it every autumn when they killed the cattle and swine that would feed them through the winter. The average citydweller might never see meat that was not already rendered into its component parts; the farmer had raised that "meat" from a baby, and had resisted his children's efforts to name it and make a pet of it.

Killing a cow was easier than killing a man? Not when the farmer had delivered the cow as a calf, had agonized over its illnesses, had called it to its food every day for all of its life, brought it all unaware into the killing shed, and stared into its eyes before killing it. Whereas the man he faced was a stranger, was hidden in his helm, and wanted to kill *him*. Then wanted to take his land, his goods, and his women. A farmer would have no difficulty in making the decision to kill a man.

No, he was happy to see farmers here. It was the citydwellers, the craftsmen, that he was concerned about. It was one thing to train and look proficient—it was quite another thing to hold yourself together in combat.

He glanced at his charge; Selenay was looking white about the lips. He wondered why.

:She understands now what we're facing,: Kantor replied. *:It's hit her, in her gut, in her heart, just how* big *our army is, and by extension, how big theirs is, and all that this implies.:*

Ah. Well, he felt sorry for her, but better now than later. Better now, when she would have time to gather the courage he knew she had and compose herself before the eyes of those who would fight for her sake.

:For the sake of Valdemar,: Kantor corrected.

:It is the same,: he countered, as he spotted the convocation of larger, fancier tents that marked the center of the army, and the seat of its leadership. What with bodyguards, sentries, servants and all, it had been too big a convocation to house in any farmhouse.

:A philosophical difference, perhaps,: Kantor replied, *:to you. A real one to us.:*

They reached the periphery of the tents, a boundary marked by another set of sentries stationed every few paces around the edge. The edge was defined by what appeared to be ornamental swags of rope hung between stakes. It *wasn't* ornamental, and it was a device suggested by Alberich. Hidden amid the fringe and bullion were bells, very loud bells, and anyone who so much as brushed against those ropes would raise a very audible alarm. One couldn't climb over it or crawl under it. A small thing, but one more barrier between his charges and harm.

The Lord Marshal was taking no chances. It was the Lord Marshal who had suggested the second innovation, a layer of black felt lining the inside of the tents, so no one would be silhouetted against the canvas by lights within. Another small thing, but it would make the King, his Heir, and the officers less of a set of targets once night fell. Unless a spy was able to watch them closely, one wouldn't even know when they were *in* their tents.

The Lord Marshal himself was there to greet them, and Alberich moved closer to Selenay as they all dismounted. This would be another good time to strike at her, in the moment when everyone was a trifle relaxed at the end of the journey.

But Kantor had made a statement that needed to be answered. *:She is not Valdemar? Then let her* become *Valdemar,:* he said fiercely. *:Men fight better when the symbol of what they fight for is before them. Why do you think we carry a shrine of Vkandis before us when we wage war?:*

He actually took Kantor aback for a moment. *:An interesting observation,:* the Companion replied, and left it at that.

It was as well that he did, for Alberich's attention was elsewhere now—scanning every face and every body around them, even—no, especially—among the servants of the highborn. *That* was the place for a traitor to slip in, among the servants. He watched without seeming to watch, a good trick he had acquired in the taverns of the worst part of Haven. There were a great many tricks he had acquired there, or learned from Dethor, and he had taught most of them to Selenay's Six, and Sendar's too, or at least as many as he could impart to them in the short time he had to school them.

He was pleased to see that they were using those lessons; pleased to see that the ones guarding Sendar were doing likewise. They were more obvious in their watchfulness, but there was no harm there; they drew attention to themselves, and if there was anyone watching *them,* he would spot the watchers…

Layers upon layers of care and misdirection, of planning and deception, and upon them Selenay and Sendar's lives might depend.

The moment passed; the King and Heir moved into the circle of guards and canvas. Thin protection, or so it seemed, but stronger than one might guess, for they were out of the milling crowd, where a knife could be employed suddenly and without warning, and into a more controlled place where more watchers watched the watchers.

He joined them, in the background, always in the background. Now, more than ever, he needed to be unnoticed.

How ironic, that he, who had trained for most of his life to be a leader, should now require of himself to be insignificant.

How ironic that he should find, as he dropped back to be a shadow-Herald in his dark gray leathers, that he preferred the place in the shadows to the one in the light. He watched young Selenay as, white-lipped, but with her head held high, she took her place beside her father at the planning table.

And then he turned his attention to those around his King and his charge. He knew what the strategy for the initial stages of battle would be, at least for now; it had been discussed and discussed until it was tattered. He knew, and he feared that the enemy knew.

But it had been too late to prevent them from knowing when the strategy was decided—and as he himself had told Dethor, "No strategy survives the first engagement." You could plan and plot all you liked, but when your plans depended on the enemy doing what you *thought* he would do, it wasn't likely that he'd cooperate with you.

Now all they could do was see what he did, and trust that they could move to counter it, whatever "it" turned out to be. Chances were, it wouldn't be anything they had planned for. The Tedrel Warlords had not survived this long by being stupid. If anything, they were entirely *too* clever; that very cleverness had caused any ruler who might consider hiring them to take a good long look and realize that they were in many ways as much a danger to the one who had hired them as they were to the enemy they were sent against. So no one, in all the time they had been roaming, had ever before hired the *entire* nation. Broken up into Companies, they were safe to have inside your borders. Only the Sunpriests, in an act of monumental hubris, had gathered all the Companies together in one place.

Now the Sunpriests were well aware of their folly, too late to do them or Valdemar any good.

We cannot simply turn them back, he thought with anguish. *If we do, they will only turn on* my *people—*

And of all of those here in this camp, he was the only one who would care if they did.

But what else could he have done, except to act as he had? He hauled his divided attention back to where it belonged, and kept it on Selenay and those around her. The tents were dark, thanks to the felt lining them; the only light came from the entrance and the unlined canvas tops. The bases had been rolled up to ankle-height to allow air to circulate. The interior of the one they were in was sparsely appointed—that would change when the baggage train caught up with them—and for now, the only seating was on folding stools. Sendar was offered one of these and refused it; Selenay did not.

Talamir called for food and drink, and when it came, made sure that both the King and Heir availed themselves of it. Sendar was, of course, completely immersed in all the reports of the commanders, even though there was nothing new in them. Selenay was looking wan, but Alberich did not suggest that she retire to her own tent. She had to harden herself; they *all* had to harden themselves, to go beyond what they thought they could do until there was no more strength left, then find more strength, somewhere, somehow.

As if she had heard his thought, she turned her head toward him and met his eyes. Then she rose and took her place at her father's side, paying every bit as much attention to the reports as he was. Although the King did not even glance at her, Alberich watched as he placed his hand on her shoulder, tacitly welcoming her presence, and showing any who doubted that she belonged there.

Good. Now no one would suggest that she get some rest, dismissing her as irrelevant to their discussions.

A movement—an *odd* movement—caught his eye. Without turning his head, he identified the movement as someone pulling slightly away, rather than leaning *toward* the group. His peripheral vision was excellent, better perhaps than anyone guessed, for he had no trouble telling who it was without betraying his interest by looking at the man.

It was Orthallen, who was serving as the commander for the militia of his sector. His brows were furrowed, his posture tense.

And he was frowning at Selenay.

1 5

Orthallen—

There were some singular holes in Alberich's intelligence regarding Orthallen. At that moment, Alberich wished that he'd spent a little more time trying to fill them.

But in the very next instant, Orthallen's frown vanished, to be replaced by his usual, affable expression, apparently leavened by worry. And if Alberich hadn't *seen* the transformation, he would have thought that the expression was genuine. Now, however, he was aware that it was a mask, one that Orthallen could don in the blink of an eye, and very seldom dropped.

A mask over what, one wonders…

Alberich forced himself to be charitable. *All* he saw was a frown, which might have been occasioned by anything. That Orthallen didn't approve of anyone as young as Selenay being privy to every bit of war planning going on. That Orthallen didn't like the prospect of a Queen instead of a King. That Orthallen didn't approve of a female being involved in war planning. That Orthallen had indigestion.

Perhaps not that last, although being on the doorstep of the final campaign of a nasty war was enough to give anyone worse than indigestion.

The likeliest was that Orthallen had suddenly been confronted with the fact that he would one day be serving a Queen instead of a King. And given the urgency of the current situation, "one day" might be a great deal closer than he thought. And he didn't like the prospect.

It had been some time since Valdemar had had a Queen; there wasn't anyone now alive who remembered the last one—it had been a good long time, after all, and *she* had been a co-Consort, ruling with her King, Sendar's grandfather.

Sendar's Queen, who'd had no interest in being co-Consort, had died when Selenay was a mere infant, and Orthallen had a good reason to be wary of the problems associated with a female ruler. Women *did* die in childbirth, and even if Selenay wedded someone Chosen, who could be a co-Consort, there could be trouble if she died; the Kingdom had been left to the Council to rule while Sendar had gotten over his beloved wife's death. If that had happened when there was a crisis like *this* one looming, the result could have been a disaster.

Could have been, but *would not* have been. Perhaps Orthallen couldn't understand that; he wasn't a Herald, he didn't know what deep wells of comfort the Companions were, and he might not understand just how totally Heralds were driven by duty. If Sendar had had to deal with a crisis, even in the moment of his beloved's death, he would have. That he gave himself over to mourning was only because he knew he had the luxury of doing so.

Nevertheless, Alberich did not like that frown on Orthallen's face; there was something about Orthallen's expression that he couldn't pin down, and his instincts said it was more than just one older man concerned about the possibilities that a young woman Heir represented.

It must have come as a distinct shock to him, seeing her here, seeing her being briefed instead of being sent to a tent to rest. It's one thing to see "the child" sitting at a Council table, it's quite a different thing to see her sitting here. After all, just because Selenay had a Council seat, it didn't follow that she was truly a part of the Council's deliberations. The seat *could* have been nothing more than show, for certainly Selenay's vote went with her father's every time. Given Orthallen's patronizing attitude toward the Heir, the shock of realizing that she *was* a power to be reckoned with and had a mind of her own must have been unpleasant. But was it unpleasant enough to cause that particular *kind* of frown? It hadn't been the look of a man surprised and a little offended; it had been the expression, calculating and angry, of one who had not realized that there was a roadblock to his plans. Or so Alberich *thought*, but everything he thought he'd observed was all in retrospect, for the expression hadn't been there more than a moment. It was distinctly frustrating not to be able to quantify his feelings, but since he'd been working in the slums of Haven, his instincts had sharpened, and he'd come to depend on what they told him.

Therefore, he would keep an eye on Lord Orthallen.

So he delegated a portion of his mind to doing just that, and turned the rest of his attention back to the briefing that Sendar was getting. The Lord Marshal and his Herald Joyeaus were getting to the end of things Alberich already knew, and they looked as if there was more to say. A great deal more. And that it was bad news.

"The ForeSeers are reporting difficulty, Majesty, as are the FarSeers," Herald Joyeaus said. Her thin face was set in an expression of solemn thoughtfulness, for this development was something new—though not unexpected, at least, not to Alberich. The fact was, he was surprised that it had taken so long for the Tedrels to block attempts to FarSee what they were doing. Possibly they had not realized that the Heralds could do such a thing with the amount of accuracy they had. Possibly they had been blocking attempts to scry magically, and had not until now reckoned on the Gifts. Possibly they had been saving their mages for this moment.

Or possibly it had taken them this long to buy or coerce magical expertise...

It seemed to take the rest by surprise, though, all but the Lord Marshal, who looked grim. "Exactly what do you mean by 'difficulty,' Joyeaus?" Sendar asked.

Joyeaus' mask didn't slip, but Alberich didn't have to be an Empath to know that she was very worried. "As you know, Majesty, my own strongest Gift is FarSeeing, and although when I Look elsewhere I have no difficulties, when I Look across the Border, I might as well be Looking into fog. In concert with two others, I made further attempts, but we managed no more than glimpses, which were confusing at best. The ForeSeers tell me that they are unable to See *anything* when they attempt to scry into the future—"

"But as we all know, ForeSeeing is chancy at best," Sendar finished for her. "The most probable answer to that is that there are so many possibilities branching from this moment that they are unable to see even one clearly. I am more concerned by the report from the FarSeers. Can FarSeeing be blocked?"

Officers and Councilors began murmuring nervously among themselves and shifting their weight. Alberich pulled at his collar, feeling stifled suddenly and wondering if he was the only one who found the rising tension in the tent to be edging close to panic.

"I—" Joyeaus hesitated. Alberich was astonished that she did so. How could she not *know* that it could be blocked? How could she not have *expected* that enemy mages would do so? And yet, from the way she looked, and the way Sendar acted, it seemed that the possibility had never even occurred to them.

Alberich didn't want to step out of the shadows and draw attention to himself, but he didn't seem to have a choice. No one else saw the blindingly obvious. He cleared his throat; the sound was shocking in the silence that had followed Sendar's question. Every head in the tent swiveled in his direction.

"Herald Alberich?" Sendar prompted.

"Senior, high-rank Sunpriests, such powers have," he said carefully. "And unscrupulous others with magic for hire are, in the Southern Kingdoms. Among the Tedrels, there may be magicians, though specifically I have not of such heard."

They looked at him as if he had spoken in Karsite, not Valdemaran. Maybe in a way he had. He cursed his lack of fluency, and the need to speak without composing what he was going to say.

He tried again, this time coming directly to the point. "Assume you must, that others than Heralds Gifted are. Surely Sunpriests are, for this I know! Surely Tedrels are, for they are a nation, and *some* must Gifted be! *Yes.* Blocked your Gifts *can* be!"

Joyeaus blinked, and looked as if she was coming out of a daze. "He's right, Majesty," she said. "We have been remiss in assuming that *only* Heralds are Gifted—and that just because we don't know ways of blocking Gifts, it doesn't follow that someone else hasn't found a way."

"So the Gifts are useless?" asked one Councilor, his voice sounding strained.

"No, no—only FarSight and ForeSight!" Joyeaus hastened to say. "Mindspeech works perfectly well, and Fetching as well, at least as far as we can tell. We've never *depended* on ForeSight, it's too rare a Gift and too erratic anyway."

I can vouch for that, Alberich thought grimly.

"And we've never depended *entirely* on FarSight either," Selenay put in, her high, young voice carrying over the muttering (and, yes, there was rising panic in those voices) of those around her. "We'd be fools to depend on *any* single source of intelligence, gentlemen! You may depend upon it, there are other ways of finding things out at a distance. In eluding—" she added, with a touch of irony, "—common spies."

"Animal Mindspeech," replied someone. Alberich couldn't tell who, precisely, for the background chatter distorted the sound. The voice was female, though, and very confident. "The Chronicles say that the Hawkbrothers of the Pelagiris Forest use Animal Mindspeech with their birds as spies. Surely we can do the same? Or listen through the ears of a horse or hound?"

The muttering subsided, and what there was of it sounded less panicky. Sendar turned to Joyeaus. "Deal with it, Joyeaus. Find the Heralds with Animal Mindspeech; see what you can do. Ask Myste what's in the Chronicles. Perhaps the Heralds of our generation have not needed to worry about their Gifts being blocked, but there's no reason to think it hasn't happened in the past somewhere, and if anyone will know where, when, and what was done about it, it will be Myste."

"Sire." Joyeaus bowed and edged her way out of the crowd.

No wonder the voice had sounded familiar, and he felt that familiar apprehension whenever he thought of the half-blind Herald-Chronicler-in-training. Well, at least he'd given her enough skill to get herself out of trouble if she had to, and he could count on her strong instinct for self-preservation to keep her out of the fighting itself.

Unless, of course, there was no other choice. But if *that* happened, everyone in a white uniform with a mount that was even vaguely pale in color was going to be in danger. The Tedrels knew better than to let a single Herald escape alive.

It has to be Sunpriests that are helping them, though. No mage worth the name would serve Karse or the Tedrels. No mage worth the name will serve where the Mercenary Guild won't. Even one of the blood-path mages wouldn't serve the Tedrels, in part because the Tedrels themselves would know better than to trust one of *that* sort. You didn't want a blood-path mage around; when sacrifices ran short, they tended to grab whoever was closest...

That didn't make things any better, however. The Sunpriests had *power.* Everyone knew about the invisible creatures they commanded that stalked the night, able to see into a man's very soul and discern if he was a heretic and a traitor, and thus, their lawful prey. He himself had *heard* them, howling in the distance.

:Then why didn't they take you?: Kantor asked, with none of the ironic humor he might have put into such a question.

:Because I am no heretic,: he replied, with none of the sharpness *he* might have put into a reply, because Kantor was not teasing him, and deserved candor. *:I follow the Writ as well as I may; and though I often fail, failure does not make a heretic,* blasphemy *does. They hunt those who would deny Vkandis, not the sinner. If they hunted sinners, there would be no man or woman safe in Karse, and precious few children. And as for their other prey, I am no traitor to Karse or my people.:* There was heat in his last sentence, though; he couldn't help himself, and Kantor reacted to it.

:Peace, I only asked to see what it was that these creatures that haunt your darkness

might seek,: he said soothingly. *:I suspect in part it is a feeling of guilt, and in part, the fear that such guilt would cause. Especially in those who think that such creatures can read their souls, and know that the Sunpriests would not approve of what is there.:*

Well, that was a novel suggestion. And it was one he would think about in depth—and perhaps discuss with Myste, since she was here— but later. For now, since the mere mention of the fact that other peoples had as much or more magic at their disposal as the Heralds did seemed to cause Sendar and the others to act as if they were momentarily stunned, he had other things to worry about. *:Take it as read, you and the other Companions, that the Sunpriests are going to try to block whatever Gifts we use,:* he advised. *:I don't know how well Sendar and Joyeaus understood what I was trying to tell them—:*

—and even now he truly didn't understand how the possibility hadn't even occurred to them.

:We probably can't do anything about FarSight and ForeSight, but I defy them to block Mindspeech with the Companions boosting it,: Kantor said with determination. *:And we* might *even be able to boost the other Gifts on an irregular basis.:*

Good enough. Now for the rest; he waited until there was a gap in Sendar's orders, and interrupted.

"Majesty," he said clearly, with a touch of sharpness. "If blocking FarSight the enemy suddenly is, when until *now* he has not, then is it not that he does not *want* to be seen? And steps is taking, of that to make certain? And that would be—why?"

Sendar stared at him a moment, his brow furrowed, and again Alberich cursed his lack of expertise in Valdemaran. But it would have taken him a quarter-candlemark to work out how to say it clearly, and they didn't have the time—

The others just stared at him, probably trying to untangle his mangled syntax as well. Selenay, who was far more used to the way he spoke, uttered an oath that would have made one of the muleteers blush.

"They're moving!" she said—no, shouted—before her father could rebuke her for her language. "Father, the Tedrels, they *knew* we'd be watching them, they didn't care until this moment since all we'd see is their troops building, but now they don't want us to see them because they're *moving!*"

Sendar swore, in language even stronger than Selenay's (and there was no doubt in Alberich's mind where she'd learned to curse so fluently). But he put up his hand to quell the raised voices around him, stilling an incipient panic with a single gesture.

Alberich hoped that Selenay was taking note. This was the sort of thing a Monarch needed to be able to do by sheer force of personality.

"Even if they could fly—which they cannot—they could not be at our Border before three days have elapsed," Sendar pointed out. "Since they must move on their feet and those of their horses, it will be longer than that. We have a dual task—to find another way to gain the intelligence that FarSight would have given us, and to prepare the army to meet them. The former is in the hands of Joyeaus and Myste, and if any two Heralds can find what is needed in the past, *they* can. So, my friends, let us bend our minds to the latter, for it is time to finish our strategies. That is what *we* can do."

Alberich withdrew a little, for at the moment he was best as an observer. *No battle plan survives the first encounter with the enemy,* he reminded himself. He'd reminded Myste of that truism often enough as well; with luck, she'd remember it and she and Joyeaus would add several more layers to their plotting.

And if he paid a little more attention to Orthallen than the rest, well, that also was part of his responsibility. It was not only an enemy that could do damage. Sometimes the danger came from within, and the one who brought it could even have all of the best intentions in the world.

It was a very small tent—more like a pavilion, actually, showing old and much-faded colors on its canvas—pitched among the slightly untidy cluster of those belonging to Heralds assigned to the King and his officers. No two of these tents were alike, taken as they were from whatever was available after the Guard, the officers, the King and his servants were done picking over the available canvas, but this one stood out for both its inconvenient size and its shabby state. As the sun dropped toward the horizon, Alberich looked at it askance. Surely not.

"My home away from home," Myste said, gesturing at the canvas square with its peaked top. She held the flap open to let him in.

"This must be the oddest campaign tent I have ever seen," Alberich remarked, as he squeezed himself into the tent that Myste had taken, ducking his head to avoid the low cross-beams. "It's certainly the smallest—"

Myste shrugged. "That's probably why no one else was particularly eager to take it. I think it must have been cut down after the canvas around the bottom started to rot and stitched together with replacements, because the floor is newer than the sides and top."

He *had* expected something entirely different, a tent that was more a semiportable library. Well, there were books, but nowhere near as many as he'd expected. His glance at the neat packing case that served as a bookcase as soon as the cover was unstrapped made her smile. "I brought copies of War Chronicles, and some odd bits, and nothing more than would fit in that case," she said. "Only copies. If the army retreats and I have to flee with nothing more than the uniform on my back, may the Tedrels have joy of them."

He didn't tell her what he thought the Tedrels would use the paper for, he just folded his legs under him and sat on the canvas floor. "And this is interesting—"

He pointed at the arrangement where anyone else would have had a cot or a bedroll. He *thought* there might be a cot under there, but one third was propped up to serve as a chair back and the opposite end dropped down, and the rest had a strange tray raised over it on some sort of folding legs, with everything needed for writing arranged atop it; a brazier no bigger than the palm of his hand, stacks of very cheap wood-pulp paper, graphite sticks, and pen and ink, and a lantern she could hang on the tent pole overhead. Which she did at that very moment, raising the chimney after it was hung to light it with a coal from the tiny brazier. And a moment later, she sprinkled the coal with a powder that sent up a haze of insect-repelling incense.

She grinned as she saw what he was looking so closely at. "That's my invention. Bed, chair, and table in one, and it all comes apart and fits together. It even makes part of its own case. My clothes and bits are packed in the back half under the cot, and the desk is the top. And since we've got messengers going to Haven twice a day anyway, they take what I've written with them whenever they go. No matter what happens, we won't lose more than half a day's rough notes from meetings and anything else I know about, and if everything goes pear-shaped, Elcarth will at least have a record of what led up to it." She swung the "desk" away on a pivoting arm, and sat down.

He hoped that losing a half-day's rough draft would remain her only concern.

For all that the bed thing was amazingly compact, there wasn't much room left in her tent. He'd seen her rooms at the Collegium. She was a woman addicted to clutter and a collector of *things*. This sparse minimalism was totally unlike the Myste he knew. She gave him a side glance as if she guessed what he was thinking, and a half smile, which swiftly sobered. "Joy and I have had our little conference and we have some plans, and you were right, there *have* been times when Gifts have been blocked, and—oh, do hold back your surprised look—by Karsites. But there are things we can do, and they have never managed to block Mindspeech on our side of the Border. Or battle line, whichever came first. Another point of interest, if you will, is that since Lavan Firestorm's time, apparently they have been unable to coax those night-stalking things you were talking about anywhere near the Border because they haven't appeared at all over here. Now, can I count on that continuing, do you think?"

Alberich chewed on his lower lip and considered what he knew. He had only heard the things in the distance, and had never asked any Sunpriest about them. But then, one didn't ask *them*. Interest in what they sent out might cause them to suspect guilt, or worse, heresy. But it did occur to him that although he had never heard them *too* near the Border, the reason for that was probably less than arcane. The Sunpriests would not risk *themselves* anywhere near the Border, and they probably had to be within a certain proximity to their charges to control them.

And if the Tedrels were providing a screen of bodies, they wouldn't hesitate to follow.

However, the situation at the moment suggested that the Sunpriests had a great deal more to concern themselves over than their ancient enemies.

"I think—I think perhaps that even if the Sunpriests *could* send their servants across the Border, at this point they *wouldn't*. I believe that they hold them back in reserve to make certain the Tedrels, after conquering Valdemar, do not turn on them as well." He raised an eyebrow. "Consider, if you will, the troops we know are flanking the Tedrels, the ones my spies said are *not* to cross the Border. No, I think the Night-demons will stay within Karse."

"That is a distinct relief." She made a note amid the rest on the desk at her side. Then closed her eyes for a moment. She looked tired, and he wondered how long she had been here, for he hadn't noticed her among the Heralds around the King.

"It is one small blessing," he replied. "Another is that *our* troops have limited choice of ground, given where we think they must come. And a greater blessing is that our troops will be fresh."

"All they have to do is stop overnight, their troops will be just as fresh as ours," she pointed out. "They know *we* won't cross the Border. But frankly, all I know about battles and war is what I've read, and everything

I've read just makes me want it all to go away."

"Unless he is a madman," Alberich said soberly, "I believe you will find that even the great generals feel the same."

She looked down at her hands. "May I ask you a horrible favor?"

He was going to say, "It depends on the favor," but something about the way she had asked that question made him answer, unequivocally, "Yes," instead.

She fixed him with that glittering gaze of eyes shielded behind thick, glass lenses. "Shielded" was a good thought—she probably used those lenses as shields to hide what *she* was thinking.

"May I stop pretending that I'm brave and cheerful around you? I feel as if I can trust you, more even than the rest of the Heralds, I mean; you've seen me at my worst, I suppose, and you seem to know, somehow, why I *have* to be here." She shrugged, helplessly. "And I do. It's important that a Chronicler be here, and it can't be Elcarth, since he can't make himself detached enough—but it's also important that someone be here who knows history, because things that have been done in the past are likely to solve a problem now. I daren't pretend I'm anything other than insanely optimistic around anyone else; Joy is not entirely certain I should even *be* here—or at least she wasn't until this afternoon—and if they have any idea how terrified I am, they'll be certain I'll freeze up at the worst moment and try to send me back."

He felt his expression softening, and for once, he let it. How odd to see her looking vulnerable! It wasn't that she ever attempted to look warrior-tough, but she wore this facade of cool indifference, even when he'd been training her—when she wasn't wearing an aura of annoyed irritation. He didn't think he had *ever* seen her look so helpless, much less on the verge of tears. He held up his hand to stop her. "Of course you can," he said, with sympathy that surprised even him. "And although I did not expect to see you here, I understand what you can do that no one else can; the amount of information you must carry about in your mind is astonishing."

"Not so much that, as I know where to look for things. I can ask Elcarth to find what I need, and he can Fetch handwritten notes down here." She shook her head. "I *can't* do that from up there in Haven. It depends on being *in* a meeting and seeing a problem and knowing where to look for an answer. And telling people that there *is* an answer, right then, before they get hysterical. You have to *be* there to know what priority to put on the problem; reports don't tell you that. But nobody wants me here; they look at me and see a half-blind, clumsy liability who's likely to be in the way, or worse, need rescuing. So I have to put up a facade so they don't find another reason to send me back."

He hesitated. "As the Weaponsmaster, I am concerned that you are the person least able to defend herself here."

"Which is why I'm *petrified,*" she replied, in a very small voice. "And I want to go *home*. But I can't, and I won't, and I won't ask anyone else to look out for me."

"I never thought for a moment that you would." The tent was *so* small, he could easily reach over and pat her shoulder, which he did, awkwardly. Her face crumpled, but she didn't cry. Just as well. Women in tears unnerved him. She did put her own hand up to hold his on her shoulder, though, and he didn't mind—

:*Bollocks. You like it.*:

:*You stay out of my head,*: he said sharply. :*Or at least be quiet about being there.*:

Kantor wisely did not reply.

"Don't think I want *you* to take care of me either," she continued, even though she was shaking. "I don't! I *can* take care of myself, even if I'm not a good fighter, I won't freeze up, and *will* be sensible and be the first to run away, if the time comes to retreat!"

"I didn't think you would ask, not for a moment. As your Weaponsmaster, although I am concerned, I am certain that I have trained you well, and I trust you to be intelligent enough to do what you must." He tightened his hand on her shoulder. "But as your Weaponsmaster, you need not be brave with me. In fact, if you have concerns and feel you cannot voice them to others, do tell me. The night stalkers, for instance; that was a reasonable thing to consider."

She sighed, and some of her shaking eased. "I'm not a brave person," she said reluctantly. "Actually, I'm rather a coward. I'm afraid of so much, it's easier to say what I'm *not* afraid of. I think about what can go wrong all the time, it keeps me awake at night, and it makes me want to dig a hole and hide in it. And even if things don't go wrong, it's still going to be horrible—people dying and blood and pain—and it's one thing to read about battles, but it's something else to have one happening around you."

There were so many things he could have said—that she was right to be afraid, that she would be less afraid if she stopped thinking so constantly about all the dire possibilities—

He said none of them, for none of them seemed quite right. And after a moment, she let go of his hand and he took it back. With a touch of reluctance... which felt a bit odd.

:Because you don't know how to act around a woman who might be more than a friend, but isn't either out of bounds or a whore,: Kantor said bluntly.

Well—that was true enough. But this was no time to try and learn how. Later, perhaps, if there was a later. *And now who is dwelling on the dire possibilities?*

She took a deep breath, squared her shoulders, and turned those glittery lenses in his direction with a wan smile. "Thank you for being my friend as well as my Weaponsmaster and fellow Herald, Alberich. It helps to have someone human I can be at ease with."

He nodded. "As you help me. Think of the relief I feel, not only to drop my mask, but to have someone with whom I can speak my native tongue." He managed a wry smile. "Perhaps you can help me with my Valdemaran, so we don't have a repetition of that scene in Sendar's tent. Only Selenay understood me!"

Myste shook her head. "At least it made *her* look very competent, and gave her credit a strong boost. Poor little Selenay! I hope she can find someone to take her mask off with."

"If no one else, it will be me," he promised, reading the request for exactly what it was. Then he deemed it time for a change of subject. "Now what else have you found in those Chronicles?"

"All the routes that your people have *ever* used to come at us." She reached under her cot, and pulled out a roll which proved to be a map. "I traced them all on this."

"Very useful." The hilly, sometimes mountainous terrain along the Border only permitted so many practical routes for an invading force, and here they all were, or at least, as much about them as the Valdemarans knew, since most of Karse was unknown land to them. But *he* knew the Border, if not as well as he'd like, certainly better than anyone here, and perhaps with the help of some of the FarSeeing Heralds or the ones with Animal Mindspeech who could see through the eyes of a high-soaring hawk, he would be able to fill in the terrain on the other side a bit, and they'd know which paths and passes to watch.

"Myste, I shall be sure and let it be known that you are *monumentally* useful," he said. And was rewarded with a genuine smile. "Now I shall go and present this to Sendar so that I can do that."

"And I shall write up the next lot of notes to dispatch." She tucked her legs under the tray and pulled it toward her, and that was how he left her, head down, lamplight shining down on it, an island of peace in the midst of frantic preparations for war.

But his night was not yet over. He went to Selenay's tent, and found her toying with the remains of her dinner—a dinner which, for the most part, looked uneaten. Her two guardians were right with her, and her tent was ringed with regular Guardsmen.

He nodded with satisfaction as they challenged him, then sent one of their number to fetch someone from Selenay's bodyguards who could verify his identity. That was quite right; they should never assume that someone was who he said he was if *they* didn't know him on sight. One of the two bodyguards recognized him the moment she put her head out of the tent, of course. Only then was he allowed inside the perimeter they had established.

Selenay gladly put aside the plate at his entrance. There were several lamps suspended overhead here, which didn't matter, since the felt lining on the walls made it impossible for anyone to see silhouettes on the canvas. He noted the arrangement of the cot in the middle of the tent—now folded—with approval. "Is there any news?" she asked, her expression somber and a little pinched.

He shook his head. "That I have heard, nothing. But for you, a task I have."

She actually brightened at that. "Good. I feel as if there is something I should do, but I can't think of anything." She reached up and tucked a strand of hair self-consciously behind her ear. "I don't think there are many people besides you and father who think I should even be here."

He regarded her gravely. "Come. Among the troops, we must walk. Speak to them, you shall, this night and every night. Of their homes and families, must you ask; speak you must as your heart tells you, to put heart in them, to put a face—*your* face—on Valdemar."

"You mean, make myself some kind of mascot?" she asked, as he gestured to her guardians to take up their weapons and follow. "Create a symbol?"

"Of a sort. Speak of Valdemar, you must; not just of the evil that comes to tear her, not of fear alone, but of hope." Hope. *He* hoped she was up to this; Sendar would likely be making his own forays among the troops, but there was a limit to his time. Selenay had more of that available to her, and Selenay was a handsome young girl, golden-blond and fresh-faced, and not unlike the pretty girls the men and women wearing the uniform tabards of the Valdemaran army would see at home. He wanted to put *that* face on the abstract notion of "my land, Valdemar." He wanted them to see that their leaders served *them*, as much as they served their leaders. When they saw their leaders, remote and at a distance, he wanted them to remember the night *this* one walked and talked with them.

"But what should I say?" she asked, sounding a little desperate, as they left her tent. He motioned to the sentries to stay in place. Mounted on Companions, they were as safe as they would be in a knot of guards. Kantor waited for them; Caryo came out of her lean-to, and Alberich helped Selenay throw her saddle on her.

"Ask, first. Ask of home and family. Ask of their welfare. Then, think, and as your father would, speak." She had spent all of her life listening to her father's speeches; it was time she learned to make some of her own. In fact, there was very little she could say that would be *wrong.* Her mere presence out here with the troops, asking after their well-being and their background, would be enough. She would be showing the concern of their monarch, putting a face and a voice under the crown. And word of that would spread.

They rode down the torchlit paths between the tents at a walk, so that the two bodyguards could keep pace afoot, until they came to the first campfire of common footsoldiers. As fighters did, the world around, they had gathered around their common fire, and there was talk, some rough joking, a small cask of beer to be shared. It all stopped, when two Companions loomed up out of the darkness. It ceased altogether, when they dismounted, their officer (good man! thought Alberich) recognized Selenay and scrambled to his feet, then tried to drop to one knee. "Highness!" he stammered, as Selenay prevented him from going down by taking his elbow and keeping him erect.

"Just Selenay—ah—lieutenant?" she replied, her cheeks going pink.

"Lieutenant Chorran, Ma'am," he said, his cheeks pinker than hers, his eyes anxious under an unruly thatch of dark hair.

"Well, then, Lieutenant Chorran, would you make me known to your men?" she replied with admirable composure. If Alberich hadn't known this was her first foray out into an army camp, he would never have guessed it.

She stood, hands clasped gravely behind her back, as Lieutenant Chorran introduced her to every one of the round-eyed men encircling the fire. When he was done, she picked one at random. "So, Nort Halfden—what part of the world are *you* from?" she asked, as if his answer was something she burned to hear.

"Boarsden, Ma'am, east of Haven," he replied, looking as if he was having to concentrate to keep from tugging his strawberry-blond forelock at her.

"I know it; good grain country." She smiled at him, and he looked about to faint, yet couldn't help beaming with pride. "And perfectly *lovely* morel mushrooms in the forest in the spring."

"Aye, Ma'am!" he enthused, losing a little of his shyness. "That there be!" She gave him a nod of encouragement, and he warmed to his subject. "Why, there's a copse just by our duck pond that—"

That was all it took; he was off about his father's farm, and that led her to single out others who looked as if they were losing their awe of *her* to want to boast about their own lands. A leading question or two was all it needed; she just gave them a cue, and let them run on. This lot was all farm folk, though from differing parts of Valdemar; companies were made up of men (and women, though it would have to be a sturdy wench who was in the pikes) who came into the force at about the same time, so that they all worked through training together and got to know one another well. Alberich approved of the arrangement; it created cohesiveness.

When Selenay showed interest in their lives, their homes, and their families, they swiftly warmed to her. When she showed them that she was not that different from them, they took her to their hearts. The firelight shone on their young faces, and Alberich tried not to think about how *very* young they were, how it was certain that some of them would not be going back to those homes and families. It wrung his heart; he reminded himself that they would only be worse off if war had come to their little farms, and they had to face it all untrained.

"But what about now?" she asked finally, looking around. "Your lieutenant is obviously a fine officer—"

"The best, Ma'am!" said one stoutly, and young Chorran blushed.

She nodded with earnest satisfaction. "If there is anything you need, then I'm sure she'll see to it. But are you getting enough to eat—"

"Well, no one and nothin' is gonna fill up Koan, there—" said one fellow slyly, and the rest laughed; this was evidently a joke of long standing among them. "But barrin' that, it ain't home, here, but we're all right, Ma'am."

She looked at each earnest, friendly face in turn, and Alberich watched them watching her, intent on her. It was clear that she had it, that subtle charisma that marked her sire. She had more than their attention; she had won their loyalty.

"My father and I want you all to get home again," she said softly, as the firelight made a golden halo of her hair, giving her, had she but known it, a slightly ethereal look. "We want that more than anything. And we want you to go right on gathering mushrooms every spring, chestnuts and potan roots every fall, telling tales beside the fire every winter. But that isn't going to happen if *they* win."

Nods all around, each of them looking as if they were hearing this for the first time, even though it was hardly news to any of them.

"But we have what *they'll* never have," she continued, holding her young head high, her pride in *them* showing in every word. "*They* don't have a home and they don't want to trouble to build one for themselves; they want to steal ours. *They* don't have families, even, so Alberich says." She gestured at Alberich, who contented himself with looking somber. "And I'd feel sorry for them, I'd even invite them to come settle if they'd just *asked* us! That's what we're all about, is Valdemar—we *don't* keep people out if all they want is peace! That's the way we've always been, haven't we?"

Murmurs of assent, with a growl under it.

Good.

"But since these Tedrels don't *want* peace, don't *want* to build, and only want to steal our land and homes from us—there's only one way we can meet them," she continued, with a look of fierce pride that would have been incongruous on such a young face, but for the circumstances. "We didn't begin this war, but by all that is holy, I swear we will *end* it!"

It wasn't the best speech he'd ever heard, but it did exactly what Alberich wanted it to; it galvanized them. Partly it was Selenay's personality, partly it was that they *wanted* to find a figurehead for their cause. They cheered for her, and that was what counted; she thanked them in a way that made them cheer for her again, and when she mounted Caryo, she was glowing with enthusiasm and flushed with pleasure.

Then it was off in another direction, to another campfire, wandering in a random fashion, skipping some groups that seemed to be intent on some business or entertainment of their own, going on to others who might need her speech more. Selenay was beginning to run out of energy and wilting a little when Alberich called a halt to the visits for the night, and led her and her guardians back to her tent.

"Did I—" she asked quietly, as the encampments quieted and the fighters around them let their fires die down and sought their bedrolls.

"Well, you did," he assured her. "Very well. And tomorrow, again you will do so, and the next night, and the next. Each time, a different direction, a different set of fires. And know, all will, that their Princess cares for them, and thinks of them, and their King cares for them and his daughter sends to see they are well. So for you they will fight—"

"Not for me!" she exclaimed. "For Valdemar!"

"But Valdemar, *you* are," he countered. "A face they need, upon the idea. That face, you are."

She might have continued to voice her objections, but they had reached her tent, and he bundled her inside without standing on ceremony as soon as she had unsaddled Caryo and rubbed her down. "Sleep now," he told her. "Think and argue on the morrow."

And there he left her, too tired, really, to do more than he had told her to do. She let the tent flap fall shut behind her, Caryo ambled into the lean-to that served as her stable, and he mounted Kantor again.

:She has the spirit in her,: he told his Companion with intense satisfaction as they reached his tent, and he dismounted to free Kantor of his burden of gear. *:And she found words enough that were right to do the job.:*

:Caryo helped. But you're right. And this is something that's needed.: Kantor flicked an ear back in his direction. *:She's putting heart in them.:*

He heaved the saddle onto its stand, and hung the bridle up beside it, taking up a wisp of straw to give the Companion a quick rubdown. *:And they in her.:* That was the beauty of the thing; even as she gave them something tangible to fight for, they gave *her* confidence, and helped her to find her courage. The more courageous *she* felt, the more heart she'd put in *them. :There. That should hold you until morning.:*

The Companion gave himself a brisk shake, and walked into his own lean-to. *:You're wasted as Weaponsmaster,:* Kantor said thoughtfully, from out of the shadows under the canvas. *:You should have been a Councilor.:*

: Vkandis forbid!: he exclaimed indignantly. *:I would rather muck out stalls!:*

:There—it's a similar occupation,: countered Kantor, and his mental chuckle followed Alberich all the way to his bed.

1 6

For days, there had been nothing but drill and drill for the men, plan and replan in the commanders' tent. Every day Selenay sat at her father's side and listened, putting in a word or two that was always apt, always to the point. Every night she and Alberich and her bodyguards went out to another set of campfires, talking to another set of fighters. He tried to see to it that she had words with every sort—from the young Knights of the heavy cavalry to the archers and pikemen, from the half-wild hill folk serving as scouts to the massive brutes of the heavy foot. He had his own ears to the ground, and he was satisfied with what he heard—as he'd hoped, the men and women she spoke with *talked*, and soon it spread like wildfire across the entire army that the King and his pretty daughter were "right folk" worth fighting for, who knew their people and *cared* for their people and would be right in there slogging it out *with* their people when the day came. The mood in the army shifted imperceptibly and took on a focus. *That* was what he wanted; Selenay had helped to make it happen. Now there was a sense of the lightness of the cause, and a certainty of purpose. *Now* their leaders were not some impersonal images somewhere. The King and Heir had personalities and faces, and were well on the way to becoming "beloved."

"Beloved" was excellent; men (and presumably women too) fought fiercely for something that was "beloved." And should anything happen to Sendar, his daughter stood a fighting chance of being able to take up the reins without a pause or hesitation. Nor, should the worst happen, was there now any chance that another contender could take the throne away from her—not that any Herald would try, but he had to operate on the assumption that there could always be someone willing to attempt a coup. Certainly, the common people, the Guard, and the army would support her without a second thought, should a would-be usurper appear. He hadn't revealed *that* part of his plan to anyone, not even Kantor—though he had the feeling Kantor had guessed it and approved. As Sendar would approve, if he ever learned it himself.

Selenay, of course, would be horrified, which was why she would never hear of it.

Now he sat in Kantor's saddle, under a clear, summer sky, with dew still wet on the grass. The planning was over; it was too late now to wonder if they had overlooked anything.

For now it all came down to this: two massive armies, both rested, facing each other across firm ground. The Tedrels had taken their time getting here, and they seemed unsurprised to find the Valdemaran Guard waiting for them. "Seemed" was the operable word, since there was no way of knowing for certain if they were surprised or not; when the Tedrels began to move, Sendar ordered the spies out and back home.

(And they made it; somehow, they all made it, though not entirely intact. A couple were injured escaping, but escape they did, and the last of them had come over the Border two days ago.)

Alberich hoped that was a good omen. He could use a good omen, for he was not at all confident about this final confrontation. Of all the times to have some handle on the future, this would have been the best, for the sake of his own spirits, if nothing else—so of course, he got no inklings at all. If the Tedrels, or the Sunpriests, were blocking ForeSight, they were doing a good job of it, if he couldn't even get a *hint* of what this day would bring. All he *felt* was akin to having an enormous wave cresting a furlong above him, about to crash down on him, and the sense that nothing he could do would get him out of the way. Which was, in a figurative sense, exactly what was about to happen. He wouldn't describe the feeling as "impending doom" precisely, but it certainly was a sense that events were about to overwhelm him.

Last night, the Tedrels had camped just over the horizon; the glow of their campfires had been clearly visible from the edge of the Valdemaran camp. It had made for an uneasy night on this side of the Border. Alberich doubted that anyone had gotten very much sleep. There had been scouts of all sorts out all night, and double the usual guards—the Tedrels were not altogether predictable, and a night attack had not been out of the question. A lot of people had slept (or tried to) in their armor.

This morning, there they were, having marched into place in the predawn, deliberately arranging their ranks on the other side of the valley, quite as if they were setting up for a review or a parade, looking as if they'd shown up for an appointed meeting.

It might just as well have been an appointed meeting. Alberich had no doubt that they had known since they began moving in this direction exactly where the Valdemaran army was. There was no reason why the Tedrels should not have spies of their own, and every reason why they should. Alberich had done his best to find them, but he doubted he'd made more than a significant dent in the population.

And, when it all came down to cases, it was rather difficult to hide the movement of the entire Valdemaran army from much of anyone in a country that had as much freedom as Valdemar; the Tedrel spies had no doubt counted most of the Valdemaran troops and reported them on the move. Alberich could only hope that the Tedrels believed those troops were made up of old men and inexperienced boys and girls—basically, the last possible lot of conscripts left out of a depleted population.

Working in Valdemar's favor, of course, there weren't many options open to where the Tedrels came across the Border, given where they had made their base, deep in the hills. The fact that Valdemar had known *where* that base was, and had moved to block the only real access point right at the Border itself, might (he hoped) have come as a slight surprise.

Or not. If the Tedrels really, truly thought they had superior numbers, there was no reason why they should care where the battlefield was as long as neither side had a critical advantage.

Alberich surveyed the Tedrel nation from his place at Selenay's side, and hoped that his sinking heart didn't make itself known in his expression. They filled their side of the battlefield, from one side of the valley to the other, and there seemed no end to them. A hundred thousand? Two hundred thousand? More?

Surely not more. *Sunlord help us if it is.*

Beside him, with Selenay's silver-and-blue battle banner streaming above her, Myste sat stock-still, the mask of her lenses making it impossible to tell what she was thinking, but her skin was nearly as white as her Companion's hide. Myste had volunteered to take Selenay's banner, and Alberich had agreed, given that it was unlikely Selenay's party would see real combat—and if they did, it was because they were fighting their way to retreat.

Talamir had the King's battle banner, much larger than Selenay's; both were affixed in a socket behind the saddle and didn't need a free hand the way Karsite banners did.

It was easy to tell which were the real Tedrels and which the mere recruits. Behind those shock troops, whose mounted officers had to constantly ride their lines to keep them in their places, the *real* Tedrels had formed up, rank on rank of them, unmoving and unmoved, silent, waiting. Their armor glittered in the morning sun, each man a minute scale upon the body of some massive beast, poised to claw and rend its way to Valdemar's heart. So far away as to be just barely visible to the naked eye, fluttering above the heads of the enemy at the top of the next ridge, were the purple battle banners of the Tedrel commanders.

Alberich hoped that the King and Lord Marshal were proud of *their* fighters, who stood rock-steady in the face of so numerous a foe. Two or three moons ago, many of these young people had been following plows, sweating at a forge, or tending beasts—or hauling nets, tending shops, working at a craft. Now they stared at the enemy, knew they were about to fight for their lives against battle-tested and hardened mercenaries, and did not flinch.

There was no sign of Sunpriests. Alberich strained his eyes in every direction to be sure, but they simply weren't there, and his heart, which had sunk down into the soles of his feet, rose as far as his ankles. *Thank you, Lord Vkandis, giver of life, awful in majesty...*

"Sire?" the Lord Marshal said quietly, at Sendar's right. "Your orders?"

"This side of the valley is Valdemar; that side is Karse," said Sendar in a low but clear voice. "We will not provoke this fight. Though they have attacked us every summer for the past three years, we will not provoke them, and we will not cross the Karsite Border. If they insist on having this confrontation, they must break the peace and the Border, for we will not."

Sendar sounded completely calm, quite composed, as if he did not care whether the Tedrels came or not. Alberich glanced at Selenay's Six; all were mounted, surrounding her, the Guards on ordinary horses rather than Companions.

Well, not *quite* ordinary horses; these were the big, ugly, fighting horses out of Ashkevron Manor, trained by horse-talkers who were trained by Shin'a'in, or so it was claimed. Knights of Valdemar dreamed of being able to own a single one of these beasts in a lifetime, and Alberich had never seen more than three in all of the time he'd been in Haven, but Ashkevron Manor had sent enough of their finest to mount every one of the bodyguards that wasn't a Herald. They carried their armor, a set of hinged plates that protected vulnerable head, chest, and flank, as if it weighed no more than a bit of barding. Each of the Guards had been schooled by one of the horse-talkers in how to handle their brutes and had not just learned to ride them, but had bonded in a sense with them; the results were impressive. They were pleasant enough in corral and under saddle, but Alberich pitied the man who met them in a fight. A single touch of the knee and a shouted command, and an enemy would be pulp. And if the horses were attacked first, their attacker would be pulp *without* the signal or the command.

Those horses were much heavier than any Companion save Kantor. So the Guards (and Crathach, the Healer) were in the point position for both the King and Heir, carrying wide shields to ward off missiles coming from the front. The Companions wore lighter armor of chain and leather, probably proof against arrows, probably not against axes. Everyone was armored, even lean Jadus; everyone had a shield, even though Jadus wouldn't use one in a fight. If—no, say *when*—arrow storms fell, they'd all trained in locking those shields overhead in the formation called "the turtle," to protect Selenay and Sendar. The archers would have to be in range first, though—that was what the Heralds, used to judging their firing distance, would be watching for.

Where's their cavalry? he wondered suddenly, as he realized that the *only* mounted troops in sight were the officers commanding the front ranks. *I know they have cavalry; they've had them before. So where are they?*

No time to say anything about his sudden thought; at that moment, a far-off trumpet sounded, and with a roar, the Tedrel shock troops flowed down the side of the hill carrying with them a wall of sound, their running feet making the ground shake. In a moment, they had crossed the little stream at the bottom, and so—broke the peace, and began the war.

As they pounded toward the waiting lines, the Valdemaran front ranks braced; spearmen butting their weapons on the ground and kneeling. Behind them, the pikemen also braced their longer weapons and stood fast. And behind *them*, the archers waited, arrows to bow, for their officers to call the first volley.

"Hoi!" The call came, a little ragged, as the first line of shouting men, their running feet pounding the meadow grass flat, set foot on Valdemaran soil. The sound of a thousand bows snapping, a thousand arrows swishing into the air was like a wind, a perilous wind; the archers aimed up, so as to clear their own ranks, and not at any specific targets, for with the enemy so thick, enough arrows would hit to make a difference—

The wind went up, the deadly rain came down, and hoarse battle cries turned to screams of pain as arrows found seams in plate, or chain-mail insufficiently fitted or tended, heads without helms or helms without visors. And some men went down, and the ranks behind them stumbled over their bodies, but it wasn't enough to blunt the charge. Screams of pain joined the sound of battle cries and pounding feet.

Now Alberich entered that singular state of hyperawareness that a fight put him into; he saw *everything*, but was affected emotionally by nothing. His feelings just vanished for the moment, leaving his mind clear and his body ready to act or react. He knew he would pay for this later, when all of that suppressed emotion hit him, but for now, he tightened his hands on his weapons, and watched, and waited—and, in a terrible sense, *enjoyed*.

The noise was incredible; it battered the senses, and it had a strange effect on the mind. He knew this of old, knew that the quickening of his pulse and the sudden surge of bloodthirstiness was due to the very noises that assailed his ears. Whether any of the others were affected in the same way, he didn't know for certain, but he suspected they were, more or less. Certainly the men of his company had been, some more than others. At the first sound of battle, some of them had nearly gone mad with blood-lust—but those did not last very long. They were first into the fight, charging in with no care for themselves. "Spear catchers," was what seasoned commanders called that sort.

"Hoi!" The best archers of Valdemar were good, none better; they could, if need be, get off two more volleys while the first was hitting the enemy. Again, the whirring, as much like the sound of an immense flock of birds as a wind, again the death-dealing rain rattled down—and still they fell, and still they came. Behind the ranks of charging men *their* archers walked in, slowly, and now it was *their* turn to come into play.

The spearmen and pikemen were protected by their armor and helms and stood fast; the Valdemaran archers dropped back beneath shields on orders from their officers, and the first of the Tedrel troops hit the line of spears and pikes with a shock.

The avalanche of sound as the two lines met was indescribable, and even Alberich winced. Screaming, shouting, the clash of weapon on weapon; there was nothing as dreadful as the sound of army meeting army. Some of the Tedrel fighters ran right up on the spears like maddened boars, screeching as they died; the rest hacked at the shafts with heavy broadswords and axes, shouting furiously, while more pikemen came up from the rear to take the place of those who'd lost their weapons.

A rain of Tedrel arrows fell on the pikemen and the archers behind them, but the pikemen had good armor and helms meant to defend against arrows, and the archers were under their shields. And the moment the hail of arrows stopped, the archers popped out from under cover and let fly a volley of their own. This volley fell on the Tedrel archers, who were lightly armored and not as fast as their Valdemaran counterparts. This time, the hail of arrows took a higher toll; more screaming, and louder now.

Men of both sides fell and died, or fell wounded, crying out in agony. The innocent little rill that marked the Border went from muddy to bloody.

Though Sendar watched it all, it would be up to the Lord Marshal to issue orders. Wise man, was Sendar; he knew he was no more than a fraction of the strategist under actual battle conditions that his underlings were. The Lord Marshal had faced these troops in his own person for the past three years, while Sendar had only gotten his reports. The Lord Marshal had the direct experience of the battlefield that the King did not, and Sendar knew it.

And at the moment, as the sun climbed into the sky and then reached its zenith, the Lord Marshal was looking for something, peering down at the battlefield with a frown on his heavily-bearded face.

"The cavalry," Alberich heard him saying, as if he was thinking aloud. "Where are their *cavalry?*"

And in the same moment, he turned to his Herald, and there was urgency in his voice. Alberich felt both relief that the Lord Marshal had noted the same thing *he* had, and a heart-sinking moment of dread. "Mindspeak the flanks," the Lord Marshal ordered, "and ask the ones with the birds. Find out if the cavalry is behind their lines, still, or if they're trying to get us in a pincer."

Alberich strained to hear the answer, which came within the instant. "No and no, my Lord," the Herald replied. "There is no sign of mounted troops of any sort."

Now Sendar turned his head to fix the Lord Marshal with a look of surprise. "Then where *are* they?" he demanded. "Surely they haven't put all of their mounted troops afoot!"

The hair on the back of Alberich's neck stood up, and he got a sick feeling in the pit of his stomach. It traveled rapidly over his entire body, and at that moment, he *knew* his Gift hadn't deserted him. In fact, it was about to come down upon him with a vengeance. He slid down out of his saddle as dizziness engulfed him, so that he wouldn't have as far to fall when it hit him—which it was going to, in less than a heartbeat—

He clutched Kantor's saddle, as his Companion turned his head to look at him. A flash of blue came between him and the rest of the world—

A woman, barefoot, bareheaded, running, but she couldn't outrun the horseman behind her—

Another flash—

A man, looking up from his weeding, eyes wide, then unseeing, as the lance took him through the heart—

—like blue lightning—

Children, screaming, being herded into a pen by a dozen horsemen, while the rest set fire to the village—

"Sunlord save us—" he muttered in Karsite, automatically reverting to the language he knew best. The visions, thank the God, were silent, silent, and he could still hear, dimly, the sounds of the battlefield and the people around him.

"What?" Myste snapped behind him, in the same tongue. Thank the God she did—he wasn't sure he could even understand Valdemaran at this moment, much less respond in it. The visions shook him like a terrier with a rat.

The visions caught him up again and threatened to pull him in so far he would not be able to tell the others what he Saw; he struggled against them, against a Gift that was running away with him. *:Kantor!:* he cried, and a steadying presence held him out of the chaos of a hundred, a thousand disasters playing out at once inside his head. He could still *see* them, but at least he could manage to get a few words out.

"The cavalry has flanked us on either side, but not to attack *us*," he babbled in Karsite, thanking Vkandis yet again that Myste was there. Myste, who knew Karsite, who could tell the King, tell the Lord Marshal—"They're clearing the countryside—burning the villages, killing the adults, rounding up the children—"

He knew why, but he didn't have time to explain; the visions took him again, despite all of Kantor's help. *A man pinned to the door of his own house by a spear. A child being wrenched from its mother's arms, and the woman tossed into the flames of her burning barn. The Tedrel cavalry, riding across the land like a wave of locusts, clearing it for its new masters, keeping only the young children, whom they would then take into their own ranks and turn into Tedrels—*

He struggled to speak, but his throat and mouth were not his own, not now while the visions held him. He knew dimly that he had gone rigid as a plank, jaw clenched, unable even to whimper.

Fire. Murder. Fear. Death. It went on forever. He was the helpless observer, unable to do anything save—sometimes, in brief moments when the visions released him—babble a report of what he saw, and *where* it was. Names came to him, the names of villages? Villages that were not going to exist shortly—but he called them out anyway. How much was *now* and how much *soon?* How many places were far enough distant that help *might* come in time?

He was engulfed in a sea of horror, until, without warning, the visions let go of him entirely, and he dropped back into his own time and place.

Head swimming, he looked up through streaming eyes to find that he was clinging with both hands to Kantor's stirrup and the pommel of the saddle, that he had buried his face in Kantor's shoulder.

Sendar and the Lord Marshal were arguing at the tops of their lungs, while Selenay's gaze switched from one to the other. *Her* face was white and pinched, and her hands in their armored gauntlets shook.

"But then, we'll *have* no reserves!" the Lord Marshal shouted.

"And what good will reserves do us if every creature older than a child on this side of the Border is dead?" Sendar shouted back. He whirled and turned to Talamir. "This is a royal command, King's Own. You *heard* where the attackers are, now deploy the reserves and every Herald not in combat to the rescue!"

Talamir bowed his head and closed his eyes for a moment, while Taver stood as steady as a statue. "Done, Majesty," the Herald said in a perfectly calm and slightly distant voice. "But you do realize that this will leave us seriously outnumbered on this field?"

Alberich was aware of movement, massive movement, behind them. The reserve troops were moving out, to the right and the left, the cavalry first. Ahead of them, on the swiftest steeds of all, two wings of Heralds, already speeding out of sight over the crest of the ridge, like a flock of swift, white birds. Behind them, the troops pulled out, leaving their rear unprotected.

"Of course I realize it," Sendar growled; and drew his sword, with a bright metallic *scrape.* It glittered wickedly in the sun, matching the hard gleam in the King's eyes. "We need to end this—*now.* Or we won't have a country left when we win the war." There was something wild in the King's eyes that Alberich recognized; something he had felt himself, down in the taverns of Haven...

That feral look matched the savageness that *he* felt, when he let himself work out his frustration on the bodies of those two-legged beasts that populated Haven's criminal underground.

But he was only one Karsite Herald, and replaceable—not easily, perhaps, but replaceable. He could—marginally—rationalize risking himself. *This* was the King of Valdemar.

He's not—Alberich thought with sudden terror.

:He is!: said Kantor, grimly.

No—Sendar couldn't—Someone had to *stop* him!

And as Alberich struggled to pull himself up, the Companion gave a kind of twist and a shove with his nose just under Alberich's rump. That got Alberich most of the way into the saddle, and a gut-wrenching effort of arms and legs got him seated securely enough to turn and try to stop Sendar before he could move—

But the King was already gone, halfway down the hill, though Alberich had no idea how he could have gotten that far in so short a time.

Too late—He could do nothing for Sendar. But *Sendar* was Talamir's responsibility. Alberich had another.

"*Stay here!*" he roared to Selenay and her bodyguards, who were only just starting to react. The King's Six had—*Vkandis be thanked*—acted in concert with the King. They must have realized the moment he drew his blade what he intended to do; they rode with him, knee and knee, with Talamir at Sendar's right and Jadus at his left, a flying wedge that penetrated the ranks of those between them and the struggling front lines. A roar went up as the King, his banner bearer, and his escort of Heralds and Guards (and Healer!) entered the zone of fighting.

Alberich and Myste imposed themselves as a barrier between Selenay and the path to her father's side; the rest of her escort crowded in, hemming her and Caryo in among them. "Stay *here!*" he bellowed at her, trying to get her attention. "Selenay! Heed me!"

She had no intention of doing any such thing. He could see it in her eyes, wild with fear and grief beneath her light helm. She hit out at them with mailed fists, flailing at them as she sobbed and cursed; she sawed at Caryo's reins, she even tried to fling herself off Caryo's back and follow on foot. But there were no divided loyalties among those who were protecting *her*. However suicidal Sendar's action might be, however much their hearts and minds cried out to follow him and protect him, their *duty* was with Selenay. To keep her safe. And if there was one thing that a Herald understood—or a Guardsman—

—*or the Sunsguard*—

—it was duty.

She wept and fought their restraining hands; she hit and screeched at them, with the background of the chaos of battle nearly drowning out her screams. She actually caught Alberich a glancing blow across his chin, and Herald Keren a direct hit that would leave her with a black eye soon. She called them cowards, traitors, and worse. She ordered them to let her go, pleaded with them, threatened them with imprisonment, whipping, death. He paid no attention to what she said, not because she didn't mean it, because of course, she *did*, but because it was irrelevant. No matter how much she cursed them now or hated them later, they *would* keep her here, out of the fighting.

Satisfied that her bodyguards had her pinned, if not under control, he edged Kantor out of the tangle and let Myste take his place. The danger to *her* was not less with Sendar down on the battlefield. If anything, it was greater.

He pulled his own sword and stood lone guardian for a moment over the group, his eyes raking over the hilltop, looking for help. He was in luck; there were still a few of the Royal Guard who stood hesitantly nearby, milling a little in confusion. *They* were not mounted, not swift enough to follow Sendar on his headlong plunge toward the fighting-zone; they were torn between trying to battle their way toward him and staying to guard the Heir. Alberich solved their hesitation for them.

"To Selenay!" he roared at them; given clear orders, they gratefully obeyed, and made a second line of defense in a half-circle around her, weapons at the ready, a line of four archers kneeling in front of another five swordsmen.

He turned back to the group around Selenay; she was still in danger, if the enemy archers took it into their heads to shoot. Perhaps only the fact that the Tedrel commanders wanted her alive had kept them safe so far, for they were the *only* members of the command group still on the ridge. Everyone else, the Lord Marshal included, had followed Sendar. He wanted to look—but Selenay's safety came first.

"Get her *down!*" he shouted, "On the *ground!*" and enforced his order with Mindspeech. No telling which of them would hear—but the Companions would. *Caryo* would. *"On the ground, unhorsed, get her down! Form the turtle!"*

The others fell back a little, as Myste half-lunged and half-fell off her Companion, taking Selenay and the banner with her, while Caryo helped by giving a buck and a twist to dislodge her rider. Myste and Selenay disappeared as Keren and Ylsa spilled off their mounts and formed the turtle over them with their shields. The Guardswomen looked uncertain for a moment. "You four, ahorse stay—help me!" he shouted at them, and they stayed mounted. *:Kantor, I want the Companions and us between the enemy and Selenay, but behind the Royal Guard. Make a circle.:*

:Right.: The Companions, now without riders, made a square of their bodies around the turtle. "Yourselves space out," Alberich ordered. "Bunch not, but knee to flank go—Companion, Guard, Companion."

Garbled and heavily accented as his words were, they evidently figured out what he wanted; with riderless Companions between them, they wedged themselves into the circle, facing outward. Under the turtle of shields, there was still a lot of movement and raised voices, but nothing was coming out, so Alberich dismissed the struggle from his mind.

He looked sharply toward the battlefield; in the middle of the fighting, where it was at its most heated, the King's banner still waved. But— but *their* lines were now on the verge of the little stream, not behind it. Sendar's charge had carried the entire line of battle forward; insane as the move had been, it looked as if it might have had the desired effect.

He saw the faint movement above the heads of the milling fighters on the other side of the stream, behind the Tedrel lines, and acted on instinct.

"Shields up!" he shouted, and put his over his head as example. The others did the same.

Just in time; arrows clattered down on them, force in no-wise spent by their long journey. The movement he'd seen *had* been the arrows arcing up to clear the battle lines from the Tedrel side.

The arrows fell harmlessly, thanks to his instincts; the shields, their armor, their mounts' armor, kept anyone from being hurt, and under the turtle, Selenay was completely safe. It sounded like being caught in a terrible hailstorm, however, and the first volley was followed within a moment by a second, a third—

:She's stopped fighting. I think the arrows have scared her.: said Kantor.

Good. One less thing to worry about.

"The turtle stay under! Shields up!" he ordered, as another rain of arrows clattered onto the upheld shields. He did not look behind him to see if he was being obeyed; he knew that even if Selenay rebelled, the Heralds would make sure she stayed put. Myste would sit on her to make certain of that.

An unfamiliar mind-voice touched his inward "ear." *:For once being clumsy paid off; if I'd tried to hang onto her and pull her onto my saddle, she'd* *probably have gotten away from me, but she couldn't do anything about my falling off with her.:*

:Myste?: He was astonished. She'd never tried to Mindspeak to him before.

:Don't worry, she can't get away from me now; I outweigh her by quite a bit. She might be a little squashed, but she can't get me off of her.: Although he was nothing like an Empath, he was astonished by the complex emotional overtones that came with her words. Amusement at her own expense, pain, anger, grief, frantic worry for herself, more worry about Selenay and Sendar, and over all, terror held rigidly in check. And yet, her thoughts were so clear, he could hardly believe it. *:Even if they get this far, they'll have to get through me to touch her, and there's a lot of me to act as a shield.:*

He didn't ask if she was all right; she wasn't, none of them were. *:Are you hurt?:*

:My lenses are broken, and I think I broke my ankle, but that's the least of our worries. Don't call anyone, and don't try and get me out of here for now. I won't be moving anyway until this is over, or unless you have to haul her out of here and run for it. Promise me, though, if that happens, make sure I get back in my saddle? I'm curious about these Tedrels, but not that curious.:

:You have my word.: He wanted to try and summon a Healer for her, for she must be in excruciating pain, but she was right, and with luck her armored boot would hold her ankle well enough in place that no further damage would occur until they had the luxury of worrying about it. Given the kinds of terrible wounds being inflicted out there in the zone of fighting, a broken ankle counted as "minor." There was no doubt that Myste *knew* what the right answers were, and was giving them, even though she probably was howling inside with terror and the "right" answers were the last thing she wanted to supply.

Probably? Given the level of terror and pain he sensed, she was howling deep in her own heart, all right. Years ago, when she refused to learn weapons' work, this was the *last* thing he would have expected out of Trainee Myste.

And in that, he had done her a tremendous disservice…

And I'll make it up if we live.

He turned his attention back to the battlefield, and for the first time, felt his heart rise, just a little.

The tide of battle was turning.

Sendar's charge had paid off in unexpected ways. The Tedrels had given up whatever battle plan they'd originally had, and were concentrating on trying to take him down. This had the effect of concentrating all of their attention on the center of the line, and gathering in fighters from the rest of the field as they *all* tried to be the one to take the King. Those who had been hired or recruited were the worst, for their motive was profit, not the gain of a new homeland. Even if the true Tedrel commanders had not put a price on King Sendar's head, these men would *think* there was, and anticipate a golden reward for killing him.

In the meantime, pulling away toward the center meant that the Valdemaran forces were able to draw in to enclose the Tedrels on three sides. The thick press of Tedrels toward the King gave the Valdemaran archers somewhere to aim for, and they were taking advantage of that— those that were not already aiming for the *Tedrel* archers.

When the enemy is in range, so are you... And there was only so much room in the King's immediate vicinity. The vast majority of those struggling to get at him could not actually fight *anyone* because of the press of their fellow fighters; they were tied up without being of any use. But the long Valdemaran pikes could reach *them*, and so could the spearmen, the archers, and the warhammers.

The sight of their King in danger was enough to put extra strength in the arms of Valdemaran fighters. The sight of the King within reach had drawn the Tedrel leaders down off *their* hill.

And when you are in range, so is the enemy!

The Lord Marshal was in the thick of the fighting, and so was Talamir; there was no one to ask permission of.

He hesitated. But only for a moment.

To the Hells with permission. I'll apologize later.

:Are there any Heralds with bows and *the Fetching Gift left here?:* he asked Kantor, with an idea so impossible, it just might be able to work.

:Ah—: Kantor paused; it was going to take a lot longer for Companion to speak to Companion in all of this mess. And he didn't want to distract anyone who was right in the middle of the melee either. He waited, watching the line of fighting swaying, slowly, like a sluggish snake. Retreating a little *there*, bulging a little *there*—

:Four. And they've pulled out of combat for the moment.:

:Have them shoot for the Tedrel commanders, and put Fetching Gift behind it.: Whether they could even *do* that, he had no idea, but if they could, it would be something no Sunpriest would think of guarding against, if it even *could* be guarded against.

If there are any Sunpriests still helping them. He had to wonder, in the back of his mind, if the reason his Gift had suddenly broken through was because the Karsite Sunpriests had abandoned their erstwhile allies as soon as the Tedrels were fully occupied with Valdemar…

He hoped so. If the priests decided to mix in with this, it would make things so much worse.

At this distance, he couldn't see anything other than the dark purple blot under the purple Tedrel battle banners; he couldn't make out individual arrows, and he *wouldn't* see anyone fall if they were hit, so he didn't even trouble to try to watch for it. He would know if anything happened by the tide of battle. *:If there are any Animal Mindspeakers still here, ask if they can spook the Tedrel horses.:* One more bit of damage; the officers were all ahorse, and even if his arrow trick didn't work, if he could drive them off, there would be less control on the battlefield.

He didn't want to interfere any more; the rest of the Heralds were the only way the various parts of the Valdemaran Army had to communicate with one another. Things were falling apart on their side badly enough as it was.

Instead, he kept his shield above his head, although there were no more hails of arrows. The Valdemaran archers were doing that much, forcing the Tedrel archers to duck under cover, or even into a full retreat. And he kept Kantor turning in a slow circle, watching not only to the front, but to the rear and the sides, looking for a suicidal charge into *their* ranks, assuming that there could still be an attempt to capture or kill Selenay. Of course, the Tedrels might not realize Selenay was still here; her battle banner was on the ground, dropped when Myste lunged for her, and the only white uniform on this hilltop was Alberich's.

All the more reason to keep the four of them on the ground.

Then it came—

A flash of blue.

On the left; attackers, fresh, unwounded, and seasoned, hidden in a ditch full of bushes and about to emerge.

It wasn't *much* warning, but it was enough; he turned to the left, spotted movement and shouted, pointing with his sword to get the attention of Selenay's guards.

And they just popped up out of nowhere, a band of twenty, thirty—forty?—more?—suddenly *materializing* as if conjured—but they hadn't been, of course; they'd found cover and slipped through the lines, avoiding detection by avoiding fighting. It was a trick he'd used himself, and so had the bandits he'd fought.

And now, at last, he had something he could vent his own anger and fear against.

His blood pounding in his ears, he howled a curse at them; Kantor didn't need the touch of a heel. Kantor was just as eager for blood as *he* was. What Sendar could do, *he* could do, and for as good a cause—keeping Selenay safe.

Buying some time for her guards to react.

Before the Guardsmen on foot could rearrange their line of defense to meet the attackers, *he* was racing toward the ambushers. Not so far to go, after all; ten of Kantor's long strides at most before he crashed into the first knot of them.

Lightly armored, of course, *much* more lightly than he, to facilitate slipping through cover.

First mistake.

He got a brief glimpse of a swarthy face beneath a light cap helm—a true Tedrel, then. This *was* a group sent to capture the Heir. He swung his blade at the same time as he got that glimpse of *target,* and he felt the shock of his sword meeting flesh as he slashed across the line of the eyes. The man fell; Kantor made a ferret-quick turn to trample him. Then he and Kantor were among them, and for the first time, he learned what it was like to fight with a Companion as a partner.

He gave himself up to it. In fact, he gave himself up *totally* to it, to the terrible joy of killing, for the first time in his life. He would probably be sick later, but now—

Now, these beasts, these fiends, were here to murder his friends, his brothers and sisters, to enslave his country. They were going to take or murder that sweet, cheerful girl he'd come to admire so much, who was so very old for her few years, and yet so charmingly young. They, and others like them, were killing innocent, ordinary farmers like those boys and girls he and Selenay had met around the fires, old men like Dethor and women like Myste, mothers like his—

Now he and Kantor would kill *them.*

He felt Kantor's rage along with his own; Kantor reveled in. the shock that traveled up his arm with every good blow—he rejoiced in the impact of Kantor's hooves on flesh. They moved as one in an awful and glorious dance of death, as Kantor's white hide and his white uniform and armor were spattered, splattered, drenched in red, as red blood ran down his sword arm and soaked into Kantor's legs. Kantor danced on bodies that *crunched* and screamed; he reared and kicked, hooves connecting with heads and bodies, before and behind. They were surrounded; Alberich didn't care. *Let* them waste their force on him! *He* was expendable; Selenay was not.

He used his shield as a weapon as well as protection, the heavy metal frame as a club.

And his sword made short work of those too-light cap helms, when he struck them at all. Mostly he went for the faces—the eyes, those dark and fierce eyes that held no pity and no remorse, only a flicker of terror when the blade came at them. He reveled in the terror. He wanted more of it.

He howled in protest when they slashed at Kantor's rump; Kantor screamed in rage as they cut through his armor into his leg.

They fought as he had never before fought in his life, without effort, with endless strength and energy, and in a white heat of rage that slowed time and sped his reactions.

And still they fought—and continued to fight—

The briefest possible flicker of blue hazed his vision for a moment, but not even his Gift could conquer *this* unbridled rage.

But something was going to happen—

Something *awful* was going to happen—Then a sickening blow to the soul—

—that should have sent him to his knees—

—told them both that Sendar—

—Sendar, his patron—Sendar, his King—

For a moment, just a moment, *he* leaped skyward, out of his body, and found himself looking down on the field of battle where tiny creatures fought and died. There *he* was, the sole target of a circle of Tedrel elite, who had forgotten their primary mission in the face of *his* attack. He continued to fight like a night-fiend, despite the fact that *he* wasn't "there" anymore.

Another blow, nauseating and disorienting, struck him; his attention snapped to the battle line.

Sendar was cut off from the rest of the Valdemaran forces, with only his bodyguards for protection. *He* fought like a demon, and so did they, but even as Alberich realized what peril they were in, three of the bodyguards went down, leaving only Crathach, Jadus, and Talamir to fight with him. There was a blur of motion just *under* the noses of the Companions. A shriek of pain that came from the soul of Taver as well as the body, and Taver flung up his head.

Then a burly hulk with an ax swung at Talamir.

No—*not* at Talamir—at Taver! At the exposed neck—

—of the King's Own Companion—

Nothing could have survived that blow to the neck, no matter how heavily armored. Taver went down, blood gushing from the severed throat, neck snapped, Talamir with him, leaving the King's right flank open.

No!

Alberich howled in protest, uselessly, silently—but suddenly Jadus was there, between the King and the axman, and the ax came down—

This time, not across a Companion's neck, but across Jadus' leg. The Companion, reacting to his Chosen's agony, shied sideways, leaving Sendar unprotected.

As if in a nightmare where time slowed to a crawl, yet nothing could be done to stop what was happening, Alberich saw a hundred fighters moving at the same time. Saw the mob close in, like a pack of rabid dogs, shoving Crathach into Sendar's side, hemming in the horse and Companion so that neither could move.

Watched as too many weapons to count pierced first Sendar's Companion, then Sendar.

Flicker of blue—and a wave of sickening horror *smashed* him back into his body. But he knew what he had seen was real.

Sendar, the King of Valdemar—

—was dead.

That was when a shriek of berserk rage tore the throat of every man and woman in the army, and sent them against their foes in a killing frenzy such as no Valdemaran had experienced in three centuries or more. He and Kantor rode that wave of bitter, mindless hatred, rode it and used it and let it use them, until it ran out—

—and the foes ran out—

—and left them, like every other surviving fighter on the Valdemar side, exhausted and sickened; blinking at the carnage around them, peering at death through eyes that streamed with agonized tears, in grief and mourning that would never entirely be healed.

1 7

The taste of blood was in his mouth; the sweet-sickly stench of it in his throat. His nostrils felt choked with it.

He thought, vaguely, that he *should* be on his knees, throwing up what little there was in his stomach. But instead, all he could feel was grief and numbness.

:Selenay——: prompted Kantor, with unutterable weariness, turning his head in the direction of the Heir.

No, not the Heir, he reminded himself, with a stabbing sensation in his heart. *The Queen.*

He wiped blood and sweat away from his eyes, and peered through a haze of exhaustion toward her circle of protection. He hadn't prevented all of the Tedrels from getting to her and her guardians, after all—just a great many of them. Another clot of bodies marked where the Royal Guardsmen and her bodyguards had taken care of the ones that had gotten by him. Four of the Royal Guardsmen were dead, the rest wounded, two of the four mounted bodyguards were down.

Kantor stumbled to them; he half fell out of the saddle. His leg slash and half a dozen other wounds burned with a fire of their own, but he knew from the way they felt that though they hurt like demons were poking him, they were relatively minor. He wasn't going to bleed to death any time soon, and his injuries weren't going to incapacitate him. Therefore, as he had countless times when he was injured, he would carry on, if need be, until he dropped.

Berda and Locasti were on the ground with their greathearted horses standing over them like guard dogs. Locasti sat up just as he got there, holding her head in both hands; a dented helm told him what had happened to her. It was a *good* helm, that, double-walled, with extra space between the inner and outer wall on the top of the head—a helm inside a helm, so to speak. Good job it was built that well; it had saved her from a cracked skull or worse.

Berda rolled over on her side, moaning, and Lotte slid down off her mount to help her; blood spewed from the knee joint of her armor. But she was still alive, and Lotte was down beside her, tearing off the thigh armor to get a belt around the leg even as he reached them. Lotte had a slash of her own down her arm that she didn't seem to notice—or else she didn't care, knowing that it was minor compared to that leg wound.

She's going to lose that leg, he thought dispassionately, looking at the joint laid half-open. *Better that than her life. Much better that than losing Selenay...*

:They're telling me all over the field that what's left of the Tedrels are routed,: said Myste into his mind, with a deceptive calm that overlaid hysteria. *:The others are telling me that they're disengaging and scattering to the four winds. And our reserves have caught up with their cavalry and they're cutting them to finely-chopped bits. I think we can get up now.:*

That was when he realized that she was Mindspeaking Keren and Ylsa—and the Companions—as well as himself. The Companions spread out, and the little armored shell at the heart of their circle opened up.

"Your guard drop not," he croaked, as Keren and Ylsa stood up, Ylsa hauling a weeping Selenay up by main force. Myste stayed where she was.

"We don't intend to," Keren said grimly, and put her back to Selenay, shield up, facing out.

Alberich dropped heavily to one knee before the Queen, who stared at him without comprehension, her face contorted with grief, tears pouring down her cheeks. Perhaps it was without recognition as well; his Whites were saturated with drying blood, the white leather-and-plate armor over it blood-streaked and crusting. He must look like something out of a nightmare.

"Majesty," he said in a harsh voice from a throat made raw with screaming. "To your people, you must show yourself. *Now.* Your banner must fly. Know they have a Queen, they must."

He really, truly didn't expect her to understand him. He didn't think she would even *hear* him, much less realize what he had just said.

But as Ylsa's armored hand fell on her shoulder in a gesture as much of comfort as a hand in a gauntlet could convey, he watched sense come into her eyes, watched with awe and wonder as she somehow—out of what reserves, he could not even begin to imagine—pulled herself together. She pulled off her gauntlet and wiped her streaming eyes with the back of her hand, then straightened. "You're right, of course," she said, in a flat voice. "Myste?"

"Working on it." He saw that Myste had hauled herself to her feet—
—no, *foot*, for the other one was held clear off the ground—

—and her Companion was lying down on the ground so she could get into the saddle. She did so with a grunt of pain, leaned over and picked up the bloody, muddy battle banner by a corner of the fabric. Her Companion heaved herself to her feet, rider and all, and Myste manhandled the banner back into its socket. In the next moment, Selenay mounted Caryo, and pulled off her helm so that her golden hair shone in the westering sunlight.

:Heralds of Valdemar—: Myste Mindcalled, the voice echoing painfully in Alberich's skull. That was a *strong* Mindcall. *:Behold your Queen.:*

"Alert remain!" Alberich growled to the remaining bodyguards, and dragged himself back up into the saddle, though a gray film of exhaustion seemed to fog everything.

He made a trumpet of his hands, and shouted what Myste had called out to those with Mindspeech. He was used to bellowing battlefield orders—he put every bit of that into his shout.

"Valdemar! Behold your Queen!"

From that vantage, he watched as slowly, slowly, heads turned toward them, in a wave of motion starting from those nearest the group on the hill until it reached even to where there were knots of fighting still going on.

Myste was right, though; from where he sat, there was more fleeing than fighting, and as combat broke off, those who could still move took advantage of the momentary distraction of their opponents to escape.

There was still a pool of purple between the Valdemaran lines and the hilltop, but it wasn't moving, and the battle banners were nowhere to be seen. Could the Tedrel High Command actually be *dead?*

:I think so—: Kantor told him, after a moment. *:Yes. Your idea worked. The Fetching-Heralds did it, when Sendar died.:*

He winced; for a moment he had difficulty breathing. *If only they could have done it before—*

So many "if onlys." Never had a victory felt so much like a defeat.

:The Lord Marshal?: he asked Kantor.

:Coming.:

A strange silence fell over the battlefield; the sunlight glittered on helms, but there wasn't a single raised sword or spearpoint to be seen. The pressure of thousands of eyes was a palpable force that even Alberich, in his exhaustion, felt.

Then it began, weakly at first, but gathering strength, a sound—
—a cheer—

Wordless, inarticulate, torn from the throats of exhausted men and women, grew and grew from a thread to a river, from a river to a torrent, to a wall of sound that surrounded them.

'They came, walking, then running, sometimes dropping weapons, but all, all cheering; some weeping while they cheered, but all of them saluting her, their Queen—Valdemar incarnate.

And when they reached her, they reached for her, hands outstretched to touch her, touch Caryo, assure themselves that she *was* alive, was real. She reached out to them, touching hands, faces, and as each one of them got that assurance, he made way so that others could discover for themselves that their hope still lived.

Caryo began to move forward, one slow and infinitely careful step at a time, taking her through the sea of upturned faces and reaching hands. Alberich and her remaining four bodyguards followed, though what they could do in this press of bodies if anything happened—

:Let anyone so much as breathe harm on her and the army will tear him to pieces,: Kantor said. *:She's safer now than she has ever been.:*

The Lord Marshal's horse swam through the river of humanity to meet them, and Alberich was immensely grateful to see him. Alberich knew *nothing* of Courts and politics, and without missing a beat, he and Kantor dropped back to ride just behind and to her right, as the Lord Marshal took the place on her left. He wasn't sure where they were going, except farther into the battlefield, until they got there—and he was having enough trouble staying alert and concentrating on Selenay's back to think about it.

It was slow going, wading through that surging sea of humanity. It must have taken at least a candlemark to get from where they'd been to where they were going. And by that time, the handful of men and women who had not been pressing toward the young Queen had accomplished a great deal...

They passed through a protective ring of Guardsmen into a clear space; the men working there among the fallen stopped what they were doing and respectfully dropped to their knees. There was another pile of Tedrel bodies laid to one side—a very large pile. The bodies of several Guardsmen had been laid out respectfully in a neat row, their weapons in their dead hands clasped on their chests. And the blood-drenched, white bodies of two Companions—*Idiot. Of course she'd come here first.*

Selenay slid from Caryo's back to kneel at her dead father's side.

They'd already laid him on a stretcher, with his banner draped as a pall across his body. She pulled the fabric down to reveal his face.

Alberich couldn't watch; he felt as if he was intruding on what should have been a private moment. He wondered if she hated him for keeping her away from her father's side; if she would ever forgive him for keeping her "safe" at the moment. But as he turned away, he caught sight of Healer Crathach sitting on the churned-up, bloody ground with Talamir's head in his lap, both hands resting on the Herald's forehead.

Kantor stepped carefully to the side, to stand over them. Crathach looked up as if he had felt Alberich's gaze on him. His eyes were haunted, but fierce.

"He wants to die," Crathach said, in a low voice, hoarse with shouting, screaming, and weeping. "He wants to follow Taver. But I won't let him, not now. Selenay needs him. We can't afford an untrained Queen's Own, not now; she needs someone with every bit of international, Court, and political experience possible."

"Hold to him, then," Alberich agreed. "Jadus?"

"They've already taken him to the Healers' tent. There's nothing left of his leg to save, but he'll live." Crathach growled. "Bloody hell. Those bastards knew *exactly* what to do at the worst possible time. We were holding our own until they got us too crowded together for the hooves to come into play, then sent a man in to hamstring the Companions."

Alberich bit back an oath. No wonder the two Companions had gone down so easily! And no wonder Sendar had faltered just long enough for the fatal blow to fall. "Stand fast, can you?" he asked.

"As long as I have to—the new Grove-Born should be coming as fast as he can; I just have to hold until he comes." What he was saying made no sense to Alberich's weary mind, but it was too much to try and think about. Jadus and Talamir were going to live; that was all that counted. A pair of stretcher carriers came up, then, and Crathach let them take Talamir up, though he kept one hand on the Herald's head the whole time. They carried the Herald away, with Crathach, as it were, attached.

Alberich found himself swaying in the saddle, and dragged his attention back to Selenay. She had drawn the fabric over her father's face again, and now she stood up.

"Gently bear him away, and prepare him for his journey," was all she said, but there was a rush of volunteers, most of them still weeping, and when the stretcher was picked up there was not a finger's width of it that did not have an eager hand supporting it.

As the body was taken through the crowd, men fell silent, removing their helms and standing with heads bowed until it had passed them. Selenay stood looking after it, with the last scarlet rays of the sun turning her golden hair to a red-gold crown.

Then she mounted Caryo again, summoned Alberich and the Lord Marshal with a glance, and rode from the silent field back to the encampment. For a moment, a curtain of gray haze came between Alberich and the world; it cleared up in the next heartbeat, but it was a sign he couldn't ignore.

Alberich signaled Kantor to drop back a pace, putting him even with Ylsa. "You and Keren—" he began.

"We've already figured *you're* in no shape to protect anything," the rangy Herald told him bluntly. "We're on it. And what's more, the minute she dismisses you, there'll be a Healer waiting to take *you* off."

"Ah—my thanks," he managed. Let them decide for themselves what he was thanking them for. He urged Kantor up again. They passed through the camp, and as they did, it was through another corridor of battered fighters. Some wanted to touch her or Caryo, some just saluted her respectfully. Some murmured things like "The Gods bless you, Majesty," and others gazed in worshipful silence. A tiny shard of Alberich's mind that was still able to think was both pleased and sorrowful at these demonstrations. Pleased, because his work with her among the fighters had born such fruit—and full of remorse because the harvest had been gathered too soon.

They moved now through a blue haze of twilight; he was grateful, for it cloaked the injuries, hid the wounds of men and beasts in soft shadows from which the color had been leeched. And he was grateful, too, for the fact that he needed only to sit Kantor's saddle for the moment. He wasn't certain he was up to much else. When they reached the command tent, she paused, and did not dismount as he had expected she would. Instead she turned Caryo so that they faced the crowd of quiet men and women who had followed her.

Someone brought torches and stood to either side of her, so that she was clearly illuminated. Her young face looked years older than it had this morning; her cheeks smudged and armor and surcoat dirtied from the struggle to escape from Myste, Keren, and Ylsa. And still she looked, he thought, every inch a Queen. "We have fought a terrible foe today, and we have won," she said to all of them, her voice carrying across the stillness. "And it has been at a cost that none of us would willingly have paid. I do not speak of the loss of my—my father only; I do not speak of your gallant friends and comrades only. But many, if not all of you, know that our battle plans changed without warning, and that King Sendar made a strange and some might say, suicidal charge toward the enemy that ended in his death and that of many, many others. There was a reason for that, and I believe that you should all hear *why* my father acted as he did today."

She told them all then what had happened up there on the hillside; why Sendar had sent away the reinforcements, and why he had subsequently made of himself such tempting bait that the main Tedrel army threw away their own plans and strategy, and were lured into defeat. All this was new to those straining to catch her every word—and there was one telling omission. She did not say it was Alberich who'd had the visions; she let them think it had been Sendar himself.

He was astonished, amazed—it was a brilliant stroke, for it made Sendar just that little bit larger than life, that much more of a hero, while at the same time it kept Alberich's Gift a secret among the very few that he knew could be trusted with it. If he'd thought of it himself, it was exactly what he'd have asked her to say. Since *she* thought of it, he could not have been more proud of her.

"We have lost a great King this day," she said, when the murmurs of wonder had died away. "We have lost a King who cared so deeply for the lives of his people that he flung his own down to save them; we have lost a wise and compassionate leader, and a great-hearted man as well. And I have lost, not only a father, but my best and truest friend."

Her voice caught on a sob, but she stopped for a moment, wiped her eyes, and went on. "But Valdemar lives, and I live, and together, we will make certain to be worthy of his sacrifice. There is much to do now, and much that will need to be done in the future, but we have proved today that together there *is* no foe that can stand against us, and no matter the odds, we *will* prevail!"

A great roar went up as she dismounted and gave Caryo into the willing hands of waiting aides. Keren and Ylsa were a fraction of a moment behind her, flanking her as she walked into the command tent.

Alberich did not so much dismount as fall out of the saddle, and he had to cling to it for a moment before his head cleared. Kantor swiveled his head to peer at him, but before the Companion could say anything, more aides came to take Kantor away with the other three Companions. Alberich set his jaw, swayed for a moment, and followed Selenay into the tent, intending to stay discreetly on the sidelines. That gray haze clouded his vision, but he had fought it away before, and he would fight it away now.

That was his intention, anyway—

What *happened* was that he got three paces inside the door flap, that grayness turned to blackness, and he passed out cold at Selenay's feet.

He came awake all at once, and blinked up at white, sun-washed canvas.

"It's about time," Myste said dryly, as he realized he was not alone and this was not his tent. "Layabout. Come on, get up and get out of that cot; they need it for someone who's *really* hurt."

He sat up; it was a *big* tent, and it was full of more cots like his. He had been put in one right beside the tent wall; his nearest neighbor was—

"Jadus—" he said.

The lean Herald turned to face them without raising his head from the pillow, and grimaced. "In the flesh, most of it. They had to take the leg."

Jadus' eyes had that half-focused look of someone powerfully drugged; Alberich was surprised he could speak at all. "The saying should be, better the leg than the life."

He shouldn't have said that; he knew it as soon as the words were out of his mouth. Too late. "Better mine than *his,*" Jadus replied, voice thick with sorrow. "But I didn't get to make a choice."

"Seldom does anyone." Alberich reached across and put one hand on Jadus' arm. He didn't have the words of comfort he wanted, not even in his own language, but Jadus seemed to understand that he meant to offer whatever support he had without words.

"Thank you," Jadus told him, in a tone that said he meant the words. "You know—they just dosed me. I believe I need to sleep… now…"

His eyelids dropped, and in a moment, he *was* asleep.

"Poor man. I hope we can find something he can teach at the Collegium—" Myste began, but Alberich interrupted her.

"Bah! A sad day indeed it will be, the day a Herald needs two legs to do his duty!" He would not hear of it, a healthy man, certainly no older than the late King, being given makework, just because he lacked half a limb. "And of legs speaking—"

He looked down at hers; one of them was in a rather odd boot. A very *thick* boot. "I note that *you* manage, having not quite a whole leg. Unless a phalanx of slave boys you have, to carry you a litter upon."

She smiled faintly. "Yes, I broke my ankle. No, I'm not letting it stop me, though let me tell you, it *still* hurts like seven hells, and it's only because the Healers are very good that I'm not screaming now. Between their off-and-on magics and some truly vile concoctions, even if it hurts, I tend not to care, if that makes sense. And this plaster boot they've granted me lets me get around." She looked wistful for a moment. "Though, come to think of it, I wouldn't *mind* a squad of litter-carrying slave boys… ah, never mind. I'm supposed to tell you that Selenay sent me for you."

"Me?" He stared at her; he wasn't certain he'd heard her correctly. One of his last thoughts before he passed out, after all, was how long she would hate him—

"Of course, you. You saved her life, she knows that. *Everyone* knows that. You did it twice over, in fact, once by keeping her from following Sendar, and again, when that lot of infiltrators popped up." She spoke matter-of-factly, in such a way that he could not doubt her. "And you did more than that, although there aren't too many who know it was you that caused Sendar to send the reinforcements out to save the countryside. Ah—" She hesitated. "Just so you know, Selenay wants to keep it that way, except for those of us who were there."

He didn't feel up to stumbling his way through Valdemaran anymore, and reverted to Karsite. "Myste, I have *no* objection to that. He might just as well have had the visions as I; what did or could I do about them? I just blurted them out to you, and not even in a tongue he could understand. *He* understood what they meant, and in his greatheartedness, elected to save his land rather than his own life. He charged the front line, knowing what he was doing, and knowing full well that he had less chance of surviving that charge than a rabbit charging a pack of foxes. Let his people think whatever they want; he deserves all of it."

"I told her you'd feel that way." She nodded. "Anyway, Selenay did indeed send me this morning to stay here with you until you woke, and tell you to come to her when you did. A bit melodramatic, that, passing out at her feet, wasn't it?"

He winced. "I hope I was discreet about it."

"You weren't, but I don't think anybody cared; actually, those of us who were still able to think were trying to figure out if we'd have to get Crathach to mind-blast you to get you to stop being so infernally noble and self-sacrificing." She lifted an eyebrow at him. "You saved us from that by neatly falling over."

Well, he was cleaned up, at least; *someone* had done him that tremendous favor, and left him to sleep off his exhaustion in a clean white shirt and trews. The rest of his Whites were beside him on a chair. He started to reach for them—

"No," he said aloud. "I put them on for Sendar, but I do not think I will wear Whites again. Not unless there is a pressing reason."

Myste pursed her lips, but looked curiously satisfied, as if she thought she had been particularly clever. "I thought you might say that. So I stopped by your tent, and brought these."

She pulled a basket out from under his cot—and there were *his* form of the Heraldic uniform; the dark gray leathers he had worn up until they had left Haven.

"Are you certain you are not an Empath?" he asked.

"No, I'm a Herald with work to do, and now that you've been informed that Her Majesty wants you, I need to go do it." She softened her words with a slight smile, then suddenly reached out and took his hand.

"But I won't always have work to do," she said, giving it a slight squeeze. "And I find you excellent company because I don't have to pretend or mince words around you."

Then she picked up a crutch from beside her stool, stood up, and hobbled off.

He stared after her with bemusement.

:You really don't *know what to do with a woman who isn't either untouchable or a whore, do you?:* said that familiar, faintly mocking voice in his mind.

:Well, why don't you *teach me?:* he shot back, stung, and reached for his familiar gray leathers.

:I might. But you'll have to ask me nicely.:

His ears burned.

Changing swiftly, he headed out of the tent, intending to pause only long enough to tell one of the Healers that he would not be needing that cot beside Jadus anymore.

But the first Healer he ran into was a very familiar face, and one he had not expected to see tending to the wounded.

"Crathach!" he exclaimed, and seized the man's arms, grasping him by the elbows with both hands. "But—Talamir—"

"Come see for yourself," the Healer said, taking *him* by the elbow. Crathach led him out of the ranks of the Healers' tents, and into the ring of command tents. Alberich could not help but notice some gaps, where tents *had* been—and felt a stab in his heart.

But one tent still stood. Crathach led him to it. As with many tents used by Heralds, it was fully large enough for a Companion to fit inside, for Heralds sometimes preferred to know that their partners were as comfortable as *they* were. Inside, Talamir lay quietly in his cot, and lying beside him on a worn rag rug was a Companion.

For one moment, Alberich's heart stopped. There was only *one* Companion that had that special look, that faint aura of otherworldliness—

Taver?

He stopped himself from blurting it just in time. The Companion lifted his noble head, and looked into his eyes.

:Not Taver, Weaponsmaster. I am Rolan.:

"Your pardon," Alberich murmured, a little unnerved.

The Queen's Own's new Companion nodded his acceptance of the apology. *:It was a natural thought, and no harm was done. I am pleased to see you. We will probably be seeing a great deal of each other in the future, but if you will forgive me, I have* my *charge to tend for now.:* The Companion turned his gaze back toward the quiet figure on the cot.

Talamir no longer looked like a corpse, but he had aged, and aged greatly, in—what? Less than two days? He had looked no older than Sendar, middle-aged at worst, before the battle; now he looked *old*, thin and worn out with long struggle, his face etched with lines of pain. And he looked fragile. Alberich felt his heart wring with pity, and wondered if, perhaps, it *would* have been better for him if he'd been allowed to die.

But that was not his decision to make—

Vkandis be thanked.

Crathach tugged at his sleeve, and they left the tent to the Companion and his charge. "He did what I could not," Crathach said. "How he got here in so little time—well, I can't guess. But he did what I couldn't. I could only hold him just out of reach of death's gate; Rolan dragged him back to life, then full awareness, and made him stay."

"He has awakened, then?" Alberich asked, still in a murmur, with a glance back at the tent.

"Several times. He's quite sane, now, and he doesn't seem to want to die, but he's fragile, Alberich, very fragile. I've told the Queen that he's not to do much for a while, and she agrees." Crathach tilted his head to one side, and gave him a penetrating look.

"Hmph." Alberich traded him look for look. "Then, until you say, so shall I *sit* upon him, if need be."

"I knew I could count on you." Crathach slapped him on the back. "Now, I think the Queen wants you."

"So I believe, and I shall my leave take of you." He hoped Crathach would say something that might give him a clue to the Queen's mood.

But Crathach didn't seem to have any more idea than he did. "Ever since Rolan arrived, I've been too busy to go near the command tent," he replied and sighed. "And at the moment, my services as a Healer are in far more demand than those as a bodyguard."

Alberich grimaced. "Wish I could, that otherwise it were."

Crathach nodded. "And I. It is good to be able to use one's Gifts, but—" He could only shrug helplessly.

They parted then, but having seen Talamir alive, if not exactly *well,* Alberich's heart felt a little lighter.

But now it was time to face the Queen. And he was not looking forward to that. For no matter what Myste said, *he* was not at all sanguine about his reception. Surely Selenay would never want to see his face again, after what he'd done to her. If nothing else, she would never forgive him for keeping her away from her father's side, and who could blame her?

Probably she wanted to see him only so that she could tell him she wanted him to return immediately to Haven and confine himself to the salle from now on…

It was in this mood that he presented himself at the command tent.

The guards—*his* choice, he saw, with pride—let him past. He tried to slip in unnoticed, but Keren spotted him, and bent down to whisper in Selenay's ear. She looked up sharply.

"Herald Alberich—" she said.

Silence descended like a warhammer.

He cleared his throat awkwardly. "You summoned me, Majesty."

"I did. Come here, Herald Alberich." Queens did not say "if you please." Queens issued orders, and their subjects obeyed. As did he. He made his way between two ranks of officials and highborn who parted to let him pass, thanking his luck that the tent was not all *that* large, for to have to pass a gauntlet of only a double-handful of watchers was bad enough. She was sitting in her father's chair, at his table, and she watched him with a measuring gaze as he approached.

"Don't kneel," she said sharply, as he started to bend. "And look at me." She tilted her head to one side and looked him up and down. "You've gone back to your shadow-Grays, I see. Good; if you've no objection, except when we need you in Whites for—ah—*formal* occasions, I should like you to keep to them. It will serve very well to make it clear that while you are taking Talamir's place for some little while, you are not the Queen's Own."

He blinked. Surely he had not heard that correctly. "Majesty?" he faltered. "I am—what?"

"Crathach tells me that Talamir will not be fit for duty for a while. Until he is, I wish you to take his place, here, at my side." She smiled wanly. "At least until you resume your duties at the Collegium, that is. Crathach thinks Talamir will be ready by the time we reach Haven. I should like Keren to go back to what *she* does best in my bodyguard; meanwhile I need someone here beside me in the capacity of adviser as well as guard, someone with a level head who knows when his Queen needs to be dragged out of her saddle and sat upon."

"Yes, Majesty," he managed, and changed places with Keren, who looked only too happy to relinquish her position.

She resumed the business that he had interrupted, which seemed to concern those enemy fighters who had thrown down their weapons and scattered. Some of them, it was thought, had come north rather than south, and were trying to hide themselves in Valdemar.

There were several arguments ongoing as to the best way to hunt them down; brutal, savage plans, most of them. Apparently it was not enough that the entire command structure had been wiped out. There were plenty who wanted every single person who had so much as carried a bucket for the Tedrels hunted out and strung up on the nearest branch high enough to haul them off the ground, and the corpses left to hang there until they rotted away.

Selenay listened impassively until the various angry speeches had been made, then looked at Alberich.

"Well?" she asked. "Have you any suggestions?"

He supposed that, by all rights, he *should* have been just as full of righteous anger, but he wasn't. He was just—tired. Tired of death, sick of the stench of it in his nostrils. He didn't want any more deaths, not if he could help it.

"Real Tedrels—if any live—dare not the Border to cross," he said slowly. "And I think the Sunpriests a most—unpleasant—fate will accord them, should they foolish enough be, in Karse for to stay, for heretics by the measurement of the Sunpriests the Tedrels most surely are. Say I would, that their welcome will *not* be warm, except, of course, that it rather *too* warm will be."

It took a moment for the others to realize what he had said, and more to figure out what he had *meant.* The Fires, of course; there wasn't a chance that any real Tedrels would be spared the Fires. Someone in the back snickered, although he had not meant it as a joke.

"As for the rest—" He shrugged. "The worst of mercenaries, and the most foolish of fortune hunters they are. Perhaps some are here, in Valdemar. The first—will swiftly run afoul of constables and Guards, or even of farm folk, and in trouble they soon will be, and have them you will. Now, how to tell are we *which* are those that fought here, and which mere outlanders? Arrest all, who with an accent speak?" He raised his eyebrow. "Then, without acting Queen's Own you will be—"

She blinked, but nodded, and some of the muttering stopped. He had to say this much for most of the people she had about her now, they weren't stupid.

"What is Valdemar if not just?" he asked rhetorically. "Leave some Guards, perhaps, to deal with them as found they are, but I think you need not hunt them. Live off the land, they cannot; when their swords they cannot hire out, leave they shall, or break the law, and so you have them, as *lawbreakers*, which can be proved. The second, either a lesson will have learned, or will not, and thus also—" He spread his hands.

"So you're saying we shouldn't track them down?" Lord Orthallen asked smoothly, as if the question was of no matter to him. "Just leave them as a menace to the countryside?"

"I say find them you will, without hunting. Hide, they cannot, and with nothing more than what on their bodies they have, little have they to live on, and only one trade they know."

"But what if they try and pass themselves off as laborers?" someone asked angrily.

Alberich raised an eyebrow. "To *escape* labor it was, that most turned to sell-swording. Wish them joy of it, I do—and find may they, only the hardhearted as masters."

"Please," said Selenay in an exasperated tone of voice, "Do *think* this through! Do any of you *want* to keep this army together, spending the treasury dry to feed them and keep them in wages, just to frighten the locals by riding over their fields and interrogating anyone who looks the least bit out of place? And how do you propose to tell one of these Tedrels from—oh, say a hillman out of Rethwellan looking for work? Or a poor brute of a Karsite who's taken advantage of this to cross into Valdemar for sanctuary? Or *are* you actually proposing, as Alberich said, to string up every man with a foreign accent from the nearest tree?"

"I repeat, begin with me, you would have to," Alberich pointed out gently.

There were some embarrassed coughs.

"I won't even *begin* to point out how my father would have responded to such an idea," she continued, looking at all of them and making a point of staring each in the eyes until he either dropped his gaze or met hers with agreement. "It is so totally foreign to *everything* Valdemar has always stood for! I agree with Alberich; if anyone *has* crossed to our side of the Border, the likeliest thing is that they'll try to get over to Rethwellan and be of no concern to us. If any stay, they will either settle and fit in, or *not* and break the law, and we can deal with them on that basis."

"Well, Majesty—" Lord Orthallen began.

But he was interrupted.

"Dammit, I *will* see Her Majesty!" snapped a querulous, aged female voice that he knew and had *not* expected to hear. And a moment later, the owner of that voice, someone he knew—as well as he knew himself—

—pushed her way in past everyone.

He should know Herald Laika, though he'd last seen her just before she left to infiltrate the Tedrels in her guise of an old washerwoman. After all, he'd helped form half of the "memories" that now made her what she was.

:And given that fact, you shouldn't be surprised that she's as stubborn as a mule and as intractable as a goat,: Kantor put in, as she bullied her way right past the Lord Marshal, made a pretense at a courtly curtsy, then stood glaring at Selenay with her hands on her hips.

Selenay stared at her blankly and without recognition; well, she *wouldn't* recognize Laika, though she might know the name, for as far as Alberich knew, neither she nor Caryo would have seen Laika before.

"Herald Laika, Majesty," Alberich said carefully. "One of our four Herald-agents, behind Tedrel lines, she was. Within the camp; infiltrated, was she, as a washerwoman. And very valuable."

"Damn right," the old woman grunted. "And that's why I'm here. I want to know what the *hell* you're going to do about the children?"

Selenay blinked. "I beg your pardon, Herald Laika, but we do already have people—Healers and others—out trying to find the children whose parents were killed by the Tedrel cav—"

"Not *those* children!" Laika exclaimed. "Not the children of *Valdemar!* I'm talking about the Tedrel children! What are you going to do about the *Tedrel* children?"

1 8

"What Tedrel children?" Selenay asked, blankly.

Alberich was going to explain, but Laika saved him the effort. "This wasn't just a mercenary company, this was a *nation,*" she said, with the irritation of a teacher whose student hasn't studied her subject sufficiently. "Granted, they'd made a vow never to wed or have families until they had a land of their own again, but that sure as hellfires didn't stop them from *breeding.*"

Selenay's eyes widened, and her mouth made a silent "O" shape.

"What's more, they used to pick up every stray boy-chick they could get their hands on and throw him in with the rest!" Laika continued. "Not to mention the ones they kidnapped, not a few of 'em from our own people. They didn't have much use for girls until they were of breeding age, but boys—oh, my, yes! *That's* why they were taking such pains to keep *our* littles alive, so they could turn *them* into Tedrels. Now you've got a camp full of orphans and other youngsters over there that the Karsites are *not* going to want. You've killed off their fathers and protectors, if they even *have* mothers, their mothers are probably halfway to Rethwellan by now and might not have waited about for them, and what are you going to do about it?"

"Won't the Karsites just take them?" Selenay asked, looking to Alberich.

"Probably—no," he said, reluctantly. "Karse needs no extra mouths that come not with hands that can work. And—they are heretics, and the children of heretics, and what is more, even their own blood, to the Sunpriests' eyes, they are *not*—or no longer are—Karsite."

He did not elaborate on what that meant, but there was something very unpleasant stirring in the back of his mind; something like a— protovision. An intimation, not of what *would* be or what was *about* to be, but what *might* be.

A vision of the Fires of Cleansing. And the fuel that fed them.

"I don't want to sound utterly callous and hardhearted, Herald, but, not to put too fine a point upon it, what *can* we do?" the Lord Marshal asked. "They're on Karsite land, in Karsite hands."

She looked at him as if he was an idiot. "And this stopped Vanyel? This stopped Lavan Firestorm?"

The Lord Marshal wasn't about to back down. "That was in another situation entirely," he retorted. "And if you're referring to the 'Demonsbane' legend, Vanyel was on *Hardorn* land, not Karsite."

Alberich cleared his throat. "Ah—Herald Laika—a question. Suppose I must, that *you* have these children been among. Think you, they can *be* anything but Tedrel?"

"Most of 'em aren't now," she replied, and shook her head. "Some of 'em, in fact, a lot of 'em, are Karsite orphans—some of 'em are camp followers' children. And, dare I repeat myself, *some* of 'em are ours, grabbed every time they hit Valdemar in the past three years! But like I said, they don't have much use for girls that aren't breeding age, so they don't pay any attention to 'em, and boys aren't useful until they're thirteen and old enough to take into a Tedrel lodge for training, so they're all right up until then. Basically, they're not Tedrel, they're not Karsite, they're not anything, really. When I was in there, they had a lot of the camp followers that were tending to all of them, and most of *those* were girls out of Rethwellan, Seejay, and Ruvan, with a couple of Karsites. So that's what they've been raised as."

"Raised as nothing, then," Selenay ventured.

"Pretty much. A pretty weird mix, they all speak a kind of Tedrel-pidgin with words from all over. The girls don't *ever* get taught pure Tedrel tongue; that's a man's mystery. The kiddies have got some little religious cult they've made up on their own that isn't like anything I've ever heard of. Like I said, they aren't Tedrel, they aren't anything." She sighed. "What they are, is dead needy for adult attention. Even an old hag like me, they swarmed over."

"But babies—without mothers—" someone put in doubtfully.

"Babes in arms—" She shrugged. "That little, the Tedrels don't take. The ones born to the camp followers, well, they may be whores, but they're still mothers; the ones that'll bolt, they'll take the children they can manage to carry and run for Rethwellan. That leaves the orphans, or ones whose mothers don't care, and there's a couple hundred, anyway, of an age we *could* rescue. No more than a thousand…"

Selenay glanced at Alberich, who was thinking furiously. "Karse—I think *might* be busy—elsewhere—"

Elsewhere hunting down all the escapees on their *side of the Border and either conscripting them as bound slaves or making sure no one else ever does—*

"—and," he continued, "if the rescue and evacuation were made quickly, might not know it had been entered at all."

"And a thousand children?" Selenay gulped.

"It's not an *unmanageable* number," the Lord Marshal put in. "It's not as if it would be a thousand captives; most of them couldn't run far."

Laika snorted. "Show 'em food and smiles, and most of 'em won't run at all. And don't forget—*some of them are ours*. And if word gets out that we left *Valdemaran* children to starve or hope for the mercy of the Sunpriests…" She let that particular statement sink in without elaborating. "What's more, they aren't more than a day's march inside Karse! When the Tedrels moved this time, they were preparing the full-on invasion, remember. They thought we were going to go over with just a push, and they had everything and everyone set to move straight across the Border."

"Surely not," Lord Orthallen said skeptically. "Surely they were not going to put all of *that* so close to the battle lines."

Laika smiled grimly. "And what makes you think they were unaware that the moment the fighters left the base camp, the Karsites were likely to grab everything? Believe me, that was the talk all over the camp— everyone wanted to be sure that *they* didn't get left behind. The last camp they made would be where they left all the non-combatants and the baggage and all. In fact, there was talk about setting it less than a half-day's march from the Border, figuring that the closer it was to Valdemar, the less likely it was that the Karsites would come calling. The campfire glow we saw in the farther sky last night was probably from their *full* camp, not their battle camp."

"I thought they looked rather too well-rested," murmured the Lord Marshal.

"Then that means we won't have to break the Border so much as— bend it a little," Selenay said speculatively. "I suppose one *could* consider what is in that camp to be legitimate war loot?"

Now it was the Lord Marshal's turn to smile grimly. "One could, Majesty," the Lord Marshal said. "And in fact, one *should*. Why, after all, should the Karsites have the benefit of this—war booty—when it is Valdemar that suffered?"

Alberich merely raised an eyebrow. "How can we, calling ourselves civilized, leave children to suffer? And welcome in Karse, they will *not* be."

Now Selenay looked to the rest of her advisers and commanders. "I—honestly, gentlemen, ladies—I think we should do this. I know we *can;* I think we should."

"Bringing life out of death?" asked the Chief Healer. "I don't think there is any doubt. *Sendar* would."

Selenay smiled wanly. "My father would have been at the head of the expedition," she said softly.

That seemed to decide them all, and the prospect of having a positive task to organize also seemed to galvanize them, lifting them somewhat out of the slough of depression that most of the encampment had sunk into.

The mood in the tent suddenly lifted, and even Selenay's voice took on more life than it had held since before the battle.

"We'll need wagons to carry the children, won't we?" she asked, breathlessly. "How many? Where will we get them?"

"We already have them, Majesty," said the Chief Healer, catching fire from her enthusiasm. "We were going to send some of the wounded north—leg injuries, not so serious, but needing some recovery—but they'll gladly wait for a little to save these children! The horses are harnessed right now, the wagons are provisioned, we haven't loaded the wounded yet—why, we can be ready to go on the instant!"

She turned to Alberich. "Would—you—"

"Of course he would!" the Lord Marshal exclaimed. "Great good gods, who else! You used to patrol here, didn't you, man? And you won't be doing without him for more than a day or two—"

"What about us?" Laika interjected. "Oh, good gods, not as leaders, but we know the Karsite language and we came across here to get out, and the children know *me,* at least."

"Give me a moment, and I'll send a messenger about the wagons," the Chief Healer put in, and they were off with the bit between their teeth. Alberich simply stood there, while all the decisions were made for him. They seemed to accept without question that Alberich should serve as the leader, and that Laika and the other three spies should be in the rescue party, and that it would consist of Heralds, Healers, and wagons. Heralds to act as eyes, ears, and if need be, guards; Healers to soothe the children, and wagons to carry them. The decision to go was made so swiftly that if, as Laika asserted, the camp was no farther than a half-day's march away, Alberich reckoned that they *might* get there and back by this same time on the morrow.

And it slowly dawned on him that no one, no one at all, even *thought* about the question of his loyalty. *Of course* he would lead the rescue; he was the best person for the job. *Of course* he would bring these children—some of them Karsite—back to Valdemar. And *of course* he wouldn't even consider taking the opportunity to defect back to his homeland. He was a Herald, wasn't he? Divided loyalties didn't even come into it.

Perhaps there were a few who thought differently, but there always would be. There would have been had he come from Hardorn, or Menmellith, or Rethwellan, or anywhere else other than Valdemar.

Within a candlemark, the whole thing was organized and ready to go, with plenty of volunteers. He hadn't been surprised by the ones among the Heralds or even the Healers, but the fact that the teamsters had lined up to a man had come as a bit of a surprise.

He was a little uneasy about leaving Selenay on her own, though. Still—

She was essentially on her own from the moment her father died. She has trained for this for years, hasn't she? If she couldn't handle the reduced Council *now*, when there was so little opposition and she was the darling of the army, what would she do back in Haven?

And as for her bodyguards—they were taking their job just as seriously now as they had before the battle. If any true Tedrels had survived, *now* would be the time for an assassination attempt, for now, whoever still lived had nothing to lose, and such men were the most dangerous of all.

Selenay saw them off, but she kept things brief. "Go safely and swiftly," she said, and impatient to be off, they took her at her word. She didn't linger to watch them rattle across the little stream at the Border either; when he looked back, she was gone.

Not only was he not surprised, he was pleased. It wasn't as if she didn't have more than enough on her hands, for the aftermath of a war generally left both sides in shambles. There were hundreds of decisions to be made, and in the end, only the Queen could make them. Then, when one factored in all of the messages and dispatches arriving from Haven moment by moment, every one of them requiring *her* attention, he was certain she would be getting very little rest between now and when he returned.

Which might be just as well. It would give her very little time to brood, and might exhaust her enough that she would actually sleep instead of lying awake, staring at the darkness behind her eyelids.

It was a strange sensation, crossing onto the Karsite lands of the hills, where he had once ridden at the head of a troop of Sunsguard. "A close watch keep, for bandits," he warned everyone when they first set out. "Driven away by the battle, they were perhaps—but like vultures, return to feast upon the slain they shall." He had to wonder, though, as they rode through empty valleys, and over hills bare of the usual flocks of sheep and goats, if the Sunsguard had actually sealed off this area. If that was the case, and bandits *had* fled the coming conflict, they could easily have run right into the Sunsguard. He hoped so. He truly hoped so. Not only because it meant that *they* would not encounter any trouble going there and back, but because the scum that had fattened on the misery of the shepherds of these hills for so long well *deserved* to be cut down like the plague rats they were.

It was easy enough to know where to go, despite the fact that there was no road to follow. The marching feet of so many thousands of men had *left* a road across the landscape, the tough and wiry vegetation hereabouts pounded flat, then into dust. This was a tough country, of scrubby vegetation and endless hilly moors, punctuated (as he used to tell Dethor) by endless rocky hills, yet it had its own beauty. The gorse was in bloom, and the heather, and drifts of purple, white, and yellow spread hazy blotches of color across the face of those hills. The weather elected to smile upon them today—or the Sunlord Himself did—for the sun beamed down upon them, neither too brazenly hot, nor thin and chill, out of a sky whose blue was interrupted only by the occasional white, fluffy cloud like one of those missing sheep. Once or twice, they caught sight of wild goats on the ridges, or heard the bray of an equally wild donkey, but otherwise it was nothing but wind and birdsong.

He had no idea how low his spirits had been in the wake of the battle until they were well away from the battlefield, and he could allow himself to pretend it had never happened. But the clean wind swept through his heart and soul; he was going to a *rescue*, not a battle, and he felt as if the wind was carrying away his sadness, a little at a time.

And this was home... the breeze felt right, the hills *smelled* right, they were the right color of gray-green, and the right sort of rocks poked up through the thin soil. He might never see these hills again, so he absorbed the changing landscape, stowing it away in his memory to take out on those nights that would surely come, when he felt himself to be entirely alien in an alien land.

Finally, he had to remind *himself* to stay alert; this was no pleasure jaunt. Things could still go wrong at any moment. If the Sunsguard wasn't busy picking off former Tedrels, they could be here at any moment...

:This is a handsome land,: Kantor observed, ears pricked forward to catch every sound. *:Hard, but handsome.:*

:I think so,: he agreed, secretly pleased by Kantor's compliment. *:Ah— we'll be coming up to a spring here shortly, if my memory of this area is any good. There aren't a lot of good watering places here; warn the others that we'll be stopping for a moment.:*

His memory *was* good—and interestingly enough, the Tedrels had not made use of the spring he recalled, for they had to deviate from the track and go over a hill to the east to get to the half-hidden water source. When they did, they found no sign that anyone had been there, and the Tedrels would surely have trampled the bank of the stream that the spring fed, and muddied the basin.

But Alberich was taking no chances. Just to be sure that they *hadn't* been here and tampered with the water (which would have been entirely like them) he called over one of the Healers.

"Test this, for fouling or poison, can you?" he asked the green-clad woman.

"Hmm." She gave him a sidelong glance, but bent to test the water, taking up a single drop on the end of her finger and touching it to her tongue. "That would have been like those bastards, wouldn't it?" she said absently. "Spoil what's behind them so the Karsites couldn't follow."

"My thought," he agreed gravely.

"Well, it's clean; you can bring them all in." She stood up; he waved at the wagons, and the teamsters brought their charges in to drink at the stream fed by the spring, while the humans drank at the source. Tooth-achingly cold, the water tasted of minerals. The horses adored it. Fortunately, they were not so thirsty that they were in any danger of hurting themselves by drinking too much, too fast.

He kept an eye on the crests of the hills around them; the disadvantage of stopping here (or anywhere) for a drink was that doing so made them very vulnerable. But this spring, flowing as it did out of the side of a hill, at least was not as exposed as the stream it fed, that ran along the bottom of the valley. He put a lookout on the crest of the hill, which was all anyone could reasonably do, and trusted also to his Gift and that of the FarSeer that was with them to warn of any danger approaching.

But all that appeared was a herd of sheep and a dog—and a very brief glimpse of the shepherd, who turned his flock aside and back over the hill when he saw them.

:At least he'll know the water's safe,: Kantor pointed out, as he rounded everyone up, anxious to be gone now that they had been spotted. *:I don't think he's likely to say anything to anyone for a while. Days, probably.:*

Considering the taciturn nature of the lone shepherds here, Alberich was inclined to agree. The Sunpriests hated them, for they could not be controlled as easily as villagers. They thought their own long thoughts alone out here, for moons at a time, and could not be compelled to come for the regular temple services. You could not leave sheep to tend themselves while you hiked to the nearest village for SunDescending, SunRising, Solstice and Equinox, after all, and sheep tended to run astray when *they* felt like doing so, not on any schedule. If there was to be wool for the wheel and the loom, and mutton and lamb for the table, the shepherds had to be left to their own ways and thoughts. The priests were not amused, but they could do nothing about it.

On a rock beside the mouth of the spring, he left the thank-token for whoever actually owned the resource. It might even be that shepherd—but whoever laid claim to the water rights would find the proper toll for the use of his water. Alberich had packed several such needful things in Kantor's saddlebags before they'd left. In this case, it was something virtually every hillman would find useful, the more especially since the confiscation of so many weapons by the Sunpriests; a Tedrel crossbow and a quiver of quarrels for it, all wrapped in oiled canvas to keep them safe. There was nothing about any of the tokens Alberich had brought that said "Valdemar" and nothing—such as, for instance, a bit of gold—that would be difficult for a poor hill-man to explain.

These were, after all, *his* people still. He would have a care to what happened to them when he was gone again.

And on they went, taking to the pounded track once again, as the sun sank on their right and the light edged into gold, and golden-orange and the shadows of the hills grew long and stretched across their path.

That was when he sent Laika and a younger Herald out on a long scout ahead. If Laika was right, they should be getting near to the camp. And *he* began the usual futile attempt to probe at the near-future, like a man probing at an old wound to see if it still hurt. As usual, his Gift was silent.

Which was, in a way, a good thing, since it wasn't *warning* him about anything.

The sun was dropping nearer the horizon now, and the sky to the left had turned a deeper blue, while the sky to the right, with long banks of cloud across the path of the sun, was turning red. It would be sunset soon, and they still hadn't found that camp. He was beginning to be concerned. They would have to decide very shortly whether to go on under the full moon, able to see all right, but risking ambush, or make camp themselves—

:*Alberich!*: came a Mindcall; it jerked him out of his preoccupation with scanning the hilltops for trouble, and made his heart race in sudden alarm.

:*Steady on, Chosen. That wasn't trouble*—: Kantor said. And in the next moment, he knew that his Companion was right, of course. If it had been *trouble*, there would have been warning and alarm in that mind-voice.

It was from the youngster who had gone out with Laika. And the next words that came were excited, not fearful. :*Alberich, get up here—you have to see this to believe it!*:

The excitement communicated itself to Kantor, who tossed his head in sudden impatience to be gone, ears pricked forward, muscles tensing.

"Laika and Kulen, something have seen!" he called to the rest. "Keep to the track—summoned I have been."

Kantor evidently felt that was enough; he launched from a swift walk into a flat gallop, speeding over the top of the hill, down across the next valley, and over the next hill, and the next, and the next—

And that was when Alberich saw *why* there had been so much excitement in Kulen's mind-voice. Because, coming slowly toward them, flowing over the hill like a dusty, moving carpet, was an army.

An army of children.

Not just children, he saw, after his first astonished look. There were some adult women among them. But not many, and *they* were burdened with infants, slung across their backs *and* their chests, carried in baskets, even.

It was clearly the children themselves who were in charge here—and it made Alberich's heart leap into his throat to see how carefully they were tending to each other. There were carts pulled by donkeys and ponies full of the very smallest, led by those old enough to control a beast. There were more carts that the tallest and strongest were towing *themselves*. And those old and strong enough to walk by themselves were doing so, in little groups, each shepherded by one older child.

And now that Alberich was here, Laika was not going to wait any longer; she and her Companion raced toward the oncoming horde, and after an initial reaction of alarm, several of the children recognized her, and dropped the bundles they were carrying to race toward *her*, cheering as they went.

:Kantor—:

:I've told them,: Kantor replied joyfully. *:They're putting on some speed.:*

By the time Alberich and Kantor got to the front of the mob, Laika was engulfed in children, all babbling in that strange polyglot tongue she had told him about. He remembered what else she had told him as they rode on the way—that these poor children were starved for adult attention, that she used to tell them stories, and had made herself a kind of extended grandmother to a great many of them. The dry, bare bones of her narrative did not prepare him for seeing this, and he felt his eyes stinging with tears. At least *he* had had his mother, lonely though his childhood had been—

He felt a tugging at his sleeve, and looked down at a little girl who had the features of one of his own hill folk. "Aunty Laika says you were of the people of the Sunlord," the child whispered in Karsite, peering up at him hopefully. "And that you are of the White Riders of the Ghost-Horses now—"

"I am both," he told her, immediately dropping to the ground to put his eyes on a level with hers. "This is my Ghost-Horse; his name is Kantor."

:Ghost-Horse? Where did she come up with that? I like that a great deal better than "White-Demon" or "Hell-horse,": Kantor said, lowering his nose to touch the hand she stretched out to him.

"Have you really come to take us somewhere safe?" she asked, as he marveled that a child of *Karse* should ever reach toward a Companion without fear.

"We have—but who told you of all this?" he asked, trying to make sense of the puzzle. "Who told you about Ghost-Horses and White Riders?"

If it was Laika, he was going to have a few choice words with her. That sort of story could have gotten her killed and the other three Heralds exposed.

"Oh, it was Kantis, of course," the child told him blandly, in a tone that put the emphasis on *of course.* "Kantis has told us about the White Riders *forever,* and he promised us that some day they would come and take us where there are always good things to eat and a soft bed to sleep in, and no one would make us walk when we're tired, and that we'd all have a mum and a da, though we'd have to share—"

Before he could ask her *who* Kantis was, much less *where* he was and how he had come up with this unlikely tale and convinced them it was going to be true, she caught sight of something past his shoulder, and with a squeal of glee, ran off.

He looked around; what she had seen, and what had set the rest of the children running, was the first lot of Heralds and wagons topping the hill, brushed by the scarlet and gold of sunset. And in a moment, he was nothing more than a rock in a flood of children who found a little more energy in their weary bodies to run. They flowed around him like the largest flock of sheep in the world, faces transmuted by hope—and it was all he could do to hold back his tears.

And of course, faced with this oncoming flood of children screaming, not in fear, but with delight, the Heralds and Healers and teamsters reacted just as any decent human beings would—tumbling out of the seats and off their mounts to open their arms and their hearts, to open the boxes and bags of provisions they had brought, to stuff little hands and mouths with food and drink and toss little bodies into wagons padded with blankets, even as more little bodies were helping even littler ones to climb up as well. They couldn't understand what the children were saying, but they didn't need to know to understand what was needed.

And many of *them* were smiling with tears in their eyes. How could they not? After leaving that grim scene of battle aftermath behind them, how could they *not* want to ease their own aching hearts with the warmth of a joyful child?

And it was all sorted out in a remarkably short period of time. Those carts that *had* been drawn by children were fastened to the backs of the wagons. With the children themselves sharing out the provisions in a generous way that made Alberich marvel, *everyone* got enough to fill his empty belly. The few camp followers who had come with the children rather than fleeing, burdened with abandoned infants, were provided with seats and clean linens for the babies, and in lieu of milk, sugar-water for them to suck to at least stop their crying and ease their hunger. The last of the teamsters, finding no need for their empty wagons, asked permission to go on under guard and see what they could get out of the abandoned camp. After a moment of thought, Alberich gave his permission—although, with un-childlike forethought, the little ones were *all* carrying loot in their bundles: whatever was small, valuable, and light.

They gave it up to the Heralds without a second thought, and that pained him. Did they think they would have to *pay* for their rescue?

"No," Laika said, when he asked her that. "No, this is just something that this mysterious Kantis told them to do."

He relayed that information back to the army via Kantor, along with his recommendation that at least a portion of it be kept in trust for the children themselves. That was all he could do about it, but they seemed far more interested in eating and sleeping than in the jewelry and coins they'd lugged along, so he dismissed it from his mind.

As if the One God had decided to ease their way further, the full moon rose before the last light of twilight faded. With the broad track to follow, there was no chance of getting lost, and not much chance that a horse would make a misstep and hurt himself; accordingly there was never even a *thought* but that they would turn around and head back to the Border.

Bit by bit, as Laika and the other three talked to the older children, a broad picture began to form of what had happened.

One of the first Karsite orphans scooped up by the Tedrels when they first made their alliance and moved into Karse was a boy they all called Kantis. It was *he* who had somehow concocted the odd "cult" that Laika had noticed among the children—a cult that admitted no adult members, and whose members were sworn to secrecy with a solemn oath that, apparently, not even the boys who were later initiated into the Tedrel lodges ever broke.

Most of the cult that Kantis had created had a very familiar ring to Alberich, for it was virtually identical to the simple forms of Vkandis' rites that he had learned as a child from his mentor Father Kentroch, even to calling the God by the name of Sunlord. But there were more interesting additions...

Kantis had, from the beginning, it seemed, included a kind of redemption story, told whenever times were particularly hard for the children. He told them all that "some day" the Keepers (as he called the Tedrel adults) would abandon them and never return. And on that day, the White Riders and their Ghost-Horses would come for them and take them all away into a new land. This would *not* be the home of the Sunlord, he had assured those who, out of bitter experience, had feared that this meant they would all have to die. No, this was a very real land, where they would all make families with a shared set of parents, where they would always have enough to eat and a warm, safe place to sleep, and where they would never have to follow the drum again.

The children stolen out of Valdemar only reinforced Kantis' stories, when they identified the White Riders as Heralds.

Somehow, he had impressed upon them the need to keep all of *this* utterly secret, even more so than the redemption story.

And somehow, he had known the very moment when the Tedrels

lost their battle, for even before the remnants of the army came running back to the camp to take what they could carry and flee, he was telling the children that *now* was the time. He organized them, told them they should get what they wanted and whatever "shiny things" they could find in the adult camp, hide the ponies and donkeys until the last of the adults were gone, and prepare to march north, themselves, as soon as the last of the Keepers fled away.

Which was exactly what they had done. Those camp followers who had not run off with skirts stuffed full of valuables and some protector or alone had been bewildered by the stubborn insistence of the children on their goal, but had gone along with it, seeing no other options before them. Most of *them* were heartbreakingly young by Alberich's standards, and not yet hardened from "camp follower" to "whore."

They must have set out from the remains of the camp about the same time that Alberich and his group set out from Valdemar. The entire story was mind-boggling. And he wanted, very badly, to meet this boy, this so-clever, so-intelligent boy calling himself "Kantis," and speak with him.

But though he rode up and down the line, he could not actually find the boy. One child after another asserted that yes, Kantis was certainly with them—somewhere—but no one could tell him what group Kantis was with or where he'd last been seen. He might have been a figment of their collective imagination—he might have been a ghost himself—for he had somehow utterly vanished from among them the moment that they spotted Laika and Kulen.

1 9

The wagons loaded with the most portable of the Tedrel wealth caught up with them much sooner than Alberich had anticipated. This was in part because the portable wealth was *very* portable indeed, and in part because the section carrying the children was moving slowly. The poor things were exhausted, and even packed together like so many turnips in a sack, once stuffed with food and water, they fell asleep. So, since the treasure wagons were going to have to catch up with the main part of the group anyway, Alberich took their pace down to a steady walk.

Laika came up beside him; now that night had fallen, he was able to relax his guard. Laika, sharing his memories of Karse, was similarly relaxed. Nighttime held no terrors for Alberich now, not after so many years in Valdemar. *If* the Sunpriests unleashed their demons—and given how quiet the night was, he rather thought that said demons were fully engaged in pursuing stray Tedrels at the moment—he didn't think they would bother to do so here. So far as the Sunpriests knew at this point, there was no one in this part of the hills but the children, and why waste their most dangerous and powerful nighttime weapon on a lot of children?

Children who couldn't escape on their own, and would soon be facing the Fires anyway...

He had to unclench his jaw over that thought. And he sent up a silent prayer—not the first, and he doubted if it would be the last—that one day the Sunpriests would be answering for their transgressions, and one day it would be priests like his old mentor Kentroch, and like Father Henrick and Geri, who would be ruling in Karse again.

One of the other Heralds came riding up, looking nervously over his shoulder. "Herald Alberich, shouldn't we be putting outriders all around?" he asked. "I mean—"

"Peace; at ease be, protected we are by the priests themselves," Alberich said, and exchanged a glance with Laika. She laughed.

"Karsites won't stir out of their doors after dark," she said, with the air of *one who knows*. "Their priests have a habit of sending some sort of creepy-howly thing out at night, to make sure nobody's out doing something they shouldn't."

"Even the Sunsguard stirs not," Alberich added, with sardonic amusement. "So that now, should even a priest order them out, they will not go."

"Caught in their own trap," Laika said. "And serve 'em right. So by the time sun's up, *we'll* be so close to our people that even if they catch on we're here, our folks can mount a big enough rescue to squeak us across without losing so much as a hair."

Alberich considered how much the Tedrels had drained from the country, and sighed with pain. "*If* they scout or FarSee us, we take—so far as they will know—useless mouths only. We leave—think, they will—the camp unplundered." Privately, he doubted that even the Sunpriests would trouble themselves with FarSeeing this part of Karse; they would use their power to track down the Tedrels and Tedrel recruits. They must know that Sendar was dead, but they must also know that now was not the time to attack Valdemar themselves. Valdemar had just fought a terrible battle, and were exhausted, yes, but the Karsite Sunsguard was drained and weakened by the demands of the Tedrels. The current Son of the Sun—

He set bandits against Valdemar, then hired the Tedrels to do his work for him, Alberich thought somberly. *And now, thanks to the drain that the Tedrels put on his resources, the Sunsguard must be even more depleted. He hasn't got the* means *to attack us.*

No, the Sunsguard would be mopping up what was left, with the priests assisting, then they would all descend on the Tedrel base camp with an eye to getting back what had been drained from them.

"Believe me, there is no way the plunder in that camp can be exhausted, even by us and the Tedrels that were left," Laika told them both. "There'll be enough there to satisfy priestly greed even after our wagons come back. It isn't only the Karsite treasury they've been draining; they've got the accumulation of some twenty or thirty years' worth of loot from other campaigns they've fought, and they've been saving it all, waiting for the day when they'd have their own land again." She scratched her head, thinking, and added, "I'll give the bastards this much; they had discipline. Almost a quarter-century of honest pay, extortion, and booty, and they didn't spend a clipped copper coin more than they had to. *Every* fighter had his own store of loot, but beyond that, every true Tedrel war duke had a treasury tent, waiting for the day when he could finance the building of his own fortified keep in the heart of his own principality."

Alberich was greatly pleased to hear *that*. If the wagons sent onward came back so well loaded, then perhaps the children's little hoards could be kept solely for their use when they were older.

If the ride out had been a mixed pleasure, the ride back was an unalloyed—if bittersweet—one. With all worry about encountering Sunsguard gone, under a glorious full moon and a sky full of stars, and buoyed on the energy of the successful rescue, there was nothing in the way of opening themselves up to pure aesthetic enjoyment of a tranquil ride through peaceful countryside. The teamsters, once the situation was explained to them, relaxed and sat easily on the seats of their wagons. Even the babies only whimpered a little, now and then. Timeless and dreamlike, they moved on across ground that seemed enchanted and drunk with peace. It was as if the One God was granting them all a reprieve from their grief, the sorrow that would confront them when they crossed back into Valdemar, giving their hearts a rest so that they could all bear it better when at last it came.

Just about the time when the moon was straight overhead, he heard the wagons coming up behind them, the sound of the wheels echoing a little among the hills. Since they were near to the spring they'd used on the way in, he called a halt there once the whole party was together again. The children didn't even wake up.

"More about these children, tell me," he asked of Laika, when they were on the move again and a comfortable sort of fatigue began to set in. The moon, silvering the grass around them, turned the landscape into a strange sculpture of ebony and argent; with hoofbeats muffled by the soft earth and grass, they seemed to be moving in a dream, and he asked the question more to hear a human voice than for the information itself.

"You'll find they're a funny lot," she replied. "You'd think, being mostly not taught anything, that they'd be wild. But—well, once they got out of babyhood, they pretty much had to teach themselves and take care of each other, and by the gods, that's what they do. Maybe it was because so many of 'em lost their whole families, but they've got a kind of motto—*nobody left behind*—and they stick to it. The older ones see that the little ones get fed and clothed, the little ones do what they can to help the older ones. I think they're the next thing to illiterate, but they'll drink up anything you teach them like thirsty ground. They *all* found out that the Tedrels themselves may not do anything for them, but if they made themselves useful, they got rewards beyond whatever the Tedrels dumped in their section of the camp, so that's another thing they learned to do, how to make themselves useful. Then when that Kantis child showed up, he *really* organized them. Of course—I didn't get to see much of that, since I was an adult." She coughed. "Very secret, that cult was. No grownups were to hear about it."

"So—when into our camp we bring them, they will helpful be?" he hazarded.

"I would be greatly amazed if they didn't swarm the place, doing all sorts of little chores. Anybody expecting a bunch of terrified, wild little beasts is going to get a shock. Having 'em around is a lot like having a tribe of those little house sprites some old stories talk about; they can't do heavy labor, but by the gods, when they get determined to do something, it gets *done.* I had to fish more of 'em out of my wash tubs than I care to think about." She chuckled a little, then sobered. "Listen, *you* have the Queen's ear; make sure no one breaks them up into little groups right away—let 'em sort themselves out. They've made up little family groups of their own, and it's all they've got. Make sure none of us take that away from them."

"I shall," he promised. It wasn't a difficult promise to make.

The caravan moved on, ghosting through the darkness. And even at the slow pace, they reached the Border again a little after sunrise.

The children *were* awake by then, and peering eagerly ahead. Alberich had elected to come into the camp, not from the south directly, but indirectly from the west, saving the children the sight of the battlefield. They might have run tame in the Tedrel camp for most of their lives, and they might be inured to the aftermath of battle, but he didn't think they had ever seen a *battlefield.* Even now, there would still be much of horror about it. The result of so great a conflict was not cleaned up in a day or two... and it was no sight for these little ones.

So they actually made a detour upcountry, leaving the trampled "road" that the Tedrels had left until they struck an old track that crossed the Border at a ford, and joined up with one of the Valdemaran roads used by Border patrols. The old track showed some wear, so *someone* was still using it; it was rutted and gave the teamsters some hard times, but they took it in good part, knowing they were nearly home. Whenever a wagon got stuck, the children (if it was one that was carrying children) all piled out and the largest children mobbed it, put their young shoulders to it, and helped in the front by hauling on the horse's harness. No wagon remained stuck for long, with that kind of help.

For Alberich, crossing the Border brought on a mood of melancholy and depression. Not despair—but his heart sank with every pace they came nearer the camp. For a little, he had been allowed to forget, but only for a little and now—

They had all lost so much... so much.

And yet, just as they approached the camp with what seemed like half the inhabitants waiting for them, and in the very moment that the blackest depression descended on him, the children changed the complexion of everything.

They had been clinging to the sides of the wagons, peering over and around each other, trying to see ahead—when they saw the lines of white-clad Heralds and Companions, they could not hold themselves back. They *boiled* out of the wagons, spilled over the sides, tumbled to the ground, laughing and shouting, and ran to those who waited. "White Riders! White Riders!" they shouted (virtually the only Karsite they knew), pouring into the camp and running up to anyone who looked even halfway friendly, as if these were not strangers, but friends and beloved relations.

There were a great many of these children, he realized, as more of them spilled out of the wagons and carts. More than the "thousand" that Laika had promised. But no one seemed to mind. Certainly no one called him or Selenay to account for it, not then, and not at any time thereafter.

And in the days following, as the bodies were burned or buried, as the wounded were taken north, as the encampment was disassembled and troop after troop of fighters sent north again, it was the children who kept them all sane. They were everywhere, poking their noses into everything, trying to learn Valdemaran, trying to help where they could, and just being children, some for the first time in their short lives.

Not even Selenay was proof against their sheer exuberance at being *here*, a place that they seemed to consider an earthly paradise, and before long she had "adopted" a half dozen (or they adopted her), making them her pages and promising that they would be allowed to join her Royal Household in that capacity once they all reached Haven. Nor was she the only one; every wagon going north seemed to hold a handful of children going to a new home. Fighters, teamsters, Heralds—servants and highborn—everyone who *could* take in two, three, or four children did so.

"I never would have believed it, no matter who had told me, if anyone had claimed that bringing these children here was the best thing we could have done," Selenay told him on the third afternoon of the return, watching a child dash away with a message to be given to the next dispatch rider going out of the camp. Her eyes were still shadowed with sorrow, but her lips curved in a faint, fond smile. "I thought that it was something that had to be done, but truth to tell, I was dreading the mess they'd make for us."

They'd taken down the black felt linings for the tents, and the painted canvas glowed with afternoon light. That, too, was a mixed blessing. More light raised the spirit a little—but the black felt had gone for use as shrouds...

"And I," he agreed. "Most unnaturally helpful, they seem."

She had to smile at that, just a little. *"You* don't see them at their worst. They're still children, they still fight, and get into things they shouldn't and have tantrums. But for all of that, I'm afraid that in years to come, they're going to be held up as the good examples that every naughty child in Valdemar *should* behave like."

"Or perhaps, as children being, a year from now and they will no better nor worse than others become," Alberich suggested.

She flicked a fly away with the feather end of her quill. "Perhaps." She put pen to paper, and signed another order. "Who knows? I'm no ForeSeer."

"And I—See not that far, when I See at all," he admitted ruefully. *If I had been, could I have changed any of this? Or was it all too big for any one man to change?*

"Speaking of the children, I've given some thought to what to do with them, the ones that haven't managed to get themselves adopted already, that is," she said, looking up at him. "And I wanted to ask you what *you* think."

"Keeping them to their own—ah—'families,' you are?" he asked, a little anxiously, because he had seen, just as Laika had told him, how they sorted themselves out into their own little "families," and stayed together. It had been the smallest of those groups of two, three, or four children that were the ones that found homes first.

"Of course," she replied. "It doesn't take an Empath to realize we shouldn't tear apart what few bonds they have! But that's where the problem lies, you see; there aren't too many families or even childless couples prepared to take in six or a dozen children at once, much less ones that don't even speak our language. So my first thought was to—well—

send them to school." She folded both hands over the papers on her little desk and looked anxiously at him to see what his reply would be.

He nodded; that made perfect sense. "Like—the Academy?" he hazarded.

She nodded. "Or the Collegia. Oh, obviously, they can't actually go to the Collegia, we haven't nearly enough room for them, but something *like* the Collegia. And there are a lot of Valdemaran orphans to deal with, too—though those are having to go to the Houses of Healing, I'm afraid; they need MindHealers right now, not schooling…"

Her face darkened for a moment, but she took a deep breath and went on. "So I've written to all of the major temples, the ones with both day- and boarding-schools, and asked if they would take in some of the 'families' for a year, teach them Valdemaran and some basic reading and writing, until I've got these orphan collegia built." She waited for his response. He pondered what she had told him. "*Your* project, this is?"

She nodded. "If I have to," she said, with some of the same mulish stubbornness of her father, "I'll pay for it out of my own household budget—"

He raised an eyebrow. "Doubt do I, with the current mood of the Council, you will have to."

And now she had the good grace to blush. "Then better to push it through now than wait," she said, raising her chin. "Given that the booty from the Tedrels has furnished the means to restore all the damage they did down here, there isn't a great deal for the Council to complain about."

That was certainly true. Laika had been correct about that, as well.

"So build housing for these children—but *homes?*" he prompted.

"I'm going to look for childless couples, and ask *them* to serve as surrogate parents," she said, warming to her subject. "More than one couple, of course, for each house! It will probably take a year to get that all sorted out, find couples that like each other enough to share that kind of responsibility, get the houses built. But then we can keep them all together, we can probably even put Valdemaran children in *with* them—"

"That," he interjected, "a most good idea is. Help each other, they can. And good it would be, for Valdemaran children to know, Tedrel children are no different than they."

She sighed deeply. "I was hoping you would say that. Then it's settled; I'll put it up to the Council, first thing. Maybe *they* won't think it's as important as some of their other business, but I do."

So the "prophecy" is going to come true after all, that the children of the Tedrels were going to have real homes, though they would share "mothers and fathers." Once again, he wondered about that mysterious child called Kantis; since arriving back in camp, he'd been too busy to look any further for him.

And by now, he could be gone.

"Well, this will be the last one of *these* that I sign here," Selenay said, signing the last of the papers waiting for her signature and seal, and putting it in the pile of completed work. She closed her eyes for a moment, and it cost him to see how worn and tired she looked. "I won't miss this place."

"Nor I." He could not wait to be gone, truth to tell. If this had been Karse, rather than Valdemar, the aftermath would have been left for the locals to clean up. But it wasn't. So now there was a neat cemetery with rows of wooden markers out there where the churned-up ground had been—and a pit full of ashes where everything that wasn't Valdemaran had been disposed of. There had been too many burials for single ceremonies; each day at sunset had ended with a mass ceremony at which the names of the interred fallen for that day had been read. He had come to hate sunset, as each sunset brought fresh pain or the renewal of old, as names of those he hadn't known were gone, and those he had known were dead, were read out. He woke each morning, it seemed, with the scent of death in his nostrils, and went to sleep at night with a heart too heavy for tears.

Only Sendar and a few of the highborn were going north to find burial. It was too bad, but there were not many who could afford the expense to bring their loved ones home—and the horror of transporting *that* many bodies, stacked in the beds of wagons like so much cargo—and in the heat of summer—did not bear thinking about. There wasn't a teamster in the country who could be induced to use his wagon and team for that. But that was always the case in war...

The highborn had already been taken north in their expensive, sealed coffins, by the family retainers, in black-felt-draped wagons bedecked with family crests. Only the King was left, to make his final journey in the company of his daughter and those who had known him best.

It would be an honor guard, and it was an honor to be included in it. And here was the one factor that leavened, just a little, the sadness of the journey for Alberich. No one, *not one person,* had objected to his presence at Selenay's side. Talamir had already been sent north with the wounded, and there was no Queen's Own to ride with her. But she wouldn't need the Queen's Own on the journey, only bodyguards. The Council had gone on ahead, and now that the most urgent needs had been answered, all decisions were being held until Selenay reached Haven. So when it came down to it, Selenay only needed her bodyguards, not Alberich.

Yet no one said a word when she posted the final list of who was to accompany her, and chief on the list was "Herald Alberich, acting Queen's Own."

"Are we on schedule?" she asked, packing up her writing case with greater care than the simple task warranted.

"Ahead, a little," he told her. "In readiness, all will be, for leaving at dawn."

She closed and locked the case, then sighed. "I suppose I'll be expected to make a speech."

"Yes." He did not elaborate on that; he felt horribly sorry for her, but it was *her* duty, and she knew it. But there was another aspect to this journey of grief that he didn't think she had considered. Not only the army mourned its King, but the country. "It is wondered, Majesty, if pausing you will be at each village?" They'd left it to *him* to ask that delicate question, that and any others that might come up. He was acting Queen's Own, after all; delicate questions, it seemed, were a part of the job.

"At each village?" she asked, looking blank.

"A speech to make?" he elaborated.

She frowned, and looked as if she had suddenly developed a headache. "Oh, gods. I don't *want* to… but people are going to want to pay their respects, aren't they? But each time we stop, it's just going to make this whole thing drag out longer, and—" The frown turned into a look of despair, and he sensed that if he told her she *should* make all those stops, she'd do it, but it might break her.

He racked his brain for an answer, and finally thought he had a compromise. "Majesty—perhaps not a *stop*, and not a speech. But—spectacle. Something for memory and showing honor. A Herald sent ahead to warn each place that we come, then… drop pace to a slow walk? With—ah—muffled drums? Lowered banners? Through each place's center, though a detour we make? No speech, but—" he sought for the word, desperately, "—on your part, to be the icon of grief? You need speak not, only mourn, publicly—"

She looked as if he had taken a huge burden off of her shoulders.

"The very thing—would you go see to it for me, get it all organized?"

She must be near the breaking point, or she wouldn't delegate that to me. "At once, Majesty," he promised. "Please—be eating would you? Little have you had since morning."

That got a thin ghost of a smile from her. "Except for the accent, you sound like Talamir. Or my old nurse. All right, Nanny Alberich, I'll go get something to eat, and I promise I'll get some sleep, too. Maybe I'll have Crathach give me something to make me sleep, and go to bed early."

"That, most wise would be," he said. "And eat you must. Too thin, you are. How are you to get a husband, so thin you are?"

She stared at him for a moment in utter silence as he kept his face completely expressionless. Then, weakly, she began to laugh.

He allowed himself a smile.

She wiped away a tear, but he could see that some of the lines of grief and worry around her eyes had eased. "And they say you have no sense of humor," she said.

"Nor do I. All know this," he assured her. "Go now, and something impossible demand of the cooks."

"Impossible?" That caught her off guard. "Why?"

"First, that a reason they will have, at last to complain. Cooks must complain; in their nature, it is. Second, that injured their pride has been, that you have asked for nothing. Their pride is in that their masters demand much of them. Third, *concerned* they have been, that you have asked for nothing. They fear you need them not. Fourth, they worry *for* you." He raised an eyebrow. "But be certain, though impossible, it is something you *want*. Suspect I do, that they will create it."

"Ah." She blinked. "Do you know *everything* that is going on around here?"

He shook his head at that. "Not I. But Kantor I have, as Caryo *you* have. Our Companions know much, and what they know not, generally, they can discover. Sendar made use of that, often and often."

"I'd better get used to doing the same, then." This time her smile was a little stronger, as she picked up her writing case and stood up. "And I'll think about impossible things to eat on the way to my tent. Can you find Crathach and send him to me, while you're doing all the other things I've asked you to?"

"Without difficulty." He returned her smile. "Ask Kantor, I shall."

They left the tent together. She picked up her escort of Ylsa and Keren at the door of the command tent, and went her own way in the golden light of another perfect evening, while Alberich started off on the last of the errands she had set him.

The last turned out to be the first; Crathach was nearby, and heartily approved of Selenay's wish to sleep early. Most of the rest were trivial and easily discharged. That left the organization of what were essentially funeral corteges through every hamlet, village, and town on the road to Haven. But rather than solve that one himself, he asked Kantor to have all the Heralds that were left in camp—save only Selenay's bodyguards—meet him back at the command tent, and bring with them the remaining highborn, officers, and Bards. The latter because Bards tended to be very good at concocting ceremonies, and he suspected they would have some ideas.

They did. And it didn't take very long either, since this was only going to be a procession. The greatest amount of time was spent in deciding what the order of precedence was going to be, and then, what places in the procession would belong to whom. He left them at it, after about a mark; *his* place would be with Selenay, and if they settled their differences without any interference from him, even if not everyone was happy, they couldn't attach any blame to him *or* the Queen.

And nothing would be required of her except to follow the wagon carrying the coffin on foot, with Caryo walking beside her. Certainly no speeches. The focus of attention wouldn't be on her, but rightfully, on the King's remains, which should be something of a relief. So he hoped, anyway. If she wept, all the better. He hoped she would weep; she hadn't done nearly enough.

By this time, it was full dark, and the camp was quiet; with an early start planned for the morrow, most people had, if their duties allowed, made an early night. He moved down the now-familiar lanes of tents in the light of the torches stuck on either side of his path, thinking that this place would look very odd when all of the canvas had been struck and there was no sign of what had stood here but trampled grass.

:*I'm glad to be leaving,*: Kantor said.

:*So am I.*: At least in Haven, there would not be the ever-present reminders that *this* was the place where they had lost a King.

His tent had been moved inside what had been the royal enclosure to adjoin Selenay's, and out of habit, he glanced at hers to see if there was any light showing.

There wasn't, and with a feeling of relief, he nodded to the guards at the tent door, and entered his own. They didn't trouble to leave guards inside the tent' anymore; Selenay's little pages all slept in bedrolls spread out across the floor, and anyone trying to get in would probably step on one of them. He certainly wouldn't get in quietly; those children slept lightly and the least little sound sent half a dozen heads shooting up. Any intruder would set off more noise than disturbing a flock of geese.

A lantern had been lit for him, and hung from the center pole, showing that most of his baggage had already been packed up and presumably put on the wagon. There wasn't much left; only a bedroll, a set of clean linen and the towels and soap he'd need in the morning, and Kantor.

Most Heralds' tents were big enough for their Companion, Myste's being an exception, but she had obviously gotten last choice on accommodations. Somewhat to his surprise, it wasn't at all unusual for Heralds to share their tents with their Companions, rather than using the canvas shelters. Kantor took up roughly half the space; that first night in his own tent again, bowed down by grief, he had craved Kantor's company with a need that was almost physical, and Kantor had obliged by leaving the canvas shelter at the side and moving into the tent proper. And at first, despite that craving, it had still seemed unnatural in a way to have a—horse—in his tent. Now it was just as in the old days when he had shared tent space with another Sunsguard; it no longer seemed at all odd to see him there.

:Excuse me. I believe I am far better company than any *of the Sunsguard you ever shared tent space with,:* Kantor said indignantly.

He felt instantly contrite. *:I beg your pardon. Indeed you are. Did anyone leave anything here for me to eat?:*

Selenay's swarm of little ones had adopted him as well, and lately had taken to fetching food for him at the same time that they got meals for her, leaving them in his tent, well-covered and protected against the depredations of insects and other pests.

:As a matter of fact, they did, and—I don't suppose you'll share?: Kantor asked hopefully.

Since his appetite had suffered as much lately as Selenay's, Kantor's hope was well-founded. *:I don't know why not.:* He sat down on the bedroll and saw that the usual covered platter and cup had been left for him, cleverly balanced on two more cups in a pan of water, which prevented insects from crawling into it.

He took them out, and shoved the pan of water over to Kantor's side of the tent. Taking the cover off the platter explained why Kantor had hoped he'd share.

Selenay had asked for the impossible, gotten it, and had seen to it that *he* got some of the cook's largesse. Perfect for the heavy weather and a failing appetite were two sallats, a savory one and a sweet, the former a bed of greens with cheese, bits of chicken, fragrant herbs and spiced vinegar, the latter of chopped fresh fruit and nuts, with honey-sweetened cream. How had she known he'd like such things, too?

:Pfff. She asked me via Caryo, of course; she doesn't need being told something twice. I'd like some of that cress, please, and some spinach.:

With the empty platter and cup left outside his tent door, he stretched out along his bedroll, and listened to the sounds of the camp. He had been a soldier for too long not to be able to sleep when he needed to, but he had also been a soldier for too long not to be able to assess the mood of the camp just from the night noises.

Tonight, he sensed mostly weariness and relief. They had been here long enough, and, through work and time, what had been terrible anguish had muted to bearable sorrow. Now it was more than time to go home and take up their lives again. Except, perhaps, for Selenay, the time for grief was over, and the time to move on had come.

And that was as it should be.

When morning came, he was barely able to get dressed and out of his tent before Selenay's servants swarmed all over it. Her tent had already been struck, and she was finishing a strong cup of *chava* and a buttered roll while in her saddle, as he escaped from the collapsing tent still tying the laces at the collar and cuffs of his shirt.

One of the "pages" handed him a similar cup and roll and waited, impatiently, for the empty cup. Another brought Kantor a bucket of grain; the Companion immediately plunged his nose into it and began his own breakfast. Prudently, Alberich ate and drank *before* getting into the saddle; there wasn't a chance he'd be given a chance to finish unless he did.

The *chava* wasn't scalding hot, as he had feared it might be, but the heavy admixture of cream and sugar, and the color, like thin mud, warned him that it was probably from the bottom of the pot.

It was; even with the help of cream and sweetening, it nearly made his hair stand on end. But it certainly woke him up. He handed the empty cup to the page, who took it and vanished; the second whisked off the bucket the moment Kantor lifted his head from it.

All around them, tents were falling in the thin gray light of predawn. Selenay gave her cup to a page just as Ylsa and Keren walked their

Companions into what had been the royal enclosure. Alberich was in the saddle a moment later.

Selenay looked around at the vanishing camp. "Is breaking camp always like this?" she asked, a little dazed.

"A camp, we Sunsguard seldom had," Alberich admitted.

"I got the impression last night that everyone was pretty impatient to be out of here. But don't take my word for it." Keren shrugged. "I don't usually serve with the army."

"That speech you should make before we leave, I fear," Alberich told Selenay in an undertone. "But it will be the last, until Haven we reach. This, I can promise."

She grimaced, but nodded. "I hope you two know where I'm supposed to be?" she asked the other two.

"That's why we're here," Ylsa told her. "They sent us to fetch you."

Selenay gestured broadly with one hand. "Well, lead on, since you know where we're going."

The procession—for procession it would be, even when it wasn't going through a village—had already begun to form up on the road. Keren and Ylsa went straight to the front of it, where the rest of Selenay's guards were waiting. The funeral wagon would *not* be immediately behind her, but would be the first of the string of wagons.

Bard Lellian, in charge of the ceremonial part of the journey, came up and introduced himself.

"Majesty, I have devised something I hope will meet with your approval," he told Selenay, ignoring the rest of them in a way that told Alberich that his single-minded focus was due to anxiety, not an intention to slight them. "It will not be the ordeal that stopping for speeches would have been. You will merely have to drop back and take your place on foot behind the coffin when we reach any sort of town, along with the rest of the notables who have been deemed of high enough rank to follow you afoot. That is all; simply follow afoot, and—do whatever you feel impelled to do."

Selenay's relief at the simplicity of the arrangements was obvious.

"Then, when you have dropped back, the riders here at the front will all divide to either side of the road, let the wagon and the walkers pass, and fall in behind the last of the walkers, except for two Bards with muffled drums," the Bard finished. "Those will ride in front of the wagon." He peered anxiously at her; he was not a young man, but he didn't seem to know Selenay very well. "I hope that meets with your approval?"

:He's a specialist in this sort of thing,: Kantor confided. *:Funeral dirges, memorial ballads, funerary rituals—rather a melancholy profession, I would think, but apparently it suits him. This is the first time he's had anything to do with the Royals, though, and he's nervous.:*

"I think it is very fine," she told him, and he smiled with relief. "You must have worked terribly hard to come up with something this— appropriate—at such short notice."

Now he blushed with pleasure, and murmured a disclaimer. She raised her head to assess the state of preparations even as he thanked her.

:We seem to be ready to move out,: Kantor told his Chosen.

"Would you sound a call for silence, please?" Selenay asked the Bard, who snatched up the trumpet at his saddle bow, and played a four-note flourish.

Silence fell immediately, and Selenay rode Caryo up onto the bank beside the road so that everyone could see her.

"This seems to be a moment that requires a speech," she said, into the waiting silence. "But a speech, to me, means something that has been prepared for the ears of strangers, and after all that we have been through together, I think that none of us are strangers now." She paused and looked up and down the road, and Alberich knew that she was making certain each and every one of those in this cortege felt she had made eye contact with *him*. "Perhaps some day, when our losses are not so fresh, our wounds are not so raw, we will be able to look back on our victory *as* a victory, with more pride than sorrow. And we *should*. It was not only my father's sacrifice that won the day, it was the sacrifice of every single person who perished or was wounded, and every one of you who held a weapon, who wielded your Gifts, who tended a beast, kept us fed, or served any other task here. The victory belongs to all of you, and never, ever let anyone tell you differently."

She took a breath, blinked hard, and continued. "And even if the enemy had won here, he would never have taken Valdemar, for Valdemar is more than land; Valdemar is the people, and the spirit that lives in those people, and that spirit can never be conquered." Now she looked at the sealed coffin, draped in black, and covered with a pall upon which the arms of Valdemar were embroidered—a pall that had once been Sendar and Selenay's battle banners, and which were still stained with blood. Not just Sendar's blood either, but that of all those who had been with him, whether wounded, or fallen. "He knew that, and he trusted to that spirit to carry on, no matter what happened to him. You have shown that spirit is alive in all of you, and he could have no better tribute than that, nor would he have asked for anything more." Another pause. "And I do not ask for anything *less.*"

:*Well said, my Queen,:* he Mindspoke to her, and was rewarded by a brief flicker of her eyes in his direction.

"Now it is time for all of us to tender him our final service," she finished. "Now—let us bear him gently home."

And she rode down the bank to her place at the head of the procession, and lifted her hand in signal.

Alberich took his place at her side, with Keren and Ylsa to the right and left. She dropped her hand, and they moved forward on the road to Haven.

And though there had not yet been a ceremony, or a coronation, everyone in that procession knew that *this* was the moment when the Heir truly took up the reins of power. And so, in silence but for the sound of hooves and feet and wheels on the road, the reign of King Sendar ended, and the reign of Queen Selenay began.

2 0

The journey north accomplished for Selenay what the cleanup of the battlefield had done for everyone else; it allowed her to indulge in the full expression of her mourning—in public. Until the moment of departure, she had held her grief firmly in check, perhaps feeling that with so many others suffering, she should not further burden them with her own grief. If she wept, she did so only in private; everyone knew she mourned, but she did so quietly. But on this journey, her public duty was to mourn, to be the symbol of Valdemar's grief, and at last she could give free rein to all of the anguish she had held inside.

It seemed that everyone along their route wished to pay their final respects to the King; farmers left their fields, shepherds their flocks, tradesmen their crafts. Villagers and townsfolk lined both sides of the road, and the road itself was carpeted with rushes, flowers and herbs whenever they entered a town, so much so that the wheels of the wagons were muffled and cushioned against bumps. People carrying baskets and great bouquets of blossoms, and even hand-woven garlands and blankets of flowers, brought them up and placed them on the wagon as it crept past them at a slow walk, until it overflowed with blooms and foliage, and nothing of the black-draped coffin could be seen. And *they* wept, which had the effect of freeing Selenay's tears.

It was exhausting for her, but at the same time, it was exactly what she needed. Alberich and Crathach saw to it that she got plenty to drink, plenty of clean handkerchiefs, and the occasional arm about her shoulders. The Healer concocted soothing eyewashes to rinse her sore eyes and face with whenever they stopped. She ate with growing appetite, which was no bad thing, and was so emotionally exhausted by the time they camped for the night that she slept soundly and without waking. Her little pages saw to it that she had everything she needed, faithful as hounds. And each day that passed saw a little easing of the tension within her that had kept her so near to the breaking point.

It was not that she ceased to care, or became numb, as the days passed. It was more as if the worst of her grief was a finite thing, a barrel that had only *seemed* bottomless until she began allowing it to flow freely.

By the time they reached Haven, and the procession made its slow and solemn way through the city to the Palace, that pinched and overstrained look had left her. She wore her sorrow and her loss like a cloak, with grave dignity, rather than being bowed down beneath their intolerable burden.

She needed that release, for as the journey reached its end, she was about to undertake her final ordeal; the entrance to Haven marked the day of Sendar's official funeral. Haven had been waiting too long to put it off for even one more day—and that wasn't a bad thing. The funeral, though it would be exhausting for all concerned, especially Selenay, would put closure to everything.

They all camped overnight just outside the walls at the Royal and Home Farms, and servants from the Palace brought them all formal mourning garments, Formal Whites, Greens, and Scarlets. The line for the bathing facilities and even to use the horse troughs and pumps for a bath was a long one, and Alberich (as did many others) elected to bathe in the river instead; the faint, weedy fragrance of the river water was no match for the strong horse soap they used on themselves as well as their mounts. When they arrived at the gate of the city in the early morning, they looked as if they had all come straight from the Palace itself, and the wagons carrying tents, belongings, and a small mountain of dirty clothing had already gone up the hill, leaving only one single wagon, the one that had carried Sendar to his final rest.

The Court joined them at the first gate; the Lord Marshal, the Seneschal, and the heads of Bardic, Healers' and Heralds' Circles all walked with her behind the coffin, while the rest joined the riders. The coffin itself was transferred by a hand-picked group of the Guard, with great solemnity and ceremony, to a more ornate carriage used solely for state funerals before Sendar made his last journey through the streets of his capitol.

And Talamir joined them as well; Alberich was glad enough to relinquish his place at the young Queen's side and join the rest of her bodyguards.

But Talamir did not so much ride to meet Selenay as *appear*. It was a very strange moment for Alberich, when the official greetings were over and suddenly, in a pause and a pocket of silence that seemed created for him, there was Talamir.

And Talamir was changed, vastly changed.

It was more than just the twenty years that had been added, overnight, to his appearance. It was more than just that his hair had gone silver-white, like the mane of a Companion. After all, Alberich had found gray roots to the hair at his temples this very morning, when he had stolen a moment at an unoccupied mirror. It was much, much more than that. There was an otherworldly *stillness* about the Queen's Own, a distant look in his eyes as if he was always *listening* to something no one else could hear, and a faint translucency about him, as if his flesh was not quite solid enough to contain all of the light of his spirit. And a sadness that had nothing to do with the all-too-mortal grief he displayed so openly for his King.

It made Alberich shiver a little, and he sensed he wasn't the only one—but not everyone seemed to notice the change. Selenay didn't, for one. But perhaps she was too young, too involved with her own grief, or both—

Alberich was just glad to acknowledge Talamir's thanks, and drop back farther into the procession, selfishly grateful to Talamir for having recovered quickly enough to take his proper place back; it hadn't been a position *he* had been comfortable with. He hated being in the public eye, on show. Now, in the Formal Whites that the young Queen had asked him to don for the funeral, he was just one Herald among many.

Besides, now we're into Haven, we come into Court protocols and precedence, all the pomp and ceremony that I know nothing about. The arrival of the state funeral coach had been the first sign that he was rapidly getting out of his depth of experience.

He and the other Heralds—and the Royal Guards that were left—rode alongside the walkers, between them and the crowds of onlookers and mourners. Here, as out in the country, the streets were carpeted with flowers and the green herbs of mourning, rue and rosemary, but there were far, far too many people here to allow folk to pile more flowers on the carriage; it would have been covered within a single block. That was all right; they seemed content enough to strew their blossoms in the path of the carriage and the procession.

The muffled drums, augmented now by more mounted and walking musicians, made a dull throbbing through the too-quiet streets. That was the strangest part of all, the *quiet* in the city. Alberich was used to the noise of Haven, but today, the silence was broken only by the sound of people sobbing, and even that was muffled, as if the mourners did not want to spoil the solemnity of the occasion by being too vocal.

They stopped three times in the course of the morning, at three of Sendar's favorite temples, for memorial services that were mercifully brief—just long enough that the walkers could rest before carrying on. Similar services were being held all over the city, and would be all day, and well into the night, but *these* comprised the official funeral for the citizens of Haven.

And it took most of the day to get from the city gates to the Palace Gates. They took one break at noon, at one of the huge Guildhouse Squares; Selenay and her entourage retired to the Needleworkers' Guildhouse for rest and a meal, while Sendar's coffin lay in state in the enormous Guildhall of the Woolmerchants' Guildhouse, and lines of folk, some of whom had traveled for a day to be here, filed past.

Then the procession began again after two candlemarks, stopping twice more for two more memorial ceremonies. And at long last, they entered the Gates of the Palace. By then, they were all exhausted, even those who had only joined the procession when it entered Haven.

Sendar was to be interred in the crypt beneath the floor of the Palace Chapel, along with the rest of his line; all was in readiness there, and had been, presumably, for days. The Guard now marched off to their barracks, leaving a much shrunken company to enter the chapel behind the coffin. They all filed inside, where at least it was possible for those who had been walking for so long to sit down.

Candles had already been lit all over the chapel, although the last light penetrated the western windows, and the interior was overly warm, with the golden and reddish light making it appear warmer still. Incense warred with the scent of lilies for supremacy. The chapel was packed solid, shoulder to shoulder; Alberich, who had been riding all day rather than walking, took a standing position up against the wall beside the Royal pew. He was glad to be *there*, truth to tell; the stone wall felt cool against his back.

It *could* have been awful; speaker after interminable speaker eulogizing the King, until grief turned to benumbed boredom. And that would have been a terrible thing to do to Selenay. But someone had been wise; there were no interminable eulogies, only a few, brief speeches by those who had known and loved Sendar the best, punctuated by some of the most glorious music that Alberich had ever heard. Not for nothing was this also the site of Bardic Collegium; the Bards had exerted themselves to the utmost, and even though he had thought that the depths of his grief had been plumbed and exhausted, it was the music that brought tears again to his eyes. Anyone who could have listened to such music and not wept must have had a heart of stone.

Needless to say, when it came time for the last of the speakers—Selenay—she mounted the podium with reddened eyes and tear-streaked cheeks. But her voice was clear and steady as she spoke.

"Sendar was my King as well as my father," she said simply. "He was outstanding at both tasks. It can't have been easy to rule this unruly land of ours, and at the same time govern an ungovernable child, being father *and* mother to her—but he did it, and did it well. I will spend the rest of my life missing him; wishing he could be here to see—so many things. I suspect Valdemar will miss his steady hands on the reins, too. I can only pray that I can be as wise and compassionate a ruler as he was; I doubt very much if I can ever equal him as a parent. And I would gladly give my own life to have our positions reversed." She raised her head a little. "Nevertheless, such a sacrifice demands more than just words; it demands deeds. It demands that we *be* worthy of it; it demands that we all go beyond what we think is enough, making our own sacrifices in the name of a better life for all of Valdemar. That, in the truest essence, is what *he* did. That is what *I* will do. That is what he would expect of all of us; he deserves, and should have, nothing less than excellence as a fitting tribute to his memory. Only then can we be worthy of such a great and terrible gift—the life of a King."

She sat down in silence. And it seemed to Alberich that she had surprised many of her listeners—nonplussed some—and actually startled others. They were not sure how to react to her. This was *not* the speech of a young woman, overwhelmed with grief, that they had expected to hear...

More music filled the silence, then, a final prayer, and the service was over. A small and very intimate party followed the coffin down into the crypt for the final interment; Alberich was not part of that procession, nor did he wish to be. He had been an integral part of a funeral that had stretched on for far too long, from the Border to Haven, and—meaning no disrespect to Sendar's memory—he was weary of it, and wanted only to rest.

:Believe me, Selenay feels the same,: Kantor told him, the weariness in *his* mind-voice clear as cut crystal. *:She's going straight to bed, and she told Caryo that she is going to sleep for a week! We' re already bedded down, and Caryo and I intend to stay here and rest. I told Caryo to stay as long as Selenay stays asleep.:*

:Good,: he said, and meant it. He remained where he was only long

enough to see them all emerge from the crypt, see that the Seneschal cut short the line of those wishing to offer condolences, and watch Selenay vanish through the private door at the rear of the chapel that led straight into the Royal Suite with Talamir, Crathach, and the Seneschal in close attendance. Then he made good his own escape. Perhaps he should have stayed to listen to the Court gossip and read what he could out of expressions and what was *not* said, but—

—but that, frankly, was Talamir's job.

Then he recalled what Talamir had looked like, and wondered if Talamir was even capable of descending to such mundane and petty depths now. *All right. I had better start to learn it. But not tonight.*

The air in the chapel had been warm, and now it felt stifling; too hot, too heavy with the mingled scents of candle wax, incense, and lilies. He was only too glad to get out into the night. It was sultry and humid out there, but not as suffocating as the Chapel had been.

And he was unsurprised to be intercepted at the door by Dethor, who must have stationed himself right at the exit. He'd sensed the old Weaponsmaster lurking somewhere about, but he figured that Dethor would wait until *he* was free before greeting him.

"By your Sunlord, boy, it is *good* to see you," was all the old man said, but Alberich felt something inside him warm at the welcome. He seized Alberich's shoulders in both hands, and stared into his eyes, while the last few mourners filed out of the chapel door behind them. "I wish I could tell you just how good it is."

"I think that I may know, for as good it is to see you," he replied quietly, and sighed. "A thousand things, I wish to tell you—"

"And all of them can wait. A good cleanup for you, and then your own bed," Dethor told him firmly. "That's why I came here to get you. Falling on your nose won't honor Sendar or help his daughter, and besides, she's got all of the Collegium and every Herald that could get here to keep an eye on her tonight."

He felt compelled to protest weakly. "But—duties I have—"

"Which are in Talamir's hands, at least as far as Selenay is concerned. Do him good." Dethor gave him a little push to send him on the path down toward the salle. "As for your duties as Weaponsmaster, the Court and Collegia are in a week of official mourning. No Council meetings unless there's an emergency, no Court functions, no classes, no lessons. The only thing on anyone's plate is planning the coronation, and *that* is for the Seneschal and Bardic Collegium, not us. Not even Selenay, actually; all *she* has to do is go through what they plan out for her. For you lot, this is a week of rest."

"Ah." He absorbed that with relief—when something that Dethor had said at the beginning of the explanation struck him as odd. "Dethor— Weaponsmaster's Second, I am, not Weaponsmaster—"

"Not as of today, you're not," Dethor said smugly.

"With the Dean's approval, *I* just retired, and *you* are Weaponsmaster."

"Ah—" he said. It was all he could say. He felt completely stunned and utterly blindsided. This, he had *not* expected!

"Glad you agree," said Dethor with satisfaction. "Which is just as well, since it's too late for you to back out. Come along. It's a shower bath for you, and then bed. Worry about whatever it is you're going to worry about *tomorrow.* "

:You might as well surrender now,: Kantor said sleepily. *:He still outranks you. Retired Weaponsmaster outranks the current Weaponsmaster.:*

And in fact, there was a sweet relief in doing just that, surrendering and letting someone else give the orders. He had *never* thought he would be comfortable in doing that—but he had never trusted anyone the way he now trusted these friends—these brothers—his fellow Heralds. As *they* trusted him; had trusted him with the safety and life of their Queen, and their own.

As they had trusted him to go home to Karse—and come out again.

"In your hands, I put myself," he said, and gave in gracefully to the inevitable.

"I find it somewhat ironic," Selenay said, a good two weeks and a bit later, as Alberich stood beside her, on her left. "That one of the first things I do is ask you to keep to your shadow-Grays, and yet circumstances keep forcing you into Whites."

They stood outside the doors of the Great Hall, and from the other side came a hum of voices and a sense of expectation. On her right was Talamir, in that same set of Formal Whites Alberich recalled from the first moment he'd actually *seen* the Queen's Own. Now he wore a set of Whites every bit as elaborate as Talamir's, and very uncomfortable he felt in them, too. It wasn't as if they were ill-fitting; quite the contrary, they fit him better than any clothing he'd ever worn. They should. It had taken two cobblers, three tailors, and five fittings to ensure that they did, and the wonder was, it had all been done in just under a fortnight. No, it was that same reaction he'd had to Talamir's Whites; this was a set of clothing for a highborn courtier, not a common man like him.

:I believe at the time you were thinking, "a foppish highborn courtier," or something of the sort,: Kantor observed.

:So I was. I still think so. And the moment all this is over, I am changing out of these ridiculous garments as quickly as humanly possible.

He refrained from tugging at his high collar. It wasn't tight; he only felt as if it *should* be. "Only for one day, it is," he replied. "Tomorrow, Alberich the Grim I shall again be." He did *not* add how much it would take to induce him back into the cursed Whites.

"Is that what the Trainees call you?" Talamir asked with interest. Talamir's health had improved vastly, and continued to do so, but there was still something that was otherworldly about him—more so at some times than others—as if only part of him was still here, among the living. And it wasn't as if he was absentminded, or that his mind wandered; actually, he was, if anything, sharper than ever. He noticed *everything* but said very little. Perhaps that was part of it; he stood aside from life, an observer rather than a participant. The things that irritated and annoyed other people, Talamir did not even comment upon; Alberich wondered if there was even anything he was afraid of anymore.

There were times when he seemed so distant and remote that he didn't quite seem human…

Fortunately, today he was very much in the moment, and the most like his old self that he'd been since before the last battle.

"Oh, that they call me, other things among," Alberich replied. "And 'Great Stone-Face,' or 'Herald Stone-Heart.'" He permitted himself a sardonic little smile. "They take me, perhaps, for granite."

Talamir and Selenay both blinked at him. "Was that a *joke* I just heard?" Talamir asked, in utter disbelief. "A *pun?*"

"Not possible," he replied blandly. "No sense of humor have I. All know this."

It was too late for any retort, for the trumpets sounded just beyond the double doors of the Great Hall. The doors themselves were opened from inside, and Selenay stepped forward, followed closely by her two escorting Heralds.

The Great Hall was crowded as full as it could be with every highborn and notable who had been able to get here in time for the funeral and subsequent coronation. All six of Selenay's little Tedrel pages, decked out in the dark blue of the Royal livery, preceded her as she paced up the narrow path between the two halves of the audience, in time to the music. Each of them had a basket of fragrant herbs, which they scattered in her path with meticulous care. Initial rehearsals had them either dumping handfuls and running out halfway up to the dais, or being so stingy with each leaf that they still had full baskets when they got there, so they were taking immense care to do it *right* this time. The looks of fierce concentration on their little faces were quite endearing.

All of the doors and windows were flung open to the summer day outside the Hall, so at least it wasn't as close in here as it could have been. But the crowd glittered like the contents of an overturned jewel chest, garbed in so many colors that, after a fortnight of the stark blacks and whites of mourning, it hurt Alberich's eyes to look at them. The sunshine pouring in the windows glanced off gold and jewels, and the crowd glittered with every tiny movement.

Selenay set the pace, they only had to follow her; she looked meditative, as if she was taking a stroll in the gardens, not walking up to the throne that she would officially take in a few moments. Alberich thought that *she* looked as beautiful and fragile as a snow spirit in the gown that had been made for this moment, a gown of some soft, silky, draping stuff based on Herald's Whites, but with winglike sleeves and a train that trailed out behind her, glittering with tiny moonstones and gold beads, and a chaplet of moonstones and beads in her unbound hair. He would much rather that she had worn her armor, truth to be told. He would have preferred to see her marching up to the throne like a conquering battle maiden. Who would take this sweet young *girl* seriously as a monarch?

The army. Anyone who was with us on the battlefield. Perhaps those who heard her eulogy for her father. But the others? Highborn and notables from across the land? They knew only what they saw—a girl, a mere girl, come to govern.

Well, she'd better learn how to handle them. It was her job to *make* them take her seriously.

With perfect timing, they reached the dais just as the music ended. And in a silence remarkable for a room holding so many people, the three of them ascended it.

Waiting for them there were the chief members of the Council, ranged in a half circle behind the throne—the Seneschal, the Lord of the Treasury, the Lord Marshal, and the chiefs of the Heraldic, Bardic, and Healer's Circle. Representing all of the various and varied religions of Haven was the Patriarch Pellion d'Genrayes; Alberich didn't know which sect and temple he represented, but he *looked* every inch the part—white-haired, bearded, in robes of purple and white that were absolutely stiff with white embroidery, and an imposing staff capped with a huge globe of amber.

"Who comes before the throne of Valdemar?" the Lord Marshal thundered, placing his hand on the hilt of his purely ornamental sword.

"I, Selenay, daughter of Sendar, and rightful Queen of Valdemar," she replied, in a voice as cool as mountain snow. "In the name of the gods, I lay claim to the throne of Valdemar."

"By what tokens do you claim the throne?" asked the Seneschal, who looked nothing near as imposing as the Lord Marshal. Truth be told, he *looked* as if he should be asking, "Have we got the order of precedence right?"

Selenay answered the challenge as her father's daughter should. "By the token of my blood, of the line of Valdemar, first King of this land. By the token of my Choosing, by the Companion Caryo. By the token of my mind, trained to rule this land as wisely as the first King. By the token of my heart, that is given to the service of the people of this land. And by the token of my right hand, that will wield the sword of war or the staff of peace over it as need be." She held her head high, and her voice remained steady and clear.

"And who vouches for these things?" the Lord Treasurer asked.

"I vouch for her blood, of the line of Valdemar, for my Healers saw her born of Sendar's consort," said the Chief Healer.

It was the Chief Herald's turn. "And I, that she is Chosen by the Companion Caryo, for my Heralds saw her trained and granted Whites."

"I," the chief Bard said, somehow putting far more theatrical flourish into the words than anyone else, "vouch for her mind, for my Bards have tested her training, and found it complete."

Now it was Talamir's turn; his voice trembled a little, but only a little, and Alberich didn't think that anyone noticed but him. "I vouch for her heart, for I am the Queen's Own, and her heart is open to me."

Now, tradition said that the last lines were to be spoken by the Lord Marshal himself, but Selenay had asked for Alberich to take the final part. "Who else could *but* you?" she had asked, and he could not find it in him to deny her. He had drummed his response into his brain until he woke to find himself reciting it in his sleep; this was *no* time to let his Karsite syntax mangle what he was going to say.

"And I," he said, in a voice that sounded harsh to his own ears, "vouch for her hand, strong in defense, gentle to nurture, for I am the Queen's Champion, and I have tested her will and her spirit in the fires of adversity."

The Lord Marshal nodded, and stepped back. "Then come, Selenay, daughter of Sendar. Come and assume your rightful place, Queen of Valdemar."

Selenay took the last few paces until she was within touching distance of the throne, then turned, and faced the gathering. Her pages scrambled to gather up the train of her gown and arrange it at her feet. Alberich moved farther to her left and took the gold wand that served as the seldom-used scepter from the hands of the Seneschal, as Talamir did the same on the right and took the crown from the Seneschal. Selenay removed the bejeweled chaplet with her own hands, and gave it to the Treasurer.

With infinite care, Talamir placed the simple gold crown, hardly more than an engraved circlet, on her golden head, and stepped back to take his place behind the throne. Alberich gave the scepter into her hands, and looked for a moment deeply into her eyes.

She looked back at him fearlessly. A world of question and reassurance passed between them in that look, and he could not have told which of them comforted the other more. But he knew then, in that moment, that no matter what hardships, what trials came in the future, she would not break under them. He *had* seen her tested in the fires of adversity, tested and tried and tempered, and she had come out of it full of strength, true as steel, and as tough and flexible.

:As have you,: Kantor said, a universe of love and pride coloring the words. *:And those who don't see it, haven't eyes. The rest are proud that you are one of us, Herald Alberich.:*

He stepped back and took *his* place, next to Talamir, and the Lord Marshal called out the very same words that *he* had used, all those many days ago, on the road to Haven.

"Valdemar—behold your Queen!"

And the cheer that erupted from those gathered below her held nothing feigned or uncertain.

EPILOGUE

Alberich had wanted to come to the Temple of the Lord of Light and visit Geri for nearly a moon, but there had just been too much to do. It wasn't just his full duties as Weaponsmaster, although that was a time-devouring job in and of itself. When you added his continued forays into the darker streets of Haven, *then* his informal, but very necessary lessons with Talamir, lessons detailing the intricacies of the life of the Court and the highborn courtiers that made it the very hub of their existence, as well as all the eddies and swirls of intrigue within it—

There just hadn't been enough marks in a day.

Working with Talamir had been the hardest, although Talamir was, during these sessions, the *most* like his former self that he ever was these days. Alberich walked into the lessons with a shiver, and out of them with a feeling of relief and the strong sense that he'd been in the naked presence of someone who'd been done no favors by being brought back to life, and who lived each moment longing to return to the path he'd been taken from so that he could finish the journey.

But Crathach had been right; there *was* no one else that could serve as the Queen's Own that Selenay needed right now. And Talamir knew that.

Perhaps that was why he was driving Alberich so hard. Transferring the full weight of the job of—intelligence master, for lack of a better tide—onto Alberich's shoulders meant there was one less thing holding Talamir back from that delayed journey.

Finally, it had been the fact that he *hadn't* been to the temple in far too long that had decided him. Talamir was busy with some delegation or other paying respects to Selenay, and the scum of Haven could stew without him for one night.

Kantor heartily approved, which eased his conscience somewhat. And truth to tell, it felt very good to ride down into the city *without* wondering which persona he should don, if there was going to be any trouble that night, or whether he was going to have to explain himself to the constables and City Guard *again*. He felt relaxed, as he seldom did, as Kantor stopped inside the walls of the temple's outer court and waited for him to dismount.

On a pleasant evening like this one, he had expected the court to be full of the Sunlord's worshipers, and indeed it was. As the priests intended, the court was serving its function as the neighborhood gathering place. Older children who had not yet gone to bed played games along one wall, a number of folk were using the "free" lantern and torchlight to read by, sitting at the benches on the opposite wall to where the children played. There were little knots of gossip and courtship, awkward flirtation and some friendly rivalry, and even a pair of old men playing a game of castles on a portable board. Alberich wouldn't have been surprised to see a hot pie seller there, though no doubt, if one had appeared, Geri would have run him off. There were *some* things that were just a shade too undignified for the forecourt of a temple.

None of them paid any attention to Alberich. He was now a fixture at the temple—though he doubted that anyone knew him for the Queen's Champion, in his dark gray leathers. They probably thought he was just someone's private guard. Anyone could have a white horse, after all, and what would the Weaponsmaster of Herald's Collegium be doing down here, in this little neighborhood temple, anyway? Those with Karsite blood took great pride in the fact that one of their own was a Herald, but no one would ever dream that a Herald would come here to worship the Sunlord, however devout he was.

People, he was coming to think, mostly saw what they *expected* to see. And if they saw something that ran counter to their expectations, they tended to rationalize it away.

Useful, that, for a man in his position, though he would never trust his life to that principle. People were *also* likely to figure out the one thing you wanted to keep hidden from them at the worst possible moment.

The door to the temple lay open to catch the coolness of the night breezes, and he simply walked in. And stopped to stare.

For there was Geri, and around him was a gaggle of children, one of which he *recognized* as the little Karsite girl who had talked to him on the night of the rescue. They were all wearing a version of the warm yellow tunics and trews worn by novices in the service of Vkandis, brand new, and a bit oversized. And they all acted as if they were completely at home here.

Geri was giving them a Valdemaran lesson, with the flock of them tucked out of the way in the side chapel used for long vigils and private meditations. Alberich realized after a moment of complete blankness that this little temple had taken in all of the *Karsite* children that had been taken by the Tedrels. And if the hour seemed rather late for lessons, well, that might be the case for anyone other than a Temple of Vkandis—the Sunlord had rites and rituals going on from the dawn to sunset, and only after darkness fell was Geri going to be free to give these little ones the language class they needed before they could hope to learn anything else.

I'll have to ask Myste if she can get down here and give him a hand, he thought, watching them all. *I wonder if there are any other Karsite exiles who've got the time to help? Geri won't push it, but* Myste *will.*

He quickly moved back into the shadows, lest he disturb them, and watched. And felt something extraordinary unfold inside him. Something so extraordinary, that at first, he didn't recognize it for what it was.

Happiness. Pure, unalloyed happiness. Of *all* of the things he had done or had a hand in doing, this was the one that had brought nothing but good for all concerned, with nothing whatsoever to regret or wish he had done differently.

The children responded to Geri with all of the warmth that he would have expected; Geri was one of the kindest souls in the world, and children liked him even when he had to discipline them for something. But these children in particular were blossoming for the young priest like flowers in the sun—already he could tell a vast difference between the too-eager, too-helpful, anxious, pinch-faced little things they had been, and the bright-faced creatures they were now. It was wonderful. This was how Karsite children *should* look. And even as he reveled in the pleasure of knowing that *he* had had a key hand in making it possible for them to be here, he also knew a moment of sadness at the fact that even in Karse, most Karsite children were not this free, not this happy...

Sunlord, gentle giver of light, make it possible for them, too—

A small hand tugged at his sleeve, and he turned and looked down.

"I heard you were looking for me?" said a very small, *very* red-haired boy, with amazing blue eyes that looked oddly old in such a young face.

For a moment, Alberich stared at him, trying to work out what on earth the child could mean. Then it struck him.

"You are the boy they called Kantis?" he asked.

The child nodded. "And you're Alberich, the White Rider, the one who was promised to us. Right?"

"Well—" He squatted down on his heels, so that he could look the boy straight in the eye. "I would say that it depends on just who was doing the promising. And where he got his information."

The child grinned at him. "It would be me that was doing the promising, but the promise wasn't *mine*, it was the Prophecy. And it all came out of the Writ, of course. I know the Writ very well!" He struck a pose, and began to recite. "Alcar, Canto Seven, Verse Nine—*And the children shall be reft from the people, and they shall suffer in the hands of the infidel, but those that keep faith shall endure and the rulers of light shall redeem them.* Porphyr, Canto Twelve, Verse Twenty-two—*And lo! in the moment of despair, I shall be with you, I shall guide you, as you were a child, out of the camp of iniquity and into the hands of the saviors, and great spirits of white shall succor you.* Werthe, Canto Fifteen, Verse Forty-nine—*And a rider of the purest white spirit shall—*"

Alberich held up his hand to stop the flow of words. "I would say that you do, indeed, know the Writ very well," he admitted gravely. "But I am not at all certain that there is anything in those verses that *I* would recognize as being part of the—the Prophecy."

He was going to add, *if there ever was a Prophecy*, except that what this child had done, and the hope he had given the others, the way he had organized them and kept them going—how had that been so wrong? Even if it had all been a childish tale concocted out of the scraps of Writ he knew, the tales the Valdemaran children babbled, and his fertile imagination, it had essentially saved them.

"But I suppose it depends on how you interpret them," he finished instead. And smiled. "I wanted to meet you primarily because I wanted to thank you for helping all of the others so much."

The boy looked at him unblinking, but with a smile playing about his lips. "Isn't that what we're all supposed to do? Help each other? No matter who we are and where we come from? That's what the Writ says, in the Great Laws."

Where had the child learned *that?* Not from any of the Sunpriests that Alberich had served… "Absolutely right." He stood up, and gazed down at the child. "You are a very remarkable fellow."

"And so are you, Alberich of Karse, Herald of Valdemar." The child's voice suddenly deepened, and seemed to fill his ears, his mind, and his world shrank to the boy's young face and the voice that resonated all through him. He couldn't move. And he didn't want to… "A man of such conscience and honor is a remarkable man indeed; so remarkable, that it would seem that his prayers reach a little farther than most."

Alberich could not look away from those blue eyes, eyes which held an impossible golden flame in their depths. He wasn't afraid, though. Far from it. He had never felt such peace before in his life.

"A man of conscience and honor—who has found a fitting place in his exile, among those who value that honor, and honor the conscience." The boy nodded. "It is written that exiles do not last forever, for those who are true to their word, their family, and their home. But remember, always, that the Writ tells us that a man's home is where his family is, Herald Alberich. And also, that friends are the family one can choose…"

The child backed away a few paces, as Alberich felt his pulse hammering in his throat, as if he had run a very long distance. He hardly knew what to think; he couldn't have actually *said* anything if his life had depended on speaking.

The boy turned, and walked a few more steps away in the direction of the door, then looked back over his shoulder.

"And if you think what *I* am is remarkable, wait some few years. And you will see what my daughter can do. Or should I say, my daughter who will be my Son?" Then he laughed and ran off, a high, utterly childlike laugh that broke the spell that had held Alberich motionless.

He still couldn't think; his thoughts moved as if they were flowing through thick honey. But—he needed to run after that boy—

"Alberich!" Geri called, and he turned—

The priest had broken up the class, and apparently had spotted Alberich in the back of the temple. "I was hoping you'd come to see what we've done! We took *all* of the Karsite children when the Queen's people came to ask if we had room for any. You know, we just couldn't turn them away, and they've been a delight to have here. What's more, they are making remarkable progress!"

"Like—that boy?" he replied, feeling his heart still racing with an emotion that held both excitement and fear. No—not *fear*, but an emotion like fear. It took him a moment to recognize it as hope…

"Boy?" Geri looked puzzled. "What boy?"

"The boy I was—" he gestured, but there was no sign that there had ever been anyone there. "—talking—to—"

They both scanned the now-empty temple, but there was no sign of any children now. "It must have been one of the youngsters from the courtyard," Geri replied, looking puzzled. "All of the Karsite children were with me."

"Are any of the children who come here in the evening named Kantis?"

he ventured, not knowing whether he wanted to hear the answer.

But Geri only shrugged. "I haven't a clue, there are so many of them, and they just swarm the place in weather like this. Some of them aren't even worshipers of the Sunlord. They just come to play with our children."

Alberich licked dry lips and thought furiously. It *might* just have been a child playing a prank; it would have been natural for the Karsite children to tell others about Kantis and their peculiar prophecy. Children sometimes played the most elaborate jokes, *especially* on adults, when they thought they could get away with it. Although the families who worshiped here were fluent in Valdemaran, they all spoke Karsite at home, and children picked up languages easily. It would have been *easy* for one to pick out some passages from the Writ that matched that "Prophecy." Wouldn't it?

And who was he, to be the recipient of a visitation from the Sunlord Himself? No one. If anyone should have gotten a visitation, it should be Geri. Not him.

And—no. I won't worry this to death. If it was *the Sunlord in His aspect as Child of the Morning, or if it* wasn't, *it is all the same to how I should continue to act.* That was Free Will again, the Gift of the Sunlord, to choose or not choose a path. He would choose the same path he always had, that of honor. *And in either case, because pearls of wisdom drop from innocent mouths, I shall take the advice to heart, for it comes from the Writ, and I shall take comfort from it for the same reason.*

"It probably was one of the youngsters from outside; if you see him again, make sure to get him to talk to you, for he is remarkably well-spoken," he said, and slapped Geri on the back. "I am dying for a decent glass of tea. Why don't you tell me what you've been doing with these children, and give me some idea of how I can help?"

After all, wasn't that what everyone was supposed to do? Even an exile in a strange land—

Exile? The Writ—and the boy—were right. When he had come here, perhaps, but among these people, he had found those who understood that a man had to hold to his word and his honor. People who were the truest sort of friends—and as the Writ said, the sort of friends who became one's family.

Which meant that he wasn't really an exile after all.

It was good to be home.

EXILE'S VALOR

A VALDEMAR OMNIBUS

BOOK TWO
OF EXILES of VALDEMAR

Dedicated to the members of the NYFD, lost 9/11/01

Engine 1: Andrew Desperito; Michael Weinberg
Engine 4: Calixto Anaya Jr.; James Riches; Thomas Schoales;
Paul Tegtmeier
Engine 5: Manuel Delvalle
Engine 6: Paul Beyer; Thomas Holohan; William Johnston
Engine 8: Robert Parro
Engine 10: Gregg Atlas; Jeffrey Olsen; Paul Pansini
Engine 21: William Burke, Jr.
Engine 22: Thomas Castoria; Michael Elferis; Vincent Kane;
Martin McWilliams
Engine 23: Robert McPadden; James Pappageorge; Hector Tirado,
Jr.; Mark Whitford
Engine 26: Thomas Farino; Dana Hannon
Engine 33: Kevin Pfeifer; David Arce; Michael Boyle; Robert Evans;
Robert King, Jr.; Keithroy Maynard
Engine 37: John Giordano
Engine 40: John Ginley; Kevin Bracken; Michael Dauria; Bruce
Gary; Michael Lynch; Steve Meteado
Engine 50: Robert Spear, Jr.
Engine 54: Paul Gill; Jose Guadalupe; Leonard Ragaglia;
Christopher Santora
Engine 55: Peter Freund; Robert Lane; Christopher Mozzillo;
Stephen Russell

1

Muted light, richly colored, poured gold and sapphire into the sparsely furnished sitting room in Herald Alberich's private quarters behind the training salle.

Now that the colored window was installed, and the protective blanket taken off, it made that little room look entirely different. Alberich hardly recognized it.

The four Journeymen glassworkers who had helped their Master install the piece were gone now, leaving Alberich alone with the artist himself.

Both of them gazed on the finished product in silence, while behind them a warm fire crackled on the hearth. It was a staggeringly beautiful piece of stained-glass work; in fact, Alberich thought, it would not be exaggerating to say it was a masterpiece. Not that he had expected less than a fine piece from the Master of the Glassworkers Guild, but this was over and above those expectations.

The artisan responsible for its creation stepped forward and gave the top right-hand corner a final polish with a soft cloth, removing some smudge not visible to ordinary eyes. He flicked off an equally invisible dust mote as well, and stepped back to view the expanse of blues and golds with a critical eye. A man gone gray in his profession, he was tall, but not powerful, with wiry, knotty muscles rather than bulging ones. His expression was unreadable, a square-jawed, hook-nosed fellow whose face might have been stone rather than flesh.

"It'll do," he grunted finally, his long face betraying nothing but a flicker of content.

"A work of power and beauty, it is," Alberich replied, unusual warmth of feeling in his voice. "It is exceeding my expectations, which were high already. Your skill is formidable, Master Cuelin."

"It'll do," the artisan repeated, but with just a touch more satisfaction in his own voice. "I'll not praise myself, but it'll do."

This was such understatement that Alberich shook his head. In so many ways, this was a piece of artwork that went far, far beyond even the monumental works that only the great and wealthy could afford, be they individuals or organizations. It was the care to every detail, as much as the design, that showed that expertise. For instance, to protect the fragile leaded glass, made up of pieces no larger than a coin, the panel had been installed against the existing window. Now, the bars holding those old panes in place *could* have cast distracting lines across the new pattern—except that Master Cuelin had taken that into account in his design, and the shadows had been integrated in such a way that unless you looked for them, you did not notice them.

Yet Master Cuelin seemed no more than mildly pleased that everything had worked out as he had planned. Alberich knew that tone; not only from working with Master Cuelin on this window, but from working with others who shared the same obsessive drive to excellence that marked the man's work. No point in heaping him with effusive praise, for it would only make him uncomfortable, and he would begin to point out "flaws" in the work not visible to anyone but him.

"Very happy, you have made me," he said instead. "Never shall I weary of this piece." And although he had paid Master Cuelin already, when he shook the man's hands in thanks, a heavy little purse that had been in his hand slipped quietly into the Master's. That was the way of doing business, in Karse, when one was pleased with special work. Some things, Alberich felt, were probably universal—an extra "consideration" for work that exceeded expectation being one of them.

Evidently the custom held true in Valdemar, because Master Cuelin did not seem in the least surprised; he said nothing, only pocketed the purse with a nod of thanks. He dusted off his hands on the side of his brown leather tunic—all of his clothing, tunic, breeches, even his shirt, was leather, because leather wasn't likely to catch fire.

"Well, if you're that satisfied, Herald Alberich, I'll be off," the Glassmaster said. "I've that lazy lot of 'prentices to beat back at my studio, for no doubt they'll have ruined the cobalt plate I laid out for them to cut for the new 'Pothecary Guild window, aye, and muddled the designs I set them to copy, and complain I've assigned them too much work."

Alberich shook his head, in mock sadness. "It is ever so," he agreed, and sighed. "The younger generation—"

"We were never like that, eh?" Master Cuelin barked a laugh and slapped Alberich's back. The Weaponsmaster allowed a hint of a smile to show, and the Glassmaster winked. "Well, 'tis heavy work we have before us—you know what the old saw is, 'A boy's ears are on his backside, he heeds better when he's beaten!'"

Since there was nearly the identical saying in Karse, Alberich nodded, and with another exchange of pleasantries, he escorted the Glassmaster out. Indeed, some things were universal.

But since it was not yet time for the next class of Heraldic Trainees to arrive for their weapons' training, he returned to his sitting room in the back of the training salle to admire his newly installed possession once more.

This was more than mere ornament; while there was a Temple of Vkandis Sunlord down in Haven proper—though for obvious reasons, it was referred to even by Karsite exiles as "the Temple of the Lord of Light"—Alberich seldom was able to get there for the daylight ceremonies. Certainly he was never able to arrive for the all-important SunRising rite.

Contrary to what the current Karsite priesthood wished their followers to think, it was very clear in the Writ—now that Alberich had seen copies of the old, original versions—that any follower of the Sunlord could perform the rites, with or without a Sunpriest. It was what was in the heart, not the words, that mattered, and prayerful meditation at any time was appropriate. And now Alberich had an image here, a proper image, that would put him in the proper frame of mind.

There had been a plain glass window here, but the presence of such an expanse of clear glass had made Alberich, on reflection, rather uneasy. It was fine for the former Weaponsmaster, Herald Dethor, to have such a thing, but Dethor didn't have to think about potential Karsite assassins peering through it—or the far more common, but equally annoying habits of the young, idle, and foolish offspring of Valdemaran nobles daring each other to spy on the dreaded Weaponsmaster from Karse. Not that they'd see anything except Alberich reading, pacing, or staring at the fire, or occasionally entertaining a visitor, but it made him irritated to think of them watching him. It wasted their time, annoyed the Companions, and made the back of his neck prickle for no good reason. If he sensed someone watching him, he wanted to know there was danger, not adolescent curiosity behind it.

But he hadn't wanted to block off the window either. Very useful light came in there by day, although the view was nothing spectacular, just one of the groves of Companion's Field. It had been Herald Elcarth who had suggested the stained-glass panel when he had mentioned the annoyance of looking up to see lurkers in the bushes one night.

It had nearly been *former* lurkers in the bushes, and it was a good thing for them that he had Kantor out there to warn him it was only some Unaffiliates and a Bardic Trainee, because his hand had been on the one-handed crossbow he kept under the table, and he had no problem with shooting out a window. Especially not his own window. A bit of broken glass was a small price to pay for your life.

He hadn't mentioned that to Elcarth, however, though he *thought* he saw some understanding in the other's nod. Perhaps that was why the Herald had suggested the stained-glass panel. And at that moment, Alberich had realized how he could bring a kind of Vkandis chapel into his own home, make this place truly *his* home, and solve that problem of the huge window in a single stroke.

Elcarth hadn't known where to obtain such a thing, but Herald Jadus had. In fact, Jadus had pointed him to the particular glassworks involved in creating most of the stained- and etched-glass windows for the various Temples in and around Haven, whenever a generous patron was moved to donate such a thing.

Until he went to the workshop and saw some of the designs, Alberich hadn't been entirely certain of the exact shape and image of the design, only that it should have some link, somehow, to the Temples that he had felt most comfortable in. As soon as he realized what Cuelin specialized in, heraldic (rather than Heraldic) designs, he had realized what his window surely must show.

The Sun-In-Glory of the God of Karse, of course; Vkandis Sunlord in a form that few in Valdemar would recognize as such, and no one who mattered would likely take offense to. Particularly as *this* Sun-In-Glory would be laid out, not on the usual field of reds as in a similar window in Karse, but on a field of Heraldic blue.

If Master Cuelin realized just what the pattern was, he hadn't said anything. Alberich would not have wagered on his being ignorant, though. He had been doing religious glasswork for far too long not to have learned virtually every symbol of every deity worshiped in Haven, and every possible variation and nuance of each symbol. Vkandis *was* worshiped here, and by Karsite exiles—just not under that name. The "Lord of Light" was what He was called here; all things considered, a title and a name less likely to evoke hostility from the good neighbors of those exiles.

Alberich would not have taken it much amiss had Master Cuelin delegated the work to his apprentices either—but he hadn't. He'd attended to it all himself. And the result was glorious, well worth the cost of the one indulgence that Alberich had permitted himself since he'd been made Weaponsmaster.

:Very nice for us, too,: his Companion Kantor commented, as Alberich sat down and allowed himself to drink in the color and composition. *:We get the best view of it at night, when the light is coming from inside. Clever of you to station lanterns with reflectors shining outward at the bottom corners. Gives us a lovely piece to look at.:*

:And prevents any shadows falling upon it and telling people what goes on in my sitting room,: he pointed out. *:After paying no small fortune for such a piece, I've no mind to have it shattered by an ill-considered crossbow bolt from outside, because I was foolish enough to show a target.:*

Since there was no graceful reply to that, Kantor wisely declined to make one.

The leaded glass was thicker and heavier than the window it had been mounted against, and Alberich realized after a moment of sitting there that the drafts he'd become accustomed to were gone. Well. An unforeseen advantage.

And a third—as he bathed in the golden light from the Sun-In-Glory, despite the fact that on the other side of the glass, there was a bleak winter landscape under overcast skies, he understood why Master Cuelin had insisted that the Sun dominate the panel. No matter what the weather outside, the light coming in would be warm and welcoming. Already Alberich felt his spirits become a little lighter.

:For which my gratitude to Master Cuelin knows no bounds,: Kantor observed dryly. *:Anything that sweetens your temper makes me grateful.:*

:Indeed?: Alberich countered. *:Alas, that he cannot do me the return favor of creating such a thing for you, since you spend your days out of doors. Perhaps I should query Bardic Collegium about the possibility of serenading you on a thrice-weekly basis to sweeten your temper?:*

:Then who would chastise the greenlings properly?: Kantor asked airily. *:Disciplining the youngsters requires a certain acidity of temper to deliver correction with the appropriate degree of sting.:*

Alberich shook his head. He should learn never to try and exchange barbs with his Companion; Kantor would always win. Kantor was at least as old as his Chosen, probably a few years Alberich's senior, and twice as witty.

Not that there wasn't some truth in what Kantor said; Kantor was to the young Companions what Alberich was to the Heraldic Trainees, in a way. Not so much the trainer in fighting technique, for a great deal of *that* was in the hands of the riding instructors, but as the disciplinarian of the Companion herd. Normally that would be in the hands—or rather, authority, backed by speech, and occasionally hooves and teeth—of the Companion to the Queen's Own Herald, the Grove-Born Rolan. But Rolan's Herald was Queen's Own Talamir, who had very nearly died in the last battle with the Tedrels on the Border with Karse; Talamir's original Companion Taver *had* died, and one never spent much time in Talamir's presence without realizing that in many ways it had been no great service to Talamir that he had been brought back to life again. Though Kantor had never said as much in so many words, Alberich got the distinct impression that most of Rolan's time was taken up in making sure that Talamir remained—well—*sane*. So a good portion of Rolan's duties to the herd had been delegated to those best suited to the task.

Not all of those duties had gone to Kantor either.

Some were the provenance of some very wise old Companion mares, thus ironically echoing the hierarchy in a real horse herd, where the leaders were the oldest mares, not the stallion, as Alberich very well knew.

:Hmm. And human herds, though ye know it not.:

:Your point being—?: Alberich replied. *:Though you'd best not let Queen Selenay discover you think of her as an old mare, wise or not.:*

He sensed Kantor's snort of derision. *:Selenay should be perfectly happy to be compared to a Companion mare.:*

Alberich let that one go. There was no use trying to explain to Kantor that no nubile young woman was going to appreciate being compared to a mare, ever, under any circumstances.

Particularly not when her Councilors—some of them, anyway—were very diligently trying to make her into one. Of the brood-stock variety…

Which was one reason why he had welcomed Master Cuelin's arrival this afternoon to install the window, as the perfect excuse to avoid the afternoon Council meeting. *That* particular item was on the table for discussion, and it was a subject that Alberich was particularly anxious not to get embroiled in. For one thing, no matter how publicly he'd been lauded and laden with honors after the Tedrel Wars, no matter how trusted he was by most—by no means all—Valdemarans of note, he was still the outsider. He was, and always would be so. It could not be otherwise. And for another, well—

—well, it was a subject where nothing he said or did was "safe." Someone would take exception, whether he urged that Selenay remain single, or weighed in on the side of those who wanted her to wed, and at this point, he didn't need to add any enemies to a list that was already long enough.

The atmosphere of the Council Chamber this afternoon was unwontedly subdued. Usually there had been at least three arguments by this time, and the kinds of icy, polite catcalling that made people who were not used to Council debates blanch and wonder if a duel was about to break out. Today, however, was different. The atmosphere hadn't been so edgily cordial since the first tentative sessions after Selenay's coronation. Around the horseshoe-shaped, heavy wooden table not a voice had been raised. The representatives of the Bardic, Heraldic, and Healer Circles, in their red, white, and green uniforms respectively, had been extremely quiet, as had the Lord Marshal's Herald and the Seneschal's Herald, and of course, the Queen's Own Herald, Talamir.

As for the rest—well, they had been nervous. They didn't really know her, although she had been in their midst all of her life. They were her father's Council, really, not hers. They were his friends, advisers, and peers, and none of them had expected to serve her at all, much less so quickly. So they often argued and battled among themselves, as if she wasn't even there, or was no more than a token place holder.

Except on the rare occasions when what they wished to do was going to have to involve her. Then they generally acted as they did today; becoming very quiet, and rather nervous. These elder statesmen and women were apparently unaware that they gave themselves away, acting as they did.

Queen Selenay knew why they were nervous, of course. They didn't know she knew, which might have been funny under other circumstances. In the throne that had been her father's, with the chair at her right hand empty, Selenay watched her Councilors behaving as if they were good little schoolchildren debating beneath the strict disciplinarian eye of their teacher.

This was, of course, because they were shortly going to unite in a totally uncharacteristic burst of single-mindedness and do their level best to force their Queen to do something she had no intention of doing whatsoever.

Marry. Worse than that, to marry someone *they*, not she, had chosen. The potential candidates were as sad a collection as nightmare could have conjured. The youngest was ten, the oldest ninety. Among them were a number of young men, but even these were impossible. Some she had heartily detested from the moment she'd met them, others she didn't even know, and from their reputations, had no desire to know. A very few might be reasonable fellows, some were pleasant enough company on a casual basis, but that was no reason to marry any of them. Some were even Heralds, or at least, Trainees—but the Heralds all had lives of their own that she was not a part of, and as for Trainees—well, they seemed like mere infants to her now.

Her Councilors, however, did not see it that way.

It hadn't been like this when her father had sat in this throne, but Sendar had *ruled* as well as reigned. She reigned, but only the backing of the Heralds made it possible for her to command much of anything. She knew that; she had expected it from the moment she took the Crown. She was much too young to be a Queen, much too young to command the respect of men and women old enough to be her parents. Not even the white uniform proclaiming her a full Herald managed to gain her that respect.

Well, there were ways around that. But she was getting weary of the artful dodges, of setting her words in the mouths of others, and she had not even reigned a year. And these marriage plans were more than a mere inconvenience; they were an attack on her autonomy. Her good Councilors would not be happy with a mere Prince Consort. They wanted a King.

She tapped her index finger idly on the stack of papers just under her right hand, and smiled a grim little smile. Her Councilors—the non-Heraldic ones, anyway—were not aware that she had come prepared for this afternoon's meeting. She knew what every man and woman around the table was about to put forward, for not all of them had been close-mouthed about it, and Talamir had gotten wind of it and let her know what was planned. That had given her ample time to prepare for what they were about to unleash on her. They had no idea that she had come forewarned and forearmed.

For that matter, other than Talamir and Elcarth, she wasn't sure the other Heralds at the Council table were aware that she'd been engaged in laying the groundwork to defend her freedom.

It was nothing less that she had done, for her Councilors were determined that she should not reign alone—and each and every one of them had a particular candidate to place in the running, sometimes more than one. All of them, of course, with the best interests of the Kingdom foremost in their minds, or so, at least, they would tell themselves. Of course, every candidate would have blood ties or ties of obligation to the Councilor who put him forward, but never mind that. They would put such things out of their minds, telling themselves that they were doing this for Valdemar, and not for any selfish reasons. *There was no Heir! Selenay had been an only child, and the Crown now rested on her fragile head alone! She must marry, and produce children, quickly!*

Of course, if the chosen spouse happened to be helpful to friends and families, well…

Every one of them had given over whatever disputes they had to settle on that list of potential Consorts, arguing and trading without any consideration for what *she* wanted, until they had mutually agreed on enough men that if they couldn't bully her into taking one, they could wear her down until she agreed out of exhaustion.

When Talamir told her what the plans were, Selenay had gone straight to Herald-Chronicler-Second Myste, who was surely the only person in Haven who had the esoteric knowledge to help her out of the trap. And although she had not really expected a great deal of sympathy from Myste, the Herald had amazed her by reacting with indignation to the plans.

"By Keronos!" Myste had exclaimed, her eyes behind the thick lenses of her spectacles going narrow with speculation. "That's obscene! You haven't been Queen a year, girl! Shouldn't they at least wait until you've settled, and gotten comfortable with your place?"

"Apparently not," Selenay had replied, seething with anger. "And apparently none of them want to see a foreigner brought in as Consort either—or at least, they don't seem to have taken much thought about that particular possibility. Insane, I'd call it. Not that I particularly *want* a foreign Consort, but Father used to have serious talks with me about the possibility of needing to cement a foreign alliance with a marriage."

"Idiots," Myste had muttered under her breath, pushing her lenses up on her nose. "The hand of a Queen's too damned valuable to waste. What if, as your father said, we need an alliance?"

"What if we just need to keep five or six princes dangling on promises?" Selenay had countered. "And besides—"

She didn't add the "besides," which was that she wanted to be able to love her husband, not merely tolerate being in the same room with him. Myste probably guessed it, for she'd given Selenay a shrewd look, but she hadn't said anything, except: "Well, if they haven't got the sense to see past their own interests, it's up to some of the rest of us to see to it that they can't meddle."

And Myste had outdone herself on the Queen's behalf, spending every spare moment locked away with dusty law and record books going back generations. The result was the pile of neatly written papers under Selenay's hand.

Aside from the two exceptions of Talamir and Elcarth, there wasn't a single person around the Council table that had the slightest inkling that they were about to see what Selenay could do when she was *not* in a mood of sweet cooperation. In point of fact, no matter who was brought up, the various candidates for potential spouse were going to be mown down like so many stands of ripened grain...

Myste had not even told Alberich; she had sworn herself to secrecy before Selenay had even asked. There was no tighter-lipped creature in Valdemar than Myste when she opted to take that particular path.

It's too bad Alberich isn't here, Selenay thought, still tapping. *He might enjoy watching me dispose of this idiocy.* She missed his craggy, scarred face at the table today; although he did not have an official position on the Council, as Talamir's right-hand man (and in no small part, hers as well), he could and did sit in on it whenever he chose. When he did, he usually took Elcarth's seat as the representative of the Heraldic Circle. The Weaponsmaster knew of the plans, of course, though not how she intended to counter them. And she thought that he would take great pleasure in how she was going to discomfit them all.

Or maybe not. In Selenay's limited experience, a confirmed bachelor like Alberich had a tendency to panic when confronted by the question of potential matrimony, regardless of whether it was his or someone else's.

Besides, he's probably concerned that if I flatten every other possible consort, someone will suggest him as an alternative. The mere thought made her stifle a smile. While the Heralds would welcome the idea, and possibly even the Bard and Healer would as well, the rest of her Councilors would have apoplexy. They'd suggest she take an illiterate fisherman from Lake Evendim before they suggested Alberich. Not that she'd mind an illiterate fisherman from Lake Evendim half so much as she disliked some of the so-called "candidates" for her hand her Councilors were going to suggest.

The Councilors had been well aware from the moment they started their plotting that this was a subject their Queen was *not* going to entertain gladly, which was why they were intending to surprise her with it, in hopes of taking her off guard.

As they disposed of some final trivial business, they kept glancing at her out of the corners of their eyes, and there was a certain nervous tone to their voices that would have been amusing if she had not been so very angry with them. Her father had not been dead a year, and already they were at her to marry! As if she could not rule by herself, or at the very least, rule with the true counsel of those who were loyal to her (and not merely devoted to their own interests), and rule well and wisely!

:You can rule with more wisdom than some of their choices,: her Companion Caryo said into her mind. *:Not that some of their choices would be allowed to rule at all. They wouldn't be Chosen by a Companion if every living male in Valdemar were to drop dead this moment.:*

A stinging indictment indeed, coming, from Caryo.

And there was the real rub. What some of her Councilors seemed to keep forgetting was that any husband she took would be nothing more than Prince Consort unless he was also a Herald. Only *then* could he be a co-ruler.

Of course, they probably assumed that a young woman would be easily led by her husband to give him whatever he wanted, which would certainly make him the power behind the throne, if not an actual monarch. Some of them probably assumed that she could *make* a Companion Choose him, if she wanted it badly enough.

:The more fools they,: said Caryo.

:Well, they have a poor opinion of how strong a woman's will can be.: Selenay reflected, as she gathered her nerve, that it was a very good thing that Caryo was of a mind with her. It would be great deal easier to resist both bullying and blandishment with Caryo behind her.

:And don't forget, you have Myste, too,: Caryo reminded her.

Yes, indeed. Myste, her secret weapon, who not only had supplied her with this vast and intricate report, but was currently mewed up in the library with every book of Valdemaran genealogy in Haven at her fingertips, and a page to bring her whatever she needed for as long as this meeting lasted. No, her Councilors surely could never have reckoned on Myste.

The last of the minor business was disposed of. The Councilors put up their papers, some of them poured themselves wine, and there was a great deal of coughing and shuffling of feet. Then, as she expected, really, it was Lord Gartheser, more portly now than he had been before the Tedrel Wars, and more florid of face, who cleared his throat awkwardly and put the subject on the table.

"About the matter of Your Majesty's marriage—" he said, and stopped.

Selenay smiled sweetly, a smile that went no farther than her lips, as she looked down each side of the horseshoe-shaped table before she allowed her eyes to rest on Gartheser.

He makes a poor conspirator, she thought. It was from him that Talamir had learned what was coming, though Gartheser himself was probably completely unaware that he had betrayed anything. But he gave himself away, according to Talamir, in a hundred ways, by little nervous tics, by being unable to meet a person's eyes, by dropping far too many hints when he was satisfied with himself. At that point, both Talamir and Alberich had gone to work, and no secret was secure when those two were ferreting it out.

Though it occurred to her that Talamir had probably not done nearly as much work as Alberich. Talamir's sympathy was probably at least in part with the Council. Well, give credit where it was due; he had told her in the first place.

"My marriage?" she asked, in feigned innocence. "I wasn't aware I had been betrothed, much less that there was a marriage in view. Certainly King Sendar never said anything of the sort to me."

"Ah, well, Your Majesty, that's the whole point," Gartheser managed. "You haven't one, you see. Betrothed, that is."

She took her time and looked carefully around the horseshoe-shaped table again, making sure to look each one of her Councilors steadily in the eyes. The silence was deafening. No one moved. "Indeed."

"And you—that is, we thought—that is—" Gartheser couldn't look her in the eyes anymore. He dropped his gaze and stared at his hands, and stumbled to a halt.

"We have some candidates in mind, Selenay," Lord Orthallen took up the thread smoothly. Orthallen looked the part of the senior statesman; he had retained a fine figure, and the silver streaking in his dark blond hair in no way detracted from his handsome appearance. Women younger than Selenay threw themselves at him on a regular basis, though she had never heard so much as a whisper to indicate that he was unfaithful to his wife. "You really must marry as soon as may be, of course. A young woman cannot rule alone."

"Indeed," she said levelly, hiding her rage with immense care. She wanted to scream at them, then burst into tears, and nothing could be more fatal at this moment.

But the others took that lack of objection on her part as the signal that she was going to be properly malleable, and took heart from it. Only Elcarth and Talamir understood that Selenay had her own plans.

Elcarth winced a little at her tone; Talamir's lips quirked, just a trifle.

"The first, and indeed, the most eligible candidate is my nephew Rannulf," Gartheser said brightly, "who—"

"Is not eligible at all, I'm afraid," she interrupted smoothly, with feigned regret. "He's related to me within the second degree, on his mother's side, through the Lycaelis bloodline. You know well that no King or Queen of Valdemar can wed a subject who is within the third degree of blood-relationship. That is the law, my Lord, and nothing you nor I can do will change that." She raised her eyebrows at them. "The reason is a very good one, of course. I shall be indelicate here, for there is no delicate way to say this. As my father told me often, the monarchs of Valdemar cannot afford the kinds of—difficulties—that can arise when a bloodline becomes too inbred."

And with you and yours marrying cousins and cross-cousins with the gay abandon of people blind to consequences, that's the reason half of your so-called "candidates" are dough-faced mouth-breathers who couldn't count to ten without taking their shoes off, she thought viciously.

:*Harsh. With justification, but harsh,*: Caryo observed sardonically.

Gartheser blinked, his mouth still open, and stared at her. Finally, he shut it. "Ah," he said at last. "Oh—are you quite sure of that?"

She opened Myste's report to the relevant page. "Rannulf's mother is Lady Elena of Penderkeep. Lady Elena's mother was my father's cousin through his mother. That is within the second degree."

"Oh—" Gartheser said weakly.

"Then there is my nephew, Kris—" said Orthallen quickly.

"Related to me within the third degree on *both* sides of his family, as his mother was a cousin-by-marriage of my father, and his father was a cousin-by-blood to my father," she said briskly, already prepared for that one. "Besides being so young that there is no question of consummation for *at least* eight years." She smiled dulcetly at Orthallen. "Which does rather negate the entire reason for marrying with such remarkable speed in the first place, before my year of mourning is over. Doesn't it?"

To her great pleasure, Orthallen was left so stunned by her riposte that his handsome face wore an uncharacteristic blank look. Not that she wanted to humiliate him—she was really awfully fond of him, after all—but it gave her no end of satisfaction to make him understand, in no uncertain terms, that just because she was fond of him, she was not going to allow him to manipulate her into something she did not want to do.

And blessings upon Myste; she suspected that not even Orthallen knew about the nearness of her blood relation to his nephew. He proved it in the next moment by saying, cautiously, "I assume you have the particulars of these degrees?"

She went to the second page of Myste's notes and gave him the genealogical details, chapter and verse, in a no-nonsense, matter-of-fact tone of voice.

"Ah," he said. And wisely said nothing more.

So it went. Every single candidate that any of them brought up, she cut off at the metaphorical knees. Including the ones that she had not given Myste to research; that was why Myste was shut up in the library. She would leaf through her thick sheaf of papers to give Myste the chance to trace pedigrees, then pretend to read what Myste Sent to her.

At last they ran out of names—or at least, of names that they could all agree on. Now the daggers were out, and the looks being traded across the tabletop were wary. Any new candidates would be men and boys that had already been rejected, because one or another of the Councilors objected to them for reasons of his or her own. She could sit back and let them play against each other, which was the better position to be in.

At least, that was true among the highborn Councilors; the Guildmasters were a different story entirely. None of them—and no candidate outside of the nobility—would be related to her, which eliminated that argument.

However, she thought she could count on the highborn Councilors to fight tooth and nail against any common-born man being put up as a potential Prince Consort. There was an advantage to snobbery.

Mind, if she did happen to fall in love with a commoner, she wasn't going to let snobbery stop her—

That would open up a whole new set of problems which she wasn't going to think about right now. The current set was more than enough to deal with.

It's too bad Alberich isn't there now, she thought, letting her anger begin to die. *This is the part he'd really enjoy—watching them cut the legs out from under each other.*

Ah well. She hoped the installation of his window had gone well. She was looking forward to seeing it. It would be the only part of her day she was able to look forward to.

Why would anyone want to be a Queen?

* * *

"Oo *wouldn't* want t'be a Queen?" demanded the rather drunken tart sitting at the table next to Alberich's. "Larking about, doin' whatever ye please, gettin' waited on 'and an' foot—"

Not from Haven, thought Alberich to himself. *Though you have the accent, it isn't quite good enough, my girl. And you aren't nearly as drunk as you seem. What's your game, and who put you up to it, I wonder.*

Now perhaps, at any other time, perhaps in another year or so, she might have gotten away with such an ill-considered remark. But not now. Not when barely six months had passed, and Selenay had been making herself very popular with little gestures like the "Queen's Bread." People down here had a lot of trouble keeping their children fed, and one guaranteed free meal a day, at the trifling cost of lessons in rudimentary literacy and numeracy, was a small price to pay. A youngling down here couldn't earn the price of that breakfast himself in the course of a morning. It was good economics to send your younglings to a temple until noon, *then* put 'em to work.

"'ere now!" A man just near enough to have overheard the speech stood up, glaring at her. "Our Selenay ain't like that, ye owd drab, an' if you was a man, I'd'a thrashed ye fer that!"

The woman shrank back, and well she should have. He was big and broad, and looked as if he knew very well how to handle that cudgel at his belt. "No offense meant, I'm very sure," she said, hastily. "I didn' mean Queen Selenay! I just meant, *a* Queen, in a gen'ral sort of way."

The man glared at her. He *was* as drunk as the whore pretended to be, and he was at the very least going to say his piece. "*Our* Selenay ain't no layabout!" he insisted. "Why, I *seen* 'er, I even *talked* to 'er, couple'a nights afore the last battle. Come right to our fires, she did, 'avin' a word with our officers, seein' we 'ad good treatment!"

"Oh, yeah, an' she talked t' you, did she, ye old liar!" jeered someone else—

Ill-advisedly.

The drunk rounded on the skeptic with a roar, and grabbed the man's shirt in one hamlike fist. Only the intervention of the "peacekeeper" that the proprietor of the Broken Arms had seen fit to hire prevented mayhem from breaking out. But there was the start of a fight, and under cover of it, the woman slipped out.

Alberich followed.

She wasn't at all difficult to follow, the silly wench. She paid absolutely no attention to what was behind her. The man she accosted just outside in the alleyway next to the tavern was a little more careful, but not enough to spot Alberich. He was a darker shadow in the alley—people always thought that wearing black would make them blend in with shadows, but it didn't; it made them into man-shaped black blotches in an *almost* black place. Alberich was wearing several shades of very, very dark brown and gray. Each leg was a slightly different color. So was each arm. And his tunic was blotched. There was nothing about him that was man-shaped, when he stood in shadow.

"I'm not doin' that no more!" the woman shrilled at her contact, just as Alberich eased within listening range. "You go do your own dirty work from now on!"

There was a murmur, too low for Alberich to make out the words.

"I didn' get but a word out," she said sullenly, "an' up jumps this drunk bear and nearly thrashes me!"

More murmuring, and the clink of coins. The woman departed, muttering.

Alberich followed the man.

There had been a lot of money exchanged there for such simple services—a lot for this part of town, at any rate. Alberich hoped that his new quarry would try another quarter, one where such a payment would be the norm rather than the exception. And lo! As if his wish had flown straight to the ear of Vkandis, that was precisely what his quarry did.

It wasn't a *wealthy* part of town; working class was more like it, but working class that got work regularly, of the sort that came with weekly pay packets and a little something extra on the holidays. A place, in short, where there were City Guards and constables on patrol regularly.

A place where Alberich could manage to do something to get them both arrested.

Which, as soon as a constable hove into view, Alberich did.

He nipped back around the corner so as to be able to intercept his quarry coming, apparently, from the opposite direction. It wasn't hard; he knew this part of Haven better than the back of his hand. There were few yards with high fences and even fewer with dangerous dogs tied up in them. Once he came back around, he saw that the constable was strolling along at a leisurely pace that would take him past his quarry before Alberich reached the man. Good. He didn't want the constable to actually see what was going on between him and the stranger, only *hear* it and make some inferences that, as it happened, would be entirely unwarranted.

:You're enjoying this,: Kantor accused.

:Hush. I'm busy.:

The fact was, he *was* enjoying this. It was the first hint of trouble, real trouble, *his* sort of trouble, that he'd had in moons.

As he approached the man, he stared at him—easy enough to do, since there were streetlamps here. Then he contorted his face into an expression of rage and roared.

"You! You bastard! *Thought you could ruin my sister and run away, did you?"*
And then he flung himself at the startled man.

As he had expected, the man was not startled for long, and he was armed. So what the surprised constable saw when he turned was a man with a knife attacking an unarmed man. Since he couldn't know which of the two of them the accusation had come from, he assumed—as any good constable would—that the man with the knife was the attacker, not the defender.

That Alberich was in no danger from a mere knife was something he couldn't know. So, to his immense credit, he waded in himself, wielding his truncheon and blowing a whistle for dear life to summon help. He was aiming most of his blows for the head of the knife wielder, and Alberich helpfully positioned the target so that, by the time the help arrived, his quarry was out cold and he was able to protest feebly that *he* didn't know what the madman was talking about, he'd just jumped for him with a knife, screaming about a sister...

"We have to stop meeting like this, Herald," said Captain Lekar of the City Guard, with a feeble attempt at humor. "People are going to start talking."

"I fervently hope not," Alberich replied, rubbing his wrists where the conscientious constables had tied them—being too wise ever to take one potential miscreant's word over another's. He warmed his hands on his cup of tea, but did not drink from it. The herbal teas consumed by the night shift of the City Guard were not drinkable, even by the standards of a former Karsite Sunsguard. "If talk they do, my personae will in danger be."

"Yes, well, I wish you'd find some other way of catching your lads without getting the both of you thrown in jail," the Captain replied wearily.

Since this was only the third time that Alberich had used that particular desperation ploy, he held his peace. "Keep him safe," was all he said. "Speak with him under Truth Spell I wish to, when he awakens."

The Captain did not ask why. The Captain did not want to know why. The Captain was an old friend of Herald Dethor, Alberich's mentor in this business, and he knew very well that he did not want to know why. And Alberich knew that he knew, and both were content with the situation.

Now, if this had been Karse—he reflected soberly, as he left the City Jail by an inconspicuous exit, making certain that there was no one to see him leave.

:If this was Karse, and you were an agent of the Sunpriests, that man would be in extreme pain for a very long time, and at the end of it, he would be dead,: Kantor said.

:He may still be dead when this is over,: Alberich replied, grimly, making his way toward the stable of the Companion's Bell. *:But if he is, at least it won't be by my hands.:*

:If he's lucky, we'll find out he's just a troublemaker.: Kantor didn't sound as if he really believed that would be the case.

Yes, and if that happened to be true, well, there was no law against speaking out—or having someone else speak out—against the Monarch. Laws like that only made for more trouble; some people always had to have a grievance, and making grumbling illegal was a guaranteed way of ensuring that grumbling turned into resentment, and resentment into anger. If that was the case, he'd be let go, with the vague memory of having proved he didn't know anything about anyone's sister to the satisfaction of the City Guard.

If it was not the case—

Well, there was one Herald in the Circle who had no trouble with dirtying his hands with difficult jobs. Alberich would find out who had sent this fellow down into the dark parts of Haven to foment discontent. And he would follow that trail back as far as it would go.

And the man would *still* be let go—but this time with the very clear memory of having been questioned under Truth Spell by a Herald. Chances were, he would cut and run, and hope his employers never found him. That would be convenient, because it would take the problem off of his hands.

And if he didn't run—his employers would probably take the problem off Alberich's hands a little faster.

He collected Kantor and the two of them made their way up to the Collegium—Alberich feeling the effects of the truncheon blows that *had* connected with him, and Kantor brooding. Alberich didn't press him as to the subject of his brooding; whatever it was, Kantor would talk about it when the Companion was good and ready and not one moment before.

And in fact, as Alberich hung up his saddle, Kantor finally spoke. *:I hope this doesn't mean it's all starting again.:*

Alberich sighed. *:My good friend—I hope this doesn't mean it never finished.:*

2

"Why is it always me?" Myste asked, as Alberich made his second trip of the night down into Haven, this time with her in tow. The scholarly Herald pushed her lenses up on her nose and shivered beneath her cloak.

"Because you have the strongest Truth-sensing ability in the Collegium," Alberich said. "And because the two of us can speak in Karsite. If our naughty boy doesn't understand Karsite, he won't know what we're talking about, and it will make him nervous, and if he does, you'll know it, and we'll have him where we want him."

"Bloody hell," she said with resignation, and pulled the cloak tighter around herself. She hated cold, she hated winter, and she hated being dragged out of her study, and he knew all of that. He also knew that unless someone dragged her out of her study periodically, she would hibernate there for as long as the cold lasted. Which was, so far as he was concerned, just as valid a reason for making her his assistant in this case.

The city jail was not bad as such places went. It was clean, insofar as you could keep any place clean considering the standards of hygiene of the inhabitants. It smelled of unwashed bodies, with a ghost of urine and vomit, for no matter how many times the cells were cleaned, *someone* was always fouling them again. It did *not* smell of blood. If anyone was so badly injured as all that, they went under guard to a separate set of cells that had a Healer in attendance. And it went without saying that no one here—at least, among the jailers—spilled the blood of the prisoners.

Of course, the conditions were spartan and crowded, and no prison was a good place. But compared with those jails that Alberich had seen in Karse—not to mention the ones that were rumored to exist…

Myste grimaced as they rode in at the stable, and grimaced again as they walked in through the front door. Alberich was wearing his Whites—no one looked at a Herald's face, they only saw his Whites. The prisoner would see the Whites and not even *think* that the man inside the white uniform might be the madman that had attacked him.

They were taken to a little room, windowless, lit by a single lantern, that held a single chair. The chair was for the prisoner, whose legs would be tethered to it; Myste and Alberich would be free, so that they could evade any attacks he might try.

The prisoner was brought in and his legs shackled to the legs of the chair. He was as pale as a snowdrift when he saw who was there to speak with him.

Slowly, and carefully, Alberich outlined exactly what he had observed, while the man listened, jaw clenched, eyes staring straight ahead. "So," Alberich finished. "What have you to say for yourself?"

He half expected the man to flatly deny everything, but after a long, tense silence, he spoke.

"I cannot tell you what you want to know."

A candlemark later, Alberich and Myste left the jail. There was a frown of frustration on Herald Myste's round face.

Alberich didn't blame her. The man certainly *had* been paying people to try to foment discontent against the Queen—quite a few of them, in fact, but with, by his own admission, limited success. And he had been doing so on the orders, and with the money, of someone else.

The only problem was, he didn't know this "someone else." He had never even seen the man's face.

Myste had not even needed to cast the Truth Spell to force the truth out of the man; her own innate Truth-sensing Gift had told her he was telling them everything he knew. He himself had a grudge against the Crown in general, and Selenay in particular, for when she had served her internship in the City Courts of law with Herald Mirilin, she had made a ruling against him. So there was his personal motive—

But who had sought out this man with a grievance against Selenay? Who had supplied him with the money and the idea to foster rebellion? And why?

Only one thing was absolutely certain; the trail came to a dead end now. It was unlikely that the man would ever be contacted again, for someone astute enough to find him in the first place would certainly be sharp enough to discover he had been arrested and know not to use him again.

"Now what will you do?" Myste asked, as they neared the Collegium.

"Keep looking," he said, and shrugged.

There seemed nothing more he could say. Or do.

* * *

The closing in of winter always brought one definite disadvantage to the weaponry classes; much of the time practices and lessons had to be held in the salle instead of out of doors. This limited the kinds of lessons that could be given and the way that practices could be held. Every season brought its difficulties for a Weaponsmaster; in spring and summer there were torrential rains to deal with, it was difficult to muster enthusiasm for heavy exercise in high summer, and in the winter, of course, there was the cold and the snow. Well, if the job had been easy, anyone could have done it.

Alberich still held some outdoor archery classes in the winter, but when, as today, snow was falling thickly, with a wicked wind to blow it around, there wasn't much point in keeping the youngsters at the targets. Yes, they *would* find themselves having to fight for their lives under adverse conditions, but adverse conditions affected the enemy, too. And as for needing to hunt, well, no Herald was going to starve because he or she could not hunt in a blizzard; Waystations were stocked with sufficient supplies, and every Herald on circuit carried emergency rations. During their last year, each Trainee would get an intense course in survival hunting and disadvantaged combat, and there was no point in making the youngsters utterly and completely miserable for the sake of showing them what it was like to be utterly and completely miserable. Not even the Karsite Officers' Academy did that to its students, and having seen what life was like at the Collegia, Alberich knew that the lessoning he'd gotten at the Academy was harsh, and not at all conducive to training youngsters like these.

Besides, with the Tedrels gone, and Karse itself essentially neutralized for a while, the only enemies that Heralds were likely to encounter in the field were bandits and brigands.

Now, as Alberich well knew from long experience, bandits and brigands are humans; they are essentially lazy, or they wouldn't be trying to steal rather than earn an honest living, and they are just as attached to their own creature comforts as any other humans. Given a choice in the matter, *they* wouldn't attack under adverse conditions either. By night—certainly. In ambush, definitely. In a blizzard? A flood? A raging storm? Not likely. In fact, in all of the time that Alberich himself had led his men of the Sunsguard against the bandits on the Karsite border, never once had he encountered a band moving against a target when the weather was foul. That didn't mean it was impossible, just unlikely. That made the circumstance something to guard against, but not something that required extensive training.

So, when the snows began to fall in earnest just after the noon meal, Alberich herded the next class to arrive into the salle itself. Which occasioned the inevitable delay in the cleaning of boots at the door, and the taking off of cloaks and gloves and hanging them up to dry along the oven wall before anything could get started. And then, because this was a mixed class of Trainees from all three Collegia and some Blues as well, there was more delay as Alberich sorted them out into the limited space inside the salle.

Although there was no fire actually in the room—far, far too dangerous to have a fireplace in an area where someone could fall or be thrown into it—the salle was kept reasonably warm by a huge brick "oven" in one corner. A relatively small fire deep inside it was set alight in the first really cold days of autumn and never allowed to go out, night or day. That fire heated the great mass of bricks that made up the oven and chimney and the wall, and that mass, in turn, radiated heat into the room. It also wasted heat along the outside of the same wall as well, but unfortunately, that couldn't be helped... and anyway, that outside wall was a nice place for the Companions to come and warm themselves on a cold and sunless day. The salle wasn't cozy—but no one was going to freeze without his cloak.

You could—and Alberich occasionally had—actually bake meals in that oven, if said meals were the sorts of things that required slow baking. You could—and Alberich did, quite often during the winter— leave a pot of soup or stew in there as well, to stay warm during the day. It was off limits to the Trainees, however, not by virtue of any orders but by common sense. You couldn't open the cast-iron door without burning your hand unless you used a heavy leather blacksmith's gauntlet, and Alberich prudently never left any of those lying around outside; you had to go into his quarters to get one, or, like the servant who tended the fire now and again, you brought one with you.

Of course, on a day like today, every youngster in the class was doing his or her best to get close to the oven and the warmest part of the room, which meant that unless the Weaponsmaster took a hand in it—*and* remembered who had gotten that choice part of the room last—there were going to be difficulties right from the start of the lessons.

Especially today, when devilment seemed to have infected all of them. There was pushing and shoving, teasing and a few insults and counterinsults, and the general restlessness that showed he was going to have to be an autocratic brute today. He gave a purely internal sigh; what *was* it about adolescents that made them run wild at utterly unpredictable intervals? Maybe it was that all of the students in this class were boys. Girls were a steadying influence, at least in these classes. The boys in this age group didn't seem quite so willing to run about like idiots when there were girls around.

Well, run—that was a good idea. He ought to have them run first. It would warm their muscles up and might exhaust a little of that too-plentiful energy. It would give him a chance to make a mental partner-list and decide who to assign where.

"Run!" he ordered, barking out the single word. "Full speed. Around the salle, ten times."

Grumbling, and in a straggling line, they ran, while he tried to remember who of this lot had gotten the prime spot during the last indoor lesson, and who hadn't gotten it in a decent while. By the time they finished their warm-up run, he thought he had it sorted, and before they could get up to any immediate devilment, he separated the most likely troublemakers and paired them up with the more tractable for this practice session.

"Short swords, no shields," he ordered. "Single line for equipment, by pairs. No pushing." Those who had headed for the storage room, eager to be at their practice, got the best choice of equipment, while the stragglers got what they deserved. Not that any of it was bad—Alberich saw to that—but those who got first choice got the padded armor and helms that fit them best, and those who brought up the rear paid for being laggards by getting equipment that Alberich would make them add extra padding to, so there would be no slippage.

With his pairs of youngsters distributed across the salle and trading blows, Alberich began his slow walk up and down the lines, giving the call.

Every blow had a corresponding number, starting from "one" for a straight thrust to the center of the enemy's body, and the two students in a pair were designated "odd" and "even." Alberich called out sequences of blows, beginning with "odd" or "even" for the students to follow, rather like a dancing instructor calling out a sequence of dance steps. Beginning students, of course, were taught one blow at a time, and specific parries for each. At the level these students had reached, the active student was given a pattern to follow, and the defensive student could use any sequence of parries he or she chose. Alberich began slowly, but as muscles warmed up further, and reactions quickened, he slowly sped up the pace of the call. And, as the students concentrated on what they were doing, the clatter of wooden sword on sword, which had started out rather ragged, became a single beat, just a fraction off the rhythm of the call.

Meanwhile, Alberich circled the floor like a hunting cat, watching the students, alert for any weaknesses, any bad habits. He wasn't going to interrupt the call just yet to correct them—this was part of the business of making blow-counter sequences automatic and instinctive—but he watched for them and noted them for later.

Now that they were up to speed, he added the next variation to the call. They had been fighting toe-to-toe. Now he ordered them to move.

"Odd! Five-seven-a*dvance*-four-two-*retreat*—five-seven-*step right*-one-eight. Even! Four-three-*step left*—" Now it really did look like a dance, and with movement added, some parries were not always working, some blows were getting through. Still, he was not going to make corrections just yet; this was the point in the practice where experience was the teacher, and there was nothing quite like the experience of a good bruise to drive the lesson home.

Again, he sped up the call, forcing them to move a little faster than they were used to. But now they were beginning to tire. The response was getting ragged again, and some of the students began dropping some of the sequence as weary muscles failed to keep up with the cadence. Time to stop, and go on to individual lessons.

"*Rest!*" he barked, and at that welcome command, the points of a dozen wooden practice blades dropped to the wooden floor with a loud *thwack*.

"Kiorten and Ledale, center! The rest, circle!" That order called the first of his pairs into the middle of the floor, with the rest around them to observe. It was not as unfair as it might have seemed, to order a pair straight into the next part of the lesson when the rest were getting a breather. Kiorten and Ledale were the strongest and had the most endurance; a Blue and a Heraldic Trainee, and as alike as brothers. They were still relatively fresh after the call. That endurance needed to be tested; they needed to learn what it was like to fight real combat while they were tired.

Now Alberich took up a wooden long sword, to separate them when he saw something that needed either correction or scoring. The two combatants squared off, standing warily, balancing on the balls of their feet. They'd fought often, of course. Though Alberich made a point of rotating partners in practice, he tended to put these two against each other more often than not, just to keep things even. They enjoyed the practices, too, and he had more than a suspicion that they practiced against each other recreationally.

He held his sword out between the two; they tensed, waiting. "One—" he counted, "two—three—*heyla!*"

He pulled back the sword and jumped back in the same instant, and they both went on the offensive, which was what he expected from them. They were aggressive fighters, and neither one had learned yet that immediate offense wasn't necessarily the wisest course to take.

He didn't separate them, even though they immediately tangled up in the middle of the wooden floor, with Kiorten seizing his opponent's sword in his free hand and Ledale grabbing the front of Kiorten's padded jerkin with *his*. Neither could do anything against the other when they were bound up like that, and a moment later, they broke apart by themselves, circled for a moment, then began an exchange of blows.

Kiorten got a hit, and Alberich stopped the combat for a moment. "Na. Let me look—" He made a quick judgment of position and strength. "Ledale, you are losing the free hand; struck it truly, Kiorten has. Tuck it behind you. Heyla." Let Ledale judge for himself that he had left that hand out there as an easy target. With the wooden blade, the blow probably only stung a bit, but had it been a real short sword, even with an armored gauntlet, the hand would have been seriously injured.

But Ledale wasn't taking this lying down; he launched himself at his opponent with a flurry of blows that drove Kiorten back, and scored a hit himself that made Alberich stop the combat again. "Na—a flesh wound, but you bleed. If this goes on, you weaken. Heyla."

It didn't go on for very much longer. Ledale was at a disadvantage with that hand tucked behind him; it made him turn a little too far to the right, leaving his body more open to attack. Kiorten saw that, and saw also that Ledale was going to go aggressive again. So this time, he wisely *let* it happen, and by the way he avoided the blows, led Ledale in the direction he wanted, until he got a good opening for a body shot. He had to commit everything to that, but he made the full commitment, and the sword *thwacked* home against Ledale's torso with an impact that made him grunt in pain.

"Enough!" Alberich called, although he hadn't really needed to. Ledale backed up immediately, saluted his opponent, and pulled off his helm in surrender.

"Curse you!" he said amiably, though his face was a little white. "I'm going to have a bruise the size of my head for a week, even assuming you haven't cracked my ribs!"

"See the Healers," Alberich directed brusquely, as Kiorten pulled off his helm and extended his hand for his defeated opponent to shake. "After lessons." He knew full well that no ribs were cracked; if they had been, the lad would not have been able to breathe, and what was more, the Trainee's Companion would immediately have told Kantor, who would have told Alberich. "Ledale, observe. Kiorten, you drop your point too often; go to practice lunges at the mirror. Aldo and Tirana, center."

Two more students came out of the circle to face off against each other in the center, while Ledale took a vacant spot in the circle and his erstwhile partner obediently moved to the side of the room to face one of the full-length mirrors set into the back wall of the salle, and began lunging with his sword fully extended, watching his reflection the way he would watch an opponent.

Those mirrors had utterly shocked Alberich the first time he had seen them. Mirrors were expensive, appallingly expensive, and that much mirrored glass at that size represented a sum of money that had made his head swim. But when he'd gotten over the shock, he had to admit that putting those mirrors there was a brilliant idea, for nothing enabled a student learning *anything* involving body movement to correct himself like being able to see for himself as well as feel exactly what he was doing right or wrong.

Right now, however, he kept his attention on the two students before him; a pair of the children of the nobly born. Trainees, that is, not Blues, though a pair of Blues would have worked just as hard as these two. Things had certainly changed there—perhaps not in the attitude of those highborn toward him, but at least in the fact that they no longer expressed their contempt for him aloud. And no longer permitted their children to act on that contempt. The Blues for the most part now worked just as hard in his classes as any Heraldic Trainee, and there were no more sneers or other expressions of disrespect in his presence.

As for what happened outside his presence, he cared not at all. If they respected him, well and good. If they feared him, perhaps that was just as good. If neither, as long as they behaved themselves *in* his class, it mattered not what they thought, nor their parents. Let them revile him behind his back if it pleased them, so long as they maintained respect to his face. Discipline in the salle was what he demanded; so long as he got that, they might actually learn a thing or two from him.

These two, Grays both, were going at it with the same concentration and will—if not skill—as the previous pair. And with a touch less aggression; not so bad a thing, since he preferred to see caution over bravado. When one finally defeated the other, he sent them to observe, rather than to the mirrors.

The third pair, Healer and Heraldic Trainees, also bouted and retired; one went to the mirrors, the other to point practice on a ball suspended from the ceiling. The fourth pair, however—

Well, both of them were high-spirited most times, and today, truly full of bedevilment. One was a Heraldic Trainee, the other a Bardic Trainee, and between them, the two were responsible for half the pranks that were pulled at the two Collegia. Both were slender and agile, both possessed of so much energy that their teachers sometimes despaired over trying to get them to hold still long enough to learn something, and envied their inexhaustible verve at one and the same time.

So Alberich knew he was going to have to be sharp to keep these two within bounds today.

If he could. Adain, the young Bard, and Mical were harder to keep control of than a bushel of ferrets today; he saw that within moments of their bout.

The two went at each other with the same concentration and will as the first two, and a great deal more energy and enthusiasm. As a consequence, *they* didn't stay inside the circle of observers, and those who had been quietly practicing found themselves scrambling out of the way as their combat ran from one end of the salle to the other.

Alberich had heard some rumors that these two were in the habit of experimenting with new moves—well, here was the proof that the rumors were true. It looked less like a practice bout and more like an acrobatic exhibition. Very few of their blows actually connected with anything. They weren't actually parrying each other, they were tumbling and spinning and jumping about so much that they never even got near each other with their wooden blades.

"*Stop!*" Alberich roared, just as Adain, by more luck than anything else, bound Mical's blade in a complicated corkscrewing parry—

—and with a wild flip of his arm, disarmed his opponent and sent the wooden sword flying—

—straight at one of the precious panels of mirror.

Alberich opened his mouth to shout, and knew it was already too late.

It was one of those moments when time slows to a crawl, and the coming disaster is observed in painful detail without anyone being able to actually do anything about it. Adain's grin of triumph slowly turned to one of horror, Mical clawed the air in futility after his lost sword as it headed straight for the mirror, its own reflection seeming to fly to meet it in midair. As the heavy, weighted stick flipped over and over in midair, Alberich just braced himself for the inevitable.

And, with a terrible crash, it came. The weighted end hit with the sound of a hundred hand mirrors hitting a pavement; the mirror spiderwebbed—and shattered.

A profound and dreadful silence fell over the salle, broken only by a belated series of musical *chinks*, as a few of the shards that were left detached themselves and landed on the wreck of the rest of the mirror.

Chink. Chinker-chink Chink.

"Uh-oh," said Adain, in a very small voice.

Chink.

Alberich stood behind the two miscreants with his arms crossed over his chest, as they faced the desk of the Acting Dean of Herald's Collegium. Elcarth was not alone; the Dean of Bardic Collegium, Bard Arissa, had joined him for this particular conference. While Elcarth, slight and birdlike, with an inquisitive face and mild manner, was not normally the sort of person who might inspire trepidation in a student, the look he wore today would have frozen the marrow of anyone's bones.

The two boys huddled unhappily in their chairs. It was the first time within his knowledge that Alberich had seen these two subdued. Their shoulders, under gray and rust-colored tunics respectively, were hunched with misery; their dark heads were both bowed, and two sets of hazel eyes were bent upon the floor.

"What, precisely, possessed you two to demonstrate your—new fighting techniques today?" That was Bard Arissa, a slim, autocratic woman, dark as a gypsy and resplendent in her full formal Scarlets, and you could have used the edge in her voice to cleave diamonds.

"It seemed like a good idea?" Adain suggested, in a whisper.

"And why did you not ask Herald Alberich if you could show him these things in private?" asked Elcarth, his voice like a wintry blast from the snowstorm outside.

"Um. He's very busy?" Adain seemed to be doing all the talking;

Mical was sitting like a stone. Alberich knew why; Mical was from a family prosperous enough to possess one or two real glass mirrors and he knew just how expensive they were, although he probably had no idea that the price increased exponentially with the size. Adain was highborn; until he came to the Collegium, he had never had to pay for anything himself in his life, and he had no idea what even a hand mirror cost, much less one of the huge panels in the salle. Mical thought he knew, and he was scared, just thinking it would cost about the same as a good horse; Alberich knew better, knew that you could buy a nice house with a garden in a good part of Haven for less than one of those mirrors.

"Never, to my knowledge, did you inquire of me, these new moves to observe," Alberich said from behind them. "My duty it is, to make time for such things."

"You wanted an audience," Arissa said, in that same hard, sharp voice—which, given that she was a Master Bard, was certainly deliberate. And, given that she was a Bard, and so was one of the miscreants, her statement about their motive was probably correct. "You couldn't bear not to have an audience. You wanted to show off what you thought you could do."

Alberich's surmise that she had uncovered what had really driven the match today was borne out by the way that both the boys winced.

"Well," she continued, "you *got* an audience. I trust you're pleased. You've made fools out of yourselves in front of that audience, not to mention the damage you did in the salle."

Now it was Elcarth's turn. "Speaking of damages... are either of you aware of just how difficult—and expensive—it is to replace a mirror of that size?"

Identical head shakes.

Elcarth named a figure. Both of them went white as the snow falling outside. Even Alberich was impressed, hearing the exact cost; it made what he had paid for his stained-glass window look like pin money by comparison.

"Now," Elcarth continued. "Naturally, some of this is going to come from your stipends. We shan't take *all* of your stipends, but you're going to be down to less than half of what everyone else gets."

Mical finally said something. "But—we could never pay all that back, not even if we stayed Trainees for a hundred years!" He gulped audibly.

"Which is why you are *both* going to be spending all of your free time working for the Master of the Glassworker's Guild until he finishes the new mirror," Arissa said flatly. "We intend for you to see why, at first-hand, such things cost so dearly. We intend for you to have a very proprietary interest in the replacement. When the mirror is finished, I trust you will have an entirely new understanding of your folly."

"And a new set of muscles," Elcarth added enigmatically. "Now you may go, and reflect on the fact that you will not have any time to get up to any more clever ideas for the duration. This will be your last evening with any leisure in it, because you'll be spending your mornings, your afternoons, and half of your evenings down at the glassworks for a while. Enjoy it."

As if they could, with a sentence like that one hanging over their heads. The two rose, heads hanging, and shuffled out of the room, the very image of dejection.

Elcarth sighed once they were gone, and ruffled a hand through his hair. "I wouldn't mind so much if they'd gone about their little project sensibly," he said. He motioned to Alberich to sit; Alberich did so. "Consulting with their instructors, for instance. Not that all of that gymkhana nonsense would have *worked*, mind you. I wonder where they got such a notion?"

"Out of their imaginations, I suppose," growled Arissa, sitting on the other chair. "Which are entirely too active if you ask me. Or perhaps out of some idiot play or other; the two of them are always running down into Haven to see some fool drama whenever there's one to be seen. I presume they're going to be put to working the bellows at the glassworks for the next moon or so? It could be worse; this could be summer."

"It will be summer before they see the end of their labor," Elcarth said. "I intend to leave them down there for more than a moon. Master Cuelin tells me his apprentice is ready to go on to more complicated work, and he doesn't have a junior apprentice to start on the bellows or do any of the other simple labor in and around the place. So our lads can serve until he gets one. It could have been worse. At least it was only one mirror panel, not two or more."

"How often does this occur?" Alberich asked curiously. "Assume, I must, that accidents do happen. Stupidity probably rather more often than accident."

Elcarth shrugged. "About once every hundred years or so. I mean, we designed the salle to minimize the possibility of an accident, and you Weaponsmasters rarely permit flying objects in the salle itself. It does happen, and it isn't always a Trainee's fault, though I must say that this time is probably going into Myste's Chronicles for sheer wrongheadedness. The panels are all a standard size, and the glassworks has the dimensions in their records from the last time, so Master Cuelin won't even have to come up here to take measurements. I can't tell you how long it's going to take to replace the mirror, though. The Master will have a lot of failures before he gets a success."

"I would interested be, to watch," Alberich admitted. "Or at least, to hear from the Master how such a thing is made."

"Then deliver the criminals yourself in the morning, after breakfast," Elcarth told him. "Someone will have to escort them the first time."

Alberich took quick account of his schedule, and smiled thinly. "So I shall," he decided.

Arissa laughed, her voice full of ironic humor. "Oh, they'll enjoy seeing *your* face tomorrow morning!"

The snow was still falling all that afternoon, into the night, and the next day, and Alberich had sent word up to the Collegia that the Trainees were to have a day-and-a-half holiday from their weaponry classes while the salle was cleaned. A small army of Collegium servants were scouring the salle floor for the tiniest slivers of glass, and would not leave until the floor had been swept several times over, then washed down, huffed and lightly sanded, so that it wasn't slippery. The one proviso to this "holiday" was that the Trainees were to spend the class time out of doors, but with this much snow, he doubted that would be much of a trial for them. The first lot was already building a snow fort when he and Kantor left to escort the two troublemakers to their appointed labors, while snow continued to fall from a sky that was the same color as a pigeon's breast, and looked just as soft.

When Alberich got to the grounds of Herald's Collegium, the two boys were waiting for him on the road that ran among the buildings, mounted, Adain on his Companion and Mical on a sorrel gelding from the Palace stables. There was a conspicuous absence of Trainees anywhere near them; they waited alone in their disgrace.

As Alberich and Kantor approached, he observed that Adain and Mical looked just as subdued as they had last night, and even Adain's Companion drooped a little. They kept the hoods of their cloaks well up, and aside from a soft, "Good morrow, Weaponsmaster Alberich," he got nothing more out of them. Not that he intended to try to get them to talk. It would do them good to contemplate their sins in silence.

Snow drifted down now as fat, slow flakes; there wasn't even a breath of wind, and the air smelled damp. Most of the trees bore burdens of snow along their black, bare branches, and large mounds bore testament to bushes hidden under heaps of the stuff. Nothing had spoiled the pure whiteness yet, except for where the road had been cleared by the Palace gardeners.

By midmorning, people would be out playing in it. And the two boys would be painfully aware of that. A good thing; better they should have to reflect on their sins in sorrow than congratulate themselves that today would have been a miserable one to be out in anyway.

Alberich led them away from the Palace and toward the wall that surrounded the entire complex. They left from the Herald's Gate, the guarded postern at the Collegium side of the Palace grounds. Outside the walls, the road hadn't been cleared as yet. Heavy as the snow on the road was, the Companions made easy going through it, and the horse was able to follow in Kantor's wake. By the time they got down through the manors of the highborn and the very wealthy, there were crews out starting to clear the road. Traffic was limited to a few riders and people on foot; except for a few main thoroughfares, the streets hadn't been shoveled out yet either. Fresh snow was nearly up to the knee, and drifts blocked many smaller side streets and alleys. But people were already out with shovels and teams of horses pulling scrapers, and work was going apace.

After all, it was in the interest of a shopkeeper to get the street in front of his place of business cleared quickly. So as they passed farther down into the commercial parts of Haven, there were more clean pavements and more activity. And by the smoke coming from the chimney of the glassworks as they arrived, things were busy in there as well.

Alberich dismounted and gave a hard rap on the door to the glassworks courtyard with his fist. Two of the apprentices met them at the door; one took charge of their mounts, and with an evil grin, the other took charge of the miscreants. Alberich understood the reason for the grin perfectly; the apprentice would now be put to doing something far more interesting and less labor intensive than mere manual work, while Adain and Mical took his place at the bellows. The furnaces were always going in a glassworks; the fire needed to be quite hot indeed and at an even temperature. The least-skilled job was that of keeping the bellows pumping air into those furnaces, so that the molten glass was always ready to use, cane for decoration could be melted, and glass being blown into vessels could be reheated.

Alberich knew from his previous visits where to find Master Cuelin;

in the Master Workshop. That was where he headed. The glassworks itself was a dangerous place, and he was extremely careful as he made his way through it.

Even now, in the dead of winter, it was very warm in here. Surrounding the furnaces were stations for molding glass, for those who decorated finished vessels, for beadmakers, for glassblowers. The floor was of pounded dirt, the benches and tables made of metal and stone. There was very little that could catch fire, logically enough. It was surprisingly dark here, too; Alberich supposed there was a reason for that. Perhaps it made the hot glass easier to see while it was being shaped.

Glass was both blown and molded here, and all manner of things were made. The most common pieces were molded disks and the thick "bullseye" glass for inferior windows, made by dropping hot glass into molds and pressing it. That was a job for an apprentice; it was relatively easy, relative being the proper word when you were talking about glass, a substance that ran like melted wax and would burn you to the bone if it got on you. Beadmakers formed their amazing little works of art on mandrels at their own little benches—or spun out long, thin tubes of colored glass to be chopped into bits and sand-polished in big drums when cool. Glassblowers formed the molten stuff into every shape imaginable, and decorators took the finished vessels and shapes and embellished them with ribbons of colored glass.

Alberich had been here once before, when he had commissioned his window, and then, as now, it had occurred to him how like a glassworker Vkandis Sunlord was. The glass had no notion of what it was going to be; it was melted in the heat of His regard, then molded or shaped, polished, turned into something that bore little or no resemblance to the grains of sand it had been.

Sometimes mistakes happened. And when they did, He gathered up the broken shards with infinite patience, put them back in His furnace, and began again.

The more conventional analogy—and the one that the Sunpriests favored—was to compare Him to a swordmaker. But it had come to Alberich that He was really nothing like a swordmaker; for one thing, the vast majority of the people He made were not creatures of war. And for another, few of them were tempered and honed. Most of them were simply made, humble creatures of common use, as perfectly suited to their lives as a thick pressed-glass window. Some were merely ornamental, like a bead. Some were honed and polished like the glass scalpels the Healers used for the most careful surgery. But they all came from the same hands, and the same place.

Better window glass was made in the same way as mirror glass, and required a glassblower as well. Alberich had been rather surprised by that when Master Cuelin told him; it had not occurred to him that one would use the same technique that created a goblet or a vase to make a flat pane of glass.

But, in fact, that was precisely how it was made. Glass was blown into a bubble of the right thickness, the bubble was then rolled against a flat and highly-polished metal plate to form a cylinder, the ends were swiftly cut off the cylinder and the cylinder slit up the middle while the glass was still soft enough to "relax," and the resulting pane unrolled itself onto the plate and cooled flat. A master of the craft created a flat, rectangular pane of even thickness with irregularities so few as to be trivial.

But of course, the larger the pane—or mirror—the more difficult the task of blowing and cutting. Something the size of the mirror in the salle was going to be extremely difficult to do.

And in fact, it was Master Cuelin himself who was taking the first tries at it. A pile of rejected shards to one side testified that he had already tried and failed a time or two this morning.

"Ah, I give over," he said, as Alberich arrived. "I thought I'd give it a try, but I've not the lungs anymore. I'll stick to my colored glasses and let young Elkin here do what he does best."

But "young" Elkin—who was older than Alberich—shook his head. "It won't come quick, Master Cuelin," he said honestly. "I've never done aught that big. I'll need to work up to it."

"I wouldn't expect anything else, my lad," Cuelin told him. "Give it time; you'll manage. Kernos knows so long as you don't make the mess of it that I just did, we can find buyers for the smaller panes and mirrors while you work your way up to the right size."

"Are you sure of that, Master?" the other craftsman asked, surprised.

Cuelin laughed, and pulled off his leather gauntlets. "Certain sure. You just wait; as soon as word gets out that we're replacing a salle mirror up there on the hill, there'll be a stream of highborn servants at the door. 'If you'd happen to have a spare window glass, so-by-so, Master Cuelin… if you're like to have a mirror for milady's dressing table…' *They* know we have to work our way up to a pane that big, and *they* know they'll get a bargain they wouldn't get if they'd commissioned those glass panes and mirrors special. Then it'll be the polishing, and then the silvering, and that'll be a bit tricky as well. Master Alberich, I want to show you something that'll catch your interest, aye, and you, too, Elkin—I had the Collegium servants bring me down the old glass, and when I got it, this is what I found."

He held up a shard of silvered glass. "This'll be from the top of your mirror—" and a second, "—and this'll be from the bottom. Now, what d'ye think of that?"

The top shard was clearly thinner than the bottom. Alberich scratched his head. "Glass not so good as you can make it?" he hazarded.

Cuelin laughed. "Oh, flattery! No, no, it was fine glass, and we'll be hard put to match it. But I'll reckon that mirror was over two hundred years old if it was a day, Master Alberich. Maybe more. And when it was made, top to bottom was the same thickness."

He wanted Alberich to look puzzled; with some amusement, Alberich obliged him. "Then, how?" he asked.

"Glass never quite *sets*, Master Alberich," Cuelin told him. "It's like slow water, my old Master told me. Believe it or not, it keeps flowing— oh, slow, too slow to notice, but over a century or two, or three, you look, you'll see that any glass has got thicker at the bottom than it is at the top. Mind, most of it doesn't stay unbroken long enough to find that out, 'specially with lads like your two troublemakers about, but there you have it. You can tell the age of a piece by how thick it's got on the bottom compared to the top."

Alberich examined the two shards, then passed them on to Elkin, and blinked at that, and tried to get his mind wrapped around the idea of something that flowed that slowly. "I am—astonished," he admitted after a moment. "Astonished."

"Wonderful stuff, is glass," Master Cuelin said with pride and pleasure. "And I'll see to it your lads get their heads stuffed full of more than they ever cared to learn about it. No point in exercising their arms and leaving their heads to come up with more mischief. I'll send them back up the hill on time for their classes, though, no worry. And—" he took a slip of paper out of a pocket in his tunic and consulted it, "—I see I'm to expect them back down here at fourth bell, and keep them until our suppertime. We eat late, mind."

"Correct," Alberich said. "Be here, they will be. Fed, they will be when they arrive, then they must study for the morrow, then bed."

Cuelin laughed. "If they've strength enough to hold up their heads without falling into their books, I'll be main surprised."

Alberich took his leave of the Master with better humor than he had arrived in; clearly Cuelin understood boys, and was quite prepared to handle them as they needed to be handled. Mical's horse and Adam's Companion were comfortably housed, as the Weaponsmaster saw when he went to fetch Kantor, so Alberich left them in peace. The horse was happy enough; the Companion still looked subdued.

:An interesting place. Have you ever thought of glasswork as a hobby?: Kantor asked, as Alberich mounted.

:I think I would not be good enough to satisfy myself: Alberich replied truthfully. They rode out into the street; already, the industrious craftsmen here had gotten it cleared, and the snow had been piled up along the walls. *:Why was the boy's Companion so quiet?:*

:Because he is as much to blame as the children,: Kantor told him. *:Apparently, he was in league with them. He is very young.:*

Alberich snorted. *:He must be. I thought your kind had better sense.:*

Kantor sighed gustily. *:Those of us who are older, are. Some of us, like Eloran—are young.:*

:Have you got any plans for delivering some sort of chastisement to Eloran?: Alberich asked after a moment, while he tried to sort out the meaning behind his words and couldn't come up with anything.

:Oh, yes,: came the reply. *:Rolan and I have devised something quite—appropriate.:*

And since nothing else was forthcoming, Alberich's curiosity had to remain unassuaged.

3

Selenay looked out of a window in the Long Gallery on the way to her Lesser Audience Chamber and sighed with regret. The garden was alive with color and movement against the snow—the brilliantly colored cloaks, coats, and hoods of the younger members of her Court as they chased one another, flung snowballs, and generally forgot any pretense of dignity. Young men who had lately fought the Tedrels had cast aside their adulthood for a few hours as they fired snowballs at pages safely ensconced behind the sturdy walls of a snow fort. Young ladies giggled and joined the pages in flinging missiles back at their suitors. Others were on the way to frozen ponds with skates slung over their shoulders, or moving toward the artificial hills in the "wild" garden with sleds. Selenay would have given a year of her life to be down there with them.

Alas. The Queen had an audience with the ambassador from Hardorn, and there was no time for frolicking in the snow, no time for skating, no time for a fast run on a sled.

Curse it.

She nodded to the guards on either side of the door of the Lesser Audience Chamber and went inside. She'd had the room repainted in softer colors than her father had favored, though she couldn't do much about the leather paneling, which had been there for decades and would probably be there for decades more. It was easy to keep clean and looked far more luxurious than anything she could install to replace it; she'd settled for painting the trim an ashen brown with silver-gilt touches here and there. The Ambassador and his entourage were already waiting, as was Talamir. Bless him. It was clear he had been keeping the Ambassador properly entertained; although such gentlemen were notable for being able to conceal any evidence of impatience, the smile Ambassador Werenton turned on her was quite genuine and warm, and his eyes were relaxed. He wore the fine shirt, tunic, trews, and floor-length, open vest in the current Valdemaran style, which was a little disappointing. She'd wanted to see what the Hardornan mode was, for the talk was that the new Queen was quite a fashion setter.

She gave him her hand; he bowed over it, and she was pleased to note that his hand was warm and dry, not cold or clammy. She took her place on the small, velvet-covered throne on the sketchy dais, and motioned to him to sit. This was a room meant to welcome rather than awe; the warm ocher of the leather-covered paneling and the aspect of it, situated so that it looked out into a sheltered courtyard, made it surprisingly comfortable for a formal room. The furnishings were all upholstered in leather that matched the paneling, and the floor carpeted; there was a fine fire in the fireplace, and servants with mulled, spiced wine to serve. Everything that could have been done to relax the Ambassador and his entourage had been—more of Talamir's work, no doubt.

"Ambassador Werenton, it is good to see you again," she said warmly. "And I am glad that you were able to reach our Court before this snow closed us in."

"As am I, Majesty," he replied. "And my King wishes me, first, to tender his sympathies for your loss, and second, offer his apologies that he was not able to send me sooner."

She smiled at him, and hoped that her weariness with all of the official expressions of condolence did not show. She knew very well that the King of Hardorn could have cared less about who was on the throne of Valdemar. He knew that Valdemar would *always* favor allies and peace over conquest. In fact, so long as that attitude prevailed, the King of Hardorn would not have cared if the Council had elected a horse to wear the crown. "Please, Werenton—the message of condolence arrived with the usual promptiness of our friends and allies, and I can certainly understand how your King would be otherwise too occupied with his own defensive preparations against Karse to think about sending you to our Court."

"If Valdemar had fallen—or even been pushed back—" Werenton said apologetically, and shrugged. "We share a border with Karse, as you know. The King was prepared, at need, to unite our force with yours if it had come to that. As it was, the defeated Tedrels spread into our land, and we were forced to deal with them as one would any other plague."

The King would not have bestirred himself unless his Border Lords forced him to, she translated to herself. *In fact, it probably wouldn't have been the King of Hardorn who united his forces with us at all; it would have been the local Hardornen border-levies.*

"And your King was right to concern himself first with them, and concern himself with other things second," Selenay agreed. "I am glad it never came to the point of asking our allies for help."

She knew, and probably the Ambassador did, too, that the reason her father hadn't asked Hardorn for troops was precisely because there was no telling what the Tedrels were going to do for certain. Yes, Karse had hired them to take Valdemar. But if Hardorn's border troops had been removed to bolster Valdemaran forces, leaving that border unguarded, the Tedrels would probably have taken southern Hardorn and come at Valdemar from the eastern flank. The King of Hardorn was a good man, and served his people well—but he was not a very good strategist, nor were any of his military advisers, sad to say. All of them were old men, and more accustomed to dealing with the odd bandit force than a real campaign. Karse's long-standing and increasingly hostile feud with Valdemar had ensured that Hardorn had been very little troubled over the past two reigns. Her father had deemed it wise not to distract Hardorn's king with—as he had put it—"conflicting needs."

She had better say something flattering, before her mouth let something unflattering escape. "And am I to understand that congratulations will shortly be in order?" Selenay continued, with a slight smile.

"We do expect the birth of an heir before spring, yes," Werenton admitted. He did not mention that the young Queen was only a little older than Selenay, nor that the King was older than Sendar had been. Nor did Selenay make anything of it. She was just grateful that the King of Hardorn had married *before* the death of her own father. Now at least there was one old man who was out of the running as a potential suitor. Had he still been single—his previous wife having died without producing a living heir—there soon would have been advisers on both sides of the Border clamoring for a match between them.

"I will have to rack my brain to find a unique birth gift, then," Selenay replied. "I'm sure that by now His Majesty has an entire room given over to silver rattles and ivory teething rings."

The Ambassador smiled politely, as if to suggest that a royal infant could not possibly have too many silver rattles and ivory teething rings.

Selenay spent the better part of two candlemarks with the Ambassador, mostly taking her lead from Talamir or the Ambassador himself as to when subjects currently under negotiation needed to be mentioned. There were some, of course. Hardorn badly wanted to take back some land that Karse had overrun half a century ago, but if they did, the King wanted to be sure that Valdemar wouldn't take it amiss. Valdemar wanted warning if this was going to happen, so that when Karse reacted (though given how unsettled things were there at the moment, Karse might not even notice for a year or two) there would be extra guards on the Border again. Hardorn wanted to know what Valdemar was going to do with all those "Tedrel" children. Valdemar politely told Hardorn it was none of Hardorn's business, but that, in fact, the children were more than halfway to being Valdemaran by now. Hardorn suggested polite skepticism; Valdemar offered examples, and pointed out the general ages of the children. There were some matters of trade to discuss, some concessions that both of them wanted. No few of these would have to go before the Council, and, presumably, an equivalent body in Hardorn, but in a simple, convivial discussion like this one, it was possible to get a feel for how such overtures would be met when presented formally.

Finally—and none too soon, in Selenay's opinion—the Ambassador gave signs that he had said all he needed to, and she politely decreed the audience was at an end. He withdrew; she turned to Talamir as soon as the doors had closed behind him and his entourage.

Talamir shrugged wearily—he did everything wearily these days. He seemed to have aged twenty years since the end of the Wars. His hair had gone entirely to silver-gray, and that lean, careworn face had lines of pain in it that had not been there a year ago. The eyes had changed the most, though; now they were an indeterminate, stormy color with the look in them of someone who has looked into places that mortal men are not supposed to see.

Still, most of the time he was the same Talamir she remembered, stubborn and difficult to move once he had decided on a thing.

"No hidden agendas, I think, Majesty," he said judiciously.

"Other than the obvious; that the King waited to see if I'd survive six months on the throne on my own before sending a formal envoy," she said, with a feeling of resignation. All of the envoys had been like this; it was disheartening to think that there were probably bets being placed on how long she would remain Queen *and* sole ruler of Valdemar.

"Well, you *could* have wedded immediately," Talamir pointed out. "From his point of view there was no harm in waiting to see if you did before sending the Ambassador."

"Or I could have been toppled by one of my own nobles, or assassinated by a leftover Tedrel." She did not add *After all, I'm only a woman*, but the unspoken words hung in the air between them.

"Well, you weren't," Talamir replied unexpectedly. "And those of us who knew you also knew you wouldn't be. And if some foreign monarch is foolish enough to think that your youth and sex means that you are weak or foolish, well, I pity him. He'll take a beating at the negotiation tables."

She flushed, feeling suddenly warm with pleasure. "Thank you for that, Talamir," she replied. So Talamir really *did* think she was capable! It was a welcome surprise; she would not have been at all surprised if he had still been thinking of her as "little" Selenay, who needed a firm hand on the rein and a great deal of looking after.

He gave a little bow, and smiled; he still had a charming smile. "Credit where credit is due," he said simply. "And by this point, I'm sure the Throne Room is filled with impatient petitioners—"

"So on to the next chore." She thought longingly of the fresh snow outside, and ruthlessly pushed away the longing. Queens did not desert their Court to frolic carelessly when there were duties to be done. Queens had responsibilities. "Time to get to it; the sooner we clear the work out, the less likely it is I'll incur the wrath of the cooks by delaying luncheon." She rose, and shook out her skirts, still startled, even after all this time, to note the trimming of black on her Royal Whites where the silver of the Heir or the gold of the Monarch should be. "Speaking of wrath," she continued, as Talamir went to hold the doors of the chamber open for her. "What's the outcome of that little disaster down at the salle?"

Talamir coughed, to hide a smile, she thought. "Alberich escorted the two miscreants down to the glassworks just after breakfast," he told her. "They will be spending from now until—we're thinking—Vernal Equinox pumping the glassworks' bellows every free moment that they have. We're loath to keep them down there once the weather begins to get significantly warmer, because work switches to the nighttime once it becomes hellish to keep the furnaces going at full heat in the hottest part of the day. But we also want them to feel they're really being punished when the weather turns and all their friends are enjoying themselves outdoors again."

"Poor things!" she said, feeling rather sorry for them, seeing as she was in a similar situation with no hope for a reprieve.

Talamir coughed again; this time it sounded a bit disapproving. "Selenay, do you have any notion how much the Crown's treasury is going to have to pay the glassworkers for a new mirror? You could replace every horse in the Royal Guard with Ashkevron war stallions for less than the cost of that mirror. Personally, I think they're getting off lightly."

"If those mirrors cost so much, how on earth did the Crown manage to pay for all of them when they were first installed?" she asked, as the two of them, flanked by a couple of guards, made their way down the gallery that overlooked the snow-covered gardens.

"If the legends are correct, no one paid for them at all," Talamir replied. "The Herald-Mages made them, supposedly. Just as whenever one was broken, the Herald-Mages fixed them."

"How very convenient," she said dryly. "Did the Herald-Mages fix plumbing, too? I've had an Artificer in my bathing room twice now, and that drip still isn't fixed. When I was trying to sleep last night, that was all I could hear."

"Sendar used to say he found it soothing," Talamir said quietly.

I am not my father, Selenay thought, and felt a surge of resentment as well as sadness. But she was not going to say it. "Just have someone send a different Artificer, please," she replied instead. "If I have to move into my old rooms for a few days until it's fixed, I've no objections. If I have to listen to that drip for many more nights, I'm going to go mad."

With classes canceled for the day, Alberich found himself with unexpected free time on his hands. In light of the frustration of pursuing inquiries to dead ends recently, he decided he had a good idea of how to fill some of it. At this point, all of his usual sources of information had run dry. It was time to find some new ones, but to do that, he would have to create new identities.

What I am looking for is not going to be found around Exile's Gate, he decided.

It was with a distinct feeling of pleasure that he noted that Kantor had followed his thought, and had altered his course, heading, not for the Collegia, but for the Companion's Bell. This was a prosperous tavern that played host to Heralds quite regularly—and to Alberich quite a bit more often than to most, although, if you had asked the staff, they would have said, truthfully, that they didn't see him there very often.

There was a secret room in the back of the stables where Herald Alberich would retire, and someone else would emerge, by way of a door that no more than a handful of people knew existed. In that room was a chest of disguises, which were apparently tended to by someone in the

Bell, for no matter what state they were in when Alberich left them there, the next time he returned they would be clean—or at any rate, cleaner, since the apparent dirt and real stains were an integral and important part of some of them. Furthermore, any damage he'd done to them would be repaired, and the clothing neatly put away, back in the chest.

He'd inherited that room and that chest from Herald Dethor, his predecessor as Weaponsmaster, and he'd put quite a bit of wear on the disguises he'd found there. Enough that it was time to do something about the situation, before he found himself literally without anything to wear.

He'd have to do it in disguise, though. Even though he flatly refused to wear Herald's Whites, his own gray leathers were distinctive enough to mark him as the Collegium Weaponsmaster. If the Weaponsmaster was noted visiting the used-clothing merchants, it would be a short step for anyone keeping an eye on him to determine that he was purchasing disguises. Why else would he be making a great many purchases of used clothing?

So, after leaving Kantor tucked into an out-of-the-way stall in the section of the stables reserved for Companions, Herald Alberich retired into that room, and a persona he had never used until now emerged into the alley behind the inn.

His clothing was well made, of good materials, but a little out of style, as befitting a prosperous merchant or craftsman from one of the farther or more rustic reaches of the kingdom. Good thick boots with a significant amount of scuffing and wear to the tops suggested that he was used to doing a great deal of walking in rough country. Leather breeches with little wear on the seat but a great deal to the legs and knees added to that impression. His heavy wool cape with an attached hood was significantly old-fashioned, though the material was very good, and it was lined with lambs-wool plush, which was quite a luxurious fabric. Beneath the cape was a knit woolen tunic that went down to his calves— also significantly out of fashion, for it should have been (but was not) worn with a sleeveless leather or cord-ware jerkin if he'd been living in Haven for any length of time. All of this gear looked homemade rather than tailor-made, and every bit of it made him look rustic.

If he spoke slowly and took care with his syntax, despite the odd accent he still had, he'd be taken for a farmer or craftsman—or, just possibly, a country squire—from some agrarian part of Valdemar with its own regional accent. It was a fine guise, and very useful for what he was about to do—which was to buy used clothing.

Such was easy enough to acquire, and it was easier to put mending and patching onto gently used clothing than it was to repair clothing that was getting far past its useful lifespan. It was easier to put on stains than remove them. That so-helpful, completely invisible accomplice at the Companion's Bell was quite literate, as Alberich had proved to himself by leaving some instructions with one of those disguises, and returning to find that those instructions had been carried out to the letter. So he would buy appropriate outfits, and leave instructions on how the items were to be abused if they looked insufficiently used.

And finally he would have things that fit him, rather than Dethor. His predecessor had been slightly shorter and significantly broader in the waist than Alberich, with much shorter legs.

It will be good not to have to wear my breeches down around my hips to keep them from looking too short.

He spent a very profitable morning, going from shop to stall to barrow, examining items with all the care that any thrifty fellow from the hinterland would use, exhibiting all the suspicion that he was being cheated by a city sharper that any Haven merchant would expect from a shrewd bumpkin, eager to get his money's worth. He never bought more than one piece from any one place at the same time—though he *did* come back, later, if he'd seen more than one item that he wanted. In this persona, Alberich was not particularly notable. There were several men like him, engaged in similar errands, up and down the quarter where used clothing was sold. Most were alone, though a few had wives or older children with them. Whenever he had a collection of three or four items, he went back to the Bell, and left them, so that he was never observed carrying great piles of clothing.

By doing this, he was able to acquire disguises for a good dozen personae, including one or two that were just a touch above his current character; good, solid citizens who would be welcome in any decent house or tavern in the city. Anything else, he'd get from the Palace; he had a notion he'd like to have a set of Palace livery, perhaps a Guard uniform, and clothing appropriate for the lower ranks of the highborn.

And, under the guise of purchasing something for his wife, he bought some women's clothing as well. Not that he'd ever tried to impersonate a woman, but—well, he might need to.

:You'll never pull it off: Kantor said critically as he stowed these last purchases away, hanging them up, rather than putting them in the chest, as even with all of the old guises taken out and left with a note to get rid

of them, there was no more room in that chest. *:You'd need a wig. And how would you hide that face of yours?:*

:I've seen plenty of ugly women in this city,: he objected.

:I'm sure you have, but none that looked as if they'd been through a fire, then fought in a dozen taverns and a war,: Kantor argued. *:And you don't act like a woman; you don't know how to act like a woman. If you need to find out something only a woman can, then get a woman to do it. Myste would probably fit those skirts.:*

:But—: he started to argue—then stopped. Myste *would* fit those skirts. And she was a native of Haven. And she'd come into the Heraldic Circle as an adult, which meant that she was used to being a civilian, acting like a civilian, and she had all the knowledge that an ordinary citizen of Haven had. He wouldn't want to take her down into the area around Exile's Gate, but—

:But she'd go if you asked her to. Think about it anyway. There's Herald Keren, too. She'd go, and she'd fit in anywhere that was rough, including around Exile's Gate. Good gods, some of the clientele of those fishers' taverns in the ports of Evendim would frighten the whey out of the loungers in the Broken Arms!: Kantor sounded very sure of himself, but Alberich saw no reason to doubt that he was right. Keren was a tear-away of the first order, and back in the day, if the Sunsguard had permitted women to take up arms, he'd have had no objection to her in his cavalry unit. She made a fearless bodyguard for Selenay.

:I'd have to find a way to persuade Ylsa to stay away, though. The two of them together would be a dead giveaway to anyone who knows anything about the Heralds.:

:Pointing that out ought to be enough to persuade Ylsa,: Kantor replied with a hint of humor. *:Wild they might be, stupid, they aren't.:*

Well. Two excellent ideas in one morning, one from his own mind, and one from Kantor!

:And didn't I tell you, back when we first came here, that you and I were a good match?: Kantor asked smugly.

:So you did. And you were correct. So very correct that I don't even mind hearing you say 'I told you so.' :

Kantor's only reply was a sort of mental snicker.

Alberich finished writing notes on what he wanted done—or not—to each of the new disguises, left them piled atop the chest or hung up on pegs around the room, went to the stable-side door, and blew out the lamp.

:Don't worry, you won't be seen. No one here but us Companions,: Kantor told him, and he slipped the catch, moved out into the stable, and shut the door carefully behind himself. It locked itself with a soft *click.*

There were, indeed, two other Companions in stalls with Kantor.

One was partnered with Herald Mirilin, who was one of the two Heralds assigned permanently to dispense justice within Haven. The other assigned to that duty was Jadus, who, since losing his leg, could not ride for very long or very far—but whose insight and understanding of human nature made him very suitable for this job. Jadus' Companion was not here, though; the third Companion was not one he recognized.

:Not a Herald you know either. Someone just in off circuit, and an old friend of Mirilin's.: And something about the tone of Kantor's mind-voice told Alberich that the "old friend" was female and that neither Mirilin nor the newcomer would be found in the common room. But that they *would* be found with each other.

Heh. So Mirilin was human, after all. Mirilin, with a woman! Now that was a thought to hold onto. From the way that Mirilin usually acted, Alberich had the idea that he'd be very embarrassed if he was caught playing truant with a woman and no matter if the woman was another Herald.

:I believe,: he said, as Kantor turned his head to wink one blue eye at him, *:that I will have one of the Bell's delicious pigeon pies. And I believe I will linger over it.:*

It would do him no end of good to see the expression on Mirilin's face when the Herald finally did emerge…

Kantor snickered. There was no other word for it. The sound wasn't even remotely horselike.

:I'll see to it that their Companions "forget" to mention you're here.:

Mirilin and the stranger strolled into the smaller common room—the one usually used by Heralds—with a careless and casual air, as of people who expect to find a room empty. And since Alberich had deliberately set himself in the most secluded corner of the room—which happened to be right beside the cheerful fire—Mirilin and his friend would not be able to see him until they were already well into the room.

"Heyla, Mirilin," he said calmly, and was rewarded when Mirilin actually jumped a little, startled. The other Herald, an attractive little redhead, didn't jump, but did look surprised.

The Herald peered at his corner. To Alberich's further pleasure, he flushed and looked extremely discomfited. Not that there was anything at all wrong with two Heralds having a quiet mark or two alone together, far from it! But being discovered by the enigmatic Alberich—

That same Alberich that Mirilin had openly and avowedly not trusted at all when he first became Selenay's bodyguard? And who was now one of the great heroes of the Wars? And if Mirilin was not acting as a Justiciar in the Heraldic Court, shouldn't he be up the hill at the Collegium at the moment?

Again, there was no reason why Mirilin should *not* take a mark or two out of the day to please himself—but someone like Mirilin would feel guilty that he had, and moreover, he probably wouldn't want anyone to know he had done so.

"Ah. Herald Alberich? What are you doing in Haven?"

"Delivering our miscreants to their place of punishment," he replied. "Heard of the incident in the salle, I presume you have?"

"A broken mirror, wasn't it?" Mirilin said, after a moment. "And a couple of Trainees with more enthusiasm than sense?" Mirilin was regaining his composure, which made Alberich smile a little. After all, he only wanted to discomfit the fellow a trifle, not humiliate him.

Alberich uttered a dry chuckle. "Well put. And no more free time, in which to devise more such mischief, will they have until well into spring. Pumping the bellows at the glassworks, Dean Elcarth has decreed, is to be their task."

Mirilin smiled and winced at the same time. "Well—at the least, they'll have stout muscles when spring comes."

"Make the punishment fit the crime—I like that," said the woman— not as young as Alberich had first thought. She wasn't as old as Mirilin, but she was older than Alberich. "Are you the new Weaponsmaster, then?" She left Mirilin and approached Alberich, her hand extended, somewhat to Mirilin's consternation. "Sorry I haven't met you before this; I've been on one circuit or another for almost six years, and when I come in, I usually stay here rather than at the Collegium. When I'm off, I'm a bit of a carouser, and why disturb people's sleep when I can have all the fun I like and not upset anyone down here? I'm Ravinia. Mindspeech and Animal Mindspeech."

Alberich rose, took her hand, and bowed slightly over it. "And I am Alberich," he told her, releasing it. "ForeSight, for whatever good it does."

She smiled at him. Mirilin was very clearly discomfited again. Perhaps because the lady he had come here to meet was being so very friendly to someone he—used to—not trust very much? "So you are indeed the very famous Herald Alberich; it's a pleasure to meet you at last. Since I'm staying at least a moon this time, I expect you'll see me at the salle. I could use some sparring practice; can you find me partners at short notice?"

:Is she flirting with me?: he asked Kantor incredulously.

:No. She really does need sparring practice. Find some of the mid-level Guards from Selenay's bodyguard. Or Keren or Ylsa.: Kantor chuckled. *:She's not flirting; she's being direct. And she doesn't mistrust you. She hadn't met you at a time when you were under suspicion. You are not Alberich of Karse to her; you are Herald Alberich.:*

"You will welcome be, and partners can be found," he replied, and decided to end Mirilin's discomfort by taking himself off. "Rude I do not wish to seem, but my task and meal both being over, returning I must be."

"Certainly," Ravinia agreed. "I expect we'll meet again in the next day or two."

"Excellent." He nodded at Mirilin. "And fare you well, in your afternoon's tasks, Mirilin. Perhaps the heavy snow will thin the plaintiffs."

Mirilin shrugged. "I wouldn't count on it, but I wouldn't be upset if you were right." But there was a change in Mirilin. A subtle one, but there it was. Perhaps because, for the first time, he saw Alberich through the eyes of someone *he* trusted. And he saw the man before him as *Herald* Alberich.

Alberich took that as a dismissal, and took himself off, keeping his chuckle strictly internal. *Well, well, well.*

Of course, neither of them could know that *he* knew the two of them hadn't just accidentally arrived at the Bell at the same time—but Mirilin suspected Alberich knew. And Alberich was never going to let on one way or another.

:They let the stablehands take their Companions in,: Kantor told him. *:They had a great deal of—catching up to do.:*

:Indeed,: Alberich replied. It was interesting that Mirilin was clearly embarrassed, but Ravinia was not.

:Sheiteny says that Ravinia isn't embarrassed by much,: Kantor observed dispassionately. *:A very cool one, she says.:*

:I can believe that.: Alberich paused at the door to swing his cloak over his shoulders, and pushed out into the stable yard. Snow was still falling, but at least it was not much more than token flakes, and a single stable boy with a broom was doing a reasonable job of keeping up with it. He crossed the yard and walked into the stables again, and a bay horse in the stall nearest the door peered over the side of the partition and snorted at him.

:I trust that the boys are already on their way back up to the Collegia?: he added.

:Halfway there, and just in time for their classes,: Kantor confirmed, as he picked up saddle and blanket from the side of the stall, and heaved

them onto Kantor's back. *:Just about in the state of sore-muscled, worn-out wretchedness you'd hoped for. Not utterly miserable, certainly not feeling any desperation, but definitely feeling—chastised.:*

:Good.: He didn't *want* them to be desperate, but he wanted them to *feel*, well and truly, that they were being punished for making not one, but several bad decisions. Not the least of which was that they made the choice to act recklessly in a place where mistakes would be magnified. Elcarth had made an excellent decision as to their punishment, and he and the Dean of Bardic had made it crystal clear that the boys were being punished by their respective *Collegia*, not by Alberich alone.

He finished putting on the last of the tack, and Kantor backed out into the aisle so that Alberich could mount. *:What had you planned for this afternoon?:*

:I believe I'll have a talk with Keren about that suggestion of yours,: he replied. *:And perhaps with Myste—though I had rather speak to Keren first.:*

:Good. Mind you, I'd feel better if you had more than one set of hands and eyes helping you—:

:But the more people there are in on a secret, the harder it becomes to keep it.: He felt Kantor's sigh of resignation beneath his legs as they trotted out into the stable yard, under the arched gate that led to the street, and onto the thoroughfare itself. Kantor didn't argue with him, though. The Companion knew just as well as anyone that if Alberich was going to do the covert part of his job effectively, it *had* to be kept secret. Heralds were humans—as witness Mirilin!—and humans talked, gossiped, let things slip by accident. That was one of the reasons why Alberich needed to do his job in the first place.

The ride up to the Collegium was uneventful, and now that substantial inroads had been made on clearing the snow, it was a bit faster than the ride down had been. And Alberich noted as they rode that it wasn't only the Trainees that had been infected by a spirit of play—there were snow fights and sliding, the building of snow sculptures and castles, and he saw no few people going by with skates over their shoulders. As they came into the region of private houses, larger and representing more wealth, the closer they came to the Palace, there was even more sign of merrymaking in the snow.

:Well, it isn't often that Haven sees a snowfall as heavy as this one has been.:

:Personally, I have never seen anything of the sort,: Alberich admitted. *:There are snows in my hills, but they are thin and dry.:*

:This is winter weather typical for the North of Valdemar, not so much here,: said Kantor. *:I wonder—:*

There was a long pause, as they wove their way among the houses of the highborn, and laughter and shrieks of pleasure and excitement echoed behind the walls and fences.

:You wonder—?: Alberich prompted his Companion.

:Well, it's dreadfully soon… and the Court is technically still in mourning… but a snowfall like this doesn't come very often, and there's going to be a hard cold spell coming behind it.: Kantor gave the impression to Alberich that he was musing aloud, though Alberich wondered for a moment where he was getting his weather information. *:The Terilee is going to freeze solid when that cold spell comes—that hasn't happened in fifty years. I just wonder if it's occurred to Selenay to decree an Ice Festival.:*

Although Alberich had never heard of an Ice Festival before, the name pretty much told him everything he needed to know. *:If the river freezes solid, isn't something like that bound to happen spontaneously anyway?:* The very novelty of the frozen river would bring skaters—the skaters would draw vendors of food and drink, and those would attract musicians, skate sharpeners, skate vendors, and probably more merchants than that. On the whole— well, it wouldn't be a bad thing for an official Festival to take place, official mourning be damned. The Wars had dragged on for years. Sendar's death had cast a pall over the entire country, but there was only so much grieving that you could do before you just wearied of it. Selenay's coronation had been a triumph, but it had been a shadowed triumph.

:Well, you can hear it beginning for yourself,: Kantor agreed, tossing his head in the direction of yet more laughter. *:And once the river freezes, people will come flocking down to the banks. If it were me, I'd go ahead and make the decree so that what is going to break out anyway gets some time limits to it. And while we're at it, something like this would create a number of excellent opportunities for you to nose about and listen.:* Kantor paused, perhaps to gather his thoughts. *:If anyone is going to try and foment discontent, oddly enough, a Festival is a good place to do so. You can say things then that people will dismiss as the drink talking—but the words will still stick in the memory, and should Selenay or her Council do something that people don't agree with—those words will be remembered.:*

:We really do think too much alike,: Alberich agreed, as they turned in at the gate, with a friendly nod to the Guardsman on duty. *:So, to whom should we drop hints, and when?:*

:Leave that to us Companions,: said Kantor. *:It's what we're good at.:*

The area around the salle was extremely quiet without streams of Trainees coming and going. When Dethor had moved out, Alberich had gotten the carpenters to put in a good, stout, one-Companion "stable" up against that oven wall for Kantor to stay in when he chose. It was immensely more convenient not to have to go all the way up to the Companions' stable in order to tack him up—and this way, he and Kantor could come and go without any fuss or anyone noticing. Kantor himself always went up to the main stable to eat and drink, and Companions being Companions and not horses, the interior of this secondary stable didn't need to be cleaned. Alberich being Alberich, he saw to Kantor's tack himself, except for the fancy "show" or "parade" tack, so it wasn't really any inconvenience to the stablehands, either, for Kantor to have his everyday kit down here. Alberich dismounted at the door of the little lean-to addition, and Kantor followed him inside. It was pleasantly warm, thanks to that brick wall.

:I'm going up to the stable,: the Companion said, as Alberich took off his halter and he shook his head and neck vigorously. *:I'm going to have some consultations.:*

Alberich bent to unbuckle the girth. *:I'll probably be here for the next mark or two. I want to think a few things over myself.:*

Kantor tossed his head, and when Alberich had a good grip on the saddle and blanket, walked out from underneath them. *:I'll let you know if anything gets started.:*

And with that, the Companion trotted back out into the snow, leaving Alberich to wipe down the tack and hang it up to dry.

It was less quiet in the salle than Alberich had thought it would be. He'd forgotten that there was going to be a crew of cleaners making sure that there was not the tiniest bit of glass left behind, then setting the floor to rights again. The soft murmur of voices was rather pleasant. He slipped in without disturbing them and went back into his own quarters.

The glory of his window took him by surprise—a blaze of gold and blue, color in a room that had been pale and faded in winter light before the window had been put in.

It was going to be a while before he got used to the change, but the shock was one of pleasure, and he found that he liked it. He sat down where he got the best possible view of the glass, and was bathed in the golden light coming from the Sun-In-Glory.

Ah... It felt good. It felt right, to have the light of Vkandis about him. It felt like a blessing, and perhaps it was. If that was so, well, this was a good place for him to be when he was thinking about important decisions.

Now, the question about Keren and Myste was, should he take one or both women into his confidence concerning his covert work? Myste had the better knowledge of Haven; Keren would fit into rougher places. As he weighed the abilities of one against the other, it became clear that if he was going to do this, it *would*, eventually, have to be both. Neither had the ability or the skills to move in all the places that he could. But he thought that he would approach Keren about this first. It was, after all, the rougher places of Haven where most of his prowling was done.

That made him feel easier. Later, perhaps, he could ask Myste, if he thought he'd need her. She wasn't much good at anything physical, and he wasn't sure just how well she could conceal her feelings. He really didn't want to involve her if he didn't have to.

No matter how good a notion Kantor thought it was. Companions weren't *always* right.

4

"Bloody hell!" Herald Keren said, in sheer admiration. She shook her head. "All this time? You've been running around in Hell's own neighborhood all this time? By yourself? Bloody hell!" Keren had held Alberich in high esteem for his skill, but he sensed that this had not been anything she would have pictured him doing. "So where's your wheelbarrow, then?"

"Pardon?" he said, puzzled, as Ylsa choked. But neither of them explained, so he decided it was one of those colloquialisms he wouldn't understand even if he knew what she'd meant, and dismissed it from his mind.

Keren was probably Alberich's age, though with someone from Lake Evendim it was hard to tell. They were all lean, tall, and had the sort of face that appears not to change a great deal between the ages of twenty and sixty. She had been a Herald for several years by the time Alberich came to Haven, and people swore she'd looked pretty much the same as she did now on the day she arrived. She was an oddity among the female Heralds, as she wore her brown hair cropped close to her head, but then, the only "hairstyle" she was interested in was how to braid up a Companion's mane and tail for parade.

"Since Dethor his Second made me, prowling the streets I have been," Alberich confirmed. Keren grinned at him, with a glint in her eye that made her partner Ylsa sigh and cast a glance up toward heaven.

Ylsa was cut of similar cloth to Keren, though her hair was an ash-blonde and her jaw square rather than Evendim-narrow. Apparently they had been together from the time they were yearmates as Trainees. Ylsa tended to be the one who exercised more caution than Keren did; hardly surprising, really, since Myste claimed the Lake Evendim fishers were all descended from pirates. "And just how often have you been doing this?" she asked.

"Of late, perhaps every two or three nights. But during the worst of it, nightly, could I manage it."

"Bloody hell! When did you sleep?" Keren demanded.

"Infrequently, apparently," Ylsa muttered.

He had known he would have to let Ylsa in on the secret of his double life the moment he'd decided to recruit Keren; he had learned as a commander that the only way to ensure perfect cooperation from his men—or now, his women—was to make certain their partners knew what was toward. And although by the strictest Karsite creed what was between Ylsa and Keren was not to be thought of, Alberich had been a leader of men for far too long not to know that things that were not to be thought of were commoner than the Sunpriests admitted.

Back when he'd been a Captain of the Sunsguard, two of his men had had just such an "understanding" between them, though the rest of the troop had not known, and Alberich doubted that even the two in question ever realized he had discovered their association. They had been very good at keeping it all to themselves, but Alberich had been better at reading subtle body language than they were at concealing it from him. Never once had it affected their performance; never once had they allowed it to affect their behavior in the troops. After careful soul searching on Alberich's part, he had finally decided that what did not affect the troops did not matter, and ignored it.

Several more of the men had clandestine marriages with women in one or another of the villages—ordinary fighters were not permitted to marry, at all, under any circumstances, only officers. Needless to say, those "understandings," too, had been kept very quiet. Strange, that whoring was tolerated, if preached against, but an honest marriage was absolutely forbidden... on the grounds that it was a distraction to the soldier.

This had all conflicted with what the Sunpriests decreed, and as their leader, his responsibility was to report every irregularity to the Sunpriests. Except that if he did that, he'd earn the hatred of half of them, and see the other half cashiered before six months was over. Eventually he had come to a decision on his own about what the men did or did not do. If some behavioral trait of one of his people did not affect performance and honor adversely, it mattered not at all. If it affected performance and honor positively, it mattered a very great deal.

So when confronted by similar "irregularities" as a Herald, he followed the same course, and that seemed to be the right way to go. It certainly fell right into line with the credo that "there is no one right way."

So far as he could judge, Keren and Ylsa were good partners. Keren gave Ylsa a boost to thinking imaginatively. Ylsa steadied Keren down, something that hellion badly needed. If they had lovers' quarrels, they kept it to themselves, or at least, never involved anyone but a counselor. And although Keren was permanently stationed at the Collegium— there hadn't been a better riding instructor in the past fifty years, so it was said—and Ylsa was a Special Messenger, which took her out of Haven all the time, neither of them complained about being separated far too often. If they'd been Sunsguard, he'd have called them fine soldiers, and written them up for commendations. As it was, since there was no such thing as officers in the Heraldic Circle and thus absolutely nothing he could say or do that would get them any advance in rank, he merely considered it a pity that there weren't more Heralds like them.

"And you want me to help you out?" Keren continued, still with that glint in her eyes.

"From time to time. Not often. But there are some things women tell not to men. And some places men are welcome not." He shrugged. "That there is the greatness of threat to Valdemar that there was once, I think not. That there is the threat still existing, however, I do think. I know not why there was that man paying for grumblings against the Queen, for instance, and this troubles me. Valdemar was not impoverished in the Wars as it could have been—"

"Thanks to you," Ylsa pointed out. "If you hadn't gone after those children, and got the lion's share of the Tedrel loot in the process, we would have been."

He waved that aside. "Still, seasoned fighters were lost; Valdemar hires not from the Mercenary Guild, so weakened will Valdemar be for some time. A weakened land is a land that others may seek—to exploit."

"Hmm." Ylsa sat back in her chair, and stroked her chin speculatively. "That could be... though we've friends on the east and south."

"There is the north," Keren pointed out. "Northern barbarians are always a danger, and the gods only know what Iftel might do— just because it's been quiet for centuries doesn't mean it won't suddenly roar up and turn into a menace. And there's always the west. Pirates on Evendim. Bandit bands large enough to qualify as armies. Weird stuff out of the Pelagirs. Gods only know what comes farther into the west than the Pelagirs."

"Even so." Alberich nodded. "The Northern Border and the Western are—"

"Fluid," Ylsa supplied him. "And what's more, Selenay inherited a Kingdom where war has allowed other problems to be ignored. And I suspect you know that at first hand." She raised an eyebrow at him; Special Messengers saw a lot, and were chosen as much for their ability to keep their mouths shut as their riding prowess.

He shrugged. "Indeed. The enemy I fear most lies within our borders. In Haven, the City Guard short-handed still remains. Opportunists come in all stripes, and all ranks. Perhaps this is why someone seeks to agitate against Selenay. While we look to that as trouble, we miss some other evil he may do. Where there are fortunes to be made, men will seek to make them, be the source never so vile."

"And once you start selling one vile thing, further vileness comes easier. Especially when the price is good enough." Keren shook her head. "Well. How would you like me to start?"

"By learning to act a part," Alberich told her immediately. "The hellion will not always welcome be, where I would ask you to go. Sometimes, the serving wench. Sometimes, the whore."

Keren snickered at that. "Me! I'd never pass as a whore! Nobody'd look twice at me!"

"You are not old, not raddled with drink, have all your teeth, most of your mind, and no disease," Alberich said pragmatically, before Ylsa could jump in. "In the quarters where I go, that is enough."

Keren snorted. "*Most* of my mind! I like that!"

Ylsa laughed. "You're a Herald. You are volunteering to spy in the worst parts of Haven, dear. That's not exactly anything I see sane people queuing up to do."

Keren made a face. But she didn't argue.

"So. There it is. Can you act a part?" Alberich asked. "Can you act *those* parts?"

Keren scratched one eyebrow thoughtfully. "I'm pretty sure I can, at least, as long as you don't expect me to bed anybody. Not for days and weeks at a time, but then, you aren't going to want that, I suppose."

"No," he agreed. "If it must come to days and weeks, another solution sought must be. Not you nor I can be spared our assigned duties. A few hours at most, is what we will need. And no—if the whore you play, it is *my* whore you will be."

"For a few hours, I can manage anything," Keren decreed. "I suppose I could even manage pretending to be a lady."

"I'd pay money to see that!" Ylsa chortled.

"If it is a lady I need, to Talamir I should take myself," Alberich told them both. "Better to find one within the Court who is a friend—and I assume that he has more than one such already."

"Probably," Ylsa agreed, and Keren nodded. "There are highborn Heralds, too—*probably* no one would tell them anything directly, and since everyone would know they were Heralds, they'd be useless as spies, but people do gossip, and gossip alone might be worth something."

So, there it was. He had agreement, not only from Keren, but from her partner—which basically meant that Ylsa agreed not to interfere. He felt a little of the weight lift from his shoulders. "Well, then, I thank you both." He stood up, and motioned them both to remain seated. "I shall myself let out. Not soon will this be—nothing have I that needs a female, at the moment."

"Better to have the gaff in your hand before you try to land the sturgeon," Keren observed. "Take me with you a time or two when you've not got something on the boil, and I can get used to playing your doxy."

"I shall," he promised, and let himself out of their somewhat cramped quarters. They shared a room meant for one—well, it probably wasn't as crowded as it could have been, since both of them tended to keep personal possessions at a minimum and Ylsa was often away. But it felt very claustrophobic to him.

All things considered, he wasn't unhappy about being down in the salle. If he wanted or needed more room, he could just add on, as apparently generations of Weaponsmasters had done before him. Quarters in the Heralds' Wing were best described as "tight" by his current standards, and he wasn't at all certain he would care to have neighbors on either side of his walls either.

That went very well, he decided, and knew that it could have turned out a flat failure. Keren might not have been interested—Ylsa might well have objected. And Keren's suggestion of going about in persona when there was nothing particularly that he needed to do was an excellent one. It would establish *her* personae and allow him to correct her, if need be, at a time and place where breaks in the particular persona would not be dangerous. Better to clear all that up before it could be fatal. Prowling the slums when there was nothing in particular he was watching for could be tedious at times; at least with Keren along, it might be less tedious. And having her with him when he changed into one of his varied costumes would also be useful. She could double-check the face paint he wore to cover his scars. The stuff was a damned nuisance; it had to be peeled off when he was done with it, and in hot weather it itched, but it was the only way he could keep from being recognized.

He'd better warn her about the food and drink in The Broken Arms, though, before they entered what passed for its door. There were some things even Keren's famously iron stomach could not digest safely.

Perhaps I should lure those whom I suspect there, and buy them meals. After a single bite I would have the truth out of them in no time.

Selenay chased the last of her servants out and closed the door to her bedchamber, even though she hadn't the least intention of going to sleep. It had been a long day, and unfortunately, it had also been a very dull one. It had not helped that every moment of it, she had been poignantly aware that just outside the Palace walls, virtually every creature of Court and Collegia—with the possible exceptions of the two scamps who'd broken the salle mirror—was taking the time to have some winter fun in the heavy snow. Even the oldest of codgers was out there, standing by one of the braziers, watching the younger folk skate or stage snowball fights. It made her feel very forlorn.

It had also made her miss her father very much. Sendar had loved the winter; had he still been alive, he'd not only have chased her out to play, he'd have contrived a way to join her. At night, during a full moon, he'd have huge bonfires in the gardens, and serve ice wine to the skaters. He was always the first one to inaugurate a sled run, and, as he said so often, "Royal dignity be damned."

She bundled up in a fur-lined robe over her nightdress, and took a book to the window seat in her bedroom, though she had no intention of reading it. Instead, she rubbed a clear patch through the frost on a windowpane with her sleeve, and looked out over the gardens.

The moon was just up, shining through the branches of the trees as if it had been trapped there. It was just a half-moon, with a little haze around it, and a faint golden cast to its face. Light from other windows in the Palace made golden rectangles on the surface of the snow beneath, with the occasional shadow passing across them as she watched. She had retired early tonight, but life in the rest of the Palace went on as usual. Even as she watched, she heard a giggle from outside, and a vaguely feminine form bundled up in a cloak and hood ran across the snow, followed by a second, then a third, scudding across the white snow like clouds across the moon. Three of the young ladies of the Court, out for a moonlight frolic? Were they meeting young men, or just having some girl-fun? Slipping out to skate on the frozen ponds by moonlight? Or were they servants, or even Trainees? They couldn't be Heraldic Trainees, for the cloaks had been too dark to be Grays, but they could be Bardic or Healer Trainees…

Perhaps not Healers, who tended to be *very* serious indeed, and not likely to be out for a moonlit frolic in the snow. But Bardic, perhaps. Or even—well, no, probably not three of the common-born female Blues, either, the ones who got into the Collegia on merit. Those young ladies, fewer than the males by far, tended to be even more serious than the Healer Trainees, spending their evenings in study, except for taking the rare night off to go to the Compass Rose. Their positions were hard-won; many of them had come here over parental opposition, and they were not going to hazard what they'd gained by frittering it away.

Selenay sighed, feeling a wistful kinship to that handful of young women. She was in a very similar position, or at least, it seemed that way to her. She, and they, were prisoners to their duty and their responsibilities.

Except that they were self-imprisoned; she was bound by blood and rank as well as duty. Surely self-imposed bonds were less galling than ones imposed from the outside.

She sighed again, more deeply, and rested her chin in her hand, and wondered what it would be like to be ordinary.

:That rather depends on what it is that you mean by "ordinary,": Caryo replied. *:An ordinary Herald, for instance?:*

:I suppose,: she replied, unable to even think of what her life would be like without Caryo.

:You've had some taste of it, when you accompanied Herald Mirilin down to the City Courts in Haven,: Caryo reminded her. *:The real difference between you and the other Heralds is that you can never escape being Queen, and they can sometimes escape being Heralds for a candlemark or two.:*

:Exactly.: Selenay was relieved that Caryo hadn't started in on a lecture about how she should be grateful, that there were hundreds of young women in her Kingdom who had gone to bed hungry and would wake up with no better prospect of breakfast than they'd had of supper. That there were young women who had done extremely unpleasant things in order to get a supper, or a bed, and would do the same tomorrow. She knew that; knew that very well, no matter how much Talamir and Alberich tried to shelter her from it. She also knew that there wasn't anything much she could *do* about it with the limited resources at her

behest. She knew that children went to bed hungry and cold, or even curled up in a doorway without a bed at all. She was doing what she could about that, with what she had—the mandatory schooling was a help, as were the "Queen's Bread" meals she'd managed to get instituted, so that at least every child had one meal in a day that it could count on...

But never mind that now. She was just grateful that Caryo understood.

:Of course I understand. The wild songbird that's had its wings clipped and been clapped in a cage doesn't feel much like trilling, no matter how comfortable the cage is, nor how good the food in its cup.:

She felt her throat close a little, and blinked back the urge to cry—she was tired of weeping, tired of feeling sad and beaten and alone. That was a pretty accurate summing up. And no matter where she looked, it seemed that someone around her was trying to install yet another set of bars.

She wanted some fun again. She wanted to be irresponsible for just a little while. She wanted to tell the Council, the courtiers, the petitioners, to just *wait* for a candlemark or two while she went skating and sledding.

It felt almost as if she was being punished, and not only had she done nothing to deserve being punished, she'd done everything she was *supposed* to be doing!

She didn't remember her father being so hedged about—

—wait a moment—

She blinked, and ran through that thought again.

I don't remember Father being so hedged about that he couldn't take a candlemark or two—

But the Councilors would be furious. There were so many things they wanted her to attend to, it often seemed that they even begrudged her the time she took to eat and sleep.

Just who is the Monarch here, anyway, me or them? Are people going to die because I take a little time to relax and have some fun?

:Exactly so,: Caryo agreed calmly. *:It would be one thing entirely if you neglected your duties to spend all of your time in pleasure and games. But since the moment the Crown was put on your head, the most you've stolen was a candlemark or two at bedtime to read.:*

:But how do I—: she began, then stopped, thinking back to her father. All right; Sendar'd had the authority to simply stop everything and say, "I'm going out for such-and-such." She didn't. So—

:I'll have to schedule it. Won't I?:

:Better still, decree it, in such a way that it becomes a duty—in their eyes—to take some pleasure.: And as she tried to work out how she could decree a

few candlemarks off to go skating, Caryo added helpfully,: *There is a cold spell—a very cold spell—on the way. It's already frozen the verges of Evendim out to almost a furlong from the shore. It'll freeze the Terilee solid, and it should last for a fortnight at the least.:*

She blinked. She could barely remember the last time the Terilee had frozen solid. And when it had—

:I declare an Ice Festival?: she hazarded.

:Announce there will be one if the Terilee freezes, and make the announcement public,: Caryo agreed. *:Your Councilors will be so certain it won't that they'll just smile and ignore the decree. Then, when it does, it'll be all over the city, and they won't be able to cancel it.:*

:But—what does one do—:

:Leave that to the merchants, for the most part,: Caryo said wisely. *:Once you make the decree, they'll do exactly what they do for a Midwinter Fair, except that they'll prepare to set the booths and tents up on the ice. And you know, merchants being merchants, if you don't decree a Festival, they'll do this anyway. At least by making a royal occasion out of it, you can set a time limit on it. All you need to do is send someone to rummage through the attics for some prizes for skating contests and other competitions, and arrange for a Royal Pavilion out there with some provisions and cooks for the highborn. And talk to the Deans. Perhaps the young Bardic Trainees could perform gratis? Certainly there should be at least one day off from classes.:*

The more she thought about it, the more excited she became. *:But what if the ice starts to break—:*

:Just find some people that know ice to be ice wardens; if it starts to break up, there'll be plenty of warning.:

Competitions. There ought to be skating races, of course, short and long. Perhaps something for trick skating? A prize for the best ballad on a winter theme. One for the best spiced cider and mulled wine?

:And hot meat pie,: Caryo said, with a mental shudder. *:There are so many wretched hot pies, any encouragement to make them better would be a boon to your people.:*

Ice fishing. There should be a prize for the biggest fish caught ice fishing.

:One- and two-horse sledding races.:

That was just about all she could fit in a single day, she thought with regret. And she wouldn't dare to take more than one day off herself—

:So have all of the elimination contests before the Royal day,: Caryo advised. *:That way there will be some real anticipation building up, and you won't have to taste more than five or six final entries in the food and drink contests.:*

Or listen to more than five or six ballads on the subject of winter…

:And end with a feast and entertainments by moonlight on the ice, with the feasting supplied by the Crown,: Caryo said. *:Have a Royal Ball at the Pavilion to coincide with the common feast. It will be very romantic. Some of your young ladies have been trying to get their young men to come to the question since you were crowned, and if this doesn't do it, nothing will.:*

She thought of those giggling girls out in the snow, and sighed wistfully. The last year of the Tedrel Wars had put paid to a great many romances, and placed obstacles in the paths of many more. Young men who had survived that last battle had sometimes not had the heart for much after what they had been through. She could certainly understand *their* frustration!

Not that she had anyone she wished would come to the question with her. Far from it. No, she wished mostly that for once a "courtship" didn't consist of her Council shoving names and portraits at her. It would be so nice to listen to poetry, even bad poetry, about the beauty of her eyes. It would be wonderful to listen to stammered, clumsy compliments in the moonlight, and to pull away from an attempted kiss at the last possible, and most coquettish, moment.

Was it so wrong of her to hanker after romance, to long for a circle of adoring young men who *didn't* adore the crown rather than the girl? Oh, she knew that most young women of her Court went off to arranged marriages rather than romantic ones, but still, they usually weren't bartered off to the highest bidder like prize cattle. They usually had some choice in the matter.

Well, she had one choice, she supposed. She could always say "no." They could badger her and nag her, but they couldn't force her to marry anyone.

:Think about your festival,: Caryo advised. *:You've taken all the steps you need to about the marriage plans. Think about something pleasant.:*

But would Talamir and Alberich approve? They were in charge of her safety, after all…

:Alberich has already supposed that you were going to do just this, and has been making his own plans,: Caryo said instantly. *:Or so Kantor tells me.:*

What? Her head came up, like a hound suddenly sniffing something it did not expect on the breeze. But how—

:Partly knowing you, partly knowing you need some pleasure in your life about now, but mostly, I suspect, that ForeSight of his giving him a nudge in the right direction. It doesn't always have to be a disaster that he ForeSees. And when it isn't—

he probably doesn't realize that it's ForeSight.:

Well, that made perfect sense to her. And it was comforting, knowing that someone she trusted as much as she trusted Alberich thought this was a good idea.

:Oh, yes. For the people as much as for you. There's been too much sadness. When you mourn for too long, you start to forget how to feel joy.:

She bent her head at those words, feeling sadness overcome her again for a moment, and felt Caryo sighing with her. That struck to the heart of the matter, and had been something she had not felt comfortable voicing aloud. It had felt somehow disloyal to her father's memory to be weary of weeping for him. And yet, how many tears could she, should she shed?

So Alberich, who had been as loyal to Sendar as anyone could have asked, felt she was ready, and Valdemar was ready, to let go and move on?

Perhaps she didn't need to feel guilty, then.

But Talamir?

:Rolan says that Talamir will have no problem with this.:

Well, she wouldn't expect Talamir to participate; it would be unkind. She wouldn't really *need* the Queen's Own for something like this, just some good bodyguards. Alas. She wished she could have done without *those* as well.

But probably the monarchs of Valdemar hadn't been able to do without bodyguards since—well, for as long as she could think. Certainly as long as there had been difficulties with Karse.

So, there was one good thing; if she had to have bodyguards, they could at least be people she knew would be able to enjoy the Festival with her.

:Heh,: Kantor said, just as Alberich was choosing a book to read by his fire before going to bed. *:I doubt that you're going to be surprised at this. Caryo has just told me that Selenay has decided to hold that Ice Festival.:*

He settled down in his favorite chair, and adjusted the lamp behind him so that the light fell properly on the page. His window had an interesting look to it, with the light falling on it rather than through it. Rather like colored stone set in a mosaic. No doubt the Glassmaster had considered this as well, when he'd chosen the glass and the colors.

He hoped no one would ever take a shot at him from the other side of it. Getting those colors matched would be impossible. He'd probably have to have the whole thing made again.

At least it would take less time to craft a new window than that blasted mirror.

:Good,: he said firmly. *:It will be good for her, and good for Haven. But we'll need to slip it past the Councilors, so tell Caryo to suggest that Selenay wait until she's holding public audience, then make a decree tomorrow that if the Terilee freezes solid, there will be the Festival.:*

:What difference will that make?: Kantor asked.

Alberich sipped his hot wine. *:First, the decree will be in public, which will make it more difficult for the Councilors to object. Secondly, they'll applaud this in public as being a grand gesture, and think in private that it's about as likely as pigs flying. Then, since the decree will have been posted all over the city, when the river does freeze solid, it will be too late for them to do anything about forbidding any such festivities.:*

He was rather pleased with this. He wanted Selenay to have a victory without having to fight for it. The more of those she got, the more her Councilors would become accustomed to the idea that she *was* the Queen and *was* a ruler. Sooner or later, she was either going to have to rule in truth, or become the mouthpiece for her Council, a figurehead, but not a leader.

The sad part was, he could see even the *Heralds* who were on her Council gently maneuvering her into that role, all the while telling themselves that it was for her own good, that she was still too young to take the burden of the Crown, that they would just *guide* her…

It was always easier to hold power than to give it up. That was how the Son of the Sun and his strongest Priests had come to rule Karse. And look where that had gotten them.

Kantor seemed to be following his thoughts. *:Good idea. I'll tell Caryo.:* And after a moment, *:Who do you want for Selenay's bodyguards? I doubt she'll be able to take more than a day away from her duties, but she'll need guards when she does.:*

Bodyguards… someone out there was trying to cause trouble over Selenay's rule, and even if he was doing it as a distraction, it was *still* possible that his words would find fertile ground in some poisoned mind and bear unexpected fruit. Maybe she wasn't in quite as much danger as she had been during the Tedrel Wars—

But maybe she was. He was in charge of her safety. He could not take the chance. So… that meant very good bodyguards, all over again.

Good question, who he should assign; assuming that the Collegia would be taking a full set of holidays, the various teachers and their assistants wouldn't be needed up here, but the Royal Guard *would*, in its full strength, both at the Palace and at the Festival. They would be busy keeping watch over all the highborn; he needed someone watching over Selenay and only Selenay. *:Might as well make it Keren and Ylsa for the daylight hours.:* He gave some more thought to what this Festival should involve, for lowborn and high as well. *:I suppose she'll have a feast and entertainment for the highborn in a pavilion on the ice the same evening that she attends the games? Or should I say, there will be two feasts, one for the common folk, and one for the Court? And I mean* all *of the highborn, as many as can come at short notice in winter? It would be good for building loyalty.:*

Kantor was taken by surprise by that question. *:I don't think she'd even considered a Court Feast for the entire roster of the highborn throughout the Kingdom, but it's a good idea. A very good idea. I'll pass it on.:*

Alberich felt a certain amusement that he, born poorest of the poor, and bastard to boot, should be the one to be making suggestions about what the great and grand would find appropriate. Still. He'd been raised on tales of it, after all. Virtually every child had. And he'd been watching *this* Court for years now. *:A grand feast for the Court will help lighten things considerably. Midwinter was shadowed; the first one without Sendar, and Selenay still in mourning. I don't think anyone had the heart for it. But this won't have any memories, any connotations. It's the sort of thing that ought to make the Councilors happy with the whole idea, since they'll be able to haul in all their so-called eligible candidates for her hand and hope that one of them charms her.:*

He added that last with just a touch of sourness. Sourness, because, truth to tell, it annoyed him to see these supposedly sensible men trying to force the poor young woman into a destiny of *their* choosing. And because they were wasting so much time and effort on the project, time and effort that could be going to some task more useful. If they would put half the concentration they put into working together that they put into finding a mate for the Queen, three quarters of the current difficulties besetting the Kingdom would vanish overnight.

And for just a little while, it was a relief to think about something other than plots and intrigues. He had never been very comfortable in dealing with plots and intrigues, except for his singular talent of being quiet and unreadable. He was better at it now, but that didn't mean he enjoyed it.

Well, except for the occasions when he had an excuse to let off some of his tension by breaking a few heads. Hmm. This Festival just might give him a chance at that form of relief—

He quickly sealed *that* thought away from Kantor.

:She can be impartially charming right back to any would-be suitor without giving any of them hope,: Kantor agreed. *:I wish that more of them were worth being charming to.:*

:So do I.: The fact that so many potential mates had been systematically disqualified by Selenay in public meant that anyone who was dredged up and hauled in for the Ice Festival was bound to be marginal at best. Unsuitable in the extreme, unless some distant cousin out of the back of beyond happened to get dragged out of his manor, Chosen on the spot, and proved to be the man of Selenay's dreams. If she even had any dreams on the subject. It was hard for Alberich to tell. Selenay's mind was often opaque to him; he didn't have a great deal of experience with young women. Come to that, he didn't have a great deal of experience with women in general.

:And whatever suitors are hauled in will probably be stone-deaf and ninety at worst,: Kantor sighed. *:Poor Selenay! It will be a shabby lot of dancing partners she'll be getting.:*

Another aspect that hadn't occurred to him. With things so subdued at Midwinter, she hadn't seemed to want any dancing. The Selenay he remembered had loved dancing. Well, maybe he could do something about that.

:I think at an occasion like an Ice Festival, she ought to dance every other dance with a Herald, don't you?: he asked Kantor. *:In fact, isn't there some sort of mandate about that, somewhere? So that no highborn can claim two dances with her in an evening?:*

:If there is, Myste can find it,: Kantor replied, with a chuckle. *:And if there isn't—:*

:Myste can still find it,: he replied, thinking with real pleasure of how Myste and Selenay together had foiled the entire Council plan to get her safely betrothed to someone of *their* choice. It had been a thing of beauty, according to Myste. He was just glad that he had kept himself out of it, so that when he'd been asked, he'd been able to truthfully disclaim any knowledge of it all.

Not that he'd wanted to be anywhere near the room at the time the entire thing unfolded. Whenever certain members of the Council were thwarted, they always looked at the Karsite as the source of their troubles. Funny. They suspected *his* hand behind even this without his being anywhere near the Council Chamber that day; they'd entirely overlooked Myste. *:I'm not entirely certain about all those cross-cousin links Myste* *was finding. Surely the highborn of Valdemar aren't that closely inbred.:*

:Chosen! You don't think Herald Myste would concoct information, do you?: Kantor asked, pretending to be aghast at the thought.

:You're forgetting she was a clerk before she was a Herald,: he replied. *:They spend a quarter of their lives writing things down, a quarter finding what other people have written down, a quarter hiding what was written down, and a quarter making sure if it should have been written down and wasn't, it is now.:*

Kantor had no real reply for that, but Alberich didn't really expect one. And no, in the case of something important, he really did not think that Myste would stoop to forgery. But in the case of something like this, where nothing was hanging on a little judicious creativity but Selenay's all-too-rare pleasure, Myste could and would unbend her rigid ethics in order to ensure that the "tradition" existed, even if it hadn't been a tradition until a few moments ago when he'd thought of it.

Apparently Kantor agreed. *:Consider it a tradition that's been in place for centuries. You know, Myste is very good at aging documents.:*

Well, she had to be; she had to know how to forge them in order to detect forgeries. And it wasn't as if she'd be doing anything really unethical, like forging the Great Royal Seal. She could just insert it in a list of protocol from the last Ice Festival, hand it to the Seneschal as the guide to how he should conduct the feast at the end, and no one would be the wiser. And Selenay would get dancing partners that she could relax with. In fact, he'd handpick them. Or rather, he'd handpick them after consulting with someone who knew which Heralds were adequate dancers.

Which reminded him of something else.

:Don't the wretches generally sneak off to some private, Heralds-only party as soon as they can when there is an enormous fete like this one?: he demanded, recalling that they had done *just* such a thing at Selenay's Coronation.

:Um——: Kantor began, with overtones of guilt.

:Well, not this time, and that is an order, and have Talamir enforce it,: he said firmly. *:Not until Selenay is ready to leave. By Vkandis' Crown, if she doesn't get to enjoy most of this affair, it'll be no fault of mine, and it won't be for lack of good company, friends among the rest, as well as dancing partners!:*

:Yes, sir!: Kantor replied, for once with no hint of mockery or irony whatsoever in his mind-voice.

Hmph. He settled into his book with a feeling of satisfaction, as Kantor and the other Companions—and whatever Heralds would be involved in the plot—coordinated themselves. Myste, Talamir, the Seneschal's Herald, presumably. Those here at the Collegium who were young

enough to make decent conversation with her, good dancers, or both—
—and he wouldn't have to worry about a Herald as a risk to her safety either. Not that it was likely that anyone would try anything in so great a throng, but—

Grand, something else to worry about.

:What about—: Kantor interrupted his pretense at reading. *:—if we concoct another point of protocol? That any final-year Trainee of appropriate age and gender can serve as the Queen's dance partner?:*

He thought about that for a moment; it would effectively double the number of young faces at the occasion, and what was more they would be people Selenay already knew and would feel comfortable around. It wasn't that long ago that she'd been a Trainee herself.

:Perfectly reasonable. While we're at it, throw the doors open for the Bards and Healers as well. No reason why they can't be included. Every reason why they should be.: And Bards and Healers were just as trustworthy as Heralds. With any luck, there would be so many of them that no one else would even get a chance at taking a dance with Selenay.

He felt Kantor's approval. *:Good. Bards make better dancers anyway.:* And, once again, he sensed Kantor's withdrawal.

He felt himself smiling; there was something to be said for this particular kind and purpose of conspiracy. It made everyone who was involved in it feel good. And it got their minds moving in directions that had been sadly unfamiliar for far too long. Poor Selenay had been spending the last six moons and more thinking only of the welfare of those around her and dependent on her. It was about time that they all returned the favor.

:If Keren and Ylsa are going to be her bodyguards, shouldn't she have an official escort?: Kantor said, coming "back" from wherever he'd "been."

Good God, another sticking point, another point of vulnerability. Not one of the suitors—oh, no. That would be opening the door to all sorts of potential trouble *and* danger. But who? *:Since this is a Festival, what about a Bard?:* he asked, thinking about all the really handsome-looking Bards he'd seen in and around the Collegia. *:Besides, with a Bard around, you never lack for conversation. It's their job to be witty.:*

:Good idea. Then she can't be accused of favoritism for the Heralds, but she won't be stuck with one of the suitors.: Kantor "vanished" again, and Alberich was left alone with his book.

He might even manage to get a page or two read, in between thinking of yet more security holes, and coming up with schemes to block them. While she was up *here*, behind her walls, she was secure. But down there, for the God's sake, out on a solid sheet of ice—

But her people love her. Even down there, in the worst part of Haven, there was anger when that whore tried to make trouble. He had to take comfort in that; had to remember that this was *not* Karse and Selenay *could* move among her people without fear.

Most of them, anyway—

He sighed, and put down the book. No point in trying to read now. It was time to start making some lists, or his mind would be buzzing and he'd get no sleep at all this night.

"When do you sleep?" "Infrequently."

He sighed, and fetched a pen and paper.

5

Clear sky of a brilliant, cloudless blue, and it was cold enough to freeze the—Well, it was colder than Alberich had ever been without also being wet clear through. It got cold in Karse, but never quite like this, a dry, biting cold that didn't penetrate so much as stab. He was grateful for the extra pairs of socks he was wearing, as well as for the peculiar contraptions that Keren had cobbled up for everyone at the Collegium, leather straps with five or six tacks in them that you could strap on over your boots to give you traction on the ice. She said that people used them for ice-fishing on Lake Evendim. Well, he would take her word for it, because if it was cold enough to freeze that lake this thick every winter, he never wanted to go there.

He'd never learned to ice skate, and at this point in his life, he was a bit dubious about the odds of his success if he started, so it was a good thing he had these so-called ice cleats on his feet. They kept him from measuring his length on the slippery river ice more than once.

He just wished there was something for sun glare off of ice and snow that made him wear a squint that was beginning to feel permanent. He had his hood up and a hat on top of it to shade his eyes, but that did nothing for the reflected glare. It was also beginning to give him a headache.

Still, this Ice Festival was something to be seen, and worth the cold and the rest of it. He didn't often get out during the day down in Haven in one of his disguises, and for once, he wasn't even down here on "business."

Whoever the jolly lad had been who'd been paying for people to foment dissension over the Queen, evidently getting his hireling arrested had frightened him off. Not a rumor, not a sign, not a *breath* of trouble had there been since then. Talamir reckoned that the whole scheme *had* been hatched up to create a distraction at some point—and that the hatcher of said plot had gotten cold feet when his agent had been unmasked.

Maybe, maybe not—but thanks to the Festival, Selenay's star was very high with the common folk, and grumbling was going to get someone's head broken. And *that* would quickly bring the City Guard and constables, which meant that Alberich's job was being done for him, at least in part. So—if this excursion, intended so that Alberich could listen to people talking, spend some time in and around the places where liquor flowed freest and tongues were loosest, wasn't entirely pleasure, it wasn't entirely business either.

As he traveled with the flow of the crowd down the improvised "street" of booths that had been built on the solid ice of the Terilee, he was covertly watching the reactions of those around him to his current guise. This costume represented more of a middling class of working man, someone who was, unlike many of his personae, *not* a particularly dangerous fellow, and he wanted to make sure he had the nuances down. The last thing he needed to do was to alert people when what he wanted was for them to be careless and at their ease around him. Normally he would have worn a clever cosmetic paste that covered his scars, but that wouldn't pass muster in the daylight. Fortunately, it didn't have to, not when he and almost all of the other people down here had their faces wrapped in scarves against the cold. He was experimenting with false beards and other facial hair, but those didn't stick too well in the cold.

That meant a lot of work on his part: moving easily, schooling his eyes and eyebrows into a vacantly pleasant expression. People reacted to the language of body and expression without even realizing that they were doing so; he knew very well how to read those things now. He'd been good as an officer, but now, thanks to no end of schooling, he was very, very good. That instruction had been not only at the hands of his mentor Dethor, but with the help of Jadus, who before becoming a Herald had been a Trainee of Bardic Collegium, where the Trainees were taught drama and acting as part of the curriculum. It had taken him years to get to this point, where he was willing to try going about among the middle classes, attempting to be unnoticed.

He thought, judging by the way that he was jostled, shoved, and occasionally grumbled at, that he was succeeding. None of his bully-boy personae would have been blundered into like this; the folks of the daylight hours would have taken one look at him and given him a wide berth. Assuming they didn't report him to the City Guard as a suspicious person. It was too bad he couldn't find a thief, especially a pickpocket, to teach him how to blend in. If there was one person whose very life depended on blending in, it was a petty thief.

He'd been on the. lookout for those, just to keep his hand in at spotting them, but oddly enough, he hadn't seen any. Possibly that was because they were keeping to the nighttime hours in order to work the crowd in more safety, but possibly the issue was that they were no better on the ice than he was. If you had to run for it—well, you couldn't run for it.

:If I was a petty thief,: Kantor observed, *:I would work the booths on the bank and stick to the nighttime. A couple of hours past sunset, and it's not only dark enough to make a good getaway, people are a lot drunker than they are now.:*

:Glad you aren't out here?: Alberich asked.

:Profoundly. I shudder to think of me on the ice. Keren hasn't yet come up with cleats for us, and neither has the blacksmith managed shoes that will work out there.: Kantor did not mention how much he disliked the cold; that was a given. Alberich had taken pity on him, and hadn't even ridden him down to the Bell today; he'd borrowed an ordinary horse from the Palace stables.

Alberich snugged the hood down around his ears, adjusted the scarf, and pulled the floppy felt hat down tighter. There was another thing to feel grateful for, and that was the quality of his costume. The good, thick, homespun wool with the old-fashioned hood was better than anything that the young bucks were sporting out here, and his clumsy-looking boots had room for three pairs of socks.

As he had predicted, the Councilors had thought the idea of the river freezing solid enough to hold the Ice Festival extremely amusing when Selenay brought up the idea before them. They ignored it in Council, and chuckled as she issued the proclamation in front of the Court. Well, the ones that weren't Heralds did, anyway; the Heralds already knew it was going to happen, but nothing would have convinced the Councilors of that. The news got down into Haven, and with a feeling of anticipation, people began making quiet preparations.

Then the cold wave rolled in silently at night, and everyone woke to find ice in the water jugs on their bedside tables, ice so thick on the glass of windows that you couldn't see out, and down along the river, reports that it was frozen over.

And all of the townspeople, who had, of course, been certain that anything the Queen made a proclamation about would come to pass, had sent watermen out to test the thickness of the ice daily. It had taken three days until everyone was certain that it was strong enough for the festivities. No one wanted accidents, however much they wanted a holiday.

Then, overnight, an entire Fair sprang up, with the more timid arraying their tents on the banks, and the bolder setting up right on the ice. Predictably, the merchants on the ice were heavily weighted in favor of hot food and drink stalls, while the ones on the banks featured fairings and other goods. The Midwinter Fairs, not only in Haven but all around the countryside, had been something of a failure, for the weather had been bleak and no one had had much heart for frivolity; this was going to more than make up for it, if the merchants had any say in the matter.

There were stalls doing a brisk business in crude skates, basic wooden blades with simple straps to hold them to the soles of the shoes. They could be made for you right there on the spot and fitted to your shoes or boots. There were several more booths set up to wax or smooth the blades. Then there was a knife grinder who'd set up to sharpen the blades of good steel skates. Those were blacksmith-made, of course; no one in the crowd that Alberich was moving in now could afford such things. Those with the money for steel skates who hadn't already gotten a pair were queuing up to get theirs, though, and the blacksmith who'd had blades going a-begging at Midwinter was getting double the price for them now. There were two kinds; you could get the ones that strapped on as the wooden skates did, or, if you really had money to spare, you could bring the blacksmith a pair of your boots or shoes, and he'd fasten the blades permanently to the soles. Anyone with those, though, was someone dedicated to the sport.

A kind of protocol had sprung up in the first day of the Festival about who got what part of the ice, since there were both skaters and walkers among the booths. Skaters got the middle of the lane, and those who were slipping and staggering about on their own shoes kept to the sides. The lane had been laid out wide enough that there was room for both, though occasionally a skater would go careening into the crowd, and the walkers would curse and try to cuff the skater. Most of the time people took it in good part, and if they saw someone skidding toward them, they often did their part to rescue him before he cracked his skull.

The contests had begun as soon as the booths were set up; informal races at first, which soon weeded out those whose bravado exceeded their skill. By the time that the Palace had sent down real judges, the would-be competitors had been winnowed down to a manageable number.

There had been those whose skill exceeded the limits of their equipment, but Selenay had a good plan to take care of that. She'd ordered preliminary races and games among those with the cheap wooden blades only, and the winners of those got steel skates—still of the strap-on sort, but made stoutly and of good steel—as prizes. That put the competition on something like a level field when the real contests started.

The booths began at the largest bridge across the river, where there were steps built into the banks. The racecourse began and ended where the booths did; going up-river for a set distance, carefully marked on both riverbanks, then returning. Anyone who cared to come to the bank along the race route could see the races; some enterprising souls along the bank were renting their rooms for the final day of racing, so that people could watch in comparative comfort. Alberich couldn't quite see the point of that—being crowded up to a window that gave you less of a view than the worst spot on the bank itself—but then, from what he was hearing, there would be so much in the way of drinking and carousing going on in those rooms that no one would be paying much attention to the races anyway.

Then there were the competitions in trick skating, being held in a particularly smooth section. Real seats had been set up there, and there were contests in jumping over barrels, fancy skating in singles and pairs, and sprint racing. When the trick skaters weren't performing or competing, someone had come up with a strange game involving two teams of eight men each, armed with brooms, a ball, and two goals. There didn't seem to be many rules, except that the participants evidently needed to be drunk enough not to care when they fell down or crashed together, but not so drunk they couldn't manage to play. Fights frequently broke out, but no one got seriously hurt, as far as Alberich had been able to tell. There were black eyes, a few lost teeth, and broken brooms, but no broken bones. Perhaps that was due at least in part to all the padding that the players wore in the way of extra clothing. The games tended to have no set duration, lasting either until everyone was too tired to go on, or the fancy skaters wanted to use the ice again and got the Guard to chase the gamers off. Whereupon the gamers would pick up their goals—made of eel traps—and move to rougher ice until the good patch was free again. To Alberich's inexperienced eyes, the game looked something like a game played on ponyback by some of the hill shepherds, who had allegedly got it from the Shin'a'in.

There weren't any prizes for the broom-ball game, so the people playing it were doing so purely for the sheer enjoyment of the mayhem they were engaging in. And, perhaps, for the hot wine and mulled ale that their supporters brought out for them whenever they took a break.

It never failed to amaze Alberich how much effort some people would go to for a "free" drink.

Skating competitions weren't the only ones that had been announced.

Ice and snow sculptors had been hard at work, too, with their creations ranged wherever the artists' fancy had chosen to put them, with the traffic left to deal with them. Alberich had never considered ice as a sculptural material before, and he'd never seen anything made of snow other than a child's snowman, but these pieces were quite astonishing, and he thought that it would be a pity when they finally melted. There was one entire snow castle, with blocks of ice for windows, and furniture made of ice and snow, and a clever tavernkeeper inside selling ice wine in glasses made of ice. Some people were said to be paying him for the privilege of sleeping on the ice beds, but to Alberich's mind that was going more than a bit too far for novelty. Still, the place was pretty at night, with light from colored lanterns making the walls glow from within.

Probably the most popular places of all were the warming tents, prudently set on the riverbank, where braziers of coals kept the worst of the cold at bay and allowed frozen feet and hands to thaw out. Sellers of hot wine and hot pies provided the tents, and the benches inside. The Crown supplied the fuel (a gesture of good will that was much appreciated, for otherwise it would have cost something to be admitted), so even someone without the penny for a pie could get warmed up. And if you were clever, you brought your own drink in a metal can, and your own pies from home, to warm at the brazier.

The pies themselves were something new to Alberich—not that he'd never seen them before, but in this cold, they served a new and dual purpose. The pie itself served as a hand-warmer, in fact; most people made or bought sturdy offerings with a hard crust that could stand a great deal of abuse, wrapped them in a scrap of cloth as soon as they came right out of the oven, and tucked them into pockets and muffs to act as a heat source until the owner got hungry. By that time, the pie would probably have suffered enough that the owner could gnaw through the tough crust without losing a tooth—and if it had gotten too cold, you could always rewarm the thing without worrying too much about it. Or, as one old fellow said to Alberich, "Wi' my wife's cookin', a little char improves the flavor."

And the pies were as universal as the snow and ice, even for the denizens of the Collegia. If they presented themselves to the Collegia cooks before coming down, the Trainees were given pies as well, for the same dual purpose, but nothing like the common sort, which could have stood duty as paving stones. Alberich had one in each pocket right now, as a matter of fact, providing a comforting source of heat for both hands.

:You know, that might be another reason why there are so few pickpockets,: Kantor said. *:Your purse is somewhere inside your coat or your cloak and hard to get at. Your pockets are full of pies of a dubious nature.:*

Besides testing his disguise, a matter of curiosity had brought Alberich down here today. The Dean of Bardic Collegium had intercepted him yesterday to tell him that she thought she knew where the two mirror breakers had gotten their mad ideas for gymnastic fighting. Her information had brought him down to the booths at the bridge end where, as part of the Festival, a troupe of players had set up a tent to display their talent. There weren't many of those—it was, to be honest, too cold for anything but unaccompanied singers to be performing out-of-doors, and as for the sort of acrobats and dancers that plied their trade at Fairs, they'd be risking their skins to bounce about in their usual skimpy attire. This set of players, however, usually performed several times in a week at one of the bigger inns off the Trade Road; they'd moved to this venue just for the Festival, and as Alberich neared the canvas walls that held their makeshift theater, he saw that the move must have been very profitable for them. He joined the end of a longish line just forming up for the afternoon performance with some interest.

Well, "tent" was something of a misnomer, he discovered, as he got to the entrance, paid his entry fee, and filed inside with the rest. Only the area over the back half of the stage was roofed over and curtained, the rest was simply canvas walls to prevent the show from being viewed by those who had not paid, with an overhead scaffolding of rigging for stage effects and nighttime lighting reaching out into the area of the audience. Crude benches in rows fronting the stage were supplied to the public, and the show must have been popular, for the tent was half full when Alberich arrived, and by the time of the show, the benches were packed and so was the standing-room area along the walls.

The drama was called—or so the banners outside proclaimed—"The Unknown Heir." The banners could have fit any one of a hundred standard stories, and probably served for every play these actors ever put on. They looked superficially new, but Alberich could tell that they'd been freshly touched up just for the Festival.

The audience was ready to be entertained, and when the back curtains finally parted and a single actor took the stage, they erupted in cheers that must have gladdened his heart.

Alberich sat back on his bench, arms folded under his cloak, and prepared to see just what it was that had "corrupted" two Trainees.

First came the declamation of the Prologue. The plot, what there was of it, concerned a highborn child, stolen from his cradle and sold to slavers, subsequently bought or rescued (the prologue was rather unclear on the subject) by a troupe of poor but noble actors, and raised by them to adulthood. All of this was laid out in a spirited fashion by that single actor before any of the real action took place.

Alberich had to admit that the fellow knew what he was doing; he had the right mix of flamboyance and humor to keep the audience's attention. He finished his piece, gave an elaborate bow, and retired to great applause.

Then the curtains parted on "A Sylvan Glade," represented by two rather sad little trees in pots, and a painted backdrop, against which marched the troupe, portraying the actors on their way from one town to the next. The real action opened immediately with the Unknown Heir and his adoptive family being attacked by bandits, and the Heir proceeding to single-handedly, acrobatically, drive the bandits off. But not before the bandits had managed to mortally wound the Heir's adoptive father—though how they got a knife blade through the four or five layers of costume he was wearing was beyond Alberich's comprehension. This worthy managed an amazingly long set-piece while dying in his "son's" arms. He explained the young man's circumstances, presumed highborn heritage, and handed over the medallion the child had inexplicably still been wearing (even though it was solid gold) when taken from the hands of his kidnappers. It was an astonishing monologue, especially from the lips of someone stabbed through the heart quite some time ago.

None of this evidently stretched the credulity of most of the audience.

With tears and histrionics, the Heir proclaimed that he would regain his rightful place, and wreak revenge for his father's death.

Riotous applause called up many bows from the actors before the action resumed.

The rest of the play consisted of one improbable fight scene after another, taking advantage of the acrobatic abilities of—Alberich guessed—roughly four of the actors in question. And there was no doubt in his mind before the first act was over that this was, indeed, where the two miscreants had gotten their misguided ideas, and given the wild applause that these bizarre fights managed to garner, he was a lot less surprised that the boys had become enamored of the idea of fighting like *that*.

As the Heir and his Best Friend—both in love with the same girl, of course—battled their way through throngs of evil henchmen attempting to keep them from claiming the Heir's rightful place as the Duke of Dorking, Alberich had to admire their stamina, if not their style. In the conclusion to the first act, the Heir plummeted off the top of a "cliff" to flatten half a dozen evildoers, then engaged four at once, sword-to-sword, and after being disarmed, defeated his enemies with a bucket. In the second act, the Heir and the Friend, ambushed in a Peasant Hovel, made the most creative use of a ladder, a table, and a stool that Alberich had ever seen. In fact, what they most closely resembled was not a pair of fighters at all, but a pair of ferrets trying not to be caught. In the third act, the Best Friend met the end that Alberich had expected from the first, after yet another acrobatic exhibition, dying in the arms of the Heir and bravely commending the Heir and the Girl to one another, with the Heir vowing revenge once again—

:*You know,*: Kantor commented, :*I'd steer clear of that man. People trying to kill him seem to keep missing and hitting his friends instead.*:

But it was in the fourth act that something entirely unexpected happened, and it had nothing to do with the script.

Now, Alberich had noticed something a bit odd just before the play began. In the front benches, just off to one side, was a group of young men in clothing far finer than anyone else here was wearing. When the action started, he quite expected them to begin jeering and catcalling, but to his surprise, they did nothing of the sort. In fact, they were quiet and attentive to a degree all out of keeping with the quality of the drama unfolding. And it wasn't as if they weren't *used* to better fare, either; he recognized two of them from having seen them moving in the fringes of Selenay's Court.

Now, that was odd. So odd, in fact, that he felt a tingle of warning and kept his eye on them all during the play.

Then came the fourth act, and the "Grand Climax and Exhibition of Sword-play with Astonishing Feats of Strength and Skill, Never Before Seen on Any Stage" which was laid in the Grand Hall of the Duke of Dorking's Castle. The Heir's enemies held both the Heir's real parents *and* his True Love captive and were engaging in a spot of gloating.

And the Heir swung in over the heads of the front of the audience on a rope.

Alberich had to give them credit; it was a spectacular entrance. Not a very bright one for a real fighter, since while the Heir was swinging about on a rope he was an easy target for anyone with a knife, crossbow, spear, or lance, all of which were in evidence among his enemies—but it was a spectacular entrance. The Heir let go the rope, did a triple somersault in the air, hit the stage, and came up fighting.

No mistaking that move, which was one the boys had tried (in vain) to copy. The actor might be a phony fighter, but he was a superb athlete and tumbler.

There was more of the same wildly unrealistic combat and Alberich noted in passing that the actor who *had* been playing the Best Friend was now, with the assistance of a beard, playing the Chief Villain. And then—

—then came the break with everything Alberich had expected.

If he hadn't been watching so closely—*and* watching the audience, in particular, his lot of young nobles—he might have thought it an accident.

But in the middle of the duel with the Chief Villain, a prop-sword went clattering across the stage, right under the lead actor's feet. He apparently stepped on it, because the next thing that happened was that his right foot shot out from under him, he staggered and tried to catch his balance, and then he went blundering right over the edge of the stage and down onto the audience in the first row—landing atop the same young highborn that Alberich had noticed—to the gasps and shrieks of the crowd.

But all was not as it seemed.

The thing was, someone as good a tumbler as that actor was shouldn't have gone off the edge of the stage at all. What was more, he *hadn't* stepped on or tripped over the sword—

No, as Alberich saw, just before he surged to his feet along with the rest of the audience, the actor had actually kicked it off to the side before making that spectacular "fall."

Furthermore, the young men he'd landed among *had been tensed and ready to catch him.*

If he'd *really* fallen by accident, they'd have scattered instinctively away from his path, not gathered under him, broken his fall, and set him down.

He was up in a trice, as the audience applauded, bowing to them, apologizing to his "victims," even brushing one of them off—

Which was when Alberich distinctly saw a folded set of papers pass from the actor to the young highborn man, vanishing inside the latter's cloak before he could blink.

:Great Gods!: Kantor exclaimed, as Alberich struggled to keep his expression precisely like that of everyone else around him. *:What in the nine hells—:*

:I don't know,: Alberich said, as the actor got back up on the stage and resumed the play. *:But I am going to find out.:*

"—and I do not know who it was," Alberich told Talamir, feet stretched out toward the fire in Talamir's somewhat austere chamber. He had come here directly from the Festival, so directly that he hadn't even had a chance to properly thaw out, though he had stopped long enough to change out of his disguise at the Bell. But Kantor had warned Rolan that Alberich needed to speak to Talamir, who had in his turn informed Talamir that Alberich was coming and was in serious need of defrosting. And Talamir had arranged for hot drinks and a well-stoked fire as well as getting free long enough for this quick meeting.

"A young man you've seen in the Court. No one you clearly recognized." Talamir frowned. "I wish the young people were a little more distinctive, or at least wore the same badges they put on their retainers' livery. Your description doesn't resonate with me either."

Alberich shrugged. "That being the case, until I discover, I am going to have to spend more time around the Court than it is usual. Most probably, it is you who shall have to identify him for me, once his face I see."

"I can do that, certainly, but what do you suppose was the meaning of this?" Talamir asked, leaning over to refill Alberich's tankard. Alberich shifted a little, and shrugged.

"What it probably *wasn't*, much more easily can I say, than what it was," Alberich replied, absently taking another drink and half-emptying the tankard again. "Not an assignation do I think; better ways there are, of passing love notes, than the midst of a play. Not contraband of the usual sort; papers, these were, nothing more."

"Unless the contraband is too large to hand off, and the papers were directions telling where it was," Talamir observed. "It could be something else less-than-legal. Stolen goods, perhaps a valuable horse— or—perhaps money to pay for it?"

"Only papers," Alberich countered. "And what would the purpose be, of the poorer actor paying the highborn, rather than the reverse?" He shook his head. "No. And I think not, the papers were directions to something stolen. Which leaves—information. Paid for by the highborn, gotten by the actor. So—why the exchange in the midst of the play?"

"Because our highborn fellow does not want to be seen making clandestine visits to a mere player." Talamir seemed very certain of that point. "Someone like that would never come up the hill or be allowed even in the gates of one of the manors. Let me tell you, there is *nothing* more certain about the Great Houses than access to them."

"Surely as an actor, easy would it be to feign to be the servant?" Alberich hazarded.

Again Talamir shook his head. "Every servant in a Great House will either have worked for the family for generations, have come from the family's country property, or have been personally vouched for by other servants. Every delivery person will be from a particular set of shops and will be known to the servants. Even the folk who come to take off the trash are personally known to the servants—what the highborn discard is picked over by dozens of lower servants before it gets to the bins outside, and then the right to cart off what is left is jealously guarded."

"Hmm." Alberich blinked; he hadn't known that. Well, so much for ever trying to insinuate himself into a Great House as a servant! "And the boy could not come to the actor in a more secret way?"

"Hah." Talamir raised an eyebrow. "Not where they are. And people take note when they see someone richly dressed hanging about a 'common' venue. No matter how careful he was, someone would see him. Unless, of course, he was as practiced in deception as you are, which is highly unlikely."

"And the resources have, as well," Alberich reminded the older Herald. "Without the Bell, my movements could not possible be."

Talamir's lips formed into a thin line. "The question is, what information, why, and to whom is it going?"

"And does the Crown have interest?" Alberich added. "It could be, we need do nothing about it. It could be, this is only to do with the rivalries among the titled."

Talamir looked thoughtful as Alberich put the empty tankard aside on a little table that stood between their chairs. "It could be, I suppose," he admitted. "But it seems a great deal of trouble to go to simply to acquire information about a rival. And why the connection with a troupe of common players?" He shook his head. "No. I don't like it. I scent something else here."

Alberich was willing to bow to his experience. "So, you think it is something surely to do with a larger issue? Still, it could signify only that someone has an interest, and is not hostile."

"Or not. The Karsites are not our only enemies." Talamir looked pensive. "Or it could be agents of a putative ally, who wishes to learn more than we've told him. In which case—we need to establish if there is any harm in letting him continue to operate."

Alberich snorted at that. "Allies can cause as much harm as enemies, and are less suspected."

"Hmm. There are times, my suspicious friend, when I am glad that you are who and what you are," Talamir replied after a long silence. "That had not occurred to me."

Alberich shrugged. "I am, what I am," he replied. "In Karse, one keeps one's friends close, and one's enemies closer."

"And in Karse, suspicion is no bad thing." Talamir pinched the bridge of his nose and closed his eyes in a grimace. "Let us start with the obvious. You might as well add yourself to Selenay's bodyguards tomorrow. The entire Court will be down at the Festival, and I've no doubt that your mysterious young man will be in the midst of the throng. You'll have your best chance to spot him then, and I can identify him for you."

That was a shortened version of "You'll show him to Kantor, who'll pass the image to Rolan, who'll show it to me, and I'll put a name to him." Alberich nodded.

But he wasn't happy. "Hoped I had, the crush to avoid," he sighed. He still wasn't comfortable rubbing elbows with the titled, even when he was playing so "invisible" a part as that of a bodyguard.

"Well, you can't," Talamir retorted, with an unusual level of assertion. "I won't be around forever, and it is well past the time when you began taking up the duty of spy within the Court as well as down in Haven."

If anything, that made Alberich even more uncomfortable—because no matter what he did, he *couldn't* take Talamir's place within the circles of the Court. For one thing, even if he'd been Valdemaran, he wouldn't fit. For another, no one was ever likely to confide anything in *him*. He just didn't have the face for it.

But he held his peace. There were more ways of undoing a knot than splitting it with an ax. There were Heralds permanently assigned to the Collegium who might serve as his eyes and ears among the highborn, especially the women. Ylsa, perhaps. And there were Trainees coming up who were highborn themselves who might be trusted to play clandestine agent.

"My best, I will ever do," was all he said, and he and the Queen's Own got down to the business of trying to find other ways for Alberich to set eyes on the young man in question again—just in case, against all probability, he did *not* show his face at the Festival.

Because in Alberich's experience, the thing that you planned for always turned out to be the one that was least likely to happen—and the one that you had never thought of was the one that landed in your lap.

6

Selenay's day at "her" Festival dawned cloudless, bright, and bone-chillingly cold. Alberich and the others had planned on forgoing Formal Whites for the sake of warmth, but the ever-resourceful seamstresses had provided the entire escort with heavy woolen capes lined and trimmed with white fur, white fur mittens (fur inside and out), and heavy stockings trimmed at the top with fur, which would make the boots look as if *they* had been lined and trimmed with fur. As a result, they all looked smartly turned out and entirely festive.

When they had all arrived to escort Selenay down to the river, one wag suggested that they ought to have their capes festooned with the same bridle bells as were on the Companions' parade tack, a suggestion which had earned him a handful of snow down his back. After that, he kept his thoughts on costume to himself.

They made quite a little parade, going through town. Fortunately, no one had thought it necessary to make a real procession out of it, though people were lining the streets, waving and cheering, the whole way.

"I think your people love you, Your Highness," said one of Lord Orthallen's hangers-on, patently hoping to curry favor, for he still had his mouth open to continue with a compliment when Selenay laughed.

"I think they love the Queen's Bread they're getting today, and the feast I've arranged for tonight," she replied, and Alberich smothered a smile. For this, the final official day of the Festival (although people would probably stretch things out for as long as the ice held), she'd arranged for bread to be distributed in the morning until the supplies ran out, and meat, wine, and bread for the same time as the Court Feast this evening. If the fountains weren't running with wine instead of water, it was because it was too cold; instead, there would be hot wine available in huge cauldrons along the bank, alongside fires where various beasts were roasting on spits, and more of the bread that had been baked well in advance, and stored cold. Although the notion of "whole roasted oxen" was a romantic one, for practicality's sake, what was going to be offered was just about any beast that could be spitted and roasted and would provide enough meat to satisfy a portion of the crowd. There were quite a few sheep, for instance, and a great many pigs, domestic and wild.

Selenay had been as generous as her purse would allow. If anyone had seen these creatures alive, he would have been well aware that they were all, well, not exactly prime. Most of them had come from the Royal Farms, and were past breeding or working age. Still, they'd been well tended all their lives, and if they were going to provide somewhat tough eating, well, as one old man once told Alberich, "Forbye, much chewin' makes it last the longer, and tough be tasty." Most of the people who would be swarming the fires didn't taste meat more than a few times in a year, and it was almost never anything like beef or mutton.

And as for those who could afford better, well, they could take their purses and go buy it.

In fact, the fires were already being set up for the cauldrons, and the carcasses turning over *their* flames when they arrived at the river. It occurred to Alberich, as the scent of roasting meat filled the air, that the food merchants were not going to do badly out of this, after all. The meat wouldn't be ready for hours, but people would be hungrier with the scent of it in their noses.

For all that he disliked the crush, the sidelong glances, the discomfort of his position as Selenay's shadow, Alberich could not begrudge the Queen a single moment of her day of relative freedom. All he had to do was to catch a glimpse of her face to know that she was enjoying herself for the first time in—well, in far too long. She was smiling a great deal, even laughing, and there was a glow on her that made her look more alive than she had in months.

It didn't take a MindHealer to know why either. This day at her Ice Festival was, perhaps, the only time she had spent since her father's death that wasn't shadowed with memories. Sendar had never presided over such an occasion; guided only by old Chronicles, her friends, and her own imagination, this was something that Selenay had created for herself. It had taken Alberich a little aback to see her *smiling*.

With special nail-studded shoes to give traction on the ice (for the blacksmith had finally come up with something that worked as well as the ice cleats) the Queen, her escort of Heralds, and their Companions came down onto the rock-hard river just about a candlemark after dawn to view the ice sculptures. When a winner had been chosen and rewarded, she went on to watch the children's races and present medallions, money, and skates to the winners. Alberich enjoyed that; the children were enthusiastic and excited without turning it into the cut-throat competition he'd seen watching the preliminary races of the adults. The losers were disappointed but consoled by the sweet cakes Selenay passed out to all the competitors, and the winners so bursting with joy that they could hardly contain themselves.

By midmorning she was ready to taste the three finalists in the meat pie, the mulled ale, the spiced cider, and the hot and ice wine competitions. Then, fortified, she returned to the exhibition area for the fancy skating.

By this time, Alberich was both cold and frustrated, for he hadn't yet seen the young highborn fellow he'd been hoping to identify. When Selenay retired to the Royal Pavilion set up on the ice for a hot meal and a chance to catch her breath, *he* left her in the guard of Keren and Ylsa, and went prowling.

Selenay never had her noon meal in the presence of her Court; by the time she had a chance for that respite, she was generally sick to death of most of them, and wanted nothing more than a little privacy to go along with her food. She wasn't going to change that habit now, so Alberich had a good candlemark to roam about the Royal Enclosure to see what, if anything, could be seen.

There wasn't much. Just a few of the younger set who were already sport-mad, and some of the older ones who never missed a chance to hover in the presence of royalty, and had done so even in Sendar's time. Alberich decided that he would have the best luck if he sidled in near the former and tried to eavesdrop on their conversation, so he got a skewer of basted meat from one of the cooks serving up food *al fresco*, and stood just behind a likely pair, slowly eating and staring off at nothing in particular, doing his best to be ignored.

"...Jocastel may think he's clever, taking the whole house for the day," one of them sniffed, "but they shan't see anything but the middle of the races."

"Well, none of them will, except for Redric. He took that warehouse." The other nodded at a warehouse on the opposite bank, whose docks were festooned with greenery and a few pouting girls wrapped up to the eyes in expensive furs.

"Oh, yes. Well, trust *him*. That entire set is gambling-mad. They'll be there all day."

"And so will Jocastel's, and I doubt that any of *them* will be watching even the middle of the races." A knowing tone crept into the young man's voice. "Redric may have snared most of the ladies, but Jocastel got the keys to his father's wine cellar."

The first one snorted. "Idiots. The lot of them. You can guzzle wine anytime, but when is there likely to be another Ice Festival in our lifetimes? The last one was over fifty years ago, and every champion skater who could get here in time is going to be in the races today! Listen, the big races will begin as soon as the Queen comes back out—*I'm* for hunting down one of those broom-ball tournaments I've heard of. The Terilee might thaw, but the pond up at the old pile will hold for months yet, and I've a mind to get a bunch of the lads together and try the game out ourselves!"

"Oh, now there's a plan!" enthused the second, and both of them moved away, gesturing at each other.

Well, that explained why there was no one here to speak of… a gambling party in a warehouse, a drinking party in a rented house, and that pretty much accounted for most of the youngsters of the Court.

Alberich wandered over to the vicinity of a quintet of older men, who were glaring at the young ladies on the dock with disapproval and muttering at each other. "What are their fathers thinking?" grumbled one, just as Alberich got within earshot. "The idea! Going off to some rented hovel unescorted—"

"Oh, it isn't the daylight hours that I would be concerned about," said another sourly. "But who's to say what's going to happen when the Feast is going on and some of them slip off, unsupervised?"

Alberich eavesdropped shamelessly a little more, learning only that most of the "younger sets" weren't even planning to come down to the Royal Enclosure until the sun set. The older courtiers would be trickling in during the late afternoon, but they weren't the ones Alberich was concerned with.

He returned the skewer to the care of the cooks, and drifted back to Selenay's Royal Pavilion feeling heartily annoyed at humankind in general and that feckless lot of highborn in particular. Hang it all! Why couldn't all those eager parents insist that the young men come down here to dance attendance on the young—and eligible—Queen? Why were they allowing their offspring to gamble and drink away the afternoon without even trying to steal moments of Selenay's time? What were they thinking?

:They're probably thinking that if Selehay hasn't indicated her interest in any of them by now, there's no point in freezing their manhoods off to try to impress her today,: Kantor observed dispassionately.

:Hmph.: Alberich nodded to the Guards at the entrance, and pulled back the door flap, feeling entirely disgruntled. *:Then there's no damned point in my being here now.:* The Royal Pavilion had been set up with a kind of antechamber to keep out the coldest air; he parted a second set of door flaps just inside the first.

:Yes, there is. It will get everyone used to seeing you playing bodyguard, so that no one will think twice about it tonight,: Kantor retorted.

It wasn't much warmer inside, but at least there were carpets laid over the ice, and braziers of coals on sheets of slate atop them that provided little pockets of warmth. The light in here was a lot more restful than out on the frozen river, too; the pitiless sunlight glowed through the painted canvas rather like the light coming in through his precious colored window. And it was out of the wind.

"Alberich!" Selenay called from amid a heap of furs and cushions piled on a high-backed settle that had been brought down from the Palace, her cheeks glowing, her eyes sparkling. "What's to do between now and the Feast?"

"More races," he replied. "The really serious ones; all the champion skaters that could get here in time are going to be competing. Out there will be some intense rivalry; the prizes for the adult races are considerable, and to claim one bragging rights will bestow for a decade."

"Really!" She looked entirely pleased. "How exciting! Have we referees along the course?"

"Absolutely," Keren replied, before Alberich could answer. "Not only is there the prospect that someone is likely to cheat, there's the fact that if someone goes down, there might be a fight over it. He'll probably claim he was fouled, and he might take a part of the field with him. We have this sort of thing every Midwinter where I'm from."

"And there is, I hear, much gambling over the outcome," Alberich added. "So, more incentive there is, to cheat."

"And if someone's accused of cheating?" Selenay looked from Keren to Alberich and back again. "What do I do? Whoever is accused will deny it, no doubt."

"Depends on how and where in the race, and if a referee saw it,"

Keren said judiciously. "Let the referee handle it, unless enough people got taken down. Then, if you're inclined, you can have 'em run the race over again. Presumably, everybody'd be equally tired, so they'd all be on the same footing. If I were a betting person, I'd lay odds you'll have to rerun at least one race this afternoon. This is going to be the climax of the Festival for a lot of people—not even the Feast is going to eclipse it. Feelings will be running high."

"Which is why I have plenty of the Guard stationed on the course and off it," Selenay replied, nodding. "The Seneschal warned me about that, after he watched the semifinals."

"You won't be able to jail everyone who starts a fight—" Keren began dubiously.

Selenay laughed. "And we won't try! Instead, anybody who gets out of hand is going to find himself hauling wood and chopping wood for the spits and the cauldrons!"

Keren laughed, too. "Good enough! Work the energy out of a hothead and leave him too tired to fight!"

"That was the plan," the Queen agreed, looking pleased with herself. "So, besides the races, is there anything else for me this afternoon?"

"Only a skating pageant," Alberich replied, having seen the preparations going on for the thing nearly every day since the Festival began. "Like a street pageant."

"Only instead of *you* riding along the street and stopping at every display, you'll be the one sitting, and the groups doing the displays will pass in front of you, stop, and make their presentations," Keren said helpfully.

Selenay made a face. "I suppose," she sighed, "that everyone would be very disappointed if I didn't watch the whole thing."

Alberich didn't blame her. There were only so many badly rhymed paeans to one's beauty and goodness, sung by shrill and slightly-out-of-tune children's choirs, that a sensible person could stand.

"Very," said the Seneschal, who had just entered the Pavilion himself, in his firmest voice.

"Can I watch it on Caryo instead of in the grandstand?" she asked hopefully. "It's warmer on Caryo—"

"But the purpose of the pageant is as much for you to be seen as for you to view the presentations," the Seneschal pointed out, in a tone that made it very clear that Selenay would not be watching the affair from her saddle.

She sighed. "I hope you have lots of these furs," she said.

* * *

The races were just as exciting as Keren had predicted. And a great deal more dangerous for the participants than Alberich had anticipated. In fine, the contestants were no longer holding back, at all, to save something for the climax. This *was* the climax, and every one of them was determined to go home bearing the champion's medal. The putative honor of entire villages depended on the results, at least for the next year or so, and the skaters were in competition not only for themselves, but for all of their backers.

They wore a lot less for the actual racing than Alberich would have thought wise, but then, moving at the speeds these folks did, perhaps they burned up so much energy they simply didn't feel the cold once they got moving. Or maybe their exertions kept them warm. Whichever it was, when it came time to form up along the starting line, they all left off coats and cloaks, keeping only thin, knitted woolen trews bound closely to their calves, and thin, sleeved, knitted woolen tunics, with scarves wrapped close around face and mouth, and knitted hats and gloves. They all looked somber, focused, and purposeful. By this point, anyone left in competition had steel blades on their feet, and they were wickedly sharp, too. It was when he was looking at those blades glinting as the skaters warmed up before the first race, that Alberich suddenly realized that the races could be *dangerous* as well as competitive. These folk were wearing knives on their feet, and if they went down in a heap…

Well, they must know that. Presumably, they would take care if they did go down. Or at least as much care as could be taken. The idea just made him shake his head, though; he couldn't imagine taking the chance of getting a leg or arm slashed to the bone for the sake of a race.

Interestingly enough, it was the longest of the races that started first, because by the time this race, of several leagues, ended, the shorter races would be long over. They called it simply the Long Race, and those who competed in it were specialized skaters indeed, and would not take part in any other race today. It was a lonely sort of race—far, far down the river and back again, a test of endurance as well as speed, and the organizers had supplied each of the volunteer referees stationed along the route with a fire, blankets, and restoratives so that they could go to the rescue of any racer who failed.

That race began with a preliminary scramble, but as the skaters passed out of sight beyond a bend in the river, it was clear that the pack had quickly sorted itself out, and the race had turned into an orderly skate in which each man would play out a strategy that he had predetermined for himself.

Then the fast races began. First the sprints, which were *very* fast indeed, and just as contentious as Keren had promised. There were falls, and the predicted fights among both skaters and spectators, and some sorting out by the Guard, Selenay declared that two races would be rerun.

Then came the longer races, which was where Alberich got a good look at the sort of pace that could rival that of a Companion at full gallop. The skaters bent low over their feet, with their hands clasped behind their backs, making strong, sure, gliding strokes that were most like the oarstrokes of men in sculls. Only at the beginning and the end did any real fight for position take place, although there were some minor exchanges back in the pack. It was fascinating to watch, and the slightest mishap could change everything. More than once, a bit of bad ice caused a fumble that could drop a skater one or more places, and once, a fall took out the entire back half of the pack, with the resultant scrambling that meant there was no chance that any of them could fight for one of the top positions.

The dock at that warehouse was full of people the entire time, and highborn though they might have been, they were shouting, gesticulating, and jumping up and down just as much as any of the commoners on the banks until all but one of the races was over.

And the crowd settled down to wait, eyes straining to the bend in the river, ears cocked for the first sounds of approaching blades.

Then, at long last, the first of the exhausted endurance skaters hove into view—that is, Alberich assumed they were exhausted, though the ones in the lead showed no signs of it, just gliding on with long, sure strokes, swinging their arms for added momentum, looking neither to the left nor the right. The crowd bellowed encouragement, and in the last few furlongs, the final bits of strategy played out; and a skater who had been steadily in third place, hanging so close to the man in front of him that it looked as if they were bound together with a rope, suddenly pulled away. As people screamed and shouted, he put on a final burst of energy; he passed the man in second place. The man in first heard the shouts and made the mistake of looking behind him, faltering for just a moment.

That was just enough.

The fellow behind him somehow found the strength to surge ahead.

And he crossed the finish line with scarcely the length of his forearm ahead of the man he had just passed.

The crowd went mad, and flooded toward the skaters, screaming wildly, while the rest of the skaters staggered over the finish line.

Only then did the exhaustion hit the skaters, as friends swarmed the ice with blankets and cloaks, and legs gave out, sometimes with breathless cries of pain...

Alberich found himself shouting and screaming along with the rest.

There was a brief period for the skaters to recover; then, wrapped warmly in their cloaks again, there came the moment of their glory, when Selenay rewarded the first three finishers with medals, purses, and pairs of the finest skating blades made.

It was at that point that, much to his shock, Alberich realized that he had screamed himself hoarse.

The skaters were all taken away to recover, and Selenay and her bodyguards settled into the reviewing stand, her ladies around her, and Alberich *under* the stand to ensure nothing could get to her from that point. Then came the pageant. And Selenay sat in the reviewing stand, patient as a statue, with a footwarmer under her boots and a handwarmer tucked into a muff someone had brought for her, smiling, while her servants showered the participants with sweets and small coins by way of reward. Alberich felt sorry for her; she was musical by nature, and the kind of cold they were experiencing did not do good things to instruments. Nor did all the screaming that the singers had been doing during the races help the quality of their voices.

Yet when the afternoon wound to a close, and the sun sank over the river, lending everything a tinge of red, he thought that Selenay looked as if she would have gladly sat through another three or four pageants rather than see the day come to an end.

But, of course, it hadn't. Not yet. As the horns sounded to signal that the common folk could begin queuing up to the roasting beasts and simmering cauldrons, Selenay retired once again to the Royal Pavilion to exchange her clothing for a gown created for this particular event. A floor of wood had been laid over the ice, and a special tent pitched over it. Tapestries and hangings brought down from the Palace to hang against the walls of the tent provided further insulation from the punishing cold. While it would not be *warm* within the canvas walls, it would not be nearly as cold as it was outside.

Outside, there was music, and a peculiar and very attractive kind of ice dancing, skaters carrying torches either in round dances or following one another in a close file through intricate figures that were made up on the spur of the moment by the skater in the lead. Inside, there was also music, and fires in firepits, and candles and oil lamps wherever it was safe to put them. Outside, the common folk feasted on meat and bread and well-watered wine drunk hot. Inside—

Inside, it would be another Court Feast like so many others, the only novelty being the cold.

Alberich waited on guard just inside the main entrance to the Royal Pavilion until the Queen appeared, newly attired and ready for her Feast. When she emerged, he saw that Selenay's gown—white, of course—was of heavy quilted velvet, with a fur-lined surcoat and a heavy gold belt at her hips. Her hair was surmounted by a fur hat rather than her crown, with one of the great cloak brooches of the Royal Regalia pinned to the front of it, a great blazing diamond surrounded by lesser diamonds, and instead of slippers, she wore boots. Most of the garments would be like that tonight, he thought, and the wind would shake the canvas walls, reminding all the courtiers present that although they might mock winter by holding their feast on the ice, the winter could take them if it chose.

Still. When Selenay emerged from the back of the Pavilion, she was still smiling, and Alberich thought that she looked both charmingly young and utterly regal. He took her arm himself, and led her out into the torch-lit darkness. He brought her over the treacherous ice as far as the door to the Feasting Tent, where her official escort took over. He found himself a little reluctant to let her go, but that could have been because of the man she had chosen to partner her at the Feast.

Her official escort for the Feast was Lord Orthallen, who had had his tailor copy Selenay's garb in a lush and warming golden brown. He looked extremely handsome, and the surcoat—his ending at his calves, rather than trailing behind in a train as Selenay's did—suited him very well. To Alberich's mind, he looked rather smug as well.

:Hmm,: Kantor commented. *:He does, doesn't he? One wonders why.:*

Well, it could only be because Selenay was showing him such preference tonight. Alberich hoped so. Fortunately, Orthallen was safely wedded, and there was no way that he could divorce his faithful, fruitful, and obedient wife without a major scandal—so there was no way that he could imagine this sign of preference to be anything but Selenay's choice to honor her "Uncle" Orthallen in what was, essentially, a meaningless gesture.

Meanwhile, he had a job to perform, and he set about doing it, following immediately behind the pair as they walked up the aisle between the rows of lower tables. The two Heralds he'd chosen to play bodyguard at the High Table were already waiting there, flanked by Royal Guardsmen in their blue formal uniforms.

He and the other two Heralds he'd picked as bodyguards for tonight—Alton and Shanate—had taken the precaution of purloining some dinner from the cooks before the Feast began, just as the Guardsmen had. So they were able to keep their minds on the surroundings and not the food.

Not that there was even the slightest hint of trouble. Just a great many excited, animated people, who were showing clearly with their high spirits that this entire Festival had been a very good idea. No one looked at *this* High Table with that shadowed glance of regret. The very different setting kept any memories of Sendar's High Feasts from intruding.

So did the food, though not as much as the setting. There were some novelties, which was only to be expected; a soup served iced rather than hot, many small ice sculptures on the tables, and clever combinations of chilled food seasoned with hot spices. There were sherbets and shaved ice with fruit and syrup spooned over the top—something that would not have survived more than a moment in the heated Great Hall. There were other concoctions that were actually doused in liquor and set afire, that made a fine show as well, though those made Alberich more than a little wary until they'd been doused.

With Orthallen on Selenay's right, and Talamir on her left, unfortunately Selenay could not have gotten much novelty in conversation. Well, she couldn't have everything. And she did appear to be enjoying herself.

On the whole, Alberich thought about halfway through, he and his fellow bodyguards had gotten the better part of the meal—by the time the stuff got to the table, with the exception of dishes served flaming, quite a bit of it was lukewarm at best.

He scanned the tables for his suspect, but the full Court wasn't here—it wouldn't have been possible to serve them all under these conditions for one thing—so those at the table were the most important members of the most important families, and his *young* highborn wasn't among them. Alberich stifled his disappointment. The time to really look for the elusive fellow was coming.

Finally, the last subtlety was served and eaten, Selenay and her escort parted company with smiles, and everyone cleared back to huddle around the firepits and braziers to let the servants swarm over the place and clear out all of the tables and most of the benches, setting some against the tapestries so that those who were not dancing would have a place to sit. Now the evening could really begin.

And now people literally poured into the grand tent; the Royal Pavilion was even now being laid out with refreshments to save room here, for this was where the dancing was to be held. The small dais where the High Table had stood now held a single proper seat—Selenay's portable throne, which she took as soon as it had been set up. The musicians, teachers at Bardic Collegium all, sat near her, on stools, where she could give them any instructions she might have on what sorts of dances to play.

The musicians carefully tuned their instruments, and at a nod from Selenay, the first notes cut across the milling crowd. Those courtiers who did not care to dance cleared away to the side; the rest, including most of the younger ones, taking the floor, forming up into four rows of couples, waiting expectantly for Selenay to take the lead spot.

And Selenay's first dancing partner came forward, a very tall, very clever-looking fellow in full Bardic Scarlet. He bowed over her hand; she stood up, and they took their positions.

Every dance had been arranged in advance, of course. The only deviation would be if Selenay elected to sit any of them out, at which time her partner would be expected to attend her and offer conversation. Alberich doubted that Selenay would do any such thing, though; she loved dancing, and she'd been keyed up all day without having much of an outlet for her energy.

If ever his young nobleman was going to appear, it would be here. But not, Alberich thought, among those nearest to the Queen.

And in fact, the evening was half over before he caught a glimpse of the young man. It was only a glimpse, too—too quick to be certain, much less to pass the sight along to Kantor. But Alberich was good at remembering details, and the young man was wearing a hat that was reasonably identifiable. Alberich kept his eye on that hat, watching as it swam through the crowd, as it swayed and bent in a dance, as it huddled with several more hats off to one side—

And, for one horrible moment, he thought it was going to duck out of the entrance.

But it hesitated, then bowed to an elegant plume. It joined with the plume—escorting it?—and the pair moved along the side of the dancing-floor until, at last, they moved out onto it.

As luck would have it, it was a round-dance, and eventually the figures brought the hat, and its owner, into Alberich's line-of-sight.

He felt Kantor absorb the young man's image through his own eyes; felt Kantor "absent" himself for a moment.

Then Kantor "returned."

:Devlin Gereton, third son of Lord Stevel Gereton,: Kantor reported. *:Talamir will tell you what he knows about the young man, and his family, later. It isn't much; it's an old family, but not particularly prosperous, and they haven't done much to draw attention to themselves or distinguish themselves. There's only one thing; there's no reason why this young man should be so interested in common plays or actors. His eldest brother's a sound amateur poet, and the only thing that Devlin is known for is that he has a good ear for poetry and letters and is considered a budding expert in drama.:*

Well. Wasn't that interesting.

Wasn't that very interesting indeed…

7

Selenay woke just before dawn; if she had had any dreams, she couldn't remember them.

Yesterday everything had gone perfectly. With one exception. One glaring, aching exception.

Her father hadn't been there.

A weight of crushing depression settled over her.

She opened her eyes and lay quietly in her bed as thin, gray light crept in through the cracks in her curtains. She closed her eyes again, and hot tears spilled from beneath her lids and down her temples to soak into her hair.

Her throat closed, and a cold, hard lump formed in it. Selenay tried to fight back the sobs, but one escaped anyway, and she turned over quickly and muffled her sobbing in her pillows. She didn't want to wake her attendants, or alert the servants on the other side of the door. She didn't want anyone to know she was crying.

They wouldn't understand. They would think that she should be thrilled, not choked with tears. After all, her Festival had been a triumph, and people would talk about it for years. The Court had loved it. The common folk had adored it. Even the Seneschal and Keeper of the Treasury had been happy, for she had been very frugal, extracting the maximum benefit from every coin she'd spent, either overseeing the preparations herself, or sending people with stern demeanor and sharp eyes to do so for her. The Feast for the common folk had been a wild success, going on long into the night as folk brought or bought food of their own to extend that supplied by the Crown.

As for the entertainments for her Court, their Feast and dancing had been as much of a success, and for once, she'd had nothing but perfect dancing partners. Alberich had been right; having Heralds and Bards (and even a few Healers) alternate with her young nobles had made all the difference. Her gown—the first time she'd been out of mourning—had made her look beautiful; she hadn't needed dubious compliments to tell her so, for her mirror and the frank gazes of the Bards and Heralds had made that clear enough.

But Sendar hadn't been there, and it might just as well have been a total failure because of that. She'd tried to lose herself in the preparations, then to immerse herself in the happiness of other people, and she'd actually forgotten for a little—just a little. She'd smiled and even laughed, and when she'd come back here to her rooms, she'd been so tired she'd fallen straight asleep.

But she'd known, the moment that she awakened, that one day, one week, hadn't changed anything, hadn't filled the emptiness, hadn't given her back the part of herself that was gone.

Her father would have loved this. He'd have reveled in her triumph. He would have had so many ideas for the Festival, so many more than she had—

The brief respite she'd had was just that—a moment of forgetfulness, nothing more. And now, with nothing but day after day of gray sameness stretching ahead of her, she missed him so much she thought she was going to break beneath the weight of grief.

So she sobbed into her pillow, inconsolable. How *could* anyone console her for this? She and her father should have had years and years together; she should have had him to cast stern eyes over would-be suitors, to advise her how to deal with the Council, to scold her for working too hard and send her to read a book or ride. And if she ever married—he should have been there to see it, to see his grandchildren, to spoil them as he'd often threatened to do. All of that was gone, taken from her before it ever had a chance to happen.

She didn't want anyone to hear her crying; they wouldn't understand. They'd tell her stupid things—that it had been long enough, that she needed to "pull herself together," that it was "time to move on."

How could they know? How many of *them* had a beloved father cut down in front of their eyes? How many of *them* were facing what she faced, the rest of her life without the man who had been father *and* mother to her, and friend, and counselor? None of them understood. None of them could. None of them wanted to. What they wanted, was for her to be something else, some biddable creature they called "Selenay" that had no feelings but the shallowest, and no thoughts of her own. *Her* feelings were an inconvenient obstacle to that.

Or worse than telling her to "get over this," they'd spew some kind of platitude about how he was surely watching her from somewhere and was proud of her, but would be unhappy that she was still mourning for him. How could they know? How could anyone know?

It wasn't fair. It wasn't right. Sendar had been *good;* he'd given up so much, he'd always done so much for others—it wasn't *fair!* She'd always thought that when you did good, good came to you. What kind of a cruel god would do this to her, and to him?

For that matter, she wasn't entirely certain that there *were* any gods out there, not after this. And if there weren't any gods, then that meant that when you *died,* you just died, and her father wasn't "out there," looking after her. He was just gone, and all those platitudes were nothing but empty lies…

Damn them. Damn them all, and their needs, and their platitudes, and their plans. They would never, *could* never, understand. She'd lost her best friend as well as her father; she had been cheated out of *years* of things that they all took for granted.

How could she possibly ever "get over" that? There would be a great, gaping wound in her for the rest of her life that would never be properly filled!

Except with tears, the tears that never seemed to heal anything inside her.

She had tried, these past moons at least, to do things that would keep her moving, keep her busy, keep her too concentrated on things outside herself to think. For a while, the sheer desperation of having to learn how to rule, of having to outwit her Council when they tried discreetly to shunt her aside or maneuver her into something she didn't want to do, had filled that need to keep moving. She would work and plan and learn until she fell asleep, exhausted, and wake early to work again—and that had helped, at least, to keep things at bay. Keep moving, keep busy, keep her mind full, keep it all at a distance. Then, just as the urgency of all that began to ease, there'd been the preparations for the Festival to fill the silences, to force her to work, think, and not remember.

But now—now she had awakened this morning, knowing there was nothing, nothing between her and that vast, aching void that used to be filled with her father's presence.

And anyone who found her crying like this would just never understand. They'd wonder why, after yesterday, she could be unhappy. Even if she tried to explain, they'd stare at her without understanding, then tell her that it was time she moved on, that it was time to leave her grief behind her. As if she could!

:Of course you won't,:. Caryo said, very, very quietly. *:And you shouldn't. That would be wrong. How can you leave it behind you when it's a part of you?:*

The feeling that Caryo had somehow put comforting arms around her only made her sob harder. But Caryo didn't seem to think there was anything wrong with that.

:They keep telling me stupid things like "Time will heal it—": she said, around the sobs that shook her entire body.

There was an ache in Caryo's mind-voice that matched the aching of her heart. *:Time doesn't. All that Time does is make it more distant, put more space between you and what happened. It doesn't heal anything. I don't know how or what does the healing, but it isn't Time.:*

:Oh, Caryo, I miss him so much!: she cried.

:So do I.:

Somehow, that was exactly the right thing for Selenay to hear; it let loose another torrent of weeping, but this time, it seemed as if she was weeping herself out, until at last she lay there, curled in her bed, her nose stuffed and her eyes sore, her pillow soggy—

:Turn your pillow over, love.:

She sniffed hard and obeyed without thinking, and closed her aching eyes. She was exhausted now, limp with crying, and if the ache in her heart didn't hurt any less, at least she was too tired to cry any more.

:I keep thinking, if only I'd gone after him—:

:If only. Those must be the two saddest words in the world,: Caryo sighed. *:The best thing that I can tell you is that there is nothing that could have happened that would have allowed you to follow him. And there was not one scrap, one hint of knowledge or even ForeSight that any of us had that would have let us guess what he was going to do, or enabled us to prevent it. If there was ever a moment in history where a man took his own fate in his own two hands, that was it.:*

:Then I wish I could go back—: But there was no use in pursuing that line of thought. She couldn't. No one, not even in the tales of before the Founding, had ever said anything about being able to go back into the past and change things.

:I don't want to get up, Caryo.: And she didn't. She didn't want to move. She didn't want to leave her bed. Ever. The weight of depression pressed down on her and filled her with lethargy. She wanted to close her eyes, and fall into oblivion, and never come out again. She didn't exactly want to die—but if only there was a way to *not live*—

And Caryo didn't say any of the stupid things that other people might, about how she "had" to live for Valdemar, or how she was being hysterical, or overreacting. *:If you don't get up, I'll miss our morning ride,:* she said instead, wistfully, as if she was deliberately misunderstanding the "I don't want to get up" as merely meaning "this morning," and not "forever." Maybe she was.

But—the thought of the morning ride, another of those times when she could forget, for a little, as Caryo moved into a gallop, and she could lean over that warm, white neck and let the movement and the rush of air and the rhythm all lull her into a kind of trance, that same state of *not being* that she was just longing for—that broke through the lethargy. It was hard to tell why, but it did; it made her decide that she *had* to get up, to keep moving, to try for another candlemark, another day. And as she forced her legs out from under the covers, it occurred to her that as long as she just kept moving, even if she didn't find any peace or escape in movement, she might at least find a little more distraction.

Distraction. She had to distract anyone from knowing she'd been crying, or they'd want to know why, and then there would be all that stupid nonsense that she didn't want to hear.

She slipped out of bed and went to the table where a basin and pitcher waited; she splashed some of the cold water into the basin, and bathed her face until she thought that most of the signs of her tears were gone. Her eyes were probably still red, but with luck, no one would remark on it. After all, with all of the snow glare out there yesterday, probably they'd think it was that. If anyone said anything, she'd claim it was snow glare. And maybe she could claim a headache, too, and cut the Council session short.

She blew her nose, and went back to her bed, and crawled back into it, feeling as exhausted as if she hadn't slept at all.

:Just close your eyes,: Caryo advised. *:They'll expect you to sleep late after last night. You really did look lovely, you know. All of the young Heralds, at least, were saying so. I can't speak for the Bards; they don't have Companions to gossip about them, but the Heralds were very taken with how you looked.:*

:They were?: That was—if not comforting, at least it was satisfying. Nice to know that she did look as good as she had thought.

:Believe it or not, even Alberich thought so. In fact, I think he might have had just a twinge of jealousy when he handed you off to Orthallen.:

Well, that penetrated the lethargic depression, a bit. *:Alberich? Surely not.:* And anyway, it was probably only that he disliked Orthallen. Well, apparently the feeling was mutual, and there wasn't anything she could do about that. When two men decided to take a dislike to one another, there really wasn't anything to be done about it. It was like trying to get a pair of dominant dogs to be friends; no matter what you did, each of them was going to be certain that *he* should be head of the pack, and all you could do was to try and keep them separate as much as possible. Orthallen was one of the few people who *didn't* say anything stupid about her father. He didn't even say that she ought to be over her grief by now, and that made him one of the few people she felt comfortable being around, even if he did tend to treat her as "little Selenay" instead of the Queen.

Besides, it wasn't Alberich that she wanted to make jealous.

Though, on second thought, there really wasn't *anyone* in her entire Court or the Heraldic Circle she wanted to make jealous. Honestly, if the whole business of trying to get her to marry someone who was tied to a whole pack of special interests was put aside, the real reason she didn't want to marry any of the Council's choices was that they all *bored* her. There wasn't one of them that was worth spending an entire afternoon with, much less a lifetime. There wasn't a single unattached male in the entire Court that even gave her a flutter of interest.

She was just so tired of it all; tired of the ache in her soul, tired of the loneliness, tired of trying to outmaneuver the people she *should* have been able to lean on. It seemed as if her entire life was nothing more than dragging herself through an endless round of weariness and grief, and she just wanted an end to it all.

She buried her face in her pillow, not to muffle more sobs, but to block out—everything. If only for a moment.

It was when she woke again to the sounds of her servants and attendants bustling around the room that she realized she must have fallen asleep again. And if she didn't feel *better*, at least she felt a little less tired.

Enough so, that she felt she could probably face the day. She didn't want to, but she could.

:I think,: she told Caryo, as they came to get her out of bed and dress her, *:I think we'll have our morning ride before breakfast.:*

:Good,: Caryo said simply. *:I'd like that. Thank you.:*

Keep moving. That was the only answer. Just keep moving…

And if that wasn't an answer, at least it was a way to keep her from just—stopping. Stopping and never starting again.

* * *

For Alberich, the day after the Festival's climax began just as any ordinary day did—the only differences being that now, at least, he didn't have to concern himself with making preparations for Selenay's appearance, and now that he knew the identity of the young man he'd been looking for, he could concentrate on thinking of ways to find out what was going on.

But as far as the young Trainees went, apparently, the end of the Festival meant restlessness and discontent. They'd had an unexpected break in their routine, and as Alberich was woefully aware, any break in a youngster's routine generally meant trouble in getting him back into that routine.

As a consequence, the first class of the morning was a disaster. Far too much time was wasted in trying to get his students back on track after the excitement of the Ice Festival. And they fought him every step of the way, performing their warmups lethargically, running through the initial exercises in a state of distraction, and wasting time in chattering about the pleasures of the day before.

And part of him was still puzzling over the question of Devlin Gereton, why he would be receiving information from a play-actor, and what that information could be. It took real effort on his own part to put that aside and concentrate on getting some results out of the class.

But it was a futile effort. The Trainees were utterly disinclined to settle down and work, and finally, in desperation, he decided that if all they could do was chatter about ice sports, well, he'd *give* them an ice sport they would never forget!

After all, they were going to have to learn to work together, in coordinated teams…

"Silence!" he barked. "Weapons *down.*"

Startled, they shut off the chatter, dropped weapon points, and stared at him.

"Weapons put away. Get the staves," he ordered grimly. "Now. Then on with cloaks, and follow me."

Now looking apprehensive and guilty, they obeyed. He snatched up his own cloak, hid a little surprise inside it as he did so, and stalked out, followed by a suddenly subdued tail of Trainees of all four colors.

Out into the snow they went, out past the practice grounds and into Companion's Field, following a path beaten by others into the thigh-deep snow. It was another cloudless, bone-chilling day, and sunlight poured pitilessly down through the skeletal branches of the trees. He led them to one of the frozen ponds in Companion's Field, one that had been cleared off so that it could be used for skating, but was far enough from the Palace and the Collegia that it wasn't in use very much. In a welcome release for his temper, he kicked three basket-sided holes in the snow at the edge of the ice, one at each point of an imaginary equal-sided triangle laid on the pond, then divided the class into two teams. He made sure that the Trainees were fairly evenly distributed between both teams, and he made a point of dividing up friends as much as he could. If they were mad for sport, well, he'd give them bloody sport indeed...

:Chosen, I hope you aren't releasing a wolf from a trap, here,: Kantor said, full of amusement. *:Are you sure you know what you're doing?:*

:No,: he said honestly. *:But at least they'll get some stave practice out of this.:*

Then he dropped what he had picked up onto the ice in front of them.

It was one of the little round cushions that they used over their knuckles when they were practicing bare-fist fighting. They looked at it, then at him, then back down at it, without any comprehension at all.

"Pah. You are two teams of fighters now. *There* are your goals. First team—there, second team, there." He pointed. He thought he saw comprehension beginning to dawn. He hoped so. They'd *all* seen the broom-ball competition. He hoped they weren't so dense that they couldn't figure this out! "The third goal neutral is. Either team may score there. The cushion, into the opposite goal, or into the neutral goal, you are to put," he said icily and moved carefully off the slippery surface of the ice with as much dignity as he could muster, heaving a sigh of relief when he reached the bank and could stand there with his arms folded over his chest, under his cape.

"But is this like broom-ball? What are the rules?" someone asked, and "But we don't have skates!" protested another.

"There are rules in war? I think not," he retorted. "Skates you will be carrying in the field? Enough. No rules. The cushion, in the goal, you will put. How it comes there, your problem is. Hit it, you may. Kick it, carry it, I care not. You have staves. Use them. Fight with them. *No rules.*"

He hadn't been altogether certain what their response would be. On the one hand, they were Trainees, and had a modicum of training in organization. On the other hand, they were overstimulated adolescents with too much restlessness to settle down. They *could* settle in and make some rules, assigning tasks and responsibilities before they set to their new version of broom-ball.

They *could.* But they didn't.

With a yell, someone broke and swatted at the cushion with his stave, and the melee began as someone else jumped for the cushion, and half of the other team piled onto the one making the move. It was, in a sadistic sort of way, rather entertaining for the onlooker. Staves went everywhere— though not as successfully as if the fighting had been on solid, unslippery ground. Bodies went everywhere. Most of them ended up sprawled on the ice. The cushion tended not to get anywhere near a goal.

He had been counting on the ice to ensure that no one was able to get in any dangerously hard blows with the staves, and the ploy worked. Even the ones that were good skaters found the going slippery, and none of them were used to trying to stay balanced on the ice while simultaneously swatting with a stave. And all of them were fairly good at stave work to begin with, so if someone swung for an opponent instead of the cushion, there was a good chance that he'd find the blow blocked. But none of them were doing much in the way of coordination or teamwork; it was pretty much every man for himself, and Alberich had ensured that the little amount of teamwork that *might* have occurred naturally was sidelined by breaking up friends onto opposite teams.

It got pretty wild out there, though, before it was all over. He didn't know if any of *them* were keeping track of the number of goals that were made. He certainly wasn't. All he was interested in was to make sure that no one was injured beyond falls and bruises and bumps on the head. Putting them on the ice had another effect; even when someone connected with a stave, most of the force of the blow went into sending the opponent flying like a giant version of the cushion. Oh, they were going to be aching and stiff when it was over.

:There's going to be competition for the bathtubs today,: Kantor observed, sounding highly amused. *:And calls for liniment, I suspect.:*

:They wanted excitement,: he told his Companion.

:So they did.:

If they were going to act like a lot of wild hill brats, then by the Sunlord, they were going to learn why discipline and organization were necessary if you wanted to win a fight.

By the time that class was over—more to the point, by the time he broke up the melee that the "game" had turned into and sent them all back to their other classes—it didn't appear that the lesson had sunk in yet.

But he was relatively certain that eventually it would, as they thought back over the chaos on the ice. Certainly they were, one and all, winded, weary, aching in every limb, and there wasn't one of them that wasn't sporting some sort of injury. There were a hefty number of black eyes, and lots of bruises in places that didn't show. And a strain or two, and lumps on the skull. And he would have laid money on the fact that not one of them was going to give the other instructors any trouble for the rest of the day.

But most of all, for the sake of the lesson in teamwork, it was painfully clear that no one had any idea who had won.

So when the next class showed the early symptoms of the same "disease," he administered the same "cure." It was only when he got the final-year students that he got any signs of sense and steadiness out of them, and managed to run a normal class.

He didn't have the option of thinking much past the fact that at least he'd gotten some work *out* of them, and a lesson of sorts *into* them. After classes were over, some of the Guard appeared for a little training, and he was able to work out some of his own frustration in a satisfying series of bouts. When the last of the adults had gone, and the last of the daylight faded, leaving the salle in blue gloom, he was more concerned with a hot shower than anything else.

He went back into his quarters and got himself cleaned up, coming out of his bathing room to find that the servants had come and gone from the Collegium, leaving behind both his dinner and a visitor.

"What in the bloody blue blazes did you infect your students with today?" Myste demanded, peering at him through her thick glass lenses, pausing in the midst of laying out plates, cups, and cutlery. "They look like they've been through the Wars, and they're chattering like magpies about some ice exercise you invented."

He stared at her for a moment, bemused both by her presence and by the question. He hadn't thought much beyond exhausting the worst offenders; it hadn't occurred to him that they'd actually *take* to the exercise. Well, not really, anyway. Maybe some of the Blues, the courtiers' children, who hadn't anything better to do with their time. "They would not settle," he replied after a moment. "So, to exhaust them, I decided. And to show them, organization is needed, a battle to win."

"Well, your little experiment in ice warfare is being talked about over all three Collegia," she said in a rueful tone, as if she could hardly believe it. "And the ones that hadn't tried it yet were mad to, while the rest are trying to come up with rules, so-called 'proper' equipment, scoring. It's all anyone could talk about over luncheon *and* dinner, and they want to do it in their free time—"

He interrupted her with a gust of incredulous laughter. "No—they mean to make a *sport?*"

"Evidently." She shook her head, and dished out food for both of them. Then she sat down, next to the fire, with a bowl of stew in hand. "I suppose we should be grateful. It's new, it's a good alternative to tavern hopping and getting into pranks, *and* it's exercise."

"And they will weary of it, soon enough," he said. "If they do not, when the ice melts, over it is." He couldn't believe that anything as ridiculous as the foolish melee he'd put them through had suddenly become an all-consuming interest.

"Hmm." She ate a little, chewing thoughtfully, as the fire crackled beside her. "I think what's likeliest to happen is that they'll all try it, but the only way to keep from getting bruised up and battered over it is to have a lot of rules, and maybe purloin the padding and helms used for weapons practice into the bargain. But having a lot of rules means that they'll have to *agree* over the rules. No two sets of would-be players are going to have the same idea of what the rules should be. And in the end, they won't have agreed before the ice melts."

"Probably," he agreed, feeling relieved and irritated at the same time. Cadets would never have been allowed such foolishness. But then again, as he had noted before, Heraldic Trainees were not Karsite Cadets… "I had noted that on the river, the players of the broom-ball game required much drinking of wine and beer to continue the game past the first few goals."

"And without that, it isn't *nearly* as much fun." She chuckled. "Right. That's what I'll tell the others. They were afraid it was going to take over the Collegia."

He thought about that for a moment. Thought about the fact that a certain level of madness seemed to come out of the confinement of winter. And thought about all the high spirits generated by the Festival. "It will, probably, for a short time," he decided. "But that gives a painless punishment as well. For those of the Collegia at least, who will not settle and study, *forbid* them from playing. Make playing contingent upon good marks. Blues, we can do little about, if they are highborn children. But then again—time, they have, to waste. At least melees on ice harm them only."

"Oh—ouch. Very good indeed," Myste laughed. "That should do the trick."

They finished dinner quickly; so much time spent out in the cold used up a lot of energy, and he was wolf-hungry.

Only after they had cleared the dishes away into the hampers did it occur to him to wonder why she had come there tonight. It couldn't have been because she wanted his company—could it?

At that thought, he got a very odd feeling in the pit of his stomach. Not unpleasant, no, but—fluttery. It disconcerted him. It disconcerted him so much that he just blurted out what was in his head.

"Why are you here?" he heard himself saying, and could have hit himself for how it sounded.

But she didn't seem to take offense at his words or his tone.

"Well—" she began, and hesitated. "Mixed motives, actually. I wanted to find out what you'd done with the youngsters. I must say that the ones who *had* gotten your lesson were nicely subdued for my classes; it was only the ones that hadn't gotten to 'play' that were wound up like tops. And, um—" another hesitation, "—I, um, enjoy your company. And one other thing—" she added, hastily, before he could decide if she was blushing or not. "Keren slipped a little. Well, she didn't really *slip*, so much as I browbeat it out of her when she brought me a dress, of all things, to mend for her." She laughed. "I mean, Keren? In a *dress?* Please! That was odd enough, but a dress that looked like *that?*"

"Like what?" he asked, unthinking.

"A dockside whore," she replied, with cheerful bluntness, and it was his turn to flush. "She said she didn't want to take it to the Collegium seamstresses, because it was supposed to be a secret, and then tried to backtrack. Well, needless to say, I got the whole story out of her."

"So you know?" he asked, feeling a little guilty that he hadn't told her before this, seeing that he'd been thinking about asking for her help anyway.

"Hmm. I guessed, before this. Too many evenings when you weren't here in the Complex, too many times when you knew things you shouldn't have about parts of Haven you weren't supposed to have ever visited," she said thoughtfully. "I mean, I can put two and two together— and unlike some of our colleagues with some rather lofty ideas about Heraldic duties and honor, I know a bit about the practicalities of life. Anyway, I just wanted you to know that if I can help, without getting in the way, I'd like to. Keren might fit in some of the wilder parts of Haven, but I know the craftsmen's districts inside and out."

That stopped him cold. It hadn't occurred to him that Myste might want to *volunteer.* Or that she would actually have some inside knowledge that he *didn't.* He'd thought he would have to persuade her, then train her.

"It's not as if I'd have to act a part, like Keren," she continued. "I'd just have to be what I was before I was Chosen. An accountant, a clerk, ordinary. Believe me, people like me are just invisible as long as we keep our mouths shut. No one thinks anything about having us around. We're a kind of servant, and no one ever pays any attention to the servants."

He didn't know how true the latter statement was, but the former was true enough. "There could be danger in this," he warned.

She raised an eyebrow. "You might not think it, but there's danger in being an independent clerk. You don't always know just who is hiring you, or for what—or at least, not until they ask you to run two sets of books, or you get a look at papers you weren't supposed to see. That never happened to me, personally, but I know those it did happen to. And there's stories about people turning up missing after taking certain jobs." She chuckled weakly. "Well, that's probably what most of the people who knew me think is what happened to me. I know for a fact that none of them realize I was Chosen."

Well, she was on that last battlefield for the Tedrel Wars, and she'd volunteered for that, too. She'd faced danger there, certainly enough. "I might then ask you for help," he said carefully.

"Ask, and you'll have it," she said. And then seemed at a loss for anything else to say.

But he didn't want her to leave. They sat in awkward silence for a long time. And when the silence was broken, they both broke it at once.

"Can you tell me—"

"What of interest have you—"

They both broke off, flushing. Alberich was just a little angry— at himself. Surely he was more than old enough to have a simple conversation with an interesting woman without blushing like a boy! Particularly this one, that he had shouted at, cursed at, and forced to learn things she adamantly did not want to learn!

"You first," she said, gesturing.

He paused. What *did* he want to say? It suddenly occurred to him that there was a lot he didn't know about her. He might as well start with that.

"So. What was Myste, the clerk, like?" he asked. "What was her life?"

She laughed. "Boring. But—" Her eyes grew thoughtful behind those thick lenses. "But you don't know much of anything about the ordinary person in Valdemar, of the middling classes, do you? I know a lot about all of that, in Haven, in particular. So even if I'd be bored by it—"

"Please," he said, with a slow smile. "Tell me."

And so, she did. And being Myste, she got as much about Alberich of

Karse out of him, as he did about Myste of Haven.

It was, on the whole, an equitable exchange. And perhaps, best of all, it was one that would take some time in telling.

8

The Ice Festival had taken place a fortnight after Midwinter. Now, another fortnight later, the deep cold finally broke with a gray day, vastly warmer than the ones that had brought the Ice Festival, and with a dampness to the air that warned of snow. By a candlemark after sunrise, the snow had begun, and it fell, thick and soft, all day and into the night. Alberich, for one, was very happy to see it, for it meant that all the frozen ponds were covered over, and at least until the would-be athletes shoveled them clear again, there would be no more ice melees.

Or, as the Trainees had decided to call it, *Hurlee.* Yes, they had given it a name. They had agreed on that much, and more. It had taken on a life of its own.

He had, unwittingly, created a monster. Yet at the same time, it was a very useful monster. If, at times, it seemed that the vast majority of the free time of both Trainees *and* young courtiers was taken up with creating rules and scoring for this combative game, and arguing over both endlessly, at least they were learning about teamwork, cooperation in combat, and negotiation. If they seemed obsessed, at least, as several teachers said with a sigh, there were worse things to get obsessed about, and the slightest *hint* that falling marks would occasion being forbidden to play or even *discuss* the game often worked miracles.

Still, it seemed that there was nowhere in Court or Collegia that one could go to *escape* the wretched game. Even some of the younger Guards had started to take it up. For all Alberich knew, it was spreading down into Haven by now, and many older members of the Court, decidedly unamused by the racketing teams of youngsters surging here and there and practicing on every open bit of ice, or even *creating* unauthorized bits of ice to practice on, often gave Alberich unfriendly glares when he saw them.

The cushion had been replaced by first a child's bean-bag, then a tough leather ball filled with heavy buckwheat in its husks, of the sort that jugglers practiced with. The staves now had small scoops on one end. The holes in the snow were now nets, and the teams had been stabilized at five members each, one of which was supposed to guard his team's net.

Combat with the staves was still very much allowed; Alberich had the feeling that no few little feuds were being worked out during the games. Half-helms of padded leather and elbow, kidney, and kneepads had been agreed upon. Skates were *not* allowed, on order of the Healers, who didn't want to deal with the results. Other additions were being argued about, or rather, forcefully argued *for* by Healer's Collegium, which did not want an influx of Trainees and other youngsters with missing teeth or broken jawbones. At this point, Alberich had washed his hands of the entire project and disclaimed any involvement with it. Like the other instructors, *he* had declared that inattention and falling marks would be grounds for being forbidden to play.

He was rather desperately hoping that a thaw would put an end to it, and depressingly afraid that, given the new changes in it, they would be able to play without ice.

At least, by this point, it was very clear that no more than half of the Heraldic Trainees, and substantially, very substantially *less* than a quarter of the Healers' and Bardic Trainees, were going to actually be playing this game. The rest lacked the coordination and, after the initial excitement was over, the inclination. That did not, however, mean that the rest weren't interested. Oh, no. They were still just as mad about watching it as the rest were about playing it.

But he could not spare much time to worry about a mere game. He had decided to start taking Keren out on some of his prowls through Haven. And he had yet to come up with a plan to let him discover just what Devlin and that actor were up to.

The main stumbling block was that he could not think of a way to shadow the young courtier *or* the actor without alerting them to the fact that someone was watching them. For one thing, he was more than a little wary about trying to disguise himself around the actor, at all. He could fool ordinary folk, but an actor? The fellow might have a style that was ridiculously flamboyant, and exaggerated, but that, Alberich suspected, was for the benefit of his audience, which was not going to react to a subtle performance. The man could not have come up with so clever a plan for passing information if he was not clever and subtle himself. And if Alberich tried to pass himself off as someone who had business being around either Devlin or the actors—

It seemed impossible; Alberich was certain he'd be caught. He might be able to pass off his Karsite accent as Hardornan or Rethwellan down in the slums, but actors had an ear for accents, and might even be able to correctly identify his. And just how many Karsites were there in Haven? Not many; not many that still had their accent. The paste he used to disguise his scars passed muster after dark, but actors knew about makeup and false hair—he'd never get by an actor without him noticing. How many Karsite Heralds were there? A sufficiently clever man could easily put two and two together.

As for getting in close, that *was* impossible. The man—*finally* Alberich had learned who he was (Norris Lettyn), and where his troupe was operating from (the Three Sheaves in the Cattle Market area)—seldom went anywhere outside of the inn, and never consorted with anyone except his fellow actors and exceedingly attractive, buxom, adoring women. Neither of which Alberich was—nor were Keren or Myste. They might be able to feign the adoration, but the kind of ladies that Norris kept company with were the sort that made men turn in the street and stare after them.

Not surprisingly, no few of them were ladies of negotiable virtue, but the price they placed on their services was very, very high. They were nothing like the common whores of the Exile's Gate neighborhood. And Alberich could not make up his mind if Norris was paying for their company, or getting it on the basis of his reputation, popularity, stunningly handsome face, and muscular body. If he was paying for it—where was a mere actor getting the money? On the other hand, someone who looked like Norris did generally have women fawning on him, and Alberich saw no reason to suppose that expensive courtesans were any less likely to fawn than supposedly "honest" women.

Thanks to Norris' face and flamboyant style, the troupe was certainly prospering, as was the inn to which they were attached. They didn't even have to give plays every day for the public anymore. Once every two days, the courtyard was packed with spectators for one of the repertoire of plays they put on, and it certainly wasn't because of the high literary standards of the things. Moving to that tent on the riverbank during the Festival had been a shrewd move—putting on their play there spread their reputation to the entire city, and the city evidently followed them back to their home ground when the Festival was over. Norris even was beginning to get something of a following among the highborn of the Court—while the plays they put on for the public were hardly great literature, evidently they had in their repertoire a number of classical works, and the troupe had been hired to give private performances at least twice now. There would, without a doubt, be more of those, though how lucrative they were in contrast to the public performances, Alberich had no way of telling.

Which created another problem. It seemed to Alberich that Norris was living somewhat beyond his means, but without getting close to the man, there was no way to know that for certain. *He* didn't know how Norris was paid, or if, now that he had a bit of a following among the highborn, he was getting gifts or patronage.

If so, then young Devlin would have the perfect excuse to add to that patronage, and even visit the actor openly. So Alberich still did not know what was being exchanged, whether or not it mattered to the Crown, nor how dangerous it was, and at the moment he had no way of finding these things out.

And there was another thing that worried him, that had nothing to do with the Devlin problem. It seemed to him that Selenay was not looking entirely well. It wasn't that she looked *ill*, exactly, but that she looked far more subdued than he liked. It was the death of her father, of course; it couldn't be anything else. The Festival had been an all-too brief diversion from her grief, he suspected. He wished he could do something for her, but the honest truth was that *he* was completely unsuited to that sort of task. All he could do was what he was good at, and let others—Talamir, who was, after all, Queen's Own—do their job without any interference.

Assuming that the Hurlee players didn't drive him utterly mad before spring.

"The problem is," Myste said, over a good slice of beef in the Bell, "you don't understand the sports-minded." Both of them were in disguise; he as a middling craftsman, she in some of her old garb from her previous life, including the spectacles she had worn then, lenses held in frames of wire. This was the first time he had brought Myste down into Haven to try out her disguise, but it was more for his benefit than for hers. He wanted to look like an ordinary craftsman in the audience at the Three Sheaves, and if he didn't have to talk, he stood a better chance of passing as Valdemaran.

"The bloody-minded, not the sports-minded," he muttered under his breath, then said, louder. "And you do?" It seemed unlikely. Bespectacled Myste held as much aloof from the Hurlee madness as he did, as far as he could tell.

"As a matter of fact," she retorted, "I do. *I* was raised here, in an ordinary family, and not in a Cadet School. People with a bit of leisure time. Ordinary folk *like* sport, even if they don't play a game, or at least, don't play it well. That's why they like to cheer on those who do."

"That, I do not understand, at all," he admitted, reluctantly.

She sniffed. "You ought to. It's part of what makes it easy for a sufficiently unscrupulous leader to get his people involved in a needless war. Look, it's like this, as I reckon it. People like to be in groups, on one side, so they can tell themselves that their side is better than the other. They can get the excitement and the thrill of being worked up about just how much better they are than the other side is. And when they're in a group doing that, then the excitement is doubled just because everyone else is doing the same."

"That, I understand," he said darkly. "So you are saying that being sports-minded, a little like being in a war is?"

"Without the bloodshed," she replied, and sighed. "Without the consequences. People like competition, but at the same time, they like cooperation almost as much. With something like Hurlee, you get to either be *on* a team, or *for* a team, and you get cooperation, like being in a special tribe. But then, your team goes against someone else's team, and there's your competition. It satisfies a whole lot of cravings all at once. It's like a bloodless war, and then you get to go out and buy each other beer afterward, and you get cooperation all over again."

He shrugged. It made sense, he supposed. He thought about how he had been shouting at the end of the last skating-race, along with everyone else. If even *he* could get caught up in a sport to that extent, then what Myste said made sense.

And there wasn't any warfare going on. People who had been used to living with a conflict and an enemy now found themselves with nothing of the sort. Maybe those who had actually *fought* were perfectly comfortable without having an enemy, but those who hadn't—particularly all those youngsters—might be looking for a focus for all that energy.

So maybe that was why Hurlee had suddenly become an obsession. And probably, as Myste expected, within a couple of months it would turn into a sport like any other. At least, now that the rules had been agreed on, and things had sorted out into a round-robin of regular teams with exact rosters, the situation wasn't quite so out-of-hand. Certainly the whole scheme of forbidding participation if marks fell off was working—miraculously, even with the highborn Blues, and heretofore, if their parents weren't concerned with marks, there had been no way to effectively discipline them.

Maybe Hurlee wasn't so bad after all.

"So where exactly is it that we're going?" she asked.

"The Three Sheaves Inn," he told her. She nodded, though she looked surprised. He had explained his situation with regard to young Devlin and his contact Norris, and the difficulty he found himself in trying to get close enough to make some sort of judgment about it. "I thought, at the least, into the play-going crowd we can insert ourselves. Good for me, for open my mouth I cannot, without myself betraying, so you can do the speaking for us both. Good for you, it would be, and it may be that an opportunity you will see that I cannot."

"Fair enough," she agreed, and glanced out the window into the thickening gloom of twilight. "And I might. You never know. Besides, I wouldn't mind seeing this actor fellow; if he's setting young hearts afire."

Alberich snorted. "Not just young," he corrected, and finished the last of his meal.

"All the better, then." She chuckled at the expression on his face, and pushed off from the table without another word.

"Now, something did occur to me," she said, as they moved out into the cold, snowy streets, passing a lamplighter who was climbing up to light one of his charges. "Had you considered paying one of those low-life pickpockets you hang about with to snatch young Devlin's purse when you think he's carrying what you're looking for? Tell him you want the papers, he gets anything else."

Since it had *not* occurred to him, he almost stopped dead in the street to stare at her. "Ah. No," he managed at last.

"Should be easy enough," she pointed out. "I suppose you'd have to make up some cock-and-bull tale about *why* you wanted it done. And you'd have to work the whole setup just for the other lad to do the snatch-and-run so he'll get away clean, maybe even interfere with some of the constables to keep them from nobbling him. But between what you paid the fellow and what he'd get off Devlin, I'd have to think that it'd more than pay him to keep his mouth shut about it."

His mind was already at work on the problem. He could sacrifice one of the problematic personae if he needed to. If one of *them* was never seen again after getting the papers, it wouldn't matter if the thief in question couldn't keep his mouth shut, because there'd be no one to betray, it was definitely an idea, and a good one. Not perfect, but—

—but it opened up a whole new set of ideas. It hadn't occurred to him to make use of the criminal element. There were other possibilities here. If, for instance, he could discover which room in the inn Norris used, perhaps he could send someone to search it…

"You do know that someone might recognize me at this inn, don't you?" she continued conversationally. "Not as a Herald, of course—I'm certain nobody actually knows that's where I went when I quit my job. My Choosing was pretty quiet, actually, and since I was right in Haven, I persuaded Aleirian to let me finish out my work for the day, hand in my notice, and slip out without a fuss."

"Modest of you—" he began.

She laughed. "Hardly. I didn't want anyone who wanted a favor showing up at the Collegium looking for me. Anybody who knew me would recognize me as Myste Willenger, the accountant and clerk, not Herald Myste. Except for the Wars, I haven't set foot outside the Collegium Complex since I was Chosen."

"Really? Well, that would not harm anything." He pulled the hood closer around his neck; this damp cold seemed to be more penetrating than the dry cold of Festival Week. "In fact, it might be a good thing."

"Reestablish myself in my old haunts?" She glanced at him sideways. "Well, if you want me to do that, I can. I'll think up something to tell anyone who asks where I've been—"

He had to snort at that. "Where else, but for the Army working?" he asked. "At least until the Wars ended."

She stared at him a moment, and stumbled over a rut, then smiled. "You've got a good head for this," she said. "You're right, of course. All those soldiers needed feeding, supplying, paying—that needs clerks."

"And now, half of them disbanded are, and no more need for extra clerks." That was certainly true enough. Just as it was true that an Army the size of the one that Sendar had assembled had required a vast force of people to support it.

"Which is why I'm back—" Her smile spread. "But of course, the reason I'm not back at my *old* job is because I was replaced. Which I was, but when I was Chosen. So—"

"A job you must have." He frowned over that thought.

"Not necessarily—"

"No, wait—an idea I have. The Bell. That is safe enough. A note I will leave; it will be arranged, should anyone ask." Not that anyone would; no one was likely to ask about a minor clerk and accountant, but it was best to cover every contingency. "For the master, you do the records, and the taproom clerk you are, also. You board there as well." This was common enough. Just because people were *supposed* to be literate didn't mean they were good at reading and writing. Often enough, they were willing to pay someone else to write a letter for them—and of course, any legal documents absolutely *required* a clerk to draw them up.

"That'll do." She sighed with satisfaction. "I like to have everything set out, just in case."

"As do I. Alike, we think, in that way." And before he could say anything else, although there were a couple of half-formed ideas in the back of his head, it was too late to say anything.

Because the Three Sheaves was looming before them, and with it, a good-sized crowd milling about at the door, waiting to get into the courtyard for the performance. They joined it, and at that point, kept their conversation to commonplaces.

The one excellent thing about having Bardic Collegium right on the grounds of the Palace was that there were always fine musicians available at a moment's notice. The Hardornan Ambassador from King Alessandar had expressed an interest that afternoon in hearing some of the purely instrumental music that Valdemarans took for granted, and Selenay had been able to arrange for that wish to be gratified with an impromptu concert after dinner. Ambassador Isadere was finally rested enough from his journey and formal reception to show some interest in the less formal pastimes of the Court—which meant, to Selenay, the ones where she wasn't required to pay exclusive attention to him, or indeed, to anyone. Bardic Collegium responded to her request for an instrumental ensemble with what almost seemed to be gratitude; she'd been puzzled by that at first, but then, after a moment of thought, she realized that she had not made such requests more than a handful of times since she'd become Queen, whereas her father had called on Bardic, either for simple musicians or true Bards, at least every two or three days. Perhaps they took this as a sign that things were getting back to "normal."

Well, even if *she* didn't feel that way, was it right for her to impose her depressed spirits on everyone else?

No, it wasn't. No matter what she *felt* like, wasn't it her duty to put on a sociable mask?

Besides, entertainments like this meant she wouldn't really have to put on more than the mask. When she thought about it, she realized that anyone who was really listening to the music wouldn't require anything from *her* except that she not be dissolved in tears.

So when she sent a note back to Bardic thanking them, she asked if it would be possible for them to supply musicians of the various levels of expertise to her as they had to her father—and as often. The immediate response was that they would be overjoyed to do so, and would even save her the trouble of trying to decide on informal entertainments by setting them up with her household, as they had done for Sendar.

With great relief, she let them know that this was perfect. And she led her Court into the Great Hall for the concert, then settled into her seat, enthroned among the courtiers, with Ambassador Isadere at her left, thinking that tonight was turning out to be something of a respite after all. And the gods knew she needed one. She wasn't feeling up to an evening of bright conversation with her foreign guests tonight; she'd been fighting melancholy all day, knowing that it would take next to nothing to make her break out in tears. Now, with not only the ambassador but his entire entourage listening with rapt attention to the musicians, she could lean back in her chair and wait for the evening to be over.

Or so she thought.

"Majesty, are you well?" whispered Lord Orthallen. He leaned over the arm of his chair toward her, his voice pitched so that it would not disturb anyone else, and to his credit, he really did look concerned.

She smiled faintly at him, and nodded. He raised an eyebrow, as if he didn't entirely believe her, but turned his attention back to the music.

She glanced over at Herald Talamir, who did not appear to have noticed the interchange. But then, it was difficult to tell, these days, what Talamir did and did not see. It was even more difficult to tell what he thought about what he saw.

In fact, he was sitting back in his chair, eyes half-closed, and he looked exactly like a statue—except that there was nothing of the solidity of a statue about him. How he managed this, she could not tell, but these days Talamir didn't entirely seem to be in the *here and now,* as it were. His manner was often preoccupied, as if listening to and watching something no one else could hear or see. And to her mind, there was a suggestion of translucency about him, the spirit somehow shining through the flesh. When there was something that really *required* his attention, he was almost like his old self, but when there wasn't, he was almost like a ghost made flesh, and not altogether contented with that state.

He made a great many people uneasy, without any of them being able to articulate why. He made Selenay uneasy, as a matter of fact; she could never glance at him—except in the times when he *was* very much in the here-and-now—without an involuntary shiver.

And yet, there were plenty of people who saw no difference in him at all. People like Orthallen, for instance; they acted in Talamir's presence now exactly as they had acted in Talamir's presence before the last battle.

Before he died, and was dragged back to life...

That was the crux of it, of course. Heralds, Healers, and Bards almost all sensed it. Talamir was a man in two worlds now, and most of his concentration seemed to be taken up with the unseen world. That was why Selenay just could not bring herself to confide in him, even though that was what the function of the Queen's Own was supposed to be.

How could I sit there and tell him things? she wondered wearily. *Even if he wasn't a man, and as old as my father. It would be like trying to share girl-secrets with a particularly unworldly priest...*

And anyway, Talamir had been her father's closest friend—which was only as it should have been, of course, but how could she tell him how much she missed her father and cry on his shoulder, when surely Talamir missed him as much, or more? It would be too cruel, too cruel for words. Talamir had already suffered so much pain, losing his own Companion to death as well as Sendar and so many other friends—No, it would be too cruel to inflict further pain on him that way.

As for sharing her scarcely articulate longing for, well, *romance*—

Oh, no. He would never, ever understand. And she'd get a grave, well-considered, perfectly reasonable lecture about her duties as Queen, and how great power required great responsibility.

As if she didn't know, as if she didn't feel all that with every pulse of blood through her veins.

But that didn't stop her from wanting it. Even though most of the younger members of her Court were probably going to make arranged marriages in the end, that didn't stop them from flirtations and even outright courtship. After all, there was always the chance that both sets of parents would be pleased to find that an alliance had been made.

And even if they weren't, well, as one young lady had tearfully put it, unaware that Selenay was eavesdropping from the other side of the

459

hedge, "It will give me something to remember when I'm wedded to that awful old man—"

But a Queen couldn't have flirtations. And of course she knew that only too well. Knowing she *couldn't* was bad enough, but being reminded of that fact by someone like Talamir would only make it worse. Her father would have understood; *he'd* been able to marry for love. He'd always said he didn't want to see her sacrificed to a marriage of state, but with him gone, and with no telling what needs might arise, she had to count on sacrificing herself.

She felt a lump rising in her throat and closed her eyes against the sting of tears, fighting them back. This was neither the place nor the time to display weakness.

It was at that moment that she felt, with a sense of shock, someone press a folded bit of paper into her hand.

Her eyes flew open in time for her to see Lord Orthallen, removing his hand from hers. Their eyes met, and he nodded gravely, then sat back again.

For one brief moment, an incredulous thought came into her head. *A love note? From Orthallen?*

No, surely not. He was married. He was older than her father. And besides, every other Councilor would spontaneously combust with rage at the very idea.

She looked down at the scrap of paper, and opened it.

Selenay, you used to call me your "Lord-Uncle," and told me all your childish woes, she read. *And if I have, in recent days, often forgotten that you are no longer my "Little Niece" but my Queen and fully adult, please forgive an old man for clinging to his illusions longer than he should have. I have seen you fall into melancholy more than once these past few days; I think you might be in need of a friend with whom you can unburden yourself freely; if that is the case, will you honor your father's friend by putting me in that place as he did, so that this old man can begin to see the grown lady of reality instead of the child of the past? Perhaps we can help each other in our shared sorrow.*

Selenay blinked. This was unexpected. First of all, Lord Orthallen was, above all else, a very proud man. He seldom apologized. Secondly, he had been one of those on her Council that had seemed the most adamant about keeping her from taking the reins of power into her own hands—

But this *was* an apology, and a tacit admission that he was ready and willing to see her as the Queen in fact as well as in title.

And the part about shared sorrow—that made the lump in her throat swell all over again. Orthallen had been her father's good and trusted friend. She hadn't thought about how *he* must be feeling. But that pride of his might well have prevented him from making any great show of his own grief...

And who better to *talk* to? He was safe enough, with a wife he honored; he had never, ever given rise to a single rumor about his fidelity (unlike far too many men in her Court). She had known him all her life; she'd cried on his shoulder before this.

Who else was there, really—and she was beginning to think that if she didn't find *someone* she could talk to, someone besides Caryo, that is, she was going to crack. Talking to Caryo was a little too much like talking to herself. And besides, even Caryo was getting tired of how depressed and burdened with grief she was.

She looked up and met his eyes. He tilted his head to the side, in grave inquiry. She nodded. He smiled; it was a sad, weary smile, the same sort that she often found on her own lips of late.

She smiled back, folded the piece of paper, and put it into her sleeve pocket for safekeeping, feeling a little better already. Better enough, at least, to give the musicians her full attention for the rest of the concert.

Rather than joining the people in the courtyard on their benches, Alberich paid out enough for seats on the second-floor balcony that ran along the inside walls facing the courtyard, a balcony that made up a sort of makeshift gallery. It was marginally warmer here, and the folks in the cheap seats were notoriously rowdy. When the troupe had been playing in that tent, there had been no balcony, and the expensive seats had been in the first several rows. Not so here.

The courtyard was entirely enclosed by inn buildings. Behind the stage and the curtains that closed off the back of it, were the stables. Not the sort of place where anyone would care to sit, so using that wall as the back of the stage wasted no valuable space that could have accommodated paying customers. The other three wings were the three stories of what was a typical market inn, with an arched passage in the middle of what was, in this configuration, the "back" of the courtyard leading out into the street outside. The ground floor of that wing, divided as it was by the passage, held two separate dining rooms, a taproom for the common sorts of folk, the drovers, the shepherds, the farmers who came to the market, and the second an actual set of dining rooms, one large dining room for the better-off sort, and several private parlors for the "gentry," or at least, those with enough money that the innkeeper's servants called them "m'lord" and "m'lady," whether or not they had any right to the title.

Above that, in the second and third stories, since that wing both had the noisy dining areas on the first floor, and faced the Street, were the cheapest of the sleeping rooms. These were the sort where strangers packed in several to a room together, on pallets laid so closely together that the room might just as well have been one big bed.

The right and left wings held more expensive sleeping rooms on the second and third floors, with the kitchens on the ground floor of the left-hand wing, and the servants' quarters on the ground floor of the right-hand wing.

When there wasn't a play on, the balconies gave access to those rooms. Now, however, there were benches there, where those willing to spend a bit extra could sit along the balcony railing. The view was good from here, and you weren't going to find yourself harassed by someone who'd paid less than the cost of a pint for his seat.

Normally, at least with most acting troupes, the truly expensive seats were *on* the stage itself, to the left and the right. Not with this lot—their energetic acrobatics made that a dangerous place to be, and the entire stage was free of any such obstructions.

Myste laid her arms along the balcony rail and parked her chin on them, peering down at the stage with interest. The courtyard was lit almost as well as the Great Hall of the Palace, with torches in holders on every supporting beam, and shielded lanterns around the stage. The thing about holding a play at night meant that the players could actually do some things with the scenery—like a paper moon with a lantern behind it, or using foxfire smeared all over someone's face if he was a ghost. Or, as had occurred in the scene they'd just watched, the softer, dimmer light had made the shabby costumes and tinsel and paste gems of the "lords and ladies" at a grand Festival look positively genuine. *:This isn't as bad as I thought it would be,:* she remarked to Alberich in Mindspeech.

:True,: he replied. *:This is actually one of the plays they do privately.:* It was a tale of unlucky lovers, who came from feuding families, who met by accident at some celebration, and of course, were lifebonded at first sight. The troupe were playing on current events by making the place of their first meeting the Ice Festival—which worked out very well, since it allowed them to bundle up in their warmest costumes. And of course,

the feud allowed for several of the signature acrobatic fight scenes.

Down there on the stage, the feud had been acted out by means of a confrontation in the first scene, then several of the youngsters of both clans had gotten caught up by accident in the party following a wedding. The hero and heroine had met and fallen instantly in love, and had retired. Down on the stage, the stagehands were scuttling about in the pause for the scenery change between the first and second acts.

:I suppose they're both going to end up dead in the end,: Myste sighed.

Alberich had seen this play before. *:Well, it is a tragedy.:* And in fact, that was exactly what was going to happen. Hero and heroine would be wedded in secret in the second act. In the third, the feud would escalate into open warfare, isolating them from one another as the city turned into a battlefield. In the fourth act, the lovers would arrange a desperate meeting, intending to flee the city and seek the help of the King. The heroine's brother would discover the hero waiting with horses, and challenge him. The hero would attempt to placate him, but to no avail. He would find himself forced into the duel, the brother would disarm him, and just as the heroine arrived, fatally wound him. She would run screaming toward them both; startled, the brother would turn, and she would be accidentally impaled on his sword, and the lovers would die in each other's arms.

Not before forgiving the stricken brother, however, and extracting his vow to end the feud for all time.

Not the worst of plays, by any means, and with enough action to please the male members of the audience.

:I see at least a dozen people I know down in the audience,: Myste remarked. *:The most interesting thing is, though, that—Look, see that bald-headed fellow down there, stage left? The one who seems to be in charge of the scene changing? I know him very well. The last time I saw him, he was the butler for an officious little mercer I did regular work for. I wonder how he got this job?:*

:Really?: Well, that could be interesting, if he happened to recognize Myste.

And even as that thought passed through Alberich's mind, the man looked up at their gallery, blinked, and peered upward at them, through the torch smoke and lantern light.

He gave a tentative wave. Myste nodded, and waved back. He grabbed a passing boy, said something to him, pointed at Myste, and shoved him in the direction of the stairs. A few moments later, the boy clambered toward them.

"'Scuze me, mum, but Laric wants t'know, if you're Myste, Myste Willenger, the clerk?" the boy asked.

"That I am," Myste replied, without a moment of hesitation.

The boy grinned. "Well, mum, then Laric 'ud like ter talk with you arter the play, if you've time, an' could use some work," the boy continued. "'Cause he's got a job that needs doin'."

Myste grinned. "Tell him, thanks. Who can't use extra work?"

The boy grinned back. "I'll tell 'im, mum."

With that, he scrambled back down the stairs, presumably to find the now-vanished Laric. Myste settled down for the second act, with a smile like a cat in cream.

:Well. How about that for an opportunity dropping into our laps?: she asked.

Alberich could only shake his head in amazement.

9

Alberich and Myste lingered after the end of the last act, assuming that Laric would seek them out as soon as the audience cleared out. It was a reasonable assumption; both of them assumed he would not have interrupted his urgent work to send up a boy if he hadn't intended to get to Myste as soon as he could. It wasn't comfortable, sitting out there in the cold, on the hard benches, but both Alberich and Myste had the feeling that it just might be worth the wait.

And they were right. As soon as the actors took their final bows, the audience began to shove its way out. Once the actors were gone, the audience lost interest in what, to Alberich, was actually more interesting than the play itself. In the torchlight, there had been a certain— something—that had given an illusion of reality to the play. Now the illusion was coming apart, bit by bit, and it was fascinating to Alberich to see how it had been put together in the first place.

First, the lamps at the edge of the stage were blown out and gathered up, and the stagehands began clearing away the properties on the stage, carrying them back behind what *had* looked like a false front of several buildings made rather solidly of wood. But it was now apparent that it wasn't wood at all, nor solid, but another canvas backdrop of the same sort that the troupe had used during the Festival. With no one being careful about how they moved around it, the thing rippled and waved as people went behind it. Two other bits of business that stood on either side of the canvas, hiding the edges, looked a bit more solid. They were only a single story tall, though they had a pair of doors in them that the actors had used to come and go. As two stagehands hauled off the "horses" that the hero and heroine were to have escaped on, Laric dashed out of one of the doors in the scenery onto the edge of the stage, and peered up at the balcony. "Heyla!" he shouted, and waved at her. She waved back. "Myste! Stay right there for a bit while I tie things up!"

Myste nodded vigorously; evidently that was enough for Laric, who dashed back through the false door again. "Tie things up, hmm?" she said cheerfully to Alberich. "I hope that isn't literal."

"That, I could not tell you. I know nothing of—all this," Alberich admitted, waving vaguely at the stage. And at precisely that moment, the painted cloth at the back of the stage, depicting the outer walls of several buildings, dropped down to the stage with a bang, along with the pole it was fastened to along the top. Behind it was another, with a forest or garden scene; it came down next. And finally, a third, showing stalls of a market and sky—that was the setting for the Ice Festival. Down it came, revealing the bare front of the stables, which was three stories tall, like the rest of the inn, though Alberich could not for a moment imagine what they would need three stories for.

Well, this was a busy place, with a lot of animals coming and going. Maybe they needed all that space for hay and straw storage.

A cheerful-looking little boy had been up at the top, where there was a crane and a pulley with a rope still hanging from it. Apparently that was what the backdrops had been fastened to. Now he slid down from the upper loft of the stables on the rope there, and he and another stagehand began rolling up the three backdrops on their poles. With another *bang*, one of the two pieces of scenery that screened each side of the backcloth fell over, and two more men came up to haul it away. The second one followed in short order. In a remarkably short period of time, not only had the sets and properties vanished into the stable, so had the stage itself, which apparently came apart, although it seemed solid enough even with all of those actors leaping about on it. That explained how the troupe had been able to get a stage into their tent that could take the amount of abuse they had been delivering with every performance. Alberich watched in fascination until there was nothing to be seen but a perfectly ordinary-looking inn courtyard with the stables at the rear.

And that was when Laric emerged from the stable door again and wearily climbed the nearest staircase, heading in their direction. He mopped his red face with a handkerchief the size of a small sail as he came. He was a very big man, with an imposing belly, red-faced, with hair going thin at his temples and surprisingly honest eyes. Not that Alberich was going to trust how someone *looked* to tell him anything about that person's real nature.

His clothing was ordinary enough: a sheepskin vest over a heavy knitted tunic and moleskin breeches. He wore shoes, rather than boots, but most city dwellers did. If you *had* to go out in fresh snow that hadn't been shoveled or packed down yet, and you didn't have boots, you just wrapped your feet, shoes and all, in canvas, and tied it around your calves with twine.

"Damme, but if makin' an honest livin' ain't the hardest work going!" he exclaimed as they both stood up. "Myste, where you been? I got hauled in to stage manage for this idiot lot, and just when I had some work for ye, ye ups and vanishes!"

She shrugged. "Army needed clerks," she said simply. "Now it don't, so they let me go. Back I came. Got some work at the Companion's Bell, but it ain't full-time."

"Well, that's a break fer both of us," he said genially. "Who's yer friend?"

"Bret," she said, without batting an eye. "Carter. From down-country, on the border. Army don't need carters now, neither; nothing more to haul down *or* up."

"Ah, hard luck, man," the stage manager said, with sympathy.

"Don't feel too sorry for him!" Myste laughed. "The Army may not need 'im, but damn-near everyone else does! He paid *my* way in tonight!"

"Owed her one," Alberich said, gruffly, but with as much good humor as Myste, and doing his level best to minimize his accent. "Bet 'er a meal an' a raree-show, an' she picked this. Warn ye, man—don't play cards with this one!"

He hoped that someone who *wasn't* an actor wouldn't think twice about his accent, and took the chance on actually saying something. It was worth the risk; the big man let out a belly-laugh without a single look askance.

"Myste! You conned another country boy! Listen, man, you're lucky the stakes wasn't more than just a meal and a seat at a play!" Laric responded, wiping his eyes with that kerchief. "I learned that one a long time ago!"

"Well, a man looks at her face, he don't think of card sharp!" Alberich replied. "He thinks pen pusher!"

"Which she is, she is, but she's got some *system,*" Laric replied earnestly. "It ain't cheatin', but she's got the cards in her head, somehow, an' she can figger the odds of what's coming up—" He shook his head. "*I* can't make it work, but she can. So we know better'n t' play against her."

"You get along, Bret," Myste said, in a kindly tone of voice. "You got a load in the morning, and we might be a while. I can get back by myself."

:I'm safe enough with Laric,: she added. *:Just go wait at the Bell, and I'll catch up with you.:*

"Right-oh," he responded, as if he was just a casual friend, and left—though with a lot more reluctance than he showed. He didn't like leaving her alone, even if she knew the man. He didn't like the idea that she would be walking back to the Bell alone, even though this neighborhood and the ones between here and the Bell were safe enough.

But he had no excuse to linger, once Myste had "dismissed" him, and no place to wait for her to finish her business with the stage manager. Now he was sorry he hadn't scouted this area beforehand and found some place he could have holed up nearby. If she was going to actually get involved with these people—

Still. She had her "throwaway purse," just like he'd taught her. If someone tried to rob her, she'd toss that purse away and run in the opposite direction. And the Three Sheaves was very public. Even near the sleeping quarters, there were people coming and going all night. If something happened, her Companion would be out of the Bell's stable in a trice and on the way to help. Surely she couldn't get into trouble… he hoped.

He returned to the Bell alone, going in through the hidden door in the back of the stable to the secret room. There he changed his disguise for his gray leathers, and waited impatiently in the Heralds' common room for her to return, sitting right at the window so he could see her when she did. Or at least, see her if she came anywhere near the front.

:She won't,: Kantor reminded him. *:She'll use the back, just like you did. Alberich, she's more used to moving around in a city than you are.:*

Well, that was true enough. Especially this city, at least the reasonable parts of it.

It felt like half the night, rather than just a candlemark or so, before he "heard"—rather than saw—the Herald-Chronicler at last:.

:I'm back. Everything went smoothly; it's a distinct advantage to go disguised as yourself. Don't get yourself in a knot, Alberich,: she said cheerfully. *:I've got good news for you. Just let me change into my uniform.:*

He signaled a girl and ordered hot wine for both of them, knowing that by now she must be frozen. She was, thankfully, faster at changing her clothing than most women he had encountered. The hot wine he ordered was barely on the table when she came in, lenses glittering in the lamplight—and fogging up in the transition from cold outside to warm and humid inside.

"So," she said, without preamble, sliding onto the bench across from him. She took off her lenses to polish them on a napkin before replacing them on her nose. "Here's what we've got. You want to know how Norris started up this whole show in the first place?"

"All information is useful," he admitted.

"So I've learned." She took a sip of wine. "There were a lot of people displaced by the Tedrels as you know, and quite a few of them ended up here in Haven. Your boy Norris is supposed to be from near the Rethwellan Border, and managed to get separated from the entertainment troupe he'd been with. Laric didn't say how, and I didn't ask. Supposedly, he hitched up with a caravan, doing acrobatics to amuse everyone around the fire at night, and ended up at the Three Sheaves along with the caravan. Supposedly, the rest of his group was going to come up to Haven and find him, and they never did. He wasn't minded to sign up with the Army, but he was running up a big bill at the inn, when he got the idea to put together his own new troupe from some of the other ragtags of entertainers that were drifting in so he could *pay* that bill without getting put to work in the kitchen. That's the story, anyway; I suspect at least part of it's true. He's definitely an actor, and he's better than anyone else of the bunch. He's got 'em all charmed, that's for sure, and now that they're doing just as well as he promised they would, there isn't a one of them will hear a word against him. I don't know if he's from Rethwellen, because he's damn good at putting on and taking off accents. He did at least four in my presence."

Alberich almost choked on his wine. "You *saw* him? You talked to him?"

Myste shrugged. "It was after I made the bargain with Laric; we were looking over the office I'm going to use. He swanned in with two women on his arms. Laric told him I was going to be checking the books. He looked at me, saw a dowdy lump, wafted a little charm in my direction just to keep his hand in, and promptly forgot me as soon as he turned around and headed out the door. I *told* you that it's useful being a clerk. Nobody ever pays any attention to us. Even that business with card counting; Lane's the only one who ever caught on I was doing it. Everybody else just figured I was lucky."

"Evidently so," Alberich managed. How close a call had it been? He wished he had been there to see Norris' reaction with his own eyes.

"Anyway, here's the thing; the innkeeper is the one taking in the receipts at the door, because he takes his room and board for the troupe right off the top, and now that they've gotten popular, Laric thinks he's skimming. But nobody else can manage to cipher for the numbers that they're bringing in of an evening now. So from now on, I'm going to go every night they're putting on a play—which is once every two nights—and go over the books, the head-count, and the innkeeper's tally." She grinned. "And I'm doing it all from the room next to Norris', which is Laric's office. Which means that I'll be in a position to tell you when he's there, where he's gone if he isn't, when he's likely to be back, and to leave my own window open for someone to come and go. If you want to search his room for papers, I can make it happen."

Alberich stared at her. "And for how long will this go on?"

"That, I don't know," she admitted. "Laric wants me to come regularly at first, then taper off. He thinks, and I agree with him, that if the innkeeper *is* skimming, it's going to be better not to confront him on it, just bring *me* in. They know what I was at the Three Sheaves, and they'll know why I'm in Laric's office with the tally boards. If the innkeeper knows we're watching him, he'll be honest, and by comparing the take over time, we'll know if he's *been* honest in the past. And knowing that Laric has me on tap will probably keep him honest when I stop coming around."

"So, earliest on the best of our chances will be." Alberich didn't like that particularly, but there was an old saying that beggars didn't get to pick what they were given. And another that it didn't pay to inquire too closely about the age of a gift horse.

:*Or, in my case, the color of his eyes,*: Kantor said wickedly.

And Myste was right. The best way to find out what Norris was passing was to search his room for the papers before he got rid of them. Which meant that Alberich was going to have to find a way to copy them, because they might be in code, and he certainly wasn't going to be able to memorize them even if they weren't—

"Is there, perhaps, a way to copy such things?" he asked.

"Several," she assured him. "Rubbings, if he's using graphite or a crayon, damp-paper transfer if he's using ink. I can show you. We do that all the time to make emergency copies. Of course," she added judiciously, "when you do that, you get a mirror-image, but that's no great problem."

Alberich took in a deep breath, and let it out in a sigh. "Myste—very well have you done. Thank you."

She made a face. "Well, if you're doing the dangerous bit—and I assume it'll be *you* climbing in that window and not some lowlife from around Exile's Gate that you hired—I'm doing the tedious part. Here I was, pleased I'd finally gotten *out* of doing accounts, and here I am back into it!" Then she sighed and looked out the window. "And on top of my real work, too."

"Worse, it could be," Alberich reminded her. "On the battlefield, we could be."

She gave him a wry glance. "Well," she admitted. "There is that. I'll try to keep it in mind when I'm trying to hide you or throw you out a window because your lad Norris came back early."

And there just wasn't much he could say to that, so wisely, he said nothing at all.

But as Myste had pointed out, just because they were involved in this after-hours clandestine work it did not make their normal duties go away. He had his full set of classes to train, and as the season edged toward spring, the snow began to thaw, and the blustery winds began to blow, it became more and more of a challenge to hold classes out of doors. At least that wretched game of Hurlee was put on hold, for the ice on the ponds was getting rotten and not to be trusted, but the ground was alternately frozen mud or slushy snow, so the game couldn't be transferred to some sort of playing field. And, oh yes, he had already heard that there were plans afoot for *that*, though the players would have to run, rather than sliding. The next thing he'd probably hear was that the Heraldic Trainees were going to try it Companion-back...

Meanwhile, the replacement mirror finally arrived and was installed. The two miscreants who began that particular adventure were as responsible for creating the new one as destroying the old one, being the ones who had spent an interminable amount of time polishing it to rid it of as many defects as possible. Both Deans decreed that their term of punishment at the glassworks was at an end, although they would still be serving double-chores at the Collegium for well into the summer. They had missed the entire Hurlee season, and whenever an animated discussion of the game began, their faces were a study in adolescent disappointment. Alberich wasn't at all surprised. If ever there were two rascals who might have been born to play a game like Hurlee, it was those two. And it occurred to him that this, alone, might be the worst punishment that could have been inflicted on them. They had missed out on the creation of the game, they had missed out on becoming some of the first experts. From now on, the best they could hope for was to play catch-up to some other ascendant star.

And in a way he felt just a little guilty, for if it hadn't been for his own curiosity about where they had picked up their wild ideas, he would never have investigated the actors, and never have known that there was something going on.

He still didn't know *what* it was, of course, but at least he knew there was something. Now he had a fighting chance to discover what it was, and whether or not it was dangerous.

Nevertheless, he had an important duty to perform, right there at the Collegium, and it was one that he could not give less than his total attention to during the hours when he was teaching, and no few of the hours outside of that time.

He was training those who would one day become Heralds how to stay alive, when other people wanted them dead.

And that was a massive task.

It began with the youngest or the least experienced—not necessarily the same thing, as his tutelage of Myste had proven—and the basic skills of hand and eye coordination, and familiarity with weapons. And while they were learning these things, he was studying them, to determine what their lifelong weaknesses would be (for there had never been a person born who had so perfect a physique that he *didn't* have one) and how to make them aware of the fact.

Then, he would move them into the next stage of their training—how to compensate for those weaknesses.

By then, they were roughly halfway through their years as Trainees; they had mastered basic skills, and they were as strong and flexible and coordinated as they were ever likely to get. There were exceptions to that last, of course, but those were the exceptions that proved the rule. If they had found him a hard master before, he was harder still at that point, because no one, *no one*, ever likes having a weakness pointed out, and human nature is such that when one *is* pointed out, the natural reaction is to try to deny it exists.

Which was why he would go from master to monster at that point, until not even the most persistently self-delusional could continue to believe anything other than that the problem was real, and something had to be done about the problem.

Sometimes the weaknesses were physical—restricted peripheral vision, for instance. Sometimes they were mental. Often, they were emotional, and the biggest lay in the very natures of those who were Chosen as Heralds. These youngsters did not *believe* in the goodness and decency of their fellow man, they *knew* it. It was fundamental to their souls.

And he had to, somehow, prove to them that their fellow man was very likely to plant a knife in the middle of their backs without destroying that deep and primitive *knowledge*. As Heralds, they had to go into every day expecting that the people around them would all act as ordinary, fallible, but decent human beings who, given the chance, would act decently and humanely. They also had to be prepared for the eventuality that those around them would do nothing of the sort—and be able to cope with such a contradiction without going a little mad.

Not that all Heralds weren't already a little mad, but—not *that* kind of mad.

Then, once the weaknesses had been identified and acknowledged, he had to train them to compensate for the weaknesses.

It would have been infinitely easier to do this had his students been, say, Karsite Cadets. Only physical and mental weaknesses would have to be dealt with, because emotional weaknesses literally did not matter to the Sunsguard so long as they were locked down tightly—and he could have proven those weaknesses to them with sheer, brute force, by persistently attacking them at those weak points until even a blind man could see what was wrong. Persuasion always took a lot longer than hammering something home.

He was generally in that last stage only with those who were in the last year of their Trainee status—it was far, far easier to work with these Trainees, who were quite ready for Whites if only they had a little more experience and skill. For them, he was a mentor, not a monster.

It had occurred to him, and more than once, that here in the Collegium the Trainees were put through a kind of forced-maturation process that sent them out into the greater world at eighteen, nineteen, or twenty with the mental and emotional skills of someone well in his thirties or older.

Alas, most of his time was spent in being the tyrant with the heart of stone.

This was never more true than when the energy level of those in his class was such that the students were near to bouncing off walls as they entered the door of the salle, and he turned them right around and took them outside to run their drills in the mud, the slush, the half-frozen snow, and no matter if it *was* too wretched out to be doing any such thing. Cold, dampness, and dirt weren't going to harm them any; if they got too cold, he knew the signs and always sent them back into the salle to warm up at the oven. Not that there was any chance of getting cold enough to fall ill, unless something odd happened to keep them standing about soaked to the skin.

The Blues, of course, were exempt from this if they chose. However, if they declared their unwillingness in such a way as to be insubordinate, rather than merely electing not to show up for lessons, he had a weapon to either bring them to heel or get rid of them entirely.

Such as today—with one of the classes that was in their middle, and most difficult period of development.

And they roared into his salle already in full antagonist mode.

The battle lines were already drawn; Blues versus Trainees, one ringleader facing off for each side. The insults were flying. Blows would follow, in a moment.

Except that Alberich waded right into the middle of it, and sent both of them to the floor with a blow to the ear, and the silence that descended was absolute.

"Well," he said crisply. "Before it begins, I care not how it started, nor *who* started it. You brought it into my salle. You will take it out again. There will be no second mirror to be replaced."

A nervous titter came from behind him. He didn't turn to look. Neither boy had moved, and he gave them both looks that should have turned them to ice. "I said," he enunciated carefully, "you will take it outside. You wish to fight? Well enough. Outside. It ends when I say it ends, and *I* will be the judge of the winner."

The Trainee on the floor had the sense to go pale; he, at least, must have some inkling of what Alberich meant—which was to let the fight go on until they were both too exhausted, bruised, and battered to stand. There would be no winner, short of one of the two being knocked unconscious, which, with the bare hands of a pair of boys fundamentally unskilled in bare-hand fighting, was unlikely. This was, actually, *why* Alberich did not teach bare-hand fighting to anyone who had not passed into that third and final stage of development...

But the Blue was one of Alberich's personal headaches. Arrogant, assertive and, unfortunately, skilled enough to have earned the right to a part of that arrogance. Alberich would have gladly rid himself of the boy— Kadhael Corbie—if he could have. Unfortunately, that was out of his hands. Kadhael was in the class unless and until he took himself out of it.

The boy looked him up and down, and sneered. "No," he said.

Someone gasped.

Alberich did not move, and did not change his expression by so much as a hair. "I do not believe I heard you correctly," he said evenly, trying to suppress the thrill of glee the boy's insolent answer gave him. "What, precisely, did you say?"

"I said, *no.* No, I am not going outside. No, I am not fighting by your rules. Who are you to give *me* orders, old man?"

Alberich smiled—and Kadhael took one look at the smile and suddenly realized that he had made so fundamental a mistake that there was not going to be any evasion of the consequences.

"I," he said quietly, and with the perfect and precise control of Valdemaran grammar that came upon him in moments of stress "am the Collegium Weaponsmaster. As such, *when I choose to exercise my rank,* within the four walls of my salle and on its grounds, I outrank, by Valdemaran law, every man, woman, and child in Valdemar save only the Monarch. And within these four walls, the Monarch is my equal, not my superior."

And it was all perfectly true. How else could he properly *teach* the sons and daughters of the highborn? How else could he train high-ranking Guards? How could he drill the greatest warriors and nobles of the realm? How could he *ever* train the Heirs, if he did not outrank them? To properly train, there would be injuries. They might be serious. And the Weaponsmaster could not be held responsible for such injuries. To *be* trained, the Weaponsmaster must know his orders would be obeyed, and the only way to be sure of that was to see that his rank on these grounds was higher than anyone else's in the land.

Which was why—though he had not learned this until *after* Dethor had retired—he had that special status within the salle and on the grounds.

Kadhael looked as if the blow Alberich had given him had knocked every particle of sense right out of his head. He stared, he gaped, he looked as if he could not rightly understand a word of what had been said. "But—"

"And since you choose not to abide by the laws of this, *my* Kingdom," Alberich continued, still smiling. "I banish you. Now and forever."

"What?" Kadhael stammered.

"Out. Go. Do not *ever* present yourself as my pupil. You may tell your father why you are not here, or not. I care not. I will report this matter to the Queen, the Lord Marshal, and the Provost Marshal—since you are not a Trainee, I shall not trouble any of the Deans with it."

"You can't *do* this!" Kadhael protested wildly, paling. Alberich knew why. Kadhael's father had watched Alberich fight and train the Guards for months before the boy had been sent to the salle with a class. Kadhael's father *knew* that there was not enough money in Valdemar to purchase the services of a trainer as good as Alberich.

Kadhael's father would be very, very unhappy about this.

"I can. I have." Alberich eyed the boy consideringly. Should he?

:Oh, go ahead, do,: Kantor answered.

He bent down, and grabbed the boy by the back of his tunic and hauled him to his feet. Without much effort, be it added—Kadhael was just about Alberich's size and weight, but he was still an uncoordinated adolescent, not a trained, honed warrior. Alberich tightened his grip *just* enough that the fabric half-choked the boy, eliminating any more babble out of him.

"I will, because you do not seem to understand your own tongue properly, repeat myself," Alberich said, with no anger whatsoever. "You are banished from the salle and the grounds. You are no longer a student here. You are leaving now, and you will never return. If you do, I will personally thrash you until you cannot stand, and throw you off the grounds again. Training here is a privilege, not a right. You have just proved you do not deserve to enjoy that privilege."

And with that, he frog-marched the boy out the door, down the path, to the very edge of the training grounds. And with great care and utmost precision, he pitched the insolent brat right into the biggest, muddiest patch of slush that he thought he could reach.

He did not even wait to see if Kadhael went headfirst into it, or managed to somehow save himself. He turned on his heel and marched back into his salle.

No one had moved. This was good. He wasn't going to have to discipline anyone else—yet.

He raked them all with his stony gaze. "More objections, do I hear?" he asked, raising one eyebrow.

Silence.

"Then outside you will go. All of you." He turned a stern gaze on the Trainee, who was still sitting on the floor—Osberic, that was the boy's name. "Osberic," he continued, and the Trainee flinched. "Since no opponent you have now, yet equally of guilt you are to have brought a *fight* within my walls, it will be me that you face. Fetch two staves, and follow. Even practice swords, I will not ruin in this muck."

He would not be *too* hard on him. Putting him on his face or back into the mud two or three times would be enough.

:He started the fight,: Kantor put in. *:Not that Kadhael wasn't trying to goad him into starting it, but he did start it.:*

All right. Four. Teach the boy to hold his temper.

:Good answer. I'm going to watch.:

Alberich smiled as he walked out into the cold again and saw that there was no sign of Kadhael, other than a vaguely human-shaped depression in the slush. *:Please do.:*

The boys had formed up in a rough circle, and Osberic came up to Alberich with two fighting staffs and a hangdog look. Alberich took one without looking at it.

"Consequences, Osberic," he said as he squared off against the boy, who began circling him warily. "Say I will not, that a Herald loses not his temper—but aware a Herald is, that consequences there are for doing so."

His staff shot out at ankle-level, tripping Osberic. Down he went.

He picked himself back up, and aimed a blow at Alberich's head. Alberich blocked it, riposted, and let the boy block him. "So think you—had there a fight been, what consequences there would be?"

"Uh—" Osberic tried again, was blocked again. "Lord Corbie would get me in trouble?"

"Wrong." Alberich flipped the staff at Osberic's ankles; the boy dodged, and Alberich flipped the other end around to thwack him in the buttocks and send him into the slush again. "Lord Corbie would protest to the Queen, who would be forced to go to the Dean, who would have to answer to why discipline was so lax among the Trainees that a highborn fought a Trainee."

Osberic picked himself up, flushing. "My fight would get the *Heralds* in trouble?"

"Correct." Alberich let the boy try a few more blows; not bad, but he wasn't going to get through Alberich's defenses any time soon. "And who else?"

"The Queen?" Osberic hazarded.

"Correct. Now, why will there be *no* trouble for what I did with Kadhael Corbie?"

Osberic didn't answer, being a little too busy fending off a flurry of blows from Alberich, only to trip over a hardened lump of snow and land on his backside in an icy puddle.

:That should count,: Kantor said from the sideline.

:I agree.:

"Because," Alberich continued as Osberic picked himself back up for the third time, "a proper and correct order gave I. Insolence I was given. My proper authority I exerted—no temper, no beatings, no punishments, and only when more insolence and refusal was I given, did I remove Kadhael with prejudice. To his father he will go, yes, but his father will likely box his ears. Now, know you why *I* am drilling you thus?" Osberic came at Alberich yet again, Alberich let the boy drive him back.

"To punish me!" Osberic shouted, his cheeks burning with humiliation. "To make me look stupid in front of everyone!"

"No, that would the act of a bully be," Alberich told him. "So that, should Lord Corbie protest it was *you* who began the fight, *I* can tell the Queen that you were punished, and all here will swear to that. This is not for *you*, it is for the Heralds, that all know that we tend to the misdeeds of our own in proper measure." He then neatly sidestepped the last rush and tripped Osberic as he went past. Once again, Osberic measured his length in the mud. "A Herald cannot merely *right* be, Osberic. A Herald must guided by the *law* be. He cannot dispense the law, if he follows it not himself. He cannot dispense the law, if he thinks himself immune from it. He cannot dispense the law, if he will not deal it to his fellows in the same measure as he does to those whom he has in charge."

"Yessir, Herald Alberich," Osberic groaned from the ground.

"And that is why, for fighting, you have also been punished in this way," Alberich continued. "Now, back into the salle. There is work to be done."

They were all quick to follow the order, but none so quick as Osberic.

10

Kadhael Corbie disappeared from the Court and Collegia entirely. Not that Alberich would have noticed his absence, having banned the boy from the salle, but it wasn't long before there were murmurs and speculations among his students and the Court—and being that it was his business to know things, he heard every one of them. Rumor had it that the boy's father was so enraged that he had gotten himself thrown out of Alberich's class and forbidden to enter the salle that he'd sent the boy straight down to the family manor, there to languish in what the young lords and ladies called "rustification." Since it was said to be a particularly dull and cheerless place, lacking in anything that a young man might find amusing, and since rumor also had it that Lord Corbie had sent orders for his son to be confined to the house and grounds until further notice, Alberich was perfectly satisfied that the punishment fit the crime.

On the other side of the table, Lord Corbie went to Selenay and also demanded the punishment of "the Trainee who started it," and allegedly was nonplussed to learn that "the Trainee" had already been punished. And that the punishment fit *his* crime, since all he had done was to bring a fight into the salle and after being reprimanded, had behaved with the proper respect for the Weaponsmaster. The trouncing—with lecture—at the hands of the Weaponsmaster in front of his peers was deemed both painful and humiliating enough, even for Lord Corbie.

And Lord Corbie had been quite taken aback to learn that it had all happened within moments of Kadhael's expulsion.

Without knowing much about the man, but intuiting a great deal from the behavior of his son, Alberich doubted that humiliation of Kadhael at the hands of "that foreigner" would ever be forgotten or forgiven, but at least there was nothing overt that Lord Corbie could do about the incident. Alberich had exercised *precisely* the correct amount of authority: he'd been defied, he banished the offender. Not from any other classes at any other part of the three Collegia, only from his own. He had indeed ejected the boy by force—because the boy would have gone on defying him if Alberich hadn't physically thrown him off the premises. He had not exceeded his authority, and in point of fact, Alberich *could* have given the boy a taste of what Osberic had gotten, and hadn't. In fact, Kadhael had gotten off lightly at Alberich's hands, and not only was there no denying it, but both the Lord Marshal and the Provost Marshal (who was in charge of discipline on and off the Collegia grounds) said loudly and publicly that *they* would have boxed both his ears until he was deaf.

Nevertheless, Lord Corbie would not like the man who had rejected his son; he would not like the Collegium nor the organization that had given him the authority to do so.

One more enemy… but Alberich was used to those by now. He would have to watch his back, but when had he ever done anything else? And sure enough, within days, there were rumors in the Court about how the Weaponsmaster was abusing his pupils, abusing his authority, treating Heraldic Trainees with indulgence and punishing Blues arbitrarily. A few Blues were quietly absent from his class after that. But there was not a great deal that he could do about that—nor, truth to be told, wished to do.

As for Osberic—according to Kantor, that very evening, when the Trainee's bruises started aching and he started feeling particularly sorry for himself, his Companion had given him a good talking-to. Whether this was delivered in the form of a lecture or with sympathy, Kantor didn't say—but one thing was certain: when Companions took it upon themselves to correct their Chosen, the lesson tended to stick. Osberic was certainly properly contrite the next day, and if there was still a great deal of moaning about Alberich's hardheartedness, at least no one among the Heraldic Trainees was claiming he was a bully or a sadist. Hardhearted, he could live with. In fact, the more hardhearted they thought him, the better off they would be in the long run.

Though shortly after the Kadhael incident, there was one little lad who would not have agreed with that estimation.

He was one of the "Tedrel orphans," brought in by the Companion Cheric the very same day as Osberic and Kadhael's chastisement. It took a day or two to get him settled into the Collegium, so Alberich didn't see him until his mentor, Trainee Rotherven, brought him by himself to the salle, shortly after the last class of the day.

Alberich was overseeing a set of Guards working out with maces, when the door to the salle opened and a final-year Trainee came in with a very small boy at his side. Alberich left the two to continue their bout, and walked over to the door where they waited politely.

"This is a new Trainee, Weaponsmaster," Rotherven said, leading the young boy by the hand—a *very* young boy indeed, no more than seven, if Alberich was any judge. He was rather angular, with an unruly thatch of no-colored hair, but very intelligent eyes, and a look about him that was vaguely familiar. And when he got a good look at the Weaponsmaster, the boy gaped at him with shock—then awe—then spun to look up at his mentor with a look just short of accusation.

"You did not tell me this was the Great Rider!" the child exclaimed, and Alberich knew immediately by the trace of a Karsite accent that this must be one of the children brought out of the Tedrel camp after the end of that final battle.

"Great rider?" Rotherven said, his brow furrowed with puzzlement. "But—"

"Never mind, I understand him," Alberich interrupted. He looked down at the boy with some bemusement. So *that* was why the boy looked vaguely familiar; he was Karsite, or at least, half Karsite. Most of the hill-folk shepherds were mongrels by Sunpriest standards anyway. "So," he said—in Karsite, "we have another of the Sun's children come to be a White Rider, eh?" This one must not have been too damaged by his experiences, or he wouldn't have been Chosen so very young. "There are others here, not as White Riders, but as Selenay's pages. You won't be alone."

"Oh." Relief suffused the boy's features. "I did not know that, Great Rider—"

Alberich looked up at Rotherven. "Selenay has perhaps five or six Tedrel orphans; in her service as pages they are. See that this lad meeting them is, please. Perhaps a playfellow he will find among them."

Then he looked back down at the boy and continued the conversation in Karsite. "Also, there is Priest Gerichen, a true man of the Sunlord. You may go with the others to the Temple of the Sunlord if you wish—though they do not call it that here, but rather, the Temple of the Lord of Light. And if you do not wish to do so, you need not. You are free to serve who you wish, here."

"I still serve the Sunlord, Great Rider," the boy said quietly. "The Sunlord of the Prophecy."

"Then you will find His House yonder in Haven, and Gerichen at His altar," Alberich replied, suppressing a smile at the child's solemn demeanor. It was quaint and charming, but a little sad also. Those children had been forced to grow up far too quickly. "I have it on the best authority that He approves of the White Riders and all they stand for, and that there is nothing in the pledges that a White Rider must make that run counter to His will. Quite the opposite, in fact. In serving as a White Rider, you will also serve Him. You will be a hope and an example to our people, and repay some of the debt to those who saved and succored us, as I try to do."

The child's face took on a look of fierce pride and determination. "I will not fail you, Great Rider!" he said, in tones that made it a vow. "I will not fail the Prophecy!"

Rotherven's expression of bemusement, as he looked from Alberich to the boy and back again, made Alberich very glad that he had a great deal of practice in keeping his own face under control, or he might have laughed aloud.

"It is a great responsibility," Alberich replied, as gravely as if the child was three times his actual age. "And a signal honor."

"I do know that, Great Rider," the child said, nodding. "Cheric has told me so. And it is—all I could ever wish to be."

"Excuse me, Herald Alberich, but I was supposed to tell you that young Theodren here is one of the orphans," Rotherven said, then laughed self-consciously, "but obviously you already know that."

"I do, but I thank you," Alberich replied, and turned back to the boy. "So. I am glad to see you, Theodren. You will be learning weapons at my hands—as any other Trainee. And you must call me Herald Alberich, not Great Rider. I am no greater than any of the other Heralds—the White Riders. We are all brothers and sisters."

"Yes, Herald Alberich." The boy gave an odd little salute that he must have learned from the Tedrels. "I was afraid, when my friend Rotherven said I was to be given over to weapons lessons. Now I am not." He smiled. "I was afraid the training would be like—the bad place."

"It will be hard, but not like that other place, I promise you," Alberich said, and turned back again to Rotherven. "He will be in the beginner's class, of course—just following luncheon, that would be."

"Yes, sir." The Trainee's expression told Alberich everything he needed to know; evidently Theodren had been properly terrified when he'd been told he was to learn weapons' work, and Rotherven's solution had been to bring him directly to Alberich so that he could see his teacher for himself. Or, perhaps, the suggestion had come from Rotherven's Companion, who had been no mere colt when Rotherven was Chosen. "Thank you for talking to him; I think he'll settle now, and I was a bit worried about him—"

Alberich nodded. "You have done exactly what was needed, bringing him here. My thanks." And to Theodren, "This young man is also my pupil, and he will be as a brother to you as well as a Brother Rider. You may give him your trust. He will also see that you meet the others brought out of the camp that are now in Selenay's service, and perhaps you may find a friend or two among them, as well."

The child's eyes shone with gratitude. "Thank you, Herald Alberich."

Then Theodren looked up at Rotherven, and said, in Valdemaran that was much better than Alberich's, "Thank you for bringing me to the salle, Rotherven. Herald Alberich is the chief of those who came to save us, and I am honored to be taught by him."

It was so formal, and so charming, that Rotherven couldn't help but smile. It was a kind smile, and Alberich knew at that moment that the older boy had been a good choice to watch over Theodren. "Well, good. And now you've met all your teachers, so let's get some dinner. You'll be back here after luncheon tomorrow."

Alberich escorted them to the door of the salle, then watched the two of them off up the path back to the Collegium. As they disappeared into the twilight shadows, he felt Kantor coming up beside him. He put his hand on Kantor's shoulder, and felt the Companion's silken hide beneath his palm, warm and smooth.

:Cheric can't Mindspeak him very clearly yet, and the little lad was petrified,: Kantor told him. *:He thought he was about to be put into one of those vile Boy's Bands that the Tedrels used to "toughen" the boys. Nasty training, if you could call it training. Kept them on short rations, more or less forced them to steal if they were going to keep from going hungry, but beat them within an inch of their lives if they got caught. Weapons' training with real, edged weapons—if you got hurt or died, too bad. Every infraction was punished with a beating, in fact. Small wonder he was terrified.:*

:Well, I'm glad he recognized me. I only hope he doesn't hero-worship me,: Alberich sighed. *:Though it might be pleasant for me, it would do him no good.:*

:I wouldn't necessarily agree with that.: Kantor nudged him affectionately. *:You could do with a little hero-worship.:*

:Adoration is for the Sunlord. I am content with respect,: Alberich replied, but

rubbed Kantor's ears with affection. :*So long as I have the friendship of my Companion and a few good comrades, I am content.*:

:*Piff. I can think of one other thing you could do with.*: Kantor's eyes sparkled with mischief, and Alberich had a very good idea what he was talking about, but he pretended otherwise. After all, it was usually Kantor who managed a jest on Alberich, rather than the other way around.

:*Yes, indeed,*: he replied blandly. :*I could do with my dinner.*:

And he laughed aloud at Kantor's exasperated snort.

The following day was very much business as usual, although during the day he found himself looking forward much more than usual to dinner, because Myste had sent down a note asking if she could join him then. He didn't know why, and she didn't tell him; probably it had something to do with the players. Since she clearly was comfortable with them and was not going to have to *act* in order to fit herself into a persona, he had elected to leave her to get used to the situation, and her "employers" to get used to her, before he asked her to actually do anything. He'd told her to let him know when she thought she was ready, and that was probably why she wanted to meet him over dinner.

And yet—well, he wouldn't be disappointed if it wasn't the business of the actors that brought her.

When she arrived with the servant that brought his dinner, as usual, helping to carry the baskets, he did note that her step was definitely light, and that there was more than a mere suspicion of a smile on her face. But she only spoke of commonplace things—more rumors about Kadhael, in fact, and more slurs about Alberich himself—until the servant had gone. And when he bent to uncover the first of the supper dishes, she held out a hand, forestalling him.

"Dinner can wait for a moment," she said, as always when she was with him, speaking in Karsite. It was an effective hedge against anyone who might, somehow, have gotten in close enough to be listening. Not that Alberich expected anyone to manage, for he'd have to get past the Companions to do so, but sometimes Trainees dared each other to particularly stupid pranks and it would be just his luck for one of them to sneak in to eavesdrop on the Weaponsmaster and overhear something he shouldn't.

"I assume you have a reason?" he replied.

She nodded. "First, I want you to see these."

And she handed him a folded packet of paper; the paper itself was odd, thin, very light, very strong. He unfolded it.

And knew immediately what it was, because it was in cipher, and there was only one place at the moment where Myste would have gotten a packet of papers in cipher. They were the same papers—or more of the same—that he'd seen passed from Norris to Devlin!

"No, they're not," Myste said immediately, as if she had read his mind. Not that she needed to; she would know exactly what he was thinking at that moment. "In this case, it's a packet that was passed the other way, from Devlin to Norris."

He looked from it, to her, and back again, speechless for a moment. "But—how did you—"

Her grin widened, and she sat down with an air of triumph. "He gave them to me."

Alberich also sat down, then. He had to. His knees wouldn't hold him. "If you're joking—"

"I'm not," she replied with satisfaction. "I swear I'm not. He gave them to me with his own lily-white hands. And do you know *why?*" She laughed, a rich and satisfied chuckle. "Because, my friend, he wanted me to copy them for him."

Alberich had thought himself too surprised to react to anything by that point, but he felt his mouth gaping open, and shut it, and swallowed. "I think," he said at last, "that you must tell me this from the beginning."

But first, he leaned over and poured both of them a full cup of wine. He had a strong need for a drink, just now. Myste laced the fingers of both hands together over her knee, and looked as satisfied as a cat with a jug full of cream in front of her. "Sometimes," she said, with a touch of pardonable smugness, "the person you need to keep an eye on someone isn't a spy, or a tough bully-boy. Sometimes it is *exactly* the kind of middle-aged, dowdy, forgettable little frump that no one looks twice at."

"You aren't dowdy or forgettable," he said without thinking. "Or a frump."

She looked inordinately pleased at that, but didn't interrupt her story. "It didn't take me long to get their books straight, and yes, the innkeeper has been skimming, and yes, he stopped *immediately* when he knew I was there to check on him. So since I was there anyway, both the players and their other staff started coming to me for other little things. You know, the odd letter from home to be read or written, arranging with a goldsmith to put something away for a rainy day, that sort of thing. And

King Norris would come sailing by now and again, vaguely note that I was there, and be off again—and whenever he came by, I always made sheep's eyes at him, which is exactly what he expected. Women throw themselves at him all the time, and if I *hadn't* acted infatuated, he might have suspected something. Well, that was how things stood, right up until last night, when we had an—interesting situation."

"Oh?" Alberich prompted.

"They'd done a reduced-cast play for a private audience in the afternoon, and all the leads had to hurry back to the inn to do the main play that evening," she said, her lenses gleaming. He didn't have to see her eyes to know that there was great satisfaction in them. "So I'm sitting there in the office with folded hands, nothing much to do, and in comes Norris himself and for once, he's *looking* for me. 'Can you make a fair copy of something without knowing the language?' he asks. I gave him a look—"

She tilted her head slightly, and showed Alberich the expression of dazzled infatuation she must have given Norris.

"—and I said, 'Of *course* I can, I'm a clerk! If we stopped to actually read what we're copying, we'd never get half the work done that we do! Eye to hand to paper, and no stopping at the brain, that's us—' And before I can say anything else, he dropped this in front of me." She indicated the packet. "And some paper—if you can believe it—that's even lighter than this is. 'I'm in a hurry,' says he, 'and I haven't time to do this myself. I need *that* transcribed in the smallest hand you can manage onto that paper, then burn the original. And I need it by the time I'm off the stage tonight.' I looked at him like I didn't care so long as the job was for *him*, and didn't ask why. He didn't tell me, he just rushed straight out, and I heard the wardrobe mistress screeching for him, so he must have been late for costuming. The rest is easy enough. I made his copy and tossed the original out the window to Aleirian, who carried it away."

"Good God," he breathed. "I wouldn't have thought of that."

"I didn't," she admitted. "Aleirian did. Anyway, then I kept an ear out to gauge the progress of the play, copied as many pages of the original again in the original size as I could fit in the time left, made them the top sheets in a stack of blanks, and when he got offstage and came for his papers, he saw *that* packet merrily burning away and assumed I'd burned the original the way I was told. He was damned careful, too; he stayed there until all the papers were burned, then broke up the ash until there wasn't a fragment the size of the head of a nail. Then he went off. I assume that he must have gotten the originals at that private performance. And I guess that my copies must have gone out that night, because he just flew out the door with them. It wouldn't have been hard. You could have rolled the lot up and hidden them practically anywhere."

"I can probably find out who and where when we know what is in these," he replied absently, unable to believe his good luck. "What did he do when you gave him the copy, besides watch the papers burn?"

"Well, he made an excuse for hanging about while he made sure the papers were gone by pouring charm all over me until I was practically gagging on it," she replied, a chuckle in her voice. "And I gazed at him adoringly like he expected me to, and hung on his every word, and vowed that if I could ever do something for him again, he had only to ask. He went away never thinking twice about having entrusted me with papers in cipher."

Surely they couldn't be *that* lucky. "You're sure it wasn't some sort of trap—" he said warningly.

"Well, of course anything is possible," she replied. "But he wasn't expecting a Herald, or Aleirian, or, well—Alberich, I know that kind of man. I ran into them all the time when I was a girl and my best friend was the prettiest girl in our quarter." She sighed, and for a moment, that good humor and sparkle faded. "The first time, and even the second and third, that a handsome boy came and poured that kind of charm and flattery all over me, I fell for it—but after three times of being fooled and finding out that they were only being nice to me because they wanted to meet my friend, I became immune to it."

His mouth formed a silent "Oh."

She shrugged. "It's one of those things that plain girls learn, Alberich. You just get used to it after a while. Well, your lad Norris might be one of the best in Valdemar at charming people, but someone like me—" She shook her head. "Actually, he's never encountered someone like me, I suspect, because we *won't* throw ourselves at him; we know better. He'll never even see the plain ones who are on to his little game—they might be at the performances, and they'll certainly admire his acting ability, but so far as lingering on the off chance they'll meet him, it will never happen. So he looked at me and saw a plain, frumpy little mouse with a little mouse's job, who looked at him with eyes of adoration, and figured he knew *exactly* what I was and how he could use me. And best of all, he wouldn't have to actually do more than give me a bit of attention, because someone like me would never, ever expect someone like *him* would want to romance me." The cynical laugh she uttered at that moment made him wince, and he wondered then about the young girl in lenses who'd been tricked three times by manipulative boys. "Oh, no, a crumb of attention to cherish in the darkness of my little closet of a room, that's all he needed to give. I'd be his slave forever, and never demand anything out of him."

"Myste—" He swallowed. "I apologize."

She started, and stared at him. "For what?" she asked.

"For people like him." He shook his head. "I am sorry."

She laughed again, but this time the humor was back in her voice. "Good gods, Alberich, don't be. Trust me, the injuries to my heart, such as they were, scabbed over a long time ago, and the scar is a useful reminder. If I *hadn't* been hurt and used by all those heartless boys back in the day, I'd never have been able to see right through your lad Norris, would I? So don't think I'm living with a tragic past! Good gods, compared to at least half of the others that have gone through these walls, it's a teacup tragedy at worst, and a farce at best." She winked at him. "Besides, I saw my pretty best friend not long ago. She's tripled in size, she's had a baby a year, and her handsome husband chases tavern girls. Have pity for her, not me."

"Ah." He felt a good deal better. At least she wasn't likely to reject him out of hand if—

"Besides," she chuckled again, "it gives me an appreciation for men who blurt out 'you're not a frump,' and not some carefully rehearsed speech, who say it without even *thinking* about it, and who then go on to apologize for the vagaries of their sex."

"Ah—" He felt his face burning. "Er—"

"I think you might be sitting too near the fire," was all she said then. "Now, about dinner? We shouldn't let it get cold."

Lord Orthallen had asked, had *requested,* in writing, an informal meeting with Selenay. She had invited him to dinner, in her own suite. Not alone, of course; they'd be surrounded by servants, but it would certainly be informal. She was intensely curious; the note had a certain apologetic tone to it that she couldn't quite put her finger on.

The first course arrived, and was complimented, without her curiosity being satisfied. She sipped her wine as the second course was plated and served. She felt she could afford to be patient.

"My dear Selenay," said Lord Orthallen at last, over the third course. "I have done you a grave disservice."

She motioned to a page to refill his wineglass. "Yes, my lord," she said somberly, "I think you have." She was not going to pretend that she did not know exactly what he was talking about. *He* had been the prime instigator of that wretched plot to get her married off, and she was not in the least happy about it, and what was more, she intended for him to know it.

He sighed, and grimaced a little. "In my own defense, I was trying to protect Valdemar from being in the precarious position of having no Heir. But I am afraid—truly and sincerely, Selenay, I *was* afraid, I was dreadfully afraid, and I still am. I never dreamed we would be in this position. Sendar should have been King for decades yet. You are a very young woman, and we have just fought a hideous war—"

"And Valdemar needs to look strong, not vulnerable, I know, Orthallen," she replied with spirit, and with some heat. "But didn't it occur to you that rushing me into a marriage is going to do the very opposite of making us look strong? *Why* would I suddenly wed the first candidate presented to me, if I wasn't desperate? I might as well send out letters to every likely ally we have, saying that I'm up for sale to the highest bidder!" She frowned at him, and he looked pained.

"I know, I know," Orthallen replied, flushing. "And if I had possessed any sensitivity or common sense where you are concerned, I would have come directly to you, rather than laying it all out in front of the Council—"

"So it *was* your idea." Selenay gave him a hint of the anger she felt in her gaze. She'd been certain it was all along, as had some of the others, but now, at last, he had admitted it.

"To my shame." He nodded. "Not that the men we presented are not fine—"

"My lord," she said, interrupting him with exasperation as well as a feeling of real depression, "although I would give a very great deal to be like other young ladies and at least be able to *dream* of finding a great romantic love, I am not, and I know it." She heard her own voice retaining its steady, reasonable tone, despite the lump in her throat, and felt a moment of pride at her own self-control. "I am Queen, and when I wed—which I must, for the people would not accept an Heir born out of wedlock—it is for Valdemar, not myself. But my father *did* find a lady who suited him well enough that he never remarried, and I at least hope to be able to find a friend, if not a lover. I will not find such a Consort by being rushed into an imprudent marriage. And I cannot find one if I have twelve dozen potential husbands shoved at me every time I turn about!"

Orthallen flushed again. "Sendar might not have been in love with your mother when they agreed to marry," he said quietly, "but he came to love her, deeply, and she him. And they were great, good friends before they wed."

She spread her hands wide, ignoring the fork in one of them. "So you see that I am right."

"Indeed, I do see," he agreed. "And I was wrong, very wrong. I was just afraid that—" he laughed, self-consciously, "—well, there are a number of fine young foreign princes out there, younger sons, whose fathers would be very happy to cement an advantageous alliance with us. Perhaps too advantageous. Especially if one of them managed to make you infatuated with him. My thought was that—Well, at the least, we could keep your interest here at home."

She sniffed. He took the hint. "Well, you have given me every reason to agree with your point of view, and I believe you have convinced me. I will approach my fellow Councilors and suggest that the subject should be tabled for the foreseeable future—and I will insist that our Queen is wise enough to choose her own future husband *without* our help."

She exhaled a long sigh of genuine relief. "And I thank you for that, Orthallen. You cannot know just how much easier that makes me feel."

"Oh, perhaps I do, a little," he replied genially. "Your father was none too pleased at the prospect himself, and he was not even King when the idea of marriage was first broached to him."

As the meal progressed, Orthallen first told her about her father's reluctant search for a prospective bride, and how he had eventually settled on her mother when after a month went by *without* her throwing herself at his feet, he asked her why—or rather, why not. After all, every other young woman of rank and spirit had...

"And she told him that she would, on the whole, prefer to be his sister than his wife!" Orthallen laughed, shaking his head. "And when he asked her why, she told him that she had more desire for his library than for him!"

All this was new to Selenay; she stared at him, not quite believing it. "And what did he say?"

"That *he* would rather at least have someone he could talk to, and that anyone who wanted his books that badly was someone who could hold an interesting conversation." Orthallen smiled. "She certainly intrigued him; and I think most of what intrigued him at first was that she wasn't *trying* to intrigue him, she really felt that way. She was inordinately shy, you know. And then, when she proposed to him, she made him agree that she would participate as little as possible in Court life before she'd even entertain the merest idea of marriage with him."

"But she was happy?" Selenay felt she had to know.

"Oh, very," Orthallen assured her. "And by the end of a year of marriage, as much in love with Sendar as any woman could be. And he with her. Remarkable, really. Usually the most one can expect from a marriage of state is an easy partnership—a business relationship, of a kind."

Her heart sank a little at that, and Selenay couldn't help wondering if that was what she was fated to have. And she changed the subject.

Nevertheless, before the dinner was half over, she found that she had confided a great deal in Lord Orthallen, and not the least of those confidences involved her own, barely-articulate wishes for— well—romance.

She was rather surprised at herself for spilling so much into his willing ears, and even more surprised when he seemed sympathetic and not at all dismissive.

:He's certainly easier to talk to than Talamir,: she said to Caryo, after he'd gone.

:On that subject, a doorpost would be easier to talk to than Talamir,: Caryo replied sadly. *:At least Orthallen is well rooted in the here-and-now, enough to know that a young woman, Queen though she is, deserves to at least be able to dream. Poor Talamir.:*

Poor Talamir, indeed. But at least now, and with Caryo's tacit approval, Selenay had someone she could confide in.

And to her mild surprise, she found that it helped, a little.

Enough that she went to sleep that night, for the first time since the end of the Wars, without first lying awake for a candlemark staring into the darkness.

1 1

Something teased at the back of Selenay's mind for the next several days, making her feel restless, full of nervous energy. Perhaps it was the season; spring was *almost* upon them, the early crocuses were already pushing their way up through the flower beds, the last of the snow was gone, the really wretched end-of-winter rains had begun, and now the days were long enough to make you believe that winter might actually end, after all. The air still felt raw, and other than the optimistic crocuses there was no sign of anything growing, but there were moments when the sun felt warm as a hand on the cheek, and when there was a hint of green-scent in the wind.

Winter would end. Spring would come, and after it, summer, and a year would have gone by without her father. Time, they said, was a great healer. Some of her depression eased a little more with the lengthening days, certainly. Maybe it was due to the season, maybe she was just getting used to Sendar not being there anymore; there was no longer the blow to the heart when she entered the Throne Room and did not see him there, nor quite the feeling of emptiness when she took what had been *his* chair at the Council meetings. Not all of it—oh, by no means. But enough that she was sleeping the night through, and not waking up to weep in the darkness.

Sometimes she even slept until her maids woke her, and it was a deep and thankfully dreamless sleep.

Orthallen was as good as his word. At the next meeting of the Full Council, before it was called officially into session, he asked for a moment to address the group personally. "This is not Council business, precisely," he said. "But it is something that I would like the Council to hear."

They all looked at Selenay; she nodded. The Seneschal called the meeting to order, and gestured to Orthallen. And when he had the silent regard of everyone around the table, he cleared his throat awkwardly, which was not like him at all. That alone got him the full and alert attention of everyone sitting there.

"My lords, my ladies, I believe that we have been pressing the Queen on an issue that really has no urgency at all," he said, looking embarrassed. "And by that, I mean the issue of her choosing a spouse immediately. After due consideration, and more thought, I believe we have been overly hasty."

Selenay inclined her head, accepting what he had said without saying a word herself. This was not the time to add her own thoughts. She wanted Orthallen to explain it all to the rest of the Council in his own words. Though there was one thing that struck her as odd, and that was the phrasing Orthallen had used. Spouse was a peculiar choice of word, when it came to the Queen of Valdemar. Why not say Consort, which was the traditional title if the ruler was the Queen, and the husband was not a Herald?

Perhaps it was because she had shown no real interest in any of the Heralds, but Orthallen did not want to make that too obvious. Now if she'd had a candidate among the Heralds, she'd have made her choice known immediately. It was a given that unless her husband was also a Herald, he could never be King and co-ruler. But still—given that none of the candidates *were* Heralds, why not just say 'Consort?'

Maybe it was just that Orthallen was keeping the options open in their minds, eliminating neither the possibility of Consort nor King. *It's been a long time since Valdemar had a Queen. Maybe it's just slipped their mind that no husband of mine can rule unless he's a Herald.* It might be just as well not to remind those of the Council who had forgotten that fact.

"It should be obvious to all of us by this time, that while the Queen is a *young* woman, she is not only capable, she is wise enough to know when she needs advice and guidance. She could lawfully have replaced all of us, and has not, because she trusts us as her father trusted us, and believes that we, who were her father's advisers, are capable in ourselves." He coughed, as a murmur went around the table. "We may be flailing about in the wake of our loss and casting for solutions to situations that are not actually problems."

Selenay exchanged looks with the other Heralds on the Council: Kyril, the Seneschal's Herald, Elcarth, and Talamir. Although Orthallen had included the rest of the Councilors in this "admission," it was a signal departure for him to admit to making a mistake.

And they *had* been flailing about, as if she herself was a problem, before there had been any evidence of anything of the sort!

Orthallen cleared his throat again, and continued, reluctantly. She held her breath. Was he? Was he going to admit it? "Furthermore, by seeming to cast about frantically for a suitable candidate, we may be giving an impression of weakness to those who do not wish us well. As if we do not trust our Queen and our own ability to carry on in the absence of her father. We could be giving the same impression as a herd of sheep, milling about anxiously without a shepherd, and I do not need to tell you that there are wolves about."

Another murmur, and Selenay stifled a smile, hearing Orthallen borrowing so heavily from her own argument. *He did. He admitted I'm right. I may only get apologies from him in private, but at least he's admitting that I'm right in public.* It was a triumph, but she was not going to gloat over it.

"I know that I was the one pressing most eagerly for such a wedding— or betrothal, at least—but I should like to urge that we drop the subject for now." He shrugged, and no few of the other Councilors looked as embarrassed as he did.

"If you recommend so, Orthallen," Lord Gartheser said hesitantly. "You know more about foreign affairs than the rest of us do."

"I think it would be the wisest course." And in that moment, Orthallen all but said, *I was wrong.* But he went on quickly, making an attempt to regain the face he had lost. "In all events, having the Queen so blatantly unattached can also work to our benefit. There are a number of young men of rank, of valuable connection—princes, even—in other lands, who are also unattached. No doubt, their rulers will soon see that there is a way to bring Valdemar into close alliance by the closest of ties. So let us table this search for now, and get on with the business of the realm."

Nods all around the table, a few reluctant—well, not surprising that the oldest Councilors were less than comfortable about a *Queen*, and a young one at that, and the oldest men were the ones least inclined to trust her to rule alone. *Only time will cure that*, she decided. *Time—or perhaps a change of Councilors.* It wouldn't hurt for the Bardic and Healer representatives to retire, for instance. It would be better if there were more women on the Council. *A woman who has made her own way in the world will be more inclined to see me as a leader and less as someone needing to be led.* Perhaps she should also add an entirely new seat or two. Someone from one of the newer Guilds, perhaps? To have more people whose wealth was self-made rather than inherited could be of real benefit.

Orthallen moved on to some dispute between the Guilds of the

Mercers and the Weavers while Selenay's thoughts were elsewhere. She quickly brought her own attention to bear on the situation; it would not be a good idea to undo all of Orthallen's work by seeming to be lost in other thoughts. She did notice that several of the Councilors actually waited to hear her opinion before voicing theirs, which was a pleasant change. The rest of the meeting proceeded in the same atmosphere, and if she felt a momentary resentment that she'd had to get Orthallen's "approval" before being granted the respect she was due, at least now she had that respect. And though it might be temporary, having gotten it once, it would be easier to regain it.

But once the meeting was over, as she and she and her escort of Guards and ladies wound their way back to her quarters, she allowed her thoughts to tend in other directions. Orthallen's comment about foreign princes—*that* struck a chord, and told her that *that* was what had been nagging at her all this time, since the Councilor had first voiced that idea over dinner.

What foreign princes? Certainly there had been no hints of such a possibility before now. No envoys had presented themselves, no inquiries had been voiced via ambassadors.

But perhaps they had all been waiting until her year of mourning was over. That would only be appropriate, really.

Assuming there are such mythical creatures, she told herself, as she entered the door to her suite, and the Guards took up their stations outside.

But they might not be mythical—

Surely, though, if there were such young men wandering about unpartnered, she would be aware of them. Granted, her knowledge of highborn families outside of Valdemar was sketchy to say the least, but the only royal that she knew of was the King of Hardorn, and *he* had married an allegedly lissome young creature out of his own Court a little more than a year ago.

But would Orthallen have mentioned the possibility twice if it didn't exist?

So just what foreign princes *were* there, out there? She dismissed her ladies, and selected a gown to be worn at dinner while her maids drew a hot bath.

Did the Shin'a'in have princes? She couldn't remember anything of the sort. *:Caryo, is there such a thing as a Shin'a'in prince?:*

:I've never heard of one.: Caryo sounded surprised. *:I think they don't have things like Kings and Princes. I think they are an alliance of Clans.:*

That tallied with the little that Selenay recalled, but perhaps some of the Clans were big enough that their Chiefs would qualify as princes. There were a great many Shin'a'in after all. It was an—*interesting* possibility.

She stepped into the bath that had been prepared for her, and chased the maids away while she soaked. As she relaxed in the hot lavender-scented water, she had a silly little vision of a strong, wild warrior, raven hair down to his waist, riding into Haven dressed in black furs and leathers, astride—bareback, of course—a horse as black as his hair. And wouldn't that make a pretty picture, the two of them riding together, she all in Whites on Caryo, he on his midnight steed…

She gave herself a mental shake. Ridiculous, of course; what Shin'a'in nomad would ever leave the Plains, much less do so with the intention of marrying a foreign, civilized queen? Besides, even if he came here looking for her, he wouldn't stay. The Shin'a'in never stayed away from the Plains for long, and *she* could scarcely leave Valdemar. What would the Shin'a'in get out of such a marriage, anyway? Valdemar was too far from the Plains for there to be any advantage in an alliance at all. No, no, no—too easy to burst that particular bubble of illusion.

But who else did that leave? Rethwellan? Were there unmarried princes in Rethwellan? If there were, well, they at least shared a border with Valdemar, and it would be an advantage to them to have such an alliance, if only for trade advantages. Menmellith? Menmellith was a principality of Rethwellan, but she couldn't really recall anything at all about their ruling family. Not Karse, of course—

Could there be interest as far away as Jkatha or Cee-jay, which were just names on a map to her? Surely not; Valdemar didn't even trade directly that far away, so why would any stray princeling come wandering up here?

But there might be places she had never heard of. To the North—well, Iftel was out of the question; no one ever came past their borders except a few favored traders who were remarkably close-mouthed about the place.

The bath was cooling; time to finish and get out, before someone came in here to scrub her. Stupid; she'd bathed herself for the last fourteen years and more, so what was it about being a Queen that rendered her incapable of bathing herself now?

But the splashing as she emerged from the bath seemed to be some sort of signal that caused maids to swarm around her with towels and robes and scents and lotions. And for once, involved in her own thoughts, she let them fuss over her.

Once she was properly clothed in a lounging robe, they messed about with her hair while she continued her ruminations. North, other than Iftel, were the barbarians above the Forest of Sorrows. Surely not. *Surely not.* The idea of a greasy, violent, fur-clad brute was even more repulsive than some of the octogenarians the Council had suggested.

Were there little secretive kingdoms out in the West, in the Pelagiris Forest or past it? It was possible. There were certainly *people* out there, and not just the halfmythical Hawkbrothers. There were entire villages that looked to the Hawkbrothers for protection, so maybe there were kingdoms in the West. But still—what possible advantage could they have in an alliance with Valdemar? Nothing that she could imagine.

Or were there men in other kingdoms who were like the Great Dukes of Valdemar, who held enough power that they qualified as princes? There might well be; she hadn't had time to study such things. In such a case, for a younger son, there would be a great deal of prestige and advantage in marrying a Queen, even if it left the young man as nothing more than a Consort without ruling powers. His children would rule, if they were Chosen, and that might be enough. Separate trade agreements could be made with the family, and *that* might be enough. There was a great deal of difference between royal marrying royal, and royal stooping to wed a rank below hers. In that case, the advantages to be gained were almost all on the side of the lower rank.

:Surely there's something in the archives of letters from ambassadors and trade envoys,: Caryo said helpfully. *:Or Seneschal's Herald Kyril will know where to look. I should think that someone would know if we might expect a spate of foreign suitors.:*

A foreign prince—or more than one—the idea gave her a kind of fluttery feeling of excitement inside. Oh, they might well all be as impossible or even repulsive as the candidates she'd been presented with so far, but—at least they would be someone different.

And surely one would be older than an adolescent and younger than a graybeard. Maybe even handsome—though she wouldn't necessarily care, as long as he wasn't a monster. Someone she didn't know, that she couldn't predict, someone with entirely new ways and manners. Even if she didn't want to marry him, it would be interesting to have him in her Court.

It would be more than interesting—it would be fascinating! She licked her lips, and hardly noticed the maids tugging at her hair.

I mustn't get my hopes up, she told herself. *There might not be any such thing. If they exist, they might all be old. Or feeble-minded. Or already married.* She shuddered involuntarily, as she realized that she'd had a narrow escape without realizing it. If King Alessandar *hadn't* gotten wedded to his sweet young thing—if he'd still been alone—

Well, he would not have let the opportunity to propose slip past, no matter how many sweet young things were in his Court. And the Council would *never* have allowed her to reject his suit. Hardorn and Valdemar had been allies for so very long that there had even been cases of Heralds coming to the rescue of Hardornans in the past. Even Herald Vanyel had done so; that was how he earned his title of "Demonsbane." There would have been no way to gracefully turn down such a proposal.

Bright Havens, what a narrow escape!

She suddenly needed to *know*, and know with certainty, if there really was a possibility of a foreign suitor.

I have to know. And I truly have to know if there are any unwedded Alessandars just waiting for my year of mourning to be over—

Well, there was one person to ask, and it wasn't Herald Kyril, however knowledgeable Kyril might be. No, Orthallen would be the one to ask. After all, he was the one who had brought it all up in the first place. If there had been such a position in her Council as Foreign Minister, he surely would have been the one to fill it; his knowledge of the lands outside of Valdemar was as exacting as hers was vague.

A foreign prince… An easy thought to kick off daydreams, and it was a good thing that she was safely away in her own suite where no one would notice if her attention wandered.

When the maids were finished with her, she chased them out, all but one, whom she sent off with a note to Orthallen. They would discuss this tonight, after her dinner with the Court, for certain.

Alberich had a meeting of his own after dinner, and he had, with some regret, decided against inviting Myste to share it. No, there could only be one invitee to this "gathering," and it had to be the Queen's Own.

Talamir was, for once, very much alert and in the *here and now* as he examined the documents that Myste had purloined. Alberich had been reluctant to let them out of the salle; he was even more reluctant to let them out of his sight. Fortunately for all concerned, Talamir had no trouble in getting about, though he was still—well—fragile.

It was hard on a man to have been through all that Talamir had— dying and being dragged back to life again must have been unthinkably grim. At Talamir's age, it had been more that, and Alberich was still surprised that he was reasonably sane afterward. In a way, he was doing far better than anyone had any right to expect.

:Yes, he's fragile, rather than frail,: Kantor agreed. *:And a good half of that is mental, I'd say.:*

Except when something that required all of his attention was before him. Then he was the old Talamir again. It was the old Talamir that had appeared, unescorted, at the door of Alberich's rooms. It was the old Talamir, alert and in possession of all of his wits and wiles, who heard him out, and examined the documents with great care. Alberich hoped—wildly, he knew, but stranger things had happened—that Talamir would recognize the cipher, even be able to read it a little. The odds were very much against it, but—well, ciphers and secret messages were not part of the training of a Karsite Cadet, and the denizens of the vile dens down near Exile's Gate that he usually trafficked with were barely literate. Asking them to manage a cipher would be like asking a pig to dance on a tightrope.

"Well," the Queen's Own said, putting the pages down carefully. "I don't know enough about ciphers to make any sense of this. In fact, there's something we should consider, and that's the possibility that this might not even be in Valdemaran."

Curses. Oh, well.

"Actually," Alberich said with extreme reluctance, "it probably is not. If consider we do that it was intended for someone in another land, in that language it would be. Which could be anything."

"So we have two puzzles to crack; the cipher itself, and which language it's in. Still—" Talamir rested his index finger along his upper lip, his eyes opaque with thought. "Still, we're very much further on than we were before. If someone is going to this extreme to send messages in cipher, I think we can be pretty certain it isn't just Guild secrets or messages to a mistress. I will need to take these to an expert, I think."

"I should, the originals prefer to keep here," Alberich ventured, wondering how Talamir would take that. "Evidence, they may become."

"Oh, certainly!" Talamir waved his hand dismissively, as if the idea of taking the originals was out of the question. "I would rather you did, too. Myste can make copies for me to give to—" He hesitated a moment. "Well, forgive me, if I just tell you it is a fellow whose hobby is ciphers, one I've taken such problems to before this. Odd little chap, but solid and true, and you'd be surprised if you knew who he was. I won't tell you his name, though, if you don't mind."

"Safer for *him*, if you do not," Alberich agreed. "Secrets are secrets between two, in danger between three, and often lost between more than three."

Talamir nodded, but with an air of assurance that he had been certain that Alberich would understand before he'd asked the question.

"And, if you don't mind my saying it, it would be safer for Myste if she can get away from those actors," Talamir replied. "But I doubt either of us could persuade her."

"Of that, you may be sure," Alberich sighed, having spent several marks fruitlessly attempting to persuade her to do just that. *"If I leave now, they'll be suspicious, and you'll never get a chance to follow Norris and find out who he's meeting!"* she'd said, which, alas, was true enough. *"And if he trusted me once, he'll likely trust me again. Think of what else I could get! What if he really runs out of time some day, and asks me to do the ciphering!"* "More of these, she hopes to obtain," he added.

"Well, the more samples, the better. If they change the cipher key, my man will spot that much right off." Talamir pushed the papers across the table to Alberich. "Put those somewhere safe, and I'll come and get the copy—"

"Tomorrow, Myste says," Alberich began. "Two copies—"

Talamir smiled. "Good! Then instead of my coming alone, let's have a little get-together with Jadus, and Crathach, too. With the originals hidden, you should be all right bringing the copies up to the Collegium— we can meet in Jadus' rooms. No one would see anything amiss in that, and you can safely give me the copies then. Clandestinely, if you like. Or just come along to my rooms to 'remind me' of our gathering, and pass me the copies then."

"That is the best plan. And I should like to see the others. Jadus is—I have not seen much of him—" Alberich said, feeling guilty.

"Because it isn't easy, learning to get about on one leg, and once he got his strength back, he's been working hard at it," Talamir replied. "He hasn't had much time to spare for any of us but Crathach, my friend, but I think he's well on the road to feeling useful again. He won't be doing any dancing, but there'll be a vacancy for a Herald in the Courts of Justice in Haven, and he'll do well there."

Alberich was relieved; Jadus probably would do well there, for his sound common sense if nothing else, and his soft ways would put frightened people at their ease. But when the time came for stern justice,

Jadus was not a man to be put off by anything, or anyone.

"Tomorrow night, then," Alberich agreed, and gathered up the papers.

Talamir stood. "I don't want to see where you put them, so I'll take my leave now." He glanced at the stained-glass window, and raised an eyebrow. "Now I see why you put that bit of artwork in. Or one reason, anyway."

"Yes. We cannot be watched, through such a thing," Alberich replied.

"Hmm. And when I think of all the people who said you were the last person to put in Dethor's shoes…"

"Myself, included," Alberich replied. Talamir gave him a penetrating look, then shrugged.

"I wouldn't have picked Myste as a spy either," he said. "Good night, Weaponsmaster."

When he was gone, Alberich folded the papers into their original packet, and felt carefully under the table until he found the catch that released a little drawer inside one of the thick legs. Dethor had shown it to him, so he was reasonably sure that no one else knew about it. There were hiding places like this all over the private quarters of the salle, but this was the only one that he could use without getting up. Probably there was no one out there trying to make sense of the shadows on the other side of the colored glass, but just in case there was, there would be no way to tell that Alberich had hidden something. It only looked as if he was reaching for his drink.

And there was another set of papers on the tabletop, just in case the shadows had betrayed that Talamir had been looking at papers. This was a report about bandit activity along the Karsite Border, something that Alberich could reasonably have an interest and expertise in. If someone came to the salle in the next mark or so, Alberich would take great pains to mention that report. It wasn't just that he was taking precautions about the papers Myste had stolen, he was protecting *himself.* There were a great many people in Court circles who distrusted "the Karsite," besides those who had no reason to love him because he did not cosset their children. Sometimes he grew very tired of it all.

Layers upon layers; he envied Jadus and Glcarth and all the others who didn't have to live their lives weaving webs of subterfuge. He wished—

Well, it didn't matter what he wished. He would, as a gambling friend of his had often said, play out the cards he had been dealt.

Complications, complications.

"My life is full of complications," he said aloud. There was no answer. Vkandis knew it was true enough.

Another complication: Myste herself. She'd been on his mind all day. There had been *no* doubt in his mind that Myste had been discreetly flirting with him last night. And he'd liked it. He'd even tried a little clumsy flirting back—

:Not as clumsy as you think,: Kantor put in. *:I was pleasantly surprised. You've got a light touch, when you care to use it.:*

He felt himself blushing, but it was at least partly with pleasure. But what would the other Heralds think of this, if they realized that she and he were attracted to one another?

:If they bothered to take any notice, they'll wait to see if you mind teasing, then give you both a bit of a word about it, now and again,: Kantor told him. *:Other than that, they'd probably begin a betting pool as to when the two of you decided to stop flirting and get down to something serious.:*

:Serious—: he ventured.

:Bedding,: Kantor said bluntly.

Alberich bit his tongue. Quite by accident—Kantor had startled him. *:But—:*

:Sorry. Didn't mean to shock you. But if this gets past flirting, Myste is going to expect it to go there. Heralds are—well, by the standards of a Karsite, they're flagrantly immoral and utterly hedonistic when it comes to the ways of man with maid. Not that she is. Myste, I mean. She's not a maid.:

Maybe he should have been shocked, but he wasn't. Startled, yes, but not shocked. Well, not that Myste wasn't a maid, anyway.

In fact, he was relieved. It had been a long time since he'd—well— and then it had been someone he'd paid. He didn't have any practice in the more polite forms of congress, and he was probably going to step on his own feet more than once if things—got past flirting. And the ache in certain parts of him let him know in no uncertain terms that his *body* certainly wanted it to get past flirting. *Far* past flirting.

As for how she came to be not a maid, well that was her business.

Unless she made it his. And then it was even more her business…

:Good man. Slow and cautious. She's in no hurry and neither should you be.:

:As long as she doesn't run in terror from my face,: he said dryly, *:I doubt there is anything else about me that cows her. Underneath, that woman is someone that would appall people if they only knew her. There are things she will not compromise on. And things that she would kill over, if it came to that.:*

Which was, of course, how she was getting away with purloining secrets out from under the very noses of the owners, and with their cooperation. At some point, perhaps in that last battle, Myste had found, or gotten, her courage. Now he doubted that anything could effectively stand in her way if she believed in or wanted something badly enough.

Like me—?

He sat firmly on *that* thought and crammed it back into the little mental cupboard it had come out of.

Back to business. *:What do you Companions know about ciphers?:* he asked. After all, better to cover all possible avenues with this one.

:Nothing much,: Kantor said with regret. *:Nobody here at the Collegium for sure, and I think not anybody alive. Just because we're good at Mindspeech doesn't mean we're good at everything. Working ciphers takes a particular kind of mind—the kind that can see patterns where the rest of us would see only chaos.:*

Well, he'd had to ask. *:Should I just leave all this to Talamir, then?:*

:He knows more about who to trust in this than you do. I think I know who he'll be taking the papers to, and no one is safer.:

Well, that was a dismissal if he had ever heard one. Time to stop worrying about that end of the situation, and think about the part he could do something about.

Such as discovering just who, besides young Lord Devlin, his contact in the Court, Norris was meeting.

1 2

It was spring, at long last, and the gardens were bursting with greenery and blossoms, as if to make up for last year's sorrowful season. With every breeze, the ornamental cherries carpeted the ground beneath their boughs with pink and white petals; the air was full of a hundred different scents. Kingdom business be hanged; Selenay was going to walk in her gardens before the season ripened any further into summer.

So she told the Seneschal at their morning meeting over breakfast that she wanted him to shorten the usual afternoon audiences by half.

"If I stay within walls for much longer I'm going to shred something," she said a little crossly, expecting him to object. "I'm tired of never seeing the sun except through windows, and I am exceedingly tired of hearing *people whining*. I would like to hear birds for a change, and if I must hear voices, I would prefer it to be the voices of people who are not complaining to me, at least for a candlemark or two."

But he only nodded his graying head, and regarded her kindly. "If Your Majesty will recall," he told her, "your father was exactly the same, in the spring."

And now that he had reminded her, she *did* remember it, but not as a memory of him ordering shorter audiences, but as seeing him in the gardens every fine afternoon, and walking there with two or three friends in the evening, too. But she—

I was taking classes, or practicing, and he'd always done that, every spring, so it never struck me as odd, she decided. *I didn't know then that the business of government takes up so much time, and that he must have been stealing time from it for a little while.*

Or perhaps, it wasn't that he had been stealing time at all, though she would certainly have to, and the only place where she felt she could in good conscience take it was from the Audiences. Now that she thought about it, her father had definitely had more "leisure" time than she seemed to.

But then, he had been King for all of her life (obviously) so he'd had some practice at it. Maybe it would get easier as she went along; perhaps the more practiced she became, the less of *her* time it would take… perhaps, some day, she would have some candlemarks of leisure for herself.

She felt guilty; then decided that feeling guilty was stupid. If she was ready to rip someone's throat out now, how would she be *without* taking some time, at last, for herself? A pox on that. Bridges were not going to fall down, nor buildings collapse, because she walked in her garden and played at games a little while with her ladies.

"Well, then schedule fewer petitioners for the foreseeable future," she ordered, adding, "if you please."

Surely some of those people can manage to sort out their troubles by themselves.

"Certainly, Majesty," the Seneschal said, with a little smile. "If Your Majesty will forgive my voicing my own opinion, you are just a trifle too accessible. Restricting your availability will make people think before they request an audience for which they might have to wait several days."

She blinked, then nodded. And here she had thought he was going to disapprove! But the prospect of a simple walk in her gardens was enough to elevate her spirits for the entire morning, even though the Exchequer occupied her for most of that time with budget and tax allotments. Just the simple knowledge that she *was* going to escape his stuffy little office was enough to set her to work with more energy than she'd had in weeks for such things.

And the audiences did not seem as tedious either. And when the Seneschal announced that she would not be seeing any more petitioners that day, it was all she could do to keep from leaping up out of the throne and flying out the Privy Door behind the dais to get to her chambers and out of her robes of state.

She changed into a simple, split-skirt gown without calling for her maids, collected a ball and racquets, then gathered up her rather startled ladies-in-waiting, and bustled them all down the hall like a goose-girl hurrying her geese to the pond.

And when they were out into the garden, she acted like a child newly freed from lessons, dropping every bit of her dignity to lead them all in a game of "tag," then taking each of them on in turn at racquets. In fact, she wore some of them out with her energy, until they all begged, laughing, for a moment of rest.

Which she graciously gave them. And while they sprawled on the lawn, or lounged on benches, she walked alone among the flower beds. She hadn't intended to actually pick any flowers, but this spring there was a superabundance of blossoms, and she found herself taking one here, one there, not deliberately selecting anything, just picking them from places where the blooms seemed crowded or scents were especially intoxicating. *I'll put them in my bedroom,* she decided, feeling an unaccustomed glee. *Just stick them all in a vase full of water. No formal flower arranging, no careful selection of "harmonious colors." The kind of bouquet—no, bunch of flowers!—I used to pick for myself as a child!*

She didn't—thank goodness—have to think twice about wandering about here alone either. It was safe enough for her to be unguarded here in the Queen's Garden. There were Royal Guards all around the grounds, and the grounds themselves were walled off, of course. No one could come here who wasn't a member of the Court or Collegia, and it was a matter of etiquette not to invade the Queen's Garden when the Queen was in it unless you were specifically invited.

So she was a little surprised to look up from picking another bloom and see the Rethwellan Ambassador, followed at a slight distance by a young man she did not recognize, coming toward her on the path.

He dropped to one knee when he reached her, and she automatically extended her hand for him to kiss, then gave it a slight tug, indicating that he should rise.

"Ambassador Brenthalarian, whatever is it that brings you here?" she asked. "I hope you aren't going to trouble my afternoon with a problem—"

"Nothing of the sort, Majesty," the Ambassador said smoothly. "Indeed, I only wished to inquire if your Majesty would be willing to receive King Megrarthon's second son, Prince Karathanelan. He has come bringing His Majesty's belated personal condolences, for you have already had His Majesty's official ones."

"Yes, I recall," she replied, looking at him with a feeling of interest tinged with excitement. So—here was her answer to the question "what foreign princes were there?" before she had even asked anyone about it. A foreign prince, from Rethwellan! Princes did *not* travel abroad unless they had very compelling reasons for doing so…

She cast a surreptitious glance at the young man who waited just out of earshot, and felt another thrill, this time of pleasure. He was handsome. *Very* handsome. His coloring was an intriguing mixture—dark chestnut hair, quite curly and almost shoulder length, and blue eyes that were a lighter color than her own, the color of a sky with a thin, high haze of cloud over it. He had a long nose, high cheekbones, and a narrow face with a cleft chin. He looked—

:Like centuries of inbreeding,: Caryo said sardonically.

:Oh, hush, silly!: she replied keeping a watch on him out of the corner of her eye. *:What he looks like is not like a Valdemaran, which is a refreshing change. I think he's lovely.:*

"When could the Prince come to Court, do you think?" she asked, pretending that she had not already guessed that the Prince was right here in her own garden. The Ambassador knew very well that she knew, and so did the Prince, but greeting him straightaway would spoil the game. And it was likely to be a very amusing little game. *Surely this is one of the "foreign princes" that Orthallen was talking about!* "I would, of course, be delighted to receive him at any time."

"Then in that case, gracious lady, let the Prince prevail upon your noble nature and present himself!" the young man said, flinging himself at her feet in the most romantic posture possible. "My curiosity brought me here, but my heart will not allow me to remain outside of your regard for a single moment more!" He seized her hand and kissed it, and she flushed with pleasure. He spoke very good Valdemaran, with scarcely a trace of accent.

"Then, welcome, Prince Karathanelan," she said, tugging his hand. He took the hint and rose gracefully. "How could I be less than gracious enough to welcome you when confronted with such a gallant gentleman?"

She was trying to be queenly and dignified, but she felt her flush turning into a blush. He gave her a sidelong glance and smiled. "You are as gracious as you are beautiful, Queen Selenay," the Prince replied. "Will you permit me to conduct you back to your ladies?"

"With pleasure," she said. And now it was the Rethwellan Ambassador's turn to smile.

The Prince offered his arm; she took it. The first play of the game was over, and it had been *very* pleasant. Selenay could hardly wait to see what the next move would be.

One of the most difficult things Alberich had ever done was to put that cipher out of his mind and concentrate on the rest of his duties. And yet, there was nothing he could *do* about the message except to guard the original. He'd sealed the panel of its hiding place shut to make certain that it wouldn't be tampered with, and short of locking it in a strongbox and burying the strongbox under the floor of his room, he couldn't make it any safer. So at this point, there was nothing *he* could do about it. No man could be an expert at all things, and it was a bit late in his life to begin studying ciphers.

Instead, he went on with his own double life. He taught his students, and drilled those Heralds and Guards who came to him for extra tutoring and practice by day. And when his work for the day was over, and everyone assumed he was resting in his own quarters, he went out into the city by night in one of his assumed personae.

There was one distinct improvement in his clandestine tasks, however, and that was that the City Guard and constabulary were back up to full strength. He no longer needed to ferret out ordinary criminals; they had their *own* agents for that again. In fact, he knew one or two City Guards who did such things by sight, and they knew him. If he spotted them in one of his haunts of a night, he would move on to a different spot, knowing that they were probably on the trail of something or someone, and the very best thing he could do would be to get out of their way. There was, after all, no point in spoiling someone else's hunt, and too many hunters in one spot sometimes made the "game" shy of being around.

And he suspected that they did the same, on seeing him.

At any rate, with the Tedrel Wars over and Karse busy with its own internal problems, the market for information on Valdemar's strengths and weaknesses had dried up somewhat. He also suspected that the market for information of interest *to* Valdemar was not what it had been. For now, anyway, there just was not as much trafficking in that sort of thing going on. Now the highest prices were being paid for more mundane information—usually having to do with who was in possession of what valuable goods, and how strongly a treasure was guarded, and so on. The most interesting trafficking he saw now was the manufacture of new identities, and he had the strong suspicion that the people who were buying these identities had once called themselves "Tedrels." How they managed to get as far north as Haven he could not imagine; even he hadn't done it without having a Companion. The journeys must have been terrifying. He was not, however, concerned. Selenay was in no danger from them; there were no Tedrel leaders for her to be taken to as hostage or as forced-bride, and he doubted that any of the men purchasing new lives for themselves wasted a moment of thought on her.

Well, as long as they stayed on the right side of the law, he'd be hanged if he turned any of them in, or the people who were helping them (for a price) either. And if they broke the law, well, he might be the one to catch them, but it was up to the Guard and constabulary to deal with it.

Information trafficking was mostly going the other way now, and even those prices were deflated. He could almost feel sorry—almost—for the fellows whose sole stock in trade was in intelligence.

On the other hand, this made two of *his* personae very popular fellows with those selling information about Valdemar's neighbors, since both those personae were still buying. Though for information about Karse, he was relying on Geri and the informal network that the Sunpriests who had escaped to or been born in Valdemar had built over the years.

As a consequence, he had known well in advance of today that one of the younger Princes of Rethwellan was arriving "secretly" with the intention of paying court to the Queen. He had told Talamir, and neither of them had seen any reason to spoil the surprise by informing Selenay. "Let her have a little romance," Talamir had opined, and his opinion was seconded by Herald Kyril. "She is sensible enough to know that whatever courting or romantic attention he pays her is only an illusion, and that he is here purely for the purpose of making an advantageous alliance. She will bear in mind, I am sure, that he would pay her the same compliments if she was stooped and squint-eyed. This will amuse her, and she has had little enough pure amusement since the Ice Festival."

Illusion or not, romance was not in Alberich's area of expertise, nor were the doings of princes. He would leave that to Talamir, and had said as much. His personal opinion was that the arrival of this princeling was a damned good thing for *Talamir.* Between the discovery of the ciphered papers and the advent of the Rethwellan Prince, Talamir was looking more centered than he had since the Coronation.

Alberich had filed that observation away for further thought, but there was one conclusion to be made from it that was obvious—Talamir needed real things to do, too, things he could get his metaphorical teeth into, things that focused him on what was going on around him. Alberich made up his mind to find more such tasks.

Now, following that actor fellow—*that* was something he could do.

Though once the weather turned and spring was well and truly in bloom, he began to wonder where the man got his energy, and whether he *could* manage to follow him without dropping over.

It wasn't only that Norris was performing every evening with the full company at the inn and rehearsing new productions every afternoon—

That is, when he wasn't performing with a reduced company at special private performances of an afternoon—

No, it was that once those evening performances were over, he scarcely had time to wipe the paint from his face and change out of his costume before he was off somewhere. Most of the time it was with a female. Alberich couldn't call them "ladies," though some of them had that title, even if they acted more like cats in heat. When he wasn't with a female, he went roistering off with a gang of male friends, drinking and carousing through several taverns—and usually then ended up in a woman's bed in some bawdy house anyway.

It was astonishing. Because then, no matter how late he'd been out, there he was again, looking alert and fresh and ready to go, no later than noon, to rehearse with the company.

"I know not how he does it," Alberich said, as he accompanied Myste, in his guise as "her friend from the Army, the carter," back to the Companion's Bell where she was ostensibly staying. They had just watched Norris drink enough to make Alberich's head reel, then take three whores up to his room. Only one thing was certain; he wouldn't be going anywhere tonight. Thank the Sunlord. Alberich didn't think he could have made another late night of it himself.

"Nor does anyone else," Myste admitted. "Especially not his head for drink! That man can drink any three under the table, and I am not exaggerating, because I've seen it with my own eyes. And the next day, you'd never know he'd taken a drop."

Alberich licked his lips thoughtfully. "A useful talent, for an agent."

"Damn right it is." She tucked her hair behind her ears, and adjusted her lenses. "What's more—and this is a woman's intuitive observation, so take it with whatever grains of salt you choose—I don't see that he has anything that you could exploit as a weakness. Not even for women."

Alberich gave her a dubious glance. "Pardon?"

"He *uses* them," she elaborated, "but he has no *use* for them. I think, they're like food for him—he satisfies his appetite, and he does have a hearty appetite, but once he's through, he pays no more attention to them than he would to the shepherd's pie he just finished eating. He pushes away the leftovers, and wants them cleared away. I've watched him with his women, remember. Quite a lot more than he thinks I have, actually. I have yet to see him show any emotional attachment to anyone, woman *or* man. He acts as if he does, says all the right things, and it is superb acting, yes—actually quite a bit better and far more subtle than anything he does on stage. But so far as I can tell, there's nothing genuine behind the words and the gestures."

"Well," Alberich said thoughtfully. "Well, well, well. I think it is good that I have never tried to come too near to him, or I might have been swiftly found out. But that makes me concerned for you—"

She nodded. "It makes *me* concerned for me, too, believe me, and the only things I have in my favor are that he thinks I'm besotted and under his thumb, that I'm not ornamental to look at so he spends as little time as he can get away with doing so, and that he does not think that women in general are particularly intelligent. I expect," she added thoughtfully, "that he regards *me* rather in the line of a trained dog. Quite clever at performing the tricks I've been taught, and utterly devoted to my masters, but not really capable of thinking for myself."

"Which would make, I think, other women his lap dogs," Alberich pointed out, continuing the analogy. "Good for ornament, and sensually pleasant, but otherwise utterly useless."

She laughed aloud at that. "Oh, I wish some of his light'o'loves could hear you say *that* of them! How he manages to keep them from tearing him to bits in jealousy is beyond me."

"Perhaps they are in truth as utterly besotted as he thinks you to be," Alberich observed. "Or else, he has the gift of golden speech."

"Both, I think." She shook her head. "You know, as often as I see it, I'm still amazed at how self-deluded a lot of women are. A man says one thing, and does something else, and they believe the words and not the actions."

"That behavior is not restricted to women," Alberich pointed out. "Are his fellow actors not equally deceived in thinking him a grand fellow?"

"Hmm. That's true enough." They were nearly at the Bell, but neither of them made the turn that would take them into the alley and the back way. "Alberich, I don't believe we're alone."

"So you have noticed." Someone had been following them for some time. Alberich had been certain of it about a third of the way back.

"I'm not usually good at this, but I heard a footstep that I know just before I said something. It's Norris."

Well, that put a different complexion on things. "So the three bawds—?"

"A ruse. Maybe he isn't as sure of me as I thought. So—hmm. Now what do we do?"

"You go up to your room, and I say good night. Then I see what your friend does next."

They had, because Alberich always liked to plan for every possible contingency, planned for this one as well. Myste *did* have a room here—in fact, it was one of several that Heralds could use if they needed one; if, for instance, there was a major convocation of Heralds and all the beds at the Collegium were full. They were very spartan in nature, hardly more than closets with bunks in them, identical to the servants' rooms and exactly the sort of thing that a clerk would get in trade for his services to an inn. So when they reached the door of the Bell, they parted company as old friends rather than anything more intimate, and Myste used her key to the side entrance where the long-term residents and inn servants had their rooms. Albench clumped off, made certain that their follower hadn't followed *him*, then reversed his coat to the matte-black side, and ghosted back.

Sure enough, there was Norris, hidden, and hidden relatively well, in a shadow across the street. After a moment, one of the little windows in the garret rooms glowed as a candle was brought inside. Alberich was about to suggest to Myste with Mindspeech that she go to the window, when she did just that without his needing to prompt her. She not only went to it, she opened it, and sat in it for several moments, as if enjoying the warm, spring night. Even though she was probably dying to peer down into the street to look for their follower, she did nothing of the sort; instead, she took off her lenses, rubbed her eyes as if she was tired, and sat back with her head against the side of the window frame and her eyes—as far as Alberich could tell—closed.

:Is the kitty still stalking me?:

: Yes, he is,: Alberich replied.

:Persistent beast. I don't suppose you can think of anything that will make him go away?:

:I am working on just that,: he told her, although in truth, he was coming up rather dry as to ideas.

After all the times when his admirers have been a nuisance to get around, this is one time when I wish some of them would appear, he thought crossly.

:How many would you like?: came Kantor's interested query.

He blinked. *:Why do you ask?:*

: Because there is an entire table full of young women from the audience this evening here. They wanted to get a table there, but you know how it is—:

Yes, indeed, Alberich knew very well how it was. Norris' company was, by far, the most popular in Haven in a very long time. On the nights when there were plays, it was impossible to get a table in his inn, either before or after the play. The innkeeper had taken to doing the unheard of—making *reservations* for tables. There were people who had waited as long as three weeks before being able to take their pre-play dinner or after-play supper in Norris' presumed presence.

:—*at any rate, all they've done is talk about Norris since they got here. They're very loud, and I think, a bit tipsy.*: There were distinct overtones of snigger in Kantor's voice. :*I can't imagine how they'd be useful to you, though.*:

:*Oh, I can*—:

He slipped away from his hiding place, went into the alley, in through the secret room at the back of the stables, and changed into, not his clothing, but his uniform. This was not even his gray Weaponsmaster's garb, but the Heraldic Whites that he seldom, if ever, wore. He had kept a set down here for just this reason. He wanted to be noticed this time, but he wanted all the attention to be on his clothing, not his face.

Then he strolled openly into the Bell, and listened for the sound of female voices. It didn't take him long to hear them, for as Kantor had said, they were both loud and tipsy, the latter probably being the cause of the former.

:*All right, Myste,*: he Mindspoke. :*Yawn, stretch, put out your candle and go to bed. You shouldn't have to stay there much longer.*:

:*I'm alive with curiosity.*:

The Bell had more than one public room; there was the main tavern area, and several supper rooms that were intended more for eating in than drinking. He entered the room where the young—and not so young—women were, as if looking about, possibly for a place to sit.

They were, so far as he could tell, not highborn. But they definitely were prosperous; their gowns were all new, of good quality, and they wore a moderate amount of silver jewelry. Middling well-off merchant or craft families, he guessed; the younger ones had probably persuaded their families to let them see the players, and the older ones had come along as chaperones, and they *all* had fallen under the spell of the handsome leading man. They were already planning their next outing to see him perform!

A Herald always got noticed, even in Haven, and when he entered the room, they all looked up and at him. He concentrated very hard on his words, and his accent. This was not the time to sound like a foreigner. If Norris went to the effort of trying to track back who betrayed him— Alberich just wanted to be "a Herald." He gave a little bow, and said, "Your pardon, my ladies. I wouldn't want to interrupt your party—"

One of the older ones giggled; it was one of the young ones who called out, "Oh, that's quite all right, Herald, you weren't interrupting anything. We were just talking about the play we've been to."

"The play be hanged!" said one of the tipsier ones. "It's that actor Norris' way of filling out tights that *we* were talking about!"

Some of them laughed hilariously, some with embarrassment, and Alberich smiled. "He's a fine actor, that one," he said agreeably. "Very impressive indeed. I think all of us managed to get to one or more of his performances during the Ice Festival." Then he added, as if the idea had suddenly struck him, "He wouldn't be waiting for any of you, would he?"

Oddly enough, it was one of the drunker ones who caught the implications of that last question, which slipped right by most of them. "What d'ye mean, waiting for one of us?" she asked, not quite slurring her words. "Y'mean, now? Right now?"

"Why, yes," Alberich replied, feigning surprise. "I saw him just across the street, lingering in the doorway, as if he was waiting for someone to come out of the Bell—"

Well, that was *all* he needed to say, and the only thing he needed to *do* was to press himself against the wall to get out of the way of the avalanche of gowns heading for the door.

They piled past him and rushed for the front exit. A moment later, and there was something like a little chorus of squeals as they tumbled out into the street. "Is that—" "It is!" "It's him!"

:You wicked, wicked man!: Myste chortled, as the sounds became a bit inarticulate and much louder.

There was a single, masculine voice, saying desperately over the torrent of giggles and little shrieks, "Ladies! Ladies!" and the owner was clearly getting nowhere.

Alberich strolled out to the door, and stood there with his face in shadow, leaning against the doorpost with his arms crossed, enjoying the havoc he had created. Norris was in the center of a tight knot of women, all of them breathlessly telling him of their admiration at the tops of their lungs, all of them trying to elbow each other aside to get closer to him. He looked like a very desperate man at the moment.

:Oh, this is choice,: Myste said. *:I can't resist.:*

From overhead and to the right came her familiar voice. "Will you please be *quiet?*" If Alberich hadn't known Myste so well, he would have been certain that she was angry, not trying with might and main to hold back gales of laughter. "People are trying to *sleep!*"

Her window slammed shut.

Then Myste's plaint was joined by several other, genuinely irritated voices, calling down to the gaggle of women surrounding Norris to *shut up!* and *go away!* and *I'll get the constables on you, see if I don't!*

And it wasn't long before a constable *did* appear, and suggest to Norris (as the apparent center of the disturbance), that "It would be very nice, sir, if you and your friends were somewhere else right now."

And there was nothing else that Norris could do at that point, except to bow to the inevitable. He was going to be stuck with these women for the next candlemark at least. And the only way he was going to get rid of them was back at his own inn, where he knew the ground, and could slip away from them under the guise of attending to nature's call or something of the sort—or getting one of the cast to find one of his regular bawds to come down and drag him back to his room. The one thing that would embarrass them enough to go away even in their present state of intoxication *would* be the presence of a real whore.

But it would have to be done there, not here—

Somehow, perhaps by sheer force of personality, he got the group moving, and away they went, still surrounding him on all sides, chattering like a flock of noisy little birds, and he with the look of a man being nibbled to death by ducks.

When they were all out of both sight and hearing, he Mindcalled up to Myste. *:I think you can come out now.:*

:Just a moment. I was not exactly dressed. I wanted to add some verisimilitude to the illusion that I had gone to bed.:

Now he wished he'd looked up when she leaned out of her window.

Then it struck him; there'd been a hint of—something—in her mind-voice. Was it what he thought it was? Should he? Did he dare?

:If you didn't read that as an invitation, you're denser than I thought,: said Kantor.

He couldn't clear his throat in mind-voice, but he managed a combination of eagerness and diffidence. *:I don't suppose you would care for me to come up instead?:*

He heard the purr in her mind-voice, and almost tangled his own feet together, trying to whip himself around and head for the stairs. *:Ah, yes. Indeed I would. Please, do.:*

1 3

The journey back up to the Palace was surreal. Dreamlike, as the four of them made their way through peace-filled, cool air scented with honeysuckle. Alberich held onto the moment fiercely; no matter what had happened in the past, or what would happen in the future, he'd had this night, this time. His heart was, for the moment, at peace, and he could not have been more content with his lot. He hoped—he thought—Myste felt the same.

They parted with a touch of lips and hands at the branching of paths, one leading up to the Heralds' Wing at the Palace, the other to the salle. He and Kantor moved off into the velvet night.

:I told you that you were worrying too much,: Kantor said, when he and Alberich were finally settled back in their respective "beds," in, and beside, the salle.

:Hmm. You were right.: Still—no, there was no "still." Kantor was right. The benefit of being Gifted; there was no question of how one's partner felt. There had been a little initial fumbling, but—

No "buts."

He sighed, and started to settle into sleep—

Then something popped up into his mind and jolted him into wakefulness again. *:Now,* why *did she tell you "Thank you, you were right"*—?:

:Ah. You weren't supposed to hear that.: Kantor sighed. *:I gave her some advice, some time back. Through her Companion, of course, but she knew it was from me, because she asked me directly.:*

:Yes?: He decided that, no matter what it was, he wasn't going to be annoyed. After all, look what it had gotten him.

:I told her, "He won't *make the first move; you'll have to. And don't be subtle. In this situation, he's trying so hard to be a gentleman that he won't notice if you're subtle." But if you're wondering, I don't think this was planned, I think she just seized the opportunity when it was too good to be passed up. I know she's felt diffident*

about approaching you here, in your own place, and more than a bit shy about inviting you up to the Collegium where—:

:Where everyone would notice and gossip.: Alberich finished for him, and mulled it all over. No, he definitely was not going to be annoyed. *:Thank you. You were right.:*

Of course, now that the first move had been made in the game…

He chuckled to himself in the darkness. The *next* time she showed up here, it wasn't all going to be business. Not that he was going to forget his duty, far from it.

Now he did let his doubly tired body relax. And his last thought was, perhaps not oddly, *Norris is a fool.*

Selenay sat at her open window, and breathed in the honeysuckle-scented air dreamily. Karath—he had insisted almost immediately that she call him Karath—had been officially presented at Court two days ago. He had gone out of his way to be charming, and Selenay was by no means the only one to have been affected by that charm. But his attention had been directed, like a focused beam of light, on her.

This was not the first time that she had been the focus of someone's attention, but it *was* the first time the attention had been completely positive, and universally directed to the sole object of pleasing her. Heady stuff.

And it didn't hurt at all that Karath was so very good to look upon…

No, not at all. But there was more, as impossible as it seemed. Karath understood her.

It was magical, how well he understood her. Already they had shared commiserations on how heavy the burden of duty was for a royal child, and how unfair it was that they had less freedom than the lowest of their subjects. How very unfair…

And he had looked straight into her eyes and said, "It is a sad pity that you have no one to share your burden with."

Oh, she had laughed at that, and demurred that she had an entire Council to help her, but his words had rung very true, and she wondered if there was something behind them. As if—could it be—

No, of course not. He's a Prince of Rethwellan. If he can charm me into giving Rethwellan advantages, he will. He may even be courting me with an eye to a marriage of state. Right now, though, he's simply being friendly; he's a Prince, and there can't be too many people that he can confide in. It isn't as if he has a Companion to talk to, or even someone like Lord Orthallen. He was, she thought, a very proud young man. It would be hard for him to confide in anyone that he considered below him. *Yes, that is certainly it.* She rested her head against the window frame, feeling suddenly melancholy, for herself, for him.

No, there could be nothing more to it than that. *Besides, he can't possibly stay for very long. He'll have to return home soon.*

The thought made her feel cheated, somehow, and even more melancholy.

But after a moment, she shook it off resolutely. The Seneschal had decided that having a Prince of the blood here was an occasion of great import, and had arranged that his days should be enlivened by all manner of amusements, and that it was Selenay's duty to take part in at least some of them. The Vernal Equinox was in a few days, and although it was the wrong season for hunting, it was the best season for other sorts of outdoor excursions. They were all going to watch a new version of the Hurlee game, played Companion-back by the oldest of the Trainees. Others had been trying to come up with warm-weather variations on Hurlee, but this was by far the most exciting and successful. And there were those who were trying to get horses to do what the Companions were doing, but it would probably take a couple of years to train horses to put up with balls rolling under their hooves and sticks whizzing about their ears. For now, at least, the only mounted version of the game would be played by Heralds or Trainees.

It made an excellent excuse to sit out on lawns, with hampers of refreshments, in the warm sunshine, rather than in the stuffy Audience Chamber, listening to even stuffier old men complain about each other.

There would be supper in a pavilion on the lawns after the game, and then, a concert of music under the stars in the gardens. *It will be the most fun I've had since the Ice Festival. Actually, it will be much more fun than the Ice Festival; I won't be on show to an entire city.*

She smiled as she thought about it. To think that she would have most of a day devoted to something other than Kingdom business! But her Councilors all seemed very much in favor of the idea, even those who were reserved in their assessment of Karath.

Maybe he will stay longer…

After all, Orthallen was convinced that he had come here with every intention of courting her. It was a time-honored means of cementing alliances, marriage. He *was* the younger Prince; he wouldn't be in line for the throne at this point, not even if his older brother died, because

Faramentha already had a young son of his own. So—

She shivered, but with delight and anticipation, not dread. Oh, no, definitely not *dread*. Not like she'd felt with every other would-be suitor that had presented himself or been presented so far.

Now, wait and see, she cautioned herself. *Don't start chasing hares until the hounds have the scent. Orthallen could be misreading this. He might just be very kind.*

But if he *was* courting her—it was just a bit difficult to be loverlike when he never saw her except in the company of ten or twenty other people.

The question was, did she *want* him to court her? Actually, more to the point, did she want to marry him? She thought—perhaps—but she still wasn't entirely sure. It probably wouldn't be too much of a battle to convince the Council, but the rest of her subjects might not care for the idea of a foreign Consort. And while he had beautiful manners, and was extremely sympathetic, it was all words so far. She had no idea if he was truly attracted to her, Selenay, or was just being properly diplomatic and sympathetic to the Queen. *He* was one of the handsomest men she had ever seen, but how did she look to him, really? And how would she ever be able to say what he really felt with the constant audience that was around her?

If only there was a way to get rid of the audience—the courtiers, the ladies, all of them. If only there was a way that she could just slip away from them all, long enough for the two of them to be alone for just a little.

And then, she had an idea. It was a terribly romantic idea. And it just might work.

I'll have a masquerade, she thought with delight. *I'll have it when the year of mourning is officially over. Out in the gardens, spread out everywhere, with everyone in costume and masked. I'll have the same costume made up for me and all of my ladies, except I'll let him know by some little token which one is me. If he can't manage to get me alone for a little, then he won't be trying.*

Yes, that would do it. That would do it indeed. She chuckled at her own cleverness.

And meanwhile, she had tomorrow to look forward to, a half a day and all evening with nothing before her but to relax and enjoy herself. And perhaps Karath would show something more of his intentions.

She went to her bed and fell asleep, still smiling.

There were three stands set up along the three sides of the triangular playing field; the best one, reserved for the Queen and her Court, was on the side between the Scarlet and Green goals with a good view of both. Out on the field, the two teams faced each other, Scarlet and Green goalkeepers standing warily alert on their respective goals, the two goalkeepers on the neutral, third goal, watching each other as much as the teams.

There was a tension-filled silence as one of the referees placed the ball on the ground between the two teams, then ran off, well out of the way of what was coming.

A trumpet blast—

A single shout swelled a thousand throats, and the game was on.

"Explain to me what I am seeing, please," Karath asked, watching as the tide of riders collided, the ball somewhere under the churning hooves of the Companions. One half of the riders were wearing Bardic scarlet, the other, Healer Green—not because they actually were Bards and Healers, but because the two teams had been "sponsored" by the two other Collegia. It would, after all, have been impossible to tell which rider was on which team, otherwise.

"The players are all Heraldic Trainees, and they usually wear gray," Selenay said, as there was a loud *crack*, and the ball suddenly seemed to fly out of the scrum on a pair of invisible wings. "This came out of a game the Trainees made up over the winter, called Hurlee—" She interrupted to cheer, as the Bardic goalkeeper made a last-minute save, her Companion rearing and pivoting on hind hooves, letting her catch the ball in her net. The goalkeepers had nets, rather than club-ended sticks.

"Anyway, we wouldn't be able to tell the teams apart, so Bardic Collegium sponsored the team in red, and Healers the team in green." She shouted again, as the Bardic goalkeeper threw the ball back into play, and one of her own people caught it while it was still in flight and sent it whizzing toward the Healer goal with a mighty blow of his stick. The whole field went charging after it.

"But how are the horses so well-trained?" Karath asked.

"They aren't horses, they're Companions," she answered automatically. "Um—they're—" She searched for a way to explain it to an outsider. "They have Mind-magic, and so do the Trainees, and it's like having a partner. They can speak to one another."

"Ah, magic," Karath said wisely. "Of course. Like the Hawkbrother mages who control their birds in the strange places in the Pelagirs."

Actually, it's not like that at all, she thought, but that was probably as close as he was going to get until he'd been here a while, and saw for himself.

Or until a Companion Chose him. "That's close enough, I suppose," she said instead, and turned her attention to the game.

It was absolutely vicious in its way; Alberich had insisted that the original version of Hurlee be played with no holds barred, and nothing short of murder against the rules, and this version was no different, with one single exception. No one was allowed to deliberately thrust a stick among the legs of the scrumming Companions. The idea of a Companion with a deliberately broken leg was just too horrifying. But the Companions were *certainly* allowed to ram each other, and shoulder each other out of the way; the riders could hit at each other with their sticks, and try to pull each other out of the saddle. Companions and riders alike wore hard helmets of leather over steel; the Companions wore neck guards, the riders wore padding and guards of their own.

It was war out there; Selenay, who had seen war firsthand, recognized it for what it was. Relatively bloodless, perhaps, but nonetheless, war. Which was why both Weaponsmaster Alberich and the new Equitation Instructor, Herald Keren, approved of it. You could study mounted combat all you liked; you could even practice as much as you dared, but you got no *sense* of what combat was really like—

Well, the fourth- and fifth-year Trainees certainly were now. By the time the first third was over, that was obvious. There was plenty of danger; one player was already out with a broken arm, and a second sidelined while the Healers made sure that the crack on the head hadn't resulted in a concussion. A third was playing with a broken nose, and there were two with black eyes, and no one would know until it was over how many bruises and strains there were. No Companions were injured, but that was always possible, too.

The second third began after a brief pause for water—both drunk and poured over heads—and a quick change of players. Then they were off again, with no less vigor than before.

"It seems very dangerous!" Karath shouted to her, over the cheers and shrieks. She glanced at him; he seemed just as excited as everyone else. His color was high, and he had a wide smile of enjoyment.

"It is!" she shouted back. "Our Weaponsmaster is using it for war-training!"

"Aha!" He nodded vigorously, then cheered wildly with everyone else as the Scarlet and Green goalkeepers on the neutral goal got into a clinch, and a Scarlet rider nipped in right under their noses and slammed home a goal.

Hurlee on ice had been exciting. This was beyond exciting—this was intoxicating. Even Selenay, who had been in the thick of war, was caught up in it, drunk as any of them on it, free to feel it, knowing that this time, there was no fear that anyone would die. One rider was actually knocked unconscious by the ball before it was over, and there was a broken wrist and a second broken arm, both caused by being unseated and falling badly. But Selenay knew that the Healers would soon put all of them to rights, and when the Healers were done with them, the congratulations they would get at the hands of the rest of the Trainees—and everyone else with an interest in the game—would soon make the pain just a memory. The Scarlets took the lead and held it for most of the game, but at the very end, in the final third, the Greens took the victory away from them by a single point.

When the winded and the exhausted winners and losers both had been mobbed and rushed off the field to their own celebratory feast, Selenay found herself hoarse with screaming and nearly as tired as if she had been out there on the field herself.

"My word!" the Prince said, his eyes still wild with excitement. "That's altogether more thrilling than any tournament I've ever seen! You say your Weaponsmaster is using this for war-training?"

Selenay nodded, and sat down so that everyone else could. Protocol, after all—while the Monarch was on her feet, no one else could sit. There was some little time before the *al fresco* dinner, which would be served out in the gardens, and she wanted to give her staff plenty of time to have it set up before she led the ravenous hordes toward the food. Meanwhile, pages were going around with wine and fruit, and she availed herself of both. Karath sat down in the place of honor beside her, though he still looked as if he would like to go find a Hurlee stick and try the game for himself.

Not Selenay. She enjoyed watching the game, but once it was over, she couldn't help but think about why Alberich was so in favor of it. She didn't want any of those youngsters to have to see what she had seen. There had been too many no older than they who had not returned from the Wars.

"Indeed, he is, Your Highness," the Seneschal said, as both the Rethwellan Ambassador and the Ambassador from Hardorn leaned closer in order to hear. "He and the Equitation Instructor have found it an invaluable substitute for melee and skirmish training. They say they have found that both the mounted and foot versions are equally valuable. And it is all the better for the fact that the Trainees *want* to do it, and several of them spend a great deal of their free time in practice at it. We are restricting the mounted version to the final-year students, however, given the level of expertise required, and the danger involved."

"Better a broken bone or two now, than something worse in combat," Selenay said, sobered by her recollection of another spring day—nearly this time last year—

Then she shook off her melancholy. This was supposed to be a day given over to relaxation and pleasure, and she was not going to spoil it. "Well, gentlemen, you can tell your friends and kin back in your homelands that we here in Valdemar know how to provide both novelty *and* entertainment for our guests," she said lightly. "I do believe that was the first ever public game of mounted Hurlee."

"And I hope you will convey my admiration to your Weaponsmaster for finding so clever a solution for a training dilemma," the Prince said with a smile. "Though I will confess, if *that* is the level that he trains to, he is fully as expert as our own Weaponsmaster at home—though perhaps not *quite* to the exacting standard of Swordmistress Tarma shena Tale'sedrin, the famed Shin'a'in who trained my father and older brother."

"But not you?" asked the Hardornan Ambassador, and Selenay had the oddest sensation that *he* knew something about Karath that he would like very much for Karath to reveal. Something unflattering…

Though *why* he would wish for such a thing—

Ambassadors are always jockeying for favor. I suppose he thinks that if Karath appears less than perfect, I will lose interest in him. Absurd.

The Prince frowned, and for just a moment, a shadow passed over his face. But in the next moment, he was all smiles again, and Selenay wondered if she had even seen it. "Alas, no," he replied smoothly. "The Swordmistress retired and closed her school before I was old enough in my mother's eyes to be sent away to it. And at any rate, from all I have heard, the lady is extremely ascetic in her ways and strict in her discipline; some might say, she is overzealous in both regards. And I—well—" He shrugged. "I am not much like my brothers. While I feel that every man of breeding should be adept at the use of arms, I fail to see why he should undergo the same rigorous training as someone who intends to live by them. Personally, I am afraid that the Swordmistress and I would be doomed to perpetually clash, so perhaps it is just as well. It would be a terrible scandal for a Prince of the blood to be thrown out of a school for mercenaries as an abject failure, or worse, a *discipline problem.*"

The Rethwellan Ambassador laughed, politely, but it sounded strained. Selenay was baffled. If *that* was all the Hardornan Ambassador had been angling for, she failed to see what was so unflattering about it. Not even a Trainee who was unsuited to the martial arts was required to do more than learn how to defend him or herself. Why, look at Myste! Most of *her* training had been in the best ways of running away!

She decided to steer the subject away from the area that Karath was finding uncomfortable. "The Swordmistress—is that a Shin'a'in name?" Selenay asked, curiously, thinking wistfully of her earlier daydream of a wild Shin'a'in Clan Chief coming here to claim her hand. "I've never seen a Shin'a'in, though I believe some of our people in the south have traded with them."

"It is, indeed, Majesty," Karath replied. "Why do you ask?"

"Oh, only that I had never heard of Shin'a'in living outside the Dhorisha Plains, and I often think I would like to meet one, someday," she confessed. "I believe one came as far as Lord Ashkevron's manor in my father's day, to help the Lord with his horses, but it was before I was born."

"It is true that they do not often venture off their traditional grounds," the Rethwellan Ambassador said, after waiting for a few polite moments for all of them to nibble a little at their fruit and sip from their goblets of wine. "We see them from time to time selling horses, but as soon as the beasts are sold, they swiftly return to their homeland. The city of Kata'shin'a'in is the only spot off the Plains where you will see them regularly. The Swordmistress is somewhat of an anomaly; she lives—or *lived*, since she was quite old, when last I heard—with her blood-oath sister, who had a school of sorcery alongside the school for swordsmen. Perhaps one day I will be able to entertain you with some tales of their adventures. They are rather famous in Rethwellan."

"I would enjoy that," Selenay said, wondering to see that faint shadow pass over the Prince's face again. "But today, it is incumbent upon me to entertain *you*, gentlemen, and I believe that it is time that we all went to supper."

She rose, and they all, perforce, rose with her. "And high time, Majesty," the Seneschal said lightly. "Watching the Hurlee game was nearly as exhausting as *playing* it, and just as stimulating to the appetite. These refreshments were welcome, but I swear, if you put butter on a brick, I would eat it at this point!"

"Pray, don't say that," she chided with a laugh. "Our guests will be afraid to try the pastries!"

She led the way down out of the viewing stands and into the gardens, with the rest of the Court trailing after. She wondered if she should ask the Prince about that Shin'a'in Swordmistress—perhaps there was some problem there that she should know about.

Well, perhaps not. Probably he was piqued that his older brother had the privilege of training under so famous a teacher, and he had not. She could understand that. As difficult as Alberich was, there was absolutely no doubt that he was the best Weaponsmaster that Valdemar and the Collegium had seen in a very long time. If she had a sibling who'd been able to train under Alberich, while she was not allowed to for whatever reason, *she* would be horribly jealous, too.

The meal was laid out along tables in the shade, protected from insects by tents of fly-gauze. Nothing was intended to be served hot. A guest had but to tell a page what he wanted, and go to find a good seat on the lawn, near the pavilion where the musicians were tuning up, and the page would bring him a laden plate and a cup of wine. It was all finger food of the sort that could be eaten with nothing but a little recourse to a napkin, and most of it was light and cool, meant to tease the palates of the diners with its subtlety. It wasn't the sort of heavy feast they'd shared at the Court Feast of the Ice Festival. Selenay made her selections, and went to take her seat. She wished that she could sprawl on a carpet or cloth, as she had on these occasions when she was only the Heir, but she was Queen now, and such an undignified pose would not be proper for her. Instead, she followed her page to a rustic seating arrangement of a garden bench softened with cushions inside a bower facing the pavilion, with a semicircle of chairs placed around it for her particular guests.

She was pleased to see that Talamir was already there, waiting for her. He hadn't attended the Hurlee game, pleading a need to see to something or other, but she had been a little concerned that the real reason was that he was feeling ill again. As the anniversary of her father's death—and that of his first Companion, Taver—approached, he had been looking distinctly frail.

But he seemed well enough now, and very much in the moment. He conducted her to her seat with all the gallantry of which he was capable (which was a very great deal) and to Karath's evident annoyance, took his traditional place at her left hand, leaving Karath to take the remaining chair at her right.

"I trust your business is taken care of?" she asked, as he made sure that she had all she needed before sending the page off for his own supper. She tried something sweet and spicy wrapped in a lettuce leaf; bits of spiced meat with crunchy little bits of vegetable in a light sauce, and decided that she would have *that* often this spring and summer. The cooks seemed to have outdone themselves; she hadn't recognized most of the dishes on the tables.

"More so than I expected, Majesty," he replied, with a definite twinkle in his eye. "I would hesitate to say anything, except that you will hear about it from any one of a dozen gossips before the end of the day. Apparently our Weaponsmaster is not as invulnerable to the darts of emotion as he thought. But he is skilled enough in deception that even *I* thought that his meetings with the Chronicler were all business until today."

Selenay wrinkled her forehead in puzzlement, trying to make out what Talamir was getting at. "Alberich? And—Myste—" And all at once it dawned on her. "Alberich? And *Myste?* Oh, my word!" She began to laugh delightedly, as the Prince and the two Ambassadors looked puzzled. "Oh, but how lovely! Talamir, you must pledge me on your word that you will *not* tease him about it! Above all things, I do *not* want the poor man frightened off, just when he's taken the first steps into this venture."

"Not I, nor any other Herald, Majesty," Talamir promised. "We're too pleased, to tell you the truth. And we would rather that the Trainees didn't find out about it either—or at least, not until the relationship is so long established that they'll be as terrified of saying anything about it as they are of offending him in any other way."

Selenay turned to her guests, still smiling at the thought that somber Alberich, who seemed as destined to remain chaste as any sworn priest, should finally have found a lady who clearly found *him* fascinating. She and Myste were uncommonly well-acquainted, despite the differences in their age and backgrounds, and Myste had dropped more than one little remark after they had all returned from the Wars that had told Selenay that the Herald-Chronicler had definite leanings in the Weaponsmaster's direction. *He* treated her as she wanted to be treated, with respect for her learning and as an equal in intelligence. If they occasionally exasperated one another, that was only to be expected with two such strong personalities. But she had thought Alberich impervious to anything but friendship.

Apparently not. "You are puzzled, gentlemen; it is only a little romance among our Heralds, but a rather unlikely one, or so I would have thought until now. The season seems to have affected our Weaponsmaster, whom we all thought to be a man of iron. And the great irony is that the lady in question is the only Herald he was never successful in teaching the martial arts to—the Chronicler, Herald Myste."

The Prince smiled vacantly, clearly finding the subject of no particular interest, but the Hardornan Ambassador chuckled right along with Herald Talamir. "Well! So the spring has managed to melt the heart of stone after all! Good for Herald Alberich! And twice as many kudos to your Herald Myste; my guess would be that she was the one to do the stalking. These old warriors are as shy as partridge in hunting season when it comes to the matters of the heart."

Talamir laughed. "That, sir, would be telling Heraldic secrets. I will leave it to your imagination."

"And on that note, I beg that we listen to the music and enjoy our repast," Selenay said firmly. "Or else we will start to sound like a gaggle of village gossips."

The sun was just setting, making the gardens a wondrous place indeed. The day-blooming flowers wafted the last of their perfumes over the guests as they closed their blossoms for the night; the night bloomers were just beginning to open. As twilight closed over the garden, a soft breeze sprang up; the musicians kept to soft, lyrical melodies, and servants made their way about, lighting the torches unobtrusively. Selenay set her empty plate and cup aside, and suddenly felt a hand brushing hers, as if by accident.

Then it happened again; she glanced aside at the Prince, who caught her gaze for just a moment, touched the tips of her fingers with hers, and gave her a quick, conspiratorial wink.

She felt her heart give a leap, and an answering smile crossed her lips before she turned her attention back to the musicians.

But she sighed, and watched him covertly out of the corner of her eye. His *apparent* attention was on the musicians, too, but she had the feeling that she was being watched behind the screen of his long lashes and half-closed lids.

The breeze touched her cheeks, cooling the heat that had suddenly suffused them. She was glad for the shadows within the bower, so that her blushes would not betray her. *Surely that wasn't just the gesture of a gallant...*

She reached for her wine cup, and her fingers touched something else. Trying to appear as casual as she could, she managed to get both objects, and found that she was holding both her cup, and a red rosebud from which all of the thorns had been carefully removed. He turned his head slightly, lowered his gaze to the flower meaningfully, smiled, and looked back to the musicians.

Now her whole body seemed to vibrate with a thrill that she had never felt before. To cover it, and to moisten her mouth gone suddenly dry, she sipped at the wine. Then she put the cup back down—but kept the rose.

The half-planned masquerade took on a new importance and urgency in her mind. She would give him the setting. And she would see if he reacted to it.

And then—

Then things would fall as they fell.

1 4

Selenay stood very quietly in the exact middle of her dressing-room, while three maids fussed and fluttered around her, making sure that every detail of her costume was just so. In a few moments, she and her ladies would be going down into the gardens to perform the masque that would open the Midsummer Masquerade. In fact, there was music drifting through the open windows of her suite right now, making her both impatient and nervous at the same time.

She stared fixedly at herself in the mirror on the wall opposite her. Her costume was identical to the ones her ladies would be wearing; all of them would wear floating, ethereal dresses composed of many layers of pale green silk gauze, the topmost layer embroidered with tiny sprigs of leaves and flowers, fitted to the waist and flaring outward like the petals of a trumpet flower. It had a hint of a train, with long, trailing butterfly sleeves and a round neckline that showed just enough bosom to suggest, rather than reveal. With it, she wore soft silk slippers dyed to match the gown. None of them would wear jewels, not even she, only a loose, trailing belt of ivy, and bracelets and anklets of flowers. All would be masked, the strange, featureless silver masks of the legendary Moon Maidens, ovals without even eye holes—a cunning layer of silver gauze where the eyes should be was perfectly easy for the dancers to see through, but gave no hint of the eyes behind the masks. Their hair, which otherwise would give their identities away, was covered with more silk gauze in the form of a wrapped coif with floor-sweeping veils crowned with chaplets of more flowers. And the only difference between Selenay and the rest of them was her secret; she wore a single rosebud tucked into the ivy at the waistband of her gown. She had not told the Prince this; he would have to discover it for himself. In fact, she had not told *anyone* this. And since no one was to unmask before midnight, she would be indistinguishable from any of her ladies except for that one detail.

Which meant, if she chose, she should be able to slip away from the rest without being missed and throwing everyone into a panic.

She surveyed herself in the mirror, and was satisfied with what she saw. In designing this costume, she and her seamstresses had taken every flattering aspect of every dress she had ever worn, and combined it into a single gown. In the past, as often as not, she had carefully selected her clothing to serve as armor. This gown, however, was meant to be a weapon. Now the only thing that remained to be seen was if the weapon would be used. She already knew, just from what she saw in the mirror, that it would be effective.

Was it so silly of her, to want to be *wooed* like an ordinary woman? To know that the man who asked for her hand wanted *her* as well as what she represented? She was sure, now, that Karath was here for the purpose of courting her, or else he would have gone home by this time. There had been several opportunities for him to leave, including when his own Ambassador was recalled because of an emergency in his family. He could have gone back to Rethwellan then, with the man who had brought him here in the first place. He hadn't. In fact, he had stayed even though the Rethwellan Embassy was virtually empty but for a few servants. Even though half of his guards had gone back to protect the Ambassador on his journey, and she had loaned him some of her own Guards until either the old Ambassador returned, or a new one with the rest of the entourage came to take his place.

She knew that most of her Councilors were devoutly praying for such a match. It would all but secure the southern Border, since Rethwellan would be obliged to help defend it if the Karsites somehow found the means to attack again. It would bring many, many trade advantages, since Valdemaran goods would probably be exempted from the onerous taxes on imported stuff. It would mean easy access to several great trade markets of the south. No one could or would object to a Rethwellan Prince on the grounds of either consanguinity or unequal rank.

But she didn't want a *trade alliance*, or a military advantage. She wanted a Consort, a partner, a confidant. Someone she could talk to; someone who—

—Well, someone she could love. Someone who would love her. Who would treasure Selenay as well as the Queen, as her father had treasured her mother.

She thought, if things worked out as she hoped, that she would be able to tell if that was true of Karath. She knew already that she was deliriously infatuated with him. How could she not be? Nearly every woman of the Court was half in love with his handsome face and charming manners. Every time he looked at her, she felt a shiver of delight; every time she thought about him, she went hot and cold all over. She had dreams of him at night that made her wake full of aching desire.

They had shared several conversations now, which were, if not completely private, certainly *mostly* private. He really did understand the terrible burden of the crown, of being unable to ever have much real privacy, of having to be everything to everyone. They had talked about all the times when, as children, they had lost entire holidays being on show for the people. They'd spoken of the difficulty of finding real friends. She thought that he understood these things as not even a Herald could. If he wanted her, well, he *had* her. But only if he truly wanted her; she was not going to go into this *now* unless she had him just as truly.

He would have to say so. More than that, he would have to convince her that he meant it. Otherwise—

Well, in the end, she still might marry him. But it would not be for a while, maybe not for years. If this was to be nothing more than an alliance marriage, then she was *not* going to throw her heart after him.

:That's the first sensible thing you've thought of,: Caryo said. She started; Caryo had been uncharacteristically silent lately, and had not—until now—said a single word about the Prince.

:What was the point? I don't like him; I don't know why. But you—you're in love with him. Or with his face and manners and fine words, anyway, and you're not going to send him away just because I don't like him. I'd have to give you a lot better reason than that, and I don't have one.:

Selenay bit her lip and stared at her mirror. *:But if you don't like him—:*

:I'm also not going to try to stop you from doing something you really want to,: Caryo said, irritation clear in her mind-voice. *:And if he can convince you that he's as much in love with you as you are with him—well, there's nothing more to say. It won't be the first time that someone in a bride's family hasn't gotten along with the groom. If human families can put up with such a thing, so can I.:*

Selenay found herself horribly torn between annoyance at Caryo and gratitude—annoyance, that Caryo would have the infernal gall not to like Karath, and gratitude that she was not going to stand in the way of what her Chosen wanted. She settled, finally, on the gratitude. There was no point in being annoyed, anyway. Caryo would do what Caryo did; the two of them didn't always see eye to eye.

:It hasn't happened,: she reminded Caryo. *:And what would be better—him,*

or someone that was beholden to one or more of my Council, someone we couldn't trust not to have a dozen people whispering in his ear?:

:Who's to say your precious Prince doesn't have that baggage already?: Caryo countered, then softened. *:I suppose that you're right. And besides, if he doesn't take the bait tonight, and he can't convince you—:*

:Then even if I eventually marry him anyway *for alliance purposes, it won't be until I've managed to control my own feelings,:* Selenay said firmly. *:If I am doomed to an alliance marriage, it will be with all my armor on.:*

She said that, but underneath her words was the yearning, the hope, that she'd never be required to live up to those words. What was more, she wasn't entirely certain that she could. She thought that she covered it well, however. Certainly Caryo seemed mollified.

:Then, in that case—go, and see whatever is to be seen with clear eyes,: Caryo told her, and slipped out of her mind.

She heaved a sigh of relief. That could have gone very badly, and the one thing that she could not bear would have been for Caryo to be angry with her.

On the one hand, if Caryo never could grow to like Karath, well, too bad. There were even Heralds who didn't particularly care for one another, and not even all the Companions got along in perfect accord.

On the other hand, maybe she would mellow over time. When Alberich had first been Chosen, there had even been a group of young Companions who had tried to attack him. Now there wasn't one of them that wouldn't defend him to the death, and when he got into it with one of the Trainees—as he had over the broken mirror—even the Companions of those Trainees backed the Weaponsmaster.

If Karath truly loved her, then with luck Caryo would come around eventually. It could be just a matter of time and patience.

She dismissed the whole situation from her mind. Tonight would be hers—more truly than that moment on the battlefield when she became Queen, more truly than the moment of her coronation, because in both cases, it had been the Queen, not Selenay, who had received the accolades, whose life had been forever altered. Tonight, it would be Selenay, and not the Queen.

She glanced at the windows, and was gratified to see that the last rays of sunset were gone, and the light outside was deepening into twilight. It was nearly time for the masque. All the guests would have been assembled by now, and would be waiting for the appearance of the Moon Maidens to begin the real festivities.

"Are my ladies ready?" she asked one of the maids.

"In the antechamber, Majesty," the girl said promptly.

She nodded. "Good. Then that's enough fussing with the gown; it is never going to be more perfect than it is now. Hand me my mask."

Wordlessly, one of the maids gave it to her; she fitted it over her face, and the maid tied it in place over the coif, then settled the long, trailing veil over her hair, now so tightly braided and coiled under the coif that once the chaplet was pressed down over the veil and coif, not a hair was to be seen.

The world as viewed through the eye holes of the mask was clear enough, perhaps a little obscured, as if by a thin mist, but no worse than that. The face presented to the mirror, however, was a featureless silver oval, more than a bit uncanny.

The legend of the Maidens of the Moon was right out of Rethwellan, not Valdemar, and told of a young prince—supposedly one of Karath's ancestors—who met a maid dancing in his garden by the light of the full moon and fell in love with her, only to discover that she was one of the twelve daughters of the King of the Moon. He went through many harrowing adventures to get to the Moon-King's kingdom to claim her, only to be faced by a final test—pick her out from among her twelve identical sisters as they danced before him. She hoped that was enough of a hint to Karath of what he was expected to do tonight.

"Let's go down," she told the maids, and went out to her antechamber to collect her eleven ladies.

But she was not the one in the lead; she let Lady Jenice have that honor. She was determined not to give Karath any more hint than that rosebud—and not to give *anyone* else any hint, so that no one could prevent her from escaping from the throng with him if he chose right. She had instructed all of her ladies to speak only in whispers and never to so much as hint as to their identities, pointing out that the whole purpose of a masquerade was to keep everyone guessing (insofar as that was possible) until the unmasking. And everyone taking part in the masque had agreed with alacrity. One or two of her ladies, she suspected, had certain suspicions of their own lovers and were thinking to see if they could be caught out. One or two she *knew* were hoping to use the opportunity for some clandestine flirtations of their own. The rest were all simply intrigued by the idea, which was more than enough to keep them in the spirit of the game.

She saw with more than a little amusement that she was not the only one of them to be wearing a flower tucked in the ivy-belt, but none of those flowers was a rosebud. Good! One more point of confusion, if Karath was not serious enough to be paying attention.

The guests were all in the garden by now, and she could hear the musicians playing incidental music. She and the other ladies would perform their dance on the torchlit terrace above the gardens, giving everyone a good view. She felt a flutter in her stomach, a nervousness greater than she'd felt even at her own coronation. Her hands felt cold and clammy, and her face flushed. She was glad that she wasn't going to have to *say* anything, or she was sure she would have stammered and stumbled over the words.

The ladies lined up at the terrace door in two lines, forming six pairs. Selenay joined her left hand to her partner's right—that would be Lady Betrice, though you wouldn't be able to tell that if you didn't know it. A maid ran outside to let the Bard in charge of the entertainment know that they were ready. Someone giggled nervously.

From outside, muffled by the closed terrace doors, she heard the Bard's staff pounding three times on the stone of the terrace, and a single trumpet sound a brief, silvery fournote call for attention. The chattering stopped; so did the music.

"My Lords and my Ladies!" the Bard called into the sudden silence. "In honor of His Highness, Prince Karathanelan of Rethwellan, Her Majesty, and her Ladies will now perform the Masque of the Moon Maidens!"

The doors were pulled open from outside by two pages; the music began, and the twelve ladies danced onto the stone terrace above the gardens to the strains of a solemn pavane. Selenay felt her heart pounding and concentrated fiercely on the steps of the dance, watching the lady in front of her. *One-two-three, dip-two-three, turn-two-three, pause*—

To her immense relief, Selenay realized that she couldn't see a thing down below the terrace, that the light from all of the lanterns and torches quite obscured all of the courtiers and guests below. She could concentrate on the intricate patterns of the dance quite as if it was no more than just another rehearsal, even though her heart was pounding as if she was running, and her hands still felt as if she'd been holding them in ice-rimmed water.

In a way, it was just as well that this was *not* an easy dance, nothing like any of the normal dances of the Court. It began as a round dance in slow gigue-time, then moved into a double-round of two circles of six ladies with the pattern changed to a slow gavotte. Then it moved into a triple-round of three circles of four, back in a gigue. There were extra bows and flourishes of the veils and the long sleeves, extra circlings and glidings between the figures of the dance. In and out and around Selenay wove her steps, turning and bowing, touching the fingers of her next partner, then releasing them, turning again to face a new partner. Then it became a line dance as a pavane, then a six-couple line dance in a chassone, then a double line of three couples in minette, then three square dances as a pavane. And each time the dance changed, they struck a new tableau for a hold of six bars of music, until the music came around again to the first round dance, at the end of which they struck a twelve-person tableau. Selenay wasn't even in the center of that final tableau, she was over at the far right. There was literally no way of telling *which* of the ladies she was; she was quite certain of that.

As the music ended, the applause from below was enthusiastic, and very gratifying. She felt herself flushing with pride, and she was certain that she wasn't the only one. They all broke their tableau and stepped to the edge of the terrace in a line, holding hands, and took their bows, bending their knees and bowing their heads in a graceful acknowledgment of the applause. It sounded quite genuine, which was delightful, actually, since most masques in her experience were more endured than enjoyed, and the accolades tended to be dutiful rather than enthusiastic.

Then they came down the steps from the terrace to the lawn to mingle with the rest of the guests as dance music began. And here was the hard part—other than getting through the Masque itself. Somehow she had to carry herself like one of the rest, neither with too much authority nor too little, neither with diffidence nor haughtiness. She decided to avail herself, first thing, of one of the fans laid out on a table just where the terrace steps ended, for the use of those who found themselves overly warm. A fan was an excellent thing; it served as a kind of shield as well as something to occupy the hands.

But before she could do more than pick one up, someone grabbed her free hand. Startled, she found that she had been seized by one of the more exuberant young courtiers and was being pulled into a rowdy country-style ring dance. She couldn't tell who it was, of course; he was wearing an ornate and rather antique uniform or livery, and a mask made in the shape of a rooster's head. It was clear he had taken her for one of her ladies and not the Queen.

Don't resist! she reminded herself, and allowed him to pull her into the circle. Everyone was laughing, sometimes tripping over the little uneven parts of the ground, and acting altogether like a lot of children. And somewhat to her surprise, she found herself having—fun!

And in a moment she understood why; she was anonymous, and she had been chosen by this young man for what he could see of her body, not because she was Selenay. Of course he assumed she was one of Selenay's ladies at least, but behind the anonymity of his mask and hers, they were able to act freely. As she romped her way around the ring, she realized that she hadn't felt this lighthearted since she'd been a Trainee, and just Selenay, who happened to sleep over in the Palace and not in a room on the Girl's Side of the dormitory floor.

She was very glad, however, that all the parts of her costume had been fastened securely. It wouldn't do to have the coif and veil, or worse, the mask fall off, and reveal her for who she was.

She took the precaution, in a moment between dances, to knot her sleeves and tie up her veil all the same. No point in getting them tangled and pulled off either.

A kind of madness infected her, and she was not the only one. That was the thing about a masquerade; you could be as wild and silly as you liked under the anonymity of a mask. Especially if you had one of the more common masks; as she whirled through the steps of another dance, she saw: at least two roosters, three Horned Men, and no less than five bears. She, of course, was one of a dozen Moon Maidens, and there were cats, Wild Women, goddesses and butterfly masks that were no less popular.

Another dance struck up immediately, this one a brasle, where two lines of dancers ran at each other, then seized new partners and whirled madly until it was time to run at each other again. She went through four rounds of that, when suddenly she was seized by someone in a costume she did not at all recognize.

He wore a half-mask of gold surmounted by a huge hat crowned with feathers, the costume an elaborate doublet and trews of silk and velvet in reds and yellows. And as the young man paused in their heady rush, he bent over and whispered, "I am the Moon Prince. Have I chosen aright, Selenay, my Moon Maiden?"

She pulled back, startled, and he laughed in Karath's voice and boldly plucked the rosebud from her belt. "I see by this token that I have!" he said, the mouth beneath the half-mask grinning. "Here—run with me!"

He took her hand; she hesitated only long enough to snatch a handful of her skirt so she could run more freely, and the two of them sprinted hand-in-hand off into the depth of the gardens, laughing like a pair of children.

She didn't know where they were going; she didn't care. They ran through torchlight and shadow, the sounds of music and merriment fading behind them. She more than half expected him to run toward Companion's Field, or some other remote place, but instead, he ran toward the Palace. Once again, he had chosen correctly; there was no one in this part of the garden at all, and little light. They were right beside the windows of the Collegium kitchen, which at this hour was dark. There, in the shadows of a thick clump of bushes, he finally stopped, and pulled her into his arms.

"Won't you unmask now, Selenay?" he murmured, confronted with the featureless oval of her disguise. And as if to set the example, he pulled off his hat, which proved to be fastened to his half-mask.

She put up her hands to the back of her head and loosened the chaplet, but he was too impatient to wait for her fumbling fingers. He carefully took off the chaplet, then the veil, and untied the mask himself, discarding each on the ground beside his hat. With every item he removed, her heart pounded a little faster.

When he had laid her face bare, he looked into her eyes for a long moment.

Then, suddenly, his arms were around her again, his lips crushed against hers, and she felt a heat rise in her and overwhelm her. She felt as if she was made of butter, melting against him, pressing her body into his, wanting nothing so much as to have the kiss go on forever and ever.

But—too soon for her desire—she felt his arms loosen, and he lifted his face from hers to stare down into her eyes again. There was just enough moonlight for him to see her upturned face; his was all in shadow, and she strained to hear his voice.

"By the gods, Selenay, I have wanted to do that from the moment I saw you!" he breathed.

She lifted her face wordlessly to his, but he shook his head, and with every evidence of regret, loosened her from his grasp.

"No," he said, "I dare not, or I will not stop, with but a kiss."

"No?" she asked, feeling obscurely disappointed. "Then—"

"But I can do this," he said, interrupting her. He dropped to his knees, clasping both her hands in his. "Here if is only you and I, not our countries, not our Councils, only ourselves to satisfy. We will please only ourselves; we will answer only to our own will, here. Selenay, I ask this for myself, and for myself—would you, will you, grant your hand to me in marriage?"

He had read her riddle; more than that, he had answered her invitation *and* her challenge and met it, his Prince to her Moon Maiden. And now—now, away from all witnesses, all eyes, he had asked her to wed him specifically for himself, and not for his country.

If this wasn't the answer to her questions, she could not imagine what could be.

"Yes," she whispered. "With all my heart."

He leaped to his feet and took her in his arms again, and her whole body thrilled to the caresses that he bestowed on it. She would quite willingly have torn off her own gown and melded her body with his there and then. It was his restraint that stopped anything more from happening.

And though a great deal of her was frustrated and disappointed, the rest of her was grateful and full of admiration at his self-control.

"Here," he said, as he actually stepped away from her, then took her hand and bestowed a tender kiss on the palm. "You may be only one Moon Maiden among twelve, but we should not take the risk that you are missed. Let me help you mask again."

And so she stood, burning with desire for him, as he, clever as her best maid, masked her hot cheeks with the silver ovoid again, and placed the veil over her head, and the chaplet atop it. Then he retrieved his own mask and resumed his guise as well. "Shall we walk?" he asked. "My own lady?"

A shiver went up her spine at the caress in his words.

"To cool ourselves," she murmured in reply, and he laughed.

"I think that cooling is what we both need, my Moon Maiden!" he chuckled. "It is just as well that our masks will hide our faces, or they would surely betray us to anyone with eyes in his head!"

He took her hand, and led her back toward the festivities, at a far more decorous pace this time. She was glad of the night air and the chance to get her pounding heart to quiet itself. Her hand trembled in his, and he felt the trembling, and tightened his fingers about hers for a moment.

They passed other couples on their way to the dancing-lawn, making use of the little bowers and grottoes of the gardens, standing or sitting together. They also passed places shrouded in darkness from which little sighs and murmurs came that made her cheeks flush again, and a stab of envy lance through her.

But Karath took no notice, or at least, did not appear to. They sauntered on together, like any couple on a leisurely stroll, until they stepped onto the lawn below the terrace and into the full glare of the torchlight.

She did not know what she would have done then, but the situation was taken out of their hands by a wild game of crack-the-whip that crossed their path the moment they stepped onto the torchlit grass. The trailing girl seized Karath's hand in passing, and since he still had Selenay's she was perforce now the running, laughing, end of the "whip" until she in her turn could grab another hand.

Before long, the scampering line was too unwieldy to be a whip, and became a dancing, running snake, winding its way among the more sedate and older courtiers, who either laughed indulgently or frowned and snorted behind their masks. Around and around they went, in and out of the ornamental bushes, until everyone that had any youth in his body had been caught up in it; the musicians seemed to have been infected by the excitement, for they did not stop or even pause in their playing, until Selenay was out of breath, her side aching, the corners of her mouth actually hurting from all of the laughing and smiling she was doing. When they snaked around a potted rosemary tree, she finally let go of Karath's hand and that of the person behind her so that she could drop out of the line. The person behind her ran up and grabbed Karath's hand to keep the line going, and he was soon out of her sight.

With her hand pressed to her side, breathing hard, she sought out a stone bench that was too exposed to be a choice of lovers, and sat down on it. She wished she had the fan that she had lost, somewhere back when the dancing began. But at least the breeze was cool, and her gown was light; she fanned herself with a piece of her veil, and took deep breaths, waiting for the stitch in her side to pass.

But she had not been there long before Karath appeared again, and wonder of wonders, he brought a fan for her! He handed it to her with a graceful bow, and she thanked him and wafted herself with it, wondering gratefully if there was *any* other man here who would have thought of such a thing.

He took a seat beside her on the bench, and covered her free hand with his own. "One thing only, my own lady," he said, quietly, his voice barely audible over the music. "Is it your pleasure that we make our choice known tonight, or would you——"

"Tonight!" she said quickly. "If we wait, if I go first to the Council—— there will be objections, however trivial, and the Councilors will want to argue it over for days and days! But if we simply *tell* them, at the unmasking, they will accept what they must."

"You are as wise as you are beautiful," he said warmly, patting her hand. "I would not have thought of that. And—how fitting, for any who might recognize *my* costume if we are standing together at the unmasking—"

"Or better still," she said, suddenly seeing it all in her mind's eye, "—on the terrace!"

His eyes sparkled behind his mask. "Oh, well thought! How soon before midnight strikes?"

That, she could answer, for there was a time-candle visible from where they sat. She pointed, and they could both see that there would be just enough time for them to slip into the Palace and get into place before the trumpeter marked the moment of unmasking.

Giggling with a giddy exhilaration, she now led *him* in through an unguarded door in the public part of the Palace, then back through the maze of corridors to the terrace door where she had so lately stood. There was no one there now, not even a page, and the doors stood open. Together, hand in hand, they walked out onto the terrace at the exact moment that the trumpeter sounded the call of midnight.

With a cheer, the masks came off—all but theirs. With an instinct for the drama of it, they both waited until the rest of the guests noticed that there was a couple standing alone on the brightly lit terrace where the Masque had taken place—

—that one of the figures was a Moon Maiden—

—began to grasp that the other *must* be Prince Karathanelan—

And at that moment, he pulled off his mask and flung it behind himself, as she pulled chaplet, veil, mask, and coif all off, shaking her hair loose so that it fell down around her shoulders. And as the guests saw that it was *her,* he again pulled her to him, and bent down in their first public embrace and kiss.

She closed her eyes, as her ears filled with the great cheer that went up as her arms went around him.

And she thought, in that moment, that there could be no happier person in all of Valdemar than she.

1 5

From the moment it was announced, Alberich had deliberately planned to avoid the masquerade. This was precisely the sort of gathering at which he felt most uncomfortable. And after all, it was primarily a Court function, and not one at which he expected anything significant would happen either. Those older members of the Court upon whom he had his eye were unlikely to use such an occasion for any conspiratorial gathering; both he and Talamir were agreed on that. Of all the times and places in which one could talk with fellow conspirators, an occasion such as this, where there were dozens of people milling about, all masked so that you could not know just who, exactly, was around you, was not ideal. And furthermore (although many popular plays and romances would have attempted to persuade otherwise), a gathering that was held out of doors where you could never be sure there was not someone hiding and listening to you, was probably a very bad choice for passing on secret information.

Alberich hated this sort of entertainment with a passion. And since Selenay was going to be costumed identically with eleven of her ladies, at least until the moment of unmasking, this was probably one of the few times when she would be safer without a bodyguard. Unless, of course, all *twelve* of them were to be granted bodyguards. So he had said, decidedly, that he was not needed nor wanted. Talamir had agreed with him, and had suggested that he might wish to actually relax that evening for a change.

He had, in fact, decided to keep an eye on Norris that evening.

He already knew where to find him; there was not a performance tonight, and with all of the young nobles up at the masquerade, there was little chance that Norris would be meeting any of *them* down slumming with the actors tonight. No, if he met up with anyone above his own station, it would be because there was something more than drinking going on. This was one of the things that Alberich was going to keep a watch out for; someone who *should* be at the masquerade who was not.

If anybody had asked him what he was hoping to discover, he would have told them that he was not, in fact, hoping for anything. He knew better than to expect a result from any given evening; results never came when you expected them. You got ready for them in case they cropped up, and you watched for them to make sure you didn't miss them when they came, but you never expected them.

Since Myste would not be there tonight as it wasn't a performance night, he decided to trot out a new persona, one that was designed to blend in as well as Myste did—the aging, cranky scholar. His station would be shabby middle-class, genteel poverty, but poor because he spent all his money on books, travel to confer with other scholars, and paying to print his own monographs on obscure subjects. He wore clothing that was of good material, but not new, a long-sleeved, high-collared, belted tunic and trews of heavy linen in a rusty black, with a shirt of white linen, and the flat scholar's cap. Not shabby, but also neither well cared for nor well fitted. He had an old leather satchel stuffed full of papers and books. He brought a reading book with him, parked himself in an out-of-the-way corner of the common room, and apparently kept his nose in it while he ate, in an absentminded fashion. He had engaged a room, but it was a very small one and did not come with candle or lantern, so it was perfectly reasonable for him to take his book here to read. He had debated getting a set of lenses like Myste's, but decided against it. If *he* were checking to see if someone was in disguise and snooping about, the first thing he would do would be to arrange to knock their lenses off to see if they were real. A pair of plain clear glass lenses would be a dead giveaway. And for once, his scars were an asset rather than a liability; by enhancing them rather than trying to conceal them and at the same time enhancing those creases that would, in time, become frown-lines, he was able to age himself credibly by nearly thirty years.

He did not know for certain that Norris would be here tonight, but with no play on, there was a good likelihood that he would at least spend the afternoon in rehearsals, then have some dinner here, where he was fed for free, before going out anywhere. And at any rate, even if the man didn't start his evening here, there was a good chance that by careful listening, Alberich would pick up some gossip about him or his whereabouts.

But his luck was truly in tonight; not only did Norris begin his night here, but the rehearsal ran long, so that Norris came down from his room about two candlemarks after sunset, dressed in quiet elegance, all fawn-skin breeches and fine linen shirt open at the throat, thigh-high boots nearly as tight as the breeches.

He stepped up to the bar and ordered himself a drink. And shortly after that, so carefully timed that Alberich did not for a moment think it was coincidence, someone came looking for him.

Except that the man didn't exactly come *looking* for him, the way an admirer would. He didn't begin by asking the doorkeeper if Norris was about, for instance, and he didn't come up to him openly, as a simple admirer would.

The stranger cast a glance around the common room; his eye lit on Norris, standing beside the bar and chatting, mug in hand. Since Alberich was watching Norris very carefully, he saw the actor catch the stranger's eye and hold it for just a moment. Then the newcomer took a seat of his own, in the same out-of-the-way corner that Alberich was already in. It was an awkward little cul-de-sac beneath the stairs, big enough for only a couple of two-person tables. Alberich already had the most exposed of the tables; the stranger took the one that was the least exposed to the rest of the room.

Alberich went on reading. He did not even look up as the man brushed by him, nor when the serving wench brought him his order. Norris didn't pay any great amount of attention overtly either—but after some time, the actor left the bar and drifted over in his direction. By this time, the common room was at its most crowded, and virtually the only seats left were at two-person tables like the ones Alberich and the stranger each had. Somehow Alberich didn't think that Norris was going to ask if he could join the scholar.

Norris paused for a moment beside Alberich; Alberich's neck prickled, but he didn't look up from his book. Surely it wasn't possible that the actor was going to sit at *his* table!

Surely it isn't possible that he recognized me?

The actor certainly gave Alberich a good look-over. Alberich did just what his persona would have done: he read, outwardly oblivious to anything going on around him. Norris moved on, and said to the stranger, "Friend, would you mind if I sat at this table?"

"Be my guest," the man said with every sign of indifference. And that would have been perfectly ordinary, if it hadn't been that both of them pitched their voices just a little louder than if they'd been talking merely to each other, and not for the benefit of anyone who happened to be nearby.

Alberich turned his page, and furrowed his brow. It was appropriate to furrow his brow at this point; the author was taking a slightly controversial stance, and one that someone like Alberich was bound to disagree with. Alberich had chosen this book quite deliberately; he was very familiar with it, and if challenged, could converse knowledgeably about the contents. And tonight, he just might have to. Despite the heat in the overcrowded room, he felt a chill of apprehension.

He heard the scrape of a stool on the floor; the sounds of someone sitting down behind him. He didn't actually *hear* anything then, but the serving wench materialized, as they all did, whenever Norris summoned them, however imperceptible the signal was to anyone else. The actor ordered dinner, and when it came, there was a pause as the wench flirted a little with Norris then was summarily shooed away.

"Is it all right?" said the stranger, in a very, very soft voice.

"Safe as houses," Norris replied, casually. "Safer than my room. Can't tell who might be on the other side of the wall there."

Well, thought Alberich, *that's what you get for insisting on the big corner room.* Norris had recently demanded—and gotten—one of the better chambers at the inn. Even with Myste keeping a jaundiced eye on the take, the innkeeper was doing a phenomenal amount of business thanks to the ongoing presence of the actors here, and couldn't afford to offend Norris at this point. The problem with the new room, however, was that while Norris had one of his fellow actors as a neighbor on one side, the other was a room that anyone could rent, and it was often taken by someone who wanted to be near the actor. That would practically *guarantee* a snoop with her ear to the wall.

"What about *him?*" persisted the stranger, and Alberich knew, by the prickling feeling on the back of his neck, that the man was pointing at *him* in some way. Probably with a little jerk of the chin; less obtrusive, unless you were watching for something of the sort.

"Hmm." There was a scrape; Norris this time; Alberich could tell from the position of the chair.

He's going to do something. Alberich thought he could guess what, and a moment later, it came. And now he had to do something that was against all of his instincts; he had to relax, not tighten his muscles in anticipation. The scholar would be deep in the book and would not even be aware of the rest of the world. You should be able to come up behind him and shout in his ear without his noticing.

There was the sound of a stumble, and Norris blundered into him, spilling his drink, knocking the book out of his hand, nearly knocking him over. Alberich did not try to save himself; he let the chair go over, and himself with it, as with a cry, he lurched for his book. Norris was there before him, picking it up, all apology, offering his hand, and when Alberich was on his feet, dusting him off.

"Horribly clumsy of me, I beg your pardon—" While Norris babbled on, he was managing to get a look at the book, in fact, at the place where Alberich had been reading. And thank the Sunlord for that, since it meant he was *not* looking closely at Alberich's disguise instead! He handed it back to Alberich so quickly, though, that it was unlikely anyone like the scholar would have realized that the actor had examined the book before relinquishing it. But an actor had to be a quick study; the man probably had both pages memorized by now.

Alberich snatched it away, glared angrily at him, and fussed over the book, making certain that none of the pages were bent, nothing stained. "You clumsy oaf!" he shrilled, pitching his voice to a whiny falsetto. "Curse you, fellow! Where did you think you were going?"

"I'll buy you a new drink," Norris was saying, as the serving wench bustled up with a towel to clean up the mess.

"If you've so much as creased a page, you'll buy me a new *book*, young man," Alberich replied querulously. "Copies of Canton's *Lives of the Philosophers* do not grow on trees!"

"No, they don't, I'm sure," Norris said agreeably, as the serving wench brought another drink and Norris paid her for it. "And I would be devastated to think I had ruined one. I particularly admire his scholarly treatise on Loyal Hestalion, for instance."

Alberich simply gave him a good long stare, as if suspiciously certain that Norris was only trying to jolly his way past Alberich's anger. "It's *Lowal* Hestalion, young man, as you would know if you had actually read the book, rather than making something up to try and worm your way into my favor. And what is more, the man may be sound enough on other biographies, but his treatise on Hestalion is little more than a repetition of scurrilous rumor!"

Norris threw up his hands and laughed. "Caught! Well, I most sincerely apologize again, I *have* restored your drink, and I hope I haven't foxed your book, so are we quits?"

"The book appears to be intact," Alberich said icily. "I believe I am also intact. And I beg the pleasure of your absence."

"Yes, *sir!*" Norris laughed, and went back to his place while Alberich ostensibly and ostentatiously reburied himself in his book.

"So, there, you see," Norris said under the sound of the conversations all around them. "Nothing but a bookworm. We could burn down the place around him, and he wouldn't notice."

"Good enough. The game's in play tonight," the stranger said. "We think it will play out well."

"Good news," Norris said with satisfaction. "And my reward?"

"You'll get it when the bond is sealed," the stranger replied. "Even if all goes well, there will be opposition. We may need you before then. And don't forget, we'll also need you after, for a time, anyway."

"No, you won't," Norris growled, sounding irritated now. "The boy's a natural seducer. And the girl's untried. And *I* absolutely the finest instructor in the arts of seduction that was ever born. You say he's showing his hand tonight. If he doesn't have her well enchanted before the week is out, and wedded within the moon, I'll eat my hat without salt."

"All well and good, but he'll still need pretty speeches, and he's not bright enough to make them up on his own," the stranger said, irritation in his own voice. "Until there's an heir in the offing, we're not safely home."

"And *I* don't get my theater." Norris sighed, as if much put upon. "All right, then, I'll stay available. But he'd better not drag this on too long. It doesn't take *that* long to get a girl with child, and after that, keeping her bound will be up to him. I've never seen a woman born yet that didn't make every excuse in the world for the father of her child."

"After that, we'll have what we need," the voice purred. The tone made the hair on Alberich's head stand up. There was something very sinister about it, that made Alberich wonder uneasily just what it was that the voice and his cohorts needed.

And he felt very sorry for the girl in question.

But it seemed that, whatever was going on here and now, it had little or nothing to do with the security of Valdemar. Evidently Norris had been coaching some unscrupulous young man in how to seduce a young woman into marriage. He could almost picture her in his mind as he carefully turned another page in his book, some young, lonely, plain thing, but wealthy—for surely only great wealth could be the cause for such a scheme.

Would there be any way to warn her, assuming he could find out who she was?

Probably not. Even coming from a Herald, she probably wouldn't believe anything that anyone told her against her beloved. Not if she was as infatuated as Norris thought. And he was a practiced seducer, after all.

But he didn't fool Myste, a little voice in the back of his mind reminded him.

Yes, well, Myste had been fooled at least once in her past, when she was younger. You had to have experience in something before you could recognize danger when you saw it, and since the stranger called the unknown young woman a "girl," she probably wasn't old enough to have experience in much of anything. Poor thing.

He turned a page of his book, groped for his drink without looking at it, and took a sip. Well. Norris was very generous; this was much better beer than the stuff Alberich had ordered the first time around.

The scrape of a stool signaled someone's departure, and it turned out to be the stranger. He eased his way past Alberich, being exceptionally careful not to jar him. Alberich ignored him entirely, though he would very much have liked to get a good look at him. The best Alberich could manage was a quick glance at the man's profile. It looked faintly familiar, in the way that someone looked if seen once or twice. It could be anybody Alberich had seen around here. Alberich filed the face in the back of his mind.

Now Norris was alone—but not for long.

There was a bit of a commotion at the door, the sound of high, shrill voices, and a flash of bright color. Alberich heard Norris chuckle under his breath, and buried his nose even further in the book.

But Norris was the one who got up, and sauntered over to the trio of women who were clearly what Alberich's mother had been mistaken for.

Now, Alberich knew he was no expert when it came to women's dress, especially not here in Valdemar, but there were some commonalities among the ladies of negotiable virtue everywhere, and this lot showed every one of the sartorial signs. There were flounces and ribbons and curls and painted cheeks and lips, all done to excess. Colors were bright (including hair color, for all three sported hair of colors not normally found in nature), there was a great deal of cleavage, a great deal of bare arm and shoulder, and even a scandalous amount of leg showing. Jewelry was positioned the way a general arranged his best troops, with the intent of directing the enemy's sight to a particular object.

"Well, my lovelies," Norris said genially, as they clustered around him like gaudy butterflies around a tall flower. "What brings you here?"

By this time, Norris had the attention of everyone in the room, and very well knew it. He was playing for the crowd, and the crowd sensed it was going to get a free show—short, maybe, but nonetheless, free.

"You," said the boldest, flirting acid-yellow hair at him. "We've a bet on that you can't take all three of us at once."

The entire room howled with laughter, in which Norris joined, throwing back his head and roaring. "In that case," he shouted, and Alberich at last looked up with an affronted expression on his face, "you're doomed to lose, my bawd!"

"In that case," cried the second of the trio, with hair the same blue-black as a raven's wing, boldly twining herself around him, "we win!"

In the barrage of laughter that followed *that* sally, Norris seized the bold one, picked her up in his arms, and trailing the other two, went straight up the stairs to his room.

Now it was entirely possible that all that had been a ruse to cover Norris' exit through a window, but Alberich didn't think so. For one thing, that new corner room would be cursed difficult to get out of without being seen. For another, Norris had looked as surprised as anyone else with the whores' replies. So there it was. He might as well go home, since not even Norris could—Well, it would take him the rest of the night, if he was going to make good on his boast and not lose the bet. And that was one sort of bet that a man like Norris could not bear to lose.

He shut his book and went over to "his" room. He took off his tunic and turned it inside-out; now it was brown moleskin. He stuffed the hat in the satchel of books and papers. Now he looked like a well-off working man, probably enjoying a night out. He saturated a rag with sendal oil and used it to take off his "wrinkles," then doused his head in the basin to wash his hair clean of the streaks of gray he had painted in. He rumpled up the bed, making sure it looked slept in, and left other signs of recent occupation. And when he was certain that no one was watching, he went out the window. The room was already paid for. No one would raise a hue and cry, finding it empty in the morning. He had told them that he expected to be away by first light. They'd simply assume he had been as good as his word.

Still, he did have one thing; that rather sordid business about the unknown young woman. There might be something in that worth investigating later.

I suppose I can get some sort of list of wealthy young women who have full rights to their fortunes somewhere, he reflected. *And whichever one posts the banns in the next moon or so would probably be the one I'm looking for.*

He was so involved in his own thoughts that he actually wasn't even thinking about his Companion—until Kantor himself startled him.

:Great good gods!: exclaimed Kantor in his mind, surprising him so much that he stumbled over his own two feet. He recovered without falling, but he was thoroughly irritated when he answered back.

:What?: he snapped.

:The masquerade!: Kantor exclaimed. *:Selenay—at the masquerade—she just picked Karathanelan in front of everyone at the masquerade!:*

:Picked him for what?: Alberich began with even more irritation, and then, of course, it dawned on him. Kantor would hardly be this shocked over the young Queen choosing a dancing partner. *:She chose the Prince of Rethwellan as her Consort? But—:* Now he was bewildered a little, by all that he did not know about Valdemar. *:Can she do that? Just pick someone like that?:*

:She can, and she has,: was Kantor's reply. *:We had better get back up the hill and quickly. Every Herald in Haven is going to want to say something about this.:*

Since Alberich was already moving as fast as he could without being obvious, he saved his breath for running. Which he did when he got into the alleys where no one was there to see him. It seemed to take forever before he was safely in his little room at the back of the Bell's stables, though he knew rationally that he'd made good time.

In a remarkably short period of time, Alberich was back in his gray leathers, and they were cantering through the streets, heading for the Collegium.

:What happened, exactly?: Alberich asked, moving easily with Kantor's gait, and keeping a sharp eye out for unwary pedestrians.

Kantor told him.

:Didn't Caryo guess what was going to happen?: he demanded. *:Why didn't she warn the rest of us? We could have gone to more pains to investigate him!:*

:I don't know,: Kantor said, mirroring Alberich's irritation. *:Maybe she thought it would all blow over. This shocked everyone; no one guessed Selenay would do this. I suppose she didn't even confide in her own Companion.:*

He kept his thoughts on *that* subject to himself. All right, granted he wasn't the most competent when it came to matters of the heart and particularly of romance, but there were some things that were obvious. He hadn't set eyes on this Prince himself, but he'd heard from plenty of people that the boy was absurdly good-looking. When you took a young woman like Selenay, who surely cherished her own *dreams* of romance even though she knew very well she was unlikely to fulfill them—and you presented her with a handsome young man of the proper birth and with all of the advantages that a foreign minister could ask for—well, what did you *expect* to happen? The only reason that he, Alberich, had been blindsided was because the young man himself had given no outward signs—*that Alberich knew of*—that he was interested in a marriage alliance with Selenay and Valdemar.

Clearly both he and Selenay had played these cards very close to the chest, if even Caryo had thought it would all blow over.

:So what does anyone know about this prince?: he demanded.

The way cleared; they were in among the manors of the highborn now. And the highborn were all still at the masquerade, so the way was clear. Kantor broke into a gallop.

:I don't know anything more than you do,: Kantor replied. *:But you'll shortly find out.:*

Alberich cut his questions short. But behind his silence, they were piling up, like stones before an avalanche.

"—and that is all any of us know," Myste concluded. Since she was the Chronicler, she had elected to be the one to collect all of the information there was about the Prince, and all of the information there was *concerning* the Prince and concerning the reaction this unique declaration was going to have on the Council.

Myste sat down on a bale of hay. They were meeting in the stables—the *Companions'* stables. The building had the advantage of being big enough to hold all of them, and away from prying eyes and eavesdropping ears.

No one seemed particularly ready to break the silence that followed Myste's words. Finally, someone coughed.

"And Caryo doesn't like him, but can't say why…" said the Herald who taught some of the law classes. "I am reluctant to place too much weight on this. Not even all of the Companions get along all the time; there are Companions that dislike anyone who isn't a Herald, including their Chosen's own relatives. I would even hate to speculate."

"It could just be his natural arrogance that gets her back up," Talamir suggested. "The boy *is* arrogant. It's to be expected, in someone with that much rank and privilege, who is also that confoundedly good-looking."

"It could be jealousy," said someone else, in what sounded like the voice of experience. "Just as Peled said. We're not perfect, and neither are *they.* I know the first time I flirted with an outsider, my Jandal got as jealous as anything."

Someone sighed. "I don't suppose it would do any good to reason with her about it—"

"Not if you don't want her to call for a priest and wed the boy on the spot," Keren said flatly. "For those of you who don't happen to have experience with first love—"

"Infatuation, Keren, surely!" exclaimed someone else.

"First love, first infatuation, it doesn't matter because it's a strong emotion either way," Keren snapped back. "She's young, she *just* lost her father, and we can guess that he's been playing all the parts she needs right now in a single package—part comforter, part protector, part lover. *And,* may I add, her Council has been putting pressure on her to *make* some kind of marriage. With all of that going on, not only won't she hear anything bad about the boy, she'll turn on the one who tries to criticize him. *I've* seen that, time and time again, in my village. The fastest way to get a girl to marry someone is to tell her you don't want her to."

She nodded with an air of finality. Alberich saw her looking at him, and just shrugged. If anyone thought *he* had any insights on what would work with Selenay, they were going to be sadly disappointed.

"So what are we going to do?" asked someone in a small voice that sounded very bewildered in the darkness.

Now Talamir cleared his throat—and rose to the occasion.

"We will support her, and her choice," he said firmly. "No matter how hasty or ill-thought we believe it to be. Think! The worst, the very worst, he can do is to make her unhappy—at which point, since Valdemar law supports divorcement, he may well find himself packed back to Rethwellan with his tail between his legs!"

There were some chuckles at that. Weak, but laughter, nonetheless. And at least in Alberich's case, a sigh of profound relief. This was the old Talamir, seeing the larger picture and finding the cleanest path through what could turn out to be a quagmire.

"The best that he can do is to make her happy, and if he does that, even if we still do not care for him, who are we to object?" Talamir went on, the shadows cast by the lantern beside him making him look as ancient as a Grove oak. "Remember, *unless he is Chosen by a Companion* and becomes a Herald, he will never be more than the Queen's Consort, who will have only as much power, or as little, as she grants him—and all of it behind the throne." Talamir looked around, managing to meet the eyes of every Herald there. "So let us determine to put a good face on things," he continued. "Offer her our congratulations, singly, and as a group. Support her choice. Make sure that she knows that we are *there*, as we always have been, for Herald Selenay as well as the Queen."

And that seemed to be about all that anyone could offer.

Alberich went back to the salle, feeling very uneasy. He hoped that would be enough.

He was afraid that it wouldn't be.

But the game had been played out before any of them even knew it was *in* play at all. Now they could only ride along with it, and wait.

1 6

The game was played...

Something about that phrase nagged Alberich as he fell into an uneasy sleep, but it wasn't until he woke the next morning that he realized where he had heard it last.

And it was only after the recollection jolted him that he realized that there might be a connection between where he had heard it first, and Selenay.

He had the flash of memory as he moved into wakefulness, and it brought him alert all at once, his mind moving from a standing start into a full gallop.

The game is about to play—It had been that stranger talking to Norris last night. He could hear the voice clearly in his mind. It had been a well-educated voice, and if there was one thing that it was hard for the well-educated to do, it was to counterfeit being a member of a lower class than their own.

The similarity of phrases was what had given him that shock to the system. What if the girl they had been talking about, the one Alberich had assumed was simply wealthy and plain, had actually been *Selenay?* And that the young man being tutored in seduction had been the Prince of Rethwellan?

It fit. It certainly fit. Untried, sheltered, accustomed to flattery but *not* to the kind of practiced seducer Norris was, she would be easy prey for a man of Norris' experience—or one coached by him.

And Selenay, alone in all of the Court, was the only young woman who would have been sheltered from such men. There was the irony; if she had spent any time among her peers, she would have *seen* attractive young men use their looks in such an unattractive way—and young women do the same.

Or—perhaps not. She *had been* the Heir, and even in the Court, that might have protected her.

Odd as it might seem, the cads in Court circles saved their wiles for two sorts of women—the lower-class girls that they seduced and abandoned, and the unattractive, wealthy ones they seduced and wedded and abandoned on their estates in the country, while *they* came back to Court to enjoy themselves unencumbered by the inconvenient wife. They wouldn't have dared to use those ploys on Selenay.

Still, she had been sheltered in another way. From the time she had been Chosen, she had been at the Collegium, and not the Court. She never saw the intrigues among her peers, because she was among another set of "peers" for whom intrigue was simply out of the question. Even when the occasion had called for it, *she* hadn't spent much time socially in Court circles, *she* spent her social time among Heralds. Or at least, she had until she'd become Queen.

But there should have been one creature above all who would have—or should have—*realized* what was happening before this. And even if she hadn't been able to stop it, she should have been able to warn the rest of them!

:Kantor,: he called.

:I follow you,: his Companion replied. *:I hope you don't mind; you jarred me awake and I just followed your thought.:*

Once he would have been angry; not now. Now, in fact, he was grateful. Kantor had become the perfect partner, in a way; the shield-brother, the man you could depend on to fall in at your side and match you, move for move.

:That's the way it's supposed to work.:

Well, he could see that. Clearly, it didn't always.

:You're thinking Selenay and Caryo.: There was a moment of hesitation. *:You can't understand why Caryo didn't nip this in the bud, especially since she doesn't much like Prince Karath. And why she didn't realize how far things had gotten.:*

:Exactly,: Alberich replied.

:You and I are—exceedingly compatible now. We are about the same age, with similar experience. Selenay and Caryo—aren't. I mean, they're compatible, but their experiences are vastly different.:

Alberich blinked in surprise. That hadn't occurred to him as a possibility.

:Think of Caryo as a maiden aunt, or a virginal, scholarly sister who is much, much older than Selenay. She's—well, to be honest, she's rather sexless. Kind-hearted and stalwart, protective absolutely, ready to comfort when Selenay is hurt or angry, but as thick as two short planks when it comes to romance and especially sex.:

Oh… This was beginning to make him feel a little ill.

:Caryo is the sort of person whose shoulder you cry on when your father dies, the wise and clever person you could ask for help with political and administrative problems. Not the person you go to when you're moon-calfing over a boy. And as for sexual attraction—you'd be horribly embarrassed even to hint that you had such a thing to her, because she would be horribly embarrassed if you brought it up.

Now, suddenly, it all made sense. Terrible sense.

At least, insofar as he understood young women, and insofar as Caryo being in the dark about all this right along with everyone else. *:Dear God…:* he replied, aghast. *:We've all been blindsided.:*

:Our own damned fault,: Kantor agreed. *:We, the Companions, should have known. We know Caryo better than anyone but Selenay—and she was exactly the right Companion for a girl who was bound and determined not to think too hard about anything that wasn't involved in being the Heir and a Herald. If Sendar was still alive—:*

:If Sendar was alive, he'd have sent the boy packing, after making him look ridiculous and unpalatable in Selenay's eyes first. That's the only way to handle such things.: Alberich was at least on surer ground there; as an officer, he'd had to break up many an ill-timed romance.

:But with Selenay alone, we didn't think about how Caryo should change, and you Heralds didn't think that Selenay would find herself looking for something outside of her duties.:

:We were fools,: Alberich said flatly. *:She was clearly drowning in duty and we thought a festival or two would be enough.:*

:Blindsided. And there is only one way to deal with it, and that is to go along with it, just as Talamir said last night. Yes, even if it turns out that this Rethwellan princeling is a rounder and a cad who has been studying how to seduce our Queen.:

The very thought made him angry, made him want to get hold of the blackguard and beat him with the flat of his sword—but Kantor was right. And Talamir was right. Hadn't he *just* been watching plays all this winter and spring that proved that very point? The best way to get a young woman set on a particular young man, and vice versa, was to oppose the match. The only way to separate her from someone who was not good for her was to be reserved on the subject of the young man, while being supportive of *her.* Then, when things began to go wrong, and only then, did you make it clear that you were "on her side." The only difference between a cliché and a truism was the skill and intricacy with which the latter was presented. And, unfortunately, Norris was a much better actor than the tawdry plays he presented for the common folk would have suggested. If he was, indeed, coaching the Prince—

:Have you talked with Caryo about this?: he asked his Companion, as he rolled over on his back and stared up at the ceiling.

:Not yet. Right now she's very hurt that Selenay didn't even hint of this to her. And, frankly, angry with herself for not seeing it. And she should be.:

Well, *he* wasn't going to be the one to say anything, but Kantor was right. In retrospect, Selenay had virtually handed everyone a map to her feelings with that masque, and all anyone had thought, if they'd thought at all, was how clever she was to have devised something that would entertain and honor all at the same time. Kantor was right; in this case, Caryo *had* been as thick as two short planks. And so had they.

:Least said, soonest mended,: the Companion said philosophically. *:I am keeping my thoughts to myself until Caryo is ready to talk to the rest of us. But I think that where Selenay is concerned, our voices must be raised in a song with but a single refrain—:*

:Which is, "All we want is your happiness," I think,: he replied. *:It's true enough.:* At least the feeling behind that phrase would be absolutely genuine. All any of them *did* want was Selenay's happiness. They just wanted it without the Prince's presence involved.

:Meanwhile, I don't think you should give up chasing Norris,: Kantor continued. *:Now I think that young Devlin was probably his contact in the Court to pass him information about Selenay herself. So I don't think you should take your eyes off Devlin either.:*

He smiled grimly up at the ceiling. *:Ah, now, nor do I. In the first place, Norris might* not *have been tutoring the Prince. In the second place, if that was indeed what was toward, we may someday need the evidence. Because what I overheard makes me think that once there's a wedding, the Prince will slip. Selenay might excuse him a time or two, but she won't put up with it forever. And* then *we can prove to her how she was manipulated.:* Then, because he was honest, he had to add, *:If she was. He might really be in love with her; he might be everything he seems. But my gut says he isn't.:*

He felt Kantor's satisfaction. *:You're better at this business than you were.:*

He sighed. *:I could wish that there was no reason to be. The Weaponsmaster is all I ever cared to be.:*

:We play the game we're put into, Chosen,: said Kantor, which seemed to be about the only possible answer.

After that, however, it seemed as if a whirlwind had suddenly engulfed them, and the whirlwind's name was Selenay.

Alberich never had a chance to voice any opinion at all, because it was never asked of him. Selenay simply seemed to *assume* that because she was enchanted by the Prince, everyone else was, too. She had never before had anything that she wanted, really and truly *wanted* so much as Prince Karath—except, perhaps, for her father to be alive again. But the latter was impossible and the Prince was entirely within her reach. She was lonely, she was in love, and at the moment, there was no more potent combination. She could not imagine living without him, and she was taking steps so that she wouldn't have to.

Alberich was not present at the Council meeting that day after the masquerade where she *announced*—not asked, not even for advice— *announced*, arbitrarily and making it clear that she would brook no opposition, that she and the Prince were going to wed. And that it would be within the month. He was told about it later that evening by Elcarth.

Elcarth, Kyril, Jadus, and Talamir were all in Alberich's quarters, which made it a bit crowded once Myste, Keren, and Ylsa joined the group. Elcarth was looking more than a bit dazed, Kyril a little grim, and Talamir very—quiet and contained. Inhumanly so, actually. It made the hair on the back of Alberich's neck rise.

But they all had other considerations at the moment.

"You ladies wouldn't have known her father when he was at his most stubborn," Elcarth said, rubbing his hands over his temples. "When there was something he *knew* he wanted done, and he wasn't going to take 'no' for an answer. He was a force of nature, and there was no point in getting in his way, any more than there is in standing in the path of an avalanche and expecting it to stop because you want it to. It was like seeing her father all over again, with the addition that she was positively *fixated* on getting her way in this, as if it not only would be, it *had* to be, or the world would end."

"She simply rode right over the top of any opposition," Kyril seconded. "Not that there was very much, not when Orthallen and Gartheser threw in on her side. But still—I've never seen her like this, she became a petty tyrant, in fact. It was as if anyone who said anything contrary to her just didn't exist—"

"She was afraid," Talamir said, into the silence. "Fear can make anyone a tyrant."

The men looked at him blankly; Alberich was among them. He couldn't imagine how Talamir had come to *that* conclusion; there was no logic in it.

But Keren and Myste exchanged an eloquent glance, and after Keren nodded, Myste spoke up.

"She was afraid that if she didn't force this through, now, she would lose him, you mean," Myste said. It was a statement, not a question. "And if she loses *him*, it will break her, and she knows it."

"I think so." Talamir passed a hand over one eye, and looked, for a moment, impossibly frail.

"How can it break her?" Elcarth asked, aghast. "Great good gods, she's been through much worse than having a love affair end!"

"She does not precisely *confide* in me, so I can only judge by what I see and sense, based on what I know. I have never been in love myself," he added, somewhat wistfully, "so all I can do is guess. But as for why it will break her—it is precisely because she has been through so much in this last year. I believe that she sees Prince Karath as—as a sort of lifeline."

"I think—maybe—it's *because* he's an outsider," Myste put in. "I mean, she thinks she can't unburden herself to the rest of us, because we're a part of that burden. And anyway, he's made himself indispensable now. If she loses him, it will be that proverbial last pebble that starts the avalanche. Maybe he's only a pebble, but sometimes that's all it takes."

"Think about it, think back to how you *felt* with your first loves, not what you know now. The first time a youngster falls in love, there's no way to tell the difference between love and infatuation from the inside," Ylsa added sadly. "So as far as Selenay and this situation are concerned, right now, the difference is negligible."

"You mean, we treat it as love even though it might be—is probably—infatuation." Kyril looked pained. "But—"

"Remember what I told you about supporting her," Talamir warned.

"But if she goes on like this, overruling everything before anyone even has a chance to object—" began Elcarth. But both Talamir and Alberich were shaking their heads. Talamir gestured to Alberich.

"I think she will not, for there is no fear there for her," Alberich said. "Such things do not rouse her passion or her fear, for they do not affect her love."

"Precisely." Talamir nodded. "Why should she be afraid about a matter of budget, or of setting a law? None of this is going to wrench her love out of her arms. We should be far more concerned that she stops *caring* about these things, frankly."

"Actually," Jadus spoke up, making everyone turn to look at him, "I think the best thing we could do is get this wedding over and done with, if it could be done *tomorrow,* I'd say to do it."

"Because—" Alberich said slowly, *feeling* his way toward the words, "—if mere infatuation it is, the sooner reality comes, the better. So—let the Prince but think he has her, then revert to whatever his true self is, he will."

Just as that stranger with Norris said. He is not bright enough to make up his own speeches. When he has her, his control over himself will lapse.

"Something like that," Jadus agreed. "And when she *has* him, she won't fear she'll *lose* him anymore, so whether it's love or infatuation, she'll start thinking again instead of reacting with her emotions."

"That's what I meant by treating infatuation the same as if it was love," said Ylsa. "Even if *we* are certain it's infatuation, she's certain it's love, and that he shares it, and if you don't give the emotion the same respect as if it is love, she'll stop listening to you."

"Oh, gods," Elcarth groaned. "It's *hard.*"

"Because we all assume we know better than she does, we're so much older and wiser," said Myste dryly. "Believe me, that's exactly what she's most afraid of. She doesn't want to hear about our experience, she doesn't want to think that this intense emotional storm that is making her feel so good for the first time in months is based on anything less than truth. And hellfires, for all we know, she could be in the right. The Prince may be the best thing for her. He may *be* in love with her, and she with him. He's only a second son; there is no way that he is going to be able to aspire to anything but chair-warming at home; at least here, while he may not be a King, he'll be more than a hanger-on. Even if he isn't in love with her, he may see her as *his* escape from mediocrity, and he may treat her with all the respect and tenderness we could ask because of it. But until we have evidence to the contrary, *and* she's ready to look at that evidence, then—"

"—then?" prompted Alberich.

Myste sighed. "Then I believe we need to be planning a wedding."

The "we" turned out to be entirely rhetorical. With the opposition melted to nothing, and perhaps fearing tacit disapproval, if not of the marriage itself, at least of the haste with which she was insisting it be conducted, Selenay turned to the Court rather than the Heralds for her wedding plans.

Now, Alberich had no more notion of how such things were done than any other sisterless bachelor. A month seemed to him to be a perfectly reasonable length of time to plan even a royal wedding. After all, what did one need? A place, a priest, some new clothing, perhaps, and a feast— surely no more time was needed for that than for the Ice Festival.

Evidently not. And although he was *the* most certain man even among the Heralds that this Rethwellan upstart was nothing more than opportunism wrapped in a cloak of glamour, he was relieved to find himself excluded from the planning. Because the entire Court went absolutely mad…

It was sheer bedlam. Just for a start, apparently *every* female of rank had to have a new gown. And every female of rank with any male relatives was bound and determined to shovel their males into new clothing as well. So there was a steady stream of seamstresses and tailors, jewelers and fabric merchants, furriers and shoemakers, going to and from the Palace and the manors around the Palace, from dawn to well past dusk, clogging the roads and getting in everyone's way.

Then there was the question of *where* to hold the ceremony, for there were at least four enormous Temples in Haven that demanded the privilege. That debate alone occupied the Council for an entire day, and was only resolved when, in desperation, the Seneschal suggested that the entire ceremony be held outdoors, on the Palace grounds.

And there was the question of how long the public celebration would be, for an occasion like this warranted feeding the populace at large for a whole day, at least, if not more; there was the problem of food, of course, and since it was now summer, the added problem of spoilage. A week was out of the question, but a day seemed too meager.

And once that was settled, there were the particulars of the wedding feast *and* the wedding breakfast here at the Palace, and why the Council should be involved in *that*, Alberich could not imagine, but evidently they felt they had to decide even the most minute details of the menu.

The next question that threatened civil war within the Court itself was that of precedence and who would serve as which ladies in attendance. It actually came to hair-pulling in the public gardens on one notable occasion. Myste solved this question when not even the Seneschal could, by tracing forward the pedigrees of everyone who had served as ladies in attendance at Sendar's wedding.

"I had the advantage," she admitted later to Alberich, "having that genealogical research at my fingertips to eliminate all those suitors." Having Myste settle the question did earn the Herald-Chronicler a few enemies among Selenay's ladies who discovered themselves placed farther *down* the chain than they wanted, but earned the gratitude of everyone else, including the entire Council.

Although there was no question of who would perform the ceremony (the Lord Patriarch, of course), the question of *which* ceremony would be held was a pressing one. The Queen had her own personal choice of deities that she worshiped, but this was done privately, not publicly. There was no state religion in Valdemar. In fact, the Valdemaran credo was: "There is no one right way." And while this made for great tolerance and freedom—it also made for a problem. How to perform what was essentially a religious ceremony without offending any of the myriad religions and their adherents became a matter of hysteria, until Myste in exasperation unearthed a previous wedding that quoted from every major religion in Valdemar, including (to Alberich's shock) that of the Sunlord. At that point, as far as Selenay was concerned, Herald Myste could do no wrong.

"And I'll play on that later, if I have to," she told Alberich darkly.

The list of difficult questions, it seemed, only grew longer and longer with each passing day. It had been a very long time since a reigning Queen of Valdemar took a Consort, and many things had changed since that time.

Alberich held himself lucky to be well out of it. He understood vaguely that Lord Orthallen got himself put in charge of it all with the help of the Seneschal, and that things were being sorted out, and that was all he cared to know about it. He might not care for Lord Orthallen himself, but there was no doubt whatsoever that the man was a superb diplomat and administrator.

Nevertheless, the whole business was shattering discipline on the Collegium side. The Ice Festival had been bad enough; this was worse. He had to get positively savage with some of the youngsters in his classes, when the excitement over at the Palace started to ooze into the Collegia and some of the Trainees even had the temerity to *skip weaponry classes.*

It was all the fault of the Blues, actually. There was absolutely no point in expecting much of anything out of the highborn Blues, though, and he knew it. Half the time, they weren't even at their classes, having been pulled out for various reasons having to do with The Wedding (he was coming to think of it with capital initials). And the other half of the time, their minds weren't on anything that anyone was trying to tell them anyway. Some of them weren't worth the water in a bucket with a hole in it, but others had friends among the Heraldic Trainees, and unfortunately, they were the ones playing the part of the tempters, luring their Trainee friends away with the siren song of "Oh, come on! It won't hurt to skip just this once!"

The Blues were a lost cause, and Alberich knew it; even parents would look at poor marks this one time and say to themselves, "Oh, but it was all the excitement of the wedding."

As for the Trainees, at least he and the other instructors had ways and means of enforcing their authority. In Alberich's case, there was the threat of humiliation when a truant came back to class. The shame that the runaways would find themselves repeating a class brought some back into line, the threat of "no Hurlee" or other games got the attention of others. But in the end, what saved them all was that Selenay finally got around to declaring a fortnight holiday for all three Collegia, which at least solved the problem of keeping absent minds on study and would-be truants in their seats.

And it gave Alberich an opportunity all unlooked for, to get back down into Haven and concentrate all of his attention on Norris.

And on a new problem.

The sound of music and laughter from the common room and taproom of the Bell was loud enough to reach all the way to the stables. Wedding fever had begun even down in Haven; the banners that had greeted the coronation were being hung again, more decorations were being hung every day, and it seemed to be all anyone could talk about. And of course, where there was an event, there would be commerce—medallions, flags, and banners to wave, portraits and statues, dozens of songs (most bad). There were even stalls with pairs of Selenay and Karathanelan dolls appearing—either dressed as the Moon Maiden and the Prince, or in what were fondly supposed to be the Queen and Prince's wedding finery.

And even the quiet Bell was abuzz. Alberich wasn't terribly unhappy about all the fuss—it made it easier to slip in and out, rather than more difficult—a good thing, since for a change he was here in broad daylight. He was actually in his secret room, changing into one of his personae, when he heard the stable-side door open behind him.

His heart leaped into his throat. He whirled with a knife in his hands, one small part of him wondering *how* anyone had gotten past Kantor, when he saw it was Myste.

He slipped the knife back in its hiding place, hoping she hadn't seen it, and was going to say something—something irritated, actually, since she wasn't supposed to burst in on him like this—when he caught the look of worry on her face. That, and the fact that she was wringing her hands together, made him bite back what he had been about to say.

"I'm in trouble," she said, and for one, startled moment, he flashed on the only thing *that* phrase meant, back in Karse—

"They want me to become their full-time clerk, accountant, and treasurer," she continued, oblivious to whatever expressions had flitted across his face in that brief moment. If any had. He'd probably looked like an idiot with his mouth hanging open.

Then what she'd *said* penetrated, and he realized that the situation was quite serious indeed. "Oh, hellfires," he said. *They want her to work for them and only them, and how is she supposed to do that and continue being Herald-Chronicler? Scratch that; spending that much time with them, how is* she *going to manage without getting caught?*

"Norris has found a backer, and he's getting a theater for the company. The gods of actors and idiots only know where he's getting the money from, but it's quite certain. And the fellow that handles all the business matters—you met him, remember?—wants me to do all of the money things for them. It's a full-time job, I can pledge you that, between managing the take at the door, getting everyone and everything paid for, taxes, hiring things like cleaning women and laundresses." She shook her head frantically. "Thank the gods I got wind of this *before* they actually asked me. I think they're waiting—wisely, may I add—to be sure that the money for the theater is in hand before they say anything to an outsider." Now her voice took on the tones of a wail of fear. "But what am I going to *do?*"

She wasn't panicking, but she looked as if she was in knots. "Sit down, for one thing. You look as pale as a shirt." She did as he ordered, while he sucked on his lower lip and thought, hard. "All right, you *can't* take that job; I couldn't take it and stay undiscovered with a trained actor like Norris watching me. Which means we have to come up with some reason *why* you can't take it."

The moment he said, "You can't take the job," he saw relief suffuse her features. And he was very glad that it was Myste in front of him now, and not Keren, who would have been offended at the very thought that she couldn't keep up the deception. "I think we have these options to get Myste the Clerk out of range before the offer can actually be made. You can 'take another position'—tell them tonight, even, that you've been offered a job, say, on some Great Lord's staff but on his estate, so you have to leave. You can send them a letter saying that some wealthy elderly relative you didn't even know of before today is sick, and wants you to move in and take care of her, and if you do, you'll inherit everything. Or Myste can have a terrible accident and die."

"Myste *will*, if we can't figure out something," Myste said darkly, but looked infinitely more relaxed. "Well, the first one won't do, because every Great Lord is going to be *here* until the wedding is over, and I want to be able to tell them I'm leaving tonight. I'd just as soon not close off all options by killing my old self, so that leaves the second. And I want it to be by letter; I don't want to take the chance on arousing any suspicion by giving them a chance to start asking questions about my story."

"The best choice, I think," he agreed. "No one is going to seriously suggest that you give up a grand inheritance in favor of a position with a theater company that doesn't even have a theater yet. And in case Clerk Myste ever has to come back to Haven, it can either be as a visit after your wealthy aunt has died, or it can turn out that the wealthy aunt wasn't as wealthy as she made herself out to be, and you are back looking for work."

"Excellent," Myste replied, and closed her eyes and sagged back against the wall. "And I have to leave immediately. Better yet, I'm already gone. My aunt sent a coach, and I left in it. I don't mind telling you, I was panicked. Especially after last night."

Alberich nodded; he could well understand Myste's concern, for last night she had gotten to copy another one of those encrypted messages from Norris to—well, whoever they were *to*.

And that gave him an idea. "Writing a letter is perfect," he said. "In fact, write *two*. One to the manager of the company and one to Norris. If you were as infatuated as he thinks you are, he'd think it strange if you didn't send him a personal goodbye. As your old friend, I'll take them both over, and you can go back up the hill as soon as you change."

"What—" Myste began, and then she nodded. "Right! So that Norris *doesn't* suspect, after last night, that I'm a spy who is running off now that I have what I need. I think I know just the tone. The brokenhearted farewell letter of the hopelessly infatuated woman who knows she had less chance with him than a lapdog, but can't bear not to tell him about how her soul will be empty forever without him. It'll take some clever writing—"

"And hold out the offer that if he is ever in—Three Rivers, I think that's far enough, and rustic enough—or if he ever finds himself down on his luck, he can call on you for anything he needs." Alberich chuckled a little as Myste made a face. "You might as well spread it on thick."

"Oh, I will." She stood up and went to the small chest that held writing materials. "This won't take very long."

And it didn't. By the time he was finished changing into his guise as the carter, she had finished both letters, sanded them to dry the ink, folded, and sealed them with a blob of candlewax and her thumbprint. On the outside of one, she made a little drawing of a pen, and on the other, a mask. "The mask goes to Norris," she said, handing them to him.

"Good. Would it sound loutish of me to say that I am relieved that this is over for you? And that I have never liked having you in this position?" he asked, taking them and stowing them in his pouch.

"No, and not half as relieved as I am," she replied, and unexpectedly kissed him. "I make a good historian. I make a mediocre spy."

"But if it had not been for you—" He kissed her back, feeling warm and peculiarly *protective*. It was a very pleasant sensation, now that she was going to be out of danger. He had deliberately not thought about her being *in* danger while all of this was going on. It wouldn't have done any good in the first place, and in the second, well, it might have done both of them quite a bit of harm. They were, first and foremost, *Heralds*. They had duties. Only she could do what she was doing, and they both knew it.

But now he certainly knew what people meant by the phrase, "having your heart hostage to fortune." It was not a feeling that he had welcomed.

"I still make a mediocre spy," she replied. "And I hope you never need my peculiar mix of talents again."

"Oh, I shall—but I hope not as a spy." He raised an eyebrow and she flushed, but laughed. "Don't forget to tell the innkeeper before you leave the Bell where Clerk Myste is going, and that she left in a private coach for Three Rivers a candlemark ago."

"I won't," he promised. He gave her a little bow, and slipped out the back way.

The last thing he was going to do, especially after this, was to go directly from the Bell to his destination. Instead, he cut through back alleys and even through a few unfenced yards to get him to the part of town where the tanners and dyers had their workshops, before he finally headed for the inn. He never came at it from the same direction twice if he could help it, and today it would be especially important that there be no association between himself and the Companion's Bell.

Other than that his "friend" Myste had lived there, of course.

He discharged the first errand by leaving the letter in the room that served as an office, for the business manager was out on some errand or other. But as for the second—the troupe was rehearsing in the stables, and he had heard Norris' voice when he passed by. Now he went in, and waited patiently until there was a break in the action and Norris left the group that was declaiming at each other to get himself a drink of water from the barrel Alberich stood beside.

"Message for you, sir," he said, making sure that his voice was pitched low, his tone harsh, rather than high and shrill as the "scholar" had been. He thrust the folded paper at Norris, who took it automatically, but with a look of annoyance.

Still, the man did open it, and read it, his mouth twitching with amusement. Alberich was rather surprised to find himself wanting to punch that mouth and make him eat that amusement...

"So, the little mouse has got herself a granary, eh?" he said, carelessly. "Well, I can hardly blame her for running off to secure it. Lads!" he called to the rest of the group, whose heads all turned in his direction. "That drab little clerk of ours has fallen into the cream! Some rich auntie's got sick, and she's run off to nurse and inherit!"

"Cor, I could do with a rich auntie," said a beardless fellow enviously.

"Hey, Norris, if she's rich enough, reckon she can afford you?" catcalled another, as Norris made a face.

"She'd have to be richer than the head of the Goldsmiths Guild," Norris scoffed back.

Throttling down the urge to throttle Norris, Alberich started to turn away to leave. Because if he stayed a moment longer, he might hear something that would make him lose his temper.

"Say, fellow, could I get you to run a similar errand for me?" Norris asked. "For, say, a silver penny?"

Alberich turned back. "Aye," he said curtly. "As long as it don't take me out o' town."

"Oh, it won't." Norris pulled an embroidered handkerchief— masculine in style, rather than feminine—from a pocket in his trews. "A friend of mine left this here by accident last night. I'd like you to take it back to him. He lives at a rather grand place on Hoberd Hill. It's the one with the wyvern gateposts; you'll know it when you see it."

Alberich took the handkerchief and the penny, successfully concealing his surprise. Because he knew that address; knew it very well indeed.

It was the location of the Rethwellan Embassy.

All the time he was on his way, he wondered what exactly he would learn when he got there. He knew what the handkerchief business was about, of course, for sewing a packet of papers between two identical handkerchiefs to conceal them was an old play. The bit of fabric had been neatly folded, but he'd felt the thin papers when he put the object in the belt pouch that had lately held the letters. Myste had written these last night, he was certain of it, for the paper was very thin and light.

So this time Norris was prepared to send his—whatever he was sending—openly. Probably more instructions to the Prince on how to handle a woman. Couple that with Myste's certainty that Norris had found a "backer," and it was clear that Norris was under the impression that his job was complete. So maybe he was willing to take a risk he would not otherwise have dared.

Or perhaps he doesn't care now.

Or both. Or—one more possibility—Norris knew that his "handler" would be as busy with the wedding preparations as everyone else, and figured he could afford to be lazy this time, for he wouldn't be caught.

When Alberich reached the Embassy—he went around to the "tradesman's" entrance. Not for the likes of him, those wyvern-carved doorposts and the imposing worked-iron gate. Oh, no.

He followed a narrow passage between the walls until he came to the back of the property, where there were signs of life. Quite a bit, actually, which was hardly surprising considering that the Prince was marrying the Queen of his host country. It took Alberich a while to get the attention of someone who looked as if he was in charge of things.

"What do you want, fellow?" asked the harried-looking man in Rethwellan livery—who then interrupted himself to shout, "Look, how many times must I remind you, the Prince does *not* like lilies!"

"Actor by the name of Norris sent this," he said, thrusting the folded cloth at the man, who took it, then gave it a second, startled glance. "Says someone up here left it down at his inn."

"Ah—yes. Of course." From the man's expression, Alberich knew that they must be the Prince's own handkerchiefs—and that the man had not expected to get them in quite this way—*and* that he knew very well there was something inside them. "Thank you, my man; I'll see it gets to the Pr—owner. Ah—" He fumbled in his belt pouch, came up with a couple of coins, and thrust them at Alberich without looking at them. "Here. For your trouble."

So you think about the tip and forget about wondering why I needed to march up here to return a handkerchief. "Thankee, sir," he said, with a little bow. "I'll be off out of your way."

"Yes, yes, of—*No! No, no, no!*" The man was off, chasing down a couple of fellows with what looked like a rolled-up carpet. Alberich absented himself.

Quickly.

Because he didn't want anyone here to get a good look at him, he didn't want the man to think about questioning him, and above all, he wanted to get back to talk this over with Talamir.

For what the man had almost said was, "I'll see that it gets to the Prince."

17

It would have been a satisfactory end to the tale for Selenay to have realized, at the very altar, that the Prince was a cad who was manipulating her for his own purposes. It would have been equally satisfactory for Talamir and Alberich and Myste to have presented her with the evidence they had gathered, including the decoded papers outlining—well, *something* rotten—in time for her to come to her senses and send the blackguard packing.

In fact, nothing of the sort happened.

The papers were still not decoded, and even if they had been, Selenay would neither have looked at them nor believed what was in them. No one who saw her could have doubted that she was insanely, deliriously happy. The Prince appeared to hang on her every word, *she* certainly did on his. The wedding plans swiftly turned into preparations, without even an incident that could have been thought of as ill-omened, and with no more problems than any other major undertaking. In the end, of all things, it was probably the Tedrel Wars that were due the credit for organizing so much, so well, in so little time. After putting together armies and encampments and battle plans, then seeing to it that everything... was smoothly executed, Selenay's people had more than enough experience to pull off a Royal Wedding in a moon.

Alberich stayed away from the Palace as much as possible; during the last week he never even left the salle. Myste brought him some meals from the Collegium kitchens, for there were no servants to be spared to bring them to him; others he simply prepared for himself. They assiduously avoided the topic of the wedding, concentrating instead on any other matters that could possibly be considered useful.

And in a curious and careful exploration of each other. In fact, with the shining example of what *not* to do so blatantly in front of them, somehow they had both come to the conclusion, simultaneously, that they ought to take a very long time in simply talking about things. It was very curious. Alberich suspected that their Companions had a hand in it. But he wasn't going to object…

These long talks provided the pleasant interludes in what was otherwise a period that was not so much ridden with anxiety as resignation.

He knew that he wasn't the only one who felt this way. Most of the other Heralds that he knew, if they were not actually supposed to be taking part in the proceedings, were avoiding the Palace altogether. The feeling that they all seemed to share was most adequately described by one of the fellows from the south, who had seen some terrible mudslides when he'd been a child. "You see it start," he said, "and it's so slow, and so big, it seems impossible that it can be happening. And then you realize that it's actually impossible to stop—and impossible for you to get out of its way. And if you aren't in the path, all you can do is stand there and watch, knowing that there isn't one damn thing you can do except try and pick up the pieces when it's all over."

He had simply made sure that the Guards he trained as the Queen's bodyguards, who were suffering no such misgivings, were at their absolute peak of performance and knew in their guts as well as their heads that no matter what happened, they were always to protect Selenay from *anyone* that threatened her. Including her husband. When people came to the salle looking for a workout, if they were up to his level of expertise, he gave them one. If they were not, he found them partners, and supervised.

Then the day of the wedding arrived; it was a Collegium holiday, with all the Trainees serving as helpers, additional servitors, or actually participating with their families. It was very quiet at the salle, and Alberich made himself a solitary breakfast, then took the time to give the salle a thorough cleaning and checking. The wedding breakfast was for family, the highest ranking Court members, and the three highest ranking Heralds. After the breakfast would come the preparations. No one needed to turn up in the gardens for hours yet.

By midmorning everything was in perfect shape, and he was sitting on a bench outside, in the sun, working on mending training equipment while Kantor watched. Every so often, a bit of breeze carried a snatch of music from the Palace gardens, but otherwise he could have been all alone out here. He had thought about going down into the city, but couldn't bring himself to face the crowds partaking of the public festivities.

Finally, he couldn't put it off any longer. He went back to his quarters, donned his Formal Whites, and made his way to the gardens.

Any checking of invitations was going on at the gates in the wall around the Complex itself; anyone on the grounds was already part of the festivities. There were far, far more people crowding into the gardens than Alberich felt comfortable around, and the ones who were not in formal uniforms of white, scarlet, or green were, for the most part, so laden with ornaments and so vivid with embroideries that they hurt his eyes. And the sound of dozens and dozens of people all chattering brightly at the tops of their lungs was nearly enough to drive him mad.

Fortunately for his sanity, the Heralds actually had a job to do and a place to go until the moment of the ceremony itself. The Queen's Garden was the assembly point, and he made his way there.

The first person to greet him was not, somewhat to his disappointment, Myste. It was Keren, looking unexpectedly sharp in what was clearly a brand new set of Formal Whites.

"Like me new duds?" she asked, in a heavy Evendim accent, and laughed at his expression. "Never had a set of Formals made for me before; just had a set that was a hand-me-down from the stores. Neither has Myste, actually. We're both odd sizes, and neither of us had the money for a tailor the way the highborn Heralds have. And somewhere along the line somebody figured this out in time to have some tailored up for us." She backed up a pace and looked Alberich over critically. "Now you, you've got the proper military bearing and figure. Must have been a doddle to find a set to fit you."

"I suppose," he replied, noting that her eyes were a little too bright, and figuring that Keren was using inconsequential chatter to cover her unease. "There is, it seems, some merit in being average."

"You, average? Bite your tongue," said Myste, worming her way between two Heralds Alberich didn't recognize. "You couldn't be average if you tried."

He was saved from having to answer anything by the sound of the trumpet that signaled their part of the ceremony.

Heralds at the entrance to the garden formed into a double line and began filing out; the rest of them joined one or the other line in no particular order. Somehow Alberich, Myste, and Keren ended up at the end of their lines; this didn't displease him on the whole. He did not particularly want to be near the center of attention.

The Heralds lined both sides of the path that Selenay and her wedding party would take from the door of the Palace to the bower where the Lord Patriarch waited. Alberich was actually nearest the door in his line, and Keren was directly opposite him. At a mental signal that was passed via their Companions, they smoothly and simultaneously unsheathed their swords and crossed them overhead, forming an arch of shining steel.

As the swords left their sheaths, the chattering stopped. There was a moment of absolute silence.

Then the musicians struck up the processional march, the door of the Palace opened, and the first of the ladies in attendance emerged.

There were twenty of them, strewing rose petals on the path from silver baskets. Last of all came Selenay.

He could not have told what she was wearing, though he knew that even Heralds who were female would be discussing it for days if not weeks; he *was* only a man, after all. It was white—no surprise, she *was* a Herald as well as Queen. It was made of some soft, shining stuff, overlaid with some gauzy stuff, and embroidered with gold and pearls. She was swathed in what seemed like furlongs of veil, which made it difficult to see her face; he thought, as she passed, that she looked terrifyingly happy, though. She stared straight ahead, both hands holding a huge bouquet of white flowers and ivy.

Her step was firm and brisk, and in a moment, she was past him, and all he could see was the back of her gown. It trailed for quite some distance on the ground behind her, and there were two of the little Tedrel orphans carrying her train. And one of them was that little lad in Formal Trainee Grays, an exact duplicate of Formal Whites, except done in gray. He looked terribly solemn and a little scared, but when he saw Alberich he brightened, and Alberich raised his free hand in a formal salute that made him look still happier as he passed.

Fortunately, the children were too young to have been infected with the doubts that plagued their elders.

The Heralds held their pose until the entire wedding party had assembled at the altar. Then, with another signal passed by the Companions, they pulled their swords into a formal salute, and simultaneously sheathed them. As the musicians ended the processional with a flourish, they turned as one to face the altar.

Alberich was just as glad that all he could see was the back of the Herald in front of him. He was reminded of all of the ceremonies he had attended as a member of the Sunsguard, after he had realized how many of Vkandis Sunlord's Priests were corrupt and venial creatures with no more calling than a cat. Then, as now, he had made his mind a blank, and set his face in an expression of bland attentiveness.

The ceremony, which made reference to every deity worshiped in all of Valdemar *and* Rethwellan, was a long one. Before it was over, long before, in fact, he sensed the restlessness of some of his fellow Heralds who had not spent their youths in military training. Anyone who had been a soldier got used to standing at attention for unconscionably long periods of time...

This should have been a joyful occasion. It struck him as inexpressibly sad that it should have become one that was merely endured.

At long last the final vows were spoken, somewhere up there ahead of him. The rings were exchanged, Selenay's veil lifted, the first marital kiss given.

Bells rang out all over the Complex, which signaled the bells of the city below to begin pealing. A cheer rose over the assembled crowd—

And it might have been noticed that the Heralds were not cheering, except that someone had decided that they should form the sword-arch again at full attention. Whether that someone had been Talamir or even Myste, the action made certain that no one was going to have to try and force out something he didn't really feel.

The procession came back through the arch, led by Selenay and her new Consort. He had his arm around her possessively, but Selenay was between him and Alberich, so the Weaponsmaster didn't get much of a look at him. They all retired back into the Palace to be divested of parts of their costumes—veils and trains being highly impractical for outdoor receptions and feasts—and make a first appearance on a balcony above the gardens.

Once again, the Heralds saluted—each other, this time—and sheathed their swords. But now the double line swiftly broke apart, to be absorbed into the milling crowd, some heading for the formal gardens, others on errands of their own.

Myste was one of the latter; Alberich gathered that she had some little wedding duties to attend to in the matter of protocol. He loosened his collar and, feeling heavy in spirit, swiftly separated himself from the throng and headed back down to the salle.

Once there, he stripped himself of the detested finery as quickly as he could, and donned a set of his oldest and most comfortable leathers.

:What did you have in mind for the rest of the day?: asked Kantor.

:I suppose—: he began, then heard footsteps on the path and looked

up to see Elcarth approaching—with a bottle in one hand.

"We might as well stay out here," he said, by way of greeting. "The others will be here shortly."

"Others?" Alberich inquired, raising an eyebrow.

"You'll see soon enough," Elcarth told him, with a sardonic twist to his lips.

And within the candlemark, Jadus, Keren, and Ylsa all arrived bringing *their* bottles. And last of all, bringing up the rear, came Myste, with Healer Crathach, more bottles, and a hamper between them.

The last evidently came as a surprise to the rest; Myste and Crathach set down the hamper and the Healer surveyed them all, hands on hips, as they tried not to look guilty. "Myste advised me of what you were likely to do," he said, and Alberich tried not to wince or feel betrayed. "Or shall I say, the state you were likely to get yourselves into." But Crathach was only warming up to his theme.

"Now, all things considered, I am somewhat in sympathy with the idea of finding a bit of ease in drink, at this particular time. But I told her that you were *not* going to undertake this without me. We are going to get drunk," he announced. "We are going to get *genteelly* drunk, pleasantly drunk, and we will remain in that state with careful application of food as well as drink. We will not drink ourselves sick, we will not drink ourselves stupid, or maudlin, or unconscious, and I will make personally sure that when we finally seek our beds, we will do so in a state that will permit us to sleep and wake without hangovers. Are you with me?"

They set out a kind of *al fresco* area under the trees, since none of them really wanted to be inside, and at any rate, Alberich's little sitting room would have been horribly cramped with all of them crammed into it. "I certainly don't need to be up there now. There are a couple dozen people who'll be giving me their notes," Myste said sourly, jerking her head in the direction of the gardens. "Including Talamir."

"I can't figure Grandfather on this at all," Keren replied, waving vaguely at the Palace; Alberich wondered if she'd gotten a start on all of them back in her own quarters, for although she walked and moved perfectly well, and her speech was clear, she had a glazed quality to her eyes as she passed him a full mug of wine.

"Grandfather?" he asked. Keren had her nose in her mug, so it was Myste who answered.

"Talamir is Keren's grandfather; her people marry off early, and it's usually arranged between families," Myste replied. "Since he was the only boy in his, he had to take a break during his Trainee period to go home and fulfill his—ah—obligation."

"Four breaks, to be precise," Keren added, with a smirk. "Fortunately for me, I'm half of a twin set, and traditionally only one of us had to do the duty. So when I was Chosen, that left my brother Teren as the one."

"But is Teren also not a Herald?" Alberich asked, puzzled.

"He got Chosen after he'd provided the family with a litter," Keren replied and shrugged. "What can I say? With so many close relational ties, my people have to be more pragmatic about marriage. You marry who's available, and if it turns out there's a love match, all well and good, but if not, nobody cares who you sleep with for love or pleasure as long as no one is harmed by it."

"About your grandfather—Talamir," Alberich prompted, wanting to change the subject back to its original topic.

Keren lay back on the old, worn rug she'd appropriated, and stared up at the branches waving overhead. "I don't understand why he isn't *doing* something about this," she said finally. "I mean, it's wrong, we all know in our bones that it's wrong, though—"

"We can't put a finger on why," Elcarth interrupted. "That's the reason, I think. We don't *have* a reason, and somewhere down inside, we're all uncertain that the only thing we can object to is that the Prince is an outsider."

"But none of us objected to Sendar's choice of wife," Jadus said slowly. "None of us had this feeling of wrongness about her, and she was not a Herald."

"But she was Valdemaran," said Crathach, and turned to Alberich. "And have you anything to contribute?"

Alberich shrugged. "No ForeSight, if that is what you mean," he admitted. "Only the same feeling, that this marriage will prove to be a grave mistake." He did not mention the things he had learned about the Prince's contacts with the actor, in no small part because it was not yet proven. But he exchanged a look with Myste, who gave a small shrug.

"Which could all too easily be nothing more than prejudice," Ylsa pointed out shrewdly. "He certainly has gone out of his way to be agreeable to everyone."

"Too agreeable?" Keren asked, then snorted. "As if it matters."

"Well," Myste said slowly, "it does. If we aren't just making a mountain out of nothing, if this is going to turn into a bad situation, then the best thing that we can do for the Queen is to support her in every way. Including keeping an eye on *him,* so that if he does something against her, or against Valdemar, we can do something about him."

"That's more or less what Grandfather said," Keren admitted. "But of all things I hate, I hate having to play a waiting game the most."

"Don't we all," Jadus replied, and that seemed all that anyone could say.

They passed the remainder of the evening assiduously avoiding the entire subject—but it was with them, as an unseen presence, a kind of specter at the feast, the whole time. Alberich left them early, feeling that not all the wine in the world could wash away his unease, and feeling wearier than he ever had in his life. He sought forgetfulness in sleep, and for the first time in his life, actually found it. Whatever was wrong, it was not immediate enough even to give him uneasy dreams.

The Collegium was back in session; things were getting back to normal again. The last of the classes was over for the day, and Alberich was working with Kimel of the Guard, while two more of Kimel's fellows waited their turn to bout with him. They were outside, on the practice grounds, rather than inside the salle—whenever possible, since the mirror incident, Alberich preferred to run practices that were, by their nature, unpredictable on the grounds outside.

Alberich caught movement on the path long before the Prince and his entourage arrived; he sensed it, identified it as "outsiders" by the lack of Whites or Guard uniforms, and dismissed it as currently unimportant, all in a heartbeat. The group of seven or eight paused a prudent distance outside the edge of the practice ground and watched.

There was some murmuring, but nothing more than that; certainly there was no hint of scorn or scoffing in the tones of the muttered conversation. Perfectly acceptable, that was. Alberich finished the bout in a draw with Kimel. He probably could have beaten him; he usually did but caution made him decide not to do so in front of outsiders. The two of them drew back and saluted, and only then did Alberich turn his attention to the audience.

It could not have been clearer that the one in the middle was Prince Karathanelan. The man was, Alberich supposed, handsome enough. He could certainly see that Selenay would have no reason to find the arrangement of his features less than pleasing. The cut and style of his clothing was a bit different from roughly half of the young men around him; the effect was of "foreignness," but was reasonably flattering. The others were apparently friends of his from Rethwellan; Alberich had heard something of them, that a number of the Prince's landless friends from Rethwellan had arrived in time for the wedding, and that Selenay had already granted them holdings of their own from unclaimed properties on the Border with Karse and Rethwellan. Alberich wished them joy of their new lands. They weren't the most prosperous even at the best of times, being mostly sheep country.

What Alberich didn't like was the posture of those around him. These were sycophants; nothing more. They devoted themselves to pleasing someone stronger; if any of them had ever had an original thought in his head, he had quickly suppressed it. A man who surrounded himself with men like these, in Alberich's experience, was a man who had a great deal of difficulty in understanding that the world did not happen to run itself to his desire.

There were a great many Sunpriests like that...

Still, the look on the face of the Prince suggested that he had some respect for Alberich's ability.

Alberich gave him a sketchy sort of salute, while the Guards gave him the full bow due to his position as Consort. He waited, resting, to see what the Prince would do or say.

Although a brief shadow passed over the Prince's face, aside from that flicker of displeasure, the Prince's expression did not change, and his voice, when he spoke, was polite and pleasant enough.

"You are the Weaponsmaster?" he asked. "The Karsite?"

"Weaponsmaster Herald Alberich," Alberich confirmed. "Karsite-born, yes, Your Highness."

The Prince looked him over carefully. "And Karsite-trained, I am told. Interesting." As he was surveying Alberich, the Herald was doing the same for him.

:There's muscle there,: he observed to Kantor.

:No matter what he's been doing since he got here, he's not soft,: Kantor agreed.

"I should like to bout with you," the Prince said abruptly.

Alberich did not bother to point out that the Prince was hardly dressed for a round of vigorous exercise; he was clearly one of those who did not trouble himself over the ruin of a suit of clothing. He merely glanced at the two Guardsmen, who quickly effaced themselves with a little nod, making it clear that they were perfectly willing to yield their time to the Prince. One of them picked up a set of practice swords and offered them to the Prince, as some of his entourage helped him to take off his elaborate doublet and relieved him of some of his jewels.

"Would Your Highness make a choice of practice weapons?" the Guardsman asked.

But the Prince waved them off. "Live steel is the choice of men," he said, with a touch of arrogance that made the Guardsman flush.

:*Stupid. Overconfident*,: Kantor said acidly.

:*Testing me*,: Alberich countered, as he took up his own sword from where it was lying with the Guardsmen's. :*And he knows that there is no way that I would dare harm him. He has me at a disadvantage, he thinks*.:

The question was whether that advantage was real or only in the Prince's mind. There was muscle under that silk, but somehow Alberich doubted whether the Prince had ever had a Weaponsmaster who really tested the Prince to the limits of his ability. There was too much sly arrogance there.

Nevertheless, Alberich was not at all certain that he wanted to show the Prince which of them was the superior fighter. The Prince was the enemy here, but he was an enemy who had not yet truly shown his hand. He knew far more about the Prince, he would warrant, than the Prince knew about him. So there was a distinct advantage in leaving the Prince with the impression that his expertise was less than it actually was.

All that flashed through his mind in a few moments, as he made sure that his weapons were in good condition and his own muscles thoroughly warmed up.

Then they faced off, and the combat began.

It was no real challenge; Alberich was not only able to react automatically to the Prince's blows and feints, his mind was free to *think* about what he was doing, despite the fact that they were using live steel weapons.

The Prince's style of fighting was a curious combination of aggression and stealth that told Alberich far more about the Prince's personality than the Prince would ever guess. He did not—quite—engage in the underhanded moves of the streetfighting bravos that Alberich had encountered in his own nighttime prowlings, but the things that he did left Alberich with no doubt that he was perfectly well acquainted with such tactics. And while Alberich himself made no bones about teaching his Trainees those moves, he doubted that the Prince had any notion of this. So he pretended that he had not noticed those little suggestions of a feint, and proceeded exactly as if he was fighting in the "classical" style.

And he thought that he saw the Prince's lips tighten in a self-satisfied little smile when Alberich failed to respond to those feints.

So much for the testing; having established the perceived limits of Alberich's expertise, the Prince abruptly switched tactics, and went for a very aggressive, straight-on attack. Alberich kept up a purely defensive strategy, and did not respond to any of the openings that the Prince gave him. This was surely puzzling Kimel and the other Guards, but Alberich wasn't working for their benefit, only for this audience of one. The impression he wanted to leave the Prince with was that Selenay's Weaponsmaster was skilled, competent, strong, but limited in his vision—and thus, in what he was teaching the Trainees.

I'll have to have someone watch the boy when he *practices,* he realized. There was a lot he could guess from what the Prince had done so far, but if it ever truly came to a fight between the two of them, he wanted to be sure of what the Prince could and could not do.

Gradually, the Prince's style began to drift, and for a moment, there was a nagging sort of familiarity to it that Alberich could not pin down. It was flamboyant, definitely overconfident, and grew more so as time went on.

Then, as the young man committed to a traveling lunge with a shout, a lunge that would have gotten him into a world of difficulty if he had not had lightning reflexes and stupendous athletic ability, Alberich realized where he had seen this style, and *knew* who had been teaching him.

Norris.

Should I let him beat me? he wondered, then.

:I wouldn't,: Kantor cautioned. *:He might guess that you did. And besides, you want him wary of you, yet sure he can beat* you *if he really puts his mind to it. Wait until he gets a little careless, and take advantage in such a way that it can be a draw*—there!:

But Alberich had already spotted the momentary distraction, and drove in, so that the two of them ended up body-to-body with their blades hopelessly entangled. A draw.

And the Prince withdrew with a salute that was not—quite—mocking.

"An excellent bout, Weaponsmaster!" he said jovially, removing the practice helm and tossing it carelessly to Kimel, who caught it unthinkingly. "Thank you!"

Alberich gave him a grave bow without speaking, and as the Prince and his chattering entourage sauntered back up the path to the Palace, he disarmed and turned his attention back to his Guardsmen.

Kimel gave him a questioning look, but said nothing. The others took their lead from him. Alberich nodded.

"Sometimes," he said quietly, "it is as well, not to reveal all."

Kimel grunted and nodded. "I wondered," he said and left it at that.

But Alberich was not quite done. "I would be grateful, should anyone an eye to that man keep, should he be found in weapons' practice."

Kimel nodded again, and this time, so did the other Guardsmen. "We'll see to it, Weaponsmaster," he said, and Alberich clapped him on the shoulder with a feeling of satisfaction. The undercurrents of that simple conversation had said more than the words themselves. Kimel and the others had seen the hints of underhandedness and had not liked what they'd seen. And perhaps they had already observed some things in the Prince that made them uneasy. For the first time, Alberich had some coconspirators who were *not* among the Heralds (or in Crathach's case, the Healers).

And that would be very useful indeed.

Nevertheless, this was hardly something that needed to be pursued immediately; it was unlikely, having had this round of exercise, that the Prince would choose to go find another sparring partner and continue the practice. That was not how Alberich was reading his nature. He would bask in the admiration of his friends and sycophants, none of whom had or ever could have taken Alberich to a draw, and after he tired of the admiration, he would probably either find another subject or move into a dissection of the bout. But he would not, now that he was warmed up, follow it up with more practice. Nor would he make much of an effort to find out what his cronies knew about Alberich.

So the immediate need was to continue the practice that had been interrupted, perhaps now with an eye to drilling in the counters to those abortive moves that the Prince had displayed.

"So, Rusken," Alberich said, picking up a wooden blade and gesturing to the Guardsman, "your turn it is, I believe?"

Dutifully, though her heart was not in it, Selenay forced herself to concentrate on the dull details of the Council meeting when what she really wanted to do was to lapse into a daydream. She felt like a cat full of cream; she wanted to smile and purr and generally make a spectacle of her contentedness.

And of course, she could do nothing of the sort. She had to look grave and attentive, and pay attention to her Council debating over the details of the trade agreements with Rethwellan that were a consequence of her marriage, when she didn't want to think about trade at all, she wanted to think about tonight, and what would happen when she and Karath were alone at last.

No wonder that people would do and say nearly anything for love!

She had known that it would not be pleasurable at first; she'd had plenty of instruction from a sympathetic Healer named Anelie during the weeks before the actual wedding. But the "at first" had not been long—

Ruthlessly she dragged her attention back to the meeting, in time to nod gravely as the Councilors finally agreed on a trade package, then went on to the relatively simple matter of signing off on the grants of property that Karath had asked her to settle on his friends. It was a small enough thing. There were properties along the southern Border whose owners were no longer among the living thanks to the Tedrel Wars, and here were landless second sons out of Rethwellan, who were eager to take responsibility for them. The Councilors had no great objections, and the papers were quickly written up.

So ended yet another tiny problem—with the income from these properties, those landless second sons would now be able to support themselves in Haven at least half of the year. Karath would have friends here, something that had worried her—though he did seem to be getting along very well with some of her own young courtiers.

That was, in fact, where he was now; out hawking with some of the young men of the Court. He had also said something about wanting to test the mettle of her famed Weaponsmaster; she hoped that Alberich would go easy on him.

The Council meeting went on for what seemed to be an interminably long time. Yet she had to admit that there was a great deal of business to take care of, as much had been set aside in the rush attending on the hasty wedding and the week she had stolen for herself thereafter. But it was concluded at last, when it appeared that if it was *not* concluded, the Councilors would be forced to do without their dinner.

And as this was not an emergency, sending the pages out for cold viands and drink and continuing the business—even if Selenay herself had been prepared to put up with it—was not to be thought of. The Councilors liked their comforts, too, and were not prepared to do without them, having been forced to do so for the last months of the Tedrel Wars.

She took her leave of her Councilors, and all but flew to her quarters and the hands of her maids; as she changed her clothing and submitted to their attentions, she heard, with an internal thrill, the sounds of laughter as Karath approached the door. He and his friends must have had a grand day while she had been working. And after all, why not? He was not co-Ruler and could not be unless he was Chosen, which was looking less and less likely as time passed, so why shouldn't he be spending his time in sport? In fact, by socializing with the courtiers, he would be taking the burden from her of doing the same.

"Ho, Selenay!" he cried, bursting through the door, waving some of his friends, who laughingly tried to follow, back into the hall. "I have met your Weaponsmaster, and tried his blade!"

She leaped up from her seat, as the maid who had been fixing her hair waved her hands in fruitless protest. He enfolded her in his arms and kissed her; her lips parted beneath his and his tongue teased hers as she tasted the salt on his mouth.

She felt herself melting, as always; it was he who pulled away first. "And what came of that, my Prince?" she asked breathlessly.

"Oh," Karath said carelessly, "I think, had I exerted myself, I could have taken him. But he is a fine swordsman, conservative, but fine. I am sure he is a good Weaponsmaster."

Selenay almost said something then, for that certainly did *not* sound like Alberich—Alberich, conservative?—but then she thought better of it. Alberich was certainly doing *her* a favor, letting Karath think himself the finer fighter, and where was the harm in that? In fact, now that she came to think of it, she felt a surge of warmth toward dour Alberich, that he would compromise his own reputation in order to make Karath feel the superior.

So she resolved not to say anything about it, she simply smiled and said, "I doubt it not," and let him lead her in to dinner.

The contest turned out to be something of a topic of conversation among Karath and his friends, with a great deal of gesturing and boasting. She discovered, with a flush of pride, that Karath was very much considered to be the superior swordsman among his cronies, and she thought, given the apparent sincerity of their talk, that this was not just flattery. That he had fought Alberich to a deadlock was considered to be amazing by those of his friends who were Valdemaran, and their admiration was considerable. Karath warmed under their regard, and expanded on the theme, describing other bouts he was particularly proud of. She smiled and paid little attention to the chatter, which sounded to her ears very like that of the younger Trainees when they first began to gain some success in arms, and concentrated instead on merely watching him. He was hardly insensible of her regard, and looked as if it gave him a great deal of pleasure.

Bless him—let him preen and strut a little! He had never been forced to *use* that sword of his, and if she had her way, he never would. It was all still a game to him, and not the deadly business that she knew it was; she took great pleasure in that.

From dinner, the Court went out into the gardens, where there was music and some simple dancing. He remained assiduously at her side, showing by means of a smile or a casual, whispered remark that he was as eager to withdraw as she was. But of course, this sort of thing was as much of a duty as the Council sessions, and she carefully exchanged pleasantries and conversation with, not only the Rethwellan Ambassador, but all the other notables present.

It did give her a great deal of pleasure, however, to be able to tell Karath's friends over the course of the evening that they were to receive official word of their grants from the Council on the morrow. She loved the way that Karath smiled and accepted their effusive thanks graciously.

Finally, it seemed that to her that they had distributed their attention enough for one evening, and when she whispered to Karath, "My lord, shall we withdraw?" he smiled knowingly and nodded.

It was not the custom in Valdemar, much to her relief, for the Monarch to leave a social gathering with any fanfare. So they simply drifted off under the ever-watchful eyes of her Guards, and took the private entrance back into the Royal Suite.

Once there, her maids descended on her like a swarm of ants, while he sauntered off to his dressing room to the like attentions of his servants. The days were long gone when she could dress and undress herself; being Queen apparently meant wearing gowns that it was impossible to get into or out of without help. But once her maids had taken down her hair and gotten her stripped down to her shift, she dismissed them all, slipped into a silken bed gown, and with a shiver of anticipation, got into bed to await Karath.

He was not long in coming. With a knowing grin when he saw her waiting for him, he extinguished the last candle, and she felt the mattress take his weight in the sudden darkness.

In the next moment, he had slipped the gown from her shoulders, and his lips were on hers, insistently; his tongue probing at her mouth.

Her lips opened immediately as she felt her skin flush, and for a moment, his hands cupped the sides of her face as his tongue teased hers.

But then his hands were moving lower, caressingly, clever fingers making her skin tingle, and when his hands reached her breasts; she gasped at the sensations he awoke in her body, and with that now-familiar feeling of melting, lay back into the softness of the mattress.

As one hand slipped still lower, his mouth took over where his hands had been, evoking still more intoxicating thrills of pleasure, and she moaned softly under his caresses. By this time, she was nearly mindless, all of her attention bound up in the sensations that he was creating in her body, feeling herself on fire with pleasure and desire and an urgency driving her towards that peak she now not only knew existed, but which had become so very necessary to her life.

So that, when he finally took her, she was all animal, crying out as she raced toward the goal, nothing else mattering in all the world but their bodies moving together to that moment when she exploded in pleasure, convulsed and paralyzed at the same time, a cry escaping from her that she could not have stopped and didn't want to.

And before she had fallen from that pinnacle of sensation, he had come to his own shuddering climax, so that they fell together, tangled in sweat-gleaming limbs, into dreamy, euphoric lassitude, and then, when he had pulled the covers over them both, sleep.

1 8

Karath was eating and talking at the same time, and it always amazed Selenay that he managed to eat as much as he did and still look trim and fit. At the moment, he was eating his way through the plate of breakfast pastries like a fire going through dry timber. Selenay was just as happy to let him have all of them to himself; a little dry toast and some tea was all that she could bear to stomach at the moment, and her stomach was not altogether pleased about *that*. And alas, this was no mere illness, which she could expect to recover from in a day or so. Oh, no.

She had, somewhat to her dismay, discovered that eternal truth that most women learn, soon or late. The pleasures of the bedroom, undertaken without precautions, end in babies. Three days of discovering that she could not rise in the morning without recourse to a basin had told her that much.

Of course, in her case, the pleasures of the bedroom were *supposed* to end in babies, and in fact, were required to end in babies. As many as possible, in fact—but at least the typical "heir and a spare," so that there were two chances of being Chosen. That was, after all, what her Council had been nattering about for *months*—why they'd wanted so desperately to find her a husband in the first place. When she let them know—well, they'd be thrilled. At least, right up until the moment that it occurred to them that there was some risk in childbearing. Not that she was worried; she was in the best of health and positively surrounded by Healers. She'd been in a lot more danger of injury watching a Hurlee game.

I just didn't think it would happen so quickly, she thought mournfully, and told her stomach sternly to behave itself while Karath went on with his meal and his one-sided conversation, utterly oblivious to her discomfort. Of course, the Healers would have things that could help in this case— but that would mean going to the Healers, and then they would know she was pregnant, and then *everyone* would know she was pregnant, and that would open up an entirely new set of things for the Council to natter at her about—

Yet another worry. Why was it that she always seemed to add concerns, and never seemed to actually get rid of any?

Karath's chattering, usually about things that interested her only vaguely, like hawking and the recent exploits of his friends, tended to pass through her head at the best of times like an express coach, without stopping to unload any information. This morning, as preoccupied as she was with keeping her scant breakfast down, she almost missed what he was saying entirely. Except that one word caught her distracted attention, forcing her to bring her mind back to the breakfast table, and she blinked and finally *looked* at him.

"Forgive me—I was woolgathering for a moment," she said apologetically. "What was it you just said?"

He pouted a little. He pouted, as he did everything, beautifully. It was distinctly unfair. If she'd been able to pout that prettily, she would never have to fight her Council.

"Sometimes I wonder if you ever hear anything I say in the morning," he complained. "You always seem distracted at breakfast. I *said,* I think I'd like to have that handsome black stallion that just came into the Royal Stables as our wedding gift from Lord Ashkevron for my coronation mount."

Coronation mount? Hadn't he been paying attention at all?

"I thought that was what you said," she replied, choosing her words with great care. "You can certainly have the stallion all to yourself since *I* have no use for him, but Karath, I thought it had been explained that there won't be a coronation for you. You can't be crowned King of Valdemar."

"Why not?" he asked, pouting even more, though his eyes were getting stormy. "Don't you Valdemarans crown your Kings in a public ceremony?"

"We do." She felt a cold nausea that had nothing to do with pregnancy as she realized that they were about to have their first fight. Good gods—she *knew* all this had been explained to him! It had been in the marriage contract! Hadn't he even read it? "But you can't be King."

His mouth suddenly went from a pout to a hard, angry line. "Why not?" he asked tightly. "You are the ruler here. Your Council doesn't have any power except to advise you. I've seen what you can do when you want to. You've handed out properties and titles to anyone you choose without even *telling* them. You can make me King if you wanted to. You can tell your Council, just like you told them that you were going to marry me."

"No, I can't," she said, the nausea rising into her throat. "And it has nothing to do with the Council. It's the law that's keeping you from it, and not even the Queen is above the law. You *can't* be King, because you aren't a Herald. Only a Herald can be a King or a Queen in Valdemar."

He snorted with exasperation, as if he suspected she was prevaricating. "Then make me a Herald!" he exclaimed angrily. "If that is all that it takes, just make me a Herald and get it over with! I don't know why you haven't bothered to do it already!"

"I can't *make* you a Herald!" she replied, now getting a little angry herself. Hadn't he listened to anything anyone had told him since he had arrived here? Or did he only listen when what he heard was what he wanted to hear? "Heralds aren't made, they're Chosen."

"Then *Choose*—" he began, but she interrupted him.

"They aren't Chosen by a person, they're Chosen by their Companion," she told him flatly, a chill over her words that he seemed oblivious to. "So you can't be a Herald because none of them have Chosen you." She didn't bother to add that he would then have to go through the Collegium like anyone else before he became a full Herald and could be crowned co-Consort and King. If he really had ignored something so fundamental as needing to be a Herald before becoming a King, he would never grasp having to be schooled for four or more years first.

"You're telling me," he said, slowly and incredulously, "that the reason I can't be King is because I don't have a white horse?"

"They aren't horses," she began, but he was already pushing away from the table.

"There must be fifty or a hundred of those beasts in that field next to the Palace," he said, a dangerous edge to his voice. "They can't all belong to somebody. We'll see about this nonsense."

He stalked out, and she *might* have tried to stop him—except at that moment she lost her battle with her stomach, and with that, her will to try to break him of his delusions gently evaporated.

Let him stand around in Companion's Field with a carrot in his hand for the rest of the day, if he elected to. He'd only look silly, and maybe when he was tired, hot, and ready to come back to the Palace he'd be more reasonable.

* * *

:Chosen—: Kantor said, just as Alberich was correcting one of the younger Trainees' aim with his bow, nudging his feet into a better stance, showing him how to aim along the shaft, then elevate to allow for the arrow dropping in flight. *:I don't want to interrupt you, but there is about to be something of a crisis. And we are the closest—we, and Keren and Dantris, of course—to the situation.:*

Calmly, Alberich stepped back and let the Trainee shoot, not changing his expression by a hair. *:What crisis? What situation?:*

:Prince Karathanelan is coming to Companion's Field; he has three friends, they are all mounted, and they all have ropes. He thinks he's going to catch and break a Companion so he can be made King. Evidently when Selenay convinced him just now that he couldn't be crowned unless he was a Herald, he put his own interpretation on being Chosen.:

Hardly surprising, if he was the sort of Prince that Alberich thought he was.

The arrow hit the target this time, at least, which was an improvement over the Trainee's last several shots. *:I fail to see the crisis. Surely you aren't going to try to tell me that he can catch one of you if you don't want to be caught?:* It wasn't as if the Prince could pin a Companion in a corner; the fence around the Field was mostly to keep people out, not Companions in. In fact, Alberich would not have put it past a Companion to leap the wall around the Complex, at need.

And besides that, any Companion in danger of being caught against his will would be instantly rescued by the entire herd. No horse would stand there and face a charging Companion herd, no matter what his rider wanted.

:Of course not,: Kantor replied, now coming into view through the trees, trotting toward him. *:But I believe Caryo intends to be caught, so she can kick the fewmets out of him. And other than you and I and Keren and Dantris, I think the rest are inclined to let her have her way. She has put up with a great deal since he arrived here, and done without much of the company and attention of her Chosen.:*

:Ah.: That put an entirely different complexion on things. At the least, if the Prince was damaged, Selenay would be distressed. If he was embarrassed, he'd make her miserable. And even if Caryo was not the sort to have murder on her mind, accidents could happen. He didn't bother to ask if the other Companions had tried to reason with her; Caryo was as stubborn as any Companion born, and as Kantor had pointed out, she'd had to put up with a lot of aggravation since Selenay met the Prince. This was one insult too many. "Students!" he

said aloud, as Kantor reached him. "Some small trouble there is that I must attend. Trainee Telbren, you are in charge." And as he finished the sentence, Kantor stood steady and he vaulted onto Kantor's bare back. As soon as he had his balance, the Companion whirled on his rear legs and broke into a gallop. Which *looked* like more of an impressive feat of horsemanship than it actually was; Companions were legendary for their ability to keep their Chosen in the seat.

They were also legendary for their speed, but as they came out of the trees, bearing down on four strangers mounted on mere horses, he saw it was already too late. There was Caryo, neatly "caught," standing meekly with four ropes and a saddle and bridle on her—

His heart sank. *Oh, no. They used a horse-bridle.* If there had been *any* chance that the Prince might be forgiven his *faux pas* by the other Companions, given that Caryo was burning to teach him a lesson, it had just flown swiftly away. No Companion would ever forgive the insult of having a bit stuffed into his or her mouth, nor forgive the insult to a fellow Companion.

—and there was the Prince, down off his horse and approaching her with a swagger, grabbing the reins and preparing to mount.

"Highness!" he shouted, as a second white streak that could only be Keren and Dantris came into sight from the direction of the riding arena. "Highness, *look out*—"

But it was far, far, too late.

If he had blinked, he would have missed it. As it was, in one way, he was glad he had not, though in another, he *wished* he had.

From meek, docile, and trussed up, Caryo turned into a whirling, spinning—and quite deadly, if she chose—fury. In that brief moment, the merest breath, she expertly yanked three of the four ropes out of the hands of their holders and freed herself from their control, probably leaving the palms of those hands bloody and torn in the process, though they were in too much shock to register the pain immediately. The fourth rope was in the Prince's hands, and instead of ripping it out of his hands, she wound it around herself as she whirled and used it to pull him in closer, he being not bright enough to *let go*—

—and as soon as he was in range, both hind feet lashed out in a precisely calculated kick—

—which landed right in the Prince's midsection. He went flying backward through the air, most spectacularly.

Caryo rid herself of all four ropes, though he could not make out how she did it. She simply seemed to give a kind of shrug, and they loosened and fell off, and she stepped out of the loops lying on the ground. She spit out the bit, shrugged off the bridle as easily as she had the ropes, then she bucked off the saddle and kicked it after the Prince, and went galloping away, head high, tail flagged. Evidently, with the probable intervention of two Heralds and their Companions at hand, she considered that the single kick was enough.

Behind her, three young courtiers were bent over their hands and their saddle-bows, cursing and gasping. The Prince was on the ground, also gasping; not a surprise, given that the hammer blow of hooves to his gut must have driven every bit of air that had been in his lungs out of them. But he could have had broken ribs—

:He doesn't,: Kantor said. *:Though he'll have black-and-blue hoofprints on his belly for days. Caryo didn't actually kick him; it was more like a calculated and very powerful shove.:*

Keren got to the Prince first; rolled him on his side, then slammed him across the back until he could breathe again, then helped him to his feet, talking the whole time. Alberich reached them just in time to hear her finish.

"—terrible insult. Like putting a slave collar around *your* neck, Highness," she said. Alberich could tell, though, that the Prince wasn't listening. He was red-faced now, and it was with anger.

"I will hunt that beast down this moment, and I don't care who it belongs to," he said between clenched teeth. "And I will *destroy* it."

Enough was enough. Alberich seized both his shoulders, turned him so that he was looking right into Alberich's eyes, and shook him twice. Hard. Like a wolf with a snake. "Then on trial for murder and treason you will be, and pay for both with your life!" he rasped harshly. "To kill a Companion is *murder* by Valdemaran law. To kill the Queen's Companion, *treason.* Do not force your bride to hang you, Prince, for she will."

Evidently Alberich's words penetrated, for the Prince gaped at him in shock.

"For a *horse?*"

"For a *Companion.*" Blessed Sunlord, just how stupid was this fool? "They—are—not—horses," he continued, emphasizing each word with a hard shake. "No matter what your eyes tell you. Your eyes lie." He had done some reading since the Prince arrived, on Myste's insistence, and now he was glad that he had. "Have you broken ribs? A broken pelvis? No. Because it was a Companion that kicked you—shoved you with her hooves, rather—and not a horse. Think! Had it been a *horse* that had done this, would you not in blood and broken bones be lying? In your own land, lives the Shin'a'in Tarma—so I know that you know of this. The Companion is like to her *kyree* Warrl. Be grateful she did no more than kick you for your insults."

He saw the Prince's eyes widen, then narrow again, at the comparison. He also heard Kantor's snort of disgust at being compared to a *kyree*. But Kantor knew better than to object, since at least now the Prince had some basis for comparison that he *might* believe.

"So—" Karathanelan got out around clenched teeth. "How do I get one of them to let me ride it?"

"Choose you, you mean?" Alberich replied, letting go of the young man's shoulders. "After this?" He shook his head, and wondered at the monumental hubris that would permit the Prince to even think of such a thing. He considered trying to explain that it *might* happen—if the Prince were to have such a complete change of character as to be a different person. He opted for the simpler choice, for Karathanelan would never believe that he needed to change his character. "After such an insult to all Companions as this—never. Not even if the Queen was to come here and beg them upon her knees."

And satisfied at least that the fool was in no condition to try any more foolishness, he gave the merest sketch of a bow, and turned on his heel. Two steps took him to Kantor, and he mounted and rode off. There were more important matters to tend to than the petulant Prince.

At least for now.

Myste was laughing so hard that there were actually tears coming from the corners of her eyes, and her lenses fogged. "Oh, gods," she gasped. "Oh, *gods.* I wish I'd seen it!" She mimed the Prince's ungraceful arc through the air with one hand. "*Eeeeeeeee—thump!* Oh, I wish I'd seen it!"

"No, you don't," Alberich contradicted her sourly. "The Prince has a good memory, and although he probably will not dare to touch another Companion, he is *going* to find a target for his anger. More than one, I suspect; anyone who actually witnessed his disgrace is going to find themselves on his short list of people he'll mark for punishment and revenge. With his reputation and manliness so utterly refuted, he will want to make someone pay."

"And what could he do to a Herald?" Myste scoffed.

"I don't know," he replied. "And that is what concerns me. He has already tried to have me dismissed from my post as Weaponsmaster today—for 'putting violent hands on a Prince of the Blood,' if you please. It was only the reaction of the Council to that statement that persuaded him that I am out of his reach for now." He shook his head. "Kyril stood up and said that he was lucky I had not finished the task Caryo started. And that for laying violent hands on a Companion, *he* could have found himself in the Palace dungeons."

"The Palace doesn't have dungeons," Myste said without thinking.

"I know that, and you do, but the Prince apparently does not." Alberich shrugged. "That is not relevant. The point is, he has already sent his three 'friends' packing. He tried to disgrace me. Keren has been warned, and is going to try to stay out of his sight." He grimaced. "Poor Selenay."

"Why 'poor Selenay'?" Myste asked, surprised.

"Caryo is *her* Companion," he reminded her. "I do not think that he will harm her physically, but there are other ways he can make her unhappy." Many other ways, actually. He wondered how Caryo had broken the news to Selenay, for surely she would not have waited for the Prince to tell his version of the tale first.

She shrugged. "I suspect that after he hears the news, he won't be inclined to take any of his pique out on her. If he wants a validation for his masculinity, he'll surely have it."

"The news?" He looked at her blankly. "What news?"

"She's going to have a baby, of course." Myste *tsked*. "Men. I suppose you think it isn't important."

But her words made his blood run cold, as he remembered that overheard conversation with Norris. "On the contrary," he said. "It is very important. If what we suspect about the Prince is, in fact, true—"

Myste lost her sarcastic smugness, and went a little pale. "I'd forgotten about that. Once the baby's born, if he can't be King—"

"—there is nothing in the laws of Valdemar that say that a Regent must be a Herald," Alberich finished grimly for her. "And even now you would find it difficult to persuade most of the members of the Council that he should not be Regent for his own child should something happen to Selenay."

Selenay had thought she was prepared for an unpleasant time with her husband—insofar as it was possible to be prepared, after getting a shock like that from Caryo. Bless her heart, Caryo had *not* said, "I told you so," she had only given the bald facts of the matter, and all she said in her own defense was, *:I was afraid if he managed to catch one of the youngsters, someone would have gotten seriously injured before it was over. And I admit, I wanted to put him in his place. I didn't exactly kick him, though, Selenay. There's nothing broken but his pride.:*

She could scarcely countenance, not only that he had tried to force a Companion to his will, but that he had done so in the mistaken belief that he would then be a Herald and could be crowned King and co-Ruler. It was as if every lesson in Valdemaran law that he had been given had soared over his head. Hadn't he even bothered to listen a little?

Apparently, it was only to what he wanted to hear.

When Caryo first told her, she was so furious she could not even see, and had to sit down as her knees went weak. Rage and an empty stomach do not combine well.

She raged inwardly at him, nevertheless. How *dared* he lay violent hands on a Companion? How *dared* he think that such a despicable act would actually gain him the Crown? If he had come to her at that moment, she might have snatched up some old sword hanging on the wall and beaten him with the flat of it.

But as a little time passed, she regained control over her temper. Though she was still going to give him a lashing, it would be with her tongue and not a whip or a sword blade. And she had the first phrase ready on the tip of her tongue when he finally appeared.

She had thought that after such a monumental act of stupidity, Karath would have come to her contrite and looking for forgiveness. In fact, she could not imagine any other scenario.

Instead, he burst in through the door, slammed it behind him, and proceeded to shout at her, quite as if she were somehow to blame for all this, and as if this business of not being made King was somehow her fault, something she had concocted to keep him from his rightful place, and as if the debacle with Caryo had been something that she had planned to humiliate him.

And that made her furious all over again.

His ranting was like a spark in dry grass; she pounced on the first available pause for breath, and *then* she made her riposte.

"If you think I'm going to take your side in this, you are very much mistaken, Karath. I told you—and if I told you once about how things are here, I told you a dozen times!" Selenay shouted at the angry face of her husband. "The *Council* told you! Your own *Ambassador* told you! For the gods' sake, Karath, it was *in the marriage contract* that you signed! In *both* languages! Just how *stupid* are you to have missed it that many times?"

She knew the moment that the words left her mouth that they were the wrong thing to say, but she couldn't help it. Just how stupid *was* he? Or did he live in some fantasy world where because he wanted something, it would simply be given to him?

Well, maybe that was the way things had been back in Rethwellan, but that wasn't the way it was in Valdemar.

"Stupid enough to have wedded *you!*" he shouted back. "Such a fine bargain I have made for myself! I have wedded no power, no responsibility, and no rank but that which I was born with! And for this, I have what? A wife with neither the face nor the form to stand out in a crowd—with common tastes and common, petty morals, a little girl who thinks more of her horse than of her husband! For this bargain, I take a cold, naive, ignorant *virgin* who grasps her little power as a miser does gold, who does not even know how to properly pleasure a man!" And before she could retort, he stormed out, and before the astonished eyes of her Guards, who had no doubt heard it all, he slammed the door behind him, leaving her feeling as if he had dealt her a blow.

She was left staring at the door he slammed behind him, torn between wanting to throw herself to the ground, weeping, and wanting to strangle him.

The latter won out, but not by much, and as she paced back and forth across her sitting room, there were tears streaking her cheeks as well as anger making her clench her jaw until it ached.

Her heart ached, too; ached bitterly, for every insult he had thrown at her felt like a blow.

She managed to get some control over herself in order to put herself into the hands of her maids; tonight she took extra care with her appearance, for surely he who was so conscious of the trappings of status would not absent himself from dinner where he sat at her right hand. Common, was she? She would show him. She would make him mad to take her in his arms again, and she would, by the gods, make him *beg* for the privilege. And apologize, not only to her, but to Caryo.

But the chair at her right remained empty all evening.

She put on a good face, of course, replying lightly to Talamir's query that he was probably passing the time with the friends who had come up from Rethwellan, to whom she had given titles and property. "They are probably celebrating, now that it is official," she said, with a false lightness. "And after all, Talamir, you can hardly expect a young man to hover over his wife every moment of the day! At some point every young man *I* have ever known, be he never so devoted, has longed for the company of his old friends!" Her laugh sounded hollow to her own ears, but Talamir made no sign that he had noticed her unhappiness. "Just because we are wedded, this does not mean that we are joined at the hip!"

"No, of course not," Talamir agreed, and nothing more was said on the subject in her hearing.

But as the dinner wore on, she was able to think less and less clearly. By the time the sweetmeats were served, *she* would almost have been ready to ask forgiveness of *him* if it would put things back the way they had been yesterday. She kept listening, dreading that she would hear something about the debacle in Companion's Field, but evidently no one was going to talk about it where she could overhear.

Maybe that was why he wasn't here! He didn't want to have to answer any questions about what he'd done; he didn't want to have to explain himself…

She felt a great surge of relief, then, and was able to talk normally, able to think of something besides wondering where he was. She was still angry at him, especially for the cruel things he had said to her, but she was ready to forgive him, so long as he asked for forgiveness.

Except that he did not appear in their quarters after dinner. Tonight she had retired to her suite as soon as dinner was over, letting her Court amuse itself for a change.

And he did not appear as the hour grew later and later; she filled the time with attending to her private correspondence, something she had neglected badly over the past fortnight or two. But her heart was not in it, and time after time, she had to throw out a letter that was ruined by tears falling on it.

He had not come when her maids arrived to help her prepare for bed, and he still had not arrived when they blew out the candles, leaving her alone in the dark in that great bed.

And when she realized that he wasn't *going* to come, the anger ran out of her.

What was wrong? How could he not understand, at least by now, how she was powerless in the face of the law? How could he not realize by now the enormity of the insult he had given Caryo? Of course he had been angry, but how could he have flung those horrible insults at her? She thought he had *understood* her, as no one had ever understood her before. Hadn't they shared all those long conversations about how miserable it was to be a child of royal birth? Hadn't he commiserated with her about it as no one else had ever done before? Hadn't he told her how he had dreamed of finding someone he could care for as well as merely marry for the sake of an alliance, and had given it up as an idle dream until he met her? How many times had he sworn that to her? How many times had he shared his dreams with her, and how many times had she discovered to her joy that they were the same as hers?

What had gone wrong? How could he have changed so? What had she done to make him turn away from her?

She had no answers for any of this, and she waited, fruitlessly, in her cold, lonely bed, until at last she cried herself to sleep.

Alberich contemplated the glass image of the Sunlord—defined at the moment by the lines of leading rather than the colors of the glass—and tried to think of all of the possible paths that the Prince might take after this afternoon.

The most obvious, of course, was the most direct; wait until the baby was born, and engineer an "accident" that would kill or incapacitate Selenay. There was no law in Valdemar that the Regent had to be a Herald; as Regent, it was even possible that he would have the same power as the Monarch, just without the title.

But that was only one of a number of courses he could take—

:Chosen, the Royal Guard Kimel is coming down the path,: Kantor warned, breaking into his train of thought. *:I can't imagine he'd be coming to see anyone but you at this time of night.:*

Forewarned, Alberich got up to meet the young man as soon as he entered the salle, greeting him at the door. But it wasn't until he got to Alberich's private quarters that the Herald could see his expression, and it was both grim and troubled.

"Master Alberich," the young man said, when he'd taken the proffered seat and been offered, and refused, any refreshment. "I overheard a conversation this evening that—that I do not much like."

"Did you?" Alberich replied noncommittally.

The Guard nodded. "It was during the hour of dinner for the Court. I was on duty when I heard two voices raised in argument on the other side of the wall where I was standing—I happened to be in the gardens, and there was an open window right above my head."

"Assume, I must, that you overheard something that might of importance be?" Alberich prompted.

"Two men arguing," Kimel replied. "And one of them was the Prince." He coughed. "I knew about what happened this afternoon, and I guess he'd gone to someone to complain about it." He frowned as he concentrated on what he was going to say. "I didn't recognize the voice, but he got not much sympathy. In fact, the person he was talking to gave him a regular dressing-down about it. The man said that the Prince was on the verge of 'spoiling it all,' though he didn't say what 'it' was."

"Go on," Alberich told him. Surely there was more to this story!

"Well, then the Prince said something about the unfairness of it all, and the other man told him to be patient, and that Selenay was—" here Kimel blushed, "—well, anyway, what he went on to say was 'once the child is born, there is no law preventing you from becoming Regent, when something happens to Selenay. All you have to do is to be patient.' And the Prince muttered something, and the man laughed, and they all went out of the room."

So. There it was. "You may have done Her Majesty a great service, Kimel," Alberich said gravely.

"I am in a position to do more," the young Guard replied, to Alberich's surprise. "So long as I wear my uniform, and look as if I am guarding *something*, no one ever notices me. I could make sure that if I am not on duty elsewhere, I can follow the Prince all over the grounds of the Palace. Perhaps I might discover who he was speaking with."

"If you did, invaluable, it would be," Alberich said, hardly able to believe the luck.

"Then I will." That seemed to be all that Kimel felt urged to say on the matter; he remained a little longer, but not much, and excused himself.

:Well?: he said to Kantor when the young man was gone.

:I think we've gotten an ally, who will at least be watching out for Selenay. I don't know how useful what he learns or overhears will be.:

:It's better than nothing, which was all we had,: Alberich pointed out.

:Yes, Chosen. It is at that.:

1 9

Everyone knew the obvious that night—that the Prince had not attended the Queen at dinner. By morning, though, there was a better bit of gossip to take its place—that the Prince had not spent the night with the Queen, nor even (it was said) in the Palace.

By breakfast, that gossip had inflated further, with the addition that the Prince had returned at last, from somewhere outside the Palace walls. And he had gone to his own suite, not the Queen's.

Valdemaran royal marriages, like most royal marriages, were not always for love. Hence, the Consort always had his (or her) own suite of rooms within the larger Royal Suite. It had its own entrance; the one who occupied it could come and go without disturbing the Monarch. It would not be the first time that the Monarch's spouse had elected to take up residence in his own private space. The trouble was, this defection of the Prince would have gone unnoticed except that this was supposed to have been a love match. Selenay herself had virtually bullied the marriage through the Council. And now, it seemed, it was already falling apart.

So tongues were wagging from the first, and Alberich did not think it possible that Selenay was unaware of the gossip. She'd have to be blind and deaf, and she was neither. It made him sick inside to think how unhappy she must be, but there was little he could do about it.

She was paying a heavy price for her infatuation; this was going to be a very expensive lesson in thinking things through. However unhappy the Prince was with his wife and his situation, Alberich doubted that Karathanelan was going to relinquish what he *did* have willingly, once he realized the alternatives. Even if Selenay became so unhappy as to wish to dissolve the marriage, such a move could not be made without the agreement of the other party—and the Prince would never agree.

No, unless the Prince actually committed an overt act of treason, Selenay was stuck with her bad bargain. And if she was unhappy now, when the last of the infatuation wore off, she was going to be even less happy.

Alberich wished there was something he could do, but he knew that, in this case, there really was nothing. He was entirely the wrong person for her to confide in on two counts. First, the task required someone who was a close friend, which he was not—someone, perhaps, that was Selenay's yearmate at the Collegium. Second, his sex was against him; he knew instinctively that to become a confidant and adviser in this situation, a man just would not do.

Which, unfortunately, left Talamir out of the running as well. Perhaps she was confiding in her Companion; perhaps at this point Caryo was about the only one she could confide in. He hoped that Caryo was wise enough to know not to criticize the Prince herself at this point—because Selenay would feel impelled to defend him, and that would only prolong the agony, so to speak.

The Prince continued to shun the company of his Queen; one or two days stretched into a week with no sign of him in or around the Palace from the time he rose until the time—which was usually very late—he returned from wherever he had just spent his day. Alberich grew increasingly weary of the words, "They say—" as the days passed. But not weary enough not to listen, for there were several nuggets of information to be mined from the dross.

One of them sent him out in disguise one evening, to an establishment known as "The Silver Horn," which catered to "the discriminating tastes of gentlemen." Or at least, it catered to those with money who cared to call themselves gentlemen; certainly you could find both the highborn and the monied lowborn there, although there were special places within the establishment to which money alone did not guarantee entrance. Alberich already had a persona established here, that of an elderly, semideaf gentleman with a substantial fortune—elderly, because that way he would not be looked on askance for not making use of the opulent rooms up the parlor stair and the ladies who inhabited those rooms, as jewels graced a setting. Alberich would, every now and then, dodder in, partake of a splendid meal, and sit enjoying the entertainments on offer in the more public rooms—generally scantily clad young ladies singing or dancing, though it was said that they performed far more interesting maneuvers elsewhere in the establishment—until he apparently nodded off. Then, if he had overheard nothing of importance, he would "wake," and dodder off again. He found the place far more useful than the Court for obtaining information about the goings-on of the highborn.

The Horn provided something of an educational tradition with the aristocracy. Young men were often brought here by brothers or even fathers for their first (so far as the parent knew) sexual experiences. Then, as they grew older, they would come here by themselves or with friends to make a night of it—fine meals, gambling, entertainment, and then a romp. It wasn't cheap—but Alberich wasn't paying for this out of his own pocket. And there were times when he felt as if, given the number of candlemarks he had spent in the Broken Arms and other, even fouler dens, lurking on street corners in the freezing dark, getting soaked with rain or baking in the hot sun, that he had earned an occasional evening in the Horn. Even if all he did was have a meal and lurk.

He had heard that friends of the Prince were going to introduce him to the pleasures of the Horn, and as a consequence both of that, and of an internal prodding too vague to really be called ForeSight, after the third night in which the Prince did not appear, Alberich began haunting the Horn nightly. He was a forgettable enough character that no one really noticed. And the Prince did, indeed, appear that first night, and every night subsequent.

Unfortunately, to Alberich's vast disappointment, the Prince kept himself to the "exclusive" areas for the most part, and Alberich never saw more of him than his back as he swaggered through the public rooms and into the private areas.

It seemed, after three nights, that Alberich was wasting his time, that all the Prince was doing was roistering. Fine, he *could* bring this to Selenay, but what good would it do?

Yet that vague prodding only strengthened as the nights went on, and although he never got a glimpse of ForeSight, after the fourth night he *knew*, with absolute certainty, that if he kept up his watch, something significant would happen.

And then, on the seventh night, it was not the Prince who became the center of attention when he walked in the door.

It was the actor, Norris. And with him was young Devlin.

Alberich was in a shadowy corner, slumped in one of the Horn's supremely comfortable chairs, fingers interlaced over his "paunch," chin on his chest, seeming to doze. This time he had chosen a seat *because* of the feeling that this was where he needed to be—again, it was a feeling and not a vision, nothing concrete, but he was certain that it was linked to his ForeSight, and he acted on it. One of the young ladies had made certain to tuck a cushion on either side of him so that he wouldn't put a crick in his neck; he had muttered vague and sleepy thanks, and she had giggled and left him alone. Now everyone seemed to have forgotten he was there, which gave him ample opportunity to watch the room from mostly closed eyes.

When Myste had absented herself from the theater, Alberich had continued to keep an eye on the actor at a distance, through other contacts, but there did not seem to be any sign of further chicanery. In fact, Norris was so busy, Alberich couldn't see how he managed to find the time to sleep, much less write letters and find ways to pass them to anyone. In addition to rehearsing and performing, he spent every waking moment at the site of his new theater, obsessing over details and virtually flogging the workers into going faster.

But here he was, and as soon as they saw him, those young ladies who were not otherwise occupied left what they were doing and clustered around him with exclamations and coos of delight.

The odd thing was, although he put on a very good show of being pleased, and it was clear that young Devlin was nervously gratified to have him here, Alberich got the distinct impression that he very much would rather not be there.

Then again, as busy as the man was, Alberich wondered where he had found the time to come here in the first place.

The only possible corner of the room that could have been considered secluded was the one in which Alberich had ensconced himself. Norris accepted refreshments, teased and flirted with the ladies, but took none of them up the stairs, which was so entirely out of keeping with everything that Alberich knew about the man that he was immediately on alert. Devlin did not move from his side either, and it seemed to Alberich that the young noble was keeping a sharp watch on the door.

And perhaps three-quarters of a candlemark later, the Prince strolled in, with an escort of young sycophants.

Except that one of them apparently was not as much of a sycophant as the Prince had thought, because before Karathanelan could vanish, as usual, into one of the private parlors, that young man steered him over to Norris' chair. Devlin and the other young man exchanged a glance; Devlin nodded, and within moments, the newcomer gathered up the Prince's escort and hustled them into the private parlors.

"Highness," Devlin said with a bow to the Prince. "Our patron wishes you to have a discussion with my friend." And at that, he took himself off, going, not into the back like the others, but back out the front door.

Alberich was torn between following—for surely he was going to report to someone!—and staying to listen. But his own internal urging said *stay,* so stay he did.

And Norris, looking up indolently at the Prince, indicated with a nod that Karathanelan should take a seat beside him. "Run away, my beauties," the actor said, in an amused tone of voice. "We gentlemen need to discuss things too delicate for your tender ears."

With giggles and pretty pouts, as the Prince glared his outrage, the ladies did as they were told. "Sit down," Norris said, and then, when the Prince did not move, repeated, with force, *"Sit down.* Now."

"I shall do nothing of the sort!" the Prince said tightly. "I *will* have you horsewhipped and thrown into the street for your insolence!"

"You won't if you know what's good for you," Norris said, without turning a hair. "I am here at the behest of, and doing a *very great favor* for, our mutual sponsor, and if you *don't* sit down, I am going to walk out of here and tell him why I did so. You can see what will happen to you without his protection then, but I don't recommend it."

The Prince sat down.

"That's better," Norris said pleasantly.

"What about *him?"* the Prince growled, nodding at Alberich.

"Nothing to worry about." Norris dismissed Alberich with a shrug. "He's older than dirt, half senile, mostly deaf. I tested him—" Norris grinned then. "If he'd been conscious when I tipped little Kassie's skirts up, he'd have at least twitched."

Yes, and you aren't quite as clever as you think, Alberich told him mentally. *Because a real agent wouldn't have reacted even if you'd taken the girl on the spot.* He wasn't sure *he* would have had the ability to remain "asleep," but then again—he'd yawned through worse, down in the Broken Arms.

"Now," Norris continued, losing the grin. "Before we begin, I'll trouble you to remember that I have no loyalty to you, or to anyone else who has not paid my fee. Once bought, however, I stay bought; this is good business, and it is why our patron brought me here, but remember that I do not give a damn what happens to *you.* My part of your education should have been over moons ago, and it would have been, if you hadn't been such an idiot a week ago."

"Idiot?" the Prince hissed. "I think not—"

"Exactly," Norris interrupted. "You *don't* think. If you did, you would realize that you are expendable, fellow-my-lad."

The Prince started, and looked at Norris as if he thought the actor had run mad.

Norris wagged a finger at him. "Turnabout is fair play. Sauce for the goose will serve for the gander. If your bride has done her dynastic duty by getting with child so quickly, *you* have done your work at stud, and she doesn't *need* you anymore. Didn't that ever occur to you over the past few days, while you've been doing your best to make her hate you?"

Alberich couldn't see the Prince's face, but he sounded smug. "She cannot be rid of me. I would not agree to the dissolution of the marriage."

"Which just shows how much of a fool you are," Norris countered flatly. "Certainly, a marriage can't be dissolved without the consent of both parties—*if you were an ordinary couple*. But you aren't, you are in a foreign land, and the law can be whatever she gets the Council to agree to. And if you should be so indiscreet as to do something treasonable, she wouldn't even have to dissolve the marriage. She could simply arrange for the Council to make her a widow." Norris examined his nails critically. "They hang traitors to the Crown in Valdemar, you know."

"She—couldn't!" the Prince gasped, as if it hadn't occurred to him.

"She could," Norris replied matter-of-factly. "And you're skirting perilous close to it, let me tell you; if your lovely bride had chosen, your little folly in the matter of a mount would have had you facing a High Court already. In fact, the only reasons you haven't been charged with treason already are because our patron is protecting you, and because our patron is fairly certain that your wife is still weeping over your misbehaving and hasn't yet gone from tears to anger. Which is why our patron brought me here. Because you mean nothing to me, I owe you nothing, you can do nothing to me, and I can and will tell you what no one else around you would dare." He leaned forward and shoved his index finger at the Prince. "Now, you listen to this; you'd better believe it, and you'd better act on it. Our patron's patience is not inexhaustible, and he won't continue to support and protect you while you run about like a tomcat. You're wasting those very expensive lessons of mine; you can be replaced, and you *will* be, once your wife decides that she's going to stop crying herself to sleep in an empty bed and start doing something about the situation. You might survive the experience, but I'd bet not; our patron has enemies of his own, and they'd be perfectly happy to bring you down and replace you with one of their own choices. And he won't go down to save *your* worthless hide."

Alberich "snored" gently, and wondered just who the "mutual patron" was. More than that, what did this mysterious entity expect to get out of his patronage of Karathanelan? If he could "protect" the

Prince, surely he could get whatever he wanted for himself.

The Prince was silent for a long moment. "I don't like this. How do I know that this is true?" he said at last.

"I don't care what you think about it," Norris replied impatiently. "And I don't have to prove anything to you. I already have what I wanted out of the bargain, and I don't particularly care whether or not you believe me. *You* are wasting *my* time, not the other way around. Time to wake up and deal with the mess you've made, lad, before you find yourself neck-deep and no way to get out."

Norris' very indifference seemed to work as a powerful argument with the Prince. "What do I do?" he asked at last, grudgingly.

Norris snorted. "Do I have to draw you a map?" But when the Prince looked at him blankly, he sighed. "Apparently I do. All right then, the first thing you do is go apologize to your wife for whatever you said to her and everything you've done since you quarreled with her. Groveling to her, if need be, until you get her forgiveness."

"I will never—" the Prince began hotly.

"You will if you want to keep your head on your neck," Norris hissed. "And once you've groveled enough, you tell her that now that you've come to your senses and have looked back on your unspeakable conduct these past several days, you realized tonight how unsatisfactory all these other women you've been bedding are, compared to her."

The Prince sniggered. Norris shrugged. "Of course that's ridiculous, but that's what she wants to hear, and believe me, it is the *only* thing you could say that will make her forgive you for sleeping with anyone else. Then you will have to go *right* back to your first lesson with her, and woo her all over again. Only it will be a little easier this time, because she knows what you can do in bed, and you won't be handicapped by having to hold back with her to save her virtue. Remember what I taught you, and everything our patron managed to find out. *Use* that. Make her feel that you are the only person in the whole world who could possibly understand her. I wrote you the scripts; drag them out again."

The Prince seemed to think it over, and finally said, grudgingly. "If this is what our patron wants…"

"Hang our patron. This is the only thing that will keep you out of a dungeon cell," Norris said bluntly, as Alberich mentally cursed. If only he could have counted on the Prince's arrogance to push things and keep pushing them, until Selenay was ready to be rid of him!

Well, it looked as if that was a vain hope.

"Very well." The Prince got up, but did not offer his hand to Norris. "You and our patron have been right in the past. I must assume that you are right now. Fare you well."

"Right," Norris replied, waving him away indolently. "Just see that you remember what I've told you, the next time you're tempted to assert yourself."

Alberich continued to "doze" until the Prince was inside the door to one of the private parlors, and Norris was surrounded again by his bevy of beauties. Then, with a "start," he "woke," surveyed the room indulgently, then levered himself up out of his chair to totter away.

Part of him wanted to string up Norris as soon as the Prince had been dealt with. But part of him, which had been listening to the conversation with keen interest, had a better idea.

:I think we should hire him when this is over,: he said, knowing that Kantor had been following everything that had transpired.

:You what?: Kantor asked, incredulously. Kantor had no need to ask who "he" was.

:I think we should hire him as our agent,: Alberich amended. *:Mind, I wouldn't tell him just who is hiring him, but he could be damned useful to us.:*

:But he said himself he could be bought!: Kantor protested—then stopped. *:And he said that once he was bought, he stayed bought. Didn't he.:*

:That was exactly what he said,: Alberich replied. *:I think he could be a valuable agent. More valuable alive and working for us, than in prison. If we could even find something to charge him with. Which I doubt.:*

:Emotionally, I don't like it,: Kantor replied unhappily. *:But logically— you're right. He's an amoral beast, but better he's been bought by us. At least then we can control him.:*

:As much as such a one is ever controlled,: Alberich finished. And sighed. *:And this assumes that his patron—whoever that is—loses interest in him. If he's the sort who stays bought, we'll never get him otherwise.:*

:Good,: Kantor said firmly. *:I'd rather we didn't. I'd rather we could have him thrown in jail.:*

:Which we can't, because he hasn't done anything wrong,: Alberich pointed out. *:All he's done that we know of is to give the Prince lessons on how to woo and win the Queen. Which is hardly illegal. And we can't even prove that he did that much, really, not to satisfy a law court. But oh, how I wish he hadn't been here tonight!:*

:I know exactly what you mean,: Kantor said glumly.

* * *

Karathanelan might have been an arrogant, self-centered beast, but apparently he was bright enough to know when he was getting good advice.

He was also phenomenally lucky.

Because the next day, the *very* next day, word came from Rethwellan that his father, the King, was dead.

Now, that might not have been thought of as luck, except that word also came from Rethwellan that the King had *already* been buried, that Karath's presence was not required at home, and that, in fact, his brother the new King, Faramentha, suggested strongly that he should remain in Valdemar at the side of his new bride and do his mourning in private.

Even while the Rethwellan Embassy was being swathed in black, Karath hurried to the Palace, and in full view of everyone as Selenay herself was hearing the news, flung himself weeping at her feet.

Selenay canceled the rest of her audiences that day, and took him with her back to her chambers. Alberich could not know, of course, *what* the Prince told her, aside from the "script" that Norris had provided for him, but he could guess. What would appeal to Selenay more, than to have her beloved husband suddenly bereft of his own father?

Certainly he went about after that in heavy mourning, and certainly Selenay was as unshakably attentive to him as he was to her. To Alberich's disgust, he was more firmly in Selenay's good graces than he had been before, always by her side, and playing the devoted husband. Selenay spent a disturbing amount of time gazing at him or into his eyes with every sign of being firmly under his spell.

And in public, at least, he was as devoted as she could ever have wished.

In public, he was also playing the tragic figure of the mourning son and rejected brother. When a new Ambassador came from Rethwellan to replace the old one, he showed a very chilly face to the man, who was, in his turn, no better than icily polite.

Which meant nothing to Alberich, until Talamir enlightened him, one late summer evening.

"Oh, do *think* about this for a moment," Talamir told him, with unusual impatience. "The Prince was not told of his father's death until Faramentha was firmly on the throne. And he was not recalled. What does that tell you?"

"Ah." Alberich shook his head. "I was thinking too much of our own side of this, and not beyond our Borders. Faramentha does not trust his brother. And the Prince holds Faramentha in enmity."

"So—?"

"So—whether or not the old King was privy to Karathanelan's plans, the new one is not, probably."

Talamir nodded. "And unless I miss my guess," he added shrewdly, "the Prince's grief is not all sham. Not that he is brokenhearted over being rejected by his brother, nor mourning terribly for his father—"

"If he is," Alberich was moved to point out, "the ladies of the Horn have not noticed."

"Precisely. But if there is one thing the Prince cares about, it's his own well-being. And with his father dead and his brother, who despises him, on the throne?"

"He has nowhere to go if he fails here—" Alberich felt cold. "I do not like this."

"Neither," Talamir said delicately, "do I."

But there was not much either of them could do about it. Karath had too many good cards in his hand, and Selenay's own condition was aiding him; by summer's end, as the first leaves began to turn, Selenay was deep in work, and when she wasn't working, she was generally asleep, or at least, resting. Her pregnancy was hard on her, not so much that it was difficult, but that she was finding it exhausting, according to Crathach, who made no secret that he disapproved of her getting with child so quickly. This left ample opportunity for the Prince to comport himself as if he was a bachelor.

But he went about it so discreetly that most of the Court had no idea.

Unfortunately, one of the things that was wearing Selenay out was that he still had not given up the notion of being crowned. Even though he was not fighting with her about it, using less aggressive means to get his point across, roughly once a fortnight, he would find some other reason to bring the tired old plaint back up, or some new scheme to get around the law. This, Alberich heard from Talamir, usually when Alberich came up to the Collegium to report on whatever new information he might have gathered on his prowls in Haven. The city was quiet of late, as the season passed from summer into autumn; even the criminal element was up to no more than the usual trouble. There seemed nothing that required Alberich's intervention. Stalking Devlin to try and find the identity of the "patron" was proving to be fruitless; where Devlin went, none of Alberich's personae was welcome. As for Norris, the actor was so busy with his new theater that even *he* was beginning to look a little frayed about the edges.

"He's come up with another one today," Talamir said, lowering himself wearily down into a chair by the hearth. He looked ancient tonight, and very transparent; Alberich wondered what he had been doing to wear himself so thin.

He wants to be gone, came the unbidden thought. *He's faced with things he can't do anything about, and he just wants to be gone—from problems, from life. And he wants it with all of his heart.*

He might want it—but he wasn't pursuing it, at least. Duty held him here at Selenay's side, however poorly suited he thought himself to the task.

At that moment, Alberich pitied the Queen's Own.

"This time, what?" Alberich asked, knowing that the "he" could only be the Prince, and that the "another one" was yet another ploy to pressure Selenay into somehow getting him a crown.

"That she's shaming him in front of his family—or so he says," Talamir said wearily. "According to him, that she hasn't made him King means that she thinks he is unworthy of a crown, and now he says that this is why his own brother has rejected him and kept him from his father's side when the King was dying."

"Ah. So now he attempts guilt?" Alberich replied.

"I would guess," said Talamir, and shook his head. "At least she came to me with this, looking for reassurance. And I planted another seed."

"Perhaps you can use the papers soon?" Alberich hazarded. They finally had a translation of them; it took long enough to break the code. When they had, as Alberich had suspected, they proved to be instructions on what to do and say to Selenay to win her, with some very intimate details. Some were things that Alberich blinked at; things that one would have thought were the sort of confession that Selenay would not have given to anyone—girlish daydreams, actually, about the sort of man she was looking for, and the loneliness of being who she was, the despair that she would never have the kind of marriage her father had enjoyed.

Where had all of that come from? Even Talamir had been surprised at the bitterness and anguish of some of it.

But maybe Selenay had been pouring her woes into the ears of one of her servants. Alberich would have *thought* they were trustworthy, and probably they were, but he supposed there was no reason why they shouldn't tell others what Selenay had told *them.*

Some of what had been written were intimate glimpses into Selenay personally, and what to say to her to play to her sympathies, but others— well, Alberich had found himself blushing at the step-by-step instructions for seduction; they did not merely border on the pornographic, they *were* pornographic. And Alberich was no longer surprised that Norris was so popular with the ladies, nor that Selenay was so deeply infatuated with the Prince. How could she not be, if the Prince was following these instructions, meant to make Selenay believe that here, past all her hopes, was not only her soulmate but a lover who could guarantee the satisfaction of a female partner, closely and with all his attention? Part of him wanted to burn the wretched papers, but they were useful, very useful. If ever Selenay's attachment began to fade, at the right moment, showing her these things could turn her fading infatuation to distaste. Only she could know how closely the Prince followed his "scripts"—but the more closely he had, the more obvious it would be that he *was* following a script, and that there never had been any real feeling behind his act.

"Not until after the child is born," Talamir sighed. "Crathach says that he doesn't want any more stress on her right now; between matters of state and the Prince's continuous pressure, she's got more than enough on her. He's playing the 'bereft orphan' very convincingly, and of all of the acts he could contrive, that's the one that will make her excuse him nearly anything."

Alberich counted up the months in his mind. "Spring, then," he said with a sigh. "But the Prince himself will, perhaps, overstep before then?"

But Talamir shook his head. "No, I think that this 'patron,' whoever he is, has found a way to clamp controls down over the Prince. More than just Norris, I mean, or even young Devlin. Devlin can't be more than a messenger. It astonishes me. And I wish I knew how real the threat to Selenay is."

Alberich nodded. There was the real question, truth be told. There were actually a number of interpretations that could be placed on what Norris had said to his control.

First, it could be all bluster. It was one thing to say that the Queen was dispensable; it was quite another to actually *act* on those words. Norris was, when it all came down to cases, a commoner. Whatever he knew about life at Court he could only learn from brief glimpses and the rather unrealistic views of life among the highborn that he got from his plays, or just perhaps by whatever his patron told him—assuming the patron told him anything at all about life at Court. Selenay was surrounded night and day by Guards that Alberich himself had trained and could vouch for, and by the Heralds as well. To actually assassinate her, someone would have to get past them *and* Selenay's own impressive self-defense abilities, and it was guaranteed that whoever tried would not survive the attempt. So the enemy would have to find someone highly skilled, clever, and suicidal—not an easy task. Poison was out of the question; Healers checked everything that she ate and drank, and even if someone managed to slip poison past them, there were no "instantaneous" poisons other than some rare snakebites; Healers would almost certainly be able to save her. Norris (and, presumably, his "patron") might simply be counting on the hazards of childbearing to remove Selenay. To Alberich's mind, that was as foolish a hope as finding an assassin; Selenay was in excellent health and by no means delicate. Women gave birth without complications every day *without* the small army of Healers to attend them that Selenay had.

"I wish I could hazard a guess," Talamir replied. "It seems a preposterous idea on the face of it. The ForeSeers are no real help either."

Alberich knew what *that* meant. Too many future possibilities to sort out. That, or so he had been told, was why *he* never got any visions inspired by ForeSight that extended into the future by more than a candlemark. His Gift evidently operated in the same fashion as he did— if there were too many choices, his Gift elected not to show any of them, so that he could concentrate without distractions pulling him in a dozen directions at once. It only showed him things he could actually act on.

"It is that I think, sometimes, our Gifts are more hindrance than help," he said sourly.

"Some of them, at any rate," Talamir agreed. He looked broodingly off over Alberich's left shoulder for a long moment, staring at nothing, but doing it in a way that tended to raise the hackles on the back of Alberich's neck. What was he looking at, so intently, with that expression of focused detachment? Alberich was used to that "listening" look that Heralds got when they were conversing with their Companions, and this wasn't *that* expression. It also wasn't the absentminded look most people got when they were engrossed in their own thoughts. The closest analogy that Alberich could come to was that odd look that cats sometimes got, when they stared intently at something that apparently wasn't there. It was a Karsite tradition that when they did that, they were looking at spirits. Talamir's look was very like that.

But if the Queen's Own was seeing ghosts, he hadn't said anything about it to anyone.

Alberich repressed a shiver and coughed quietly to bring Talamir's attention back to the present.

Talamir blinked, and picked up the conversation where it had left off.

"I have to think at this point that your actor's conversation was a deliberate attempt on his part to remind his control and his patron that *he* knows where all the skeletons are," Talamir said. "I think he was trying to extract more money from them to buy his silence in case anything *did* happen to the Queen."

Alberich thought that over. It was plausible. More plausible than any of his own theories. Norris might stay bought, but when you did that, there was less incentive for your "employers" to try to keep you in their pocket once they had what they initially wanted.

And theaters were more expensive to maintain than a stable full of racehorses.

"A dangerous ploy, that one," Alberich observed. "He could be removed before a danger he becomes."

"Perhaps, perhaps," Talamir admitted. "But that is the best fit for what you overheard."

Alberich nodded his agreement, but not without a sense of relief. If *that* was all it was…!

They finished their business, and Alberich made his way back to the salle through the dark. Not alone, of course; the moment he crossed over the fence into Companion's Field, Kantor joined him.

:You're still troubled.,: his Companion observed.

:I don't like it, for some reason,: Alberich admitted. *:Unfortunately, I don't know why.:*

:Well, what can you do about it?:

He pondered that for a moment, trying to think of all of the times Selenay *could* be vulnerable. Not when holding Court, not at Council meetings. Probably not in the gardens or in her own quarters, or at meals or entertainments—unless the harpists suddenly produced arrows and used their instruments as bows.

Not very likely.

But before the arrival of the Prince, Selenay had occasionally donned the working Whites of a common Herald, and gone off for a long ride, down to the Home Farms, outside the walls of Haven, usually accompanied only by Talamir and sometimes not even him. And then, if ever—

:You know, I believe I am going to start attending the Hurlee practices,: he said slowly. *:I believe I will begin working with the Hurlee players. She might object to an escort; she won't object to a crowd of cheerful youngsters flattering about sport. In fact, she might even enjoy their company. But it will not take much*

to turn them from gamesmen to melee-experts.:

:Hurlee is cursed like a melee already,: Kantor observed.

:And that is the point,: Alberich replied. *:Furthermore, unless she is really craving privacy, Selenay won't think anything of a Hurlee team riding along with her. They're only Trainees, not Guards.:*

:So she won't object,:

He smiled. *:I believe she will welcome them.:* Then he sobered. *:The hard part will be in training them to be weapons at her side, without any of them realizing that is what I am doing.:*

:If anyone can,: Kantor said firmly, *:you can.:*

He sighed, and hoped his Companion was right.

2 0

A harsh, cold wind blew across the Hurlee ground, rattling the last of the sere, brown leaves still clinging to the trees. A helm and neck-brace weren't much help in protecting from the cold; the wind ripped gleefully down the Weaponsmaster's collar and the sudden chill brought back memories of long patrols in the lonely hills of Karse in weather worse than this, when he would wake cold, patrol until he and his men were warm only where their bodies were in contact with their horses' hides, then gather around smoking fires where you warmed little bits of yourself, while the rest stayed achingly cold. Now—well, he had come from a warm salle, and he would be going back to it; this was just minor discomfort, inconsequential.

Alberich gravely surveyed the twelve best Hurlee players in the Collegium now gathered before him; in their turn they gazed fearlessly back at him. They were all superior athletes, all either in their last or next-to-last years, and all were old enough to give Alberich respect untempered with fear. They were past that half-fearful, half-awestruck stage, past thinking him an unreasonable taskmaster. They knew him now, knew what he was about, knew why he did what he did with them. There were those that were this lot's yearmates that still had not grasped those truths; that was why he had picked his candidates so carefully.

And if they suspected what he was about with them now was going to be something more than turning them into vicious Hurlee players— well, he reckoned *they* only thought to the moment when they were to get their Whites, and assumed that he was fitting them better to be Heralds in some of the more dangerous sectors. And it was true enough that this training would serve that end, so they were not entirely wrong.

The real purpose was a secret held by him, Talamir, Kantor, and Rolan—and the Companions of these dozen young Grays. After careful consultation with Kantor, he and Talamir had elected to include the

Companions, but not the Trainees, because of the risk that someone would let something slip. No secret was ever safer, and he and Kantor felt that to get the best result, he needed the informed cooperation of the Companions. Other than that, no one else had been told. Not even Myste knew, though of course, he would tell her eventually for the sake of the Chronicles. Just not now; later when the danger was past, and his fears were proved false—or true.

The twelve sat shivering in their saddles, waiting for him to speak. They wore more than the usual Hurlee protections; shin, knee, and calf-guards, kidney-belts, elbow-guards, armguards, neck-braces. And they were finding, as he already knew, that none of these protections helped against the teeth of the wind.

There were no observers today. No one wanted to sit in the cold, in the open, with no shelter on a day like this. Not even to watch the best Hurlee players in Haven. It seemed an especial irony that rather than being overcast, the sun shone down among swiftly-moving scuds of cloud in a mostly-blue sky. It gave no help against the cold.

"Two teams of six for now," he said, and pointed. "Harrow. You sit out, throw in the ball, referee. I will play this third and the next."

When Hurlee had first been turned into a game and not a form of exercise, it had started with as many players as could be crowded onto the field, but now the official tally was twenty-four on the field, twelve to each side. Two of the twelve were goaltenders, two played close to the goals, and another two were "rovers" outside the scrum, on the alert for a miss-hit ball or a pass from one of their own side. Alberich was paring the teams down again to two goaltenders and four others; four roaming players, one on the home goal, one on the shared goal.

"A new rule," he continued. "The Companion a fair target is." He was counting on any ambushers being armed with swords rather than any other exotic weapons—it would be easy enough to incapacitate Companions by thrusting the shafts of spears among their legs in a melee—a broken leg would send a Companion down as easily as a horse. But it was still possible, more than possible, for a Companion to be killed by a sword thrust. He would have to teach them to avoid the possibility.

And as for the stroke that had killed the King and his Companion, and killed Rolan's predecessor—well, that would be coming in later lessons.

"Yes," he repeated, with a little more force. "The Companion a legal target is." *That* startled them, though the Companions all nodded or snorted and pawed the ground to indicate willingness. Well, *they* knew, and knew why; this only surprised their Chosen. It startled and shocked them, as if he had suggested that they should practice assassination techniques on infants. Still, they were all intelligent, and in a moment, they nodded too. And this probably confirmed their suspicions; that he was fitting them for dangerous missions, missions in which their Companions would *most definitely* be targets, the targets of people who were out to kill them, not incapacitate them.

Well, he was. *If* he needed them, it would be facing people who would probably strike at their Companions first. The Prince might be willfully ignorant when it came to the Companions, but his comrades weren't. And they would know what the Tedrels had known; kill the Companion, and the Herald is lost as well.

"And Companions—you are to target opposing riders," he continued, and he thought he caught a wicked glint in one or two blue eyes. "Pull them down, out of the saddle; knock them over. Chase them to the boundaries." The Companions would be quicker to adapt than their Chosen; at least at first. The Companions of this lot were all full adults, more experienced than their riders.

"So—" He held up his stick; the "traditional" beginning to a Hurlee game was for all players to raise their sticks and crack them together. Belatedly, the rest of them cracked theirs against his. "Harrow—throw in the ball and referee. Signal no fouls, only danger or hurt. We play."

Harrow had a whistle, but under these rules, he wasn't to blow it except to start game play unless someone was injured. These were real no-holds-barred conditions, with the Hurlee stick becoming a weapon— club, spear, staff, whatever suited. As the two teams lined up against each other, staring at each other, waiting, it occurred to him to be amused at himself. Whoever would have thought that his impulse to give a set of overexcited youngsters something to burn off some energy with would have turned into this?

Harrow's whistle cut through the cold air, and the "game" began.

As he had expected, the Trainees promptly forgot the new rule about targeting Companions. *He* hadn't, though, and Kantor charged straight into the Companion of the opposing team's captain, using his greater bulk and muscle to literally knock the other off his feet. The others scattered before that charge; Kantor in a full charge was a terrifying sight. Kantor angled sideways at the last moment, ramming the other with his chest, as Alberich thrashed at the rider with his stick, and missed, the rider ducking under the blow. The shock of the meeting jolted through him. The Companion went over, knocked right off-balance, his rider remembering his equitation classes and jumping free at the last minute, and as Alberich charged down on him, he brought up his stick defensively in time to deflect the blow Alberich was aiming at his head.

Alberich and Kantor galloped past and Kantor whirled with a hip-wrenching reversal of direction, charging for the opposing team's goalminder. Meanwhile, thinking just a little faster on his feet than the rest, Alberich's shared goalminder followed the Weaponsmaster's example and slapped his counterpart's Companion over the rump with his stick. Trumpeting indignation, the offended Companion leaped out of the way, giving Alberich's team a clear shot at the goal.

Which they took.

Harrow whistled to stop play, and ran in to fetch the ball.

The first play was over, and the only "casualty" was one rider unhorsed, one Companion slapped. And the second would likely not happen again. Alberich felt his heart swell with pride. They were good. They were more than good. They were brilliant: adaptable and clever.

And before time to change came up, they were all playing by the new rules without having to think about it too much.

Not that any of them had *much* of a chance against Alberich, because he was not holding back for their benefit. He wanted them to feel what it was really like, fighting against an adult, and an experienced and cunning one as well. *He* had tested the Prince's skills himself, and he was not going to assume that the Prince's chosen accomplices, should he try this thing, were going to be any less skilled. But unless the Prince somehow recruited people from the Tedrel Wars, none of *them* would have had anything like real combat experience, nor anything like what he and these Trainees were practicing.

When change-up came and Harrow signaled them, for the sake of making it a bit fairer as far as scoring was concerned, he switched sides; Harrow came in, and a player from the other team came out. And the game began again, except that this time, they all were playing like they meant it.

And at the third change-up, Alberich sat out altogether, and ran a critique from the sidelines. By this time, they were playing by the new rules *without* having to concentrate on them, and the riders suddenly found themselves confronted by something that had never happened to them before.

Their Companions were no longer entirely mindful of their Chosen.

Not when they were busy avoiding dangerous blows themselves. That meant that there were moments out there when they were no better off than if they'd been riding a superbly trained horse. Those were the moments of greatest danger, just as they had been in real combat. Those were the moments when, if they thought about it at all, these young Trainees got their first taste of real, bone-chilling fear.

When he brought the game to an end, they were all—himself included—absolutely exhausted, bruised, and battered. And there was a light of grim, ready-to-drop satisfaction in their eyes.

:And you're warm,: Kantor observed, with weary humor. *:Though you won't stay that way if you start making a speech.:*

Alberich ignored him. "Good," he said, and their eyes lit up. "Very good. Look, you. This a special class will be. Every day, this time, until I say. For now, we Hurlee a-saddle, but the next step will be—unhorsed, and you Hurlee aground until you can get mounted again. And those mounted will try to separate you from your Companion. And *you* will be trying to take the Companion down from the ground. So be thinking on this."

"Yes, Weaponsmaster," they said in a ragged chorus.

Harrow, quicker than the others, looked pale, but asked, "You mean, we're trying to repeat what killed the King and the Monarch's Own Companion?"

"You are striving to *prevent* that," Alberich corrected gently. "And it will take time. So here you will be, every day, for two candlemarks or a full game, whichever arrives first."

"But what if we've got a class or work scheduled?" one of them piped up, voice trembling only a little.

"See Talamir; he will tend to it," Alberich ordered. "This class, precedence has." And several of them exchanged meaningful glances. Sober ones, too, he was proud to see. So, they knew; somehow in this first round of mock-combat, they had learned that deadly lesson, that fighting was dirty, foul, and ugly—that combat meant hurt. That *they* could be hurt, which was a difficult lesson for any young person to grasp.

He did not think that they had yet come to grips with the other lesson—that they could *die.* But at least they knew that there was no glory to be found in this, and there was a great deal of danger.

He hoped.

:Oh, they know. And they're thinking furiously, trying to come up with the reason for all of this,: Kantor told him. *:Don't worry; we'll encourage the "right answer.":*

Good. He needed them to concentrate on that "answer." Because by the time the snow was falling, he'd have them practicing in full armor.

And by the time it melted, he would have them practicing in sets of custom-made armor that would not show under Trainee Grays. When that armor arrived, he wanted them to be firmly fixated on their own answer, and not his.

He raised his stick; automatically, they raised theirs, and they all clashed together overhead. "Good game," he said with satisfaction. "Same time tomorrow."

Fat, fluffy flakes of snow fell thickly from a sky that was a uniform, featureless gray from horizon to horizon. The damp, still air seemed oddly warm, but perhaps it was only because there was no wind blowing at the moment. Already the new snow was a thumb's-breadth deep everywhere, covering the old, crusty, knee-deep stuff, softening the harsh, bare bushes and skeletal tree limbs.

It covered everywhere, except the Hurlee field, which was a churned-up mess of dirty snow, clods of earth, and grass. There was not a single spot on the field that wasn't pounded down with hoofmarks.

Despite the muffling effect of the falling snow, the game was loud enough. Not because of the shouting of spectators (there weren't any), nor the shouts of the players themselves (mostly they just grunted). No, it was the clash of stick on armor.

Every one of the players wore armor, including Alberich; thigh-, shin-, and foot-guards, breast and back-plates, shoulder-, neck-, and arm-guards, and, of course, the helm. It wasn't articulated plate of the sort that a knight might wear; the Trainees wore protective plates riveted onto leather. Much lighter and easier to move in—relatively.

Easier to fit under or over other garments, anyway. Under the armor, they wore padded gambesons, and over it, padded surcoats. The Companions were armored, too, at least for these practice sessions—a face-plate to protect their heads, articulated plate along their necks, and leg-guards. Alberich didn't want any of them injured either—

He was on home-goal guard this session, which gave him more opportunity to watch the rest as they skirmished. And they had made amazing progress in the past few moons.

I should have expected it, I suppose, looking back on how all those young Trainees drove themselves before the last Tedrel War. He felt a warmth toward them that was almost paternal; challenge them, and they rose to the challenge. Let them but *think* that there was a challenge in the offing, and they rose to it. And they'd go through fire to meet it.

Most of the noise was coming from sticks connecting with the Companions' armor, since *they* weren't wearing any padding over it, and he wondered if perhaps he shouldn't order the armor off. When the day came that they began riding guardian on Selenay, there was no way to disguise what was essentially horse-armor, so the Companions would have to do without. If it was making the Companions dependent, possibly careless—

:*It's not; they just aren't ready yet to have us dodging underneath them. Not with all that extra weight.*:

Kantor's assurance was all he needed; he stopped worrying about it. This was only the third session under armor, and they still weren't used to it. Fortunately, the custom-made and fitted armor he had ordered up for them was going to be lighter than this stuff. Not as strong or protective, but it should easily be good enough against the kinds of light court-blades that the Prince and his friends sported, if Alberich's worst fears came true.

And if the Prince and his friends elected to attempt to hire professionals rather than doing the dirty work themselves, Alberich would hear about it. There was no job involving dirty work in Haven that at least one of his personae didn't hear about, either via the rumor vine, or directly.

If the Prince decides to hire out his evil work, wouldn't it be a great irony if he approached me directly?

Just as he thought that, the melee surged toward his goal; he judged his moment, and as soon as they drew near enough to be a threat to the goal, Kantor charged the rider nearest him. The Companion's powerful muscles surged under him. Kantor's unusual weight and size—quite as large as any warhorse—was next to impossible for another Companion to stand up to. The best they could do was to try and turn aside at the last moment so that he slid along a flank—or to dodge out of the way.

But there was nowhere for this Companion to dodge to, and no room to turn. Kantor hit him hard, and the shock of the meeting jarred both his body and Alberich's. *They* bounced back; Kantor anticipated the shock and caught himself without a slip. The other Companion's hooves scrabbled desperately in the snow as he tried to stay upright; the rider dropped his stick, grabbed the hold on the pommel, and hung on grimly.

And Kantor charged again, while Alberich swung at the rider.

It was a short charge, more of a push, but the other Companion's hind feet slid right out from under him, at the same time that Alberich's stick connected with the rider's helm with a solid *clang* that vibrated up the stick and into Alberich's arm.

Down they both went, the Companion sliding over sideways with a squeal of pain, the rider just—falling. Not jumping free, not even trying. And Alberich knew as soon as they started to fall that they were both hurt.

Blessed Sunlord...

So did Shanda, who was refereeing; she gave a blast to her whistle as the two hit the slushy ground, and the scrum instantly *stopped.*

What have we done?

The rider groaned, and tried to rise as Alberich leaped off Kantor's back and ran for him. The Companion got to his feet, with a lurch and a scramble, whining under his breath with pain, but when he stood, it was on only three legs.

:Not broken,: Kantor relayed instantly, *:but it's a bad sprain.:*

Alberich unfastened Harrow's helm strap and lifted the helmet from Harrow's head. "Look at me," he commanded, and it didn't take a genius to see from the unequal size of the boy's pupils that he'd been concussed. And it didn't take a genius to see why either; the padding had come loose and slid down the back of the helm to bunch up against the neck protector.

Shanda was on the case already; she and her Companion were dragging up the two-horse stretcher they kept at the side of the field. Alberich didn't have to give them a single order.

They worked as if they had rehearsed for this disaster; half of them lifted Harrow straight up off the ground without moving his back or neck, and placed him on the stretcher. Within a moment, they were heading toward Healer's Collegium with Harrow held securely by the straps around the stretcher.

Meanwhile the other half of the Trainees left behind were buckling Harrow's Companion onto the saddles of two more Companions so they could take some of his weight and he wouldn't have to put that injured leg to the ground. In another moment they, too, were on their way to the Healers, picking their way through the uneven snow.

Alberich was left to pick up the helm and stare numbly after them. He felt sick, but what could he do? There were injuries like this even in normal practice, much less the risky stuff he was asking them to do now. And if he didn't push them—if they didn't push themselves—if it came to a real fight, they might not live through it. He wasn't going to apologize—

But what were they thinking?

"Find us a substitute, Weaponsmaster," called Brion over his shoulder as the second lot limped toward the Collegium with Harrow's Companion. "We're not good enough yet, and this just proves it. Get us a substitute, or get us just a referee and *you* substitute, and we'll pick this up tomorrow."

The words both startled and gratified him, and for a moment, he actually felt his eyes burn. "I will!" he called after them, hoping that they didn't notice the slightly choked quality caused by the lump in his throat. "But session is ended for today, I think."

:Tell the others with Harrow, will you?: he asked Kantor.

:Certainly.: There was a pause. *:Harrow says to tell you he apologizes for not checking his helm better, and that this is all his fault.:*

That called for an apology. *:Tell him that he is right but that it is also my fault for not checking the equipment first myself and that I also beg his pardon for my carelessness.:*

:That ought to scare him out of his bed,: Kantor chuckled. *:You, apologizing!:*

But as Alberich hung the faulty helm on the pommel of his saddle, and turned to mount Kantor's saddle and head for the salle, he caught sight of movement out of the corner of his eye.

For one horrible moment, he thought it was someone from the Court. Perhaps one of the Prince's people—

Which could be a disaster.

Then he saw the color of the mount and the rider's clothing and had another sickening feeling. This was another Trainee and Companion, and they'd seen the accident. If he thought he was being portrayed as a monster before—

:No Companion thinks you're a monster.:

He hadn't seen them there; he'd thought there had been no one watching. In a moment, he recognized them, with something of a start. The Trainee was young Mical, his Companion Eloran—two of the unholy trio whose antics had broken that mirror in the salle and had inadvertently sent him down the road to discovering what the actor Norris had been up to.

What were *they* doing here?

But Mical's punishment was long since over; what could he possibly have been doing out here? It wasn't for pleasure; he looked practically blue with cold, and he must have been here the entire time they'd been playing.

"Weaponsmaster Alberich?" the boy called, as soon as he was within easy conversational distance. "Can we volunteer to be that substitute?"

Alberich raised an eyebrow, making certain that none of his considerable surprise showed on his face, although his jaw ached with the effort of keeping it from dropping. He knew very well that young Mical had a reputation as a demon Hurlee player, despite the late start that he and Eloran had on it because of the punishment work he'd been doing. But that was regular Hurlee, not this—this combat version. Surely no one sane would volunteer for this, not after today, not seeing that the *Weaponsmaster* would injure one of the Trainees and apparently not think twice about it. And Mical had at least three more years to go in his training, not one or less than one.

"How long have you watching been?" he asked, keeping his tone flat. He expected to hear a slightly cocky "Long enough," but once again he got a surprise.

"A little more than two moons," Mical replied. "It took me a while to get my chores scheduled so I had the candlemark free. I heard about it, and I started watching. At first it was—well, because it was *Hurlee.*" He emphasized the game as if invoking the name alone would explain everything. "Then I stayed."

Kantor snorted. *:Well, well. This is interesting.:*

"This no kind of game is," Alberich told him, harshly. "Not anymore. Not *this* group. There is this, serious injury today. More, there are likely to be."

"I *know* that, Weaponsmaster," Mical replied, head up, eyes blazing. "But I'm good, *really* good at regular Hurlee, and I want to help." His Companion moved forward until he was nearly nose-to-nose with Alberich, and the rest of his speech was made in a whisper. "I know why you're doing this," he continued, and if his hands and voice trembled a little, his gaze was firm. "That is, I think I know *what* you're doing. You're training up a bunch of people who are always at the Collegium until they graduate into Whites, and who nobody is going to even consider as adequate protection. Not even the Queen, so we could go anywhere. You think that if the Queen ever leaves the Palace grounds, someone is going to try to kidnap her. Maybe even the Prince's friends, to try and get the Queen and the Council to agree to make him a King."

Since that was very near to what Alberich *was* afraid of, he actually started, and stared at the boy, and this time he didn't even try to keep his jaw from dropping. "But—how—" he began.

Mical shrugged. "Healer Crathach is my second cousin, and my uncle knows people who know the Prince's set. I'm good at putting things together, and my Gift is Touchreading." At Alberich's puzzled look, he explained. "If I pick up something barehanded, and I want to know, sometimes I can tell where it's been and what it's been doing going back to when it was first made." He gulped. "I haven't had it working for long, not so I could trust it. Otherwise I'd have told you."

Alberich blinked again. So did Kantor. *:I was under the impression that Mical's Gift was fairly unreliable.:*

"My Gift-teacher still thinks it's unreliable," Mical continued. "But in the last moon it's been getting a bit more under control, and that was when I noticed something. If someone has been handling what I pick up very recently, and feeling strongly about something, it's pretty dead-accurate. I can pick up bits of what they've been thinking about. When I realized there was something strange about this Hurlee team, I—" He flushed. "I started snooping on you. You've been awfully worried lately, and you've been doing a lot of repairs on the practice equipment." His chin firmed. "I know this *is* dangerous; you just cracked Harrow's skull for him, and that was just in practice! But I still want to help."

Alberich thought about it for a long, long moment, as the snow fell all about them, sealing them off from the rest of the world inside a wall of white curtains.

"All right," he said at last. "Come down to the salle with me. I will need to measure you, and get you armor. And your gods be with you."

Mical went off with his measurements taken, a set of armor of the approximate size ready for him, and an admonishment to say nothing of his speculations, not even to his fellows on the team. "Tell them that you are the substitute, you may," Alberich told him. "If you care to."

Mical just shook his head. "They aren't my yearmates, and it'll be better coming from you," he replied, showing a maturity that Alberich hadn't expected. "If *you* say it, they'll just figure you picked the best you could think of. If I do, it'll sound like I'm boasting."

It sounded as if young Mical had learned a lot more in that glassworks than how to make mirrors.

And there had not been one single attempt on Mical's part to suggest some of the stage-fighting techniques he had been so enamored with a year ago. He'd done a great deal of physical growing in the past year, too; he'd gone from weedy adolescent to a young powerhouse with muscles as hard as rocks. It was no wonder that he was reputed to be such a demon Hurlee player. Evidently pumping those bellows had been very good for him.

But as Alberich brooded over his solitary supper, he was still worried. The boy might be big and strong, but he was still a boy, still three years younger than the rest of the team. He'd volunteered, but did Alberich have the right to accept him? He thought of poor Harrow, even now being taken care of by the Healers. He would be throwing young Mical into the middle of a team that was already playing a deadly game; *they'd* had moons of practice at it, and Mical and Eloran didn't.

:But he's been watching,: Kantor reminded him.

:Watching isn't the same as playing: Would Mical just end up in a bed next to Harrow in the next day or two?

:Eloran is getting some special coaching, this minute,: Kantor told him. *:This business is half the Companion's job, remember. And Eloran is a lot faster than Harrow's Companion.:*

Another shock; this was a day full of them. *:I thought all of you were fairly equal—:*

:Oh, no. Not that any of us is the Companion equivalent of Myste—: There was a snicker in that, and Alberich could hardly blame him. Poor Myste! By now she was so notorious that Selenay just had a page assigned to her to follow around behind her, picking up the things she dropped and gathering up the things she put down and forgot. Well, she might forget where she left her spare pair of lenses; she *never* forgot a fact, a law, or a precedent.

:Some of us have different priorities,: he replied truthfully.

:As do we. At any rate, Eloran is a little nimbler than Lekaron, with slightly better reactions. That should make up for lack of experience.: But he detected a hint of doubt in Kantor's mind-voice, and oddly enough, that comforted him. If Kantor was having feelings of guilt, at least it meant that Alberich wasn't being overly nice about this situation.

:They're terribly young,: he said gloomily.

:Lavan Firestorm and his Companion weren't any older.:

:And Lavan never got the opportunity to grow any older.:

Kantor was silent for a moment. *:Lavan never really got the opportunity to volunteer. Mical did.:*

There was that. But could someone that young have any real idea of what he was volunteering for? Bad enough to take the Trainees he *had*— all adolescents to one extent or another thought they were immortal, that death was something that happened to someone else; the older lot at least were well aware that they could be horribly hurt. But fifteen-year-olds *truly* thought that they were immortal, yes, and invulnerable, that even injuries would nod and pass on by. And in spite of what he'd seen, was this truly informed consent?

:When do you trust someone?: Kantor asked, seemingly out of the blue.

:Excuse me?:

:When do you trust someone? Is it by age, or maturity? What is the magic number? When do Trainees start to think like adults?:

He understood what Kantor was saying, of course, and his head agreed with it. Mical had been there on the worst day the team had experienced. He'd watched them for two moons at least. And he'd evidently learned some sobering lessons in the glassworks.

He'd shown every sign of acting in a measured and mature fashion this afternoon. So when did Alberich stop doubting and start trusting?

:When my gut decides to go along with my head, I suppose,: he replied glumly. *:And my gut is going to be screaming, "but he's only a child!" for a little while longer at least.:*

He might have said something more, but at just that moment, a bell rang out, cutting across the winter night.

And for one, horrible moment, he thought it was the Death Bell, and his thoughts fastened on Harrow—

But no, it wasn't. It was the Great Bell at the Palace—not the Collegium Bell, that sounded the candlemarks and the meals, but the huge, deep-toned Bell that sounded only for major occasions. So what—

A moment later, his question was answered.

:It's time! It's Selenay!: said Kantor, and given the gravid condition of the Queen, that was all Kantor needed to say.

Selenay had gone into labor. By dawn, Valdemar would have an Heir-Presumptive.

And from that moment on, the Queen would be standing between Prince Karathanelan and his ambitions.

Alberich shivered. It had begun.

2 1

"I'm sorry, Weaponsmaster," Mical sighed. He pushed the papers away from him, and reluctantly, Alberich took them and folded them up, tightly. "All I get from them is—" he screwed up his face, "—the writer was in a hurry, really annoyed with something, and wanted to get this over with. I *think* he was that actor fellow—the one we all thought was so—interesting." He paused again, then smiled wanly. "And about the only thing that I can tell you besides that is that he thought the person he was writing to was very, very thick."

Alberich sighed. It had been a long shot, of course. He'd hoped that somehow the secret instructions from Norris to the Prince would have some link to the unknown patron. But—no luck, it seemed. Whoever the patron was, Norris had not been thinking of *him* when he'd been writing the Prince's "scripts."

"My thanks, regardless, Mical," he said. He saw Mical glancing with longing at the door, and he found a bit of sympathy for the boy. It was the first fine day in—well, since autumn. And Mical, no longer under punishment duty, was probably afire to be out in it. "Go along—"

He hadn't so much as gotten the words out when Mical was out the door like a shot.

"Frustrating," said Myste redundantly. "We've got one end of the path—Norris to Karath. We have the other, Devlin to Norris. But we still don't have the so-called 'patron' who links it all into a neat circle."

"Nor will we," Alberich said with grim certainty. "I believe it was the same person who was paying for unrest against the Queen earlier. I even believe it was the same person who was selling information out of the Council during the Wars. And I have my suspicions who that person is. Unfortunately, I do not have a shred of proof. He is too clever at covering his tracks and hiding his identity. He is *probably* in disguise most of the time when he deals with underlings."

This "certainty" was not true ForeSight, but it came with the scent of ForeSight on it. He would have liked to confide his suspicions to someone who had some other Gift that might be used to spy upon this person, but unfortunately, the suspicion was so wild that he knew that even the Heralds would have stared at him with incredulity.

Yes, even Talamir. Even Myste.

Even, perhaps, most of the Companions.

:But not me,: said Kantor, with equal certainty. *:So you and I will watch and wait and bide our time—quietly. We'll catch him eventually.:*

"So all we can do is keep a guard on Selenay?" Myste asked mournfully.

"It seems so," he replied. She sighed.

:I wish I could tell her,: he said to his Companion.

:You can when it's over,: Kantor replied. *:You're used to keeping secrets.:*

And that, alas, was only too true.

It was just too bad that Selenay had not realized that little fact before all of this had begun, and had confided in *him* rather than—well— whoever she had, who had been so *poor* at keeping them.

Selenay tried to concentrate on the reports in front of her, but her eyes kept drifting to the window, and her thoughts drifting off into nothingness. It was only two moons since the baby's birth. Two moons. Spring was just beginning outside those windows, and she was stuck inside. And when she managed to wrench her eyes and her thoughts back to the job at hand, an angry wail from the next room cut across her concentration and she winced, and shoved down the surge of angry irritation that made her want to go into the nursery and put a pillow over baby Elspeth's face—

And immediately, she felt sick with guilt—

horrible thought. She was a horrible mother. How could she think such things about the baby? She should have been all moony-eyed and willing to bear with *anything*. She should be longing to hold Elspeth, to cradle her for hours and hours, she should be spending every waking moment hovering over the cradle, gazing down at the little mite with adoration.

Instead, she had thoughts of wanting to smother the poor thing. She was unfit to be a mother. She should never have had a child...

:That's not a child,: Caryo said testily. *:It's a stomach with a warhorn attached*

*to one end, and a mechanism that produces more excrement than a full-grown cow
attached to the other.:*

Selenay was glad that there wasn't anyone in the room to see her as
she choked on a laugh. There was some truth to that, though Selenay
herself seldom had to attend to the latter. Still. The former—

Elspeth's wails scaled up a notch. Selenay's own nurse, old Melidy,
was in charge of the nursery, but she seemed to have her hands full with
Elspeth, who had an awfully robust set of lungs for something so small,
and the need to demand attention *constantly.*

Do all babies cry so much?

At least baby Elspeth's demands were reasonable; milk, comfort, a
clean napkin. Unlike her father...

Selenay's irritation increased, as did her headache.

He'd been pouting again this morning. He didn't even have to *say*
anything anymore, just pout and look aggrieved and put-upon. His
pouts didn't seem quite so attractive anymore either, and his bereft-
orphan pose was beginning to look a great deal more like a pose than
like her own, real grief. She knew what true mourning looked like, from
the inside, and—well, all his protestations to the contrary, it had begun
to look to her as if his father's death and brother's estrangement were
things he really didn't feel deeply about.

If at all.

Oh, come now! said her conscience. *You can't blame him for wanting to be a
King, now that his brother is King of Rethwellan. And he's been thoroughly agreeable
since Elspeth was born. Didn't he say he had sent for* his *old nurse for her, so that
old Melidy wouldn't have to do all the looking-after by herself? And with two Chief
Nursery Attendants on the job, there shouldn't be any more of this howling while
you're trying to get some work done.*

Agreeable he might be, but she couldn't help the feeling that it
was all on the surface. He certainly wasn't about whenever something
needed doing. When they retired for the evening and she wanted to tell
him about the annoyances of the day, just to get them off her chest, *he*
would launch off into some hunting story or other, ignoring her hints
that another topic—*any* other topic—would be welcome. And what
had happened to Karath the lover? All very well to speak tenderly of
wanting to give her plenty of time to recover from Elspeth's birth, but
just how long did he think she needed?

Besides, it wouldn't hurt her to be held and comforted, now and
again. She could do with more of the commiseration about the burdens

of the Crown that he used to give her, and less complaining that he wanted the crown himself.

He's the father of your child, she reminded herself. Though as Elspeth's wails turned into distinctly angry howls, that was seeming less and less of a good thing.

Finally, just when she thought that her head was going to split, she heard the sound of feet running into the nursery and the howls cut off—and lest she worry that someone *else* had put a pillow over the baby's face, she heard suckling and cooing noises. The wet nurse had been found, it seemed. Her Highness was now satisfied.

If only *His* Highness could be satisfied so easily.

She sighed, and pinched the bridge of her nose to try and ease the pain in her head. Demands for attention, demands for service, wanting everything now, this moment, totally self-centered…

Perfectly reasonable in an infant.

Not so attractive in her father. And unfortunately, at this late date he was unlikely to grow out of it. Things seemed dreadfully clear, all of a sudden—when she wasn't looking into those beautiful eyes, and listening to that honey-sweet voice whispering in her ear. When she had been sleeping alone for far too long. When she realized that the demands were never, ever going to stop, and she began to understand Caryo's antipathy to him—and wonder which Karath was the real one.

What was I thinking? she thought with despair. *What have I done?*

She dropped her head into her hands, and for a moment, gave way to the despair.

She who had been afraid of being trapped had trapped herself. She was trapped within the hard shell of the Crown, trapped with an infant she had not really planned for, trapped with a husband who was—

Face it, Selenay—who is beginning to look like someone who put on a show for you.

She wanted, suddenly, to get away, away from the Palace, away from the Crown. Not forever, just for a few candlemarks, where she could be just Selenay, not the Queen, not a mother, just herself. She needed to be able to think clearly, and she couldn't even think at all with the baby fussing in the next room. Something had changed between her and Karath; she needed to figure out what it was, and somehow get things back to the way they had been before that terrible quarrel.

If she could. She had to think about that, too. She had to be able to step back from the whole situation and try to look at it objectively, as if this was Selenay sitting in judgment in the City Courts.

If only she could go somewhere that held no memories of the Prince, where she could be herself entirely again, the Selenay she used to be.

I'll do it. To the seven hells with these reports. They can wait a few candlemarks more. She pushed away from her desk and stood up. :*Caryo? Would you be amenable to a ride to the Home Farms? Just the two of us?*:

This was the best day for practice that they had gotten in a long time. Spring rains hadn't yet begun, the ground was good and dry, and although the air was chill, it was not cold enough to be uncomfortable even if you weren't moving.

Alberich watched his teams as they writhed in a knot of flying sticks and flailing bodies; the view was excellent from the sidelines, and he allowed himself a moment of grim satisfaction. They were good. And they were ready. He had believed in them, and they had repaid that belief in full.

Even young Mical, that most unlikely of prodigals.

The boy had flung himself into his self-appointed niche with the controlled energy of a tightly-wound spring, and a concentration Alberich suspected he never would have had if he had not spent those moons in the glassworks. You dared not lose your concentration around hot glass, for if you did, the best you could expect was the total ruin of all your work. And the worst—the worst could cost a limb, or a life, or worse than just your life, if you were a glassblower. He didn't know if the Collegium Healers could do anything about scorched lungs before the patient died of the injury. He did know that it was one of the nastier and more painful ways to die.

Although no such disaster had occurred at the glassworks while the two Trainees had been serving their time there, Mical had probably been witness to several minor accidents, and certainly had been told all of the horror stories. It was amazing to see the level of steadiness and concentration he had attained—

It was nevertheless true that steadiness and concentration couldn't make up for a difference of three years of age and growth. The boy was *not* the most skilled of the skirmishers. Although in the normal Hurlee games Mical was a star player, in these practices he was merely at the level of all the others. Still, given that they were three years older than he, and had several moons of learning and practice that he *hadn't* had, that was absolutely astonishing.

Part of it, Alberich was sure, was a natural ability in combat, or exercises that were combatlike. Alberich had taught a few youngsters who possessed that near-magical combination of reflexes, strength, coordination, cleverness, and the instinct for combat; Mical was definitely one of that number. Take, for instance, the way that he and Eloran worked together, moving through the pack, smooth as an otter in a fast-flowing stream. Never a wasted moment, often managing to anticipate the next blow and thwart it by the simple expedient of not being there when it fell—

—the next blow—

Flash of blue.

Alberich clung to his pommel as the Foresight Vision slammed him between the eyes.

Selenay—

But it wasn't a long one.

It didn't need to be, actually. He had spent the last several moons anticipating exactly what it showed him; all it needed to give him was the *where* and the *when.*

Where—

Outside the city walls, on the Home Farms. He recognized that spot, along the riverbank, beyond the point where he and Selenay had fished for eels. It was secluded there, quiet, and out of sight of any of the farmworkers.

When—

Soon—

Too soon. Moments at most. Terror rose in him.

:Not for us!: Kantor said fiercely, before he could even begin to panic, as the players suddenly froze in place, their Companions relaying to them what Alberich and Kantor already knew. "Weapons!" cried Harrow. "No time!" shouted someone else, and suddenly they were all in motion, Alberich and Kantor in the lead, flying across the grass, leaping obstacles, scattering Trainees and courtiers out of their way, and out of the main Palace Gate before Alberich even had time to *think* about what they were doing.

They knew! How did they know?

No—no they didn't know—or hadn't known *consciously* before this moment. But the peak of readiness they had attained was such that at this point they had been ready for *anything.*

:Warn Caryo!: he told Kantor urgently—and needlessly, of course—

:I—the trap's sprung. Don't panic. We can get there in time—: And with grim

satisfaction, *:They weren't expecting her to fight.:*

Alberich had his sword, for even in the Hurlee practices he never left the salle without putting it in a saddle sheath. The teams, however, had no weapons. But they *did* have their modified Hurlee sticks, special sticks sheathed in metal, of a wood so hard they called it "iron-wood," so dense and tough that even without the metal sheath it dulled blades that tried to cut it. And they were all in their fitted armor, which Alberich had insisted they wear as soon as it was available.

And the *Companions* were armored.

In all the time that Alberich had been a Herald, he had not understood what it was like to be in the saddle when Kantor was at full gallop. He had *heard* about the extraordinary speed of a Companion, but he had never fully experienced it for himself. When Kantor had rescued him from the burning shed and carried him out of Karse, he had been drifting in and out of awareness.

It was exhilarating and terrifying.

Already the troop was down in the crowded streets of Haven, and the houses and shops blurred past as the hapless bystanders pressed themselves against the walls in an effort to get as far out of the way as possible. Somehow the crowds were parting before them like a school of minnows in front of a pike.

Thank the Sunlord! Being in the lead as he was, he could see them making way, as if something invisible was shoving them to either side of the street ahead, just in time to avoid being trampled. But if someone *didn't* get out of the way in time—

:They will. You leave that to us.:

Somewhere behind them, the Palace and Collegia were aboil; of course, only he and his teams had been *instantly* ready to respond, but the rest, every man and woman who was in Whites and no few in Grays were scrambling to join the rescue, getting weapons, saddling up—some, like Keren, probably not even bothering with a saddle.

How did that bastard know? The vision had shown him the Prince and a mob of his hangers-on; how had he *known* that Selenay would be there, and alone, when even *he* hadn't known she'd left the Palace?

He must have had a small army of watchers on the Palace, waiting for her to leave under *exactly* the right circumstances, following her to see where she went, sending back the message he had been waiting for. This was not spur-of-the-moment or something conceived in passion. This had been long in the planning, probably from the moment he came into Valdemar.

Or else someone else had planned it all for him.

No time to think about that now. He had to try and remember what the vision had shown him—

Swiftly, as swiftly as Kantor was running, he worked out a rough plan. They'd have to be fools not to expect rescue coming from the Heralds. But they wouldn't be looking for it so soon.

Alarm bells were sounding all over the city; if the Prince had thought he was going to be able to carry this off quietly, he was going to get more than one rude surprise. At least the alarms had the effect of clearing the streets entirely. Kantor somehow redoubled his speed, and they shot through the gates going at such a rate that even Alberich was dizzy. And he was *not* going to think about what would happen if any of them tripped and fell—

There was no finesse in this. Down the road, in at the gates of the Home Farms, riders clutching their weapons in grim silence, hooves pounding like thunder—so loud they couldn't hear the fighting ahead of them—

—so loud that the ambushers surely thought it *was* thunder—

And they didn't even pause as they sighted their target. Just as the team had been taught, just as they had practiced for moons and moons, they crashed in among the milling ambushers, exactly as if it was a Hurlee skirmish. They broke into the mob around Selenay, and their sticks went to work.

In that first and last glimpse, Alberich got the sudden, heart-sinking realization that there were more of them than he had thought there would be, or than he had Seen. A lot more. The odds were roughly two-to-one, in fact.

Hard on the heels of that realization was another—he hadn't *heard* about this down in the rough parts of Haven because the Prince hadn't needed to recruit anyone for this plan. He'd brought them with him, in the guise of servants, of hangers-on, of sycophants.

And last of all—even as he raised his stick and Kantor ran straight into the horse of one of these pseudo-servants, he looked up and saw Selenay lose her sword—

—to Norris. Norris, who had regarded women as mere objects of convenience, and would no more hesitate to kill her than he would hesitate to kill a fly.

There was a bulwark of fighters three deep between him and her. There was no way he could fight his way to her in time.

And that was when he saw the incredible, the miraculous, the totally insane.

Eloran, coming in at full gallop from the *side*, where there was no one in the way; crashing into Norris' horse.

Just as Mical rose in his stirrups, pushed off, and with the momentum of Eloran's charge behind him, flung himself out of his saddle at Norris. *Somehow* he wrapped his arms around the actor when he hit, pinning Norris' sword to his side as they tumbled out of the saddle to the ground. *Somehow* he managed to stay uppermost. They went over the side of the horse and out of sight.

Selenay took advantage of the moment of confusion that followed to get Caryo a little farther into the open, where the Companion's hooves came into play. That cleared a little more space for her to fight, and as Alberich's stick connected with the man in front of him, Kantor shoved through to her side.

"Here!" he shouted, and tossed his sword, hilt-first, at her.

"Here! Alberich!" he heard from somewhere below, and as Kantor pirouetted on his hindlegs, Mical thrust a sword up at him from the ground, hilt first, doing so left-handed, holding his right tight to his belly. Norris wasn't moving, so the blade was presumably the actor's. Alberich snatched it, and Mical scrambled out of the way. Eloran rammed his way in beside his Chosen, and, even one-handed, Mical was able to haul himself back up into the saddle.

From the way he was holding that arm, however, he wasn't going to be a further factor in the fighting.

Then it all stopped having anything to do with thought, as the mob closed in around them again, and he and Selenay fought side-by-side against the tightening circle. Kantor kept himself interposed as much as he could between the fighters and Caryo. *He* was armored; Caryo was not.

Norris' sword wasn't much better than a Hurlee stick, but at least it had a pointed end and not a blunt one.

And that was just about all that Alberich had time to think about.

Then, for what seemed like forever, it was all shouting, blow and counterblow, screams and blood and last-minute parries, and far too many people trying to kill his Queen.

Until suddenly the fighting melted away from in front of him, and those who were not on the ground groaning (or dead) were in full retreat, as the reinforcements came pounding up on their Companions with swords in their hands and rage on their faces.

And it was at that moment that he looked down and realized that the last man he had bludgeoned to death with that pathetic excuse for a sword was the Prince.

He had not even known who it was he was fighting.

Mical had a broken wrist; there were some slices and cuts to the others, but his was probably the most serious injury. Alberich could have wept with relief; his gamble of putting them into armor had worked, for the Prince's ambushers had foolishly worn none at all.

Mical had done the impossible, and Norris' phenomenal luck had run out just before the Prince's had, for when Mical had hit him and taken him down to the ground, he had not been able to compensate for his attacker's weight. All of his agility and training had, after all, counted for naught. He'd broken his neck as they hit the ground together.

Alberich limped over to where Crathach was tending to the boy, who looked up at him, too weary and full of pain to care about much of anything. "That, one of your fool play-acting moves was," Alberich growled. "Yes?"

The boy nodded.

"And practiced it, you have been?"

Mical hesitated. "Um. *Sort* of. With a straw-man. Eloran and I didn't think it was really going to work, so we'd kind of given up on it, but when we came up on the ambush and saw Norris with Selenay——" He shrugged and hissed with pain. "I *knew* I couldn't fight him; it's not just stage-fighting he knows and he's better than me. The important thing was to immobilize him long enough for you to get to her."

He would have said more, but Alberich held up his hand. "Enough. Good reasoning. Right action. *Never* do it again. Your neck broken, it could have been, not his."

Mical turned a bit green, and not from the pain. Alberich didn't blame him. This was his first kill, and it had literally been with his bare hands; not an easy thing for a boy of fifteen to cope with. Alberich turned on his heel and left him with Crathach, who was better suited to helping him deal with the emotional ramifications than the Weaponsmaster himself was. Alberich went to find the rest of his team, make sure *they* were all right, and if not, see that they were under someone's wing before he went looking for the Queen.

He found Harrow last of all; the boy was staring down at one of the ambushers' bodies, running his hands reflexively up and down the

Hurlee stick. Just as Alberich came up to him, he looked at his hands and realized what he was doing. With an expression of repulsion, he threw the thing away.

"I am *never* playing again!" he said to Alberich, who nodded, understanding all that the youngster could not put into words. That it wasn't a game anymore; that it would be forever tainted for him. That he could never even think of Hurlee without knowing that he had killed at least one man with his stick.

"Go to see Crathach," was all he said, and then made sure that he did so.

:Why do I think that Hurlee is now going to fade away into the mists that hold all old fads?: Kantor asked, rhetorically.

:Oh, someone might revive it again, when this lot has gone on into Whites. Not until then. And that's not a bad thing; it won't be such an obsession when it comes around for the second time.: He, personally, wouldn't be sorry to see it go. The business of the Collegia was learning, after all, not gamesmanship. And there were other ways to teach teamwork.

Selenay was sitting a little way away, under a tree; when Alberich came up to her, Talamir was speaking earnestly to her in a low voice. Alberich caught the name "Norris" and the word "script" before they both looked up at him.

She had been crying quietly, and she rubbed the tears from her face with the back of her hand. "So it was an act from beginning to end," she said bitterly. "Every bit of it."

"Tailored precisely to you, Majesty," Alberich agreed, since she seemed to be waiting for a reply. "Sorry, I am."

"I don't want your pity!" she snapped, then wilted. "Damn. I apologize. It's not your fault. And I probably wouldn't have listened to you before—" The tears started again; she seemed unaware of them. "It's not fair. I'm glad you killed him."

"Majesty, I am not," Alberich replied, and she looked up at him, startled. "In death, he has escaped the consequences of his actions. And left you to deal with them. I am not glad. And what His Majesty of Rethwellan will say and do, I know not."

"Leave that to me," Talamir said instantly. "Although, given not only what Karath claimed but what my agents have verified for me, there was definitely no love lost between the King of Rethwellan and his brother." He brooded a moment. "No. No love lost at all. He seems to have been—more welcome in his absence than his presence, and it was not by *his* doing that he was not told of his own father's death until it was long past the moment when he could have been recalled for the funeral."

Alberich nodded; that wasn't much of a surprise. "So, King Faramentha, not so displeased to hear of this will be?"

Talamir shrugged. "I believe that if we are discreet, or as discreet as we may be, having roused all of Haven, this will probably be no more than a matter of some delicate maneuvering. In fact, I suspect it will be of more import that it is clear that we do not hold His Majesty responsible for his brother's actions than that we—were forced to eliminate a Prince of Rethwellan."

Alberich caught a little movement from the corner of his eye. Selenay was staring at him. "And when I think of what you've been doing so quietly all this time, Alberich—and to think that at one point I thought you were just jealous because he was as good a swordsman as you and that was why you weren't up at the Palace anymore—you're—"

She was about to say it. He cut her off.

"Selenay, no hero am I," he told her firmly but gently. "For heroes, look to young Mical, who I think was certain he would be killed when the actor he attacked. Or Myste, who is no great dissembler, and could not have herself defended, had Norris discovered her intent."

"If you are no hero, then what are you?" she demanded.

He managed a smile—the first genuine smile he had felt on his face since she'd married. "Your Weaponsmaster. Your Herald." And he held out his hand. "I hope, your friend and brother. Nothing more."

She took it, and looked long and hard at him, and he knew then that at one point she herself must have had something of a crush on him, now long past—but that she was afraid that he might now be the one with secret feelings for *her.*

It wouldn't have been the first time such a thing had happened. He was just as glad that the whole notion was so absurd. "I always wanted a brother, growing up," she said aloud, and let go of his hand.

"Good." He smiled again. "Then if my advice you will take, you will make of Myste and Mical great heroes, and let your Shadow Herald stay where best he is suited."

"And I will second that," Talamir agreed, and gave Alberich a look that the Weaponsmaster had no trouble interpreting. *You can go now.*

:Hmph. We know when we aren't welcome.:

:Don't be absurd,: he chided Kantor. *:Do you really want her weeping and*

raging at us? Then do you want to be embroiled in the political maneuvering this is going to cause?:

:Well—: Kantor admitted. *:No.:*

:Good.: He scratched his head, encountered a patch of someone else's dried blood in his hair, and grimaced. *:I want a bath. Let's go home.:*

"I may never forgive you," Myste said, her head on his shoulder. It was the first time she'd been in his quarters since the rescue, and he was mortally glad to have her there.

He would be even gladder to have her in his bed—but not quite yet. For now, it was enough to have her in his arms.

"For telling Selenay to make you a hero?" he asked, amused, and shifted a little on the couch so that his position was a little more comfortable. "Someone has to be."

"But why *me?*" she demanded.

"Because you earned it," he replied, staring into the stained-glass face of Vkandis Sunlord. "Because people need heroes. But primarily because you are the *least* likely hero I can think of."

"Well, there I agree with you, but wouldn't that—"

"Hear me out," he interrupted. "People need heroes, and Heralds are that. But Heralds aren't very *ordinary.*"

"Hmm." She did think about it. "I see your point. Most of them are athletic, and even if they aren't handsome, the Whites at least make them look distinguished."

"But you, my dear Chronicler, represent someone who is just like them, or like people they know. And *you* went and did something very dangerous, something that your Whites would not protect you from, something that not even your Companion could have protected you from."

"Hmm." She pushed her lenses up on her nose. "I see your point. And Mical?"

"Everyone likes to have heroes who are young, handsome, and a touch reckless." He laughed. "It won't spoil him. He knows if he gets too much above himself it's back to the glassworks for another couple of moons."

She chuckled. "To think all this began over a broken mirror! Isn't that supposed to mean bad luck?"

"It was bad luck," he pointed out. "For Norris and Karathanelan. Because if it hadn't been for Norris, the mirror would never have gotten broken in the first place."

She fell silent then, leaving him alone with his thoughts. Comforting as it was to think that they had closed the circle, he knew that this was not in the least the case. *Someone* had been Karathanelan's patron, and Norris'; someone who was high in Court circles and privy to some very personal information about Selenay. And they still didn't know who that was.

No, the game wasn't over yet. And if or when *that* person was uncovered, there would, without a doubt, be more troubles on the way.

But at least for a little while, there would be some breathing space. And in the end, that was all anyone, Herald or Queen or ordinary citizen, could ask for.

"Now," he breathed into her hair, "would you like to find out how a hero is rewarded?"

Her response was everything he could have wished for—and he knew that for a few marks, at least, the world would be completely all right for both of them. It would not remain that way for long—

—but it was enough that it remain that way for now.

TAKE A THIEF

A VALDEMAR OMNIBUS

BOOK THREE
OF EXILES of VALDEMAR

To the memory of Gordon R. Dickson
Gentleman and scholar

1

"**G**errup."

Skif's dreams shattered, leaving him with vague fragments of being somewhere warm, cozy, and sweet-scented. A toe scientifically applied to Skif's rib cage with enough force to bounce him off the back wall of the under-stair cubby he called his own reinforced the otherwise incomprehensible order that he wake up. He woke, as ever, stiff, cold, and with a growling stomach.

It was the beginning of another beautiful day at the Hollybush Tavern. *An' good mornin' to you, too, bastard.*

He scrambled to his feet, keeping hunched over to avoid hitting his head on the staircase, his ratty scrap of a blanket clutched in both hands. His uncle's eldest son looked him up and down, and grunted—probably disappointed that Skif was awake enough that a "pick-me-up" cuff to the side of the head wasn't going to be necessary this time.

Skif squinted; Kalchan was a monolithic silhouette against the smoky light from the open kitchen door, narrower at the top and swiftly widening where shoulders would be on an ordinary human, his only distinguishing characteristics from neck to knee being a pair of pillowlike arms and the fat bulging in rolls over his waistband. Skif couldn't see his face, which was fine as far as he was concerned. Kalchan's face was nothing he cared to examine closely under any circumstances.

"Breffuss," Kalchan grunted, jerking his head over his shoulder so that his greasy locks swung in front of his face. Skif ducked his head and quickly folded his blanket, dropping it on the pad of rags over straw that served him as a pallet. He didn't need to dress; in the winter he slept in every stitch of clothing he owned. Satisfied that Skif was on duty, Kalchan went on to awaken the rest of the tavern staff.

Yah, an' do not a hand's worth of work, neither.

"Breakfast," was what Kalchan had said, but he hadn't meant that it

643

was time for Skif to partake of that meal.

As soon as he was out of the way, Skif scuttled out into the kitchen and began the tedious business of lighting the fires, hindered by the fact that his uncle's penny-pinching ways were reflected in every aspect of his purchases. For firewood, he relied on the rag-and-bone men who swept out fireplaces and ovens in more prosperous households, sifting out the ashes for sale to the tanners and soap-makers, and selling the clinkers and partially-burned ends of logs to people like Londer Galko, keeper of the Hollybush Tavern. Nor would Uncle Londer actually buy a decent firestarter, much less keep a candle or banked coals going overnight; Skif had to make do with a piece of flint and one of some other rock. The fact that at least half of this "firewood" had been doused with water before the ragmen picked it up—which was, in fact, the law—didn't make it any easier to light.

Before he could do anything about a fire, Skif went to the pile of sweepings from the floor of the common room that he'd collected last night after the last drunken lout had been rolled out the door. Every bit of dust and fluff that looked as if it might possibly catch fire became his tinder. At worst case, he'd have to sacrifice a precious bit of the straw stuffed into his boots for warmth.

Heh. Sommun' been trackin' in straw. Hayseed from country, prolly. Oh, ayah—here be nice dust bunny, too.

Swearing under his breath, Skif hacked his two bits of rock together, trying to generate sparks, hoping one of them would land in the tiny patch of lint and fluff. When one finally did, and finally cooperated with his efforts, he coaxed it into a tiny flame, then got the flame to take hold of the driest of the wood. He nursed it tenderly, sheltering it from the drafts along the floor, begging it to take. Finally, he set it on the sooty hearth, surrounded it with what was left of the dry wood from last night, and slowly fed it until it was large enough to actually cook over.

Only when the kitchen fire was properly started did the slattern used by Uncle Londer as a cook, dishwasher, and general dogsbody finally shuffle down the stairs from the loft where she slept into the room, scratching head and buttocks at the same time without ever dislodging any of the vermin who called her "home." Skif often wondered why so few people who ate here died. Perhaps it was only because their stomachs were already full of the acidic potions his uncle sold as wine and beer, and once a stomach was full of that rotgut, nothing that came in from the food lived long enough to cause sickness.

The kitchen door stood open to the cold courtyard; Kalchan came in that way every morning, bringing the day's supplies. Uncle Londer never bought more of anything for the inn than he absolutely had to. Now Skif braced himself to head outside into the cold.

Where 'ud it hurt if 'e bought for a week? Wouldn' 'e get it cheaper that way?

Skif ran out into the courtyard to unload the wagon—hired for the purpose by the candlemark, together with a boy to drive it. The quicker Skif unloaded the thing, the less Uncle Londer would be charged—and if he didn't save Uncle Londer every possible pennybit, he'd learn about it when Kalchan's fist connected with his head.

The boy stared at the ears of his donkey, studiously ignoring Skif, who was so much lower in the social scale than he was. This boy had a coat, new boots, both clean.

Ah, stuck up! Skif thought, and stuck out his tongue at the unresponsive back.

First off, a half-sack of flour, followed by a tub of tallow grease thriftily saved from cookshops where they skimmed off the grease from roasting and frying, and resold to those who could not afford butter and candles. Maisie would be put to taking peeled rushes and dipping them in the melted grease to make the tallow dips that served the tavern as lights, and the cook would use the same grease in baking and on the bread.

Skif moved it carefully and set it down beside the flour; sometimes the stuff was still liquid underneath, and he didn't dare spill it.

Then came a bucket of meat scraps, which would serve for the soup and meat pies.

I don' wanna know what that meat came from. Reckon it might meow...

Next, a peck of withered, spotty turnips, another of dried beans and peas that were past their best and smelled of mold. Last of all, two barrels of beer and one of wine. Both represented the collected dregs from barrels all over the city, collected last night from one of the large merchants who supplied goods to other inns and taverns. Needless to say, this was the cheapest conceivable form of beverage; it even cost less than the sweet spring water collected from outside Haven. It was so awful that Guild cooks wouldn't even use the stuff in sauces; stale and loaded with sediment, it smelled sour even through the wood of the barrel. Skif got the barrels off the wagon quickly, and the boy turned the wagon just as quickly and sent his donkey trotting out into the street. Skif lugged the food into the kitchen where old Moll, the cook, took charge of it all. Only she or Kalchan were allowed to touch the food and drink once it came off the wagon.

Skif had no intention of touching any of it. He never ate here—not that Uncle Londer encouraged him to.

He wasn't done yet; he had to bring in enough water from the courtyard pump to fill the half-barrel in the kitchen—one bucket at a time. He stumbled on the rutted, frozen dirt of the courtyard; his boots, stuffed with straw for extra warmth, were far too big for him. He didn't care; better too big than too small.

Leastwise they don' pinch.

Now Skif went out into the common room to ready it for the first customers, lighting the fire there with a brand from the kitchen fire, arranging bits of wood on either side of the hearth to dry, taking the benches down off the tables, and the shutters off the windows. The oiled paper in the windows didn't do a great deal to keep out the cold, but with snow in the street outside, there was some light getting in this morning, so it was just as well that oiled paper hindered more than it helped in that direction. Skif would never want to see what the common room looked like in the full light of the sun.

As horrible as the food and drink here in the Hollybush were, there were two customers waiting for Skif to open the door. He knew them both by sight; two men who would down a minimum of six mugs of foul beer and choke down a slice of stale, burned bread with a scraping of nameless fat before shambling off somewhere, not to be seen until the next morning. Presumably, they had jobs somewhere and this was *their* breakfast.

They slumped down on the benches nearest the door, and Skif yelled for Maisie, the fourth member of Uncle Londer's tavern staff. As usual, she emerged from her own cubby of a blocked-up stair that once led to the second floor (which, unlike Skif's, had a flap of patched canvas for a door) followed by Kalchan. As usual, she said nothing, only scuttled into the kitchen for the customer's beer and bread, her face set in a perpetual mask of fear. Kalchan hitched at his trews and grinned, showing yellowed teeth, and followed her into the kitchen.

Skif shuddered. As awful as his position was here, Maisie's was worse.

This was a tavern, not an inn, and the kitchen and common room were all there was of the place. The tenement rooms upstairs, although they belonged to Uncle Londer, were not available for overnight guests, but were rented by the month. There was a separate entrance to the rooms, via a rickety staircase in the courtyard. This limited the tenants' access to the inn and the fuel and food kept there. Uncle fully expected his tenants to pilfer anything they could lay their hands on, and they responded to his trust by doing so at every possible opportunity. Not that there were many opportunities; Kalchan saw to that.

Now Skif was free to leave at last for the lessons that every child was required by Valdemar law to have until he was able to read, write, and cipher. Not even Uncle Londer had been able to find a way to keep Skif from those lessons, much as he would have liked to.

Skif didn't wait around for permission from Kalchan to leave, or his cousin would find something else for him to do and make him late. If he was late, he'd miss breakfast, which would certainly please Kalchan's sadistic notion of what was amusing.

See ya—but not till dark, greaseball!

He shot out the door without a backward look, into the narrow street. This was not an area that throve in the morning; those who had jobs were usually at them by dawn, and those who didn't were generally out looking for something to put some money in their pockets at least that early, or were sleeping off the results of drinking the vile brews served in the Hollybush or other end-of-the-alley taverns. The Hollybush was, in fact, located at the end of the alley, giving Uncle Londer the benefit of giving custom no chance to stumble past his door.

There were other children running off up the alley to lessons as well, though not all to the same place as Skif. He had to go farther than they, constrained by his uncle's orders. If Skif was going to have to have lessons, his uncle was determined, at least, that he would take them where Uncle Londer chose and nowhere else.

Every child in this neighborhood was running eagerly to their various teachers for the same reason that Skif did; free and edible breakfast. This was an innovation of Queen Selenay's, who had decided, based on her own observation, that a hungry child doesn't learn as well as one with food in his belly. So every child in Haven taking lessons who arrived on time was supplied with a bacon roll and a mug of tea in winter, or a buttered roll and a piece of fruit in summer. Both came from royal distribution wagons that delivered the supplies every morning, so there was no use in trying to cheat the children by scrimping. But if a child was late, he was quite likely to discover that his attendance had been given up for the day and someone else had eaten his breakfast, so there was ample incentive to show up on time, if not early, for those lessons, however difficult or boring a child might find them.

Skif had no intention of missing out on his share. His stomach growled as he ran, and he licked his lips in anticipation.

Unless luck went his way, this might be the only really edible food he'd get for the rest of the day—and there was no doubt in his mind that the rest of the children in his group were in the same straits.

The narrow, twisting streets he followed were scarcely wide enough for a donkey cart. The tenement houses, three stories tall including the attics, leaned toward the street as if about to fall into it. There was not enough traffic to have worn away the packed, dirty snow heaped up against the walls of the houses on either side, and no incentive for the inhabitants to scrape it away, so there it would remain, accumulating over the course of the winter until it finally thawed and soaked into the dirt of the street, turning it to mud.

But that would not be for several moons yet. There was all of the winter to get through first. At least the cold kept down the smell—from backyard privies, chicken coops, pigeon houses, pig sties. The poor tried to eke out their meager foodstuffs any way they could. Pigeons were by far the most popular, since they could fly away by day to more prosperous parts of town and feed themselves at someone else's expense. There were clouds of them on every available perch, sitting as close together as possible for warmth, and whitening the broken slates and shingles of the rooftops with their droppings. Of course, with all the snow up there, the droppings were invisible in winter.

Skif was finally warm now, his breath puffing out whitely as he ran. He had no coat, of course, but no child in his neighborhood had a coat. There were three ways to get warm in the winter—work until you were warm, do something that kept you near enough to the fire that you weren't freezing, or—be as creative about finding warmth as Skif was.

After six turnings, he was in a slightly more respectable neighborhood. The streets were marginally wider, a halfhearted attempt to remove the snow had been made, and there were a few dark little shops on the first floors of the tenement houses. More chimneys sported thin streams of smoke, and at the end of this final street, just before it joined one of the main thoroughfares, was the Temple of Belden. It wasn't a large temple as such things went; it had only four priests and a half-dozen novices. But the Order of Belden was a charitable Order, which was just as well, since there wasn't much scope for anything but charity down here.

As such, one of the charitable acts performed here was to educate the poor children of the area. But Skif wasn't here because he had chosen the place, or even because Uncle Londer had picked it from a number of options. He was here because his second cousin, the middle son of his uncle's brood of three, was a novice here.

Cousin Beel had as little choice about his vocation as Skif did; Uncle Londer wished to impress his social superiors with his sense of charity, and so Beel became a novice. Beel seemed to like the life, though— or, he liked it as much as this curiously colorless young man could like anything. Beel was as forgettable as Kalchan was remarkable.

Skif pushed open a little side door in the chapter house next to the Temple. The door opened directly into a public room with several tables and benches in it; there were thirty or forty other children that took lessons there, and about half of them were already sitting on the benches, waiting for their meal. Skif slid in beside one of the smaller girls, a tiny big-eyed thing called Dolly. She smiled up at him in welcome; he was her protector and kept her from being harassed by any of the more aggressive children who would try to bully her outside of classes for anything that they thought they could get from her.

He took her cold little hands in his and held them until they warmed while they waited for the last of the children to straggle in. Skif heard her stomach growl while they waited; his answered hers, and she gave a little giggle.

Finally, a small bell rang somewhere in the Temple marking the end of the First Service, and a door at the back of the room opened. Beel and one other novice entered, carrying baskets. The delicious aroma of bacon wafted gently to where Skif sat, trying not to fidget; every eye in the room was riveted on those baskets as Beel and the other novice left and returned with steaming pots of tea and thick clay mugs.

Cor! Can they move any slower?

It seemed an eternity before the last of the paraphernalia of breakfast finally was brought in and arranged to Beel's liking. Only then were the children permitted to come up to him, one at a time, and receive their rolls and mugs. By then, of course, the rolls were stone cold and the tea at best lukewarm.

It didn't matter. So long as the rolls weren't frozen hard as stones, so long as the tea wasn't a block of ice, there wasn't a child here that wouldn't devour every crumb and drink down every drop. Some of them began eating and drinking while they walked back to their places, but not Skif, and not Dolly either, for she followed his example. It wasn't for the sake of manners; Skif didn't have any, no more than any of the others. It was because he had figured out that if he ate over the table, he could catch every crumb, and he did. When they were done, he and Dolly licked their fingers and picked up the tiniest fragments from the wood.

Lukewarm as the tea was, it was still warmer than the room. The mug served double duty as a hand warmer until the tea was gone. They weren't allowed to linger over it, though, not with two novices standing over them.

Then Beel's fellow novice collected the empty mugs and vanished, leaving Beel to his teaching duties.

Skif should, in fact, not be here at all. He read and wrote as well as any of the children at these tables, and the law said only that children had to be able to read, write and figure to a certain level before their compulsory education was complete, not at what age a child could be released. Skif enjoyed reading and even took a certain aesthetic pleasure in writing; it would have been hard for him to feign being bad at either. Beel probably would have quickly caught on before long and sent him back to the tavern where he'd quickly be slaving for Kalchan—and doing without his breakfast. But figuring had never come easy to him, and it was boring besides. He still couldn't add two numbers of two figures each and come up with the same answer twice in a row, and in all likelihood neither answer would be the right one. Needless to say, although he pretended that he was trying, his progress was glacial. He had to make *some* progress, of course, or even Beel would suspect something, but he was going to put off the evil day when Beel would pronounce his education complete for as long as he could.

In the meantime, since he was so good at reading and writing, during those lessons Beel saw no reason why he should not take some of the workload off of his own shoulders, and Skif was put to tutoring the youngest children, including Dolly. He didn't mind; he was big enough to be able to bully those who weren't at all interested in learning things, and Beel had no objection to his delivering admonitory cuffs to the ear if it became necessary to keep discipline. That was the main thing that was hard about being the tutor; littles like Dolly who wanted to learn just needed some help over the rough spots.

It was turn and turn about then, and time for one of the other boys to tutor Skif—along with children three years his junior—in figures. For Skif, this was the worst part of the day, and not because he himself was a discipline problem; being anywhere other than the tavern was an improvement and he wasn't eager to get himself kicked out.

It was horribly cold in this room—there was a fire, but it didn't get things much above freezing and by now they were all suffering from icy hands and feet. He was bored. And breakfast had long since worn thin. Only in summer was this part of the day bearable, for as cold as the temple buildings were in winter, they made up for it by being pleasant in summer, and smelled of ancient incense rather than the reek of privies, of garbage, and of the muck of all of the animals hidden away in back courts.

There!

The heads of every child in the room, Skif's included, came up as the bell summoning the faithful to Midday Service rang from the top of the Temple. If they'd been a pack of dogs, their ears and tails would have quivered. Novice Beel sighed.

"All—" he began, and the children literally leaped from their seats and stampeded for the door before he could finish. "—right—" Skif heard faintly behind him as he scooped up Dolly and shoved his way with the rest through the open door with her held protectively in front of him.

Once outside, he broke away from the mob of children, bringing Dolly with him. The rest streamed in every direction, and Skif hadn't a clue what made them all so anxious to get where they were heading to do so at a run. Maybe it was the prospect of finding a little warmth somewhere. Without a word, he wrapped his arm around Dolly's thin shoulders and turned her in the direction of her home. Since a few days after her first appearance in the schoolroom, when he'd caught some of the older children teasing and tormenting her, he'd played her guardian. Her father brought her in the morning on the way to his work at the docks, but Skif was her escort home, where she would join the rest of the children in her family and her mother at their laundry. In winter, despite having to struggle with soaking, heavy fabric and harsh soap that irritated and chapped the skin, a laundry wasn't a bad place to work, since you could always warm up in the room where the washing coppers were kept hot over their fires. Dolly never lingered once they arrived; she only cast Skif a shy smile of thanks and scampered inside the building, where a cloud of steam poured out into the street from the momentarily open door.

His self-appointed duty complete, Skif was now free for as long as he could keep out of the way of his relatives.

Kalchan would work him until he dropped, not serving customers, since that was Maisie's job, but doing everything else but cooking—and "everything else" included some things that made Skif feel sick just to think about. On the other hand, out of sight was definitely out of mind with Kalchan, and so long as Skif didn't claim meals, his eldest cousin probably thought he was in lessons during the daylight hours. Fortunately Beel had suffered enough under his older brother's fist as a child that he didn't go out of his way to enlighten Kalchan as to Skif's whereabouts out of school.

That did leave him some options. Sometimes he could find someone with errands to run; sometimes he could shovel snow or sweep crossings for a pennybit. There was refuse to haul off for the rag-and-bone men if they came up short a man. But none of that was to be counted on as a source of food or money to buy it, and Skif had finally hit on something that was.

It took him far out of his own neighborhood, and into places where his ragged, coatless state was very conspicuous. That was the drawback; before he reached his goal, he might be turned back a dozen times by suspicious folk who didn't like the look of him in their clean and prosperous streets.

Eventually he left the tenements and crooked, foul streets and penetrated into places where the streets were clean and kept clean by people whose only job was to sweep them. The transition was amazing to him, and even more amazing was that there were single families that lived in buildings that would serve to house a dozen or more families in *this* area. He didn't even try to venture onto those streets; there were all sorts of people there whose only job was to keep people like *him* out.

Now he went to the alleys, slinking from bit of cover to bit of cover. There was plenty of cover here; permanent rubbish bins where ashes, broken crockery, bits of wood, scraps from food preparation too small or too spoiled for anyone from these houses to consider useful were left for the rubbish collectors. This was where the wood—and possibly some of the foodstuffs—bought by Uncle Londer came from. Skif knew better than to rummage in those bins; they "belonged" to the rubbish collectors who guarded their territories jealously, with curses, kicks, and blows. But the rubbish collectors didn't care who they saw in their alleys so long as he left the bins alone, and they ignored Skif as if he was invisible. Sometimes there were other things left back here as well, usually weeds, bags of dead plants and leaves, sticks and trimmings from gardens. It all made places for a small boy like Skif to hide. These alleys were faced by blank walls that rose well above Skif's head, but not all of those walls were as impervious as they seemed.

He had skipped over three or four social strata now; he'd known better than to look for a mark among people like Dolly's parents or the small merchants. Such folk feared to lose what they'd built up and were as penurious in their way as his uncle; they didn't share what they had, and when they caught someone trying to get a bit for himself, punished him with fury. No, when Skif decided that he was going to help himself to the bounty of others, he knew he'd need to find someone who had so much that he couldn't keep track of it all, and so many servants that it wasn't possible even for them to do so.

The drawback was that in such a rich household, there were privileges that were jealously guarded, and as he knew very well, even those things that the owner thought were refuse had value. The cook and her staff all had the rights to such things as fat skimmed from the cooking, the burned or otherwise "spoiled" bits, and "broken meats"—which last were cooked leftover items that had been cut into or served from without actually having been on someone's plate. Depending on the household, unless such items were designated to go to the poor, the cook and helpers could sell such items from the back door, or give them to relatives who were less well-provided-for, or a combination of all of these things. "Scrapings"—the leftovers scraped from plates into a slop bucket by the dishwashers—belonged to the dishwashers in some households, or were fed to household animals in others, and again could be sold or carried off, if not fed to animals. Stale bread and cake were the provenance of the pastry cook, sometimes a different entity from the head cook, who had the same options.

All these leftover items were jealously guarded from the time they became leftovers. But from the time they left the hands of the cooks until the moment that they were brought back to the kitchen, no one was paying any great amount of attention to the quantities on platters in a so-called "great" household.

And that was where Skif had found his little opportunity to exploit the situation.

He noted the first breach in the defenses by the cloud of sweet-scented steam rising over the wall; this was a huge household that had its own laundry. Making sure that he wouldn't be spotted, he kicked off his boots and hid them inside the wall, squeezing them in through a place where he'd found a loose brick. It had occurred to him more than once that he was probably using someone *else's* hiding place—bricks in well-tended walls like this one didn't just "come loose" by accident. He wouldn't be the least surprised to learn that someone (or several someones) in this great house had once used the place to store small articles purloined in the course of duties, to be retrieved and carried off later.

Now barefooted, he climbed nimbly over the top and into the open laundry yard, full of vats of hot water, bleaches, and soap in which household linens soaked before being pounded by a dozen laundresses, rinsed, and hung up to dry. Between the vats, sheets and towels were strung on lines crisscrossing the yard. The bleaches were so harsh that these vats were kept in the open, and away from the rest of the laundry where the clothing was cleaned, for a careless splash could ruin a colored tunic forever. The steam and the hanging linens gave him cover to get into the room where the livery for the pages was stored once it had been laundered, and on his way through, he grabbed a wet towel out of one of the vats to take with him. The pages—there were at least twenty of them—went through a dozen sets of livery apiece in a week, for the servant who had charge over them insisted on absolute cleanliness.

This room—which they called a "closet," although it was as big as the Hollybush's common room—held only shelves that were stacked with tabards, tunics, and trews for every possible size of boy. They didn't wear boots or shoes, perhaps because they were so young that they would probably outgrow boots or shoes too quickly; instead, they wore colored stockings with leather bottoms, which could fit a wide variety of feet. Hence, Skif's current barefoot status.

The rest of the livery was designed to be oversized on practically any child, so Skif would have no difficulty in fitting into whatever was clean. Within moments, his own clothing was hidden under piles of discarded but clean tabards too worn to be used for anything but really dirty jobs, but too good to be relegated to duty as rags. A quick wipe all over himself with the damp towel—a dirty boy would stand out dreadfully among the clean pages—and a quick change of clothing, and Skif was now a page.

Just in time for luncheon.

Now properly outfitted, and hence invisible to the rest of the staff, he dropped the filthy towel in a pile of others waiting to be cleaned, trotted out of the laundry just as if he was on an errand. He crossed a paved court to the kitchens, slipped inside the door, and joined the line of pages bringing common food into the lord's Great Hall. He made certain to take a platter heavily laden with a pile of what looked like boiled baby cabbages no bigger than his thumb; by the time it got to the table, two of them were in his pockets.

This Lord Orthallen must be a very important person. Every day he entertained a horde of people at his table, perhaps fifty or sixty of them, besides the dozen or so of his own immediate family. That was just *guests;* there was a small army of his own servants and retainers at still lower tables, but they had to serve themselves from great bowls and platters brought from the kitchen by one of their own number.

Skif and the other pages served only the guests, who got foods that were designed to be eaten with one's own knife and hands. After the tiny cabbages, he purloined a dainty little coin-sized meat pie, a soft roll of white bread, a cube of cheese, more cheese wrapped in pastry, a small boiled turnip, and an apple. That was all his pockets would hold. He made certain that he was in the procession of pages that got the platters going to those who sat below the lord's salt—he didn't have the manners to serve at the head table and he knew that he'd be recognized for an interloper. Those who sat lower were too busy eating, gossiping, and watching their betters to pay attention to the pages.

Once his pockets were full, Skif made certain to "accidentally" get some grease on the front of his tabard—an accident that occurred to at least three of the pages at every meal, since many of them were young and they were all rushing to and fro. As he expected, he was sent to the laundry to change.

Once there, he swiftly changed back into his own clothing, left the soiled uniform with others like it, and went back up—but not over the walls and into the alleys.

After all, why should he? He had nothing particular to do out there. His friends were all too busy working or on schemes of their own to get themselves fed to have any time for play—playing was what the fortunate children of the rich did. For the moment, he wanted a warm place to rest and eat, and there was one right here at hand.

There was an attic over the laundry, a loft area that was barely tall enough to allow him to walk hunched over, where old tubs and some of the laundry stores were kept. It got more than enough heat from the laundry below to be comfortably cozy and more than enough steam to keep down the dust. Here, Skif curled up inside an overturned wooden tub for extra concealment and dug into his purloined food.

He could, of course, have eaten three times what he'd stolen—but it was twice what he'd get at the tavern, and not only entirely edible, but tasty to boot.

With his stomach relatively full, he curled up in the tub for a nap. Here, and not in his cubby at the Hollybush, was where he could sleep in comfort and security. And he did.

2

No matter how comfortable he was, Skif slept like a cat, with one eye open and one ear cocked, in case trouble stole upon him, thinking to catch him unaware. So even though he didn't know *what* woke him, when he woke, he came alert all at once, and instead of jumping to his feet, he stayed frozen in place, listening.

Wood creaked slightly, somewhere in the loft. Was it a footstep? The sound came again, a trifle nearer, then fabric brushed against something harder. There was someone up here with him.

Now, it wouldn't be one of the laundry servants on proper business; they came up the stair, clumping and talking loudly. It *might* be a servant or a page come up here to nap or escape work—if it was, although Skif would have a slight advantage in that the other wouldn't want to be caught, he had a profound disadvantage in that he didn't belong here himself, and the other could legitimately claim to have heard something overhead and gone to investigate. If that was the case, he'd be stuck under this tub until the other person left.

It might also be something and someone entirely different—a thief, who wouldn't want to be found any more than Skif did, who might flee, or might fight, depending on the circumstances, if Skif came out of hiding.

He didn't know enough yet; better to wait. It was highly unlikely that the other would choose Skif's particular tub to hide himself or anything else underneath. It was out of the way and smallish, and Skif had chosen it for precisely those reasons. Instead, he peered under the edge of it, as the surreptitious sounds moved closer, thanking his luck that it wasn't dusty up here. Now would be a bad time to sneeze.

It sounded, given the direction the sounds were coming from, as if the unknown had gotten into the loft the same way that Skif had, through the gable window at the end. Skif narrowed his eyes, waiting for something to come into his area of vision among the slats of the wooden tubs. The light was surprisingly good up here, but the sun was all wrong for Skif to see a shadow that might give him some notion of who the other intruder was. The creaking gave Skif a good idea that the fellow moved toward the stairs, which meant he was at least *thinking* of using them to descend into the laundry itself. That wasn't an option Skif would have chosen—unless, of course, the fellow was a thief, and was planning on purloining something from the laundry itself. There was plenty of stuff to steal in there; silk handkerchiefs and scarves, the embroidered ribbons that the young ladies of the household liked to use for their necks and hair and the young men liked to give them, the gossamer veils they wore in public—all light, easy to carry, presumably easy to sell. The only reason Skif hadn't helped himself before this was that he didn't know where to dispose of such things and was not about to share his loot with Kalchan.

A foot slid slowly into view; not a big foot, and most importantly of all, not a foot clad in the soled sock of a page or liveried indoor servant. This was a foot in a half-boot of very flexible black leather, laced tight to the ankle and calf, much worn and patched, not much larger than his own, attached to a leg in rusty black trews with worn places along the hem. This foot, and the person who wore those trews, did not belong here. No one in Lord Orthallen's service wore anything of the sort.

Skif made a quick decision, and struck. Before the other knew he was there, Skif's hand darted from under the tub, and Skif had the fellow's ankle held fast in a hand that was a lot stronger than it looked.

Skif had half expected a struggle, or at least an attempt to get free, but the owner of the ankle had more sense than that—or was more afraid of the attention that the sounds of a struggle would bring than anything Skif could do to him. So now, it was the other's turn to freeze.

Skif mentally applauded his decision. He thought he had a good idea of what was going through the other fellow's mind. Now, the arm that Skif had snaked out from beneath the tub was clad in a sleeve that was more patch than whole cloth. So Skif obviously didn't belong here either, and the two of them were at an equal advantage and disadvantage. For either to make noise or fuss would mean that both would be caught—and no point in trying to claim that one had seen the other sneak over the wall and followed to catch him either. An honest boy would have pounded on the back entrance to report the intruder, not climbed up after him. No, no—if one betrayed the other, both of them would be thrown to the City Guard.

So the other fellow did the prudent thing; he stayed in place once Skif let go of him so that Skif could slip out from under the tub. Like it or not, for the moment they were partners in crime. Skif, however, had a plan.

There was a moment when the other *could* have tried to knock Skif out and make a run for it, but he didn't. Such an action would have been noisy, of course, and he still might have been caught, but with one unconscious or semiconscious boy on the floor to distract those who would come clambering up here, he might have been able to get away. Skif breathed a sigh of relief when he was all the way out from under the tub and was able to kneel next to it, looking up at the interloper.

What he saw was a boy of about fifteen, but small for his age, so that he wasn't a great deal taller than Skif. His thin face, as closed and impassive as any statue's, gave away no hint of what he was thinking. His eyes narrowed when he got a good look at his captor, but there was no telling what emotion lay behind the eyes.

His clothing was better than Skif's—but then again, whose wasn't? Skif wore every shirt he owned—three, all ragged, all inexpertly patched by his own hands, all faded into an indeterminate brown—with a knitted tunic that was more hole than knit over the top of it all. His linen trews, patched as well, were under his woolen trews, which for a change had been darned except for the seat which sported a huge patch made from an old canvas tent. This boy's clothing was at least all the same color and the patches were of the same sort of material as the original. In fact, unless you were as close as Skif was, you wouldn't notice the patches much.

He had long hair of a middling brown color, and a headband of dark braided string to keep it out of his eyes. His eyes matched his hair, and if he'd been fed as well as one of the page boys his face would have been round; as it was, the bones showed clearly, though not nearly as sharply defined as Skif's.

There were other signs of relative prosperity; the other boy's wrists weren't as thin as Skif's, and he showed no signs of the many illnesses that the poor were prone to in the winter. If he was a thief—and there was little doubt in Skif's mind that he was—this boy was a good enough thief to be doing well.

The two of them stared at each other for several moments. It was the older boy who finally broke the silence.

"Wot ye want?" he asked, in a harsh whisper.

Until that moment when he'd seized the other's ankle, Skif hadn't known what he wanted, but the moment his hand had touched leather, his plan had sprung up in his mind.

"Teach me," he whispered, and saw with satisfaction the boy's eyes widen with surprise, then his slow nod.

He squatted down beside Skif, who beckoned to him to follow. On hands and knees, Skif led him into the maze of tubs and empty packing crates until they were hidden from view against the wall, next to the chimney.

There they settled, screened by stacks of buckets needing repair. From below came the steady sounds of the laundry, which should cover any conversation of theirs.

"Ye ain't no page, an' ye ain't got no reason t'be in the wash house. Wot ye doin' here?" the boy asked, more curious than annoyed.

Skif shrugged. "Same as you, only not so good," he replied. He explained his ruse to get fed to the boy, whose lips twitched into a thin smile.

"Not bad done, fer a little," he acknowledged. "Noboddie never pays mind t'littles. Ye cud do better, though. Real work, not this pilferin' bits uv grub. I kin get through places a mun can't, an ye kin get where I can't. We might cud work t'gether."

"That's why I want ye t'teach me," Skif whispered back. "Can't keep runnin' this ferever. Won' look like no page much longer."

The boy snorted. "Won't need to. Here, shake on't." He held out his hand, a thin, hard, and strong hand, and Skif took it, cementing their bargain with a shake. "M'name's Deek," the boy said, releasing his hand.

Skif was happy to note that Deek hadn't tried to crush his hand in his grip or otherwise show signs of being a bully. "Call me Skif," he offered.

Deek grinned. "Good. Now, you stay here—I come back in a tick, an' we'll scoot out by th' back t'gether." He cocked his head down at the floor, and it was pretty clear that there wasn't anyone working down in the laundry anymore. It was probably time for supper; the laundresses and some of the other servants ate long before their betters, and went to bed soon after sundown, for their work started before sunrise.

Skif nodded; he saw no reason to doubt that Deek would play him false, since he was sitting on the only good route of escape. He and Deek made their way back to Skif's tub; Skif ducked back inside, and Deek crept down the stairs into the laundry.

Deek came back up quickly, and the quick peek of silk from the now slightly-bulging breast of his tunic told Skif all he needed to know. As he had expected, Deek had managed to slip downstairs, purloin small items of valuable silk, and get back up without anyone catching sight of him.

As long as he took small things, items unlikely to be missed for a while, that weren't such rare dainties as to be too recognizable, it was quite likely that the owners themselves would assume they'd been mislaid. No specially embroidered handkerchiefs, for example, or unusual colors of veils. He beckoned to Skif, who followed him out over the roof, both of them lying as flat as stalking cats as they wiggled their way along the tiles, to minimize the chance of someone spotting them from below. From this position, they couldn't see much; just the lines of drying linens in the yard, the tops of bushes past the linens that marked the gardens, and the bulk of the magnificent mansion beyond. If anyone looked out of the windows of the mansion, they *would* be spotted.

Not likely though.

The pipe-clay tiles were infernally cold after the warm wash-house attic, and Skif clenched his teeth together to keep them from chattering. As he slid belly-down along them, they kept finding tears and rents to protrude through, right against his bare skin. The edges of the tiles caught on his rags, too; he had to move carefully, and make sure that nothing had snagged as he moved, to keep from dislodging one of them and sending it down with a betraying clatter. It seemed to be getting a little darker, although the sky was so overcast that Skif couldn't tell where the sun was. That was good; the closer it was to dusk, the less likely anyone would see them.

Already his bare feet ached with cold. The most risky part of this procedure was the moment that they got down from the roof onto the top of the wall. The roof actually overhung the wall, so that they had to dangle over the alley and feel with their toes for their support. And of course, this put them in clear view of anyone in the alley.

But as Skif already knew, it was too early for scrap collectors and too late for the rag-and-bone men, too late for tradesmen and too early for those delivering special items that Lord Orthallen's cooks did not have the expertise to prepare in time for an evening's feast. There was no one in the alley.

Deek went first; Skif followed. He slipped his legs over the edge of the roof and lowered himself down, hanging on grimly to the lead gutters, groping after the rough stone of the wall somewhere underneath the overhang with his benumbed toes.

When he finally got his feet on it and set them solidly, he eased himself down and under the overhang, his arms hurting with the strain. Deek crouched there, waiting for him with great patience, and he paused for just a moment to shake some feeling back into his fingers.

From the wall, they climbed down to the alleyway; Skif noted with concealed glee that Deek came down the same route that he himself used. "Wait a mo—" he said, as Deek made to move off, and retrieved his boots from the hidden nook.

Deek's mouth dropped open. "Cor! That be right handy, that do!" he whispered in amazement.

Skif just grinned, and shoved his boots on quickly. They still couldn't afford to be caught here; someone might search them. Deek wasted no more time, but led Skif off in the opposite direction from which Skif had come. He didn't go that way for long, however; just far enough to get back into a more modest area. Then he cut back in the direction that Skif had expected. He didn't slow down, not for a moment, and Skif had to stretch his legs to keep up with him. For all that, he didn't look like a boy who was somewhere he shouldn't be; he strode with his head up, paying close attention to anything that stood out like a landmark, quite as if he had an errand he'd been sent on. Skif tried to emulate him.

As they worked their way back toward the south and east, Deek started to talk, quietly enough so that it wasn't likely they'd be overheard. "'Sjest me an' a couple boys, an' Bazie," Deek said. "Bazie, he's the clever cuz what tells us how t'nobble. Cain't do it hisself; ain't got no legs. But 'e kin show us, an' he innerduces us t'the fence, so we gotta place t'sell the swag."

"He gonna have a prollem with me?" Skif wanted to know.

Deek shook his head. "Nah," he said decisively. "We bin one short since Larap tookt off on 'is own. No flop an' no feed, though," he added, casting a look aside at Skif. "Not lessen' ye bin wi' th'gang a sixmun."

"Gotta flop," Skif replied shortly. "An' I kin feed m'self. I kin wait."

But secretly, he was astonished at his good luck. That he even had a *chance* for a new place to sleep and meals—if he could just get out of Uncle Londer's clutches. Anything would be better than the Hollybush!

Deek laughed, and slapped Skif on the back, as they turned a corner and entered a working-class neighborhood where they could leave the alleys and take to the streets. This wasn't one anywhere near the Hollybush, and Skif wondered just how far they were from the tavern.

Far, I hope, he thought. *Don' want Kalchan catehin' wind uv this.*

Each turning that Deek made took them deeper into the kind of areas that Skif called home, though nothing looked familiar. The streets grew narrower, the buildings shabbier and in worse repair. Another corner turned, and they came unexpectedly into a little square, where there was a market going at full shout, with barrows and stalls everywhere. Deek ignored the noise, the hagglers, the confusion of people and barrows; he pushed in between a rag-and-bone man selling bundles of half-burned wood, and a barrow full of broken and cracked pottery, leading Skif into a narrow passage between two buildings not much bigger than his own slim shoulders.

Then, with an abrupt turn in the half dark, he darted into an opening in one wall and up a staircase. Skif followed, taking care where he put his feet, for there was plenty of debris on the rickety wooden stairs, some of it slippery. The stairs were steep, and switched back and forth, with landings on each floor that led to two or three closed doors.

At the top, however, there was only a single door, which Deek opened without knocking. Skif followed him inside, only to be confronted by a long hallway with more doors, lit from above by a single skylight with some translucent stuff in it that let in enough light to make out the doorways. Deek went straight to the end of the hall, much to Skif's bafflement. There was nothing there but the blank wall, an expanse of water-stained plaster with a couple of old, rusted hooks on it.

Deek paused at the end, and grinned back over his shoulder at Skif. "Figger it out, yet?" he taunted, then pulled on a hook.

A door separated itself from the cracked plaster, the lines of the door previously completely hidden in the cracks.

Deek motioned to Skif to go inside, and closed the door behind him. Now they went down a stair, more of a ladder than a staircase, one somehow sandwiched between the walls of buildings on all four sides; and in a moment, Skif realized that this must be an air shaft, and at some point someone had jury-rigged a stair inside it. There were windows looking into the shaft, but most of them had shutters over them to keep out the cold air. They climbed down and down until they passed through the bottom of the shaft, and Skif knew that they were below street level. If he hadn't already guessed that, the sudden increase in dampness would have given it away.

There was a door at the bottom of the stair; Deek knocked on this one in a definite pattern that Skif didn't quite catch. The door swung open, and Deek grabbed his arm and pulled him inside.

Another boy, this one older than Deek, with hair of a mousy blonde color, closed the door behind them. Skif stood at Deek's side, and took it all in without saying a word.

It was warm down here, warm and humid. The source of the warmth was a—

—copper wash boiler. Which was also the source of the moisture. It sat in a brickwork oven in the far corner of the stone-walled room, a chimney running up the corner behind it, with a fine fire burning beneath it, and presumably, laundry soaking in it. Hanging just below the ceiling were strings of drying wash.

Silk objects hung there, expensive silk, mostly scarves and handkerchiefs, a few veils, some lady's stockings and finely-knit silk gloves—and a few perfectly ordinary shirts and tunics and trews, stockings, all darned and patched.

Well, hey, if they're washin' the swag, they might's well wash their own stuff, I guess.

The fire beneath the cauldron, despite the name of "wash boiler" was not hot enough to boil the water, only to keep it warm. Next to the cauldron was a remarkable figure, seated on a stack of flat cushions, busily darning the heel of a silk stocking with fingers as fine and flexible as a woman's. He was bald, shiny-pated in fact, with enormous shoulders and chest muscles beneath a shabby tunic. The legs of his equally patched trews were folded under at the knee, as Deek had implied. He didn't look up from his work.

There were two more boys in the room, one stirring the laundry with a stick, the other cracking and peeling hard-boiled eggs at an old table with one broken leg propped up and crudely nailed to an old keg. Skif tried not to look at the eggs; his pilfered lunch had long since worn thin. Besides the table and the stool the boy sat on, of furnishings there were none. There were boxes in various states of repair, old kegs, half-barrels, and a wide variety of cushions, quilts, and other linens. Anything that was made of fabric, unlike the rest of the contents of the room, was neatly patched and darned and in good repair—and clean, very clean. There was plenty of light here, from a motley assortment of lamps and candles. And there was definitely one thing missing—the usual smell of poverty, compounded of dirt, mildew, grease, mouse, and sweat.

The man finished his darning and, with a gusty sigh, tossed the stocking in with the rest of the laundry in the wash boiler. Only then did he look up. His eyes, a startling black, seemed to bore right into Skif's brain.

"Where ye get this'un?" he asked Deek, turning his gaze on Skif's companion.

If Deek had possessed such a thing as a cap, he'd probably have snatched it off and held it diffidently in front of him in both hands. As it was, he ducked his head. "'E caught me, Bazie," Deek told the man. "'E wuz in th' wash-house loft, an' 'e caught me cummin' in." Then, having gotten the difficult bit over with—admitting that he'd been caught by a mere child—he continued with more enthusiasm, describing Skif's own "lay" and his wish to be taught. The other two boys pretended not to listen, but Skif caught them watching him surreptitiously.

"Figgered 'e cud take Larap's place, mebbe, if'n 'e makes it past sixmun," Deek concluded, looking hopefully at his mentor.

Now Bazie transferred his unwavering gaze to Skif. "Ye livin' rough?" he asked, and Skif knew that he'd better tell the truth.

"At Hollybush," he replied shortly. "Kalchan's m'cuz, Londer's m'nuncle."

Evidently Bazie knew the Hollybush, since he didn't ask where or what it was. His gaze became even more piercing. "Bonded?"

With relief Skif shook his head. "Nuh-*uh!*" he denied vigorously. "Ma didn' bond me 'fore she croaked. Londer's pretty het 'bout it, but ain't nothin' 'e kin do now. An' 'e niver cud put me out, 'cuz 'e took me in, on th' rolls an all, reckonin' t' get me bonded."

A bonded child was just short of property; required to serve in whatever capacity his "guardian" chose until he was sixteen, for the privilege of being sheltered and fed. Skif's mother had neglected (perhaps on purpose) to bond her toddler to her brother when her man left her and she fell ill—she worsened and died before Londer could get the bond signed and sworn to. It was too late now; no notary would swear to a faked bond. Well—no notary would swear to a faked bond for the pittance of a bribe that was all that Londer would offer.

By the point when Skif's mother died, Londer was already on record with the same Temple Beel served at as the responsible party for his sister and nephew (hoping to get Skif's bond). As such, he was technically required by law to care for Skif until the age of twelve without any benefit. At twelve, which was no more than a couple of years away, he *could* turn Skif out, but he probably wouldn't. Skif was still supplying free labor at no real cost to him, and as long as that was going on, Londer would let sleeping dogs lie.

Now, the fact was that although Skif was under no obligation to serve at the Hollybush for his keep, the *only* thing he could coerce out of Kalchan and Londer was a place to sleep. The food they offered him— the leavings from customers' meals—a pig wouldn't touch. If he wanted to eat, he had to either find alternate ways of getting meals (as he had) or do even more work than he already was. And as long as he wanted to sleep at the Hollybush, which though wretched, was infinitely better and safer than trying to find a place on the street, he had to obey Kalchan's orders whenever he was around the tavern. There were a lot of things that could happen to a child on the street—"living rough"—and most of them were far worse than being beaten now and again by Kalchan, who had no taste for little boys or girls.

'Course, if 'e thunk 'e cud get away wit' it, 'e'd hev no prollem sellin' me. Kalchan would sell his own mother's services if he thought he wouldn't get caught. As it was, on the rare occasions when Skif got dragooned into "helping," he often had to endure the surreptitious caresses and whispered enticements of some of the customers who had wider ideas of pleasure than Kalchan did. As long as Kalchan didn't actually accept money in advance for the use of Skif's body, there was nothing that Skif could report to Temple or Guard.

And as long as Kalchan didn't take money in advance, the customers could only try to entice a boy; they wouldn't dare try to force him in public. The likelihood of one of them cornering Skif somewhere private was nonexistent. There wasn't a wall built he couldn't climb, and he knew every dirty-fighting trick there was for getting away from an adult.

After some time, during which Skif felt very uncomfortable, Bazie nodded. Now, at last, he showed a faint sign of satisfaction. "'E might cud do," he said to Deek. "Give 'im a try."

Deek grinned, and elbowed him.

"Wouldn' mind puttin one i' th'eye uv that bastid Londer," Bazie continued, a gleam in his own black eyes. "Yew work out in one moon, yer in."

Deek sucked in his breath; he had told Skif it would be *six* moons, not one, before he'd be accepted into the gang. Skif was amazed himself, and tried hard not to grin, but failed.

Bazie raised an eyebrow. "Don' get cocky," he cautioned. "'Tis as much t' put one i' the eye uv Londer."

Skif ducked his head. "Yessir," he said earnestly. "I unnerstan' sir." But he couldn't help feeling excited. "Ye'll be teachin' me, then?"

"Ye kin start now, at boiler," Bazie grunted, gesturing to the boy at the cauldron. "Ye take Lyle's stick."

Skif was not at all loath. For the second time today—the first had been when he was asleep in the washhouse loft—he was warm. Stirring a cauldron full of laundry was nowhere near as much work as toting rubbish for the rag-and-bone men.

Lyle was happy enough to give over the stick to Skif, who industriously stirred away at the simmering pot. Every so often, at Bazie's imperious gesture, he'd lift out a kerchief or some other piece of fabric on the stick. If Bazie approved, the second boy took it and hung it up to dry; if not, it went back in the pot.

Meanwhile Deek sorted his loot by color into baskets along the wall; Bazie, darning yet another silk stocking, noted Skif's incredulous stare as he did so, and snorted. "Ye think'm gonna ruin goods w' dye runnin'? Think agin! We gets twice fer th' wipes 'cause they's clean an' mended, boy—thas a fair piece fer damn liddle work wi' no risk!"

Well, put that way—

Skif kept stirring.

Lyle began taking down kerchiefs that were dry; Bazie continued to mend, and Deek picked through one of the baskets, looking for more things that needed fixing. The third boy finished peeling the hard-boiled eggs, and stood up.

"'M off, Bazie," he said. He was clearly the oldest, and Bazie looked up from his mending to level a measuring gaze at him.

"Ye mind, now," the man said, carefully. "Ye mind whut I said, Raf. Ye slip *one*, an' move on. No workin' a crowd on yer lone."

The boy Raf nodded impatiently with one hand on the doorknob. As soon as Bazie finished speaking, he was already out the door. Bazie shook his head.

"He don' lissen," the man said with gloom.

"Ah, he lissens," Deek assured their mentor. "'E's jest inna hurry. They's a street fair a-goin' by Weavers, an' 'e wants t' get to't afore they pockets is empty."

Bazie didn't seem convinced, but said nothing to Deek. "Lemme see yer hands," he said to Skif instead, but shook his head sadly over the stubby paws that Skif presented for his inspection. "Ye'll not suit th' liftin' much," he decreed. "Least, ye'll nivver be a master. Ye got t'hev long finners fer the liftin'. Kin ye climb?"

Deek answered for him. "Like a squirrel, I seen 'im," the boy chimed in cheerfully. "An' look at 'is nose an' feet—'e ain't gonna get big for a good bit yet, maybe not fer years."

Bazie examined him carefully from top to toes. "I thin' yer right," he said after a moment. "Aye. Reckon ye got a matey, Deek."

"That'll do," Deek replied, with a grin, and turned to Skif. "We'll be learnin' ye th' roof walkin', then, wi' me. In an' out—winders, mostly."

"An' ye live t' see summer, ye'll be doin' the night walks," Bazie said with a little more cheer. "Won't be wipes yer bringin' 'ome then, nossir."

Deek snorted, and Skif felt his heart pounding with excitement. "Not likely!" Deek said with scorn. "Wipes? More like glimmers!"

"Ye bring 'ome the glimmers, and we'll be findin' new digs, me lads," Bazie promised, his eyes gleaming with avid greed. "Aye that, 'tis us'll be eatin' beef an' beer when we like, an' from cookshop!"

Lyle, however, looked worried, though he said nothing. Skif wondered why. It was clear from the wealth of kerchiefs—"wipes"—and other things here that Bazie was a good teacher. Skif saw no reason why that expertise shouldn't extend to second-story work and the theft of jewelry.

He'd never actually seen any jewelry that wasn't fake, all foiled glass and tin, but he could imagine it. He could imagine being able to eat all he liked of the kinds of food he served to Lord Orthallen's guests, too, and possessing fine clothing that wasn't all patches and tears—

"'Nuff moon-calfin'," Bazie said sharply, recalling them all to the present. "Boy—Skif—be any more i' the pot?"

"Jes' this," Skif said, fishing out the last of the garments on the end of the stick. Bazie examined it, and grunted.

"That'll do," he decreed, and Lyle took it to hang it up. "Deek, next lot."

Deek brought over the next batch of wash, which was of mingled saffrons, tawnys and bright yellows, and dumped it in the cauldron. Lyle got up and took the stick from Skif without being prompted and began energetically thrusting the floating fabric under the water.

"Ye kin hev two eggs, boy, an' then Deek'll get ye 'thin sight uv Hollybush," Bazie declared. "Eat 'em on th' way."

"Yessir!" Skif said, overjoyed, mouth watering at the idea of having two whole boiled eggs for himself. He picked a pair out of the bowl, tucking them in a pocket, and followed Deek out the door and up the rickety staircase.

Once down on the street he and Deek strolled along together like a pair of old friends, Deek putting in a laconic comment now and again, while Skif nibbled at his eggs, making them last. He'd had boiled eggs before this—they were a regular item at Lord Orthallen's table—but not so often that he didn't savor every tiny bite. Once Deek darted over to a vendor's wagon and came back with a pair of buns, paying for them (somewhat to Skif's surprise) and handing one to his new "mate."

"Why didn' ye nobble 'em?" he asked in a whisper.

Deek frowned. "Ye don' mess yer nest," he admonished. "Tha's Bazie's first rule. Ye don' take nuthin' from neighbors. Tha' way, they don' know what we does, an' 'f hue-an'-cry goes up, they ain't gonna he'p wi' lookin' fer us."

Well, that made sense. It had never occurred to Skif that if your neighbors knew you were a thief, you'd be the first one they looked for if something went missing. He ate his bun thoughtfully, as Deek pointed out landmarks he could use to find his way back tomorrow.

"I got lessons," Skif pointed out reluctantly, and Deek laughed.

"No worries," the boy replied. "Bazie won' be 'wake 'till midday. Ye cum then. Look—ye know this street?"

Skif looked closer at the street they had just turned onto, and realized that he did—he had just never come at it from this direction before. "Aye," he told Deek, "Hollybush be down there—" and pointed.

"G'wan—" Deek gave him a little push. "See ye midday."

The other boy turned on his heel and trotted back through the gloom of dusk along the way they'd come, and in a moment Skif couldn't make him out anymore.

With a sigh and a bowed head, he trudged toward his uncle's tavern and the cold welcome that awaited him. But, at least, tonight he had something to look forward to on the morrow.

3

Kalchan never asked him where he'd been, so long as he came back before dark. He just welcomed Skif back with a cuff to the ear, and shoved him into the kitchen. By now, the kitchen was full of smoke, and the cook coughed and wheezed while she worked. It wasn't just the fault of the chimney, which certainly could have used a cleaning—the cook routinely burned the bottom crust of the bread, burned what was on the bottom of the pot, dripped grease on the hearth, which burned and smoked.

Skif didn't have to be told what to do, since his duties were exactly the same thing every day. Poor half-witted Maisie, on the other hand, had to be told carefully how to go about her business even though it was all chores she'd done every day for the last however-many years. That was why, if Skif wasn't back by dark and the time when the big influx of customers came, he'd get more than a cuff on the ear. If you gave Maisie one thing to do, then interrupted her with something else, she became hysterical and botched everything.

First, the water barrel had to be filled again—not because anyone had used much of it in cleaning, but because like everything else in the Hollybush, it was old, used, and barely functional. It had a slow leak, and it cost nothing to have Skif refill it. To have it mended would have meant paying someone.

So back and forth Skif went, doing his best not to slosh the icy water on himself, particularly not down his boots. When the barrel was full, the next chore was to take the bundle of twigs on a stick that passed for a broom and sweep the water and whatever else was on the floor out into the courtyard, where the water promptly froze (in winter) or turned into mud (in summer). Since Skif was the one who went into and out of the courtyard most often, it behooved him to at least sweep it all to one side if he could.

Next was to bring wood in from the woodpile in the courtyard and mend the fire in the common room, which was also full of smoke, but not as bad as the kitchen. Then he collected the wooden plates left on tables, carried them to the kitchen and thriftily scraped the leavings back into the stew pot over the fire. It didn't matter what went in there, since it all blended into the anonymous, lumpy brown muck, well flavored with burned crud from the bottom, that was already there. A quick wipe with a rag, and the plates were "clean" and ready for the next customer.

Mugs were next; he'd figured that it was better to take plates in stacked and not try to mix mugs and plates, for if he tried, he'd drop something and get beaten for breaking it. These were crude clay mugs with thick bottoms to make the customer think he was getting more beer than he was. Those didn't even get a wipe with the rag, unless they'd been left in a plate and had greasy gravy all over them; they were just upended and stacked beside the plates. There was no tableware to bother collecting; Londer wouldn't have anything that could be so readily stolen. In this, however, he was exactly like every other tavern keeper around this area. Customers ate with their own wooden spoons, usually hung on the belts beside their money pouches. Some ate with their personal belt knives, although these useful implements were used less often. The food in cheap taverns was generally soup or stew, and didn't need to be cut up—nor was there often anything in the bowl or on the plate large enough to be speared on the point of a knife. Those who had no spoon shoveled the food into their mouths with improvised implements of heavy black bread. Black bread was all that was ever served at the Hollybush; made of flour that was mostly made of rye, buckwheat, and wheat chaff, like everything else associated with Uncle Londer, it was the cheapest possible bread to make. The strong taste covered a multitude of culinary sins, and since it was already black, it had the advantage of not showing how badly it was burned on the bottom.

When mugs and plates were collected, it was time to add to the stew in the cauldron. The cook put Skif to work "chopping vegetables" while she cut the meat scraps. The stew kept going day and night over the fire had been depleted by lunch and early dinner, and now had to be replenished. Londer's picks at the market were like everything else; more of what better inns and kitchens threw out. With a knife that had been sharpened so many times that it was now a most peculiar shape and as flexible as a whip, Skif chopped the tops and tails of turnips, carrots, whiteroots, and beets and flung them into the cauldron, along with the leftover crusts of burned bread too hard to serve even *their* customers. The cook added her meat scraps, and began stirring, directing him to deal with the bread she had removed from the bake oven built into the side of the chimney. There were only three rather lumpy loaves, but they wouldn't need more than that. The bread was used mostly as an implement, and secondarily to soak up the liquid part of the stew so that every drop paid for could be eaten.

Skif sawed at the bread—better bread would not have held up under the treatment he gave Kalchan's loaves, but this stuff was as heavy and dense as bricks and just about as edible. Every slice was thriftily measured out to the minimum that the customers would stand by means of two grooves cut in the tabletop, and once cut, was "buttered" with a smear of fat and stacked up waiting to be slapped onto a plate. No one ever complained that it was stale; Skif was not certain it would be possible to tell a stale slice from one freshly cut off of *these* loaves.

When the bread was done, it was time to go get plates again; business was picking up.

Skif could not imagine what brought all these customers to the Hollybush, unless it was that Kalchan's prices were cheaper than anyone else's. It certainly wasn't the food, which would have poisoned a maggot, or the drink, which would have gagged a goat. And Maisie was no draw, either; plain as a post, with her dirty hair straggling down her back and over her face, she skulked among the tables like a scared, skinny little starling, delivering full plates and empty mugs while Kalchan followed in her wake, collecting pennybits and filling the mugs from his pitcher. Only Kalchan dispensed drink; the one time that Skif had dared to do so in Kalchan's momentary absence, his cousin had left stripes on his back with his leather belt. No one actually ordered anything—there wasn't anything to order by way of choice. You sat down at a table and got beer, bread, and stew—or beer alone, by waving off Maisie's proffered plate or sitting at the fireside bench with the steady drinkers. When customers were done, Skif came around and collected their plates and mugs. If one wanted more, he waited until Maisie came around again and took another laden plate from her; if not, he took himself off. This way Kalchan never had to worry about a customer complaining he hadn't been served when he'd paid, or about a customer sneaking off without paying. The only exceptions to this rule were the folk occupying the two benches in front of the fireplace. They got beer, period, and signified they wanted refills by holding up their mugs to Kalchan. When they were done, they left their mugs on the floor—which were usually claimed by another bench warmer before Skif could collect them.

Skif made his rounds in an atmosphere thick with smoke and the fug of unwashed bodies, grease, stale beer, and burned food. Light came from tallow dips held in clamps on the wall, and from the fire in the fireplace. It wasn't much, and all the smoke dimmed the light still further. He couldn't have made out the faces of the customers if he'd wanted to. They were just an endless parade of dark-shrouded lumps who crammed food into their mouths and went their way without ever saying anything to him if he was lucky. Every so often one would fondle Maisie's thigh or breast, but if Kalchan caught him at it, he would have to pay an additional pennybit for the privilege.

There wasn't any entertainment in the Hollybush. Kalchan didn't encourage self-entertainment either, like singing or gaming. Most of the customers didn't know each other, or didn't care to, so conversation was at a minimum. As for fighting—it was wisest not even to consider it. Kalchan discouraged fighting by breaking the heads of those who fought with the iron-headed club he carried at his side, and dumping the unconscious combatants outside. The drunks here were generally morose and quiet, and either stumbled out of the door on their own two feet when their money ran out, or passed out and were unceremoniously dumped in the street to free up space for another customer. Once in the street, an unconscious former customer had better hope that friends would take him home, or the cold would wake him up, because otherwise the thieves would strip him of everything of value and drop him in a gutter.

Difficult as it was to believe, customers kept coming in, all night long. The benches and tables were never empty until just before closing; Skif and Maisie never had a moment to rest. He'd tried once to reckon up how much money—in the tiniest of coins, the pennybit—Kalchan took in of a night. There were four pennybits to a penny; beer was two a mug, bread and stew were three for a plate. Just by way of comparison, a mug of good, clean water from something other than a pump in dubious proximity to a privy cost two pennybits (but it wouldn't get you drunk—and a mug of sweet spring water was three) and a bun like the one that Deek had bought him this afternoon was a full penny. So you could have something wholesome, though not much of it, for the same price as a full meal in the Hollybush. Evidently, bad as it was, there were enough people who felt they were getting value for their money to keep coming. The two fireside benches sat four each, and the four tables accommodated six eaters. Unless they planned a night to get drunk, the tables cleared pretty quickly. Skif figured that there were probably a couple hundred customers in here over the course of a day.

That was where Skif's grasp of numbers broke down—but he reckoned that the Hollybush brought in a couple hundred pennies in a night, and maybe a third of that during the day. Uncle Londer obviously had a good thing going here. His costs were low, buying cheap as he did, and the hire of his help was even lower. Maisie was a half-wit; Uncle Londer paid some relative of hers for her services. Whatever he paid, it wasn't much, and she never saw any of it; all she got was food and a place to sleep. Skif's labor was free, of course, and he seldom ate here. And the cook—

Well, he didn't know what the cook got. He never saw her getting paid, but she stayed, so she must have been getting something. It couldn't have been *that* much; even he could cook better than she did.

Maybe the attraction for her was the unlimited supply of beer. He never saw her without a mug somewhere nearby, and she had the yellowish color of someone who was drinking herself to death, although her shuffling footsteps were steady and she never seemed drunk.

The upshot was, this place was mostly profit for Londer, that much was for sure. Skif wasn't going to feel at all guilty about vanishing in a moon. Uncle Londer could just find himself another boy or do without.

What Kalchan was getting out of the situation was less clear; certainly he had Maisie's dubious charms to enjoy whenever he cared to, he did get real food rather than tavern swill, and he had his own special butt of drink that no one else touched, but what else was he getting? Every night after he locked the front door, he waddled down to his father's home with the night's takings, and came back empty-handed except for the box that held his own dinner. *He* slept in the common room on a greasy featherbed piled high with blankets that were stored during the day in the unused staircase. Was Londer splitting the profit with his son? If he was, what in Havens was Kalchan spending it on? It wasn't clothing, it wasn't women—not even the shabbiest streetwalker would touch Kalchan with a barge pole without a lot more up front than the penny or two Kalchan was likely to offer.

It had occurred to Skif recently that maybe Cousin Kalchan was just as stupid as he looked, and Uncle Londer gave him nothing in return for his labors at the Hollybush. If so, he didn't feel in the least sorry for him.

By the time that Kalchan dumped the last of the bench warmers outside and locked the front door, Skif was absolutely dead on his feet. Not tired—he'd had that nap in the wash house—but aching from neck to toes and longing for a chance to sit down.

Kalchan threw the bolt on the front door, and waddled out the back; when Skif heard the door slam shut behind him, he dropped down onto a bench to rest for a moment. The cook brought in three plates of stew and bread, and dropped them on the table. Skif took one look at the greasy, congealing mess, and pushed it toward Maisie, who had come to rest across from him and was already shoveling her food into her mouth as if she was afraid it was going to be taken from her at any moment. The cook had brought her own mug and picked up the beer pitcher that Kalchan had left on a table, shaking it experimentally. Finding there was still beer in it, she took it, her mug, and her plate to the fireside and settled down facing the remains of the flames, her back to her fellow workers.

Maisie finished her plate, picked up the platter in both hands and licked it, then went on to Skif's portion. She never said thank you, she never said anything. She never even acknowledged his presence.

Skif shuddered, got to his feet, and plodded into the now-deserted kitchen.

From his cubby, he took a tiny tin pot and a packet of *chava* leaves that he'd filched from Lord Orthallen's kitchen. Dipping water out of the barrel, he added the leaves and brewed himself a bedtime cup of bitter *chava*. The stuff was supposed to be good for you and make you feel relaxed and calm; at any rate, at this time of year it made a nice warm spot in his belly that let him get off to sleep.

He drank it quickly to get it down before Kalchan came back and then retreated to the cubby. The tin pot was shoved into the farthest corner where he kept a few other things that Kalchan didn't think worth taking—his own wooden spoon, a couple of pretty pebbles, some bird feathers, a spinning top he'd found. Then he wrapped himself up in his cast-off blankets, pillowed his head on his arms, and waited for Kalchan to get back, feigning sleep.

The only light in the kitchen came from the fire, and it was dying. It was the cook's job to bank it for the night, but she forgot more than half the time, which was why he had to start it again in the morning. When Kalchan came back, grunting and snorting, it was hardly more than a few flames over glowing coals. Kalchan pulled the door shut and dropped the bar over the inside, paying no attention to Skif.

Which meant that it had been a good night by Kalchan's standards. If it hadn't been, he would either have hauled Skif out and knocked him around a bit before letting him get back to his bed, or he'd have bawled for the cook and had her *lay* into Skif.

Kalchan's return was the cook's signal to go on up to her loft. She shuffled in, dropped the curtain over the door, shoved ashes over the coals, and limped up the stairs. There was some sound of fumbling with cloth overhead, then silence.

Meanwhile, Kalchan settled down to his dinner, which he had brought back from his father's kitchen. In theory, half of that dinner was supposed to be Skif's, but in all the time he'd lived here, he'd never gotten a morsel of it. Kalchan "shared" it with Maisie—that is, he dropped tidbits to her as if she was a dog, in return for which—

Skif generally tried to be asleep by that time, the moment when Kalchan's bedding was arranged to his satisfaction beside the fireplace, and Maisie was arranged to his satisfaction in it. And tonight, both exhaustion and the unusual circumstance of having had three decent meals in a day conspired to grant him his wish for slumber.

He woke from the oddest dream that morning—a dream he couldn't quite fathom, unless it had come from yesterday's encounter with Bazie. He had been climbing like a spider along the ledge of a building, several stories up. It was the dead of a moonless night, and he was dressed all in black, including a black hood that covered everything except for a slit for his eyes. And he had the impression that there was a girl behind him, although he hadn't seen any girls at Bazie's.

It was an interesting dream, though, wherever it had come from.

He heard Kalchan snorting and moving around in the next room, slowly waking up; it must be morning, then. Somehow Kalchan had the knack of being able to wake up at exactly the same time every morning, although it usually took him some time to go from sleep to full wakefulness. The one and only time that knack had failed him, he'd been dead drunk after swilling himself senseless on the free wine given out at some Guild Midwinter Feast three years ago. Not that Kalchan belonged to any Guilds, but he'd somehow managed to get himself invited or sneak in, and he'd certainly drunk far more than his share. He'd gotten back to the tavern on his own two feet, but had fallen straight onto the bedding that Skif and the cook had laid out in anticipation of his return, and he hadn't awakened until noon. Then, between anger at losing a whole morning's custom, and the temper caused by his hangover, he'd beaten Skif black and blue, blacked Maisie's eyes, and kept them all working and away from the temple largesse of Midwinter Day. All taverns closed the afternoon of Midwinter Day—there was no point in remaining open, since there was a Feast laid on at the temples for anyone who attended the Service beforehand. It was the one time of the year that Skif, Maisie, and the cook got a chance to stuff themselves sick on good, toothsome food, and Kalchan kept them from it, and beat them again the next day for good measure. That had marked the lowest point of Skif's life, and if he'd been bigger or older, he'd have run away and damn the consequences.

They never let him oversleep by that much again, not even though it meant a beating for awakening him. Not even broken bones would keep Skif from a Temple Midwinter Feast.

He was already up and waiting for Kalchan to unbar the kitchen door by the time his cousin waddled into the room. Kalchan looked at him with nothing other than his usual irritated glare, and performed that office, then turned and went back into the common room, leaving Skif to start the fire or go wait for the pony cart in the yard as he preferred.

For a wonder, when the cook had remembered to bank the fire, she'd actually done it right. There must not have been as much beer in the pitcher as she had thought. There was one coal left, not a lot, but enough to get some flames going with the help of lint, straw, and a little tallow. For once, Skif was done with his morning duties early, and he dashed out before Kalchan noticed.

That meant he was waiting at the temple door long before any of the other pupils, and decided against his usual custom to go into the sanctuary and watch Beel and his fellow priests perform the service. Not that he cared one way or another about religion, but the sanctuary was a place to get out of the cold and to sit down.

For a service like this one, where no one was really expected to come join in the worship, there was no grand procession up the center of the temple. Instead, a few priests came in from doors on either side of the altar, lit candles and incense, and began very quiet chanting. If you knew the chants and wished to join, you could—otherwise, you could observe and pray, according to your own nature.

He was the only person in the sanctuary other than the priests, and he had found a marginally warm place in the shadows of a pillar, so they probably didn't even notice him. They certainly didn't make any effort to pitch their voices to carry, and the distant murmur, combined with the fact that he could lean up against the pillar, allowed him to drop into a drowse again.

He drifted back into the dream of this morning; it seemed to be a continuation of the same story. This time he and the girl were crouched together in a closet, listening to something in the next room. The murmur of the priests at their devotions blended with the murmurs in the dream. Then the dream changed abruptly, as dreams tended to do, and he found himself incongruously staring deeply into a pair of large, deep blue eyes that filled his entire field of vision.

Blue eyes? *Whose* blue eyes? He didn't know anyone with blue eyes.

Abruptly, the bell signifying the end of the service rang, and he started awake.

Huh, he thought with bemusement. *Haven't dreamed this much in—can't 'member when. Must've been ev'thin I 'et!*

He got to his feet when the priests were gone, sauntered out of the sanctuary, and joined the rest of the pupils now gathering for their lessons.

But today was going to be different. For the first time ever, he put real effort into his attempts to master numbers. If he was going to have a position with Bazie's gang, he *didn't* want the authorities looking for him to clap him back into lessons. There was always a chance that they would catch him. If that happened, his uncle would know exactly where to find him.

No, the moment that Bazie had a place for him, he wanted to be able to pass his test and get released from school. Then he could disappear, and Uncle Londer could fume all he wanted. At the moment, he couldn't see how hanging with Bazie's gang could be anything but an improvement over the Hollybush.

His determination communicated itself to his tutor, and the younger boy put more enthusiasm into the lesson than Skif had expected. By the end of it, he'd made more progress in that single morning than he had in the four years he'd been taking lessons.

When lessons were over and the bell rang, he got ready to shoot out the door with the rest, but before he could, he felt a heavy hand on his shoulder, holding him in his seat.

Beel. He must have noticed something was different. Skif's stomach knotted, and his heart sank. He was in trouble, he must be—and for once, he didn't know why, or for what reason. And that made it worse.

"You can all go—" said Beel, whose hand, indeed, it was—but Beel's hand kept Skif pinned where he was.

Only when the room had emptied did Beel remove his hand from Skif's shoulder, and the young priest came around in front of him to stand looking down at him soberly.

"Skif—do you do work at the tavern in the afternoons?" Beel asked, a peculiarly strained expression on his face.

What?

Skif hesitated. If he told the truth, surely Beel would tell his father that Skif was a regular at playing truant from the Hollybush, and he would be in trouble. But if he didn't—Beel was a priest, and might be able to tell, and he would be in worse trouble.

But Beel didn't wait for him to make up his mind about his answer. "I want you to do something for me, Skif," he said urgently, his eyes full of some emotion Skif couldn't recognize. "I want you to promise me that today you *won't* go near the tavern from the time lessons let out until the time darkness falls."

The look Skif wore on his face must have been funny, since Beel smiled thinly. "I can't tell you why, Skif, but I hope that you can at least trust the priest if you can't trust your cousin. My father… is not as clever as he thinks he is. Someone is angry, angry at him, and angry at Kalchan. I think, unless he can be persuaded to curb his anger, that he is going to act this afternoon. You have nothing to do with all this, and you do not deserve to be caught in the middle."

And with those astonishing words, Beel turned and left, as he always did, as if nothing out of the ordinary had ever transpired between them.

After a moment, Skif shook off his astonishment and slowly left the building. Once out in the sunlight, he decided that whatever Beel was hinting at didn't really matter, because he had no notion of going back to the tavern during the day anyway. He was going to meet Deek, and get his first lessons in the fine art of thievery!

Deek wasn't lurking anywhere on the way to the building where Bazie's "laundry" was, but Skif remembered the way back to Bazie's, including the secret passages, perfectly. He suspected that this was his first test, and when he rapped on the door in an approximation of Deek's knock, it was Deek himself who opened it with a grin.

"I tol' ye 'e'd 'member!" Deek crowed, drawing Skif inside.

"An' I agreed wi' ye," Bazie said agreeably. "If 'e hadn', 'e wouldn' be much use, would'e?"

There was new laundry festooning the ceiling today—stockings and socks. Only Lyle was with Bazie and Deek; the third boy was nowhere to be seen.

"J'eet yet?" asked Lyle, as Deek drew him inside. At Skif's head shake, the other boy wordlessly gestured at the table, where half of a decent cottage loaf of brown bread waited, with some butter and a knife. Beside it was a pot of tea and mugs. Buttered bread, half eaten, sat on a wooden plate next to Bazie. All in all, it was the sort of luncheon that wouldn't disgrace the table of a retiring spinster of small means.

Not that Skif cared what it looked like—he'd been invited to eat, and eat he surely would. He fell on the food, cutting two nice thick slices of bread and buttered them generously, pouring himself a mug of tea. Bazie watched him with an oddly benevolent look on his face.

"Eat good, but don' eat *full* afore a job," he said, in a manner that told Skif this was a rule, and he'd better pay close attention to it. "Nivir touch stuff as makes ye gassy, an' nothin' that'll be on yer breath. Whut if ye has t' hide? Summun smells onions where no onions shud be, or wuss—" He blew a flatulent razz with his lips, and the other boys laughed. "Oh, laugh if ye like, but I heerd boys been caught that way! Aye, an' growed men as shoulda knowed better!"

Skif laughed, too, but he also nodded eagerly. Bazie was no fool; no matter that what his gang purloined was small beer compared with jewels and gold—it was obviously supplying them with a fair living, and at the moment, Skif wouldn't ask for more.

"Nah, good gillyflar tea, tha's the stuff afore a job," Bazie continued with satisfaction. "Makes ye keen, sharp. Tha's what ye need." He waited while Skif finished his bread and butter and drank a mug of the faintly acidic, but not unpleasant, tea. He knew gillyflower tea from the temple, where it occasionally appeared with the morning bread, and it did seem to wake him up when he felt a little foggy or sleepy.

"Nah, t'day Deek, I don' want wipes," Bazie continued. "I got sum'thin' I been ast for, special. Mun wants *napkins*. Ye ken napkins?"

Deek shook his head, but Skif, who had, after all, been serving in Lord Orthallen's hall as an ersatz page, nodded. "Bits uv linen—'bout so big—" He measured out a square with his hands. "Thicker nor wipes, kinda towels, but fine, like. Them highborns use 'em t' meals, wipes their han's an' face on 'em so's they ain't all grease an' looks sweetly."

"Ha!" Bazie slapped his knee with his hand. "Good boy! Deek, where ye think ye kin find this stuff?"

Deek pondered the question for a moment, then suggested a few names that Skif didn't recognize. "We h'aint touched any on 'em for a while."

"Make a go," Bazie ordered. "I needs twa dozen, so don' get 'em all in one place, eh?"

"Right. Ye ready?" Deek asked, looking down at Skif, who jumped to his feet. "We're off."

"Not like *that'e* ain't!" Lyle protested. "Glory, Deek, 'e cain't pass i' them rags!"

Bazie concurred with a decided nod. "Gi'e 'im summat on ourn. 'Ere, Lyle—i' the cubberd—"

Lyle went to the indicated alcove and rummaged around for a moment. "'Ere, these're too small fer any on' us—"

The boy threw a set of trews and a knitted tunic at Skif, who caught them. They were nearly identical to Deek's; the same neat and barely visible patches, the same dark gray-brown color. Happy to be rid of his rags, Skif stripped off everything but his smallclothes and donned the new clothing.

Now Bazie and Lyle nodded their satisfaction together. "We'll boil up yer ol' thin's an' mend 'em a bit—ye kin 'ave 'em back when ye git back," Bazie said. "We don' wan' yer nuncle t' wonder where ye got new close."

"Yessir," Skif said, bobbing his head. "Thankee, sir!"

Bazie laughed. "Jest get me napkins, imp."

Now properly clothed so that his ragged state wouldn't attract attention, Skif was permitted to follow Deek out into the streets.

They walked along as Skif had already learned to, as if, no matter how fine the neighborhood, they belonged there, that they were two boys who had been sent on an errand that needed to be discharged expeditiously, but not urgently.

Deek, however, knew every illicit way into the laundries and wash houses of the fine houses on these streets, and he led Skif over walls, up trees, and across rooftops. Together they waited for moments when the laundresses and washerwomen were otherwise occupied, and dropped down into the rooms where soiled linens were sorted for washing.

It was Skif who picked out the napkins from among the rest—no more than two or three lightly soiled squares of linen at each place. He chose nothing that was so badly grease-stained that it was unlikely it could be cleaned, nor did he pick out items that were new.

Once retrieved, Deek did something very clever with them. He folded them flat, and stuffed them inside the legs of his trews and Skif's, so that there was no way to tell that the bits of fabric were there at all without forcing them to undress. When they had the full two dozen, with no close calls and only one minor alarm, Deek called a halt, and they strolled back to Bazie's.

Skif was tired, but very pleased with himself. He'd kept up with Deek, and *he'd* been the one to pick out the loot Bazie wanted. Nothing new, nothing over-fine, nothing that would be missed unless and until a housekeeper made a full inventory. Not likely, that; not in the places that Deek had selected.

They made their way up, over, and down again, and back to Bazie's den. This time when Deek knocked, it was Bazie himself that opened the door for them, and Skif watched with covert amazement as he stumped back to his seat like some sort of bizarre four-legged creature, supporting himself on two wooden pegs strapped where his legs had been, and two crutches, one for each arm.

"Aaa—" Bazie said, in a note of pain, as he lowered himself down to his seat and quickly took off the wooden legs. "When ye brings back th' glimmers, young'un, I'll be gettin' proper-fittin' stumps, fust thing." He gestured in disgust at the crude wooden legs. "Them's no better nor a couple slats. How's it that a mun kin be sa good wi' needle an sa bad wi' whittlin'?"

He put the crutches aside, and looked at them expectantly.

"Here ye be, Bazie!" said Deek, taking the lead, and pulling napkins out of his trews the way a conjure mage at a fair pulled kerchiefs out of his hand. Skif did the same, until all two dozen were piled in front of their mentor.

"Hah! Good work!" Bazie told them. "Nah, young'un—ye look an ye tell me—wha's the big problem we got wi' these fer sellin' uv 'em?"

That was something Skif had worried about. Every single napkin they'd taken had been decorated with distinctive embroidered initials or pictures on the corners. "Them whatchacalls in th' corners," Skif said promptly. "Dunno what they be, but they's all different."

"They's t' show what owns 'em, but ol' Bazie's gotta cure for that, eh, Deek?" Bazie positively beamed at both of them, and took out a box from a niche beside his seat. He opened it, and Skif leaned forward to see what was inside.

Sewing implements. Very fine, as fine as any great lady's. Tiny scissors, hooks, and things he couldn't even guess at.

His mouth dropped open, and Bazie laughed. "Ye watch, an ye learn, young'un," he said merrily. "An' nivir ye scorn till ye seen—"

Bazie took out the tiniest pair of scissors that Skif had ever seen, and a thing like a set of tongs, but no bigger than a pen, and several other implements Skif had no names for. Then he took up the first of the napkins and set to work on it.

Within moments, it was obvious what he was doing; he was unpicking the embroidery. But he was doing so with such care that when he was finally done, only a slightly whiter area and a hole or two showed where it had been, and the threads he had unpicked were still all in lengths that could be used.

"Nah, I'll be doin' that t' all uv them, then into th' bleach they goes, an' no sign where they come from!" Bazie rubbed his hands together with glee. "An' that'll mean a full five siller fer the lot from a feller what's got a business in these things, an' all fer a liddle bit uv easy work for ye an me! Nah, what sez ye t' that, young'un?"

Skif could only shake his head in admiration. "That—I'm mortal glad I grabbed fer Deek's ankle yesterday!"

And Bazie roared with laughter. "So'm we, boy!" he chuckled. "So'm we!"

4

Skif did not go out again, nor did Deek. Instead, they emptied out the cauldron of its warm, soapy, green-gray water, pouring it down a drain hole in the center of the room, and refilled it with fresh. This was no mean feat, as it had to be done one bucketful at a time, from the common pump that everyone in the building shared—which was, predictably, in a well house attached to the side of the building to keep it from freezing. Bazie had special buckets, with lids that kept the water from slopping, but it still made for a lot of climbing.

No wonder Bazie was ready to bring me in! Skif thought ruefully, as he poured his bucketful into what seemed to have become a wash cauldron without a bottom. His arms ached, and so did his back—this business of becoming a thief was more work than it looked!

"How often d'ye empty this'un?" he asked Bazie, who was mending a stocking as dexterously as he had unpicked the design on the napkins.

"Once't week," Bazie replied. "We saves all th' whites fer then. Wouldna done it early, forbye th' napkin order's on haste, an' ye're here t' hep."

Skif sighed, and hefted the empty bucket to make another journey. This was like working at the Hollybush—

He had no doubt that he would be the chief cauldron filler until Bazie took on another boy, so he had this to look forward to, once a week, for the foreseeable future.

On the other hand, Bazie appeared to feed his boys well and treat them fairly. Skif had plenty of time to think about the situation, to contrast how Raf, Deek, and Lyle all acted around Bazie and how well fed (if a bit shabby) they looked. So Bazie wasn't running a gang that was wearing silks and velvets and had servants to do their work. So he and the rest of the boys had to do a hauling now and then. They were eating, they were warm, and Bazie was a good master. What was a little hard work, set against that?

So he hauled and dumped, hauled and dumped, while his arms, back, and legs complained on every inward journey. When the cauldron was at last filled, Bazie let him rest for just long enough to drink another mug of tea. When the tea was gone, Bazie put him to building up the fire beneath the cauldron, then adding soap and a pungent liquid that he said would whiten the worst stains. When the water was actually boiling, at Bazie's direction he added the napkins, then other articles that *should* have been white. There wasn't a lot; pure white was a very difficult state to attain, so the boys didn't steal anything that should be white.

"Dunno how them Heralds does it," Bazie said, half in wonder and half in frustration. "Them Whites, 'sall they wears, an' how they nivir gets stains, I dunno."

"Magic," Deek opined cheekily, and Bazie laughed.

"Gimme stick," Deek told Skif. "Take a breather." Deek took over then, stirring while Skif lay back on a pile of straw-stuffed sacks that served as cushions, letting his aches settle.

Lyle arrived, tapping his code on the door, and Deek let him in. Raf was right behind him. Both boys began emptying their pockets and the fronts of their tunics as soon as they came in. Skif sat up to watch as Bazie supervised.

What came out of their clothing wasn't kerchiefs and other bits of silk this time, but metal spoons, knives, packets of pins and needles, fancy pottery disks with holes in the middle—

"Ah," Bazie said with satisfaction. "Wool Market good, then?"

"Aye," the boy named Raf said. "Crowd." This was the one that Skif hadn't seen much of yesterday, and if someone had asked him to point Raf out in a crowd he still wouldn't be able to. Raf was extraordinarily ordinary. There was nothing distinctive in his height (middling), his weight (average), his face (neither round nor square), his eyes and hair (brown), or his features (bland and perfectly ordinary). Even when he smiled at Skif, it was just an ordinary, polite smile, and did nothing; it seemed neither warm, nor false, and it certainly didn't light up his features.

Bazie watched him as he examined the other boy and mentally dismissed him—and Bazie grinned.

"So, young'un, wot ye think'o Raf?" he asked.

"Don' think much one way or 'tother," Skif said truthfully.

Bazie laughed, and so did Raf. "Na, ye don' see't, does ye?" Bazie said.

"Wall, he wouldn' see it now, would'e?" Raf put in. "If'n 'e *did*, that'd be bad!"

The others seemed to think this was a great joke, but it was one that Skif didn't get the point of. They all laughed heartily, leaving him sitting on the stuffed sacks looking from one to the other, perplexed, and growing irritated.

"Wha's the joke?" he asked loudly.

"Use yer noggin—" Lyle said, rubbing his knuckles in a quick gesture over Skif's scalp. "Raf's on the liftin' lay, dummy. So?"

"I dunno!" Skif retorted, his irritation growing. "Whazzat got ter do wi' wot I think uv 'im?"

"It ain't wot yer think uv 'im, 'tis 'is *looks,*" Deek said with arch significance, which made the other two boys go off in gales of laughter again, and Bazie to chuckle.

"Well, 'e ain't gonna ketch no gurls wi' 'em," Skif replied sullenly. "'E don' look like nothin' special."

"And?" Deek prompted, then shook his head at Skif's failure to comprehend. "Wot's special 'bout *not* special?"

Finally, *finally,* it dawned on him, and his mouth dropped open in surprise. "Hoy!" he said. "Cain't give no beak no ways t' find 'im!"

A "beak," Skif knew, was one of the city watchmen who patrolled for thieves and robbers, took care of drunks and simple assault and other minor crimes. Anything major went to the Guard, and anything truly big went to one of the four City Heralds—not that Skif had ever seen one of these exalted personages. He'd never seen a Guard either, except at a distance. The Guards didn't bother with the neighborhoods like this one, not unless murder and mayhem had occurred.

Bazie nodded genially. "Thas' right. Ain't no better boy fer learnin' th' liftin' lay," he said with pride. "Even'f sommut sees him, 'ow they gonna tell beak wot 'e looks like if'n 'e don' look like nothin'?"

Now it was Skif's turn to shake his head, this time in admiration. What incredible luck to have been born so completely nondescript! Raf could pick pockets for the rest of his life on looks like his—he wouldn't even have to be particularly *good* at it so long as he took care that there was nothing that was ever particularly distinctive about him. How could a watchman ever pick him out of a crowd when the description his victim gave would match a hundred, a thousand other boys in the crowd?

"'E's got 'nother liddle trick, too," Bazie continued. "'Ere, Lyle— nobble 'im."

Not at all loath, Lyle puffed himself up and seized Raf's arm. "'Ere, you!" he boomed—or tried to, his voice was evidently breaking, and the words came out in a kind of cracked squeak. He tried again. "'Ere, you! You bin liftin'?"

Now Raf became distinctive. Somehow the eyes grew larger, innocent, and tearful; the lower lip quivered, and the entire face took on a kind of guileless stupidity mingled with frightened innocence. It was amazing. If Skif had caught Raf with his hand in Skif's pocket, he'd have believed it was all an accident.

"Whossir? Messir?" Raf quavered. "Nossir. I'm be gettin' packet'o pins fer me mum, sir…" And he held out a paper stuck full of pins for Lyle's inspection, tears filling his eyes in a most pathetic fashion.

Bazie and Deek howled with laughter, as Lyle dropped Raf's arm and growled. "Gerron wi' ye."

As soon as the arm was dropped, Raf pretended to scuttle away with his head down and shoulders hunched, only to straighten up a few moments later and assume his bland guise again. He shrugged as Skif stared at him.

"Play actin'," he said dismissively.

"Damn *good* play actin'," Bazie retorted. "Dunno 'ow long ye kin work it, but whilst ye kin, serve ye better nor runnin' from beaks." He set his mending aside and rubbed his hands together. "'Sall right, me boys. 'Oo wants t'fetch dinner?"

"Me," Raf said. "Don' wanta stir washin', an' don' wanta sort goods."

The other two seemed amenable to that arrangement, so Raf got a couple of coins from Bazie and took himself off. The napkins in the cauldron were finally white enough to suit Bazie, so Skif got the job of pulling the white things out and rinsing them in a bucket of fresh water, while Lyle hung them up and Deek sorted through the things that Lyle and Raf had brought back.

Presently he looked up. "Six spoons, two knifes, packet uv needles, three uv pins, empty needlecase, four spinnin' bobs," he said. "Reckon thas 'nuf wi' wot we alriddy got?"

Bazie nodded. "Arter supper ye go out t' Clave. Ye kin take napkins t' Dooly at same time. An' half th' wipes. Lyle, ye'll taket' rest uv th' goods t' Jarmin."

"Kin do," Lyle replied genially, taking the last of the napkins from Skif. "Young'un, git that pile an' dunk in wash, eh?"

He pointed to a pile of dingy shirts and smallclothes in the corner with his chin. "Thas ourn," he added by way of explanation. "Ye kin let fire die a bit, so's it's cool 'nuf fer the silks when ourn's done."

Skif had wondered—the stuff didn't seem to be of the same quality as the goods that the boys brought back to Bazie. Obediently, he picked up the pile of laundry and plunged it into the wash cauldron and began stirring.

"Ye moght be a wonderin' why we does all this washin' an wimmin stuff," Bazie said conversationally. "I tell ye. Fust, I tell m'boys allus t' nobble outa the dirty stuff—'cause thas inna pile, an nobody ain't counted it yet. See?"

Skif nodded; he *did* see. It was like playing a page at Lord Orthallen's meals. Food was checked before it became a dish for a meal, it was checked for pilferage before it was taken to the table, and it was checked when it came back to the kitchen as leftovers. But there was that moment of opportunity while it was in transition from kitchen to table when no one was checking the contents. So, dirty clothing and linen probably wasn't counted—why should it be? But if you stole something off a wash line, or out of a pile of clean clothing intended for a particular person, it would be missed.

"So, we gets stuff tha' way, but if's dirty, it ain't wuth so much. 'F it were just th' odd wipe we git from liftin' lay, wouldn' be wuth cleanin'—an' thas why most on liftin' lay don' clean whut they nobble, 'cause they gotta get glim fer it now so's they kin eat." Bazie peered at Skif to see if he was following. "Us, we pass *straight* onta couple lads as has stalls in market, 'cause what we got's clean an' got no markin's on't. Looks jest like wha' ye'd sell t' market stall an' yer ol' mum croaked an' ye're droppin' 'er goods. We spread it 'round t' several lads so's it don' look bad."

That made perfect sense. The used-clothing merchants buying the things had to know they were stolen, of course—either that, or they were idiots—but there was no other way to tell. And once Bazie's loot was mixed up with all the other things in a merchant's stall, it all looked perfectly ordinary. Servants often got worn, outgrown, or outmoded clothing from their masters as part of their wages or as a bonus, and most of that ended up with a used-clothing merchant. Then those who wished to appear well-to-do or seamstresses looking for usable fabric for better garments would find bargains among the bins. Pickpockets unlike Bazie's gang, who lifted used kerchiefs and the like—and outright muggers, who assaulted and stripped their victims bare—would have to sell their soiled goods to a rag man rather than directly to a stall holder.

"Me old mam made me learn th' sewin'," Bazie continued. "'M a pretty dab 'and at un. Mended stuff's wuth more'n tore-up, an' unpickin' the pretties makes 'em plain—well, like napkins. All it costs's time—an' hellfires, I got time!"

"Smart," Skif said, meaning it. Bazie looked pleased.

"*Some* lads thinks as is sissy stuff, 'an' couldn' stick i' wi' us," Deek put in, scornfully. "*Some* lads, sayin' no names but as rhymes with *scare-up*, thinks is a waste uv time."

"*Some* lads'll end up under the beak inside a moon," Lyle said lazily. "'Cause *some* lads kin ony think uv glim an' glimmers, an' don't go at thin's slow. I don' care, long's I gets m' dinner!"

Bazie laughed, as Skif nodded agreement vigorously. "Thas m' clever lads!" Bazie said approvingly. "Roof over t'head, full belly an' warm flop—thas' th' ticket. Glim an' glimmers kin wait on learnin t' be better nor good."

"Righto," Deek affirmed. "Takes a mort'o learnin'. They's old thieves, an' they's bold thieves, but they ain't no old, bold thieves."

That seemed excellent advice to Skif, who stirred the cauldron with a will.

It wasn't until he began pulling garments out with the stick that Skif noticed his own clothing was in with the rest—and that Bazie had neatly mended and patched it while he was gone. He'd resewn Skif's clumsy work to much better effect, and Skif felt oddly touched by this considerate gesture.

Raf returned as he started on the next lot of purloined scarves, carrying a packet and another loaf of bread. "They's mort'o doin's over t' Hollybush," he said as he handed Bazie the packet.

Skif's head snapped around. "What doin's?" he asked sharply.

"Dunno fer certain-sure," Raf replied. "Summun sez a couple toughs come in an' wrecked t' place, summun sez no, 'twas a fight, an' ev'un sez summun's croaked, or near it. All I knows' theys beaks an' a Guard there now. Figgered ye shud know."

Bazie mulled that over, as Skif stood there, stunned, the wash stick still in his hands. "Reckon five fer supper," he said judiciously. "Huh."

"I cud go wi'im arter dark," Lyle offered. "We cud reck th' doin's."

Bazie shook his head. "Nay, no goin' near—Raf! Ye good fer goin' out agin? Hev a drink i' th' Arms?"

The grandly named "King's Arms" was the nearest rival to the Hollybush, and its owner had no love for Kalchan or Uncle Londer. One reason for the rivalry was economic—the Arms didn't serve the kind of swill that the Hollybush did, and charged accordingly. Many, many of the poorest customers opted for quantity over quality, and their custom went to Kalchan. If anything bad had happened to the Hollybush or its owner, the buzz would be all over the Arms.

"Oh, aye!" Raf laughed. "They don' know me there, an' leastwise ye kin drink th' beer 'thout bein' choked."

"Arms beer's nought so bad," Bazie said complacently. "Here—" He flipped a fivepenny coin at Raf. "Get a drink and fill me can, an' come on back."

Raf caught the coin right out of the air, picked up a covered quart beer pail, and saluted Bazie with two fingers. "I'm be back afore the bacon's fried," he promised.

Skif could only wonder what had happened—and how Beel had known that it would. And what if Beel *hadn't* given him that timely warning? He could have walked straight into a fight, or a trap, or who knew what trouble.

A shiver ran down his back—for his own near miss, and not for anything that might have happened to Kalchan. In fact, he sincerely hoped that Kalchan was at the very least cooling his heels in the gaol. Given all the rotten things that Kalchan had done—just the things that Skif knew about—he had a lot coming to him.

He shook his head and went back to his stirring. Bazie had been watching him closely, and seemed satisfied with what he saw. "Ye mot not hev a home," he ventured.

Skif shrugged. "Hell. Bargain's a bargain. Ye said, a moon, I'll not 'spect a flop a'fore that. 'F nobuddy's there, I kin sneak in t' sleep. I kin sleep on roof, or stairs, or summat." He managed a weak grin. "Or even Lord Orthallen's wash house."

Bazie now looked *very* satisfied; evidently Skif had struck exactly the right note with him. No pleading, no asking for special consideration— he'd got that already. Just matter-of-fact acceptance.

'Sides, 'tis only for a moon. That ain't long. Even in winter.

Actually, the wash house wasn't a bad idea. Skif had slept there once or twice before, when Kalchan had decided that in addition to a set of stripes with the belt, he didn't deserve a bed, and locked him out in the courtyard overnight. From dark until dawn the only people there would be the laundry maids, who slept there, and none of them would venture up to the storage loft after dark. The ones that weren't young and silly and afraid of spirits were old and too tired to do more than drop onto the pallets and snore. It would be cold, but no worse than the Hollybush.

The only difficulty would be getting in and out, since beaks and private guards were on the prowl after dark in force.

Well, he'd deal with the problems as they came up and not before. *Hard on me if I can't slip past a couple beaks.*

He didn't have very long to wait for his news; by the time the next batch of laundry was in the cauldron, Raf returned with Bazie's pail of beer and a mouth full of news.

"Well!" he said, as soon as Deek let him in. "Ol' Londer did hisself no good this time! What I heerd—'e cheated a mun, sommun wi' some brass, an' th' mun got a judgment on 'im. So's the judgment sez the mun gets Hollybush. On'y nobuddy tol' yon Kalchan, or Kalchan figgered 'e weren't gonna gi'e up, or Londer tol' Kalchan t' keep mun out. So mun comes wi' bullyboys t'take over, an' Kalchan, 'e sez I don' think so, an lays inta 'em wi' iron poker!"

"Hoo!" Skif said, eyes wide with glee. "Wisht I'da been there!"

"Oh, nay ye don'—cuz it went bad-wrong," Raf corrected with relish. "Th' cook, she comes a-runnin' when she hears th' ruckus, lays in w' stick, an th' girl, she tries t' run fer it, an' slippet an starts t' scream, an' that brings beaks. So beaks get inta it, an' they don' love Kalchan no more nor anybuddy else, an' they commences t' breakin' heads. Well! When 'tis all cleared up, they's a mun dead wi' broke neck, an' Kalchan laid out like cold fish, t'cook ravin', an' t'girl—" Raf gloated, "—t'girl, she turn out t'be bare fifteen, no schoolin', an' pretty clear Kalchan's been atop 'er more'n once!"

"Fifteen!" Skif's eyes bulged. "I'da swore she was eighteen, sure! Sixteen, anyroad!"

Then again—he'd simply assumed she was. There wasn't much of her, and she wasn't exactly talkative. She had breasts, and she was of middling height, but some girls developed early. Wasn't there a saying that those who were a bit behind in the brains department were generally ahead on the physical side?

"Thas' whut Londer, 'e tried t'say, but they got th' girl's tally from Temple an' she's no more'n bare fifteen an' that jest turned!" Raf practically danced in place. "So ol' Londer, he got it fer not schoolin' th' girl, an' puttin' er where Kalchan cud tup 'er, an not turnin' over Hollybush proper. Cook's hauled off someplace, still ravin'. Girl's taken t' temple or summat. Kalchan, he's wust, *if* 'e wakes up, which Healers sez mebbe and mebbe not, 'e's'up fer murder *an* fer tuppin' the girl afore she be sixteen."

Skif had to sit down. Kalchan and Uncle Londer had always come out on top of things before. He could scarcely believe that they weren't doing so now.

"Good thing ye weren' there," Bazie observed mildly. "Kalchan 'ud say t'was *you* was tuppin' girl."

"Me? Maisie?" Skif grimaced. "Gah, don' thin' sough! Druther turn priest!"

"Well, wouldna' be call fer th' law if 'twas you. Couple kids foolin' 'round's a thing fer priests, not the law. Summun old's Kalchan, though, thas different, an' reckon 'f ol' Londer don' 'ang 'is boy out t' dry, he'll say 'twas you." Bazie rubbed his chin speculatively. "Don' 'magine girl 'ud conterdick 'im."

"Don' fergit, she's in Temple," Lyle piped up. "Dunno 'f they'd git 'er t'talk. Mebbe use Truth Spell."

"It don' matter," Skif decided. "I don' want nothin' t'do wi' em. I ain't goin' back."

Londer wouldn't know where he was, nor would Kalchan, who was, in any event, in no position to talk. The trouble was Beel knew he had stayed away. So would Beel send anyone looking for him? And should he tell Bazie about all of this?

Reluctantly, he decided that he had better.

"This's gettin' complisticatered," he said unhappily, and explained about Beel, and Beel's warning.

The others all sat silent for a moment, their eyes on him.

"This Beel, 'e knows nowt 'bout us?" Bazie asked, his head to one side, quizzically.

Skif shook his head. "'E ain't niver sed much t'me afore this," he replied. "I allus figgered 'e wuz jest Londer's eyes. Niver reckoned on 'im warnin' me." He considered the odd conversation a little further. "Must've known, an' didn' warn his Da neither. Niver reckoned on 'im stickin' t' th' law—an' ye kin bet Londer wouldn't. Huh. Turned on 'is own Da!"

Bazie nodded slowly. "Niver know wut bein' in temple'll do wi' a mun," he said sagely. "Gets t'thinkin' 'bout 'is own soul, mebbe. Starts thinkin' 'is ol' man cud stan' bein' took down a peg, mebbe figgers th' ol' man cud stand t' get held 'countable. Figgers a kid don' need t' get mixed up in't."

"Point is, ain't nobuddy knows out us," said Raf. He stared intently at Skif for a very long and uncomfortable moment. Finally, the older boy seemed to make up his mind. "Bazie, I sez we votes now. Young'un ain't behind wi' helpin', an' Deek sez 'e's good over roof. Bring 'un in."

Bazie looked at the other two as Skif blinked with bewilderment. What on earth was he getting at?

"Aye!" Deek exclaimed. "In by me!"

"Makes three," said Lyle lazily. "'E's already done more'n a couple days than You Know did in a week."

Now Skif realized what they were saying, and his heart leaped as he looked to Bazie, the leader, the teacher—

"Oh, I'd already reckoned," Bazie said with a smile. "'E might's well jump in. Lyle, ye take 'im wi' ye t' Jarmin, so's Jarmin gets t' know 'is face, an' 'e gets t' know th' proper pay fer th' goods."

He clapped Skif on the back. "Yer in, young 'un. They's room 'nuf an' a bed nobuddy got, an' plenty t' go 'round. Ye're well-come."

"Hey! Les' eat!" Deek exclaimed, before Skif could really get it fixed in his mind how his life had just been turned around, that he had just been fully accepted into the gang. That he never had to go back to Kalchan and the misery of the Hollybush again.

And no more lessons!

Bazie laughed, and distributed the labor. Skif was set to cutting the loaf and buttering the slices, Deek to frying slices of fat bacon over the fire beneath the cauldron, Lyle to get the plates and pot of mustard, Raf to pour small beer for all of them. Skif was a bit surprised by that last. Kalchan never shared beer with anyone—but Raf divided the quart equally among the five of them with Bazie's approval.

It was the first friendly meal that Skif had ever shared with anyone; the first time he had ever, within memory, eaten in a leisurely manner.

While they ate, Bazie decided what goods they would take to each buyer as soon as darkness fell. It would be better to take their bundles of goods out under the cover of night, just to be certain that no one in their building saw them toting around unusually bulky packages. Once they were out in the street, of course, they would just be three boys carrying out errands, but their neighbors in the building shouldn't be given the excuse to be nosy.

As soon as dinner was polished off and the last of the laundry hung up to dry, Skif and Lyle packed up the goods for Jarmin, the old clothes seller. Evidently Jarmin was a man who catered to those with a taste for finer things; almost all of the fancier goods were going to him. When everything had been selected, they each had a fairly bulky bundle wrapped in oilcloth. Bazie showed Skif how to use a piece of rope to make a crude backpack of it, to keep his hands free.

"Take a stick," he cautioned Skif; Lyle had already selected a stout cudgel from six or so leaning over in a corner near the door. "Plenty uv folk out there'll beat ye jest hopin' ye got summat they want."

Like I don't know that! Skif thought—but he didn't make any comments, he just selected a stick for himself.

The packs made negotiating the stairs a little awkward, but they got out all right, and Lyle strode down the street with the air of someone who had a place to get to in a hurry. Skif had to trot to keep up with him. For all that Lyle acted lazy back in the room, he could certainly put out some energy when he chose to!

He didn't waste any breath on talking either. What he *did* was to keep his eyes moving, up and down the street, peering at doorways, watching for trouble. Skif followed his example. Until now, he hadn't been out on the street much at night, and he was very conscious of how vulnerable two boys were. There wasn't much light. Nobody wasted much money on streetlamps around these neighborhoods. What little there was came from windows and a few open doors, and from the torches people carried with them.

They didn't have a torch, but Skif didn't really want one. Certainly having a torch or a lantern made it easier to see your way, but it also made it very clear how many people were in your group and whether or not you had anything that looked worth stealing. Plus you couldn't see past the circle of light cast by the torch, which made it easier for you to be ambushed.

The street was anything but deserted, despite the darkness. People came and went from cookshops and taverns, groups of young toughs strolled about looking for whatever they could get into, streetwalkers sauntered wherever there was a bit of illumination, with their keepers (if they had one) lurking just out of sight of potential customers. There were ordinary working men and women, too, coming home late from their jobs. For a bit it would only be a *little* more dangerous to be out on the street than it was during the day.

Skif had figured that this "Jarmin" would be somewhere nearby, but apparently he was wrong. They must have gone a good ten blocks before Lyle made a turn into a dead-end street that was very nicely lit up indeed.

If the dim and sullen Hollybush had been at one extreme of the sorts of taverns frequented by the poor, this was at the other. The whole back of the cul-de-sac was taken up by a tavern blazing with tallow-dip lights; that had torches in holders right outside the door, and light spilling from parchment-covered windows. There was music, raucous laughter, the sounds of loud talk. A group of men were betting on a contest between two tomcats out in the street, and with them were three or four blowsy females of negotiable virtue, hanging on their arms and cheering on the two oblivious cats.

On either side of the tavern were shops, still open. Skif never got a chance to see what the one on the left sold, because they turned immediately into the one on the right.

This was their goal; an old-clothes shop that specialized in fancy goods of all sorts, but mostly for women. Skif had a shrewd idea where most of the females from the tavern spent their hard-earned coins.

Jarmin, a perfectly ordinary, clerkly sort of fellow, had an assistant to help him, and when he saw Lyle entering the front door, he left the customer he was attending to the assistant and ushered them both into the rear of the shop.

"Have you got sleeves?" Jarmin asked, as soon as he dropped the curtain separating front from back behind them. "I particularly need sleeves. And veils. But particularly sleeves. And I don't suppose you've got silk stockings—"

Lyle shrugged out of his pack, and Skif did the same. "Aye, Jarmin, all uv that. This's Skif; 'e's wi' us now. I'm be showin' 'im th' way uv things."

"Yes, yes." Jarmin dismissed Skif entirely, his attention focused on the packs. "You know, if you just have some good sleeves and stockings, I can sell a dozen pairs tonight, for some reason—"

"All or nowt, Jarmin. Ye know that. Ye takes all or nowt." Lyle had gone from lazy boy to shrewd salesman in the time it had taken to reach this place, and Skif marveled at him as he bargained sharply with the fretful shopkeeper. At length they arrived at a price that was mutually satisfactory, and Skif tried to look as indifferent as Lyle did. It was hard, though; he'd never seen so much money before in all his life.

Aye, but that's from how much work? A week, mebbe? An' there's five uv us t'feed.

Lyle divided the cash between them. "Just i'case," he said darkly, and showed Skif how to wrap it so that it didn't clink and tuck it inside his tunic where it wouldn't show. Only then did they ease out of the shop, where already Jarmin had frowsty girls crowding around the counter demanding shrilly to see the new goods.

If Lyle had set a brisk pace going out, he did better than that coming back. Only when they were safely in the building and heading up the stair did he finally slow down, with Skif panting behind.

"Sorry," he said apologetically. "Hate goin' out. Got caught once, 'fore I worked fer Bazie."

"No worries," Skif assured him. "I don' like it much, neither."

In fact, he didn't feel entirely comfortable until he was safely back in Bazie's room, where they pulled out their packets of coin and turned the lot over to a grinning Bazie.

"Good work," he told them both. "Fagged out?"

"'Bout ready t' drop," Skif admitted; now that they were back in the warmth and safety, the very long day, with all of its hard work and unexpected changes in his life suddenly caught up with him.

"Not me!" Lyle declared, and made a growling face. "Ready t' match ye at draughts, ol' man!"

Bazie chuckled. "Show th' young'un 'is cupbard, then, an' I'll get us set."

Lyle pulled on Skif's sleeve, and took him to the side of the room opposite the laundry cauldron, where he opened what Skif had taken to be shutters over a window. Shutters they were, but they opened up to a cubby long enough to lie down in, complete with a straw-stuffed pallet, blankets, and a straw-stuffed cushion. By Skif's standards, it was a bed of unparalleled luxury, and he climbed up into it without a moment of hesitation.

Lyle closed the shutters for him once he was settled, blocking out most of the light from the room beyond. Within moments, he was as cozy and warm as he had ever been in his life, and nothing was going to keep him awake. In fact, the sounds of laughter and dice rattling from the other room couldn't even penetrate into his most pleasant of dreams.

5

If Skif thought he was going to get off easy by no longer attending lessons at the Temple, he got a rude awakening the next day.

He was used to getting up early, and he woke—or so he guessed—at or near his usual time. For a moment, he was confused by the total darkness, scent of clean laundry and the lack of *stench*, and most of all, by the fact that he was warm and comfortable. He had never awakened warm and comfortable before. Even in the middle of summer, he was generally stiff from sleeping on the dirt floor, and except in the very hottest days and nights, had usually had all the heat leached from his body by the floor. Initially he thought he was still dreaming, and moaned a little at the thought that now he was going to have to awaken to Kalchan, cold, and misery.

Then he sat up, hit his forehead on the inside of the sleep cubby before he got more than halfway up, and remembered where he was. He lay back down—he hadn't hit his head that hard, since he hadn't tried to get up very fast.

I'm at Bazie's. Ol' Kalchan's in trouble, deep, 'n so's m'nuncle. An'I don't never have t' go back t' th' tavern!

He lay quietly on his back, stroking the woolen blanket with one hand, tracing the lines of each patch. It must have been patched and darned by Bazie; the seams were so neat and even. No one else was stirring, though, and for the first time he could remember, he lay back in his bed and just luxuriated in the freedom to lie abed as long as he cared to. Or as long as the others would let him—but it looked as if the rest were in no hurry to get about their business.

What was this new life going to be like? The other three boys seemed content and well-nourished, and he couldn't see how a legless man like Bazie could force them to stay if they didn't want to. There would be hard work, and a lot of it; he knew that much from yesterday, when he'd hauled

696

water all afternoon. Danger, too. Despite the fact that the other boys had a cavalier attitude about being caught, there was a lot of danger involved in the life of even a petty thief, and the penalties were harsh. Plenty of people meted out their own punishments on those they nobbled, before the beaks were called, which generally meant a bad beating first, then being clapped in gaol, then any of a variety of punishments.

Official punishments were many and varied, none of them very appealing. *Which's the point, I s'pose.* A thief could be transported to work in someone's fields, could be sent to work as a general dogsbody for the Guard, could be left in gaol, could get lashes—it all depended on the judge. That was for the first time you got caught. After that, the punishments were harsher.

But he wouldn't think about that until after he'd been caught for the first time. If he was. If he was clever, fast, smart—he might never be. *Why not? I bin keepin' from gettin' caught 'till now, an' I'm just a young'un. Ye'd think I'd just get smarter as I get bigger.*

There would be a lot of learning time, though, a great many menial chores as well, and he couldn't expect to share in the profits even his own hauls brought in for a while. That didn't matter; life here would be a paradise compared with what his life had been like at the tavern. In fact, he didn't much care if all he did was wash the stuff the others brought in for the next year! It wouldn't be any harder than working at the tavern, and he'd be full and warm all the time, with a bed like he'd never had before and clothing that wasn't more hole than fabric.

He lay in the darkness contemplating his future until he heard someone stirring, heard the shutters of another bed open, and the pad of feet on the floor. He turned on his side and saw a flicker of light through the cracks in the shutters of his cubby. He pushed them open cautiously, and looked out.

"Heyla, 'nother lark, eh?" Raf said genially. "Come gimme 'and, then."

Skif hopped out and shut the cubby doors behind him. Raf was bent over the fire under the wash cauldron, coaxing a flame from the banked coals. "Take yon tallow dip, take a light from here, an' light them lamps," he ordered, jerking his head at a tallow dip on the otherwise clean table behind him, barely visible in the dim and flickering light from the hand-sized fire. Skif picked it up, lit it at Raf's little fire, and went around the walls to relight the lamps he vaguely recalled hanging there. There were a lot of oil lamps—four!—and all of them were cobbler's lamps with globes of water-filled glass around the flame to magnify the light, the most expensive kind of oil lamp there was. Skif was impressed; he hadn't paid any attention before, other than to note absently that although this room didn't have any windows there was plenty of illumination. It was interesting; Bazie didn't spend money on luxuries, but in places where it counted—the good soap for the laundry, for instance, and the lighting, and decent fuel for the fireplace under the wash boiler—Bazie got the best.

When he was done, he blew out the tallow dip and put it with the others in a broken cup above the firebox. By this time the shutters of another cubby, one just above Skif's, had been pushed open by a foot, and Deek's tousled head poked out.

"Eh, Bazie?" he called, yawning. "Yon ge'op? Me'n Raf'r op. Young'un Skif, too."

"Aye," came a muffled reply, and the shutter to a third eased open. This one was larger—taller, rather—and Bazie was sitting up inside, peering out at them, the stumps of his legs hidden under his blanket. Satisfied that the fire was well started, Raf got up, and Deek swung himself out and down onto the floor. The two of them went to Bazie's cubby and linked hands. Bazie put an arm around each of their shoulders and swung himself onto the "chair" made by their hands.

They carried him to a door beside the one that led outside—one that Skif hadn't noticed before. Bazie let go of Raf's shoulder, which freed one of his hands, and opened it, and they carried him inside. There was evidently another room there that Skif had no notion existed.

The door swung open enough to see inside. The room was a privy! Skif gaped, then averted his eyes to give Bazie a little privacy—but it wasn't just *any* privy, it was a real water closet, the kind only the rich had, and there was a basin in there as well. The boys shut the door and left their leader in there with the door closed until a little later, when a knock on the door told he was finished. They carried him back to his usual spot beside the fire, directly under one of the lamps.

"And mornin' t'ye, young'un," Bazie said genially.

"Mornin' Bazie," Skif replied, wondering with all his might just how anyone had gotten a water closet built down here, and where Bazie had gotten the money to do so. And why—

"Skif, ye're low mun now—'tis yer task t' fetch water fer privy an' all," said Bazie, which answered at least the question of where the water for flushing came from. "An' t'will be yer task t' keep it full. Which—" he added pointedly, "—it needs now."

"Yessir," Skif said obediently, and went for the buckets. Well, at least one thing hadn't changed—here he was, fetching water first thing in the morning!

It took about three trips to fill the tank above the privy and the pitcher at the basin, and another trip to fill the water butt that served for everything except the wash boiler. By that time all three boys were up and tidying the room at Bazie's direction. After a breakfast of hard-boiled eggs and tea, he ordered them all to strip down and wash off, using the soapy laundry water and old pieces of towel which were dropped back into the wash cauldron when they were done. Then, much to Skif's utter amazement, instead of putting their old clothing on, they all got *new,* clean clothing—smallclothes and all—from the same cupboard as his outfit from yesterday had come out of. Their old clothing went straight into the piles waiting to be washed.

"What's on yer mind, young'un?" Bazie asked as he tried to keep his eyes from bulging.

"D'we—get new duds *ev'ry* day?" he asked, hardly able to believe it.

"D'pends on how hard ye bin workin'," Bazie replied, "But aye, an' it'll be ev' third day at least. Ye're dirty, ye stan' out. Ye canna stan' out—an' mind wut I tol' ye 'bout *smell.*"

Skif minded very well, and he couldn't believe how thorough Bazie was; it was brilliant, really.

"(Thas' why yon fancy privy—" Raf said with a chuckle.

"Heh. 'Twas coz *ye* didn' fancy carryin' me t' t'other, up an' down stair," Bazie countered, and they both laughed. "but aye, could'a had earth closet, or jest dropped privy down t'sewer 'thout it bein' water closet, but there'd be stink, ye ken, an' that'd be on us an' on t'goods we washed, eh? So we got mun t' put in water closet when' we took't this place."

Raf sighed. "Took a mort'o th' glim, it did," he said wistfully. "Didn' know ye'd saved tha' much, ye ol' skinflint."

"Kep't fer when we needed't," Bazie replied. "Yer wuz liddler nor th' young'un. Had Ames an' Jodri an' Willem then—an' we made 't up quick now."

"Wut happened t' *them?*" Skif asked cautiously, fearing to uncover some old, bad news.

But Bazie laughed. "Ames's off! Took't up wi' some travelin' show, run's t' cup'n'ball lay, liftin' i' th' crowd. Jodri, 'e's on 'is own, took't t' sum place t'South. An' Willem made th' big 'un—got hisself th' big haul, an' smart 'nuff t' say, *thassit.* Bought hisself big 'ouse uv flats, like this'un, on'y in better part uv town, lives i' part an' rents out t'rest. Set fer life." Bazie chuckled, and Skif sighed with relief. If Bazie wasn't lying—and there was no reason to think that he was—then his "pupils" had done well for themselves.

And so should he.

It also spoke well that Bazie was perfectly pleased about their success and didn't begrudge them their independence.

"Nah, young'un, ye did good yestiddy, but 'tis in m'mind that mebbe ye shouldn' be seed fer a bit?" Bazie made a question out of it, and Skif was in total agreement with him.

"If th' Guard's got inta it—what wi' th' girl Maisie an' all—mebbe they lookin' fer me," Skif replied. "Ol' Kalchan, well, 'e got hisself in bad deep, an' Guard'll be lookin' fer witness t' whut 'e done. An' ol' Londer, *'e'll* be lookin' fer me t'shet me up."

"No doubt. Mebbe—permanent." Bazie lost that expression of pleasant affability that Skif had become accustomed to. "I know sumthin' uv ol' Londer, an'—mebbe *'e* wouldn' dirty 'is 'ands personal, but 'e knows plenty as would take a 'int 'bout gettin' ye quiet."

Skif shuddered. He had no doubt about that. "'F I'm not 'bout, 'e'll let ol' Kalchan 'ang. Specially 'f Kalchan don' ever wake up. An' 'e'll say, 'e didn' know nothin' 'bout th' girl, an' no one t' say otherwise."

Londer had three sons, after all. He could afford to lose one.

Hellfires, 'e'll prolly get a girl and breed him a couple more, just t'be on th'safe side, Skif thought with disgust. He rather doubted that his uncle's long-dead spouse had enjoyed a love match with the man, for Londer never mentioned or even thought of her so far as he could tell. And Londer wouldn't have any trouble finding another bride either. All he had to do was go down to the neighborhood where the Hollybush had been or one like it, and he could buy himself a wife with a single gold piece. There were dozens of husbands who would sell him their own wives, or their daughters, brothers who would sell sisters, dozens of women who would sell him their own selves.

Well, that was hardly anything Skif could do something about.

"I think ye're gonna be m'laundry maid fer a fortn't or so, young'un," Bazie said. Skif was disappointed by that, of course, but there really wasn't any way around it. He had to agree, himself. *He* didn't want to get picked up by the Guard, and he surely didn't want his uncle looking to keep him quiet. There wasn't going to be any excitement in washing up scarves and veils—but he figured he might as well put a good face on it.

"Nawt s'bad," he replied, as cheerfully as he could. "Don' mind doin' laundry, 'specially bein' as it's pretty cold out there."

Raf, Lyle, and Deek looked pretty pleased over the situation, though. Well, they should be, since it got them out of hauling water, washing, and taking out whatever trash couldn't be burned.

"Cheer up," Raf said, clapping him on the back. "Bazie's nawt s'bad comp'ny, eh, Bazie? An' 'tis warm enuf in 'ere, real cozy-like. Better nor that there 'Ollybush, eh?"

"Oh, aye, an' 'e ain't 'eerd all me tales yet," Bazie laughed. "So I got an audience wut won' fall asleep on me!"

One by one, the other boys went out to prowl the streets and see what they could filch, leaving Skif alone with Bazie. Little did Skif guess what lay ahead of him when he finished all the chores Bazie set him— including, to his utter shock, washing the stone floor!—and the last of what Bazie referred to as their "piece goods" were hung up on the lines crisscrossing the ceiling to dry.

Lunchtime had come and gone by then, and the boys had flitted in and out, leaving swag behind to be cleaned and mended, when Bazie said, "Right. Skif, fetch me th' book there—i' th' shelf next t' loaf."

Obediently, Skif went to the set of shelves that held their daily provisions—Bazie never kept much around, because of the rats and mice that couldn't be kept out of a room like this one—and found the book Bazie wanted. It wasn't difficult, since it was the *only* book there, a battered copy of a housewife's compendium of medicines, recipes, and advice lacking a back cover. He brought it over and started to hand it to the old man.

"Nay, nay—" Bazie said. "Sit ye down, 'ere, where light's best, an' read it. Out loud."

Puzzled, but obedient, Skif opened it to the first page and began to read. It was hardly the most fascinating stuff in the world, but Bazie followed his every word, frowning with concentration as he sounded out a few terms that were unfamiliar to him, and correcting him on the one or two occasions when he didn't say the words quite right.

"That'll do," Bazie said with satisfaction when he finished the chapter. "Ye read good 'nuff. Na, get ye bit uv charcoal from fire, an' copy out that fust receipt on table."

"On table?" Skif asked, flabbergasted. "That'll make right mess!"

"An' ye kin wash't off, after," Bazie countered, in a tone that brooked no argument. So Skif fished out a burned bit of stick and did as he was told, with Bazie leaning as far forward as he could to see just how neat Skif's writing was.

"That'll do," he said again, when Skif finished. "Wash that, but don' drop th' charcoal. Ye're gonna do sums."

"*Sums?*" Skif squeaked, turning around to stare at the old man. "*Sums?* Wut good're sums gonna do a *thief?*"

"They're gonna make sure ye ain't cheated by fence, tha's wut," Bazie replied, as sternly—no, far *more* sternly—than ever Beel was. "Ye thin' I'm gonna let ye tak' th' swag t' fence if ye cain't even tell if 's cheated ye? 'Ow ye think me other boys did so well, eh? 'Ow ye think Raf an' Lyle an' Deek knows wut's wut?"

"Aw, Bazie—" Skif wailed.

"An' none uv yer *'Aw, Bazie.'* I ain't havin' no boys here wut cain't do th' bizness. Get th' coal in yer 'and an' sit ye down." The look in Bazie's eye warned Skif that if he argued, he might find himself out on the street, promises or no promises. With a groan, he bent over the scrubbed table, and prepared to reveal the depth of his ignorance.

And it was abysmal. It wasn't long before Bazie called a halt to the proceedings, with Skif wondering the whole time if Bazie wasn't going to reconsider, now that he knew what a dunce his "new boy" was.

"Skif, Skif, Skif," Bazie sighed, looking pained. "Oh, lad—tell me 'ow 'tis summun as smart as ye are got t' be so iggnerent."

"I didn' wan' miss me breakfust," Skif said humbly, head hanging in shame. "T Queen sez ever' young'un whut's still takin' lessons gets breakfust. Niver did like sums, so's easy 'nuff not t' learn 'em."

Silence from Bazie for a moment, then, much to Skif's relief, a chuckle. "Well, 'tis 'onest 'nuff answer, an' nay so stupid a one," Bazie replied. "Well, young'un, ye're 'bout t' learn them sums, an' learn 'em t'hard way."

"The hard way," Skif soon learned, was to get them by rote.

Bazie drilled him. And drilled him. And then, when he grew hoarse and Skif thought he *might be* done for the day, at least, Bazie paused only long enough for a mug of hot tea to lubricate his throat and began the drill all over again. Only when Skif was mentally exhausted did Bazie give over, and at that point, Skif was only too pleased to haul water instead of reckoning his four-times table.

Shortly after that, Lyle returned with the makings of dinner and helped Skif put together a satisfying meal of bacon, day-old bread, and apples. As the bacon fried and the bread toasted, the other two appeared with a new lot of loot. Raf brought in more sleeves—this lot was a bit worn and threadbare about the hems, but Bazie examined them and gave it as his opinion that he could make a sort of trim out of some of them that would serve to cover the worn parts, making them look new.

Deek brought back only a couple of scarves and kerchiefs, but a great deal of news for Skif.

"Yer Nuncle Londer's 'angin' 'is boy Kalchan out t' twist on 'is own, which I guess we all figgered," he announced, as Skif and Lyle tucked thick slabs of bacon between two pieces of toasted bread and added mustard before handing them around. "It don' look like ol' Kalchan's gonna be much like hisself, though. Healers say 'is skull wuz fair cracked, an' they figger 'is brains is addled. They reckon 'e'll be good fer nowt but stone pickin' fer 'is life, an' I reckon they'll put 'im out wi' sum farmer or 'tother."

Skif snorted. "'E wuz no prize anyroad," he countered. "But if 'e's addled, reckon 'e cain't conterdick Nuncle Londer." But it was an odd thought. Kalchan, who never turned his hand to any physical labor if he could help it, eking out the rest of his life in the hard and tedious work of picking stones out of farm fields to make them easier to plow. Such work was endless, or so he'd heard; it seemed that no matter how many stones one dug out of a given field, there were always more working themselves to the surface.

Serves 'im right. It might not be a punishment that accurately fit the crime, but it suited Skif. His only regret was that, once again, Uncle Londer was going to escape the consequences.

But it don' bother me 'nuff that I wanta go talk t' Guard about it.

The new owner of the Hollybush had already moved his own people in. The cook was gone, no one knew where, but possibly still in Guard custody. The Hollybush was back in business, but with slightly better food and drink and slightly higher prices, or so Deek's sources had told him. The new people were a hard-faced woman who acted as cook, and her henpecked husband who managed the drink, and their three grown children. Rumor had it that the two daughters, who acted as serving wenches, could be had for a modest price, plying their trade in the curtained-off alcove that had served Maisie as a sleeping cubby. Given that there were probably no wages being paid to the children, plus the added income brought in by the daughters, the place would probably remain profitable despite higher prices that would drive some customers elsewhere.

What was important to Skif was that there was no point in going back after his meager belongings; by now anyone who was grasping enough to serve as madam to her own daughters would have claimed everything usable for herself.

Well, they were welcome to it.

"'F I nivir 'ear uv m'nuncle agin, 'twill be too soon," Skif proclaimed loudly. "An' whoivir's got the 'Ollybush kin 'ave it, much good may't do 'em. 'Eard awt uv Maisie, though?"

"Yer cuz Beel, wut's wi' th' Temple, took 'er, they sez," Deek told him. "Cleaned 'er up, 'ad 'Ealers wi' 'er. They sez she's t'work i' Temple, i' kitchen, mebbe scrubbin' an' cleanin'."

"She nivir did me 'arm," Skif observed slowly. "Nawt thet she 'ad more'n a scatterin' uv wits t' begin wi'. Ol' Beel—'e dun me a good turn, reckon 'e's dun wut 'e cud fer Maisie."

"Like I sed," Bazie put in, when comment seemed called for. "Niver know wut a mon'll do, when 'e gets in temple. I reckon ol' Londer ain' gonna be too pleased wi' yon Beel from 'ere on."

Skif smiled slowly. "Reckon yer right, Bazie."

The next several days passed much as the first had. Skif had originally been more than a little cautious around Bazie, especially when he found himself alone with the man. Crippled or not, Skif was in Bazie's control, and there was always the possibility that Bazie's interests in his boys went beyond the obvious. But Bazie never once showed anything but an honest friendliness that was both nurturing and practical. If Skif had ever known a real father, he would have recognized the odd feelings he was having now as being those of a son for a caring father—and he would have seen that Bazie's actions were like those of a caring father for his sons. He only knew that he liked Bazie enormously, and he trusted the man more and more with every moment. For his part, Bazie pretty much took care of his own needs, requiring only to be carried to and from the water closet. Skif was impressed by how calmly self-sufficient he was. He had guessed by now that Bazie was at least forty or fifty years old, and yet he never *seemed* old.

There was one thing, however, that Bazie always insisted on which seemed rather odd to Skif. One of his daily chores was to set a handful of wheat to soaking, and rinse the sprouting grains from previous days. When the sprouts got to a certain length, Bazie would eat them. He didn't seem to like them very much, but he doggedly munched them down.

"'F ye don' like tha' muck, why'd ye eat it ev' day?" Skif finally asked.

"'Cuz I like m' teeth," Bazie said shortly. "'F I don' eat tha' muck, seein' as I niver sees th' sun, 'twon't be long 'fore I lose m'teeth an' gets sick. Tha's wut Healer tol' me fust time m' teeth started bleedin' an' I got sick. Mucky grass 's cheapest stuff 'round, so's tha's wut I eat in winter. Summer, 'course, they's good stuff i' market."

As the days pa'ssed, Skif finally grew bold enough to voice some of his curiosity about this most curious of situations. Besides, getting Bazie to talk made a welcome break from being drilled in sums as he scrubbed or stirred the laundry kettle.

At first, his questions were about commonplaces, but eventually he got up the courage to start asking more personal things. And, finally, he asked the most important of all.

"Bazie—wut 'appened t' yer legs?" he ventured, and waited, apprehensively, for a hurt or angry reply.

But Bazie voiced neither. Instead, he gazed at Skif for a moment. "'Tis a long story, but 'tothers 'ave 'eard it, an' likely they'll figger it oughta be me 'as tells ye." He paused. "Ye ever 'ear uv th' Tedrel Wars?"

Skif shook his head.

"Thought not." Bazie sighed gustily. "Wuz back yon twenny yearn, easy, mebbe thutty. Well, I wuz in't. Tedrel meres—tha's mercenaries, they's people wut fights wars fer money, fer them as don' figger on doin' the fightin' thesselves—they wuz paid t'come up from south, t' fight 'gainst Valdemar fer Karse. On'y 'twasn't t' be known thet they wuz doin' it fer Karse; they wuz a lot uv promises made 'bout Tedrels gettin' t' hev t'half uv Valdemar when they won." He shook his head. "Daft. 'Course, I didn' know thet. I wuz young 'n dumb, didn' think about nawt but loot an' wimmin."

"You wuz with 'em?" Skif asked, turning to look at him, mouth agape.

"Oh, aye. Stupid." He shook his head. "Furst fight, practic'ly, got m' legs took off at knee. Didn' know then if 'twas good luck thet I lived, or bad. Got took up wi' rest uv prisoners, an' when war wuz over, didn' hev nowhere t' go. On'y I wuz in meres cuz I wuz caught thievin' an' had t' 'ide, so me'n a couple other young fools decided we stick t'gether an' see 'f I cud teach 'em wut I knew 'bout thievin'. So we did, an' I did."

"Wut 'appened to 'em?" Skif asked.

Bazie shrugged. "Went back 'ome when they had th' glim, an' by then, I 'ad young Ames 'n Jodri, an' I reckoned I 'ad a good thing. I teach the young 'uns an' they share th' swag. Works out." He smiled—a little tightly. "Sorta like gettin' some uv th' loot I wuz promised. Heh.

Mebbe I ain't got part uv Valdemar, but Valdemar's still feedin' me. An' I'm still alive, so I reckon I'm doin' all right."

Skif pondered all of that; it was kind of interesting. "So, how come ye take such good care uv us, eh?" he asked.

Bazie laughed aloud. "An' ye'd do what if I didn'? Run off, right? 'Sides, I kinda like the comp'ny. 'Ad a good fam'ly an' I miss it. Me da wuz a good 'un, on'y 'e got 'urt, an' died, an' I 'ad t' do wut I culd fer me an' mum an'm' brothers—till they got sick an' died i' plague. Allus wished I'd 'ad family uv me own, on'y they's nuthin' but hoors wi' merc army, and wut wimmin 'ud hev a fam'ly wi' me now?" He shrugged. "So I reckon I make me own fam'ly, eh?"

"They sez, i' temple," Skif ventured, "thet friends is th' fam'ly ye kin choose. I sure *hellfires* wouldn' hev chose m' nuncle, nor Kalchan. Reckon this way's a bit better."

He was rewarded by a beaming smile from Bazie—and perhaps, just a hint of moisture in his eyes, hastily and covertly removed with a swipe of the hand. "Aye," Bazie agreed. "Reckon tha's right."

Skif quickly turned his questions to other topics, mostly about life as a mercenary, which Bazie readily answered.

"'Tis a life fer the young'n stupid, mostly, I'm thinkin'," he admitted. "Leastwise, wuz wi' Tedrels. Seems t' me, if yer gonna fight, mebbe ye shouldn' be fightin' fer things summun else thinks is 'portant. But 'twas lively. Did a mort'a travelin', though 'twas mostly on shank's mare. Got fed reg'lar. Seems t' me that lot uv lads joined thinkin' they wuz gonna get rich, an' I knew thet wouldn' 'appen. Reg'lar merc, 'e don' get rich, 'specially not Tedrels."

"Why?" Skif wanted to know.

Bazie laughed. "'Cause Tedrels wuzn't Guild mercs, tha's why! Tedrels, they sez, useta be in they own land, but got run out. So they took up fightin' fer people, th' whole lot uv 'em. By time I 'id out wi' em, Tedrels took wut nobuddy else would, cuz th' fights they took't weren't real smart. Ain't no Guild merc comp'ny wud fight 'gainst Valdemar! And ain't no Guild comp'ny wud fight *for* Karse. They's bunch uv fanatics, an' they ain't too good t'their own folk." He pondered for a moment. "Ye know, I kinda wondered 'f they figgered t' use us up, so's they wouldn' hev t' pay us. But I guess Cap'n wuz pretty desp'rate, so they took't th' job." He shook his head. "I'druther be'n 'onest thief. I figger'd t' make m'self scarce when th' coast wuz clear, on'y it niver wuz, an' they allus 'ad an eye lookin' fer deserters."

"Huh. So how come they ain't no problem gettin' folks fer Guard, 'f goin't' fight's a dumb thing?" Skif wanted to know.

"Oh, th' Guard, that's different," Bazie acknowledged. "They's got 'onor. When they ain't 'elpin' beaks, they's watchin' Border, cleanin' out bandits an' slavers." He shook his head. "Got no use fer bandits an' slavers. Us, we on'y take frum people kin afford a bit took't frum 'em. Tha's rule, right?"

Skif nodded; he'd already been given that rule numerous times. Here in the poorer part of town, the only legitimate targets, by Bazie's rules, were the people like Kalchan and Uncle Londer. Most thefts were out of the pockets and possessions of those who had the money to spare for luxury.

"Bandits an' slavers, they's hurtin' people nor better orf than us'n," Bazie declared. "So, bein' in Guard's 'onor'ble. An' Valdemar Guard takes care uv their own, so's not so daft t' join op."

This was getting altogether too confusing and complicated for Skif, and evidently Bazie saw from his expression that he was sorely puzzled.

"Don' worry 'bout it fer now," he cautioned, "'Tis all complisticated, an' real 'ard t' 'splain. 'Ellfires, sometimes I cain't figger it out."

Skif pursed his lips, but decided that Bazie was probably right. There was just far too much in life that was altogether too complicated to try and work out. Like religion—if the Gods cared so much about people, why did they allow the Kalchans and the Londers—and worse—to go on doing what they did? Why wasn't everybody fed and warm and happy? Why were there rich people who had *piles* more things than they needed, and people like him who didn't have anything?

It was all far more than he could wrap his mind around, and eventually he just had to give up on it all.

Maybe someday he'd have some answers. For right now, he had food in his belly, a warm place to sleep, and friends.

And what more could anyone ask for, really? Gods and honor and all the rest of that stuff could go hang. He would put his loyalty with those who earned it.

6

Skif was excited; finally, two weeks after he had officially joined the gang, something he had been hoping for all along happened. Bazie decided that when the boys returned from their own forays into the streets, although his talent probably lay in the area of burglary, he ought to have training in "the liftin' lay"—the art of the pickpocket.

All three of the boys were enthusiastic when Bazie put it to them. "'E might's well as not!" Raf exclaimed. "Ain't no 'arm, an' 'e might 'ave th' touch arter all."

Deek nodded. "'Sides, Bazie, any mun kin run shake'n'snatch. An' fer that, we orter 'ave a new'un anyroad."

So Raf and Deek got out some bits and pieces from various cupboards, and began to put together a most peculiar object. When they were done, there was something like a headless man standing in the middle of their room, one hung all over with bells.

"There!" Bazie said, looking at their handiwork with pleasure. "Mind, yon's not wut a mun wants t' 'ave in 'is place when beaks come callin'. Dead giveaway, that. But I do sez, I done good work wi' that lad. Ye'll no find a better 'un this side uv th' Border."

So Bazie had built this thing in the first place? It was very sturdy, in spite of being assembled from a lot of apparently disparate bits. In the mannequin's pockets were handkerchiefs, around his "neck" was a kerchief, and he had two belt pouches slung from his belt and a third tucked into the breast of his tunic.

Skif could not imagine how anyone could get at any of these tempting articles. Even the belt pouches were slung right under the mannequin's stuffed arm. But Raf, their expert, was about to show him.

"Watch close, young 'un," Bazie chuckled. "Yon Raf's slick."

He strolled up to stand beside the mannequin, looking from side to side as if he was observing the traffic in a street. Meanwhile—without ever so much as glancing at his quarry—his hand moved very, very slowly toward one of the handkerchiefs just barely hanging out of a pocket. Thread by thread, almost, he delicately removed it, and when it fell free of the mannequin's pocket, he whisked it into his own so quickly it seemed to vanish. As slowly as it had seemed to move, the whole business had not taken very long—certainly it was reasonable to think that a target would have remained standing beside the thief for that period of time, especially in a crowd or at the side of a busy street with a lot of traffic on it.

"Tha's th' 'ard way," Bazie told Skif, who watched with wide eyes. "Raf, 'e's th' best I ivir showed. 'E's got th' touch, fer certain-sure."

Now Raf sidled up to the other side of the mannequin, still casual and calm; he pretended to point at something, and while the target's attention was presumably distracted for a moment, out came a knife no bigger than a finger, and between one breath and the next, the strings of both belt pouches had been slit and knife and pouches were in Raf's pocket.

And all without jingling a single bell.

Now it was Lyle's turn, and he extracted the remaining handkerchief without difficulty, although he was not as smooth as Raf. "I'm not near that good," Deek said. "So I'm got t' do th' shake'n'snatch. Tha' takes two."

He got up, and he and Lyle advanced on the mannequin together. Then Lyle pretended to stumble and fell against it, setting all the bells jingling; as it fell into him, Deek grabbed for it. "'Ey there, lad!" he exclaimed. "Steady on! An' you—watch where yer goin', you! Mussin' up a gennelmun like that!"

Skif would have expected Deek to pretend to brush the mannequin off, and get hold of his goods that way, but Deek did nothing of the sort. He simply set it straight. They both moved off, but now the mannequin no longer had the kerchief around its neck, and Deek held up both the kerchief and the pouch that had been tucked inside its tunic triumphantly.

"Tha's th' easy road, but riskier," Bazie noted. "Chance is, if mun figgers 'e's been lifted, 'e'll send beaks lookin' fer th' shaker—tha's Lyle."

"An' I'm be clean," Lyle pointed out. "Ain't nothin' on me, an' beak'll let me go."

"But if 'e knows th' liftin' lay, it'll be Deek 'e'll set beak on, an' Deek ain't clean. Or mun might even be sharp 'nuff t' figger 'twas both on 'em," Bazie cautioned. "Ye run th' shake'n'snatch, ye pick yer cony careful. Gotta be one as is wuth it, got 'nuf glim t' take th' risk, but one as ain't too smart, ye ken? An' do't when's a mort uv crowd, but not so's ye cain't get slip-put away."

Skif nodded solemnly.

"Na, 'tis yer turn. Jest wipes, fer now."

Skif then spent a humbling evening, trying to extract handkerchiefs from the mannequin's pocket without setting off the bells. Try as he might, with sweat matting his hair from the strain, he could not manage to set off less than two. And here he'd thought that he'd been working hard, hauling water and doing laundry, or going over walls and roofs with Deek! That had been a joke compared with this!

At length, Bazie took pity on him. "That'll be 'nuff, lad," he said, as Skif sagged with mingled weariness and defeat. "Ye done not bad, fer th' fust time. Ye'll get better, ye ken. Put yon dummy i't' corner, an' leave 'im fer now. Time fer a bit uv supper."

Skif was glad to do so. It was beginning to occur to him that the life of a thief was not as easy as most people believed, and most thieves pretended. The amount of skill it took was amazing; the amount of work to acquire that skill more than he had imagined. Not that he was going to give up!

I'll get this if 't kills me.

"So, wha's news, m'lads?" Bazie asked, deftly slicing paper-thin wafers of sweet onion. This was going to be a good supper tonight, and they were all looking forward to it. Deek and Skif had done well for the little gang.

Lyle sliced bread and spread it with butter that Skif had gotten right out of a fancy inn's kitchen that very morning. He and Deek had been down in the part of town where the best inns and taverns were, actually just passing through, when one of those strokes of luck occurred that could never have been planned for.

The inn next to the one they had been passing had caught fire—they never found out why, only saw the flames go roaring up and heard the hue and cry. Everyone in the untouched place they'd stopped beside, staff and customers alike, had gone rushing out—either to help or to gawk—and he and Deek had slipped inside in the confusion.

Somehow, without having a plan, they'd gotten in, snatched the right things, and gotten out within moments. For one thing, they had gone straight to the kitchen as the best bet. Taking money was out of the question; they didn't know where the till was. There was no time to search for valuable property left behind in the confusion. Without discussion, they had gone for what they needed, where they knew they would find something worth taking.

The kitchen.

Like the rest of the inn, it was deserted—when the chief cook left, everyone else had taken the excuse to run out, too. There must have been a big delivery not long before, since the kitchen was full of unwrapped and partially unwrapped parcels of food.

It was like being turned loose in the best market in town. Skif had grabbed a wrapped block of butter, a cone of sugar, and a ham, and a handful of the brown paper the stuff had come wrapped in. Deek had gone for a whole big dry-cured hard sausage, a string of smaller ones, and half a wheel of cheese. Then out the back and over the wall they went, into an alley that was full of smoke and hid them beautifully. As soon as they were in the smoke, Skif and Deek pulled out the string bags they always brought with them just in case something in the nature of foodstuffs presented itself. Quickly wrapping up the articles in paper under cover of the smoke, they stuffed their booty into the bags, then came running out of the smoke into the crowd, coughing and wheezing far more than was necessary, acting like innocents who'd gone shopping for their mums and been caught in the alley. No one paid them any mind—they were all too busy ogling the fire and the bucket brigade or craning their necks to see if the fire brigade had gotten to the burning inn yet. Skif and Deek had strolled homeward openly, carrying enough food to last them all for weeks. All of it luxury stuff, too—not the sort of thing they got to taste more than once in a while. They had eggs a lot, since they were pretty cheap, with just about anyone who had a bit of space keeping pigeons or chickens, even in the city. Bread was at every meal; bread was the staple of even the poorest diets.

Roots like tatties and neeps were cheap enough, too, and cabbage, and onions—even old Kalchan had those at the inn. Dried pease and beans made a good soup, and Kalchan had those, too, though more often than not they were moldy.

Skif had eaten better with Bazie than he ever had in his life, even allowing for what he'd snitched from Lord Orthallen's kitchen. Good butter, though—butter that was all cream and not mixed half-and-half with lard—they didn't see much of that. Deek's cheese wasn't the cheap stuff that they generally got, made after the cream had been skimmed from the milk. And as for ham and sausages—sausages where you didn't have to think twice about what might have gone into them—well, those were food for the rich. And sugar—

Skif had never tasted sugar until he started snitching at Lord

Orthallen's table. Bazie had a little screw of paper with some, and once in a while they all got a bit in their tea. Now they'd be able to sweeten their tea at every meal.

Each of them had a slice of bread well buttered, with a thin slice of onion atop, and a slice of hard sausage atop that. The aroma of sage and savory from the sausage made Skif's mouth water. Bazie had put some of his sprouting beans on his slice, and had taken a second slice of buttered bread to hold it all together. Skif hoped the sprouts wouldn't taste bad with all that good stuff in and around it. They were going to eat like kings for a while.

"Kalchan croaked." That was from Lyle, with his mouth full. "They sez. Nobuddy sez nothin' 'bout Londer. I ast 'round 'bout Skif. Don' seem nobuddy's lookin' fer 'im now. Reckon they figger 'e saw t'set-to an' run off."

"Huh." Skif shrugged. "Tol' ye about th' fire. Tha's all we saw." Deek nodded agreement, but his mouth was full, so he added nothing.

"White shirt's sniffin' 'round Little Puddin' Lane," said Raf. "Dunno why; askin' a mort'uv questions, they sez."

Huh. Wonder what Herald wants down there? There wasn't anything down in that part of town that a Herald should have been interested in; Little Pudding Lane was just a short step above the neighborhood of the Hollybush so far as poverty went.

"Stay clear uv them for now," Bazie advised. "They got ways'uv tellin who's lyin'."

"No fear there!" Raf promised. "Ain't gonna mess wi' no witchy white shirt!"

Be stupid to, Skif reflected. Not that he'd ever actually seen a Herald, except once, passing at a distance. Even then, he wasn't sure it had been a Herald. It could just have been a pale-colored horse.

Bazie shrugged. "Dunno they be witchy, jest sharpish. Ah, like's not, 'tis summat got nawt t'do wi' likes uv us. When any'un seed a white shirt down *hare*, eh?"

"Not so's I kin 'member," Raf, the oldest, said at last. Skif and Deek both shook their heads.

"Saw 'un onct, passin' through," Lyle offered, and grinned.

"Passin' fast, too! Reckon had burr under 'is saddle!"

"White shirt's don' bother wi' us," Bazie said with certainty, and finished the last bite of his supper with great satisfaction. "Slavers, raiders, aye. Big gang'uv bandits, aye. E'en summat highwayman, e'en footpad, 'f 'e's stupid 'nuff to murder along'uv robbin'. But us? A bit'uv cheese here, a wipe there? Nothin' fer them. 'Tis th' beaks we gotta watch for. But all th' same—" he finished, brow wrinkling, "steer clear'uv 'em. They nivir done me no 'arm, e'en wi' me an' the' rest fightin' 'em, but they nivir done me no favors either, an' Karsites allus said they was uncanny." He laughed. "Well, *demons* is wut they said, but figger the source!"

When Skif went to bed that night, though, he wondered what would have brought a "white shirt"—a Herald—down as close to their territory as Little Pudding Lane. It had to be something important, for as Bazie said, the Heralds didn't bother themselves about petty thieves as long as it was only a crime against property and not against a person.

Bazie had strict rules about *that;* too—not the least because if by some horrible accident someone was hurt, it could be a hanging offense. It made no sense to court that kind of trouble all for the sake of some loot you could get another time. Better to drop everything and run if it all went bad. Even if you were one of a team, there was no point in coming to the rescue when *that* would only mean that two of you would be caught instead of one.

The worst that would happen to any of them would be some time in gaol, and perhaps a beating administered by the victim; only Raf had a previous offense against him, and he would take care to give another name if he was caught. Bazie had coached Skif on this with great care. The very best ploy was to get rid of anything you had on you, so you'd be clean. If you couldn't do that, the next best was to act scared, and cry and carry on and say that you were starving, had no job, and couldn't get one, then produce a convincing cough as if you were very sick. None of them were so well fed that they looked prosperous, though none of them ever went hungry either, and they could probably carry the story off as long as the beaks didn't get involved. Lyle, with his innocent face and ability to make his eyes seem twice their size, had gotten away with that more than once.

Wish I could, Skif thought with envy. But—Lyle was another on the liftin' lay, and it was easier to get away with that when you were caught out on the street than it was when you were caught in someone's house.

Raf was sitting up with Bazie, although Deek and Lyle had already gone to bed. Their voices came easily through the shutters of his bed. "Lissen, Bazie, Midwinter Fair's a-comin', an' I'm thinkin' we should be workin' it in twos," Raf said quietly. "One liftin', an' one t'carry. Mebbe I'm bein' nervy, but I don' like t'idea uv yon white shirt sniffin' round."

"You reckon?" Bazie sounded interested. "Hadn' tried that afore, hev we?"

"Ain't's risky. Reckon I take's the young'un, Lyle take Deek. An *ev'ry* time we gets a lift, we takes it t' carrier. Carrier brings it here. Then no matter how wrong't all goes, ain't no'un caught wi' more'n one lift on'im." Raf sounded very sure of himself, and truth to tell, Skif agreed with him. It would be a lot more work that way for the carrier, who would have to run back and forth between wherever the Fair they were working was being held, and here, but Raf was right. No matter what happened, no matter what went wrong, no one would be caught with more loot than a single kerchief or pouch.

"Som'thin' got ye spooked?" Bazie asked shrewdly. Skif could imagine Raf's shrug. "Can't 'magine white shirts lookin' fer lifters."

"Mebbe. Somethin' i' th' air. Not like white shirts t' be i' this t' th' chancy parts'uv town. Somethin's up. An'—" Raf paused. "Lots'uv forners pretendin' not the forners lurkin' about, i'taverns, askin' questions, little too casual-like."

"Na, ye stay clear'uv *them*, boy!" There was real alarm in Bazie's voice. "Tha's stuff fer th' highborns! Ain't no call t'get mixed up wi' them!"

"Eh." Raf agreed, but he still sounded worried. "Bazie, ye gotta wonder—how long afore *their* bizness gets down amongst us? Ye know, whut they sez—rotten apple falls fastest and futhest."

"On'y thin' you an' me an' the likes'uv us got t' 'ave t'do wi' *them* is t' get out uv way when they falls."

And that seemed to be the end of that. Skif was asleep before Raf helped Bazie into bed.

When the Midwinter Fairs began, the first thing they had to do was try and figure out which ones they would work, because every other thief and pickpocket in Haven would be doing the same. Bazie had a shrewd way of eliminating them, based on the number of beaks assigned to each, the general level of prosperity, and the number of drunks by midafternoon. He wanted a moderate number of beaks, a slightly-better-than-middle level of prosperity, and a high level of drunks. So, not too surprisingly, he decided that they should work the Fair associated with the Brewers Guild. He also picked one very large Fair held just outside the city, where there were going to be a large number of tent taverns because it was playing host to a series of contests among performers. Not Bards;

in fact, Bards were excluded. These were to be contests among ordinary musicians with no Gifts.

He chose a third Fair for no reason that Skif could tell, but Raf and Deek grinned over it so broadly that he figured he'd get the joke when he saw it.

The last chosen was the first Fair of the seven days of Midwinter Festival; Lyle went out with Deek early in the afternoon, with Skif and Raf following about a candlemark later.

It was an overcast day, the still air with a soft feeling about it, and humid. The clouds hung low, so low they looked about to touch the roofs of the buildings to either side of the narrow street. Skif kept looking up as they walked down the streets, heading for the square where the Fair had been set up. Weather like this meant snow, the kind that packed together easily.

He wasn't disappointed; it came drifting down shortly after they got on their way, big, fat, fluffy flakes of it.

"Is snow good or bad fer bizness?" Skif asked anxiously. Midwinter had never been more than a date to him before this; he'd avoided the Fairs, since he hadn't any money to spend and kids as ragged as he'd been back in the bad Kalchan days were generally chased away by stall holders and beaks. Why bother to linger about the edges of a place you wouldn't be allowed into? So he hadn't any idea what to expect, or whether weather would make any difference in the number of people crowding the aisles between the stalls.

Raf cast a glance upwards and smiled. "*This* kinda snow's good," he opined. "Gets people playful, belike. Gets 'em thinkin' 'bout fun, an' not 'bout keepin' an eye out. Na, snow wit' a nasty wind, tha's diff'rent. Or colder, tha's diff'rent, too. This's near-perfek. Perfek 'ud be sun, right arter this kinda snow." He scratched his head speculatively. "This weather 'olds, reckon there'll be drink stalls an 'ot food stalls down t'river, too, an' aside summa th' ponds i' fancy parks. People'll be skatin', makin' snow stachoos an' forts, 'avin' snowball fights."

"Kids?" Skif asked. "Littles?"

Raf laughed. "Na, growed people, too! Graybeards, even! I seed 'em!"

Skif could only shake his head at the notion of full-grown adults having the leisure to pursue snow sports.

They heard the Fair long before they saw it, a jangle of instruments, laughter, loud voices, echoing down the narrow street. And when they saw it, it was just a patch of color at the end of the street. Only as they approached it did the patch resolve into people, waving banners, and a couple of tents bedecked with painted signs on canvas.

Obviously, there was far more to it than that to account for all the noise, but that was all they could see at the end of the street.

This was usually the cattle market, where larger livestock was bought and sold once every fortnight. Part of the market—the part where really *fine* horses and stud bulls and prize milch cows were sold—was actually underneath a building on ten tall stone pillars. It was like a fine house where the ground floor had been reserved for stalls for beasts. Skif didn't know what went on in the building atop those pillars, but it was probably some sort of commerce. The rest of the place was just an open square, which on market days had rough wooden pens set up for the more plebeian stock; sheep, goats, donkeys, mules, and those cattle and horses without aristocratic lineage.

As they came to the end of the street, the Fair filled that square and even edged onto the walkways around the perimeter. And the first thing that met Skif's astonished eyes was a woman, in a flounced dress so short he could see her legs up to the thigh, balancing along a rope strung from the eaves of a shop to the staircase of the stone cattle stalls.

"Na, young'un," Raf said in his ear. "Iff'n ye kin do *that*, ye kin call yersel' a roof walker, eh?"

Skif shut his open mouth and followed Raf into the aisles of the Fair. Within a very short time, it became perfectly obvious to him why Bazie had picked *this* Fair for them to prowl. There were next to no women among the patrons, and very little besides food and drink for sale. The drink was *all* alcoholic; mulled ales, wines, and ciders, cold beer, cold wine, and cold spirits of wine, which Skif had only heard of, never seen. The food was all hot, spicy, or salty. The rest of the stalls were uniformly for either entertainment or games of chance. And there were more entertainers in this place than Skif had ever seen in his lifetime. Jugglers, acrobats, musicians—that was only the start of it. There were trick riders, most of them women and attired very like the girl on the rope overhead—a man who did the most astonishing things with a loop of rope—a fire-eater—a sword swallower. And girl dancers, whose costumes were even more abbreviated than the riders! Which was probably why most of the patrons here were men and boys...

The dancers, of which there were two different troupes, and a set of raree shows promising to display the most amazing oddities, held pride of place in the stone cattle stalls. They'd used their tents to fashion canvas-walled rooms beneath the roof, firmly anchored to the stone sides of the stalls, making it impossible to lift the corner for a free look, to the acute disappointment of the boys swarming the place. The rest of the entertainers had to make do with their tents!

Raf found a good place for him to stand out of the way, just beside the stone staircase, where he also had a fine view of the ropedancers. He disappeared into the crowd.

Wake up now, he told himself sternly. *Ye're here t'work, not gawk.*

It was hard, though—so many distractions, what with the dancers going across the rope when the crowd tossed enough in their dish to make it worth their while, with the glimpses of men on stilts at the farther edge of the Fair, the music coming from the dancers' stalls, and the enthusiastic bawling of the tent men, each proclaiming that nothing had ever been seen like the wonders in *his* tent.

Well, certainly Skif had never seen anything like this.

Just as he was starting to get cold, Raf reappeared with a cunningly-made paper cone full of hot chestnuts, which they shared—and under cover of which, Raf passed Skif a fat belt pouch. After Skif had peeled and eaten enough nuts to warm hands and stomach, Raf took back the half-empty cone and loudly told him to run on home.

After a brief whining plaint, Skif trotted off, exactly like a younger brother chased off by an elder. And once away from the Fair, he broke into a loping run. In no time at all he had left the pouch with Bazie to be examined and counted, and he was on his way back, more than warmed up by his exertions.

It took longer for Raf to return the second time; Skif hoped that this meant he was being very careful. He also hoped that by the time he brought back Raf's second or third lift, Bazie would tell him that they'd collected enough for the day. Although this Fair was exciting and completely fascinating, Skif couldn't help being nervous about the composition of the crowd—mostly male, and mostly drinking. It wouldn't take much for an ugly situation to develop.

The ropedancers didn't seem to mind his being there, though, which was a plus; he'd been afraid they might chivvy him off. While he waited for Raf to appear again, he watched them closely, trying to figure out how they did it. There were four of them; two girls, a young man, and a little boy; the latter didn't walk the rope himself, he seemed to be there mostly to balance on the shoulders of the young man.

Reckon since ye cain't see up his skirt fer an extra thrill they figger they gotta have th' little 'un there t'make it more dangerous.

Of the two girls, the youngest was the most skilled; while the older one just walked the rope, stopping midway for some one-footed poses, the younger one had an entire repertoire of tricks. So far Skif had seen her balance on one foot while she drew the other up with her hands to touch her heel against the back of her head, dance a little jig in the middlemost part of the rope, jump up and come down on the rope again, and make three skips with a jump rope out there. It was even-up between her and the older one for the dancers called out most often—the older one was, well, *older,* and had breasts and all, but the younger one was more daring.

It soon became obvious to Skif that the young man and the little boy were there to draw the crowd—they were the ones that went out for free. The girls didn't dance unless there was enough money collected in the tin bucket hung at the side of the stone staircase—and there was an older man with them who emptied it every time one of them went out. Skif thought there was a distinct family resemblance there with all of them.

Just then, Raf came up again, this time with a pair of waxed paper cones full of hot mulled cider. He handed one to Skif.

"Be kerful drinkin'," he cautioned, in a lowered voice. "They's summut in bottom."

"Seen Lyle?" Skif asked in a normal tone. "'E sed 'e'd be 'ere, didn' 'e?"

"Oh, aye, an' 'is mum's gonna be right riled," Raf said cheerfully, as Skif sipped the hot, spicy liquid, fragrant with apples. "'E's 'ad a pair uv beers an' 'e's a-workin' a third."

Lyle's gotten two lifts and Raf saw him working a third? That was good news. By this point Skif understood why Raf had warned him. There was something hard and heavy at the bottom of the cone, heavy enough that if he didn't finish the cider quickly and carefully, the cone might start to disintegrate and leak. "I'm gonna go 'ome an' see'f Mum'll be lettin' us stay past dark," he offered.

Raf gave him a nod. "I be over t'orse dancers," he said, and wandered away as Skif trotted off again.

He continued to sip at the hot cider until he could actually see what was in the bottom. It looked like jewelry—chain, with a seal attached. And from the taste now in the cider, it was silver. He ducked into a blind alley and fished the thing out, dumped the last of the cider and then, thinking, put it back into the paper cone. Nobody as poor as he was would waste waxed paper by throwing it away—it was too useful as a spill for starting fires. So he screwed the thing up into a spill shape with the chain and seal inside, and went on his way again.

Bazie was pleased with the lift, but gave no hint that he was ready for them to stop, so back Skif went again.

Raf had warned him that he might be noticed—by the ropedancers themselves, if no one else—if he went to the same spot a third time. The new meeting point was the tiny corral holding the trick riders; Raf had pointed out a good place the first time they'd gone past, where a farm cart full of hay was pushed up against the corral fence. That was where Skif went, propping hands and chin on the lower railing as he watched one of the riders riding—standing—on the back of a remarkably placid horse.

A heavy hand gripped his shoulder.

Skif jumped—or tried to; with that hand on his shoulder, he couldn't do more than start. Heart racing, he turned his head, expecting a beak. *I'm clean!* he thought, thanking his luck that he was. *I'm clean! 'E cain't do more'n tell me t' get out!*

But it wasn't a beak that held his shoulder. It was his cousin Beel.

"Beel!" he squeaked.

"I'm pleased you recall one family member, Skif," Beel said gravely. "I'd like to know where you have been."

Skif thought quickly. "Wuz runnin' errand, came back, an saw t'fight," he said, trying to look absolutely innocent. "Saw beaks in't, an—well, 'ad t'spook, Beel. Couldn' do nothin', so I 'ad t'spook."

Beel nodded. "But then where have you been? Why didn't you come to—"

Skif took a chance and interrupted. "Beel—I *cain't* go back t' Nuncle Londer," he whispered. "Them beaks, they want me t'tell 'em stuff 'bout Maisie—but ye *know* tha's stuff Nuncle don' want me t'tell!"

The corners of Beel's mouth turned down, but he took his hand from Skif's shoulder. "It would be wrong of me to—put temptation in the path of anyone, let alone my own father," he said reluctantly. He didn't say what temptation, but they both knew what it was. "Just tell me—no, don't tell me where you are and what you're doing—but are you continuing with your lessons, at least?"

Skif groaned, and Beel smiled reluctantly. "Am I! They's wus'n you! Set me a sum, I dare ye!"

"Twelve plus fifteen," Beel asked instantly, knowing that Skif couldn't have added that when he'd run.

"Twenny—" Skif screwed his eyes shut and concentrated. "Twenny-se'en!" He looked up at his cousin triumphantly. Beel lifted his hands, conceding defeat.

"But what should I say if my father asks if I've seen you?" the priest wondered out loud, worriedly. "Lying—"

Skif clambered up into the hay. "Tell 'im ye seed me i' cattle market, then ina farm cart frum t'country," he suggested pertly. "An 'twon't e'en be a fib!"

Now Beel smiled ruefully, and shook his head.

"You're too quick and facile for your own good, Skif," he said. "You worry me. But all right—if my father thinks you've gone and hired yourself out as farm labor, he's not going to bother trying to find you." He rested one hand on Skif's head—in a blessing?—and moved off into the crowd.

Fortunately no one else seemed to have been paying any attention to this interchange. Skif clambered down out of the cart—reluctantly, for the hay had been soft and warm—before anyone from the trick riders' group could scold him for being up there.

He was still sweating, just a little. That had been a narrow escape. How could he ever have guessed that Beel of all people would show up here? This was *not* the sort of atmosphere he'd expect a priest to seek out!

He looked anxiously for Raf, hoping the older boy hadn't been caught. After much too long a wait, he spotted Raf working his way through the crowd coming toward him. The relief was enough to make him feel light-headed.

"Time t' go," Raf said as soon as the two of them were together. "Wut I got now'll gi' Bazie 'nuff, an' I sore yer cuz 'ere."

"I did more'n see 'im," Skif said, as they worked their way out to the street together. He explained what had happened as they walked together toward home.

"Aw, hellfires!" Raf responded, making a motion of wiping his forehead. "Tha's a close'un!"

"Too close," Skif agreed. "I took't chance on Beel bein' a good'un—ye ken 'e warned me, afore th' to-do. An' 'e is, I guess."

"Well, I saw 'im doin' some beggin' fer Temple; guess tha's 'ut brung 'im there," Raf said. "I'd made lift, an' I nipped off t' look fer ye."

It had been far too close a call and Skif's heart was still beating hard. But at least they'd made some good lifts today, and no harm done.

Skif had managed—by luck and a glib tongue—to squeak out of danger again.

7

It was a good, dark night—not quite moonless, but it had been a day moon, shining in the blue sky half the afternoon, and it would be down before Skif was done with tonight's job. Right now, the shadows were perfect for getting into his target. Skif sniffed the air appreciatively, but silently; it was crisp and cold, with a hint of wood smoke, but not as much as there would have been if all of the fireplaces in his target house were running. With a dry autumn this year, there was no treacherous ice on the roof or tops of the walls. In the fall the first bit of cold kept people off the street at night and tucked up in a cozy tavern, instead of wandering about, taking a chance of getting run off by the Watch for the fun of gawking at the show homes of the rich. All except for the rich themselves, of course, who were making the rounds of their estates—if they had them—or their friends' estates. It was hunting season, and no one who was anyone would be caught dead in Haven at this time of year, not when they could go out to the country and use the slaughter of wild game as an excuse to have house parties.

It was very strange. Granted, wild game was a luxury, and featured prominently in the menus of the rich. But surely their foresters and servants could do a better job of going after it than people who didn't hunt for a living.

Still, all to the good. A smart lad with the wit to go and hold horses outside the Great Houses always knew who was having a country-house party and who was going to it. When the master was away, the servants left behind took their own sort of holiday, and getting into and out of a place was child's play.

Well, it was if the "child" was Skif.

Hidden in a join of two walls, where one stuck out a little farther than the other and left a vertical slot of dark shadow, Skif waited until the Watch passed. There was always the Nightwatch to reckon with, in the fine neighborhoods. When he'd worked by day, snatching things out of the laundries of many of the fancy houses he now robbed, he hadn't had to worry about the Nightwatch.

Not that he worried too much about them now—so long as he knew the schedule. He kept his head turned away as they passed with their lantern to keep from having his night vision ruined, then nicked across the top of Jesolon's wall to the top of Kalink's.

The home of the arrogant "new money" grain merchant Kalink was his goal tonight. The irony was that *this* Kalink wasn't even the one who made the money—that had been the work of the old man, who according to gossip had been perfectly content to live quietly, if comfortably, in the country until he died. Not the son, though. Gossip grudgingly admitted he had as good a head for business as the old man, maybe better, but *he* wasn't going to molder in the countryside, not he! He got himself a show-wife, long on looks and short on wits, and had this brand new manor house built right up against Jesolon's, first tearing down the smaller place that had been there. He hadn't been content to simply add on—no, nothing was good enough for him but brand new, nor would he hear any advice on the subject. It didn't matter to *him* that having walls run right up to the side of a house just made a road for a thief to walk on—hadn't he the very latest in locks and catches and other theft-foiling hardware? Hadn't he ornamental ironwork on all the windows?

Hasn't he left enough room between them bars to put a donkey through? Skif snickered to himself, as he slipped over the roof of the stable to the uneven triangle of shadow just against the wall of the house that the moon wouldn't reach at this time of night. He managed it all without a hint of sound, not the rattle of a stone, not the slip of a slate. In his all-black "sneak suit," with hands in black gloves and face wrapped in a black scarf, smeared with charcoal where the scarf didn't reach, the only part of him visible was his eyes.

Oh, yes, indeed, Kalink was "new money" in Haven and proud of it. Proud enough to have halved the space where his garden had been in order to put in a stable for a single horse, the fool! True enough, a horse was a very expensive, very conspicuous luxury in the city, but *one* horse would only pull a cart (which there was no room for) or a tiny, two-wheeled, half-carriage called a "gig," that would only carry two people at a time (and which barely fit in the stable with the horse). Your servants couldn't use it for real shopping, it was fair useless for transporting anything large or heavy, if you had a country estate or summer home as Kalink did, you still had to hire a wagon to carry your baggage when you went back for hunting season or summer. You had to drive it yourself, for there wasn't room for a driver. It was good for two things—for arriving at a fancy "do" with the wife, and for the wife or a daughter to go off with a servant to drive to make her daytime social calls. If wife or daughter couldn't drive, the only way your women could use it for *their* shopping was if they arranged for whatever they bought to be delivered.

Which was, of course, what Kalink's brainless bit of a show-wife always did, though she did have wit enough to be able to drive herself, so she took her personal maid instead of a manservant. Skif's lip curled in contempt. *Very* nice.

And in exchange for this ostentatious bit of status-flaunting merchandise, you lost half your garden, and had to have an extra boy around to drive and to tend the creature from dusk to dawn, just to keep the beast from stinking up the neighborhood and drawing flies.

The show-wife had a weakness for jewelry, and brainless though she might be, she had a true expert's eye for picking out the best. And a boy who volunteered to hold m'lady's horse while she browsed through the goldsmiths' row in search of more of the stuff heard a lot.

Especially when m'lady was discussing with her new maid what to do with her purchases. And since m'lady was in a hurry to go on her social calls as well as brainless, and the maid was new and didn't know where the concealed cupboard for the valuables was, m'lady told her all about it right then and there instead of waiting until she was back home and showing her.

Now came the only tricky part. Skif wasn't going to take his eyes off the garden below, or the garden next door, so he had to reach up over his head and feel for the ledge of the gabled window there, then pull himself up onto the windowsill by the help of the bars there and the strength of his arms alone. Quietly. Smoothly. So that no movement of a shadow-within-a-shadow would draw the attention of someone he hadn't spotted.

The Nightwatch had some good, sharp men on it—not many, but some. That was why Skif took no chances by turning his back. And when he'd finished with Kalink, he'd never hit this neighborhood again, no matter how juicy it seemed.

With hands wrapped around the bars on the window, he drew himself up into the enclosure; like the work of the ropedancers, it looked smooth and easy, but it was hard work. Hard enough to make his arms scream as he pulled himself up, braced himself, pulled himself farther up, braced, then finally got himself up onto the windowsill. He wedged his thin body between two of the bars, and waited. Watching, listening, for any sign of another shadow down below, now slipping out of cover to go and fetch his fellow thief catchers.

Nothing.

Just for good measure, he waited until fingers and toes were chilled, but not numb and clumsy, and only then did he slip the special, paper-thin, flexible knife blade from the sheath strapped to his ankle and slip the catches—for there were two, which was Kalink's idea of being clever—of the window beside him. He didn't open the window, though. Not yet.

From out of the breast of his tunic came a tiny bladder full of lamp oil, which he used on the bottom edge of the window to ease its passage; this was no time to have it stick. Then he squirted the last of it on the hinges—no time to have them groan either! Only then did he push the two halves of the window open, shove his body sideways between the bars, and feel with his foot for the floor, all of it moving as slowly as a tortoise. When he was certain that his footing was secure, he put all of his weight on it, brought the other leg in through the window—and closed it, putting on one of the catches to hold it shut. There were plenty of jobs that had been ruined because the thief forgot to close the window behind himself on a cold night, and some servant felt a draft.

Skif knew where he was; the room used by the show-wife's maid. He'd watched over the course of several nights when Kalink and his wife were at some party or other, knowing that the girl would have to stay up to help her mistress undress. The windows of the master's bedroom might have fancy locks on them, but the maid's cubby wouldn't, and it was a guarantee that the maid's room would give off right onto the master's bedroom. That was one of Bazie's first lessons when Skif began doing *real* work—the layout of the fancy houses.

The weak point in a house was always the personal maid's room, or the manservant's, but the maid was the easiest target. The personal maid—she had special status, because she had to be able to do more than just run errands. Fine sewing and embroidery, hairdressing, getting her mistress into and out of her fancy clothes and doing it unobtrusively—that was just the start of her duties. She might have to cook sweet and soothing dainties if her mistress was indisposed and the cook had gone to bed, she certainly had to be able to do a bit of nursing if her mistress was ill, pregnant, or elderly. Depending on where her loyalties were, she might be the master's spy on his wife—or run discreet messages and make assignations with her mistress's lovers. She had to know how to make and apply beauty treatments, even cosmetics. And she had to be available day or night, except when the mistress was out of the house and hadn't taken her along.

All that required a room of her own, adjoining the master's bedroom—or the mistress's, if husband and wife didn't share a bed. And since the last thing the mistress would tolerate was the ability of her maid to go sneaking off without the mistress knowing about it, the maid generally had to go through the master's bedroom to get to the rest of the house. That prevented the maid from entertaining men in her own room, and greatly curtailed her ability to slip off and be entertained by them elsewhere. A good lady's maid was something no woman wanted to lose, so it was worth the effort to keep her from the lure of masculine company.

After all, she might get married, or pregnant, or both. Then what would her mistress do?

Dismiss her, of course, and go on the hunt for another; this was a quest more fraught with hazard and emotional turmoil than the search for a new cook. One could train a new maid, of course, but then one would have to be willing to put up with a great deal while the girl was in training.

Skif remained crouched on the floor and waited while his eyes adjusted to the deeper darkness in this tiny room. He reached out cautiously and encountered the rough wool of a blanket to his right.

So—the bed was there. He moved carefully to avoid making the floorboards creak, and edged over to the bed. Making sure not to lean on it, he located the head and the foot, then eased down to the foot and felt for the wall.

From the wall, he found the door, and eased it open, creeping through it practically on hands and knees.

His nose told him that he was in the bedroom, and that the room was the exclusive domain of the mistress, for the aroma of perfume and scent in here was far heavier than most men would tolerate. So—the mistress and master slept separately. He'd rather expected that; the show-wife, whether she knew it or not, shared her husband's attentions with a lady of—earthier—qualities. Kalink kept her in a nice little set of rooms near the cattle market, where she had once been a barmaid. The show-wife was just that; a trophy to be displayed before other men and eventually got with an heir.

Well, this was his goal. He grinned to himself. Old Kalink thought he was being so clever! Most hiding places for valuables were in concealed wall cupboards, but according to the wife, Kalink had the brilliant notion to put *his* in the floor, under the bed. Well, *Kalink* thought it was a brilliant idea. Skif would not only be able to get at it with ease, he'd be hidden while he went through the goods at his leisure.

The bed was easy enough to see, even in the dim light from the three unshuttered windows, for the curtains hadn't been drawn since the mistress wasn't home. There was plenty of moonlight in this enormous room, which faced south and west—poor little maid, she had her window on the east side, where the sun would smack her right in the eyes if she hadn't gotten up by dawn. Skif kept his head down, though, and still moved cautiously, traveling crabwise below the level of the windows. The bed was one of those fashionable, tall affairs that you needed a set of steps to get into—

—so that you could get to the safe-cupboard under it, of course—

—and Skif slid beneath it with plenty of room to spare.

Now, for the first time, he drew an easy breath. If he found what he thought he was going to find, this one haul of loot would keep him and the two new boys Bazie had taken in, and do so in fine style for a year or more.

Which we need. They ain't liftin' enough t'keep us in old bread.

He slipped off one glove, and felt along the floorboards for the tell-tale crack that would show him where the edge of the lid was, and whatever sort of mechanism there was to lock it shut.

He was the last of the old lot; Deek had undergone an unexpected growth spurt that turned him into a young giant and made his intended occupation of house thief entirely impractical. He served as a guard for a traveling gem merchant now—who better to watch for thieves than a former pickpocket? Last Skif had heard, he was on his way to Kata'shin'a'in.

Raf had gotten caught, and was currently serving out his sentence on the Border with Karse, for he'd made the mistake of getting caught with his hand on the pouch of a Great Lord.

Lyle had given up thievery altogether, but only because he'd fallen in love instead. He'd gone head over heels with a farmer's daughter one Fair Day in the cattle market, and she with him, and over the course of six weeks had managed to charm her old father into consenting to marriage. Lyle had taken to country life as if he'd been born to it, which amazed all of them, Lyle himself not the least.

Bazie had gotten two new boys just before Lyle fell to the love-god's arrows, and it was left to him and Skif to train them up. That was why Skif was going for a big stake *now;* the boys weren't up to the lifting lay yet, and only one was adequate at swiping things out of laundries. Skif had the feeling that Bazie had taken them more out of pity than anything else; Lyle had brought them in after finding them scouring the riverbanks—mudlarking—for anything they could salvage. Thin, malnourished, and as ignorant as a couple of savages, even Bazie wasn't about to try and pound reading, writing, and reckoning lessons into them. *That* fell on the head of some poor priest at the nearest temple.

Skif traced the last line of the lid of the safe-cupboard and found the keyhole easily enough. No one had made any effort to hide it, and he slid his lock pick out of a slit pocket in his belt and went to work by touch.

Before very long, he knew for a fact that Kalink had been cheated, for this was the *cheapest* lock he had ever come across in a fancy house. It wasn't the work of more than a few moments to tickle it open, and ease the lid of the safe-cupboard open.

With the lid resting safely on the floor, Skif reached into the cupboard and began lifting out heavy little jewel cases, placing them on the floor until he had emptied the cupboard. What he wanted was gold and silver.

Gold was soft; with a hammer and a stone, Skif could pound chains and settings into an amorphous lump, which any goldsmith would buy without a second thought and at a reasonable price. Silver wasn't bad to have; you could cut it up with a chisel and render the bits unidentifiable. He'd rather not have gemstones; you couldn't just take them to a goldsmith, and you wouldn't get more than a fraction of their worth.

So he opened each box and examined its contents by feel; rejecting out-of-hand all gem-studded rings, earrings, and brooches. He selected chains, bracelets, pendants, anything that was mostly or completely made of metal. The emptied boxes went into the bottom of the cupboard, with the rest stacked on top. With luck, the theft wouldn't even be uncovered for days after Kalink and his wife returned. By then, of course, everything would have been disposed of, melted down—it might even become part of whatever baubles the mistress picked to replace what was lost!

Each piece he selected, he wrapped in one of Bazie's purloined silk handkerchiefs to cut down on sound and stored in one of the many pockets of his "sneak suit." It didn't do a thief a great deal of good to be chiming and chinking when he moved!

He hesitated once or twice, but in the end, opted to be conservative in what he chose. He had no way of getting rid of that triple rope of pearls, for instance, nor the brooch that featured a huge carven cabochon. And when his fingers told him that the piece he was holding was of finely-detailed enamel, he couldn't bear the idea of destroying something that so much work and creativity had gone into. The same for the wreath of fragile leaves and flowerlets—a clever way of getting around the fact that a commoner couldn't wear a coronet. But the rest of what he chose was common enough, mere show of gleaming metal, without much artistry in it.

He replaced the last box and eased the lid back down on the cupboard. Now came the fun part: getting out.

He didn't want the maid to get into trouble; that was hardly fair. If he left the window in her room with the catches undone, she'd be the first to be blamed. So after he slid out from under the bed, he crept across the mistress's room to try the next door over.

It was a bathing room, and he laughed silently. *Good old Kalink! Nothing but the best for him for certain-sure. Nothing but the latest!* There was an indoor privy, everything flushed away with water after you'd done, and a boiler to heat bath water, all served from a cistern on the roof. Good place to leave open.

He opened the catch on the window and pushed open the shutters that served this room instead of ironwork. Let Kalink presume that this was how his thief got in, and wonder how on earth he came up the wall from the yard, or down the wall from the steeply-pitched roof.

Now he returned to the maid's room. He'd go out the way he came, but he had a trick to use on the kind of simple bar catches on that window. A loop of string on each of them let him pull them closed again once he'd closed the window behind him.

By now the moon was down, and there wasn't a chance anyone could see him. In moments, he was down in the alley, running like a cat, heading for his next destination. He didn't dare be caught in *this* outfit! There would be no doubt in anyone's mind of what his business was!

But there was a remedy for that, too. Two streets over was that wonderfully handy cavity in Lord Orthallen's wall, and that was where he'd left a set of breeches and a tunic. In the safety of the utter blackness, he pulled the bricks loose and extracted them. The hood of his shirt became a high collar, the scarf around his face and throat went around his waist beneath the tunic. He wiped the charcoal from his face with the inside of the tunic, and in very little time, a perfectly respectable young lad was strolling down the street with a bundle under his arm. He could be anyone's page boy or young servant on any of a dozen errands, and he even passed patrols of the Nightwatch twice without any of them stopping or even looking at him.

If they had, they'd have found nothing worse than a bundle of gentleman's underthings. And if he was asked, he'd mumble and hide his face and say he couldn't *rightly* say, but his mistress had told him to take them quietly to a certain gentleman and there wasn't anything else he could tell them.

The Watch would, of course, assume that the gentleman in question had been forced to make a hasty exit from a bedroom where he'd had no business being and had left the least important of his clothing behind. As it was no business of the Watch to oversee the morals of anyone, Skif would be sent on his way, perhaps with a laugh.

The closer he got to his destination, the more relaxed he felt. Already he was planning where to take the metal, how to show the two boys to pound the gold and silver into flat, indistinguishable sheets.

Hunger caught up with him then; he hadn't eaten much, following Bazie's dictum that a full stomach made for a slow thief. Bazie wasn't actually expecting him for some time yet, since it was always his habit to go home by as circuitous a route as possible. A thief might be expected to hurry back to his den to hide his loot—and so a thief who feared pursuit *would* do. But no one knew that Skif carried a small fortune about his person, nor did any sign of it show. No one knew that the Kalink household had been robbed this night. There was no pursuit.

So why hurry back? *A thief runs when no one chases him,* was another of Bazie's dictums, and he was right. If Skif *looked* guilty, acted guilty, the Watch *might* detain and search him, just on principle.

So, as soon as he reached a street of inns and taverns—the same one, in fact, where he had robbed the kitchen of a burning tavern so very long ago—he drifted to the busiest, a hostelry called the "White Rider" with a sign of a Herald and his Companion.

The place was packed full, with not one, but two musicians, one at each fireplace, holding forth. It was, of course, impossible to hear either of them in the middle of the room. Skif found a place on a bench next to a weary woman and her brood of four children, got the attention of a serving girl by grabbing her apron as she went by, and ordered food. He tried ordering wine—he always did—and the girl smirked. When she came back with his meat pie and drink, the drink was cider. He sighed and paid her.

While the wealthy were *out* of the city, the common folk came in. A great deal of business happened here in the fall, before the snows made it hard to travel. Skif picked out half a dozen different accents just from where he was sitting.

There could not have been a more vivid contrast to Skif's old home: too cold three seasons of the year, full of sullen silences, always in semi-darkness. Here it was cozy, and the air vibrated with talk and sound. There were plenty of lights, and there was no problem seeing what you were eating. The tabletop got regularly wiped down with clean rags, and although the floor was collecting a fair bit of debris over the course of the evening, Skif had no doubt it would start out the next day being swept clean enough to eat off of. The cooking aromas were all tempting, and there was no reek of stale beer and wine. If the customers themselves were a bit whiffy, well, it had been a hard day for some of them.

Skif relaxed further, his belly full of good food and cider. The woman gathered up her herd and left, to be replaced by a couple of equally weary fellows who could have been any sort of craftsman or farmer. Or possibly skilled laborers, come for one of the hiring fairs.

They both seemed rather concerned, huddling together to murmur at each other, and finally the one nearest Skif asked him politely what the least expensive meal was.

Skif gave them a friendly grin, and his recommendation.

They's a right couple 'uv conies! he thought, wondering which of the lads who worked this inn on the liftin' lay would lighten their pockets before they found work. Not that it was inevitable of course, but it was likely. You had choices in the liftin' lay; you could work half a dozen of easy marks like these two, or you could go for one big score who'd be cannier, better guarded. In either case there was about the same amount of risk, for each time you worked a mark in a crowd, you increased the risk of getting caught.

Well, that wasn't his outlook. He didn't work the liftin' lay anymore, and the two lads back with Bazie were too ham-handed for it right now. He finished the last of his cider, shoved the pottery mug to the middle of the table, and extracted himself from the bench, taking his bundle with him.

From here on, his story—if he was caught by the Watch—would change. Now he was bringing his father's clothing home from the pawnshop. It wasn't at all unusual for a family to have articles of clothing in and out of pawn all the time, and in some families, in more often than out.

And as he stepped out into the street, sure enough, a Watchman across the street caught sight of him, frowned, and pointed his truncheon at him.

"You! Boy!" he barked. "Halt there!"

Obediently, and with an ingratiating, cringing smile, Skif obeyed.

"What've ye got there?" the Watchman asked, crossing the street. Skif held out his bundle, hunching his shoulders, and the Watchman poked it with his truncheon. "Well? Speak up!"

"'S m' Dad's shirt 'n' smalls, m'lor'," Skif sniveled. "Jest got 'em f'om Go'den Ball, m'lor'." With the fall hiring fairs going on all over Haven, the set of good linen smallclothes that had been in pawn all summer *would* come out again, for someone who was going to a hiring fair would be dressed in his best.

Then they'd go right back in again, if the job was only until winter and the end of hunting season.

"Open it," the Watch demanded. Skif complied; no one paid any attention to them as he did so, firstly because you didn't interfere with the Watch, and secondly because you didn't want the Watch's attention brought down on you.

The Watchman's eyes narrowed suspiciously. "If yer Dad's smalls 've been in the nick, what're ye doin' eatin' at yon Rider?" he demanded.

A stab of alarm mixed with chagrin pierced Skif, but he didn't show it. Even as he opened his mouth, he had his answer. After all, this was Quarter-Day, or near it—servants and laborers with year-round jobs got paid four times a year. "'Tis out'a me *own* wages, m'lor!" he said with a touch of indignation. "M'Dad got a busted arm an' m'Ma didn' say nothin' till now, when I got me Quarter-Days!" Now he let his tone turn grumbling. "Reckon a lad kin hev a bit uv dinner when 'e's missed 'is own so's 'e kin help out 'is own fambly on 'is own half-day!"

There; just enough story to let the Watchman fill in the rest on his own—a son in service, a father injured and out of work, neither parent saying anything until the boy had the money to retrieve the belongings they'd put in pawn to see them over the lean time. Common servants got a half a day off—which usually began well into the afternoon and was seldom truly a "half-day"—once every fortnight or so. Servants as young as Skif usually didn't leave their employer's houses except on the half-day off after they'd gotten paid. Servants like Skif pretended to be wouldn't have gone out during dinner time either, which was probably why the Watchman had been suspicious, for why would a common servant spend his wages on food he could have gotten for free at his master's table? Or if he was visiting his parents, why hadn't *they* fed him?

But—Skif's story had him visiting his parents, discovering the situation, and going out after the pawned clothing. Presumably there was nothing in the house to eat, his job wouldn't include the benefit of "broken meats" to take home to his relatives, and as a result, he was missing a meal to do his duty to his parents. Skif was rather proud of his fabrication.

The Watchman grunted. "Wrap it up, then, boy, and keep moving," was all he said. Skif ducked his head and tied up the bundle again, then scuttled away.

The back of his neck was damp with sweat. That had been a close one! He made a mental note not to use that story or that inn again any time soon.

But with the haul he'd just made, he shouldn't have to.

Better be careful. Be just my luck now t' get hit with some'un pullin' a smash'n'grab. That was the crudest version of the liftin' lay, a couple of boys careening at full speed down the street, one after the other. One would knock a mark over, while the other came in behind and scooped up whatever he dropped. If that happened to Skif, while the Watchman's eye was still on him, the Watchman would be suspicious all over again if Skif didn't pursue his attackers, or refused to swear out charges against them. And at the moment, he couldn't afford the suspicions that might lead to being searched!

So he clutched his bundle tightly and raised his eyes to look up and down the street for the little eddies of activity that would mark a couple of smashers on a run.

And that was when he saw the red glow above the rooftops.

Fire.

He picked up his pace.

A *big* fire.

And from the look of it—somewhere near home. There would be a crowd, a mob—and a mob meant opportunity, even in a neighborhood as poor as his, for fire drew spectators from all over. He might not be an expert at the liftin' lay, but he was good enough to add to his take in the kind of crowd drawn by a big fire.

He moved into a trot. Get home, empty out his pockets, then go out in the mob—

He joined a stream of running, shouting spectators and would-be helpers, all streaming toward the fire like so many moths attracted to the light. Now he could see the lick of flames above the rooftops. He was jostled on all sides and had to concentrate to keep hold of the bundle and keep his own head cool while everyone around him was caught up in the fever of the moment.

And he couldn't help notice that he was getting nearer and nearer to his own home. Excitement began to take on a tinge of alarm. *Hellfires! It's close! Wonder who—*

He turned the corner with the rest of the mob—and stopped dead. His building. *His* home. Now nothing but flames.

8

This was no place for a Herald. But then Herald Alberich was no ordinary Herald.

He hunched over his drink and rubbed at eyes that watered from the smoke filling the room, his ears filled with the droning of drunks, his nose wrinkling at the stench of too many unwashed bodies, burned food, and spilled beer. He had been in this part of Haven to meet an informant in a disgusting little hole of a tavern called "The Broken Arms"—an obvious and unsubtle reference to what would happen to a patron who displeased the owner. The sign above the door, crudely and graphically painted, enforced that—human arms do not normally bend in four places.

The informant had never showed his face, which didn't really surprise Alberich. He'd never reckoned the odds to be better than even at best. The man might have gotten cold feet; or he might even be entirely cold at this point—cold and dead. If so, it was fifty-fifty whether Alberich would ever find out what had happened to him. Bodies didn't always turn up. Even when the river was frozen over, there were plenty of ways in which a corpse could vanish without a trace. The people Alberich suspected of intrigue against the Queen were powerful, and had a very great deal to lose if they were unmasked. They had the ways and means to insure that more than one petty informant vanished without a trace if they cared to make it so.

The Herald sipped his stale beer, and watched the rest of the customers from beneath lowered eyelids. In the back of his mind, he felt his Companion fretting at the situation, and soothed him wordlessly. He knew that no one was going to recognize him, no matter what Kantor thought. Alberich did not stand out in this crowd of ne'er-do-wells, pickpockets, and petty thieves.

He probably wouldn't had he not bothered to disguise himself; he never *would* wear the traditional uniform of Herald's Whites even when presiding over the classes of Heraldic Trainees in his capacity as the Collegium Weaponsmaster, preferring instead a leather uniform of a slightly darker gray than the color used by the Trainees.

Herald's Whites—let those with fewer sins on their souls wear the Whites. He'd have worn black, if the Queen hadn't expressly forbidden it.

"Bad enough that you look like a storm cloud," she'd told him. *"I won't have them calling you 'Herald Death.' You stand out quite enough as it is from the rest of the Heraldic Circle."* He didn't point out to her that they might as well call him "Herald Death," that his business *was* Death, the ways and means of dealing it out. He simply bowed and let her have her way. She was the Queen, after all.

But at the moment, he was not on official duty, and he wore nothing like a uniform; his clothing was as drably no-colored, as tattered and patched as that of any man around him. His unfashionably short hair was concealed beneath an ancient knitted cap of indeterminate shape and origin. Only his sword and knives—themselves both disguised beneath plain, worn leather sheaths—would have told a different story about him.

Or perhaps not; to a slum-dwelling bullyboy, his sword was his life, and many of them bore weapons of superior make. A blade that bent or snapped, or wouldn't hold an edge, wasn't the sort of tool to risk your life on. Alberich was supposed to be that sort of sell-sword, a man whose blade went to the man with the price of it, with no questions asked on either side.

In the absence of his informant, Alberich was going to have to pretend he was here for the same reason as everyone else; to get drunk. He would probably have to use this tavern again, and he definitely needed to keep in character; he didn't dare break this carefully constructed persona. It had taken too long to build.

Most of the beer was going to hit the floor, though. Like many of the patrons here, he had his own mug, a leather-jack, tarred on the inside to make it waterproof and kept tied to his waist when not in use. Only, unlike theirs, his had a hole in the bottom; he seldom took an actual sip when the mug went to his lips. He relied on the slow but steady leak and the crack in the table he sat at to conceal where the rest of it got to. No one in this place was going to notice beer on the floor under the layer of rushes that hadn't been changed for a year or more. Only when his mouth dried or he needed something to wash the stench of the place from his tongue did he actually drink. The beer, stale and flat, was still preferable to the taste left behind in breathing the miasma of this miserable tavern.

Impatience made his head throb, and he forced himself to look bored instead of pained. He was wondering just how many more mugs of the noxious stuff he'd have to down before he pretended to stagger out, when the street outside erupted into what sounded like a riot.

Shouts—*screams!* His heart rose into his throat, and his pulse hammered in his ears as every nerve in his body reacted to the alarm.

He—and virtually everyone else in the tavern—jumped to their feet and ran for the door. He wasn't slow to react, but there were still plenty of people who were between him and it. He ran right into a wall of jostling bodies.

He told himself that this was a good diversion to get out and back to the Collegium, but he couldn't help himself. The noise out there was of panic and fear, and he *had* to respond. For the rest, of course, any disturbance held a potential for profit…

Sweat stink mingled with a different kind of smoke—this was coming from the street outside. The noise now was like nothing he'd heard off a battlefield. He shoved his way through the crush at the door ruthlessly, elbowing one man in the ribs and brutally kicking another in the knee to get them out of the way. Both men swore and turned on him; both shrank out of the way when they saw who it was. He had a formidable reputation here; another reason why he was reluctant to sacrifice this persona. He could virtually come and go as he liked unmolested, and it had taken him no few knife fights to build that reputation. He had yet to draw his sword in here, which was a mercy, though his opponents only thought he was showing his contempt for them by meeting their swords with his knives. The poor fools had no idea that he was saving them from almost certain death at his hands if he pulled the longer blade. It wasn't his skill he was worried about, it was theirs; he'd seen drunken brawls end fatally when one idiot slipped and rammed himself onto another's sword. It had happened while he watched far too often to want to see that happen with him holding the blade. And it wasn't because he liked them that he spared their wretched lives, it was because if he killed a man, even by accident, the Watch would come, and there would be questions, and there would go his hard work in establishing Rokassan among the bullyboys.

That was why it was Alberich here, and not another Herald. He was… practical.

He delivered another elbow blow to a set of ribs, this time with enough force to it to make the man in his way whuff, curse, and bend over, and Alberich was out into the not-so-open street.

It should have been dark and relatively empty. It wasn't. It was filled wall-to-wall with a churning mass of spectators and a growing number of those who actually were doing something. A lurid red glow reflected off their filthy, upturned faces as the wretched denizens of this neighborhood organized themselves into lines of hands that passed buckets of water away toward Alberich's right.

The source of the glow was as hellish as any Sunpriest sacrificial fire Alberich had ever seen in Karse.

An inferno that had once been a building raged madly against the black of the night sky. It was one of the nearby tenement blocks, and it was a solid sheet of flame from its foundation to its roof. It couldn't have been more fully involved, and Alberich was struck motionless for a moment at the sight, for he couldn't imagine how it had *gotten* that way so quickly—short of a Red-Robe Priest's demon calling. For one horrible moment he wondered wildly if a Red-Robe *had* infiltrated the capital of Selenay's Kingdom—

But then an acrid whiff told him the real reason the building was so thoroughly engulfed.

Tar. Someone had been painting the sides of the building with tar. The heavy black smoke roiling over the tips of the highest flames confirmed it. A sudden wind drove it down into the street, and screams turned to coughs and gasps.

Now, that wasn't uncommon in this part of the city. Landlords didn't care to spend more than they had to on maintenance of these old buildings, and when they got word that an inspection was in the offing, they frequently created a new and draftless facade by tarring and papering the exterior with any of a number of cheap substitutes for real wooden siding. The work could be done in a day or less, and when finished, presented a less ramshackle appearance that generally fooled overworked inspectors into thinking that the building was in better shape than it actually was. With so many buildings to inspect and so little time, the inspector could easily convince himself that *this* one didn't need to be looked at any closer, and move on. The work would hold for a while, but soon the paper would disintegrate, the tar soak into wood left unpainted for so long that it soaked up anything, and the place would revert to its former state. A little darker, perhaps, and for a while the tar would fill in the cracks that let in the winter winds, but nothing more.

Still… it seemed odd to Alberich that the thing should be blazing with such fiendish enthusiasm. Slum landlords were as stingy with their tar and paper as they were with everything else, and to burn like this, someone must have laid the stuff on with a trowel—

"*Stop him! Stop that boy!*"

Alberich sensed, rather than saw, the swirl in the crowd that marked someone small and nimble bouncing off the legs of those around him. Then a wiry, hard body careened into his hip.

He was running to the fire. Somehow, Alberich knew that—and his ForeSight showed him what would happen if the boy made it through the crowd.

A small body writhing in the flames, screaming, dying—An echo of the sacrificial fires of Karse. His gorge rose.

Automatically he reached out and snared the tunic collar of the boy before he could get any farther.

The boy turned on him, a spinning, swirling fury. "Let me go!" he screamed. "*Let me go!*" He spat out a stream of invective that rivaled anything Alberich had ever heard, and flailed at Alberich's arm with hard little fists. "I gotta get in there, ye bastid! *I gotta!*"

Screaming and writhing in the flames...

Alberich didn't bother arguing with the brat, who was red-faced and hysterical, and he didn't have time to calm him. No doubt his family was in there—

Gods. He pulled the boy off his feet, and the brat still fought.

Well, if they were, they were all dead, or they were somewhere out in the street, sobbing over the loss of their few possessions. Nothing could survive that inferno, but there was no reasoning that point. Alberich couldn't let the boy go—

But there was work here; he might not be dressed in Whites, but he knew his duty, which was to help to save the buildings around the doomed one. He couldn't do that if he was playing nursemaid. With a grimace of pity, Alberich pulled his dagger as the boy continued to struggle toward the blaze, and tapped him behind the ear with the pommel nut the first moment the target presented itself.

The boy went limp. Alberich was still near enough to the door of the tavern to struggle back and drop him just inside, as far out of harm as possible in this neighborhood. Then he joined one of the many bucket brigades coalescing out of the mob. Until the Guard and the pumps and hoses arrived, they had to help convey water to soak down the buildings to either side of the fire to keep it from spreading. Already Kantor was raising the alarm for him, and help could not be more than a few moments away.

But he felt a moment of pleasure at the way people around him were responding to the emergency. So they weren't *all* villains, even though that was all he'd met since he began frequenting The Broken Arms. Even in this neighborhood, people could work together.

With one accord, the water throwers wisely concentrated their efforts on the buildings that were merely in danger and let the blazing tenement burn itself out. Anything and everything that could hold water was being pressed into service, with men and strong women sending the heavy, laden vessels toward the fire and smaller women and children passing the empties back to be filled again. Alberich's concentration narrowed to a few, vital tasks. Breathing. Taking the bucket. Passing it on with a minimum of spillage. Turning back for another.

Before he lost track of anything but the pain in back, shoulders, and arms and the cold that soon penetrated his soaking wet hands, legs, and feet, Alberich saw buckets, pots, pans, and even a chamberpot making the circuit up and back, up and back, while people shouted incoherent directions, and the flames laughed at their efforts.

Skif woke stiff and cold, with his head aching so much it hurt to open his eyes. He would just as soon have rolled over and gone back to sleep, but the pounding pain behind one ear and the cold prevented him from doing so—as did the sudden and electrifying realization that he wasn't in his bed.

He sat up abruptly, despite a stab of agony that made him yelp.

The cold, gray light of the street coming in at an open door next to where he sat completely disoriented him. Where was he?

This isn't home—

Then it all came back, in a rush. The triumph of the successful run. The fire.

The man who'd grabbed him, keeping him from—from—

With an inarticulate howl of grief, he scrambled to his feet and staggered out into the street.

He coughed in the miasma of fog and stale smoke that met him like a wall. He fought through it, staggered a few paces—and stared, unbelieving, at the absolute ruin of his home.

Gone. All gone. A few blackened timbers stuck up out of the wreckage, marking where the staircase had been. The rest—was an unidentifiable pile of charred wood and still-smoldering wreckage.

The vultures were already hauling away whatever they could claw out, for in this place, even charcoal could serve to help eke out firewood and grant a few more hours of warmth. They had baskets, barrows—their clothing and faces black with soot.

Somewhere under there was his home—Bazie—and the boys.

Another howl tore itself out of his throat, and he hurled himself at the burned-out building, scrambling over what was left of the wall to the corner where the secret stair should have opened to Bazie's little den. It was underground—surely it was safe, surely they were safe—

They have to be safe!

But he couldn't help thinking... how long it took them to get Bazie out on the rare occasions when he emerged from the room. What a struggle it was to get him to the latrine, much less up the stairs. And that was on a bright spring day, not amid choking smoke and flames—

He began to dig, frantically, first with his bare hands, then with a piece of board until that broke, then with the blade of a shovel he found, still hot enough to blister. His throat closed, his gut clenched. He welcomed the pain in his hands—he should have been there! If he'd been there—if only—

He dug, with his eyes streaming tears and his heart breaking, dug and dug and dug until finally he was too exhausted to dig anymore.

He collapsed among the wreckage, and wept, leaning against a broken beam, until his sides ached and his eyes burned, and still he could not weep himself free of the pain.

Gone. All gone... I should have been here. All gone... it's my fault. All gone, all gone...

Around him, people continued to scavenge, oblivious to his grief, or ignoring it. His grief turned to anger, then, and he stood up and tried to scream at them for the plundering ghouls that they were—but his throat was raw and his brain wouldn't work and all he could do was moan.

In the end, it was Jarmin, unlikely Jarmin, clerkly proprietor of the shop who bought their plundered silks, who found him there, whimpering like a whipped dog. Jarmin, who stepped mincingly into the wreckage, looked him up and down and asked, without any expression at all, "Got swag?"

Skif, shocked out of his grief for a moment by the sheer callousness of the query, began to shake his head. Then, suddenly remembering that triumph that seemed to have happened a hundred years ago, nodded.

Jarmin took him by the elbow and hauled him to his feet. Shock sealed his mouth and made him docile, though his aching eyes still streamed tears, his gut ached, and deep inside he wanted to strike out at whatever was nearest.

To strike out at himself.

Gone, all gone!

They picked their way to the street, with Jarmin still holding tightly to Skif's elbow, and once there, Jarmin headed determinedly toward his own shop. Skif just went along, too heartbroken to think, too full of bottomless mourning to care if Jarmin was about to lead him off somewhere to kill him for his loot.

Let him. I deserve it, I wasn't there.

They entered the shop, all of its tawdriness only too apparent by day. The girls were nowhere to be seen as Jarmin shoved Skif before him, past the counter, through a flap of hanging cloth, then up a narrow staircase that ended in a room just under the roof. A single dirty window covered with oiled parchment let in enough light to see by. There was a pallet there, and blankets, and some storage boxes; nothing else. Jarmin had to stoop to fit under the rooftree, and he shoved Skif roughly down onto the pallet, and gestured impatiently at his tunic.

Skif read the gesture for the demand that it was, and slowly undid his clothing to pull out the jewelry he'd taken last night. He laid it out on the pallet. Jarmin squatted down beside him and examined it piece by piece, grunting a little, but otherwise saying nothing.

Now he's gonna kill me. Skif could form the thought, but couldn't muster anything beyond the grief to care what happened to him. Care? No, that wasn't true. He cared. He deserved death. If he'd gotten back sooner, if he hadn't been so determined to bring back every damned piece that couldn't be traced—

I'd have been there. I'd have noticed in time. I'd have gotten them out.

Gone. All gone.

He just sat where he was, staring at his own hands, while Jarmin turned the jewelry over and over in his hands.

Finally, the fence pulled the kerchief off his own neck and bundled it all up. He shoved the ends under his belt and knotted them, got up slowly and painfully, then descended the staircase. It looked from where Skif sat as if he was sinking into the floor...

Tears began again, burning his eyes and his raw cheeks, and Skif didn't even bother to wipe them away. His nose closed up, his gut spasmed, and his thoughts ran around and around in a tight little spiral, like a mouse in a trap. Gone. *My fault, I should have been there.*

A moment later Jarmin was back again, a bundle of cloth under one arm, a jug in his hand.

"Here," he said gruffly. "These ought to fit you." He dropped the clothing down next to Skif, who stared at it without comprehension. "Even swap; the swag for these, food, and this room for three moons. After that, you get another place or start paying." As Skif stared at him as if he was speaking in a foreign tongue, he glanced at the jug in his hand as if he was surprised by its presence. "Oh, aye. And you get this."

He shoved it at Skif until Skif took it from him perforce.

"Go on. Pop the cork and drink it," Jarmin said fiercely.

Numbly, Skif obeyed. The cork came out with difficulty; the liquid inside tasted of cherries and burned like fire, burned him from his tongue to his gut, all the way down.

He knew as soon as he tasted it what it was, though he had never done more than sip a bit before this, the dregs left in some rich man's glass; spirits-of-wine, and worth its weight in silver. He gasped at the fire in it, but didn't spill a drop; it would bring blessed oblivion, which now he wanted more than he'd ever wanted anything. It went to the head quickly; in a few swallows, he was dizzy. A few swallows more, and he had trouble holding the jug. Jarmin, his eyes gleaming fiercely in the half light, steadied it for him and helped him lift it to his mouth.

"Keep drinking, boy," he heard, as from a far distant land. "'Twon't take the hurt away, but it'll numb it for a while."

Numb... Numb was good. Maybe if he was numb, he wouldn't keep seeing Bazie and the boys... and the flames.

He swallowed again, the stuff burning its way down into his belly. Now he was more than dizzy; the room swam around him and tilted disconcertingly. Jarmin took the jug, corked it, and set it aside as he sagged down onto the pallet.

The room was definitely moving, but he didn't care. He just didn't want to have to watch it, so he closed his eyes. "Best thing for you, boy," he heard, then footsteps on the stair.

He didn't actually pass out; he hadn't drunk quite enough for that. But every time the numbness and the dizziness started to wear off, he heaved himself up onto his elbow and took another long pull at the jug until it came back again. Now and again he tired of simply feeling the room circling him and opened his eyes to watch the ceiling rotate. When the light started to fade, Jarmin appeared again with a lantern and bread and sops, a chamberpot, and a big jug of water. He made Skif eat and drink all of the water before he took the lantern and the plates away. Skif took some more pulls on the jug, then, and as shrill voices and the cajolery of the girls drifted in through the window, he let the liquor take him away to a place where nothing mattered anymore.

Jarmin told him later that he'd stayed drunk for a week. Sometimes he cried, but only when he was alone. Sometimes he heard someone moaning, and dimly realized that it was himself. All he knew was that the jug was, temporarily, his best friend. Jarmin kept it full, but insisted on his eating and drinking water, an annoyance he put up with because it meant that Jarmin would top off the jug.

He retained enough of sense and the cleanliness Bazie had drummed into him to make proper use of the chamberpot. It never seemed to stink, so Jarmin must have kept it clean as well.

Jarmin also came up to talk to him now and again. For a while, he ignored the words and the man because he didn't want to go to the place where words meant something. For a while, that is, until something Jarmin said jarred him back into *thinking.*

"Word is," Jarmin said, into Skif's rosy fog, "that fire was set."

Set? Skif opened his eyes with an effort. "Wha?" he managed, mouth tasting of old leather and liquor.

Jarmin didn't look at him, and his tone was casual. "Word is that the landlord got a surprise inspection, and was going to have to fix the place. Or get fined. Going to cost him dearly, either way. So he burned it instead, and is calling it a terrible accident."

Understanding—and anger—stirred sluggishly. "He—*burned* it?"

Jarmin shrugged, as if it all mattered not a whit to him. "Word is, that's the case. Don't know who the landlord is—was," he corrected. "*You* know how it is. Probably some high-necked merchant, or even highborn. Couldn't possibly be connected with us, nor where we live. Couldn't soil himself by openly owning the place, but takes our copper right enough. So long as no one knows where he got it. But he wouldn't want to have to spend good coin either, not when burning it costs him less and allows him to sell the lot afterward."

Anger burned away the fumes of the liquor—hot as the flames that had destroyed his only family. "He burned it?" Skif repeated, sitting up, fists clenching.

"Word is that. *Who*ever he is." Jarmin shrugged, then with a sly look, pushed the jug toward Skif.

Skif pushed it back, still dizzy, but head getting clearer by the moment.

He burned it. Or ordered it burned, whoever he is.

"No warning, of course," Jarmin continued casually. "Because that would tip off the inspectors that he didn't mean to fix it. And the highborn don't care how many of us burn, so long as an inconvenient building is gotten rid of. That is how it is."

There was light in the window and relative quiet on the street. It must be day, and the girls were asleep. Skif was still drunk, and he knew it, but he was getting sober, more so with every breath, as his anger rose and rose, burning like the flames that had taken his family. He looked down at himself, and saw that he was still wearing the filthy clothing he'd been brought here in. The pile of clean stuff still lay at the foot of the pallet. "Wanta bath, Jarmin."

"Comes with the room," Jarmin said indifferently. "I'll tell madam. Get yourself downstairs when you can."

He descended the stairs, and Skif waited until he could stand without too much wavering. Then he picked up a shirt, trews, and socks, and followed.

Jarmin was behind the counter tending to a customer, but waved him out the door. Skif tottered out, blinking owlishly at the daylight, and the door of the brothel next to Jarmin's shop opened. An oily-looking fellow beckoned to him, and Skif went in.

He wasn't given any time to look around the shabby-luxurious "parlor" where customers came to choose from the girls if they hadn't already picked one. The oily fellow hustled him into the back where there was—

A laundry.

Only the remains of the liquor and the firmest of controls kept Skif from breaking down right there and then. The urge to wail was so great he practically choked.

There were several tubs, two of which had girls in them, three of which had laundry. Before he could lose his head and bawl, a burly woman with work-reddened hands and a tight, angry mouth stripped him before he could open his mouth and shoved him into the last of the tubs. She didn't give him a chance to wash himself either; she used the same brush and lye soap that she used on the linen on *his* hide, with the same lack of gentleness.

The bristles lacerated his skin, his scalp. He didn't let out a single sound as she scrubbed as if she intended to take his skin off, then made him stand, rinsed him with a bucket of water cold enough to make him gasp, and bundled him in a sheet. His own clothing went into one of the tubs with laundry in it, and she handed him the plain trews, socks, and shirt he brought with him, leaving him to clothe himself as she turned back to her work. He noticed that the girls didn't get the same ungentle treatment. They were allowed to bathe themselves and did so lazily, completely ignoring his presence.

Well, that was all right. He didn't want any stupid whores fussing over him like he was some sort of animate doll. He didn't want their sympathy. He didn't want anyone's pity.

Hard. I gotta be hard. That's what I gotta do.

He dried himself off—the laundress snatched the sheet away from him before he could lay it down and popped it back into a tub—and got the clothing on. It was rather too big, but that hardly mattered. All he had left now were his own boots, which he pulled on, and left without a backward glance.

His head was clear enough now, and while the laundress had scrubbed him, his grief had somehow changed, shrunk, condensed down into a hard, cold little gem that formed the core of a terrible anger that seemed almost too large to contain in so small a compass as his heart.

Revenge. That was what he wanted, more than anything in the world. And he wasn't going to rest until he got it.

He walked into Jarmin's shop, and the old man gave him a sharp glance, then a nod of satisfaction. "You'll do," was all he said, and tossed him a pouch.

It clinked. Skif opened it and found a little money; mostly copper, a bit of silver. He tucked it inside his shirt. It was little enough. Jarmin was cheating him, of course. The room, the food, the clothing, the baths— none of that was worth a fraction of what he'd stolen! Jarmin wasn't *giving* him anything.

And Skif didn't want anything but this—the expected cheating, the usual grifting. No more kindness. No more generosity. He could move on from here without looking back or regretting anything. This was a business transaction for Jarmin. Save one of the best thieves he knew and ensure a steady supply of goods for his shop—as simple as that.

So he didn't thank the man for the money; he just nodded curtly and went back out into the street. He knew what the money was for—tongues weren't loose without money. And Skif was going to have to find a lot of tongues to loosen. It was going to take a long time, he already knew that. That was fine, too. When revenge came, it would come out of nowhere. The enemy would never know who it was that hit him, or why.

Just as disaster had come upon him, and with equal destruction in its claws. When he was finished, whoever had killed Bazie would be left with nothing, contemplating the wreckage of what had been his life, with everything he valued and loved gone in an instant.

Just like Skif.

Skif smiled at the thought. It was the last smile he would wear for a very long time.

9

Smoke drifted over the heads of the customers; it wasn't from the fireplace, but from the tallow dips set in crude clay holders on the tables and wedged into spaces between the bricks around the room. Skif sat as far from the door as it was possible to be, in the "odd" corner of The Broken Arms, a kind of rectangular alcove just before the walls met, into which someone had wedged a broken-legged stool, making a seat hemmed in on three sides with brick. The brick was newer here, so this might be an old entrance; gone now, since the next building over was built right up against this one. Or maybe it had been a window slit; you couldn't have used it as a door, not really. It was too short and too narrow. Maybe a former fireplace, before the big one was put in, before this room became a tavern. No, it wasn't big enough for a man to be comfortable sitting here, but it was perfect for him. Here he could spend hours unnoticed, the wenches had gotten so used to it being empty.

Before things got so crowded, he'd bought himself a jack of small beer and a piece of bread and dripping, so his stomach was full but not full enough to make him drowsy. Meanwhile the number of customers rose, and the place got warmer. This nook was a good place to tuck himself into when he wanted to eavesdrop on conversations. Eavesdropping was almost as good as paying for information, and it cost nothing. He'd become adept at being able to sort one set of voices from all of the babble and concentrate on them. Once in a while one of the wenches would notice that he was there, and like this afternoon, he'd buy a mugful of small beer and a piece of bread so that they'd leave him alone, but that was only when the place was less than half full. When it was crammed tight, as it was now, he'd be overlooked all night.

He'd already wedged himself up onto the seat, knees just under his chin and his arms wrapped around them, so not even his feet were in anyone's way. Every bench and stool at every table was full; not a surprise with rain coming down in barrel loads outside. Not a good night for "business," except within walls.

Not that anyone in the Arms was going to do any business. That sign over the door wasn't there for a joke. That was what made and kept the Arms so popular; when you walked in here, you knew you'd come out with your purse no lighter than the cost of your food and drink. The women wouldn't try and get you drunk so they could talk you into paying for wine for them either. The wenches here weren't hired for their looks, gods knew—absolute harridans, most of 'em. They'd been hired because they knew the liftin' lay, and how to spot someone at business. One whistle from one of them, and the miscreant would find himself on the street with his own arms looking just like the ones on the sign. It was a good dodge for the wenches, for certain-sure; a young thing, plain though she might be, would still have an excuse to come sidling alongside of a fellow with a bit of an invitation. An old hag wouldn't; and though her fingers might still be wise, they weren't as nimble as a young thing's, so if she tried the old dodge of stumbling into a fellow, the odds were that he'd be clapping his hand to his belt pouch before she could get into it. *And* if he didn't, and she got it, her feet wouldn't carry her as far or as fast anymore. The older you got in the trade, the likelier it was you'd be caught that fatal third time, and unless she got herself a gaggle of littles to teach the trade to—taking everything they lifted, of course—there wasn't much an aging woman could do to turn a penny. There weren't a lot of women who learned the high roads or the ketchin' lay, professions that could keep you going for a long time, so long as you were limber enough to climb or bold enough to cosh.

Not that Skif held with the ketchin' lay. Bazie'd turned up his nose at it; didn't take a mort of skill nor brains to take a cosh to a fellow's head and make off with his goods. And the Watch and the Guards didn't give a third or even second chance to anyone caught at *that* trade; caught once, you saw ten years of hard labor for the Guard.

The women Skif knew didn't hold with the ketchin' lay either, though he wasn't sure what the difference was between laying a fellow out with a cosh and taking his goods when he was drunk dead asleep. Whatever, *that* was still another trade, and an old hag couldn't ply it either.

So it was good business all around for "Pappa" Serens. He had the reputation now, and always had himself a full complement of cheap serving wenches, seeing as he gave them all bed space, drink, board, and a couple of coppers now and again. They got free access to the cheapest beer after closing, as much as they cared to drink, and to the dregs of every barrel and mug of whatever price during the hours of custom, so long as they didn't get drunk. Every one of Serens' four "girls" had her own pottery pitcher back in the kitchen, and no mug belonging to the tavern ever went back out to the custom without being drained—every drop—into one of those pitchers. Since by this point in their lives what they were mostly interested in was a warm bed and enough drink to knock them out every night, nobody was complaining about the low wages. The drinking killed them off, of course, but the moment that one was carried out the door on a board, another came in on her own two feet to replace her.

Serens supplied a unique commodity for this part of the city. You could go to a dozen taverns to lift skirts, to a dozen more for a cheaper drunk than you got here, even to a couple for a bigger meal at the same price. The Arms, however, was the only place Skif knew of where you could set yourself down without worrying about fingers at your belt pouch, have beer that wouldn't choke you and a meal that wouldn't sicken you, and talk *about* anything *to* anyone, unmolested. The wenches were ugly, but they kept their mouths shut, and their eyes on their own business. There were occasional fights, but it was generally some young bullyboy trying to prove something, it usually went outside, and the older, wiser sell-sword he'd picked would settle him down quick enough. And if it didn't go outside and racketed among the benches, Seren himself, big as a bull and quick as a stag, would settle it, and The Broken Arms would have another gutter-side advertisement of how the proprietor treated those who broke the rules.

Tonight, with waterfalls pouring from the clouds outside and the wind in the right direction so that the chimney drew properly instead of sending smoke into the room, there wouldn't be any disturbances. Everyone was too comfortable to want to find himself out in the dark and rain. Skif could stay here tucked up until closing. And he would; right now his doss was a stable garret, cheap enough and cool enough even by day, now it was summer, but boring. Worse, with the rain pouring down; it'd lull him to sleep and mess him up. He slept by day, not by night, and he didn't need to find himself starting to nod in the middle of a job because he'd let his sleeping and waking patterns get messed up.

Besides, if he wasn't going to be able to work tonight, he might as well see if he couldn't pick up something interesting.

In the months since the fire, he'd made some progress finding out who was responsible—not anywhere near as fast as he'd have liked, but not so little that he was disappointed. He'd traced the money and responsibility up the line from the immediate "landlord" to whom they'd paid their rent, through two middlemen, both of whom were worse off for the loss of the building and neither of whom actually owned it. There, he'd come to a dead-end, but *someone* had given orders it be burned and *someone* had carried out those orders, and there weren't too many who were in the business of burning down buildings. Skif had, he thought, identified them all.

He had no intention of going up to any of them and confronting them about it. In the first place, there was nothing he could offer in the way of a bribe or a threat to get them to talk. In the second place, doing so would likely get him dead, not get him answers. So he was taking the slow and careful path, much though it irked and chafed him; coming here as often as he could to listen to their talk. For here was where all dubious business was conducted, and here was where the one who was really responsible might come to commission another such job.

In point of fact, as luck would have it, one of Skif's targets sat not a foot away from him tonight, making it absurdly easy to pick out his words from amidst the babble all around him.

So far it had been nothing but idle talk of bets won and lost, boasting about women, tall tales of drinking bouts of the past. On the other hand, the man hadn't been talking to anyone but his cronies. He was a professional, and well enough off by the standards around here; he didn't *have* to spend his evening in the Arms. He could get himself a woman, have a boy deliver a good tavern meal to his room, or find a better class of place to drink in. So maybe, just maybe, he'd come here tonight to make a contact, or even a deal.

When he got up to ask someone at one of the two-person tables if he'd move to the seat *he* had just vacated—for a monetary consideration—and take his comrade with him, Skif felt a thrill of anticipation and apprehension. He *was* meeting someone!

The door at the front of the tavern opened and closed, and there was a subtle movement in the crowd. It wasn't that the tavern patrons actually moved away from the newcomer, but they *did* make room for him to pass. They hadn't done *that* for anyone since Skif had been sitting there, which meant that whoever had come in was respected, but not feared. So he wasn't one of those half-crazed bullies, he wasn't someone that people feared could be set off into a rage. But they gave him room. You earned that here.

When the man made his way to Skif's part of the tavern, Skif knew why people gave him room. He didn't know the man's name, but he knew the face—closed, craggy, hard. The man was a sell-sword; he didn't start quarrels, but those that others started with him, he finished, and he was so good he never actually drew his sword when fights were picked with him. After the third bullyboy to go outside with him wound up in the dust, finished off by a man with two knives against their swords, no one picked another fight with him. Defeat was one thing; anyone could have a bad day and get beaten in a fight. Humiliation was another thing altogether. You could live down a bad day; you lived with humiliation forever, if only inside your own head.

So nobody bothered *this* man anymore.

He took his seat at the little table across from Skif's target with an attitude that said—quite calmly—that he had expected that the seat would be free and would be *kept* free for him.

But to Skif's disappointment, even though he strained his ears as hard as he could, he couldn't make out anything more than an occasional word, and none of them had anything to do with the fire.

"Rethwellan" was one word. "Vatean" was another. The first was a country somewhere outside of Valdemar; the second he recognized as a merchant—a very wealthy merchant—and a friend of the great Lord Orthallen. Skif still filched food from Lord Orthallen on a regular basis; he'd gone back to it in the wake of the fire, after his three moons had run out. It was hard to go back to the roof road, and the liftin' lay didn't pay enough for him to have a room, buy drinks to loosen tongues, and eat, too. So all this winter past, he'd lifted silks and fenced them, lived in a little box of a garret room tucked into the side of the chimney of a bakehouse—wonderfully warm through the rest of the winter, that was—and went back to mingling with the servants in Lord Orthallen's household to get his food. Only now he knew far, far more. Now he knew how to slip in and out of the household, knew how to conceal more and *what* to conceal. He knew what delicacies to filch and trade for entire meals of more mundane foodstuffs. That, perhaps, was the best dodge.

With educated eyes, he soon learned how to get into and out of the storage rooms without being caught. The easiest way was to bribe one of the delivery boys to let *him* take what had been ordered to Lord Orthallen's manse. Now these days he no longer bothered to disguise himself as a page. While the cook or the butler was tallying what had come in on his pony cart, he would carry foodstuffs into the storage room and leave a window unlocked. Then he would come back once the frantic work of preparing a meal had begun, slip in, help himself to whatever he wanted, and slip out again. He wasn't buying a lot of food anymore.

When the bakehouse room became unendurable in late spring, he packed up his few possessions and found his new room over a stable that supplied goats and donkeys for delivery carts. Cheap enough, with windows on both sides, it caught a good breeze that kept it cool during the day while he was sleeping. The animals went out each day at dawn—when he got back from his work—and came back at sunset, by which time he was ready to leave. The goats and donkeys took their pungent smells and noise with them, and by the time he had finished eating and was ready to sleep, there was nothing but the sound of the single stableboy cleaning pens and very little smell. It was a good arrangement all around, and if his landlord never asked what he did all night, well, he never asked why on nights of moon-dark a certain string of remarkably quiet donkeys with leather wrapped around their hooves went out when he did and arrived back by dawn.

By spring he had gone back to roof work, although he kept his thefts modest and more a matter of opportunity than planning. What he did mostly was *listen,* for it was remarkable what information could be gleaned at open windows now that the weather was warm. Some of that, he sold to others, who trafficked in such information. Why should *he* care who paid to keep a secret love affair *secret,* or who paid to avoid tales of bribery or cheating or other chicanery quiet? It was all incidental to his hunt for Bazie's murderer, but if he could profit by it, then why not? When a valuable trinket was left carelessly on a table in plain sight, though, it usually found its way into his pocket, and then to a fence. His own needs were modest enough that these occasional thefts, combined with his information sales and garden-variety raids on laundry rooms, kept him in ready coin.

The beauty of it all was that the three activities were so disparate that no one who knew one of them was likely to connect him with the other two. If it became too dangerous to filch silks, he could step up his roof work. If he somehow managed to get hold of some information that proved dangerous, he could stop selling it, and filch more laundry. And if rumors of a clever sneak thief sent the Watch around on heightened alert, he could stop going for the trinkets and confine himself to listening at chimneys, which sent up no smoke in this lovely weather, but did provide wonderful listening posts.

Unfortunately, although he had cultivated acute hearing, it wasn't good enough to enable him to hear what it was that the dour sell-sword was saying.

However, it did seem as if the man was *buying*, not selling, information. When the surreptitious motion that marked the passing of coins from hand to hand finally took place, it was the sell-sword who passed the coins to Skif's target, and not the other way around.

Might could be I could sell 'im a bit, it's Lord Qrthallen he's wantin't' hear about, Skif thought speculatively. He decided to investigate chimneys at the manse at the next moon-dark. They might prove to be useful.

"Fire," he heard then, which brought him alert again, and he closed his eyes and put his head down, the better to concentrate.

"Bad enough," the sell-sword grunted. "Ye'd'a seen me a-passin' buckets that night."

Skif's target, who Skif knew as "Tain Kelken," but who the sell-sword addressed as "Jass," laughed shortly. "Could'a bin rainin' like 'tis now, an' ye'd nawt hev got it out," he replied, with a knowing tone. "Reckon when a mun hev more'n twenny barrels uv earth tar an' wax painted on mun's buildin', take more'n bucket lines t'douse it."

Earth tar! Skif had heard rumors that the reason the fire had caught and taken off so quickly was because it had been tarred—but this was the first he'd heard of earth tar and *wax!* Ordinary pine tar, or *pitch,* as it was also called, was flammable enough—but the rarer earth tar, which bubbled up from pits, was much more flammable. And to combine it with wax made no sense—the concoction would have been hideously expensive.

Unless the point was to turn the building into a giant candle.

Only one person could know that about the fire. The man who'd set it.

Now Skif had that part of the equation, and it took everything he had to stay right where he was and pretend he had dropped into a doze with his forehead on his knees. Anger boiled up in him, no matter that he had pledged he would not do anything until he knew the real hand behind the fire. The bullyboy sounded proud of himself, smug, and not the least troubled that whole families had died in that fire, and others been made bereft, parentless, childless, partnerless.

And my family—gone. All gone.

"And just how would you know that?" the sell-sword asked. His tone was casual… but there was anger under it as deep and as controlled as Skif's. The bullyboy didn't hear it, so full of himself he was; maybe only someone with matching anger would have. It shocked Skif and kept him immobile, as mere caution could not have.

"That'd be tellin', wouldn' it?" the bullyboy chuckled. "An' that'd be tellin' more'n I care to. 'Less ye've got more'v what brung ye here."

The sell-sword just grunted. "Curious, is all," he said, as if he had lost interest. "Don' 'magine th'lad as ordered that painted on 'is buildin' would be too popular 'round here."

"What? A mun cain't hev a coat've sum thin' *good* put on 'is property 'thout folks takin' it amiss?" the man known as both Jass and Tain said with feigned amazement. "Why man, tha's what's painted on ships t'make 'em watertight! Mun got word inspectors weren't happy, 'e puts the best they is on yon buildin'! Is't *his* fault some damnfool woman kicks over a cook-stove an' sets the thing ablaze afore he kin get th' right surface on't, proper?"

"You tell me," the sell-sword sneered. Evidently he didn't care much for the man he faced. Maybe Taln-Jass couldn't tell it, but there was thick-laid contempt in the sell-sword's voice.

The bullyboy laughed, and Skif seethed. "That'd be tellin'. An' I'm too dry t'be tellin'."

Skif thought that this was a hint for the sell-sword to buy his informant a drink, but a scrape of stools told a different story. "This rain ain't liftin' afore dawn," the arsonist said. "I'm off."

"Sweet dreams," the sell-sword said, his tone full of bitter irony that wished the opposite.

Laughter was his only answer. Skif opened his eyes to see his target turn and shove his way out through the crowd to the door. The sell-sword remained seated, brooding.

Then his back tensed. He stood up, slowly and deliberately, and for a moment Skif thought he was going to turn around to look behind him to see who might have been listening to the conversation.

Skif shrank back into his alcove as far as he could go, and tried to look sleepy and disinterested. Somehow he did not want this man to know that *he* had heard every bit of the last several moments.

But evidently the sell-sword trusted in the unwritten rules of the Arms. He did not turn. He only stood up, and stalked back out through the crowd, out the door, and into the rain.

Two tenants of a nearby, more crowded table took immediate occupation of the little table. And Skif breathed a sigh of relief, before he settled back into his smoldering anger. Because now that he knew who the tool was—that tool would pay. Perhaps not immediately, but he *would* pay.

When the rain died, Skif left; there was still a drizzle going, but not enough to keep him in the Arms any longer. His mind buzzed; his anger had gone from hot to cold, in which state he was able to think, and think clearly.

Somehow, he had to find the next link in the chain—the man who had paid for the arson. But how?

Loosen the bastard's tongue, that's what I gotta do. As Skif dodged spills out of waterspouts and kept when he could to the shadows, he went over his options.

No point tryin' to threaten 'im. Alone, in his stable loft, he could indulge himself in fantasies of slipping in at a window and taking the man all unaware—of waking the scum with the cold touch of a knife at his throat. But they were fantasies, and Skif knew it. Knives or no, unaware or not, the bullyboy was hard and tough and bigger than Skif. Much bigger.

So what were his real options? Drink? Drugs?

Not viable, neither of them. He couldn't afford enough of the latter to do any good, and as for the former—well, he'd seen that particular lad drink two men under the table and stagger out with his secrets still kept behind his teeth. The closest he ever got to boasting was what he'd done tonight.

Just stick on 'im like a burr, Skif decided, and ground his teeth. It wasn't the solution he craved. *Watch 'im, an stick to 'im. If he takes up summat to 'is rooms, I gotta figger out which chimbley leads 't his, or—*

Suddenly, an idea struck him that was so brilliant he staggered.

I don' need all that dosh fer shakin' loose words loose no more! He knew who had set the fire! So the money he had been using to pay bribes could be used for—

For a room in th'bastard's own place!

Above, below, or to either side, it didn't matter. So long as Skif had an adjoining surface, he could rig the means to hear what was going on no matter how quiet the conversation was. Bribes weren't all he'd been paying for—he'd been getting lessons at spycraft. How to follow someone and not be detected. How to overhear what he needed to. In fact, so long as Skif had a room *anywhere* in the arsonist's boarding house, he'd be able to eavesdrop on the man. It would just take a little more work, that was all.

He lifted his face to the drizzle and licked the cool rain from his lips, feeling that no wine could have a sweeter taste. *I'm gonna get you now,* he thought with glee. *An'once I know what you know—*

Well.

Knives weren't the only weapons. And poisons were a sight cheaper than tongue-loosening drugs.

"I don' need a lot've room," Skif said to the arsonist's scrawny, ill-kempt landlord, who looked down at him with disinterest in his watery blue eyes. "No cook space, neither. Mebbe a chimbley an' a winder, but mostly just 'nuff room t' flop."

"I mebbe got somethin'," the landlord said at last. Skif nodded eagerly, and did not betray in the slightest that he already *knew* the landlord had exactly what *he* wanted, because Skif had bribed the tenant of the highly-desirable room right next to his target to find lodgings elsewhere. Young Lonar hadn't taken a lot of bribing—he was sweet on a cookshop girl, and wanted some pretties to charm her out of her skirts and into his bed. Skif simply lifted a handful of jingling silver bangles from a dressing-table placed too near an open window; they were worth a hundred times to Lonar what Skif would have gotten for them fenced.

It had taken him time to work this out, time in which his anger kept ice water flowing in his veins and sparked his brain to clever schemes. First, finding out the arsonist's exact room. Next, casing the place, and discovering who his neighbors were. Then picking the most bribable, and finally, the bribe itself.

Lonar had one room—Skif had even been in it several times already. It was ideally suited for Skif's purposes; the back of the arsonist's own fireplace and chimney formed part of one of the inner walls. From the look of the bricked-up back and the boarded-up door in the same wall, the room and the arsonist's had once been part of a larger suite, and the fireplace had been open between the two rooms, giving each a common hearth.

"Ten copper a fortnight," the landlord said tersely. "No cookin', no fires. Chimbley oughter be enough t'keep ye warm'o nights."

In answer, Skif handed over enough in copper and silver to pay for the next six moons, and the man nodded in terse satisfaction. This wasn't unusual behavior, especially out of someone who had no regular—or obvious—job. When you were flush, you paid up your doss for as long as you could afford. When you weren't, you tried to sweet-talk the landlord as long as possible, then fled before he locked up your room and took your stuff.

Probably he expected that Skif would be gone by the end of those six moons.

Be nice, but I ain't countin' on it.

The landlord handed over a crude chit with an "M"—for Midwinter Moon—on it. That was how long Skif had; if the landlord tried to cheat him by claiming he'd paid for less time, he could show it to a court to prove how long his tenancy was supposed to be. There was, of course, no key to be handed over, not in a place like this one. Tenants were expected to find their own ways of safeguarding their belongings. Some were more interesting than others.

Skif pocketed his chit, picked up his pack and bag, and ran up the narrow stairs to the second-floor landing. Three doors faced it; his own was in the middle. His room wasn't much bigger than a closet between the two sets of two rooms each on either side. The door was slightly ajar, and Skif slipped inside quickly, closing it behind him and dropping a bar across it. The room itself wasn't much wider than the door.

Lonar hadn't left anything behind but dirt. The walls, floor, and ceiling were a uniform grime color. Impossible to tell if there was paint under the dirt. Closed shutters in the far wall marked the window. From the amount of light leaking in around them, it didn't look as if they were very weathertight. Not that it mattered. Skif wasn't here for the decor. He was, however, here for the walls.

Never mind how well the shutters fit, it was the window itself that featured prominently in Skif's plans.

He flung open the shutters to let air in, and unrolled his pallet of blankets on the floor, adding his spare clothing beneath as extra padding, and untied the kerchief in which he had bundled the rest of his few belongings. Including the one, very special object that he had gone to a lot of trouble to filch.

A glass. A *real* glass.

He set it in the corner out of harm's way, and laid himself down on his pallet, closing his eyes and opening his ears, taking stock of his surroundings. Bazie would have been proud of him.

Not a lot of street noise; this house was on a deadend, and most of the other places on the street also supplied rooms to let. Skif identified the few sounds coming from outside and ignored them, one by one.

Above him, footsteps. Four, perhaps five children of varying ages, all barefoot. A woman, also barefoot. That would be Widder Koil, who made artificial flowers with paper and fabric. Presumably the children helped as well; otherwise, he couldn't imagine how she alone would earn enough to feed them all. The voices drifted down from above, edgy with hunger, but not loud.

Below, nothing. The first-floor tenant was still asleep; he was a night carter, one of the few tenants here with a respectable and relatively well-paying job.

To the left, the wall with no fireplace, four shrill female voices. Whores, four sisters sharing two rooms; relatively prosperous and without a protector. They didn't need one; the arsonist slept with at least two of them on a regular basis, and no one wanted to chance his anger.

And to the right…

Snores. The chimney echoed with them.

Not surprising; like Skif, the arsonist worked at night. The question was, which of the two rooms was the man's bedroom?

Skif's hope was that it was not the one with the fireplace, but there was no way of telling if the man was snoring very loudly in the next room, or not quite as loudly in the fireplace room.

At least I can hear him.

Well, there was nothing more to do now. He let his concentration lapse, and consciously relaxed the muscles of his face and jaw as he had learned to do when he wanted to sleep. He would be able to learn more in a few candlemarks. And when his target went out tonight, so would he.

He woke all at once, and knew why. The window above his head showed a dark-blue sky with a single star, his room was shrouded in shadows, and next door, the snoring had stopped.

Jass-Taln was awake.

He sat up quickly and felt in the corner for his precious glass. He put it up against the wall and put his ear against the bottom of it.

The man moved like a cat; Skif had to give him that much grudging credit. He made very little noise as he walked around his rooms, and unlike some people, he didn't talk to himself. No coughing, no sneezing, no spitting; how ironic that a cold-blooded murderer made such an ideal neighbor.

Ideal. Unless, of course, you actually wanted to hear what he was up to.

Now there was some noise in the fireplace! Skif frowned in concentration, isolating the sounds.

Whittling. Shavings hitting the bricks. The sound of a hand scraping the shavings together, then putting them in the grate. Then the rattling and scratching of a handful of twigs. A log coming down atop them.

A metallic *clunk* startled him, though he should have expected it. Taln-Jass had just slapped a pan down onto the grill over his cooking fire.

A while later; the sound of something scraping and rattling in the pan. Eating sounds. Frequent belches.

All of which were sweeter than any Bard's music to Skif's ears. The trick with the glass worked, just as his teacher had claimed it would! And it sounded as if the room with the fireplace was the arsonist's "public" room, for all of these noises were nearer than the snores had been. Which meant that when the man brought clients here for private discussions, it would be the room nearest Skif where those discussions would take place.

A fierce elation thrilled through him, and he grinned with clenched teeth. Who needed drink, drugs, or even threats when you could listen to your target at will, unnoticed?

Now all he needed was time and patience, and both were, at last, on his side.

1 0

Although Skif's patience was taxed to the uttermost by the lack of any concrete progress in his quest, he at least was collecting a great deal of personal information on his "neighbor," Jass. The arsonist, it soon developed, had as many names as there were moons in the calendar.

Not only was he known by the two Skif knew, but he was addressed variously as "Hodak" by his landlord, "Derial" by the whores, and various nicknames derived from the slight squint of one eye when he was thinking, his ability to move silently, the fact that a small piece was missing from his ear, and some not-very-clever but thoroughly obscene epithets that passed for humor among his acquaintances.

Skif decided on "Jass." Easy to remember, it had no associations for him other than his target. But he was careful never to personally address the man at all, much less by name, since he wasn't actually supposed to know any of his names. The few times they met on the stairs or the landing, Skif ducked his head subserviently and crammed himself to the wall to let the arsonist pass. Let Jass think that Skif was afraid of him— all that meant was that Jass had never yet gotten a look at anything other than the top of Skif's head.

A man of many trades was Jass. Over the course of three fortnights, Skif listened in to his conversations when he had someone with him in his rooms—pillow talk and business talk, and boasts when deep in his cups. He wasn't "just" an arsonist. If he had been, he'd have gone short more often than not, as that wasn't a trade that he was called on to practice nearly often enough to make a living at it. Together with all four of the whores he practiced a variation on the ketchin' lay where one of the girls would lure an unsuspecting customer into Jass' clutches where the would-be lecher soon found himself hit over the head and robbed.

He was also known for setting fires, of course—though, so far since Skif had moved in, they were all minor acts of outrage, designed to frighten shopkeepers into paying for "protection" from one of the three gangs he worked for, or to punish those who had refused to do so. On rare occasions, he sold information, most of which Skif didn't understand, but seemed to have to do with intrigues among some of the city's wealthier folk. Where he got these tidbits was a mystery to Skif, although there was a direct connection with the darker side of Haven, in that the information generally was about who among Jass's cronies had been hired by one of the upright citizens, and for what dirty job.

The craggy-faced sell-sword was not the only one interested in Jass' information. There were at least three other takers to Skif's knowledge, two of whom transacted their business only within the four walls of Jass's fireplace room.

But to Skif's growing impatience, not once had Jass been commissioned by the same person who had put him to igniting the tenement house.

Skif might have learned more—this summer brought a rash of tiny, "mysterious" fires to blight the streets of Haven—but he had to eat, too. Frustratingly, he would sometimes return to his room after a night of roof walking only to hear the tail end of a conversation that *could* have been interesting, or to hear Jass himself come in after a long night of—what? Skif seldom knew; that was the frustrating part. He might learn the next day of a fire that Jass *could* have been responsible for, or the discovery of a feckless fool lying coshed in an alley, who had trusted in the blandishments of a face that drink made desirable that *might* belong to one of Jass' girls. But unless Jass boasted, and boasted specifically, there was no way of telling what could be laid at his door and not someone else's.

Midsummer came and passed, remarkable only for Midsummer Fairs and the fine pickings to be had at them, and Skif was no closer to uncovering the real culprit behind the fire. Day after day he would come awake in the damp heat of midday with a jolt the moment that the snoring in the other room stopped, and lie on his pallet, *listening*. Sweat prickled his scalp, and he spread himself out like a starfish in a vain hope of finding a hint of cooler air. He longed for the breezes of his stable loft, but still he lay in the heat, waiting for a word, a clue, a sign.

He had thought that he knew how to be patient. As days became weeks, and weeks tuned to moons, he discovered he knew nothing at all about patience. There were times when his temper snapped, when he *wanted* to curse, rail at fate and at the man who was so obstinately concealing his secrets, to pound the floor and walls with his fists. That he did none of these things was not a measure of his patience, but rather that he did not *dare* to reveal himself to Jass by an overheard gaffe of his own.

The more time passed, the more his hatred grew.

But at least he was not alone in hating and despising Jass. The sell-sword was no friend to the arsonist either, not if Skif was any judge. Twice he had caught the man glaring at Jass' back with an expression that had made Skif's blood turn cold. Twice only—no more than that, but the second time had been enough to convince Skif that the first was no fluke. Whatever he had done to earn the sell-sword's enmity, Skif was certain that only the fact that Jass was, and remained, useful to the man kept Jass alive and unharmed.

One stifling day, Skif lay on the bare boards of his room dressed in nothing more than a singlet, eyes closed and a wet cloth lying across them in an attempt to bring some coolness to his aching head. He could only breathe in the furnacelike air, and reflect absently on how odd it was that this part of town actually stank less than some better-off neighborhoods. But that was simply because here, where there was nothing, *everything* had a value. Even nightsoil was saved and collected—tannery 'prentices came 'round to collect urine every morning, paying two clipped-pennybits a pot, and the rest went straight into back-garden compost heaps. People who had birds or pigs collected their leavings for their gardens, and as for the dung from horses and donkeys—well, it was considered so valuable that it barely left the beast's bum before someone scuttled out to the street and scooped it up. Nothing went to waste here, no matter how rotten food was, it went into *something's* belly. As a consequence, the only stench coming off these streets and alleys was of sweat and grime and stale beer, but nothing worse than that. Why, Skif could hardly bear to walk in the alley of a merchants' neighborhood in this weather!

Jass' snores still echoed up the chimney; how could the man sleep in heat like this?

The faintest breath of air moved across the floor, drifting from the open window to crawl under the crack beneath the door. Drops of sweat trickled down Skif's neck and crept along his scalp without cooling him appreciably.

A fly droned somewhere near the ceiling, circling around and around and bumping against the grime-streaked paint in a mindless effort to get beyond it. It could have flown out the window, of course, but it was determined to find a way through to the next story of the house, no matter how unlikely a prospect that seemed.

Skif felt a curious kinship with the fly. At the moment, his own quest seemed just about as futile.

And he was just as stupidly, bullheadedly determined not to give it up.

He wondered if perhaps—just perhaps—he ought to start spending the day somewhere other than here. Somewhere in a cellar perhaps, where he would be able to doze in blessed coolness. So long as he managed to awaken before Jass did, and get back here…

But as sure as he did *that*, Jass would change his habits and start sleeping, at least in part, by night, so that he could conduct some of his business by daylight.

At least I'm savin' money an eats, he thought wryly. In this heat he had no appetite to speak of, and spent most of his food money on peppermint tea. It was easy enough to make without a fire; just put a pot full of water and herb packets on the windowsill in the sun, and leave it to brew all day. And it cooled the mouth and throat, if not the body.

Skif found himself thinking longingly of rain. A good thunderstorm would cool the city down and wash the heaviness out of the air. Rain was his enemy—he wouldn't, couldn't work in the rain—but it would be worth not working for one night.

In weather like this, anyone who could afford to went off into the country anyway. Houses were shut up, furniture swathed in sheets, valuables taken away with the rest of the household goods. Only those few whose duties kept them here remained; Lord Orthallen, for one— he was on the Council, and couldn't leave. Which was just as well for Skif's sake, since his larder was supplying Skif's peppermint and the sugar to sweeten it.

Next door, the snoring stopped. Jass was awake at last.

No sounds of cooking this past fortnight; Jass was eating out of cookshops rather than add to the heat in his rooms by lighting a fire.

Within moments Skif knew that there was no point in lingering around this afternoon; Jass would be going out and probably not returning until after nightfall, if then.

No point in Skif staying inside either. He wasn't going to sleep, not here. He might as well see if there was somewhere, anywhere in the city where there was a breath of cooler air.

In loose breeches, barefoot, and with his shirtsleeves rolled up, he was soon out into the street, where virtually everyone looked just as uncomfortable and listless as he. For once, the narrow streets proved a blessing; not much sun got past the buildings to bake the pounded dirt and add to the misery.

It occurred to him that temples, constructed of thick stone, just might harbor some lingering coolness in their walls. In fact—the temples over in wealthier parts of Haven usually had crypts beneath them, which would *certainly* be as cool as any wine cellar, and a deal quieter.

Aye, but then I get preached at, or I get asked what I want. They find me i' the crypt, they run me out, sure as sure. Them priests is like ants, always where ye don' want 'em. Wisht I could find me a temple crypt wi'nawt about.

Well… maybe he could; there were plenty of the highborn who had their own chapels, and private crypts, too, in the city cemeteries. There, he'd run little risk of being disturbed.

Some might have second thoughts about seeking a nap among the dead, but Skif wasn't one of them.

A candlemark later, Skif slipped down the stairs of a private chapel in one of the cemeteries reserved for the highborn. The chapel was above, where those who were queasy about any actual contact with the dead could pray; Skif headed down into the family crypts. Said lordling was gone, the house shut up, with only a couple of maids and an old dragon of a housekeeper. So there wouldn't be any impromptu visits by the family. The chapel had been locked, but that was hardly going to stop Skif.

He'd picked this place in particular because the family was known for piety and familial pride—and because there *hadn't* been a death in more than a year. Napping among the dead was one thing; napping among the recently interred was another. And family pride, Skif hoped, would have seen to it that the crypt was kept clean and swept. He didn't mind the dead, but spiders were something else and gave him the real horrors.

It was darker than the inside of a pocket down here, but his hunch had been right. It was blessedly cool, and he pressed his overheated body up against the cold marble walls with relief while he waited for his eyes to adjust. Some light did filter down the staircase from the chapel windows above, and eventually Skif was able to make out the dim shape of a stone altar, laden with withered flowers, against the back wall. He sniffed the air carefully, and his nose was assaulted by nothing worse than dust and the ghosts of roses.

There were two rows of tombs, each bearing the name and station of its occupant graven atop it. No statues here; this family wasn't *quite* lofty enough for marble images of its dead adorning the tombs.

Skif yawned, and felt his way to the stone table at the back of the chapel, meant for flower offerings. Just in case someone came down here, he planned to take his nap in the shadows beneath it.

Stone didn't make a particularly yielding bed, but he'd slept on stone plenty of times before this; it would be no worse than sleeping on the floor of his uncle's tavern, and a lot quieter.

He was very pleased to note that his hunch had paid off; even beneath the table there wasn't much dust. He laid himself out in the deep shadow with his back pressed against the wall and his head pillowed on his arm. The stone practically sucked the heat right out of his body, and in moments, for the first time in days, he fell into a deep and dreamless sleep.

It seemed only heartbeats later that something jolted him awake.

He froze, his eyes snapping open, and saw the wavering light of a single candle illuminating the staircase he had only just crept down.

"Yer certain-sure there ain't gonna be nobody here?"

That's Jass! Skif thought in shock. *What's he doing here?*

Surely not grave robbing—the amount of work it would take to get into one of these tombs was *far* beyond anything the Jass that Skif knew would be willing to do! Even supposing there was anything of value interred there...

"I'm quite sure," said a smooth and cultured voice. "Rovenar and his family are at his country estate, and none of his father's friends are still alive to pay him a graveside visit. Besides, it would hardly matter if anyone *did* come. I have the key; Rovenar trusts me to see that no one gets in here to work any mischief in his absence. If anyone should appear, I am simply doing him that favor, and you, my servant, have accompanied me."

"Servant?" Jass growled. It was amazing how well the stairs worked to funnel sound down here; Skif would have thought they were in the same room with him.

The voice laughed. "Bodyguard, then." The voice was clearly amused at Jass' attitude toward being taken as a servant.

It occurred to Skif that if he was seeing the light of a candle up there, it must be later than he'd thought when he was initially startled awake. It must have been the turning of the key in the lock on the chapel door that woke him, and he blessed the owner who had put in a door that locked itself on closing.

Whatever brought Jass and the unknown gentleman here, it had to be something out of the ordinary.

"What'd ye want t' meet *here* for?" Jass grumbled. "Place fair gives me th' creeps."

"It is cool, it is private, and we stand no chance of being overheard," the voice replied. "And because I have no mind to pay a call on *you*. I pay you; you can accommodate yourself to me."

Skif winced. Nothing could have been clearer than the contempt in those words.

But either Jass was inured to it, or he was oblivious to it.

Mebbe he just don't care. Anyone who'd been entrusted with the key to a lordling's chapel had to have money, at least, and the song of that money must ring in Jass's ears, deafening him to anything else.

"So wut's th' job *this* time that you don' want ears about?" Jass asked bluntly. "It better pay better nor last time."

"It will," the voice said coolly. "Not that you weren't paid exactly what the last job was worth—and I suspect you made somewhat more, afterward. I'm given to understand that you are considered something of an information broker."

"Ye never give me enuff fer quiet," Jass said sullenly.

Skif felt as if he'd been struck by lightning. *Bloody 'ell! This's where Jass gets 'is stuff about th'highborns!*

"I don't pay for what I don't require," the voice countered. "Just remember that. And remember that when I *do* pay for silence, I expect it. Don't disappoint me, Jass. You'll find I'm a different man when I've been disappointed."

A shiver ran down Skif's back at the deadly menace of that voice, and he was astonished that Jass didn't seem to hear it himself. Jass was either oblivious or arrogant, and neither suggested he'd be enjoying life for very much longer unless he realized he was treading on perilous ground. "Th' job," he simply prompted impatiently, quite as if *he* was the one in charge and not his client.

"Simple enough," the smooth, cultured voice replied. "Another fire, like the one I commissioned last winter. But this time, I don't want any cleverness on your part. No earth tar, no pine tar, no oil or mineral spirits; *nothing* to encourage the blaze. The warehouse will be left open for you, so start it from the inside."

Skif froze; he couldn't have moved to save his life. There it was— everything he'd been looking for. Except that he couldn't see who Jass was talking to, and he'd never heard that voice before.

Jass growled. "Ain't gonna burn good," he complained. "Might even save it, if—"

"Nonsense," the voice replied firmly. "In this heat and as dry as it's been? It'll go up like chaff. People were suspicious the last time, Jass. There were enquiries. I had a great deal of covering up to do. It was exceedingly inconvenient for me, a considerable amount of totally unexpected work. What's more, some of that work went to saving *your* neck. Some of the tenants didn't get out—and if the fire had been traced back to you, they'd have hanged you for murder."

Jass actually laughed, but it had a nasty sound to it. "Well, they didn't, did they? Tha's cuz there weren't no witnesses. I seen t' that. Tha's why people didn' all get out. 'Cause I quieted 'em."

Skif's heart turned to ice.

"And that is supposed to show me how clever you are?" The man snorted. "You're very good at what you do, Jass, and my lord Orthallen gave you high recommendations, but you've become arrogant and careless. Stick to what you're told to do. Don't try to be clever. And if you get caught, I'll wash my hands of you, don't think I won't."

"Jest gimme th' job," Jass growled, and the voice related details and instructions.

Jass thinks if 'e's caught, 'e kin turn 'is coat an' tell on milord, there, savin' 'is own neck. But Skif was *listening*, as Jass was not, and he knew that if Jass was ever caught, his life wasn't worth a bent pin. If there was even the *chance* that the Watch was on to Jass, his employer would ensure his silence in the most effective way possible.

It wouldn't take much—just another interview in an out-of-the-way place like this one. Only Jass would not be meeting "milord," and there would be an extra corpse in the cemetery.

There was a metallic chink as money passed from one hand to another, and Jass counted it.

"Remember what I said," the voice warned. One set of footsteps marked the owner's transit to the door of the chapel, and Jass got up to follow. "Don't get creative. Just set the fire, and get out."

"Awright, awright," Jass sneered. *"My lord."*

The light vanished; the candle must have been put out. The door swung quietly open on well-oiled hinges, with only a faint sigh of displaced air to mark it opening. Then it shut again with a hollow sound, and the key rattled in the lock.

'E's gettin'away! I dunno 'oo 'e is, an 'e's gettin'away!

Skif practically flew up the stairs, no longer caring if he was discovered, so long as he could see who that voice belonged to!

Too late. Not only were they gone, he couldn't even hear footsteps.

He flung himself at the windows—hopeless; not only was it dark outside, but the windows didn't open and they were made of colored glass as well. There was no way he could see *anything* through them—except for one single blob of light, a lantern, perhaps, receding into the darkness. He returned to the door, but you couldn't just *open* it from within once you got inside, it had to be unlocked from the inside as well as from the outside. Cursing under his breath, he got out his lock picks again, knowing that this would cost him yet more time, in the dark and fumbling in his hurry.

He cursed his clumsy fingers and the lock picks that suddenly turned traitor on him; at last he heard the *click* of the tumblers and wrenched the wretched door open.

There wasn't a single light to be seen within the four walls of the cemetery. They'd gotten far enough away that they were out of sight among the tombs, and by now Jass and his employer would have gone their separate ways, with nothing to show the connection between them, nothing to prove that "milord" *wasn't* just paying a sentimental or pious visit on the anniversary of someone's death.

No! Skif wasn't going to give up that easily.

From here there was only a single path winding among the chapels, crypts, and trees, and Skif tore up it. There were only two entrances, and he thought he knew which one "milord" would take. He had to catch the man before he left the cemetery—he had to! He had to *know*—

With his heart pounding and his eyes burning with rage, he abandoned everything but the chase. At a point where two private chapels faced one another across the path, where he might have slowed, just in case there was someone lurking in the shadows, he only sped up.

And at the last moment as he passed between them, too late to avoid the ambush, he sprung a trap on himself.

A trap that took the form of a cord stretched at knee-height along the path.

Skif hit it, and went flying face-first into the turf. The impact knocked the breath out of him and left him stunned just long enough for the ambusher to get on top of him and pin him down.

He fought—but his opponent was twice his size and had probably forgotten more dirty tricks than Skif knew. Ruthless, methodical, he made short work of one young boy. Before he could catch the breath that had been knocked out of him by the fall, Skif found himself gagged, his hands tied behind his back, pulled to his feet, and shoved into one of those two chapels.

The door shut with an ominous brazen *clang.* Skif's feet were kicked out from beneath him before he could lash out at his captor, and he went to the floor like a sack of meal.

There was a rattle of metal, and the shutter of a dark lantern opened. Skif blinked, eyes watering at the light, as the craggy sell-sword who had bought so much information from Jass peered down at him.

"Well, well. A trap for a fox I set, and I catch a rabbit," the man said, looking down at Skif with no humor in his face whatsoever. He wasn't talking like one of the denizens of Haven's rough streets anymore; he had an accent that Skif couldn't place. "Now, why is it, I wonder, that wherever I find Jass, also you I find?"

Skif glared at him over the gag, daring him to try something. Not that he had the slightest idea of what he was going to do if the man made a move...

But the man only stooped swiftly, and seized one of Skif's ankles. Kick as hard as he could, Skif could do nothing against the man's greater strength; at the cost of a bump on the head that made him see stars, he gained nothing and found himself with both ankles trussed and tied to his wrists, which were in turn tied behind his back. Only then did the man take off the gag, taking care not to let his hands get within range to be bitten.

He squatted easily beside Skif, sitting on his heels. "I believe it's time speech we have, you and I," he said, frowning. "And it is that I hope for your sake that you *aren't* Jass' errand boy."

He stared hard at Skif for a long time; Skif worked his jaw silently, and continued to glare at him, although he was beginning to feel a little—odd. As if there was something messing about inside his head.

So if 'e wants ter talk, why don't 'e get on wi' it? he thought furiously. And at that exact moment, the man smiled grimly, and nodded to himself.

"What were you doing here?" the sell-sword asked as soon as Skif's mouth was clear of the threads the cloth had left on his tongue.

"Sleepin'!" Skif spat, and snarled in impotent fury. If it hadn't been for this bastard, he'd have found out who Jass' employer was! He made up his mind not to tell the man one word more than he had to.

"In a cemetery?" The man raised one eyebrow.

Skif found angry words tumbling out of his mouth, despite his resolution not to talk. "Wha's it matter t'you? Or *them*? They's not gonna care—an' it's a damn sight cooler an' quieter here than anywheres else! Them highborns is all playin' out i'country, *they* ain't gonna know 'f I wuz here!"

"You have a point," the man conceded, then his face hardened again.

"But why is it that you just *happen* sleeping to be in the same place where Jass goes to have a little chat?"

"How shud *I* know?" Skif all but wailed. "I drops off, next thing I knows, he's up there yappin't' summun an' *I* wanta know who!"

If he'd had his hands free, he'd have clapped both of them over his mouth in horror. His tongue didn't seem to be under his control—what was happening to him?

"Oh, really?" The man's other eyebrow arched toward his hairline. "And why is that?"

"Becuz Jass' the bastid what set th' big fire an' burned me out—an' the mun whut was with 'im wuz th' mun what *paid* 'im t' do it!" Skif heard himself saying frantically. "I know'd it, cuz I 'eerd 'im say so! 'Is boss set 'im another fire t' start right whiles I was listenin'! An' I wanta know who *he* is cuz I'm gonna get *'im,* an' then I'm gonna get Jass, an—"

"Enough." The man held up a sword-callused palm, and Skif found his flood of angry words cut off again. Just in time, too; there had been tears burning in his eyes, and he didn't want the man to see *them.* He blinked hard to drive them away, but he couldn't do much about the lump in his throat that threatened to choke him.

Wut in hell is happenin 't 'me? But the man darted out a hand, quick as a snake, and grabbed Skif's shoulder and shook it. That hand crushed muscle and bone and *hurt—*

"Now, to me you listen, boy, and engrave my words on your heart you will—" the man said, leaning forward until all Skif could see were his hawk-sharp, hawk-fierce eyes. "You playing are in deeper waters than you know, and *believe* me, to swim in them you cannot hope. Your nose out of this you keep, or likely someone is to fish you out of the Terilee, with a rock around your ankles tied, if find you at all they do."

Skif shuddered convulsively, and an involuntary sob fought its way out of his throat. The man sat back on his heels again, satisfied.

"Jass will to worry about shortly, much more than the setting of fires have," the man said darkly. "And he *will* answer for the many things he has responsible been for."

"But—"

"That is all you need to know," the man said forcefully, and the words froze in Skif's throat.

The sell-sword pulled out a knife, and for one horrible moment, Skif thought that he was dead.

But the man laid it on the floor, just out of reach, and stood up. "Too clever you are, by half," he said, with a grim little smile. "Now, about my business I will be. The moment I leave, getting yourself loose you can be about. Manage you will, quite sure I am."

He dropped the shield over the dark lantern, plunging the chapel into complete blackness. In the next moment, although Skif hadn't heard him move, the door opened, a tall, lean shadow slipped through it, and it closed again.

Skif lost no time in wriggling over the stone floor to the place where the man had left the knife. When he was right on top of it, he wriggled around until he could grab it. As soon as he got it into his hands, he sawed through the cord binding his wrists to his ankles. Not easy—but not impossible. The man had left him enough slack in his ropes to do just that.

Once that was cut, he managed to contort his body enough to get his arms back over to the front of himself and then sawed through the bindings at ankle and wrist. It was a good knife; sharp, and well cared for. If it didn't cut through the cords holding him as if they were butter, he wasn't forced to hack at them for candlemarks either.

But all the time his hands were working, his mind was, too.

Who—and *what*—was that man? How had he managed to get Skif to tell him everything he knew? Why did he want to know so much about Jass? *Why'd 'e lemme go? Why'd 'e warn me off?*

Not that Skif had any intention of being warned off. *Oo's 'e think 'e is, anyroad? Oo's 'e think 'e was talkin' to?* If there was one thing that Skif was certain of, it was his own expertise in his own neighborhood. However clever this man thought he was, he wasn't living right next door to his target, now, was he? He hadn't even known that Jass was the one who'd set that fire—Skif had seen a flicker of surprise when his own traitorous mouth had blurted *that* information out. He might think himself clever, but he wasn't as good as all that.

But 'ow'd 'e make me talk? More to the point, could he do it again if he got Skif in his hands?

Best not to find out.

'E won' catch me a second time, Skif resolved fiercely, as he cut through the last of the cords on his wrists and shook his hands free.

He stood up, sticking the knife in his belt. No point in wasting a good blade, after all. His anger still roiled in his gut; by now Jass was far off, and his employer probably safe in his fancy home.

I'll know 'is voice, though, if I ever hear it agin. Small consolation, but the best he had.

He slipped out the door of the chapel and closed it behind himself, not caring if he left this one unlocked or not. Around him the dead kept their silence, with nothing to show that there had ever been anyone here. Crickets sang, and honeysuckle sent a heavy perfume across the carefully manicured lawn. Jass had picked a good night for a clandestine meeting; the moon was no bigger than a fingernail paring.

Skif made his way to the spot where the wall was overhung by an ancient goldenoak—he hadn't come in by a gate, and he didn't intend to leave by one either. All the while his mind kept gnawing angrily on the puzzle of the sell-sword. *Bastid. Oo's 'e t' be so high i' th' nose? Man sells any thin' 'e's got t' whosever gots the coin!* Hadn't he already proved that by buying information from Jass? *An' wut's 'e gonna do, anyroad? Where's 'e get off, tellin' me Jass's gonna go down fer the fire? Why shud 'e care?*

Unless—*he* had a wealthy patron himself. Maybe someone who had lost money when the fire gutted Skif's building?

Or maybe Jass' own employer was playing a double game—covering his bets and his own back, hiring someone to "find out who set the fire" so that Jass got caught, the rich man could prove that he had gone far out of his way to try and catch the arsonist. Then no matter what Jass said, who would believe him?

The thought didn't stop Skif in his tracks, but it only roiled his gut further. The bastards! They were all alike, those highborns and rich men *and* their hirelings! They didn't care who paid, so long as *their* pockets were well-lined!

Skif swarmed up the tree by feel, edged along the branch that hung over the opposite side, and dropped down quietly to the ground, his heart on fire with anger.

Revenge. That's what he wanted. And he knew the best way to get it, too. If he didn't have a specific target, he could certainly make all of them suffer, at least a little. Just wait until they all came back from their fancy country estates! Wait until they returned—and came back, not just to things gone missing, but to cisterns and sewers plugged up, wells and chimneys blocked, linens spoiled, moths in the woolens, mice in the pantry and rats in the cellar! He'd cut sash cords, block windows so they wouldn't close right, drill holes in rooftops and in water pipes. It would be a long job, but he had all summer, and when he got through with them, the highborn of Valdemar would be dead certain that they'd been cursed by an entire tribe of malevolent spirits.

No time like right now, neither, he thought, with smoldering satisfaction as he fingered the sharp edge of his new knife.

So what if he didn't have a specific target. They were all alike anyway. So he'd make it his business to make them all pay, if it took him the rest of his life.

1 1

Skif had every intention of beginning his campaign of sabotage that very night, but when he tried to get near the district where the homes of the great and powerful were, he found the Watch was unaccountably active. There were patrols on nearly every street, and they weren't sauntering along either. *Something* had them alerted, and after the third time of having to take cover to avoid being stopped and questioned, he gave it up as hopeless and headed back to his room with an ill grace.

He got some slight revenge, though; as he turned a corner, a party of well-dressed, and very drunk young men came bursting out of a tavern with a very angry innkeeper shouting curses right on their heels. They practically ran him over, but in the scuffle and ensuing confusion, he lifted not one, but three purses. Making impotent threats and shouting curses of his own at them (which had all the more force because of his personal frustrations), he turned on his heel and stalked off in an entirely different direction.

Once out of sight, he ducked into a shadow, emptied the purses of their coins into his own pouch, and left the purses where he dropped them, tucking his pouch into the breast of his tunic. Then he strolled away in still another direction. After a block or two, there was nothing to connect him with the men he'd robbed. That was a mistake that many pickpockets made; they hung onto the purses they'd lifted. Granted, such objects were often valuable in themselves—certainly the three he'd taken had been—but they also gave the law a direct link between robber and robbed.

As he walked back toward his room, he managed to get himself back under control. Taking the purses had helped; it was a very small strike against the rich and arrogant bastards, but a strike nevertheless. *Just wait till they get to a bawdy house, an' they've gotta pay*—he thought, with grim satisfaction. *They better 'ope thet friends is willin' t'part with th' glim!* Skif had seen the wrath of plenty of madams and whoremasters whose customers had declined to pay, and they didn't take the situation lightly—nor did they accept promissory notes. They also employed very large men to help enforce the house rules and tariffs. When young men came into a place in a group, *no one* was allowed to leave until everyone's score had been paid. Those who still had purses would find them emptied before the night was over.

The thought improved his humor, and that restored his appetite. Now much fatter in the pocket than he had been this afternoon, he decided to follow his nose and see where it led him.

It took him to a cookshop that stood on the very border of his neighborhood, halfway between the semi-respectable district of entertainers, artists, musicians (not Bards, of course), peddlers, and decorative craftsmen and their 'prentices, and his own less respectable part of town.

I've earned a meal, he decided; taking care not to expose how much he had, he fished out one of the larger coins from his loot and dropped the pouch back into his tunic. Best to get rid of the most incriminating of the coins.

He eased on in; it was full, but not overcrowded, and he soon found space at the counter to put in his order. With a bowl of soup and a chunk of bread in one hand, and a mug of tea in the other, he made his way back outside to the benches in the open air where there were others eating, talking, or playing at dice or cards. Hot as it was, there were more folk eating under the sky than under the roof.

As was his habit, he took an out-of-the-way spot and kept his head down and his ears open. He was very soon rewarded; the place was abuzz with the rumor that *someone* had broken into the home of the wealthy merchant, Trenor Severik, and had stolen most of his priceless collection of miniature silver figurines. Severik had literally come home in time to see the thief vanishing out the window. Hence, the Watch; every man had been called out, the neighborhood had been sealed off, and anyone who couldn't account for himself was being arrested and taken off to gaol. It seemed that one of those arrested was an acquaintance of several of those sitting near Skif.

"Hard luck for poor Korwain," one of the artists said, with a snicker. "He couldn't say where he'd been—*of course.*"

His friends nearly choked on their meals. "I told him that woman was trouble," said another, whose dusty beard and hair bedecked with stone chips proclaimed him to be a sculptor. "Two sittings, and she's got me backed into a corner, tryin' to undo m'britches!" He shuddered, and the rest laughed. *"Patron of arts,* she calls herself! My eye!"

"Heyla, we tried to warn you, so don't say we didn't!" called a fellow with a lute case slung over his back. "Korwain knew it, so he's only got himself to blame!"

"That's what happens when you let greed decide your commissions for you," put in another, whose mouth looked like a miser's purse and whose eyes gloated at a fellow artist's misfortune. "I'd rather live on bread in a garret and serve the Temples than feast on marchpane and capon and—"

"Your paintings are so stiff they wouldn't please *anyone* but a priest, so don't go all over pious on us, Penchal!" catcalled the first artist.

That set off an argument on artistic merit and morality that Skif had no interest in. He applied himself to his soup, and left the bowl and mug on the table while the insults were still coming thick and fast, and rapidly building to the point where it would be fists, and not words, that would be flying.

At least now he knew why the Watch was up, and he wouldn't dare try anything for days, even a fortnight. Why would anyone bother to steal the collection of silver miniatures, anyway? They were unique and irreplaceable, yes, but you'd never be able to sell them anywhere, they were too recognizable, and you wouldn't get a fraction of their value if you melted them down. Oh, a thief could hold them for ransom, Skif supposed, but he'd certainly be found out and caught.

The only way the theft made sense was if someone had gotten a specific commission to take them. It was an interesting thought. Whoever had made the commission would have to be from outside Haven; what was the use of having something like that if you couldn't show it off? Anyone in Haven would know the collection as soon as it was displayed. The client could even be outside Valdemar altogether. So the thief, too, might be from outside Valdemar…

Huh. That'd be somethin', he thought, keeping an eye out for trouble as he made his way back home. *Have'ta be some kinda Master Thief, I guess. Somebody with all kinds uv tricks. Wonder if they's 'prentices fer that kinda work?* He'd never heard of a Master Thief, much less one that took on proteges, but maybe that sort of thing happened outside of Valdemar. *Like mebbe they's a whole Guild fer Thieves. Wouldn' that be somethin'!*

He amused himself with this notion as he worked his way homeward. He never, even when he had no reason to believe that he was being followed, went back home directly. He always doubled back, ducked down odd side passages, even cut over fences and across back gardens—though in the summer, that could be hazardous. In *his* neighborhood, no one had a back garden for pleasure. People used every bit of open ground to grow food in, and often kept chickens, pigeons, or a pig as well. And they assumed anyone coming over the fence was there to steal some of that precious food. Those that didn't have yards, but did have balconies, grew their vegetables in pots. Those that had nothing more than a window, had window boxes. Even Skif had a window box where he grew beans, trailing them around his window on a frame made of pieces of string. It was just common sense to augment what you could buy with what you could grow, but that did make it a bit more difficult to take the roundabout path until after the growing season was over.

It wasn't as late as he'd thought; lots of people were still up and about, making it doubly hazardous to go jumping in and out of yards. The front steps of buildings held impromptu gatherings of folks back from their jobs, eating late dinners and exchanging gossip. Most of the inns and cookshops had put benches out onto the street, so people could eat outside where it was cooler. It was annoying; Skif couldn't take his usual shortcuts. On the other hand, so many people out here meant more opportunities to confuse a possible follower.

With that in mind, he stopped at another cookshop for more tea and a fruit pie. More crust than fruit, be it added, but he didn't usually indulge in anything so frivolous, and the treat improved his temper a bit more. Not so much that he forgot his anger—and the burning need to find out who Jass' boss was—but enough so that he was able to look as though nothing in his life had changed in the last few candlemarks.

He paid close attention to those who sat down to eat after him, but saw no one that had also been at the previous cookshop. That was a good sign, and he quickly finished his tea and took the shortest way home.

Jass wasn't back yet. Neither were his girls—which meant that Jass probably wasn't going to set his fire tonight. Skif watered his beans and stripped for bed, lighting a stub of a candle long enough to actually count his takings.

His eyes nearly popped out of his head, and he counted it twice more before he believed it.

Gold. Five gold crowns, more than he'd ever had in his life! He'd thought the tiny coins were copperbits, not gold, and he'd paid for his meal and his treat with larger silver royals so as to get rid of two of the most conspicuous coins in his loot. He'd never dreamed the men could have been carrying gold.

Gold. Gold meant—everything. With gold, he suddenly had the means to concentrate *entirely* on finding Bazie's murderer. He wouldn't have to work the entire summer. With gold, he had the means to offer the kind of bribe that would loosen even the most reluctant of tongues.

With gold—he could follow up on the only real clue he had that wasn't connected to Jass.

"…my lord Orthallen gave you high recommendations…"

Gold could actually buy Skif a way into Orthallen's household—you didn't just turn up at a Great Lord's doorstep and expect to be hired. You had to grease palms before you got a place where you could expect to have privileges, maybe even collect tips for exemplary service. Gold would purchase forged letters of commendation—very rarely did anyone ever bother to check on those, especially if they were from a household inconveniently deep into the countryside. Those letters could get Skif into, say, a position as an under-groom, or a footman. A place where he'd be in contact with Lord Orthallen's guests, friends, and associates. *Where he could hear their voices.*

This one encounter changed everything…

Maybe.

It was one plan. There were others, that would allow Skif to hang onto the unexpected windfall. Jass wouldn't have been paid for the job entirely in advance—he'd have to collect the rest, and maybe Skif could catch him at it. There were other places where Skif could go to listen for that familiar, smooth and pitiless voice.

But the idea of insinuating himself into a noble household was the kind of plan that the craggy-faced sell-sword would not be able to anticipate. If he knew anything at all about Skif, he'd know that in the normal course of things, pigs would fly before someone like Skif would get his hands on enough money to buy his way into Lord Orthallen's household.

So Skif carefully folded the five gold coins into a strip of linen and packed them with his larger silver coins in the money belt that never left his waist. Then he blew out his candle, laid himself down, and began his nightly vigil of listening for Jass and Jass' business.

Because while gold might add to his options, if Bazie had taught him anything at all, it was to never, ever *abandon* an option just because a new one opened up.

* * *

But Jass didn't come back that night, nor the next day. Skif fell asleep waiting to hear his footsteps on the stairs, and woke the next morning to the unaccustomed sound of silence next door. He waited all day, wondering, with increasing urgency, what was keeping the man from his own rooms.

By nightfall, though, he knew why.

At dusk, a three-man team of the Watch came for Jass' two girls, *escorting* them off, rather than taking them off under guard, so it wasn't that they were arrested or under suspicion. Skif was at his window when they showed up, and he knew before they ever came in view that *something* was wrong, for the whole street went quiet. People whisked themselves indoors, or around corners, anything to get out of sight, and even the littles went silent and shrank back against their buildings, stopping dead in the middle of their games, and staring with round eyes at the three men in their blue-and-gray tunics and trews. The Watch never came to *this* part of town unless there was something wrong—or someone was in a lot of trouble.

Skif ducked back out of sight as soon as they came into view, and when he heard the unmistakable sound of boots on the staircase, huddled against the wall next to the door so that no one peering underneath it would see his feet.

What're they here for? For me? Did that feller turn me in? Did summun figger I lifted them purses? His mind raced, reckoning the odds of getting out via his emergency route through the window if they'd come for *him*, wondering if that sell-sword had somehow put the Watch onto him. And if he had—*why?*

The footsteps stopped at his landing, and his heart was in his mouth—his blood pounding in his ears—every muscle tensed to spring for the window.

But it wasn't his door they knocked on—and they knocked, politely, rather than pounding on it and demanding entrance. It was the girls' door, and when one of them timidly answered, an embarrassed voice asked if "Trana and Desi Farane" would be so kind as to come down to the Watch Station and answer a few questions.

Skif sagged down onto the floor, limp with relief. Whatever it was, it had nothing to do with him.

Now, everyone knew that if the Watch had *anything* on you, they didn't come and politely invite you to the Watch Station. When someone came with that particular request, it meant that you weren't in trouble, though someone else probably was. But if you were asked to come answer questions and you refused, well… you could pretty much reckon that from then on, you were marked. And any time one of the Watch saw you, they'd be keeping a hard eye on you, and they'd be likely to arrest and fine you for the least little thing. So after a nervous-sounding, unintelligible twitter of a conversation among all four of the sisters, Trana and Desi emerged and five sets of footsteps went back down the staircase.

Now he had to see what was up! When Skif peeked out around the edge of the window, he saw that two of the Watch were carrying lit lanterns, making it very clear that the two girls weren't being manhandled, or even touched. And he could see that the two girls had taken long enough to lace their bodices tight, pull up their blouses, and drop their skirts where they were usually kirtled up to show their ankles. They were definitely putting on a show of respectability, which only made sense. That was the last he saw of them until just before dark.

They returned alone, but gabble in the street marked their arrival, waking Skif from a partial doze.

Their sisters must have been watching from the window; they flew down the stairs to meet them, and half the neighborhood converged on them. Skif took his time going downstairs, and by then the block was abuzz with the news that Jass had been found dead in a warehouse that afternoon, and the girls had been brought in to identify the body. There was no question but that he was the victim of foul play; he'd been neatly garroted, and his body hidden under an empty crate. He might not even have been found except that someone needed the crate and came to fetch it, uncovering this body.

Damn…. Skif couldn't quite believe it, couldn't quite take it in. *Dead? But—*

By the time Skif drifted to the edge of the crowd to absorb the news, Trana and Desi were sobbing hysterically, though how much of their sorrow was genuine was anyone's guess. Skif had the shrewd notion that they were carrying on more for effect than out of real feeling. Their sisters, with just as much reason to be upset, looked more disgruntled at all of the attention that Trana and Desi were getting than anything else.

Skif huddled on the edge of the crowd, trying to overhear the details. There weren't many; he felt numb, as if he'd been hit by something but hadn't yet felt the blow. Before a quarter candlemark had passed, the landlord appeared.

He had tools and his dimwitted helper; he pushed past the crowd and ran up the stair. The sounds of hammering showed he was securing the door of Jass' room with a large padlock and hasp. An entire parade, led by the girls, followed him up there where he was standing, lantern in one hand, snapping the padlock closed. "There may be inquiries," he said officiously when Desi objected, claiming that she'd left personal belongings in Jass' rooms. "If the Watch or the Guard wants to inspect this place, I'll be in trouble if I let anyone take anything out."

There wouldn't be any inquiries, and they all knew it; this was just the landlord's way of securing anything of value in there for himself.

But if they knew what I knew—Skif thought, as he closed and bolted his own door, and put his back to it.

He began to shake.

Of all the people who could have wanted Jass dead, the only one with the money to get the job done *quietly* was the smooth-voiced man in the cemetery. What had the sell-sword said? "*You're in deeper waters than you can swim*—" Or something like that. Deep waters—his knees went weak at how close he'd come last night to joining Jass under that crate. If he'd been caught down in that crypt—

Skif sat down on his bedroll and went cold all over. There was at least one person in Haven who knew that there was a connection between Skif and Jass. And that craggy-faced sell-sword just might come looking for him, to find out exactly what, and how much, Skif knew.

I got to get out of here. Now!

The thought galvanized him. It didn't take him long to bundle up his few belongings. More and more people were showing up to hear the news directly from the girls, and the more people there were moving around, the better his odds were of getting away without anyone noticing. He watched for his chance, and when a group of their fellow lightskirts descended on Desi and Trana and carried them off to the nearest tavern, the better to "console" them, he used the swirl of girls and the clatter they generated to his advantage. He slipped out behind them, stayed with them as far as the tavern, and then got moving in the opposite direction as quickly as he could.

He didn't really have any ideas of where he was going, but at the moment, that was all to the good. If *he* didn't know where he was going, no one else would be able to predict it either.

The first place that anyone would look for him would be *here*, of course, but as Skif trudged down the street, looking as small and harmless as he could manage, he put his mind to work at figuring out a place where someone on his track was *not* likely to look. What was the most out of character for him?

Well—a temple. But I don' think I'm gonna go lookin' t' take vows—was his automatic thought. But then, suddenly, that didn't seem so outlandish a notion. Not taking vows, of course—but—

Abruptly, he altered his path. This was going to be a long walk, but he had the notion that in the end, it was going to be worth it.

Skif made his eyes as big and scared as he could, and twisted his cap in his hands as he waited for someone to answer his knock at the temple gate. This temple was not the one where his cousin Beel was now a full priest; it wasn't even devoted to the same god, much less the same Order. This was the Temple and Priory of Thenoth, the Lord of the Beasts, and this Order took it on themselves to succor and care for injured, sick, and aged animals, from sparrows and pigeons to broken-down carthorses.

It existed on charity, and as such, was one of the poorest temples in Haven. And one thing it could always use was willing hands. Not everyone who worked here in the service of Thenoth was a priest or a novice; plenty of ordinary people volunteered a few candlemarks in a week for the blessing of the God.

Now, what Skif was hoping was that he could hide here for the sake of his labor. He hoped he had a convincing enough story.

The door creaked open, and a long-nosed Priest in a patched and dusty brown robe looked down at him, lamp in one hand. "If you be seekin' charity, lad, this be'nt the place for ye," he said, wearily, but not unkindly. "Ye should try the—"

"Not charity, sor," Skif said, putting on his best country accent. "I be a norphan, sor, mine nuncle turn me out of the far-um, and I come here t'city a-lookin' for horse-work, but I got no character. I be good with horses, sor, an' donkeys, an' belike, but no mun gi' me work withouten a character."

The Priest opened the door a little wider, and frowned thoughtfully. "A character, is't? Would ye bide in yon loft, tend the beasts, and eat with the Brethren for—say—six moon, an' we give ye a good letter?"

Skif bobbed his head eagerly. "Ye'd gi' me a good character, then? Summut I can take fer t'work fer stable?"

He's taken it! he thought with exultation.

"If ye've earned it." The priest opened the gate wide, and Skif stepped into the dusty courtyard. "Come try your paces. Enter freely, and walk in peace."

Skif felt his fear slide off him and vanish. No one would look for him here—and even if they did, no one would dare the wrath of a God to try and take him out. So what if his story wasn't quite the truth?

I don'mind a bit' uv hard work God can't take exception t'that.

The priest closed the gate behind them, and led Skif into and through the very simple temple, out into another courtyard, and across to a stabling area.

As he followed in the priest's wake, Skif was struck forcibly by two things. The first was the incredible poverty of this place. The second was an aura of peace that descended on him the moment he crossed the threshold.

It was so powerful, it seemed to smother every bad feeling he had. Suddenly he wasn't afraid at all—not of the sell-sword, not of the bastard that had arranged for Bazie's building to burn—

Somehow, he knew, he *knew,* that nothing bad could come inside these walls. Somehow, he knew that as long as he kept the peace here, he would not ever have to fear the outside world coming in to get him.

That should have frightened him... and it didn't.

But he didn't have any leisure to contemplate it either, once they entered the stable. Skif had ample cause now to be grateful for the time he'd spent living in that loft above the donkey stable where he'd gotten acquainted with beast tending—because it was quite clear that the Order was badly shorthanded. One poor old man was *still* tottering around by the light of several lamps, feeding and watering the motley assortment of hoof stock in this stable.

Skif didn't even hesitate for a moment; this, if ever, was the moment to prove his concocted story, and a real stableboy wouldn't have hesitated either. He dropped his bedroll and belongings just inside the stable door, and went straight for the buckets; reckoning that water was going to be harder for the old fellow to carry than grain or hay. And after all, he'd had more than his share of water carrying when he'd been living with Bazie...

The old man cast him a look of such gratitude that Skif almost felt ashamed of the ruse he was running on these people. Except that it wasn't exactly a ruse... he was going to do the work, he just wasn't planning on sticking around for the next six moons. And, of course, he was going to be doing some other things on the side that they would never know about.

As he watered each animal in its stall, he took a cursory look at them. For the most part, the only thing wrong with them was that they were old—not a bad thing, since it meant that none of them possessed enough energy or initiative to try more than a halfhearted, weary nip at him, much less a kick.

Poor old things, he thought, venturing to pat one ancient donkey who nuzzled him with something like tentative affection as he filled its watering trough. And these were the lucky ones—beasts whose owners felt they deserved an honorable retirement after years of endless labor. The unlucky ones became stew and meat pies in the cookshops and taverns that served Haven's poor.

"Bless ye, my son," said the old priest gratefully, as they passed one another. "We be perilous shorthanded for the hoof stock."

"Just in stable?" Skif asked, carefully keeping to his country accent.

The priest nodded, patting a dusty rump as he moved to fill another manger. "With the wee beasts, the hurt ones, there's Healer Trainees that coom t'help, an' there's folks that don't mind turnin' a hand with cleanin' and feedin'. But this—"

Skif laughed softly. "Aye, granther, this be work, eh?"

The old priest laughed himself. "'Struth. They say there's a pair of novices coming up, come winter, but till then—"

"Till then, I'll be takin' the heavy work, granther," Skif heard himself promise.

When the last of the beasts were watered and fed, the old man showed him his place in the loft, and left him with a lantern, trudging back to the Chapter House. Like his last bed above a stable, this was in a gable end with a window supplied with storm shutters, piled high with hay, that looked out over the courtyard. He spread out his bedroll, stowed his few possessions in the rafters, blew out the lantern, and lay down to watch the moon rise over the roofs of Haven.

This's been—about th' strangest day of m'life, he thought, hands tucked behind his head. What was just about the strangest part of it was that he had literally gone from a state of fearing for his very life, to—this.

There was such an aura of peace and serenity within these walls! What might have seemed foolish trust under any other circumstances— after all, he was just some stranger who'd shown up on their doorstep, and at night, yet—was perfectly understandable now that Skif could see the poverty of the place himself. There literally was nothing to steal. If he didn't do the work he'd promised, he wouldn't be fed, and he'd be turned out. There was no reason for the Brethren not to trust him.

He should have been feeling very smug, and very clever. He'd found the perfect hiding place, and it was well within striking distance of the manors of the high and mighty.

Instead, all he could think was that, as workworn and weary as both the priests had seemed, there had also been something about them that made his cleverness seem not quite as clever as he'd thought it was. As if they had seen through his ruse, and *didn't care*. And that didn't make any sense at all.

I've got to think this through—he told himself, fighting the soporific scent of cured hay, the drowsy breathing of the animals in their stalls beneath him, and the physical and emotional exhaustion of the last day and night.

It was a battle he was doomed to lose from the start. Before the moon rose more than a hand's breadth above the houses, he was as fast asleep as the animals below.

Skif started awake, both hands clutching hay, as a mellow bell rang out directly above his head. For a moment he was utterly confused—he couldn't remember where he was, much less why he'd been awakened by a bell in the pitch-dark.

Then it all came back, just as someone came across the courtyard bearing a lit lantern.

Hellfires! he thought, a little crossly, yet a little amused. *I shoulda known this lot'd be up afore dawn! Mebbe I ain't been so smart after all!*

"Heyla, laddie!" called the aged voice of last night from below. "Be ye awake?"

"Oh, aye, granther," Skif replied, stifling a groan. "I be a-coomin' down."

He brought last night's lantern down with him, and he and the old man made the morning rounds of the stable in an oddly companionable silence. The old man didn't ask his name—and didn't seem to care that Skif didn't offer it. What he *did* do was give Skif the name and history of every old horse, donkey, mule, and goat in the stable, treating each of them like the old friend it probably was.

When they finished feeding and watering, the old man led Skif into the Chapter House, straight to a room where others of the Order had stripped to the waist and were washing up. Not wanting to sit down to breakfast smelling of horse and goat, Skif was perfectly willing to follow their example. From there they all went to breakfast, which was also eaten in silence—oat porridge, bread, butter and milk. Skif was not the only person who wasn't wearing the robes of the Order, but the other two secular helpers were almost as old as the priest who tended the stable. There *were* younger priests, but they all had some sort of deformity or injury that hadn't healed right.

One and all, either through age or defect, they seemed to be outcasts, people for whom there was no comfortable niche in a family, nor a place in the society of other humans. Maybe that was why they came here, and devoted themselves to animals...

Yet they all seemed remarkably content, even happy.

After breakfast, it was back to the stable, where Skif mucked out the stalls while the old priest groomed his charges. Even the goats were brushed until their coats shone—as much as the coat of an aged goat could. Then it was time for the noon meal, with more washing-up first, then the old man had him take the couple of horses that were still able to do a little work out to help carry a few loads about the compound. He and his charges hauled firewood to the kitchen, feed grains to bird coops, rubbish out to be sorted, muck to bins where muck collectors would come to buy it.

The place was larger than he'd thought. There were mews for aging or permanently injured hawks and falcons, a loft for similarly injured doves and pigeons, kennels for dogs, a cattery, a chicken yard that supplied the Order with eggs, a small dairy herd of goats, and a place for injured wildlife. It was here that Skif caught sight of a couple of youngsters not much older than he, wearing robes of a pale green, and he realized with a start that these must be the Healer Trainees he'd heard about. It was, quite literally, the first time he had ever seen a Healer of any rank or station, and he couldn't help but gawp at them like the country bumpkin he was pretending to be.

Then it was time for the evening meal—all meals were very plain, with the noon and evening meal consisting of bread, eggs, cheese, and vegetables, with the addition of soup at the noon meal and fruit at the dinner meal. Then came the same feeding and watering chores he'd had last night, and with a start, he realized that the entire day had flowed past him like a tranquil stream, and he hadn't given a single thought to anything outside the four walls of the Order.

And realized with an even greater start that he didn't care, or at least, he hadn't up until that time.

And he felt a very different sort of fear, then. The place was changing him. And unless he started to fight it, there was a good chance that it wouldn't be long until no one recognized him. And possibly even more frightening, he had to wonder how long it would be before he wouldn't even recognize himself.

1 2

Skif decided that no matter how tired he was, he was not going to put off the start of his vendetta any longer. And he wasn't going to let the deep peace of this place wash away his anger either.

When he finished watering the animals for the night and the old priest tottered back to the Chapter House, he blew out his lantern, but perched himself in the loft window to keep an eye on the rest of the Priory.

One by one, lights winked out across the courtyard. Skif set his jaw as a drowsy peace settled over the scene, and hovered heavily all around him. He knew what it was, now—this was the Peace of the God, and it kept everyone who set foot here happy and contented.

Granted, that wasn't bad for those who lived here; there were no fights among the animals, and there was accord among those who cared for them. But this peace was a trap for Skif; it would be all too easy to be lulled by it until he forgot the need for revenge—forgot what he was. He didn't want to forget what he was, and he didn't want to become what this place wanted him to be.

When the last light winked out, he waited a little longer, marking the time by how far above the horizon a single bright star rose. And when he figured that everyone would surely be asleep, he moved.

For someone like Skif, there was no challenge in getting over the walls, silently as any shadow. He knew where to go first, too. If he could not strike at his foe directly, he could at least strike at someone who was near to his real target. Serve the rich bastard right, for trusting someone who would murder innocent people just because they were in his way. Besides, all those rich bastards were alike. Even if this one hadn't actually murdered poor folks, he probably wouldn't care that his friend *had*.

And my Lord Rovenar was oh, so conveniently away on his family estate in the country.

Lord Rovenar's roof was fashionably paved in slate. It was with great glee that Skif proceeded to riddle the entire roof with cracks and gaps. The next time it rained, the roof would leak like a sieve.

There was also a cistern up here, a modern convenience that permitted my lord and his family to enjoy the benefits of running water throughout the mansion. Skif hastened the ruin of the upper reaches of the building by piercing the pipes leading downward, creating a slow leak that would empty the cistern directly into the attics, and from there into the rest of the house.

Besides rainwater, the cistern could be filled by pumping water up from the mansion's own well. But by the time Skif was finished, any water pumped up would only drain into the attics with the rest of it.

So much for vandalism on the exterior. Skif worked his way over to an attic window, which wasn't locked. After all, the servants never expected anyone to be up on the roof, and certainly wouldn't expect that anyone who *did* get up on the roof would dangle himself over the edge, push open the shutters with his feet, and let himself inside.

His night had only just begun.

When he let himself out again, this time from a cellar window, his pockets were full of small, valuable objects and the trail of ruin had continued, though most of it would take days and weeks before it was discovered. Skif had left food in beds to attract insects and mice, and had ensured that those pests would invade by laying further trails of diluted honey and crumbs all over the house around the baseboards where it was unlikely that the maids—slacking work in the master's absence— would notice. He left windows cracked open—left shutters ajar. Insects would soon be in the rooms, and starlings and pigeons colonizing the attic. The skeleton staff that had been left here would not discover any of this, for his depredations took place in rooms that had been closed up, the furnishings swathed in sheets. My lord would return to a house in shambles, and it would take a great deal of money and effort to make it livable again.

He ghosted his way across the kitchen garden and over the wall, using a trellis as a ladder. But once on the other side, he laid a trail of a different sort—all of those valuable trinkets he'd filled his pockets with. He scattered them in his wake, and trusted to greed to see to it that they never found their way back to their true owner again. He took nothing for himself, if for no other reason than that it would prevent anyone from connecting *him* with the trail of damage.

He slipped easily back over the Temple walls and got into his bed in the loft in plenty of time for a nap. When the bell sounded and woke him, if he wasn't fully rested, at least he didn't look so exhausted that anyone commented on it.

Although the meals he'd shared with the Brethren yesterday had been shared in silence, evidently there was no actual *rule* of silence, for the noon meal brought a flurry of gossip from the outside world.

"The Master Thief struck again last night," said one of the younger priests to the rest of the table. "The streets are full of talk."

"And he must be from somewhere outside Haven, so they say," added another with a shake of his head. "Singularly careless, he was; he left a trail of dropped objects behind him, I heard. I can vouch that there are so many people scouring the alleys for bits of treasure that some of the highborn have asked the Guard to drive them back to the slums."

"I hope," said the Prior, with great dignity, "that the Guard declined. The alleys are public thoroughfares; they do not belong to the highborn. Neither is the Guard answerable to those with noble titles who are discomfited by the poor outside their walls. There cannot be any justification for such a request."

"Since there are still treasure hunters looking in every nook and cranny, I suspect they did decline," the young priest said cheerfully. He seemed highly amused, and Skif wondered why.

The Prior shook his head sadly. "I know that you have little sympathy when rich men are despoiled of their goods, Brother Halcom."

"If the gods choose the hand of a thief to chastise those who are themselves thieves, I find it ironic, but appropriate, sir," Brother Halcom replied evenly. "This Master Thief has so far robbed two men who have greatly oppressed others. You know this to be true."

"Nevertheless, the thief himself commits a moral error and incurs harm to his soul with his actions," the Prior chided him gently. "You should spend less time gloating over the misfortune of the mighty and more in praying that this miscreant realizes his errors and repents."

Brother Halcom made a wry face, but the Prior didn't see it. Skif did, however, and he noted when the young priest rose from the table that his leg ended in a dreadful club foot. The priest had spoken in the accents of someone who was highly educated, and Skif had to wonder how much Brother Halcom knew *personally* about the two who had "officially" been robbed.

And whether he knew anything about the one that Skif had despoiled…

For one moment, he wondered if the young man had really meant what he said. He'd sounded sympathetic.

Fah. He'll have no time fer the likes of me, no doubt, he thought, hardening his heart. *Well look who's stuck muckin' out the stalls, an who's playin' with the broke-winged birds! Push comes t' shove, money an' rank stands together 'gainst the rest of us what always does the dirty work anyroad.*

He finished his meal and went back out to clean kennels.

With the Master Thief out last night—and everybody and his dog hunting for the goodies that Skif had let fall—the last thing Skif was going to do was to go out again tonight. No, things would have to cool down a bit before he ran the rooftops again. It gave him a great deal of pleasure, though, to lie back in the sweet-smelling hay and contemplate last night's work. The only thing that spoiled his pleasure was the thought that this unknown Master Thief was going to get all of the credit for *his* work.

On the other hand, it would probably anger the Master Thief to be saddled with the eventual blame for all of the vandalizing Skif had done.

And at the moment, no one would be looking for a mere boy; they'd be trying to catch a man. This Master Thief was proving rather useful to Skif's campaign.

I s'pose I oughta be grateful to 'im, Skif thought, but he didn't feel grateful.

In fact, after a while, he realized that he wasn't as satisfied with last night's work as he thought he should be. It just wasn't enough, somehow. He was thrashing around at random, blindly trying to hit the one he *truly* wanted to hurt and hoping that somehow in the chaos he'd connect with a blow. And even then—how did putting holes in someone's roof measure up to burning down a building and committing cold-blooded murder in the process?

It didn't, and that was that. *I want him,* Skif thought angrily. *I want the bastard what ordered it!*

Nothing more—but nothing less. And right now, he was settling for less.

Still, that Brother Halcom had a point, too. He'd seemed to think that the two highborn nobles that had been robbed had pretty much deserved it and probably Lord Rovenar had done a dirty deed or two in his life, and Skif had been nothing more than the instrument of payback. That wasn't a bad thought.

Brother Halcom knew the highborn…

Brother Halcom *might* know enough to give Skif a clue or two to the identity of the one highborn that Skif really wanted. So maybe Skif ought to see if he could get Brother Halcom to talk.

Finding someone to hurt that he *knew* deserved it might feel better than this random lashing out.

And maybe, just maybe, Brother Halcom would know who the smooth-voiced highborn was.

Skif watched Brother Halcom from a distance for a full week before making a tentative approach. He learned two things in that time; Brother Halcom was from a highborn family, and he was here because he wanted to be. Not that his family hadn't tried to get their "deformed" offspring out of sight, but they'd chosen a much more comfortable— and secluded—Temple for him to enter. Halcom had stood up to them, and threatened to make a scene if he wasn't allowed *his* choice.

That gave Skif a bit more respect for the man, and Halcom's value rose again in his eyes when he realized that Halcom didn't shirk the dirty work after all. He just did the small things, rather than the large. He did his share of cleaning—usually cleaning up after the Healer Trainees when they'd finished treating a sick or injured animal. When there was a beast that needed to be tended all night, it was Halcom, like as not, who stood the vigil. And when an animal was dying, it was Halcom who stayed with it, comforting it as best he could.

Finally, Skif found a moment to make a cautious overture to the young priest. Halcom had hobbled out to the stable to assist, not a Healer Trainee, but a farrier who often donated his time and expertise, and Skif was also called on to help. The injury was a split and overgrown hoof on a lamed carthorse; Halcom was asked to hold the horse's head, since he, more than anyone else, was able to keep animals calm during treatment. And Skif was there to hold the hoof while the farrier trimmed it and fastened a special shoe to help the hoof heal.

When the farrier had left, and Skif had taken the horse back to its stall, Halcom seemed disinclined to leave. "You've been doing good work here, friend," Halcom said, looking around at the rest of the stable without getting up from the hay bale he was sitting on. "I'm glad you came here. Poor old Brother Absel just isn't up to the heavy work anymore."

"Thankee, sor," Skif said, keeping to his persona of country bumpkin, and bobbing his head subserviently. "Would ye might be a-givin' me a character, too? That be what'm here for."

"I could probably do better than that, if what you want is stable work," Halcom admitted, but with a raised eyebrow. "I've no doubt I could recommend you to several people for that. Is that what you want?"

"Oh, aye, sor," Skif replied, feigning eagerness.

"Balderdash," Halcom countered, startling Skif. "You're better than that. You don't *really* want to be a lowly stablehand for the rest of your life, do you?" His eyes gleamed with speculation. "You are much too intelligent for that. What are you aiming at? Master of Horse? Chief Coachman?"

"Ah—" Skif stammered, before he got his wits together. "But I've got no training, sor. Dunno much but burthen beasts, and never learnt to drive."

Halcom waved that aside as of no consequence. "Nor have most boys your age when they go into service. As small as you are, though— learning to handle the reins could be problematic. I'm not sure you could control a team."

"I be stronger nor I look, sor," Skif said, stung.

Halcom laughed, but it didn't have that sly, mean sound to it that Skif had half expected. "Oh, you'd make a fine smart little footman, sitting up beside your master on a fashionable chariot, but I'll tell you the truth, lad, there is not a single highborn or man of means and fashion that I'd feel comfortable sending you to in that capacity. The good men have all the loyal footmen they need—and the others—" He shook his head. "I won't send you to a bad master."

"Ye might tell me who they be, sor?" Skif offered tentatively. "If I didna know it, I might take a place I was offered—"

"So you can avoid them?" Halcom nodded thoughtfully. "That's no bad idea. Clever of you to think of it." And he proceeded, with forthright candor, to outline the character of every man he thought Skif ought not to take service with. He was so candid that Skif was, frankly, shocked. Not at the litany of faults and even vices—his upbringing in the worst part of Haven had exposed him to far worse than Halcom revealed. No, it was that Halcom was not at all reticent about unrolling the listing of faults of his "own kind."

As Halcom spoke, Skif found himself at war within himself. He *wanted* to trust Halcom, and he had sworn never to trust anyone. More than that, he wanted to *like* Halcom. It seemed to him that Halcom could easily become a friend.

And he did *not* want any more friends.

"That leaves plenty of good masters to take service with, mind,"

Halcom pointed out when he was finished, and smiled. "And for all my differences with my own family, I can quite cheerfully recommend you to take service with them. They're quite good to those who serve them well."

Huh. It's only their own flesh'n blood that they muck about with, eh? Skif thought. *Guess you'n'me have more in common than I thought.*

"It was your own uncle that turned you out, wasn't it?" Halcom said suddenly, startling Skif again with his knowledge of Skif's "background." Halcom laughed at his expression, wryly. "I suppose we have more in common than either of us would have suspected."

"'Twas your nuncle sent ye off?" Skif ventured.

Halcom nodded, and his face shadowed. "My existence was an embarrassment," he admitted sourly. "My uncle feared that my presence in his household would cast a shadow over some pending betrothal arrangements he was negotiating. My father—his younger brother—has no backbone to speak of, and agreed that I ought to be persuaded to a vocation."

"What?" Skif asked indignantly. "They figger you'd scare the bride?"

"My uncle suggested that the prospective bride's father might rethink his offer if he thought that deformity ran in my family," Halcom said bluntly, his mouth twisting in a frown. "Since my parents are dependent on his generosity for a place, I suppose I can't blame them…" He sighed deeply, and his expression lightened. "In the end, really, I'm rather glad it happened. I had very little to do with myself, I'm really not much of a scholar, and—well, needless to say, I'm not cut out for Court life either. I've always loved animals, and neither they, nor my fellow Brothers, care about this wretched leg of mine. And I *did* manage to shame my uncle into making a generous donation when he dumped me here."

Skif nodded his head, concealing as best he could that he was racked by an internal struggle. He really, truly *wanted* to be Halcom's friend. And he really, truly, did not want to make another friend that he knew he would only lose.

I ain't stayin' here forever, he told himself sternly. *He wouldn' be so nice if he knew what I was. Hellfires, he'd turn me straight over to th' Watch if he knew what I was!*

But he could almost hear the place whispering to him. It wanted him to stay. He could have a friend again. No one here would care what he had been, only what he was now, and what he might become. Oh, he'd never be rich—but he'd never starve either.

He steeled himself against the seductive whispers of peace. Him?

Bide in a place like this? Not when he had a debt to repay! Not when there was someone out there that was so ruthless he would do anything to anyone who stood in his way!

Besides, this place would put him to sleep in a season. He'd turn into a sheep inside of a year. And if there was one thing that Skif had no desire to become, it was a sheep.

"Well, I imagine you've heard more than enough to send you to sleep about *me*," Halcom said, hauling himself to his feet again. "And I still have my charges to attend to. I won't keep you from your own duties any more, lad—but do remember what I've told you, and that if you want a second letter of commendation to go with the Prior's when you leave, I will be happy to write one for you."

That last, said as Halcom turned to go, had the sound of a formal dismissal, superior to inferior.

There, you see? he taunted that seductive whisper. *I ain't a friend to the likes of a highborn, even if his people did cast 'im off. A mouse might's well ask a hawk t'be his friend. Hawk might even say yes—till he got hungry.*

Another week passed, and the city was struck with a heat wave that was so oppressive people and animals actually began dying.

The Queen closed the Court and sent everyone but her Privy Council out of the city. But there was nowhere for the poor and the working classes to go, and even if there had been, how could ordinary people just pack up and leave? How would they make a living, pay their bills, feed their children? Life in Haven went on as best it could. As many folk as could changed their hours, rising before dawn, working until the heat grew intolerable, enduring as best they could until late afternoon, then taking up their tasks again in the evening. The Prior knew a clever trick or two, though, and the Brethren began going through the poorer neighborhoods, teaching people what the Prior had taught them—for although it was the Lord of the Beasts that the Brethren served, nevertheless, Man was brother to the Beasts.

Water-soaked pads of straw in windows somehow cooled the air' that blew through them, so long as there was a breeze. And if there wasn't, the cheapest, more porous terra-cotta jars filled with water and placed about a room also helped to cool the air as the water evaporated from them. Stretching a piece of heavy paper over a frame, then fastening that frame by one side to the ceiling and attaching a cord to a corner created a huge fan that would create a breeze when the winds themselves didn't oblige; there were always children to pull the cord, and they didn't mind doing so when the breeze cooled *them* as well. And the same cheap terracotta that was used for those jars could be made into tiles to be soaked with water and laid on the floor—also cooling a room or the overheated person who lay down on them. It helped; all of it helped.

People were encouraged to sleep on flat rooftops or in their gardens or even in parks by night, and in cellars by day.

But there was always someone greedy enough to want to make a profit from the misfortune of others. Suddenly the dank and dark basement rooms that had been the cheapest to rent became the most expensive. Not all landlords raised the rents on their cellars, but many did, and if it hadn't been so stiflingly hot, there might have been altercations over it.

But it was just too hot. No one could seem to get the energy even to protest.

Skif was terribly frustrated; it was nearly impossible to move around the city by night without being seen! And yet, with all of the wealthy and highborn gone, it should have been child's play to continue his vendetta! Why, the huge manors and mansions were so deserted that the Master Thief must have been looting them with impunity, knowing that no one would discover his depredations until the heat wave broke and people returned to Haven.

Hellfires, Skif thought grumblingly, as he returned from an errand to the market, through streets that the noon heat had left deserted. *It'd be easier to make a run by day than by—*

Then it hit him. *Of course!* Why not make his raids by day? He was supposed to be resting, like everyone and everything, during the heat of the day. No one would miss him at the Priory, and there would be no one around to see him in the deserted mansions, not with the skeleton staffs spending their time in the cool of the wine cellars, most of them asleep if they had any sense!

That's pro'lly what the Master Thief's doing! he thought with glee. He was delighted to have thought of it, and enjoyed a moment of mental preening over his own cleverness.

Well, he certainly would *not* be wearing his black "sneak suit" for these jobs. His best bet was to look perfectly ordinary. The fact was, he probably wouldn't even need to get in via the rooftops; the doors and windows would all be unlocked. After all, who would ever expect a thief to walk in the kitchen door in broad daylight?

He brought the bag of flour and the basket of other sundries he'd been sent for to the kitchen and left it on the table. The Brother who acted as cook had changed the routine because of the heat. A great many things were being served cold: boiled eggs, cheese, vegetables and so forth. Actual cooking was done at night and in ovens and on brick stoves erected in the kitchen courtyard. The biggest meal of the day was now breakfast; the noon meal was no longer a meal, but consisted of whatever anyone was able to eat (given the heat, which killed appetites), picked up as one got hungry, in the kitchen. Big bowls of cleaned, sliced vegetables submerged in water lined the counters, loaves of bread resided under cheesecloth, boiled eggs in a smaller bowl beside them. There was butter and cheese in the cold larder if anyone wanted it, which hardly anyone did.

Skif helped himself to carrot strips and celery and a piece of bread; he ate the bread plain, because he couldn't bear the thought of butter either. The place might just as well have been deserted; the only sign that there had been anyone in the kitchen was the lumps of bread dough left to rise under cloths along their shelf.

Skif wasn't all that hungry either, but he ate and drank deeply of the cooled water from yet another terra-cotta jar. Then he went straight back out, as if he had been sent on a second errand. Not that there was anyone about to notice.

He sauntered along the streets, watching the heat haze hovering above the pavement, keeping to the shade, and noting that there still were a few folk out. They paid no attention to him, and he gave them no more than a cursory glance.

There was not so much as a hint of the Watch. No surprise there; what was there for them to do? There would be no fights, and it was too hot for petty theft, even if there was anything open at noon to steal from.

Where to hit? That was the question. He had no clear target in mind, and he wasn't as familiar with who belonged to which great mansion as he would have liked. Finally, he decided, for lack of any other ideas, to bestow his attentions on one Thomlan Vel Cerican, a charming fellow who had amassed a great deal of wealth by squeezing his poor tenants and giving them as little in the way of decent housing as he could get away with. He was one of the landlords who had responded to the current heat wave by evicting tenants from the newly-desirable basement rooms and charging a premium rate for them—sending the evicted to live in the attics.

It seemed as good a reason as any to wreak as much havoc as humanly possible on him. If he hadn't burned his own buildings to avoid having to make repairs, it was only because he had balked at actually destroying anything he owned.

So Skif's steps took him in the direction of the great homes of those who aspired to be counted among the highborn, not those who had actually gotten to that position.

There was still no sign of Watch, Guards, or anyone else. He strolled along the street, not the alley, and nothing met his interested gaze but shuttered and curtained windows behind the gates. These houses, while imposing, did not boast the grounds and gardens of those of the true nobility. Land was at a premium within the second set of city walls.

There were three sets of walls, in fact—four, if you counted the ones surrounding the Palace and the three Collegia. Each time that the city of Haven had outgrown its walls, a new set had been built. When that happened, land within the previous walls became highly desirable. Now, between the first set and the Palace walls, only the highborn, those with old titles, had their mansions (and indeed, manors), which had enormous gardens and landscaped grounds. Between the second and first, those who had newer titles, most less than a generation old, and the wealthy but not ennobled kept their state. Lesser dwellings had been bought up and razed to make way for these newer mansions. There were gardens, but they were a fraction of the size of those of the Great Lords of State. But there were parks here, places where one could ride or stroll and be observed. Between the third walls and the second lived most of the rest of the city, although the populace had already begun to spill outside the walls, and many of those whose wealth was very recent had taken to building mansions that aped those of the Great Lords of State, but outside the walls altogether, where land was cheaper.

Eventually, Skif supposed, another set of walls would be built, and then it would be his neighborhood that would be razed to make way for the mansions of the wealthy.

Skif passed one of the parks, and decided to take a rest near a lily-covered pond. It was deserted, the air shimmering with heat above the scorched lawns between the trees. His target was on the other side of this park, and it occurred to him that it wouldn't be a bad idea to observe it from the comfort of the park while he cooled off a little.

Even though he had sauntered along in slothful fashion, he was still sweating. He pulled his linen shirt away from his body and threw himself down in the shade of a huge oak tree beside the pond. The ground was marginally cooler than the air or his body, but there were no signs that anyone was actually sleeping here at night, despite the suggestions of the authorities.

Skif wasn't surprised. The Watch probably was discouraging the poor from moving into the parks in this section of the city, even though there were more of them here than between the second and third walls. The Watch was answerable directly to the wealthy folk living here— as opposed to the Guard, which was answerable to the Crown. Even though *they* were not here to witness the poor camping out of a night in "their" park, not one of the moneyed lot who lived around here even wanted to consider the prospect. The local Watch probably had orders to clear out campers as fast as they arrived.

Skif turned his head to peer between bushes nearby, thinking he heard something. Some zealous Watchman, perhaps? If so, he'd better be prepared with a story about why he was here.

He had heard something, but it wasn't a member of the Watch.

There was a horse wandering loose around the park, taking nibbles out of the grass, sampling the flowers. It was a handsome creature, white as snow, and still wore a saddle and bridle. Reins dangled from the bridle—no, it was a bitless hackamore, he saw. No one would leave reins dangling like that—your horse could all too easily catch a leg in them, stumble, fall and perhaps break a leg.

But if you didn't tie the reins off properly when you left a horse waiting, the horse could jerk them loose and wander off, leaving them dangling just like these were.

For one wild moment, Skif thought—*Is that a Companion?*

But no—if it had been a Companion, there would certainly be a Herald somewhere about. And besides, the saddle and hackamore were old, very plain, well-worn. Everyone knew that Companions went about in elaborate blue-and-silver tack, with silver bridle bells and embroidered barding. There were plenty of white horses around that weren't Companions. It was something of an affectation in some fashionable sets to ride white horses, or have a carriage drawn by matched teams of them.

No, some idiot hadn't tied his horse properly. Or, far more likely given the worn state of the tack, some groom had taken his master's mare out for some exercise and had combined the chore with some errand of his own. He hadn't tied the horse up, and she'd pulled her reins loose and wandered away. That groom would be in a lot of trouble—but since there wasn't anyone combing the park looking for this beast, evidently he hadn't missed her yet.

Well, his loss was Skif's gain.

Working at the Priory had given him a *lot* more familiarity with horses than he'd had before. He'd even learned to ride. And faced with this opportunity for profit on four legs, he grinned broadly.

You're mine! he told the grazing mare. *Lessee; horse fair's runnin' over on the east side. Or I kin take her out of the walls altogether an' sell her. Or I kin take her t' Priory an'collect th' reward when she shows up missin'…*

The last option wasn't a bad notion, though the first was the real money maker.

The horse moved around the bushes and out of his sight; knowing that she was probably some high-strung well-bred beast, he got up slowly and began to stalk her. If he, a stranger, was going to catch her rather than spooking her, he'd have to catch her by surprise.

When she actually moved between two thick, untrimmed hedges, he could hardly believe his good luck. She couldn't have gotten into a better situation for him to corner her!

Knowing that a horse is averse to backing up, he ran around to the front of the hedges, and struck.

Making a dash out of cover, he grabbed for the reins and the saddle in the same movement, hauling himself into the saddle before she had time to do more than snort. And somehow, before he realized it, he was in the saddle and in control!

For just about a heartbeat.

Because in the next moment, the horse tossed her head, jerking the reins out of his hand, and set off at a gallop, and all he could do was cling desperately to the pommel of the saddle.

1 3

All Skif could do was hold on, with every aching finger, with knees and thighs, wrists and ankles. If he could have held on with his teeth, he would have. If he could have tied his *hair* to the saddle, he would have.

He'd lost the stirrups almost at once, shortly after he lost the reins. That didn't give him a lot of options; either cling on like a burr, or try to jump off. But the mare was going so fast, he knew if he jumped, he'd get hurt.

Badly, *badly hurt*—

And that was if he was lucky. He'd seen someone who'd been thrown from a galloping horse, once. The poor fool had his back broken. Healers could fix that, he'd been told, if the Healer got to you quickly enough, if you were important enough to see a Healer. He'd seen countless people thrown from runaway wagons, and they always ended up with broken arms and legs. That was bad enough.

She was at the gallop, head down, charging along as if she'd gone mad, pounding down the paved streets, the occasional bystander gawking at them as they tore past. No one tried to stop the runaway horse, and all that Skif could do was hang on tight and trust to the fact that as hot as it was, she'd tire soon. She'd have to tire soon. She was only a horse, just a fancy horse, she couldn't run forever—

He closed his eyes and crouched over the saddle, gripping her with his thighs and holding onto the pommel of the saddle with all his might. Her mane whipped at his face, it was like being beaten with a fly whisk, and he gasped with every driving blow of her hooves that drove the pommel into his gut. She'd be slowing any moment now.

Any moment now…

Oh, please—

He cracked his eye open, and closed it again.

She wasn't slowing. If anything, she was running faster. People, shops, pavement blurred past so fast he was getting sick. His eyes watered as some of her mane lashed across them.

How was that possible?

Hellfires! I stole a racehorse! Of all the stupid, idiot things to have done—

He opened his eyes again, just in time to see a wagon pull across the street in front of them and stop.

She's got to stop now—

She raised her head a little, and her ears cocked forward.

She's not gonna stop!

The driver stared at them, then abruptly dove off the seat. The mare increased her pace; he felt her muscles bunch up under his legs.

She's gonna jump it!

She shoved off, her forequarters rising; he clawed desperately at the saddle as his weight shifted backward. He screamed in terror, *knowing* he was going to fall, then the wagonbed was underneath him—

She landed; he was flung forward, his nose and right eye slamming into her neck. He saw stars, and his head exploded with pain. Somehow, some way, he managed to hang on. The thought of falling off terrified him more than staying on.

She didn't even break stride as she continued her run and careened around a corner; sweat flew off her, and she didn't even seem to notice. She was off around another corner, pounding through a half-empty market, then toward the last of the city walls.

No—

But she wasn't listening to what he wanted.

She plunged into the tunnel beneath the walls, and for a moment her hooves echoed in the darkness, sounding like an entire herd of horses was in here with him.

There were Guards on the wall! Surely, surely they would stop her— Then she was out, with no sign of a Guardsman.

Skif dared another glance, out of the eye that wasn't swelling. Through his tears all he could see was a road stretching ahead of them, the road leading away from Haven. He couldn't even tell *which* road; all he knew for certain was that they were flying down a roadway, and people were scattering out of their way, shouting curses after them.

The mare wove her way in and out of the traffic with the agility of a dancer. He actually felt the touch on his ankle as they brushed by other riders, the whiplike cut of a horse's tail as it shied out of the way. And somehow, she was getting faster.

He knew if he tried to throw himself off now, he'd die. It was just that simple. No one, not even an experienced rider, could slip off a horse at speeds like this and live. He wouldn't just break bones, he'd break his neck or his skull and die instantly. All he could do was what he had been doing; hang on, try not to get thrown, and hope that when she stopped, he'd be able to get off of her without her killing him.

He gritted his teeth together, hissing with the pain of his eye and nose, so full of fear there was no room in his head for anything else.

The sounds of shouting and cursing were gone. He dared another glance. There were no more buildings beside the road now, nothing but fields with tiny farmhouses off in the distance. The road still had plenty of traffic, though, and the mare wove her way in and out of it with a nonchalance that made the hair on the back of his head stand up. People weren't shouting and cursing at them because they were too busy trying to get out of the way.

He had never been so terrified in his entire life.

He squeezed his eyes tight shut again, and for the first time in his life, began to pray.

Skif was limp with exhaustion, dripping with sweat and aching so much that he wasn't sure he even cared what happened to him now.

He also had no idea where he was. The mare had gotten off the main road and was still running, though not at the headlong pace she'd held through the city. This was a normal gallop—if anything this mare did was normal!

This was a country road, rutted dirt, with trees on both sides that met over his head, forming a tunnel of green. If his eye and nose hadn't hurt so much—and if he hadn't been so terrified—he'd never been anywhere like this before in his life.

He had no idea how far they were from Haven. A long way; that was about all he could tell. So in addition to the rest of it, he was hopelessly lost, and completely outside familiar territory.

And the sun was setting.

He wanted to cry.

He *did* cry; tears leaking silently out from the corners of his eyes. His nose felt as if it was the size of a cabbage, and it throbbed.

The mare suddenly changed direction again, darting into a mere break in the trees, down a path so seldom used that there weren't even any cart tracks in it. She slowed again, to a trot.

Now he could hear what was going on around him; birds, the wind in the trees, the dull thud of the mare's hooves on the turf. So this was what people meant by "peaceful countryside"? Well, they could *have* it. He'd have given an arm for his loft room right now.

He could probably have gotten off her back at this point—but for what? He didn't even know where he was! Here they were in the middle of a complete wilderness, with no shelter, nothing to eat, and no people, so where would he go? Somehow he had to convince this devil beast to get him back home—

Now she slowed to a walk, and all he could do was slump over her neck, as the light coming through the trees took on an amber cast. She was sweating, but no more than one of the horses he was familiar with would have been after a moderately hard job. She should have been foaming with sweat. Foaming? She should be collapsed on the ground by now!

Head bobbing with each step, she ambled down the path, and then, with no more warning than when she'd started this run, she stopped.

Skif looked up through eyes blurring with exhaustion and tears of frustration and fear.

Now what?

They stood in a tiny clearing, in front of the smallest building he had ever seen. They were completely surrounded by trees, and the only other object in the clearing was a pump next to the building with a big stone trough beneath it. He couldn't hear anything but birds and the wind. If there were any humans anywhere around, there was no sign of them. For the first time in his life, Skif was completely alone.

He'd have given anything to see a single human being. Even a Watchman. If the Watch had showed up, he'd have flung himself into their arms and begged them to take him to gaol.

Every muscle, every bone, every inch of Skif's body was in pain. His nose and eye hurt worst, but everything hurt. He sat in the saddle, blinking, his bad eye watering, and choked back a sob. Then he slowly pried his fingers, one at a time, away from the pommel of the saddle.

He looked down at the ground, which seemed furlongs away, and realized that he couldn't dismount.

It wasn't that he didn't *want* to, it was that he couldn't. He couldn't make his cramped legs move. And even if he could, he was afraid to fall.

Then the mare solved his problem by abruptly shying sideways.

He didn't so much slide off the saddle as it was that the horse and her saddle slid out from underneath him. He made a grab for the pommel again, but it was too late.

He tumbled to the ground and just barely managed to catch himself so that he landed on his rump instead of his face, in a huge pile of drifted leaves.

It hurt. Not as badly as, say, hitting hard pavement would have, but it still hurt.

And it knocked what was left of his breath out of him for a moment and made him see stars again.

When his eyes cleared, he looked around. He sat in the middle of the pile of old, damp leaves, dazed and bewildered at finding himself on the ground again. "Ow," he said, after a moment of consideration.

The mare turned, stepping lightly and carefully, and shoved him with her nose in the middle of his chest.

He shoved back, finally roused to some sensation other than confusion. "You get away from me, you!" he said angrily, "'f it wasn't for *you*, I—"

She shoved at him again, and without meaning to, he looked straight into her eyes. They were blue, and deep as the sky, and he fell into them.

:Hello, Skif,: he heard, from somewhere far, far away. *:My name is Cymry, and I Choose you.:*

And he dropped into a place where he would never be alone or friendless again.

When he came back to himself, the first thing he did was stagger to his feet and back away from the Companion. Never mind the wonderful dream he'd been in—it was a dream. It couldn't be real. Something was terribly wrong.

His Companion Cymry looked at him and he felt her amusement.

His Companion. And that was just not possible.

"Are you outa your *mind?*" he croaked, staring at her.

:No,: she said, and shook her head. *:I Choose you. You're a Herald—well, you will be after you go through the Collegium and get your Whites. Right now, you're just a Trainee.:*

"Like hell!" he retorted feelingly. "You are crazy! Or—I am—" It occurred to him then that all this might just be some horrible dream.

Maybe when he'd jumped onto the horse, it had thrown him, and he was lying on his back in that park, knocked out cold and hallucinating. Maybe he hadn't even seen the horse, the heat had knocked him over and he was raving. None of this was happening—that must be it—

:Don't be stupid,: Cymry replied, shoving at him with her nose. *:Be sensible! Do you ever have black eyes and a broken nose in a dream? It's not a dream, you're not unconscious, and you are Chosen. And you're going to be a Herald.:*

"I don't bloody well think so!" he said, trying to back further away from her and coming up against the wall of the little building. "If you think I am, *you're* crazy. Don' you know what I *am?*"

How could this be happening? He didn't *want* to be a Herald! Oh, even Bazie had spoken about them with admiration, but no Heralds were ever plucked out of a gutter, not even in a tale!

:Of course I do,: she replied calmly. *:You're a thief. A rather good one for your age, too—:*

"Well, then I can't be a Herald, can I?" He groped for words to try and convince her how mad, how impossible this was. Even though, deep inside, something cried out that he didn't want it to be impossible. "Heralds are—well, they're all noble an' highborn—"

She snorted with amusement at his ignorance. *:No they aren't. Not more than a quarter of them at most, anyway. Heralds are just ordinary people; farmers, craftsmen, fisherfolk—ordinary people.:*

"Well, they're heroes—"

:And none of them started out that way,: she countered. *Most of them started out as ordinary younglings, being Chosen by a Companion. There wasn't anything special about them until then—not visibly, anyway.:*

"They're *good!*"

She considered that for a moment, head to one side. *:That rather depends on your definition of "good," actually. Granted, they are supposed to uphold the law,:* she continued thoughtfully. *:But in the course of their duties, plenty of them break the law as much as they uphold it, if you want to be technical about it.:*

"But—but—" he spluttered, as the last light pierced through the tree trunks and turned everything a rosy red, including Cymry. "But—Heralds are—they do—"

:Heralds are what they have to be. They do what the Queen and the country need,: Cymry said, supremely calm and confident. *:We Choose those who are best suited to do those things and supply those needs. And what makes you think that the Queen and country might not need the skills of a thief?:*

Well, there was just no possible answer to that, and even though his mouth opened and closed several times, he couldn't make any sounds come out of it.

She paced close to him, and once again he was caught—though not nearly so deeply—in those sparkling sapphire eyes.

:Now look—I'm tired and hungry and sweaty. So are you.:

"But—" They were in the middle of nowhere! Where was he—? How was he—?

:This is a Waystation, and as a Herald Trainee—don't argue!—you're entitled to anything in it.: She whickered softly. *:I promise, there's food and bedding and just about anything you might need in there. There's also a bucket of water inside to prime the pump with. I suggest that before it gets too horribly dark, you pump up some water, clean both of us up, and get us both some of the food that's waiting. You* are *hungry, aren't you? You* can *eat and rest here for the night, and we can talk about all of this.:*

She cocked both of her ears at him, and added, *:And while you're at it, it wouldn't hurt to make a poultice for that black eye you're getting. It's becoming rather spectacular.:*

Herald Alberich, Weaponsmaster to Heralds' Collegium and sometime intelligence agent for Queen Selenay, put down the brush he'd been using on Kantor's mane and stared at his Companion in complete and utter shock.

Companions didn't lie—but what Kantor had just told him was impossible.

"You must be joking!" he said aloud, in his native tongue.

Kantor turned his head to look at his Chosen. *:As you well know,:* he said, with mock solemnity, *:I have no sense of humor.:*

"In a pig's eye," Alberich muttered, thinking of all of the tricks his Companion had authored over the years—including the one of smuggling himself past the Karsite Border to Choose and abduct one Captain Alberich of the Karsite Army.

:But I assure you, I am not joking. Cymry has managed to Choose that young scamp you've caught eavesdropping on you over the past couple of months. He is a thief, and she'll probably be delivering him to the Collegium some time tomorrow. So I suggest you prepare your fellow Heralds. He promises to make things interesting around here.: Kantor arched his neck. *:But before you do that, you might take that brush along my crest; it still itches.:*

"What in the name of Vkandis Sunlord are we supposed to do with a thief?" Alberich demanded, not obliging Kantor with the brush.

:What you always do with the newly Chosen. You'll train him, of course.: Kantor turned his head again and regarded his Chosen with a very blue eye. *:Hasn't it occurred to you that a skilled thief would be extremely useful in the current situation that you and the Queen have found yourselves in? Scratch a thief, you'll find a spy. Set a thief to take a thief, and you have been losing state secrets.:*

"Well—'"

:Of course it has. All you have to do is appeal to the lad's better instincts and bring them to the fore. I assure you, he has plenty of better instincts. After all, he's been Chosen, and we don't make mistakes about the characters of those we Choose. Do we?: Kantor didn't have any eyebrows to arch, but the sidelong look he bestowed on Alberich was certainly very similar.

"Well—"

:So there you are. About that brush in your hand—:

Belatedly, Alberich brought the brush up and began vigorously using it along Kantor's crest. The Companion sighed in blissful pleasure, and closed his eyes.

And Alberich began to consider just how he was going to break the news about this newest trainee to Dean Elcarth and the rest.

Assuming, of course, they weren't already having similar conversations with *their* Companions.

It was a good thing that Bazie had taught him how to cook. Yes, there was food here, but it wasn't the sort of thing the ordinary city-bred boy would have recognized as such.

:I'd have told you what to do,: Cymry said, her head sticking in the door, watching him, as he baked currant-filled oatcakes on a stone on the hearth. He'd also put together a nice bean soup from the dried beans and spices he'd found, but he didn't think it would be done any time soon, and he was hungry now. *:I wouldn't let you starve. I'm perfectly capable of telling you how to use just about anything in this Waystation.:*

"Somehow I ain't s'prised," he replied, turning the cakes deftly once one side was brown. "Is there anything ye *can't* do?"

:I'm a bit handicapped by the lack of hands,: she admitted cheerfully.

She—and he—were both much cleaner at this point. Beside the pump, there had been a generous trough, easily filled and easily emptied. After she'd drunk her fill, and he had washed and brushed her down as she asked, he'd had a bath in it. Then he emptied it out and refilled it for her drinking. The cold bath had felt wonderful; it was the first time in a week that he'd been able to cool down. He'd also washed up his clothing; it was hanging on a bush just outside. It was a lot more comfortable to sit around in his singlet, since there wasn't anyone but Cymry to see him anyway.

She'd told him which herbs to make into a poultice that did a lot to ease the ache of his eye and nose, and more to make into a tea that did something about his throbbing head. She already knew, evidently, that he could cook, and had left him alone while he readied his dinner over the tiny hearth in the Waystation. Now he couldn't imagine why he hadn't figured out she was a Companion immediately.

Unless it was just that the idea of a Companion wandering around in an old worn set of tack was so preposterous, and the idea of a Companion deciding to make a Herald out of a thief was still more so.

:I told them to tack me up in the oldest kit in the stables that would fit me:, she offered, as he scooped the oatcakes off their stone and juggled one from hand to hand, waiting for it to cool enough to eat. He gave her a curious stare.

"Ye—ye *kidnapped* me!" he accused.

:Well would you have come with me if I'd walked up to you and Chosen you?: she asked, her head cocked to one side. *I am sorry about your nose, but that was an accident.:*

"But—"

:I've known for several weeks that you were my Chosen,: she said, as if it was so matter-of-fact that he shouldn't even be considering any other possibility. *:I've just been waiting for the opportunity to get you alone where I could explain things to you.:*

"But—"

:You've already lost this argument you know,: she pointed out. *:Three times, in fact.:*

He gave up. Besides, the cake was cool enough to eat. And he was hungry enough by this point to eat the oats raw, much less in the cakes he'd just made.

He put a second poultice on his eye and nose and lay back in the boxbed that filled most of the Waystation. It had a thick layer of fresh hay in it, covered over with a coarse canvas sheet; it was just as comfortable as his bed in the Priory, and although he wasn't sleepy yet, he didn't really want to venture out into the alien environment outside his door. He heard things out there; all manner of unfamiliar sounds enlivened the darkness, and he didn't much care for them. There were wild animals out there, owls and bats and who knew what else. There could be bears…

:You don't for one moment think that I would let anything *hurt you, do you?:* The unexpected fierceness of that question made him open his good eye and turn his head to look at her, where she lay half-in, half-out of the doorway.

"I don' know anything 'bout you," he admitted, slowly. "Nothin' at all 'bout Companions."

:Well, I wouldn't.: She sighed. *:And you're about to learn a great deal about Companions.:*

"No, I ain't. They're gonna take one look at me an' throw me out," he replied, stubbornly.

:No, they aren't. They already know who you are, what you are, and that I'm bringing you in tomorrow.:

"What?" he yelped, sitting up straight, keeping the poultice clapped to his eye with one hand.

:Well, not everybody, just the people who need to. The Dean of the Collegium— that's the Herald who's in charge of the whole of Heralds' Collegium. Herald Alberich, the Weaponsmaster. The Queen's Own and the Queen. A couple of the other teachers. They all know, and they aren't going to throw you out.: She was so matter-of-fact about it—as if it shouldn't even occur to him to doubt her. *:As to how they know, I told them, of course. Actually I told them through their Companions, but it amounts to the same thing.:*

He flopped back down in the bed, head spinning. This was all going much too fast for him. Much, *much* too fast. "Now what am I gonna do?" he moaned, mostly to himself. "I can't ever go back—th' Watch'd hev me afore I took a step—"

:You couldn't go back anyway.: Cymry replied.

"But—"

:Skif—do you really, really *want me to leave you?:* The voice in his mind was no more than a whisper, but it was a whisper that woke the echoes of that unforgettable moment when he felt an empty place inside him fill with something he had wanted for so long, so very, very long—

"No," he whispered back, and to his profound embarrassment, felt his throat swelling with a sob at the very thought.

:I didn't think so. Because I couldn't bear to lose you.: Her thoughts took on a firmer tone. *:And I won't. No one tries to separate a Companion and her Chosen. That would be—unthinkable.:*

He lay in the firelit darkness for a long time, listening to the strange night sounds in the woods outside, the beating of his own heart, and his own thoughts.

Then he sighed heavily. "I guess I gotta be a Herald," he said reluctantly. "But I still think there's gonna be trouble."

:Then we'll face it together. Because I am never, ever going to let anyone separate us.:

In the morning, gingerly probing of his nose and the area around his eye—and the fact that he could actually open that eye again—proved that the poultice had done its work. He cleaned himself up in the cold water, and donned his shirt and trews—wrinkled and a little damp, but they'd have to do. They both ate, he cleaned the things he'd used and shut the Waystation up again. He'd been stiff and sore when he woke up, but he knew from experience that only moving around would make that kind of soreness go away. Besides, at the moment, he couldn't wait to get back to the city where he belonged. Whatever people saw in "the country" was invisible to him. The silence alone would drive him crazy in a day.

There was just one problem, of course—and that was that he wasn't going *home*, he was going to this Collegium place. As he mounted Cymry's well-worn saddle—with a great deal more decorum this time—he shook his head slightly. "I still think there's gonna be trouble," he predicted glumly.

:Skif, there will always be trouble where you are,: she replied mischievously. *:We'll just have to try to keep it from getting out of hand!:*

Without a backward glance, she started up the forest trail, going in a few paces from a walk to a trot to an easy lope. It was very strange, riding her, now that he knew what she was. For one thing, she wasn't a horse—he didn't have control over her, and that was the way it was *supposed* to be, not an accident. But as they moved out of the woods and onto roads that had a bit of morning traffic, he began to notice something else.

Now that they weren't charging down the road in a manner threatening to life and limb, people *paid attention* to Cymry, they clearly knew what she was, and they looked at her, and by extension her rider, with *respect*.

Or at least they did until they saw his black eye.

But even then, they looked at him with respect only leavened with sympathy. And since they weren't galloping at a headlong pace, but rather moving in and out of the traffic at a respectable but easy trot, some people actually began to call greetings to him and her.

"New-Chosen, aye, lad?" said a farmer, perched so high on the seat of his wagon that he was eye-to-eye with Skif. And without waiting for an answer, added, "Here, catch!" and tossed him a ripe pear.

Startled, he caught it neatly, and the second one that the same man tossed to him, before Cymry found another opening in the traffic and moved smoothly ahead.

:If you'd cut that up into quarters, I'd like some.:

He was only too pleased to oblige, since he had the feeling that was what the farmer intended anyway. The little eating knife he always kept in his belt was accessible enough, and since he didn't have to use the reins, he didn't have to try and cut the pears up one-handed. She reached around and took each quarter daintily from his hand as he leaned over her neck to hand it to her.

Everywhere he looked, he met smiles and nods. It was a remarkable sensation, not only to be noticed, but to elicit that reaction in total strangers.

He did feel rather—naked, though. He wasn't at all comfortable with all of this *noticing.*

:Don't worry. You'll blend in once you're in your Grays. You'll be just another Trainee.:

He was getting used to her talking in his head—*Mindspeech,* she called it—and he was starting to get vague pictures and other associations along with the words. When she talked about being "in his Grays," he knew at once that what she meant was the uniform of the Heraldic Trainees, modeled after the Heralds' own uniforms, but gray in color.

:That's so people don't expect you to know what you're doing yet,: she told him, looking back over her shoulder at him with one eye. *:And by the way, you don't have to actually talk to me for me to hear and understand you.:*

So she knew what he was thinking. That wasn't exactly a comforting thought. A man liked to have a little privacy—

:And when you're a man, I'll give it to you.:

"Hey!" he said, staring at her ears indignantly, and garnering the curious glances of a couple driving a donkey cart next to him.

:Oh, don't be so oversensitive! I won't eavesdrop! You'll just have to learn not to "shout" all your thoughts.:

Great, now he would have to watch, not only what he did and said, but what he thought… This Herald business was getting more unpleasant all the time.

:It's not like that, Skif,: she said coaxingly. *:Really it isn't. I was just teasing you.:*

He found a smile starting, no matter how he tried to fight it down. How could he possibly stay angry with her? How could he even get angry with her? And maybe that was the point.

He wasn't sure how long it had taken them to get from the park where he'd found her to the Waystation where they stopped, but it took them most of the morning to get back to Haven. The Guards on the walls paid absolutely no attention to him, although they had to have seen him careening down the road yesterday. Cymry didn't volunteer any information as he craned his neck up to look at them, then bestowed a measuring glance at the two on either side of the passage beneath the wall. He wondered what they were thinking, and what they might have said or done yesterday.

They sure didn't try to stop us, anyway. Not that it was likely that they'd have had much luck—not with only two Guards on the ground and Cymry able to leap a farm wagon without thinking about it. Maybe it was just as well they hadn't tried. He might have ended up with both eyes blackened.

Once they got inside the city walls, though, people stopped paying as much attention to them. Well, that wasn't such a surprise, people saw Heralds coming and going all the time in Haven. On the whole, he felt a bit more comfortable without so many eyes on him.

Their progress took him through some areas he wasn't at all familiar with as they wound their way toward the Palace and the Collegia. He didn't exactly have a lot to do with craftsmen and shopkeepers—his forte was roof walking and the liftin' lay, not taking things from shops. That had always seemed vaguely wrong to him anyway; those people worked hard to make or get their goods, and taking anything from them was taking bread off their tables. Helping himself to the property of those who already had so much they couldn't keep track of it, now, that was one thing—but taking a pair of shoes from a cobbler who'd worked hard to make them just because he took a fancy to them was something else again.

Once they got in among the homes of the wealthy, though, it was a different story. He eyed some of those places, all close-kept behind their shuttered windows, with a knowing gaze. At one point or another he had checked out a great many of them, and he knew some of them very, very well indeed. The owner of *that* one had not one, but two mistresses that his wife knew nothing about—and they didn't know about each other. He treated them all well, though, so to Skif's mind none of them should have much to complain about. Sometimes he wondered, however, where the man was getting all the money he spent on them…

:He's honest enough, but there are others,: Cymry put in. *:You see what I mean by needing your skills?:*

He furrowed his brow and concentrated on *thinking* what he wanted to say instead of saying it out loud. *:I suppose——:* he said dubiously.

But they were soon past the second wall, out of the homes of the merely wealthy, and in among the manses of the great. And Skif had to snicker a little as they passed Lord Orthallen's imposing estate. It was the first time he'd come at it from the front, but he couldn't mistake those pale stone walls for any other. How many times had he feasted at m'lord's table, and him all unaware?

They passed Lord Orthallen's home, passed others that Skif had not dared approach, so guarded around were they by the owner's own retainers. And finally there was nothing on his right but the final wall, blank and forbidding, that marked the Palace itself.

His apprehension returned, and he unconsciously hunched his head down, trying to appear inconspicuous, even though there was no one to see him.

No—there was someone.

The next turning brought them within sight of a single Guardsman in dark blue, who manned a small gate. Cymry trotted up to him quite as if she passed in and out of that gate all the time, and the man nodded as if he recognized her.

"This would be Cymry," he said aloud, casting a jaundiced eye up at Skif, who shrank within himself. "They're expecting you," he continued, opening the gate for them to pass through, although he didn't say who *they* were.

Cymry walked through, all dignity, and began to climb the graveled road that led toward an entire complex of buildings. Skif tensed. *Now I'm in for it*, he thought, and felt his heart drop down into his boots.

1 4

He sat in Cymry's saddle like a sack of grain, and waited for doom to fall on him. She had taken him up the path, through what looked like a heavily-wooded park, past one enormous wing of a building so huge it *had* to be the Palace. Eventually they came to a long wooden building beside the river in the middle of a huge fenced field—he'd have called it a stable, except that there weren't any doors on the stalls…

Then again, if this was where Companions stayed, there wouldn't be any need for doors on the stalls, would there?

It had a pounded-dirt floor covered ankle-deep in clean straw, and there was a second door on the opposite side, also open. These gave the only light. Cymry walked inside, quite at home.

The building was oddly deserted except—

Except—

For three people who were very clearly waiting for him just inside the door. One was an odd, birdlike man, slight and trim, hardly taller than Skif, with a cap of dark gray hair and an intelligent, though worried, expression. The second was taller, with a fairly friendly face which at the moment also bore a distinctly worried expression. Both of them wore the white uniform only a Herald was allowed to wear.

His "welcoming committee," evidently.

He couldn't see the third one very well, since he was standing carefully back in the shadows. The third person wasn't wearing the white uniform though; his clothing was dark enough to blend in with the shadows.

Could be sommut from the Guard, he thought gloomily. *Gonna haul me off t' gaol soon's the other two get done with me.*

:He's not, and you're not going to gaol,: said Cymry. But that was all she said. He couldn't find it in himself to feel less than uneasy about the shadowy lurker.

She stopped a few paces away from the two men, and Skif gingerly dismounted, turning to face them with his hands clasped behind his back. A moment later, he dropped his eyes. Whatever was coming, he didn't want to meet their faces and see their disgust.

"So," said the smaller one, "you seem to be the young person that Companion Cymry has Chosen."

"Yessir," Skif replied, gazing at his ill-shod toes.

"And we're given to understand that you—ah—your profession—you—" The man fumbled for words, and Skif decided to get the agony over with all at once.

"'M a thief, sir," he said, half defiantly. "Tha's what I do." He thought about adding any number of qualifying statements—that it had been a better choice than working for his uncle, that no one had offered him any *other* sort of employment and he had to eat; even that if Bazie hadn't been around to take him in and train him, he'd probably be dead now and not Chosen. But he kept all of those things to himself. For some reason, the clever retorts he had had didn't seem all that clever at the moment.

The shorter man sighed. "I suppose you're expecting me to give you an ineffective and stuffy lecture about how you are supposed to be a new person and you can't go on doing that sort of thing anymore now that you're a Trainee."

Skif stopped looking at his toes and instead glanced up, startled, at the speaker. "Uh—you're not?"

"*You* are not stupid," the man said, and smiled faintly, though his tone sounded weary. "If you've already played over that particular lecture in your mind, then I will skip it and get to the point. I am Dean Elcarth. I am in charge of Herald's Collegium. The moment you entered the gate here, so far as we are concerned, whatever you were or did before you arrived here became irrelevant. You were Chosen. The Companions don't make mistakes. There must be the makings of a Herald in you. Therefore you are welcome. But when you get in trouble, and you will, because sooner or later at least half of our Trainees get in trouble, please remember that what you do reflects on the rest of us as well, and Heralds are not universally beloved among a certain faction of the highborn. The others will give you the details as they see fit, but the sum of what I have to say is that you are *supposed* to be part of a solution, not part of a problem, and I hope we can show you why in such a way that you actually feel that in your deepest heart."

During this rather remarkable speech, Skif had felt his jaw sagging slowly. It was *not* what he had expected to hear. His shock must have been written clearly on his face, because the Dean smiled a little again. "This is Herald Teren," he continued, gesturing to the other man, who although friendlier, was looking distinctly worried. "He is, technically, in charge of you, since he is in charge of all of the newly Chosen. You'll be getting your first lessons from him, and he will show you to your new quarters and help get you set up. Under normal circumstances, he would have picked out a mentor for you among the older students— but these are not normal circumstances. So although one of the older students will be assigned as a mentor, in actuality you will have a very different, though altogether *unofficial* mentor."

"That," said a grating voice that put chills up Skif's back, "myself would be."

He knew that voice, and that accent—though when he'd heard it before, it hadn't been nearly so thick.

And when the third figure stepped out of the shadows, arms folded over his chest, scar-seamed face smiling sardonically, he stepped back a pace without thinking about it. Skif had never seen the hair before—stark black with thick streaks of white running through it—because it had been hidden under a hood or a hat. But there was no mistaking that saturnine face or those cold, agate-gray eyes. This was the sell-sword who'd spoken with (and spied on?) Jass, who had threatened Skif in the cemetery.

"You!" he blurted.

"This is Herald Alberich, the Collegium Weaponsmaster," said the Dean. "And I will leave you with him and Teren."

"But you can't b-b-be a Herald—" Skif stammered. "Where's yer, yer white—"

"Herald Alberich has special dispensation from Her Majesty herself not to wear the uniform of Heraldic Whites," Herald Teren interrupted, as Alberich's expression changed, only in that he raised his right eyebrow slightly.

And now, suddenly, an explanation for Skif's own rather extraordinary behavior in the cemetery hit him, and he stared at the Herald in the dark gray leather tunic and tight trews with something like accusation. "You *Truth Spelled* me!"

Now that he knew Alberich was a Herald, there was no doubt in his mind why he had found himself telling the man what he knew that night in the cemetery. Everyone knew about Heralds and their Truth Spell, though Skif was the first person in his own circle of acquaintances who'd actually undergone it, much less seen it.

The two Heralds exchanged a glance. "Elcarth's right," said Teren. "He's very quick."

"Survive long he would not, were he not," Alberich replied, and fastened his hawklike eyes on Skif, who shrank back, just as he had that night. "I did. Because there was need. Think on this—had you by any other been caught, it would *not* have been Truth Spell, but a knife."

Skif shivered convulsively, despite the baking heat. The man was right. He gulped.

Alberich took another couple of steps forward, so that Skif was forced to look up at him. "Now, since there is still need, *without* Truth Spell, what you were about in following that scum, you will tell me. And *fully,* you will tell it."

There was something very important going on here; he didn't have nearly enough information to know what, or why, but it was a lot more than just the fact that Jass had been killed, though that surely had a part in it. But Skif raised his chin, stiffened his spine, and glared back. "T'you. Not t'*im*. I know you. I don' know 'im."

The Heralds exchanged another glance. "Fair enough," Teren said easily. "I'll be outside when you're ready for me to take him over."

Herald Teren turned and strode out the door on the other side of the stable. Skif didn't take his eyes off Alberich, whose gaze, if anything, became more penetrating.

"Heard you have, of the man Jass, and his ending." It was a statement, not a question, but Skif nodded anyway. "And? You followed him for moons. Why?"

"'E burned down th' place where m'mates lived." Skif made it a flat statement in return, and kept his face absolutely dead of expression. "They died. I heard 'im say 'xactly that with m'own ears, an' 'e didn't care, all 'e cared about was 'e didn' want t' get caught. Fact, 'e said 'e *got rid* of some witnesses afore 'e set th' fire. Might even've been them."

Alberich nodded. "He was not nearly so free with me."

Skif tightened his jaw. "Honest—I was in the cem'tery by accident, but I was where I could 'ear real good. An' I 'eard 'im *an' th' bastid what hired 'im* talkin' 'bout a new job, an' talkin' 'bout the old one. I already figgered I was gonna take 'im down somehow—but only *after* I foun' out 'oo 'twas what give 'im th' order."

A swift intake of breath was all the reaction that Alberich showed— and a very slight nod. "Which was why you followed him." A pause. "He was more than that—more than just a petty arson maker, more even than a murderer. As his master was—is. Which was why I followed him."

Skif only shook his head. Alberich's concerns meant nothing to him—
—except—

"You *know* 'oo 'e is!" he shot out, feeling himself flush with anger.
"The boss! You *know!*" He held himself as still as a statue, although he
would cheerfully have leaped on the man at that moment, and tried to
beat the knowledge out of him.

But Alberich shook his head, and it was with a regret and a
disappointment that went so deeply into the tragic that it froze Skif
where he stood. "I do not," he admitted. "Hope, I had, you did."

At that moment, instead of simply glaring at him, Alberich actually
looked at him, caught his eyes, and stared deeply into them, and Skif felt
a sensation like he had never before experienced. It was as if he literally
stood on the edge of an abyss, staring down into it, and it wasn't that
if he made a wrong move he'd fall, it was the sudden understanding
that *this* was what Alberich had meant when he'd said that these were
waters too deep for Skif to swim in. There were deep matters swirling all
around him that Skif was only a very tiny part of, and yet—he had the
chance to be a pivotal part of it.

If he dared. If he cared enough to see past his own loss and sorrows,
and see greater tragedy and need and be willing to lay himself on the
line to fix it.

:Chosen—please. This is real. This is what I meant when I said that we needed you.:

He gazed into that abyss, and thought back at Cymry as hard as he
could—*:Is that the only reason you Chose me?:*

Because if it was—

—if it was, and all of the love and belonging that had filled his heart
and soul when he first looked into her eyes was a lie, a ruse to catch
someone with his particular "set of skills"—

:Are you out of your mind?: she snapped indignantly, shaken right out of
her solemnity by the question. *:Can't you feel why I Chose you?:*

That answer, unrehearsed, unfeigned, reassured him as no speech
could have. And something in him shifted, straining against a barrier he
hadn't realized was there until that moment.

But he still had questions that needed answering. "An' if ye find this
'master' no matter how highborn 'e is," he asked slowly, "ye'll do *what?*"

"Bring him to justice," Alberich replied instantly, and held up a hand,
to forgo any interruptions. "For murder. Of your friends, if no other can
be proved, although—"

"There are others?" Skif asked—not in amazement, no, for if the bastard, whoever he was, had been cold-hearted enough to burn down a building full of people, he surely had other deaths on his conscience.

Now, for the first time, Alberich's face darkened with an anger Skif was very glad was not aimed at him. "Three of which I know, and perhaps more. And there is that which is worse than murder, which only kills the body. Slaving, for workers, but worse, to make pleasure slaves. Behind it, he is. In small—in the selling of children, here, even from the streets of Haven. *And* in large, *very* large, wherein whole families are reaved from their homes and sold OutKingdom."

Skif heard himself gasp. There had always been rumors of that in the streets, and Bazie had hinted at it—but even his uncle hadn't stooped that low.

Worse than murder? Well—yes. He closed his eyes a moment, and thought about those rumors a moment. If the rumors were more than that, and the children—orphans or the unwanted—who vanished from Haven's streets ended up in the place where Bazie had intimated they went—

—and if there really were entire villages full of people who were snatched up and sold OutKingdom—

"Worse," he heard himself agreeing.

"And one answer there is, for such evil." Alberich's stonelike expression gave away nothing, but Skif wasn't looking for anything there. He already had his answer; forget anything else, he and this iron-spined man had a common cause.

And somewhere inside him, the barrier strained and broke.

"I'm in," was all he said. "I'm with ye." Alberich's eyes flickered briefly, then he nodded.

"More, we will speak, and at length. Now—"

There were a great many things Alberich could have said. *If you want revenge, you'd better keep your nose clean,* for instance, *or if you get yourself thrown out of here for messing up, neither one of us will get what he wants. Or you'll have to work hard at being respectable, because it's going to take someone who looks respectable to trap this bastard.*

He said none of those things. He let another of those penetrating looks analyze Skif and say something else. Something—that had warning in it, but against danger and not mere misbehavior. Something that had acceptance in it as well, and an acknowledgment that Skif had the right to be in this fight. And Skif nodded, quite as if he had heard every bit of it in words.

Alberich smiled. It was the sort of smile that said, *I see we understand one another.* That was all, but that was all that was needed.

A moment later, the sound of boots on the straw-covered floor marked Herald Teren's return. "Later speech, we will have," Alberich promised, as Teren reached them. "For now—other things."

The other things were not what Skif had expected. Not that he'd really had any inkling of what to expect, but not even his vaguest intuitions measured up to his introduction to the Collegium and his first candlemarks as a Trainee.

"If you're all right, then, follow me," Herald Teren said, and started off, quite as if he assumed Skif would follow and not bolt. Which Skif did, of course; it seemed that he was "in for it" after all, but not in the way he'd thought. His emotions were mixed, to say the least.

On top of it all was excitement and some apprehension still. Just beneath that was a bewildered sort of wonder and the certainty that at any moment they would realize they'd made a mistake—or that fearsome Alberich would call the Guards. He'd lived with what he was for so long…

Beneath *that,* though—was something still of the new image of the world and his place in it that he'd gotten during that encounter with Alberich. That—granted, the world *stank,* and a lot of people in it were rotten, and horrible things happened—but that *he,* little old Skif, petty thief, had a chance that wasn't given to many people, to help make things better. Not right; the job of making everything *right* was too big for one person, for a group of people like the Heralds, even—but *better.*

And under all of *that,* slowly and implacably filling in places he hadn't known were empty, was a feeling he couldn't even put a name to. It was big, that feeling, and it had been the thing that had broken through his barriers back there, when Cymry reaffirmed her bond with him. It was compounded of a lot of things; release, relief, those were certainly in there. But with the release came a sense that he was now irrevocably bound to something—something good. And *accepted* by that "something." A feeling that he belonged, at last, to something he'd been searching for without ever realizing that he'd been looking. And there was an emotion connected with Cymry in there that, if he had to put a name to it, he might have said (with some embarrassment) was love. It was scary, having something that *big* sweep him up in itself. And if he had to think about it, he knew he'd be absolutely paralyzed—

So he didn't think about it. He just let it do whatever it was going to do, turning a blind eye to it. But he couldn't help but feel a little more cheerful, a little more at ease here, with every heartbeat that passed.

And there was plenty to keep him distracted from anything going on inside him, anyway.

Teren led him away from the stable and toward a building that absolutely dwarfed every other structure he had ever seen. And if he was impressed, he hated to think how all those farmboys and fisherfolk Cymry had talked about must have felt when they first saw it.

The building was huge, three-and-a-half stories of gray stone with a four-story double tower at the joining of two of the walls just ahead of them. "This is Herald's Collegium and the Palace," Teren said, waving his hand in an arc that took in everything. "You can't actually see the New Palace part of the structure from here; it's blocked by this wing next to us, which is where all the Kingdom's Heralds have rooms."

"But most uv 'em don't live here, at least, not most of th' time," Skif stated, on a little firmer ground. "Right?"

Teren nodded. "That's right. The only Heralds in *permanent* residence are the teachers at the Collegium and the Lord Marshal's Herald, the Seneschal's Herald, and the Queen's Own Herald. Have you any idea who *they* are?"

Skif shook his head, not particularly caring that he didn't know. This new feeling, whatever it was, had a very slightly intoxicating effect. "Not a clue," he said. "I figger ye'll tell me in them lessons. Right?"

"Right, we'll leave that to Basic Orientation; it isn't something you need to understand this moment." Teren seemed relieved at his answer. "Now, straight ahead of us is Herald's Collegium, which is attached to the residence wing, both for the convenience of the teachers and—" he cast a jaundiced eye on Skif "—to *try* and keep the Trainees out of mischief."

Skif laughed; it was very clear from Teren's tone and body language that he meant all Trainees, not just Skif. He couldn't help but cast an envious glance at the wing beside them, though; he couldn't help but think that as a Trainee, he'd probably be packed in among all the other Trainees with very little privacy.

"Healer's Collegium and Bardic are also on the grounds, on the other side of Heralds,'" Teren continued, waving his hand at the three-and-a-half-story wing ahead of them. "You'll share some of your classes with students from there. Healer Trainees wear pale green, Bardic Trainees wear a rust red rather than a true red. There will also be students who wear a pale blue which is similar to, but darker than, the pages' uniforms. Those are a mixed bag. Some of them are highborn whose parents choose to have them tutored here rather than have private teachers, but most are talented commoners who are going to be Artificers."

"What's an Artificer?" Skif wanted to know.

"People who build things. Bridges, buildings, contrivances that do work like mills, pumps," Teren said absently. "People who dig mines and come up with the things that crush the ore, people who make machines, like clocks, printing presses, looms. It takes a lot of knowing how things work and mathematics, which is why they are here."

"Keep that away from me!" Skif said with a shudder. "Sums! I had just about enough of sums!"

"Well, if you don't come up to a particular standard, you'll be getting more of them, I'm afraid," Teren said, and smiled at Skif's crestfallen face. "Don't worry, you won't be the only one who's less than thrilled about undertaking more lessons in reckoning. You'll need it; some day, *you* may have to figure out how to rig a broken bridge or fix a wall."

They entered in at a door right in the tower that stood at the angle where the Herald's Wing met the Collegium. There was a spiraling staircase paneled in dark wood there, lit by windows at each landing. Skif expected them to go up, but instead, they went down.

"First, Housekeeping and Stores," Teren informed him. "The kitchen is down here, too. Now, besides taking lessons, you'll be assigned chores here in the Collegium. All three Collegia do this with their Trainees. The only thing that the Trainees don't do for themselves is the actual cooking and building repair work."

Skif made a face, but then something occurred to him. "Highborn, too?" he asked.

"Highborn, too," Teren confirmed. "It makes everyone equal—and we never want a Herald in the field to be anything other than self-sufficient. That means knowing how to clean and mend and cook, if need be. That way you don't owe anyone anything—because we don't want you to have anything going on that might be an outside influence on your judgment."

"Huh." By now, they had reached the lowest landing and the half cellar—which wasn't really a cellar as Skif would have recognized one, since it wasn't at all damp, and just a little cooler than the staircase.

Teren went straight through the door at the bottom of the staircase, and Skif followed.

They entered a narrow, whitewashed room containing only a desk and a middle-aged woman who didn't look much different from any ordinary craftsman's wife that Skif had ever seen. She had pale-brown hair neatly braided and wrapped around her head, and wore a sober, dark-blue gown with a spotless white apron. "New one, Gaytha," said Teren, as she looked up.

She gave him a different sort of penetrating look than Alberich had; this one looked at everything on the *surface*, and nothing underneath. "You'll be a ten, I think," she said, and stood up, pushing away from her desk. Exiting through a side doorway, she returned a moment later with a pile of neatly folded clothing, all in a silver-gray color, and a lumpy bag. "Here's your uniforms—now let me see your shoes."

When Skif didn't move, she gestured impatiently. "Go ahead, put your foot on the edge of the desk, there's a lad," she said. With a shrug, Skif did as he was told, and she *tsked* at his shoes.

"Well, *those* won't do. Teren, measure him for boots, there's a dear, while I get some temporaries." She whisked back out again while Teren had Skif pull off his shoes, made tracings of his feet, then measured each leg at ankle, calf, and knee, noting the measurements in the middle of the tracing of left or right. By the time he was finished, the Housekeeper was back with a pair of boots and a pair of soft shoes. Both had laces and straps to turn an approximate fit into a slightly better one.

"These will do until I get boots made that are fitted to you," she said briskly. "Now, my lad, I want you to know that there are very strict rules about washing around here." This time the look she gave him was the daggerlike glare of a woman who has seen too many pairs of "washed hands and arms" that were dirty down to the wristbone. "A full bath every night, and a *thorough* washup before meals—or before you *help* with the meal, if you're a server or a Cook's helper. If you don't measure up, it's back to the bathing room until you do, even if all that's left to eat when you're done is dry crusts and water. Do you understand?"

"Yes'm," Skif replied. He wasn't going to point out to this woman that a dirty thief is very soon a thief in the gaol. That was just something she didn't need to know.

"Good." She took him at his word—for now. He had no doubt he'd be inspected at every meal until they figured out he knew what "clean" meant. "Now, I don't suppose you have *any* experience at household chores—"

"Laundry an' mendin' is what I'd druther do; dishes, floor washin', an' scrubbin' is what I can do, but druther have laundry an' mendin'," he said immediately. "Can boil an egg, an' cut bread'n'butter, but nought else worth eatin'."

"Laundry and mending?" The Housekeeper's eyebrows rose. "Well, if that's what you're good at—we have more boys here than girls, so we tend not to have as many hands as I'd like that are actually good at those chores."

Her expression said quite clearly that she would very much like to know how it was that he was apt at those tasks. But she didn't ask, and Skif was hardly likely to tell her.

"This boy is Skif, Chosen by Cymry," Teren said, as Gaytha got out a big piece of paper divided up into large squares, each square with several names in it.

"I've got you down for laundry and mending for the next five days," Gaytha said. "Teren will schedule that around your classes and meals. We'll see how you do."

"Off we go, then," Teren said, and loaded Skif's arms with his new possessions.

Back up the steps they went, pausing just long enough at the first floor for Teren to open the door and Skif to look through it. "This is where the classrooms are," Teren told him, and he took a quick glance down the long hall lined with doors. "We're on Midsummer holiday right now, so all but two of the Trainees are gone on visits home. It's just as well; with this heat, no one would be able to study."

"Do what they's does in th' City," Skif advised, voice muffled behind the pile of clothing. "*They* ain't gettin' no holidays. Work from dawn till it gets too hot, then go back to't when it's cooled off a bit."

"We're ahead of you there," Teren told him. "It's already arranged. Follow me up to the second floor."

Teren went on ahead, and Skif found him holding open the door on the next landing. He stepped into another corridor, this one lined with still more doors. But it ended in a wall, and seemed less than half the length of the one on the first floor. It was a bit difficult to tell, because the light here was very dim. There were openings above each door that presumably let the light from the room beyond pass through, and that was it for illumination.

"You *won't* be living on this side of the common room," Teren told him. "This is the girls' side. The common room where you take all meals is between the boys' and girls' side. Come along, and you'll see."

He led the way down the corridor, opened a door, and Skif preceded him into the common room. There were windows and fireplaces on both sides, and the place was full of long tables and benches, rather like an inn. Skif made a quick reckoning, and guessed it could hold seventy-five people at a time—a hundred, if they squeezed in together. "How many of them Trainees you got?" he asked, as Teren held the door in the opposite wall open for him.

"Forty-one. Twenty-six boys, fifteen girls." Teren turned to catch his grimace. "That does make for some stiff competition among the ladies—or are you not interested in girls yet?"

"Never thought 'bout it," he said truthfully. "Where I come from—"

Where I come from, you den'get no girl less you pays for 'er, an' I got better things t'spend m' glim on, he thought. But no point in shocking this man. He'd probably go white at the thought.

"And this is your room," Teren said, interrupting his thoughts, opening one of the doors. Eager now to put down his burdens, Skif hurried through the door.

He was very pleasantly surprised. There was a good bed, a desk and chair, a bookcase, and a wardrobe. It had its own little fireplace—no hoping to get warmth from the back of someone else's chimney!—and a window that stood open to whatever breeze might come in. All of it, from the wooden floor to the furniture to the walls, was clean and polished and in good condition, though obviously much-used. When Skif set his clothing down on the bed, he was startled to realize that it was a *real* mattress, properly made and stuffed with wool and goose down, not the canvas-covered straw he'd taken as a matter of course.

He had never, not once, slept on a real mattress. He'd only seen such things in the homes of the wealthy that he'd robbed.

"Grab a uniform and I'll take you to the bathing room," Teren told him, before he could do more than marvel. "You need to get cleaned up and I'll take you down to the kitchen for something to eat. Then I'll take you to Dean Elcarth, and he can determine what classes you'll need to take."

It didn't seem that Herald Teren had any intention of leaving Skif alone.

With a stifled sigh, Skif picked out smallclothes, a shirt, tunic, trews, and stockings, debated between the boots and the shoes and finally decided on the latter as probably being more comfortable. With an eye long used to assessing fabric, he decided that the trews and tunic must be a linen canvas, the shirt was of a finer linen, the boots of a heavier canvas with leather soles and wooden heels. Interesting that the temporary boots were of canvas rather than leather—they'd be quicker to make up, and a lot more forgiving to feet that weren't used to boots. Or even shoes—some of the farmboys who came in to the markets went barefoot even in the city, right up until the snow fell.

Trailing behind the Herald, wondering if the man considered himself to be guide or guard, Skif left his room.

The bathing room was a shock. Copper boilers to heat the water, one with a fire under it already, pumps to fill them, pipes carrying cold and hot water to enormous tubs and commodious basins, boxes of soft, sage-scented soap and piles of towels *everywhere*—

Skif forgot Teren's presence entirely. No matter how hot it was, he reveled in a bath like no one he knew had ever enjoyed. He soaked and soaked until the aches of that horrible ride with Cymry were considerably eased and he felt cleaner than he ever had in his whole life.

In fact, it was only after he'd dried off (using a towel softer than any blanket he'd ever owned) and was half dressed in the new clothing that Teren spoke, waking him to the Herald's presence.

"Mop up your drips with the towel you used, and wipe out the tub, then drop the towel down that chute over there. Send your old clothing after it." Teren nodded toward a square opening in the wall between two basins, and Skif finished dressing, then obeyed him. How long had he been there? Had he left while Skif was filling the tub? It bothered him that he couldn't remember.

I always know where people are. Am I losing my edge?

Teren waited for him by the door, but held out a hand to stop him before he went back through it. "Hold still a moment, would you?" he asked, and put a single finger under Skif's chin, turning his face back into the light from the windows. "I thought most of that was dirt," he said contritely. "I beg your pardon, Skif. Before I take you to Elcarth, I'd like you to see a Healer for that nose and eye."

Another moment of mixed reaction—a little resentment that the man would think he was so slovenly that he'd have *that* much dirt on his face, and small wonder that the Housekeeper had been so abrupt! But that was mingled with more astonishment. A *Healer?* For a *broken nose?*

But within moments, he found himself sitting across from a green-clad Healer, a fairly nondescript fellow, who examined him briskly, said "This will only hurt for a moment," and grabbed his nose and pulled.

It certainly *did* hurt, quite as much as when he'd hit Cymry's neck in the first place. It hurt badly enough he couldn't even gasp. But the Healer had spoken the truth; it only hurt for a moment, and in the very next moment, it not only stopped hurting, *it stopped hurting.*

He opened his eyes—and both of them opened properly now—and stared into the Healer's grin. "You'll still look like a masked ferret," the fellow said cheerfully, "but you should be fine now."

"How *did* you do that anyway?" Teren asked, as they made their way back to Herald's Collegium and Skif's interview with Herald Elcarth.

"Cymry jumped a wagon, an' I hit 'er neck with my face," he replied ruefully, and found himself describing the entire wild ride in some detail as they walked.

"She made you think you'd *stolen* her?" Teren said at last, smothering laughter. "Forgive me, but—"

"Oh, it's pretty funny—now," Skif admitted. "An' I s'ppose it'll be funnier in a moon, or a season, or a year. Last night, I c'n tell you, it weren't funny at all."

"I can well imagine—" By this time, they were back down the stairs into the half basement in the Collegium again. "It'll be funnier still when you've got yourself on the outside of some lunch. Here's the kitchen—" Teren opened a door identical to the one that led to the Housekeeper's room, but this one opened onto an enormous kitchen, silent and empty. "I haven't had anything since breakfast either." He gave Skif a conspiratorial wink. "Let's raid the pantry."

1 5

"Usually, our cook, Mero, is down in the kitchen," Teren told him as they cleaned up what little mess they'd made. "Now listen, I am not telling you this because I think you're going to filch food, I'm telling you this because all boys your age are always hungry, and after the last couple of centuries running the Collegium, we've figured that out. When Mero is here, you can ask him for whatever you want to eat and if he isn't knee-deep in chaos, he'll be delighted to get it for you. When he's not here—and I know very well from my own experience how badly you can need a midnight snack—only take food from the pantry we just used. The reason for that is that Mero plans his meals very carefully—he has to, with so many inexpert hands working with him—and if you take something he needs, it'll make difficulties for him."

Skif thought fleetingly of the number of times he'd taken food from Lord Orthallen's pantry—and hoped it hadn't made difficulties for that cook.

Odd. He wouldn't have spared a thought for that yesterday.

"Now. Healed, fed, and ready for Dean Elcarth?" Teren didn't wait for an answer, but strode off, heading for the stairs.

This time they walked through the corridor that held all the classrooms; again, it was lit by means of windows over each classroom door. From the spacing, the rooms were probably twice the size of the one they'd given Skif.

Why so many and so much room?

Maybe in case it was needed. Just because they only had forty-six Trainees now didn't mean they couldn't have more at some other time. And Teren had said that the classes were shared with Bardic and Healer Trainees—and those others. That would be interesting.

They passed through the double doors that marked the boundary between Collegium and Herald's Wing, and Teren turned immediately to a door on the left. "This is where I'll leave you for now. I will see you tomorrow, and we'll start Basic Orientation. And a couple of the other introductory classes. That way, when everyone gets back and Collegium classes start again, you'll be able to join right up."

He tapped on the door; a muffled sound answered, and Teren opened it, and putting a hand just between Skif's shoulder blades, gently propelled Skif inside before he got a chance to hesitate.

The door shut behind him.

Skif found himself in a cluttered room, a very small room, but one that, from the open door to the side, must be part of a larger suite. There were four things in this room, besides Dean Elcarth; books, papers, chairs, and a desk. There were bookshelves built into the wall that were crammed full of books; books and papers were piled on every available surface. Elcarth motioned to Skif to come in and take the only chair that wasn't holding more books, one with a deep seat and leather padding that was cracked and crazed with age.

He sat in it gingerly, since it didn't look either sturdy or comfortable. He should have known better; nothing bad that he'd assumed about the Heralds ever turned out to be right. The chair proved to be both sturdy and comfortable, and it fit him as if it had been intended for him.

Herald Elcarth folded his hands under his chin, and regarded Skif with a mild gaze. "You," he said at last, "are a puzzle. I must say that Myste and I have searched through every Chronicle of the Collegium, and I cannot find a single instance of a thief being Chosen. We've had several attempted suicides, three murderers—which, I will grant, were all self-defense, and one of them was Lavan Firestorm, but nevertheless, they were murderers. We've had a carnival trickster, a horse sharper, and a girl who pretended to be a witch, told fortunes which turned out to be correct ForeSight, but also took money for curses she never performed, relying instead on the fact that she'd be long gone before anyone noticed that nothing bad had happened to the person she cursed. We've had a *former* assassin. We've even had a spy. But we've never had a thief."

Skif tried to read his expression, and didn't get any clues from it. Elcarth merely seemed interested.

"So, I have to ask myself, Skif. Why you? What is it about you that is so different that a Companion would Choose you?" He tilted his head to the side, looking even more birdlike. "Alberich, by the way, has told me nothing of why he recognized you. In fact, he didn't say much at all about you, except that he knew who you were, but until Kantor told him, he had not known you were specifically a thief."

"What d'ye wanta know?" Skif asked. The best way to limit the damage might be to get Elcarth to ask questions, so that he could carefully tailor his answers.

"More to the point, what do *you* want to tell me?" Elcarth countered. "Usually—not always, but usually—the Chosen sitting where you are start pouring out their life stories to me. Are you going to be any different?"

"I ain't the kind t'pour out m'life story to anybody," Skif replied, trying not to sound sullen, wondering just how much he was going to have to say to satisfy the Dean's curiosity. "I dunno. I ain't never *hurt* nobody. I stick t'the liftin' lay an' roof work…"

He hadn't given a second thought to whether Elcarth would understand the cant, but Elcarth nodded. "Picking pockets and house theft. Which explains why you were in *that* park in broad daylight. Taking advantage of the fact that no one was about in the heat, hmm?"

Skif blinked. How had—

"Your trail out of the city was shatteringly obvious," Elcarth pointed out. "Not to mention hazardous. From the moment Cymry left the park with you, there were witnesses, many of them members of the City Guard. But that only tells me what you do, not what you are—and it's what you *are* that is what I need to know." At Skif's silence, he prodded a little more. "Your parents?"

"Dead," he answered shortly. But try as he might, he couldn't stand firm in the face of Elcarth's gentle but ruthless and relentless questioning. Before very long, Elcarth knew something of his Uncle Londer, of Beel, and of Bazie and Bazie's collection of "boys"—and he knew what had happened to all of them. Especially Bazie. And he knew about the fire.

He managed to keep most of the details to himself, though; at least he *thought* he did. The last thing he wanted was to start unloading his rage on Elcarth. It was a handle to Skif's character that Skif didn't want the Dean to have.

But he didn't manage to keep back as much as he would have liked, though, and just talking about it made his chest go tight, his back tense, and his stomach churn with unspoken emotion. Part of him wanted to tell this gentle man everything—but that was the "new" part of him. The old part did not want him to be talking at all, and was going mad trying to keep him from opening his mouth any more than he had.

Fortunately at that point, Elcarth changed the subject entirely, quizzing him on reading, figuring, writing, and other subjects. That was what he had expected, although he didn't care for it, and his stomach soon settled again. It took longer for the tension to leave his back and chest, but that was all right. The tension reminded him that he needed to be careful.

Outside the office, the day moved on, and the heat wave hadn't broken. Thick as these stone walls were, the heat still got into Elcarth's office and both of them were fanning themselves with stray papers before the interview was over. "I think I can place you, now," Elcarth said, by late afternoon. "But I'm going to be putting you in one class you probably aren't going to appreciate."

"Figuring!" Skif groaned.

"Actually—no. Not immediately. I'm going to ask Gaytha to teach you how to speak properly." Elcarth sat back and waited for Skif's reaction.

If he'd expected Skif to show resentment, he got a surprise himself. "Huh. I s'pose I can see that—though you shoulda 'eard—*heard*— me afore—*before*—Bazie got hold of me." Actually he wasn't at all displeased. You didn't get to be a *good* thief by being unobservant, and Skif had known very well that his speech patterns would mark him out in any crowd as coming from the "bad part of town" near Exile's Gate. If he was going to consort with the highborn and be taken seriously, he'd better stop dropping his "h's".

Among other things.

And he might as well start being careful about how he spoke now. "Is that all you want with me?" he asked, watching every syllable, adding as an afterthought, "Sir."

"For now." Elcarth studied him, and Skif forced himself not to squirm uncomfortably under that unwavering gaze. "I hope eventually you'll feel freer to talk to me, Skif." He looked for a moment as if he was about to say more, then changed his mind. "I believe you have another interview before you—"

"I—" Skif began, but a tap on the door interrupted him.

"Come!" called Elcarth, and the door was opened by Herald Alberich. Who was, of course, the very last person that Skif wanted to see at this moment, when Elcarth had him feeling so unbalanced and unsettled.

Alberich looked at him for a moment, but not with the gaze of a hawk with prey in sight, but with a more measuring, even stare. "Come, I have, to take our new one off, Elcarth," he said simply. "Companion's Field, I think. Cooler it will be there."

"Well, I'm satisfied with him, so he's all yours," Elcarth replied, making Skif wince a little. But Alberich smiled, ever so slightly.

"Your Cymry is anxious to see the work of the Healer," he said to Skif. "And it is that I have evaluation of my own to make. Please—come."

He reached out and beckoned with one hand, and Skif got reluctantly to his feet.

Unlike Teren, Alberich did not seem inclined to *lead* Skif anywhere. Instead, he paced gravely beside Skif, hands clasped behind his back, indicating direction with a jerk of his chin. They left the Herald's Wing by the same door through which they'd first entered the Collegium; Skif recognized the spot immediately. There were plenty of trees here, and Skif was glad of the shade. And glad of the light color of the Trainee uniform. He hated to think what it would have been like if the outfit had been black.

"To the riverbank, I think," Alberich said, with one of those chin jerks. "You are puzzled by my accent."

"Well—aye," Skif admitted. "Never heard naught like it."

"Nor will you. It is from Karse that I am. A Captain I was, in the service of Vkandis Sunlord." With a glance at Skif's startled face, Alberich then turned his face up toward the cloudless sky. "We have something in common, I think. Or *will* have. The thief and the traitor— neither to be trusted. *Outside* the Heraldic Circle, that is."

Skif swallowed hard. A Karsite. A Karsite *officer.* From the army of Valdemar's most implacable enemy.

"But—why—"

"That is what I—*we,* for Kantor suggested this—wish to be telling you," Alberich said gravely as they approached the riverbank. His face cleared, then, as they rounded a section of topiary bushes and the river appeared, dazzling in the sun. "Ah, there they are!"

Two Companions waited for them, and Skif knew Cymry from the other immediately, though *how,* he couldn't have said. He rushed to greet her, and as he touched her, he felt enveloped in that same wonderful feeling that had been creeping in all afternoon, past doubts, past fears, past every obstacle. He pulled her head down to his chest and ran his hands along her cheeks, while she breathed into his tunic and made little contented sounds. He could have stayed that way for the rest of the afternoon...

But Alberich cleared his throat politely after a time, and Skif pulled away from her with great reluctance. "A grotto there is, in the riverbank. Cool as a cellar in this heat, and our Companions will enjoy it as well."

Cymry seemed to know exactly where they were going, so Skif let her lead him. Skif kept one hand on her neck and followed along. She led him down a steeply-sloped, grassy bank to the edge of the river itself, and there, partly out of sight from the lawn above, was a kind of ornamental cave carved into the bank, just as Alberich had said. It was just about tall enough to stand up inside, and held three curved, stone benches at the back. Nicely paved, ceilinged, and walled with flagstone, it was wonderfully cool in there, and the two Companions took up positions just inside, switching their tails idly, as Alberich and Skif took seats on built-in benches at the back.

This wasn't so bad. Without the Herald looming over him, without actually having to look him in the eyes, Skif felt more comfortable. And in the dim coolness, the Herald seemed a bit more relaxed. Alberich cleared his throat again, as soon as they settled. "So. It is you who have been telling tales for the most of today. Let someone else, for a candlemark."

"Suits," Skif said shortly, and leaned back into the curved stone bench.

"Karse," Alberich began, meditatively. "I left my land, and to an extent, my God. They call me traitor there. Think you—it is odd, that I love them both, still?"

"I dunno," Skif replied honestly. "Dunno much 'bout gods, an'—truth t'tell, I never thought overmuch 'bout anythin' like a whole *country*. Mostly didn' think 'bout much past m'own streets."

Alberich nodded a little, his gaze fixed on the river flowing outside the grotto. "No reason there was, why you should."

Skif shrugged. "Ol' Bazie, he didn' think much of Karse, an' I reckon he thought pretty well of Valdemar, when it comes down t'cases. Least—" Skif thought hard for a moment, back to those memories that he hadn't wanted to think about at all for a very long time now. "Huh. When he lost 'is legs, 'twasn't Karse as saw 'im Healed, nor the Tedrels. 'Twas Valdemar. An' he 'ad some good things t'say 'bout Heralds."

"Tell me," Alberich urged mildly, and Skif did. It was surprising, when he came to think about it, how much good Bazie had said about Valdemar and its Heralds, especially considering that he'd fought against both.

Alberich sighed. "I love my land and my God," he said, when Skif was through. "But—both have been—are *being*—ill served. And that is neither the fault of the land, nor the God."

He told his story concisely, using as few words as possible, but Skif got a vivid impression of what the younger Alberich must have been like. And when he described being trapped in a building that was deliberately set afire to execute him, Skif found himself transposing that horror to what Bazie and the boys must have felt.

But there had been no Companion leaping through the flames to save them. There had been no happy ending for Bazie.

"It was the King's Own and another Herald who came at Kantor's call," Alberich said meditatively. "Which was, for my sake, a good thing. Few would question Talamir's word, fewer dared to do so aloud. So I was Healed, and I learned—yes," he said, after he glanced at Skif. "Oh, smile you may, that into Grays I went, and back to schooling at that age! A sight, I surely was!" He shook his head.

"Why?" Skif asked. "Why didn' you just tell 'em t' make you a Herald straight off?"

"And knowing nothing of Heralds or Valdemar? Stubborn I am often, stupid, never. Much I had to unlearn. More did others have to learn of me. Selenay, after Talamir, was my friend and advocate—after them, others. More than enough work there was here, to keep me at the Collegium, replacing the aged Weaponsmaster. More than enough reason to stay, that others have me beneath their eye, and so feel control over me in their hands." He smiled sardonically. "Did they know what I learn for the Queen *here*, it is that they would send me out to the farthest Border ere I could take breath thrice."

Since Skif had seen him at work, he snickered. Alberich bestowed a surprisingly mild glance on him.

"Now, your turn, it is, for answering questions," he said, and Skif steeled himself. "But first of all, because I would know—why choose to be a thief?"

An odd question, and as unexpected as one of Alberich's rare smiles. Skif shrugged. "'Twas that—or slave for m'nuncle Londer. Wasn't much else goin'—an' Bazie was all right."

His heart contracted at that. *All right!* What a niggardly thing to say about a man who had been friend, teacher, and in no small part, savior! Yet—if he said more, he put his heart within reach of this Herald, this Alberich, who had already said in so many words that he would use anything to safeguard Valdemar, the Queen, and the Heralds…

And that's bad, how? whispered that new side of him.

Shut up! replied the old.

Skif became aware that a moment of silence had lengthened into something that Alberich might use to put a question. He filled it, quickly. "Bazie was pretty good t'us, actually." He paused. "You gonna Truth Spell me again?"

Alberich shook his head. "What I did was done in need and haste. Much there is I would learn of you, but most of it will wait. And what I would know, I think you will tell freely for the sake of your friends."

So now, for a second time, Alberich asked questions about Jass and Jass' master, this time helping Skif to pry out the least and littlest morsel of information in his memory. This time, though, the questions came thoughtfully, as slow as the heat-heavy air drifting above the riverbank and cloaking it in shimmer, each question considered and answered with the same care. Alberich was right about this much. In this case, Alberich's goals and Skif's were one, and the two voices inside him were at peace with one another.

The light had turned golden as they spoke, and the heat shimmer faded. There had been a long time since the last question, and Skif slowly became aware that lunch was wearing thin. As his stomach growled, Alberich glanced over at him again, with a half-smile.

"You know your way about, I think," the Weaponsmaster said. "Tomorrow we will meet, and you will begin your training with me, and with others."

Then, with no other word of farewell, Alberich rose and stalked out, his Companion falling in at his side like a well-trained drill partner.

"You've been mighty quiet," Skif said to Cymry in the silence.

:You were doing perfectly well without me,: she replied, with a saucy switch of her tail. *:Well. Here you are, left perfectly alone on the Palace grounds. You can go and do whatever you want; no keeper, no guardian. You could go and climb to the Palace roof if you wanted to, bearing in mind the Queen's Guard might catch you. Or hasn't that occurred to you yet?:*

It hadn't, and the revelation hit him like a bucket of cold water.

"You sure?" he gasped.

:As sure as I'm standing here.: She switched her tail again, but this time with impatience. *:They trust you. Isn't it time you started to trust them? Just start, that's all.:*

An odd, heavy feeling came into his throat. Once again, the sense that something portentous had happened, something that he didn't understand, came over him.

It was more than uncomfortable, it was unsettling, in the sense of feeling the world he knew suddenly shift into something he no longer recognized.

"I'm hungry," he announced, hastily shunting it all aside. "An' I reckon I saw some ham an' bacon in that pantry."

Cymry whickered; it sounded like a chuckle. *:I reckon you saw more than that. Go on, come back and meet me here once you've stuffed yourself.:*

Skif got up, and now that he was moving again, he felt every single bruise and strain from yesterday's ride.

Was it only yesterday? It felt like a lifetime ago…

As he got up, he actually staggered a little with stiffness. Cymry moved quickly to give him a shoulder to catch himself on, and after he'd steadied himself, he gave her a self-conscious little kiss on her forehead.

:Go on,: she said playfully, giving him a shove with her nose. *:Just don't eat until you're sick.:*

You didn't become a successful thief without learning the layout of a place on the first time through it. Nevertheless, Skif couldn't help but feeling a little self-conscious as he made his way across the grass, overshadowed by the silent building. And he couldn't help looking for those who might be looking for *him*. But there were no watchers; Cymry had been right. And when he left the heat of the outdoors for the cool of the great kitchen, he discovered it just as deserted as it had been when Teren brought him.

He opened the pantry doors and stood amid the plenitude, gazing at the laden shelves and full of indecision. Bacon or ham? White bread, or brown? It was too hot to eat anything cooked-up fresh, besides being far too much trouble, but there was an abundance of good things that could be eaten cold. His mouth watered at the sight of a row of ceramic jars labeled "Pikld Beets," but the discovery of a keg of large sour cucumber pickles made him change his mind about the beets. There were so many things here that he had only tasted once or twice, and so many more he'd seen, but never tasted—

But although Cymry had warned him playfully about eating himself sick, he was mindful of that very consideration. Too many times he'd seen people in his own streets do just that, when encountering unexpected abundance. After all, none of this was going to disappear tomorrow, or even later tonight (unless he ate it) and he wasn't going to have his access to it removed, either.

When this Cook gets back t'work—Oh, there was a thought! If there was so much here ready for snacking, what wonderful things must the Cook prepare every day? Visions of the kinds of things he'd seen in the best inns passed through his mind—minced-meat pasties, stews with thick, rich gravy, egg pie and oh, the sweets…

Eventually he made his selections, and put a plate together. He ate neatly and with great enjoyment, savoring every bite, finishing with a tart apple and a piece of sharp cheese. Then, as he had when he had eaten earlier with Teren, he cleaned up after himself and put everything away.

A glance through the windows above the great sink as he was washing up showed him that the sky had gone to red as the sun set. There would be plenty of time to spend with Cymry, and at that moment, there was nothing in the world that he would rather have been doing.

Back up and out he went, under a sky filled with red-edged, purple clouds, passing trees just beginning to whisper in an evening breeze, through the quietude that seemed so strange to him after the constant noise of the city proper. Cymry waited for him where he had last seen her, watching the sun set and turn the river to a flat ribbon of fire.

He put an arm over her shoulder, and they watched it together. How many times had he watched the sun rise or set above the roofs of the city? Too many to count, certainly, but he'd never had as much time as he would have liked to enjoy the sight, even when it was a truly glorious one like tonight.

Come to that, there had never been anyone with him who understood that it was a glorious sight until tonight. Bazie would have—but Bazie had spent most of his time in the cellar room, and there was never the time or leisure for his boys to bring him up for a sunset.

They stood together until the last vestige of rose faded from the clouds, and only then did they realize that they were not alone.

Behind them were another Herald and Companion, who must have come up behind them so quietly that not even Skif's instincts were alerted—and that took some skill.

Skif didn't even know they were there until Cymry reacted, with a sudden glance over her shoulder, a start and a little jump.

Then he looked behind, and saw the strangers.

He turned quickly, sure that they were somewhere they shouldn't have been, but the tall, elderly man standing with one arm around his Companion's shoulders (even as Skif had stood with Cymry) smiled and forestalled any apology.

"I beg your pardon, youngling, for startling you," the man said, his voice surprisingly deep for one as thin as he was. "We often come here to admire the sunset, and didn't see any reason to disturb your enjoyment. Rolan tells me that you are Skif and Cymry."

The man's uniform was a touch above the ones that Herald Teren and Dean Elcarth had worn; there was a lot of silver embroidery on the white deerskin tunic, and Skif would have been willing to bet anything he had that the trews and shirt this Herald wore were silk.

The Companion was something special as well; he was just a little glossier, just a little taller, and had just a touch more of an indefinable dignity than any of the others Skif had seen thus far did.

:This is the Queen's Own Herald Talamir and Rolan, the Grove-Born,: Cymry said hastily in his mind, in a tone that told Skif (even though he had no idea what the titles meant) that these two were somehow very, very special, even by the standards of Heralds.

"Yessir, Herald Talamir," Skif said, with an awkward bob of his head. It was a very odd thing. He had seen any number of highborn, and never felt any reason to respect them. He *did* respect the Heralds he'd met so far—but this man, without doing more than simply stand there, somehow commanded respect. But at the same time, there was an aura of what Beel might have called *mortality* and what others might have called *fey* that hung about him.

The Herald's smile widened. "And I see that you and Cymry Mindspeak. That is excellent, especially in so early a bond." Talamir stepped forward and extended his hand to Skif, and when Skif tentatively offered his own, took it, and shook it firmly but gently. "Welcome, Skif," was all he said, but the words were a true greeting, and not a hollow courtesy.

"Thankee, sir," Skif replied, feeling an unaccountable shyness, a shyness that evidently was shared by Cymry, who kept glancing at the other Companion with mingled awe and admiration. Talamir seemed to expect something more from him, and he groped for something to say. "This's—all kinda new t'me."

"So I'm told." Mild amusement, no more. No sign that Talamir had been told anything of Skif's antecedents. "Well, if you feel overwhelmed, remember that when I first arrived here, I was straight out of a horse-trading family, I'd never spent a night in my life under anything but canvas, and the largest city I ever saw was a quarter of the size of Haven. My first night in my room was unbearable; I thought I was going to smother, and I kept feeling the walls pressing in on me. Eventually, I took my blankets outside and slept on the lawn. Very few of us are ready for this when we arrive here, and—" he chuckled softly, the merest ghost of a laugh, "—sometimes *here is* even less ready for us. But we adapt, the Trainee to the Collegium and the Collegium to the Trainee. Even if it means pitching a tent in the garden for a Trainee to live in for the first six months."

Skif gaped, totally unable to imagine this elegant gentleman living in a tent, but quickly shut his mouth. "Yessir," he replied, his usually quick wits failing him.

He had no idea how to end this conversation, but the Herald solved his dilemma for him. "Have a good evening, youngling," Talamir said, and he and his Companion turned and drifted off through the dusk like a pair of spirits, making no sound whatsoever as they moved over the grass. The moon, three-quarters now, had just begun to rise, and its light silvered them with an eldritch glow.

"Is't just me," Skif asked, when he was pretty sure they were out of earshot, "or are they *spooky?*"

:*They're spooky*,: Cymry affirmed, with an all-over shiver of her coat. :*Rolan is Talamir's second Companion. Taver was killed in the Tedrel Wars, when Talamir and Jadus were trying to rescue the King. They say that everyone thought Talamir was going to follow Taver and King Sendar until Rolan came and pulled him back. Ever since then, Talamir's been—otherworldly. Half his heart and soul are here, and half's in the Havens, they say.*:

Skif shook his head. All this was too deep for him.

:*Still!*: Cymry continued, shaking off her mood. :*His mind is all here, and Talamir's mind is better than four of anyone else's. Would you like to see Companion's Field?*:

"I thought this was Companion's Field," Skif replied confusedly.

She made a chuckling sound. :*This is only the smallest corner of it. Most of it is across the river. Think you can get on my back without a boost?*:

"Please. I can pull m'self up a gutter on t'roof without usin' legs," he retorted. "I oughta be able t' get on your back!"

She stood rock still for him, and after a moment of awkwardness, he managed to clamber onto her bare back. Stepping out into the twilight at a brisk pace, she took him across the river on a little stone bridge, and they spent a candlemark or two exploring Companion's Field.

Finally, the long day caught up with him, and Skif found himself yawning and nodding, catching himself before he actually dozed off and fell off Cymry's back. Cymry brought him right back to the place where they'd met, and from there, he stumbled up to his room.

Someone had come along and lit the lanterns set up along the walls, so at least he wasn't stumbling because he couldn't see. When he got to the door of his room, he discovered that someone had also slipped a card into a holder there that had his name on it.

A sound in the corridor made him turn; his eyes met the brilliant blue ones of an older boy—hair soaking wet and wrapped in a light sleeping robe, on his way out of the bathing room. The other boy smiled tentatively.

"Hullo!" he greeted Skif. "I'm Kris; you must be the new one, Skif. It's just been me and Jeri here over Midsummer."

"Uh—hullo." He eyed Kris carefully; definitely highborn, with that accent and those manners. But not one with his nose in the air. "Jeri a girl or a boy?"

"Girl. She'll be your yearmate; got Chosen six moons ago. Oh, I made sure I left enough hot water for a good bath."

"Thanks." That decided him. Maybe he'd already had one bath today, but he was still stiff and sore, and another wouldn't hurt.

Kris was still looking at him quizzically. "I hope you don't mind my asking—but how did you get that black eye? It's a glory! If you haven't seen it, it's gone all green and purple around the edges, and black as black at your nose."

"Smacked it inta Cymry's neck," Skif admitted ruefully. "Ain't never jumped on a horse afore."

Kris winced in sympathy. "Ouch. Better go soak. Good night!"

"Night," Skif replied, and got a robe of his own to take the boy's advice.

When he got back to his room and started putting his new belongings away to clear his bed so he could sleep, he found one last surprise.

On the desk were all of his things. Every possible object he owned *except* the most ragged of his clothing from both his room next to Jass', and the Priory. Including his purse, with every groat still in it.

Startled, he tried to think at his Companion. :*Cymry!*: he "called" her, hoping she'd answer.

:*What do you need?*: she asked sleepily, and he explained what he'd found.

:*Who did that? And how come?*: he finished. It worried him…

:*Oh. That would be Alberich's doing, I expect,*: she replied. :*Usually they go send someone to tell families that the Chosen's arrived safely, and to get their belongings, if they didn't bring anything with them. Don't you want your things?*:

Well, of course he wanted his things. :*I just*—:

The fact was, he worried. Who went there. What they'd said. And how they'd known where he came from…

:*Kantor says it was all Alberich's doing, at least getting your things from your room.*: Well, that was one worry off his mind. Alberich would have gone as the sell-sword, and intimidated his way in. Good enough. :*He sent off the usual Guardsman to the Priory. They'll have told the Priory you were Chosen, and the Guardsman would have brought someone hired to take your place, so the Priory won't go shorthanded. Kantor says Alberich didn't tell your old landlord anything. Is that all right?:*

Since it was exactly what he would have wanted had he been asked, he could only agree. *:Aye. That's fine, I reckon:* In fact, he couldn't think of anything else he could possibly want.

:Get some sleep,: she told him. *:It'll be a long day tomorrow.:*

A longer one than *today?* With a sigh, he climbed into bed, feeling very strange to be in such a bed, and even stranger not hearing the usual noises of the city beyond his walls.

But not so strange that he was awake for much longer than it took to find a comfortable position and think about closing the curtains he'd left open to let in every bit of breeze. About the time he decided it didn't matter, he was asleep.

1 6

A scant week later, Skif was just about ready to face all the returning Trainees. He knew what the Heralds of Valdemar were about now—at least, he knew where they'd come from and what they did. And he was starting to get his mind wrapped around why they did it. If he didn't understand it, well, there were a great many things in the world that he didn't understand, and that didn't keep him from going on with his life.

Something had happened to him over the course of that week, and he didn't understand any of it. The things he had always thought were the only truths in the world weren't, not here anyway. He was going to have to watch these Heralds carefully. They might be hiding something behind all this acceptance and welcome.

But since a lot of what was going on with him had to do with feelings, he came to the unsatisfactory and vague conclusion that maybe it wasn't going to be possible to *understand* it. He was caught up like a leaf in the wind, and the leaf didn't have a lot of choice in where the wind took it. If it hadn't been that Cymry was a big part of that wind—

Well, she was, and despite everything he'd learned until this moment, he found himself thinking and feeling things that would have been completely unlike the boy he'd been a fortnight ago. *Soft,* was what he would have called what he was becoming now, but what he was now knew that there was nothing *soft* about where he was tending. If anything, it was hard... as in *difficult.*

And *difficult were* the things he was learning, and the things he was going to learn, though truth to tell, it was no more work than he was used to setting himself. Physical exertion? The weapons' work he was doing, the riding, none of it was as hard as roof walking. Book learning? Ha! It was mostly reading and remembering, not like having to figure out a new lock. Even the figuring—the *mathematics,* they called it—wasn't that bad. Since he could already do his sums, this new stuff was a matter of logic, a lot like figuring out a lock. The real difference was that he was obeying someone else's schedule and someone else's orders.

Yet he'd run to Bazie's schedule and Bazie's orders, and thought no worse of it, nor of himself.

For every objection his old self came up with, the new one—or Cymry—had a counter. And if there was one thing he was absolutely certain of, it was that he would not, could not do without Cymry. She didn't so much fill an empty place in him as fill up every crack and crevice that life had ever put in his heart, and make it all whole again. To have Cymry meant he would have to become a Herald. So be it. It was worth it a thousand times over.

And once again, just as when he'd been with Bazie, he was *happy*.

He hadn't known what happiness was until Bazie took him in. Moments of pleasure, yes, and times of less misery than others, but never happiness. He'd learned that with Bazie, and since the fire, he hadn't had so much as a moment of real, unshadowed happiness.

Now it was back. Not all the time, and there were still times when he thought about the fire and raged or wept or both. He wasn't going to turn his back on these people, not until he figured out what their angle was. But for the most part it was back, like a gift, something he'd never thought to have back again.

After that, he knew he couldn't leave. Out there, without Cymry, he'd go back to being alone against the world. In here, with her, there was one absolutely true thing he was certain of. Cymry loved and needed him, and he loved and needed her. The rest—well, he'd figure it all out as it came.

But he woke every day, with two persistent and immediate problems to solve. When his fingers itched to lift a kerchief or a purse, he wondered what would happen if he gave in to the urge—and when Kris and Jeri accepted him without question as one of themselves, he worried what would happen when they (and the rest of the Trainees) learned he'd been a thief. Cymry might be the center of his world, but he'd had friends before in Bazie and the boys, and he liked having them. He didn't want to lose the ones he was getting now.

He woke one morning exactly six days after he had arrived, a day when he knew the rest of the Trainees would begin coming back in, signaling the beginning of his real classes tomorrow, although it would probably take two or three more days for all of them to make it back. It helped, of course, that they all had Companions, and however long their journeys were, they would travel in a fraction of the time it took an ordinary horse to cross the same distance. He had met most of his teachers, and even begun lessons designed to allow him to fit into the classes with some of them. He had no idea how many of them—besides Alberich and Teren—knew his background either.

And eventually, it *would,* come out. Secrets never stayed secret for long. Eventually someone would say something.

He had worried over that like a terrier with a rat; in fact, he'd gone to bed that night thinking about it. And when he woke, it was with an answer at last.

Whether it would be the *right* answer was another question entirely. But he knew who to consult on it.

The Collegium cook, a moon-faced, eternally cheerful man called Mero, had turned up three days ago. The Collegium bells signaling the proper order of the day had resumed when Mero returned. So now, when Skif awoke at the first bell of the day and went down to the kitchen at the bell that signaled breakfast, he would join Kris and the girl Jeri and some of the teachers around a table in the kitchen for a real cooked meal. With so few to cook for, Mero declined help in cooking, but afterward they all pitched in to clean up. Some of Skif's daydreams about food were coming to pass—Mero even made homely oat porridge taste special.

After breakfast came Skif's first appointment of the day. It wasn't exactly a class… especially not this morning.

And this morning, he could hardly eat his breakfast for impatience to get out to the salle, where some of the weapons training was done. He cleared the table by himself so that he could leave quickly.

He ran to the salle, a building that stood apart from the rest of the Collegia, and for good reason, since it needed to be a safe distance from anywhere people might walk, accidentally or on purpose. The Trainees from all three Collegia learned archery, and even some of the Blues, the students who weren't Trainees at all. And some of those archery students were, to be frank, not very good.

Skif, although he had never shot a bow in his life, had proved to be a natural at it, somewhat to his own surprise. Seeing that, Alberich had tried him with something a bit more lethal and less obvious than an arrow. He'd tried him in knife throwing.

Skif had been terrifyingly accurate. Where his eye went, so did whatever was put in his hand. He had no idea where the skill had come from—but at least his ability to *fight* with a knife, or with the blunted practice swords, was no better than anyone else's.

Alberich had promised something in the way of a surprise for him this morning, and Skif was impatient to see what he meant, as well as impatient to speak with him.

When Skif arrived at the salle, Alberich was throwing a variety of weapons at a target set up on the other side of the room. Alberich was a hair more accurate than Skif, but Alberich's skill came from training, not a natural talent. Nevertheless, Skif watched with admiration as Alberich placed his weapons—knives, sharpened stakes, and small axes—in a neat pattern on the straw-padded target. He didn't interrupt the Weaponsmaster, and Alberich didn't stop until all the implements he'd lined up on a bench behind him were in the target.

The salle, a long, low building with smooth, worn wooden floors, was lit from above by clerestory windows. This was because the walls were taken up with storage cabinets and a few full-length mirrors. For the rest, there wasn't much, just a few benches, some training equipment, and the door to Alberich's office. For all Skif knew, Alberich might even have quarters here, since he hardly ever saw the Weaponsmaster anywhere else.

"So, you come in good time," Alberich said, as the last of his sharpened stakes slammed into the target. He turned toward Skif, picking up something from the bench where his weapons had been. "Come here, then. Let us see how these suit you."

"These" proved to be little daggers in sheaths that Alberich strapped to Skif's arms, with the daggers lying along the inside of his arms. Once on, they were hidden by Skif's sleeves, and he flexed his arms experimentally. They weren't at all uncomfortable, and he suspected that with a little practice wearing them, he wouldn't even notice they were there.

"Of my students, only two are, I think, fit to use these," Alberich said. "Jeri is one. It is you that is the other. Look you—" He showed Skif the catch that kept each dagger firmly in its sheath—and the near-invisible shake of the wrist that dropped it down into the hand, ready to throw, when the catch was undone.

Skif was thrilled with the new acquisition—what boy wouldn't be?— but unlike most, if not all, of the other Trainees, he had seen men knifed and bleeding and dead. Men—and a woman or two. Even before he left his uncle's tavern, he'd seen death at its most violent. And he knew, bone-deep and blood-deep, that *death* was what these knives were for. Not target practice, not showing off for one's friends. Death, hidden in a sleeve, small and silent, waiting to be used.

Death was a cold, still face, and blood pooling and clotting on the pavement. Death was floating bloated in the river. Death was ashes and bones in the burned-out hulk of a building.

Death was someone you knew found still and cold, and never coming back. And these little "toy" daggers were death. *Not* to be treated lightly, or to be played with.

But death was also being able to stop someone from making you dead.

"Can you kill a man?" Alberich asked suddenly, as Skif contemplated the dagger in his hand.

Skif looked up at the Weaponsmaster. As usual, his face was unreadable. "Depends on th' man," Skif replied soberly. "If you're talkin' in cold blood, I'd a took Jass down like a mad dog, just 'cause he killed m'friends, and I'd'a done it soon as I knew who his master was. In the dark. In the back. An' if somethin' happens, an' his master *won't* come up on what's due him—mebbe I'd do him, too. If you're talkin' in hot blood, if I was come at myself—someone wantin' me dead—aye, I'd kill him."

Alberich nodded, as if that was expected. "So. When are you going to display these to your friends?" he prodded. It *sounded* casual, but it was prodding.

Skif shook his head. "These—they're for serious work. Not for showin' off. 'Less you order me, Master Alberich, I ain't even gonna wear these, 'cept t' practice. That's like balancin' a rock over a door t' see who gets hit. I ain't got a hot temper, but I got a temper like anybody else. Losin' temper makes people do stupid things."

Death was a fight over nothing, and a lost temper, and blood where a simple blow would have served the same purpose. Over and over again, in the streets outside Exile's Gate, Death came when tempers worn thin by need or hurt, anger or drink, flared and blades came out. Alberich, in his guise of the sell-sword, was one of the few in those taverns that Skif had ever seen who went out of his way to avoid killing—to avoid even causing permanent harm.

Alberich gave a brief nod of satisfaction, and went on to drill Skif in the use of his new weapons. He said nothing more as the knives went into the target again and again; he was satisfied that Skif was going to be sensible, and dismissed the question as answered. That was another thing that Skif had come to realize about Alberich in the last week. Where other people—even a few Heralds—were inclined to harp on a subject that worried them, Alberich examined the subject, asked his questions, made his statements, came to his decisions, and left it alone.

If he trusted the person in question.

And he trusted Skif.

T*hat* was a very, very strange realization. But when he had come to it last night, it had been the catalyst for his own decision this morning.

"Master Alberich," he said, when the knives had been taken off and wrapped up in an oiled cloth to keep the sheaths supple and catches rust free. "I got a thought. Sooner or later some'un's gonna let it slip what I was. An' that's gonna cause some trouble."

Alberich gave him one of those very penetrating glances, but said nothing.

"But I think that you want t'keep at least part of what I can do real quiet."

Now the Weaponsmaster nodded slightly. "Have I not said it? Your skills could be—more than useful."

Skif clasped his hands behind his back. "So I had an ideer. What if we go ahead an' let *part* of it out? Just that I was on th' liftin' lay. 'Cause there's this—ain't too many as does the roof work an' th' liftin' lay, an' if people know I done th' one, they won't look for t'other." He grinned. "I can turn it into a kinda raree-show trick, y'ken? Do th' lift fer laughs. I'd like—" he continued, with a laugh, "—t'see yon Kris' face when I give 'im his liddle silver horse back, what he keeps in his pocket."

Alberich raised one eyebrow. "You have the itching fingers," he said, though without accusation.

"A bit," Skif admitted. "But—what d'you think?"

"I think that you have the right of it," Alberich replied, and Skif's spirits lifted considerably. "It *is* your skill in other things, and not as the picker of pockets, that is of primary value, at least for now. And when you have your Whites, the novelty of your past will have worn off, those within the Circle will not trouble to speak of it, and most outside the Circle will never know of it. So if there is a thing to be taken amidst a crowd of strangers, you will likely not find eyes on you."

That made perfect sense. One of the pickpockets Skif knew had spent an entire year just establishing himself as a lame old beggar who was always stumbling into people. Then when no one even thought twice about him, he began deftly helping himself to their purses, and there wasn't a man jack of the ones that were robbed that even *considered* the lame old beggar was the culprit.

Alberich's eyes looked elsewhere for a flicker of time, then returned to him. "Those who need to know what you are about," he said, "will know.

The rest will see an imp of mischief." He leveled a long gaze at Skif.

Skif shrugged. "Won't keep nothing," he said, quite truthfully. "Never took more'n I needed t'live comfortable, or Bazie did. That was Bazie's way—start t' take more, get greedy, get caught."

"A wise man, your Bazie," Alberich replied, with nothing weighting his tone.

Skif shrugged again. "So, I don' need nothing here. Livin' better than I ever did. An' you brought me my stuff."

With the purse of money, left in the loft at the Priory...

And when that money runs out, what then?

"If there is need for silver to loosen tongues, or even gold, the Queen's coffers will provide," Alberich said gravely, giving Skif a sudden chill, for it seemed as if the Weaponsmaster read Skif's mind before Skif even finished the thought. "And for the rest—for there are Fairs, and there are taverns, and perhaps there will be the giving and receiving of gifts among friends, there is the stipend."

"Stipend?" Skif asked.

"Stipend." Alberich smiled wryly. "Some of ours are highborn, used to pocket money, some used to lavish amounts of it. We could forbid the parents to supply it, but why inflict hardship on those who deserve it not? So—the stipend. All Trainees receive it alike. Pocket money, for small things. Since you *have* money already—"

He paused.

And I am not asking you where it came from, nor demanding that you give it back, said the look that followed the pause.

"—then you will have yours on the next Quarter-Day, with the others."

"Oh. Uh—thank you—" Skif, for once, felt himself at a loss for words. Blindsided, in fact. This wasn't something he had expected, another one of those unanticipated *kindnesses.* There was no earthly reason why the Heralds should supply the Trainees—him in particular—with *pocket money.* They already supplied food, clothing, wonderful housing, entertainment in the form of their own games, and the Bardic Collegium on the same grounds.

Why were they doing these things? They didn't have to. Trainees that didn't have wealthy parents could just do without pocket money.

But Alberich had already turned away. He brought out a longer knife, and was preparing the salle for another lesson in street fighting. *That,* Skif could understand, and he set himself to the lesson at hand.

* * *

"It's a fool's bet," Herald-Trainee Nerissa cautioned a fascinated Blue four weeks later. "Don't take it."

But the look in her eyes suggested that although honesty had prompted the caution, Nerissa herself really, truly wanted to see Skif in action again.

Eight Trainees, two from Bardic Collegium and six from Herald's, and three Unaffiliated students, were gathered around Skif and a fourth Blue in the late afternoon sunshine on the Training Field.

The group surrounding Skif and the hapless Blue were just as fascinated as Nerissa, and just as eager. Skif himself shrugged and looked innocent. "Not a big bet," he pointed out. "Just t'fix my window so's the breeze can get *in* and them—*those*—moths can't. He says he can, says he *has*, for himself and his friends, and I don't think it'd put him out too much."

"It seems fair enough to me," said Kris. "Neither one of you is wagering anything he can't afford or can't do." He pointed at the Blue. "And *you* swore in the Compass Rose that Skif could never pull his trick on you, because you in particular and your plumb-line set in general were smarter than the Heraldic Trainees."

The Blue's eyes widened. "How did you know that?" he gasped.

Kris just grinned. "Sources, my lad," he said condescendingly, from the lofty position of a Trainee in his final year. "Sources. And I never reveal my sources. Are you going to take the bet, or not?"

The Blue's chin jutted belligerently. "Damn right I am!" he snapped.

"Witnessed!" called four Herald Trainees and one Bardic at once, just as Alberich came out to break the group up and set them at their archery practice.

At the end of practice, once Alberich had gone back into the salle, virtually everyone lingered—and Skif didn't disappoint them. He presented the astonished Blue with the good-luck piece that had been the object of the bet, an ancient silver coin, so worn away that all that could be seen were the bare outlines of a head. The coin had been in a pocket that the Blue had fixed with a buttoned-down flap, an invention against pickpockets of his own devising, that he was clearly very proud of.

In a panic, the boy checked the pocket. It was buttoned. He undid it and felt inside. His face was a study in puzzlement, as he brought out his hand. There was a coin-shaped lead slug in it.

Skif flipped his luck piece at him, and he caught it amid the laughter of the rest of the group. He was good-natured about his failure—something Skif had taken into consideration before making the bet—

and joined in the laughter ruefully. "All right," he said, with a huge sigh. "I'll fix your window."

As the Blue walked off, consoled by two of his fellows, Herald-Trainee Coroc slapped Skif on the back with a laugh. "I swear, it's as good as having a conjurer about!" the Lord Marshal's son said. "Well done! How'd you think of slipping him that lead slug to take the place of his luck piece?"

Skif flushed a little; he was coming to enjoy these little tests and bets. Picking pockets was something he did fairly well, but he didn't get any applause for it out in the street. The best he could expect was a heavy purse and no one putting the Watch on him. This, however—he had an audience now, and he *liked* having an audience, especially an appreciative one.

"I figured I'd better have something when Kris told me that Henk had been a-boasting over in the Compass Rose, an' told me I had to uphold the Heralds' side," Skif replied, with a nod to Kris. "We've all seen that luck piece of his, so it wasn't no big thing to melt a bit of lead and make a slug to the right size. After that, I just waited for him to say something I could move in on."

"But when did you get the coin?" Coroc wanted to know. "I mean, Alberich broke us up right after he took the bet, and you didn't get anywhere near—"

Coroc stopped talking, and his mouth made a little "oh" when he realized what Skif had done.

"—you took it off him *before* the bet!" he exclaimed.

"When there was all that joshing and shoving, sure," Skif agreed. "I *knew* he'd take the bet; after all that about his special pocket, he'd never have passed it up. He figured it'd be a secret I wouldn't reckon out, and I'd lose. But even if Kris hadn't told me, I'd have figured it anyway," he added. "The button shows, when you look right, and he ain't no seamstress, that buttonhole ain't half as tight as it could be." That last in a note of scorn from one who had long ago learned to make a fine buttonhole. "Anyway, I had to have the slug, 'cause I knew once he took the bet he'd be a-fingering that pocket t' make sure his luck piece was there."

"It's a good thing you haven't shown up a Gift other than moderate Thoughtsensing," Kris laughed, "or he'd have been accusing you of Fetching the thing!"

Skif preened himself, just a little, under all the attention. If having Skif around was entertaining for his fellow Trainees, the admiration each time he pulled off something clever was very heady stuff for Skif. He'd begun beautifully, a couple of days after full classes resumed, when Kris's best friend Dirk had asked innocently where he'd come from and what his parents did. He'd put on a pitiful act, telling a long, sad, and only slightly embellished story of his mother's death, the near-slavery at his uncle's hands, his running away, and his tragic childhood in the slums near Exile's Gate. All the while, he was slowly emptying goodhearted Dirk's pockets.

"But how did you *live?*" the young man exclaimed, full of pity for him. "How did you manage to survive?"

By this time, of course, since everyone in the three Collegia loved a tale, he'd drawn a large and sympathetic audience.

"Oh," Skif had said, taking Dirk's broad hand, turning it palm upwards, and depositing his belongings in it. "I turned into a thief, of course."

Poor Dirk's eyes had nearly bulged out of his head, and this cap to a well-told tale had surprised laughter out of everyone else. Word very quickly spread, but because of the prankish nature of Skif's lifting, there wasn't a soul in Herald's Collegium, and not more than one or two doubters in Bardic and Healers', that thought him anything other than a mischief maker, and an entertaining one at that. Those few were generally thought of as sour-faced pessimists and their comments ignored.

Not, Skif thought to himself somberly as he accepted the accolades of his fellows with a self-effacing demeanor, *but what they mightn't be right about me, 'cept for Cymry.*

Except for Cymry. That pretty much summed it up. *Everyone* among the Heraldic Trainees was willing to accept Skif as a harmless prankster because he'd been Chosen, because Companions didn't Choose *bad* people. And if anyone among the teachers thought differently, they were keeping their doubts to themselves.

"Time to get to the baths," Kris reminded them. "Otherwise the hot water's going to be gone." That sent everyone but Skif on a run for their quarters. Skif lingered, not because he didn't care about getting a hot bath, but because Alberich had given him an interesting look that he thought was a signal.

He made certain that no one was looking back at him, then sidled over to the salle entrance. Alberich was, as he had thought, waiting just inside.

"Working, and working well, is your plan of misdirection," the Weaponsmaster observed calmly.

"So far." Skif waited for the rest. There had to be more; Alberich wasn't going to give him a look like that just to congratulate him on his cleverness.

"Would it be that you would know the voice of Jass' master, heard you it again?" Alberich asked.

Skif felt a little thrill run through him. So Alberich was going to use him! He wasn't just going to have to sit around while the Weaponsmaster prowled the slums in his sell-sword guise.

"I think so," Skif said, after giving the question due consideration. "But, he'd have to be talking—well, he'd have to be talking like he thought he was way above the person he was talking to."

"Condescending." Alberich nodded. "That, I believe, I can arrange. There is to be a gathering of Lord Orthallen's particular friends tonight. Get you to that place without challenge, I can do. It is for you to get yourself into a place of concealment where you can hear and observe, but not be noticed."

"Oh, I can do that!" Skif promised recklessly. "You just watch!"

"I intend to, since it will be myself at this gathering, as guard to Selenay with Talamir," Alberich replied. "I wish you at the door into the Herald's Wing at the dishwashing bell."

He turned and retreated into the shadows of the salle, and Skif whirled and ran for the Collegium.

He got his bath—lukewarm, but he hardly noticed—and ate without tasting his supper in such haste that he came close to choking once. He was in place long before the bell rang, and Alberich, arriving early, smiled to see him there. And to see him in the uniform of a page, the pale-blue and silver that all of Selenay's pages wore.

"Come," was all he said, and he didn't ask where Skif had gotten the uniform. As it happened, he hadn't stolen it, he'd won it, fair and square. Another little bet. He'd had the feeling that he might need it at some point, and he was still small enough to pass for one of the pages without anyone lifting an eyebrow.

Won't be able t'pull that much longer, though, he thought with regret. He'd learned a lot, impersonating a page in Lord Orthallen's service, and he hoped to learn more, slipping into the Palace proper.

"I trust you know how to serve," Alberich murmured, as they walked together down the corridor, servants whose duty it was to light the lamps passing by them without a second glance.

Skif just snorted.

"I should like to note," Alberich went on, as they made a turn into the second half of Herald's Wing, "that I specified you be in a place of concealment."

"Hide in plain sight," Skif retorted. "When does any highborn look at a page?"

"Unless it is his own kin—a point you have made. Well, this may serve better than having you lurking in the rafters." Alberich nodded a greeting to a Herald just emerging from his room; the other saluted him but showed no sign of wanting to stop and talk.

"Can't see nobody's face from the rafters," Skif pointed out.

They made another turning, into a section that looked immensely old, much older than the Collegium or the Wing attached to it. Skif looked about with avid curiosity; they must be in the Old Palace now, the square building upon which all later expansions had been founded. The Old Palace was rumored to date all the way back to the Founding of Valdemar, and it was said that King Valdemar had used the old magics that were only in tales to help to construct it. Certainly no one in these days would have attempted to build walls with blocks of granite the size of a cottage, and no one really had any idea how the massive blocks could have been set in place to the height of six stories. There were even rumors that the blocks were hollow and contained a warren of secret passages. Unlikely, Skif thought, but it would be impossible to tell, unless you knew where a door was, because the outer walls were at least two ells thick, and you could tap on them until you were a graybeard and never get a hollow echo.

Alberich stopped just outside a set of massive double doors. "This, the reception chamber is. The reception will be in slightly less than a candlemark. Your plan?"

"Set an' ready," Skif said boldly. "You go do whatever you're gonna do, an' leave me here."

Alberich nodded, and continued on his way. Skif checked the door of the chamber, and found it, as he had expected, unlocked.

He slipped inside.

The walls were plastered over the stone, and the plaster painted with scenes out of legends Skif didn't even begin to recognize. Candle sconces had been built onto the walls to provide light later, and there was an enormous fireplace truly large enough to roast an ox. There was no fire in it now, of course, but someone had placed an ox-sized basket of yellow, orange, and red roses between the andirons as a kind of clever fire substitute. The room looked out into the courtyard in the center of the Old Palace; here the walls were not of the massive thickness of the outer walls, and the windows ran nearly floor to ceiling, with a set of glass doors in the middle that could be opened onto the courtyard itself. There were sideboards along the wall, covered with snowy linen cloths, set up to receive foodstuffs, though none were there yet except two baskets of fruit. Candles and lanterns waited on one of the tables, though none had been put in their sconces and holders, nor lit. Skif took a tall wax taper, and went out into the corridor, lighting it at one of the corridor lamps. He then went about the room setting up the lights, quite as if he'd been ordered to do so. There seemed to be too many lanterns for the room, so after consideration, he took the extras out into the courtyard and hung them on the iron shepherd's crooks he found planted among the flowers for that purpose.

Roughly a quarter-candlemark later, a harried individual in Royal livery stuck his head in the door and stared at him. "What—Did I order you to light the lamps?" he asked, sounding more than a bit startled.

Skif made his voice sound high and piping, more childlike than usual. "Yes, milord," he replied, with a bob of his head. "You did, milord."

The man muttered something under his breath about losing one's mind as the hair grayed, then said, "Carry on, then," waving a hand vaguely at him.

Skif hid his grin and did just that. It was one of the things he'd learned impersonating a page at Lord Orthallen's. If a boy was doing a job (rather than standing about idly), people would assume he'd been set the task and leave him alone. Even if the person in charge didn't recall setting the task or seeing the boy, that person would take it for granted that it had just slipped his mind, and leave the boy to carry on.

When the upper servant appeared again, with a bevy of boys clad just as Skif was in tow, Skif was relieved to see that none of them were the boy he'd won his uniform from. That had been his one concern in all of this, and with that worry laid to rest, he paid dutiful attention to the servant's instructions. He actually paid more attention than the real pages, who fidgeted and poked each other—but then, they were yawningly familiar with what their duties were, and he wasn't.

The food arrived then—tidbits, rather than a meal, something to provide a pleasant background to the reception. He managed to get himself, by virtue of his slightly taller stature, assigned to carry trays of wine glasses among the guests. That was a plus; he'd be able to move freely, where Alberich would be constrained to go where the Queen did.

When all was in readiness, the doors into the courtyard (now nicely lantern-lit, thanks to Skif's efforts) and the doors to the corridor were flung open, the page boys took their places, and the guests began to trickle by ones and twos into the room for the reception.

1 7

Alberich stood at Selenay's right hand as she circulated among Lord Orthallen's guests. He wore his formal Whites, something he did only on the rarest of occasions. He was not at all comfortable in what, for the first two decades of his life, had been the uniform not only of the enemy, but of the demon lovers. Only three people knew that reason, however; to tell anyone but Selenay, Talamir, and Myste would have been to deliver a slap in the face to those who had rescued and cared for him and taken them into their midst.

Sometimes, though, he did wear the uniform, when the need to do so outweighed personal discomfort. In this case, he wore his Whites because he would be far more conspicuous in his favored dark gray leather than in his Heraldic uniform.

Talamir stood at Selenay's left, where he could murmur advice into her ear if she needed it. Alberich stood on her right, where his weapon hand was free.

He watched everyone and everything, his eyes flicking from one person to the next, and he never smiled. This evidently bothered some, though not all, of Lord Orthallen's guests—the ones who had never seen Alberich before and only knew of him by reputation. Those who frequented Court functions were used to the way he looked at everyone as if he saw a potential assassin.

He did, however. *Everyone* was a *potential* assassin. Of course the likelihood that any of them actually were assassins was fairly low. But he was the Herald who had saved Selenay from death at the hands of her own husband, cutting the Prince down with the Prince's own sword. He saw treachery everywhere, or feigned that he did, and when he looked at someone he didn't know with suspicion in his eyes, that person tended to get very nervous.

Sometimes he wished that he didn't have quite so formidable a reputation. Sometimes he wished that he could just *look* at someone and not have them flinch away.

That was about as likely at this point as for him to turn as handsome as young Trainee Kris.

That was what Herald-Chronicler Myste said, anyway, looking at him from behind those peculiar split-lensed spectacles of hers that forced her to pull her head back to peer down her nose when she was reading and tilt her chin down to peer through the top half when she was looking at anything past the length of her arms. "What do you expect?" she'd ask him tartly. "The man who'll cut down a prince wouldn't hesitate at putting a blade in the heart of a man of lesser rank. But for the gods' sake don't ever try smiling at them. You aren't any good at faking a smile, and when you try, you look as if you were about to jump on people and tear their throats out with your teeth."

A pity Myste was perhaps the Herald who was the most inept with weapons in the entire Circle. He could do with a dose of her good sense here tonight. Not that she'd enjoy it, of course. She would far rather be where she could avoid all this interminable nonsense, in her quarters, either writing up the current Chronicles or going over old ones, a glass of cold, sweet tea at her elbow.

Where she would probably knock it over at least once tonight. Hopefully when she did, the glass would be empty. If it wasn't, well, at least the papers on her floor were discards, unlike the ones piled all over Elcarth's office.

Alberich pulled his attention back to the reception. The heat wave had finally broken, though the thick stone walls of the Old Palace kept every room in it comfortably cool even during the worst of the heat. With the doors open, there was a pleasant scent coming from the roses in the courtyard. No one gone out there, though, for Selenay and Orthallen were in *here.* No matter how tired anyone's feet got, he wouldn't leave where the power was.

If Alberich's gaze rested more often than usual on a particular page, circulating among the guests with a tray of wineglasses, probably no one was going to notice. It was a very ordinary-looking boy: small, dark, curly-haired. If he moved more gracefully than the usual lot, that wasn't likely to be noticed either. Alberich was pleased with the way he was looking up at the people he was serving—not staring enough to make him seem insolent, just paying respectful attention. Very good, very smooth. The boy must have done something like this before, many times, though Alberich doubted it had been for any purpose other than to filch food from whatever noble household he had infiltrated.

Lord Orthallen, on whose behalf this reception was being held, also circulated among the guests quite as if he was the one who was the host, and not the Queen. This particular festivity was a reward for those who had helped Orthallen to conclude a set of delicate negotiations that would ultimately benefit the Crown substantially, according to Myste. Alberich was not at all clear on just what those negotiations were, only that they had involved a number of men (and a few women) of vastly disparate backgrounds, many of whom had personal differences with each other.

One thing they all had in common, though. They were all very, very wealthy.

That much showed in their costumes, rich with embroidery and of costly materials, and in their ornaments, heavy gold and silver and precious gems. The details didn't matter to Alberich, though Myste would have been studying them with the eye of one who would be recording every subtle detail later in her writings. That was the problem of living around a Chronicler; he never knew just what detail, what secret that *he* assumed was just between them would end up in one of her Histories, to be goggled at by some other generation of Heralds to come.

Right now, he was in the unusual position of having part of his attention devoted to something other than Selenay and her welfare. He watched that one small boy, not as a hunter watched prey, but as the prey watches a hunter, alive to every nuance in his behavior, waiting for the slightest sign that the boy recognized a voice he'd only heard once.

When he told the boy that he could arrange for him to hear words spoken in tones of condescension, he had not been promising more than he could deliver. Although these people had worked together for Orthallen's cause, they had not forgotten rank and perceived rank and all of the tangle of quarrels that had made it so difficult to get them to work together—they had merely put those things aside for the moment. And although they were now basking in the unanticipated presence of Royalty, those things still remained. Where the Queen gazed, all was harmony, but the moment that she took her attention away, the claws were unsheathed, though subtly, subtly, with a care not only for the Queen's presence, but for the watchful eye of her guardian.

Who might misinterpret what he saw. And in Alberich's case—

Well, no one wanted Alberich to misinterpret anything.

So rather than bared claws and visible teeth, there were mere hints of rivalries and competitions, mostly carried out in tone and carefully chosen words.

Oh, there would be condescension in plenty, among those able to read tone and words so exactly that they could choose to ignore what they heard or exaggerate the offense. Small wonder the crude bully Jass hadn't heard what the boy had read in his master's tone. The wonder was that the boy had read it so accurately.

Well. Every Herald, every Trainee, is a wonder, small or great.

It could be that this boy was—or would be—more of a wonder than most. There were still those—not Heralds, mostly—who doubted the wisdom of having a thief as a Trainee. And the boy was not yet committed to becoming a Herald; Alberich, so apt at reading the unspoken language of gesture and tone, knew that better than any. If it had been a case of trusting to the boy by himself to come around, to learn to trust, to understand what it was they were doing, Alberich would have been the first to say, "No. He is a danger to us, and cannot be trusted past his own self-interest." But there was more than that; there was the Companion. And so, Alberich was always the first, not the last, to say, "Peace. He will be ours, soon enough."

The boy was good; *very* good. Alberich had no difficulty in imagining him moving through a crowd of just about any sort of folk save, perhaps, the highest, and remaining completely unnoticed. He was, after all, a pickpocket; that was the way of the game. The unobtrusive prospered; the rest wound up in gaol. Watching the boy was the only entertainment he had, though, and in the end the reception was, as such things generally were, deadly dull. These people were small; in the normal course of things, no matter how wealthy they were, they would never have seen Selenay except from the back of the Audience Chamber, or at most, stood before her for a few, brief moments while she passed some judgment in their favor or against them. They would never have watched as she bent that cool, thoughtful gaze on each one alone, never have heard her inquiring as to the details of their lives. For that moment of reflected glory, they were content to be restrained and to keep their masks firmly in place, their smiles unwavering.

And although the boy had shown a moment or two of hesitation, there was no sudden recognition. The reception came to its predictable end when Selenay had had a private word with each and every one of Orthallen's guests, and withdrew, along with Talamir and Alberich. And after that, the guests would depart swiftly, there being nothing there to hold them. The boy Skif would have to extricate himself from the toils of the Page Master as best he could.

And when he did—just as swiftly as Alberich had reckoned he would—he found Alberich waiting for him in his own room.

Alberich had taken some thought to the needs of boys and had brought with him something *other* than the things, good though they were, that lay in Mero's free pantry. He had gone down to the Palace kitchen, and commanded some of the dainties that Selenay's Court feasted on. He calculated that having had such things paraded beneath his nose all night, the boy would not be emotionally satisfied with bread and cheese, however good those common viands were, and if he was anything like Alberich had judged him, he had not filled himself at dinner.

So when Skif pushed open his own door, there was Alberich, beneath a lit lantern mounted on the wall, sitting at his ease in the boy's chair, the covered platter beside him on the desk.

The boy started, but covered it well. "Didn' think t'see you afore the morrow," he said matter-of-factly as he sat down on his bed.

"Good service demands immediate reward," Alberich replied, and uncovered the platter.

Then pulled out the two glasses and half-bottle of wine from beneath the chair. The boy gaped at him—then shut his mouth and looked at the wine. There was a brief flash of greed there. But thankfully, no *need*. Good. That was one thing that Alberich had worried about. Trouble with drink started early among those who lived near Exile's Gate. Alberich had seen children as young as ten caught by the addiction of drink there.

"I didn' think we was allowed—" Skif began, though his nose twitched as Alberich uncorked it, and he was young enough that his yearning showed a little more. He must be getting very weary of the spring water, fruit juice, ciders, teas, and milk that were all the Trainees were ever offered.

"It is only half a bottle, and I intend to share it with you," Alberich replied, pouring the glasses full and handing him one. "That is hardly enough for even an innocent to be drunk upon. I suspect you've had a deal stronger in your time, already."

The boy accepted the glass and to his great credit, took a mouthful and savored it, rather than draining the glass. "So *this's* what all the fuss is about," he said, after he allowed the good vintage to slip down his throat. "*This* is what the good stuff's like."

"It is," Alberich agreed. "And now, I fear, it is spoiled you'll be for the goat piss that passes itself off as wine near Exile's Gate."

"Dunno how you drunk it, and that's for certain-sure; I allus did my drinkin' a little higher up the street," Skif replied, putting his glass down and reaching for the nearest tidbit, a pasty stuffed with morels and duck breast. Of course, he didn't know that until he bit into it, and as it melted on his tongue, the boy's face was a study that very nearly made Alberich chuckle. He didn't, though; children's dignity was a fragile thing, and this lad's rather more so than others.

"They been passin' those under my nose all night, and if I'd known how they tasted—" Skif shook his head. "This is too much like reward, Weaponsmaster. The plain fact is there were three men that sounded *something* like the one we want, and not one I'd be willin' t'finger."

"Reward is not exclusively earned by accomplishing a task," Alberich noted, pushing the platter toward the boy, but taking a pastry himself. He hadn't eaten any more than the boy had, though Selenay had nibbled all evening, and he wanted something in his stomach to cushion the wine. "Sometimes reward is earned just in the making of the attempt."

"Huh." Skif chose a different dainty, and washed it down with wine. "Now what d'we do?"

"I will try and find another opportunity to put you where you can observe some of the ones I suspect," Alberich told him. "If I do not, it is that you will go to hunt on your own. Yes?"

Skif shrugged, but Alberich read in the shrug that he had considered doing so, if he had not already made an attempt or two. "I got cause," was all he said, and left it at that.

"Meanwhile—I hunt in a place you cannot, for no boy, however disguised, would be permitted to the discourses of the Great Lords of State," Alberich continued.

Skif cocked his head to the side. "Shut the pages out, do they?" he asked shrewdly, and sighed. "Not like I ain't busy."

A most unchildlike child, Alberich reflected later, as he left the boy to finish his feast. But then, most, if not all, of the children from *that* quarter were more-or-less unchildlike. They'd had their childhood robbed from them in various ways; Skif's was by no means the most tragic. He'd *had* a loving mother, for however short a time he'd had her. He'd had a kind and caring guardian and mentor in the person of the thief trainer. That was more, much more, than many of his fellows had.

And if Selenay had even an inkling of the horrors in the twisted streets of her own capital, she would send out Heralds and Guard and all to scour the place clean. There would be a grim forest of gallows springing up overnight.

And her own people would speak her name with hate—and it would be all in vain, for half a candlemark after we'd gone, the scum would all be back again. This was the cost of welcoming any and all who sought shelter under Valdemar's banner. Sometimes what came in was not good. Not all, or even many, of the former Tedrel mercenaries who had remained in Valdemar were of Bazie's stamp.

Alberich sought his quarters—he actually had quarters both with the other Heralds and in the salle, but the latter was less convenient tonight. It was too late, or not late enough, for a visitor; his room was empty, and in a way, he was relieved. He was not fit company tonight; there was too much of a mood on him.

It was more of a relief to get himself out of the Whites and into a sleeping robe, and then into bed. There had been a double reason for the wine this evening; it was not only to prove to the boy that Alberich considered him—in some things—to be an adult. It was to make certain that tonight, at least, he would not be slipping out to snoop and pry on his own. That Taltherian wine was strong stuff; Alberich might have made certain that the greater part of the bottle went inside *him*, but there was more than enough there to ensure that Skif slept.

For that matter, there was more than enough there to ensure that Alberich slept, he realized, as he went horizontal and found a moment of giddiness come over him. It came as something of a surprise, but one he was not going to have any choice but to accept.

Then again, neither would Skif.

Which thought was a safeguard, of sorts.

Skif lay back against a bulwark of pillows propped up against the wall and stared out at the night sky beyond his open window. Not that he could see much, even with his lantern blown out; the lower half of the window was filled by a swath of cheesecloth stretched over a wooden frame that fit the open half of the window precisely. You couldn't slip a knife blade between the frame and the window frame.

Trust a Blue to be that fiddly.

It worked, though. Not a sign of moth or midge or fly, and all the breeze he could want. He thought he might want to dye the cloth black though, eventually, just to get that obtrusive white shape out of the way.

The wine Alberich had brought had been a lovely thing, about as similar to the stuff Skif had drunk in the better taverns as chalk was to cheese. He'd recognized the power with the first swallow, though, and he'd been disinclined to take chances with it. He'd stuffed his belly full of the fine foods Alberich had brought, which slowed the action of the wine considerably, which was good, because he wanted to think before he went to sleep.

He put his hands behind his head and leaned into his rather luxurious support.

Luxurious? Damn right it is. When the best my pillows have been till now was straw-filled bags? This place was pretty amazing, when it came right down to it. Maybe for some people the uniforms were a bit of a comedown, but not even the worst of his was as mended and patched as the best of his old clothing. And for the first time in his life to have boots and shoes that actually *fitted* him—

Didn't know your feet wasn't supposed to hurt like that, before.

His room had taken on the air of a place where someone lived, in no small part because of Skif's little wagers. Mindful of the impression he was hoping to create, he always wagered for something he knew wouldn't put the person who was betting against him to any hardship. So in many cases, particularly early in the game, that wager had been a cushion against a small silver coin—which, of course, Skif knew he wasn't going to lose. Skif preferred sitting in his bed to study, unless he actually had to write something out, and any Trainee could make as many cushions for himself as he cared to—fabric and cleaned feathers by the bagful were at his disposal in the sewing room as Skif well knew. Palace and Collegia kitchens went through a lot of fowl, most of which came into the complex still protesting. The Palace seamstresses bespoke the goosedown for featherbeds, the swansdown for trimming, and the tail feathers for hats. Wing feathers went off to the fletchers and to be made into quill pens. That left the body feathers free for the claiming, so there were always bags full of them for anyone who cared to take worn-out clothing and other scrap material to make a patchwork cushion or two.

Skif now had nearly twenty piled up behind him. And for those whose pockets ran to more than the stipend, some of the more top-lofty of the Blues, he'd wagered against such things as a plush coverlet, a map to hang on his wall so that he wouldn't need to be always running up to the Library, and, oddly enough, books.

The plush coverlet was folded up and waiting for winter to go on his bed, the map made a dark rectangle on one whitewashed wall, and the bookcase—the bookcase was no longer empty.

He'd never disliked reading, but he'd also never had a lot of choice about what he read. It had never occurred to him that there might be other things to read than religious texts and dry histories.

Then he discovered tales. Poetry. Books written to be read *for pleasure.* It wasn't the overwhelming addiction for him that it was with some of the Trainees, who would have had their nose in a book every free moment if they could, but for him, reading was as satisfying as a good meal, in his opinion.

And a book made a very, very useful thing to demand on a wager. It made him look a great deal more harmless in the eyes of those highborn Blues.

So now his bookshelves held two kinds of books; his schoolbooks, and the growing collection of books he could open at any time to lose himself in some distant place or time. And the room now had personality that it hadn't shown before.

But that was not what he wanted to think about; it was what had happened at that reception tonight. The whole thing had been good, in that it proved Weaponsmaster Alberich had every intention of using him. But it hadn't gotten them any results. And what could be done within the wall around the Palace wasn't anything near enough, and he knew that Alberich knew that it wasn't enough. One end of the trail might be here, but the other was down near Exile's Gate. Here, there was likely only one person, the man behind it all. There—well, there were a lot of people, there had to be, and plenty of 'em with loose tongues, if you could catch 'em right, or get enough liquor into 'em.

Now, Alberich *could* go down there, fit in, and be talked to. He'd already proved that. *But* the question was not whether he'd be talked to, the question was *who* would talk to him. Jass had spoken to him, sold him information, and now Jass was dead. Had anyone made that connection? Skif didn't know, and it was certain-sure that no one was going to tell Alberich if they had. Take it farther; if Alberich pressed too hard and in the wrong direction, someone might decide he was too dangerous to let alone. Now; old Alberich wasn't very like to get himself in serious trouble, not with Kantor to come rescue him at need, but if a white horse came charging into Exile's Gate and carrying off a fellow who was hard-pressed in a fight, there weren't too many folks down there that *couldn't* put two and two together and come up with the right number.

There was that, but there was more. The kinds of people that Alberich would talk to were the bullyboys, other sell-swords. If he was lucky, possibly, the tavernkeepers would talk to him. They wouldn't necessarily have the information he needed. There was, however, another set of people who might. The whores, the pawnbrokers, the people who bought and sold stolen goods—they all knew Skif, and *they* knew things that the folks who practiced their trades in a more open fashion might not.

Come to that, Skif knew a few of the other thieves who might trade a word or two with him. You never knew what you were going to find yourself in possession of when you were a thief. It might could be that one of them would have run across something to put Skif on the trail.

Particularly intriguing was that thread of information that Alberich had let fall—how the trade in children stolen off the streets and the trade in slaves taken by bandits might be linked. It made a certain amount of sense, that, if you assumed that the slavers were all working together.

Skif hummed to himself tunelessly as he considered that. Who would know, if anyone did? There were always rumors, but who would be able to give the scrap of foundation to the rumor?

One by one, he ran down the list of his acquaintances, those who had always seemed to know where to start, when you were looking for someone or some*thing*—most particularly, those who had pointed him on the trail of Jass. And he dragged out all of the tag bits of information he'd been given that hadn't led him to Jass, but into other paths that had seemed at the time like dead ends.

At the moment, he couldn't imagine anything more bizarre than that he, reclining at his ease in his own room of a wing attached to the Palace itself, should be running down the lists of those who owed him favors (and those whose cooperation could be bought) in the most miserable quarter of Haven. Nevertheless—

Alberich does it all the time. So I ain't the only one.

None of the things he'd been told seemed to lead him to child stealing, nor could he think of anyone he knew likely to really know anything other than just rumors. Reluctantly, he found himself thinking that if there was one black blot in the alleyways of Exile's Gate that might hide part of the answer, it was his own uncle Londer. Londer Galko always skirted the fringe of the quasilegal. Londer was not brave enough to dare the darkest deeds himself, but Skif could tell, even as a child, that he yearned to. The older Londer got, the less he dared, but the more he yearned.

Bazie had hinted, more than once, that Londer would have sold Skif in a heartbeat if Skif hadn't already been registered on the city rolls. And even then, if he could have manufactured a believable story about Skif running away—

Skif was not at all surprised now that half-witted Maisie had been illegally under-age—perhaps not for the employment at the Hollybush, but certainly for the uses that his cousin Kalchan had made of her. She hadn't *looked* under-aged, what there was of her was woman-sized, but Londer had to have known. Skif wouldn't be surprised now to learn that Londer himself had sampled Maisie's meager charms before passing her on to his son. Londer had never given his sons anything he hadn't already used (Beel being the exception, but then the idea of Londer attempting the life of a priest was enough to make a cat laugh) and Londer didn't exactly have women lining up to keep him company. In the years since running off, Skif had learned a lot about his uncle, and he'd learned that when it came to women, Londer had to pay for what he got. Since he'd already paid for Maisie, it followed that he'd probably seen no reason why he shouldn't have her first. Not that he'd shown any interest in anything too young to have breasts, but half-wits often matured early, and Londer probably wouldn't even think twice about her *real* age if he'd taken her.

Londer had more-than-dubious friends, too, even by the standards of Exile's Gate. And after the raid on the Hollybush—well, he'd lost what few friends he had around there. Not only because of Maisie, but because he had laid all the blame on his own son, and left him to rot and eventually die in gaol. Kalchan had never recovered enough even to do the idiot's work of stone picking, and Londer had done *nothing* to help him recover. Business was business, but blood was blood, and people didn't much care for a man who disclaimed responsibility for things that people knew he was responsible for because his unconscious son couldn't refute them. A good thing for Londer that his son never did wake to full sense and died within three moons. The case against Londer died with him, and Skif could only wonder who Londer was friendly with now, given how many people that callousness had offended. Or had that just freed his uncle to edge a little nearer to those dark deeds he secretly admired?

Given all of that, Londer *probably* didn't engage in child snatching for his own puerile entertainment. But that didn't mean he didn't help it along, just because he got a thrill out of doing so. He probably had been frightened enough by his brush with the law not to do anything so dangerous for his own profit either. But it was increasingly likely, in Skif's estimation, that he knew something about it. The Hollybush hadn't, by any means, been Londer's only property. He owned warehouses in places where there wasn't anyone around to notice odd things going on at night.

So, a very good place to start would be with his uncle. Skif knew the ins and outs of Londer's house, for more than once, he'd contemplated getting some of what he considered that he was owed out of his uncle. He'd eventually given up on the idea, for the fact was that anything Londer had of value was generally too big to be carried off easily. But because of that, Skif knew the house, and he knew the twisty ways of Londer's mind almost as well as he knew the house.

The best way to get information out of him would be to frighten it out. Londer was good at keeping his mouth shut, but not when he was startled, and not when he was genuinely frightened.

So Skif set himself to figuring out exactly how he could best terrify his uncle into telling Skif *everything* he might know or guess about the child stealing and the slavery ring.

In his bed, in the dead of night, Skif decided. Skif was short, even for a boy his age—but a shadowy figure dressed in black, waking you up with a knife to your throat, was likely to seem a whole lot bigger than he actually was. And a hoarse whisper didn't betray that he was too young for his voice to have broken yet.

Alberich had brought the all-black night-walking suit when he'd collected Skif's clothing. *Skif* knew a way into Londer's house that not even Londer knew about. Good old Londer! Every window had a lock, every door had two, but he forgot completely about the trapdoor onto the roof. All Skif had to do was get into the yard and shinny up the drainpipe from the gutters. Once on the roof, he was as good as inside.

Right enough, if Londer knew anything, Skif would have it out of him. But he needed a suitably convincing story for his black-clad terrorist to ask the questions he needed the answers to. *I'll say I'm lookin' for m'sister,* he decided. *That's a good story, an' Londer'll probably believe it.*

Now, getting from here to there.

He'd be able to get out of his room easily enough; no one checked beds to see that people were in them around here. The trouble was, how was he to get out of—and more importantly, back inside—the Palace walls?

:Me, of course,: Cymry replied in his head. He jumped; then smiled sheepishly. *:Nobody is going to stop a Companion and her Chosen.:*

:You don't mind?: he asked, hesitantly. After all, this wasn't precisely going to be a sanctioned excursion.

:Mind?: he felt her scorn.

:You just try and do it without me! You wouldn't have a chance.:

Well, she was probably right.

:But what do I do with you while I'm sneakin' around?: he asked.

She chuckled. *:I'll take care of that. Trust me, I can always insinuate myself into someone's nearby stable. But I'm not having you so far away that I can't come to your rescue if I have to.:*

He was both touched and a trifle irritated. Did she think he couldn't take care of himself? He'd been *taking* care of himself for the past year and more! She hadn't been around then!

Now she sounded contrite. *:Of course you can take care of yourself, I never doubted that. But your uncle might have guards—:*

He laughed, silently. *:Londer? Old cheap Londer? Not a chance. What he has got is dogs—but he's too cheap to get trained ones, so he just gets nasty ones and keeps 'em hungry to keep 'em mean. Which means—?:*

Cymry knew; bless her, she got it at once. *:They'll eat anything you throw in front of them.:*

He grinned. *:And I know where to get plenty of poppy syrup. Put 'em right to sleep inside a candlemark, then I slip inside and give old uncle a surprise.:*

:Then what will you do?: she asked soberly. *:When you leave? You aren't—:*

:I'm gonna make him drink poppy hisself.: Skif reassured her. *:No way I'm taking a chance on hitting him hard enough to make sure he stays knocked out. Besides, with that thick head of his—I'd probably break what I hit him with before I knocked him out.:*

He felt her sigh gustily. *:Good. Then this will all work. And what then?:*

:Then—: He closed his eyes, but couldn't yet see a direction for himself. *:It's early days to make any plans. I'll figure on what to do after I hear what old Londer has to say.:*

And that would have to do, for now.

1 8

Skif looked down on the silent, darkened oblong that was his uncle's yard from the roof of his uncle's house. The rooftree was not the most comfortable place he'd ever had to perch, but better to rest here than inside the house. Down there somewhere in the shadows were five lumps of sleeping canine that had been completely unable to resist juicy patties of chopped meat mixed with bread crumbs soaked in poppy syrup. Poor miserable animals, Uncle Londer would probably be even harsher with them after their failure to stop him.

This was the halfway point, and Skif paused for a breather while he could take one. He'd gotten out of the Collegium through his window, out of the Complex openly on Cymry's back, as if he was going out into the city for any perfectly ordinary reason.

Well, perhaps not *ordinary*, since Trainees as young as he was generally didn't go out to the city after dark. But he'd made sure to look serious, as if someone had sent for him, rather than overly cheerful, as if he expected to find himself in, say, the "Virgin and Stars" tavern that night. No one questioned him, and Heraldic Trainees (unlike the common-born Blues or the Bardic Trainees) were not required to give a reason for leaving the Complex at whatever hour, probably because it was generally assumed that their Companions would not agree to anything that wasn't proper.

Once in Haven, Cymry found an unguarded stable near Uncle Londer's house—unguarded because it was completely empty and beginning to fall to pieces, symptom of a sudden change in someone's fortune. There he had changed into his black clothing, feeling distinctly odd as he did so. It seemed that the last time he'd worn this was a lifetime ago, not just a couple of moons. But where he was going, that uniform was a distinct handicap.

He hadn't swathed his face and head, or blackened exposed flesh with charcoal just then. He'd still had to get the chopped meat, the bread, and the poppy syrup, and not all in the same market square, just so no one would put him and the ingredients together if they were questioned later. That was why he'd left the Collegium early. Markets stayed open late in the poorer parts of town, for the benefit of those whose own working hours were long. Skif had no trouble in acquiring what he needed, and he made his final preparations in that stable by the light of the moon overhead.

Then, and only then, did he finish dressing, and with the treated meat stuffed into cleaned sausage bladders which he tied off, and then put into a bag, he had slipped out alone into the darkness.

The key to making sure that all five dogs got their doses was to send the bladders over the wall at long intervals. The first and strongest dog wolfed down his portion, then staggered about for a bit and fell asleep. When Skif heard the staggering, he sent over the second bladder; by that time the strongest dog was in no condition to contest the food, and the second strongest got it. It took a while, but Skif was patient, and when he couldn't hear anything other than dog snores, he went over the wall and up the gutter to the roof.

Now he sat on the rooftree with his back against one of the chimneys, using its bulk to conceal his silhouette, and took deep, slow breaths to calm himself. His gut was a tight knot—a good reason for not eating much tonight. And he was thirsty, but thirsty was better than being in the middle of a job and having to—well. This would be the first time he had ever entered a house with the intention of confronting someone. Normally that was the *last* thing he wanted to do, and it had him strung tighter than an ill-tuned harp.

So he ran over what he needed to do in his mind until he thought he'd rehearsed it enough, and Mindcalled Cymry.

:I'm going in,: he told her.

:You know what to do if you get in trouble,: she replied, for they had already worked that out. Skif would get outside, anywhere outside, and she would come for him. She swore she could even get into the yard if it was needful. How she was to get over that fence, he had no notion, but that was her problem. Bazie had taught him that once you put your confidence in a partner, you just *trusted* that he knew what he was doing and went on with your part of the plan. Because once the plan was in motion, there was nothing you could do about what *he* was responsible for, anyway, so there was no point in taking up some of the attention you

should be paying to your part of the job by worrying about him.

He slipped over the rooftree to the next chimney; the hatch into the crawl space was just on the other side of it. It wasn't locked—it hadn't been locked for the past five years that Skif knew of. Even if it had been, it was one of those that had its hinges on the outside, and all he would have had to do would have been to knock the hinge pins out and he could have lifted it up from the hinge side. He left it open, just in case he had to make a quick exit and couldn't use the route out he'd planned.

The space he slipped down into was more of a crawl space than an attic, too small to be practical to store anything. He crawled on his hands and knees, feeling his way along until he came to the hatch that led down into the hallway separating all of the dozen garret rooms where Londer's servants slept, six on one side of the corridor, and six on the other.

Well, where the servants Londer had would have slept, if he'd had more than the three he kept. Like everything else Londer had, his servants were cheap because no one else would have them, and he worked them—screaming and cursing at them all the while—until they dropped. His man-of-all-work was a drunkard, so was his cook, and the overworked housemaid was another half-wit like Maisie. None of them was going to wake up short of Skif falling on them, which obviously he didn't intend to do.

Not that he was going to take any chances about it.

He found the hatch, which had a cover meant to be pushed up and aside from the hallway below. He lifted it up and put it out of the way, then stuck his head down into the hall and took a quick look around.

As he'd expected, it was deserted, not so dark as the crawl space thanks to a tiny window on either end of the hall, and silent but for three sets of snoring.

He actually had to stop and listen in fascination for a moment, for he'd never heard anything like it.

There was a deep, basso rumbling which was probably the handyman, whose pattern was a long, drawn out sound interrupted by three short *snorks*. Layered atop this was a second set, vaguely alto in pitch, of short, loud snorts in a rising tone that sounded like an entire sty full of pigs. And atop that was a soprano solo with snoring on the intake of breath and whistling on the exhalation. One was the housemaid and the other the cook, but which was which? The housemaid was younger, but fatter than the cook, so either could have had the soprano.

All three were so loud that he could not imagine how they managed not to wake *themselves* up. It took everything he had to keep from laughing out loud, and he wished devoutly that he dared describe this to one of the Bardic Trainees. They'd have hysterics.

At least now he knew for certain that the last thing he needed to worry about was making a noise up here. He grabbed the edge of the hatch and somersaulted over, slowly and deliberately, lowering himself down by the strength of his arms alone until his arms were extended full-length. His feet still dangled above the floor, so he waited for the moment when the chorus of snores overlapped, and let go, hoping the noise would cover the sound of his fall.

He landed with flexed knees, caught his balance bent over with his knuckles just touching the floor, and froze, waiting to see if there would be a reaction.

Not a sound to indicate that anyone had heard him.

Heh. Not gonna be hard figuring which rooms are empty! That had been a serious concern; he *needed* to find an empty room with a window, get into it, get the window unlocked and opened for his escape, because now that he was inside, he knew that there was no way he was going to get out the way he came in. If there had been a ladder to let down from the crawl space, that would have been ideal, but there wasn't.

By great good fortune, the room nearest the drainpipe he wanted to use was one of the empty ones—no thief could survive long who wasn't able to tell where he was inside a house in relation to the outside without ever being inside. Out of the breast of his tunic came one of his trusty bladders of oil, and he oiled the hinges to the dripping point by feel before he even tried to open the door.

There was a faint creak, but it was entirely smothered in snores; the door opened onto a completely barren room, not a stick of furniture in it. Moonlight shone in through the dirty window, finally giving him something to see by. After the absolute dark of the crawl space and the relative dark of the hallway, it seemed as bright as day.

Moving carefully with a care for creaking floorboards, he eased his way over to the window, and out came the oil again. When catches, locks, and hinges were all thoroughly saturated, he got the window open wide, checked to make sure he could reach the drainpipe from its sill, and left it that way. He did, however, close the door to the room most of the way, just in case one of the three snorers woke up and felt impelled to take a stroll. They were too dimwitted to think of an intruder, but they might take it into their heads to close the window, which would slow his retreat.

The servants' stair lay at the end of the hallway, and it was just the narrow sort of arrangement that Skif would have expected from the age of the house. In this part of the city, land was at a premium, so as little space as possible within a home was "wasted" on servants' amenities. But fortunately, whoever had built this stair had done so with an eye to *silence* in his servants, and had built it so sturdily that it probably wouldn't creak if a horse went down it.

Not even Londer's neglect could undo work that solid, not in the few years that Londer had owned the house anyway.

Down the stairs went Skif, and now he had to go on the memories of a very small child augmented by as much study of the house from outside as he had been able to manage. Londer's bedroom, as he recalled, and as study of the house seemed to indicate, was on the next floor down, overlooking the street. A curious choice, given that street noise was going to be something of a disturbance and would *certainly be* obtrusive early in the morning. But Londer wanted to see who was at his door before they were announced, and the other choice of master bedroom was over the kitchen and *under* the servants' rooms. Altogether a poor choice for someone who probably knew all about the snorers' chorus and didn't want it resonating down into his bedroom. Nor would he want the aromas of the cook's latest accident permeating his bedroom and lingering in the hangings.

He stifled another laugh as he felt his way down the stair, tread by tread.

He could only wonder what Londer had thought when he discovered the amazing snoring powers of all three of his servants.

This stair should come out beside the room just over the kitchen that Londer used for his guests. Important guests, of course, not people like his sister and her young son. They'd lived in one of the garret rooms, though Skif couldn't remember which one, since they hadn't lived there for long.

When he reached the landing, once again he stopped and listened. Aside from the now faint chorus from Snore Hall above, there was nothing.

He took a precautionary sniff of the air, for a room that was occupied had a much different scent than one that had been shut up for a while. If Uncle had a guest that Skif didn't know about, the guest became an unforeseen complication, a possible source of interference.

But the scent that came to his nose was of a room that had lain unused for a very long time; a touch of mildew, a great deal of dust. And when he emerged from the stair he found himself, as he had reckoned, in the dressing room to that unused guest suite.

The dressing room led directly to the corridor, and probably the reason that the stair came out into it at all was the very sensible one of convenience for the original master and builder of the house, who probably *would* have chosen this suite for himself. Water for baths would come straight up the stair from the kitchen in cans, to be poured into the bath in the dressing room. If the master was hungry and rang for service, his snack would be brought up in moments, freshly prepared.

This corridor was short; it ran between the old master suite to two other sets of rooms. It extended the width of the house and had a window on either end, with the staircase leading downward for the family's use on Skif's right. Three doors let out on it, besides the one that Skif stood in. The one on Skif's side led to a second bedroom separate from the master suite, probably intended for a superior personal maid or manservant. The two opposite were probably for guests or children in the original plan. One was now Londer's, and heaven only knew what he did with the other.

Skif put his ear to the door nearest him on that side.

It was definitely occupied, although the slumberer was no match for the trio upstairs. Just to be sure, Skif eased down the corridor and checked the other.

Silent and, as turning the door handle proved, locked as well.

He returned to Londer's room, took a steadying breath, and took out—

—another bladder of oil. Because he did not want Londer to wake up until Skif's knife was at his throat.

Only when the hinges were saturated did Skif ease the door open, wincing at the odor that rolled out.

Well, the old man hasn't changed his bathing habits any.

After the cleanliness of Bazie's room, the Priory, and the Collegium, Skif's nose wrinkled at the effluvia of unwashed clothing, unwashed sheets, unwashed body, rancid sweat, and bad breath. It wasn't bad enough to gag a goat, but it was close.

If this wasn't so important, I'd leave now. It made his skin crawl to think of getting so close to that foul stench, but he didn't have much choice.

Londer had his windows open to the night air, so at least he could see. And at least he wasn't going to smother in the stink.

He took a deep breath, this time of cleaner air, and slipped inside.

Londer didn't wake until the edge of the knife—the *dull* edge, did he but know it—was against his throat. Skif had tried to time his entry for when the moon was casting the most light on the streetward side of the house. In fact, moonlight streamed in through the windows, and Skif could tell from the sheer terror on Londer's face that he was having no trouble seeing what there *was* to see of Skif.

"Don't move," Skif hissed. "And don't shout."

"I won't," Londer whimpered. "What d'you want from me?"

Londer shivered with fear; Skif had never seen anyone actually *doing* that, and to see Londer's fat jowls shaking like a jelly induced a profound disgust in him.

"You can start," hissed Skif, "by telling me what you did with my sister."

Londer looked as if he was going to have a fit right there and then, and Skif thought he might have hit gold—but it turned out that Londer had just gotten rough with one of his paid women, and he thought that Skif was *her* brother. Not but that Skif was averse to seeing him terrified over it, but that wasn't the street he wanted to hound his uncle down.

So he quickly established that the apocryphal sister was one of the children snatched off the streets, and the interview continued on that basis.

Skif must have looked and sounded twice as intimidating as he thought, because Londer was reduced in very short order to a blubbering mound of terror and tears. Skif would have been very glad to have the Heraldic Truth Spell at his disposal, but he figured that fear was getting almost as much truth out of Londer as the Spell would have.

Unfortunately, there was very little to get. Londer knew some of what was going on, as Skif had thought; he knew some of the men who were doing the actual snatches, what their method was for picking a victim, how they managed it without raising too much fuss, and where they went with the victims afterward. Which, as Skif had guessed, was one of Londer's own warehouses. But who the real powers *behind* the snatches were, he had no idea; his knowledge was all at street level. Even the warehouse had been hired by a go-between.

Which was disgusting enough. Londer whimpered and carried on, literally sweating buckets, trying to make out that the poor younglings grabbed by the gang were better off than they'd be on the street. Sheltered and fed, maybe, but better off? *If* they were incredibly lucky and not at all attractive, they'd find themselves working from dawn to dusk at some skinflint's farm, or knotting rugs, sewing shirts, making rope, or any one of a hundred tasks that needed hands but not much strength.

If they were pretty—well, that was something Skif didn't want to think about too hard. There had been a child-brothel four streets over from the Hollybush that had been shut down when he was still with Bazie—there were things that even the denizens of Exile's Gate wouldn't put up with—but where there was one, there were probably more. The only reason why this one had been uncovered was because someone had been careless, or someone had snitched.

But by far and away the single most important piece of information that Skif got was that the man who was in charge of the entire ring always came to inspect the children when they were brought to the warehouse. It seemed he didn't trust the judgment of his underlings. If there was ever to be a time to catch him, that would be it.

When Skif had gotten everything he thought he could out of Londer, he took the knife away from the man's throat. Londer started to babble; an abrupt gesture with the knife shut him up again, and Skif thrust a bottle made from a small gourd at him.

"Drink it," he ordered.

Londer's eyes bulged. "Y'wouldn't poison me—"

"Oh, get shut," Skif snapped, exasperated. "I'd be 'shamed to count ye as a kill. 'Tis poppy, fool. I've got no time t' tie ye up an' gag ye, even if I could stummack touchin' ye. Now drink!"

Londer pulled the cork with his teeth and sucked down the contents of the bottle; Skif made him open his mouth wide to be sure he actually had swallowed it, and wasn't holding it. Then he sat back and waited, knowing that it was going to take longer for the drug to take effect on the man because of Londer's fear counteracting it. Meanwhile, his uncle just stared at him, occasionally venturing a timid question that Skif did not deign to answer. If he really *was* someone out to discover the whereabouts of a young sister, he'd spend no more time on Londer than he had to, and tempting as it was to pay back everything he owed Londer in the way of misery, such torment would not have been in keeping with his assumed role.

And it might give Londer a clue to his real identity.

So he stayed quiet, focusing what he hoped was a menacing gaze on the man, until at long, long last, Londer's eyelids drooped and dropped, his trembling stopped, all his muscles went slack, and the drug took him over.

Only then did Skif leave the room, taking the bottle with him.

His exit via the garret room and the drainpipe was uneventful, as was his exchange of clothing in the stable and his escape from that part of town. It almost seemed as if there was a good spirit watching over him and smoothing his way.

He said as much to Cymry, once they were up in among the mansions of the great and powerful.

:I wish you'd gotten more information, then,: she replied ruefully. *:I hate to think that much good luck was wasted on essentially trivial knowledge.:*

"Not as trivial as y'might think," he replied thoughtfully, for a new plan was beginning to take shape in his mind. It was a plan that was fraught with risk, but it might be worth it.

And he was *not* going to carry out this one alone...

"Out late, aren't you, Trainee?" said a voice at his stirrup, startling him. He looked down to discover that Cymry had brought him to the little gate in the Palace walls used by all the Trainees on legitimate business, and the Gate Guard was looking up at him with a hint of suspicion.

:Tell him the truth, loon,: Cymry prompted, as he tried to think of something to say. He hadn't expected that Cymry would try to take them in the same way they'd gone out.

"I had t'see my uncle in Haven," he said truthfully. "He didn't think he was gonna live. There was summat I needed t'hear from him."

:Very good. He really didn't think you'd leave him alive, did he?:

The Guard's demeanor went from suspicious to sympathetic. "I hope his fears weren't justified—"

Skif stopped himself from snorting. "I think he was more scared than anything else," he replied. "When I left, he was sleepin' off a dose of poppy, and I bet he'll be fine in the morning."

:Lovely. Absolute truth, all of it.:

Evidently the Guard either had relatives who were overly convinced of their own mortality, or knew people who were, because he laughed. "Oh, aye, I understand. Well, I'm sorry you're going to have your sleep cut short; breakfast bell is going to ring mighty early for you."

Skif groaned. "Don't remind me," he said, as the Guard waved him through without even taking his name. "Good night to you!"

He unsaddled Cymry and turned her loose, and slipped into his room again via the window, thus avoiding any potentially awkward questions in the hall. He'd had the wit to clean himself up thoroughly at that stable, so at least he needed to do nothing more than strip himself down and drop into bed—which he did, knowing all too well just how right that Guard had been.

Tomorrow, though... he had to arrange an interview with the Weaponsmaster. The sooner, the better.

All during his classes the next day he had only half his mind on what was going on. The other half was engaged in putting together his plan, and as importantly, his argument. Herald Alberich wasn't going to like this plan. It was going to be very dangerous for Skif, and Skif knew for certain that Alberich would object to that.

During Weapons Class, Skif managed to give Alberich an unspoken signal that he *hoped* would clue Alberich to the fact that he needed to talk privately. Either he was very quick on the uptake, or else Cymry had some inkling of what was going on inside Skif's head and put the word in to Alberich's Kantor; in either case, just as class ended, Alberich looked straight at Skif and said, "You will be at my quarters here at the salle, after the dinner hour."

The others in the class completely misconstrued the order, as they were probably intended to. So as they all left for their next class, they commiserated with him, assuming that something he had done or not done well enough was going to earn him a lecture.

"I know what it is. It's that you dragged yourself through practice. Whatever you were doing last night to keep you up, you shouldn't have been," Kris said forthrightly. "You've got rings like a ferret under your eyes. If you thought *he* wasn't going to notice that, you're crazed."

"He'll probably give you a lecture about it, is all," opined Coroc.

"I suppose," Skif said, and sighed heavily. In actuality, he really wasn't *that* tired, although he expected to be after dinner. That was probably when it would all catch up with him.

"Whatever it was, it can't have been worth one of Alberich's lectures," Kris said flatly.

Skif just yawned and hung his head, to feign sheepishness that he in no way felt.

His next class was no class at all, it was a session in the sewing room, where he couldn't stop yawning over his work. The other boys in his classes had twitted him about his self-chosen assignment on the chore roster, until he pointed out that he was the only boy in a room full of girls. They'd gotten very quiet, then, and thoughtful—and stopped teasing him.

Today he was very glad that this was his chore, because the girls were far more sympathetic about his yawns and dark-circled eyes than the boys had been. Not that they let him off any—but they did keep him plied with cold tea to keep him awake, and they did make sure he got the best stool for the purpose—one that was comfortable, but not so comfortable that he was going to fall asleep.

A quick wash in cold water while the rest of them were having hot baths woke him up very nicely, and he hurried through his dinner, now as much anxious as eager. Alberich wouldn't like the plan, but would he go along with it anyway? It was probably his duty to forbid Skif even to think about carrying it out, even though it was the best and fastest way to get the man they were both after.

Well, Alberich could forbid him, but that wouldn't stop him. He just wouldn't use *that* plan; he'd come up with something else.

So as he walked quickly across the lawn, with the light of early evening pouring golden across the grass, he steeled himself to the notion that Alberich would not only not like the plan, but would put all the resources of the Collegium behind making sure Skif didn't try it alone.

Well, I won't. I dunno what I'll do, but I can't do that one alone, so there 'tis. He didn't need Cymry warning him against it; the entire plan depended on having someone else—by necessity a Herald or Trainee—standing by. There was not one single Trainee that Skif would dare even bring down to Exile's Gate quarter in the daytime, much less at night. So it would have to be a Herald, and the only one likely to agree to this would be Alberich. Which brought him right around to crux of the matter again.

He entered the salle, and went to the back of it, where one of the mirrors concealed the door to Alberich's other set of quarters. It was no secret that they were there, but it wasn't widely bruited about either. Maybe the concealed door was older than Alberich, who knew? Skif could think of a lot of reasons why hidden rooms might come in handy.

He tapped on the wall beside the mirror, and it swung open as Alberich pushed on the door from within.

He stepped inside. Alberich closed the door behind him and brought him through a small room that served him as an office and contained only a desk and a chair. On the other side of a doorway to the left were the private quarters, a suite that began with a rather austere room that contained only two chairs, a ceramic-tiled wood stove, and a large bookcase. Alberich gestured to the nearest chair. The sole aspect of the room that wasn't austere was the huge window along one wall, made up of many small panes of colored glass leaded together, forming a pattern of blues and golds that looked something like a man's face, and something like a sun-in-glory. It looked as though it faced east, so it wasn't at its best, just glowing softly. Most of the room's illumination came from lanterns Alberich had already lit. Skif made a note to himself to nip around to the back of the salle some time after dark; with lanterns behind it, the window must be nearly as impressive as it would be from within the room in early morning.

But Alberich didn't give Skif a chance to contemplate the window, though, since his chair had him facing away from it. A pity; he'd have liked to just sit there and study it for a time. Someone had told him that the Palace chapel had several windows like this, as did the major temples in Haven, but this was the first time he'd seen one close up.

The Weaponsmaster barely waited for him to settle himself. "So, your little excursion into the city last night bore some fruit?" was Alberich's question.

Good, he's already gotten everything from Cymry and Kantor and maybe the Guard but the "who" and maybe the "why." That was a bit less explanation he'd have to give. "I visited m'uncle Londer Galko," Skif said, then smiled. "Though he didn't know 'twas me. Went masked, and in over roof. *You* know. I scared him pretty thorough, good enough I figger he told me the truth."

As well Alberich should know, since he'd been the one who brought Skif's things from his old room, and had probably examined every bit. Skif experienced in that moment a very, very odd sensation of *comfort*. It was a relief to be able to sit here and be able to be himself completely. It was like being with Cymry, only a more worldly sort of Cymry.

"That was wise." Alberich leaned forward, resting his elbows on his knees, and looked thoughtful. "I would not have thought of Londer Galko as a source of information for our needs."

"I didn' either, till I stopped lookin' for a man what needed a building burned, and started thinkin' about what I picked up while I was lookin' for him," Skif replied. "An' put that with what you tol' me about the slavers. There's summat snatchin' younglings off the streets—not many, just the ones that have-ta sleep there. More of 'em than you thought, I bet. You don't hear 'bout it, 'cause they ain't the kind that'd be missed."

"We hear more than you might think," Alberich put in, but also nodded. "Although if this is true, we are not hearing of most of them. Go on."

"Londer ain't the kind t'get his fingers where they might get burned, not after that mess with th' Hollybush, but if there's somethin' dirty goin' on, he probably knows summat about it. He likes bein' on the edge of it, not so close he gets hurt, close enough he can kind of gloat over it. So—I paid 'im a visit." Skif launched into a full explanation, frankly describing everything he had done last night, leaving nothing out. He hadn't, after all, done anything that he'd been forbidden. Nobody had put a curfew on the Trainees, no one had told him not to leave the

Collegium grounds, he hadn't stolen anything. All he'd done was to terrorize one filthy old man who'd been the cause of plenty of misery himself over the past several years.

Still—

Alberich didn't look disgusted, and he didn't look annoyed, but Skif got a distinct impression that he was poised between being amused and being angry. "You—" he said at length, leaning back in his chair and pointing a finger at Skif, "—are the sort who would find a way around *any* order, so I shall not give you one. This information interesting is— useful, possibly—"

"But if I was to go out all ragged an' kip down on th'street where I know they's been snatching?" Skif asked. "While you kept a watch? It'd be more'n useful, I'm thinkin'. We got what we need for the makings of a nice little trap. An' it's one you can't set without a youngling for bait." He stabbed his thumb at his chest. "Me. You *daren't* use anyone else."

Alberich's face went very, very still. "If you did not Mindspeak with Cymry—" he said, very slowly.

"But I do. An' you got Kantor. So 'tween them we can Mindspeak each other. An' I got some ideas that'll keep me from gettin' coshed, 'cause I know how they been workin'," Skif replied, and sat back himself. "You'll know when I get took, an' you can follow. You'll know when th' man hisself shows up. We can do more'n figger out who he is. *We can catch 'im.*"

"It is very dangerous. You could be hurt," Alberich pointed out immediately. "You can attempt to protect yourself, but that does not mean you will succeed."

"Then I get hurt," Skif dismissed, feeling his jaw tense and his own resolve harden. "It'll be worth it."

Alberich half-closed his eyes and laced his fingers together, occasionally looking up at Skif as though testing his mettle. If this long wait was supposed to test his patience as well, it wasn't going to work that way, for the longer Alberich thought, the better Skif reckoned his odds to be.

And when at last Alberich spoke, he knew he'd been right.

"Very well," the Weaponsmaster said. "Let me hear the whole of this plan of yours. I believe that you and I must do this thing."

1 9

Skif widened his eyes pleadingly and held out his bowl to anyone who even glanced at him. He certainly looked the part of a beggar boy. He hadn't worn rags like these since he'd been living at the Hollybush. It was a good thing that it was still very warm at night, or he'd be freezing in the things. They were more hole than cloth, and he couldn't imagine where Alberich had found them, couldn't imagine why *anyone* in the Collegium would have kept them.

At least they were clean. His need for authenticity didn't run to dirt and lice, and fortunately, neither did Alberich's; a little soot smeared across his forehead, chin, and cheekbones provided the illusion of dirt, and that was all that was required.

This time the place where Skif's transformation had taken place had been supplied by Alberich, not that Skif was surprised at the Weaponsmaster's resources. Alberich couldn't have walked out of the Complex in his sell-sword gear, after all.

Alberich brought him to an inn where a Herald and a Trainee could ride into the stable yard unremarked. No surprises there; the innkeeper greeted him by name, and they took Cymry and Kantor to the stable, to special loose-boxes without doors. Then came the surprise, in the form of a locked room at the back of the stable to which Alberich had the key, and which contained both a trunk of disguise material and a rear entrance onto an alley. A beggar boy slipped out that entrance into the shadows of dusk somewhat later, and after him, a disreputable sell-sword whose face would be moderately familiar in the Exile's Gate quarter. Another purpose for all that soot on Skif's features was to disguise them. It wouldn't do for him to be recognized.

Skif made his way quietly to Exile's Gate itself; then as if he had come in the Gate, he wandered the street in his old neighborhood, training his voice into a tremulous piping as he begged from the passersby. Mostly he got kicks and curses, though once someone gave him an end of a loaf, and two others offered a rind of bacon and a rind of cheese. Beggars here got food more often than coin, though there was little enough of the former. Skif went a little cold when he thought about a child trying to live on such meager fare.

He got a drink at a public pump and wandered about some more as the streets grew darker and torches and a few lanterns were put up outside those businesses that were staying open past full dark. There were streetlights, but they were very few and often the oil was stolen, or even the entire lamp. He was ostensibly looking for a place to sleep on the street, out of the way of traffic. Actually he knew exactly where he was going to go to sleep, but he had to make a show out of it, because the child snatchers were almost certainly watching him. He also kept hunched over, both to look more miserable and to look smaller. The younger the children were, the more timid they were, the better the snatchers liked them.

And behind him, going from drink stall to tavern, was Alberich. There was great comfort in knowing that.

:Kantor says Alberich is very surprised at how good you are at this.:

:A thief that gets noticed doesn't stay out of gaol long,: he replied, though he was secretly flattered. Now, if he'd *really* been trying to make his way as a beggar, *he* would never be doing it this way. He'd have bound up his leg to look as if he'd lost it, or done the same with an arm. No sores, though; people around here would stone him into some other quarter for fear of a pox. Then he'd stand as straight as he could and catcall the people passing by, a noisy banter that was impossible to ignore. He'd be cheeky, but funny, and not insulting. People liked that; they liked seeing a display of bravado, especially in a cripple. He'd be making a better go of it than this thin, wistful waif he was impersonating. And the child snatchers would avoid him. A child like that would never tame down, and would cause nothing but trouble.

In his persona of woeful beggar child, he had a single possession that was going to make this entire ruse work—a wooden begging bowl. Perfectly in character with what he was, no one would even remark on it. And it was going to keep him from being knocked unconscious, because it was much deeper than the usual bowl and fit his head exactly like a helmet. Once he curled himself up in his chosen spot for the night and pulled his ragged hood over his head, he'd slip that bowl over it under the rags. When the snatchers came along and gave him that tap on the head to keep him from waking up when they grabbed him, he'd be protected.

He also had weapons on his person; his throwing daggers were concealed up his sleeves. Alberich hadn't needed to tell him to bring them. Having them made him feel a good deal safer, although his first choice of weapon wouldn't have been one that you threw at the enemy. Or it wouldn't have been if he wasn't so certain of his own accuracy. It was very unlikely that he'd be searched. These beggar children never had anything of value on them. If they once had, it was long snatched by those older and stronger than they were.

As he trudged away from the streets where people were still carrying on the minutiae of their lives and toward the warehouses and closed-up workshops, he felt eyes on him. The back of his neck prickled. The warehouse section of Exile's Gate was where most of the children had vanished from, and he knew now, with heavy certainty, that the snatchers were somewhere out there watching him, waiting for him to settle.

Alberich was out there, too, and had taken to the same covert skulking as Skif's stalkers. He was hunting the hunters, watching the watchers, to make sure that if anything went wrong, Skif wouldn't be facing it alone.

:He's seen two of them, anyway,: reported Cymry.

He would never, ever have attempted this by himself, or even with someone who didn't also have a Companion. The key to this entire plan was that Kantor and Cymry could Mindspeak to each other, keeping Skif and Alberich aware of everything that was going on.

The buildings here were large, with long expanses of blank wall planted directly on the street—you didn't want or need windows in a warehouse. There weren't a lot of places where a tired child could curl up to sleep. But where there was a doorway that was just big enough to fit a small body, or a recessed gate, it was dark and it was quiet, and no one was likely to come along to chivvy one off until dawn. Mind, any number of adult beggars knew this too, so the first few places Skif poked his nose into were occupied, and the occupants sent him off with poorly-aimed blows and liberal curses. He lost his bacon rind to one of them, not that he fought for it.

But when he did find a place, it was perfect for the child snatchers, and thus perfect for his purposes. It was a recessed doorway, a black arch in a darkened street, with no one in sight in either direction.

He sat down on the doorstep and pretended to eat his crust and cheese rind, then with a calculatedly pathetic sigh that should be audible to his stalkers, he curled up with his back to the street and his rags pulled up over his head. If that wasn't an invitation, he'd turn priest.

As he stirred and fidgeted, "trying to get comfortable," he slipped his wooden bowl over his head, exactly as he had planned. Once he had, he felt a good deal safer, and the back of his neck stopped prickling so much. There had been the possibility that the snatchers, lured by how harmless he seemed to be and the loneliness of the street, would try for the grab before he curled up for the night. He was glad their caution had overcome their greed.

Gradually he stopped moving around, as a child would who was settling into sleep. He wouldn't find a tolerable position on this stone doorstep anyway, not after he'd gotten accustomed, not only to a bed, but to a *comfortable* bed.

Spoilt, that's what I am.

Once "asleep," he held himself still as a matter of pride, although the stone under his hip was painfully hard and his arm was getting pins and needles. Eventually, he *had* to shift off of that, but when he moved, it was only the formless stirring that a child would make when deeply asleep. He *should* be asleep; the beggar child he was counterfeiting was in the midst of one of the better moments of its short life. It had a full belly, a quiet place to lie down, it was neither too cold nor too hot. No one was going to chase it away from this shelter until morning, and if rain came, it wouldn't even get too wet. Never having known a soft bed, the stone of the doorway would be perfectly acceptable since countless feet had worn the step down in a hollow in the middle into which Skif's body fit perfectly.

Well, he hadn't had to sleep on the street, ever. That was partly because he was smart, but there was no telling how much he'd accomplished was because he'd been lucky. Mostly, he liked to think, it was because he'd been smart—though if Bazie hadn't taken him in, his life probably would have been a lot different. Harder, maybe. It depended on what he would have done after Beel warned him away from the Hollybush. If he'd gone back to Beel, he'd have had to make a statement against his uncle—

That could have gone badly for him. He'd known that even when he'd been that young—it was the reason he'd run off in the first place. Maybe he'd have been safe in Beel's Temple, maybe not. Finding out which could have been bad.

If he'd run, though... *I think maybe I'd have hidden in the storage room of Orthallen's wash house.* Then what? He didn't know. How long could he have gone on, sleeping in hidden places, stealing food from kitchens in the guise of a page?

Cymry interrupted his speculations. *:Kantor says they've all gotten together. There are three of them,:* Cymry reported, interrupting his thoughts. She sounded indignant. *:Three of them! For one little child!:*

Skif wasn't surprised. A pretty child, or one that was strong, was a valuable commodity. Having two to make the snatch and one to stand guard meant they could grab it with a minimum of damage to the merchandise. *:That's so one can be a lookout in case their target's gone inside a yard or something,:* Skif told her. *:But I have to agree. Even two seems kind of much for someone my size.:*

:It's disgusting.: He had to smile at the affronted quality in her words. *:Not that the whole thing isn't disgusting, but—:*

:I understand,: he told her. And he did. It was disgusting. He could think abstractly about a child as "merchandise," but the minute he allowed himself to get outside of those abstractions, he was disgusted.

:Skif, be ready; they're moving in.:

He heard them in the last few paces; if he'd really been asleep, particularly if he was an exhausted child with a full belly, it wouldn't have disturbed him, but he heard their soft footfalls on the hard-packed dirt of the street. They were cautious, he gave them that, but waiting for them to finally make their move was enough to drive him mad. He had to grit his teeth and clench his muscles to *stay put* when every instinct and most of his training screamed at him to get up and defend himself.

Then they were on him, all three of them in a rush.

He was enveloped in a smelly blanket. Instinct won over control and he felt the mere beginnings of a reaction—but before he could even move, much less come up fighting, someone hit him a precise blow to the head.

The bowl took most of it, as he'd anticipated, but his head and ears still rang with it. In fact, for just a moment, he saw stars. He went limp, partly with intent, partly with the shock of the blow, and when he could move again, he regained control over himself and stayed properly limp.

They didn't dally about. They bundled him up cocoonlike in the blanket, one of the snatchers threw the bundle over his shoulder with a grunt of effort, and they were off at a lope. Whoever had Skif must have been a big man, because he carried Skif as if he was nothing.

Cymry did not ask "Are you all right?" because she knew he was. And what she knew, Alberich knew. So there was no point in wasting time with silly questions, when Alberich needed to concentrate on following Skif's captors, and Skif had immediate concerns of his own to deal with. Skif concentrated on breathing carefully in that foully smothering blanket, staying limp, and keeping up the ruse that he was as completely unconscious as that blow to the head should have rendered him. This was the hardest part of the plan—to literally do nothing while his captor carried him off, and hope that Alberich could keep up with them. They only had to get to their goal, which might or might not be Londer's warehouse. Alberich had to stay with them while remaining unseen.

Not the easiest task in the world; Skif had shadowed enough people in his life to know how hard it really was.

He'd have to get the bowl off his head, too, at some point in the near future, or they'd figure out he wasn't what he seemed and he wasn't unconscious. Definitely before he got unwrapped, or he'd be in a far more uncomfortable position than he was now. So as the man jogged along, Skif worked his hands, a little at a time, up toward his head.

The blanket smelled of so many things, all of them horrid, that he hated to think of what had happened in it and to it. It wasn't so much a blanket as a heavy tarpaulin of something less scratchy than wool. Was it sailcloth? It could be. He wasn't so tightly wrapped up in it that he couldn't move. He'd been "sleeping" with his arms up against his chest, so he shouldn't have too far to work them to get his hands on that bowl…

He was glad he hadn't eaten much, since his head and torso were dangling upside down along his captor's back, the stench of the blanket was appalling, and the man's shoulder essentially hit him in the gut with every step. If there was a better recipe for nausea, he didn't know it. He'd have been sick if he hadn't been cautious about not eating much beforehand.

Bit by bit, he worked his arms higher, moving them only with the motion of the man who carried him, slowly working his hands up through the canvas towards the bowl. Then, at long last, with the tips of his fingers, he touched it.

With a sigh of relief, he pushed with his fingertips and ducked his head at the same time as the man stumbled. The bowl came off his head and fell off into the folds of the blanket. He was rid of it, and now he could—

—not relax, certainly. But wait, be still, try to ignore the reek of the blanket, and remember the next part of the plan.

:It looks as if your uncle's warehouse really is the goal,: Cymry said.

He wished he could see. *Hellfires, I wish I could breathe!*

But if Londer's warehouse was the goal, it couldn't be very much longer. Alberich was supposed to have scouted the place during the day, so he'd be familiar with the outside, at least. Skif just wished that the Weaponsmaster was as good at roof walking as he was—if only they could have switched parts—

Don't worry about your partner. If he says he can do something, and you've got no cause to think otherwise, then let him do his job and concentrate on yours.

Well, that was easy to say, and hard to do, when it all came down to cases.

It seemed forever before the men stopped, and when they did, Skif was gritting his teeth so hard he thought they might splinter with the tension. They knocked on the door, quite softly, in a pattern of three, two, and five.

:Got it,: Cymry said. *:Alberich doesn't know if he's going to try going in that way, but if he does, that will make it easier.:*

The door creaked open. "Got 'nother one?" said a voice in a harsh whisper, with accents of surprise. "Tha's third'un tonight!"

"Pickin's is good," said the man to Skif's right, as the one carrying him grunted. "Got'r eyes on two more prime 'uns, so le's get this'un settled."

"Boss'll be right happy," said the doorkeeper, as the men moved forward and closed the door behind them.

"Tha's th'ideer," grunted the man with Skif.

They moved more slowly now, and to Skif's dismay there was a fair amount of opening and closing of doors, and direction changes down passages. This place must be a veritable warren! How was Alberich supposed to find him in all of this if he got inside?

:Let us worry about that,: said Cymry—right before there was the sound of another door opening, then the unmistakable feeling that his captor was descending a staircase.

Descending a staircase? There's a cellar to this place? There isn't supposed to be a cellar here!

Skif was in something of a panic, because part of the emergency plan figured in the Companions coming in as well as Alberich, and the Companions were not going to be able to get down a narrow, steep set of stairs into a cellar.

He had to remind himself that he was *not* alone, he was armed, and he was probably smarter than any of these people. No matter what happened here, sooner or later they would *have* to take him outside this building, and when they did, he could escape.

Even if he and Alberich couldn't actually catch the head of this gang of slavers right now, so long as Skif could get a good look at him, they'd have him later.

What's the worst that can happen? he asked himself, and set himself to imagining it. Alberich wouldn't get in. He'd be held for a while, maybe with other children, maybe not. The master of this gang would inspect them; Skif could make sure he saw enough he *would* be able to pick him out again. Then—well, the question was how attractive they found him.

He had to stop himself from shuddering. Just by virtue of being healthy and in good shape, he was as pretty as most of the street urchins they'd been picking up. Which meant there was one place where they'd send him.

Now the panic became real; his throat closed with fear and he had trouble breathing. *Oh, no—oh, no—*

In all his years on the street, he had never really had to face the possibility that he might end up a child-whore. Now he did, for if he couldn't get away from these people, or they found out what he was doing—

His imagination painted far worse things than he had ever seen, cobbled up out of all the horrible stories he had ever heard, and his breath came in short and painful gasps. He went from stifling to icy cold. What if their—the *brothel* was here, in this building? They wouldn't have to take him outside. They wouldn't have to move him at all. He wouldn't get a chance to escape—they could keep him here as long as they wanted to, they could—they *would*—strip him down first and find his knives. What would they do to him then? Drug him, maybe? Kill him? Oh no, probably not that, not while they could get some use out of him—

Don't panic. Don't panic.

How could he not panic?

:Chosen—we won't let that happen. We'll get to you, no matter what—:

But how *would* they? How *could* they? It would take a small army to storm this place, and by then—

The man carrying him got to the bottom of the stair and made a turning. "This brat's awful quiet," he grunted to his fellow. "Ye sure ye didn' 'it 'im too 'ard?"

"No more'n the rest uv 'em," the other snapped. "'E's breathin', ain't 'e?"

"Aye—just don' wanta hev'ta turn over damaged goods. Milord don't care fer damaged goods." The man hefted Skif a little higher on his shoulder, surprising him into an involuntary groan, caused as much by desperation as by pain.

"There, ye see?" the second man said in triumph. "Nothin' wrong wi' 'im. 'E's wakin' up right on time."

"Les' get 'im locked up, then," said the one from the door.

There was the sound of a key turning in a lock, a heavy door swinging open. Then, quite suddenly, Skif found himself being dumped unceremoniously onto something soft.

Well, softish. Landing knocked the breath out of him, though he managed to keep from banging his head when he landed. He heard the door slam and the key turn in the lock again before he got his wits back.

He struggled free of the stinking confines of the blanket, only to find himself in the pitch dark, and he was just as blind as he'd been in the blanket. He felt around, heard rustling, and felt straw under his questing hands. The "something soft" he'd been dumped on was a pile of old straw, smelling of mildew and dust, but infinitely preferable to the stench of the blanket.

He got untangled from the folds of that foul blanket, wadded it up, and with a convulsive movement, flung it as far away from himself as possible. The wooden bowl that had saved his skull from being cracked clattered down out of the folds of it as it flew across the room.

Which wasn't far, after all; he heard it hit a wall immediately. His prison *was* a prison then, and a small one. He got onto his hands and knees, and began feeling his way to the nearest wall. Rough brick met his hands, so cheap it was crumbling under his questing fingers, a symptom of the damp getting into it.

He got to his feet, and followed it until it intersected the next wall, and the next, and the next—and then came to the door.

A few moments more of exploring by touch proved that this wasn't a room, it was a cell; it couldn't have been more than three arm's lengths wide and twice that in length.

Not a very well-constructed cell, though. Rough brick made up the walls, and the floor was nothing more than pounded dirt with the straw atop it. And when Skif got to the door, he finally felt some of his fear ebbing. The lock on this door had never been designed with the idea of confining a thief. He could probably have picked it in the pitch-dark with a pry bar; the throwing daggers he wore were fine enough to work through the hole in the back plate and trip the mechanism.

I can get out. That was all it took to calm him. These people never intended to have to hold more than a few frightened children down here. As long as they thought that was what he was, he'd be fine. If *this* was their child brothel, he could get out of it.

:Or you can jam the lock and keep them out until we get in,: Cymry pointed out, and he nearly laughed aloud at what a simple and elegant solution she had found for him. Yes, he could, he could! Then help could take as long as it needed to reach him. Even if they set fire to the warehouse to cover their tracks, he should be safe down here. He remembered once, when one of the taverns had caught fire, how half a dozen of the patrons had hidden in the cellars and come out covered in soot but safe—and drunk out of their minds, for they'd been trapped by falling timbers and had decided they might as well help themselves to the stock.

:Will you be all right now?: Cymry asked anxiously.

:Right and tight,: he told her. And he would be, he would.

He had to be. Everything depended on him now.

He would be.

He heard the men enter and leave again twice more, and each time a door creaked open somewhere and he heard the thump of some small load landing in straw. He winced each time for the sake of the poor semiconscious child that it represented.

Between the first and the second, Cymry told him that Alberich had gotten into the building, but could tell him nothing more than that. It was not long after that the men arrived with the second child—and soon after that when the cellars awoke.

There was noise first; voices, harsh and quarrelsome. Then came heavy footsteps, and then light. So much light that it shone under Skif's door and through all the cracks between the heavy planks that the door was made up of.

Then the door was wrenched open, and a huge man stood silhouetted against the glare. Skif didn't have to pretend to fear; he shrank back with a start, throwing up his arm to shield his eyes.

The man took a pace toward him, and Skif remembered his knives, remembered that he didn't dare let anyone grab him by the arm lest they be discovered. He scrambled backward until he reached the wall, then, with his back pressed into the brick, got to his feet, huddling his arms around his chest.

The man grabbed him by the collar, his arms and hands not being easy to grab in that position, and hauled him out into the corridor and down it, toward an opening.

The corridor wasn't very long, and there were evidently only six of the little brick cells in it, three on each side. It dead-ended to Skif's rear in a wall of the same rough brick. The man dragged Skif toward the open end, then threw him unceremoniously into the larger room beyond, a large and echoing chamber that was empty of furnishings and lit by lanterns hung from hooks depending from the ceiling. Skif landed beside three more children, all girls, all shivering and speechless with fear, tear-streaked faces masks of terror. Facing them were five men, four heavily armed, standing in pairs on either side of the fifth.

Was this the hoped-for mastermind behind all of this?

"'Ere's th' last on 'em, milord," said the man who'd brought Skif out. "The fust two ye said weren't good fer yer gennelmen. This a good 'nuff offerin'?"

Skif looked up from his fellow captives. For a moment, he couldn't see the man's face, but he knew the voice right enough.

"Very nice," purred the man, with just an edge of contempt beneath the approval. "Prime stock. Yes, they'll do. They'll do very nicely."

It was the same voice that had spoken with Jass in the tomb in the cemetery. And when "milord" came into the light, Skif stared at him, not in recognition, but to make sure he knew the face later. If this man was one of those that had attended Lord Orthallen's reception, Skif didn't recall him… but then, he had a very ordinary face. What Bazie would have called a "face-shaped face" with that laugh of his—neither this nor that, neither round nor oblong nor square, nondescript in every way, brown hair, brown eyes. He could have been anyone.

The man was wearing very expensive clothing, in quite excellent taste. That was something of a surprise; Skif would have expected excellent clothing in appalling taste, given the circumstances.

Milord—well, the clothing was up to the standards of the highborn, but something about him didn't fit. Since being at the Collegium, Skif had met a fair number of highborn, and there was an air about them, as if everyone they met would, as a matter of course, assume they were superior. So it was second nature to them, and they didn't have to think about it. This man wore his air of superiority, and his pride, openly, like a cloak.

So what, exactly, was he? He had money, he had power, but he just didn't fit the "merchant" mold either. Yet he *must* have influence, and *someone* must be feeding him information, or he never would have been able to continue to operate as successfully and invisibly as he had until now.

The man gestured, and one of the four men with him grabbed the shoulder of the girl he pointed at, hauling her to her feet. She couldn't have been more than eight or nine at most, thin and wan, and frightened into paralysis. The man walked around her, surveying her from every angle. He took her chin in his hand, roughly tilting her face up, even prying open her mouth to look at her teeth as tears ran soundlessly down her smudged cheeks, leaving tracks in the dirt. He didn't order her to be stripped, but then, given that she wasn't wearing much more than a tattered feed sack with a string around it, he didn't really need to.

"Yes," the man said, after contemplating her for long moments, during which she shivered like an aspen in the wind. She was a very pretty little thing under all her dirt, and Skif's heart ached for her. Hadn't her life been bad enough without this descent into nightmare? How could a tiny little child possibly deserve this?

And this was the man who had ordered the deaths of Bazie and the two boys with no more concern than if he had crushed a beetle beneath his foot. This man, with his face-shaped face—this was the face of true evil that concealed itself in blandness. No monster here, just a man who could have hidden himself in any crowd. He would probably pat his friends' children genially on the head, even give them little treats, this man who assessed the market value of a little girl and consigned her to a fearful fate. He was valued by his neighbors, no doubt, this beast in a man's skin.

Skif hated him. Hated the look of him, the sound of his voice, hated everything about him. Hated most of all that he could smile, and smile, and look so like any other man.

"Yes," the man said again, with a bland smile, the same smile a housewife might use when finding a particularly fat goose. "Pretty and pliant. This one will be very profitable for us."

"Oh—it is that I think not, good Guildmaster," said a highly accented voice from the doorway. Skif's heart leaped, and when Alberich himself walked through the door, sword and dagger at the ready, it was all he could do to keep from cheering aloud.

2 0

There was a moment of absolute silence, as even the Guildmaster's professional bodyguards were taken by surprise. But that moment ended almost as soon as it began.

The man who'd brought Skif out bolted for the door behind the Guildmaster, disappearing into the darkness. All four of the bodyguards charged Alberich, as the Guildmaster himself stood back with a smirk that would have maddened Skif, if he hadn't been scrambling to get out of the way. He pushed the three little girls ahead of him into the partial shelter of the wall, and stood between them and the fighting. Not that he was going to be able to do anything other than try and push them somewhere else if the fighting rolled over them.

Not that *he* was going to be able to do anything to help Alberich. He knew when he was outweighed, outweaponed, and outclassed. This fight was no place for an undersized and half-trained (at best) adolescent. Besides, Alberich didn't look as if he needed any help, at least not at the moment.

The Weaponsmaster had been impressive enough in the salle and on the training ground; here, literally surrounded by four skilled fighters, Skif could hardly believe what he was seeing. Alberich moved like a demon incarnate and so quickly that half the time Skif couldn't see what had happened, only that he'd somehow eluded what should have killed him—

Still—four to one—maybe he'd better do something to try and drop the odds.

Skif slipped the catches on his knives and then hesitated. The combatants were all moving too fast and in unpredictable ways. He'd never practiced against anything but a stationary target; if he threw a knife, he could all too easily hit Alberich, and if he threw a knife, he'd also throw away half of his own defenses.

:Skif, get the children out now!:

Cymry's mental "shout" woke him out of his indecision; with a quick glance to make sure the Guildmaster (what Guild was he?) was too far away to interfere, Skif grabbed the wrists of two of the three—the third was clinging to the arm of the second—and pulled them onto their feet. Then he got behind them and slowly—trying *not* to attract the eye of their chiefest captor—he herded them in front of him, along the wall, and toward the door that Alberich had entered by.

One of the three, at least, woke out of her fear to see what he was trying to do. She seized the wrists of both of the others and dragged them with her as they edged along the wall. Her eyes were fixed on that doorway; Skif's were on the fight.

It was oddly silent, compared with the tavern- and street-fights he was used to. There was no shouting, no cursing, only the clash of metal on metal and the occasional grunt of pain.

And it was getting bloody. All of the bodyguards were marked—not big wounds, but they were bleeding. It looked as if the four bodyguards should bring Alberich down at any moment, and yet he kept sliding out from beneath their blades as Skif and his charges got closer and closer to their goal. Skif wanted to run, and knew he didn't dare. He didn't dare distract Alberich, and he didn't dare grab the attention of the Guildmaster.

Ten paces... five...

There!

The girl who was leading the other two paused, hesitating, on the very threshold, her face a mask of fear and indecision. She didn't know what lay beyond that door—it could be worse than what was here.

"Run!" Skif hissed at her, trusting that Alberich had already cleared the way.

The girl didn't hesitate a moment longer; she bolted into the half-lit hallway, hauling the other two with her. Skif started to follow—hesitated, and looked back.

There was a body on the floor, and it wasn't Alberich's. While Skif's back was turned, the Weaponsmaster had temporarily reduced the odds against himself by one.

But Alberich was bleeding from the shoulder now. Skif couldn't tell how bad the wound was, and Alberich showed no sign of weakness, but the leather tunic was slashed there, and bloody flesh showed beneath the dark leather whenever he moved that arm. Skif's throat closed with fear. Somewhere deep inside he'd been certain that Alberich was invulnerable. But he wasn't. He could be hurt. And if he could be hurt—he could die.

At that moment, the Guildmaster finally noticed that his prizes had escaped.

"*Stop them!*" he shouted at his men. "*Don't let them get away!*"

Skif froze in the doorway; but he needn't have worried. No one was taking orders now. The fighters were too busy with Alberich to pay any attention to Skif, although they redoubled their efforts to take the Weaponsmaster down.

:Skif, run! Get out of there now!: Cymry cried.

"No!" he said aloud. He couldn't go—not now—he *might* be able to do something—

The lantern flames flickered, and shadows danced on the walls, a demonic echo of the death dance in the center of the room. It was confusing; too confusing. Once again Skif felt for his knives and hesitated.

Alberich was tiring; oh, it didn't show in how he moved, but there was sweat rolling down his face. He had taken another cut, this time across his scalp, and blood mingled with the drops of sweat that spattered down onto the dirt floor with every movement.

Skif *still* didn't dare throw the knives, even with one of the opponents down. He edged away from the door, and looked frantically for something else he could throw.

Alberich's eyes glittered, and his mouth was set in a wild and terrible smile. He looked more than half mad, and Skif couldn't imagine why his opponents weren't backing away just from his expression alone, much less the single-minded ferocity with which he was fighting. He did not look human, that much was certain. If this was how he always looked when he fought in earnest, no wonder people were afraid of him.

No wonder he had never needed to draw a blade in those tavern brawls.

Skif's eye fell on a pile of dirty bowls stacked against the wall on the other side of the doorway—the remains, perhaps, of a meal the child snatchers had finished. It didn't matter; they were heavy enough to be weapons, and they were within reach.

He snatched one up and waited for his opportunity. It came sooner than he'd hoped, as Alberich suddenly rushed one of the three men, making him stumble backward in a hasty retreat. That broke the swirling dance of steel for a moment, broke the pattern long enough for Skif to fling the bowl at the man's head.

It connected with the back of his skull with a sickening *crack* that made Skif wince—not hard enough to knock him out, but enough to make him stagger, dazed.

And that moment was just enough for Alberich to slash savagely at his neck, cutting halfway through it. The man twisted in agony, dropping to the floor, blood *everywhere* as he writhed for a long and horrible moment, then stilled.

Skif froze, watching in fascination, aghast. Alberich did not. Nor did the two men still fighting. They reacted by coming at Alberich from both directions at once, and in the rain of blows that followed, Alberich was wounded again, a glancing slash across the arm that peeled back leather and a little flesh—but he delivered a worse blow than he had gotten to the head of the third man, who dropped like a stone. At which point the first man who'd been felled stood up, shaking his head to clear it, and plunged back into the fray.

Skif shook himself out of his trance and flung two more bowls. Neither connected as well as the first; the first man remaining was hit in the shoulder, and the second in the back. But the distraction was their undoing, for they lost the initiative and Alberich managed to get out of their trap, nor could they pin him between them again.

The fight moved closer to the Guildmaster—Alberich got the second man in the leg, leaving his dagger in the man's thigh, and the bodyguard staggered back.

Skif threw his last bowl, which hit the man nearest the Guildmaster in the side of the face. Alberich saw his opening, and took it, with an all-or-nothing lunge that carried him halfway across the room.

Skif let out a strangled cry of horror—

If any fighter Skif had *ever* seen before had tried that move, it would have ended differently. But this was Alberich, and he came in *under* the man's sword and inside his dagger, and the next thing Skif knew, the point of Alberich's sword was sticking out of the man's back, and the man was gazing down at Alberich with an utterly stupefied expression on his face.

Then he toppled over slowly—

But he took Alberich's sword with him.

And *now* the Guildmaster struck.

Because he had done nothing all this time, Skif had virtually forgotten he was there, and had assumed that he was harmless. Perhaps Alberich had done the same. It was a mistaken assumption on both their parts.

The Guildmaster moved like a ferret, so fast that he seemed to blur, and too fast for Alberich, exhausted as he was, to react. The Guildmaster didn't have a weapon.

He didn't need one.

Skif didn't, *couldn't* see how it happened. One moment, Alberich was still extended in his lunge; the next, the Guildmaster had him pinned somehow, trapped. The Guildmaster's back was to the wall, his arm was across Alberich's throat with Alberich's body protecting his. Both of Alberich's hands were free, and he clawed ineffectually at the arm across his throat. The Weaponsmaster's face was already turning an unhealthy shade of pale blue.

"Kash," the Guildmaster said, in a tight voice. "Get the brat."

But the last man was in no condition to grab anyone. "Can't," he coughed. "Leg's out."

Given the fact that his leg had been opened from thigh to knee, with Alberich's dagger still in the wound, he had a point. The Guildmaster's gaze snapped back onto Skif.

"Well," he said, in that condescending voice he'd used with Jass, "I wouldn't have expected the Heralds to use bait. It's not like them to put a child in danger."

Skif bristled. "Ain't a child," he said flatly.

"Oh? You're a little young to be a Herald," the man countered in a sarcastic tone. Then he punched Alberich's shoulder wound with his free hand, making him gasp, and putting a stop to Alberich's attempts to claw himself free. "Stop that. You're only making things more difficult for yourself."

"What has age to do with being a Herald?" Alberich rasped.

Skif said nothing, and the man's eyes narrowed as his arm tightened a little more on Alberich's throat. "Be still, or I will snap your foolish neck for you. A Trainee, then. But still—that's *quite* out of character—unless—"

He stared at Skif then, with a calculating expression, and Skif sensed that he was thinking very hard, very hard indeed.

It was, after all, no secret that the latest Trainee was a thief. But what that would mean to this wealthy villain—and whether he'd heard that—

Then the Guildmaster's eyes widened. "Well," he said, and his mouth quirked up at one corner. "Who would have thought it. The Heralds making common cause with a common thief. Oh, excuse me—you're quite an uncommon thief. Old Bazie's boy, aren't you? Skif, is it?"

Skif went cold with shock and stared at the Guildmaster with his mouth dropping open. *How'd he know how—*

The Guildmaster smirked. "I make it my business to know what goes on in my properties, as any good landlord would," he said pointedly.

"Besides, how do you think that cleverly hidden room got there? Who do you think arranged for the pump and the privy down there?"

"But you *killed* him!" Skif cried, as Alberich tried to move and turned a little bluer for his trouble.

"I had no intention of doing so," the Guildmaster pointed out, in reasonable tones. "That was Jass' fault. If he'd *obeyed orders*, everyone would have gotten out all right, even Bazie."

Since Skif had heard the truth of that with his own ears, there was no debating the question of whether Jass had gone far beyond what his orders had been. But—

How would Bazie have gotten out in time, even so? How? The boys couldn't have carried him—

The Guildmaster interrupted his thoughts. His expression had gone very bland again. He was planning something...

"You've been very clever, young man," he said, in a voice unctuous with flattery. "I don't see nearly enough cleverness in the people I hire—well, Jass was a case in point. Now at the moment, we seem to be at a stalemate."

Alberich writhed in a futile attempt to get free. His captor laughed, and punched the shoulder wound again, and Alberich went white. "If I kill this Herald," he pointed out, "I lose my shield against whatever you might pick up and fling at me. You can't go anywhere, because Kash is between you and the door. Stalemate."

Skif nodded warily.

"On the other hand," he continued, "if you decided to switch allegiances, I could strangle this fool and we could all escape from here before the help he has almost certainly arranged for arrives."

Skif clenched his jaw. In another time and place—"An' just what'm I supposed to get out of this?" he asked, playing for time to think.

Cymry was oddly silent in his mind. In fact—in fact, he couldn't sense her at all. For the first time in weeks he was alone in his head.

"What do you get? Oh, Skif, Skif, haven't you learned *anything* about the way life works?" the Guildmaster laughed. "Allow me to enlighten you. No matter what these fools have told you, the *only* law that counts is the Law of the Street. What you'll get is to be trained by me, in something far more profitable than the liftin' lay."

"Oh, aye—" Skif began heatedly.

"No. You listen to me. *This* is what is real. These are the rules that the real world runs by." He stared into Skif's eyes, and Skif couldn't look away, couldn't stop listening to that voice, so sure of itself, so very,

very rational. "Grab what you can, because if you don't, someone else will snatch it out from under you. Get all the dirt you can on anyone who might have power over you—and believe me, *everyone* has a past, and things they'd rather not have bruited about. Be the cheater, not the cheated, because you'll be one or the other. There's no such thing as truth—oh, believe me about this—there are shades of meaning, and depths of self-interest, but there is no *truth.*"

Skif made an inarticulate sound of protest, but it was weak, because *this* was all he'd seen at Exile's Gate, *this* was the way the world as he had always known it worked. Not the way it was taught in the Collegium. Not the way those sheltered, idealistic Heralds explained things—

"And there is no *faith* either," the Guildmaster continued, in his hard, bright voice. "Faith is for those who wish to be deceived for the sake of a comforting but hollow promise. Think about it, boy—think about it. It's shadow and air, all of it. Cakes in the Havens, and crumbs in the street. *That* is all that faith is about."

The priests—oh, the priests—how many of them actually *helped* anyone in Exile's Gate in the here and now? Behind their cloister walls and their gates, they never went hungry or cold—they never suffered the least privations. Even the Brothers at the Priory never went hungry or cold...

Skif's heart contracted into an icy little knot. Alberich's eyes were closed; he seemed to be concentrating on getting what little air the Guildmaster allowed him.

"Throw your lot in with me. *I* won't deceive you with pretty fictions. You'll obey me because I am strong and smart and powerful. You'll learn from me to be the same. And maybe some day you'll be good enough to take what I've got away from me. Until then, we'll have a deal, and it will be because we *know* where we stand with each other, not because of some artificial conceit that we *like* each other." He laughed. "The smart man guards his own back, boy," the insidious voice went on. "The wise man knows there is no one that you can trust, you take and hold whatever you can and share it with *no one,* because no one will ever share what he has with you. *Hate* is for the strong; love is for the weak. No one has friends; *friend* is just a pretty name for a leech. Or a user. What do you think Bazie was? A *user.* He used you boys and lived off of *your* work, kept you as personal servants, and pretended to love you so you would be as faithful to him as a pack of whipped puppies."

And that was where the Guildmaster went too far.

Bazie, thought Skif, jarred free of the spell that insidiously logical voice had placed on him. *Bazie* had shared whatever he had, and had trusted to his boys to do the same. Bazie had taken him in, with no reason to, and every reason to turn him into the street, knowing that Londer would be looking for him to silence him.

And Beel—Beel had protected him, Beel *could* have reported a hundred times over that Skif had fulfilled his education, but he didn't. And when Beel could have told his own father where Skif was, he'd kept his mouth shut.

And the Heralds—

Oh, the Heralds. Weak, were they? Foolish?

Skif felt warmth coming back into him, felt his heart uncurling, as he thought back along the past weeks and all of the little kindnesses, all unasked for, that he'd gotten. Kris and Coroc keeping the highborn Blues from tormenting him until Skif had established that he was more amusing if he wasn't taunted. Jeri helping him out with swordwork. The teachers taking extra time to explain things he simply had never seen before. Housekeeper Gaytha being so patient with his rough speech that sometimes he couldn't believe she'd spend all this time over one Trainee. The girls teasing and laughing with him in the sewing room. The simple way that he had been *accepted* by every Trainee, and with no other recommendation but that he'd been Chosen—

Cymry.

Cymry, who had filled his heart—who still was there, he sensed her again, now that he wasn't listening to the poison that bastard was pouring into his ears. Cymry, who cared enough for him to wait while he listened—*to make his own decisions,* without any pressure from her. No love, was there? Self-delusion, was it? *Then I'll be deluded.*

Did the Guildmaster see his thoughts flicker across his face? Perhaps—

"*Kash, now!*" he shouted. The wounded bodyguard lunged, arms outstretched to grab him—

But Skif was already moving before the bodyguard, clumsy with his wounds and pain, had gotten a single step. He jumped aside, his hands flicking to each side as he evaded those outstretched arms.

And between one breath and the next—

The bodyguard continued his lunge, and sprawled facedown on the floor, gurgling in agony, one of Skif's knives in his throat.

The Guildmaster made a strangled noise—and so did Alberich.

The arm around Alberich's throat tightened as the Guildmaster slid down the wall.

Skif's *other* knife was lodged to the hilt in his eye.

But Skif's dodge had been deliberately aimed to take him to Alberich's side. The Guildmaster had been a stationary target. And at that range, he couldn't miss.

In the next heartbeat he had pried the dead arm away from the Weaponsmaster's throat, and Alberich was gasping in great, huge gulps of air, his color returning to normal.

Skif helped him to his feet. "You all right?" he asked awkwardly.

Alberich nodded. "Talk—may be hard," he rasped.

Skif laughed giddily, feeling as if he had drunk two whole bottles of that fabulous wine all by himself. "Like that's gonna make the Trainees unhappy," he taunted. "You, not bein' able to lecture 'em!"

The wry expression on Alberich's face only made him laugh harder. "Come on," he said, draping his teacher's arm over his shoulders. "We better get you outside an' get back to where th' good Healers are afore your Kantor decides he's gonna put horseshoe marks on my bum."

They got as far as the door when Skif thought of something else. "I don' suppose you *did* arrange for help, did you?"

"Well," Alberich admitted, in a croak. "It comes *now*."

:*Cymry?*:

:*Half the Collegium, my love.*:

Skif just shook his head. "Figgers. Us Heralds, we just keep thinkin' we gotta do everything by ourselves, don't we? We can't do the smart thing an' get help fixed up beforehand. Even you. An' you should know better."

"Yes," Alberich agreed. "I should. *We* do."

We. It was a lovely word.

One that Skif was coming to enjoy a very great deal.

A Herald he didn't recognize brought Skif his knives, meticulously cleaned, as the Healer fussed over Alberich right there in the street, which was so full of torches and lanterns it might have been a festival. Well, a very grim sort of festival.

It actually looked more like something out of a fever dream; the street full of Heralds and Guards, more Guardsmen swarming in and out of the warehouse, a half-dozen Heralds and their Companions surrounding Alberich—who flatly refused to lie down on a stretcher as the Healer wanted—while the Weaponsmaster sat on an upturned barrel and the Healer stitched up his wounds. Four bodies were laid out on the street under sheets; one semiconscious bullyboy had been taken off for questioning as soon as he recovered. Not that anyone expected to get much out of him. It wasn't very likely that a mere bodyguard would know the details of his master's operations.

No one had sent Skif back to the Collegium, and he waited beside Alberich, between Kantor and Cymry, listening with all his might to the grim-voiced conversations around him. Most of the Heralds here he didn't know; that was all right, he didn't have to know who they were to understand that they were important. He did recognize Talamir, though, who seemed considerably less otherworldly at the moment and quite entirely focused on the here and now.

"This is going to have an interesting effect on the Council," he observed, his voice heavy with irony.

Alberich snorted. "Interesting? Boil up like a nest of ants, when stirred with sticks, it will! Sunlord! Guildmaster *Vatean!* Suspect *him*, even I did not!"

"Gartheser is going to have a fit of apoplexy," someone else observed. "Vatean was here was here at his behest in the first place."

Hadn't they noticed he was here? This was high political stuff he was listening to!

:They know,: Cymry told him. *:But you're a Herald, even if you aren't in Whites yet. You proved yourself tonight. No one is ever going to withhold anything from you that you really want or need to know.:*

Well! Interesting...

"Gartheser will be a pool of stillness compared to Lady Cathal," Talamir observed, with a sigh. "He was a Guildmaster after all, and she speaks for the Guilds."

"Oh, *Guildmaster*, indeed," someone else said dismissively. "Becoming a Master in the Traders' Guild..." He left the sentence dangling, but everyone—including Skif—knew that the requirements for Mastery in the Traders' Guild mostly depended on entirely on how much profit you could make. Provided, of course, that you didn't cheat to make it. Or at least that you didn't get *caught* cheating.

"He was," Talamir pointed out delicately, and with a deliberate pause between the words, "quite... prosperous."

"And now, know we where the profits came from," Alberich said harshly. "It is thinking I am that Lady Cathal should be looking into profits, and whence from they come."

"*And* Lord Gartheser," said Talamir. "Since Gartheser wished so sincerely to recommend him to the Council."

"There is that," observed someone else, in a hard, cold voice. "And *now* we know where the leak of Guard movements along Evendim came from."

"It would appear so," Talamir replied thoughtfully. "Although… it is in my mind that Lord Orthallen was equally, though less blatantly, impressed with the late Guildmaster's talents…"

But a flurry of protests broke out over that remark; it seemed that the idea of Lord Orthallen having anything to do with all of this was completely out of the question.

Except that Skif saw Talamir and Alberich exchange a private look— and perhaps more than that. Looks weren't all that could be exchanged when one was a Herald, and far more privately.

I wonder what all that's about.

And Lord Orthallen had "particularly" recommended Jass to Vatean…

Well, if he wanted to know—

No, he didn't. Not at all. He knew quite enough already. All of this was going right over his head, and anyway, there wasn't anything one undersized thief could do about it even if he did know.

Or—if there *was* something one undersized thief could do about it, he had no doubt that Alberich would have a few words with him on the subject. *And maybe a job.*

So, perhaps his roof-walking days weren't over after all.

Better get myself another sneaky suit.

:I believe that Alberich already has that in mind,: said Cymry.

The little group continued to paw over the few facts they had until they were shopworn, and even Talamir, whose patience seemed endless, grew weary of it.

"Enough!" he said, silencing them all. "There is nothing more we can do until we *know* more. The boy and Alberich have told us all they know. Herald Ryvial and our picked Guardsmen-Investigators are on their way to Vatean's home even now, and if there is anything to be found there, rest assured, they will find it. Every known associate of Vatean will be under observation before sunrise, *long* before word of his death leaks out—"

"Uncle Londer," Skif interrupted wearily. Now that the excitement was wearing off, he was beginning to feel every bruise, and was just a little sick.

"And the man Londer Galko will also be observed," Talamir continued smoothly. "Because he clearly knew a great deal about the child stealing, although he is not connected with Vatean in any way."

Now he looked at Skif, and put a hand on Skif's shoulder that felt not at all patronizing. Comradely, yes, patronizing, no. "Trainee Skif is weary to dropping, Herald Alberich is in pain, and we are fresh and have constructive work ahead of us. I suggest we send them back to their beds while we get about it, brothers."

There was a murmured chorus of assent as the Healer put the last of the stitches into Alberich's scalp wound, and the Heralds magically melted away, leaving Skif and Alberich alone in a calm center in the midst of the bustle.

"You won't travel in a stretcher as you *should,*" the Healer said wearily, as if he had made and lost this same argument far too many times to bother again. "So the best I can do is order you back to the Collegium and to rest."

"Teach from a stool I will, tomorrow at least," Alberich told him.

The Healer sighed, and packed up his satchel. "I suppose that's the most I can get out of you," he said, and looked at Kantor. "Do what *you* can with him, won't you?"

The Companion tossed his head in an emphatic nod, and Skif added, "Jeri an' Herald Ylsa can run th' sword work for a week—an' Coroc an' Kris can do archery." Kantor nodded even more emphatically.

Alberich glared at him sourly, made as if to shrug, thought better of it, and sighed. "A conspiracy, it is," he grumbled.

"Damn right," Skif said boldly. And when Alberich got to his feet and made as if to mount, Kantor stamped his foot, and laid himself down so that Alberich could get into the saddle without *mounting.* When his Herald was in place, Kantor rose, and shook his head vigorously.

"You make me an old woman," Alberich complained, as Skif got stiffly into Cymry's saddle and the two of them headed up the street away from the scene of the activity, riding side by side.

"Naw," Skif denied, very much enjoying having the fearsome Weaponsmaster at a temporary disadvantage. "Just makin' you be sensible. Ye see—" he continued, waxing eloquent, "there's th' difference between a Herald an' a thief. Ye don' have t' *make* a thief be sensible. All thieves are *sensible.* A thief that won't be sensible—"

"—a thief in gaol is, yes, please spare me," Alberich growled.

But it didn't sound like his heart was in it, and a moment later he glanced over at Skif. "That was one of your mentor—Bazie—that was one of the things he told you, yes?"

Skif nodded.

"And now, revenge you have had."

True. Jass was dead, Vatean was dead; the two men responsible for Bazie's horrible death were themselves dead. Skif's initial bargain with himself—and with the Heralds—to work with Alberich because they had a common cause was over.

"Regrets?" Alberich prompted.

Skif shook his head, then changed his mind. "Sort of. There weren't no *justice.*"

"But it was your own hand that struck Vatean down," Alberich said, as if he were surprised.

It was Skif's turn to bestow a sour look. "Now, don' you go tryin' that sly word twistin' on *me,*" he said. "I know what you're tryin' t'do, an' don' pretend you ain't. No. There weren't no *justice.* Th' bastid is dead, dead quick an' easy, he didn' have t'answer fer nothing an' we ain't never gonna find out a half of what he was into. I got revenge, an' I don' like it. Revenge don' get you nothin'. There. You happy now?"

But Alberich surprised him. "No, little brother," he said gently. "I am not happy, because my brother is unhappy."

And there it was; the sour taste in Skif's mouth faded, and although the vengeance he thought he had wanted turned out to be nothing *like* what he really would have wanted if he'd had the choice, well—

I am not happy, because my brother is unhappy.

That—*that* was worth everything he'd gone through to get here.

"Ah, I'll get over it," he sighed. "Hey, I get t' boss you around fer a week, eh, Kantor? That's worth somethin'."

Once again, Kantor nodded his head with vigor, and Alberich groaned feelingly.

"This—" he complained, but with a suspicious twinkle in his eye, "—is putting the henhouse in the fox's charge."

"Rrrrr!" Skif growled, showing his teeth. "Promise. Won't have *too* much chicken."

"And I suppose you will insist on going into Whites, now that a hero you are," Alberich continued, looking pained.

"Hah! You *are* outa your head; th' Healer was right," Skif countered. "What, me run afore I can walk? Not likely! 'Sides," he continued, contemplating all the potential fun he could have over the next four years in the Collegium, "I ain't fleeced a quarter of them highborn Blues yet, nor got all I can outa them Artificer Blues!"

Alberich regarded him with a jaundiced eye. "I foresee—and ForeSight *is* my Gift—a great deal of trouble, with *you* at its center. And that no Trainee in the history of Valdemar will have more demerits against his name, before you go into Whites."

"Suits me," Skif replied saucily. "So long as I have fun doing it."

"Fun for you—yes," Alberich sighed. "Fun for the rest of us, however, extracting you from the tangles you make—"

"It'll be worth it!" Skif insisted, once again feeling that giddy elation bubbling up inside him, as he felt the warmth of *acceptance* encircle him and hold him at its heart.

And in spite of present pain and future concerns, Herald Alberich gave him a real, unalloyed smile. "Oh, there is no doubt it will be worth it," he said, and Skif had the sense that he meant more than just the subject of Skif's future mischief. He meant Skif's very existence as one of the Trainees now and Heralds to come, no matter who objected, or how strenuously, to the presence of a thief among them. He confirmed that with his next breath.

"Welcome, very welcome, to the Collegium, Skif. It seems we were always right to take a thief."

ABOUT THE AUTHOR

Mercedes Lackey is a full-time writer and has published numerous novels and works of short fiction, including the bestselling Heralds of Valdemar series. She is also a professional lyricist and licensed wild bird rehabilitator. She lives in Oklahoma with her husband and collaborator, artist Larry Dixon, and their flock of parrots.

www.**mercedeslackey**.com

THE COLLEGIUM CHRONICLES

Mercedes Lackey

Follow Magpie, Bear, Lena, and friends as they face their demons
and find their true strength on the road to becoming full Heralds,
Bards and Healers of Valdemar.

Book One: Foundation
Book Two: Intrigues
Book Three: Changes
Book Four: Redoubt
Book Five: Bastion

"Lackey makes a real page-turner out of Mags' and the collegia's
development… this book's outstanding characters, especially
Mags, will greatly please Valdemar fans." *Booklist*

"The tone, characterization, and rampant angst recall Lackey's
earliest Valdemar books… this is a worthy entry in the overall
saga." *Publishers Weekly*

"Lackey's Valdemar series is already a fantasy classic, and these
newest adventures will generate even more acclaim for this fantasy
superstar." *Romantic Times*

THE HERALD SPY

Mercedes Lackey

Mags was a Herald of Valdemar. But he had once lived the brutal
life of a child slave. When he was Chosen by his Companion
Dallen, his young life was saved, and he slowly adjusted to being
well fed, educated, and treasured as a trainee in the Herald's
Collegium at Haven. Singled out by the King's Own Herald, Mags
would thrive in his secret training as a spy. His unusually strong
Gift—an ability to Mindspeak and Mindhear anyone, not just
others who were Gifted—made him a perfect undercover agent for
the king.

Closer to Home
Closer to the Heart
Closer to the Chest

"A welcome addition to the Valdemar canon…a fast, page-turning
read." Shiny Book Review

"You can feel Lackey's passion for her characters…funny and
entertaining." The Qwillery

"Mercedes Lackey is a master storyteller and *Closer to Home* is a
masterful, satisfying visit to Valdemar." Bitten by Books